THE ANNOTATED CHRONICLES

Margaret Weis and Tracy Hickman

Dragons of Autumn Twilight

Dragons of Winter Night

Dragons of Spring Dawning

Edited by Jean Blashfield Black

Poetry by Michael Williams

Cover art by Todd Lockwood

Color plates by Larry Elmore

Interior art by Denis Beauvais, Valerie Valusek, and Jeffrey Butler

THE ANNOTATED CHRONICLES

Distributed in the United States by Holtzbrinck Publishing. Distributed in Canada by Fenn Ltd.

Distributed to the hobby, toy, and comic trade in the United States and Canada by regional distributors.

Distributed worldwide by Wizards of the Coast, Inc. and regional distributors.

Made in the U.S.A.

Cover art by Todd Lockwood
First Printing: November 1999
First Paperback Edition: October 2002
First Printing of *Dragons of Autumn Twilight*: April 1984
First Printing of *Dragons of Winter Night*: April 1985
First Printing of *Dragons of Spring Dawning*: September 1985
Library of Congress Catalog Card Number: 2001097178

9 8 7 6 5 4 3 2 1

US ISBN: 0-7869-1870-5
UK ISBN: 0-7869-2840-9
620-88778-001-EN

U.S., CANADA,
ASIA, PACIFIC, & LATIN AMERICA
Wizards of the Coast, Inc.
P.O. Box 707
Renton, WA 98057-0707
+1-800-324-6496

EUROPEAN HEADQUARTERS
Wizards of the Coast, Belgium
P.B. 2031
2600 Berchem
Belgium
+32-70-23-32-77

Visit our web site at **www.wizards.com**

PROLOGUE

The story of the writing of the DRAGONLANCE Chronicles can be fully understood only in the context of the roots from which it sprang. Those roots were a role-playing game, which hit its popular stride in the late 1970s through the early 1980s. DRAGONLANCE firmly has its roots in the ADVANCED DUNGEONS & DRAGONS role-playing games.

Role-playing games are still played around the world, of course, but none has had the popularity of the ADVANCED DUNGEONS & DRAGONS. game. Such games are quite sophisticated now, but in the early 1980s, things were quite different. Role-playing games were cutting-edge entertainment, considered a little bizarre and, in some people's eyes, downright dangerous and subversive. The average age of employees at TSR—the company that produced the DUNGEONS & DRAGONS game—was only twenty-five back then. We were pioneers, frontiersmen blazing new trails and exploring new directions—or, at least, that is how we always saw ourselves.

Reality was somewhat different. We were salaried employees of a company with occasionally bewildering internal politics. We created castles, towers, dragons, and entire civilizations inside modular office cubicles, typing on Hewlett-Packard terminals linked to a mainframe. None of us had ever seen a "mouse." If it was not on the standard keyboard, it did not exist for us. We had meetings and evaluations—just like most other companies—although the subject of those meetings could occasionally get pretty strange.

Despite layoffs, firings, management purges, and salary reductions, a group of creative people came together and developed DRAGONLANCE. These years would be the best time of my professional life. They forged not only a lasting bond with Margaret, but also with everyone known and unknown who touched this new fantasy world and made a part of it their own.

To understand the first novel, then, you need a little background in the ADVANCED DUNGEONS & DRAGONS game and how DRAGONLANCE fit into it.

The DUNGEONS & DRAGONS role-playing game is a game of make-believe. It is like playing cops and robbers. We all play "let's pretend" when we are children.

D&D is a "grown-up" form of this game. It is played almost exclusively in the players' imaginations. Characters walk across imaginary landscapes, fight imaginary dragons, and deal with incredible situations in unique ways. The outcome of actions is determined by rolling dice and consulting rules.

Of course, there has to be a rule to cover each of these different situations.

That makes for a LOT of rules—thus the ADVANCED DUNGEONS & DRAGONS system.

The rules, however, only provide a framework for telling stories—not the stories themselves. As AD&D evolved, the stories that were told were laid out in what we called "modules." Game modules are little adventure settings that give players a location, setting, and characters to interact with through the rules. These modules, in the early days, were primarily underground dungeon settings that provided maze-like environments for the players' alter-ego characters to explore, fight monsters, and collect treasure.

Some of us began to wonder if we could tell an epic story inside an adventure game.

DRAGONLANCE was the first serious attempt made to do just that—produce a game entertainment around a contiguous, epic plot. The design team was excited, eager . . .

And we didn't have a clue what we were doing.

The basic plot line was split up into twelve modules, which, together, would tell a story. *Dragons of Autumn Twilight*, the first novel in the DRAGONLANCE Chronicles, was actually being written while the first four game modules were going into production. We initially thought that the book should be written to the game designs and mirror events as we portrayed them in the game.

Our first lesson: games are fun to play but do not make very good stories.

The first book in Chronicles, as I read it through again for the first time in about a decade, is a fascinating read. I can see Margaret and I wrestling with the story to serve both the game and the novels. I see just how dependent much of the text is on the game that inspired it. There are too many characters to drag through the book properly. It was our first book together and, in many ways, shows how far we have come as writers since then.

After the first book, we were freer to build on, or ignore, some of the plot lines of the game modules (and to split the adventuring party)—altogether a much more comfortable and creative way to work.

Yet despite these flaws—and perhaps because of them—the book is all the more beautiful to me. I love these characters and this place. It is wondrous to me to see them as fresh and new as when the world began.

—Tracy Hickman, Autumn 1999

ACKNOWLEDGMENTS

Thanks to the following for their contributions to this special Fifteenth Anniversary volume, *Annotated DRAGONLANCE Chronicles:*

Michael Williams
Douglas Niles
Jeff Grubb
Roger Moore
Harold Johnson
Mary Kirchoff
Jean Blashfield Black

continent of ansalon
1 palanthas
2 high clerist tower
3 kalaman
4 godshome
5 neraka
6 sanction
7 flotsam
8 solace
9 thorbardin
10 tarsis
northern ergoth
southern ergoth
qualinesti
plain
sirrion sea

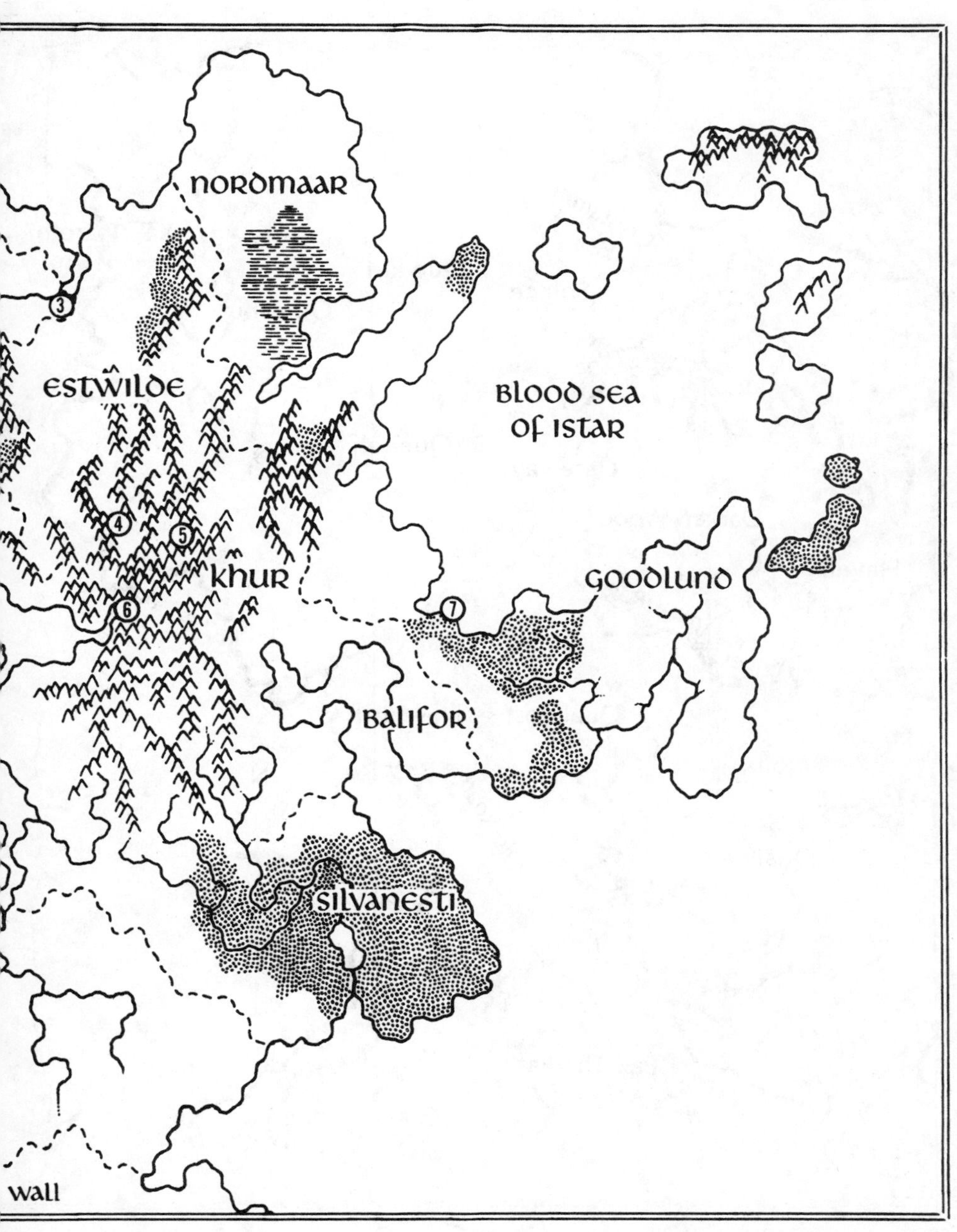
NORDMAAR
ESTWILDE
BLOOD SEA
OF ISTAR
KHUR
GOODLUND
BALIFOR
SILVANESTI
WALL
3
4
5
6
7
DIEBEL

The Lands of Abanasinia

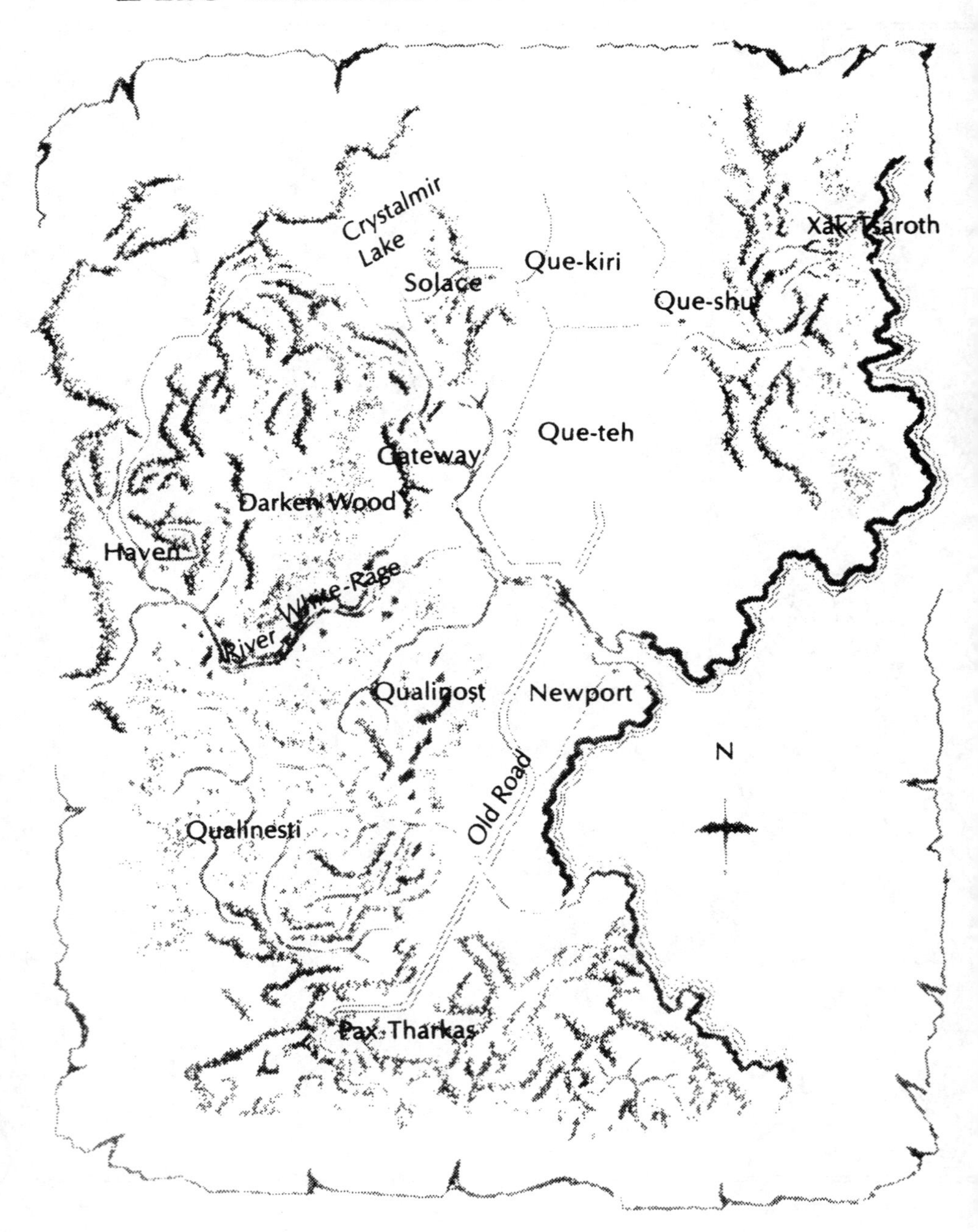

Volume I

Dragons of Autumn Twilight

DEDICATIONS

To Laura, the true Laurana
—Tracy Raye Hickman

To my children, David and Elizabeth Baldwin, for their courage and support
—Margaret Weis

When my children were little, I bribed them to leave me alone while I wrote by promising them we'd go to Disneyworld if one of my books sold well. We went to Disneyworld. David was sixteen and Lizz was thirteen, but we went. They were very patient with me. I'm so proud of both my kids.—MW

Canticle of the Dragon

Hear the sage as his song descends
like heaven's rain or tears,
and washes the years, the dust of the many stories
from the High Tale of the Dragonlance.
For in ages deep, past memory and word, in the first blush of the world
when the three moons rose from the lap of the forest,
dragons, terrible and great,
made war on this world of Krynn.

Yet out of the darkness of dragons,
out of our cries for light
in the blank face of the black moon soaring,
a banked light flared in Solamnia,
a knight of truth and of power,
who called down the gods themselves
and forged the mighty Dragonlance, piercing the soul
of dragonkind, driving the shade of their wings
from the brightening shores of Krynn.

Thus Huma, Knight of Solamnia,
Lightbringer; First Lancer;
followed his light to the foot of the Khalkist Mountains,
to the stone feet of the gods,
to the crouched silence of their temple.
He called down the Lancemakers, he took on
their unspeakable power to crush the unspeakable evil,
to thrust the coiling darkness
back down the tunnel of the dragon's throat.

Paladine, the Great God of Good,
shone at the side of Huma,
strengthening the lance of his strong right arm,
and Huma, ablaze in a thousand moons,
banished the Queen of Darkness,
banished the swarm of her shrieking hosts
back to the senseless kingdom of death, where their curses
swooped upon nothing and nothing
deep below the brightening land.

Thus ended in thunder the Age of Dreams
and began the Age of Might,
When Istar, kingdom of light and truth, arose in the east,
where minarets of white and gold

spired to the sun and to the sun's glory,
announcing the passing of evil,
and Istar, who mothered and cradled the long summers of good,
shone like a meteor
in the white skies of the just.

Yet in the fullness of sunlight
the Kingpriest of Istar saw shadows:
At night he saw the trees as things with daggers, the streams
blackened and thickened under the silent moon.
He searched books for the paths of Huma,
for scrolls, signs, and spells
so that he, too, might summon the gods, might find
their aid in his holy aims,
might purge the world of sin.

Then came the time of dark and death
as the gods turned from the world.
A mountain of fire crashed like a comet through Istar,
the city split like a skull in the flames,
mountains burst from once-fertile valleys,
seas poured into the graves of mountains,
the deserts sighed on abandoned floors of the seas,
the highways of Krynn erupted
and became the paths of the dead.

Thus began the Age of Despair.
The roads were tangled.
The winds and the sandstorms dwelt in the husks of cities.
The plains and mountains became our home.
As the old gods lost their power,
we called to the blank sky
into the cold, dividing gray to the ears of new gods.
The sky is calm, silent, unmoving.
We have yet to hear their answer.

This is what started it off—the first poem, written originally (as I recall) for an early game module. What I liked about it—and what I liked about most of the more narrative poems—was the unusual experience of having the story already known and told. As a result, my job was a fanciful, high-sounding retelling. Some people thought that the language in the narrative poem was too stylized, but that's the way bardic traditions operate: you don't write epic adventure in the language of dinner conversation.

I always liked the sixth stanza—the one about the Kingpriest.

It was, I thought, a pretty convincing description of a kind of madness.

—Michael Williams

The Old Man

The heroes' journey, a classical mythological structure, always has an older person, mentor or prophet, who sets things in motion. This grand old gentleman is part of a tradition that is older than Plato.—TRH

ika Waylan straightened her back with a sigh, flexing her shoulders to ease her cramped muscles. She tossed the soapy bar rag into the water pail and glanced around the empty room.

It was getting harder to keep up the old inn. There was a lot of love rubbed into the warm finish of the wood, but even love and tallow couldn't hide the cracks and splits in the well-used tables or prevent a customer from sitting on an occasional splinter. The Inn of the Last Home† was not fancy, not like some she'd heard about in Haven. It was comfortable. The living tree in which it was built wrapped its ancient arms around it lovingly, while the walls and fixtures were crafted around the boughs of the tree with such care as to make it impossible to tell where nature's work left off and man's began. The bar seemed to ebb and flow like a polished wave around the living wood that supported it. The stained glass in the window panes cast welcoming flashes of vibrant color across the room.

In AD&D games, inns were where everything started. It came to the point where "You are sitting around at an inn" became a cliché for starting a game.—TRH

Shadows were dwindling as noon approached. The Inn of the Last Home would soon be open for business. Tika looked around and smiled in satisfaction. The tables were clean and polished. All she had left to do was sweep the floor. She began to shove aside the heavy wooden benches, as Otik emerged from the kitchen, enveloped in fragrant steam.

"Should be another brisk day—for both the weather and business," he said, squeezing his stout body behind the bar. He began to set out mugs, whistling cheerfully.

"I'd like the business cooler and the weather warmer," said Tika, tugging at a bench. "I walked my feet off yesterday and got little thanks and less tips! Such a gloomy crowd! Everybody nervous, jumping at every sound. I dropped a mug last night and—I swear—Retark drew his sword!"

"Pah!" Otik snorted. "Retark's a Solace Seeker Guard. They're always nervous. You would be too if you had to work for Hederick, that faint—"

"Watch it," Tika warned.

Otik shrugged. "Unless the High Theocrat can fly now, he won't be listening to us. I'd hear his boots on the stairs before he could hear me." But Tika noticed he lowered his voice as he continued. "The residents of Solace won't put up with much more, mark my words. People disappearing, being dragged off to who knows where. It's a sad time." He shook his head. Then he brightened. "But it's good for business."

"Until he closes us down," Tika said gloomily. She grabbed the broom and began sweeping briskly.

"Even theocrats need to fill their bellies and wash the fire and brimstone from their throats." Otik chuckled. "It must be thirsty work, haranguing people about the New Gods day in and day out—he's in here every night."

Tika stopped her sweeping and leaned against the bar.

"Otik," she said seriously, her voice subdued. "There's other talk, too—talk of war. Armies massing in the north. And there are these strange, hooded men in town, hanging around with the High Theocrat, asking questions."

Otik looked at the nineteen-year-old girl fondly, reached out, and patted her cheek. He'd been father to her, ever since her own had vanished so mysteriously. He tweaked her red curls.

"War. Pooh." He sniffed. "There's been talk of war ever since the Cataclysm†. It's just talk, girl. Maybe the Theocrat makes it up just to keep people in line."

"I don't know," Tika frowned. "I—"

The door opened.

Both Tika and Otik started in alarm and turned to the door. They had not heard footsteps on the stairs, and that was uncanny! The Inn of the Last Home was built high in the branches of a mighty vallenwood tree, as was every other building in Solace, with the exception of the blacksmith shop. The townspeople had decided to take to the trees during the terror and chaos following the Cataclysm. And thus Solace became a tree town, one of the few truly beautiful wonders left on Krynn. Sturdy wooden bridge-walks connected the houses and businesses perched high above the ground where five hundred people went about their daily

The background history for Krynn had been plotted back in time for 3,000 years. This was due, in part, to lessons we learned after attending a seminar on J.R.R. Tolkien at Marquette University in 1983. When Aragon in the Fellowship of the Ring tells his tale about Beren and Luthien to the hobbits on Weathertop, we get a sense of the deep history of Middle Earth, as though looking at a castle on a distant hill through the mists. It is the sense of distance through time that gives the world a feeling of being real—and that these people actually come from someplace with roots.
—TRH

lives. The Inn of the Last Home was the largest building in Solace and stood forty feet off the ground. Stairs ran around the ancient vallenwood's gnarled trunk. As Otik had said, any visitor to the Inn would be heard approaching long before he was seen.

But neither Tika nor Otik had heard the old man.

He stood in the doorway, leaning on a worn oak staff, and peered around the Inn. The tattered hood of his plain, gray robe was drawn over his head, its shadow obscuring the features of his face except for his hawkish, shining eyes.

"Can I help you, Old One?" Tika asked the stranger, exchanging worried glances with Otik. Was this old man a Seeker spy?

"Eh?" The old man blinked. "You open?"

"Well . . ." Tika hesitated.

"Certainly," Otik said, smiling broadly. "Come in, Gray-beard. Tika, find our guest a chair. He must be tired after that long climb."

"Climb?" Scratching his head, the old man glanced around the porch, then looked down to the ground below. "Oh, yes. Climb. A great many stairs . . ." He hobbled inside, then made a playful swipe at Tika with his staff. "Get along with your work, girl. I'm capable of finding my own chair."

Tika shrugged, reached for her broom, and began sweeping, keeping her eyes on the old man.†

We always knew who this old man was, from the very beginning of our tale.—TRH

He stood in the center of the Inn, peering around as though confirming the location and position of each table and chair in the room. The common room was large and bean-shaped, wrapping around the trunk of the vallenwood. The tree's smaller limbs supported the floor and ceiling. He looked with particular interest at the fireplace, which stood about three-quarters of the way back into the room. The only stonework in the Inn, it was obviously crafted by dwarven hands to appear to be part of the tree, winding naturally through the branches above. A bin next to the side of the firepit was stacked high with cordwood and pine logs brought down from the high mountains. No resident of Solace would consider burning the wood of their own great trees. There was a back route out the kitchen; it was a forty-foot drop, but a few of Otik's customers found this setup very convenient. So did the old man.

He muttered satisfied comments to himself as his eyes went from one area to another. Then, to Tika's astonishment, he suddenly dropped his staff, hitched up the sleeves of his robes, and began rearranging the furniture!

Tika stopped sweeping and leaned on her broom. "What are you doing? That table's always been there!"

A long, narrow table stood in the center of the common room. The old man dragged it across the floor and shoved it up against the trunk of the huge vallenwood, right across from the firepit, then stepped back to admire his work.

"There," he grunted. "S'posed to be closer to the firepit. Now bring over two more chairs. Need six around here."

Tika turned to Otik. He seemed about to protest, but, at that moment, there was a flaring light from the kitchen. A scream from the cook indicated that the grease had caught fire again. Otik hurried toward the swinging kitchen doors.

"He's harmless," he puffed as he passed Tika. "Let him do what he wants—within reason. Maybe he's throwing a party."†

The character of this old gentleman was brought to us in part by Frank Dikos by way of Jeff Grubb. Later, Jeff would say that getting Frank and I together was like watching dueling Fizbans. Frank, by the way, is the originator and master chef behind Fizban's Fireball Chili found in Leaves from the Inn of the Last Home. *Personally, I love the stuff!—TRH*

Tika sighed and took two chairs over to the old man as requested. She set them where he indicated.

"Now," the old man said, glancing around sharply. "Bring two more chairs—comfortable ones, mind you—over here. Put them next to the firepit, in this shadowy corner."

" 'Tisn't shadowy," Tika protested. "It's sitting in full sunlight!"

"Ah"—the old man's eyes narrowed—"but it will be shadowy tonight, won't it? When the fire's lit . . ."

"I—I suppose so . . ." Tika faltered.

"Bring the chairs. That's a good girl. And I want one, right here." The old man gestured at a spot in front of the firepit. "For me."

"Are you giving a party, Old One?" Tika asked as she carried over the most comfortable, well-worn chair in the Inn.

"A party?" The thought seemed to strike the old man as funny. He chuckled. "Yes, girl. It will be a party such as the world of Krynn has not seen since before the Cataclysm! Be ready, Tika Waylan. Be ready!"

He patted her shoulder, tousled her hair, then turned and lowered himself, bones creaking, into the chair.

"A mug of ale," he ordered.

Tika went to pour the ale. It wasn't until she had brought the old man his drink and gone back to her sweeping that she stopped, wondering how he knew her name.

BOOK I

Otherwise unattributed annotations are by Jean Blashfield Black.

I

Old Friends Meet. A Rude Interruption.

And so, the first resident of Krynn we see is a goblin. Goblins are not unique to Krynn, though some say they are the Krynnish product of a joining of elves and ogres.

In AD&D, there had evolved from the rules a typical "balanced" party. The balance was found in having enough of the various skills possessed by the different character types so that you always had at least one character with the skill needed at any given time. These later evolved into archetypes of AD&D. Flint—a dwarven fighter—was one such archetype.—TRH

lint Fireforge collapsed on a moss-covered boulder. His old dwarvent bones had supported him long enough and were unwilling to continue without complaint.

"I should never have left." Flint grumbled, looking down into the valley below. He spoke aloud, though there was no sign of another living person about. Long years of solitary wandering had forced the dwarf into the habit of talking to himself. He slapped both hands on his knees. "And I'll be damned if I'm ever leaving again!" he announced vehemently.

Warmed by the afternoon sun, the boulder felt comfortable to the ancient dwarf, who had been walking all day in the chill autumn air. Flint relaxed and let the warmth seep into his bones—the

warmth of the sun and the warmth of his thoughts. Because he was home.

He looked around him, his eyes lingering fondly over the familiar landscape. The mountainside below him formed one side of a high mountain bowl carpeted in autumn splendor. The vallenwood trees in the valley were ablaze in the season's colors, the brilliant reds and golds fading into the purple of the Kharolis peaks beyond. The flawless, azure sky among the trees was repeated in the waters of Crystalmir Lake. Thin columns of smoke curled among the treetops, the only sign of the presence of Solace. A soft, spreading haze blanketed the vale with the sweet aroma of home fires burning.

As Flint sat and rested, he pulled a block of wood and a gleaming dagger from his pack, his hands moving without conscious thought. Since time uncounted, his people had always had the need to shape the shapeless to their liking.† He himself had been a metalsmith of some renown before his retirement some years earlier. He put the knife to the wood, then, his attention caught, Flint's hands remained idle as he watched the smoke drift up from the hidden chimneys below.

Being good with his hands is a dwarven stereotype. —TRH

"My own home fire's gone out," Flint said softly. He shook himself, angry at feeling sentimental, and began slicing at the wood with a vengeance. He grumbled loudly, "My house has been sitting empty. Roof probably leaked, ruined the furniture. Stupid quest. Silliest thing I ever did. After one hundred and forty-eight years, I ought to have learned!"†

Dwarves on Krynn may live to be 450 years old.

"You'll never learn, dwarf," a distant voice answered him. "Not if you live to be *two* hundred and forty-eight!"

Dropping the wood, the dwarf's hand moved with calm assurance from the dagger to the handle of his axe as he peered down the path. The voice sounded familiar, the first familiar voice he'd heard in a long time. But he couldn't place it.

Flint squinted into the setting sun. He thought he saw the figure of a man striding up the path. Standing, Flint drew back into the shadow of a tall pine to see better. The man's walk was marked by an easy grace—an elvish grace, Flint would have said; yet the man's body had the thickness and tight muscles of a human, while the facial hair was definitely

humankind's. All the dwarf could see of the man's face beneath a green hood was tan skin and a brownish-red beard. A longbow was slung over one shoulder and a sword hung at his left side. He was dressed in soft leather, carefully tooled in the intricate designs the elves loved. But no elf in the world of Krynn could grow a beard . . . no elf, but . . .

Our main character takes the stage. Margaret had some initial trouble with the character, but we soon worked it out, as you shall see later on.—TRH

"Tanis?"† said Flint hesitantly as the man neared.

"The same." The newcomer's bearded face split in a wide grin. He held open his arms and, before the dwarf could stop him, engulfed Flint in a hug that lifted him off the ground. The dwarf clasped his old friend close for a brief instant, then, remembering his dignity, squirmed and freed himself from the half-elf's embrace.

"Well, you've learned no manners in five years," the dwarf grumbled. "Still no respect for my age or my station. Hoisting me around like a sack of potatoes." Flint peered down the road. "I hope no one who knows us saw us."

"I doubt there are many who'd remember us," Tanis said, his eyes studying his stocky friend fondly. "Time doesn't pass for you and me, old dwarf, as it does for humans. Five years is a long time for them, a few moments for us." Then he smiled. "You haven't changed."

"The same can't be said of others." Flint sat back down on the stone and began to carve once more. He scowled up at Tanis. "Why the beard? You were ugly enough."

Tanis scratched his chin. "I have been in lands that were not friendly to those of elven blood. The beard—a gift from my human father," he said with bitter irony, "did much to hide my heritage."†

Tanis is, of course, another AD&D archetype: a half-elf warrior.—TRH

Flint grunted. He knew that wasn't the complete truth. Although the half-elf abhorred killing, Tanis would not be one to hide from a fight behind a beard. Wood chips flew.

"I have been in lands that were not friendly to anyone of any kind of blood."† Flint turned the wood in his hand, examining it. "But we're home now. All that's behind us."

The backstory here gives life and direction to the characters.—TRH

"Not from what I've heard," Tanis said, drawing his hood up over his face again to keep the sun out of his eyes. "The Highseekers in Haven appointed a man named Hederick to govern as High Theocrat in

Solace, and he's turned the town into a hotbed of fanaticism with his new religion."

Tanis and the dwarf both turned and looked down into the quiet valley. Lights began to wink on, making the homes in the trees visible among the vallenwood. The night air was still and calm and sweet, tinged with the smell of wood smoke from the home fires. Now and again they could hear the faint sound of a mother calling her children to dinner.

"I've heard of no evil in Solace," Flint said quietly.

"Religious persecution . . . inquisitions . . ." Tanis's voice sounded ominous coming from the depths of his hood. It was deeper, more somber than Flint remembered. The dwarf frowned. His friend had changed in five years. And elves never change! But then Tanis was only half-elven, a child of violence, his mother having been raped by a human warrior† during one of the many wars that had divided the different races of Krynn in the chaotic years following the Cataclysm.

Novels, unlike games, require proper foundation for their characters. It is not enough for us to simply say that Tanis is a half-elf; we must know why. In justifying his status, Margaret and I were led to a deeper understanding of Tanis's character, making him someone of greater depth than we knew before. —TRH

"Inquisitions! That's only for those who defy the new High Theocrat, according to rumor." Flint snorted. "I don't believe in the Seeker gods—never did—but I don't parade my beliefs in the street. Keep quiet and they'll let you alone, that's my motto. The Highseekers in Haven are still wise and virtuous men. It's just this one rotten apple in Solace that's spoiling the whole barrel. By the way, did you find what you sought?"

"Some sign of the ancient, true gods?" Tanis asked. "Or peace of mind? I went seeking both. Which did you mean?"

"Well, I assume one would go with the other," Flint growled. He turned the piece of wood in his hands, still not satisfied with its proportions. "Are we going to stand here all night, smelling the cooking fires? Or are we going to go into town and get some dinner?"

"Go." Tanis waved. The two started down the path together, Tanis's long strides forcing the dwarf to take two steps to his one. Though it had been many years since they had journeyed together, Tanis unconsciously slowed his pace, while Flint unconsciously quickened his.

"So you found nothing?" Flint pursued.

"Nothing," Tanis replied. "As we discovered long ago, the only clerics and priests in this world serve false gods. I heard tales of healing, but it was all trickery and magic. Fortunately, our friend Raistlin taught me what to watch—"

Another AD&D archetype joins the party: a magic-user.—TRH

"Raistlin!" Flint puffed. "That pasty-faced, skinny magician.† He's more than half charlatan himself. Always sniveling and whining and poking his nose where it doesn't belong. If it weren't for his twin brother looking after him, someone would've put an end to his magic long ago."

Tanis was glad his beard hid his smile. "I think the young man was a better magician than you give him credit for," he said. "And, you must admit, he worked long and tirelessly to help those who were taken in by the fake clerics—as I did." He sighed.

"For which you got little thanks, no doubt," the dwarf muttered.

"Very little," Tanis said. "People want to believe in something—even if, deep inside, they know it is false. But what of you? How was your journey to your homelands?"

Flint stumped along without answering, his face grim. Finally he muttered, "I should never have gone," and glanced up at Tanis, his eyes, barely visible through the thick, over-hanging, white eyebrows—informing the half-elf that this turn of the conversation was not welcome. Tanis saw the look but asked his questions anyhow.

"What of the dwarven clerics? The stories we heard?"

"Not true. The clerics vanished three hundred years ago during the Cataclysm. So say the elders."

"Much like the elves," Tanis mused.

"I saw—"

"Hsst!" Tanis held out a warning hand.

Flint came to a dead stop. "What?" he whispered.

Tanis motioned. "Over in that grove."

Flint peered toward the trees, at the same time reaching for the battle-axe that was strapped behind his back.

The red rays of the setting sun glistened briefly on a piece of metal flashing among the trees. Tanis saw it once, lost it, then saw it again. At that moment, though, the sun sank, leaving the sky

glowing a rich violet, and causing night's shadows to creep through the forest trees.

Flint squinted into the gloom. "I don't see anything."

"I did," Tanis said. He kept staring at the place where he'd seen the metal, and gradually his elven-sight began to detect the warm red aura cast by all living beings but visible only to the elves. "Who goes there?" Tanis called.

The only answer for long moments was an eerie sound that made the hair rise on the half-elf's neck. It was a hollow, whirring sound that started out low, then grew higher and higher and eventually attained a high-pitched, screaming whine. Soaring with it, came a voice.

"Elven wanderer, turn from your course and leave the dwarf behind. We are the spirits of those poor souls Flint Fireforge left on the barroom floor. Did we die in combat?"

The spirit voice soared to new heights, as did the whining, whirring sound accompanying it.

"No! We died of shame, cursed by the ghost of the grape for not being able to outdrink a hill dwarf."

Flint's beard was quivering with rage, and Tanis, bursting out laughing, was forced to grab the angry dwarf's shoulder to keep him from charging headlong into the brush.

"Damn the eyes of the elves!" The spectral voice turned merry. "And damn the beards of the dwarves!"

"Wouldn't you know it?" Flint groaned. "Tasslehoff Burrfoot!"†

There was a faint rustle in the underbrush, then a small figure stood on the path. It was a kender,† one of a race of people considered by many on Krynn to be as much a nuisance as mosquitoes. Small-boned, the kender rarely grew over four feet tall. This particular kender was about Flint's height, but his slight build and perpetually childlike face made him seem smaller. He wore bright blue leggings that stood out in sharp contrast to his furred vest and plain, home-spun tunic. His brown eyes glinted with mischief and fun; his smile seemed to reach to the tips of his pointed ears. He dipped his head in a mock bow, allowing a long tassel of brown hair—his pride and joy—to flip forward over his nose. Then

All AD&D game groups needed a "thief-class" character to perform various abilities and skills unique to them during the course of a game. Still, I was troubled by the idea of a race of thieves. My sole contribution to Tas and his kenderkind was their inveterate curiosity and their innocent tendency to "borrow" things for indeterminate periods of time. It was in part from this admittedly very broad concept that Roger Moore brought life to the character in his short story, "A Stone's Throw Away," in Dragon *Magazine—and launched one of our favorite characters forever onto the face of Krynn.—TRH*

he straightened up, laughing. The metallic gleam Tanis's quick eyes had spotted came from the buckle of one of the numerous packs strapped around his shoulders and waist.

Tas grinned up at them, leaning on his hoopak staff. It was this staff that had created the eerie noise. Tanis should have recognized it at once, having seen the kender† scare off many would-be attackers by whirling his staff in the air, producing that screaming whine. A kender invention, the hoopak's bottom end was copper-clad and sharply pointed; the top end was forked and held a leather sling. The staff itself was made out of a single piece of supple willow wood. Although scorned by every other race on Krynn, the hoopak was more than a useful tool or weapon to a kender—it was his symbol. "New roads demand a hoopak," was a popular saying among kenderkind. It was always followed immediately by another of their sayings: "No road is ever old."

"Kender" was originally spelled "Kinder" after the legendary "kinderkin," but it was pointed out that on the page it read more like someone who was "more kind" than referring to a unique race.—TRH

Tasslehoff suddenly ran forward, his arms open wide.

"Flint!" The kender threw his arms around the dwarf and hugged him. Flint, embarrassed, returned the embrace reluctantly, then quickly stepped back. Tasslehoff grinned, then looked up at the half-elf.

"Who's this?" He gasped. "Tanis! I didn't recognize you with a beard!" He held out his short arms.

"No, thanks," said Tanis, grinning. He waved the kender away. "I want to keep my money pouch."

With a sudden look of alarm, Flint felt under his tunic. "You rascal!" He roared and leaped at the kender, who was doubled over, laughing. The two went down in the dust.

Tanis, chuckling, started to pull Flint off the kender. Then he stopped and turned in alarm. Too late, he heard the silvery jingle of harness and bridle and the whinny of a horse. The half-elf put his hand on the hilt of his sword, but he had already lost any advantage he might have gained through alertness.

Swearing under his breath, Tanis could do nothing but stand and stare at the figure emerging from the shadows. It was seated on a small, furry-legged pony that walked with its head down as if it were ashamed of its rider. Gray, mottled skin sagged into

I wouldn't say that Tracy hated halflings as much as he was uncomfortable with what the halfling was in most of our fantasy at the time. They were tubby homebodies, stout-hearted but fearful, more at home in pastoral England than the post-apocalyptic domain of Ansalon.

The new kender were wilder than halflings, fearless, sometimes as cruel as only children can be (which became the taunt). They were savage, warrior children, ever-curious, ever alert.

But even the best-laid plans go awry, and in DRAGONLANCE*, that took the form of Janet Pack, who, in the course of dramatic readings, defined the nature of the kender and added something not initially anticipated. She, and as a result all kender since her, was cute. Extremely cute. Sweetly, lovably, frustratingly cute. And as a result, Tas and the rest of his kind are brave, fearless, taunting, and cute. And it's hard, after seeing Janet play Tas, to imagine them any other way.—Jeff Grubb*

folds about the rider's face. Two pig-pink eyes stared out at them from beneath a military-looking helmet. Its fat, flabby body leaked out between pieces of flashy, pretentious armor.

A peculiar odor hit Tanis, and he wrinkled his nose in disgust. "Hobgoblin!" his brain registered. He loosened his sword and kicked at Flint, but at that moment the dwarf gave a tremendous sneeze and sat up on the kender.

"Horse!" said Flint, sneezing again.

"Behind you," Tanis replied quietly.

Flint, hearing the warning note in his friend's voice, scrambled to his feet. Tasslehoff quickly did the same.

The hobgoblin sat astride the pony, watching them with a sneering, supercilious look on his flat face. His pink eyes reflected the last lingering traces of sunlight.

"You see, boys," the hobgoblin stated, speaking the Common tongue with a thick accent, "what fools we are dealing with here in Solace."

There was gritty laughter from the trees behind the hobgoblin. Five goblin guards, dressed in crude uniforms, came out on foot. They took up positions on either side of their leader's horse.

"Now . . ." The hobgoblin leaned over his saddle. Tanis watched with a kind of horrible fascination as the creature's huge belly completely engulfed the pommel. "I am Fewmaster† Toede, leader of the forces that are keeping Solace protected from undesirable elements. You have no right to be walking in the city limits after dark. You are under arrest." Fewmaster Toede leaned down to speak to a goblin near him. "Bring me the blue crystal staff, if you find it on them," he said in the croaking goblin tongue. Tanis, Flint, and Tasslehoff all looked at each other questioningly. Each of them could speak some goblin, Tas better than the others. Had they heard right? A blue crystal staff?

As in "Toadie." Only a hobgoblin would relish a title like "Fewmaster." —TRH

"If they resist," added Fewmaster Toede, switching back to Common for grand effect, "kill them."

With that, he yanked on the reins, flicked his mount with a riding crop, and galloped off down the path toward town.

"Goblins! In Solace! This new Theocrat has much to answer for!" Flint spat. Reaching up, he swung his battle-axe from its holder on his back and planted his feet firmly on the path, rocking back and forth until he felt himself balanced. "Very well," he announced. "Come on."

"I advise you to retreat," Tanis said, throwing his cloak over one shoulder and drawing his sword. "We have had a long journey. We are hungry and tired and late for a meeting with friends we have not seen in a long time. We have no intention of being arrested."

"Or of being killed," added Tasslehoff. He had drawn no weapon but stood staring at the goblins with interest.

A bit taken aback, the goblins glanced at each other nervously. One cast a baleful look down the road where his leader had vanished. The goblins were accustomed to bullying peddlers and farmers traveling to the small town, not to challenging armed and obviously skilled fighters. But their hatred of the other races of Krynn was long-standing. They drew their long, curved blades.

Flint strode forward, his hands getting a firm grip on the axe handle. "There's only one creature I hate worse than a gully dwarf," he muttered, "and that's a goblin!"

The goblin dove at Flint, hoping to knock him down. Flint swung his axe with deadly accuracy and timing. A goblin head rolled into the dust, the body crashing to the ground.

"What are you slime doing in Solace?" Tanis asked, meeting the clumsy stab of another goblin skillfully. Their swords crossed and held for a moment, then Tanis shoved the goblin backward. "Do you work for the High Theocrat?"

"Theocrat? "The goblin gurgled with laughter. Swinging its weapon wildly, it ran at Tanis. "That fool? Our Fewmaster works for the—ugh!" The creature impaled itself on Tanis's sword. It groaned, then slid off onto the ground.

"Damn!" Tanis swore and stared at the dead goblin in frustration. "The clumsy idiot! I didn't want to kill it, just find out who hired it."

"You'll find out who hired us, sooner than you'd like!" snarled another goblin, rushing at the distracted half-elf. Tanis turned quickly and disarmed the creature. He kicked it in its stomach and the goblin crumpled over.

Another goblin sprang at Flint before the dwarf had time to recover from his lethal swing. He staggered backward, trying to regain his balance.

Then Tasslehoff's shrill voice rang out. "These scum will fight for anyone, Tanis. Throw them some dog meat once in a while and they're yours forev—"

"Dog meat!" The goblin croaked and turned from Flint in a rage. "How about kender meat, you little squeaker!" The goblin flapped toward the apparently unarmed kender, its purplish red hands grasping for his neck. Tas, without ever losing the innocent, childlike expression on his face, reached into his fleecy vest, whipped out a dagger, and threw it—all in one motion. The goblin clutched his chest and fell with a groan. There was a sound of flapping feet as the remaining goblin fled. The battle was over.

Tanis sheathed his sword, grimacing in disgust at the stinking bodies; the smell reminded him of rotting fish. Flint wiped black goblin blood from his axe blade. Tas stared mournfully at the body of the goblin he killed. It had fallen facedown, his dagger buried underneath.

"I'll get it for you," Tanis offered, preparing to roll the body over.

"No." Tas made a face. "I don't want it back. You can never get rid of the smell, you know."

Tanis nodded. Flint fastened his axe in its carrier again, and the three continued on down the path.

The lights of Solace grew brighter as darkness deepened. The smell of the wood smoke on the chill night air brought thoughts of food and warmth—and safety. The companions hurried their steps. They did not speak for a long time, each hearing Flint's words echo in his mind: Goblins. In Solace.

Finally, however, the irrepressible kender giggled. "Besides," he said, "that dagger was Flint's!"†

I love how the nature of their relationship is established from the very beginning.—TRH

2

Return to the Inn.
A shock. The oath is broken.

I always loved treehouses as a boy.—TRH

Nearly everyone in Solace managed to drop into the Inn of the Last Home sometime during the evening hours these days. People felt safer in crowds.

Solace had long been a crossroads for travelers. They came northeast from Haven, the Seeker capital.† They came from the elven kingdom of Qualinesti to the south. Sometimes they came from the east, across the barren Plains of Abanasinia. Throughout the civilized world, the Inn of the Last Home was known as a traveler's refuge and center for news. It was to the Inn that the three friends turned their steps.

Our background design work shows through: Trade established the location of Solace in the past.—TRH

The huge, convoluted trunk rose through the surrounding trees. Against the shadow of the vallenwood, the colored panes of the Inn's stained-glass

windows glittered brightly, and sounds of life drifted down from the windows. Lanterns, hanging from the tree limbs, lit the winding stairway. Though the autumn night was settling chill amid the vallenwoods† of Solace, the travelers felt the companionship and memories warm the soul and wash away the aches and sorrows of the road.

In the original design, these were called 'Fallenwoods'—but the name didn't sound very sturdy.—TRH

The Inn was so crowded on this night that the three were continually forced to stand aside on the stairs to let men, women, and children pass them. Tanis noticed that people glanced at him and his companions with suspicion—not with the welcoming looks they would have given five years ago.

Tanis's face grew grim. This was not the homecoming he had dreamed about. Never in the fifty years† he had lived in Solace had he felt such tension. The rumors he had heard about the malignant corruption of the Seekers must be true.

Elves on Krynn can easily live 150 years, so Tanis is a young man.

Five years ago, the men calling themselves "seekers" ("we seek the new gods") had been a loose-knit organization of clerics practicing their new religion in the towns of Haven, Solace, and Gateway. These clerics had been misguided, Tanis believed, but at least they had been honest and sincere. In the intervening years, however, the clerics had gained more and more status as their religion flourished. Soon they became concerned not so much with glory in the afterlife as with power on Krynn.† They took over the governing of the towns with the people's blessing.

The name "Krynn" is from my sister-in-law Corinne. It sounded good at the time. Tracy, in most of his early writings, tended to use "Ansalon," the name of the continent, as opposed to the name of the world.—Jeff Grubb

A touch on Tanis's arm interrupted his thoughts. He turned and saw Flint silently pointing below. Looking down, Tanis saw guards marching past, walking in parties of four. Armed to the teeth, they strutted with an air of self-importance.

"At least they're human—not goblin," Tas said.

"That goblin sneered when I mentioned the High Theocrat," Tanis mused. "As if they were working for someone else. I wonder what's going on."

"Maybe our friends will know," Flint said.

"If they're here," Tasslehoff added. "A lot could have happened in five years."

"They'll be here—if they're alive," Flint added in an undertone. "It was a sacred oath we took—to meet again after five years had passed and report what we had found out about the evil spreading in

the world. To think we should come home and find evil on our very doorsteps!"

"Hush! Shhh!" Several passersby looked so alarmed at the dwarf's words that Tanis shook his head.

"Better not talk about it here," the half-elf advised.

Reaching the top of the stairs, Tas flung the door open wide. A wave of light, noise, heat, and the familiar smell of Otik's spicy potatoes hit them full in the face. It engulfed them and washed over them soothingly. Otik, standing behind the bar as they always remembered him, hadn't changed, except maybe to grow stouter. The Inn didn't appear to have changed either, except to grow more comfortable.

Tasslehoff, his quick kender eyes sweeping the crowd, gave a yell and pointed across the room. Something else hadn't changed either—the firelight gleaming on a brightly polished, winged dragon helm.

"Who is it?" asked Flint, straining to see.

"Caramon," Tanis replied.

"Then Raistlin'll be here, too," Flint said without a great deal of warmth in his voice.

Tasslehoff was already sliding through the muttering knots of people, his small, lithe body barely noticed by those he passed. Tanis hoped fervently the kender wasn't "acquiring" any objects from the Inn's customers. Not that he stole things—Tasslehoff would have been deeply hurt if anyone had accused him of theft. But the kender had an insatiable curiosity, and various interesting items belonging to other people had a way of falling into Tas's possession. The last thing Tanis wanted tonight was trouble. He made a mental note to have a private word with the kender.

The half-elf and the dwarf made their way through the crowd with less ease than their little friend. Nearly every chair was taken, every table filled. Those who could not find room to sit down were standing, talking in low voices. People looked at Tanis and Flint darkly, suspiciously, or curiously. No one greeted Flint, although there were several who had been long-standing customers of the dwarven metalsmith. The people of Solace had their

own problems, and it was apparent that Tanis and Flint were now considered outsiders.

A roar sounded from across the room, from the table where the dragon helm lay reflecting light from the firepit. Tanis's grim face relaxed into a smile as he saw the giant Caramon† lift little Tas off the floor in a bear hug.

Here is our hulking brawn-over-brains fighter archetype. The party is filling out nicely, isn't it?—TRH

Flint, wading through a sea of belt buckles, could only imagine the sight as he listened to Caramon's booming voice answering Tasslehoff's piping greeting. "Caramon better look to his purse," Flint grumbled. "Or count his teeth."

The dwarf and the half-elf finally broke through the press of people in front of the long bar. The table where Caramon sat was shoved back against the tree trunk. In fact, it was sitting in an odd position. Tanis wondered why Otik had moved it when everything else remained exactly the same. But the thought was crushed out of him, for it was his turn to receive the big warrior's affectionate greeting. Tanis hastily removed the longbow and quiver of arrows from his back before Caramon hugged them into kindling.

"My friend!" Caramon's eyes were wet. He seemed about to say more but was overcome by emotion. Tanis was also momentarily unable to talk, but this was because he'd had his breath squeezed out of him by Caramon's muscular arms.

"Where's Raistlin?"† he asked when he could talk. The twins were never far apart.

I think it was Harold Johnson who gave the brothers their names. He saw them as being the thin, wimpy mage and the burly fighter. Raistlin descended from "Wasting Man" while Caramon from "Caring Man." As the early adventures were playtested, Kate Novak was the first Caramon, but that role was soon picked up by Mike Williams, who brought a lot of Caramon's personality to the surface.—Jeff Grubb

"There." Caramon nodded toward the end of the table. Then he frowned. "He's changed," the warrior warned Tanis.

The half-elf looked into a corner formed by an irregularity of the vallenwood tree. The corner was shrouded in shadow, and for a moment he couldn't see anything after the glare of the firelight. Then he saw a slight figure sitting huddled in red robes, even in the heat of the nearby fire. The figure had a hood cast over its face.

Tanis felt a sudden reluctance to speak to the young mage alone, but Tasslehoff had flitted away to find the barmaid and Flint was being lifted off his feet by Caramon. Tanis moved to the end of the table.

"Raistlin?" he said, feeling a strange sense of foreboding.

We played the first module of the DRAGONLANCE *series as I was writing it, occasionally convening in our apartment after work. On the evening we were playing through this module, Margaret and several other work associates and friends had come over to join us. My friend, Terry Phillips, took the Raistlin character—only roughly defined at that time. When I first turned to him to ask him a question, he answered me in character—with a rasping, whispered voice filled with cynicism. I was stunned by his portrayal. Margaret, to this day, maintains that Terry actually wore black robes to that session. In that game that night, Raistlin as we know him today, was born. Thanks, Terry.—TRH*

What I noticed most was that while everyone else was shouting and clamoring to be heard, we all shut up whenever Terry spoke in that strange whisper. Which is why I added it to Raistlin's character. I'm not sure to this day if Raistlin really did have to whisper—I think not—but he knew it would draw attention. —MW

The robed figure† looked up. "Tanis?" the man whispered as he slowly pulled the hood off his head.

The half-elf sucked in his breath and fell back a pace. He stared in horror.

The face that turned toward him from the shadows was a face out of a nightmare. Changed, Caramon had said! Tanis shuddered. "Changed" wasn't the word! The mage's white skin had turned a golden color. It glistened in the firelight with a faintly metallic quality, looking like a gruesome mask. The flesh had melted from the face, leaving the cheekbones outlined in dreadful shadows. The lips were pulled tight in a dark straight line. But it was the man's eyes that arrested Tanis and held him pinned in their terrible gaze. For the eyes were no longer the eyes of any living human Tanis had ever seen. The black pupils were now the shape of hourglasses! The pale blue irises Tanis remembered now glittered gold!

"I see my appearance startles you," Raistlin whispered. There was a faint suggestion of a smile on his thin lips.

Sitting down across from the young man, Tanis swallowed. "In the name of the true gods, Raistlin—"

Flint plopped into a seat next to Tanis. "I've been hoisted into the air more times today than—*Reorx!*" Flint's eyes widened. "What evil's at work here? Are you cursed?" The dwarf gasped, staring at Raistlin.

Caramon took a seat next to his brother. He picked up his mug of ale and glanced at Raistlin. "Will you tell them, Raist?" he said in a low voice.

"Yes," Raistlin said, drawing the word out into a hiss that made Tanis shiver. The young man spoke in a soft, wheezing voice, barely above a whisper, as if it were all he could do to force the words out of his body. His long, nervous hands, which were the same golden color as his face, toyed absently with uneaten food on a plate before him.

"Do you remember when we parted five years ago?" Raistlin began. "My brother and I planned a journey so secret I could not even tell you, my dear friends, where we were going."

There was a faint note of sarcasm in the gentle voice. Tanis bit his lip. Raistlin had never, in his entire life, had any "dear friends."

"I had been selected by Par-Salian, the head of my order, to take the Test,"† Raistlin continued.

"The Test!" Tanis repeated, stunned. "But you were too young. What, twenty? The Test is given only to mages who have studied years and years—"

The Test in the Tower of High Sorcery set the world of Krynn apart from other AD&D worlds.—TRH

"You can imagine my pride," Raistlin said coldly, irritated at the interruption—"My brother and I traveled to the secret place, the fabled Towers of High Sorcery. And there I passed the Test." The mage's voice sank. "And there I nearly died!"

Caramon choked, obviously in the grip of some strong emotion. "It was awful," the big man began, his voice shaking. "I found him in that horrible place, blood flowing from his mouth, dying! I picked him up and—"

"Enough, brother!" Raistlin's soft voice flicked like a whip. Caramon flinched. Tanis saw the young mage's golden eyes narrow, the thin hands clench. Caramon fell silent and gulped down his ale, glancing nervously at his brother. There was clearly a new strain, a tension between the twins.

Raistlin drew a deep breath and continued. "When I awoke," the mage said, "my skin had turned this color—a mark of my suffering. My body and my health are irretrievably shattered. And my eyes! I see through hourglass pupils and therefore I see time, as it affects all things. Even as I look at you now, Tanis," the mage whispered, "I see you dying, slowly, by inches. And so I see every living thing."

Raistlin's thin, clawlike hand gripped Tanis's arm. The half-elf shivered at the cold touch and started to pull away, but the golden eyes and the cold hand held him fast.

The mage leaned forward, his eyes glowing feverishly. "But I have power now!" he whispered. "Par-Salian told me the day would come when my strength would shape the world! I have power and"—he gestured—"the Staff of Magius."

Tanis looked to see a staff leaning against the vallenwood trunk within easy reach of Raistlin's hand. It was a plain wooden staff. A ball of bright crystal, clutched in a disembodied golden claw carved to resemble the talon of a dragon, gleamed at the top.

"Was it worth it?" Tanis asked quietly.

Raistlin stared at him, then his lips parted in a caricature of a grin. He withdrew his hand from Tanis's arm and folded his arms in the sleeves of his robe. "Of course!" the mage hissed. "Power is what I have long sought—and still seek."† He leaned back and his thin figure melted into the dark shadow until all Tanis could see were the golden eyes, glittering in the firelight.

Here, then, is the essence of Raistlin—then and now.—TRH

"Ale," said Flint, clearing his throat and licking his lips as if he would wash a bad taste out of his mouth. "Where is that kender? I suppose he stole the barmaid—"

"Here we are," cried Tas's cheerful voice. A tall, young, red-haired girl loomed behind him, carrying a tray of mugs.

Caramon grinned. "Now, Tanis," he boomed, "guess who this is. You, too, Flint. If you win, I'll buy this round."

Glad to take his mind off Raistlin's dark tale, Tanis stared at the laughing girl. Red hair curled around her face, her green eyes danced with fun, freckles were lightly smattered across her nose and cheeks. Tanis seemed to remember the eyes, but beyond that he was blank.

"I give up," he said. "But then, to elves humans seem to change so rapidly that we lose track. I am one hundred and two, yet seem no more than thirty to you. And to me those hundred years seem as thirty. This young woman must have been a child when we left."

"I was fourteen." The girl laughed and set the tray down on the table. "And Caramon used to say I was so ugly my father would have to pay someone to marry me."

"Tika!"† Flint slammed his fist on the table. "You're buying, you great oaf!" He pointed at Caramon.

Tika was here to provide us with a female warrior for the party. Ranks are filling up now!—TRH

"No fair!" The giant laughed. "She gave you a clue."

"Well, the years have proved him wrong," Tanis said, smiling. "I've traveled many roads and you're one of the prettiest girls I've seen on Krynn."

Tika blushed with pleasure. Then her face darkened. "By the way, Tanis"—she reached in her pocket and drew forth a cylindrical object—"this arrived for you today. Under strange circumstances."

Tanis frowned and reached for the object. It was a small scrollcase made of black, highly polished wood. He slowly removed a thin piece of parchment and unrolled it. His heart thudded painfully at the sight of the bold, black handwriting.

"It's from Kitiara," he said finally, knowing his voice sounded strained and unnatural. "She's not coming."

There was a moment's silence. "That's done it," Flint said. "The circle is broken, the oath denied. Bad luck." He shook his head. "Bad luck."

An early version of the dwarf called him Flint Fieryforge and made him a rather dapper Falstaff-type character.

Flint's name was created from pure cloth. There is no connection between our Flint and the former President of TSR's younger brother with the same name. Our Flint was first.—Jeff Grubb

3

Knight of Solamnia.
The old man's party.

Raistlin leaned forward. He and Caramon exchanged glances as thoughts passed wordlessly between them. It was a rare moment, for only great personal difficulty or danger ever made the twins' close kinship apparent. Kitiara was their older half-sister.

"Kitiara would not break her oath unless another, stronger oath bound her." Raistlin spoke their thoughts aloud.

"What does she say?" Caramon asked.

Tanis hesitated, then licked his dry lips. "Her duties with her new lord keep her busy. She sends her regrets and best wishes to all of us and her love—" Tanis felt his throat constrict. He coughed. "Her love to her brothers and to—" He paused, then rolled up the parchment. "That's all."

"Love to who?" Tasslehoff asked brightly. "Ouch!" He glared at Flint who had trod upon his foot. The kender saw Tanis flush. "Oh," he said, feeling stupid.

"Do you know who she means?" Tanis asked the brothers. "What new lord does she talk about?"

"Who knows with Kitiara?"† Raistlin shrugged his thin shoulders. "The last time we saw her was here, in the Inn, five years ago. She was going north with Sturm. We have not heard from her since. As for the new lord, I'd say we now know why she broke her oath to us: she has sworn allegiance to another. She is, after all, a mercenary."

Kitiara is named after my wife, Kate—and there the similarity between the two ends. Really!—Jeff Grubb

"Yes," Tanis admitted. He slipped the scroll back into its case and looked up at Tika. "You say this arrived under strange circumstances? Tell me."

"A man brought it in, late this morning. At least I think it was a man." Tika shivered. "He was wrapped head to foot in clothing of every description. I couldn't even see his face. His voice was hissinglike and he spoke with a strange accent. 'Deliver this to one Tanis Half-Elven,' he said. I told him you weren't here and hadn't been here for several years. 'He will be,' the man said. Then he left." Tika shrugged. "That's all I can tell you. The old man over there saw him." She gestured to an old man sitting in a chair before the fire. "You might ask him if he noticed anything else."

Tanis turned to look at an old man who was telling stories to a dreamy-eyed child staring into the flames. Flint touched his arm.

"Here comes one who can tell you more," the dwarf said.

"Sturm!"† Tanis said warmly, turning toward the door.

Sturm is, in many ways, my favorite character. He represents everything I want to be. As for his archetype place in the party, he is the obligatory Paladin.—TRH

Everyone except Raistlin turned. The mage relapsed into the shadows once more.

At the door stood a straight-backed figure dressed in full plate armor and chain mail, the symbol of the Order of the Rose on the breastplate. A great many people in the Inn turned to stare, scowling. The man was a Solamnic knight, and the Knights of Solamnia had fallen into ill-repute up north. Rumors of their corruption had spread even this far south. The few who recognized Sturm as a long-time former resident of Solace shrugged and turned back to their

drinking. Those who did not, continued to stare. In these days of peace, it was unusual enough to see a knight in full armor enter the Inn. But it was still more unusual to see a knight in full armor that dated back practically to the Cataclysm!†

Additional description that didn't make the final cut: "Sturm's tooled breastplate mirrored the room in its highly polished, well-kept finish. Yet despite the obvious care given the armor, its edges were worn and nicked. The chain mail showed signs of having been often reworked. It seemed, in fact, as if Sturm must have stepped out of a display in the Solamnic emperor's legendary museum—if either the emperor or his museum still existed."

Sturm received the stares as accolades due his rank. He carefully smoothed his great, thick moustaches, which, being the ages-old symbol of the Knights, were as obsolete as his armor. He bore the trappings of the Solamnic Knights with unquestioned pride, and he had the sword-arm and the skill to defend that pride. Although people in the Inn stared, no one, after one look at the knight's calm, cold eyes, dared snicker or make a derogatory comment.

The knight held the door open for a tall man and a woman heavily cloaked in furs. The woman must have spoken a word of thanks to Sturm, for he bowed to her in a courtly, old-fashioned manner long dead in the modern world.

"Look at that." Caramon shook his head in admiration. "The gallant knight helps the lady fair. I wonder where he dragged up those two?"

"They're barbarians from the Plains," said Tas, standing on a chair, waving his arms to his friend. "That's the dress of the Qué-Shu tribe."†

Tas's parents—inveterate wanderers—had lived near the Qué-shu for a while. "Until they were run off," insists Flint.

Apparently the two Plainsmen declined any offer Sturm made, for the knight bowed again and left them. He walked across the crowded Inn with a proud and noble air, such as he might have worn walking forward to be knighted by the king.

Tanis rose to his feet. Sturm came to him first and threw his arms around his friend. Tanis gripped him tightly, feeling the knight's strong, sinewy arms clasp him in affection. Then the two stood back to look at each other for a brief moment.

Sturm hasn't changed, Tanis thought, except that there are more lines around the sad eyes, more gray in the brown hair. The cloak is a little more frayed. There are a few more dents in the ancient armor. But the knight's flowing moustaches†—his pride and joy—were as long and sweeping as ever, his shield was polished just as brightly, his brown eyes were just as warm when he saw his friends.

I believe this moustache was actually inspired by Carl Smith, a designer at the time.—TRH

"And you have a beard," Sturm said with amusement.

Then the knight turned to greet Caramon and Flint. Tasslehoff dashed off after more ale, Tika having been called away to serve others in the growing crowd.

"Greetings, Knight," whispered Raistlin from his corner.

Sturm's face grew solemn as he turned to greet the other twin. "Raistlin," he said.

The mage drew back his hood, letting the light fall on his face. Sturm was too well-bred to let his astonishment show beyond a slight exclamation. But his eyes widened. Tanis realized the young mage was getting a cynical pleasure out of seeing his friends' discomfiture.

"Can I get you something, Raistlin?" Tanis asked.

"No, thank you," the mage answered, moving into the shadows once again.

"He eats practically nothing," Caramon said in a worried tone. "I think he lives on air."

"Some plants live on air," Tasslehoff stated, returning with Sturm's ale. "I've seen them. They hover up off the ground. Their roots suck food and water out of the atmosphere."

"Really?" Caramon's eyes were wide.

"I don't know who's the greater idiot," said Flint in disgust. "Well, we're all here. What news?"

"All?" Sturm looked at Tanis questioningly. "Kitiara?"

"Not coming," Tanis replied steadily. "We were hoping perhaps you could tell us something."

"Not I." The knight frowned. "We traveled north together and parted soon after crossing the Sea Narrows into Old Solamnia. She was going to look up relatives of her father, she said. That was the last I saw of her."†

Sturm and Kitiara left Solace together when the companions parted, though they never dreamed what a situation they would find themselves in; see Darkness and Light *by Paul B. Thompson and Tonya R. Carter. For another side to their adventure, see* The Second Generation *by Weis and Hickman.*

"Well, I suppose that's that." Tanis sighed. "What of your relatives, Sturm? Did you find your father?"

Sturm began to talk, but Tanis only half-listened to Sturm's tale of his travels in his ancestral land of Solamnia. Tanis's thoughts were on Kitiara. Of all his friends, she had been the one he most longed to see. After five years of trying to get her dark eyes and crooked smile out of his mind, he discovered that his longing for her grew daily. Wild, impetuous, hot-tempered—the swordswoman was everything Tanis was not. She was also human, and love

Very early on in the creation of DRAGONLANCE, *I established a triangle model of the story: three points of the triangle that represented conflicting influences, and a fourth, central point that shifted among the other three. This model reflects itself down through the story in many levels. The three divisions of the gods—good, evil and chaos—with Krynn in the center shifting between the three. The Knights of Solamnia, the Dragon Highlords, and the people of Krynn, with our characters shifting among them. In terms of our main characters, we see Tanis being pulled by three forces as well. One of them is the urgent situation on Krynn. The second is presented here for the first time; Kitiara, who represents temptation and darkness.—TRH*

between human and elf always ended in tragedy. Yet Tanis could no more get Kitiara† out of his heart than he could get his human half out of his blood. Wrenching his mind free of memories, he began listening to Sturm.

"I heard rumors. Some say my father is dead. Some say he's alive." His face darkened. "But no one knows where he is."

"Your inheritance?" Caramon asked.

Sturm smiled, a melancholy smile that softened the lines in his proud face. "I wear it," he replied simply. "My armor and my weapon."

Tanis looked down to see that the knight wore a splendid, if old-fashioned, two-handed sword.

Caramon stood up to peer over the table. "That's a beauty," he said. "They don't make them like that these days. My sword broke in a fight with an ogre. Theros Ironfeld put a new blade on it today, but it cost me dearly. So you're a knight now?"

Sturm's smile vanished. Ignoring the question, he caressed the hilt of his sword lovingly. "According to the legend, this sword will break only if I do," he said. "It was all that was left of my father's—"

Suddenly Tas, who hadn't been listening, interrupted. "Who are those people?" the kender asked in a shrill whisper.

Tanis looked up as the two barbarians walked past their table, heading for empty chairs that sat in the shadows of a corner near the firepit. The man was the tallest man Tanis had ever seen. Caramon—at six feet—would come only to this man's shoulder. But Caramon's chest was probably twice as big around, his arms three times as big. Although the man was bundled with the furs barbarian tribesmen live in, it was obvious that he was thin for his great height. His face, though dark-skinned, had the pale cast of one who has been ill or suffered greatly.

His companion—the woman Sturm had bowed to—was so muffled in a fur-trimmed cape and hood that it was difficult to tell much about her. Neither she nor her tall escort glanced at Sturm as they passed. The woman carried a plain staff trimmed with feathers in barbaric fashion. The man carried a well-worn knapsack. They sat down in the chairs, huddled in their cloaks, and talked together in low voices.

"I found them wandering around on the road outside of town," Sturm said. "The woman appeared near exhaustion, the man just as bad. I brought them here, told them they could get food and rest for the night. They are proud people and would have refused my help, I think, but they were lost and tired and"—Sturm lowered his voice—"there are things on the road these days that it is better not to face in the dark."

"We met some of them, asking about a staff," Tanis said grimly. He described their encounter with Fewmaster Toede.

Although Sturm smiled at the description of the battle, he shook his head. "A Seeker guard questioned me about a staff outside," he said. "Blue crystal, wasn't it?"

Caramon nodded and put his hand on his brother's thin arm. "One of the slimy guards stopped us," the warrior said. "They were going to impound Raist's staff, if you'll believe that—'for further investigation,' they said. I rattled my sword at them and they thought better of the notion."

Raistlin moved his arm from his brother's touch, a scornful smile on his lips.

"What would have happened if they had taken your staff?" Tanis asked Raistlin.

The mage looked at him from the shadows of his hood, his golden eyes gleaming. "They would have died horribly," the mage whispered, "and *not* by my brother's sword!"

The half-elf felt chilled. The mage's softly spoken words were more frightening than his brother's bravado. "I wonder what is so important about a blue crystal staff that goblins would kill to get it?" Tanis mused.

"There are rumors of worse to come," Sturm said quietly. His friends moved closer to hear him. "Armies are gathering in the north. Armies of strange creatures, not human. There is talk of war."

"But what? Who?" Tanis asked. "I've heard the same."

"And so have I," Caramon added. "In fact, I heard—"

As the conversation continued, Tasslehoff yawned and turned away. Easily bored, the kender looked around the Inn for some new amusement. His eyes

went to the old man, still spinning tales for the child by the fire. The old man had a larger audience now—the two barbarians† were listening, Tas noted. Then his jaw dropped.

Barbarians, indeed! Throw another AD&D archetype on the party!—TRH

The woman had thrown her hood back and the firelight shone on her face and hair. The kender stared in admiration. The woman's face was like the face of a marble statue—classic, pure, cold.

But it was her hair that captured the kender's attention. Tas had never before seen such hair, especially on the Plainsmen, who were usually dark-haired and dark-skinned. No jeweler spinning molten strands of silver and gold could have created the effect of this woman's silver-gold hair shining in the firelight.†

A paragraph here that had to be omitted when the original manuscript proved far too long tells us something about the kender's empathy:

"The woman was listening intently to the old man's stories. She seemed absorbed in them, glad to be able to forget her own troubles for a while. Tas noted that her beautiful face was sorrowful, and there were shadows and faint lines beneath her eyes. The man may have been listening also, but his alert, dark eyes were vigilant, keeping watch as though standing guard duty in enemy territory."

One other person listened to the old man. This was a man dressed in the rich brown and golden robes of a Seeker. He sat at a small round table, drinking mulled wine. Several mugs stood empty before him and, even as the kender watched, he called sourly for another.

"That's Hederick," Tika whispered as she passed the companions' table. "The High Theocrat."

The man called out again, glaring at Tika. She bustled quickly over to help him. He snarled at her, mentioning poor service. She seemed to start to answer sharply, then bit her lip and kept silent.

The old man came to an end of his tale. The boy sighed. "Are all your stories of the ancient gods true, Old One?" he asked curiously.

Tasslehoff saw Hederick frown. The kender hoped he wouldn't bother the old man. Tas touched Tanis's arm to catch his attention, nodding his head toward the Seeker with a look that meant there might be trouble.

The friends turned. All were immediately overwhelmed by the beauty of the Plainswoman. They stared in silence.

The old man's voice carried clearly over the drone of the other conversation in the common room. "Indeed, my stories are true, child." The old man looked directly at the woman and her tall escort. "Ask these two. They carry such stories in their hearts."

"Do you?" The boy turned to the woman eagerly. "Can you tell me a story?"

The woman shrank back into the shadows, her face filled with alarm as she noticed Tanis and his friends staring at her. The man drew near her protectively, his hand reaching for his weapon. He glowered at the group, especially the heavily armed warrior, Caramon.

"Nervous bastard," Caramon commented, his hand straying to his own sword.

"I can understand why," Sturm said. "Guarding such a treasure. He *is* her bodyguard, by the way. I gathered from their conversation that she's some kind of royal person in their tribe. Though I imagine from the looks they exchanged that their relationship goes a bit deeper than that."

The woman raised her hand in a gesture of protest. "I'm sorry." The friends had to strain to hear her low voice. "I am not a teller of tales. I have not the art." She spoke the Common tongue, her accent thick.

The child's eager face filled with disappointment. The old man patted him on the back, then looked directly into the woman's eyes. "You may not be a teller of tales," he said pleasantly, "but you are a singer of songs, aren't you, Chieftain's Daughter? Sing the child your song, Goldmoon. You know the one."†

Here the prophet/mentor sets up the mythic quest.—TRH

From out of nowhere, apparently, a lute appeared in the old man's hands. He gave it to the woman who stared at him in fear and astonishment.

"How . . . do you know me, sir?" she asked.

"That is not important." The old man smiled gently. "Sing for us, Chieftain's Daughter."

The woman took the lute with hands that trembled visibly. Her companion seemed to make a whispered protest, but she did not hear him. Her eyes were held fast by the glittering black eyes of the old man. Slowly, as if in a trance, she began to strum the lute. As the melancholy chords drifted through the common room, conversations ceased. Soon, everyone was watching her, but she did not notice. Goldmoon sang for the old man alone.

The grasslands are endless,
And summer sings on,
And Goldmoon the princess
Loves a poor man's son.

This was the first song in the trilogy that adopted shorter lines, rhyme—all the things we tend to associate with song. I wish the chorus ("O Riverwind, where have you gone?") was either something else or not included. Looking back over fifteen years, I find it a little sappy. But the stanzas centered around "The grasslands are fading" strike me as much better: They let things suggest the emotion, which makes them superior to the chorus.
—Michael Williams

Her father the chieftain
Makes long roads between them:
The grasslands are endless, and summer sings on.

The grasslands are waving,
The sky's rim is gray,
The chieftain sends Riverwind
East and away,

To search for strong magic
At the lip of the morning,
The grasslands are waving, the sky's rim is gray.

O Riverwind, where have you gone?
O Riverwind, autumn comes on.
I sit by the river
And look to the sunrise,
But the sun rises over the mountains alone.

The grasslands are fading,
The summer wind dies,
He comes back, the darkness
Of stones in his eyes.

He carries a blue staff
As bright as a glacier:
The grasslands are fading, the summer wind dies.

I originally wrote music to this lyric, to these words by Michael Williams. There have been many versions, my favorite being done by a woman I used to sing folk songs with in High School, Mary Kovarik. We even cut a CD together that contains that song.—TRH

The grasslands are fragile,
As yellow as flame,
The chieftain makes mockery
Of Riverwind's claim.

He orders the people
To stone the young warrior:
The grasslands are fragile, as yellow as flame.

The grassland has faded,
And autumn is here.
The girl joins her lover,
The stones whistle near,

The staff flares in blue light
And both of them vanish:
The grasslands are faded, and autumn is here.

There was heavy silence in the room as her hand struck the final chord. Taking a deep breath, she handed the lute† back to the old man and withdrew into the shadows once more.

The lute is a rather unusual instrument for Krynn. Flutes and various horns (beloved of the armies) are more common.

"Thank you, my dear," the old man said, smiling.

"Now can I have a story?" the little boy asked wistfully.

"Of course," the old man answered and settled back in his chair. "Once upon a time, the great god, Paladine—"

"Paladine?" the child interrupted. "I've never heard of a god named Paladine."†

The design team had heard of him, of course. All the pantheon of Krynn was known before we began. —TRH

A snorting sound came from the High Theocrat sitting at the nearby table. Tanis looked at Hederick, whose face was flushed and scowling. The old man appeared not to notice.

"Paladine is one of the ancient gods, child. No one has worshiped him for a long time."

"Why did he leave?" the little boy asked.

"He did not leave us," the old man answered, and his smile grew sad. "Men left him after the dark days of the Cataclysm. They blamed the destruction of the world on the gods, instead of on themselves, as they should have done. Have you ever heard the 'Canticle of the Dragon'?"

"Oh, yes," the boy said eagerly. "I love stories about dragons, though papa says dragons never existed. I believe in them, though. I hope to see one someday!"

The old man's face seemed to age and grow sorrowful. He stroked the young boy's hair. "Be careful what you wish, my child," he said softly.† Then he fell silent.

Foreshadows events that will come all too soon. —TRH

"The story—" the boy prompted.

"Oh, yes. Well, once upon a time Paladine heard the prayer of a very great knight, Huma—"

"Huma from the Canticle?"†

The "Canticle of the Dragon," by Michael Williams (poet laureate of DRAGONLANCE), set the tone early in the book, giving foundation for the world in a very short space.—TRH

"Yes, that's the one. Huma became lost in the forest. He wandered and wandered until he despaired because he thought he would never see his homeland again. He prayed to Paladine for help, and there suddenly appeared before him a white stag."

"Did Huma shoot it?" the boy asked.

"He started to, but his heart failed him. He could not shoot an animal so magnificent. The stag bounded away. Then it stopped and looked back at him, as if waiting. Huma began to follow it. Day and night, he followed the stag until it led him to his homeland. He offered thanks to the god, Paladine."

"Blashphemy!" snarled a voice loudly. A chair crashed back.

Tanis put down his mug of ale, looking up. Everyone at the table stopped drinking to watch the drunken Theocrat.

"Blasphemy!" Hederick, weaving unsteadily on his feet, pointed at the old man. "Heretic! Corrupting our youth! I'll bring you before the counshel, old man." The Seeker fell back a step, then staggered forward again. He looked around the room with a pompous air. "Call the guardsh!" He made a grandiose gesture. "Have them arresht thish man and thish woman for singing lewd songsh. Obviously a witch! I'll confishcate thish staff!"

The Seeker lurched across the floor to the barbarian woman, who was staring at him in disgust. He reached clumsily for her staff.

"No," the woman called Goldmoon spoke coolly. "That is mine. You cannot take it."

"Witch!" the Seeker sneered. "I am the High Theocrat! I take what I want."

He started to make another grab for the staff. The woman's tall companion rose to his feet. "The Chieftain's Daughter says you will not take it," the man said harshly. He shoved the Seeker backward.

The tall man's push was not rough, but it knocked the drunken Theocrat completely off balance. His arms flailing wildly, he tried to catch himself. He lurched forward, too far, tripped over his official robes, and fell headfirst into the roaring fire.

There was a whoosh and a flare of light, then a sickening smell of burning flesh. The Theocrat's scream tore through the stunned silence as the crazed man leaped to his feet and started whirling around in a frenzy. He had become a living torch!

Tanis and the others sat, unable to move, paralyzed with the shock of the incident. Only Tasslehoff had wits enough to run forward, anxious to try and help the man. But the Theocrat was screaming and waving his arms, fanning the flames that were consuming his clothes and his body. There seemed no way that the little kender could help him.

"Here!" The old man grabbed the barbarian's feather-decorated staff and handed it to the kender.† "Knock him down. Then we can smother the fire."

The old man continues to orchestrate events, since he is the catalyst of changing events in our story.—TRH

Tasslehoff took the staff. He swung it, using all his strength, and hit the Theocrat squarely in the chest. The man fell to the ground. There was a gasp from the crowd. Tasslehoff himself stood, open-mouthed, the staff clutched in his hand, staring down at the amazing sight at his feet.

The flames had died instantly. The man's robes were whole, undamaged. His skin was pink and healthy. He sat up, a look of fear and awe on his face. He stared down at his hands and his robes. There was not a mark on his skin. There was not the smallest cinder smoking on his robes.

"It healed him!" the old man proclaimed loudly.†"The staff! Look at the staff!"

We needed a miracle to establish the return of the gods—as well as to establish a mechanism for healing characters in an AD&D game devoid of clerics.—TRH

Tasslehoff's eyes went to the staff in his hands. It was made of blue crystal and was glowing with a bright blue light!

The old man began shouting. "Call the guards! Arrest the kender! Arrest the barbarians! Arrest their friends! I saw them come in with this knight." He pointed at Sturm.

"What?" Tanis leaped up. "Are you crazy, old man?"

"Call the guards!" The word spread. "Did you see—? The blue crystal staff? We've found it. Now they'll leave us alone. Call the guards!"

The Theocrat staggered to his feet, his face pale, blotched with red. The barbarian woman and her companion stood up, fear and alarm in their faces.

"Foul witch!" Hederick's voice shook with rage. "You have cured me with evil! Even as I burn to purify my flesh, you will burn to purify your soul!" With that, the Seeker reached out, and before anyone could stop him, he plunged his hand back into the flames!† He gagged with the pain but did not cry out. Then, clutching his charred and blackened hand, he turned and staggered off through the murmuring crowd, a wild look of satisfaction on his pain-twisted face.

This makes sense to the character, if not much sense to us. Power appears to be the primary motivation of Hederick and the theocrats. He would do anything to maintain this illusion, even in the face of real miracles. How many miracles did you miss today?—TRH

"You've got to get out of here!" Tika came running over to Tanis, her breath coming in gasps. "The whole town's been hunting for that staff! Those hooded men told the Theocrat they'd destroy Solace if they caught someone harboring the staff. The townspeople will turn you over to the guards!"

"But it's not our staff!" Tanis protested. He glared at the old man and saw him settle back into his chair, a pleased smile on his face. The old man grinned at Tanis and winked.

"Do you think they'll believe you!" Tika wrung her hands. "Look!"

Tanis looked around. People were glaring at them balefully. Some took a firm grip on their mugs. Others eased their hands onto the hilts of their swords. Shouts from down below drew his eyes back to his friends.

"The guards are coming!" exclaimed Tika.

Tanis rose. "We'll have to go out through the kitchen."

"Yes!" She nodded. "They won't look back there yet. But hurry. It won't take them long to surround the place."

Years of being apart had not affected the companions' ability to react as a team to threat of danger. Caramon had pulled on his shining helm, drawn his sword, shouldered his pack, and was helping his brother to his feet. Raistlin, his staff in his hand, was moving around the table. Flint had hold of his battle-axe and was frowning darkly at the onlookers, who seemed hesitant about rushing to attack such well-armed men. Only Sturm sat, calmly drinking his ale.

"Sturm!" Tanis said urgently. "Come on! We've got to get out of here!"

"Run?" The knight appeared astonished. "From this rabble?"†

People often ask what are my favorite lines or names. This is one of my favorite lines.—MW

"Yes." Tanis paused; the knight's code of honor forbade running from danger. He had to convince him. "That man is a religious fanatic, Sturm. He'll probably burn us at the stake! And"—a sudden thought rescued him—"there is a lady to protect."†

This little scene was inspired by an old paladin AD&D character I used to play.—TRH

"The lady, of course." Sturm stood up at once and walked over to the woman. "Madam, your servant." He bowed; the courtly knight would not be hurried. "It seems we are all in this together. Your staff has placed us in considerable danger—you most of all. We are familiar with the area around here: we grew up here. You, I know, are strangers.

We would be honored to accompany you and your gallant friend and guard your lives."

"Come on!" Tika urged, tugging on Tanis's arm. Caramon and Raistlin were already at the kitchen door.

"Get the kender," Tanis told her.

Tasslehoff stood, rooted to the floor, staring at the staff. It was rapidly fading back to its nondescript brown color. Tika grabbed Tas by his topknot and pulled him toward the kitchen. The kender shrieked, dropping the staff.

Goldmoon swiftly picked it up, clutching it close to her. Although frightened, her eyes were clear and steady as she looked at Sturm and Tanis; she was apparently thinking rapidly. Her companion said a harsh word in their language. She shook her head. He frowned and made a slashing motion with his hand. She snapped a quick reply and he fell silent, his face dark.

"We will go with you," Goldmoon said to Sturm in the Common tongue. "Thank you for the offer."

"This way!" Tanis herded them out through the swinging kitchen doors, following Tika and Tas. He glanced behind him and saw some of the crowd move forward, but in no great hurry.

The cook stared at them as they ran through the kitchen. Caramon and Raistlin were already at the exit, which was nothing more than a hole cut in the floor. A rope hung from a sturdy limb above the hole and dropped forty feet to the ground.

"Ah!" exclaimed Tas, laughing. "Here the ale comes up and the garbage goes down." He swung out onto the rope and shinnied down easily.

"I'm sorry about this," Tika apologized to Goldmoon, "but it is the only way out of here."

"I can climb down a rope." Then the woman smiled and added, "Though I admit it has been many years."

She handed her staff to her companion and grasped the stout rope. She began to descend, moving skillfully hand over hand. When she reached the bottom, her companion tossed the staff down, swung on the rope, and dropped through the hole.

"How are you going to get down, Raist?" Caramon asked, his face lined with concern. "I can carry you on my back—"

Raistlin's eyes flashed with an anger that startled Tanis. "I can get down myself!" the mage hissed. Before anyone could stop him, he stepped to the edge of the hole and leaped out into the air. Everyone gasped and peered down, expecting to see Raistlin splattered all over the ground. Instead, they saw the young mage gently floating down, his robes fluttering around him. The crystal on his staff glowed brightly.

"He shivers my skin!" Flint growled to Tanis.

"Hurry!" Tanis shoved the dwarf forward. Flint grabbed hold of the rope. Caramon followed, the big man's weight causing the limb the rope was tied around to creak.

"I will go last," Sturm said, his sword drawn.

"Very well." Tanis knew it was useless to argue. He slung the longbow and quiver of arrows over his shoulder, grabbed the rope, and started down. Suddenly his hands slipped. He slid down the rope, unable to stop it tearing the skin off his palms. He landed on the ground and looked, wincing, at his hands. His palms were raw and bleeding. But there was no time to think about them. Glancing up, he watched as Sturm descended.

Tika's face appeared in the opening. "Go to my house!" she mouthed, pointing through the trees. Then she was gone.

"I know the way," Tasslehoff said, his eyes glowing with excitement. "Follow me."

They hurried off after the kender, hearing the sounds of the guards climbing the stairway into the Inn. Tanis, unused to walking on the ground in Solace, was soon lost. Above him he could see the bridge-walks, the street lamps gleaming among the tree leaves. He was completely disoriented, but Tas kept pushing forward confidently, weaving in and out among the huge trunks of the vallenwood trees. The sounds of the commotion at the Inn faded.

"We'll hide at Tika's for the night," Tanis whispered to Sturm as they plunged through the underbrush. "Just in case someone recognized us and decides to search our homes. Everyone will have forgotten about this by morning. We'll take the Plainsmen to my house and let them rest a few days. Then we can send the barbarians on to Haven

where the Council of High Seekers can talk with them. I think I might even go along—I'm curious about this staff."

Sturm nodded. Then he looked at Tanis and smiled his rare, melancholy smile. "Welcome home," the knight said.

"Same to you." The half-elf grinned.

They both came to a sudden halt, bumping into Caramon in the dark.

"We're here, I think," Caramon said.

In the light of the street lamps that hung in the tree limbs, they could see Tasslehoff climbing tree branches like a gully dwarf.† The rest followed more slowly, Caramon assisting his brother. Tanis, gritting his teeth from the pain in his hands, climbed up slowly through the rapidly thinning autumn foliage. Tas pulled himself up over the porch railing with the skill of a burglar. The kender slipped over to the door and peered up and down the bridge-walk. Seeing no one on it, he motioned to the others. Then he studied the lock and smiled to himself in satisfaction. The kender slid something out of one of his pouches. Within seconds, the door of Tika's house swung open.

Gully dwarves, whom we will meet later, tend to be more agile than other dwarves—they have to be to survive.

"Come in," he said, playing host.

They crowded inside the little house, the tall barbarian being forced to duck his head to avoid hitting the ceiling. Tas pulled the curtains shut. Sturm found a chair for the lady, and the tall barbarian went to stand behind her. Raistlin stirred up the fire.

"Keep watch," Tanis said. Caramon nodded. The warrior had already posted himself at a window, staring out into the darkness. The light from a street lamp gleamed through the curtains into the room, casting dark shadows on the walls. For long moments no one spoke, each staring at the others.

Tanis sat down. His eyes turned to the woman. "The blue crystal staff," he said quietly. "It healed that man. How?"

"I do not know." She faltered. "I—I haven't had it very long."

Tanis looked down at his hands. They were bleeding from where the rope had peeled off his skin. He held them out to her. Slowly, her face pale, the

woman touched him with the staff. It began to glow blue. Tanis felt a slight shock tingle through his body. Even as he watched, the blood on his palms vanished, the skin became smooth and unscarred, the pain eased and soon left him completely.

"True healing!" he said in awe.

Well, it's time to tally up. We've got a barbarian, a paladin-wanna-be, a half-elf bowman, a diminutive thief, a dwarf, a magic-user, and now a female cleric healer. A typical AD&D group.—TRH

Putting the game aside, I think it is the diverse nature of the party that people can relate to. In most groups of friends, each person contributes something unique. The whole is stronger than its separate parts.—MW

4

The Open Door.
Flight into Darkness.

Raistlin sat down on the hearth, rubbing his thin hands in the warmth of the small fire. His golden eyes seemed brighter than the flames as he stared intently at the blue crystal staff resting across the woman's lap.

"What do you think?" asked Tanis.

"If she's a charlatan, she's a good one," Raistlin commented thoughtfully.

"Worm! You dare to call the Chieftain's Daughter charlatan!" The tall barbarian stepped toward Raistlin, his dark brows contracted in a vicious scowl. Caramon made a low, rumbling sound in his throat and moved from the window to stand behind his brother.

"Riverwind . . ." The woman laid her hand on the man's arm as he drew near her chair. "Please. He meant no harm. It is right that they do not trust us. They do not know us."

"And we do not know them," the man growled.

"If I might examine it?" Raistlin said.

Goldmoon nodded and held out the staff. The mage stretched out his long, bony arm, his thin hands grasping for it eagerly. As Raistlin touched the staff, however, there was a bright flash of blue light and a crackling sound. The mage jerked his hand back, crying out in pain and shock. Caramon jumped forward, but his brother stopped him.

"No, Caramon," Raistlin whispered hoarsely, wringing his injured hand. "The lady had nothing to do with that."

The woman, indeed, was staring at the staff in amazement.

"What is it then?" Tanis asked in exasperation. "A staff that heals and injures at the same time?"

From an experience I had with a tarot deck once. We didn't much like each other.—TRH

"It merely knows its own."† Raistlin licked his lips, his eyes glittering. "Watch. Caramon, take the staff."

"Not me!" The warrior drew back as if from a snake.

"Take the staff!" Raistlin demanded.

Reluctantly, Caramon stretched out a trembling hand. His arm twitched as his fingers came closer and closer. Closing his eyes and gritting his teeth in anticipation of pain, he touched the staff. Nothing happened.

Caramon opened his eyes wide, startled. He gripped the staff, lifted it in his huge hand, and grinned.

"See there." Raistlin gestured like an illusionist showing off a trick to the crowd. "Only those of simple goodness, pure in heart"—his sarcasm was biting—"may touch the staff. It is truly a sacred staff of healing, blessed by some god. It is not magic. No magic objects that I have ever heard about have healing powers."

"Hush!" ordered Tasslehoff, who had taken Caramon's place by the window. "The Theocrat's guards!" he warned softly.

No one spoke. Now they could all hear goblin footsteps flapping on the bridge-walks that ran among the branches of the vallenwood trees.

"They're conducting a house-to-house search!" Tanis whispered incredulously, listening to fists banging on a neighboring door.

"The Seekers demand right of entry!" croaked a voice. There was a pause, then the same voice said, "No one home, do we kick the door in?"

"Naw," said another voice. "We'd better just report to the Theocrat, let him kick the door down. Now if it was unlocked, that'd be different, we're allowed to enter then."

Tanis looked at the door opposite him. He felt the hair rise on the back of his neck. He could have sworn they had shut and bolted the door . . . now it stood slightly open!

"The door!" he whispered. "Caramon—"

But the warrior had already moved over to stand behind the door, his back to the wall, his giant hands flexing.

The footsteps flapped to a stop outside. "The Seekers demand right of entry." The goblins began to bang on the door, then stopped in surprise as it swung open.

"This place is empty," said one. "Let's move on."

"You got no imagination, Grum," said the other. "Here's our chance to pick up a few pieces of silver."

A goblin head appeared around the open door. Its† eyes focused on Raistlin, sitting calmly, his staff on his shoulder. The goblin grunted in alarm, then began to laugh.

"Oh, ho! Look what we've found! A staff!" The goblin's eyes gleamed. It took a step toward Raistlin, its partner crowding close behind. "Hand me that staff!"

"Certainly," the mage whispered. He held his own staff forth. *"Shirak,"* he said. The crystal ball flared into light. The goblins shrieked and shut their eyes, fumbling for their swords. At that moment, Caramon jumped from behind the door, grabbed the goblins around their necks, and swept their heads together with a sickening thud. The goblin bodies crumpled into a stinking heap.

"Dead?" asked Tanis as Caramon bent over them, examining them by the light of Raistlin's staff.

"I'm afraid so." The big man sighed. "I hit them too hard."†

From another D&D game. My wife, Laura, had a character wearing Gauntlets of Ogre Power while she was trying to interrogate a goblin prisoner. Her die roll was exceptionally good—a natural twenty on a twenty-sided die—when she tried to slap the character around. She said she was sorry.—TRH

This scene was a tribute to one of my favorite books, The Three Musketeers *by Alexandre Dumas. The large Musketeer, called Porthos, says much the same thing in a similar encounter.—MW*

"Well, that's torn it," Tanis said grimly. "We've murdered two more of the Theocrat's guards. He'll have the town up in arms. Now we can't just lie low for a few days—we've got to get out of here! And you two"—he turned to the barbarians—"had better come with us."

"Wherever we're going," muttered Flint irritably.

"Where were you headed?" Tanis asked Riverwind.

"We were traveling to Haven," the barbarian answered reluctantly.

"There are wise men there," Goldmoon said. "We hoped they could tell us about this staff. You see, the song I sang—it was true: the staff saved our lives—"

"You'll have to tell us later," Tanis interrupted. "When these guards don't report back, every goblin in Solace will be swarming up the trees. Raistlin, put out that light."

The mage spoke another word, *"Dumak."* The crystal glimmered, then the light died.

"What'll we do with the bodies?" Caramon asked, nudging a dead goblin with his booted foot. "And what about Tika? Won't she get into trouble?"

"Leave the bodies." Tanis's mind was working quickly. "And hack up the door. Sturm, knock over a few tables. We'll make it look as if we broke in here and got into a fight with these fellows. That way, Tika shouldn't be in too much trouble. She's a smart girl—she'll manage."

"We'll need food," Tasslehoff stated. He ran into the kitchen and began rummaging through the shelves, stuffing loaves of bread and anything else that looked edible into his pouches. He tossed Flint a full skin of wine. Sturm overturned a few chairs. Caramon arranged the bodies to make it look as if they had died in a ferocious battle. The Plainsmen stood in front of the dying fire, looking at Tanis uncertainly.

"Well?" said Sturm. "Now what? Where are we going?"

Tanis hesitated, running over the options in his mind. The Plainsmen had come from the east and—if their story was true and their tribe *had* been trying to kill them—they wouldn't want to go back that way. The group could travel south, into the elven

kingdom, but Tanis felt a strange reluctance to go back to his homelands. He knew, too, that the elves would not be pleased to see these strangers enter their hidden city.

"We will travel north," he said finally. "We will escort these two until we come to the crossroads, then we can decide what to do from there. They can go on southwest to Haven, if they wish. I plan to travel farther north and see if the rumors about armies gathering are true."

"And perhaps run into Kitiara," Raistlin whispered slyly.

Tanis flushed. "Is that plan all right?" he asked, looking around.

"Though not the eldest among us, Tanis, you are the wisest," Sturm said. "We follow you—as always."

Caramon nodded. Raistlin was already heading for the door. Flint shouldered the wine skin, grumbling.

Tanis felt a gentle hand touch his arm. He turned and looked down into the clear blue eyes of the beautiful barbarian.

"We are grateful," Goldmoon said slowly, as if unused to expressing appreciation. "You risk your lives for us, and we are strangers."

Tanis smiled and clasped her hand. "I am Tanis. The brothers are Caramon and Raistlin. The knight is Sturm Brightblade. Flint Fireforge carries the wine and Tasslehoff Burrfoot is our clever locksmith. You are Goldmoon and he is Riverwind. There—we are strangers no longer."

Goldmoon smiled wearily. She patted Tanis's arm, then started out the door, leaning on the staff that once again seemed plain and nondescript. Tanis watched her, then glanced up to see Riverwind staring at him, the barbarian's dark face an impenetrable mask.

"Well," Tanis amended silently, "*some* of us are no longer strangers."

Soon everyone had gone, Tas leading the way. Tanis stood alone for a moment in the wrecked living room, staring at the bodies of the goblins. This was supposed to have been a peaceful homecoming after bitter years of solitary travel. He thought of his comfortable house. He thought of all the things he had planned to do—things he had planned to do together with Kitiara. He thought of long winter nights, with storytelling around the fire at the Inn, then returning home, laughing together beneath the fur blankets, sleeping through the snow-covered mornings.

Tanis kicked at the smoldering coals, scattering them. Kitiara had not come back. Goblins had invaded his quiet town. He was fleeing into the night to escape a bunch of religious fanatics, with every likelihood he could never return.

Elves do not notice the passage of time. They live for hundreds of years. For them, the seasons pass like brief rain showers. But Tanis was half human. He sensed change coming, felt the disquieting restlessness men feel before a thunderstorm.

He sighed and shook his head. Then he went out the shattered door, leaving it swinging crazily on one hinge.

5

Farewell to Flint. Arrows fly. Message in the stars.

The constellation of Takhisis, Queen of Darkness

Tanis swung over the porch and dropped down through the tree limbs to the ground below. The others waited, huddled in the darkness, keeping out of the light cast by street lamps swinging in the branches above them. A chill wind had sprung up, blowing out of the north. Tanis glanced behind him and saw other lights, lights of the search parties. He pulled his hood over his head and hurried forward.

"Wind's switched," he said. "There'll be rain by morning." He looked around at the small group, seeing them in the eerie, wildly dancing light of the wind-tossed lamps. Goldmoon's face was scarred with weariness. Riverwind's was a stoic mask of strength, but his shoulders sagged. Raistlin, shivering, leaned against a tree, wheezing for breath.

Tanis hunched his shoulders against the wind. "We've got to find shelter," he said. "Some place to rest."

"Tanis—" Tas tugged on the half-elf's cloak. "We could go by boat. Crystalmir Lake's only a short way. There're caves on the other side, and it will cut walking time tomorrow."

"That's a good idea, Tas, but we don't have a boat."

"No problem." The kender grinned. His small face and sharply pointed ears made him look particularly impish in the eerie light. Tas is enjoying all of this immensely, Tanis realized. He felt like shaking the kender, lecturing him sternly on how much danger they were in. But the half-elf knew it was useless: kender are totally immune to fear.

"The boat's a good idea," Tanis repeated, after a moment's thought. "You guide. And don't tell Flint," he added. "I'll take care of that."

"Right!" Tas giggled, then slipped back to the others. "Follow me," he called out softly, and he started off once more. Flint, grumbling into his beard, stumped after the kender. Goldmoon followed the dwarf. Riverwind cast a quick, penetrating glance around at everyone in the group, then fell into step behind her.

"I don't think he trusts us," Caramon observed.

"Would you?" Tanis asked, glancing at the big man. Caramon's dragon helm† glinted in the flickering lights; his ring-mail armor was visible whenever the wind blew his cape back. A longsword clanked against his thick thighs, a short bow and a quiver of arrows were slung over his shoulder, a dagger protruded from his belt. His shield was battered and dented from many fights. The giant was ready for anything.

Dragons may have been things of legend still in Krynn, but their legendary images apparently showed up on armor.

Tanis looked over at Sturm, who proudly wore the coat of arms of a knighthood that had fallen into disgrace three hundred years before. Although Sturm was only four years older than Caramon, the knight's strict, disciplined life, hardships brought on by poverty, and his melancholy search for his beloved father had aged the knight beyond his years. Only twenty-nine, he looked forty.

Tanis thought, I don't think I'd trust us either.

"What's the plan?" Sturm asked.

"We're going by boat," Tanis answered.

"Oh, ho!" Caramon chuckled. "Told Flint yet?"

"No. Leave that to me."

"Where are we getting the boat?" Sturm asked suspiciously.

"You'll be happier not knowing," the half-elf said.

The knight frowned. His eyes followed the kender, who was far ahead of them, flitting from one shadow to another. "I don't like this, Tanis. First we're murderers, now we're about to become thieves."

"I don't consider myself a murderer." Caramon snorted. "Goblins don't count."

Tanis saw the knight glare at Caramon. "I don't like any of this, Sturm," he said hastily, hoping to avoid an argument. "But it's a matter of necessity. Look at the Plainsmen—pride's the only thing keeping them on their feet. Look at Raistlin . . ." Their eyes went to the mage, who was shuffling through the dry leaves, keeping always in the shadows. He leaned heavily upon his staff. Occasionally, a dry cough racked his frail body.

Caramon's face darkened. "Tanis is right," he said softly. "Raist can't take much more of this. I must go to him." Leaving the knight and the half-elf, he hurried forward to catch up with the robed, bent figure of his twin.

"Let me help you, Raist," they heard Caramon whisper.

Raistlin shook his hooded head and flinched away from his brother's touch.† Caramon shrugged and dropped his arm. But the big warrior stayed close to his frail brother, ready to help him if necessary.

"Why does he put up with that?" Tanis asked softly.

"Family. Ties of blood." Sturm sounded wistful. He seemed about to say more, then his eyes went to Tanis's elven face with its growth of human hair and he fell silent. Tanis saw the look, knew what the knight was thinking. Family, ties of blood—they were things the orphaned half-elf wouldn't know about.

"Come on," Tanis said abruptly. "We're dropping behind."

They soon left the vallenwood trees of Solace and entered the pine forest surrounding Crystalmir

We see here the seeds of the unhealthy relationship that is the foundation for the Legends trilogy later. Some might think this is a "happy accident," but Margaret and I know better. As we wrote these books, we both often felt we were not so much creating a story as reporting events of some place that actually existed. The story of Caramon and Raistlin was already there—even at this early date.—TRH

Cut here was a brief scene in which they get lost in the darkness and discover that Riverwind has gone off to find a trail. Goldmoon counsels them to wait for him:

"Riverwind does not know men or their cities, but he knows trees and plants, he knows the animals. He is wise in woodlore. In Solace, he was lost and afraid, though he would not admit it. Here, Riverwind is at home. You may follow him with confidence." Even as Goldmoon spoke, Tanis heard a rustle of dry leaves on the path and saw Riverwind emerging from the brush.

The tall Plainsman cast a glance around at all of them, but he spoke only to Goldmoon. "I have found the path, Chieftain's Daughter."

Lake. Tanis could faintly hear muffled shouts far behind them. "They've found the bodies," he guessed. Sturm nodded gloomily. Suddenly Tasslehoff seemed to materialize out of the darkness right beneath the half-elf's nose.

"The trail runs a little over a mile to the lake," Tas said. "I'll meet you where it comes out." He gestured vaguely, then disappeared before Tanis could say a word. The half-elf looked back at Solace. There seemed to be more lights, and they were moving in this direction. The roads were probably already blocked.†

"Where's the kender?" Flint grumbled as they plunged through the forest.

"Tas is meeting us at the lake," Tanis replied.

"Lake?" Flint's eyes grew wide in alarm. "What lake?"

"There's only one lake around here, Flint," Tanis said, trying hard not to smile at Sturm. "Come on. We'd better keep going." His elvensight showed him the broad red outline of Caramon and the slighter red shape of his brother disappearing into the thick woods ahead.

"I thought we were just going to lie low in the woods for a while." Flint shoved his way past Sturm to complain to Tanis.

"We're going by boat." Tanis moved forward.

"Nope!" Flint growled. "I'm not getting in any boat!"

"That accident happened ten years ago!" Tanis said, exasperated. "Look, I'll make Caramon sit still."

"Absolutely not!" the dwarf said flatly. "No boats. I took a vow."

"Tanis," Sturm's voice whispered behind him. "Lights."

"Blast!" The half-elf stopped and turned. He had to wait a moment before catching sight of lights glittering through the trees. The search had spread beyond Solace. He hurried to catch up with Caramon, Raistlin, and the Plainsmen.

"Lights!" he called out in a piercing whisper. Caramon looked back and swore. Riverwind raised his hand in acknowledgment. "I'm afraid we're going to have to move faster, Caramon—" Tanis began.

"We'll make it," the big man said, unperturbed. He was supporting his brother now, his arm around

Raistlin's thin body, practically carrying him. Raistlin coughed softly, but he was moving. Sturm caught up with Tanis. As they forced their way through the brush, they could hear Flint, puffing along behind, muttering angrily to himself.

"He won't come, Tanis," Sturm said. "Flint's been in mortal fear of boats† ever since Caramon almost accidentally drowned him that time. You weren't there. You didn't see him after we hauled him out."

I once had an AD&D character with a petrifying fear of rope. It's amazing how a simple phobia can really cause other people to be creative.—TRH

"He'll come," Tanis said, breathing hard. "He can't let us youngsters go off into danger without him."

Sturm shook his head, unconvinced.

Tanis looked back again. He saw no lights, but he knew they were too deep in the forest now to see them. Fewmaster Toede may not have impressed anybody with his brains, but it wouldn't take much intelligence to figure out that the group might take to the water. Tanis stopped abruptly to keep from bumping into someone. "What is it?" he whispered.

"We're here," Caramon answered. Tanis breathed a sigh of relief as he stared out across the dark expanse of Crystalmir Lake. The wind whipped the water into frothy whitecaps.

"Where's Tas?" He kept his voice low.

"There, I think." Caramon pointed at a dark object floating close to shore. Tanis could barely make out the warm red outline of the kender sitting in a large boat.

The stars gleamed with icy brightness in the blue-black sky. The red moon, Lunitari, was rising like a bloody fingernail from the water. Its partner in the night sky, Solinari, had already risen, marking the lake with molten silver.

"What wonderful targets we're going to make!" Sturm said irritably.

Tanis could see Tasslehoff turning this way and that, searching for them. The half-elf reached down, fumbling for a rock in the darkness. Finding one, he lobbed it into the water. It splashed just a few yards ahead of the boat. Tas, reacting to Tanis's signal, propelled the boat to shore.

"You're going to put all of us in one boat!" Flint said in horror. "You're mad, half-elf!"

"It's a big boat," Tanis said.

"No! I won't go. If it were one of the legendary white-winged boats of Tarsis, I still wouldn't go! I'd rather take my chances with the Theocrat!"

Tanis ignored the fuming dwarf and motioned to Sturm. "Get everyone loaded up. We'll be along in a moment."

"Don't take too long," Sturm warned. "Listen."

"I can hear," Tanis said grimly. "Go on."

"What are those sounds?" Goldmoon asked the knight as he came up to her.

"Goblin search parties," Sturm answered. "Those whistles keep them in contact when they're separated. They're moving into the woods now."

Goldmoon nodded in understanding. She spoke a few words to Riverwind in their own language, apparently continuing a conversation Sturm had interrupted. The big Plainsman frowned and gestured back toward the forest with his hand.

He's trying to convince her to split with us, Sturm realized. Maybe he's got enough woodslore to hide from goblin search parties for days, but I doubt it.

"Riverwind, gue-lando!"† Goldmoon said sharply. Sturm saw Riverwind scowl in anger. Without a word, he turned and stalked toward the boat. Goldmoon sighed and looked after him, deep sorrow in her face.

Languages in DRAGONLANCE *are unique, although, unlike Tolkien's, they were thought out more in general terms rather than specific linguistic rules. The language of the Plains tribes seldom appears.* *—TRH*

"Can I do anything to help, lady?" Sturm asked gently.

"No," she replied. Then she said sadly, as if to herself, "He rules my heart, but I am his ruler. Once, when we were young, we thought we could forget that. But I have been 'Chieftain's Daughter' too long."

"Why doesn't he trust us?" Sturm asked.

"He has all the prejudices of our people," Goldmoon replied. "The Plainsmen do not trust those who are not human." She glanced back. "Tanis cannot hide his elven blood beneath a beard. Then there are the dwarf, the kender."

"And what of you, lady?" Sturm asked. "Why do you trust us? Don't you have these same prejudices?"

Goldmoon turned to face him. He could see her eyes, dark and shimmering as the lake behind her. "When I was a girl," she said in her deep, low voice,

"I was a princess of my people. I was a priestess. They worshiped me as a goddess. I believed in it. I adored it. Then something happened—" She fell silent, her eyes filled with memories.

"What was that?" Sturm prompted softly.

"I fell in love with a shepherd,"† Goldmoon answered, looking at Riverwind. She sighed and walked toward the boat.

Laura, my wife, actually wrote a HeartQuest multiple-choice book on this subject for TSR back in the 1980s, but the project was cancelled prior to publication. The galleys are still around the house here somewhere. . . . —TRH

Sturm watched Riverwind wade into the water to drag the boat closer to shore as Raistlin and Caramon reached the water's edge. Raistlin clutched his robes around him, shivering.

"I can't get my feet wet," he whispered hoarsely. Caramon did not reply. He simply put his huge arms around his brother, lifted him as easily as he would have lifted a child, and set Raistlin in the boat. The mage huddled in the aft part of the boat, not saying a word of thanks.

"I'll hold her steady," Caramon told Riverwind. "You get in." Riverwind hesitated a moment, then climbed quickly over the side. Caramon helped Goldmoon into the boat. Riverwind caught hold of her and steadied her as the boat rocked gently. The Plainsmen moved to sit in the stern, behind Tasslehoff.

Caramon turned to Sturm as the knight drew near. "What's happening back there?"

"Flint says he'll burn before he'll get in a boat—at least then he'll die warm instead of wet and cold."

"I'll go up and haul him down here," Caramon said.

"You'd only make things worse. You were the one that nearly drowned him, remember? Let Tanis handle it—he's the diplomat."

Caramon nodded. Both men stood, waiting in silence. Sturm saw Goldmoon look at Riverwind in mute appeal, but the Plainsman did not heed her glance. Tasslehoff, fidgeting on his seat, started to call out a shrill question, but a stern look from the knight silenced him. Raistlin huddled in his robes, trying to suppress an uncontrollable cough.

"I'm going up there," Sturm said finally. "Those whistles are getting closer. We don't dare take any more time." But at that moment, he saw Tanis shake hands with the dwarf, and begin to run toward the boat alone. Flint stayed where he was, near the edge

of the woods. Sturm shook his head. "I told Tanis the dwarf wouldn't come."

"Stubborn as a dwarf,† so the old saying goes," Caramon grunted. "And that one's had one hundred and forty-eight years to grow stubborner." The big man shook his head sadly. "Well, we'll miss him, that's for certain. He's saved my life more than once. Let me go get him. One punch on the jaw and he won't know whether he's in a boat or his own bed."

Dwarves would probably just call this characteristic being "set in their ways." Each type of dwarf claims—stubbornly, of course—to be more stubborn than the other types. Anyone listening to the argument would just sit and sigh.

Tanis ran up, panting, and heard the last comment. "No, Caramon," he said. "Flint would never forgive us. Don't worry about him. He's going back to the hills. Get in the boat. There are more lights coming this way. We left a trail through the forest a blind gully dwarf could follow."

"No sense all of us getting wet," Caramon said, holding the side of the boat. "You and Sturm get in. I'll shove off."

Sturm was already over the side. Tanis patted Caramon on the back, then climbed in. The warrior pushed the boat out into the lake. He was up to his knees in water when they heard a call from the shore.

"Hold it!" It was Flint, running down from the trees, a vague moving shape of blackness against the moonlit shoreline. "Hang on! I'm coming!"

"Stop!" Tanis cried. "Caramon! Wait for Flint!"

"Look!" Sturm half-rose, pointing. Lights had appeared in the trees, smoking torches held by goblin guards.

"Goblins, Flint!" Tanis yelled. "Behind you! Run!" The dwarf, never questioning, put his head down and pumped for the shore, one hand on his helm to keep it from flying off.

"I'll cover him," Tanis said, unslinging his bow. With his elvensight, he was the only one who could see the goblins behind the torches. Fitting an arrow to his bow, Tanis stood as Caramon held the big boat steady. Tanis fired at the outline of the lead goblin. The arrow struck it in the chest and it pitched forward on its face. The other goblins slowed slightly, reaching for their own bows. Tanis fitted another arrow to his bow as Flint reached the shoreline.

"Wait! I'm coming!" the dwarf gasped and he plunged into the water and sank like a rock.

"Grab him!" Sturm yelled. "Tas, row back. There he is! See? The bubbles—" Caramon was splashing frantically in the water, hunting for the dwarf. Tas tried to row back, but the weight in the boat was too much for the kender. Tanis fired again, missed his mark,† and swore beneath his breath. He reached for another arrow. The goblins were swarming down the hillside.

I had one fan tell me that he first started really enjoying the book when Tanis misses this shot! He said that it was the first time he ever heard of an elf missing!—MW

"I've got him!" Caramon shouted, pulling the dripping, spluttering dwarf out by the collar of his leather tunic. "Quit struggling," he told Flint, whose arms were flailing out in all directions. But the dwarf was in a complete state of panic. A goblin arrow thunked into Caramon's chain mail and stuck there like a scrawny feather.

"That does it!" The warrior grunted in exasperation and, with a great heave of his muscular arms, he pitched the dwarf into the boat as it moved out away from him. Flint caught hold of a seat and held on, his lower half sticking out over the edge. Sturm grabbed him by the belt and dragged him aboard as the boat rocked alarmingly. Tanis nearly lost his balance and was forced to drop his bow and catch hold of the side to keep from being thrown into the water. A goblin arrow stuck into the gunwale, just barely missing Tanis's hand.

"Row back to Caramon, Tas!" Tanis yelled.

"I can't!" shouted the struggling kender. One swipe of an out-of-control oar nearly knocked Sturm overboard.

The knight yanked the kender from his seat. He grabbed the oars and smoothly brought the boat around to where Caramon could get hold of the side.

Tanis helped the warrior climb in, then yelled to Sturm, "Pull!" The knight pulled on the oars with all his strength, leaning over backward as he thrust the oars deep into the water. The boat shot away from shore, accompanied by the howls of angry goblins. More arrows whizzed around the boat as Caramon, dripping wet, plopped down next to Tanis.

"Goblin target practice tonight," Caramon muttered, pulling the arrow from his mail shirt. "We show up beautifully against the water."

Tanis was fumbling for his dropped bow when he noticed Raistlin sitting up. "Take cover!" Tanis

warned, and Caramon started to reach for his brother, but the mage, scowling at both of them, slipped his hand into a pouch on his belt. His delicate fingers drew out a handful of something as an arrow struck the seat next to him. Raistlin did not react. Tanis started to pull the mage down, then realized he was lost in the concentration necessary to a magic-user casting a spell. Disturbing him now might have drastic consequences, causing the mage to forget the spell or worse—to miscast the spell.†

An example of an AD&D convention that brings unexpected depth to the story.—TRH

Tanis gritted his teeth and watched. Raistlin lifted his thin, frail hand and allowed the spell component he had taken from his pouch to fall slowly from between his fingers onto the deck of the boat. Sand, Tanis realized.

"Ast tasarak sinuralan krynawi,"†Raistlin murmured, and then moved his right hand slowly in an arc parallel to the shore. Tanis looked back toward land. One by one, the goblins dropped their bows and toppled over, as though Raistlin were touching each in turn. The arrows ceased. Goblins farther away howled in rage and ran forward. But by that time, Sturm's powerful strokes had carried the boat out of range.

Magical languages in Krynn were based structurally on Indonesian language forms, which I learned as a missionary on Java from 1975 through 1977.

I would even, occasionally, mix in actual Indonesian words, although usually I just used phonetics plugged into the grammatical construction.—TRH

"Good work, little brother!" Caramon said heartily. Raistlin blinked and seemed to return to the world, then the mage sank forward. Caramon caught him and held him for a moment. Then Raistlin sat up and sucked in a deep breath, which caused him to cough.

"I'll be all right," he whispered, withdrawing from Caramon.

"What did you do to them?" asked Tanis as he searched for enemy arrows to drop them overboard; goblins occasionally poisoned the arrowtips.

"I put them to sleep," Raistlin hissed through teeth that clicked together with the cold. "And now *I* must rest." He sank back against the side of the boat.

Tanis looked at the mage. Raistlin had, indeed, gained in power and skill. I wish I could trust him, the half-elf thought.

The boat moved across the star-filled lake. The only sounds to be heard were the soft, rhythmic splashing of the oars in the water and Raistlin's dry, wracking cough. Tasslehoff uncorked the wineskin,

which Flint had somehow retained on his wild dash, and tried to get the chilled, shivering dwarf to swallow a mouthful. But Flint, crouched at the bottom of the boat, could only shudder and stare out across the water.

Goldmoon sank deeper into her fur cape. She wore the soft doeskin breeches of her people with a fringed overskirt and belted tunic. Her boots were made of soft leather. Water had sloshed over the edge of the boat when Caramon had thrown Flint aboard. The water made the doeskin cling to her, and soon she was chilled and shivering.

"Take my cape," Riverwind said in their language,† starting to remove his bearskin cloak.

"No." She shook her head. "You have been suffering from the fever. I never get sick, you know that. But"—she looked up at him and smiled—"you may put your arm around me, warrior. The heat from our bodies will warm us both."

The point of view switches awkwardly here, since just a few pages earlier we had gone to the trouble of noting Riverwind's strange-sounding words. This seems awkward to me now that Margaret and I have been writing together for fifteen years. But this was our first book and, like a first date, things are bound to be a little clumsy.—TRH

"Is that a royal command, Chieftain's Daughter?" Riverwind whispered teasingly, drawing her close to him.

"It is," she said, leaning against his strong body with a sigh of contentment. She looked up into the starry heavens, then stiffened and caught her breath in alarm.

"What is it?" Riverwind asked, staring up.

The others in the boat, although they had not understood the exchange, heard Goldmoon's gasp and saw her eyes transfixed by something in the night sky.

Caramon poked his brother and said, "Raist, what is it? I don't see anything."

Raistlin sat up, cast back his hood, then coughed. When the spasm passed, he searched the night sky. Then he stiffened, and his eyes widened. Reaching out with his thin, bony hand, Raistlin clutched Tanis's arm, holding onto it tightly as the half-elf involuntarily tried to pull away from the mage's skeletal grip. "Tanis . . ." Raistlin wheezed, his breath nearly gone. "The constellations . . ."

"What?" Tanis was truly startled by the pallor of the mage's metallic gold skin and the feverish luster of his strange eyes. "What about the constellations?"

"Gone!" rasped Raistlin and lapsed into a fit of coughing. Caramon put his arm around him,

Valiant Warrior, or Paladine, one of the missing constellations.

holding him close, almost as if the big man were trying to hold his brother's frail body together. Raistlin recovered, wiped his mouth with his hand. Tanis saw that his fingers were dark with blood. Raistlin took a deep breath, then spoke.

"The constellation known as the Queen of Darkness and the one called Valiant Warrior. Both gone. She has come to Krynn, Tanis, and he has come to fight her. All the evil rumors we have heard are true. War, death, destruction . . ." His voice died in another fit of coughing.

Caramon held him. "C'mon, Raist," he said soothingly. "Don't get so worked up. It's only a bunch of stars."

"Only a bunch of stars," Tanis repeated flatly. Sturm began to row again, pulling swiftly for the opposite bank.

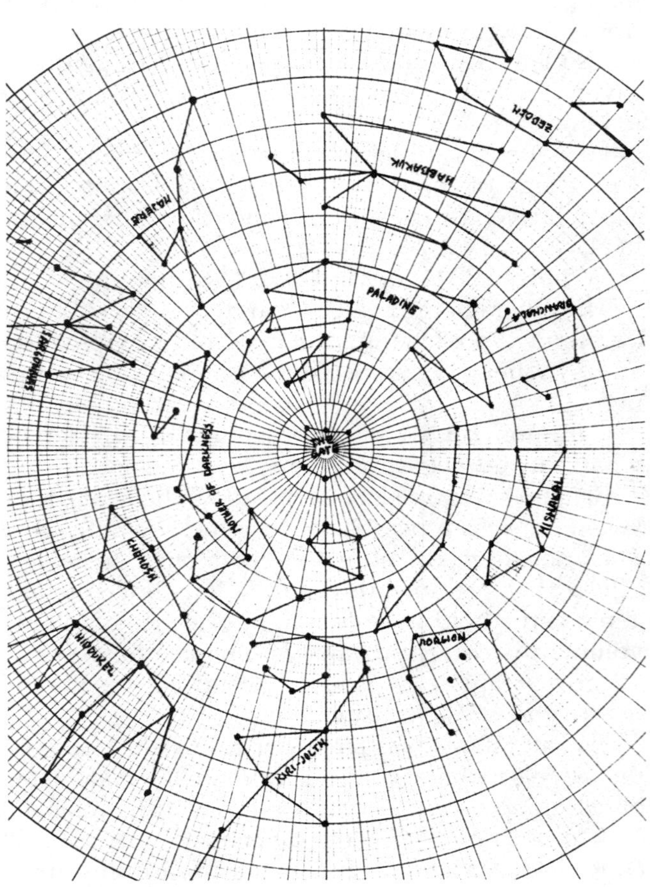

The cosmology of Krynn had been worked out in great detail prior to the novel being written. The constellations had even been plotted on a polar-celestial grid with each of the pantheon represented. The loss of the constellations is a sign that the gods have left the heavens to bring their conflict into the mortal world.—TRH

6

Night in a cave. Dissension. Tanis decides.

A chill wind began to blow across the lake. Storm clouds rolled across the sky from the north, obliterating the gaping black holes left by the fallen stars. The companions hunched down in the boat, pulling their cloaks tighter around them as the rain spattered down. Caramon joined Sturm at the oars. The big warrior tried to talk to the knight, but Sturm ignored him. He rowed in grim silence, occasionally muttering to himself in Solamnic.

"Sturm! There—between the great rocks to the left!" Tanis called out, pointing.

Sturm and Caramon pulled hard. The rain made sighting the landmark rocks difficult and, for a moment, it seemed that they had lost their way in the darkness. Then the rocks suddenly loomed ahead. Sturm and Caramon brought the boat

around. Tanis sprang out over the side and pulled it to shore. Torrents of rain lashed down. The companions climbed from the boat, wet and chilled. They had to lift the dwarf out—Flint was stiff as a dead goblin from fear. Riverwind and Caramon hid the boat in the thick underbrush. Tanis led the rest up a rocky trail to a small opening in the cliff face.

Goldmoon looked at the opening dubiously. It seemed to be no more than a large crack in the surface of the cliff. Inside, however, the cave was large enough for all of them to stretch out comfortably.

"Nice home." Tasslehoff glanced around. "Not much in the way of furniture."

Tanis grinned at the kender. "It will do for the night. I don't think even the dwarf will complain about this. If he does, we'll send him back to sleep in the boat!"

Tas flashed his own smile back at the half-elf. It was good to see the old Tanis back.† He had thought his friend unusually moody and indecisive, not the strong leader he had remembered from earlier days. Yet, now that they were on the road, the glint was back in the half-elf's eyes. He had come out of his brooding shell and was taking charge, slipping back into his accustomed role. He needed this adventure to get his mind off his problems—whatever those might be. The kender, who had never been able to understand Tanis's inner turmoil,† was glad this adventure had come along.

Tanis first met Tas in Solace when the kender was accused of thievery by an irate metalsmith named Flint. The story is in Wanderlust *by Mary Kirchoff.*

During the early days of the first book, Margaret was having trouble getting a handle on Tanis's character. His voice and actions just didn't seem right to her. In the end, she asked me about him and I told her Tanis was simple: "He's James T. Kirk of the Starship Enterprise.*" Of course, Capt. Kirk himself was also modeled after Horatio Hornblower. Anyway, the analogy worked for us. Margaret had no more trouble understanding Tanis.—TRH*

And I've become very fond of the Horatio Hornblower books by Forster.—MW

Caramon carried his brother from the boat and laid him down as gently as he could on the soft warm sand that covered the floor of the cave while Riverwind started a fire. The wet wood crackled and spit, but soon caught fire. The smoke curled up toward the ceiling and drifted out through a crack. The Plainsman covered the cave's entrance with brush and fallen tree branches, hiding the light of the fire and effectively keeping out the rain.

He fits in well, Tanis thought as he watched the barbarian work. He could almost be one of us. Sighing, the half-elf turned his attention to Raistlin. Kneeling down beside him, he looked at the young mage with concern. Raistlin's pale face reflected in the flickering firelight reminded the half-elf of the time he and Flint and Caramon had barely rescued Raistlin from a vicious mob, intent on burning the

mage at the stake. Raistlin had attempted to expose a charlatan cleric who was bilking the villagers out of their money. Instead of turning on the cleric, the villagers had turned on Raistlin. As Tanis had told Flint—people wanted to believe in something.

Caramon busied himself around his brother, placing his own heavy cloak over his shoulders. Raistlin's body was wracked by coughing spasms, and blood trickled from his mouth. His eyes gleamed feverishly. Goldmoon knelt beside him, a cup of wine in her hand.

"Can you drink this?" she asked him gently.

Raistlin shook his head, tried to speak, coughed and pushed her hand away. Goldmoon looked up at Tanis. "Perhaps—my staff?" she asked.

"No." Raistlin choked. He motioned for Tanis to come near him. Even sitting next to him, Tanis could barely hear the mage's words; his broken sentences were interrupted by great gasps for air and fits of coughing. "The staff will not heal me, Tanis," he whispered. "Do not waste it on me. If it is a blessed artifact . . . its sacred power is limited. My body was my sacrifice . . . for my magic.† This damage is permanent. Nothing can help. . . ." His voice died, his eyes closed.

The fire suddenly flared as wind whirled around the cavern. Tanis looked up to see Sturm pulling the brush aside and entering the cave, half-carrying Flint, who stumbled along on unsteady feet. Sturm dumped him down beside the fire. Both were soaking wet. Sturm was clearly out of patience with the dwarf and, as Tanis noted, with the entire group. Tanis watched him with concern, recognizing the signs of a dark depression that sometimes overwhelmed the knight. Sturm liked the orderly, the well-disciplined. The disappearance of the stars, the disturbance of the natural order of things, had shaken him badly.

Tasslehoff wrapped a blanket around the dwarf who sat huddled on the cave floor, his teeth chattering in his head so that his helm rattled. "B-b-b-boat . . ." was all he could say. Tas poured him a cup of wine which the dwarf drank greedily.

Sturm looked at Flint in disgust. "I'll take the first watch," he said and moved toward the mouth of the cave.

Balance is a fundamental principle in DRAGONLANCE*—nothing comes without a price in this world. Magic can be phenomenally powerful, but it carries an extremely high price here in Krynn. In searching for foundations in the story, we found we had to approach magic and clerics in new ways. These differences set Krynn apart from standard AD&D worlds.—TRH*

The story of Raistlin's Test in the Tower was first told in the short story "Test of the Twins," published in Dragon *Magazine number 83. Coincidentally, that issue featured a fantastic cover painting by the artist who would later do the black and white drawings for this book, Denis Beauvais.*

Riverwind rose to his feet. "I will watch with you," he said harshly.

Sturm froze, then turned slowly to face the tall Plainsman. Tanis could see the knight's face, etched in sharp relief by the firelight, dark lines carved around the stern mouth. Although shorter in stature than Riverwind, the knight's air of nobility and the rigidity of his stance made the two appear almost equal.

People often ask us where we get our names. In this case, it was inspired by a set of step-in bindings I once had as a downhill skier: Solomon Bindings.—TRH

"I am a knight of Solamnia,"† Sturm said. "My word is my honor and my honor is my life. I gave my word, back in the Inn, that I would protect you and your lady. If you choose to dispute my word, you dispute my honor and therefore you insult me. I cannot allow that insult to remain between us."

"Sturm!" Tanis was on his feet.

Never taking his eyes from the Plainsman, the knight raised his hand. "Don't interfere, Tanis," Sturm said. "Well, what will it be, swords, knives? How do you barbarians fight?"

Riverwind's stoic expression did not change. He regarded the knight with intense, dark eyes. Then he spoke, choosing his words carefully. "I did not mean to question your honor. I do not know men and their cities, and I tell you plainly—I am afraid. It is my fear that makes me speak thus. I have been afraid ever since the blue crystal staff was given to me. Most of all, I am afraid for Goldmoon." The Plainsman looked over at the woman, his eyes reflecting the glowing fire. "Without her, I die. How could I trust—" His voice failed. The stoic mask cracked and crumbled from pain and weariness. His knees buckled and he pitched forward. Sturm caught him.

"You couldn't," the knight said. "I understand. You are tired, and you have been sick." He helped Tanis lay the Plainsman at the back of the cave. "Rest now. I will stand watch." The knight shoved aside the brush, and without saying another word, stepped outside into the rain.

Goldmoon had listened to the altercation in silence. Now she moved their meager possessions to the back of the cave and knelt down by Riverwind's side. He put his arm around her and held her close, burying his face in her silver-gold hair. The two settled in the shadows of the cave. Wrapped in

Riverwind's fur cape, they were soon asleep, Goldmoon's head resting on her warrior's chest.

Tanis breathed a sigh of relief and turned back to Raistlin. The mage had fallen into a fitful sleep. Sometimes he murmured strange words in the language of magic, his hand reaching out to touch his staff. Tanis glanced around at the others. Tasslehoff was sitting near the fire, sorting through his "acquired" objects. He sat cross-legged, the treasures on the cave floor in front of him. Tanis could make out glittering rings, a few unusual coins, a feather from the goatsucker bird,† pieces of twine, a bead necklace, a soap doll, and a whistle. One of the rings looked familiar. It was a ring of elven make, given Tanis a long time ago by someone he kept on the borders of his mind. It was a finely carved, delicate ring of golden, clinging ivy leaves.

This was an in-joke among the design staff. One team member, in a zealous determination to make the world as complete as possible, had compiled an incredible collection of creatures to help populate the world. The goatsucker bird (which does, indeed, exist) struck us as particularly funny.—TRH

Tanis crept over to the kender, walking softly to keep from waking the others. "Tas . . . " He tapped the kender on the shoulder and pointed. "My ring . . ."

"Is it?" asked Tasslehoff with wide-eyed innocence. "Is this yours? I'm glad I found it. You must have dropped it at the Inn."

Tanis took the ring with a wry smile, then settled down next to the kender. "Have you got a map of this area, Tas?"

The kender's eyes shone. "A map? Yes, Tanis. Of course." He swept up all his valuables, dumped them back into a pouch, and pulled a hand-carved, wooden scroll case from another pouch. He drew forth a sheaf of maps.† Tanis had seen the kender's collection before, but it never failed to astonish him. There must have been a hundred, drawn on everything from fine parchment to soft kid leather to a huge palmetto leaf.

Tas acquired his love of maps from his father. Presumably not all kender find maps an indispensable part of wanderlust.

"I thought you knew every tree personally around these parts, Tanis." Tasslehoff sorted through his maps, his eyes occasionally lingering on a favorite.

The half-elf shook his head. "I've lived here many years," he said. "But, let's face it, I don't know any of the dark and secret paths."

"You won't find many to Haven." Tas pulled a map from his pile and smoothed it out on the cave floor. "The Haven Road through Solace Vale is quickest, that's for certain."

Tanis studied the map by the light of the dying campfire. "You're right," he said. "The road is not only quickest—it seems to be the only passable route for several miles ahead. Both south and north of us lie the Kharolis Mountains—no passes there." Frowning, Tanis rolled up the map and handed it back. "Which is exactly what the Theocrat will figure."

Tasslehoff yawned. "Well," he said, putting the map back carefully into the case, "it's a problem that will be solved by wiser heads than mine. I'm along for the fun." Tucking the case back into a pouch, the kender lay down on the cave floor, drew his legs up beneath his chin, and was soon sleeping the peaceful sleep of small children and animals.

Tanis looked at him with envy. Although aching with weariness, he couldn't relax enough for sleep. Most of the others had dropped off, all but the warrior watching over his brother. Tanis walked over to Caramon.

"Turn in," he whispered. "I'll watch Raistlin."

"No," the big warrior said. Reaching out, he gently pulled a cloak up closer around his brother's shoulders. "He might need me."

"But you've got to get some sleep."

"I will." Caramon grinned. "Go get some sleep yourself, nursemaid. Your children are fine. Look—even the dwarf is out cold."

"I don't have to look," Tanis said. "The Theocrat can probably hear him snoring in Solace. Well, my friend, this reunion was not much like we planned five years ago."

"What is?" Caramon asked softly, glancing down at his brother.

Tanis patted the man's arm, then lay down and rolled up in his own cloak and, at last, fell asleep.

The night passed—slowly for those on watch, swiftly for those asleep. Caramon relieved Sturm. Tanis relieved Caramon. The storm continued unabated all night, the wind whipping the lake into a white-capped sea. Lightning branched through the darkness like flaming trees. Thunder rumbled continually. The storm finally blew itself out by morning, and the half-elf watched day dawn, gray and chill. The rain had ended, but storm clouds still hung low. No sun appeared in the sky. Tanis felt a

growing sense of urgency. He could see no end to the storm clouds massing to the north. Autumn storms were rare, especially ones with this ferocity. The wind was bitter, too, and it seemed odd that the storm came out of the north, when they generally swept east, across the Plains. Sensitive to the ways of nature, the strange weather upset Tanis nearly as much as Raistlin's fallen stars. He felt a need to get going, even though it was early morning yet. He went inside to wake the others.

The cave was chill and gloomy in the gray dawn, despite the crackling fire. Goldmoon and Tasslehoff were fixing breakfast. Riverwind stood in the back of the cave, shaking out Goldmoon's fur cloak. Tanis glanced at him. The Plainsman had been about to say something to Goldmoon as Tanis entered, but fell silent, contenting himself with staring at her meaningfully as he continued his work. Goldmoon kept her eyes lowered, her face pale and troubled. The barbarian regrets having let himself go last night, Tanis realized.

"There is not much food, I'm afraid," Goldmoon said, tossing cereal into a pot of boiling water.

"Tika's larder wasn't well stocked," Tasslehoff added in apology.† "We've got a loaf of bread, some dried beef, half a moldy cheese, and the oatmeal. Tika must eat her meals out."

Considering that Tas was the only one to think to bring food along, it doesn't seem fair that he should have to apologize for its quality.

"Riverwind and I didn't bring any provisions," Goldmoon said. "We really didn't expect to make this trip."

Tanis was about to ask her more about her song and the staff, but the others started waking up as they smelled food. Caramon yawned, stretched, and stood up. Walking over to peer into the cook-pot, he groaned. "Oatmeal? Is that all?"

"There'll be less for dinner." Tasslehoff grinned. "Tighten your belt. You're gaining weight anyhow ."

The big man sighed dismally.

The sparse breakfast was cheerless in the cold dawn. Sturm, refusing all offers of food, went outside to keep watch. Tanis could see the knight, sitting on a rock, staring gloomily at the dark clouds that trailed wispy fingers along the still water of the lake. Caramon ate his share of the food quickly, gulped down his brother's portion, and then appropriated Sturm's when the knight walked out. Then

the big man sat, watching wistfully while the rest finished.

"You gonna eat that?" he asked, pointing to Flint's share of bread. The dwarf scowled. Tasslehoff, seeing the warrior's eyes roam over to his plate, crammed his bread into his mouth, nearly choking himself in the process. At least it kept him quiet, Tanis thought, glad for the respite from the kender's shrill voice. Tas had been teasing Flint unmercifully all morning, calling him "Seamaster" and "Shipmate," asking him the price of fish, and how much he would charge to ferry them back across the lake. Flint finally threw a rock at him, and Tanis sent Tas down to the lake to scrub out the pans.

The half-elf walked to the back of the cave.

"How are you this morning, Raistlin?" he asked. "We're going to have to be moving out soon."

"I am much better," the mage replied in his soft, whispering voice. He was drinking some herbal concoction of his own making. Tanis could see small, feathery green leaves floating in steaming water. It gave off a bitter, acrid odor and Raistlin grimaced as he swallowed it.

Tasslehoff came bounding back into the cave, pots and tin plates clattering loudly. Tanis gritted his teeth at the noise, started to reprimand the kender, then changed his mind. It wouldn't do any good.

Flint, seeing the tension on Tanis's face, grabbed the pots from the kender and began packing them away. "Be serious," the dwarf hissed at Tasslehoff. "Or I'll take you by the topknot and tie you to a tree as a warning to all kender—"

Tas reached out and plucked something from the dwarf's beard. "Look!" the kender held it up gleefully. "Seaweed!" Flint, roaring, made a grab for the kender, but Tas skipped out of his way agilely.

There was a rustling sound as Sturm shoved aside the brush covering the doorway. His face was dark and brooding.

"Stop this!" Sturm said, glowering at Flint and Tas, his moustaches quivering. His dour gaze turned on Tanis. "I could hear these two clear down by the lake. They'll have every goblin in Krynn on us. We've got to get out of here. Well, which way are we headed?"

An uneasy silence fell. Everyone stopped what he was doing and looked at Tanis, with the exception of Raistlin. The mage was wiping his cup out with a white cloth, cleaning it fastidiously. He continued working, eyes downcast, as though totally uninterested.

Tanis sighed and scratched his beard. "The Theocrat in Solace is corrupt. We know that now. He is using the goblin scum to take control. If he had the staff, he would use it for his own profit. We've searched for a sign of the true gods for years. It seems we may have found one. I am not about to hand it over to that Solace fraud. Tika said she believed the Highseekers in Haven were still interested in the truth. They may be able to tell us about the staff, where it came from, what its powers are. Tas, give me the map."

The kender, spilling the contents of several pouches onto the floor, finally produced the parchment requested.

"We are here, on the west bank of Crystalmir,"† Tanis continued. "North and south of us are branches of the Kharolis Mountains which form the boundaries of Solace Vale. There are no known passes through either range except through Gateway Pass south of Solace—"

Solace Vale lies among the Sentinel Peaks of the Kharolis Mountains. The centerpiece of the valley is Crystalmir Lake.

"Almost certainly held by the goblins," muttered Sturm. "There are passes to the northeast—" •

"That's across the lake!" Flint said in horror.

"Yes"—Tanis kept a straight face—"across the lake. But those lead to the Plains, and I don't believe you want to go that direction." He glanced at Goldmoon and Riverwind. "The west road goes through the Sentinel Peaks and Shadow Canyon to Haven. That seems to me the obvious direction to take."

Sturm frowned. "And if the Highseekers there are as bad as the one in Solace?"

"Then we continue south to Qualinesti."

"Qualinesti?" Riverwind scowled. "The Elven Lands? No! Humans are forbidden to enter. Besides, the way is hidden—"

A rasping, hissing sound cut into the discussion. Everyone turned to face Raistlin as he spoke. "There is a way." His voice was soft and mocking; his golden eyes glittered in the cold light of dawn. "The paths of Darken Wood. They lead right to Qualinesti."

"Darken Wood?" Caramon repeated in alarm. "No, Tanis!"

The warrior shook his head. "I'll fight the living any day of the week—but not the dead!"

"The dead?" Tasslehoff asked eagerly. "Tell me, Caramon—"

"Shut up, Tas!" Sturm snapped. "Darken Wood is madness. None who enter have ever returned. You would have us take this prize there, mage?"

"Hold!" Tanis spoke sharply. Everyone fell silent. Even Sturm quieted. The knight looked at Tanis's calm, thoughtful face, the almond-shaped eyes that held the wisdom of his many years of wandering. The knight had often tried to resolve within himself why he accepted Tanis's leadership. He was nothing more than a bastard half-elf, after all. He did not come of noble blood. He wore no armor, carried no shield with a proud emblem. Yet Sturm followed him, and loved him and respected him as he respected no other living man.

Life was a dark shroud to the Solamnic knight. He could not pretend to ever know or understand it except through the code of the knights he lived by. "*Est Sularus oth Mithas*"†—"My honor is life." The code defined honor and was more complete and detailed and strict than any known on Krynn. The code had held true for seven hundred years, but Sturm's secret fear was that, someday, in the final battle, the code would have no answers.† He knew that if that day came, Tanis would be at his side, holding the crumbling world together. For while Sturm followed the code, Tanis lived it.

Another language I had to invent:
Solamnic strives to be Latin-esque.—TRH

We discover later that Sturm lied about being a knight. We use this to our advantage in the second book to make him more human. As Raistlin later says in Dragons of Summer Flame, *Sturm really didn't lie—he was always a knight in his heart.—MW*

Tanis's voice brought the knight's thoughts back to the present. "I remind all of you that this staff is not our 'prize.' The staff rightfully belongs to Goldmoon—if it belongs to anyone. We have no more right to it than the Theocrat in Solace." Tanis turned to Goldmoon. "What is your will, lady?"

Goldmoon stared from Tanis to Sturm, then she looked at Riverwind. "You know my mind," he said coldly. "But—you are Chieftain's Daughter." He rose to his feet. Ignoring her pleading gaze, he stalked outside.

"What did he mean?" Tanis asked.

"He wants us to leave you, take the staff to Haven," Goldmoon answered, her voice low. "He

says you are adding to our danger. We would be safer on our own."

"Adding to your danger!" Flint exploded. "Why we wouldn't be here, I wouldn't have nearly drowned—again!—if it hadn't been for—for—" The dwarf began to sputter in his rage.

Tanis held up his hand. "Enough." He scratched his beard. "You will be safer with us. Will you accept our help?"

"I will," Goldmoon answered gravely, "for a short distance at least."

"Good," Tanis said. "Tas, you know your way through Solace Vale. You are our guide. And remember, we're not on a picnic!"

"Yes, Tanis," the kender said, subdued. He gathered his many pouches, hung them around his waist and over his shoulders. Passing Goldmoon, he knelt swiftly and patted her hand, then he was out the cave entrance. The rest hastily gathered their gear together and followed.

"It's going to rain again," Flint grumbled, glancing up at the lowering clouds. "I should have stayed in Solace." Muttering, he walked off, adjusting his battle-axe on his back. Tanis, waiting for Goldmoon and Riverwind, smiled and shook his head. At least some things never changed, dwarves among them.

Riverwind took their packs from Goldmoon and slung them over his shoulder. "I have made certain the boat is well-hidden and secure," he told Tanis. The stoic mask was in place again this morning. "In case we need it."

"A good idea," Tanis said. "Thank—"

"If you will go ahead." Riverwind motioned. "I will come behind and cover our tracks."

Tanis started to speak, to thank the Plainsman. But Riverwind had already turned his back and was beginning his work. Walking up the path, the half-elf shook his head. Behind him, he could hear Goldmoon speaking softly in her own language. Riverwind replied—one, harsh word. Tanis heard Goldmoon sigh, then all other words were lost in the sound of crackling brush as Riverwind obliterated all traces of their passing.

7

The story of the staff. Strange clerics. Eerie feelings.

Most books intended for an "adult" audience are not illustrated. But the TSR products were known for their great artwork. We decided that full-page illustrations would look too juvenile, so we decided on these half-page elegant illustrations by Denis Beauvais.—MW

The thick woods of Solace Vale were a green mass of vibrant life. Beneath the dense roof of the vallenwoods flourished thistlebrush and greenwall. The ground was crisscrossed with the bothersome tangleshoot vines. These had to be trod on with great care or they would suddenly snake around an ankle, trapping the helpless victim until he was devoured by one of the many predatory animals lurking in the Vale, thus providing tangleshoot with what it needed to live—blood.

It took over an hour of hacking and chopping through the brush to get to the Haven Road. All of them were scratched, torn, and tired, and the long stretch of smooth-packed dirt that carried travelers to Haven or beyond was a welcome sight. It wasn't until they stopped just in sight of the road and

rested that they realized there were no sounds. A hush had fallen over the land, as if every creature were holding its breath, waiting. Now that they had reached the road, no one was particularly eager to step out of the shelter of the brush.

"Do you think it's safe?" Caramon asked, peering through a hedge.

"Safe or not, it's the way we have to go," Tanis snapped, "unless you can fly or unless you want to go back into the forest. It took us an hour to travel a few hundred yards. We ought to reach the crossroads next week at that pace."

The big man flushed, chagrined. "I didn't mean—"

"I'm sorry." Tanis sighed. He too looked down the road. The vallenwoods formed a dark corridor in the gray light. "I don't like it any better than you do."

"Do we separate or stay together?" Sturm† interrupted what he considered idle chatter with cold practicality.

I wanted Sturm to be stiff and formal and rather unlikeable in this first book, so that we could see him grow and change as a character when we came to the second.—MW

"We stay together," Tanis replied. Then, after a moment, he added, "Still, someone ought to scout—"

"I will, Tanis," Tas volunteered, popping up out of the brush beneath Tanis's elbow. "No one would ever suspect a kender traveling alone."

Tanis frowned. Tas was right—no one would suspect him. Kender were all afflicted with wanderlust,† traveling throughout Krynn in search of adventure. But Tas had the disconcerting habit of forgetting his mission and wandering off if something more interesting caught his attention.

See Wanderlust *by Mary Kirchoff and Steve Winter.*

"Very well," Tanis said finally. "But, remember, Tasslehoff Burrfoot, keep your eyes open and your wits about you. No roaming off the road and above all"—Tanis fixed the kender's eye with his own sternly—"keep your hands out of other people's belongings."

"Unless they're bakers," Caramon added.

Tas giggled, pushed his way through the final few feet of brush, and started off down the road, his hoopak staff digging holes in the mud, his pouches jouncing up and down as he walked. They heard his voice lift in a kender trailsong.†

Michael Williams's irrepressible humor is demonstrated here at its best.—TRH

Your one true love's a sailing ship
That anchors at our pier.

I've come to believe that some of the lighter poems—this one, for example, and one called "Three Sheets to the Wind" in the Legends trilogy—are really the most satisfying. The mildly dirty double entendres that lurk in each stanza are probably the best things, for sheer playfulness, that I did in this trilogy ... like the last line.—Michael Williams

We lift her sails, we man her decks,
We scrub the portholes clear;

And yes, our lighthouse shines for her,
And yes, our shores are warm;
We steer her into harbor,
Any port in a storm.

The sailors stand upon the docks,
The sailors stand in line,
As thirsty as a dwarf for gold
Or centaurs for cheap wine.

For all the sailors love her,
And flock to where she's moored,
Each man hoping that he might
Go down, all hands on board.

Tanis, grinning, allowed a few minutes to pass after hearing the last verse of Tas's song before starting out. Finally they stepped out on the road with as much fear as a troupe of unskilled actors facing a hostile audience. It felt as if every eye on Krynn was on them.

The deep shade under the flame-colored leaves made it impossible to see anything in the woods even a few feet from the road. Sturm walked ahead of the group, alone, in bitter silence. Tanis knew that though the knight held his head proudly, he was slogging through his own darkness. Caramon and Raistlin followed. Tanis kept his eyes on the mage, concerned about his ability to keep up.

Raistlin had experienced some difficulty in getting through the brush, but he was moving along well now. He leaned on his staff with one hand, holding open a book with the other. Tanis at first wondered what the mage was studying, then realized it was his spellbook. It is the curse of the magi that they must constantly study and recommit their spells to memory every day.† The words of magic flame in the mind, then flicker and die when the spell is cast. Each spell burns up some of the magician's physical and mental energy until he is totally exhausted and must rest before he can use his magic again.

Another AD&D nod. —TRH

Flint stumped along on the other side of Caramon. The two began to argue softly about the ten-year-old boating accident.

"Trying to catch a fish with your bare hands—" Flint grumbled his disgust.

Tanis came last, walking next to the Plainsmen. He turned his attention to Goldmoon. Seeing her clearly in the flecked gray light beneath the trees, he noticed lines around her eyes that made her appear older than her twenty-nine years.

"Our lives have not been easy," Goldmoon confided to him as they walked. "Riverwind and I have loved each other many years, but it is the law of my people that a warrior who wants to marry his chieftain's daughter must perform some great feat to prove himself worthy. It was worse with us. Riverwind's family was cast out of our tribe years ago for refusing to worship our ancestors. His grandfather† believed in ancient gods who had existed before the Cataclysm, though he could find little evidence of them left on Krynn.

Riverwind's grandfather was named Wanderer. He was one of the very few people in Ansalon to maintain his faith in the ancient gods.—MW

"My father was determined I should not marry so far beneath my station. He sent Riverwind on an impossible quest, to find some object with holy properties that would prove the existence of these ancient gods. Of course, my father didn't believe such an object existed. He hoped Riverwind would meet his death, or that I would come to love another." She looked up at the tall warrior walking beside her and smiled. But his face was hard, his eyes staring far away. Her smile faded. Sighing, she continued her story, speaking softly, more to herself than Tanis.

"Riverwind was gone long years.† And my life was empty. I sometimes thought my heart would die. Then, just a week ago, he returned. He was half-dead, out of his mind with a raging fever. He stumbled into camp and fell at my feet, his skin burning to the touch. In his hand, he clutched this staff. We had to pry his fingers loose. Even unconscious, he would not release it.

I have often wondered just where Riverwind went for so many years when his journey apparently led him only to the eastern side of the mountains next to his home.—TRH

"He raved in his fever about a dark place, a broken city where death had black wings. Then, when he was nearly wild with fear and terror and the servants had to tie his arms to the bed, he remembered a woman, a woman dressed in blue light.

She came to him in the dark place, he said, and healed him and gave him the staff. When he remembered her, he grew calmer and his fever broke.

"Two days ago—" She paused, had it really been only two days? It seemed a lifetime! Sighing, she continued. "He presented the staff to my father, telling him it had been given to him by a goddess, though he did not know her name. My father looked at this staff"—Goldmoon held it up—"and commanded it to do something, anything. Nothing happened. He threw it back to Riverwind, proclaiming him a fraud, and ordered the people to stone him to death as punishment for his blasphemy!"

Goldmoon's face grew pale as she spoke, Riverwind's face dark and shadowed.

"The tribe bound Riverwind and dragged him to the Grieving Wall," she said, barely speaking above a whisper. "They started hurling rocks. He looked at me with so much love and he shouted that not even death would separate us. I couldn't bear the thought of living my life alone, without him. I ran to him. The rocks struck us—" Goldmoon put her hand to her forehead, wincing in remembered pain, and Tanis's attention was drawn to a fresh, jagged scar on her tanned skin. "There was a blinding flash of light. When Riverwind and I could see again, we were standing on the road outside of Solace. The staff glowed blue, then dimmed and faded until it is as you see it now. It was then we determined to go to Haven and ask the wise men at the temple about the staff."

"Riverwind," Tanis asked, troubled, "what do you remember of this broken city? Where was it?"

Riverwind didn't answer. He glanced at Tanis out of the corner of his dark eyes, and it was obvious his thoughts had been far away. Then he stared off into the shadowy trees.

"Tanis Half-Elven," he finally said. "That is your name?"

"Among humans, that is what I am called," Tanis answered. "My elvish name is long and difficult for humans to pronounce."†

Riverwind frowned. "Why is it," he asked, "that you are called half-elf and not half-man?"

The question struck Tanis like a blow across the face. He could almost envision himself sprawling

The mythos: The name Tanis is derived from the longer form of Tanthalas in the elven tongue. As the root word, "Thalas" means both "king" in the noun form and "to rule" in the verb form and the prefix "Tan"denotes "deserving," the name literally means "deserving to rule." This, in Tanis's case, was

in the dirt and had to force himself to stop and swallow an angry retort. He knew Riverwind was asking this question for a reason. It had not been meant as an insult. This was a test, Tanis realized. He chose his words carefully.

"According to humans, half an elf is but part of a whole being. Half a man is a cripple."

Riverwind considered this, finally nodded once, abruptly, and answered Tanis's question.

"I wandered many long years," he replied. "Often I had no idea where I was. I followed the sun and the moons and the stars. My last journey is like a dark dream." He was silent for a moment. When he spoke, it was as if he were talking from some great distance. "It was a city once beautiful, with white buildings supported by tall columns of marble. But it is now as if some great hand had picked up the city and cast it down a mountainside. The city is now very old and very evil."

"Death on black wings," Tanis said softly.

"It rose like a god from the darkness, its creatures worshiped it, shrieking and howling." The Plainsman's face paled beneath his sun-baked skin. He was sweating in the chill morning air. "I can speak of it no more!" Goldmoon laid her hand on his arm, and the tension in his face eased.

"And out of the horror came a woman who gave you the staff?" Tanis pursued.

"She healed me," Riverwind said simply. "I was dying."

Tanis stared intently at the staff Goldmoon held in her hand. It was just a plain, ordinary staff that he never noticed until his attention was called to it. A strange device was carved on the top, and feathers—such as the barbarians admire—were tied around it. Yet he had seen it glow blue! He had felt its healing powers. Was this a gift from ancient gods—come to aid them in their time of need? Or was it evil? What did he know of these barbarians anyway? Tanis thought about Raistlin's claim that the staff could only be touched by those pure of heart. He shook his head. It sounded good. He wanted to believe it. . . .

Tanis, lost in thought, felt Goldmoon touch his arm. He looked up to see Sturm and Caramon signaling. The half-elf suddenly realized he and the

something of a cruel joke in his early years among the Qualinesti. It became something of a prophesy in his later life.

The reality: The name—and its derivation—was created from our imaginations. Tanis was, of course, a city in ancient Egypt, but the name in our books came basically because we liked the sound of it. The subconscious may have been at work, too, as many of the names in Krynn are rather close to ancient historical names; e.g. Abanasinia and Istar.—TRH

Plainsmen had fallen far behind the others. He broke into a run.

"What is it?"

Sturm pointed. "The scout returns," he said dryly.

Tasslehoff was running down the road toward them. He waved his arm three times.

"Into the brush!" Tanis ordered. The group hurriedly left the road and plunged into the bushes and scrub trees growing along the south edge, all except Sturm.

"Come on!" Tanis put his hand on the knight's arm. Sturm pulled away from the half-elf.

"I will not hide in a ditch!" the knight stated coldly.

"Sturm—" Tanis began, fighting to control his rising anger. He choked back bitter words that would do no good and might cause irreparable harm. Instead, he turned from the knight, his lips compressed, and waited in grim silence for the kender.

Tas came dashing up, pouches and packs bouncing wildly as he ran. "Clerics!" he gasped. "A party of clerics. Eight."

Sturm sniffed. "I thought it was a battalion of goblin guards at the least. I believe we can handle a party of clerics."

"I don't know," Tasslehoff said, dubiously. "I've seen clerics from every part of Krynn and I've never seen any like these." He glanced down the road apprehensively, then gazed up at Tanis, unusual seriousness in his brown eyes. "Do you remember what Tika said about the strange men in Solace—hanging around with Hederick? How they were hooded and dressed in heavy robes? Well, that describes these clerics exactly! And, Tanis, they gave me an eerie† feeling." The kender shuddered. "They'll be in sight in a few moments."

The kender version of fear

Tanis glanced at Sturm. The knight raised his eyebrows. Both of them knew that kenders did not feel the emotion of fear, yet were extremely sensitive to other creatures' natures. Tanis couldn't remember when the sight of any being on Krynn had ever given Tas an "eerie feeling"—and he had been with the kender in some tight spots.

"Here they come," Tanis said suddenly. He and Sturm and Tas moved back into the shadows of the

trees to the left, watching as the clerics slowly rounded a bend in the road. They were too far away for the half-elf to be able to tell much about them, except that they were moving very slowly, dragging a large handcart behind them.

"Maybe you should talk to them, Sturm," Tanis said softly. "We need information about the road ahead. But be careful, my friend."

"I'll be careful." Sturm said, smiling. "I have no intention of throwing my life away needlessly."

The knight gripped Tanis's arm a moment in silent apology, then dropped his hand to loosen his sword in its antique scabbard. He walked across to the other side of the road and leaned up against a broken-down wooden fence, head bowed, as though resting. Tanis stood a moment, irresolute, then turned and made his way through the brush, Tasslehoff at his heels.

"What is it?" Caramon grunted as Tanis and Tas appeared. The big warrior shifted his girth, causing his arsenal of weapons to clank loudly. The rest of the companions were huddled together, concealed behind thick clumps of brush, yet able to get a clear view of the road.

"Hush." Tanis knelt down between Caramon and Riverwind, who crouched in the brush a few feet to Tanis's left. "Clerics," he whispered. "A group of them coming down the road. Sturm's going to question them."

"Clerics!" Caramon snorted derisively and settled back comfortably on his heels. But Raistlin stirred restlessly.

"Clerics," he whispered thoughtfully. "I do not like this."

"What do you mean?" asked Tanis.

Raistlin peered at the half-elf from the dark shadows of his hood. All Tanis could see were the mage's golden hourglass eyes, narrow slits of cunning and intelligence.

"Strange clerics," Raistlin spoke with elaborate patience, as one speaks to a child. "The staff has healing, clerical powers—such powers as have not been seen on Krynn since the Cataclysm! Caramon and I saw some of these cloaked and hooded men in Solace. Don't you find it odd, my friend, that these clerics and this staff† turned up at the same time, in

In the first draft of the manuscript, Raistlin added "and the barbarians" to the list of odd appearances.

A battle almost broke out between Riverwind

and Caramon: "Stop it!" the half-elf insisted furiously, glaring at Riverwind. Then he twisted around to face the mage who was watching them all, a sneer on his face. "No more speculation, Raistlin! We none of us know anything about this staff or these clerics or why we're out here instead of warm in the Inn of the Last Home. Everyone just sit here and be quiet!"

Apparently this episode is not bringing out the best in anyone.

the same place, when neither has been seen before? Perhaps this staff is truly theirs—by right."

Tanis glanced at Goldmoon. Her face was shadowed with worry. Surely she must be wondering the same thing. He looked back at the road again. The cloaked figures were moving at a crawling pace, pulling the cart. Sturm sat on the fence, stroking his moustaches.

The companions waited in silence. Gray clouds massed overhead, the sky grew darker and soon water began to drip through the branches of the trees.

"There, it's raining," Flint grumbled. "It isn't enough that I have to squat in a bush like a toad, now I get soaked to the skin—"

Tanis glared at the dwarf. Flint mumbled and fell silent. Soon the companions could hear nothing but the rain splatting against the already wet leaves, drumming on shield and helm. It was a cold, steady rain, the kind that seeps through the thickest cloak. It ran off Caramon's dragon helm and trickled down his neck. Raistlin began to shiver and cough, covering his mouth with his hand to muffle the sound as everyone stared at him in alarm.

Tanis looked out to the road. Like Tas, he had never seen anything to compare to these clerics in his hundred years of life on Krynn. They were tall, about six feet in height. Long robes shrouded their bodies, hooded cloaks covered the robes. Even their feet and hands were wrapped in cloth, like bandages covering leprous wounds. As they neared Sturm, they glanced around warily. One of them stared straight into the brush where the companions were hiding. They could see only dark glittering eyes through a swath of cloth.

"Hail, Knight of Solamnia," the lead cleric said in the Common tongue. His voice was hollow, lisping, an inhuman voice. Tanis shivered.

"Greetings, brethren," Sturm answered, also in Common. "I have traveled many miles this day and you are the first travelers I have passed. I have heard strange rumors, and I seek information about the road ahead. Where do you come from?"

"We come from the east originally," the cleric answered. "But today we travel from Haven. It is a chill, bitter day for journeying, knight, which is per-

haps why you find the road empty. We ourselves would not undertake such a journey save we are driven by necessity. We did not pass you on the road, so you must be traveling from Solace, Sir Knight."

Sturm nodded. Several of the clerics standing at the rear of the cart turned their hooded faces toward each other, muttering. The lead cleric spoke to them in a strange, guttural language. Tanis looked at his companions. Tasslehoff shook his head, as did the rest of them; none of them had heard it before. The cleric switched back to Common. "I am curious to hear these rumors you speak of, knight."

"There is talk of armies in the north," Sturm replied. "I am traveling that way, to my homeland of Solamnia. I would not want to run into a war to which I had not been invited."

"We have not heard these rumors," the cleric answered. "So far as we know, the road to the north is clear."

"Ah, that's what comes of listening to drunken companions." Sturm shrugged. "But what is this necessity you speak of that drives the brethren out into such foul weather?"

"We seek a staff," the cleric answered readily. "A blue crystal staff. We heard that it had been sighted in Solace. Do you know aught of it?"

"Yes," Sturm answered. "I heard of such a staff in Solace. I heard of the armies to the north from the same companions. Am I to believe these stories or not?"

This appeared to confound the cleric for a moment. He glanced around, as if uncertain how to react.

"Tell me," said Sturm, lounging back against the fence, "why do you seek a blue crystal staff? Surely one of plain, sturdy wood would suit you reverend gentlemen better."

"It is a sacred staff of healing," the cleric replied gravely. "One of our brothers is sorely ill; he will die without the blessed touch of this holy relic."

"Healing?" Sturm raised his eyebrows. "A sacred staff of healing would be of great value. How did you come to misplace such a rare and wonderful object?"

"We did not misplace it!" the cleric snarled. Tanis saw the man's wrapped hands clench in anger. "It

was stolen from our holy order. We tracked the foul thief to a barbarian village in the Plains, then lost his trail. There are rumors of strange doings in Solace, however, and it is there we go." He gestured to the back of the cart. "This dismal journey is but little sacrifice for us compared to the pain and agony our brother endures."

"I'm afraid I cannot help—" Sturm began.

"I can help you!" called a clear voice from beside Tanis. He reached out, but he was too late. Goldmoon had risen from the brush and was walking determinedly to the road, pushing aside tree branches and brambles. Riverwind jumped to his feet and crashed through the shrubbery after her.

"Goldmoon!" Tanis risked a piercing whisper.

"I must know!" was all she said.

The clerics, hearing Goldmoon's voice, glanced at each other knowingly, nodding their hooded heads. Tanis sensed trouble, but before he could say anything, Caramon jumped to his feet.

"The Plainsmen are not leaving me behind in a ditch while they have all the fun!" Caramon stated, plunging through the thicket after Riverwind.

"Has everyone gone mad?" Tanis growled. He grabbed Tasslehoff by his shirt collar, dragging the kender back as he was about to leap joyfully after Caramon. "Flint, watch the kender. Raistlin—"

"No need to worry about me, Tanis," the mage whispered. "I have no intention of going out there."

"Right. Well, stay here." Tanis rose to his feet and slowly started forward, an "eerie feeling" creeping over him.

8

Search for truth.

Unexpected answers.

"I can help you." Goldmoon's clear voice rang out like a pure, silver bell. The Chieftain's Daughter saw Sturm's shocked face; she understood Tanis's warning.

But this was not the act of a foolish, hysterical woman. Goldmoon was far from that. She had ruled her tribe in all but name for ten years,† ever since sickness had struck her father like a lightning bolt, leaving him unable to speak clearly or to move his right arm and leg. She had led her people in times of war with neighboring tribes and in times of peace. She had confounded attempts to wrest her power from her. She knew that what she was doing now was dangerous. These strange clerics filled her with loathing. But they obviously knew something about this staff, and she had to know the answer.

See "Heart of Goldmoon" by Laura Hickman and Kate Novak in Love and War.

"I am the bearer of the blue crystal staff," Goldmoon said, approaching the leader of the clerics, her head held proudly. "But we did not steal it; the staff was given to us."

Riverwind stepped to one side of her, Sturm to the other. Caramon came charging through the brush and stood behind her, his hand on his sword hilt, an eager grin on his face.

"So you say," the cleric said in a soft, sneering voice. He stared at the plain brown staff in her hand with avid, black, gleaming eyes, then reached out his wrapped hand to take it. Goldmoon swiftly clasped the staff to her body.

"The staff was carried out of a place of great evil," she said. "I will do what I can to help your dying brother, but I will not relinquish this staff to you or to anyone else until I am firmly convinced of your rightful claim to it."

The cleric hesitated, glanced back at his fellows. Tanis saw them make nervous, tentative gestures toward the wide cloth belts they wore tied around their flowing robes. Unusually wide belts, Tanis noticed, with strange bulges beneath them—not, he was sure, made by prayer books. He swore in frustration, wishing Sturm and Caramon were paying attention. But Sturm seemed completely relaxed and Caramon was nudging him as though sharing a private joke. Tanis raised his bow cautiously and put an arrow to the string.

The cleric finally bowed his head in submission, folding his hands in his sleeves. "We will be grateful for whatever aid you can give our poor brother," he said, his voice muffled. "And then I hope you and your companions will return with us to Haven. I promise you that you will be convinced that the staff has come into your possession wrongly."

"We'll go where we've a mind to, brother," Caramon growled.

Fool! Tanis thought. The half-elf considered shouting a warning, then decided to remain hidden in case his growing fears were realized.

Goldmoon and the leader of the cloaked men passed the cart, Riverwind next to her. Caramon and Sturm remained near the front of it, watching with interest. As Goldmoon and the cleric reached

the back, the cleric put out a wrapped hand and drew Goldmoon toward the cart. She pulled away from his touch and stepped forward by herself. The cleric bowed humbly, then lifted up a cloth covering the back of the cart. Holding the staff in front of her, Goldmoon peered in.

Tanis saw a flurry of movement. Goldmoon screamed. There was a flash of blue light and a cry. Goldmoon sprang backward as Riverwind jumped in front of her. The cleric lifted a horn to his lips and blew long, wailing notes.

"Caramon! Sturm!" Tanis called, raising his bow. "It's a tra—" A great weight dropped on the half-elf from above, knocking him to the ground. Strong hands groped for his throat, shoving his face deep into the wet leaves and mud. The man's fingers found their hold and began squeezing. Tanis fought to breathe, but his nose and mouth were filled with mud. Seeing starbursts, he tore frantically at the hands that were trying to crush his windpipe. The man's grip was incredibly strong. Tanis felt himself losing consciousness. He tensed his muscles for one final, desperate struggle, then he heard a hoarse cry and a bone-crushing thump. The hands relaxed their grip and the heavy weight was dragged off him.

Tanis staggered to his knees, his breath coming in painful gasps. Wiping mud from his face, he looked up to see Flint with a log in his hand. But the dwarf's eyes were not on him. They were on the body at his feet.

Tanis followed the astonished dwarf's gaze, and the half-elf recoiled in horror. It wasn't a man!† Leathery wings sprang from its back. It had the scaly flesh of a reptile; its large hands and feet were clawed, but it walked upright in the manner of men. The creature wore sophisticated armor that allowed it the use of its wings. It was the creature's face, however, that made him shudder, it was not the face of any living being he had ever seen before, either on Krynn or in his darkest nightmares. The creature had the face of a man, but it was as if some malevolent being had twisted it into that of a reptile!

"By all the gods," Raistlin breathed, creeping up to Tanis. "What is that?"

Dragonmen, or draconians, as they are here known, were another purely Krynnish creation. Originally they were intended to add a new opponent to the game, but they subsequently gained considerable depth as the story progressed. Creatures created from Dark Magic, each type died in spectacular and unexpected ways as the magic that lived in them was released in death. —TRH

Before Tanis could answer, he saw out of the corner of his eye a brilliant flash of blue light and he heard Goldmoon calling.

For one instant, as Goldmoon had looked into the cart, she had wondered what terrible disease could turn a man's flesh into scales. She had moved forward to touch the pitiful cleric with her staff, but at that moment the creature sprang out at her, grasping for the staff with a clawed hand. Goldmoon stumbled backward, but the creature was swift and its clawed hand closed around the staff. There was a blinding flash of blue light. The creature shrieked in pain and fell back, wringing its blackened hand. Riverwind, sword drawn, had leaped in front of his Chieftain's Daughter.

But now she heard him gasp and she saw his sword arm drop weakly. He staggered backward, making no effort to defend himself. Rough wrapped hands grabbed her from behind. A horrible scaled hand was clapped over her mouth. Struggling to free herself, she caught a glimpse of Riverwind. He was staring wide-eyed in terror at the thing in the cart, his face deathly white, his breathing swift and shallow—a man who wakes from a nightmare to discover it is reality.

Goldmoon, strong child of a warrior race, kicked backward at the cleric holding her, her foot aiming for his knee. Her skillful kick caught her opponent off guard and crushed his kneecap. The instant the cleric eased his grip on her, Goldmoon whirled around and struck him with her staff. She was amazed to see the cleric slump to the ground, seemingly felled by a blow even the mighty Caramon might have envied. She looked at her staff in astonishment, the staff that now glowed a bright blue. But there was no time to wonder—other creatures surrounded her. She swung her glistening staff in a wide arc, holding them at bay. But for how long?

"Riverwind!"

Goldmoon's cry woke the Plainsman from his terror. Turning, he saw her backing into the forest, keeping the cloaked clerics away with the staff. He grabbed one of the clerics from behind and threw him heavily to the ground. Another jumped at him while a third sprang toward Goldmoon.

There was a blinding blue flash.

A moment ahead of Tanis's cry, Sturm had realized the clerics had set a trap and drew his sword. He had seen, through the slats of the old wooden cart, a clawed hand grabbing for the staff. Lunging forward, he had gone to back up Riverwind. But the knight was totally unprepared for the Plainsman's reaction at sight of the creature in the cart. Sturm saw Riverwind stagger backward, helpless, as the creature grabbed a battle-axe in its uninjured hand and sprang directly at the barbarian. Riverwind made no move to defend himself. He just stared, his weapon dangling in his hand.

Sturm plunged his sword into the creature's back. The thing screamed and whirled around to attack, wrenching the sword from the knight's hand. Slavering and gurgling in its dying rage, the creature wrapped its arms around the startled knight and bore him into the muddy road. Sturm knew the thing that grasped him was dying and fought to beat down the terror and revulsion he felt at the touch of its slimy skin. The screaming stopped, and he felt the creature go rigid. The knight shoved the body over and quickly started to pull his sword from the creature's back. The weapon didn't budge! He stared at it in disbelief, then yanked on the sword with all his might, even putting his booted foot against the body to gain leverage. The weapon was stuck fast. Furious, he beat at the creature with his hands, then drew back in fear and loathing. The thing had turned to stone!†

This shows this creature to be a Baaz, smallest and most common of draconian kind. Baaz are winged but manage to conceal their wings under such clothing as capes and robes. As they are nearest in size and shape to humans, their masters often employ them as spies.—TRH

In the game material, the leader of the draconians is identified as a Kapak.

"Caramon!" Sturm yelled as another of the strange clerics leaped toward him, swinging an axe. Sturm ducked, felt a slashing pain, and then was blinded when blood flowed into his eyes. He stumbled, unable to see, and a crushing weight bore him to the ground.

Caramon, standing near the front of the cart, started to go to Goldmoon's aid when he heard Sturm's cry. Then two of the creatures bore down on him. Swinging his shortsword to force them to keep their distance, Caramon drew his dagger with his left hand. One cleric jumped for him and Caramon slashed out, his blade biting deep into flesh. He smelled a foul, rotting stench and saw a sickly green stain appear on the cleric's robes, but the wound appeared just to enrage the creature. It kept coming, saliva dripping from jaws that were the jaws of a reptile—not a man. For a moment, panic engulfed Caramon. He had fought trolls and goblins, but these horrible clerics completely unnerved him. He felt lost and alone, then he heard a reassuring whisper next to him.

"I am here, my brother." Raistlin's calm voice filled his mind.

"About time," Caramon gasped, threatening the creature with his sword. "What sort of foul clerics are these?"

"Don't stab them!" Raistlin warned swiftly. "They'll turn to stone. They're not clerics. They are some sort of reptile man. That is the reason for the robes and hoods."

Though different as light and shadow, the twins fought well as a team.† They exchanged few words during battle, their thoughts merging faster than tongues could translate. Caramon dropped his sword and dagger and flexed his huge arm muscles. The creatures, seeing Caramon drop his weapons, charged forward. Their rags had fallen loose and fluttered about them grotesquely. Caramon grimaced at the sight of the scaled bodies and clawed hands.

See Brothers in Arms *by Margaret Weis and Don Perrin for a more detailed account of the twins' military experience.*

"Ready," he said to his brother.

"Ast tasark simiralan krynawi," said Raistlin softly, and he threw a handful of sand into the air.† The creatures stopped their wild rush, shook their heads groggily as magical sleep stole over them . . . but then blinked their eyes. Within moments, they had regained their senses and started forward again!

Another AD&D Sleep spell as in Chapter 5. This magic phrase is spelled differently for no reason that I can think of except perhaps that the editors for all versions of the novels have not been well-founded in the language of magic. For any of you out there who are throwing sand in the air while uttering these words in an attempt to put your friends to sleep, you should know that neither version works anywhere outside of Krynn.—TRH

"Magic resistant!" Raistlin murmured in awe. But that brief interlude of near sleep was long enough for Caramon. Encircling their scrawny, reptilian necks with his huge hands, the warrior swept their heads together. The bodies tumbled to the ground—lifeless statues. Caramon looked up to see two more clerics crawling over the stony bodies of their brethren, curved swords gleaming in their wrapped hands.

"Stand behind me," ordered Raistlin in a hoarse whisper. Caramon reached down and grabbed dagger and sword. He dodged behind his brother, fearful for his twin's safety, yet knowing Raistlin could not cast his spell if he stood in the way.

Raistlin stared intently at the creatures, who—recognizing a magic-user—slowed and glanced at each other, hesitant to approach. One dropped to the ground and crawled under the cart. The other sprang forward, sword in hand, hoping to impale the mage before his spell was cast, or at least break the concentration that was so necessary to the spell-caster. Caramon bellowed. Raistlin seemed not to hear or see any of them. Slowly he raised his hands. Placing his thumbs together, he spread his thin fingers in a fanlike pattern and spoke, *"Kair tangus miopiar."*† Magic coursed through his frail body, and the creature was engulfed in flame.

These are apparently the mystic words of a Burning Hands spell. In game terms, Raistlin's magic has thus far consisted of two first-level spells. According to the rules of the game, this would make him at a minimum a second-level magic-user—not much progress considering all Raistlin has gone through in the Tower of High Sorcery. According to the game module DL-1 Dragons of Despair *(which covers the events of the first half of* Autumn Twilight*), Raistlin was a third-level magic-user, so he's holding one spell back.—TRH*

Tanis, recovering from his initial shock, heard Sturm's yell and crashed through the brush out onto the road. He swung the flat of his sword blade like a club and struck the creature that had Sturm pinned to the ground. The cleric fell over with a shriek and Tanis was able to drag the wounded knight into the brush.

"My sword," Sturm mumbled, dazed. Blood poured down his face; he tried unsuccessfully to wipe it away.

"We'll get it," Tanis promised, wondering how. Looking down the road, he could see more creatures swarming out of the woods and heading toward them. Tanis's mouth was dry. We've got to get out of here, he thought, fighting down panic. He forced himself to pause and draw a deep breath. Then he turned to Flint and Tasslehoff who had run up behind him.

"Stay here and guard Sturm," he instructed. "I'm going to get everyone together. We'll head back into the woods."

Not waiting for an answer, Tanis dashed out into the road, but then the flames from Raistlin's spell flared out and he was forced to fling himself to the ground.

The cart began to smoke as the straw pallet the creature had been lying on inside caught fire.

"Stay here and guard Sturm. Humpf!" Flint muttered, getting a firm grip on his battle-axe. For the moment, the creatures coming down the road did not seem to notice the dwarf or the kender or the wounded knight lying in the shadows of the trees. Their attention was on the two small knots of

battling warriors. But Flint knew it was only a matter of time. He planted his feet more firmly. "Do something for Sturm," he said to Tas irritably. "Make yourself useful for once."

"I'm trying," Tasslehoff replied in a hurt tone. "But I can't get the bleeding stopped." He wiped the knight's eyes with a moderately clean handkerchief. "There, can you see now?" he asked anxiously.

Sturm groaned and tried to sit up, but pain flashed through his head and he sank back. "My sword," he said.

Tasslehoff looked over to see Sturm's two-handed weapon sticking out of the back of the stone cleric. "That's fantastic!" the wide-eyed kender said. "Look, Flint! Sturm's sword—"

"I know, you fog-brained idiot kender!" Flint roared as he saw a creature running toward them, its blade drawn.

"I'll just go get it," Tas said cheerfully to Sturm as he knelt beside him. "I won't be a moment."

"No—" Flint yelled, realizing the attacking cleric was out of Tas's line of vision. The creature's wicked, curved sword lashed out in a flashing arc, aimed for the dwarf's neck. Flint swung his axe, but at that moment, Tasslehoff—his eyes on Sturm's sword—rose to his feet. The kender's hoopak staff struck the dwarf in the back of the knees, causing Flint's legs to buckle beneath him. The creature's sword whistled harmlessly overhead as the dwarf gave a startled yell and fell over backward on top of Sturm.

Tasslehoff, hearing the dwarf shout, looked back, astonished at an odd sight: a cleric was attacking Flint and, for some reason, the dwarf was lying on his back, legs flailing, when he should have been up fighting.

"What *are* you doing, Flint?" Tas shouted. He nonchalantly struck the creature in the midsection with his hoopak, struck it again on the head as it toppled forward, and watched it fall to the ground, unconscious.

"There!" he said irritably to Flint. "Do I have to fight your battles for you?" The kender turned and headed back toward Sturm's sword.

"Fight! For me!" The dwarf, sputtering with rage, struggled wildly to stand up. His helm had slipped

over his eyes, blinding him. Flint shoved it back just as another cleric bowled into him, knocking the dwarf off his feet again.

Tanis found Goldmoon and Riverwind standing back to back, Goldmoon fending off the creatures with her staff. Three of them lay dead at her feet, their stony remains blackened from the staff's blue flame. Riverwind's sword was caught fast in the guts of another statue. The Plainsman had unslung his only remaining weapon—his short bow—and had an arrow nocked and ready. The creatures were, for the moment, hanging back, discussing their strategy in low, indecipherable tones. Knowing they must rush the Plainsmen in a moment, Tanis leaped toward them and smote one of the creatures from behind, using the flat of his sword, then made a backhand swing at another.

"Come on!" he shouted to the Plainsmen. "This way!"

Some of the creatures turned at this new attack; others hesitated. Riverwind fired an arrow and felled one, then he grabbed Goldmoon's hand and together they ran toward Tanis, jumping over the stone bodies of their victims.

Tanis let them get past him, fending off the creatures with the flat of his sword. "Here, take this dagger!" he shouted to Riverwind as the barbarian ran by. Riverwind grabbed it, reversed it, and struck one of the creatures in the jaw. Jabbing upward with the hilt, he broke its neck. There was another flash of blue flame as Goldmoon used her staff to knock another creature out of the way. Then they were into the woods.

The wooden cart was burning fiercely now. Peering through the smoke, Tanis caught glimpses of the road. A shiver ran through him as he saw dark winged forms floating to the ground about a half mile away on either side of them.† The road was cut off in both directions. They were trapped unless they escaped into the woods immediately.

Presumably Sivak draconians, the only kind with flying abilities.

He reached the place where he had left Sturm. Goldmoon and Riverwind were there, so was Flint. Where was everyone else? He stared around in the thick smoke, blinking back tears.

"Help Sturm," he told Goldmoon. Then he turned to Flint, who was trying unsuccessfully to yank his

axe out of the chest of a stone creature. "Where are Caramon and Raistlin? And where's Tas? I told him to stay here—"

"Blasted kender nearly got me killed!" Flint exploded. "I hope they carry him off! I hope they use him for dog meat! I hope—"

"In the name of the gods!" Tanis swore in exasperation. He made his way through the smoke toward where he had last seen Caramon and Raistlin and stumbled across the kender, dragging Sturm's sword back along the road. The weapon was nearly as big as Tasslehoff and he couldn't lift it, so he was dragging it through the mud.

"How did you get that?" Tanis asked in amazement, coughing in the thick smoke that boiled around them.

Tas grinned, tears streaming down his face from the smoke in his eyes. "The creature turned to dust,"† he said happily. "Oh, Tanis, it was wonderful. I walked up and pulled on the sword and it wouldn't come out, so I pulled again and—"

Another Baaz characteristic.—TRH

"Not now! Get back to the others!" Tanis grabbed the kender and shoved him forward. "Have you seen Caramon and Raistlin?"

But just then he heard the warrior's voice boom out of the smoke. "Here we are," Caramon panted. He had his arm around his brother, who was coughing uncontrollably. "Have we destroyed them all?" the big man asked cheerfully.

"No, we haven't," Tanis replied grimly. "In fact, we've got to get away through the woods to the south." He put his arm around Raistlin and together they hurried back to where the others were huddled by the road, choking in the smoke, yet thankful for its enveloping cover.

Sturm was on his feet, his face pale, but the pain in his head was gone and the wound had quit bleeding.

"The staff healed him?" Tanis asked Goldmoon.

She coughed. "Not completely. Enough so that he can walk."

"It has . . . limits," Raistlin said, wheezing.

"Yes—" Tanis interrupted. "Well, we're heading south, into the woods."

Caramon shook his head. "That's Darken Wood—" he began.

"I know—you'd rather fight the living," Tanis interrupted. "How do you feel about that now?"

The warrior did not answer.

"More of those creatures are coming from both directions. We can't fight off another assault. But we won't enter Darken Wood if we don't have to. There's a game trail not far from here we can use to reach Prayer's Eye Peak. There we can see the road to the north, as well as all other directions."

"We could go north as far as the cave. The boat's hidden there." Riverwind suggested.

"No!" yelled Flint in a strangled voice. Without another word, the dwarf turned and plunged into the forest, running south as fast as his short legs could carry him.

9

Flight! The white stag.

The White Stag was a traditional omen of good luck and divine blessing.
According to classical myth, it draws serpents from their holes and tramples them to death.

The companions stumbled through the thick woods as fast as they could and soon reached the game trail. Caramon took the lead, sword in hand, eyeing every shadow. His brother followed, one hand on Caramon's shoulder, his lips set in grim determination. The rest came after, their weapons drawn.

But they saw no more of the creatures.

"Why aren't they chasing us?" Flint asked after they had traveled about an hour.

Tanis scratched his beard—he had been wondering about the same thing. "They don't need to," he said finally. "We are trapped. They've undoubtedly blocked all the exits from this forest. With the exception of Darken Wood . . ."

"Darken Wood!" Goldmoon repeated softly. "Is it truly necessary to go that way?"

"It may not be," Tanis said. "We'll get a look around from Prayer's Eye Peak."†

Highest of several peaks in the Sentinel Range.

Suddenly they heard Caramon, walking ahead of them, shout. Running forward, Tanis found Raistlin had collapsed.

"I'll be all right," the mage whispered. "But I must rest."

"We can all use rest," Tanis said.

No one answered. All sank down wearily, catching their breath in quick, sharp gasps. Sturm closed his eyes and leaned against a moss-covered rock. His face was a ghastly shade of grayish white. Blood had matted his long moustaches and caked his hair. The wound was a jagged slash, turning slowly purple. Tanis knew that the knight would die before he said a word of complaint.

"Don't worry," Sturm said harshly. "Just give me a moment's peace." Tanis gripped the knight's hand briefly, then went to sit beside Riverwind.

Neither spoke for long minutes, then Tanis asked, "You've fought those creatures before, haven't you?"

"In the broken city." Riverwind shuddered. "It all came back to me when I looked inside the cart and saw that thing leering at me! At least—" He paused, shook his head. Then he gave Tanis a half-smile. "At least I know now that I'm not going insane. Those horrible creatures really do exist—I had wondered sometimes."

"I can imagine," Tanis murmured. "So these creatures are spreading all over Krynn, unless your broken city was near here."

"No. I came into Qué-Shu out of the east. It was far from Solace, beyond the Plains of my homeland."

"What do you suppose those creatures meant, saying they had tracked you to our village?" Goldmoon asked slowly, laying her cheek on his leather tunic sleeve, slipping her hand around his arm.

"Don't worry," Riverwind said, taking her hand in his. "The warriors there would deal with them."

"Riverwind, do you remember what you were going to say?" she prompted.

"Yes, you are right," Riverwind replied, stroking her silver-gold hair. He looked at Tanis and smiled.

For an instant, the expressionless mask was gone and Tanis saw warmth deep within the man's brown eyes. "I give my thanks to you, Half-Elven, and to all of you." His glance flickered over everyone. "You have saved our lives more than once and I have been ungrateful. But"—he paused—"it's all so strange!"

Another of my favorite lines.—MW

"It's going to get stranger."† Raistlin's voice was ominous.

The companions were drawing nearer Prayer's Eye Peak. They had been able to see it from the road, rising above the forests. Its split peak looked like two hands pressed together in prayer—thus the name. The rain had stopped. The woods were deathly quiet. The companions began to think that the forest animals and birds had vanished from the land, leaving an eerie, empty silence behind. All of them felt uneasy—except perhaps Tasslehoff, and kept peering over their shoulders or drawing their swords at shadows.

Sturm insisted on walking rear guard, but he began lagging behind as the pain in his head increased. He was becoming dizzy and nauseated. Soon he lost all conception of where he was and what he was doing. He knew only that he must keep walking, placing one foot in front of the other, moving forward like one of Tas's automatons.

This is a reference to the episode told in Roger Moore's trend-setting short story, "A Stone's Throw Away," which appears in The Magic of Krynn.

How did Tas's story go? Sturm tried to remember it through a haze of pain. These automatons served a wizard† who had summoned a demon to carry the kender away. It was nonsense, like all the kender's stories. Sturm put one foot in front of the other. Nonsense. Like the old man's stories—the old man in the Inn. Stories of the White Stag and ancient gods—Paladine. Stories of Huma. Sturm clasped his hands on his throbbing temples as if he could hold his splitting head together. Huma . . .

As a boy, Sturm had fed on stories of Huma. His mother, daughter of a Knight of Solamnia, married to a Knight—had known no other stories to tell her son. Sturm's thoughts turned to his mother, his pain making him think of her tender ministrations when he was sick or hurt. Sturm's father had sent his wife and their son into exile because the boy—his only heir—was a target for those who would see the

Knights of Solamnia banished forever from the face of Krynn. Sturm and his mother took refuge in Solace.† Sturm made friends readily, particularly with one other boy, Caramon, who shared his interest in all things military. But Sturm's proud mother considered the people beneath her. And so, when the fever consumed her, she had died alone except for her teenage son. She had commended the boy to his father—if his father still lived, which Sturm was beginning to doubt.

Sturm and his mother, Lady Ilys, traveled to Solace in "The Exiles," by Paul B. Thompson and Tonya Carter, in the anthology called Love and War.

After his mother's death, the young man became a seasoned warrior under the guidance of Tanis and Flint, who adopted Sturm as they had unofficially adopted Caramon and Raistlin. Together with Tasslehoff, the travel-loving kender, and, on occasion, the twins' wild and beautiful half-sister, Kitiara, Sturm and his friends escorted Flint on his journeys through the lands of Abanasinia, plying his trade as metalsmith.

Five years ago, however, the companions decided to separate to investigate reports of evil growing in the land. They vowed to meet again at the Inn of the Last Home.

Sturm had traveled north to Solamnia, determined to find his father and his heritage. He found nothing, and only narrowly escaped with his life—and his father's sword and armor. The journey to his homeland was a harrowing experience. Sturm had known the Knights were reviled, but he had been shocked to realize just how deep the bitterness against them ran. Huma, Lightbringer,† Knight of Solamnia, had driven back the darkness years ago, during the Age of Dreams, and thus began the Age of Might. Then came the Cataclysm, when the gods abandoned man, according to the popular belief. The people had turned to the Knights for help, as they had turned to Huma in the past. But Huma was long dead. The Knights could only watch helplessly as terror rained down from heaven and Krynn was smote asunder. The people had cried to the Knights, but they could do nothing, and the people had never forgiven them. Standing in front of his family's ruined castle, Sturm vowed that he would restore the honor of the Knights of Solamnia—if it meant that he must sacrifice his life in the attempt.

We studied Tolkien, as I mentioned before, when we set out to create the world of DRAGONLANCE. One thing that resonated deeply was the need to ground the story firmly in a past. Huma's legend was part of that background, which we established to make the world real.
—TRH

But how could he do that fighting a bunch of clerics, he wondered bitterly, the trail dimming before his eyes. He stumbled, caught himself quickly. Huma had fought dragons. Give me dragons, Sturm dreamed. He lifted his eyes. The leaves blurred into a golden mist and he knew he was going to faint. Then he blinked. Everything came sharply into focus.

Before him rose Prayer's Eye Peak. He and his companions had arrived at the foot of the old, glacial mountain. He could see trails twisting and winding up the wooded slope, trails used by Solace residents to reach picnic spots on the eastern side of the Peak. Next to one of the well-worn paths stood a white stag.† Sturm stared. The stag was the most magnificent animal the knight had ever seen. It was huge, standing several hands taller than any other stag the knight had hunted. It held its head proudly, its splendid rack gleaming like a crown. Its eyes were deep brown against its pure white fur, and it gazed at the knight intently, as if it knew him. Then, with a slight shake of its head, the stag bounded away to the southwest.

This stag, as foreshadowed by the old storyteller in the tavern, is a traditional archetype symbol of prophecy and good omen.—TRH

"Stop!" the knight called out hoarsely.

The others whirled around in alarm, drawing weapons. Tanis came running back to him. "What is it, Sturm?"

The knight involuntarily put his hand to his aching head.

"I'm sorry, Sturm," Tanis said. "I didn't realize you were as sick as this. We can rest. We're at the foot of Prayer's Eye Peak. I'm going to climb the mountain and see—"

"No! Look!" The knight gripped Tanis's shoulder and turned him around. He pointed. "See it? The white stag!"

"The white stag?" Tanis stared in the direction the knight indicated. "Where? I don't—"

"There," Sturm said softly. He took a few steps forward, toward the animal who had stopped and seemed to be waiting for him. The stag nodded its great head. It darted away again, just a few steps, then turned to face the knight once more. "He wants us to follow him," Sturm gasped. "Like Huma!"

The others had gathered around the knight now, regarding him with expressions that ranged from deeply concerned to obviously skeptical.

"I see no stag of any color," Riverwind said, his dark eyes scanning the forest.

"Head wound." Caramon nodded like a charlatan cleric. "C'mon, Sturm, lie down and rest while—"

"You great blithering idiot!" the knight snarled at Caramon. "With your brains in your stomach, it is just as well you do not see the stag. You would probably shoot it and cook it! I tell you this—we must follow it!"

"The madness of the head wound," Riverwind whispered to Tanis. "I have seen it often."

"I'm not sure," Tanis said. He was silent for a few moments. When he spoke, it was with obvious reluctance. "Though I have not seen the white stag myself, I have been with one who has and I have followed it, like in the old man's story." His hand absently fingered the ring of twisted ivy leaves that he wore on his left hand, his thoughts with the golden-haired elfmaiden who wept when he left Qualinesti.

"You're suggesting we follow an animal we can't even see?" Caramon said, his jaw going slack.

"It would not be the strangest thing we have done," Raistlin commented sarcastically in his whispering voice. "Though, remember, it was the old man who told the tale of the White Stag and the old man who got us into this—"

"It was our own choice got us into this," Tanis snapped. "We could have turned the staff over to the High Theocrat and talked our way out of the predicament; we've talked our way out of worse. I say we follow Sturm. He has been chosen, apparently, just as Riverwind was chosen to receive the staff—"

"But it's not even leading us in the right direction!" Caramon argued. "You know as well as I do there are no trails through the western part of the woods. No one ever goes there."

"All the better," Goldmoon said suddenly. "Tanis said those creatures must have the paths blocked. Maybe this is a way out. I say we follow the knight." She turned and started off with Sturm, not even glancing back at the others—obviously accustomed to being obeyed. Riverwind shrugged and shook his head, scowling darkly, but he walked after Goldmoon and the others followed.

The knight left the well-trodden paths of Prayer's Eye Peak behind, moving in a southwesterly direction up the slope. At first it appeared Caramon was right—there were no trails. Sturm was crashing through the brush like a madman. Then, suddenly, a smooth wide trail opened up ahead of them. Tanis stared at it in amazement.

"What or who cleared this trail?" he asked Riverwind, who was also examining it with a puzzled expression.

"I don't know," the Plainsman said. "It's old. That felled tree has lain there long enough to sink over halfway into the dirt and it's covered with moss and vines. But there are no tracks—other than Sturm's. There's no sign of anyone or any animal passing through here. Yet why isn't it overgrown?"

Tanis couldn't answer and he couldn't take time to think about it. Sturm forged ahead rapidly; all the party could do was try to keep him in sight.

"Goblins, boats, lizard men, invisible stags—what next?" complained Flint to the kender.

"I wish I could see the stag," Tas said wistfully.

"Get hit on the head." The dwarf snorted. "Although with you, we probably couldn't tell the difference."

The companions followed Sturm, who was climbing with a wild kind of elation, his pain and wound forgotten. Tanis had difficulty catching up with the knight. When he did, he was alarmed at the feverish gleam in Sturm's eye. But the knight was obviously being guided by something. The trail led them up the slope of Prayer's Eye Peak. Tanis saw that it was taking them to the gap between the "hands" of stone, a gap that as far as he knew no one had ever entered before.

"Wait a moment," he gasped, running to catch up with Sturm. It was nearly midday, he guessed, though the sun was still hidden by jagged gray clouds. "Let's rest. I'm going to take a look at the land from over there." He pointed to a rock ledge that jutted out from the side of the peak.

"Rest . . ." repeated Sturm vaguely, stopping and catching his breath. He stared ahead for a moment, then turned to Tanis. "Yes. We'll rest." His eyes gleamed brightly.

"Are you all right?"

"Fine," Sturm said absently and paced around the grass, gently stroking and smoothing his moustaches. Tanis looked at him a moment, irresolute, then went back to the others who were just coming over the crest of a small rise.

"We're going to rest here," the half-elf said. Raistlin breathed a sigh of relief and sank down in the wet leaves.

"I'm going to have a look north, see what's moving back on the road to Haven," Tanis added.

"I'll come with you," Riverwind offered.

Tanis nodded and the two left the path, heading for the rock ledge. Tanis glanced at the tall warrior as they walked together. He was beginning to feel comfortable with the stern, serious Plainsman. A deeply private person himself, Riverwind respected the privacy of others and would never think of probing the boundaries Tanis set around his soul. This was as relaxing to the half-elf as a night's unbroken sleep. He knew that his friends—simply because they were his friends and had known him for years—were speculating on his relationship with Kitiara. Why had he chosen to break it off so abruptly five years ago? And why, then, his obvious disappointment when she failed to join them? Riverwind, of course, knew nothing about Kitiara, but Tanis had the feeling that if he did, it would be all the same to the Plainsman: it was Tanis's business, not his.

When they were within sight of the Haven Road, they crawled the last few feet, inching their way along the wet rock until they came to the rim of the ledge. Tanis, looking below and to the east, could see the old picnic paths disappearing around the side of the mountain. Riverwind pointed, and Tanis realized there were creatures moving along the picnic trails! That explained the uncanny hush in the forest. Tanis pressed his lips together grimly. The creatures must be waiting to ambush them. Sturm and his white stag had probably saved their lives.† But it wouldn't take the creatures long to find this new trail. Tanis glanced below him and blinked—there was no trail! There was nothing but thick, impenetrable forest. The trail had closed behind them! I must be imagining things, he thought, and he turned his eyes back to Haven Road and the many creatures moving along it. It hadn't taken them long

Richard II of England used a white hart (stag) as his personal symbol, and many pubs in England are called the White Hart.

to get organized, he thought. He gazed farther to the north and saw the still, peaceful waters of Crystalmir Lake. Then his glance traveled to the horizon.

He frowned. There was something wrong. He couldn't place it immediately, so he said nothing to Riverwind but stared at the skyline. Storm clouds massed in the north more thickly than ever, long gray fingers raking the land. And reaching up to meet them—that was it! Gripping Riverwind's arm, Tanis stabbed his finger northward. Riverwind looked, squinting, seeing nothing at first. Then he saw it, black smoke drifting into the sky. His thick, heavy brows contracted.

"Campfires," Tanis said.

"Many hundred campfires," Riverwind amended softly. "The fires of war. That is an army encampment."

"So the rumors are confirmed," Sturm said when they returned. "There *is* an army to the north."

"But what army? Whose? And why? What are they going to attack?" Caramon laughed incredulously. "No one would send an army after this staff." The warrior paused. "Would they?"

"The staff is but a part of this," Raistlin hissed. "Remember the fallen stars!"

"Children's stories!" Flint sniffed. He upended the empty wineskin, shook it, and sighed.

"My stories are not for children," Raistlin said viciously, twisting up from the leaves like a snake. "And you would do well to heed my words, dwarf!"

"There it is! There's the stag!" Sturm said suddenly, his eyes staring straight at a large boulder—or so it seemed to his companions. "It is time to go."

The knight began walking. The others hastily gathered their gear together and hurried after him. As they climbed ever farther up the trail—which seemed to materialize before them as they went—the wind switched and began blowing from the south. It was a warm breeze, carrying with it the fragrance of late-blooming autumn wildflowers. It drove back the storm clouds and just as they came to the cleft between the two halves of the Peak, the sun broke free.

It was well past midday when they stopped to rest for one more brief period before attempting the

climb through the narrow gap between the walls of Prayer's Eye Peak through which Sturm said they must go. The stag had led the way, he insisted.

"It'll be suppertime soon," Caramon said. He heaved a gusty sigh, staring at his feet. "I could eat my boots!"

"They're beginning to look good to me, too," Flint said grumpily. "I wish that stag was flesh and blood. It might be useful for something besides getting us lost!"

"Shut up!" Sturm turned on the dwarf in a sudden rage, his fists clenched. Tanis rose quickly, put his hand on the knight's shoulder, holding him back.

Sturm stood glaring at the dwarf, moustaches quivering, then he jerked away from Tanis. "Let's go," he muttered.†

A paragraph of Tanis's thoughts was cut here: Sturm was acting stranger and stranger, and Tanis wasn't certain he liked the direction the knight—or the stag—was leading them. But for now he couldn't think of anything better. North was definitely out of the question. So, apparently, were the east and the west. Tanis was glad they had been led this way—he just wondered where they would go from here.

As the companions entered the narrow defile, they could see clear blue sky on the other side. The south wind whistled across the steep white walls of the Peak soaring above them. They walked carefully, small stones causing their feet to slip more than once. Fortunately, the way was so narrow that they could easily regain their balance by catching themselves against the steep walls.

After about thirty minutes of walking, they came out on the other side of Prayer's Eye Peak. They halted, staring down into a valley. Lush, grassy meadowland flowed in green waves below them to lap on the shores of a light-green aspen forest far to the south. The storm clouds were behind them, and the sun shone brightly in a clear, azure sky.

For the first time, they found their cloaks too heavy, except for Raistlin who remained huddled in his red, hooded cape. Flint had spent the morning complaining about the rain and now started in on the sunshine, it was too bright, glaring into his eyes. It was too hot, beating down on his helm.

"I say we throw the dwarf off the mountain," growled Caramon to Tanis.

Tanis grinned. "He'd rattle all the way down and give away our position."

"Who's down there to hear him?" Caramon said, gesturing toward the valley with his broad hand. "I bet we're the first living beings to set eyes on this valley."

"First *living* beings," Raistlin breathed. "You are right there, my brother. For you look on Darken Wood."†

In "Hunting Destiny" by Nick O'Donohoe, a stag is following the companions through the Darken Wood. The stag listens as they talk about various legends dealing with Darken Wood. One legend tells of a white stag who led Huma home. Another tells of a white stag who helped turn Shadow Wood to Darken Wood. The story is in Love and War.

No one spoke. Riverwind shifted uncomfortably; Goldmoon crept over to stand beside him, staring down into the green trees, her eyes wide. Flint cleared his throat and fell silent, stroking his long beard. Sturm regarded the forest calmly. So did Tasslehoff. "It doesn't look bad at all," the kender said cheerfully. Sitting cross-legged on the ground, a sheaf of parchment spread out on his knees, he was drawing a map with a bit of charcoal, attempting to trace their way up Prayer's Eye Peak.

"Looks are as deceptive as light-fingered kender," Raistlin whispered harshly.

Tasslehoff frowned, started to retort, then caught Tanis's eye and went back to his drawing. Tanis walked over to Sturm. The knight stood out on a ledge, the south wind blowing back his long hair and whipping his frayed cape about him.

"Sturm, where is the stag? Do you see it now?"

"Yes," Sturm answered. He pointed downward. "It walked across the meadow; I can see its trail in the tall grass. It has gone into the aspens there."

"Gone into Darken Wood," Tanis murmured.

"Who says that is Darken Wood?" Sturm turned to face Tanis.

"Raistlin."

"Bah!"

"He is magi,"† Tanis said.

The word magi traditionally means "wise person." Here it also is used as another name for wizard, who, of course, is also a knowledgeable person.—TRH

"He is crazed," Sturm replied. Then he shrugged. "But stay here rooted on the side of the Peak if you like, Tanis. I will follow the stag—as did Huma—even if it leads me into Darken Wood." Wrapping his cloak around him, Sturm climbed down the ledge and began to walk along a winding trail that led down the mountainside.

Tanis returned to the others. "The stag's leading him on a straight path right into the forest," he said. "How certain are you that this forest is Darken Wood, Raistlin?"

"How certain is one of anything, Half-Elven?" the mage replied. "I am not certain of drawing my next breath. But go ahead. Walk into the wood that no living man has ever walked out of. Death is life's one great certainty, Tanis."

The half-elf felt a sudden urge to throw Raistlin off the side of the mountain. He stared after Sturm, who was nearly halfway down into the valley.

"I'm going with Sturm," he said suddenly. "But I'll be responsible for no one else in this decision. The rest of you may follow as you choose."

"I'm coming!" Tasslehoff rolled his map up and slipped it into his scroll case. He scrambled to his feet, sliding in the loose rock.

"Ghosts!" Flint scowled at Raistlin, snapped his fingers derisively, then stumped over to stand beside the half-elf. Goldmoon followed unhesitatingly, though her face was pale. Riverwind joined the group more slowly, his face thoughtful. Tanis was relieved—the barbarians had many frightening legends of Darken Wood, he knew. And finally, Raistlin moved forward so rapidly he took his brother completely by surprise.

Tanis regarded the mage with a slight smile. "Why do you come?" he couldn't help asking.

"Because you will need me, Half-Elven," the mage hissed. "Besides, where would you have us go? You have allowed us to be led this far, there can be no turning back. It is the Ogre's Choice you offer us, Tanis—'Die fast or die slow.' " He set off down the side of the Peak. "Coming, brother?"

The others glanced uneasily at Tanis as the brothers passed. The half-elf felt like a fool. Raistlin was right, of course. He'd let this go far beyond his control, then made it seem as if it were their decision, not his, allowing him to go forward with a clear conscience. Angrily he picked up a rock and hurled it far down the mountainside. Why was it his responsibility in the first place? Why had he gotten involved, when all he had wanted was to find Kitiara and tell her his mind was made up—he loved her and wanted her. He could accept her human frailties as he had learned to accept his own.

But Kit hadn't come back to him. She had a "new lord." Maybe that's why he'd—

"Ho, Tanis!" The kender's voice floated up to him.

"I'm coming," he muttered.

The sun was just beginning to dip into the west when the companions reached the edge of the forest. Tanis figured they had at least three or four hours of

daylight left. If the stag continued to lead them on smooth, clear trails, they might be able to get through this forest before darkness fell.

Sturm waited for them beneath the aspens, resting comfortably in the leafy, green shade. The companions left the meadow slowly, none of them in any hurry to enter the woods.

"The stag entered here," Sturm said, rising to his feet and pointing into the tall grass.

Tanis saw no tracks. He took a drink of water from his nearly empty waterskin and stared into the forest. As Tasslehoff had said, the wood did not seem sinister. In fact, it looked cool and inviting after the harsh brilliance of the autumn sunshine.

"Maybe there'll be some game in here," Caramon said, rocking back on his heels. "Not stags, of course," he added hastily. "Rabbits, maybe."

"Shoot nothing. Eat nothing. Drink nothing in Darken Wood," Raistlin whispered.

Tanis looked at the mage, whose hourglass† eyes were dilated. The metallic skin shone a ghastly color in the strong sunlight. Raistlin leaned upon his staff, shivering as if from a chill.

"Children's stories," Flint muttered, but the dwarf's voice lacked conviction. Although Tanis knew Raistlin's flair for the dramatic, he had never seen the mage affected like this before.

"What do you sense, Raistlin?" he asked quietly.

"There is a great and powerful magic laid on this wood," whispered Raistlin.

"Evil?" asked Tanis.

"Only to those who bring evil in with them," the mage stated.

"Then you are the only one who need fear this forest," Sturm told the mage coldly.

Caramon's face flushed an ugly red; his hand fumbled for his sword. Sturm's hand went to his blade. Tanis gripped Sturm's arm as Raistlin touched his brother. The mage stared at the knight, his golden eyes glimmering.

"We shall see," Raistlin said, the words nothing more than hissing sounds flicking between his teeth. "We shall see." Then, leaning heavily upon his staff, Raistlin turned to his brother. "Coming?"

Caramon glared angrily at Sturm, then entered the wood, walking beside his twin. The others

While the design team thought it "cool" that Raistlin have hourglass eyes, they left it up to us to explain why!—TRH

Actually, it was the artists who thought it would look great in the painting if Raistlin had hourglass eyes. I had to come up with a logical explanation. Not genetics—Caramon doesn't have hourglass eyes! That led me to the idea that Raistlin had attained them due to some sort of magical test. Which led me to an understanding of his character and also led to the development of the dread Test in the Tower of High Sorcery.—MW

moved after them, leaving only Tanis and Flint standing in the long, waving grass.

"I'm getting too old for this, Tanis," the dwarf said suddenly.†

"Nonsense," the half-elf replied, smiling. "You fought like a—"

Flint is not old for a dwarf, but his father died young, a fact that occasionally preys on his mind.

"No, I don't mean the bones or the muscles"—the dwarf looked at his gnarled hands—"though they're old enough. I mean the spirit. Years ago, before the others were born, you and I would have walked into a magicked wood without giving it a second thought. Now . . ."

"Cheer up," Tanis said. He tried to sound light, though he was deeply disturbed by the dwarf's unusual somberness. He studied Flint closely for the first time since meeting outside Solace. The dwarf looked old, but then Flint had always looked old. His face, what could be seen through the mass of gray beard and moustaches and overhanging white eyebrows, was brown and wrinkled and cracked like old leather. The dwarf grumbled and complained, but then Flint had always grumbled and complained. The change was in the eyes. The fiery luster was gone.

"Don't let Raistlin get to you," Tanis said. "We'll sit around the fire tonight and laugh at his ghost stories."

"I suppose so." Flint sighed. He was silent a moment, then said, "Someday I'll slow you up, Tanis. I don't ever want you to think, why do I put up with this grumbling old dwarf?"

"Because I need you, grumbling old dwarf," Tanis said, putting his hand on the dwarf's heavyset shoulder. He motioned into the wood, after the others. "I need you, Flint. They're all so . . . so young. You're like a solid rock that I can set my back against as I wield my sword."

Flint's face flushed in pleasure. He tugged at his beard, then cleared his throat gruffly. "Yes, well, you were always sentimental. Come along. We're wasting time. I want to get through this confounded forest as fast as possible." Then he muttered, "Just glad it's daylight."

10

Darken Wood.

The dead walk. Raistlin's magic.

The only thing Tanis felt on entering the forest was relief at being out of the glare of the autumn sun. The half-elf recalled all the legends he had heard about Darken Wood—† stories of ghosts told around the fire at night—and he kept in mind Raistlin's foreboding. But all Tanis felt was that the forest was so much more alive than any other he had ever entered.

Here, again, we see the depth in backstory—history that grounds our heroes and makes them more alive and real in our minds.—TRH

There was no deathly hush as they had experienced earlier. Small animals chattered in the brush. Birds fluttered in the high branches above them. Insects with gaily colored wings flitted past. Leaves rustled and stirred, flowers swayed though no breeze touched them—as if the plants reveled in being alive.

All of the companions entered the forest with their hands on their weapons, wary and watchful

and distrustful. After a time of trying to avoid making leaves crunch, Tas said it seemed "kind of silly," and they relaxed—all except Raistlin.

They walked for about two hours, traveling at a smooth but rapid easy pace along a smooth and clear trail. Shadows lengthened as the sun made its downward slide. Tanis felt at peace in this forest. He had no fear that the awful, winged creatures could follow them here. Evil seemed out of place, unless, as Raistlin said, one brought one's own evil into the wood. Tanis looked at the mage. Raistlin walked alone, his head bowed. The shadows of the forest trees seemed to gather thickly around the young mage. Tanis shivered and realized that the air was turning cool as the sun dropped below the treetops. It was time to begin thinking about making camp for the night.

Tanis pulled out Tasslehoff's map to study it once more before the light faded. The map was of elven design and written across the forest in flowing script were the words "Darken Wood." But the woods themselves were only vaguely outlined, and Tanis couldn't be certain if the words pertained to this forest or one farther south. Raistlin must be wrong, Tanis decided—this can't be Darken Wood. Or, if so, its evil was simply a product of the mage's imagination. They walked on.

Soon it was twilight, that time of evening when the dying light makes everything most vivid and distinct. The companions began to lag. Raistlin limped, and his breath came in wheezing gasps. Sturm's face turned ashen. The half-elf was just about to call a halt for the night when—as if anticipating his wishes—the trail led them right to a large, green glade. Clear water bubbled up from underground and trickled down smooth rocks to form a shallow brook. The glade was blanketed with thick, inviting grass; tall trees stood guard duty on the edges. As they saw the glade, the sun's light reddened, then faded, and the misty shades of night crept around the trees.

"Do not leave the path," Raistlin intoned as his companions started to enter the glade.

Tanis sighed. "Raistlin," he said patiently—"we'll be all right. The path is in plain sight, not ten feet away. Come on. You've got to rest. We all do. Look"—

Tanis held out the map—"I don't think this is Darken Wood. According to this—"

Raistlin ignored the map with disdain. The rest of the companions ignored the mage and, moving off the path, began setting up camp. Sturm sank down against a tree, his eyes closed in pain, while Caramon stared at the smaller, fleeting shadows with a hungry eye. At a signal from Caramon, Tasslehoff slipped off into the forest after firewood.

Watching them, the mage's face twisted in a sardonic smile. "You are all fools. This is Darken Wood, as you will see before the night is ended." He shrugged. "But, as you say, I need rest. However, *I* will not leave the path." Raistlin sat down on the trail, his staff beside him.

Caramon flushed in embarrassment as he saw the others exchanging amused glances. "Aw, Raist," the big man said, "join us. Tas has gone for wood and maybe I can shoot a rabbit."†

Rabbits became one of the underlying images—perhaps a subtext—of the saga.

"*Shoot* nothing!" Raistlin actually spoke above a whisper, making everyone start. "*Harm* nothing in Darken Wood! Neither plant nor tree, bird nor animal!"

"I agree with Raistlin," Tanis said. "We have to spend the night here and I don't want to kill any animal in this forest if we don't have to."

"Elves never want to kill period," Flint grumbled.† "The magician scares us to death and you starve us. Well, if anything does attack us tonight, I hope it's edible!"

Elves have a great reverence for life, though sometimes they are dismayed at the varieties it comes in on Krynn.

"You and me both, dwarf." Caramon heaved a sigh, went over to the creek, and began trying to assuage his hunger by drowning it.

Tasslehoff returned with firewood. "I didn't cut it," he assured Raistlin. "I just picked it up."

But even Riverwind couldn't make the wood catch fire. "The wood's wet," he stated finally and tossed his tinderbox back into his pack.

"We need light," Flint said uneasily as night's shadows closed in thickly. Sounds in the woods that had been innocent in the daytime now seemed sinister and threatening.

"Surely you do not fear children's stories," Raistlin hissed.

"No!" snapped the dwarf. "I just want to make certain the kender doesn't rifle my pack in the dark."

"Very well," said Raistlin with unusual mildness. He spoke his word of command: "*Shirak.*"† A pale, white light shone from the crystal on the tip of the mage's staff. It was a ghostly light and did little to brighten the darkness. In fact, it seemed to emphasize the menace in the night.

This magic word—Indonesian in form but composed of meaningless syllables—became one of Raistlin's most common magical utterances, along with its companion, "Dumak." Literally, "light" and "dark." —TRH

"There, you have light," the mage whispered softly. He thrust the bottom of the staff into the wet ground.

It was then Tanis realized his elven vision was gone. He should have been able to see the warm, red outlines of his companions, but they were nothing more than darker shadows against the starry darkness of the glade. The half-elf didn't say anything to the others, but the peaceful feeling he had been enjoying was pierced by a sliver of fear.

Raistlin first learned to use the staff to produce light shortly after undergoing the Test. See Brothers in Arms.

"I'll take the first watch," Sturm offered heavily. "I shouldn't sleep with this head wound, anyway. I once knew a man who did, he never woke up."

"We'll watch in twos," Tanis said. "I'll take first watch with you."

The others opened packs and began making up beds on the grass, except for Raistlin. He remained sitting on the trail, the light of his staff shining on his bowed, hooded head. Sturm settled down beneath a tree. Tanis walked over to the brook and drank thirstily. Suddenly he heard a strangled cry behind him. He drew his sword and stood, all in one motion. The others had their weapons drawn. Only Raistlin sat, unmoving.

"Put your swords away," he said. "They will do you no good. Only a weapon of powerful magic could harm these."

An army of warriors surrounded them. That alone would have been enough to chill anyone's blood. But the companions could have dealt with that. What they couldn't handle was the horror that overwhelmed and numbed their senses. Each one recalled Caramon's flippant comment: "I'll fight the living any day of the week, but not the dead."

These warriors were dead.

Nothing more than fleeting, fragile white light outlined their bodies. It was as if the human warmth that had been theirs while they lived lingered on horribly after death. The flesh had rotted away, leaving behind the body's image as remembered by the

soul. The soul apparently remembered other things, too. Each warrior was dressed in ancient, remembered armor. Each warrior carried remembered weapons that could inflict well-remembered death. But the undead needed no weapons. They could kill from fear alone, or by the touch of their grave-cold hands.

How can we fight these things? Tanis thought wildly, he who had never felt such fear in the face of flesh and blood enemies. Panic engulfed him, and he considered yelling for the others to turn and run for it.

Angrily, the half-elf forced himself to calm down, to get a grip on reality. Reality! He almost laughed at the irony. Running was useless; they would get lost, separated. They had to stay and deal with this—somehow. He began to walk toward the ghostly warriors. The dead said nothing, made no threatening moves. They simply stood, blocking the path. It was impossible to count them since some glimmered into being while others faded, only to return when their comrades dimmed. Not that it makes any difference, Tanis admitted to himself, feeling sweat chill his body. One of these undead warriors could kill all of us simply by lifting its hand.

As the half-elf drew nearer to the warriors, he saw a gleam of light—Raistlin's staff. The mage, leaning on his staff, stood in front of the huddle of companions. Tanis came to stand beside him. The pale crystal light reflected on the mage's face, making it seem nearly as ghostly as the faces of the dead before him.

"Welcome to Darken Wood, Tanis," the mage said.

"Raistlin—" Tanis choked. He had to try more than once to get his dry throat to form a sound. "What are these—"

"Spectral minions,"† the mage whispered without taking his eyes from them. "We are fortunate."

A little invention of my own. I rather like the idea still.—TRH

"Fortunate?" Tanis repeated incredulously. "Why?"

"These are the spirits of men who gave their pledge to perform some task. They failed in that pledge, and it is their doom to keep performing the same task over and over until they win their release and find true rest in death."

"How in the name of the Abyss† does that make us fortunate?" Tanis whispered harshly, releasing his fear in anger. "Perhaps they pledged to rid the forest of all who entered!"

"That is possible"—Raistlin flickered a glance at the half-elf—"though I do not think it likely. We will find out."

Before Tanis could react, the mage stepped away from the group and faced the spectres.

"Raist!" Caramon said in a strangled voice, starting to shove forward.

"Keep him back, Tanis," Raistlin commanded harshly. "Our lives depend on this."

Gripping the warrior's arm, Tanis asked Raistlin, "What are you going to do?"

"I am going to cast a spell that will enable us to communicate with them. I will perceive their thoughts. They will speak through me."

The mage threw his head back, his hood slipping off. He stretched out his arms and began to speak. *"Ast bilak parbilakar. Suh tangus moipar?"*† he murmured, then repeated that phrase three times. As Raistlin spoke, the crowd of warriors parted and a figure more awesome and terrifying than the rest appeared. The spectre was taller than the rest and wore a shimmering crown. His pallid armor was richly decorated with dark jewels. His face showed the most terrible grief and anguish. He advanced upon Raistlin.

Caramon choked and averted his eyes. Tanis dared not speak or cry out, fearful of disturbing the mage and breaking the spell. The spectre raised a fleshless hand, reached out slowly to touch the young mage. Tanis trembled—the spectre's touch meant certain death. But Raistlin, entranced, did not move. Tanis wondered if he even saw the chill hand coming toward his heart. Then Raistlin spoke.

"You who have been long dead, use my living voice to tell us of your bitter sorrow. Then give us leave to pass through this forest, for our purpose is not evil, as you will see if you read our hearts."

The spectre's hand halted abruptly. The pale eyes searched Raistlin's face. Then, shimmering in the darkness, the spectre bowed before the mage. Tanis sucked in his breath; he had sensed Raistlin's power, but this . . !

This is the first mention of the Abyss—of which more anon. In exclamations, the word is similar to "hell," but there the similarity ends.

Very well: "Ast," meaning "I," is the pronoun designating who is asking/demanding the magic be involved. "Bila" is the root, or operative noun. "Bilak" makes it transitive verb form. The "par" prefix and "kar" suffix transform the root "bila" into an abstract form. If "bila" means "words/ideas," then the phrase translates as "I speak (to you) concepts/thoughts," with the target of the verb implied in its transitive nature. "Suh" is an exclusive pronoun meaning "you all not including me." "Tangus" is a verb form of "sound" and "moipar" is "through." With a delineation transitive. Ergo: "You voice through (me)." Whew!—TRH

Raistlin returned the bow, then moved to stand beside the spectre. His face was nearly as pale as that of the ghostly figure next to him. The living dead and the dead living, Tanis thought, shuddering.

When Raistlin spoke, his voice was no longer the wheezing whispering of the fragile mage. It was deep and dark and commanding and rang through the forest. It was cold and hollow and might have come from below the ground. "Who are you who trespass in Darken Wood?"

Tanis tried to answer, but his throat had dried up completely. Caramon, next to him, couldn't even lift his head. Then Tanis felt movement at his side. The kender! Cursing himself, he reached out to grab for Tasslehoff, but it was too late. The small figure, topknot dancing, ran out into the light of Raistlin's staff and stood before the spectre.

Tasslehoff bowed respectfully. "I am Tasslehoff Burrfoot," he said. "My friends"—he waved his small hand at the group—"call me Tas. Who are you?"

"It matters little," the sepulchral voice intoned. "Know only that we are warriors from a time long forgotten."

"Is it true that you broke a pledge and that's how you come to be here?" Tas asked with interest.

"It is. We pledged to guard this land. Then came the smoldering mountain from the heavens.† The land was ripped apart. Evil things crept out from the bowels of the earth and we dropped our swords and fled in terror until bitter death overtook us. We have been called to fulfill our oath, as evil once more stalks the land. And here will we remain until evil is driven back and balance is restored again."

The Cataclysm, which was a central backdrop for the DRAGONLANCE Legends trilogy, was part of our designed backstory from the beginning.—TRH

Suddenly Raistlin gave a shriek and flung back his head, his eyes rolling upward until the watching companions could see only the whites. His voice became a thousand voices crying out at once. This startled even the kender, who stepped back a pace and looked around uneasily for Tanis.

The spectre raised his hand in a commanding gesture, and the tumult ceased as though swallowed by the darkness. "My men demand to know the reason you enter Darken Wood. If it is for evil, you will find that you have brought evil upon yourselves, for you will not live to see the moons rise."

"No, not evil. Certainly not," Tasslehoff said hurriedly. "It's kind of a long story, you see, but we're obviously not going anywhere in a big hurry and you're obviously not either, so I'll tell it to you.

"To begin with, we were in the Inn of the Last Home in Solace. You probably don't know it. I'm not sure how long it's been there, but it wasn't around during the Cataclysm and it sounds like you were. Well, there we were, listening to the old man talking of Huma and he—the old man, not Huma—told Goldmoon to sing her song and she said what song and then she sang and a Seeker decided to be a music critic and Riverwind, that's the tall man over there—shoved the Seeker into the fire. It was an accident—he didn't mean to. But the Seeker went up like a torch! You should have seen it! Anyway, the old man handed me the staff and said hit him and I did and the staff turned to blue crystal and the flames died and—"

"Blue crystal!" The spectre's voice echoed hollowly from Raistlin's throat as he began to walk toward them. Tanis and Sturm both jumped forward, grabbing Tas and dragging him out of the way. But the spectre seemed intent only on examining the group. His flickering eyes focused on Goldmoon. Raising a pale hand, he motioned her forward.

"No!" Riverwind tried to prevent her from leaving his side, but she pushed away gently and walked over to stand before the spectre, the staff in her hand. The ghostly army encircled them.

Suddenly the spectre drew his sword from its pallid sheath. He held it high overhead and white light tinged with blue flame flickered from the blade.

"Look at the staff!" Goldmoon gasped.

The staff glowed pale blue, as if answering the sword.

The ghostly king turned to Raistlin and reached his pale hand toward the entranced mage. Caramon gave a hoarse bellow and broke free of Tanis's grip. Drawing his sword, he lunged at the undead warrior. The blade pierced the flickering body, but it was Caramon who screamed in pain and dropped, writhing, to the ground. Tanis and Sturm knelt beside him. Raistlin stared ahead, his expression unchanged, unmoving.

"Caramon, where—" Tanis held him, trying frantically to see where the big man was injured.

"My hand!" Caramon rocked back and forth, sobbing, his left hand—his sword hand—thrust tightly under his right arm.

"What's the matter?" Tanis asked. Then, seeing the warrior's sword on the ground, he knew: Caramon's sword was rimed with frost.

Tanis looked up in horror and saw the spectre's hand close tightly around Raistlin's wrist. A shudder wracked the mage's frail body; his face twisted in pain, but he did not fall. The mage's eyes closed, the lines of cynicism and bitterness smoothed away and the peace of death descended on him. Tanis watched in awe, only partially aware of Caramon's hoarse cries. He saw Raistlin's face transform again, this time imbued with ecstasy. The mage's aura of power intensified until it glowed around him with an almost palpable brilliance.

"We are summoned," Raistlin said. The voice was his own and yet like none Tanis had ever heard him use. "We must go."

The mage turned his back on them and walked into the woods, the ghostly king's fleshless hand still grasping his wrist. The circle of undead parted to let him pass.

"Stop them," Caramon moaned. He staggered to his feet.

"We can't!" Tanis fought to restrain him, and finally the big man collapsed in the half-elf's arms, weeping like a child. "We'll follow him. He'll be all right. He's magi, Caramon—we can't understand. We'll follow—"

The eyes of the undead flickered with an unholy light as they watched the companions pass them and enter the forest. The spectral army closed ranks behind them.

The companions stepped into a raging battle. Steel rang; wounded men shrieked for help. So real was the clash of armies in the darkness that Sturm drew his sword reflexively. The tumult deafened him; he ducked and dodged unseen blows that he knew were aimed at him. He swung his sword in desperation at black air, knowing that he was doomed and there was no escape. He began to run, and he suddenly stumbled out of

the forest into a barren, wasted glade. Raistlin stood before him, alone.

The mage's eyes were closed. He sighed gently, then collapsed to the ground. Sturm ran to him, then Caramon appeared, nearly knocking Sturm over to reach his brother and gather him tenderly in his arms. One by one, the others ran as if driven into the glade. Raistlin was still murmuring strange, unfamiliar words. The spectres vanished.

"Raist!" Caramon sobbed brokenly.

The mage's eyelids flickered and opened. "The spell . . . drained me. . . ." he whispered. "I must rest. . . ."

"And rest ye shall!" boomed a voice—a living voice!

Tanis breathed a sigh of relief even as he put his hand on his sword. Quickly he and the others jumped protectively in front of Raistlin, turning to face outward, staring into the darkness. Then the silver moon appeared, suddenly, as if a hand had produced it from beneath a black silk scarf. Now they could see the head and shoulders of a man standing amid the trees. His bare shoulders were as large and heavy as Caramon's. A mane of long hair curled around his neck; his eyes were bright and glittered coldly. The companions heard a rustling in the brush and saw the flash of a spear tip being raised, pointing at Tanis.

"Put thy puny weapons down," the man warned. "Ye be surrounded and have not a chance."

"A trick," Sturm growled, but even as he spoke there was a tremendous crashing and cracking of tree limbs. More men appeared, surrounding them, all armed with spears that glinted in the moonlight.

The first man strode forward then, and the companions stared in amazement, their hands on their weapons going slack.

The man wasn't a man at all, but a centaur!† Human from the waist up, he had the body of a horse from the waist down. He cantered forward with easy grace, powerful muscles rippling across his barrel chest. Other centaurs moved into the path at his commanding gesture. Tanis sheathed his sword. Flint sneezed.

I always felt badly that the unique races of Darken Wood were never explored more fully in later books. —TRH

"Thee must come with us," the centaur ordered.

"My brother is ill," Caramon growled. "He can't go anywhere."

"Place him upon my back," the centaur said coolly. "In fact, if any of you be tired, thee may ride to where we go."

"Where are you taking us?" Tanis asked.

"Thee is in no position to ask questions." The centaur reached out and prodded Caramon's back with his spear. "We travel far and fast. I suggest thee ride. But fear not." He bowed before Goldmoon, extending his foreleg and touching his hand to his shaggy hair. "Harm will not come to thee this night."

"Can I ride, Tanis, please?" begged Tasslehoff.

"Don't trust them!" Flint sneezed violently.

"I *don't* trust them," Tanis muttered, "but we don't seem to have a whole lot of choice in the matter—Raistlin can't walk. Go on, Tas. The rest of you, too."

Caramon, scowling at the centaurs suspiciously, lifted his brother in his arms and set him upon the back of one of the half-man, half-animals. Raistlin slumped forward weakly.

"Climb up," the centaur said to Caramon. "I can bear the weight of thee both. Thy brother will need thy support, for we ride swiftly tonight."

Flushing with embarrassment, the big warrior clambered onto the centaur's broad back, his huge legs dangling almost to the ground. He put an arm around Raistlin as the centaur galloped down the path. Tasslehoff, giggling with excitement, jumped onto a centaur and promptly slid off the other side into the mud. Sturm, sighing, picked up the kender and set him on the centaur's back. Then, before Flint could protest, the knight lifted the dwarf up behind Tas. Flint tried to speak but could only sneeze as the centaur moved away. Tanis rode with the first centaur, who seemed to be the leader.

"Where are you taking us?" Tanis asked again.

"To the Forestmaster," the centaur answered.†

The Forestmaster and the centaurs of Darken Wood are more fully explored in Chris Pierson's novel, Dezra's Quest.

"The Forestmaster?" Tanis repeated. "Who is he, one like yourselves?"

"She is the Forestmaster," the centaur replied and began to canter down the trail.

Tanis started to ask another question, but the centaur's quickened pace jolted him, and he nearly bit through his tongue as he came down hard on the centaur's back. Feeling himself start to

slide backward as the centaur trotted faster and faster, Tanis threw his arms around the centaur's broad torso.

"Nay, thee doesn't need to squeeze me in two!" The centaur glanced back, his eyes glittering in the moonlight. "It be my job to see thee stays on. Relax. Put thy hands on me rump to balance thyself. There, now. Grip with thy legs."

The centaurs left the trail and plunged into the forest. The moonlight was immediately swallowed up by the dense trees. Tanis felt branches whip past, swiping at his clothing. The centaur never swerved or slowed in his gallop, however, and Tanis could only assume he knew the trail well, a trail the half-elf couldn't see.

Soon the pace began to slacken and the centaur finally came to a stop. Tanis could see nothing in the smothering darkness. He knew his companions were near only because he could hear Raistlin's shallow breathing, Caramon's jingling armor, and Flint's unabated sneezing. Even the light from Raistlin's staff had died.

"A powerful magic is laid on this forest," the mage whispered weakly when Tanis asked him about it. "This magic dispels all others."

Tanis's uneasiness grew. "Why are we stopping?"

"Because thee art here. Dismount," the centaur ordered gruffly.

"Where is here?" Tanis slid off the centaur's broad back onto the ground. He stared around him but could see nothing. Apparently the trees kept even the smallest glimmer of moonlight or starlight from penetrating through to the trail.

"Thee stands in the center of Darken Wood," the centaur replied. "And now I bid thee farewell—or fare evil, depending on how the Forestmaster judges thee."

"Wait a minute!" Caramon called out angrily. "You can't just leave us here in the middle of this forest, blind as newborn kittens—"

"Stop them!" Tanis ordered, reaching for his sword. But his weapon was gone. An explosive oath from Sturm indicated the knight had discovered the same thing.

The centaur chuckled. Tanis heard hooves beat into soft earth and tree branches rustled. The centaurs were gone.

"Good riddance!" Flint sneezed.

"Are we all here?" Tanis asked, reaching out his hand and feeling Sturm's strong, reassuring grasp.

"I'm here," piped Tasslehoff. "Oh, Tanis, wasn't it wonderful? I—"

"Hush, Tas!" Tanis snapped. "The Plainsmen?"

"We're here," said Riverwind grimly. "Weaponless."

"No one has a weapon?" Tanis asked. "Not that it would do us much good in this cursed blackness," he amended bitterly.

"I have my staff," Goldmoon's low voice said softly.

"And a formidable weapon that is, daughter of Qué-Shu," came a deep voice. "A weapon for good, intended to combat illness and injury and disease." The unseen voice grew sad. "In these times it will also be used as a weapon against the evil creatures who seek to find and banish it from the world."

II

The Forestmaster. A peaceful interlude.

Who are you?" Tanis called. "Show yourself!"

"We will not harm you," bluffed Caramon.

"Of course you won't." Now the deep voice was amused. "You have no weapons. I will return them when the time is propitious. No one brings weapons into Darken Wood, not even a knight of Solamnia. Do not fear, noble knight. I recognize your blade as ancient and most valuable! I will keep it safe. Forgive this apparent lack of trust, but even the great Huma laid the Dragonlance at my feet."

"Huma!" Sturm gasped. "Who are you?"

"I am the Forestmaster." Even as the deep voice spoke, the darkness parted. A gasp of awe, gentle as a spring wind, swept the company as they stared before them. Silver moonlight shone brightly on a

The unicorn was also an ancient symbol of good and purity. I wanted an interlude and a peaceful, idyllic setting to contrast with later events. I also wanted, if we were to use a unicorn, to place it in a proper setting and with proper reverence for what the symbol represented. —TRH

One of my favorite books is The Last Unicorn *by Peter Beagle. I used his work as inspiration of our unicorn.—MW*

high rock ledge. Standing on the ledge was a unicorn.† She regarded them coolly, her intelligent eyes gleaming with infinite wisdom.

The unicorn's beauty pierced the heart. Goldmoon felt swift tears spring to her eyes and she was forced to close them against the animal's magnificent radiance. Her fur was the silver of moonlight, her horn was shining pearl, her mane like seafoam. The head might have been sculpted from glistening marble, but no human or even dwarven hand could capture the elegance and grace that lived in the fine lines of the powerful neck and muscular chest. The legs were strong but delicate, the hooves small and cloven like those of a goat. In later days, when Goldmoon walked dark paths and her heart was bleak with despair and hopelessness, she had only to shut her eyes and remember the unicorn to find comfort.

The unicorn tossed her head and then lowered it in grave welcome. The companions, feeling awkward and clumsy and confused, bowed in return. The unicorn suddenly whirled and left the rock ledge, cantering down the rocks toward them.

Tanis, feeling a spell lifted from him, looked around. The bright silver moonlight lit a sylvan glade. Tall trees surrounded them like giant, beneficent guardians. The half-elf was aware of a deep abiding sense of peace here. But there was also a waiting sadness.

"Rest yourselves," the Forestmaster said as she came among them. "You are tired and hungry. Food will be brought and fresh water for cleansing. You may put aside your watchfulness and fears for this evening. Safety exists here, if it exists anywhere in this land tonight."

Caramon, his eyes lighting up at the mention of food, eased his brother to the ground. Raistlin sank into the grass against the trunk of a tree. His face was deathly pale in the silver moonlight, but his breathing was easy. He did not seem ill so much as just terribly exhausted. Caramon sat next to him, looking around for food. Then he heaved a sigh.

"Probably more berries anyway," the warrior said unhappily to Tanis. "I crave meat—roasted deer haunch, a nice sizzling bit of rabbit—"

"Hush," Sturm remonstrated softly, glancing at the Forestmaster. "She'd probably consider roasting you first!"

Centaurs came out of the forest bearing a clean, white cloth, which they spread on the grass. Others placed clear crystal globe lights on the cloth, illuminating the forest.

Tasslehoff stared at the lights curiously. "They're bug lights!"

The crystal globes held thousands of tiny bugs, each one having two brightly glowing spots on its back. They crawled around inside the globes, apparently content to explore their surroundings.

Next, the centaurs brought bowls of cool water and clean white cloths to bathe their faces and hands. The water refreshed their bodies and minds as it washed away the stains of battle. Other centaurs placed chairs, which Caramon stared at dubiously. They were crafted of one piece of wood that curved around the body. They appeared comfortable, except that each chair had only one leg!

"Please be seated," said the Forestmaster graciously.

"I can't sit in that!" the warrior protested. "I'll tip over." He stood at the edge of the tablecloth. "Besides, the tablecloth is spread on the grass. I'll sit on the grass with it."

"Close to the food," muttered Flint into his beard.

The others glanced uneasily at the chairs, the strange crystal bug lamps, and the centaurs. The Chieftain's Daughter, however, knew what was expected of guests. Although the outside world might have considered her people barbarians, Goldmoon's tribe had strict rules of politeness that must be religiously observed. Goldmoon knew that to keep your host waiting was an insult to both the host and his bounty. She sat down with regal grace. The one-legged chair rocked slightly, adjusting to her height, crafting itself for her alone.

"Sit at my right hand, warrior," she said formally, conscious of the many eyes upon them. Riverwind's face showed no emotion, though he was a ludicrous sight trying to bend his tall body to sit in the seemingly fragile chair. But, once seated, he leaned back comfortably, almost smiling in disbelieving approval.

"Thank you all for waiting until I was seated," Goldmoon said hastily, to cover the others' hesitation. "You may all sit now."

"Oh, that's all right," began Caramon, folding his arms across his chest. "I wasn't waiting. I'm not going to sit in these weird chair—" Sturm's elbow dug sharply into the warrior's ribs.

"Gracious lady," Sturm bowed and sat down with knightly dignity.

"Well, if he can do it, so can I," muttered Caramon, his decision hastened by the fact that the centaurs were bringing in food. He helped his brother to a seat and then sat down gingerly, making certain the chair bore his weight.

Four centaurs positioned themselves at each of the four corners of the huge white cloth spread out upon the ground. They lifted the cloth to the height of a table, then released it. The cloth remained floating in place, its delicately embroidered surface as hard and sturdy as one of the solid tables in the Inn of the Last Home.†

I believe this to be a rather helpful application of Tenser's Floating Disk spell—another AD&D staple.—TRH

"How splendid! How do they do that?" Tasslehoff cried, peering underneath the cloth. "There's nothing under there!" he reported, his eyes wide.

The centaurs laughed uproariously and even the Forestmaster smiled. Next the centaurs laid down plates made of beautifully cut and polished wood. Each guest was given a knife and fork fashioned from the horns of a deer. Platters of hot roasted meat filled the air with a tantalizing smoky aroma. Fragrant loaves of bread and huge wooden bowls of fruit glistened in the soft lamplight.

Caramon, feeling secure in his chair, rubbed his hands together. Then he grinned broadly and picked up his fork. "Ahhhh!" He sighed in appreciation as one of the centaurs set before him a platter of roasted deer meat. Caramon plunged his fork in, sniffing in rapture at the steam and juice that gushed forth from the meat. Suddenly he realized everyone was staring at him. He stopped and looked around.

"Wha—?" he asked, blinking. Then his eyes rested on the Forestmaster and he flushed and hurriedly removed his fork. "I . . . I beg your pardon. This deer must have been someone you knew—I mean—one of your subjects."

The Forestmaster smiled gently. "Be at ease, warrior," she said. "The deer fulfills his purpose in life by providing sustenance for the hunter—be it wolf or man. We do not mourn the loss of those who die fulfilling their destinies."†

As I am both a religious man and occasionally enjoy a good steak, this attitude accurately reflects my own beliefs on the subject. Moreover, it foreshadows future events as the text goes on to show.—TRH

It seemed to Tanis that the Forestmaster's dark eyes went to Sturm as she spoke, and there was a deep sadness in them that filled the half-elf's heart with cold fear. But when he turned back to the Forestmaster, he saw the magnificent animal smiling once more. "My imagination," he thought.

"How do we know, Master," Tanis asked hesitantly, "whether the life of any creature has fulfilled its destiny? I have known the very old to die in bitterness and despair. I have seen young children die before their time but leave behind such a legacy of love and joy that grief for their passing was tempered by the knowledge that their brief lives had given much to others."

"You have answered your own question, Tanis Half-Elven, far better than I could," the Forestmaster said gravely. "Say that our lives are measured not by gain but by giving."

The half-elf started to reply, but the Forestmaster interrupted. "Put your cares aside for now. Enjoy the peace of my forest while you may. Its time is passing."

Tanis glanced sharply at the Forestmaster, but the great animal had turned her attention away from him and was staring far off into the woods, her eyes clouded with sorrow. The half-elf wondered what she meant, and he sat, lost in dark thoughts, until he felt a gentle hand touch his.

"You should eat," Goldmoon said. "Your cares won't vanish with the meal—and, if they do, so much the better."

Tanis smiled at her and began to eat with a sharp appetite. He took the Forestmaster's advice and relegated his worries to the back of his mind for a while. Goldmoon was right: they weren't likely to go away.

The rest of the companions did the same, accepting the strangeness of their surroundings with the aplomb of seasoned travelers. Though there was nothing to drink but water—much to Flint's disappointment—the cool, clear liquid washed the terrors

and doubts from their hearts as it had cleansed the blood and dirt from their hands. They laughed, talked, and ate, enjoying each other's companionship. The Forestmaster spoke to them no more but watched each in turn.

Sturm's pale face had regained some color. He ate with grace and dignity. Sitting next to Tasslehoff, he answered the kender's inexhaustible store of questions about his homeland. He also, without calling undue attention to the fact, removed from Tasslehoff's pouch a knife and fork that had unaccountably made their way there. The knight sat as far from Caramon as possible and did his best to ignore him.

The big warrior was obviously enjoying his meal. He ate three times more than anyone else, three times as fast, and three times as loudly. When not eating, he described to Flint a fight with a troll, using the bone he was chewing on as a sword to illustrate his thrusts and parries. Flint ate heartily and told Caramon he was the biggest liar in Krynn.

Raistlin, sitting beside his brother, ate very little, taking nibbles of only the tenderest meat, a few grapes, and a bit of bread he soaked in water first. He said nothing but listened intently to everyone, absorbing all that was said into his soul, storing it for future reference and use.

Goldmoon ate her meal delicately, with practiced ease. The Qué-Shu princess was accustomed to eating in public view and could make conversation easily. She chatted with Tanis, encouraging him to describe the elven lands and other places he had visited. Riverwind, next to her, was acutely uncomfortable and self-conscious. Although not a boisterous eater like Caramon, the Plainsman† was obviously more accustomed to eating at the campfires of his fellow tribesmen than in royal halls. He handled cutlery with awkward clumsiness, and he knew that he appeared crude beside Goldmoon. He said nothing, seeming willing to fade into the background.

So many strange and fantastic things have happened to the companions that the simple pleasure of enjoying a meal allows the reader to share this common experience with them. This draws the reader into the world.—MW

Finally everyone began shoving plates away and settling back in the strange wooden chairs, ending their dinner with pieces of sweet shortcake. Tas began to sing his kender trailsong, to the delight of the centaurs. Then suddenly Raistlin spoke. His

soft, whispering voice slithered through the laughter and loud talk.

"Forestmaster"—the mage hissed the name—"today we fought loathsome creatures that we have never seen before on Krynn. Can you tell us of these?"

The relaxed and festive mood was smothered as effectively as if covered by a shroud. Everyone exchanged grim looks.

"These creatures walk like men," Caramon added, "but look like reptiles. They have clawed hands and feet and wings and"—his voice dropped—"they turn to stone when they die."

The Forestmaster regarded them with sadness as she rose to her feet. She seemed to expect the question.

"I know of these creatures," she answered. "Some of them entered the Darken Wood with a party of goblins from Haven a week ago. They wore hoods and cloaks, no doubt to disguise their horrible appearance. The centaurs followed them in secret, to make certain they harmed no one before the spectral minions dealt with them. The centaurs reported that the creatures call themselves 'draconians' and speak of belonging to the 'Order of Draco.' "

Raistlin's brow furrowed. "Draco," he whispered, puzzled. "But who are they? What race or species?"

"I do not know. I can tell you only this: they are not of the animal world, and they belong to none of the races of Krynn."†

The DRAGONLANCE design team wanted creatures to replace ogres, overused in fantasy literature. Conversations between Tracy Hickman and artist Larry Elmore solidified what draconians would look like. In addition to Larry, artists Clyde Caldwell, Dave Sutherland, Jeff Butler, and Denis Beauvais all made contributions to the visual feel of these dragonmen.

This took a moment for everyone to assimilate. Caramon blinked. "I don't—" he began.

"She means, my brother, that they are not of this world," Raistlin explained impatiently.

"Then where'd they come from?" Caramon asked, startled.

"That's the question, isn't it?" Raistlin said coldly. "Where did they come from—and why?"

"I cannot answer that." The Forestmaster shook her head. "But I can tell you that before the spectral minions put an end to these draconians, they spoke of 'armies to the north.' "

"I saw them." Tanis rose to his feet. "Campfires—" His voice caught in his throat as he realized what the Forestmaster had been about to say. "Armies! Of these draconians? There must be thousands!" Now everyone was standing and talking at once.

"Impossible!" the knight said, scowling.

"Who's behind this? The Seekers? By the gods," Caramon bellowed, "I've got a notion to go to Haven and bash—"

"Go to Solamnia, not to Haven," Sturm advised loudly.

"We should travel to Qualinost," Tanis argued. "The elves—"

"The elves have their own problems," the Forestmaster interrupted, her cool voice a calming influence. "As do the Highseekers of Haven. No place is safe. But I will tell you where you must go to find answers to your questions."

"What do you mean you will tell us where to go?" Raistlin stepped forward slowly, his red robes rippling around him as he walked. "What do you know of us?" The mage paused, his eyes narrowing with a sudden thought.

"Yes, I was expecting you," the Forestmaster replied in answer to Raistlin's thoughts. "A great and shining being† appeared to me in the wilderness this day. He told me that the one bearing the blue crystal staff would come this night to Darken Wood. The spectral minions would let the staffbearer and her companions pass—though they have allowed no human or elf or dwarf or kender to enter Darken Wood since the Cataclysm. I was to give the bearer of the staff this message: 'You must fly straight away across the Eastwall Mountains. In two days the staffbearer must be within Xak Tsaroth. There, if you prove worthy, you shall receive the greatest gift given to the world.' "

The old man, in another guise, is meddling once more.—TRH

"Eastwall Mountains!" The dwarf's mouth dropped open. "We'll need to fly all right, to reach Xak Tsaroth in two days time. Shining being! Hah!" He snapped his fingers.

The rest glanced uneasily at each other. Finally Tanis said hesitantly, "I'm afraid the dwarf is right, Forestmaster. The journey to Xak Tsaroth would be long and perilous. We would have to go back through lands we know are inhabited by goblins and these draconians."

"And then we would have to pass through the Plains," Riverwind spoke for the first time since meeting the Forestmaster. "Our lives are forfeit." He gestured toward Goldmoon. "The Qué-Shu

are fierce fighters and they know the land. They are waiting. We would never get through safely." He looked at Tanis. "And my people have no love for elves."

"And why go to Xak Tsaroth anyway?" Caramon rumbled. "Greatest gift—what could that be? A powerful sword? A chest of steel coins?† That would come in handy, but there's a battle brewing up north apparently. I'd hate to miss it."

I had wanted steel—a far more useful metal in this time than gold—to be the basis of exchange in the world. I wanted to make a point about the ephemeral nature of wealth, but the concept never did come across well … or work in the game either, for that matter.—TRH

The Forestmaster nodded gravely. "I understand your dilemma," she said. "I offer what help is in my power. I will see to it that you reach Xak Tsaroth in two days. The question is, will you go?"

Tanis turned to the others. Sturm's face was drawn. He met Tanis's look and sighed. "The stag led us here," he said slowly, "perhaps to receive this advice. But my heart lies north, in my homeland. If armies of these draconians are preparing to attack, my place is with those Knights who will surely band together to fight this evil. Still, I do not want to desert you, Tanis, or you, lady." He nodded to Goldmoon, then slumped down, his aching head in his hands.

Caramon shrugged. "I'll go anywhere, fight anything, Tanis. You know that. What say you, brother?"

But Raistlin, staring into the darkness, did not answer.

Goldmoon and Riverwind were speaking together in low voices. They nodded to each other, then Goldmoon said to Tanis, "We will go to Xak Tsaroth. We appreciate everything you've done for us—"

"But we ask for no man's help any longer," Riverwind stated proudly. "This is the completion of our quest. As we began alone, so we will finish it alone."

"And you will die alone!" Raistlin said softly.

Tanis shivered. "Raistlin," he said, "a word with you."

The mage turned obediently and walked with the half-elf into a small thicket of gnarled and stunted trees. Darkness closed around them.

"Just like the old days," Caramon said, his eyes following his brother uneasily.

"And look at all the trouble we got into then," Flint reminded him, plopping down onto the grass.

"I wonder what they talk about?" Tasslehoff said. Long ago, the kender had tried to eavesdrop on these private conversations between the mage and the half-elf, but Tanis had always caught him and shooed him away. "And why can't they discuss it with us?"

"Because we'd probably rip Raistlin's heart out," Sturm answered, in a low, pain-filled voice. "I don't care what you say, Caramon, there's a dark side to your brother, and Tanis has seen it. For which I'm grateful. He can deal with it. I couldn't."

Uncharacteristically, Caramon said nothing. Sturm stared at the warrior, startled. In the old days, the fighter would have leaped to his brother's defense. Now he sat silent, preoccupied, his face troubled. So there is a dark side to Raistlin, and now Caramon, too, knows what it is. Sturm shuddered, wondering what had happened in these past five years that cast such a dark shadow across the cheerful warrior.†

Raistlin took the Test, and it involved his warrior brother, too, as told in The Soulforge, *by Margaret Weis.*

Raistlin walked close to Tanis. The mage's arms were crossed in the sleeves of his robes, his head bowed in thought. Tanis could feel the heat of Raistlin's body radiate through the red robes, as though he were being consumed by an inner fire. As usual, Tanis felt uncomfortable in the young mage's presence. Yet, right now, he knew of no one else he could turn to for advice. "What do you know of Xak Tsaroth?" Tanis asked.

"There was a temple there—a temple to the ancient gods," Raistlin whispered. His eyes glittered in the eerie light of the red moon. "It was destroyed in the Cataclysm and its people fled, certain that the gods had abandoned them. It passed from memory. I did not know it still existed."

"What did you see, Raistlin?" Tanis asked softly, after a long pause. "You looked far away—what did you see?"

"I am magi, Tanis, not a seer."

"Don't give me that," Tanis snapped. "It's been a long time, but not that long. I know you don't have the gift of foresight. You were thinking, not scrying. And you came up with answers. I want those answers. You've got more brains than all of us put together, even if—" He stopped.

"Even if I am twisted and warped." Raistlin's voice rose with harsh arrogance. "Yes, I am smarter

than you—all of you. And someday I will prove it! Someday you—with all your strength and charm and good looks—you, all of you, will call me master!" His hands clenched to fists inside his robes, his eyes flared red in the crimson moonlight. Tanis, who was accustomed to this tirade, waited patiently. The mage relaxed, his hands unclenched. "But for now, I give you my advice. What did I see? These armies, Tanis, armies of draconians, will overrun Solace and Haven and all the lands of your fathers. That is the reason we must reach Xak Tsaroth. What we find there will prove this army's undoing."

"But why are there armies?" Tanis asked. "What would anyone want with control of Solace and Haven and the Plains to the east? Is it the Seekers?"

"Seekers! Hah!" Raistlin snorted. "Open your eyes, Half-Elf. Someone or something powerful created these creatures—these draconians. Not the idiot Seekers. And no one goes to all that trouble to take over two farm cities or even to look for a blue crystal staff. This is a war of conquest, Tanis. Someone seeks to conquer Ansalon! Within two days time, life on Krynn as we have known it will come to an end. This is the portent of the fallen stars. The Queen of Darkness has returned. We face a foe who seeks—at the very least—to enslave us, or perhaps destroy us completely."

The Queen of Darkness, missing from the night sky

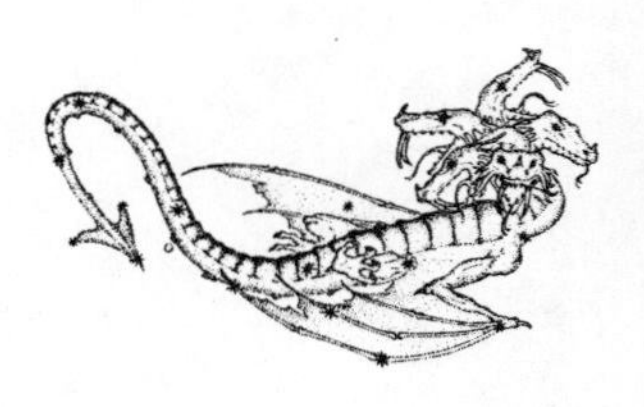

"Your advice?" Tanis asked reluctantly. He felt change coming and, like all elves, he feared and detested change.

Raistlin smiled his crooked, bitter smile, reveling in his moment of superiority. "That we go to Xak Tsaroth immediately. That we leave tonight, if possible, by whatever means this Forestmaster has planned. If we do not acquire this gift within two days—the armies of draconians will."

"What do you think the gift might be?" Tanis wondered aloud. "A sword or coins, like Caramon said?"

"My brother's a fool," Raistlin stated coldly. "You don't believe that and neither do I."

"Then what?" Tanis pursued.

Raistlin's eyes narrowed. "I have given you my advice. Act upon it as you will. I have my own reasons for going. Let us leave it at that, Half-Elf. But it will be dangerous. Xak Tsaroth was abandoned

three hundred years ago. I do not think it will have remained abandoned long."

"That is true," Tanis mused. He stood silently for long moments. The mage coughed once, softly. "Do you believe we were chosen, Raistlin?" Tanis asked.

The mage did not hesitate. "Yes. So I was given to know in the Towers of Sorcery. So Par-Salian† told me."

Par-Salian is the head of the Conclave of Wizards, who, seeing something that would affect the future of Krynn in Raistlin, allowed him to take the Test at a younger age than most wizards.

"But why?" Tanis questioned impatiently. "We are not the stuff of heroes—well, maybe Sturm—"

"Ah," said Raistlin. "But *who* chose us? And for what purpose? Consider that, Tanis Half-Elven!"

The mage bowed to Tanis, mockingly, and turned to walk back through the brush to the rest of the group.

12

Winged sleep. Smoke in the east. Dark memories.

Xak Tsaroth," Tanis said. "That is my decision."

"Is that what the mage advises?" Sturm asked sullenly.

"It is," Tanis answered, "and I believe his advice is sound. If we do not reach Xak Tsaroth within two days, others will and this 'greatest gift' may be lost forever."

"The greatest gift!" Tasslehoff said, his eyes shining. "Just think, Flint! Jewels beyond price! Or maybe—"

"A keg of ale and Otik's fried potatoes," the dwarf muttered. "And a nice warm fire. But no—Xak Tsaroth!"

"I guess we're all in agreement, then," Tanis said. "If you feel you are needed in the north, Sturm, of course you—"

"I will go with you to Xak Tsaroth." Sturm sighed. "There is nothing in the north for me. I have been deluding myself. The knights of my order are scattered, holed up in crumbling fortresses, fighting off the debt collectors."

The knight's face twisted in agony and he lowered his head. Tanis suddenly felt tired. His neck hurt, his shoulders and back ached, his leg muscles twitched. He started to say something more, then felt a gentle hand touch his shoulder. He looked up to see Goldmoon's face, cool and calm in the moonlight.

"You are weary, my friend," she said. "We all are. But we are glad you are coming, Riverwind and I." Her hand was strong. She looked up, her clear gaze encompassing the entire group. "We are glad all of you are coming with us."

Tanis, glancing at Riverwind, wasn't certain the tall Plainsman agreed with her.

"Just another adventure," Caramon said, flushing with embarrassment. "Eh, Raist?" He nudged his brother. Raistlin, ignoring his twin, looked at the Forestmaster.

"We must leave immediately," the mage said coldly. "You mentioned something about helping us cross the mountains."

"Indeed," the Forestmaster replied, nodding gravely. "I, too, am glad you have made this decision. I hope you find my aid welcome."

The Forestmaster raised her head, looking up into the sky. The companions followed her gaze. The night sky, seen through the canopy of tall trees, glittered brilliantly with stars. Soon the companions became aware of something flying up there, winking out the stars in passing.

"I'll be a gully dwarf," Flint said solemnly. "Flying horses. What next?"

"Oh!" Tasslehoff drew in a deep breath. The kender was transfixed with wonder as he watched the beautiful animals circle above them, descending lower and lower with each turn, their fur radiating blue-white in the moonlight. Tas clasped his hands together. Never in his wildest kender imaginings had he dreamed of flying. This was worth fighting all the draconians on Krynn.

The pegasi dipped to the ground, their feathery wings creating a wind that tossed the tree branches

and laid the grass flat. A large pegasus with wings that touched the ground when he walked bowed reverently to the Forestmaster. His bearing was proud and noble. Each of the other beautiful creatures bowed in turn.

"You have summoned us?" the leader asked the Forestmaster.

"These guests of mine have urgent business to the east. I bid you bear them with the swiftness of the winds across the Eastwall Mountains."

The pegasus regarded the companions with astonishment. He walked with stately mient over to stare first at one, then another. When Tas raised his hand to pet the steed's nose, both of the animal's ears swiveled forward and he reared his great head back. But when he got to Flint, he snorted in disgust and turned to the Forestmaster. "A kender? Humans? And a *dwarf!*"

"Don't do *me* any favors, horse!" Flint sneezed.

The Forestmaster merely nodded and smiled. The pegasus bowed in reluctant assent. "Very well, Master," he replied. With powerful grace, he walked over to Goldmoon and started to bend his foreleg, dipping low before her to assist her in mounting.

"No, do not kneel, noble animal," she said. "I have ridden horses since before I could walk. I need no such assistance." Handing Riverwind her staff, Goldmoon threw her arm around the pegasus's neck and pulled herself astride his broad back. Her silver-gold hair blew feathery white in the moonlight, her face was pure and cold as marble. Now she truly looked like the princess of a barbarian tribe.

She took her staff from Riverwind. Raising it in the air, she lifted her voice in song. Riverwind, his eyes shining with admiration, leaped up behind her on the back of the winged horse. Putting his arms around her, he added his deep baritone voice to hers.

Tanis had no idea what they were singing, but it seemed a song of victory and triumph. It stirred his blood and he would have willingly joined in. One of the pegasi cantered up to him. He pulled himself up and settled himself on his broad back, sitting in front of the powerful wings.

Now all the companions, caught up in the elation of the moment, mounted, Goldmoon's song adding wings to their souls as the pegasi spread their huge

When Margaret and I first wrote this book, there were some inside of TSR who were critical of the high reading level of the text. They saw the AD&D market for DRAGONLANCE *as being primarily "juvenile." After reading our pages, they asked us if we could lower the reading language. Margaret and I simply said no. We believed that our readers were smarter than that. Time has shown us correct in that faith.—TRH*

wings and caught the wind currents. They soared higher and higher, circling above the forest. The silver moon and the red bathed the valley below and the clouds above in an eerie, beautiful, purplish glow that receded into a deeper purple night. As the forest fell away from them, the last thing the companions saw was the Forestmaster, glimmering like a star fallen from the heavens, shining lost and alone in a darkening land.

One by one, the companions felt drowsiness overcome them.

Tasslehoff fought this magically induced sleep longest. Enchanted by the rush of wind against his face, spellbound by the sight of the tall trees that normally loomed over him reduced to child's toys,† Tas struggled to remain awake long after everyone else. Flint's head rested against his back, the dwarf snoring loudly. Goldmoon was cradled in Riverwind's arms. His head drooped over her shoulder. Even in his sleep, he held her protectively. Caramon slumped over his horse's neck, breathing stentoriously. His brother rested against his twin's broad back. Sturm slept peacefully, the lines of pain gone from his face. Even Tanis's bearded face was clear of care and worry and responsibility.

I have a terrible fear of heights and yet was a glider pilot when I was seventeen. My mind deals with the difference between standing atop a hundred-foot cliff and soaring at ten thousand feet in this same way.—TRH

Tas yawned. "No," he mumbled, blinking rapidly and pinching himself.

"Rest now, little kender," his pegasus said in amusement. "Mortals were not meant to fly.† This sleep is for your protection. We do not want you to panic and fall off."

This, on the other hand, probably more closely reflects Margaret's attitude.—TRH

"I won't," Tas protested, yawning again. His head sank forward. The pegasus's neck was warm and comfortable, the fur was fragrant and soft. "I won't panic," Tas whispered sleepily. "Never panic . . ." He slept.

The half-elf woke with a start to find that he was lying in a grassy meadow. The leader of the pegasi stood above him, staring off to the east. Tanis sat up.

"Where are we?" he began. "This isn't a city." He looked around. "Why—we haven't even crossed the mountains yet!"

"I am sorry." The pegasus turned to him. "We could not take you as far as the Eastwall Mountains. There is great trouble brewing in the east. A

darkness fills the air, such a darkness as I have not felt in Krynn for countless—" He stopped, lowered his head and pawed the ground restlessly. "I dare not travel farther."

"Where are we? " the confused half-elf repeated. "And where are the other pegasi?"

"I sent them home. I remained to guard your sleep. Now that you are awake, I must return home as well." The pegasus gazed sternly at Tanis. "I know not what awakened this great evil on Krynn. I trust it was not you and your companions."

He spread his great wings.

"Wait!" Tanis scrambled to his feet. "What—"

The pegasus leaped into the air, circled twice, then was gone, flying rapidly back to the west.

"What evil?" Tanis asked glumly. He sighed and looked around. His companions were sleeping soundly, lying on the ground around him in various poses of slumber. He studied the horizon, trying to get his bearings. It was nearly dawn, he realized. The sun's light was just beginning to illuminate the east. He was standing on a flat prairie. There was not a tree in sight, nothing but rolling fields of tall grass as far as he could see.

Wondering what the pegasus had meant about trouble to the east, Tanis sat down to watch the sun rise† and wait for his friends to wake. He wasn't particularly worried about where he was, for he guessed Riverwind knew this land down to the last blade of grass. So he stretched out on the ground, facing the east, feeling more relaxed after that strange sleep than he had in many nights.

We could, of course, just as easily have had the sun rise in the west on this fantasy world, but it would have served no purpose in the story and would have been just another oddity for the reader to remember. The point is that you don't need to change everything … in fact, changing everything makes a world less accessible. You need a lot of the familiar to identify with the story. —TRH

Suddenly he sat upright, his relaxed feeling gone, a tightness clutching at his throat like an unseen hand. For there, snaking up to meet the bright new morning sun, were three thick, twisting columns of greasy, black smoke. Tanis stumbled to his feet. He ran over and shook Riverwind gently, trying to wake the Plainsman without disturbing Goldmoon.

"Hush," Tanis whispered, putting a warning finger on his lips and nodding toward the sleeping woman as Riverwind blinked at the half-elf. Seeing Tanis's dark expression, the barbarian was instantly awake. He stood up quietly and moved off with Tanis, glancing around him.

"What's this?" he whispered. "We're in the Plains of Abanasinia. Still about a half day's journey from the Eastwall Mountains. My village lies to the east—"

He stopped as Tanis pointed silently eastward. Then he gave a shallow, ragged cry as he saw the smoke curling into the sky. Goldmoon jerked awake. She sat up, gazed at Riverwind sleepily, then with growing alarm. Turning, she followed his horrified stare.

"No," she moaned. "No!" she cried again. Quickly rising, she began to gather their possessions. The others woke at her cry.

"What is it?" Caramon jumped up.

"Their village," Tanis said softly, gesturing with his hand. "It's burning. Apparently the armies are moving quicker than we thought."

"No," said Raistlin. "Remember—the draconian clerics mentioned they had traced the staff to a village in the Plains."

"My people," Goldmoon murmured, energy draining from her. She slumped in Riverwind's arms, staring at the smoke. "My father . . ."

"We'd better get going." Caramon glanced around uneasily. "We show up like a jewel in a gypsy dancer's navel."†

Apparently, Caramon had some pretty interesting adventures.—TRH

"Yes," Tanis said. "We've definitely got to get out of here. But where do we go?" he asked Riverwind.

"Qué-Shu," Goldmoon's tone allowed no contradiction. "It's on our way. The Eastwall Mountains are just beyond my village." She started through the tall grass.

Tanis glanced at Riverwind.

"Marulina!"† the Plainsman called out to her. Running forward, he caught hold of Goldmoon's arm. *"Nikh pat-takh merilar!"*† he said sternly.

"Beloved!"

"No, don't go there."

She stared up at him, her eyes blue and cold as the morning sky. "No," she said resolutely, "I am going to our village. It is our fault if something has happened. I don't care if there are thousands of those monsters waiting. I will die with our people, as I should have done." Her voice failed her. Tanis, watching, felt his heart ache with pity.

Riverwind put his arm around her and together they began walking toward the rising sun.

Caramon cleared his throat. "I hope I do meet a thousand of those things," he muttered, hoisting his

and his brother's packs. "Hey," he said in astonishment. "They're full." He peered in his pack. "Provisions. Several days' worth. And my sword's back in my scabbard!"

"At least that's one thing we won't have to worry about," Tanis said grimly. "You all right, Sturm?"

"Yes," the knight answered. "I feel much better after that sleep."

"Right, then. Let's go. Flint, where's Tas?" Turning, Tanis nearly fell over the kender who had been standing right behind him.

"Poor Goldmoon," Tas said softly. Tanis patted him on the shoulder. "Maybe it won't be as bad as we fear," the half-elf said, following the Plainsmen through the rippling grass. "Maybe the warriors fought them off and those are victory fires."

Tasslehoff sighed and looked up at Tanis, his brown eyes wide. "You're a rotten liar, Tanis," the kender said. He had the feeling it was going to be a very long day.

Twilight. The pale sun set. Shafts of yellow and tan streaked the western sky, then faded into dreary night. The companions sat huddled around a fire that offered no warmth, for there existed no flame on Krynn that would drive the chill from their souls. They did not speak to each other, but each sat staring into the fire, trying to make some sense of what they had seen, trying to make sense of the senseless.

Tanis had lived through much that was horrible in his life. But the ravaged town of Qué-Shu would always stand out in his mind as a symbol of the horrors of war.

Even so, remembering Qué-Shu, he could only grasp fleeting images, his mind refusing to encompass the total awful vision.† Oddly enough, he remembered the melted stones of Qué-Shu. He remembered them vividly. Only in his dreams did he recall the twisted and blackened bodies that lay among the smoking stones.

The great stone walls, the huge stone temples and edifices, the spacious stone buildings with their rock courtyards and statuary, the large stone arena—all had melted, like butter on a hot summer day. The rock still smoldered, though it was obvious that the village must have been attacked well over a sunrise

There is nothing so horrible as that which is left to our imagination. As I have often said, writers are evokers—conjuring images in the reader's mind. Each reader has, interestingly enough, a unique experience when he or she reads—no other person in the world sees the same images, hears the same sounds. No description of detail will affect you as a reader as much as your own imagination.—TRH

ago. It was as if a white-hot, searing flame had engulfed the entire village. But what fire was there on Krynn that could melt rock?

He remembered a creaking sound, remembered hearing it and being puzzled by it, and wondering what it was until locating the source of the only sound in the deathly still town became an obsession. He ran through the ruined village until he located the source. He remembered that he shouted to the others until they came. They stood staring into the melted arena.

Huge stone blocks had poured down from the side of the bowl-shaped depression, forming molten ripples of rock around the bottom of the dish. In the center—on grass that was blackened and charred—stood a crude gibbet. Two stout posts had been driven into the burned ground by unspeakable force, their bases splintered by the impact. Ten feet above the ground, a crosspiece pole was lashed to the two posts. The wood was charred and blistered. Scavenger birds perched on the top. Three chains, made of what appeared to be iron before it had melted and run together, swung back and forth. This was the cause of the creaking sound. Suspended from each chain, apparently by the feet, was a corpse. The corpses were not human; they were hobgoblin. On top of the gruesome structure was a shield stuck to the crosspiece with a broken sword-blade. Roughly clawed on the battered shield were words written in a crude form of Common.

"This is what happens to those who take prisoners against my commands. Kill or be killed." It was signed, *Verminaard.*

Verminaard. The name meant nothing to Tanis.

Other images. He remembered Goldmoon standing in the center of her father's ruined house trying to put back together the pieces of a broken vase. He remembered a dog—the only living thing they found in the entire village—curled around the body of a dead child. Caramon stopped to pet the small dog. The animal cringed, then licked the big man's hand. It then licked the child's cold face, looking up at the warrior hopefully, expecting this human to make everything all right, to make his little playmate run and laugh again. He remembered Caramon stroking the dog's soft fur with his huge hands.

He remembered Riverwind picking up a rock, holding it, aimlessly, as he stared around his burned and blasted village.

He remembered Sturm, standing transfixed before the gibbet, staring at the sign, and he remembered the knight's lips moving as though in prayer or perhaps a silent vow.

He remembered the sorrow-lined face of the dwarf, who had seen so much tragedy in his long lifetime, as he stood in the center of the ruined village, patting Tasslehoff gently on the back after finding the kender sobbing in a corner.

He remembered Goldmoon's frantic search for survivors. She crawled through the blackened rubble, screaming out names, listening for faint answers to her calls until she was hoarse and Riverwind finally convinced her it was hopeless. If there were any survivors, they had long since fled.

He remembered standing alone, in the center of the town, looking at piles of dust with arrow heads in them, and recognizing them as bodies of draconians.

He remembered a cold hand touching his arm and the mage's whispering voice. "Tanis, we must leave. There is nothing more we can do and we must reach Xak Tsaroth. Then we will have our revenge."

And so they left Qué-Shu. They traveled far into the night, none of them wanting to stop, each wanting to push his body to the point of exhaustion so that, when they finally slept, there would be no evil dreams.

But the dreams came anyway.

13

Chill dawn. Vine bridges. Dark water.

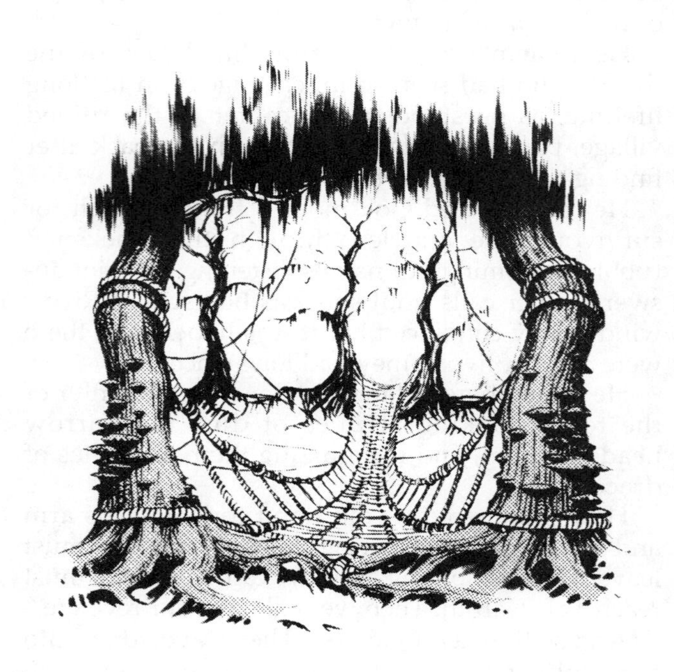

The first of many bridges—both literal and figurative—the companions will need to fight to cross.

Tanis felt clawed hands clutching at his throat. He struggled and fought, then woke to find Riverwind bending over him in the darkness, shaking him roughly.

"What . . . ?" Tanis sat up.

"You were dreaming," the Plainsman said grimly. "I had to wake you. Your shouts would draw an army down on us."

"Yes, thanks," Tanis muttered. "I'm sorry." He sat up, trying to shake off the nightmare. "What time is it?"

"Still several hours till dawn," Riverwind said wearily. He returned to where he had been sitting, his back against the trunk of a twisted tree. Goldmoon lay sleeping on the ground beside him. She began to murmur and shake her head, making

small, soft, moaning cries like a wounded animal. Riverwind stroked her silver-gold hair, and she quieted.

"You should have wakened me earlier," Tanis said. He stood up, rubbing his shoulders and neck. "It's my watch."

"Do you think I could sleep?" asked Riverwind bitterly.

"You've got to," Tanis answered. "You'll slow us up if you don't."

"The men in my tribe can travel for many days without sleep," Riverwind said. His eyes were dull and glazed, and he seemed to stare at nothing.

Tanis started to argue, then sighed and kept quiet. He knew that he could never truly understand the agony the Plainsman was suffering. To have friends and family—an entire life—utterly destroyed, must be so devastating that the mind shrank from even imagining it. Tanis left him and walked over to where Flint was sitting carving at a piece of wood.

"You might as well get some sleep," Tanis told the dwarf. "I'll watch for a while."

Flint nodded. "I heard you yelling over there." He sheathed his dagger and thrust the piece of wood into a pouch. "Defending Qué-Shu?"

Tanis frowned at the memory. Shivering in the chill night, he wrapped his cloak around him, drew up his hood. "Any idea where we are?" he asked Flint.

"The Plainsman says we're on a road known as Sageway East," the dwarf answered. He stretched out on the cold ground, dragging a blanket up around his shoulders. "Some old highway. It's been around since before the Cataclysm."

"I don't suppose we'd be fortunate enough to have this road take us into Xak Tsaroth?"

"Riverwind doesn't seem to think so," the dwarf mumbled sleepily. "Says he's only followed it a short distance. But at least it gets us through the mountains." He gave a great yawn and turned over, pillowing his head on his cloak.

Tanis breathed deeply. The night seemed peaceful enough. They hadn't run into any draconians or goblins in their wild flight from Qué-Shu. As Raistlin said, apparently the draconians had attacked Qué-Shu in search of the staff, not as part of

any preparations for battle. They had struck and then withdrawn. The Forestmaster's time limit still held good, Tanis supposed—Xak Tsaroth within two days. And one day had already passed.†

According to the first draft, Raistlin had kept a "cool head" in the face of the horror of Qué-Shu. "It was Raistlin who had calmed the frenzied and guilt-stricken Goldmoon and persuaded her to leave her father's charred body without taking time to perform the elaborate Qué-Shu burial rituals. It was Raistlin who had discovered the ancient road through the mountains and kept the group moving. It was Raistlin who kept reminding them of the time limit—two days ... two days ... It was Raistlin who had been cool-headed when the other, seasoned warriors had given way to shocked horror and grief." But, Tanis wondered, "Had it really been cool-headedness . . . or cold-bloodedness?"

Shivering, the half-elf walked back over to Riverwind. "Do you have any idea how far we have to go and in what direction?" Tanis crouched down next to the Plainsman.

"Yes," Riverwind nodded, rubbing his burning eyes. "We must go to the northeast, toward Newsea. That is where the city is rumored to be. I have never been there—" He frowned, then shook his head. "I've never been there," he repeated.

"Can we reach it by tomorrow?" Tanis asked.

"Newsea is said to be two days' journey from Qué-Shu." The barbarian sighed. "If Xak Tsaroth exists, we should be able to reach it in a day, though I have heard that the land from here to Newsea is swampy and difficult to travel."

He shut his eyes, his hand absently stroking Goldmoon's hair. Tanis fell silent, hoping the Plainsman would sleep. The half-elf moved quietly to sit beneath the tree, staring into the night. He made a mental note to ask Tasslehoff in the morning if he had a map.

The kender did have a map, but it wasn't much help, dating, as it did, before the Cataclysm. Newsea wasn't on the map since it had appeared after the land had been torn apart and the waters of Turbidus Ocean had rushed in to fill it. Still, the map showed Xak Tsaroth only a short distance from the highway marked Sageway East. They should reach it some time that afternoon, if the territory they had to cross wasn't impassable.

The companions ate a cheerless breakfast, most forcing the food down without appetite. Raistlin brewed his foul-smelling herbal drink over the small fire, his strange eyes lingering on Goldmoon's staff.

"How precious it has become," he commented softly—"now that it has been purchased by the blood of innocents."

"Is it worth it? Is it worth the lives of my people?" Goldmoon asked, staring at the nondescript brown staff dully. She seemed to have aged during the night. Gray circles smudged the skin beneath her eyes.†

None of the companions answered, each looking away in awkward silence. Riverwind stood up abruptly and stalked off into the woods by himself. Goldmoon lifted her eyes and stared after him, then her head sank into her hand and she began to weep silently. "He blames himself ." She shook her head. "And I am not helping him. It wasn't his fault."

"It's not anyone's fault," Tanis said slowly, walking over to her. He put his hand on her shoulder, rubbing out the tenseness he felt in the bunched muscles of her neck. "We can't understand. We've just got to keep going and hope we find the answer in Xak Tsaroth."

She nodded and wiped her eyes, drew a deep breath, and blew her nose on a handkerchief Tasslehoff handed her.

"You're right," she said, swallowing. "My father would be ashamed of me. I must remember—I am Chieftain's Daughter."

"No," came Riverwind's deep voice from where he stood behind her in the shadows of the trees. "You are Chieftain."

Goldmoon gasped. She twisted to her feet to stare, wide-eyed, at Riverwind. "Perhaps I am," she faltered—"but it is meaningless. Our people are dead—"

"I saw tracks," Riverwind answered. "Some managed to flee. They have probably gone into the mountains. They will return, and you will be their ruler."

"Our people . . . still alive!" Goldmoon's face became radiant.

"Not many. Maybe none now. It would depend on whether or not the draconians followed them into the mountains." Riverwind shrugged. "Still, you are now their ruler"—bitterness crept into his voice—"and I will be husband of Chieftain."

Goldmoon cringed, as though he had struck her. She blinked, then shook her head. "No, Riverwind," she said softly. "I . . . we've talked—"

"Have we?" he interrupted. "I was thinking about it last night. I've been gone so many years. My thoughts were of you, as a woman. I did not realize—" He swallowed and then drew a deep breath. "I left Goldmoon. I returned to find Chieftain's Daughter."

Cut from first draft: "Though everyone had been thinking the same thing, no one had spoken the thought aloud. Caramon flushed, embarrassed by his unfeeling brother. Sturm glared at Raistlin in disgust. The knight rose to his feet and walked over to where Goldmoon sat apart from them. Bending down, he patted her hand and spoke a few, well-chosen words of consolation. Goldmoon didn't answer."

"What choice did I have?" Goldmoon cried angrily. "My father wasn't well. I had to rule or Loreman would have taken over the tribe. Do you know what's it like—being Chieftain's Daughter? Wondering at every meal if this morsel is the one with the poison? Struggling every day to find the money in the treasury to pay the soldiers so that Loreman would have no excuse to take over! And all the time I must act as Chieftain's Daughter, while my father sits and drools and mumbles." Her voice choked with tears.

Riverwind listened, his face stern and unmoving. He stared at a point above her head. "We should get started," he said coldly. "It's nearly dawn."

The companions had traveled only a few miles on the old, broken road when it dumped them, literally, into a swamp.† They had noticed that the ground was getting spongier and the tall, sturdy trees of the mountain canyon forests dwindled. Strange, twisted trees rose up before them. A miasma blotted out the sun, and the air became foul to breathe. Raistlin began to cough and he covered his mouth with a handkerchief. They stayed on the broken stones of the old road, avoiding the dank, swampy ground next to it.

They are entering the Cursed Lands, the swamp surrounding Xak Tsaroth. It formed when the Newsea was created by the Cataclysm.

Flint was walking in front with Tasslehoff when suddenly the dwarf gave a great shout and disappeared into the muck. They could see only his head.

"Help! The dwarf!" Tas shouted, and the others ran up.

"It's dragging me under!" Flint flailed about the black, oozing mud in panic.

"Hold still," Riverwind cautioned. "You have fallen in deathmirk. Don't go in after him!" he warned Sturm who had leaped forward. "You'll both die. Get a branch."

Caramon grabbed a young sapling, took a deep breath, grunted, and pulled. They could hear its roots snapping and creaking as the huge warrior dragged it out of the ground. Riverwind stretched out flat, extending the branch to the dwarf. Flint, nearly up to his nose in the slimy muck, thrashed about and finally grabbed hold of it. The warrior hauled the tree out of the deathmirk, the dwarf clinging to it.

"Tanis!" The kender clutched at the half-elf and pointed. A snake, as big around as Caramon's arm, slithered into the ooze right where the dwarf had been floundering.

"We can't walk through this!" Tanis gestured at the swamp. "Maybe we should turn back."

"No time," Raistlin whispered, his hourglass eyes glittering.

"And there is no other way," Riverwind said. His voice sounded strange. "And we can get through—I know a path."

"What?" Tanis turned to him. "I thought you said—"

"I've been here," the Plainsman said in a strangled voice. "I can't remember when, but I've been here. I know the way through the swamp. And it leads to—" He licked his lips.

"Leads to a broken city of evil?" Tanis asked grimly when the Plainsman did not finish his sentence.

"Xak Tsaroth!" Raistlin hissed.

"Of course," Tanis said softly. "It makes sense. Where would we go to find answers about the staff—except to the place where the staff was given you?"

"And we must go now!" said Raistlin insistently. "We must be there by midnight tonight!"

The Plainsman took the lead. He found firm ground around the black water and, making them all walk single file, led them away from the road and deeper into the swamp. Trees that he called ironclaw rose out of the water, their roots standing exposed, twisting into the mud. Vines drooped from their branches and trailed across the faint path. The mist closed in, and soon no one could see beyond a few feet. They were forced to move slowly, testing every step. A false move and they would have plunged into the stinking morass that lay foul and stagnant all around them.

Suddenly the trail came to an end in dark swamp water.

"Now what?" Caramon asked gloomily.

"This," Riverwind said, pointing. A crude bridge, made out of vines twisted into ropes, was attached to a tree. It spanned the water like a spider web.

"Who built it?" Tanis asked.

"I don't know," Riverwind said. "But you will find them all along the path, wherever it becomes impassable."

"I told you Xak Tsaroth would not remain abandoned," Raistlin whispered.

"Yes, well—I suppose we shouldn't throw stones at a gift of the gods," replied Tanis. "At least we don't have to swim!"

The journey across the vine bridge was not pleasant. The vines were coated with slimy moss, which made walking precarious. The structure swayed alarmingly when touched, and its motion became erratic when anyone crossed. They made it safely to the other side but had walked only a short distance before they were forced to use another bridge. And always below them and around them was the dark water, where strange eyes† watched them hungrily. Then they reached a point where the firm ground ended and there were no vine bridges. Ahead was nothing but slimy water.

At least some of the eyes belonged to snakes in a brief episode that was cut. In addition, there was the problem they had run into before: "Flint crossed with his eyes closed, inching forward so slowly that finally Tasslehoff ran back out again and tugged the dwarf along, or he might possibly have spent the night clinging to the vines."

"It isn't very deep," Riverwind muttered. "Follow me. Step only where I step."

Riverwind took a step, then another step, feeling his way, the rest keeping right behind him, staring into the water. They stared in disgust and alarm as unknown and unseen things slithered past their legs. When they reached firm ground again, their legs were coated with slime; all of them gagged from the smell. But this last journey seemed, perhaps, to have been the worst. The jungle growth was not as thick, and they could even see the sun shining faintly through a green haze.

The farther north they traveled, the firmer the terrain became. By midday, Tanis called a halt when he found a dry patch of ground beneath an ancient oak tree. The companions sank down to eat lunch and speak hopefully of leaving the swamp behind them. All except Goldmoon and Riverwind. They spoke not at all.

Flint's clothes were sopping wet. He shook with the cold and began complaining about pains in his joints. Tanis grew worried. He knew the dwarf was subject to rheumatism and remembered what Flint had said about fearing to slow them up. Tanis tapped the kender and gestured him over to one side.

"I know you've got something in one of your pouches that would take the chill off the dwarf's bones, if you know what I mean," Tanis said softly.

"Oh, sure, Tanis," Tas said, brightening. He fumbled around, first in one pouch, then another, and finally came up with a gleaming silver flask. "Brandy. Otik's finest."

"I don't suppose you paid for it?" Tanis asked, grinning.

"I will," the kender replied, hurt. "Next time I'm there."

"Sure." Tanis patted him on the shoulder. "Share some with Flint. Not too much," he cautioned. "Just warm him up."

"All right. And we'll take the lead—we mighty warriors." Tas laughed and skipped over to the dwarf as Tanis returned to the others. They were silently packing up the remains of lunch and preparing to move out. All of us could use some of Otik's finest, he thought. Goldmoon and Riverwind had not spoken to each other all morning. Their mood spread a pall on everyone. Tanis could think of nothing to do that would end the torture these two were experiencing. He could only hope that time would salve the wounds.

The companions continued along the trail for about an hour after lunch, moving more quickly since the thickest part of the jungle had been left behind. Just as they thought they had left the swamp, however, the firm ground came abruptly to an end. Weary, sick with the smell, and discouraged, the companions found themselves wading through the muck once again.

Only Flint and Tasslehoff were unaffected by the return to the swamp. These two had ranged far ahead of the others. Tasslehoff soon "forgot" Tanis's warning about drinking only a little of the brandy. The liquid warmed the blood and took the edge off the gloomy atmosphere, so the kender and dwarf passed the flask back and forth many times until it was empty and they were traipsing along, making jokes about what they would do if they encountered a draconian.

"I'd turn it to stone, all right," the dwarf said, swinging an imaginary battle-axe. "Wham!—right in the lizard's gizzard."†

At the 1985 GenCon convention, Margaret and I—with the considerable help of Janet Pack, my wife Laura, Doug Niles, Margaret's son David Baldwin, Gary Pack, and Harold Johnson—performed a reader's theater (a GenCon first) to introduce this new series, DRAGONLANCE. Curtis Smith was our able stage manager. We all credit the lovely Lizz Baldwin, Margaret's gorgeous daughter, with bringing in our audience. This scene was one of the highlights of that presentation—and forever solidified in our minds Doug's portrayal of Flint and Janet's portrayal of Tasslehoff.—TRH

Lizz was only nine at the time. We put a sandwich board on her and sent her around the convention hall with free tickets to the play. People later told me that the only reason they came that night was so they wouldn't disappoint the sweet girl with the big blue eyes!

We were short of cast members, so I abducted friends of mine from Kansas City, Janet and Gary Pack, who were coming to visit. We handed Gary the script for Tanis as he got off the plane the day before the performance! He was a wonderful Tanis and Janet has become legendary as Tas.—MW

"I'll bet Raistlin could turn one to stone with a look!" Tas imitated the mage's grim face and dour stare. They both laughed loudly, then hushed, giggling, peering back unsteadily to see if Tanis had heard them.

"I'll bet Caramon'd stick a fork in one and eat it!" Flint said.

Tas choked with laughter and wiped tears from his eyes. The dwarf roared. Suddenly the two came to the end of the spongy ground. Tasslehoff grabbed hold of the dwarf as Flint nearly plunged head-first into a pool of swamp water so wide that a vine bridge would not span it. A huge ironclaw tree lay across the water, its thick trunk making a bridge wide enough for two people to walk across side-by-side.

"Now *this* is a bridge!" Flint said, stepping back a pace and trying to bring the log into focus. "No more spider crawling on those stupid green webs. Let's go."

"Shouldn't we wait for the others?" Tasslehoff asked mildly. "Tanis wouldn't want to us to get separated."

"Tanis? Humpf!" The dwarf sniffed. "We'll show him."

"All right," Tasslehoff agreed cheerfully. He leaped up onto the fallen tree. "Careful," he said, slipping slightly, then easily catching his balance. "It's slick." He took a few quick steps, arms outstretched, his feet pointed out like a rope walker he'd seen once at a summer fair.

The dwarf clambered up after the kender, Flint's thick boots clumping clumsily on the log. A voice in the unbrandied part of Flint's mind told him he could never have done this cold sober. It also told him he was a fool for crossing the bridge without waiting for the others, but he ignored it. He was feeling positively young again.

Tasslehoff, enchanted with pretending he was Mirgo the Magnificent, looked up and discovered that he did, indeed, have an audience—one of those draconian things leaped onto the log in front of him. The sight sobered Tas up rapidly. The kender was not given to fear, but he was certainly amazed. He had presence of mind enough to do two things. First he yelled out loudly—

"Tanis, ambush!" Then he lifted his hoopak staff and swung it in a wide arc.

The move took the draconian by surprise. The creature sucked in its breath and jumped back off the log to the bank below. Tas, momentarily off balance, regained his feet quickly and wondered what to do next. He glanced around and saw another draconian on the bank. They were, he was puzzled to notice, not armed. Before he could consider this oddity, he heard a roar behind him. He had forgotten the dwarf.

"What is it?" Flint shouted.

"Draco-thing-a-ma-jiggers," Tas said, gripping his hoopak and peering through the mists. "Two ahead! Here they come!"

"Well, confound it, get out of my way!" Flint snarled. Reaching behind, he fumbled for his axe.

"Where am I supposed to go?" Tas shouted wildly.

"Duck!" yelled the dwarf.

The kender ducked, throwing himself down on the log as one of the draconians came toward him, its clawed hands outstretched. Flint swung his axe in a mighty blow that would have decapitated the draconian if it had come anywhere near it. Unfortunately, the dwarf miscalculated and the blade whistled harmlessly in front of the draconian who was waving its hands in the air and chanting strange words.

The momentum of Flint's swing spun the dwarf around. His feet slipped on the slimy log, and, with a loud cry, the dwarf tumbled backward into the water.

Tasslehoff, having been around Raistlin for years, recognized that the draconian was casting a magic spell. Lying face down on the log, his hoopak staff clutched in his hand, the kender figured he had about one and a half seconds to consider what to do. The dwarf was gasping and spluttering in the water beneath him. Not inches away, the draconian was clearly reaching a stunning conclusion to his spellcasting. Deciding that anything was better than being magicked, Tas took a deep breath and dove off the log.

"Tanis! Ambush!"

"Damn!" swore Caramon as the kender's voice floated to them out of the mist somewhere ahead.

Tas always swore that he rescued Flint from Crystalmir Lake. A few paragraphs that were cut here might back up his claim, though Flint might prefer to forget:

"The water was cold and tasted awful. Tasslehoff sank below the surface, but, being a fairly decent swimmer, he surfaced rapidly and heard the dwarf choking somewhere near him. He also heard the draconians shouting. The kender wiped the mucky water out of his eyes, saw Flint, and reached him in a few, swift strokes. He could also see the draconians peering into the dark water.

" 'I've got you,' he panted, grasping the dwarf by the collar of his tunic. 'Quit struggling.'

"But Flint was in a state of panic and thrashed about wildly.

" 'Stop—' Tasslehoff swallowed a mouthful of water. Suddenly Flint flung his arms around the kender's neck. Flint's weight—the dwarf having refused to take off his armor—sank them both."

They all began running toward the sound, cursing the vines and the tree branches that blocked their way. Crashing out through the forest, they saw the fallen ironclaw bridge. Four draconians ran out of the shadows, blocking their path.

Suddenly the companions were plunged into darkness too thick to see their own hands, much less their comrades.

"Magic!" Tanis heard Raistlin hiss. "These are magic-users. Stand aside. You cannot fight them."

Then Tanis heard the mage cry out in agony.

"Raist!" Caramon shouted. "Where—ugh—" There was a groan and the sound of a heavy body thudding to the ground.

Tanis heard the draconians chanting. Even as he fumbled for his sword, he was suddenly covered, head to toe, in a thick, gooey substance that clogged up his nose and mouth. Struggling to free himself, he only enmeshed himself further. He heard Sturm swearing next to him, Goldmoon cried out, Riverwind's voice was choked off, then drowsiness overcame him. Tanis sank to his knees, still fighting to free himself from the weblike substance that glued his hands to his sides. Then he fell forward on his face and sank into an unnatural sleep.

14

Prisoners of the Draconians.

I wonder at the vision of draconians going out to gather grasses and then sitting around to weave this enormous piece of rattan art.—TRH

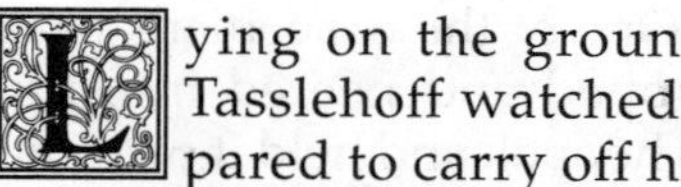

Lying on the ground, panting for breath, Tasslehoff watched as the draconians prepared to carry off his unconscious friends. The kender was well-hidden beneath a bush near the swamp. The dwarf was stretched out next to him, knocked out cold. Tas glanced at him in remorse. He'd had no choice. In his panic, Flint had dragged the kender down in the cold water. If he hadn't clunked the dwarf over the head with his hoopak staff, neither of them would have surfaced alive. He'd hauled the comatose dwarf up out of the water and hidden him beneath a bush.

Then Tasslehoff watched helplessly as the draconians bound his friends magically in what looked like strong spider webs. Tas saw they were all

apparently unconscious—or dead—because they didn't struggle or put up a fight.

The kender did get a certain amount of grim amusement out of watching the draconians try to pick up Goldmoon's staff. Evidently they recognized it, for they croaked over it in their guttural language and made gestures of glee. One—presumably the leader—reached out to grasp it. There was a flash of blue light. Giving a screeching cry, the draconian dropped the staff and hopped up and down on the bank, uttering words Tas assumed were impolite. The leader finally came up with an ingenious idea. Pulling a fur blanket from Goldmoon's pack, the draconian laid it down on the ground. The creature picked up a stick and used it to roll the staff onto the blanket. Then it gingerly wrapped the staff in the fur and lifted it up triumphantly. The draconians lifted the webbed bodies of the kender's friends and bore them away. Other draconians followed behind, carrying the companions' packs and their weapons.

As the draconians marched along a path very near the hidden kender, Flint suddenly groaned and stirred. Tas clamped his hand over the dwarf's mouth. The draconians didn't seem to hear and kept moving. Tas could see his friends clearly in the fading afternoon light as the draconians passed. They seemed to be sound asleep. Caramon was even snoring. The kender remembered Raistlin's sleep spell and figured that was what the draconians had used on his friends.

Flint groaned again. One of the draconians near the end of the line stopped and peered into the brush. Tas picked up his hoopak and held it over the dwarf's head—just in case. But it wasn't needed. The draconian shrugged and muttered to itself, then hurried to catch up with its squad. Sighing in relief, Tas took his hand off the dwarf's mouth. Flint blinked and opened his eyes.

"What happened?" The dwarf moaned, his hand on his head.

"You fell off the bridge and hit your head on a log," Tas said glibly.

"I did?" Flint looked suspicious. "I don't remember that. I remember one of those draconian things coming at me and I remember falling into the water—"

"Well, you did, so don't argue," Tas said hurriedly, getting to his feet. "Can you walk?"

"Of course I can walk," the dwarf snapped. He stood up, a little wobbly, but erect. "Where is everybody?"

"The draconians captured them and carried them off ."

"All of them?" Flint's mouth fell open. "Just like that?"

"These draconians were magic-users,"† Tas said impatiently, anxious to get started. "They cast spells, I guess. They didn't hurt them, except for Raistlin. I think they did something terrible to him. I saw him as they passed. He looked awful. But he's the only one." The kender tugged on the dwarf's wet sleeve. "Let's go—we've got to follow them."

This would mark them as Bozak draconians, although Darkness is not usually found in their spell mix. The Darkness spell is one of the more common AD&D spells, which we'll meet again, and again.—TRH

"Yeah, sure," Flint mumbled, looking around. Then he put his hand on his head again. "Where's my helm?"

"At the bottom of the swamp," Tas said in exasperation. "Do you want to go in after it?"

The dwarf gave the murky water a horrified glance, shivered, and turned away hurriedly. He put his hand to his head again and felt a large bump. "I sure don't remember hitting my head," he muttered. Then a sudden thought struck him. He felt around his back wildly. "My axe!" he cried.

"Hush!" Tas scolded. "At least you're alive. Now we've got to rescue the others."

"And how do you propose to do that without any weapons except that overgrown slingshot?" Flint grumbled, stumping along after the fast-moving kender.

"We'll think of something," Tas said confidently, though he felt as if his heart were getting tangled up in his feet, it had sunk so low.

The kender picked up the draconians' trail without any trouble. It was obviously an old and well-used trail; it looked as though hundreds of draconian feet had tramped along it. Tasslehoff, examining the tracks, suddenly realized that they might be walking into a large camp of the monsters. He shrugged. No use worrying about such minor details.

Unfortunately, Flint didn't share the same philosophy. "There's a whole damn army up there!"

the dwarf gasped, grabbing the kender by the shoulder.

"Yes, well—" Tas paused to consider the situation. He brightened. "That's all the better. The more of *them* there are, the less chance they'll have of seeing *us.*" He started off again. Flint frowned. There was something wrong with that logic, but right now he couldn't figure out what, and he was too wet and chilled to argue. Besides, he was thinking the same thing the kender was: the only other choice they had was to escape into the swamp themselves and leave their friends in the hands of the draconians. And that was no choice at all.†

There's that Ogre's Choice again.

They walked another half hour. The sun sank into the mist, giving it a blood-red tinge, and night fell swiftly in the mirky swamp.

Soon they saw a blazing light ahead of them. They left the trail and sneaked into the brush. The kender moved silently as a mouse; the dwarf stepped on sticks that snapped beneath his feet, ran into trees, and blundered through the brush. Fortunately, the draconian camp was celebrating and probably wouldn't have heard an army of dwarves approaching. Flint and Tas knelt just beyond the firelight and watched. The dwarf suddenly grabbed the kender with such violence that he nearly pulled him over.

"Great Reorx!" Flint swore, pointing. "A dragon!"

Tas was too stunned to say anything. He and the dwarf watched in amazed horror as the draconians danced and prostrated themselves before a giant black dragon. The creature lurked inside the remaining half shell of a crumbled domed ruin. Its head was higher than the treetops, its wing span was enormous. One of the draconians, wearing robes, bent before the dragon, gesturing to the staff as it lay on the ground with the captured weapons.

"There's something strange about that dragon," Tas whispered after watching for a few moments.

"Like they're not supposed to exist?"

"That's just the point," Tas said. "Look at it. The creature isn't moving or reacting to anything. It's just sitting there. I always thought that dragons would be more lively, don't you know?"

"Go up and tickle its foot!" Flint snorted. "Then you'll see lively!"

"I think I'll do that," the kender said. Before the dwarf could say a word, Tasslehoff crept out of the brush, flitting from shadow to shadow as he drew near the camp. Flint could have torn his beard out in frustration, but it would have been disastrous to try and stop him now. The dwarf could do nothing but follow.

"Tanis!"

The half-elf heard someone calling him from across a huge chasm. He tried to answer, but his mouth was stuffed with something sticky. He shook his head. Then he felt an arm around his shoulders, helping him sit up. He opened his eyes. It was night. Judging by the flickering light, a huge fire blazed brightly somewhere. Sturm's face, looking concerned, was near his. Tanis sighed and reached out his hand to clasp the knight's shoulder. He tried to speak and was forced to pull off bits of the sticky substance that clung to his face and mouth like cobwebs.

"I'm all right," Tanis said when he could talk. "Where are we?" He glanced around. "Is everyone here? Anyone hurt?"

"We're in a draconian camp," Sturm said, helping the half-elf stand. "Tasslehoff and Flint are missing and Raistlin's hurt."

"Badly?" Tanis asked, alarmed by the serious expression on Sturm's face.

"Not good," the knight replied.

"Poisoned dart," Riverwind said. Tanis turned toward the Plainsman and got his first clear look at their prison. They were inside a cage made of bamboo. Draconian guards stood outside, their long, curved swords drawn and ready. Beyond the cage, hundreds of draconians milled around a campfire. And above the campfire . . .

"Yes," Sturm said, seeing Tanis's startled expression. "A dragon. More children's stories. Raistlin would gloat."

"Raistlin—" Tanis went over to the mage who was lying in a corner of the cage, covered in his cloak. The young mage was feverish and shaking with chills. Goldmoon knelt beside him, her hand on his forehead, stroking back the white hair. He was unconscious. His head tossed fitfully, and he murmured strange words, sometimes shouting out garbled commands. Caramon, his face nearly as pale as his brother's, sat beside him. Goldmoon met Tanis's questioning gaze and shook her head sadly, her eyes large and gleaming in the reflected firelight. Riverwind came over to stand beside Tanis.

"She found this in his neck," he said, carefully holding up a feathered dart between thumb and forefinger. He glanced at the mage without love but with a certain amount of pity. "Who can say what poison burns in his blood?"

"If we had the staff—" Goldmoon said.

"Right," Tanis said. "Where is it?"

"There," Sturm said, his mouth twisting wryly. He pointed. Tanis peered past hundreds of draconians and saw the staff lying on Goldmoon's fur blanket in front of the black dragon.

Reaching out, Tanis grasped a bar of the cage. "We could break out," he told Sturm. "Caramon could snap this like a twig."

"Tasslehoff could snap it like a twig if he were here," Sturm said. "Of course, then we've only got a few hundred of these creatures to take care of—not to mention the dragon."

"All right. Don't rub it in." Tanis sighed. "Any idea what happened to Flint and Tas?"

"Riverwind said he heard a splash just after Tas yelled out that we were being ambushed. If they were lucky, they dived off the log and escaped into the swamp. If not—" Sturm didn't finish.

Tanis closed his eyes to shut out the firelight. He felt tired—tired of fighting, tired of killing, tired of slogging through the muck. He thought longingly of lying down and sinking back into sleep. Instead, he opened his eyes, stalked over to the cage, and rattled the bars. A draconian guard turned around, sword raised.

"You speak Common?" Tanis asked in the very lowest, crudest form of the Common language used on Krynn.

"I speak Common. Apparently better than you do, elven scum," the draconian sneered. "What do you want?"

"One of our party is injured. We ask that you treat him. Give him an antidote to this poison dart."

"Poison?" The draconian peered into the cage. "Ah, yes, the magic-user." The creature gurgled deep in its throat, a sound obviously meant to be laughter. "Sick, is he? Yes, the poison acts swiftly. Can't have a magic-user around. Even behind bars they're deadly. But don't worry. He won't be lonely—the rest of you will be joining him soon enough. In fact, you should envy him. Your deaths will not be nearly so quick."

The draconian turned its back and said something to its partner, jerking its clawed thumb in the direction of the cage. Both of them croaked their gurgling laughter. Tanis, feeling disgust and rage welling up deep inside of him, looked back at Raistlin.

The mage was rapidly growing worse. Goldmoon put her hand on Raistlin's neck, feeling for the life beat, and then shook her head. Caramon made a moaning sound. Then his glance shifted to the two draconians, laughing and talking together outside.

"Stop—Caramon!" Tanis yelled, but it was too late.

With a roar like a wounded animal, the huge warrior leaped toward the draconians. Bamboo gave way before him, the shards splintering and cutting into his skin. Mad with the desire to kill, Caramon never noticed. Tanis jumped on his back as the warrior crashed past him, but Caramon shook him off as easily as a bear shakes off an annoying fly.

"Caramon, you fool—" Sturm grunted as he and Riverwind both threw themselves on the warrior. But Caramon's rage carried him on.

Whirling, one draconian raised its sword, but Caramon sent the weapon flying. The creature hit the ground, knocked senseless by a blow from the big man's fist. Within seconds, there were six draconians, bows and arrows in their hands, surrounding the warrior. Sturm and Riverwind wrestled Caramon to the ground. Sturm, sitting on him, shoved his face into the mud until he felt Caramon relax beneath him and heard him give a strangled sob.

At that instant, a high-pitched, shrill voice screeched through the camp. "Bring the warrior to me!" said the dragon.

Tanis felt the hair rise on his neck. The draconians lowered their weapons and turned to face the dragon, staring in astonishment and muttering

among themselves. Riverwind and Sturm got to their feet. Caramon lay on the ground, choking with sobs. The draconian guards glanced at each other uneasily, while those standing near the dragon backed off hurriedly and formed an immense semicircle around it.

One of the creatures, whom Tanis supposed by the insignia on its armor to be some sort of captain, stalked up to a robed draconian who was staring, open-mouthed, at the black dragon.

"What's going on?" the captain demanded. The draconian spoke in the Common tongue. Tanis, listening closely, realized they were of different species—the robed draconians were apparently the magic-users and the priests. Presumably, the two could not communicate in their own languages. The military draconian was clearly upset.

"Where is that Bozak priest of yours? He must tell us what to do!"

"The higher of my order is not here." The robed draconian quickly regained his composure. "One of *them* flew here and took him to confer with Lord Verminaard about the staff."

"But the dragon never speaks when the priest is not here." The captain lowered his voice. "My boys don't like it. You'd better do something quickly!"

"What is this delay?" The dragon's voice shrieked like a wailing wind. "Bring me the warrior!"

"Do as the dragon says." The robed draconian motioned quickly with a clawed hand. Several draconians rushed over, shoved Tanis and Riverwind and Sturm back into the shattered cage, and lifted the bleeding Caramon up by the arms. They dragged him over to stand before the dragon, his back to the blazing fire. Near him lay the blue crystal staff, Raistlin's staff, their weapons, and their packs.

Caramon raised his head to confront the monster, his eyes blurred with tears and blood from the many cuts the bamboo had inflicted on his face. The dragon loomed above him, seen dimly through the smoke rising from the bonfire.

"We mete out justice swiftly and surely, human scum," the dragon hissed. As it spoke, it beat its huge wings, fanning them slowly. The draconians gasped and began to back up, some stumbling over

themselves as they hurried to get out of the monster's way. Obviously they knew what was coming.

Caramon stared at the creature without fear. "My brother is dying," he shouted. "Do what you will to me. I ask only one thing. Give me my sword so that I can die fighting!"

The dragon laughed shrilly; the draconians joined it, gurgling and croaking horribly. As the dragon's wings beat the air, it began to rock back and forth, seemingly preparing to leap on the warrior and devour him.

"This will be fun. Let him have his weapon," the dragon commanded. Its flapping wings caused a wind to whip through the camp, scattering sparks from the fire.

Caramon shoved the draconian guards aside. Wiping his hand across his eyes, he walked over to the pile of weapons and pulled out his sword. Then he turned to face the dragon, resignation and grief etched into his face. He raised his sword.

"We can't let him die out there by himself!" Sturm said harshly, and he took a step forward, prepared to break out.

Suddenly a voice came from the shadows behind them.

"Hssst . . . Tanis!"

The half-elf whirled around. "Flint!" he exclaimed, then glanced apprehensively at the draconian guards, but they were absorbed in watching the spectacle of Caramon and the dragon. Tanis hurried to the back of the bamboo cage where the dwarf stood.

"Get out of here!" the half-elf ordered. "There's nothing you can do. Raistlin's dying, and the dragon—"

"Is Tasslehoff ," Flint said succinctly.

"What?" Tanis glared at the dwarf. "Make sense."

"The dragon is Tasslehoff," Flint repeated patiently.

For once Tanis was speechless. He stared at the dwarf.

"The dragon's made of wicker,"† the dwarf whispered hurriedly. "Tasslehoff sneaked behind it and looked inside. It's rigged! Anyone sitting inside the dragon can make the wings flap and speak through a hollow tube. I guess that's how

This would indicate that the dragon was set up as a religious icon to dupe the Baaz and Bozak draconians through draconian worship of the idol. This says much about the god/worshiper relationship between draconians and dragons. It also begs the question of the wicker/basket weaving and black-lacquer painting skills of draconians. —TRH

the priests keep order around here. Anyway, Tasslehoff's the one flapping his wings and threatening to eat Caramon."

Tanis gasped. "But what do we do? There's still a hundred draconians around. Sooner or later they're going to realize what's going on."

"Get over to Caramon, you and Riverwind and Sturm. Grab your weapons and packs and the staff. I'll help Goldmoon carry Raistlin into the woods. Tasslehoff's got something in mind. Just be ready."

Tanis groaned.

"I don't like it any better than you do," the dwarf growled. "Trusting our lives to that rattle-brained kender. But, well, he *is* the dragon, after all."

"He certainly is," Tanis said, eyeing the dragon who was shrieking and wailing and flapping its wings and rocking back and forth. The draconians were staring at it in open-mouthed wonder. Tanis grabbed Sturm and Riverwind and huddled down near Goldmoon, who had not left Raistlin's side. The half-elf explained what was happening. Sturm looked at him as if he were as crazed as Raistlin. Riverwind shook his head.

"Well, have you got a better plan?" Tanis asked.

Both of them looked at the dragon, then back at Tanis, and shrugged.

"Goldmoon goes with the dwarf," Riverwind said.

She started to protest. He looked at her, his eyes expressionless, and she swallowed and fell silent.

"Yes," Tanis said. "Stay with Raistlin, lady, please. We'll bring the staff to you."

"Hurry then," she said through white lips. "He is very nearly gone."

"We'll hurry," Tanis said grimly. "I have a feeling that once things get started out there, we're going to be moving very fast!" He patted her hand. "Come on." He stood up and took a deep breath.

Riverwind's eyes were still on Goldmoon. He started to speak, then shook his head irritably and turned without a word to stand beside Tanis. Sturm joined them. The three crept up behind the draconian guards.

Caramon lifted his sword. It flashed in the firelight. The dragon went into a wild frenzy, and all of

the draconians fell back, braying and beating their swords against their shields. Wind from the dragon's wings blew up ashes and sparks from the fire, setting some nearby bamboo huts on fire. The draconians did not notice, so eager were they for the kill. The dragon shrieked and howled, and Caramon felt his mouth go dry and his stomach muscles clench. It was the first time he had ever gone into battle without his brother;† the thought made his heart throb painfully. He was about to leap forward and attack when Tanis, Sturm, and Riverwind appeared out of nowhere to stand by his side.

† He came close during their first years as mercenaries. See Brothers at Arms, *by Margaret Weis and Don Perrin.*

"We will not let our friend die alone!" the half-elf cried defiantly at the dragon. The draconians cheered wildly.

"Get out of here, Tanis!" Caramon scowled, his face flushed and streaked with tears. "This is my fight."

"Shut up and listen!" Tanis ordered. "Get your sword and mine, Sturm. Riverwind, grab your weapons and the packs and any draconian weapons you can pick up to replace those we lost. Caramon, pick up the two staffs."

Caramon stared at him. "What—"

"Tasslehoff's the dragon," Tanis said. "There isn't time to explain. Just do as I say! Get the staff and take it into the woods. Goldmoon's waiting." He laid his hand on the warrior's shoulder. Tanis shoved him. "Go! Raistlin's almost finished! You're his only chance."

This statement reached Caramon's mind. He ran to the pile of weapons and grabbed the blue crystal staff and Raistlin's Staff of Magius, while the draconians yelled. Sturm and Riverwind armed themselves, Sturm bringing Tanis his sword.

"And now, prepare to die, humans!" the dragon screamed. Its wings gave a great lurch and suddenly the creature was flying, hovering in midair. The draconians croaked and cried out in alarm, some breaking for the woods, others hurling themselves flat on the ground.

"Now!" yelled Tanis. "Run, Caramon!"

The big warrior broke for the woods, running swiftly toward where he could see Goldmoon and Flint waiting for him. A draconian appeared in front of him, but Caramon hurled it out of his way with a

thrust of his great arm. He could hear a wild commotion behind him, Sturm chanting a Solamnic war cry, draconians yelling. Other draconians leaped at Caramon. He used the blue crystal staff as he had seen Goldmoon use it, swinging it in a wide arc with his huge right hand. It flashed blue flame and the draconians fell back.

Caramon reached the woods and found Raistlin lying at Goldmoon's feet, barely breathing. Goldmoon grabbed the staff from Caramon and laid it on the mage's inert body. Flint watched, shaking his head. "It won't work," muttered the dwarf. "It's used up."

"It has to work," Goldmoon said firmly. "Please," she murmured, "whoever is master of this staff, heal this man. Please." Unknowing, she repeated it over and over. Caramon watched for a moment, blinking his eyes. Then the woods around him were lit by a gigantic burst of flame.

"Name of the Abyss!" Flint breathed. "Look at that!"

Caramon turned just in time to see the great black wicker dragon crash headlong into the blazing bonfire. Flaming logs flew into the air, showering sparks over the camp. The draconians' bamboo huts, some already ablaze, began burning fiercely. The wicker dragon gave a final, horrifying shriek and then it, too, caught fire.

"Tasslehoff!" Flint swore. "That blasted kender—he's inside there!" Before Caramon could stop him, the dwarf ran out into the blazing draconian camp.

"Caramon . . ." Raistlin murmured. The big warrior knelt beside his brother. Raistlin was still pale, but his eyes were open and clear. He sat up, weakly, leaning against his brother, and stared out at the raging fire. "What's going on?"

"I'm not sure," Caramon said. "Tasslehoff turned into a dragon and after that things get real confused. You just rest." The warrior stared into the smoke, his sword drawn and ready in case any draconians came for them.

But the draconians now had little interest in the prisoners. The smaller breed,† panic stricken, were fleeing into the forest as their great god-dragon went up in flames. A few of the robed draconians,

These small Baaz draconians are weak of both mind and character. Since they can't now do their favorite stunt of ambushing enemies, they run.

bigger and apparently more intelligent than the other species, were trying desperately to bring order to the fearful chaos raging around them.

Sturm fought and slashed his way through the draconians without encountering any organized resistance. He had just reached the edge of the clearing, near the bamboo cage, when Flint passed him, running back toward the camp!

"Hey! Where—" Sturm yelled at the dwarf.

"Tas, in the dragon!" The dwarf didn't stop.

Sturm turned and saw the black wicker dragon burning with flames that shot high into the air. Thick smoke boiled up, blanketing the camp, the dank heavy swamp air preventing it from rising and drifting away. Sparks showered down as part of the blazing dragon exploded into the camp. Sturm ducked and batted out sparks that landed on his cape, then ran after the dwarf, catching up with the short-legged Flint easily.

"Flint," he panted, grasping the dwarf's arm. "It's no use. Nothing could live in that furnace! We've got to get back to the others—"

"Let go of me!" Flint roared so furiously that Sturm let go in amazement. The dwarf ran for the burning dragon again. Sturm heaved a sigh and ran after him, his eyes beginning to water in the smoke.

"Tasslehoff Burrfoot!" Flint called. "You idiotic kender! Where are you?"

There was no answer.

"Tasslehoff!" Flint screamed. "If you wreck this escape, I'll murder you. So help me—" Tears of frustration and grief and anger and smoke coursed down the dwarf's cheeks.

The heat was overwhelming. It seared Sturm's lungs, and the knight knew they couldn't breathe much more of this or they would perish themselves. He took hold of the dwarf firmly, intending to knock him out if necessary, when suddenly he saw movement near the edge of the blaze. He rubbed his eyes and looked closer.

The dragon lay on the ground, the head still connected to the blazing body by a long wicker neck. The head had not caught fire yet, but flames were starting to eat into the wicker neck. The head would soon be ablaze, too. Sturm saw the movement again.

"Flint! Look!" Sturm ran toward the head, the dwarf pounding along behind. Two small legs encased in bright blue pants were sticking out of the dragon's mouth, kicking feebly.

"Tas!" Sturm yelled. "Get out! The head's going to burn!"

"I can't! I'm stuck!" came a muffled voice.

Sturm stared at the head, frantically trying to figure out how to free the kender, while Flint just grabbed hold of Tas's legs and pulled.

"Ouch! Stop!" yelled Tas.

"No good," the dwarf puffed. "He's stuck fast."

The inferno crept up the dragon's neck.

Sturm drew his sword. "I may cut off his head," he muttered to Flint, "but it's his only chance." Estimating the size of the kender, guessing where his head would be, and hoping his hands weren't stretched out over his head, Sturm lifted his sword above the dragon's neck.

Flint closed his eyes.

The knight took a deep breath and brought his blade crashing down on the dragon, severing the head from the neck. There was a cry from the kender inside but whether from pain or astonishment, Sturm couldn't tell.

"Pull!" he yelled at the dwarf.

Flint grabbed hold of the wicker head and pulled it away from the blazing neck. Suddenly a tall, dark shape loomed out of the smoke. Sturm whipped around, sword ready, then saw it was Riverwind.

"What are you—" The Plainsman stared at the dragon's head. Perhaps Flint and Sturm had gone mad.

"The kender's stuck in there!" Sturm yelled. "We can't take the head apart out here, surrounded by draconians! We've got to—"

His words were lost in a roar of flame, but Riverwind finally saw the blue legs sticking out of the dragon's mouth. He grabbed hold of one side of the dragon's head, thrusting his hands in one of the eyesockets. Sturm got hold of the other, and together they lifted the head—kender inside—and began running through the camp. Those few draconians they encountered took one look at the terrifying apparition and fled.

"C'mon, Raist," Caramon said solicitously, his arm around his brother's shoulder. "You've got to try and stand. We have to be ready to move out of here. How do you feel?"

"How do I ever feel?" whispered Raistlin bitterly. "Help me up. There! Now leave me in peace for a moment." He leaned against a tree, shivering but standing.

"Sure, Raist," Caramon said, hurt, backing off. Goldmoon glanced at Raistlin in disgust, remembering Caramon's grief when he thought his brother was dying. She turned away to watch for the others, staring through the gathering smoke.

Tanis appeared first, running so fast he crashed into Caramon. The big warrior caught him in his huge arms, breaking the half-elf's forward momentum and keeping him on his feet.

"Thanks!" Tanis gasped. He leaned over, hands on his knees, to catch his breath. "Where are the others?"

"Weren't they with you?" Caramon frowned.

"We got separated." Tanis drew in huge gulps of air, then coughed as the smoke flew down his lungs.

"SuTorakh!" interrupted Goldmoon in an awed voice. Tanis and Caramon both spun around in alarm, staring out into the smoke-filled camp to see a grotesque sight emerging from the swirling smoke. A dragon's head with a forked blue tongue was lunging at them. Tanis blinked in disbelief, then he heard a sound behind him that nearly made him leap into a tree in panic. He whirled around, heart in his throat, sword in his hand.

Raistlin was laughing.

Tanis had never heard the mage laugh before, even when Raistlin was a child, and he hoped he would never hear it again. It was weird, shrill, mocking laughter. Caramon stared at his brother in amazement, Goldmoon in horror. Finally the sound of Raistlin's laughter died until the mage was laughing silently, his golden eyes reflecting the glow of the draconian camp going up in flames.

Tanis shuddered and turned back around to see that in fact the dragon's head was carried by Sturm and Riverwind. Flint raced along in front, a draconian helm on his head. Tanis ran forward to meet them.

"What in the name of—"

"The kender's stuck in here!" Sturm said. He and Riverwind dropped the head to the ground, both of them breathing heavily. "We've got to get him out." Sturm eyed the laughing Raistlin warily. "What's the matter with him? Still poisoned?"

"No, he's better," Tanis said, examining the dragon's head.

"A pity," Sturm muttered as he knelt beside the half-elf.

"Tas, are you all right?" Tanis called out, lifting the huge mouth to see inside.

"I think Sturm chopped off my hair!" the kender wailed.

"Lucky it wasn't your head!" Flint snorted.

"What's holding him?" Riverwind leaned down to peer inside the dragon's mouth.

"I'm not sure," Tanis said, swearing softly. "I can't see in all this blasted smoke." He stood up, sighing in frustration. "And we've got to get out of here! The draconians will get organized soon. Caramon, come here. See if you can rip off the top."

The big warrior came over to stand in front of the wicker dragon's head. Bracing himself, he got hold of the two eyesockets, closed his eyes, took a deep breath, then grunted and heaved. For a minute nothing happened. Tanis watched the muscles bulge on the big man's arms, saw his thigh muscles absorb the strain. Blood rushed to Caramon's face. Then there was the ripping and snapping sound of wood splintering. The top of the dragon's head gave way with a sharp crack. Caramon† staggered backward as the top half of the head suddenly came off in his hands.

The name Caramon means "strength of the vallenwoods." His great-grandfather had the same name.

Tanis reached in, grabbed Tas's hand, and jerked him free. "Are you all right?" he asked. The kender seemed wobbly on his feet, but his grin was wide as ever.

"I'm fine," Tas said brightly. "Just a little singed." Then his face darkened. "Tanis," he said, his face crinkling with unusual worry. He felt at his long topknot. "My hair?"

"All there," Tanis said, smiling.

Tas breathed a sigh of relief.† Then he began to talk. "Tanis, it was the most wonderful thing—flying like that. And the look on Caramon's face—"

Perhaps Tas's topknot is the source of his strength.

"The story will have to wait," Tanis said firmly. "We've got to get out of here. Caramon? Can you and your brother make it all right?"

"Yeah, go on," Caramon said.

Raistlin stumbled forward, accepting the support of his brother's strong arm. The mage glanced behind at the sundered dragon's head and he wheezed, his shoulders shaking in silent, grim amusement.

15

Escape. The well. Death on black wings.

Smoke from the burning draconian camp hung over the black swamplands, shielding the companions from the eyes of the strange, evil creatures. The smoke floated wraithlike through the swamps, drifting across the silver moon and obscuring the stars. The companions dared not risk a light—even the light from Raistlin's staff—for they could hear horns blowing all around them as the draconian leaders tried to reestablish order.

Riverwind led them. Although Tanis had always prided himself on his own woodland skills, he completely lost all sense of direction in the black misty mire†. An occasional fleeting glimpse of the stars, whenever the smoke lifted, showed him that they were bearing north.

Murky, too.

†They hadn't gone far when Riverwind missed a step and plunged knee-deep into muck. After Tanis and Caramon dragged the Plainsman out of the water, Tasslehoff crept ahead, testing the ground with his hoopak staff. It sank every time.

"We have no choice but to wade," Riverwind said grimly.

Choosing a path where the water seemed shallower, the company left firm ground and splashed into the muck. At first it was only ankle deep, then they sank to their knees. Soon they sank deeper still; Tanis was forced to carry Tasslehoff, the giggling kender grasping him around the neck. Flint steadfastly refused all offers of help, even when the tip of his beard got wet. Then he vanished. Caramon, following him, fished the dwarf out of the water and slung him over his shoulder like a wet sack, the dwarf too tired and frightened to grumble. Raistlin staggered, coughing, through the water, his robes dragging him down. Weary and still sick from the poison, the mage finally collapsed. Sturm grabbed hold of him and half-dragged, half-carried the mage through the swamp.

After an hour of floundering in the icy water, they finally reached firm ground and sank down to rest, shivering with the cold.

The trees began to creak and groan, their branches bending as a sharp wind sprang up from the north. The wind blew the mists into wispy rags. Raistlin, lying on the ground, looked up. The mage caught his breath. He sat up, alarmed.

"Storm clouds." He choked, coughing, and fought to speak. "They come from the north. We have no time. No time! We must reach Xak Tsaroth. Hurry! Before the moon sets!"

Everyone looked up. A gathering darkness was moving out of the north, swallowing up the stars. Tanis could feel the same sense of urgency that was driving the mage. Wearily, he rose to his feet. Without a word, the rest of the group rose and stumbled forward, Riverwind taking the lead. But dark swamp water blocked their path once more.

"Not again!" Flint moaned.

"No, we do not have to wade again. Come look," Riverwind said. He led the way to the water's edge. There, amid many other ruins protruding from the

As they headed once more into the swampy Cursed Lands in the original draft, they became fearful of anything that moved. "They dodged and ducked and stabbed at shadows until everyone's nerves were frayed."

Tanis, his nerves additionally frayed by Raistlin's frequent reminders that their two days were about up, had a draconian drop on him out of a tree. "Desperately he twisted, hoping to avoid a mortal blow. There was a flash, a flare of light. The draconian gave a shriek and crumpled over, his slashing sword missing its mark.… Raistlin stood over the draconian, holding his staff in his hands like a club.…'I am not totally dependent on magic,' he said with a bitter, ugly smile."

One more extract that had to be cut, though why they should so often have concerned Tas is hard to figure fifteen years on. This time we see him weeping over those he could not save:

"Tanis, fearful of another ambush, watched the kender with wry envy, wondering if Tas ever quit finding life an enchanting adventure. Then he recalled Tas in Qué-Shu, weeping over the horror of the senseless butchery. It was a side of kenders one rarely saw and most forgot existed."

This is purposely reminiscent of Shelley's "My name is Ozymandias…" —TRH

dank ground, lay an obelisk that had either fallen or been pushed over to form a bridge across to the other bank of the swamp.

"I'll go first," Tas volunteered, hopping energetically onto the long stone.† "Hey, there's writing on this thing. Runes of some sort."

"I must see!" Raistlin whispered, hurrying over. He spoke his word of command, "*Shirak*," and the crystal on the tip of his staff burst into light.

"Hurry!" Sturm growled. "You've just told everything within a twenty-mile radius we're here."

But Raistlin would not be rushed. He held the light over the spidery runes, studying them intently. Tanis and the others climbed onto the obelisk and joined the mage.

The kender bent down, tracing the runes with his small hand. "What does it say, Raistlin? Can you read it? The language seems very old."

"It is old," the mage whispered. "It dates from before the Cataclysm. The runes say, 'The Great City of Xak Tsaroth, whose beauty surrounds you, speaks to the good of its people and their generous deeds. The gods reward us in the grace of our home'."†

"How awful!" Goldmoon shuddered, looking at the ruin and desolation around her.

"The gods rewarded them indeed," Raistlin said, his lips parting in a cynical smile. No one spoke. Then Raistlin whispered, "Dulak," and extinguished the light. Suddenly the night seemed much blacker. "We must keep going," the mage said. "Surely there is more than a fallen monument to mark what this place once stood for."

They crossed the obelisk into thick jungle. At first there seemed to be no trail, then Riverwind, searching diligently, found a trail cut through the vines and the trees. He bent down to study it. His face was grim when he rose.

"Draconians?" Tanis asked.

"Yes," he said heavily. "The tracks of many clawed feet. And they lead north, straight to the city."

Tanis asked in an undertone, "Is this the broken city, where you were given the staff?"

"And where death had black wings," Riverwind added. He closed his eyes, wiping his hand over his face. Then he drew a deep, ragged breath. "I don't

know. I can't remember—but I am afraid without knowing why."

Tanis put his hand on Riverwind's arm. "The elves have a saying: 'Only the dead are without fear.'† "

The elves said this on Krynn. The quote is attributed to Plato on Earth.—MW

Riverwind startled him by suddenly clasping the half-elf's hand with his. "I have never known an elf," the Plainsman said. "My people distrust them, saying that the elves have no care for Krynn or for humans. I think my people may have been mistaken. I am glad I met you, Tanis of Qualinost. I count you as a friend."

Tanis knew enough of Plains lore to realize that, with this statement, Riverwind had declared himself willing to sacrifice everything for the half-elf—even his life. A vow of friendship was a solemn vow among the Plainsmen. "You are my friend, too, Riverwind," Tanis said simply. "You and Goldmoon both are my friends."

Riverwind turned his eyes to Goldmoon who stood near them, leaning on her staff, her eyes closed, her face drawn with pain and exhaustion. Riverwind's face softened with compassion as he looked at her. Then it hardened, pride drawing the stern mask over it again.

"Xak Tsaroth is not far off," he said coolly. "And these tracks are old." He led the way into the jungle. After only a short walk, the northern trail suddenly changed to cobblestones.

"A street!" exclaimed Tasslehoff.

"The outskirts of Xak Tsaroth!"† Raistlin breathed.

Prior to the Cataclysm, three hundred years before the War of the Lance, Xak Tsaroth had been inland, a major trading center of such importance that even the far eastern city of Istar purchased products from its huge open-air markets.

"About time!" Flint stared all around in disgust. "What a mess! If the greatest gift ever given to man is here, it must be well hidden!"

Tanis agreed. He had never seen a more dismal place. As they walked, the broad street took them into an open-paved courtyard. To the east stood four tall, free-standing columns that supported nothing; the building lay in ruins around them. A huge unbroken circular stone wall rose about four feet above the ground. Caramon, going over to inspect it, announced that it was a well.

"Deep at that," he said. He leaned over and peered down into it. "Smells bad, too."

North of the well stood what appeared to be the only building to have escaped the destruction of the

Cataclysm. It was finely constructed of pure white stone, supported by tall, slender columns. Large golden double doors gleamed in the moonlight.

"That was a temple to the ancient gods," Raistlin said, more to himself than anyone else. But Goldmoon, standing near him, heard his soft whisper.

"A temple?" she repeated, staring at the building. "How beautiful." She walked toward it, strangely fascinated.

Tanis and the rest searched the grounds and found no other buildings intact. Fluted columns lay on the ground, their broken pieces aligned to show their former beauty. Statues lay broken and, in some cases, grotesquely defaced. Everything was old, so old it made even the dwarf feel young.

The evolution of a Sivak draconian, from rough sketch to lethal weapon of the Dark Queen.

Flint sat down on a column. "Well, we're here." He blinked at Raistlin and yawned. "What now, mage?"

Raistlin's thin lips parted, but before he could reply, Tasslehoff yelled, "Draconian!"

Everyone spun around, weapons in their hands. A draconian, ready to move, was glaring at them from the edge of the well.

"Stop it!" Tanis shouted. "It will alert others!"

But before anyone could reach it, the draconian spread its wings and flew *into* the well. Raistlin, his golden eyes flaring in the moonlight, ran to the well and peered over the edge. Raising his hand as if to cast a spell, he hesitated, then dropped his hand limply to his side. "I can't," he said. "I can't think. I can't concentrate. I must sleep!"

"We're all tired," Tanis said wearily. "If something's down there, it warned it. There's nothing we can do now. We've got to rest."

"It *has* gone to warn something," Raistlin whispered. He huddled in his cloak and stared around, his eyes wide. "Can't you feel it? Any of you? Half-Elf? Evil about to waken and come forth."

Silence fell.

Then Tasslehoff climbed up on the stone wall and peered down. "Look! The draconian is floating down, just like a leaf. His wings don't flap—"

"Be quiet!" Tanis snapped.

Tasslehoff glanced at the half-elf in surprise—Tanis's voice sounded strained and unnatural. The half-elf was staring at the well, his hands clenching

nervously. Everything was still. Too still. The storm clouds massed to the north, but there was no wind. Not a branch creaked, not a leaf stirred. The silver moon and the red cast twin shadows that made things seen from the corner of the eye unreal and distorted.

Then, slowly, Raistlin backed away from the well, raising his hands before him as if to ward off some dreadful danger.

"I feel it, too." Tanis swallowed. "What is it?"

"Yes, what is it?" Tasslehoff, leaning over, stared eagerly into the well. It looked as deep and dark as the mage's hourglass eyes.

"Get him away from there!" Raistlin cried.

Tanis, infected by the mage's fear and his own growing sense that something was terribly wrong, started to run for Tas. Even as he began to move, though, he felt the ground shake beneath his feet. The kender gave a startled cry as the ancient stone wall of the well cracked and gave way beneath him. Tas felt himself sliding into the terrible blackness below him. He scrabbled frantically with his hands and feet, trying to clutch the crumbling rocks. Tanis lunged desperately, but he was too far away.

Riverwind had started moving when he heard Raistlin's cry, and the tall man's long, swift strides carried him quickly to the well. Catching hold of Tas by his collar, the Plainsman plucked him from the wall just as the stones and mortar tumbled down into the blackness below.

The ground trembled again. Tanis tried to force his numb mind to figure out what was happening. Then a blast of cold air burst from the well. The wind swept dirt and leaves from the courtyard into the air, stinging his face and eyes.

"Run!" Tanis tried to yell, but he choked on the foul stench erupting from the well.

The columns left standing after the Cataclysm began to shake. The companions stared fearfully at the well. Then Riverwind tore his gaze away. "Goldmoon . . ." he said, looking around. He dropped Tas to the ground. "Goldmoon!" He stopped as a high-pitched shriek rose from the depths of the well. The sound was so loud and shrill that it pierced the head. Riverwind searched frantically for Goldmoon, calling her name.

Tanis was stunned by the noise. Unable to move, he saw Sturm, hand on his sword, slowly back away from the well. He saw Raistlin—the mage's ghastly face glistening metallic yellow, his golden eyes red in the red moon's light—scream something Tanis couldn't hear. He saw Tasslehoff staring at the well in wide-eyed wonder. Sturm ran across the courtyard, scooped up the kender under one arm, and ran on to the trees. Caramon ran to his exhausted brother, caught him up, and headed for cover. Tanis knew some monstrous evil was coming up out of the well, but he could not move. The words "run, fool, run" screamed in his brain.

Riverwind, too, stayed near the well, fighting the fear that was growing within him: he couldn't find Goldmoon! Distracted by rescuing the kender from tumbling into the well, he had not seen Goldmoon approach the unbroken temple. He looked around wildly, struggling to keep his balance as the ground shook beneath his feet. The high-pitched shrieking noise, the throbbing and trembling of the ground, brought back hideous, nightmarish memories. "Death on black wings." He began to sweat and shake, then forced his mind to concentrate on Goldmoon. She needed him; he knew—and he alone knew—that her show of strength only masked her fear, doubt, uncertainty. She would be terribly afraid, and he had to find her.

As the stones of the well began to slide, Riverwind moved away and caught sight of Tanis. The half-elf was shouting and pointing past Riverwind toward the temple. Riverwind knew Tanis was saying something, but he couldn't hear above the shrieking sound. Then he knew! Goldmoon! Riverwind turned to go to her, but he lost his balance and fell to his knees. He saw Tanis start to run toward him.

Then the horror burst from the well, the horror of his fevered nightmares. Riverwind closed his eyes and saw no more.

It was a dragon.

Tanis, in those first few moments when the blood seemed to drain from his body, leaving him limp and lifeless, looked at the dragon as it burst forth from the well and thought, "How beautiful . . . how beautiful. . . ."

Sleek and black, the dragon rose, her glistening wings folded close to her sides, her scales gleaming. Her eyes glowed red-black, the color of molten rock. Her mouth opened in a snarl, teeth flashing white and wicked. Her long, red tongue curled as she breathed the night air. Clear of the well's confines, the dragon spread her wings, blotting out stars, obliterating moonlight. Each wing was tipped with a pure, white claw that shone blood-red in the light of Lunitari.

Fear such as Tanis had never imagined shriveled his stomach.† His heart throbbed painfully; he couldn't catch his breath. He could only stare in horror and awe and marvel at the creature's deadly beauty. The dragon circled higher and higher into the night sky. Then, just as Tanis felt the paralyzing fear start to recede, just as he began to fumble for his bow and arrows, the dragon spoke.

Dragonfear is a magical fear induced by the aura of evil dragons. Even experienced fighters may be felled by it, at least temporarily.

One word she said—a word in the language of magic—and a thick, terrible darkness fell from the sky, blinding them all. Tanis instantly lost all grasp on where he was. He only knew there was a dragon above him about to attack. He was powerless to defend himself. All he could do was crouch down, crawl among the rubble, and try desperately to hide.

Deprived of his sense of sight, the half-elf concentrated on his sense of hearing. The shrieking noise had stopped as the darkness fell. Tanis could hear the slow, gentle flap of the dragon's leathery wings and knew it was circling above them, rising gradually. Then he couldn't hear even the flapping anymore; the wings had quit beating. He visualized a great, black bird of prey, hovering alone, waiting.

Then there was a very gentle rustling sound, the sound of leaves shivering as the wind rises before a storm. The sound grew louder and louder until it was the rushing of wind when the storm hits, and then it was the shrieking of the hurricane. Tanis pressed his body close against the crumbled well and covered his head with his arms.

The dragon was attacking.

She could not see through the darkness she had cast, but Khisanth knew that the intruders were still in the courtyard below. Her minions, the draconians, had warned her that a group walked the land,

carrying the blue crystal staff. Lord Verminaard wanted that staff, wanted it kept safe with her, never to be seen in human lands. But she had lost it, and Lord Verminaard had not been pleased. She had to get it back. Therefore, Khisanth had waited an instant before casting her darkness spell, studying the intruders carefully, searching for the staff. Unaware that already it had passed beyond her sight, she was pleased. She had only to destroy.

The attacking dragon dropped from the sky, her leathery wings curving back like the blade of a black dagger. She dove straight for the well,† where she had seen the intruders running for their lives. Knowing that they would be paralyzed by dragonfear, Khisanth was certain she could kill them all with one pass. She opened her fanged mouth.

People ask if we used our experiences in role-playing for the story. A good thing we didn't. In the first play-test, the party lowered Tanis down the well by a rope tied around his waist. He was, alas, carrying with him the blue crystal staff. The dragon at the bottom of the well heard the commotion up above, went to investigate. The dragon found Tanis, who attempted to strike it with the blue crystal staff! Tanis missed his die roll, dropped the staff into the well. The dragon killed the entire party. It would have been a short book.—MW

Tanis heard the dragon coming nearer. The great rushing sound grew louder and louder, then stopped for an instant. He could hear huge tendons creaking, lifting and spreading giant wings. Then he heard a great gasping sound as of air being drawn into a gaping throat, then a strange sound that reminded him of steam escaping from a boiling kettle. Something liquid splashed near him. He could hear rocks splitting and cracking and bubbling. Drops of the liquid splashed on his hand, and he gasped as a searing pain penetrated his being.

Then Tanis heard a scream. It was a deep-voiced scream, a man's scream—Riverwind. So terrible, so agonized was the scream that Tanis dug his fingernails into his palms to keep from adding his own voice to that horrible wail and revealing himself to the dragon. The screaming seemed to go on and on and then it died into a moan. Tanis felt the rush of a large body swoosh past him in the darkness. The stones he pressed his body against shook. Then the tremor of the dragon's passage sank lower and lower into the depths of the well. Finally the ground was still.

There was silence.

Tanis drew a painful breath and opened his eyes. The darkness was gone. The stars shone; the moons glowed in the sky. For a moment the half-elf could do nothing but breathe and breathe again, trying to

calm his shaking body. Then he was on his feet, running toward a dark form lying in the stone courtyard.

Tanis was the first to reach the Plainsman's body. He took one look, then choked and turned away.

What remained of Riverwind no longer resembled anything human. The man's flesh had been seared from his body. The white of bone was clearly visible where skin and muscle had melted from his arms. His eyes ran like jelly down the fleshless, cadaverous cheeks. His mouth gaped open in a silent scream. His ribcage lay exposed, hunks of flesh and charred cloth clinging to the bones. But—most horrible—the flesh on his torso had been burned away, leaving the organs exposed, pulsing red in the garish red moonlight.

Tanis sank down, vomiting. The half-elf had seen men die on his sword. He had seen them hacked to pieces by trolls.† But this . . . this was horribly different, and Tanis knew the memory of this would haunt him forever. A strong arm gripped him by the shoulders, offering silent comfort and sympathy and understanding. The nausea passed. Tanis sat back and breathed. He wiped his mouth and nose, then tried to force himself to swallow, gagging painfully.

This would have been fairly unusual; trolls are not among the common monsters of Krynn.

"You all right?" Caramon asked with concern.

Tanis nodded, unable to speak. Then he turned at the sound of Sturm's voice.

"May the true gods have mercy! Tanis, he's still alive! I saw his hand move!" Sturm choked. He could say no more.

Tanis rose to his feet and walked shakily toward the body. One of the charred and blackened hands had risen from the stones, plucking horribly at the air.

"End it!" Tanis said hoarsely, his throat raw from bile. "End it! Sturm—"

The knight had already drawn his sword. Kissing the hilt, he raised the blade to the sky and stood before Riverwind's body. He closed his eyes and mentally withdrew into an old world where death in battle had been glorious and fine. Slowly and solemnly, he began to recite the ancient Solamnic Death Chant. As he spoke the words that laid hold of the warrior's soul and transported it to realms of peace beyond, he reversed the blade of the sword and held it poised above Riverwind's chest.

This, or parts of it, you can find in several places—both in the two original trilogies and in novels of mine that deal with the Solamnic Knights. I was trying to do a kind of imitation of Yeats here, though it fell far short. However, I managed to catch the rhythm I wanted in lines 8 to 10.
—Michael Williams

"Return this man to Huma's breast
Beyond the wild, impartial skies;
Grant to him a warrior's rest
And set the last spark of his eyes
Free from the smothering clouds of wars,
Upon the torches of the stars.
Let the last surge of his breath
Take refuge in the cradling air
Above the dreams of ravens, where
Only the hawk remembers death.
Then let his shade to Huma rise,
Beyond the wild, impartial skies."

The knight's voice sank.

Tanis felt the peace of the gods wash over him like cool, cleansing water, easing his grief and submerging the horror. Caramon, beside him, wept silently. As they watched, moonlight flashed on the sword blade.

Then a clear voice spoke. "Stop. Bring him to me."

Both Tanis and Caramon sprang up to stand in front of the man's tortured body, knowing that Goldmoon must be spared this hideous sight. Sturm, lost in tradition, came back to reality with a start and reversed his killing stroke. Goldmoon stood, a tall, slender shadow silhouetted against the golden, moonlit doors of the temple. Tanis started to speak, but he felt suddenly the cold hand of the mage grip his arm. Shivering, he jerked away from Raistlin's touch.

"Do as she says," the mage hissed. "Carry him to her."

Tanis's face contorted with fury at the sight of Raistlin's expressionless face, uncaring eyes.

"Take him to her," Raistlin said coldly. "It is not for us to choose death for this man. That is for the gods."

16

A bitter choice.
The greatest gift.

Tanis stared at Raistlin. Not the quiver of an eyelid betrayed his feelings—if the mage had any feelings. Their eyes met and, as always, Tanis felt that the mage saw more than was visible to him. Suddenly Tanis hated Raistlin, hated him with a passion that shocked the half-elf, hated him for not feeling this pain, hated him and envied him at the same time.

"We must do something!" Sturm said harshly. "He's not dead and the dragon may return!"

"Very well," Tanis said, his voice catching in his throat. "Wrap him in a blanket. . . . But give me a moment alone with Goldmoon."

The half-elf walked slowly across the courtyard. His footsteps echoed in the stillness of the night as he climbed marble steps to a wide porch where

Goldmoon stood in front of the shining golden doors. Glancing behind him, Tanis could see his friends wrapping blankets from their packs around tree limbs to make a battlefield stretcher. The man's body was nothing more than a dark, shapeless mass in the moonlight.

"Bring him to me, Tanis," Goldmoon repeated as the half-elf came up to her. He took hold of her hand.

"Goldmoon," Tanis said, "Riverwind is horribly injured. He is dying. There is nothing you can do—not even the staff—"

"Hush, Tanis," Goldmoon said gently.

The half-elf fell silent, seeing her clearly for the first time. In astonishment, he realized that the Plainswoman was tranquil, calm, uplifted. Her face in the moonlight was the face of the sailor who has fought the stormy seas in his fragile boat and drifted at last into peaceful waters.

"Come inside the temple, my friend," Goldmoon said, her beautiful eyes looking intently into Tanis's. "Come inside and bring Riverwind to me."

Goldmoon had not heard the approach of the dragon, had not seen its attack on Riverwind. When they entered the broken courtyard of Xak Tsaroth, Goldmoon had felt a strange and powerful force drawing her into the temple. She walked across the rubble and up the stairs, oblivious to everything but the golden doors shimmering in the silver-red moonlight. She approached them and stood before them for a moment. Then she became aware of the commotion behind her and heard Riverwind calling her name. "Goldmoon . . ." She paused, unwilling to leave Riverwind and her friends, knowing a terrible evil was rising from the well.

"Come inside, child," a gentle voice called to her.

Goldmoon lifted her head and stared at the doors. Tears came to her eyes. The voice was her mother's. Tearsong, priestess of Qué-Shu, had died long ago, when Goldmoon was very young.

"Tearsong?" Goldmoon choked. "Mother—"†

"The years have been many and sad for you, my daughter"—her mother's voice was not heard so much as felt in her heart—"and I fear your burden will not soon ease. Indeed, if you continue on you will leave this darkness only to enter a deeper

Long ago, a vision of her mother had appeared to Goldmoon, telling her the old ways of the Qué-Shu were false, bidding her help Riverwind in his search for ancient gods his

darkness. Truth will light your way, my daughter, though you may find its light shines dimly in the vast and terrible night ahead. Still, without the truth, all will perish and be lost. Come here inside the temple with me, daughter. You will find what you seek."

"But my friends, Riverwind." Goldmoon looked back at the well and saw Riverwind stumble on the shaking cobblestones. "They cannot fight this evil. They will die without me. The staff could help! I cannot leave!" She started to turn back as the darkness fell.

"I can't see them! . . . Riverwind! . . . Mother, help me," she cried in agony.

But there was no answer. This isn't fair! Goldmoon screamed silently, clenching her fists. We never wanted this! We only wanted to love each other, and now—now we may lose that! We have sacrificed so much and none of it has made any difference. I am thirty years old, mother! Thirty and childless. They have taken my youth, they have taken my people. And I have nothing to show in return. Nothing—except this! She shook the staff. And now I am being asked once again to give still more.

Her anger calmed. Riverwind—had he been angry all those long years he searched for answers? All he had found was this staff, and it brought only more questions. No, he hadn't been angry, she thought. His faith is strong. I am the weak one. Riverwind was willing to die for his faith. It seems I must be willing to live—even if it means living without him.

Goldmoon leaned her head against the golden doors, their metal surface cool to her skin. Reluctantly, she made her bitter decision. I will go forward, mother—though if Riverwind dies, my heart dies, too. I ask only one thing: If he dies, let him know, somehow, that I will continue his search.

Leaning upon her staff, the Chieftain of the Qué-Shu pushed open the golden doors and entered the temple. The doors shut behind her at the precise moment the black dragon burst from the well.

Goldmoon stepped inside soft, enfolding darkness. She could see nothing at first, but a memory of being held very close in her mother's warm

grandfather claimed to have discovered. Goldmoon had not had a vision of her mother since, though she had prayed constantly for help and guidance when her days grew dark and hope dwindled.

embrace played through her mind. A pale light began to shine around her. Goldmoon saw she was under a vast dome that rose high above an intricately inlaid tile floor. Beneath the dome, in the center of the room, stood a marble statue of singular grace and beauty. The light in the room emanated from this statue. Goldmoon, entranced, moved toward it. The statue was of a woman in flowing robes. Her marble face bore an expression of radiant hope, tempered with sadness. A strange amulet hung around her neck.

"This is Mishakal, goddess of healing, whom I serve," said her mother's voice. "Listen to her words, my daughter."

Goldmoon stood directly in front of the statue, marveling at its beauty. But it seemed unfinished, incomplete. Part of the statue was missing, Goldmoon realized. The marble woman's hands were curved, as if they had been holding a long slender pole, but the hands were empty. Without conscious thought, with only the need to complete such beauty, Goldmoon slid her staff into the marble hands.

It began to gleam with a soft blue light. Goldmoon, startled, backed away. The staff's light grew into a blinding radiance. Goldmoon shielded her eyes and fell to her knees. A great and loving power filled her heart. She bitterly regretted her anger.

"Do not be ashamed of your questioning, beloved disciple. It was your questioning that led you to us, and it is your anger that will sustain you through the many trials ahead. You come seeking the truth and you shall receive it.

"The gods have not turned away from man—it is man who turned away from the true gods. Krynn is about to face its greatest trial. Men will need the truth more than ever. You, my disciple, must return the truth and power of the true gods to man. It is time to restore the balance of the universe. Evil now has tipped the scales. For as the gods of good have returned to man, so have the gods of evil—constantly striving for men's souls. The Queen of Darkness has returned, seeking that which will allow her to walk freely in this land once more. Dragons, once banished to the nether regions, walk the land."

Dragons, thought Goldmoon dreamily. She found it difficult to concentrate and grasp the words

that flooded her mind. It would not be until later that she would fully comprehend the message. Then she would remember the words forever.

"To gain the power to defeat them, you will need the truth of the gods, this is the greatest gift of which you were told. Below this temple, in the ruins haunted by the glories of ages past, rest the Disks of Mishakal; circular disks made of gleaming platinum. Find the Disks and you can call upon my power, for I am Mishakal, goddess of healing.†

"Your way will not be easy. The gods of evil know and fear the great power of the truth. The ancient and powerful black dragon, Khisanth, known to men as Onyx, guards the Disks. Her lair is in the ruined city of Xak Tsaroth below us. Danger lies ahead of you if you choose to try and recover the Disks. Therefore I bless this staff. Present it boldly, never wavering, and you shall prevail."

The restoration of truth and faith are Goldmoon's central theme and, to a great extent, the theme of this first book in the series.—TRH

The voice faded. It was then Goldmoon heard Riverwind's death cry.

Tanis entered the temple and felt as if he had walked backward into memory. The sun was shining through the trees in Qualinost. He and Laurana and her brother, Gilthanas, were lying on the riverbank, laughing and sharing dreams after some childish game. Happy childhood days had been few for Tanis—the half-elf learned early that he was different from the others. But that day had been a day of golden sunshine and warm friendship. The remembered peace washed over him, easing his grief and horror.

He turned to Goldmoon, standing silently beside him. "What is this place?"

"That is a story whose telling must wait," Goldmoon answered. With a light hand on Tanis's arm, she drew him across the shimmering tile floor until they both stood before the shining marble statue of Mishakal. The blue crystal staff cast a brilliant glow throughout the chamber.

But even as Tanis's lips parted in wonder, a shadow darkened the room. He and Goldmoon turned toward the door. Caramon and Sturm entered, bearing the body of Riverwind between them on the makeshift litter. Flint and Tasslehoff—the dwarf looking old and weary, the kender unusually subdued—stood on either side of the litter, an odd sort of honor guard. The somber procession moved slowly inside. Behind them came Raistlin, his hood pulled over his head, his hands folded in his robes—the spectre of death itself.

They moved across the marble floor, intent on the burden they bore, and came to a halt before Tanis and Goldmoon. Tanis, looking down at the body at Goldmoon's feet, shut his eyes. Blood had soaked through the thick blanket, spreading in great dark splotches across the fabric.

"Remove the blanket," Goldmoon commanded. Caramon looked at Tanis pleadingly.

"Goldmoon—" Tanis began gently.

Suddenly, before anyone could stop him, Raistlin bent down and tore the blood-stained blanket from the body.

Goldmoon gave a strangled gasp at the sight of Riverwind's tortured body, turning so pale that Tanis reached out a steadying hand, fearing she might faint. But Goldmoon was the daughter of a strong, proud people. She swallowed, drew a deep, shuddering breath. Then she turned and walked up to the marble statue. She lifted the blue crystal staff carefully from the goddess's hands, then she returned to kneel beside Riverwind's body.

"Kan-tokah," she said softly. "My beloved." Reaching out a shaking hand, she touched the dying Plainsman's forehead. The sightless face moved toward her as if he heard. One of the blackened hands twitched feebly, as if he would touch her. Then he gave a great shudder and lay perfectly still. Tears streamed unheeded down Goldmoon's cheeks as she lay the staff across Riverwind's body. Soft blue light filled the chamber. Everyone the light touched felt rested and refreshed. The pain and exhaustion from the day's toil left their bodies. The horror of the dragon's attack lifted from their minds, as the sun burns through fog. Then the light of the staff dimmed and faded. Night settled over the temple, lit once more only by the light emanating from the marble statue.

Tanis blinked, trying once more to re-accustom his eyes to the dark. Then he heard a deep voice.

"Kan-tokah neh sirakan."†

"My beloved, here am I."

He heard Goldmoon cry out in joy. Tanis looked down at what should have been Riverwind's

corpse. Instead, he saw the Plainsman sit up, holding out his arms for Goldmoon. She clung to him, laughing and crying at the same time.

"And so," Goldmoon told them, coming to the end of her story, "we must find a way down into the ruined city that lies somewhere below the temple, and we must remove the Disks from the dragon's lair."

They were eating a frugal dinner, sitting on the floor in the main chamber of the temple. A quick inspection of the building revealed that it was empty, although Caramon told of finding draconian tracks on the staircase, as well as the tracks of some other creature the warrior couldn't identify.

It was not a large building. Two worship rooms were located on opposite sides of the hallway that led to the main chamber where the statue stood. Two circular rooms branched off the main chamber to the north and south.† They were decorated with frescoes that were now covered with fungus and faded beyond recognition. Two sets of golden double doors led to the east. Caramon reported finding a staircase there that led down into the wrecked city below. The faint sound of surf could be heard, reminding them that they were perched on top of a great cliff, overlooking Newsea.

The layout was, of course, taken directly from the adventure module I had written.—TRH

The companions sat, each preoccupied with his own thoughts, trying to assimilate the news Goldmoon had given them. Tasslehoff, however, continued to poke around the rooms, peering into dark corners. Finding little of interest, the kender grew bored and returned to the group, holding an old helmet in his hand. It was too big for him; kenderfolk never wore helmets anyway, considering them bothersome and restrictive. He tossed it to the dwarf.

"What's this?" Flint asked suspiciously, holding it up to the light cast by Raistlin's staff. It was a helm of ancient design, well crafted by a skilled metalsmith. Undoubtedly a dwarf, Flint decided, rubbing his hands over it lovingly. A long tail of animal hair decorated the top. Flint tossed the draconian helm he had been wearing to the floor. Then he put the new-found helm on his head. It fit perfectly. Smiling, he took it off, once more admiring the workmanship. Tanis watched him with amusement.

"That's horsehair," he said, pointing to the tassel.

"No, it's not!" the dwarf protested, frowning. He sniffed at it, wrinkling his nose. Failing to sneeze, he glanced at Tanis in triumph. "It's hair from the mane of a griffon."†

The joke is, of course, that griffons have the back end of a lion, not the front. Thus griffons have no manes. The helm is magical, although the dwarf does not know it, and will provide any dwarf who wears it extra protection.—MW

Caramon guffawed. "Griffon!" He snorted. "There's about as many griffons on Krynn as there are—"

"Dragons," interjected Raistlin smoothly.

The conversation died abruptly.

Sturm cleared his throat. "We'd better get some sleep," he said. "I'll take first watch."

"No one need keep watch this night," Goldmoon said softly. She sat close to Riverwind. The tall Plainsman had not spoken much since his brush with death. He had stared for a long time at the statue of Mishakal, recognizing the woman in blue light who had given him the staff, but he refused to answer any questions or discuss it.

"We are safe here," Goldmoon affirmed, glancing at the statue.

Caramon raised his eyebrows. Sturm frowned and stroked his moustaches. Both men were too polite to question Goldmoon's faith, but Tanis knew that neither warrior would feel safe if watches weren't set. Yet there weren't many hours left until dawn and they all needed rest. Raistlin was already asleep, wrapped in his robes in a dark corner of the chamber.

"I think Goldmoon is right," Tasslehoff said. "Let's trust these old gods, since it seems we have found them."

"The elves never lost them; neither did the dwarves," Flint protested, scowling. "I don't understand any of this! Reorx is one of the ancient gods, presumably. We have worshiped him since before the Cataclysm."

"Worship?" Tanis asked. "Or cry to him in despair because your people were shut out of the Kingdom under the Mountain.† No, don't get mad—" Tanis, seeing the dwarf's face flush an ugly red, held up his hand. "The elves are no better. We cried to the gods when our homeland was laid waste. We know of the gods and we honor their memories—as one would honor the dead. The elven clerics vanished long ago, as did the dwarven clerics. I remember

Tanis is referring to Thorbardin, from which the hill dwarves (of which Flint is one) were barred in the years following the

Mishakal the Healer. I remember hearing the stories of her when I was young. I remember hearing stories of dragons, too. Children's tales, Raistlin would say. It seems our childhood has come back to haunt us—or save us, I don't know which. I have seen two miracles tonight, one of evil and one of good. I must believe in both, if I am to trust the evidence of my senses. Yet . . ." The half-elf sighed. "I say we take turns on watch tonight. I am sorry, lady. I wish my faith were as strong as yours."

Cataclysm. The king of Thorbardin feared that they—as well as the humans with them—would bring plague and famine in with them. The resulting bitterness has never been eased. See The Gates of Thorbardin *by Dan Parkinson.*

Sturm took first watch. The rest wrapped themselves in their blankets and lay on the tile floor. The knight walked through the moonlit temple, checking the quiet rooms, more from force of habit than because he felt any threat. He could hear the wind blow chill and fierce outside, sweeping out from the north. But inside it was strangely warm and comfortable—too comfortable.

Sitting at the base of the statue, Sturm felt a sweet peacefulness creep over him. Startled, he sat bolt upright and realized, chagrined, that he had nearly fallen asleep on watch. That was inexcusable! Berating himself severely, the knight determined that he would walk his watch—the full two hours—as punishment. He started to rise, then stopped. He heard singing, a woman's voice. Sturm stared around wildly, his hand on his sword. Then his hand slipped from the hilt. He recognized the voice and the song. It was his mother's voice. Once more Sturm was with her. They were fleeing Solamnia, traveling alone except for one trusted retainer—and he would be dead before they reached Solace.† The song was one of those wordless lullabies that were older than dragons. Sturm's mother held her child close, and tried to keep her fear from him by singing this gentle, soothing song. Sturm's eyes closed. Sleep blessed him, blessed all of the companions.

The light from Raistlin's staff glowed brightly, keeping away the darkness.

This was Sturm's first adventure, though he didn't recognize it as such at the time. See "The Exiles."

17

The Paths of the Dead.
Raistlin's New Friends.

A rather tidy Bupu, apparently cleaned up for having her picture made.

he sound of metal crashing against the tile floor jolted Tanis out of a deep sleep. He sat up, alarmed, his hand fumbling for his sword.

"Sorry," Caramon said, grinning shamefacedly. "I dropped my breastplate."

Tanis drew a deep breath that turned into a yawn, stretched, and lay back down on his blanket. The sight of Caramon putting on his armor—with Tasslehoff's help—reminded the half-elf of what they faced today. He saw Sturm buckling his armor on as well, while Riverwind polished the sword he had picked up. Tanis firmly put the thought of what might happen to them today out of his mind.

That was not an easy task, especially for the elven part of Tanis—elves revere life and, although they

believe that death is simply a movement into a higher plane of existence,† death of any creature is seen to diminish life on this plane. Tanis forced the human side of him to take possession of his soul today. He would have to kill, and perhaps he would have to accept the death of one or more of these people he loved. He remembered how he had felt yesterday, when he thought he might lose Riverwind. The half-elf frowned and sat up suddenly, feeling as if he had awakened from a bad dream.

An interesting viewpoint in light of events that will be shown in the War of Souls series.—TRH

"Is everyone up? " he asked, scratching his beard.

Flint stumped over and handed him a hunk of bread and some dried strips of venison. "Up and breakfasted," the dwarf grumbled. "You could have slept through the Cataclysm, Half-Elf."

Tanis took a bite of venison without appetite. Then, wrinkling his nose, he sniffed. "What's that funny smell?"

"Some concoction of the mage's." The dwarf grimaced, plopping down next to Tanis. Flint pulled out a block of wood and began carving, hacking away furiously, making chips fly. "He pounded up some sort of powder in a cup and added water. Stirred it up and drank it, but not before it made that gullymudge smell. I'm happier not knowing what it was."

Tanis agreed. He chewed on the venison. Raistlin was now reading his spellbook, murmuring the words over and over until he had committed them to memory. Tanis wondered what kind of spell Raistlin had that might be useful against a dragon. From what little he remembered about dragonlore—learned ages ago from the elven bard, Quivalen Soth†—only the spells of the very greatest mages had a chance of affecting dragons, who could work their own magic—as they had witnessed.

The bard is an elf, therefore no relation to Lord Soth, former human.

Tanis looked at the frail young man absorbed in his spellbook and shook his head. Raistlin might be powerful for his age, and he was certainly devious and clever. But dragons were ancient. They had been in Krynn before the first elves—the oldest of the races—walked the land. Of course, if the plan the companions discussed last night worked out, they wouldn't even encounter the dragon. They hoped simply to find the lair and escape with the Disks. It was a good plan, Tanis thought, and probably worth about as much as smoke on the wind. Despair began to creep over him like a dank fog.

"Well, I'm all set," Caramon announced cheerfully. The big warrior felt immeasurably better in his armor. The dragon seemed a very small annoyance this morning. He tunelessly whistled an old marching song as he stuffed his mud-stained clothing into his pack. Sturm, his armor carefully adjusted, sat apart from the companions, his eyes closed, performing whatever secret ritual knights performed, preparing himself mentally for combat. Tanis stood up, stiff and cold, moving around to get the circulation going and ease the soreness from his muscles. Elves did nothing before battle, except ask forgiveness for taking life.

"We, too, are ready," Goldmoon said. She was dressed in a heavy gray tunic made of soft leather trimmed with fur. She had braided her long silver-gold hair in a twist around her head—a precaution against an enemy using her hair to gain a handhold.

"Let's get this over with." Tanis sighed as he picked up the longbow and quiver of arrows Riverwind had taken from the draconian camp and slung them over his shoulder. In addition, Tanis was armed with a dagger and his longsword. Sturm had his two-handed sword. Caramon carried his shield, a longsword, and two daggers Riverwind had scrounged. Flint had replaced his lost battle-axe with one from the draconian camp. Tasslehoff had his hoopak and a small dagger† he had discovered. He was very proud of it and was deeply wounded when Caramon told him it would be of use if they ran into any ferocious rabbits. Riverwind bore his longsword strapped to his back and still carried Tanis's dagger. Goldmoon bore no weapon other than the staff. We're well armed,† Tanis thought gloomily. For all the good it will do us.

Tas named the dagger Rabbitslayer. The weapon is a blessed artifact, with the ability to inflict far greater damage to an enemy than anyone, even Tas, guesses.—MW

We now have a complete inventory of the well-accessorized dungeon crawler.—TRH

The companions left the chamber of Mishakal, Goldmoon coming last. She gently touched the statue of the goddess with her hand as she passed, whispering a silent prayer.

Tas led the way, skipping merrily, his topknot bouncing behind him. He was going to see a real live dragon! The kender couldn't imagine anything more exciting.

Following Caramon's directions, they headed east, passing through two more sets of golden double doors, and came to a large circular room. A tall, slime-coated pedestal stood in the center—so tall not even Riverwind could see what, if anything, was on it. Tas stood beneath it, staring up at it wistfully.

"I tried to climb it last night," he said—"but it was too slippery. I wonder what's up there?"

"Well, whatever it is will have to stay forever beyond the reach of kenders," Tanis snapped irritably. He walked over to investigate the staircase that spiraled down into the darkness. The stairs were broken and covered with rotting plants and fungus.

"The Paths of the Dead," Raistlin said suddenly.

"What?" Tanis started.

"The Paths of the Dead," the mage repeated. "That's what this staircase is called."

"How in the name of Reorx do you know that?" Flint growled.

"I have read something of this city," Raistlin replied in his whispering voice.

"This is the first we've heard of it," Sturm said coldly. "What else do you know that you haven't told us?"

"A great many things, knight," Raistlin returned, scowling. "While you and my brother played with wooden swords, I spent my time in study."

"Yes, study of that which is dark and mysterious," the knight sneered. "What really happened in the Towers of High Sorcery, Raistlin? You didn't gain these wonderful powers of yours without giving something in return. What did you sacrifice in that Tower? Your health—or your soul!"

"I was with my brother in the Tower," Caramon said, the warrior's normally cheerful face now haggard. "I saw him battle powerful mages and wizards with only a few simple spells. He defeated them, though they shattered his body. I carried him, dying, from the terrible place. And I—" The big man hesitated.

Raistlin stepped forward quickly and placed his cold, thin hand on his twin's arm.

"Be careful what you say," he hissed.

Caramon drew a ragged breath and swallowed. "I know what he sacrificed," the warrior said in a husky voice. Then he lifted his head proudly. "We

Maybe so, but Margaret wrote about it in The Soulforge.

Fortunately, this foreshadowing did not come to pass.—TRH

are forbidden to speak of it.† But you have known me many years, Sturm Brightblade, and I give you my word of honor, you may trust my brother as you trust me. If ever a time comes when that is not so, may my death—and his—be not far behind."†

Raistlin's eyes narrowed at this vow. He regarded his brother with a thoughtful, somber expression. Then Tanis saw the mage's lip curl, the serious mien wiped out by his customary cynicism. It was a startling change. For a moment, the twins' resemblance to each other had been remarkable. Now they were as different as opposite sides of a coin.

Sturm stepped forward and clasped Caramon's hand, gripping it tightly, wordlessly. Then he turned to face Raistlin, unable to regard him without obvious disgust. "I apologize, Raistlin," the knight said stiffly. "You should be thankful you have such a loyal brother."

"Oh, I am," Raistlin whispered.

Tanis glanced at the mage sharply, wondering if he had only imagined sarcasm in the mage's hissing voice. The half-elf licked his dry lips, a sudden, bitter taste in his mouth. "Can you guide us through this place?" he asked abruptly.

"I could have," Raistlin answered, "if we had come here prior to the Cataclysm. The books I studied dated back hundreds of years. During the Cataclysm, when the fiery mountain struck Krynn, the city of Xak Tsaroth was cast down the side of a cliff. I recognize this staircase because it is still intact. As for beyond—" He shrugged.

"Where do the stairs lead?"

"To a place known as the Hall of the Ancestors. Priests and kings of Xak Tsaroth were buried in crypts there."

"Let's get moving," Caramon said gruffly. "All we're doing here is scaring ourselves."

"Yes." Raistlin nodded. "We must go and go quickly. We have until nightfall. By tomorrow, this city will be overrun by the armies moving from the north."

"Bah!" Sturm frowned. "You may know lots of things as you claim, mage, but you can't know that! Caramon is right, though—we have stayed here too long. I will take the lead."

He started down the stairs, moving carefully to keep from slipping on the slimy surface. Tanis saw Raistlin's eyes—narrow, golden slits of enmity—follow Sturm down.†

A paragraph that was cut here added some Solamnic lore:

"Enough was enough, the half-elf decided. 'Those who do not fight as one die forlorn'—an old saying of the Solamnic knights, which accounted for their strict oaths of loyalty and fealty."

"Raistlin, go with him and light the way," Tanis ordered, ignoring the angry glance Sturm flashed up at him. "Caramon, walk with Goldmoon. Riverwind and I will take rear guard."

"And where does that leave us?" Flint grumbled to the kender as they followed behind Goldmoon and Caramon. "In the middle, as usual. Just more useless baggage—"

"There might be anything up there," Tas said, looking back to the pedestal. He obviously hadn't heard a word of what had been said. "A crystal ball of farseeing, a magic ring like I once had. Did I ever tell you about my magic ring? " Flint groaned. Tanis heard the kender's voice prattling on as the two disappeared down the stairs.

The half-elf turned to Riverwind. "You were here—you must have been. We have seen the goddess who gave you the staff. Did you come down here?"

"I don't know," Riverwind said wearily. "I remember nothing about it. Nothing—except the dragon."

Tanis fell silent. The dragon. It all came down to the dragon. The creature loomed large in everyone's thoughts. And how feeble the small group seemed against a monster who had sprung full grown from Krynn's darkest legends. Why us? Tanis thought bitterly. Was there ever a more unlikely group of heroes—bickering, grumbling, arguing—half of us not trusting the other half. "We were chosen." That thought brought little comfort. Tanis remembered Raistlin's words: "Who chose us—and why!" The half-elf was beginning to wonder.

They moved silently down the steep stairway that curled ever deeper into the hillside. At first it was intensely dark as they spiraled down. Then the way began to get lighter, until Raistlin was able to extinguish the light on his staff. Soon Sturm raised his hand, halting the others behind him. Beyond stretched a short corridor, no more than a few feet long. This led to a large arched doorway that revealed a vast open area. A pale gray light filtered into the corridor, as did the odor of dankness and decay.

The companions stood for long moments, listening carefully. The sound of rushing water seemed to come from below and beyond the door, nearly drowning out all other sounds. Still, Tanis thought he had heard something else—a sharp crack—and he had felt more than heard a thumping and throbbing on the floor. But it didn't last long, and the sharp crack wasn't repeated. Then, more puzzling still, came a metallic scraping sound punctuated by an occasional shrill screech. Tanis glanced at Tasslehoff questioningly.

The kender shrugged. "I haven't a clue," he said, cocking his head and listening closely. "I've never heard anything like it, Tanis, except once—" He paused, then shook his head. "Do you want me to go look?" he asked eagerly.

"Go."

Tasslehoff crept down the short corridor, flitting from shadow to shadow. A mouse running across thick carpet makes more noise than a kender when he wants to escape notice. He reached the door and peered out. Ahead of him stretched what must once have been a vast ceremonial hall. Hall of the Ancestors, that's what Raistlin called it. Now it was a Hall of Ruins. Part of the floor to the east had fallen into a hole from which a foul-smelling white mist boiled up. Tas noticed other huge holes gaping in the floor, while chunks of large stone tile stuck up like grave markers. Carefully testing the floor beneath his feet, the kender stepped out into the hall. Through the mist he could faintly distinguish a dark doorway on the south wall . . . and another on the north.† The strange screeching sound came from the south. Tas turned and began walking in that direction.

All from my module design for DL-1 Dragons of Despair. *We followed the original maps very carefully back then. The tendency wore off later.* —*TRH*

He suddenly heard the thumping and throbbing sound again to the north, behind him, and felt the floor start to tremble. The kender hurriedly dashed back into the stairwell. His friends had heard the sound and were flattened against the wall, weapons in hand. The thumping sound grew into a loud whoosh. Then ten or fifteen squat, shadowy figures rushed past the arched doorway. The floor shook. They heard hard breathing and an occasional muttered word. Then the figures vanished in the mist, heading south. There was another sharp cracking sound, then silence.

"What in the name of the Abyss was that?" Caramon exclaimed. "Those weren't draconians, unless they've come up with a short, fat breed. And where'd they come from?"

"They came from the north end of the hall," Tas said. "There's a doorway there and one to the south. The weird screeching sounds come from the south, where those things were headed."

"What's east?" Tanis asked.

"Judging by the sound of falling water I could hear, about a thousand-foot drop," the kender replied. "The floor's caved in. I wouldn't recommend walking over there."

Flint sniffed. "I smell something . . . something familiar. I can't place it ."

"I smell death," Goldmoon said, shivering, holding her staff close.

"Naw, this is something worse," Flint muttered. Then his eyes opened wide and his face grew red with rage and anger. "I've got it!" he roared. "Gully dwarf!" He unslung his axe. "That's what those miserable little things were. Well, they won't be gully dwarves for long. They'll be stinking corpses!"

He dashed forward. Tanis, Sturm, and Caramon leaped after him just as he reached the end of the corridor and dragged him back.

"Keep quiet!" Tanis ordered the sputtering dwarf. "Now, how sure are you that they are gully dwarves?"

The dwarf angrily shook himself from Caramon's grasp. "Sure!" he started to roar, then dropped it to a loud whisper. "Didn't they hold me prisoner for three years?"

"Did they?" Tanis asked, startled.

"That's why I never told you where I was these last five years,"† the dwarf said, flushing with embarrassment. His face darkened. "But I swore I'd get revenge. I'll kill every living gully dwarf I come across."

The whole embarrassing tale is told in Flint the King, *by Mary Kirchoff and Douglas Niles.*

"Wait a minute," Sturm interrupted. "Gully dwarves aren't evil, not like goblins at any rate. What could they be doing living here with draconians?"

"Slaves," Raistlin answered coolly. "Undoubtedly the gully dwarves have lived here many years, probably ever since the city was abandoned. When the draconians were sent, perhaps, to guard the Disks, they found the gully dwarves and used them as slave labor."

"They might be able to help us then," Tanis murmured.

"Gully dwarves!" Flint exploded. "You'd trust those filthy little—"

"No," Tanis said. "We cannot trust them, of course. But nearly every slave is willing to betray his master, and gully dwarves—like most dwarves—feel little loyalty to anyone except their own chieftains. As long as we don't ask them to do anything that might endanger their own dirty skins, we might be able to buy their aid."

"Well, I'll be an ogre's hind end!" Flint said in disgust. He hurled his axe to the ground, tore his pack off, and slumped down against the wall, arms folded. "Go on. Go ask your new friends to help you. I'll not be with you! They'll help you, all right. Help you right up the dragon's snout!"

Tanis and Sturm exchanged concerned glances, remembering the boat incident. Flint could be incredibly stubborn, and Tanis thought it quite likely that this time the dwarf would prove immovable.

"I dunno." Caramon sighed and shook his head. "It's too bad the dwarf's staying behind. If we do get the gully dwarves to help us, who'll keep the scum in line?"

Amazed that Caramon could be so subtle, Tanis smiled and picked up on the warrior's lead. "Sturm, I guess."

"Sturm!" The dwarf bounded to his feet. "A knight who won't stab an enemy in the back? You need someone who knows these foul creatures—"

"You're right, Flint," Tanis said gravely. "I guess you'll have to come with us."

"You bet," Flint grumbled. He grabbed his things and stumped off down the corridor. He turned around. "You coming?"

Hiding their smiles, the companions followed the dwarf out into the Hall of the Ancestors. They kept close to the wall, avoiding the treacherous floor. They headed south, following the gully dwarves, and entered a dimly lit passage that ran south only a few hundred feet, then turned sharply east. Once again they heard the cracking noise. The metallic

screeching had stopped. Suddenly, they heard behind them the sound of pounding feet.

"Gully dwarves!" growled Flint.

"Back!" Tanis ordered. "Be ready to jump them. We can't let them raise an alarm!"

Everyone flattened himself against the wall, sword drawn and ready. Flint held his battle-axe, a look of eager anticipation on his face. Staring back into the vast hall, they saw another group of short fat figures running toward them.

Suddenly, the leader of the gully dwarves looked up and saw them. Caramon leaped out in front of the small running figures, his huge arm raised commandingly. "Halt!" he said. The gully dwarves glanced up at him, swarmed around him, and disappeared around the corner to the east. Caramon turned around to stare after them in astonishment.

"Halt . . . " he said half-heartedly.

A gully dwarf popped back around the corner, glared at Caramon, and put a grubby finger to his lips. "Shhhhh!" Then the squat figure vanished. They heard the cracking sound and the screeching noise started up again.

"What do you suppose is going on?" Tanis asked softly.

"Do they all look like that?" Goldmoon said, her eyes wide. "They're so filthy and ragged, and there are sores all over their bodies."

"And they have the brains of a doorknob,"† Flint grunted.

Thus Flint's epithet of "doorknob" for Tas.

The group cautiously rounded the corner, hands on their weapons. A long, narrow corridor extended east, lit by torches that flickered and smoked in the stifling air. The light reflected off walls wet with condensed moisture. Arched doorways† revealing only blackness opened up off the hallway.

If you were a good game player, you'd probably have to explore beyond each of those doorways.

"The crypts," Raistlin whispered.

Tanis shivered. Water dripped on him from the ceiling. The metallic screeching was louder and nearer. Goldmoon touched the half-elf's arm and pointed. Tanis saw, down at the far end of the corridor, a doorway. Beyond the opening was another passageway forming a T-intersection. The corridor was filled with gully dwarves.

"I wonder why the little guys are lined up," Caramon said.

"This is our chance to find out," Tanis said. He was starting forward when he felt the mage's hand on his arm.

"Leave this to me," Raistlin whispered.

"We had better come with you," Sturm stated, "to cover you, of course."

"Of course," Raistlin sniffed. "Very well, but do not disturb me."

Tanis nodded. "Flint, you and Riverwind guard this end of the corridor." Flint opened his mouth to protest, then scowled and fell back to stand opposite the Plainsmen.

"Stay well behind me," Raistlin ordered, then moved down the corridor, his red robes rustling around his ankles, the Staff of Magius thumping softly on the floor at each step. Tanis and Sturm followed, moving along the side of the dripping walls. Cold air flowed from the crypts. Peering inside one, Tanis could see the dark outline of a sarcophagus reflected in the sputtering torchlight. The coffin was elaborately carved, decorated with gold that shone no longer. An oppressive air hung over the crypts. Some of the tombs appeared to have been broken into and plundered. Tanis caught a glimpse of a skull grinning out of the darkness. He wondered if these ancient dead were planning their revenge for having their rest disturbed. Tanis forced himself to return to reality. It was bleak enough.

Raistlin stopped when he neared the end of the corridor. The gully dwarves watched him curiously, ignoring the others behind him. The mage did not speak. He reached into a pouch on his belt and drew out several golden coins. The gully dwarves' eyes brightened. One or two at the front of the line edged toward Raistlin to get a better view. The mage held up a coin so they all could see it. Then he threw it high into the air and . . . it vanished!†

His childhood years as a street magician weren't wasted.

The gully dwarves gasped. Raistlin opened his hand with a flourish to reveal the coin. There was scattered applause. The gully dwarves crept closer, mouths gaping in wonder.

Gully dwarves—or Aghar—as their race was known, were truly a miserable lot. The lowest caste in dwarven society, they were to be found all over Krynn, living in filth and squalor in places that had been abandoned by most other living creatures,

including animals. Like all dwarves, they were clannish, and several clans often lived together, following the rule of their chieftains or one particularly powerful clan leader. Three clans lived in Xak Tsaroth—the Sluds, the Bulps, and the Glups. Members of all three clans now surrounded Raistlin. There were both males and females, though it was not easy to tell the sexes apart. The females lacked whiskers on their chins but had them on their cheeks. They wore a tattered overskirt wrapped around their waists extending to their bony knees. Otherwise, they were every bit as ugly as their male counterparts. Despite their wretched appearance, gully dwarves generally led a cheerful existence.

Raistlin, with marvelous dexterity, made the coin dance over his knuckles, flipping it in and out of his fingers. Then he made it disappear, only to reappear inside the ear of some startled gully dwarf who stared at the mage in amazement. This last trick produced a momentary interruption in the performance as the Aghar's friends grabbed him and peered intently into his ear, one of them even sticking his finger inside to see if more coins might be forthcoming. This interesting activity ceased, though, when Raistlin reached into another pouch and removed a small scroll of parchment. Spreading it open with his long, thin fingers, the mage began to read from it, chanting softly, *"Suh tangus moipar, ast akular kalipad."* The gully dwarves watched in total fascination.

When the mage finished reading, the spidery-looking words on the scroll began to burn. They flared, then disappeared, leaving traces of green smoke.

"What was that all about?" Sturm asked suspiciously.

"They are now spellbound," Raistlin replied. "I have cast over them a spell of friendship."

The gully dwarves were enthralled and, Tanis noticed, the expressions on their faces had changed from interest to open, unabashed affection for the mage. They reached out and patted him with their dirty hands, jabbering away in their shapeless language.† Sturm glanced at Tanis in alarm. Tanis knew what the knight was thinking: Raistlin could have cast that spell on any of them at any time.

That's the reason we don't provide any examples. —TRH

Hearing the sound of running feet, Tanis looked quickly back to where Riverwind stood guard. The Plainsman pointed to the gully dwarves, then held up his hands, fingers spread. Ten more were heading their way. Soon, the new Aghar trotted into view, passing Riverwind without so much as a glance. They pulled up short on seeing the commotion around the mage.

"What happening?" said one, staring at Raistlin. The spellbound gully dwarves were gathered around the mage, tugging on his robe and dragging him down the hall.

"Friend. This our friend," they all chattered wildly in a crude form of Common.

"Yes," Raistlin said in a soft and gentle voice, so smooth and winning that Tanis was momentarily taken aback. "You are all my friends," the mage continued. "Now, tell me, my friends, where does this corridor lead?" Raistlin pointed to the east. There was an immediate babble of answers.

"Corridor lead that way," said one, pointing east.

"No, it lead that way!" said another, pointing west.

A scuffle broke out, the gully dwarves pushing and shoving. Soon fists were flying and then one gully dwarf had another on the ground, kicking him, yelling, "That way! That way!" at the top of his lungs.

Sturm turned to Tanis. "This is ridiculous! They'll bring every draconian in the place down on us. I don't know what that crazy magician has done, but you've got to stop him."

Before Tanis could intervene, however, one female gully dwarf took matters into her own hands. Dashing into the melee, she grabbed the two combatants, knocked their heads together smartly, and dumped them on the floor.† The others, who had been cheering them on, immediately hushed, and the newcomer turned to Raistlin. She had a thick, bulbous nose and her hair stood up wildly on her head. She wore a patched and ragged dress, thick shoes, and stockings that collapsed around her ankles. But she seemed to be a leader among the gully dwarves, for they all eyed her with respect. This may have been because she carried a huge, heavy bag slung over one shoulder. The bag

It worked with goblins. . . .

dragged along the ground as she walked, occasionally tripping her. But the bag was apparently of great importance to her. When one of the other gully dwarves attempted to touch it, she whirled around and smacked him across the face.

"Corridor lead to big bosses," she said, nodding her head toward the east.

"Thank you, my dear," Raistlin said, reaching out to touch her cheek. He spoke a few words, *"Tan-tago, musalah."*

The female gully dwarf watched, fascinated, as he spoke. Then she sighed and gazed up at him in adoration.†

The character of Bupu the gully dwarf originated from an ad-lib character I created during a play test of the first game module. Everyone liked the character so much that she became part of the Raistlin legend.—TRH

"Tell me, little one," Raistlin said. "How many bosses?"

The gully dwarf frowned, concentrating. She raised a grubby hand. "One," she said, holding up one finger. "And one, and one, and one." Looking up at Raistlin triumphantly, she held up four fingers and said, "Two."

"I'm beginning to agree with Flint," Sturm growled.

"Shhhh," Tanis said. Just then the screeching noise stopped. The gully dwarves looked down the corridor uneasily as into the silence came the harsh cracking sound again.

"What is that noise?" Raistlin asked his spellbound adorer.

"Whip," the female gully dwarf said emotionlessly. Reaching out her filthy hand, she took hold of Raistlin's robe and started to pull him toward the east end of the corridor. "Bosses get mad. We go."

"What is it you do for the bosses?" Raistlin asked, holding back.

"We go. You see." The gully dwarf tugged on him. "We down. They up. Down. Up. Down. Up. Come. You go. We give ride down."

Raistlin, being carried along on a tide of Aghar, looked back at Tanis, motioning with his hand. Tanis signaled to Riverwind and Flint, and everyone started moving down the hall behind the gully dwarves. Those Raistlin had charmed remained clustered around him, trying to stay as close as possible, while the rest ran off down the corridor when the whip cracked again. The companions followed Raistlin and the gully dwarves down to the corner, where the screeching noise started up once again, much louder now.

The female gully dwarf brightened as she heard it. She and the rest of the gully dwarves halted. Some of them slouched against the slime-covered walls, others plopped on the floor like sacks. The female stayed near Raistlin, holding the hem of his sleeve in her small hand. "What is it? " he asked. "Why have we stopped?"

"We wait. Not our turn yet," she informed him.

"What will we do when it is our turn?" he asked patiently.

"Go down," she said, staring up at him adoringly.

Raistlin looked at Tanis, shook his head. The mage decided to try a new approach.

"What is your name, little one?" he asked.

"Bupu."

Caramon snorted and quickly clapped his hand over his mouth.

"Now, Bupu," Raistlin said in dulcet tones, "do you know where the dragon's lair is?"

"Dragon?" Bupu repeated, astounded. "You want dragon?"

"No," Raistlin said hastily, "we don't want the dragon—just the dragon's lair, where the dragon lives."

"Oh, me not know that." Bupu shook her head. Then, seeing disappointment on Raistlin's face, she clutched his hand. "But me take you to the great Highbulp. He know everything."

Raistlin raised his eyebrows. "And how do we get to the Highbulp?"

"Down!" she said, grinning happily. The screeching sound stopped. There was a crack of a whip. "It our turn to go down now. You come. You come now. Go see Highbulp."

"Just a moment." Raistlin extricated himself from the gully dwarf's grasp. "I must talk to my friends." He walked over to Tanis and Sturm. "This Highbulp is probably head of the clan, maybe head of several clans."

"If he's as intelligent as this lot, he won't know where his own wash bowl is, let alone the dragon," Sturm growled.

"He'll know, most likely," Flint spoke up grudgingly. "They're not smart, but gully dwarves

remember everything they see or hear if you can just get them to put it into words of more than one syllable."

"We better go see the great Highbulp then," Tanis said ruefully. "Now, if we could just figure out what this up and down business is and that squeaking noise—"

"I know!" said a voice.

Tanis looked around. He had completely forgotten about Tasslehoff. The kender came running back in from around the corner, his topknot dancing, eyes shining with merriment. "It's a lift, Tanis," he said. "Like in dwarven mines. I was in a mine, once. It was the most wonderful thing. They had a lift that took rock up and down. And this is just like it. Well, almost like it. You see—" He was suddenly overcome with giggles and couldn't go on. The rest glaring at him, the kender made a violent effort to control himself

"They're using a giant lard-rendering pot! The gully dwarves that have been standing in line here run out when one of the draco-thing-ama-jiggers cracks this big whip. They all jump into the pot that's attached to a huge chain wrapped around a spoked wheel with teeth that fit into the links of the chain—that's what's squeaking! The wheel turns and down they go, and pretty soon up comes another pot—"

"Big bosses. Pot full of big bosses," Bupu said.

"Filled with draconians!" Tanis repeated in alarm.

"Not come here," Bupu said. "Go that way—" She waved a hand vaguely.

Tanis remained uneasy. "So these are the bosses. How many draconians are there by the pot?"

"Two," said Bupu, holding Raistlin's sleeve securely. "Not more than two."

"Actually, there are four," Tas said with an apologetic glance for contradicting the gully dwarf. "They're the little ones,† not the big ones that cast spells."

Even the smallest draconians, Baaz, are the height of an average human. These tend to be picked on by their larger cousins.

"Four." Caramon flexed his huge arms. "We can handle four."

"Yes, but we've got to time it so that fifteen more aren't arriving," Tanis pointed out.

The whip cracked again.

"Come!" Bupu tugged urgently on Raistlin's sleeve. "We go. Bosses get mad."

"I'd say this is as good a time as any," Sturm said, shrugging. "Let the gully dwarves run as usual. We'll follow and overwhelm the bosses in the confusion. If one pot is up here waiting to be loaded with gully dwarves, the other has to be on the ground level."

"I suppose," Tanis said. He turned to the gully dwarves. "When you get to the lift—er, pot—don't jump in. Just dodge aside and keep out of the way. All right?"

The gully dwarves stared at Tanis with deep suspicion. The half-elf sighed and looked at Raistlin. Smiling slightly, the mage repeated Tanis's instructions. Immediately the gully dwarves began to smile and nod enthusiastically.

The whip cracked again and the companions heard a harsh voice. "Quit loafing, you scum, or we'll chop your nasty feet off and give you an excuse for being slow!"

"We'll see whose feet get chopped off," Caramon said.

"This be some fun!" said one of the gully dwarves solemnly. The Aghar dashed down the corridor.

18

Fight at the lift.
Bupu's cure for a cough.

Hot mist rose from two large holes in the floor, swirling around whatever was nearby. Between the two holes was a large wheel, around which ran a gigantic chain. A tremendous black iron pot hung suspended from the chain over one of the holes. The other end of the chain disappeared through the other hole. Four armor-clad draconians, two of them swinging leather whips and armed with curved swords, stood around the pot. They were visible only briefly, then mist hid them from view. Tanis could hear the whip crack and a guttural voice bellowing.

"You louse-ridden dwarf vermin! What're you doing, holding back there. Get into this pot before I flay the filthy flesh from your nasty bones! I—ulp!"

The draconian stopped in midsentence, its eyes bulging out of its reptilian head as Caramon emerged from the mist, roaring his battle cry. The draconian let out a yell that changed into a choking gurgle as Caramon grabbed the creature around its scrawny neck, lifted it off its clawed feet, and hurled it back against the wall. Gully dwarves scattered as the body hit the wall with a bone-crushing thump.

Even as Caramon attacked, Sturm—swinging his great two-handed sword—yelled out the knight's salute to an enemy and lopped the head off a draconian who never saw what was coming. The severed head rolled on the floor with a crunching sound as it changed to stone.

Unlike goblins, who attack anything that moves without strategy or thought, draconians are intelligent and quick-thinking. The two remaining by the pot had no intention of taking on five skilled and well-armed warriors. One of them immediately jumped into the pot, yelling instructions to its companion in their guttural language. The other draconian dashed over to the wheel and freed the mechanism. The pot began to drop through the hole.

"Stop it!" Tanis yelled. "It's going for reinforcements!"

"Wrong!" shouted Tasslehoff, peering over the edge. "The reinforcements are already on the way up in the other pot. There must be twenty of them!"

Caramon ran to stop the draconian operating the lift, but he was too late. The creature left the mechanism turning and dashed toward the pot. With a great bound, it leaped in after its companion. Caramon, on the principle of don't let the enemy get away, jumped right into the pot after it! The gully dwarves cheered and hooted, some dashing over to the edge to get a better view.

"That big idiot!" Sturm swore. Shoving gully dwarves aside to look down, he saw swinging fists and flashing armor as Caramon and the draconians flailed away at each other. Caramon's added weight caused the pot to fall faster.

"They'll cut the lummox to jerky down there," Sturm muttered. "I'm going after him," he yelled to Tanis. Launching himself into the air, he grabbed hold of the chain and slid right down it into the pot.

"Now we've lost both of them!" Tanis groaned. "Flint, come with me. Riverwind, stay up here with Raistlin and Goldmoon. See if you can reverse that damned wheel! No, Tas, not you!"

Too late. The kender, screaming enthusiastically, leaped onto the chain and began shinnying down. Tanis and Flint jumped into the hole, too. Tanis wrapped his arms and legs around the chain, hanging on just above the kender, but the dwarf missed his hold, landing in the pot helmet first. Caramon promptly stepped on him.

The draconians in the pot pinned the warrior against the side. He punched one, sending it slamming to the other side, and drew his dagger on the other as it fumbled for its sword. Caramon stabbed before the draconian could get the sword free, but the warrior's dagger glanced off the creature's armor and was jarred out of Caramon's grasp. The draconian went for his face, trying to gouge his eyes out with its clawed hands. Grabbing the draconian's wrists in a crushing grip, Caramon succeeded in wrenching its hands away from his face. The two powerful beings—human and draconian—struggled against the side of the pot.

The other draconian recovered from Caramon's blow and seized its sword. But its dive for the warrior came to an abrupt halt when Sturm, sliding down the chain, kicked it hard in the face with his heavy boot. The draconian reeled backwards, the sword flying from its grasp. Sturm leaped and tried to club the creature with the flat of his sword, but the draconian thrust the blade aside with its hands.

"Get off me!" Flint roared from the bottom of the pot. Blinded by his helm, he was being slowly crushed by Caramon's big feet. In a spurt of ferocious anger, the dwarf straightened his helm, then heaved himself up, causing Caramon to lose his footing and tumble forward into the draconian. The creature sidestepped while Caramon staggered into the huge chain. The draconian swung its sword wildly. Caramon ducked and the sword clanged uselessly against the chain, notching the blade. Flint hurled himself at the draconian, hitting it squarely in the stomach with his head. The two fell against the side.

The pot gained momentum, swirling the foul mists around them.

Keeping his eyes on the action below, Tanis lowered himself down the chain. "Stay put!" he snarled at Tasslehoff. Letting go his grip, Tanis dropped down and landed in the midst of the melee. Tas, disappointed but reluctant to disobey Tanis, clung to the chain with one hand while he reached into his pouch and pulled out a rock, ready to drop it—on the head of an enemy, he hoped.

The pot began to sway as the combatants fell against the sides in their struggles, all the while dropping lower and lower, causing the other pot—filled with screaming and cursing draconians—to rise higher and higher.†

As I recall from the playtests of the original modules, the players in the game didn't fare any better.—TRH

Riverwind, standing at the hole with the gully dwarves, could see very little through the mist. He could, however, hear thumps and curses and groans from the pot holding his friends. Then out of the mist rose the other pot. Draconians stood, swords in their hands, staring, open-mouthed, up at him, their long red tongues panting in anticipation. In moments, he and Goldmoon, Raistlin, and fifteen gully dwarves would be facing about twenty angry draconians!

He spun around, stumbled over a gully dwarf, regained his balance, and ran to the mechanism. Somehow he had to stop that pot from rising. The huge wheel was turning slowly, the chain screeching through the spokes. Riverwind stared at it with the idea of grabbing the chain in his bare hands. A flurry of red shoved him aside. Raistlin watched the wheel for an instant, timing its rotation, then he jammed the Staff of Magius in between the wheel and the floor. The staff shivered for an instant and Riverwind held his breath, fearing the staff would snap. But it held! The mechanism shuddered to a stop.

"Riverwind!" Goldmoon yelled from where she had remained by the hole. The Plainsman ran over to the edge, Raistlin following. The gully dwarves, lined up around the hole, were having a wonderful time, thoroughly enjoying one of the most interesting events to occur in their lives. Only Bupu moved away from the edge—she trotted after Raistlin, grasping his robe whenever possible.

"*Khark-umat*!" breathed Riverwind as he looked down into the swirling mist.

Caramon tossed overboard the draconian he had been fighting. It fell with a shriek into the mist. The big warrior had claw marks on his face and a sword slash on his right arm. Sturm, Tanis, and Flint still battled the second draconian who seemed willing to kill regardless of the consequences. When it finally became clear that hitting was not enough, Tanis stabbed it with his dagger. The creature sank down, immediately turning to rock, holding Tanis's weapon fast in its stony corpse.

Then the pot lurched to a halt, jolting everyone.

"Look out! Neighbors!" yelled Tasslehoff, dropping off the chain. Tanis looked over to see the other pot, filled with draconians, swinging only about twenty feet away. Armed to the teeth, the draconians were preparing a boarding maneuver. Two clambered up onto the edge of the pot, ready to leap across the misty gap. Caramon leaned over the edge of the pot and made a wild and vicious swing with his sword in an attempt to slash one of the boarders. He missed and the momentum of his swing set the pot rotating on its chain.

Caramon lost his balance and fell forward, his great weight tipping the pot dangerously. He found himself staring directly down at the ground far below him. Sturm grabbed hold of Caramon's collar and yanked him back, causing the pot to rock erratically. Tanis slipped, landing on his hands and knees at the bottom of the pot where he discovered that the stone draconian had decayed into dust, allowing him to retrieve his dagger.

"Here they come!" Flint yelled, hauling Tanis to his feet.

One draconian launched itself toward them and caught hold of the edge of the pot with its clawed hands. The pot tilted precariously once again.

"Get over there!" Tanis shoved Caramon to the opposite side, hoping the warrior's weight would keep the pot stable. Sturm hacked at the draconian's hands, trying to force it to let go. Then another draconian flew over, gauging its distance better than the first. It landed in the pot next to Sturm.

"Don't move!" Tanis screamed at Caramon as the warrior instinctively charged into combat. The pot

tilted. The big man quickly returned to his position. The pot righted itself. The draconian hanging onto the edge, its fingers oozing green, let go, spread its wings, and floated down into the mist.

Tanis spun around to fight the draconian that had landed in the pot and fell over Flint, knocking the dwarf off his feet again. The half-elf staggered against the side. As the pot rocked, he stared down. The mists parted and he saw the ruined city of Xak Tsaroth far below him. When he drew back, feeling sick and disoriented, he saw Tasslehoff fighting the draconian. The little kender crawled up the creature's back and bashed it on the head with a rock. At the bottom of the pot, Flint picked up Caramon's dropped dagger and stabbed the same creature in the leg. The draconian screamed as the blade bit deep. Knowing more draconians were about to fly over, Tanis looked up in despair. But the despair turned to hope when he saw Riverwind and Goldmoon staring down through the mist.

"Bring us back up!" Tanis yelled frantically, then something hit him on the head. The pain was excruciating. He felt himself falling and falling and falling. . . .

Raistlin did not hear Tanis's yell—the mage had already gone into action.

"Come here, my friends," Raistlin said swiftly. The spellbound gully dwarves gathered eagerly around him. "Those bosses down there want to hurt me," he said softly.

The gully dwarves growled. Several frowned darkly. A few shook their fists at the potful of draconians.

"But you can help," Raistlin said. "You can stop them."

The gully dwarves stared at the mage dubiously. Friendship—after all—went only so far.

"All you must do," Raistlin said patiently, "is run over and jump on that chain." He pointed at the chain attached to the draconians' pot.

The gully dwarves' faces brightened. That didn't sound bad. In fact, it was something they did almost daily when they missed catching hold of the pot.

Raistlin waved his arm. "Go!" he ordered.†

The gully dwarves—all except Bupu—glanced at each other, then dashed to the edge of the hole and,

All of these events were straight out of our playing the game.—TRH

yelling wildly, flung themselves onto the chain above the draconians, clinging to it with marvelous dexterity.

The mage ran over to the wheel, Bupu trotting along after him. Grabbing the Staff of Magius, he tugged it free. The wheel shivered and began to move once again, turning more and more rapidly as the weight of the gully dwarves caused the draconian pot to plummet back down into the mists.

Several of the draconians who had been perched on the edge about to jump into the other pot were caught off guard by the sudden jolt. They lost their balance and fell. Though their wings stopped their fall, they shrieked in rage as they drifted to the ground below, their cries contrasting oddly with the gleeful shouts of the gully dwarves.

Riverwind leaned out over the edge of the hole and caught hold of the companions' pot as it reached the wheel.

"Are you all right?" Goldmoon asked anxiously, leaning over to help Caramon out. "Tanis is hurt," Caramon said, supporting the half-elf.

"It's just a bump," Tanis protested groggily. He felt a large lump rising on the back of his skull. "I thought I was falling out of that thing." He shuddered at the memory.

"We can't get down that way!" Sturm said, climbing out of the pot. "And we can't stay around up here. It won't take them long to get this lift back in operation and then they'll be after us. We'll have to go back."

"No! Don't go!" Bupu clutched at Raistlin. "I know way to Highbulp!" She tugged at his sleeve, pointing north. "Good way! Secret way! No bosses," she said softly, stroking his hand. "I not let bosses get you. You pretty."

"We don't seem to have much choice. We've got to get down there," Tanis said, wincing when Goldmoon's staff touched him. Then the healing power flowed through his body. He relaxed as the pain eased and sighed. "As you said, they've lived here for years."

Flint growled and shook his head as Bupu started down the corridor, heading north.

"Stop! Listen!" Tasslehoff called softly. They heard the sound of clawed feet coming toward them.

"Draconians!" said Sturm. "We've got to get out of here! Head back west."

"I knew it," Flint grumbled, scowling. "That gully dwarf's led us right into those lizards!"

"Wait!" Goldmoon gripped Tanis's arm. "Look at her!"

The half-elf turned to see Bupu remove something limp and shapeless from the bag she carried over her shoulder. Stepping up to the wall, she waved the thing in front of the stone slab and muttered a few words. The wall shivered, and within seconds, a doorway appeared, leading into darkness.

The companions exchanged uneasy glances.

"No choice," Tanis muttered. The rattle and clank of armored draconians could be heard clearly, marching down the corridor toward them. "Raistlin, light," he ordered.

The mage spoke and the crystal on his staff flared. He and Bupu and Tanis quickly passed through the secret door. The rest followed, and the other door slid shut behind them. The mage's staff revealed a small, square room decorated with wall carvings so covered with green slime that they were impossible to distinguish. They stood in silence as they heard draconians pass in the corridor.

"They must have heard the fight," Sturm whispered. "It won't take them long to get the lift in motion, then we'll have the whole draconian force after us!"

"I know way down." Bupu waved her hand deprecatingly. "No worry."

"How did you open the door, little one?" Raistlin asked curiously, kneeling beside Bupu.

"Magic," she said shyly and she held out her hand. Lying in the gully dwarf's grubby palm was a dead rat, its teeth fixed in a permanent grimace. Raistlin raised his eyebrows, then Tasslehoff touched his arm.

"It's not magic, Raistlin," the kender whispered. "It's a simple, hidden floor lock.† I saw it when she pointed at the wall and I was about to say something when she went through this magic rigmarole. She steps on it when she gets close to the door and waves that thing." The kender giggled. "She probably tripped it once, accidentally, while carrying the rat."

Reminder: a kender is a variety of the AD&D character class called thief, which has, among other talents, the ability to perceive hidden locks. But never call Tas a thief!

Bupu gave the kender a scathing glance. "Magic!" she stated, pouting and stroking the rat lovingly. She popped it back into her bag and said—"Come, you go." She led them north, passing through broken, slime-coated rooms. Finally she came to a halt in a room filled with rock dust and debris. Part of the ceiling had collapsed and the floor was littered with broken tiles. The gully dwarf jabbered and pointed at something in the northeast corner of the room.

"Go down!" she said.

Tanis and Raistlin walked over to inspect. They found a four-foot-wide pipe, one end sticking up out of the crumbling floor. Apparently it had fallen through the ceiling, caving in the northeast section of the room. Raistlin thrust his staff down inside the pipe and peered inside.

"Come, you go!" Bupu said, pointing and tugging at Raistlin's sleeve urgently. "Bosses can't follow."

"That's probably true," Tanis said. "Not with their wings."

"But there's not room enough to swing a sword," Sturm said, frowning. "I don't like it—"

Suddenly everyone stopped talking. They heard the wheel creak and the chain start to screech. The companions looked at each other.

"Me first!" Tasslehoff grinned. Poking his head into the pipe, he crawled forward on his hands and knees.

"Are you sure I'll fit?" Caramon asked, staring at the opening anxiously.

"Don't worry," Tas's voice floated out. "It's so slick with slime you'll slip through like a greased pig."

This cheerful statement did not seem to impress Caramon. He continued to regard the pipe gloomily as Raistlin, led by Bupu, clutched his robes around him and slid inside, his staff lighting the way. Flint climbed in next. Goldmoon followed, grimacing in disgust as her hands slipped in the thick, green slime. Riverwind slid in after her.

"This is insane—I hope you know that!" Sturm muttered in disgust.

Tanis didn't answer. He clapped Caramon on the back. "Your turn," he said, listening to the sound of the chain moving faster and faster.

Caramon groaned. Getting down on his hands and knees, the big warrior crawled forward into the pipe opening. His sword hilt caught on the edge. Backing out, he fumbled to readjust the sword, then he tried again. This time his rump stuck up too far making his back scrape along the top. Tanis planted his foot firmly on the big warrior's rear end and shoved.

"Flatten down!" the half-elf ordered.

Caramon collapsed like a wet sack with another groan. He squirmed in, head first, shoving his shield in front of him, his armor dragging along the metal pipe with a shrill, scraping sound that set Tanis's teeth on edge.

The half-elf reached out and grasped the top of the pipe. Thrusting his legs in first, he began to slide in the foul-smelling slime. He twisted his head around to look back at Sturm, who came last.

"Sanity ended when we followed Tika into the kitchen of the Inn of the Last Home," he said.†

Originally, the companions who gathered at the Inn were going to be called the Innfellows.

"True enough," the knight agreed with a sigh.

Tasslehoff, enthralled by the new experience of crawling down the pipe, suddenly saw dark figures at the bottom end. Scrabbling for a handhold, he slid to a stop.

"Raistlin!" the kender whispered. "Something's coming up the pipe!"

"What is it?" the mage started to ask, but the foul, moist air caught in his throat and he began to cough. Trying to catch his breath, he shone the staff's light down the pipe to see who approached.

Bupu took one look and sniffed. "Gulp-pulphers!" she muttered. Waving her hand, she shouted. "Go back! Go back!"

"We go up—ride lift! Big bosses get mad!" yelled one.

"We go down. See Highbulp!" Bupu said importantly.

At this, the other gully dwarves began backing down, muttering and swearing.

But Raistlin couldn't move for a moment. He clutched his chest, hacking, the sound echoing alarmingly in the stillness of the narrow pipe. Bupu gazed at him anxiously, then thrust her small hand into her bag, fished around for several moments,

and came up with an object that she held up to the light, She squinted at it, then sighed and shook her head. "This not what I want," she mumbled.

Tasslehoff, catching sight of a brilliant, colorful flash, crept closer. "What is that?" he asked, even though he knew the answer. Raistlin, too, was staring at the object with wide glittering eyes.

Bupu shrugged. "Pretty rock," she said without interest, searching through the bag once more.

"An emerald!"† Raistlin wheezed.

Bupu glanced up. "You like?" she asked Raistlin.

"Very much!" the mage gasped.

"You keep." Bupu put the jewel in the mage's hand. Then, with a cry of triumph, she brought out what she had been searching for. Tas, leaning up close to see the new wonder, drew back in disgust. It was a dead—very dead—lizard. There was a piece of chewed-on leather cord tied around the lizard's stiff tail. Bupu held it toward Raistlin.

"You wear around neck," she said. "Cure cough."†

The mage, accustomed to handling much more unpleasant objects than this, smiled at Bupu and thanked her, but declined the cure, assuring her that his cough was much improved. She looked at him dubiously, but he did seem better—the spasm had passed. After a moment, she shrugged and put the lizard back into her bag. Raistlin, examining the emerald with expert eyes, stared coldly at Tasslehoff. The kender, sighing, turned his back and continued down the pipe. Raistlin slipped the stone into one of the secret inner pockets sewn into his robes.

When a branch pipe joined theirs, Tas looked questioningly at the gully dwarf. Bupu hesitantly pointed south, into the new pipe. Tas entered slowly. "This is stee—" he gasped as he began to slide rapidly down. He tried to slow his descent, but the slime was too thick. Caramon's explosive oath, echoing down the pipe from behind him, told the kender that his companions were having the same problem. Suddenly Tas saw light ahead of him. The tunnel was coming to an end, but where? Tas had a vivid vision of bursting out five hundred feet above nothing. But there wasn't anything he could do to stop himself. The light grew brighter, and Tasslehoff shot out the end of the pipe with a small shriek.

Legend has it that Raistlin placed a magical spell on the emerald to honor Bupu. The emerald will protect its owner in a life-threatening situation. The emerald may be used only by gully dwarves, gnomes, or kender.—MW

This "lizard cure" was brought home to me in 1986 when I was briefly hospitalized for kidney stones. The doctor had mistakenly overestimated the amount of Demerol I required and this non-drinking, non-smoking, drug-free Mormon was sent on a three-day ride to my own personal fantasyland. Naturally, this didn't prevent visitors. Margaret came by with something the gang had cooked up. On a leather thong was hung a hideously large rubber lizard. Bupu had sent along the lizard cure. On the third day—so they said—they wheeled me out of the hospital. The nurses were concerned about me as I sailed blissfully by them … dutifully wearing my lizard cure around my neck.—TRH

Raistlin slid out of the pipe, nearly falling on Bupu. The mage, looking around, thought for an instant that he had tumbled into a fire. Great, billowing clouds of white rolled around the room. Raistlin began to cough and gasp for breath.

"Wha—?" Flint flew out of the end of the pipe, falling on his hands and knees. He peered through the cloud. "Poison?" He gasped crawling over to the mage. Raistlin shook his head, but he couldn't answer. Bupu clutched the mage, dragging him toward the door. Goldmoon slid out on her stomach, knocking the breath from her body. Riverwind tumbled out, twisting his body to avoid hitting Goldmoon. There was a clanging bang as Caramon's shield shot from the pipe. Caramon's spiked armor and broad girth had slowed him enough so that he was able to crawl out of the pipe. But he was bruised and battered and covered with green filth. By the time Tanis arrived, everyone was gagging in the powdery atmosphere.

"What in the name of the Abyss?" Tanis said, astonished, then promptly choked as he inhaled a lungful of the white stuff. "Get out of here," he croaked. "Where's that gully dwarf?"

Bupu appeared in the doorway. She had taken Raistlin out of the room and was now motioning to the others. They emerged thankfully into the unclouded air and slumped down to rest among the ruins of a street. Tanis hoped they weren't waiting for an army of draconians. Suddenly he looked up. "Where's Tas?" he asked in alarm, staggering to his feet.

"Here I am," said a choked and miserable voice.

Tanis whirled around.

Tasslehoff—at least Tanis presumed it was Tasslehoff—stood before him. The kender was covered from topknot to toes in a thick, white, pasty substance. All Tanis could see of him were two brown eyes blinking out of a white mask.

"What happened?" the half-elf asked. He had never seen anyone quite so miserable as the bedraggled kender.

Tasslehoff didn't answer. He just pointed back inside.

Tanis, fearing something disastrous, ran over and peered cautiously through the crumbling doorway.

The white cloud had dissipated so that he could see around the room now. Over in one corner—directly opposite the pipe opening—stood a number of large, bulging sacks. Two of them had been split open, spilling a mass of white onto the floor.

Then Tanis understood. He put his hand over his face to hide his smile. "Flour," he murmured.

19

The broken city.
Highbulp Phudge I, the Great.

In the original proposal, the Cataclysm was described thus: "The face of all Ansalon was changed in one surge of cosmic force, and the peoples of the land were left to crawl out from beneath their broken dreams."

The night of the Cataclysm† had been a night of horror for the city of Xak Tsaroth. When the fiery mountain struck Krynn, the land split apart. The ancient and beautiful city of Xak Tsaroth slid down the face of a cliff into a vast cavern formed by the huge rents in the ground. Thus, underground, it was lost to the sight of men, and most people believed the city had vanished entirely, swallowed up by Newsea. But it still existed, clinging to the rough sides of the cavern walls, spread out upon the floor of the cavern—there were ruined buildings on several different levels. The building the companions had fallen into, which Tanis assumed must have been a bakery, was on the middle level, caught by rocks and held up against the sheer cliff face. Water from underground

streams flowed down the sides of the rock and ran into the street, swirling among the ruins.

Tanis's gaze followed the course of the water. It ran down the middle of the cracked cobblestone street, running past other small shops and houses where people had once lived and gone about their business. When the city fell, the tall buildings that once lined the street toppled against one another, forming a crude archway of broken marble slabs above the cobblestones. Doors and broken shop windows yawned into the street. All was still and quiet, except for the noise of the dripping water. The air was heavy with the odor of decay. It weighed upon the spirit. And though the air was warmer down beneath the ground level than up above, the gloomy atmosphere chilled the blood. No one spoke. They washed the slime from their bodies (and the flour from Tas) as best they could, then refilled their water skins. Sturm and Caramon searched the area but saw no draconians. After a few moments of rest, the companions rose and moved on.

Bupu led them south, down the street, beneath the archway of ruined buildings. The street opened into a plaza—here the water in the streets became a river, flowing west.

"Follow river." Bupu pointed.

Tanis frowned, hearing above the noise of the river another sound, the crashing and roaring of a great waterfall. But Bupu insisted, so the heroes edged their way around the plaza river, occasionally plunging ankle deep in the water. Reaching the end of the street, the companions discovered the waterfall. The street dropped off into air, and the river gushed out from between broken columns to fall nearly five hundred feet into the bottom of the cavern. There rested the remainder of the ruined city of Xak Tsaroth.

They could see by the dim light that filtered through cracks in the cavern roof far above that the heart of the ancient city lay scattered about on the floor of the cavern in many states of decay. Some of the buildings were almost completely intact. Others, however, were nothing but rubble. A chill fog, created by the many waterfalls plunging down into the cavern, hung over the city. Most of the streets had become rivers, which combined to flow into a deep abyss to the north. Peering through the mists, the companions could see the huge chain hanging only a few hundred feet away, slightly north of their present position. They realized that the lift raised and lowered people at least one thousand feet.

"Where does the Highbulp live?" Tanis asked, looking down into the dead city below him.

"Bupu says he lives over there"—Raistlin gestured—"in those buildings on the western side of the cavern."

"And who lives in the reconstructed buildings right below us?" Tanis asked.

"Bosses," Bupu replied, scowling.

"How many bosses?"

"One, and one, and one." Bupu counted until she had used up all her fingers. "Two," she said. "Not more than two."

"Which could be anything from two hundred to two thousand," Sturm muttered. "How do we get to see the Highwhoop."

"Highbulp!" Bupu glared at him. "Highbulp Phudge I. The great."

"How do we get to him, without the bosses catching us?"

In answer, Bupu pointed upward to the rising pot full of draconians. Tanis looked blank, glanced at Sturm who shrugged disgustedly. Bupu sighed in exasperation and turned to Raistlin, obviously considering the others incapable of understanding. "Bosses go up. We go down," she said.

Raistlin stared at the lift through the mist. Then he nodded in understanding. "The draconians probably believe that we are trapped up there with no way to get down into the city. If most of the draconians are up above, that would allow us to move safely below."

"All right," Sturm said. "But how in the name of Istar do we get down? Most of us can't fly!"

Bupu spread her hands. "Vines!" she said. Seeing everyone's look of confusion, the gully dwarf stumped over to the edge of the waterfall and pointed down. Thick, green vines hung over the edge of the rocky cliff like giant snakes. The leaves on the vines were torn, tattered, and, in some places, stripped off entirely, but the vines

themselves appeared thick and tough, even if they were slippery.

Goldmoon, unusually pale, crept toward the edge, peered over, and backed away hurriedly. It was a five-hundred-foot drop straight down to a rubble-strewn cobblestone street. Riverwind put his arm around her, comfortingly.

"I've climbed worse," Caramon said complacently.

"Well, I don't like it," said Flint. "But anything's better than sliding down a sewer." Grabbing hold of the vine, he swung himself over the ledge and began to inch slowly down hand over hand. "It's not bad," he shouted up.

Tasslehoff slid down a vine after Flint, traveling rapidly and with such skill that he received a grunt of approbation from Bupu.

The gully dwarf turned to look at Raistlin, pointing at his long, flowing robes and frowning. The mage smiled at her reassuringly. Standing on the edge of the cliff, he said softly, *"Pveathrfall."* The crystal ball on top of his staff flared and Raistlin leaped off the edge of the cliff, disappearing into the mist below. Bupu shrieked. Tanis caught her, fearing the adoring gully dwarf might throw herself over.

"He'll be fine," the half-elf assured her, feeling a flash of pity when he saw the look of genuine anguish on her face. "He is magi," he said. "Magic. You know."

Bupu obviously did *not* know because she stared at Tanis suspiciously, threw her bag around her neck, grabbed hold of a vine, and began scrabbling down the slippery rock. The rest of the companions were preparing to follow when Goldmoon whispered brokenly, "I can't."

Riverwind took her hands. *"Kan-toka,"* he said softly, "it will be all right. You heard what the dwarf said. Just don't look down."

Goldmoon shook her head, her chin quivering. "There must be another way," she said stubbornly. "We will search for it!"

"What's the problem?" Tanis asked. "We should hurry—"

"She's afraid of heights,"† Riverwind said.

Goldmoon shoved him away. "How dare you tell him that!" she shouted, her face flushed with anger.

I am also afraid of heights, and thus I know exactly how Goldmoon felt!—MW

Riverwind stared at her coldly. "Why not?" he said, his voice grating. "He's not your subject. You can let him know you're human, that you have human frailties. You have only one subject to impress now, Chieftain, and that is me!"

If Riverwind had stabbed her, he could have inflicted no more terrible pain. The color drained from Goldmoon's lips. Her eyes grew wide and staring, like the eyes of a corpse. "Please secure the staff on my back," she said to Tanis.

"Goldmoon, he didn't mean—" he began.

"Do as I command!" she ordered curtly, her blue eyes blazing in anger.

Tanis, sighing, tied the staff to her back with a length of rope. Goldmoon did not even glance at Riverwind. When the staff was fastened tightly, she started toward the edge of the cliff. Sturm jumped in front of her.

"Allow me to go down the vine ahead of you," he said. "If you slip—"

"If I slip and fall, you'd fall with me. The only thing we'd accomplish would be to die together," she snapped. Leaning down, she took a firm grip on the vine and swung herself over the edge. Almost immediately, her sweating hands slipped. Tanis's breath caught in his throat. Sturm lunged forward, though he knew there wasn't anything he could do. Riverwind stood watching, not a sign of emotion on his face. Goldmoon clutched frantically at the vines and thick leaves. She caught hold and clung to them tightly, unable to breathe, unwilling to move. She pressed her face against the wet leaves, shuddering, her eyes closed to block out the sight of the terrifying drop to the ground below. Sturm went over the edge and climbed down to her.

"Leave me alone," Goldmoon said to him through clenched teeth. She drew a trembling breath, cast a proud, defiant glance at Riverwind, then began to lower herself down the vine.

Sturm stayed near her, keeping an eye on her, as he skillfully climbed down the cliff face. Tanis, standing next to Riverwind, wanted to say something to the Plainsman but feared to do more harm. Saying nothing, therefore, he went over the edge. Riverwind followed silently.

The half-elf found the climb easy, though he slipped the last few feet, landing in an inch of water. Raistlin, he noticed, was shivering with the cold, his cough worsening in the damp air. Several gully dwarves stood around the mage, staring at him with admiring eyes. Tanis wondered how long the charm spell would last.

Goldmoon leaned against the wall, shaking. She did not look at Riverwind as he reached the ground and moved away from her, his face still expressionless.

"Where are we?" Tanis shouted above the noise of the waterfall. The mist was so thick he couldn't see anything except broken columns, overgrown with vines and fungus.

"Great Plaza that way." Bupu urgently jabbed her grubby finger toward the west. "Come. You follow. Go see Highbulp!"

She started off. Tanis reached out his hand and caught hold of her, dragging her to a stop. She glared at him, deeply offended. The half-elf removed his hand. "Please. Just listen a moment! What about the dragon? Where's the dragon?"

Bupu's eyes widened. "You want dragon?" she asked.

"No!" yelled Tanis. "We don't want the dragon. But we need to know if the dragon comes into this part of the city—" He felt Sturm's hand on his shoulder and gave up. "Forget it. Never mind," he said wearily. "Go on."

Bupu regarded Raistlin with deep sympathy for having to put up with these insane people, then she took the mage's hand and trotted off down the street to the west, the other gully dwarves trailing along behind. Half-deafened by the thundering noise of the waterfall, the companions waded after, glancing about them uneasily, dark windows loomed above them, dark doorways threatened. At each moment, they expected scaly, armored draconians to appear. But the gully dwarves did not seem concerned. They sloshed along the street, keeping as close to Raistlin as possible, and jabbering in their uncouth language.

Eventually the sounds of the waterfall faded in the distance. The mist continued to swirl around them, however, and the silence of the dead city was oppressive. Dark water gushed and gurgled past their feet along the cobblestone riverbed. Suddenly the buildings came to an end and the street opened into a huge, circular plaza. Through the water they could see the remnants in the plaza of flagstone paving in an intricate sunburst design. In the center of the plaza, the river was joined by another stream rushing in from the north. They formed a small whirlpool as the waters met and swirled before joining and continuing west between another group of tumble-down buildings.

Here, light streamed into the plaza from a crack in the cavern roof hundreds of feet above, illuminating the ghostly mists, dancing off the surface of the water whenever the mists parted.

"Other side Great Plaza," Bupu pointed.

The companions came to a halt in the shadows of the ruined buildings. All of them had the same thought: The plaza was over one hundred feet across without a scrap of shelter. Once they ventured out, there would be no hiding.

Bupu, trotting along without concern, suddenly realized no one was following her except other gully dwarves. She looked back, irritated at the delay. "You come, Highbulp this way."

"Look!" Goldmoon grasped Tanis's arm.

On the other side of the great flagstone plaza were great, tall marble columns that supported a stone roof. The columns were cracked and shattered, letting the roof sag. The mists parted and Tanis caught a glimpse of a courtyard behind the columns. Dark forms of tall, domed buildings were visible beyond the courtyard. Then the mists closed around them. Though now sunk into degradation and ruin, this structure must have once been the most magnificent in Xak Tsaroth.

"The Royal Palace," Raistlin confirmed, coughing.

"Shhhh!" Goldmoon shook Tanis's arm. "Can't you see? No, wait—"

The mists flowed in front of the pillars. For a moment the companions could not see anything. Then the fog swirled away. The companions shrank back into the dark doorway. The gully dwarves came to a skidding halt in the plaza and, whirling around, raced back to cower behind Raistlin.

Bupu peered at Tanis from under the mage's sleeve. "That dragon," she said. "You want?"

It was the dragon.

Sleek and shining black, her leathery wings folded at her side, Khisanth† slithered out from under the roof, ducking her head to fit beneath the sagging stone facade. Her clawed front feet clicked on the marble stairs as she stopped and stared into the floating mist with her bright red eyes. Her back legs and heavy reptilian tail were not visible, the dragon's body extending thirty feet or more back into the courtyard. A cringing draconian walked beside her, the two apparently deep in conversation.

Also known as Onyx, Khisanth's history and how she got to Xak Tsaroth, under the control of the Dark Queen, is told in The Black Wing *by Mary Kirchoff. Onyx cannot be released until a warrior approaches her, armed only with a staff.*

Khisanth was angry. The draconian had brought her disturbing news—it was impossible that any of the strangers could have survived her attack at the well! But now the captain of her guard reported strangers in the city! Strangers who attacked her forces with skill and daring, strangers bearing a brown staff whose description was known to every draconian serving in this part of the Ansalon continent.

"I cannot believe this report! None could have escaped me." Khisanth's voice was soft, almost purring, yet the draconian trembled as he heard it. "The staff was not with them. I would have sensed its presence. You say these intruders are still above, in the upper chambers? Are you certain?"

The draconian gulped and nodded. "There is no way down, royal one, except the lift."

"There are other ways, you lizard," Khisanth sneered. "These miserable gully dwarves crawl around the place like parasites. The intruders have the staff, and they are trying to get down into the city. That means only one thing—they are after the Disks! How could they have learned of them?" The dragon snaked her head around and up and down as if she could see those who threatened her plans through the blinding mists. But the mists swirled past, thicker than ever.

Khisanth snarled in irritation. "The staff! That miserable staff! Verminaard should have foreseen this with those clerical powers he touts so highly, then it could have been destroyed. But, no, he is busy with his war while I must rot here in this dank tomb of a city." Khisanth gnawed a talon as she pondered.

"You could destroy the Disks," the draconian suggested, greatly daring.

"Fool, don't you think we've tried?" Khisanth muttered. She lifted her head. "No, it is far too dangerous to stay here longer. If these intruders know of the secret, others must also. The Disks should be removed to a safe place. Inform Lord Verminaard that I am leaving Xak Tsaroth. I will join him in Pax Tharkas and I will bring the intruders with me for questioning."

"*Inform* Lord Verminaard?" the draconian asked, shocked.

"Very well," Khisanth responded sarcastically. "If you insist on the charade, *ask* my Lord's permission.† I suppose you have sent most of the troops up to the top?"

The evil dragons assumed the position of underlings in their relations with the dragon highlords. But the dragons knew who was really in control.

"Yes, royal one." The draconian bowed.

Khisanth considered the matter. "Perhaps you are not such an idiot after all," she mused. "I can handle things below. Concentrate your search in the upper parts of the city. When you find these intruders, bring them straight to me. Do not hurt them any more than necessary to subdue them. And be careful of that staff!"

The draconian fell to its knees before the dragon, who sniffed in derision and crept back into the dark shadows out of which she had come.

The draconian ran down the stairs where it was joined by several more creatures who appeared out of the mist. After a brief, muffled exchange in their own language, the draconians started up the north street. They walked nonchalantly, laughing at some private joke, and soon vanished into the mist.

"They're not worried, are they?" Sturm said.

"No," Tanis agreed grimly. "They think they've got us."

"Let's face it, Tanis. They're right," Sturm said. "This plan we've been discussing has one major flaw. If we sneak in without the dragon knowing, and *if* we get the Disks—we still have to get out of this godforsaken city with draconians crawling all over the upper levels."

"I asked you before and I'll ask you now," Tanis said. "Have you got a better plan?"

"I've got a better plan," Caramon said gruffly. "No disrespect, Tanis, but we all know how elves feel about fighting." The big man gestured toward the palace. "That's obviously where the dragon

lives. Let's lure it out as we planned, only this time we'll fight it, not creep around its lair like thieves. When the dragon's disposed of, then we can get the Disks."

"My dear brother," Raistlin whispered, "your strength lies in your sword-arm, not in your mind. Tanis is wise, as the knight said when we started on this little adventure. You would do well to pay attention to him. What do you know of dragons, my brother? You have seen the effects of its deadly breath."† Raistlin was overcome by a fit of coughing. He dragged a soft cloth out from the sleeve of his robe. Tanis saw that the cloth was stained with blood.

A black dragon's breath weapon is a stream of acid. And, as we've already seen, the dragon's favorite magic spell is Darkness, in which it can hide.

After a moment, Raistlin continued. "You could defend yourself against that, perhaps, and against the sharp claws and fangs, and the slashing tail, which can knock down those pillars. But what will you use, dear brother, against her magic? Dragons are the most ancient of magic-users. She could charm you as I have charmed my little friend. She could put you to sleep with a word, then murder you while you dreamed."

"All right," Caramon muttered, chagrined. "I didn't know any of that. Damn it, who does know anything about these creatures!"

"There is much lore on the dragons in Solamnia," Sturm said softly.

He wants to fight the dragon, too, Tanis realized. He is thinking of Huma, the perfect knight, called Dragonbane.

Bupu tugged on Raistlin's robe. "Come. You go. No more bosses. No more dragon." She and the other gully dwarves started splashing across the flagstone plaza.

"Well?" Tanis said, looking at the two warriors.

"It seems we have no choice," Sturm said stiffly. "We do not face the enemy, we hide behind gully dwarves! Sooner or later a time must come when we face these monsters!" He spun on his heel and walked off, his back straight, his moustaches bristling. The companions followed.

"Maybe we're worrying needlessly." Tanis scratched his beard, glancing back at the palace that was now obscured by the mist. "Perhaps this is the only dragon left in Krynn—one that survived the Age of Dreams."

Raistlin's lips twisted. "Remember the stars, Tanis," he murmured. "The Queen of Darkness has returned. Recall the words of the Canticle: 'swarm of her shrieking hosts.' Her hosts were dragons, according to the ancient ones. She has returned and her hosts have come with her."

"This way!" Bupu clutched at Raistlin, pointing down a street branching off to the north. "This home!"

"At least it's dry," Flint grumbled. Turning right, they left the river behind them. Mist closed in around the companions as they entered another nest of ruined buildings. This section of town must have been the poorer part of the city of Xak Tsaroth, even in its glory days—the buildings were in the last stages of decay and collapse. The gully dwarves began whooping and hollering as they ran down the street. Sturm looked at Tanis in alarm at the noise.

"Can't you get them to be quieter?" Tanis asked Bupu. "So the draconians, er, bosses won't find us."

"Pooh!" She shrugged. "No bosses. They not come here. Afraid of the great Highbulp."

Tanis had his doubts about that, but, glancing around, he couldn't see any signs of the draconians. From what he had observed, the lizardlike men seemed to lead a well-ordered, militaristic life. By contrast, the streets in this part of town were cluttered with trash and filth. The disreputable buildings erupted with gully dwarves. Males, females, and dirty, ragged children stared at them curiously as they walked down the street. Bupu and the other spellbound gully dwarves swarmed around Raistlin, practically carrying him.

The draconians were undeniably smart, Tanis thought. They allowed their slaves to live their private lives in peace—so long as they didn't stir up trouble. A good idea, considering that gully dwarves outnumbered draconians about ten to one. Though they were basically cowards, gully dwarves had a reputation as very nasty fighters when backed into a corner.

Bupu brought the group to a halt in front of one of the darkest, dingiest, filthiest alleys Tanis had ever seen. A foul mist flowed out from it. The buildings leaned over, holding each other up like drunks

stumbling out of a tavern. As he watched, small dark creatures skittered out of the alley and gully dwarf children began chasing after them.

"Dinner," shrieked one, smacking his lips.

"Those are rats!"† Goldmoon cried in horror.

"Do we have to go in there?" Sturm growled, staring at the tottering buildings.

"The smell alone is enough to knock a troll dead," Caramon added. "And I'd rather die under the dragon's claw than have a gully dwarf hovel fall on top of me."

Bupu gestured down the alley. "The Highbulp!" she said, pointing to the most dilapidated building on the block.

"Stay here and keep watch if you want," Tanis told Sturm. "I'll go talk with the Highbulp."

"No." The knight scowled, gesturing the half-elf into the alley. "We're in this together."

The alley ran several hundred feet to the east, then it twisted north and came suddenly to a dead end. Ahead of them was a decaying brick wall and no way out. Their return was blocked by gully dwarves who had run in after them.

"Ambush!" Sturm hissed and drew his sword. Caramon began to rumble deep in his throat. The gully dwarves, seeing the flash of cold steel, panicked. Falling all over themselves and each other, they whirled and fled back down the alley.

Bupu glared at Sturm and Caramon in disgust. She turned to Raistlin. "You make them stop!" she demanded, pointing to the warriors. "Or I not take to Highbulp."

"Put your sword away, knight," Raistlin hissed, "unless you think you've found a foe worthy of your attention."

Sturm glowered at Raistlin, and for a moment Tanis thought he might attack the mage, but then the knight thrust his sword away. "I wish I knew what your game was, magician," Sturm said coldly. "You were so eager to come to this city, even before we knew about the Disks. Why? What are you after?"

Raistlin did not reply. He stared at the knight malevolently with his strange golden eyes, then turned to Bupu. "They will not trouble you further, little one," he whispered.

In later years, Tika collected recipes from all over Krynn, including one from Bupu for "Rat-Dipping Fondue." After assembling the ingredients, the instructions go on: "Melt cheese, dip rat, drink wine, take nap."

Bupu looked around to make certain they were properly cowed, then she walked forward and knocked twice on the wall with her grubby fist. "Secret door," she said importantly.

Two knocks answered Bupu's knock.

"That signal," she said. "Three knocks. Now they let in."

"But she only knocked twice—" Tas began, giggling.

Bupu glared at him.

"Shhh!" Tanis nudged the kender.

Nothing happened. Bupu, frowning, knocked twice more. Two knocks answered. She waited. Caramon, his eyes on the alley opening, began moving restlessly from one foot to the other. Bupu knocked twice again. Two knocks answered.

Finally Bupu yelled at the wall. "I knock secret code knock. You let in!"

"Secret knock five knocks," answered a muffled voice.

"I knock five knocks!" Bupu stated angrily. "You let in!"

"You knock six knocks."

"I count eight knocks," argued another voice.

Bupu suddenly pushed on the wall with both hands. It opened easily. She peered inside. "I knock four knocks. You let in!" she said, raising a clenched fist.

"All right," the voice grumbled.

Bupu shut the door, knocked twice. Tanis, hoping to avoid any more incidents and delays, glared at the kender, who was writhing with suppressed laughter.

The door swung open—again. "You come in," the guard said sourly. "But that not four knocks," he whispered to Bupu loudly. She ignored him as she swept disdainfully past him, dragging her bag along the floor.

"We see Highbulp," she announced.

"You take this lot to Highbulp?" One of the guards gasped, staring at the giant Caramon and the tall Riverwind with wide eyes. His companion began backing up.

"See Highbulp," Bupu said proudly.

The gully dwarf guard, never taking his eyes off the formidable-looking group, backed into a stinking,

filthy hallway, then broke into a run. He began shouting at the top of his lungs. "An army! An army has broken in!" They could hear his shouts echo down the hallway.

"Bah!" Bupu sniffed. "Glup-phungert spawn! Come. See Highbulp."

One of the few expressions in the gully dwarf language included here. We have no idea what it means and figure we're probably happier not knowing!—MW

She started down the hallway, clutching her bag to her chest. The companions could still hear the shouts of the gully dwarf echoing down the corridor.

"An army! An army of giants! Save the Highbulp!"

The great Highbulp, Phudge I, was a gully dwarf among gully dwarves. He was almost intelligent, rumored to be fabulously wealthy, and a notorious coward. The Bulps had long been the elite clan of Xak Tsaroth—or "Th" as they called it—ever since Nulph Bulp fell down a shaft one night in a drunken stupor and discovered the city. Upon sobering up the next morning, he claimed it for his clan. The Bulps promptly moved in and, in later years, graciously allowed the clans Slud and Glup to occupy the city as well.

Life was good in the ruined city—by gully dwarf standards, anyway. The outside world left them alone (since the outside world hadn't the foggiest notion they were there and wouldn't have cared if it did). The Bulps had no trouble maintaining their dominance over the other clans, mostly because it was a Bulp (Glunggu) with a scientific turn of mind (certain jealous members of the Slud clan whispered that his mother had been a gnome) who developed the lift, putting to use the two enormous iron pots used by the city's former residents for rendering lard. The lift enabled the gully dwarves to extend their scavenging activities to the jungle above the sunken city, greatly improving their standard of living. Glunggu Bulp became a hero and was proclaimed Highbulp by unanimous decision. The chieftainship of the clans had remained in the Bulp family ever since.

The years passed and then, suddenly, the outside world took an interest in Xak Tsaroth. The arrival of the dragon and the draconians put a sad crimp on the gully dwarf lifestyle. The draconians had initially intended to wipe out the filthy little nuisances, but

the gully dwarves—led by the great Phudge—had cringed and cowered and whimpered and wailed and prostrated themselves so abjectly that the draconians were merciful and simply enslaved them.

So it was that the gully dwarves—for the first time in several hundred years of living in Xak Tsaroth—were forced to work. The draconians repaired buildings, put things into military order, and generally made life miserable for the gully dwarves who had to cook and clean and repair things.

Needless to say, the great Phudge was not pleased with this state of affairs. He spent long hours thinking up ways to remove the dragon. He knew the location of the dragon's lair, of course, and had even discovered a secret route leading there. He had actually sneaked in once, when the dragon was away. Phudge had been awestruck by the vast amount of pretty rocks and shining coins gathered in the huge underground room. The great Highbulp had traveled some in his wild youth and he knew that folk in the outside world coveted these pretty rocks and would give vast amounts of colorful and gaudy cloth (Phudge had a weakness for fine clothes) in return. On the spot, the Highbulp drew up a map so he wouldn't forget how to get back to the treasure. He even had the presence of mind to swipe a few of the smaller rocks.

Phudge dreamed of this wealth for months afterward, but he never found another opportunity to return. This was due to two factors: one, the dragon never left again and, two, Phudge couldn't make heads nor tails of his map.

If only the dragon would leave permanently, he thought, or if some hero would come along and conveniently stick a sword into it! These were the Highbulp's fondest dreams, and this was the state of affairs when the great Phudge heard his guards proclaiming that an army was attacking.

Thus it came to pass that—when Bupu finally dragged the great Phudge out from under his bed and convinced him that he was not about to be set upon by an army of giants—Highbulp Phudge I began to believe that dreams could come true.

"And so you're here to kill the dragon," said the great Highbulp, Phudge I, to Tanis Half-Elven.

"No," Tanis said patiently, "we're not."

The companions stood in the Court of the Aghar before the throne of a gully dwarf Bupu had introduced as the great Highbulp. Bupu kept an eye on the companions as they entered the throne room, eagerly anticipating their looks of stunned awe. Bupu was not disappointed. The looks on the companions' faces as they entered might well be described as stunned.

The city of Xak Tsaroth had been stripped of its finery by the early Bulps who used it to decorate the throne room of their lord. Following the philosophy that if one yard of gold cloth is good, forty yards is better, and totally uninhibited by good taste, the gully dwarves turned the throne room of the great Highbulp into a masterpiece of confusion. Heavy, frayed gold cloth swirled and draped every available inch of wall space. Huge tapestries hung from the ceiling (some of them upside-down). The tapestries must have once been beautiful, delicate-colored threads blending to show scenes of city life, or portray stories and legends from the past. But the gully dwarves, wanting to liven them up, painted over the cloth in garish, clashing colors.

Thus Sturm was shocked to the core of his being when confronted by a bright red Huma battling a purple-spotted dragon beneath an emerald-green sky.

Graceful, nude statues, standing in all the wrong places, adorned the room as well. These, too, the gully dwarves had enhanced, considering pure white marble drab and depressing. They painted the statues with enough realism and attention to detail that Caramon—with an embarrassed glance at Goldmoon—flushed bright red and kept his eyes on the floor.

The companions, in fact, had problems maintaining their serious mien when ushered into this gallery of artistic horrors. One failed utterly: Tasslehoff was immediately overcome by the giggles so severely that Tanis was forced to send the kender back to the Waiting Place outside the Court to try and compose himself. The rest of the group bowed solemnly to the great Phudge—with the exception of Flint who stood bolt upright, his hands fingering his battle-axe, without the trace of a smile on his aged face.

The dwarf had laid his hand on Tanis's arm before they entered the court of the Highbulp. "Don't be taken in by this foolery, Tanis," Flint warned. "These creatures can be treacherous."

The Highbulp was somewhat flustered when the companions entered, especially at the sight of the tall fighters. But Raistlin made a few well-chosen remarks that considerably mollified and reassured (if disappointed) the Highbulp.

The mage, interrupted by fits of coughing, explained that they did not want to cause trouble, they simply planned to retrieve an object of religious value from the dragon's lair and leave, preferably without disturbing the dragon.

This, of course, didn't fit in with Phudge's plans. He therefore assumed he hadn't heard correctly. Cocooned in gaudy robes, he leaned back in the chipped gold-leaf throne and repeated calmly—"You here. Got swords. Kill dragon."

"No," said Tanis again. "As our friend, Raistlin, explained, the dragon is guarding an object that belongs to our gods. We want to remove the object and escape the city before the dragon is aware that it is gone."

The Highbulp frowned. "How me know you not take all treasure, leave Highbulp only one mad dragon? There be lot of treasure, pretty rocks."

Raistlin looked up sharply, his eyes gleaming. Sturm, fidgeting with his sword, glanced at the mage in disgust.

"We will bring you the pretty rocks," Tanis assured the Highbulp. "Help us and you will get all the treasure. We want only to find this relic of our gods."

It had become obvious to the Highbulp that he was dealing with thieves and liars, not the heroes he had expected. This group was apparently as frightened of the dragon as he was and that gave the Highbulp an idea. "What you want from Highbulp?" he asked, trying to subdue his glee and appear subtle.

Tanis sighed in relief. At last they seemed to be getting somewhere. "Bupu"—he indicated the female gully dwarf clinging to Raistlin's sleeve—"told us that you were the only one in the city who could lead us to the dragon's lair."

"Lead!" The great Phudge lost his composure for a moment and clutched his robes around him. "No lead! Great Highbulp not expendable.† People need me!"

"No, no. I didn't mean lead," Tanis amended hastily. "If you had a map or could send someone to show us the way."

The king or chieftain or a clan of gully dwarves is the authority over the clan, but it certainly isn't an unquestioned authority.

"Map!" Phudge mopped the sweat off his brow with the sleeve of his robe. "Should say so in first place. Map. Yes. I send for map. Meantime, you eat. Guests of the Highbulp. Guards take to mess hall."

"No, thank you," Tanis said politely, unable to look at the others. They had passed the gully dwarf mess hall on their way to see the Highbulp. The smell alone had been enough to ruin even Caramon's appetite.

"We have our own food," Tanis continued. "We would like some time to ourselves to rest and discuss our plans further."

"Certainly." The Highbulp scooted forward to the front of the throne. Two of his guards came over to help him down since his feet didn't touch the floor. "Go back to Waiting Place. Sit. Eat. Talk. I send map. Maybe you tell Phudge plans?"

Tanis glanced swiftly at the gully dwarf and saw the Highbulp's squinty eyes gleam with cunning. The half-elf felt cold, suddenly realizing this gully dwarf was no buffoon. Tanis began to wish he had talked more with Flint. "Our plans are hardly formed yet, your majesty," the half-elf said.

The great Highbulp knew better. Long ago he had drilled a hole through the wall of the room known as Waiting Place so that he could eavesdrop on his subjects as they waited for an audience with him, discovering what they intended to bother him about in advance. Thus he knew a great deal about the companions' plans already, so he let the matter drop. The use of the term "your majesty" may have had something to do with this; the Highbulp had never heard anything quite so suitable.

"Your majesty," Phudge repeated, sighing with pleasure. He poked one of his guards in the back. "You remember. From now on, say 'Your Majesty.'"

"Y-yes, y-your, uh, majesty," the gully dwarf stuttered. The great Phudge waved his filthy hand graciously and the companions bowed their way out.

Highbulp, Phudge I, stood for a moment beside his throne, smiling in what he considered a charming manner until his guests were gone. Then his expression changed, transforming into a smile so shrewd and devious his guards crowded around him in eager anticipation.

"You," he said to one. "Go to quarters. Bring map. Give to fools in next room."

The guard saluted and ran off. The other guard remained close, waiting in open-mouthed expectation. Phudge glanced around, then drew the guard even nearer, considering exactly how to phrase his next command. He needed some heroes and if he had to create his own out of whatever scum came along, then he would do so. If they died, it was no great loss. If they succeeded in killing the dragon, so much the better. The gully dwarves would get what was—to them—more precious than all the pretty rocks in Krynn: a return to the sweet, halcyon days of freedom! And so, enough of this nonsense about sneaking around.

Phudge leaned over and whispered in the guard's ear. "You go to dragon. Give her best regards of his majesty, Highbulp, Phudge I, and tell her . . . "

20

The Highbulp's Map.

A spellbook of Fistandantilus.

"I don't trust that little bastard any farther than I can stand the smell of him," Caramon growled.

"I agree," Tanis said quietly. "But what choice do we have? We've agreed to bring him the treasure. He has everything to lose and nothing to gain if he betrays us."

They sat on the floor in the Waiting Place, a filthy antechamber outside the throne room. The decorations in this room were just as vulgar as in the Court. The companions were nervous and tense, speaking little and forcing themselves to eat.

Raistlin refused food. Curled up on the floor apart from the others, he prepared and drank down the strange herbal mixture that eased his cough. Then he wrapped himself in his robes and stretched

out, eyes closed, on the floor. Bupu sat curled up near him, munching on something from her bag. Caramon, going over to check on his brother, was horrified to see a tail disappear into her mouth with a slurp.

Riverwind sat by himself. He did not take part in the hushed conversation as the friends went over their plans once again. The Plainsman stared moodily at the floor. When he felt a light touch on his arm, he didn't even lift his head. Goldmoon, her face pale, knelt beside him. She tried to speak, failed, then cleared her throat.

"We must talk," she said firmly in their language.

"Is that a command?" he asked bitterly.

She swallowed. "Yes," she answered, barely audible.

Riverwind rose to his feet and walked over to stand in front of a garish tapestry. He did not look at Goldmoon or even speak to her. His face was drawn into a stern mask, but underneath, Goldmoon could see the searing pain in his soul. She gently laid her hand on his arm.

"Forgive me," she said softly.

Riverwind regarded her in astonishment. She stood before him, her head bowed, an almost childlike shame on her face. He reached out to stroke the silver-gold hair of the one he loved more than life itself. He felt Goldmoon tremble at his touch and his heart ached with love. Moving his hand from her head to her neck, he very gently and tenderly drew the beloved head to his chest and then suddenly clasped her in his arms.

"I've never heard you say those words before," he said, smiling to himself, knowing she could not see him.

"I have never said them," she gulped, her cheek pressed against his leather shirt. "Oh, my beloved, I am sorrier than I can say that you came home to Chieftain's Daughter and not Goldmoon. But I've been so afraid."

"No," he whispered, "I am the one who should ask forgiveness." He raised his hand to wipe away her tears. "I didn't realize what you had gone through. All I could think of was myself and the dangers I had faced. I wish you had told me, heart's dearest."

"I wished you had asked," she replied, looking up at him earnestly. "I have been Chieftain's Daughter so long it is the only thing I know how to be. It is my strength. It gives me courage when I am frightened. I don't think I can let go."

"I don't want you to let go." He smiled at her, smoothing wayward strands of hair from her face. "I fell in love with Chieftain's Daughter† the first time I saw you. Do you remember? At the games held in your honor."

Goldmoon and Riverwind's story, which was supposed to be experienced in my wife's HeartQuest book, was finally told in the short story "Heart of Goldmoon" by Laura Hickman and Kate Novak, which appears in Love and War.*—TRH*

"You refused to bow to receive my blessing," she said. "You acknowledged my father's leadership but denied that I was a goddess. You said man could not make gods of other men." Her eyes looked back so many, many years. "How tall and proud and handsome you were, talking of ancient gods that did not exist to me then."

"And how furious you were," he recalled, "and how beautiful! Your beauty was a blessing to me in itself. I needed no other. You wanted me thrown out of the games."

Goldmoon smiled sadly. "You thought I was angry because you had shamed me before the people, but that was not so."

"No? What was it then, Chieftain's Daughter?"

Her face flushed a dusky rose, but she lifted her clear blue eyes to him. "I was angry because I knew when I saw you standing there, refusing to kneel before me, that I had lost part of myself and that, until you claimed it, I would never be whole again."

For reply, the Plainsman pressed her to him, kissing her hair gently.

"Riverwind," she said, swallowing, "Chieftain's Daughter is still here. I don't think she can ever leave. But you must know that Goldmoon is underneath and, if this journey ever ends and we come to peace at last, then Goldmoon will be yours forever and we will banish Chieftain's Daughter to the winds."

A thump at the Highbulp's door caused everyone to start nervously as a gully dwarf guard stumbled into the room. "Map," he said, thrusting a crumpled piece of paper at Tanis.

"Thank you," said the half-elf gravely. "And extend our thanks to the Highbulp."

"His *Majesty*, the Highbulp," the guard corrected with an anxious glance toward a tapestry-covered wall. Bobbing clumsily, he backed into the Highbulp's quarters.

Tanis spread the map flat. Everyone gathered around it, even Flint. After one look, however, the dwarf snorted derisively and walked back to his couch.

Tanis laughed ruefully. "We might have expected it. I wonder if the great Phudge remembers where the 'big secret room' is?"

"Of course not." Raistlin sat up, opening his strange, golden eyes and peering at them through half-closed lids. "That is why he has never returned for the treasure. However, there is one among us who knows where the dragon's lair is located." Everyone followed the mage's gaze.

Bupu glared back at them defiantly. "You right. I know," she said, sulking. "I know secret place. I go there, find pretty rocks. But don't tell Highbulp!"

"Will you tell us?" Tanis asked. Bupu looked at Raistlin. He nodded.

"I tell," she mumbled. "Give map."

Raistlin, seeing the others engrossed in looking at the map, beckoned to his brother.

"Is the plan still the same?" the mage whispered.

"Yes." Caramon frowned. "And I don't like it. I should go with you."

"Nonsense," Raistlin hissed. "You would only be in my way!" Then he added more gently, "I will be in no danger, I assure you." He laid his hand on his twin's arm and drew him close. "Besides"—the mage glanced around—"there is something you must do for me, my brother. Something you must bring me from the dragon's lair."

Raistlin's touch was unusually hot, his eyes burned. Caramon uneasily started to pull back, seeing something in his brother he hadn't seen since the Towers of High Sorcery, but Raistlin's hand clutched at him.

"What is it?" Caramon asked reluctantly.

"A spellbook!" Raistlin whispered.

"So this is why you wanted to come to Xak Tsaroth!" said Caramon. "You knew this spellbook would be here."

"I read about it, years ago. I knew it had been in Xak Tsaroth prior to the Cataclysm, all of the Order knew it, but we assumed it had been destroyed with

the city. When I found out Xak Tsaroth had escaped destruction, I realized there might be a chance the book had survived!"

"How do you know it's in the dragon's lair?"

"I don't. I am merely surmising. To magic-users, this book is Xak Tsaroth's greatest treasure. You may be certain that if the dragon found it, she is using it!"

"And you want me to get it for you," Caramon said slowly. "What does it look like?"

"Like my spellbook, of course, except the bone-white parchment is bound in night-blue leather with runes of silver stamped on the front. It will feel deathly cold to the touch."

"What do the runes say?"

"You do not want to know . . ." Raistlin whispered.

"Whose book was it?" Caramon asked suspiciously.

Raistlin fell silent, his golden eyes abstracted as if he were searching inwardly, trying to remember something forgotten. "You have never heard of him, my brother," he said finally, in a whisper that forced Caramon to lean closer. "Yet he was one of the greatest of my order. His name was Fistandantilus."†

This is the first mention (aloud) of the name of Fistandantilus. He is—was—a legendary archmage with powers that live on … in others and in all times. Read Fistandantilus Reborn *by Douglas Niles.*

"The way you describe the spellbook—" Caramon hesitated, fearing what Raistlin would reply. He swallowed and started over. "This Fistandantilus—did he wear the Black Robes?" He could not meet his brother's piercing gaze.

"Ask me no more!" Raistlin hissed. "You are as bad as the others! How can any of you understand me!" Seeing his twin's look of pain, the mage sighed. "Trust me, Caramon. It is not a particularly powerful spellbook, one of the mage's early books, in fact. One he had when he was very young, very young indeed," Raistlin murmured, staring far off. Then he blinked and said more briskly, "But it will be valuable to me, nonetheless. You must get it! You must—" He started to cough.

"Sure, Raist," Caramon promised, soothing his brother. "Don't get worked up. I'll find it."

"Good Caramon. Excellent Caramon," Raistlin whispered when he could speak. He sank back into the corner and closed his eyes. "Now let me rest. I must be ready."

Caramon stood up, looked at his brother a moment, then he turned around and nearly fell over Bupu who was standing behind him, gazing up at him suspiciously with wide eyes.

"What was all that about?" Sturm asked gruffly as Caramon returned to the group.

"Oh, nothing," the big man mumbled, flushing guiltily. Sturm cast an alarmed glance at Tanis.

"What is it, Caramon?" Tanis asked, putting the rolled map in his belt and facing the warrior. "Anything wrong?"

"N-no—" Caramon stuttered. "It's nothing. I—uh—tried to get Raistlin to let me go with him. He said I'd just be in the way."

Tanis studied Caramon. He knew the big man was telling the truth, but Tanis also knew the warrior wasn't telling all the truth. Caramon would cheerfully shed the last drop of his blood for any member of the company, but Tanis suspected he would betray them all at Raistlin's command.

The giant looked at Tanis, silently begging him to ask no more questions.

"He's right, you know, Caramon," Tanis said finally, clapping the big man on the arm. "Raistlin won't be in danger. Bupu will be with him. She'll bring him back here to hide. He's just got to conjure up some of his fancy pyrotechnics, create a diversion to draw the dragon away from her lair. He'll be long gone by the time she gets there."

"Sure, I know that," said Caramon, forcing a chuckle. "You need me anyway."

"We do," Tanis said seriously. "Now is everyone ready?"

Silently, grimly, they stood up. Raistlin rose and came forward, hood over his face, hands folded in his robes. There was an aura around the mage, indefinable, yet frightening—the aura of power derived and created from within. Tanis cleared his throat.

"We'll give you a five hundred count," Tanis said to Raistlin. "Then we'll start. The 'secret place' marked on the map is a trap door located in a building not far from here, according to your little friend. It leads beneath the city to a tunnel that comes up under the dragon's lair, near where we saw her today. Create your diversion in the plaza, then come

back here. We'll meet here, give the Highbulp his treasure, and lie low until night. When it's dark, we'll escape."

"I understand," Raistlin said calmly.

I wish I did, Tanis thought bitterly. I wish I understood what was going on in that mind of yours, mage. But the half-elf said nothing.

"We go now?" asked Bupu, looking at Tanis anxiously.

"We go now," Tanis said.

Raistlin crept from the shadowy alley and moved swiftly down the street to the south. He saw no signs of life. It was as if all the gully dwarves had been swallowed up by the mist. He found this thought disturbing and kept to the shadows. The frail mage could move silently if there was need. He only hoped he could control his coughing. The pain and congestion in his chest had eased when he drank the herbal mixture whose recipe had been given him by Par-Salian—a kind of apology from the great sorcerer for the trauma the young mage had endured. But the mixture's effect would soon wear off.

Bupu peered out from behind his robes, her beady black eyes squinting down the street leading east to the Great Plaza. "No one," she said and tugged on the mage's robe. "We go now."

No one—thought Raistlin, worried. It didn't make sense. Where were the crowds of gully dwarves? He had the feeling something had gone wrong, but there wasn't time to turn back—Tanis and the others were on their way to the secret tunnel entrance. The mage smiled bitterly. What a fool's quest this was turning out to be. They would probably all die in this wretched city.

Bupu tugged on his robe again. Shrugging, he cast his hood over his head and, together, he and the gully dwarf flitted down the mist-shrouded street.

Two armor-clad figures detached themselves from a dark doorway and slunk quickly after Raistlin and Bupu.

"This is the place," Tanis said softly. Opening a rotting door, he peered in. "It's dark in here. We'll need a light."

There was a sound of flint striking metal and then a flare of light as Caramon lit one of the torches they had borrowed from the Highbulp. The warrior handed one to Tanis and lit one for himself and Riverwind. Tanis stepped inside the building and immediately found himself up to his ankles in water. Holding the torch aloft, he saw water pouring in steady streams down the walls of the dismal room. It swirled around the center of the floor, then ran out through cracks around the edges. Tanis sloshed to the center and held his torch close to the water.

"There it is. I can see it," he said as the others waded into the room. He pointed to a trap door in the floor. An iron pull-ring was barely visible in its center.

"Caramon?" Tanis stood back.

"Bah!" Flint snorted. "If a gully dwarf can open this, I can open it. Stand aside." The dwarf elbowed everyone back, plunged his hand into the water, and heaved. There was a moment's silence. Flint grunted, his face turned red. He stopped, straightened up with a gasp, then reached down and tried again. There wasn't a creak. The door remained shut.

Tanis put his hand on the dwarf's shoulder. "Flint, Bupu says she only goes down during the dry season. You're trying to lift half of Newsea along with the door."

"Well"—the dwarf puffed for breath—"why didn't you say so? Let the big ox try his luck."

Caramon stepped forward. He reached down into the water and gave a heave. His shoulder muscles bulged, and veins in his neck stood out. There was a sucking sound, then the suction was released so suddenly that the big warrior nearly fell over backward. Water drained from the room as Caramon eased the wooden plank door over. Tanis held his torch down to see. A four-foot-square shaft gaped in the floor; a narrow iron ladder descended into the shaft.

"What's the count?" Tanis asked, his throat dry.

"Four hundred and three," answered Sturm's deep voice. "Four hundred and four."

The companions stood around the trap door, shivering in the chill air, hearing nothing but the sound of water pouring down the shaft.

"Four hundred and fifty-one," noted the knight calmly.

Tanis scratched his beard. Caramon coughed twice, as though reminding them of his absent brother. Flint fidgeted and dropped his axe in the water. Tas absent-mindedly chewed on the end of his topknot. Goldmoon, pale but composed, drew near Riverwind, the nondescript brown staff in her hand. He put his arm around her. Nothing was worse than waiting.

"Five hundred," said Sturm finally.

"About time!" Tasslehoff swung himself down onto the ladder. Tanis went next, holding his torch to light the way for Goldmoon, who came after him. The others followed, climbing slowly down into an access shaft of the city sewage system. The shaft ran about twenty feet straight down, then opened up into a five-foot-wide tunnel that ran north and south.

"Check the depth of the water," Tanis warned the kender as Tas was about to let go of the ladder. The kender, hanging onto the last rung with one hand, lowered his hoopak staff into the dark, swirling water below him. The staff sank about half-way.

"Two feet," said Tas cheerfully. He dropped in with a splash, the water hitting him around the thighs. He looked up at Tanis inquiringly.

"That way," Tanis pointed. "South."

Holding his staff in the air, Tasslehoff let the current sweep him along.

"Where's that diversion?" Sturm asked, his voice echoing.

Tanis had been wondering that himself. "We probably won't be able to hear anything down here." He hoped that was true.

"Raist'll come through. Don't worry," Caramon said grimly.

"Tanis!" Tasslehoff fell back into the half-elf. "There's something down here! I felt it go by my feet."

"Just keep moving," Tanis muttered, "and hope it isn't hungry—"

They waded on in silence, the torchlight flickering off the walls, creating illusions in the mind's eye. More than once, Tanis saw something reach out for him, only to realize it was the shadow cast by Caramon's helm or Tas's hoopak.

The tunnel ran straight south for about two hundred feet, then turned east. The companions stopped. Down the eastern arm of the sewer glimmered a column of dim light, filtering from above. This—according to Bupu—marked the dragon's lair.

"Douse the torches!" Tanis hissed, plunging his torch in the water. Touching the slimy wall, Tanis followed the kender—Tas's red outline showing up vividly to his elven eyes—through the tunnel. Behind him he heard Flint complaining about the effects of water on his rheumatism.

"Shhhh," Tanis whispered as they drew near the light. Trying to be silent in spite of clanking armor, they soon stood by a slender ladder that ran up to an iron grating.

"No one ever bothers to lock floor gratings." Tas pulled Tanis close to whisper in his ear. "But I'm sure I can open it, if it is."

Tanis nodded. He didn't add that Bupu had been able to open it as well. The art of picking locks was as much a matter of pride to the kender as Sturm's moustaches were to the knight. They all stood watching, knee-deep in water, as Tas skimmed up the ladder.

"I still don't hear anything outside," Sturm muttered.

"Shhhh!" Caramon growled harshly.

The grating had a lock, a simple one that Tas opened in moments. Then he silently lifted the grating and peered out. Sudden darkness descended on him, darkness so thick and impenetrable it seemed to hit him like a lead weight, nearly making him lose his hold on the grating. Hurriedly he put the grating back into place without making a sound, then slid down the ladder, bumping into Tanis.

"Tas?" the half-elf grabbed him. "Is that you? I can't see. What's going on?"

"I don't know. It just got dark all of a sudden."

"What do you mean, you can't see?" Sturm whispered to Tanis. "What about your elf-talent?"

"Gone," Tanis said grimly, "just as in Darken Wood—and out by the well. . . ."

No one spoke as they stood huddled in the tunnel. All they could hear was the sound of their own breathing and water dripping from the walls.

The dragon was up there—waiting for them.

21

The sacrifice.
The twice-dead city.

Despair blacker than the darkness blinded Tanis. It was my plan, the only way we had a chance to get out of here alive, he thought. It was sound, it should have worked! What went wrong? Raistlin—could he have betrayed us? No! Tanis clenched his fist. No, damn it. The mage was distant, unlikable, impossible to understand, yes, but he was loyal to them, Tanis would swear it. Where was Raistlin? Dead, perhaps. Not that it mattered. They would all be dead.

"Tanis"—the half-elf felt a firm grasp on his arm and recognized Sturm's deep voice—"I know what you're thinking. We have no choice. We're running out of time. This is our only chance to get the Disks. We won't get another."

"I'm going to look," Tanis said. He climbed past the kender and peered through the grate. It was dark, magically dark. Tanis put his head in his hand and tried to think. Sturm was right: time was running out. Yet how could he trust the knight's judgement? Sturm wanted to fight the dragon! Tanis crawled back down the ladder. "We're going," he said. Suddenly all he wanted to do was get this over with, then they could go home. Home to Solace. "No, Tas." He grabbed hold of the kender and dragged him back down the ladder. "The fighters go first—Sturm and Caramon. Then the rest."

But the knight was already shoving past him eagerly, his sword clanking against his thigh.

"We're always last!" Tasslehoff sniffed, shoving the dwarf along. Flint climbed the ladder slowly, his knees creaking. "Hurry up!" Tas said. "I hope nothing happens before we get there. I've never talked to a dragon."

"I'll bet the dragon's never talked to a kender either!" The dwarf snorted. "You realize, you harebrain, that we're probably going to die. Tanis knows, I could tell by his voice."

Tas paused, clinging to the ladder while Sturm slowly pushed on the grating. "You know, Flint," the kender said seriously, "my people don't fear death. In a way, we look forward to it, the last big adventure. But I think I'd feel badly about leaving this life. I'd miss my things"—he patted his pouches—"and my maps, and you and Tanis. Unless," he added brightly, "we all go to the same place when we die."

Flint had a sudden vision of the happy-go-lucky kender lying cold and dead. He felt a lump of pain in his chest and was thankful for the concealing darkness. Clearing his throat, he said huskily, "If you think I'm going to share my afterlife with a bunch of kender, you're crazier than Raistlin. Come on!"

Sturm carefully lifted the grating and shoved it to one side. It scraped over the floor, causing him to grit his teeth. He heaved himself up easily. Turning, he bent down to help Caramon who was having trouble squeezing his body and his clanking arsenal through the shaft.

"In the name of Istar, be quiet!" Sturm hissed.

"I'm trying," Caramon muttered, finally climbing over the edge. Sturm gave his hand to Goldmoon. Last came Tas, delighted that nobody had done anything exciting in his absence.

"We've got to have light," Sturm said.

"Light?" replied a voice as cold and dark as winter midnight. "Yes, let us have light."

The darkness fled instantly. The companions saw they were in a huge domed chamber that soared hundreds of feet into the air. Cold gray light filtered into the room through a crack in the ceiling, shining on a large altar in the center of the circular room. On the floor surrounding the altar were masses of jewels, coins, and other treasures† of the dead city. The jewels did not gleam. The gold did not glitter. The dim light illuminated nothing, nothing except a black dragon perched on top of the pedestal like some huge beast of prey.

Apparently, Khisanth is not as disinterested in treasure as she seemed.

"Feeling betrayed?" the dragon asked in conversational tones.

"The mage betrayed us! Where is he? Serving you?" Sturm cried fiercely, drawing his sword and taking a step forward.

"Stand back, foul Knight of Solamnia. Stand back or your magic-user will use his magic no more!" The dragon snaked her great neck down and stared at them with gleaming red eyes. Then, slowly and delicately, she lifted one clawed foot. Lying beneath it, on the pedestal, was Raistlin.

"Raist!" Caramon roared and lunged for the altar.

"Stop, fool!" the dragon hissed. She rested one pointed claw lightly on the mage's abdomen. With a great effort, Raistlin moved his head to look at his brother with his strange golden eyes. He made a weak gesture and Caramon halted. Tanis saw something move on the floor beneath the altar. It was Bupu, huddled among the riches, too afraid even to whimper. The Staff of Magius lay next to her.

"Move one step closer and I will impale this shriveled human upon the altar with my claw."

Caramon's face flushed a deep, ugly red. "Let him go!" he shouted. "Your fight is with me."

"My fight is with none of you," the dragon said, lazily moving its wings. Raistlin flinched as the dragon's clawed foot shifted slightly, teasingly, digging her claw into his flesh. The mage's metallic skin glistened with sweat. He drew a deep, ragged breath. "Don't even twitch, mage," the dragon sneered. "We speak the same language, remember? One word of a spell and your friends' carcasses will be used to feed the gully dwarves!"

Raistlin's eyes closed as in exhaustion. But Tanis could see the mage's hands clench and unclench, and he knew Raistlin was preparing one final spell. It would be his last—by the time he cast it the dragon would kill him. But it might give Riverwind a chance to reach the Disks and get out alive with Goldmoon. Tanis edged toward the Plainsman.

"As I was saying," the dragon continued smoothly. "I do not choose to fight any of you. How you have escaped my wrath so far, I do not understand. Still, you are here. And you return to me that which was stolen. Yes, Lady of Qué-Shu, I see you hold the blue crystal staff. Bring it to me."

Tanis hissed one word to Goldmoon—"Stall!" But, looking at her cool marble face, he wondered if she heard him or if she even heard the dragon. She seemed to be listening to other words, other voices.

"Obey me." The dragon lowered her head menacingly. "Obey me or the mage dies. And after him—the knight. And then the half-elf. And so on—one after the other, until you, Lady of Qué-Shu, are the last survivor. Then you will bring me the staff and you will beg me to be merciful."

Goldmoon bowed her head in submission. Gently pushing Riverwind away with her hand, she turned to Tanis and clasped the half-elf in a loving embrace. "Farewell, my friend," she said loudly, laying her cheek against his. Her voice dropped to a whisper. "I know what I must do. I am going to take the staff to the dragon and—"

"No!" Tanis said fiercely. "It won't matter. The dragon intends to kill us anyway."

"Listen to me!" Goldmoon's nails dug into Tanis's arm. "Stay with Riverwind, Tanis. Do not let him try to stop me."

"And if *I* tried to stop you?" Tanis asked gently, holding Goldmoon close in his arms.

"You won't," she said with a sweet, sad smile. "You know that each of us has a destiny to fulfill, as the Forestmaster said. Riverwind will need you. Farewell, my friend."

Goldmoon stepped back, her clear blue eyes on Riverwind as though she would memorize every detail to keep with her throughout eternity. Realizing she was saying good-bye, he started to go to her.

"Riverwind," Tanis said softly. "Trust her. She trusted you, all those years. She waited while you fought the battles. Now it is you who must wait. This is her battle."

Riverwind trembled, then stood still. Tanis could see the veins swell in his neck, his jaw muscles clench. The half-elf gripped the Plainsman's arm. The tall man didn't even look at him. His eyes were on Goldmoon.

"What is this delay?" the dragon asked. "I grow bored. Come forward."

Goldmoon turned away from Riverwind. She walked past Flint and Tasslehoff. The dwarf bowed his head. Tas watched wide-eyed and solemn. Somehow this wasn't as exciting as he had imagined. For the first time in his life, the kender felt small and helpless and alone. It was a horrible, unpleasant feeling, and he thought death might be preferable.

Goldmoon stopped near Caramon, put her hand on his arm. "Don't worry," she said to the big warrior, who was staring at his brother in agony, "he'll be all right." Caramon choked and nodded. And then Goldmoon neared Sturm. Suddenly, as if the horror of the dragon was too overwhelming, she slumped forward. The knight caught her and held her.

"Come with me, Sturm," Goldmoon whispered as he put his arm around her. "You must vow to do as I command, no matter what happens. Vow on your honor as a knight of Solamnia."

Sturm hesitated. Goldmoon's eyes, calm and clear, met his. "Vow," she demanded, "or I go alone."

"I vow, lady," he said reverently. "I will obey."

Goldmoon sighed thankfully. "Walk with me. Make no threatening gesture."

Together the barbarian woman of the Plains and the knight walked toward the dragon.

Raistlin lay beneath the dragon's claw, his eyes closed, preparing himself mentally for the spell that would be his last. But the words to the spell would not form out of the turmoil in his mind. He fought to regain control.

I am wasting myself—and for what? Raistlin wondered bitterly. To get these fools out of the mess they got themselves into. They will not attack for fear of hurting me—even though they fear and despise me. It makes no sense—just as my sacrifice makes no sense. Why am I dying for them when I deserve to live more than they?

This is the voice of Fistandantilus, the evil archmage who shares Raistlin's life essence. Raistlin made this deal during the Test in the Tower. At this time, he has no memory of it.—MW

It is not for them you do this, a voice answered him.† Raistlin started, trying to concentrate, to catch hold of the voice. It was a real voice, a familiar voice, but he couldn't remember whose it was or where he had heard it. All he knew was that it spoke to him in moments of great stress. The closer to death he came, the louder was the voice.

It is not for them that you make this sacrifice, the voice repeated. *It is because you cannot bear defeat! Nothing has ever defeated you, not even death itself. . . .*

Raistlin drew a deep breath and relaxed. He did not understand the words completely, just as he could not remember the voice. But now the spell came easily to his mind. *"Astol arakhkh um—"* he murmured, feeling the magic begin to course through his frail body. Then another voice broke his concentration and this voice was a living voice speaking to his mind. He opened his eyes, turned his head slowly, and stared into the chamber at his companions.

The voice came from the woman—barbarian princess of a dead tribe. Raistlin looked at Goldmoon as she walked toward him, leaning on Sturm's arm. The words in her mind had touched Raistlin's mind. He regarded the woman coldly, detachedly. His distorted vision had forever killed any physical desire the mage might have felt when he looked upon human flesh. He could not see the beauty that so captivated Tanis and his brother. His hourglass eyes saw her withering and dying. He felt no closeness, no compassion for her. He knew she pitied him—and he hated her for that—but she feared him as well. So why, then, was she speaking to him?

She was telling him to wait.

Raistlin understood. She knew what he intended and she was telling him it wasn't necessary. She had

been chosen. She was the one who was going to make the sacrifice.

He watched Goldmoon with his strange golden eyes as she drew nearer and nearer, her own eyes on the dragon. He saw Sturm moving solemnly beside her, looking as ancient and noble as old Huma himself. What a perfect cat's paw Sturm made,† the ideal participant in Goldmoon's sacrifice. But why had Riverwind allowed her to go? Couldn't he see this coming? Raistlin glanced quickly at Riverwind. Ah, of course! The half-elf stood by his side, looking pained and grieved, dropping words of wisdom like blood, no doubt. The barbarian was becoming as gullible as Caramon. Raistlin flicked his eyes back to Goldmoon.

We don't often get to peer inside of Raistlin's mind.

She stood before the dragon now, her face pale with resolve. Next to her, Sturm appeared grave and tortured, gnawed by inner conflict. Goldmoon had probably extracted some vow of strict obedience which the knight was honor-bound to fulfill. Raistlin's lip curled in a sneer.

The dragon spoke and the mage tensed, ready for action. "Lay the staff down with the other remnants of mankind's folly," the dragon commanded Goldmoon, inclining her shining, scaled head toward the pile of treasure below the altar.

Goldmoon, overcome with dragonfear, did not move. She could do nothing but stare at the monstrous creature, trembling. Sturm, next to her, searched the treasure trove with his eyes, looking for the Disks of Mishakal, fighting to control his fear of the dragon. Sturm had not known he could be this frightened of anything. He repeated the code, "Honor is Life," over and over, and he knew it was pride alone that kept him from running away.

Goldmoon saw Sturm's hand shake, she saw the knight's face glistening with sweat. Dear goddess, she cried in her soul, grant me courage! Then Sturm nudged her. She had to say something, she realized. She had been silent too long.

"What will you give us in return for the miraculous staff?" Goldmoon asked, forcing herself to speak calmly, though her throat was parched and her tongue felt swollen.

The dragon laughed—shrill, ugly laughter. "What will I give you?" The dragon snaked her head to stare at Goldmoon. "Nothing! Nothing at all. I do not deal with thieves. Still—" The dragon reared its head back, its red eyes closed to slits. Playfully she dug her claw into Raistlin's flesh; the mage flinched, but he bore the pain without a murmur. The dragon removed the claw and held it just high enough so that they could all see the blood drip from it. "It is not inconceivable that Lord Verminaard—the Dragon Highmaster—may view favorably the fact that you surrender the staff. He may even be inclined to mercy—he is a cleric and they have strange values. But know this, Lady of Qué-Shu, Lord Verminaard does not need your friends. Give up the staff now and they will be spared. Force me to take it—and they will die. The mage first of all!"†

The chromatic dragons were taught by their ruler, Takhisis, that "Mercy is weakness, and weakness is death."

Goldmoon, her spirit seemingly broken, slumped in defeat. Sturm moved close to her, appearing to console her.

"I have found the Disks," he whispered harshly. He grasped her arm, feeling her shivering with fear. "Are you resolved on this course of action, my lady?" he asked softly.

Goldmoon bowed her head. She was deathly pale but composed and calm. Tendrils of her fine silver-golden hair had escaped from the binding and fell around her face, hiding her expression from the dragon. Though she appeared defeated, she looked up at Sturm and smiled. There was both peace and sorrow in her smile, much like the smile on the marble goddess. She did not speak but Sturm had his answer. He bowed in submission.

"May my courage be equal to yours, lady" he said. "I will not fail you."

"Farewell, knight. Tell Riverwind—" Goldmoon faltered, blinking her eyes as tears filled them. Fearing her resolve might yet break, she swallowed her words and turned to face the dragon as the voice of Mishakal filled her being, answering her prayer. *Present the staff boldly!* Goldmoon, imbued with an inner strength, raised the blue crystal staff.

"We do not choose to surrender!" Goldmoon shouted, her voice echoing throughout the chamber. Moving swiftly, before the startled dragon could react, Chieftain's Daughter swung her staff one last time, striking the clawed foot poised above Raistlin.

The staff made a low ringing sound as it struck the dragon—then it shattered. A burst of pure, radiant blue light beamed from the broken staff. The light grew brighter, spreading out in concentric waves, engulfing the dragon.

Khisanth screamed in rage. The dragon was injured, terribly, mortally. She lashed out with her tail, flung her head about, and fought to escape the burning blue flame. She wanted nothing except to kill those that dared inflict such pain, but the intense blue fire relentlessly consumed her—as it consumed Goldmoon.

The Chieftain's Daughter had not dropped the staff when it shattered. She held on to the fragmented end, watching as the light grew, keeping it as close to the dragon as she could. When the blue light touched her hands she felt intense, burning pain. Staggering, she fell to her knees, still clutching the staff. She heard the dragon shrieking and roaring above her, then she could hear nothing but the ringing of the staff. The pain grew so horrible it was no longer a part of her, and she was overcome with a great weariness. I will sleep, she thought. I will sleep and when I waken, I will be where I truly belong. . . .

Sturm saw the blue light slowly destroy the dragon, then it spread along the staff to Goldmoon. He heard the ringing sound grow louder and louder until it drowned out even the screams of the dying dragon. Sturm took a step toward Goldmoon, thinking to wrench the splintered staff from her hand and drag her clear of the deadly blue flame . . . but even as he approached, he knew he could not save her.

Half-blinded by the light and deafened by the sound, the knight realized that it would take all his strength and courage to fulfill his oath—to retrieve the Disks. He tore his gaze from Goldmoon, whose face was twisted in agony and whose flesh was withering in the fire. Gritting his teeth against the pain in his head, he staggered toward the treasure pile where he had seen the Disks—hundreds of thin sheets of platinum bound together by a single ring through the top. Reaching down, he lifted them, amazed at their lightness. Then his heart almost stopped beating when a bloody hand reached up from the pile of treasure and grasped his wrist.

"Help me!"

He could not hear the voice so much as sense the thought. Grasping Raistlin's hand, he pulled the mage to his feet. Blood was visible through the red of Raistlin's robe, but he did not appear to be seriously injured—at least he could stand. But could he walk? Sturm needed help. He wondered where the others were; he couldn't see them in the brilliance. Suddenly Caramon loomed up by his side, his armor gleaming in the blue flame.

Raistlin clutched at him. "Help me find the spellbook!" he hissed.

"Who cares about that?" Caramon roared, reaching for his brother. "I'll get you out of here!"

Raistlin's mouth twisted so in fury and frustration that he could not speak. He dropped to his knees and began to search frantically through the pile of treasure. Caramon tried to draw him away, but Raistlin shoved him back with his frail hand.

And still the ringing sound pierced their ears. Sturm felt tears of pain trickle down his cheeks. Suddenly something crashed to the floor in front of the knight. The chamber ceiling was collapsing! The entire building shook around them, the ringing sound causing the pillars to tremble and the walls to crack.

Then the ringing died—and with it the dragon. Khisanth had vanished, leaving behind nothing but a pile of smoldering ash.

Sturm gasped in relief but not for long. As soon as the ringing sound ended, he could hear the sounds of the palace caving in, the cracking of the ceiling and the thuds and explosive crashes as huge stone slabs struck the floor. Then, out of the dust and noise, Tanis appeared before him. Blood trickled from a cut on the half-elf's cheek. Sturm grabbed his friend and pulled him to the altar as another chunk of ceiling plummeted near them.

"The whole city is collapsing!" Sturm yelled. "How do we get out?"

Tanis shook his head. "The only way I know is back the way we came, through that tunnel," he shouted. He ducked as another piece of ceiling crashed onto the empty altar.

"That'll be a death trap! There must be another way!"

"We'll find it," Tanis said firmly. He peered through the billowing dust. "Where are the others?" he asked. Then, turning, he saw Raistlin and Caramon. Tanis stared in horror and disgust at the mage scavenging among the treasure. Then he saw a small figure tugging Raistlin's sleeve. Bupu! Tanis made a lunge for her, nearly scaring the gully dwarf witless. She shrank back against Raistlin with a startled scream.

"We've got to get out of here!" Tanis roared. He grabbed hold of Raistlin's robes and dragged the slender young man to his feet. "Stop looting and get that gully dwarf of yours to show us the way out, or so help me, you'll die by my hands!"

Raistlin's thin lips parted in a ghastly smile as Tanis flung him back against the altar. Bupu shrieked. "Come! We go! I know way!"

"Raist," Caramon begged, "you can't find it! You'll die if we don't get out of here!"

"Very well," the mage snarled. He lifted the Staff of Magius from the altar and stood up, reaching out his arm for his brother's aid. "Bupu, show us the way," he commanded.

"Raistlin, light your staff so we can follow you." Tanis ordered. "I'm going to find the others."

"Over there," Caramon said grimly. "You're going to need help with the Plainsman."

Tanis flung his arm over his face as more stone fell, then jumped across the rubble. He found Riverwind collapsed where Goldmoon had been standing, Flint and Tasslehoff trying to get the Plainsman to his feet. There was nothing there now except a large area of blackened stone. Goldmoon had been totally consumed in the flames.

"Is he alive?" Tanis shouted.

"Yes!" Tas answered, his voice carrying shrilly above the noise. "But he won't move!"

"I'll talk to him," Tanis said. "Follow the others. We'll be there in a moment. Go on!"

Tasslehoff hesitated, but Flint, after a glance at Tanis's face, put his hand on the kender's arm. Snuffling, Tas turned and began running through the rubble with the dwarf.

Tanis knelt beside Riverwind, then the half-elf glanced up as Sturm appeared out of the gloom. "Go on," Tanis said. "You're in command now."

Sturm hesitated. A column toppled over near them, showering them in rock dust. Tanis flung his body across Riverwind's. "Go on!" he yelled at Sturm. "I'm holding you responsible!" Sturm drew a breath, laid a hand on Tanis's shoulder, then ran toward the light from Raistlin's staff.

The knight found the others huddled in a narrow hallway. The arched ceiling above them seemed to be holding together, but Sturm could hear thudding sounds above. The ground shook beneath their feet and little rivulets of water were beginning to seep through new cracks in the walls.

"Where's Tanis?" Caramon asked.

"He'll be along," Sturm said harshly. "We'll wait . . . a few moments at least." He did not mention that he would wait until waiting had dissolved into death.

There was a shattering crack. Water began to gush through the wall, flooding the floor. Sturm was about to order the others out when a figure emerged from the collapsing doorway. It was Riverwind, carrying Tanis's inert body in his arms.

"What happened? " Sturm leaped forward, his throat constricting. "He's not—"

"He stayed with me," Riverwind said softly. "I told him to leave me. I wanted to die—there with her. Then—a slab of stone. He never saw it—"

"I'll carry him," Caramon said.

"No!" Riverwind glared at the big warrior. His arms gripped Tanis's body tighter. "I will carry him. We must go."

"Yes! This way! We go now!" urged the gully dwarf. She led them out of the city that was dying a second time. They emerged from the dragon's lair into the plaza, which was rapidly being submerged as Newsea poured into the crumbling cavern. The companions waded across, holding onto each other to keep from being swept away in the vicious current. Howling gully dwarves swarmed everywhere in a state of wild confusion, some getting caught in the current, others climbing up into the top stories of shaking buildings, still others dashing down the streets.

Sturm could think of only one way out. "Go east!" he shouted, gesturing down the broad street that led to the waterfall. He looked anxiously at

Riverwind. The dazed Plainsman seemed oblivious to the commotion around him. Tanis was unconscious—maybe dead. Fear chilled Sturm's blood, but he forcibly suppressed all emotions. The knight ran ahead, catching up with the twins.

"Our only chance is the lift!" he yelled.

Caramon nodded slowly. "It will mean a fight."

"Yes, damn it!" said Sturm in exasperation, envisioning all of the draconians trying to leave this stricken city. "It *will* mean a fight! You got any better ideas?"

Caramon shook his head.

At a corner, Sturm waited to herd his limping, exhausted band in the right direction. Peering through the dust and mist, he could see the lift ahead of them. It was, as he had foreseen, surrounded by a dark, writhing mass of draconians. Fortunately, they were all intent on escape. They had to strike quickly, Sturm knew, to catch the creatures off guard. Timing was critical. He caught hold of the kender as Tas scurried past.

"Tas!" he yelled. "We're going up the lift!"

Tasslehoff nodded to show he understood, then made a face to imitate a draconian and slashed his hand across his throat.

"When we get near," Sturm shouted—"sneak around to where you can see the pot descending. When it starts to come down, signal me. We'll attack when it reaches the ground."

Tasslehoff's topknot bobbed.

"Tell Flint!" Sturm finished, his voice nearly gone from shouting. Tas nodded again and raced off to find the dwarf. Sturm straightened his aching back with a sigh and continued on down the street. He could see about twenty or twenty-five draconians gathered in the courtyard, watching for the pot that would carry them to safety to begin its descent. Sturm imagined the confusion up on the top—draconians whipping and bullying the panic-stricken gully dwarves, forcing them into the lift. He hoped the confusion would last.

Sturm saw the brothers in the shadows at the edge of the courtyard. He joined them, glancing up nervously as a stone slab crashed down behind him. As Riverwind staggered out of the mist and dust, Sturm started to help him, but the Plainsman looked at the knight as if he had never seen him before in his life.

"Bring Tanis over here," Sturm said. "You can lay him down and rest a moment. We're going up in the lift and we'll have a fight on our hands. Wait here. When we signal—"

"Do what you must," Riverwind interrupted coldly. He laid Tanis's body gently on the ground and slumped down beside him, burying his face in his hands.

Sturm hesitated. He started to kneel down by Tanis as Flint came to stand by his side.

"Go on. I'll check on him," the dwarf offered.

Sturm nodded thankfully. He saw Tasslehoff skitter across the courtyard and into a doorway. Looking toward the lift, he saw the draconians yelling and cursing into the mist as if they could hurry the pot's descent.

Flint poked Sturm in the ribs. "How are we going to fight all of them?" he shouted.

"We're not. You're going to stay here with Riverwind and Tanis," Sturm said. "Caramon and I can handle this," he added, wishing he believed it himself.

"And I," whispered the mage. "I still have my spells." The knight did not answer. He distrusted magic and he distrusted Raistlin. Still, he had no choice—Caramon would not go into battle without his brother by his side. Tugging at his moustaches, Sturm restlessly loosened his sword. Caramon flexed his arms, clenching and unclenching his huge hands. Raistlin, his eyes closed, was lost in concentration. Bupu, hidden in a niche in the wall behind him, watched everything with wide, frightened eyes.

The pot swung into view, gully dwarves hanging from its sides. As Sturm hoped, the draconians on the ground began to fight among themselves, none wanting to be left behind. Their panic increased as great cracks ran through the pavement toward them. Water rose through the cracks. The city of Xak Tsaroth would soon be lying at the bottom of Newsea.

As the pot touched ground, the gully dwarves scurried over the sides and fled. The draconians clambered in, hitting and shoving each other.

"Now!" the knight yelled.

"Get out of my way!" the mage hissed. Pulling a handful of sand from one of his pouches, he sprinkled it on the ground and whispered, *"Ast tasark sinuralan krynaw,"*† moving his right hand in an arc in the direction of the draconians. First one, then a few more blinked their eyes and slumped to the ground in sleep, but others remained standing, glancing around in alarm. The mage ducked back into the doorway and, seeing nothing, the draconians turned back to the lift, stepping on the bodies of their sleeping comrades in their frantic rush. Raistlin leaned against the wall, closing his eyes wearily.

Sleep spell: oldest trick in the AD&D book.—TRH

"How many?" he asked.

"Only about six." Caramon drew his sword from its sheath.

"Just get in the damn pot!" Sturm yelled. "We'll come back for Tanis when the fight's ended."

Under cover of the mist, the two warriors—swords drawn—covered the distance to the draconians within a few heartbeats, Raistlin stumbling behind. Sturm shouted his battle cry. At the sound, the draconians spun around in alarm.

And Riverwind raised his head.

The sound of battle penetrated Riverwind's fog of despair. The Plainsman saw Goldmoon before him, dying in the blue flame. The dead expression left his face, replaced by a ferocity so bestial and terrifying that Bupu, still hiding in the doorway, screamed in alarm. Riverwind leaped to his feet. He didn't even draw his sword but charged forward, empty-handed. He tore into the ranks of the scrambling draconians like a starving panther and began to kill. He killed with his bare hands, twisting, choking, gouging. Draconians stabbed at him with their swords; soon his leather tunic was soaked with blood. Yet he never stopped moving among them, never stopped killing. His face was that of a madman. The draconians in Riverwind's path saw death in his eyes, and they also saw that their weapons had no effect. One broke and ran and, soon, another.

Sturm, finishing an opponent, looked up grimly, prepared to find six more coming at him. Instead he saw the enemy fleeing for their lives into the mist.

Riverwind, covered with blood, collapsed onto the ground.

"The lift!" The mage pointed. It was hovering about two feet off the ground and starting to move upward. There were gully dwarves in the top pot coming down.

"Stop it!" Sturm yelled. Tasslehoff raced from his hiding place and leaped for the edge. He clung, his feet dangling, trying desperately to keep the empty pot from rising. "Caramon! Hang onto it!" Sturm ordered the warrior. "I'll get Tanis!"

"I can hold it, but not for long." The big man grunted, grasping onto the edge and digging his feet into the ground. He dragged the lift to a halt. Tasslehoff climbed inside, hoping his small body might add ballast.

Sturm ran back swiftly to Tanis. Flint was beside him, his axe in his hands.

"He's alive!" the dwarf called as the knight approached.

Sturm paused a moment to thank some god, somewhere, then he and Flint lifted the unconscious half-elf and carried him to the pot. They placed him inside, then returned for Riverwind. It took four of them to get Riverwind's bloody body into the lift. Tas tried without much success to stanch the wounds with one of his handkerchiefs.

"Hurry!" Caramon gasped. Despite all his efforts, the pot was rising slowly.

"Get in!" Sturm ordered Raistlin.

The mage glanced at him coldly and ran back into the mist. Within moments, he reappeared, carrying Bupu in his arms. The knight grabbed the trembling gully dwarf and flung her into the lift. Bupu, whimpering, crouched on the bottom, still clutching her bag to her chest. Raistlin climbed over the side. The pot continued to rise; Caramon's arms were nearly pulled out of their sockets.

"Go on," Sturm ordered Caramon, the knight being the last to leave the field of battle as usual. Caramon knew better than to argue. He heaved himself up, nearly tipping the pot over. Flint and Raistlin dragged him in. Without Caramon holding it, the pot lunged upward rapidly. Sturm caught hold of it with both hands and clung to the side as it rose into the air. After two or three tries, he man-

aged to swing a leg over the edge and climbed in with Caramon's help.

The knight knelt down beside Tanis and was relieved beyond expression to see the half-elf stir and moan. Sturm grasped the half-elf and held him close. "You have no idea how glad I am you're back!" the knight said, his voice husky.

"Riverwind—" Tanis murmured groggily.

"He's here. He saved your life. He saved all our lives." Sturm talked rapidly, almost incoherently. "We're in the lift, going up. The city's destroyed. Where are you hurt?"

"Broken ribs, feels like." Wincing in pain, Tanis looked over at Riverwind, still conscious, despite his wounds. "Poor man," Tanis said softly. "Goldmoon. I saw her die, Sturm. There was nothing I could do."

Sturm helped the half-elf rise to his feet. "We have the Disks," the knight said firmly. "It was what she wanted, what she fought for. They're in my pack. Are you sure you can stand?"

"Yes," Tanis said. He drew a ragged, painful breath. "We have the Disks, whatever good that will do us."

They were interrupted by the shrill screams as the second pot, gully dwarves flying like banners, went past them. The gully dwarves shook their fists and cursed the companions. Bupu laughed, then she stood up, looking at Raistlin in concern. The mage leaned wearily against the side of the pot, his lips moving silently, calling to mind another spell.

Sturm peered up through the mist. "I wonder how many will be at the top?" he asked.

Tanis, too, glanced up. "Most have fled, I hope," he said. He caught his breath sharply and clutched at his ribs.

There was a sudden lurch. The pot fell about a foot, stopped with a jolt, then slowly started to rise again. The companions looked at each other in alarm.

"The mechanism—"

"It's either starting to collapse or the draconians have recognized us and are trying to destroy it," Tanis said.

"There's nothing we can do," Sturm said in bitter frustration. He stared down at the pack containing the Disks, which lay at his feet. "Except pray to these gods—"

The pot lurched and dropped again. For a moment it hung, suspended, swaying in the mist-shrouded air. Then it started up, moving slowly, shuddering. The companions could see the edge of the rock ledge and the opening above them. The pot rose inch by creaking inch, each of those inside mentally supporting every link of the chain that was carrying them up to—

"Draconians!" cried Tas shrilly, pointing up.

Two draconians stared down at them. As the pot crept closer and closer, Tanis saw the draconians crouch, ready to jump.

"They're going to leap down here! The pot won't hold!" Flint rumbled. "We'll crash!"

"That may be their intent," Tanis said. "They have wings."

"Stand back," Raistlin said, staggering to his feet.

"Raist, don't!" His brother caught hold of him. "You're too weak."

"I have strength for one more spell," the mage whispered. "But it may not work. If they see I am magi, they may be able to resist my magic."

"Hide behind Caramon's shield," Tanis said swiftly. The big man thrust his body and his shield in front of his brother.

The mist swirled around them, concealing them from draconian eyes but also preventing them from seeing the draconians. The pot rose, inch by inch, the chain creaking and lurching upward. Raistlin stood poised behind Caramon's shield, his strange eyes staring, waiting for the mists to part.

Cool air touched Tanis's cheek. A breeze swirled the mists apart, just for an instant. The draconians were so close they could have almost touched them! The draconians saw them at the same time. One spread its wings and floated down toward the pot, sword in hand, shrieking in triumph.

Raistlin spoke. Caramon moved his shield and the mage spread his thin fingers. A ball of white shot from his hands, hitting the draconian squarely in the chest. The ball exploded, covering the creature in sticky webbing.† Its cry of triumph changed to a horrifying shriek as the webbing tangled its wings. It plummeted into the mist, its body striking the edge of the iron pot as it fell. The pot began to rock and sway.

Web spell: second oldest trick in the AD&D book.—TRH

"There's still one more!" Raistlin gasped, sinking to his knees. "Hold me up, Caramon, help me stand. The mage began to cough violently, blood trickling from his mouth.

"Raist!" his brother pleaded, dropping his shield and catching his fainting twin. "Stop! There's nothing you can do. You'll kill yourself!"

A look of command was enough. The warrior supported his brother as the mage began to speak again the eerie-sounding language of magic.

The remaining draconian hesitated, still hearing the yells of its fallen companion. It knew the human was a magic-user. It also knew that it could probably resist the magic. But this human facing it was like no human magic-user it had ever encountered. The human's body seemed weak practically to the point of death, but a strong aura of power surrounded him.

The mage raised his hand, pointing at the creature. The draconian cast one last, vicious glance at the companions, then turned and fled. Raistlin, unconscious, sank into his brother's arms as the pot completed its journey to the surface.

22

Bupu's Gift. An Ominous Sight.

The dwarf's primary god is Reorx. The dwarves still believe Reorx is around. Hill dwarves are half-convinced that the Thorbardin dwarves have him all to themselves in their grand halls beneath the mountain.

Just as they pulled Riverwind out of the lift, a sharp tremor shook the floor of the Hall of the Ancestors. The companions, dragging Riverwind with them, scrambled back as the floor cracked. The floor gave way and tumbled down, carrying the great wheel and the iron pots down into the mist below.

"This whole place is caving in!" Caramon shouted in alarm, holding his brother in his arms.

"Run! Back to the Temple of Mishakal." Tanis gasped with pain.

"Trusting in the gods† again, huh?" Flint said. Tanis could not answer.

Sturm took hold of Riverwind's arms and started to lift him, but the Plainsman shook his head and shoved him away. "My wounds are not serious.

I can manage. Leave me." He remained slumped on the shattered floor. Tanis glanced questioningly at Sturm. The knight shrugged. The Solamnic Knights considered suicide noble and honorable. The elves considered it blasphemy.

The half-elf took hold of the Plainsman's long dark hair and jerked his head back so that the startled man was forced to look into Tanis's eyes. "Go ahead. Lie down and die!" Tanis said through clenched teeth. "Shame your chieftain! She at least had the courage to fight!"

Riverwind's eyes smoldered. He caught hold of Tanis's wrist and flung the half-elf away from him with such force that Tanis staggered into the wall, groaning in agony. The Plainsman stood up, staring at Tanis with hatred. Then he turned and stumbled down the shaking corridor, his head bent.

Sturm helped Tanis to his feet, the half-elf dizzy from the pain. They followed the others as fast as they could. The floor tilted crazily. When Sturm slipped, they crashed against a wall. A sarcophagus slid out into the hallway, spilling its grisly contents. A skull rolled over by Tanis's feet, startling the half-elf who fell to his knees. He feared he might faint from the pain.

"Go," he tried to say to Sturm, but he couldn't talk. The knight picked him up and together they staggered on through the dust-choked corridor. At the foot of the stairs called the Paths of the Dead, they found Tasslehoff waiting.

"The others?" Sturm gasped, coughing in the dust.

"They've already gone up to the temple," Tasslehoff said. "Caramon told me to wait here for you. Flint says the temple's safe, dwarven stonework, you know. Raistlin's conscious. He said it was safe, too. Something about being held in the palm of the goddess. Riverwind's there. He glared at me. I think he could have killed me! But he made it up the stairs—"

"All right!" Tanis said to stop the prattling. "Enough! Put me down, Sturm. I've got to rest a minute or I'll pass out. Take Tas and I'll meet you upstairs. Go on, damn it!"

Sturm grabbed Tasslehoff by the collar and dragged him upstairs. Tanis sank back. Sweat chilled his body; every breath was agony. Suddenly the remainder of the floor in the Hall of the Ancestors collapsed with a loud snapping noise. The Temple of Mishakal trembled and shook. Tanis staggered to his feet, then he paused a moment. Faintly, behind him, he could now hear the low, thundering rumble of water surging. Newsea had claimed Xak Tsaroth. The city that was dead was now buried.

Tanis emerged slowly from the stairwell into the circular room at the top. The climb had been a nightmare, each new step a miracle. The chamber was blessedly quiet, the only sound the harsh breathing of his friends who had made it that far and collapsed. He, too, could go no farther.

The half-elf glanced around to make certain the others were all right. Sturm had set down the pack containing the Disks and was slumped against a wall. Raistlin lay on a bench, his eyes closed, his breathing quick and shallow. Of course, Caramon sat beside him, his face dark with anxiety. Tasslehoff sat at the bottom of the pedestal, staring up at the top. Flint leaned against the doors, too tired to grumble.

"Where's Riverwind?" Tanis asked. He saw Caramon and Sturm exchange glances, then lower their eyes. Tanis staggered up, anger defeating his pain. Sturm rose and blocked his path.

"It's his decision, Tanis. It is the way of his people as it is the way of mine."

Tanis shoved the knight aside and walked toward the double doors. Flint did not move.

"Get out of my way," the half-elf said, his voice shaking. Flint looked up; the lines of grief and sorrow etched by a hundred years softened the dwarf's scowling expression. Tanis saw in Flint's eyes the accumulated wisdom that had drawn an unhappy half-human, half-elven boy into a strange and lasting friendship with a dwarf.†

Flint, a renowned metalsmith, was summoned to Qualinost and there befriended the young Tanis. The story is told in Kindred Spirits, *by Mark Anthony and Ellen Porath.*

"Sit down, lad," Flint said in a gentle voice, as if he, too, remembered their origins. "If your elven head cannot understand, then listen to your human heart for once."

Tanis shut his eyes, tears stinging his lids. Then he heard a great cry from inside the temple—Riverwind. Tanis thrust the dwarf aside and pushed open the huge golden doors. Striding rapidly, ignoring his pain, he threw open the second set of doors and

entered the chamber of Mishakal. Once again he felt peace and tranquillity flood over him, but now the feelings only added to his anger over what had happened.

"I cannot believe in you!" Tanis cried. "What kind of gods are you, that you demand a human sacrifice? You are the same gods who brought the Cataclysm down on man. All right—so you're powerful! Now leave us alone! We don't need you!" The half-elf wept. Through his tears, he could see that Riverwind, sword in hand, knelt before the statue. Tanis stumbled forward, hoping to prevent the act of self-destruction. Tanis rounded the base of the statue and stopped, stunned. For a minute he refused to believe his own sense of sight; perhaps grief and pain were playing tricks on his mind. He lifted his eyes to the statue's beautiful, calm face and steadied his reeling, confused senses. Then he looked again.

Goldmoon lay there, sound asleep, her breast rising and falling with the rhythm of her quiet breathing. Her silver-gold hair had come loose from its braid and drifted around her face in the gentle wind that filled the chamber with the fragrance of spring. The staff was once again part of the marble statue, but Tanis saw that Goldmoon wore around her throat the necklace that had once adorned the statue.

"I am a true cleric now," Goldmoon said softly. "I am a disciple of Mishakal and, though I have much to learn, I have the power of my faith. Above all else, I am a healer. I bring the gift of healing back into the land."

Reaching out her hand, Goldmoon touched Tanis on the forehead, whispering a prayer to Mishakal. The half-elf felt peace and strength flow through his body, cleansing his spirit and healing his wounds.

"We've got a cleric, now," Flint said, "and that'll come in handy. But from what we hear, this Lord Verminaard's a cleric, too, and a powerful one at that. We may have found the ancient gods of good, but he found the ancient gods of evil a lot sooner. I don't see how these Disks are going to help much against hordes of dragons."

"You are right," Goldmoon said softly. "I am not a warrior. I am a healer. I do not have the power to unite the peoples of our world to fight this evil and

The mythos of Goldmoon and the Disks of Mishakal have their roots in the theology and history of my own religion. Those who have studied the Mormon Church will readily see where I took inspiration for the restoration of the gods through Goldmoon.—TRH

restore the balance. My duty is to *find* the person who has the strength and the wisdom for this task. I am to give the Disks of Mishakal† to that person."

The companions were silent for long moments. Then . . .

"We must leave here, Tanis," Raistlin hissed from out of the shadows of the Temple where he stood, staring out the door into the courtyard. "Listen."

Horns. They could all hear the shrill braying of many, many horns, carried on the north wind.

"The armies," said Tanis softly. "War has begun."

The companions fled Xak Tsaroth into the twilight. They traveled west, toward the mountains. The air was cold with the bite of early winter. Dead leaves, blown by chill winds, flew past their faces. They decided to head for Solace, planning to stock up on supplies and gather what information they could before determining where to go in their search for a leader. Tanis could foresee arguments along those lines. Already Sturm was talking of Solamnia. Goldmoon mentioned Haven, while Tanis himself was thinking the Disks of Mishakal would be safest in the elven kingdom.

Discussing vague plans, they traveled on well into the night. They saw no draconians and supposed that those escaping Xak Tsaroth had traveled north to join up with the armies of this Lord Verminaard, Dragon Highmaster. The silver moon rose, then the red. The companions climbed high, the sound of the horns driving them on past the point of exhaustion. They made camp on the summit of the mountain. After eating a cheerless supper, not daring to light a fire, they set the watch, then slept.

Raistlin woke in the cold gray hour before dawn. He had heard something. Had he been dreaming? No, there it was again—the sound of someone crying. Goldmoon, the mage thought irritably, and started to lie back down. Then he saw Bupu, curled in a ball of misery, blubbering into a blanket.

Raistlin glanced around. The others were asleep except for Flint standing watch on the other side of camp. The dwarf had apparently heard nothing, and he wasn't looking in Raistlin's direction. The mage stood up and padded softly over. Kneeling

down beside the gully dwarf, he laid his hand on her shoulder.

"What is it, little one?"

Bupu rolled over to face him. Her eyes were red, her nose swollen. Tears streaked down her dirty face. She snuffled and wiped her hand across her nose. "I don't want to leave you. I want to go with you," she said brokenly, "but—oh—I will miss my people!" Sobbing, she buried her face in her hands.

A look of infinite tenderness touched Raistlin's face, a look no one in his world would ever see. He reached out and stroked Bupu's coarse hair, knowing what it felt like to be weak and miserable, an object of ridicule and pity.

"Bupu," he said, "you have been a good and true friend to me. You saved my life and the lives of those I care about. Now you will do one last thing for me, little one. Go back. I must travel roads that will be dark and dangerous before the end of my long journey. I cannot ask you to go with me."

Bupu lifted her head, her eyes brightening. Then a shadow fell across her face. "But you will be unhappy without me."

"No," Raistlin said, smiling, "my happiness will lie in knowing you are back with your people."

"You sure?" Bupu asked anxiously.

"I am sure," Raistlin answered.

"Then I go." Bupu stood up. "But first, you take gift." She began to rummage around in her bag.

"No, little one," Raistlin began, remembering the dead lizard, "that's not necessary—" The words caught in his throat as he watched Bupu pull from her bag—a book! He stared in amazement, seeing the pale light of the chill morning illuminate silver runes on a night-blue leather binding.

Raistlin reached out a trembling hand. "The spellbook of Fistandantilus!" he breathed.

"You like?" Bupu said shyly.

"Yes, little one!" Raistlin took the precious object in his hands and held it lovingly, stroking the leather. "Where—"

"I take from dragon," Bupu said, "when blue light shine. I glad you like. Now, I go. Find Highbulp Phudge I, the great." She slung her bag over her shoulder. Then she stopped and turned. "That cough, you sure you not want lizard cure?"

"No, thank you, little one," Raistlin said, rising.

Bupu looked at him sadly, then—greatly daring—she caught his hand in hers and kissed it swiftly. She turned away, her head bowed, sobbing bitterly.

Raistlin stepped forward. He laid his hand on her head. If I have any power at all, Great One, he said inside himself, power that has not yet been revealed to me, grant that this little one goes through her life in safety and happiness.

"Farewell, Bupu," he said softly.

She stared at him with wide, adoring eyes, then turned and ran off as fast as her floppy shoes would carry her.†

There are rumors in some circles that a hero who will help save Krynn will arise among gully dwarves.

"What was all that about?" Flint said, stumping over from the other side of the camp. "Oh," he added, seeing Bupu running off. "So you got rid of your pet gully dwarf."

Raistlin did not answer, but simply stared at Flint with a malevolence that made the dwarf shiver and walk hurriedly away.

The mage held the spellbook in his hands, admiring it. He longed to open it and revel in its treasures, but he knew that long weeks of study lay ahead of him before he could even read the new spells, much less acquire them. And with the spells would come more power! He sighed in ecstasy and hugged the book to his thin chest. Then he slipped it swiftly into his pack with his own spellbook. The others would be waking soon—let them wonder how he got the book.

This marks, for all intents and purposes, the end of the first game module, Dragons of Despair. *As noted elsewhere, the relationship between games and novels was new territory. In this first novel, Margaret and I were writing a novel from game material. This close adherence will gradually end. As the module ended here, it seemed that this was a logical place to break the story as well.—TRH*

Raistlin stood up, glancing out to the west, to his homeland, where the sky was brightening with the early morning sun. Suddenly he stiffened. Then, dropping his pack, he ran across the camp and knelt down beside the half-elf.

"Tanis!" Raistlin hissed. "Wake up!"

Tanis woke and grabbed his dagger. "What—"

Raistlin pointed to the west.

Tanis blinked, trying to focus his sleep-scummed eyes. The view from the top of the mountain where they were camped was magnificent. He could see the tall trees give way to the grassy Plains. And beyond the Plains, snaking up into the sky—

"No!" Tanis choked. He gripped the mage. "No, it can't be!"

"Yes," Raistlin whispered. "Solace is burning."

BOOK 2

I

Night of the Dragons.

It may have been just habit, but we seem to be starting the next phase of our adventures back at the Inn once more.—TRH

Tika wrung the rag out in the pail and watched, dully, as the water turned black.† She threw the rag down on the bar and started to lift the bucket to carry it back to the kitchen to draw more water. Then she thought, why bother! Picking up the rag, she began to mop the tables again. When she thought Otik wasn't watching, she wiped her eyes with her apron.

But Otik was watching. His pudgy hands took hold of Tika's shoulders and gently turned her around. Tika gave a choking sob and laid her head on his shoulder.

"I'm sorry," Tika sobbed, "but I can't get this clean!"

Otik knew, of course, that this wasn't the real reason the girl was weeping, but it came close. He

patted her back gently. "I know, I know, child. Don't cry. I understand."

"It's this damn soot!" Tika wailed. "It covers everything with black and every day I scrub it up and the next day it's back. They keep burning and burning!"

"Don't worry about it, Tika," Otik said, stroking her hair. "Be thankful the Inn's in one piece—"

"Be thankful!" Tika pushed away from him, her face flushed. "No! I wish it had burned like everything else in Solace, then *they* wouldn't come in here! I wish it had burned! I wish it had burned!" Tika sank down at the table, sobbing uncontrollably. Otik hovered around her.

"I know, my dear, I know," he repeated, smoothing the puffy sleeves of the blouse Tika had taken such pride in keeping clean and white. Now it was dingy and covered with soot, like everything in the ravaged town.

The attack on Solace had come without warning. Even when the first pitiable refugees began to trickle into the town from the north, telling horror stories of huge, winged monsters, Hederick,† the High Theocrat, assured the people of Solace that they were safe, their town would be spared. And the people believed him because they wanted to believe him.

Even Hederick has his own interesting tale of when things weren't going his way. See Hederick the Theocrat *by Ellen Dodge Severson.*

And then came the night of the dragons.

The Inn was crowded that night, one of the few places people could go and not be reminded of the storm clouds hanging low in the northern skies. The fire burned brightly, the ale was rich, the spiced potatoes were delicious. Yet, even here, the outside world intruded: everyone talked loudly and fearfully of war.

Hederick's words soothed their fearful hearts.

"We are not like these reckless fools to the north who made the mistake of defying the might of the Dragon Highlords," he called out, standing on a chair to be heard. "Lord Verminaard has personally assured the Council of Highseekers in Haven that he wants only peace. He seeks permission to move his armies through our town so that he may conquer the elflands to the south. And I say more power to him!"

Hederick paused for scattered cheering and applause.

"We have tolerated the elves in Qualinesti too long. I say, let this Verminaard drive them back to Silvanost or wherever they came from! In fact"—Hederick warmed to his subject—"some of you young men might consider joining the armies of this great lord. And he is a great lord! I have met him! He is a true cleric! I have seen the miracles he has performed! We will enter a new age under his leadership! We will drive the elves, dwarves, and other foreigners from our land and—"

There came a low, dull, roaring sound, like the gathering of the waters of a mighty ocean. Silence fell abruptly. Everyone listened, puzzled, trying to figure out what might make such a noise. Hederick, aware that he had lost his audience, glanced around in irritation. The roaring sound grew louder and louder, coming closer. Suddenly the Inn was plunged into thick, smothering darkness. A few people screamed. Most ran for the windows, trying to peer out the few clear panes scattered among the colored glass.

"Go down and find out what's going on," someone said.

"It's so blasted dark I can't see the stairs," someone else muttered.

And then it was no longer dark.

Flames exploded outside the Inn. A wave of heat hit the building with force enough to shatter windows, showering those inside with glass. The mighty vallenwood tree—which no storm on Krynn had ever stirred—began to sway and rock from the blast. The Inn tilted. Tables scooted sideways; benches slid down the floor to slam up against the wall. Hederick lost his balance and tumbled off his chair. Hot coals spewed from the fireplace as oil lamps from the ceiling and candles from the tables started small fires.

A high-pitched shriek rose above the noise and confusion—the scream of some living creature—a scream filled with hatred and cruelty. The roaring noise passed over the Inn. There was a rush of wind, then the darkness lifted as a wall of flame sprang up to the south.

Tika dropped a tray of mugs to the floor as she grabbed desperately at the bar for support. People around her shouted and screamed, some in pain, some with terror.

Solace was burning.

A lurid orange glow lit the room. Clouds of black smoke rolled in through the broken windows. Smells of blazing wood filled Tika's nostrils, along with a more horrible smell, the smell of burned flesh. Tika choked and looked up to see small flames licking the great limbs of the vallenwood that held up the ceiling. Sounds of varnish sizzling and popping in the heat mingled with the screams of the injured.

"Douse those fires!" Otik was yelling wildly.

"The kitchen!" The cook screamed as she flew out of the swinging doors, her clothes smoldering, a solid wall of flame behind her. Tika grabbed a pitcher of ale from the bar and tossed it on the cook's dress and held her still to drench her clothes. Rhea sank into a chair, weeping hysterically.

"Get out! The whole place'll go up!" someone shouted.

Hederick, pushing past the injured, was one of the first to reach the door. He ran onto the Inn's front landing, then stopped, stunned, and gripped the rail for support. Staring northward, he saw the woods blazing and, by the ghastly light of the flames, he could see hundreds of marching creatures, the lurid firelight reflecting off their leathery wings. Draconian ground troops. He watched, horrified, as the front ranks poured into the city of Solace, knowing there must be thousands more behind them. And above them flew creatures out of the stories of children.

Dragons.

Five red dragons† wheeled overhead in the flame-lit sky. First one, then another, dove down, incinerating parts of the small town with its fiery breath, casting the thick, magical darkness. It was impossible to fight them—warriors could not see well enough to aim their arrows or strike with their swords.

Red dragons are the largest and strongest of the evil dragons, and they make sure the other dragons know it. Their breath weapon is white-hot flame, which Solace has discovered all too well.

The rest of the night blurred in Tika's memory. She kept telling herself she must leave the burning Inn, yet the Inn was her home, she felt safe there, and so she stayed though the heat from the flaming kitchen grew so intense it hurt her lungs to breathe. Just when the flames spread to the common room, the kitchen crashed to the ground.

Otik and the barmaids flung buckets of ale on the flames in the common room until, finally, the fire was extinguished.

Once the fire was out, Tika turned her attention to the wounded. Otik collapsed in a corner, shaking and sobbing. Tika sent one of the other barmaids to tend to him, while she began treating the injured. She worked for hours, resolutely refusing to look out of the windows, blocking from her mind the awful sounds of death and destruction outside.

Suddenly it occurred to her that there was no end to the wounded, that more people were lying on the floor than had been in the Inn when it was attacked. Dazed, she looked up to see people straggling in. Wives helped their husbands. Husbands carried their wives. Mothers carried dying children.

"What's going on?" Tika asked a Seeker guard who staggered in, clutching his arm where an arrow had penetrated it. Others pushed behind him. "What's happening? Why are these people coming here?"

The guard looked at her with dull, pain-filled eyes. "This is the only building," he mumbled. "All burning. All . . ."

"No!" Tika went limp with shock and her knees trembled. At that moment, the guard fainted in her arms and she was forced to pull herself together. The last thing she saw as she dragged him inside was Hederick, standing on the porch, staring out over the flaming town with glazed eyes. Tears streamed unheeded down his soot-streaked face.

"There's been a mistake," he whimpered, wringing his hands. "There's been a mistake made somewhere."

That had been a week ago. As it turned out, the Inn was not the only building left standing. The draconians knew which buildings were essential to their needs and destroyed all those that were not. The Inn, Theros Ironfeld's blacksmith shop, and the general store were saved. The blacksmith shop had always been on the ground—because of the inadvisability of having the hot forge located in a tree—but the others had to be lowered to the ground because the draconians found it difficult to get into the trees.

Lord Verminaard ordered the dragons to lower the buildings. After a space had been scorched clear, one of the huge red monsters stuck his claws into the Inn and lifted it. The draconians cheered as the dragon dropped it, not gently, onto the blackened grass. Fewmaster Toede, in charge of the town, ordered Otik to repair the Inn immediately. The draconians had one great weakness, a thirst for strong drink. Three days after the town was taken, the Inn† reopened.

We can tell you now that, though most of the vallenwoods were burned, an excellent old specimen survived this onslaught and became the location of choice for the new Inn of the Last Home that Caramon later built.

"I'm all right now," Tika told Otik. She sat up and dried her eyes, wiping her nose with her apron. "I haven't cried once, since that night," she said, more to herself than to him. Her lips tightened into a thin line. "And I'll never cry again!" she swore, rising from the table.

Otik, not understanding but thankful that Tika had regained her composure before the patrons arrived, bustled back behind the bar. "Nearly opening time," he said, trying to sound cheerful. "Maybe we'll have a good crowd today."

"How can you take their money!" Tika flared.

Otik, fearing another outburst, looked at her pleadingly. "Their money is as good as anyone else's. Better than most these days," he said.

"Humpf!" Tika snorted. Her thick red curls quivered as she stalked angrily across the floor. Otik, knowing her temper, stepped backward. It didn't help. He was caught. She jabbed her finger into his fat stomach. "How can you laugh at their crude jokes and cater to their whims?" she demanded. "I hate the stench of them! I hate their leers and their cold, scaly hands touching mine! Someday I'll—"

"Tika, please!" Otik begged. "Have some regard for me. I'm too old to be carried off to the slave mines! And you, they'd take you tomorrow if you didn't work here. Please behave—there's a good girl!"

Tika bit her lip in anger and frustration. She knew Otik was right. She risked more than being sent off in the slave caravans that passed through town almost daily—an angered draconian killed swiftly and without mercy. Just as she was thinking this, the door banged open and six draconian guards swaggered in. One of the them pulled the CLOSED sign off the door and tossed it into a corner.

"You're open," the creature said, dropping into a chair.

"Yes, certainly." Otik grinned weakly. "Tika . . ."

"I see them," Tika said dully.

2
The Stranger. Captured!

The crowd at the Inn that night was sparse. The patrons were now draconians, though occasionally Solace residents came in for a drink. They generally did not stay long, finding the company unpleasant and memories of former times hard to bear.

Tonight there was a group of hobgoblins who kept wary eyes on the draconians and three crudely dressed humans from the north. Originally impressed into Lord Verminaard's service, they now fought for the sheer pleasure of killing and looting. A few Solace citizens sat huddled in a corner. Hederick, the Theocrat, was not in his nightly spot. Lord Verminaard had rewarded the High Theocrat's service by placing him among the first to be sent to the slave mines.

Near dusk, a stranger entered the Inn, taking a table in a dark corner near the door. Tika couldn't tell much about him—he was heavily cloaked and wore a hood pulled low over his head. He seemed fatigued, sinking down into his chair as though his legs would not support him.

"What will you have?" Tika asked the stranger.

The man lowered his head, pulling down one side of his hood with a slender hand. "Nothing, thank you," he said in a soft, accented voice. "Is it permissible to sit here and rest? I'm supposed to meet someone."

"How about a glass of ale while you wait?" Tika smiled.

The man glanced up, and she saw brown eyes flash from the depths of his hood. "Very well," the stranger said. "I am thirsty. Bring me your ale."

Tika headed for the bar. As she drew the ale, she heard more customers entering the Inn.

"Just a half second," she called out, unable to turn around. "Sit anywhere you've a mind. I'll be with you soon as I can!" She glanced over her shoulder at the newcomers and nearly dropped the mug. Tika gasped, then got a grip on herself. Don't give them away!

"Sit down anywhere, *strangers*," she said loudly.

One of the men, a big fellow, seemed about to speak. Tika frowned fiercely at him and shook her head. Her eyes shifted to the draconians seated in the center of the room. A bearded man led the group past the draconians, who examined the strangers with a great deal of interest.

They saw four men and a woman, a dwarf, and a kender. The men were dressed in mud-stained cloaks and boots. One was unusually tall, another unusually big. The woman was cloaked in furs and walked with her hand through the arm of the tall man. All of them seemed downcast and tired. One of the men coughed and leaned heavily upon a strange-looking staff. They crossed the room and sat down at a table in the far corner.

"More refugee scum," sneered a draconian. "The humans look healthy, though, and all know dwarves are hard workers. Wonder why they haven't been shipped out?"

"They will be, soon as the Fewmaster sees them."

"Perhaps we should take care of the matter now," said a third, scowling in the direction of the eight strangers.

"Naw, I'm off duty. They won't go far."

The others laughed and returned to their drinking. A number of empty glasses already sat before each of them.

Tika carried the ale to the brown-eyed stranger, set it before him hurriedly, then bustled back to the newcomers.

"What'll you have?" she asked coldly.

The tall, bearded man answered in a low, husky voice. "Ale and food," he said. "And wine for him," he nodded at the man who was coughing almost continually.

The frail man shook his head. "Hot water," he whispered.

Tika nodded and left. Out of habit, she started back toward where the old kitchen had been. Then, remembering it was gone, she whipped around and headed for the makeshift kitchen that had been built by goblins under draconian supervision. Once inside, she astounded the cook by grabbing the entire skillet of fried spiced potatoes† and carrying it back out into the common room.

There's a splendid recipe for Otik's spicy potatoes in Tika's collection in Leaves from the Inn of the Last Home.

"Ale all around and a mug of hot water!" she called to Dezra behind the bar. Tika blessed her stars that Otik had gone home early. "Itrum, take that table." She motioned to the hobgoblins as she hurried back to the newcomers. She slammed the skillet down, glancing at the draconians. Seeing them absorbed in their drinking, she suddenly flung her arms around the big man and gave him a kiss that made him flush.

"Oh, Caramon," she whispered swiftly. "I knew you'd come back for me! Take me with you! Please, please!"

"Now, there, there," Caramon said, patting her awkwardly on the back and looking pleadingly at Tanis. The half-elf swiftly intervened, his eyes on the draconians.

"Tika, calm down," he told her. "We've got an audience."

"Right," she said briskly and stood up, smoothing her apron. Handing plates around, she began to

Dezra was named for Terry Phillips's wife, who co-authored, with Margaret Weis, the short story "Raistlin's Daughter."

ladle out the spiced potatoes as Dezra† brought the ale and hot water.

"Tell us what happened to Solace," Tanis said, his voice choked.

Quickly Tika whispered the story as she filled everyone's plate, giving Caramon a double portion. The companions listened in grim silence.

"And so," Tika concluded, "every week, the slave caravans leave for Pax Tharkas, except now they've taken almost everyone—leaving only the skilled, like Theros Ironfeld, behind. I fear for him." She lowered her voice. "He swore to me last night that he would work for them no more. It all started with that captive party of elves—"

"Elves? What are elves doing here?" Tanis asked, speaking too loudly in his astonishment. The draconians turned to stare at him; the hooded stranger in the corner raised his head. Tanis hunched down and waited until the draconians turned their attention to their drinks. Then he started to ask Tika more about the elves. At that moment, a draconian yelled for ale.

Tika sighed. "I better go." She set the skillet down. "I'll leave that here. Finish them off."

The companions ate listlessly, the food tasting like ashes. Raistlin mixed his strange herbal brew and drank it down; his cough improved almost immediately. Caramon watched Tika as he ate, his expression thoughtful. He could still feel the warmth of her body as she had embraced him and the softness of her lips. Pleasant sensations flowed through him, and he wondered if the stories he had heard about Tika were true. The thought both saddened him and made him angry.

One of the draconians raised its voice. "We may not be men like you're accustomed to, sweetie," it said drunkenly, flinging its scaled arm around Tika's waist. "But that doesn't mean we can't find ways of making you happy."

Caramon rumbled, deep in his chest. Sturm, overhearing, glowered and put his hand on his sword. Catching hold of the knight's arm, Tanis said urgently, "Both of you, stop it! We're in an occupied town! Be sensible. This is no time for chivalry! You, too, Caramon! Tika can handle herself."

Sure enough, Tika slipped deftly out of the draconian's grip and flounced angrily into the kitchen.

"Well, what do we do now?" Flint grumbled. "We came back to Solace for supplies and find nothing but draconians. My house is little more than a cinder. Tanis doesn't even have a vallenwood tree, much less a home. All we've got are platinum Disks of some ancient goddess and a sick mage with a few new spells." He ignored Raistlin's glower. "We can't eat the Disks and the magician hasn't learned to conjure up food, so even if we knew where to go, we'd starve before we got there!"

"Should we still go to Haven?" Goldmoon asked, looking up at Tanis. "What if it is as bad as this? How do we know the Highseeker Council is even in existence?"

"I don't have the answers," Tanis said, sighing. He rubbed his eyes with his hand. "But I think we should try to reach Qualinesti."

Tasslehoff, bored by the conversation, yawned and leaned back in his chair. It didn't matter to him where they went. Examining the Inn with intense interest, he wanted to get up and look at where the kitchen had burned, but Tanis had warned him before they entered to stay out of trouble. The kender contented himself with studying the other customers.

He immediately noticed the hooded and cloaked stranger in the front of the Inn watching them intently as the conversation among the companions grew heated. Tanis raised his voice, and the word "Qualinesti" rang out again. The stranger set down his mug of ale with a thud. Tas was just about to call Tanis's attention to this when Tika came out of the kitchen and slammed food down in front of the draconians, skillfully avoiding their clawed hands. Then she walked back over to the group.

"Could I have some more potatoes?" Caramon asked.

"Of course." Tika smiled at him and picked up the skillet† to return to the kitchen. Caramon felt Raistlin's eyes on him. He flushed and began to play with his fork.

No wonder she was so adept at bashing with a skillet—she was totally used to handling one.

"In Qualinesti—" Tanis reiterated, his voice rising as he contested a point with Sturm who wanted to go north.

Tas saw the stranger in the corner rise and start walking toward them. "Tanis, company," the kender said softly.

The conversation ceased. Their eyes on their tankards, all of them could feel and hear the approach of the stranger. Tanis cursed himself for not noticing him sooner.

The draconians, however, had noticed the stranger. Just as he reached the creatures' table, one of the draconians stuck out its clawed foot. The stranger tripped over it, stumbling headlong into a nearby table. The creatures laughed loudly. Then a draconian caught a glimpse of the stranger's face.

"Elf!" the draconian hissed, pulling off the hood to reveal the almond-shaped eyes, slanted ears, and delicate, masculine features of an elflord.

"Let me pass," the elf said, backing up, his hands raised. "I was only going to exchange a word of greeting with these travelers."

"You'll exchange a word of greeting with the Fewmaster, elf," the draconian snarled. Jumping up and grabbing the stranger's cloak collar, the creature shoved the elf back up against the bar. The other two draconians laughed loudly.

Tika, on her way back to the kitchen with the skillet, stalked over toward the draconians. "Stop this!" she cried, taking hold of one of the draconians by the arm. "Leave him alone. He's a paying customer. Same as you."

"Go about your business, girl!" The draconian shoved Tika aside, then grabbed the elf with a clawed hand and hit him, twice, across the face. The blows drew blood. When the draconian let go, the elf staggered, shook his head groggily.

"Ah, kill him," shouted one of the humans from the north. "Make him screech, like the others!"

"I'll cut his slanty eyes out of his head, that's what I'll do!" The draconian drew his sword.

"This has gone far enough!" Sturm rushed forward, the others behind him, though all feared there was little hope of saving the elf—they were too far from him. But help was closer. With a shrill cry of rage, Tika Waylan brought her heavy iron skillet down on the draconian's head.†

There was a loud clunking sound. The draconian stared stupidly at Tika for an instant, then slithered to the floor. The elf jumped forward, drawing a knife as the other two draconians leaped for Tika.

"Skillet Bashing" for the ADVANCED DUNGEONS & DRAGONS *players out there, is a weapon specialization having a +4 to hit and a +12 damage with a +10 to any comedic events story roll. It is a specialization unique to Tika and, perhaps, Marian Ravenwood from* Raiders of the Lost Ark.*—TRH*

Sturm reached her side and clubbed one of the draconians with his sword. Caramon caught the other up in his great arms and tossed it over the bar.

"Riverwind! Don't let them out the door!" Tanis cried, seeing the hobgoblins leap up. The Plainsman caught one hobgoblin as it put its hand on the door-knob, but another escaped his grasp. They could hear it shouting for the guard.

Tika, still wielding her skillet, thunked a hob-goblin over the head. But another hobgoblin, seeing Caramon charge over, leaped out of the window.

Goldmoon rose to her feet. "Use your magic!" she said to Raistlin, grabbing him by the arm. "Do something!"

The mage looked at the woman coldly. "It is hopeless," he whispered. "I will not waste my strength."

Goldmoon glared at him in fury, but he had re-turned to his drink. Biting her lip, she ran over to Riverwind, the pouch with the precious Disks of Mishakal in her arms. She could hear horns blowing wildly in the streets.

"We've got to get out of here!"† Tanis said, but at that moment one of the human fighters wrapped his arms around Tanis's neck, dragging him to the floor. Tasslehoff, with a wild shout, leaped onto the bar and began flinging mugs at the half-elf's attacker, narrowly missing Tanis in the process.

Tanis and his companions have consistently bad luck in all the bars they frequent, usually having to beat a hasty exit. I would note, however, that they have, thus far, never had to pay for their food, drinks, or service—let alone damages. —TRH

Flint stood in the midst of the chaos, staring at the elven stranger. "I know you!" he yelled suddenly. "Tanis, isn't this—"

A mug hit the dwarf in the head, knocking him cold.

"Oops," said Tas.

Tanis throttled the northerner and left him un-conscious under a table. He grabbed Tas off the bar, set the kender on the floor, and knelt down beside Flint who was groaning and trying to sit up.

"Tanis, that elf—" Flint blinked groggily, then asked "What hit me?"

"That big guy, under the table!" Tas said pointing.

Tanis stood up and looked at the elf Flint indi-cated. "Gilthanas?"

The elf stared at him. "Tanthalas," he said coldly. "I would never have recognized you. That beard—"

Horns blew again, this time closer.

"Great Reorx!" The dwarf groaned, staggering to his feet. "We've got to get out of here! Come on! Out the back!"

"There is no back!" Tika cried wildly, still hanging onto the skillet.

"No," said a voice at the door. "There is no back. You are my prisoners."

A blaze of torchlight flared into the room. The companions shielded their eyes, making out the forms of hobgoblins behind a squat figure in the doorway. The companions could hear the sounds of flapping feet outside, then what seemed like a hundred goblins stared into the windows and peered in through the door. The hobgoblins inside the bar that were still alive or conscious picked themselves up and drew their weapons, regarding the companions hungrily.

"Sturm, don't be a fool!" Tanis cried, catching hold of the knight as he prepared to charge into the seething mass of goblins slowly forming a ring of steel around them. "We surrender," the half-elf called out.

Sturm glared at the half-elf in anger, and for a moment Tanis thought he might disobey.

"Please, Sturm," Tanis said quietly. "Trust me. This is not our time to die."

Sturm hesitated, glanced around at the goblins crowding inside the Inn. They stood back, fearful of his sword and his skill, but he knew they would charge in a rush if he made the slightest move. "It is not our time to die." What odd words. Why had Tanis said them? Did a man ever have a "time to die"?† If so, Sturm realized, this wasn't it—not if he could help it. There was no glory dying in an inn, trampled by stinking, flapping goblin feet.

Foreshadowing events to come.—TRH

Seeing the knight put his weapon away, the figure at the door decided it was safe to enter, surrounded as he was by a hundred or so loyal troops. The companions saw the gray, mottled skin and red, squinting pig eyes of Fewmaster Toede.

Tasslehoff gulped and moved quickly to stand beside Tanis. "Surely he won't recognize us," Tas whispered. "It was dusk when they stopped us, asking about the staff."

Apparently Toede did not recognize them. A lot had happened in a week's time and the Fewmaster

had important things stuffed in a mind already overloaded. His red eyes focused on the knight's emblems beneath Sturm's cloak. "More refugee scum from Solamnia," Toede remarked.

"Yes," Tanis lied quickly. He doubted if Toede knew of the destruction of Xak Tsaroth. He thought it highly unlikely that this fewmaster would know anything about the Disks of Mishakal. But Lord Verminaard knew of the Disks and he would soon learn of the dragon's death. Even a gully dwarf could add that one up. No one must know they came out of the east. "We have journeyed long days from the north. We did not intend to cause trouble. These draconians started it—"

"Yes, yes," Toede said impatiently. "I've heard this before." His squinty eyes suddenly narrowed. "Hey, you!" he shouted, pointing at Raistlin. "What are you doing, skulking back there? Fetch him, lads!" The Fewmaster took a nervous step behind the door, watching Raistlin warily. Several goblins charged back, overturning benches and tables to reach the frail young man. Caramon rumbled deep in his chest. Tanis gestured to the warrior, warning him to remain calm.

"On yer feet!" one of the goblins snarled, prodding at Raistlin with a spear.

Raistlin stood slowly and carefully gathered his pouches. As he reached for his staff, the goblin grabbed hold of the mage's thin shoulder.

"Touch me not!" Raistlin hissed, drawing back. "I am magi!"

The goblin hesitated and glanced back at Toede.

"Take him!" yelled the Fewmaster, moving behind a very large goblin. "Bring him here with the others. If every man wearing red robes was a magician, this country'd be overrun with rabbits!† If he won't come peaceably, stick him!"

Rabbit subtext again.

"Maybe I'll stick him anyway," the goblin croaked. The creature held the tip of its spear up to the mage's throat, gurgling with laughter.

Again Tanis held back Caramon. "Your brother can take care of himself," he whispered swiftly.

Raistlin raised his hands, fingers spread, as though to surrender. Suddenly he spoke the words, "*Kalith karan, tobanis-kar!*" and pointed his fingers at the goblin. Small, brightly glowing darts

For you AD&D fans, it looks like Raistlin has opted for a Magic Missile spell at this stage of the game. Another basically first-level spell. A bit on the wimpy side, isn't it? —TRH

made of pure white light† beamed from the mage's fingertips, streaked through the air, and embedded themselves deep in the goblin's chest. The creature fell over with a shriek and lay writhing on the floor.

As the smell of burning flesh and hair filled the room, other goblins sprang forward, howling in rage.

"Don't kill him, you fools!" Toede yelled. The Fewmaster had backed clear out the door, keeping the big goblin in front of him as cover. "Lord Verminaard pays a handsome bounty for magic-users. But"—Toede was inspired—"the Lord does not pay a bounty for live kenders, only their tongues! Do that again, magician, and the kender dies!"

"What is the kender to me?" Raistlin snarled.

There was a long heartbeat of silence in the room. Tanis felt cold sweat chill him. Raistlin could certainly take care of himself! Damn the mage!

That was certainly not the answer Toede had expected either, and it left him not quite knowing what to do—especially since these big warriors still had their weapons. He looked almost pleadingly at Raistlin. The magician appeared to shrug.

"I will come peacefully," Raistlin whispered, his golden eyes gleaming. "Just do not touch me."

"No, of course not," Toede muttered. "Bring him."

The goblins, casting uneasy glances in the direction of the Fewmaster, allowed the mage to stand beside his brother.

"Is that everyone?" demanded Toede irritably. "Then take their weapons and their packs."

Tanis, hoping to avoid more trouble, pulled his bow from his shoulder and laid it and his quiver on the soot-blackened floor of the Inn. Tasslehoff quickly laid down his hoopak; the dwarf—grumbling—added his battle-axe. The others followed Tanis's lead, except Sturm, who stood, his arms folded across his chest, and—

"Please, let me keep my pack," Goldmoon said. "I have no weapons in it, nothing of value to you. I swear!"

The companions turned to face her—each remembering the precious Disks she carried. A strained, tense silence fell. Riverwind stepped in

front of Goldmoon. He had laid his bow down, but he still wore his sword, as did the knight.

Suddenly Raistlin intervened. The mage had laid down his staff, his pouches of spell components, and the precious bag that contained his spellbooks. He was not worried about these—spells of protection had been laid on the books; anyone other than their owner attempting to read them would go insane; and the Staff of Magius† was quite capable of taking care of itself. Raistlin held out his hands toward Goldmoon.

It's always been my belief that Raistlin didn't know exactly what powers the Staff held. He's just good at bluffing!—MW

"Give them the pack," he said gently. "Otherwise they will kill us."

"Listen to him, my dear," called out Toede hastily. "He's an intelligent man."

"He's a traitor!" cried Goldmoon, clutching the pack.

"Give them the pack," Raistlin repeated hypnotically.

Goldmoon felt herself weakening, felt his strange power breaking her. "No!" She choked. "This is our hope—"

"It will be all right," Raistlin whispered, staring intently into her clear blue eyes. "Remember the staff? Remember when I touched it?"

Goldmoon blinked. "Yes," she murmured. "It shocked you—"

"Hush," Raistlin warned swiftly. "Give them the pouch. Do not worry. All will be well. The gods protect their own."

Goldmoon stared at the mage, then nodded reluctantly. Raistlin reached out his thin hands to take the pouch from her. Fewmaster Toede stared at it greedily, wondering what was in it. He would find out, but not in front of all these goblins.

Finally there was only one person left who had not obeyed the command. Sturm stood unmoving, his face pale, his eyes glittering feverishly. He held his father's ancient, two-handed sword tightly. Suddenly Sturm turned, shocked to feel Raistlin's burning fingers on his arm.

"I will insure its safety," the mage whispered.

"How?" the knight asked, withdrawing from Raistlin's touch as from a poisonous snake.

"I do not explain my ways to you," Raistlin hissed. "Trust me or not, as you choose."

These are two of the three ancient symbols of the Knights of Solamnia. The third is the crown.

You won't find it in the AD&D Monster Manual.

Sturm hesitated.

"This is ridiculous!" shrieked Toede. "Kill the knight! Kill them if they cause more trouble. I'm losing sleep!"

"Very well!" Sturm said in a strangled voice. Walking over, he reverently laid the sword down on the pile of weapons. Its ancient silver scabbard, decorated with the kingfisher and rose†, gleamed in the light.

"Ah, truly a beautiful weapon," Toede said. He had a sudden vision of himself walking into audience with Lord Verminaard, the sword of a Solamnic knight hanging at his side. "Perhaps I should take that into custody myself. Bring it—"

Before he could finish, Raistlin stepped forward swiftly and knelt beside the pile of weapons. A bright flash of light sprang from the mage's hand. Raistlin closed his eyes and began to murmur strange words, holding his outstretched hands above the weapons and packs.

"Stop him!" yelled Toede. But none dared.

Finally Raistlin ceased speaking and his head slumped forward. His brother hurried to help.

Raistlin stood. "Know this!" the mage said, his golden eyes staring around the common room. "I have cast a spell upon our belongings. Anyone who touches them will be slowly devoured by the great worm, Catyrpelius,† who will rise from the Abyss and suck the blood from your veins until you are nothing more than a dried husk."

"The great worm Catyrpelius!" breathed Tasslehoff, his eyes shining. "That's incredible. I've never heard of—"

Tanis clapped his hand over the kender's mouth.

The goblins backed away from the pile of weapons, which seemed to almost glow with a green aura.

"Get those weapons, somebody!" ordered Toede in a rage.

"You get 'em," muttered a goblin.

No one moved. Toede was at a loss. Although he was not particularly imaginative, a vivid picture of the great worm, Catyrpelius, reared up in his mind. "Very well," he muttered,"take the prisoners away! Load them into the cages. And bring those weapons, too, or you'll wish that worm

what's-its-name was sucking your blood!" Toede stomped off angrily.

The goblins began to shove their prisoners toward the door, prodding them in the back with their swords. None, however, touched Raistlin.

"That's a wonderful spell, Raist," Caramon said in a low voice. "How effective is it? Could it—"

"It's about as effective as your wit!" Raistlin whispered and held up his right hand. As Caramon saw the tell-tale black marks of flashpowder, he smiled grimly in sudden understanding.

Tanis was the last to leave the Inn. He cast a final look around. A single light swung from the ceiling. Tables were overturned, chairs broken. The beams of the ceiling were blackened from the fires, in some cases burned through completely. The windows were covered with greasy black soot.

"I almost wish I had died before I saw this."

The last thing he heard as he left were two hobgoblin captains arguing heatedly about who was going to move the enchanted weapons.

3

The slave caravan.
A strange old magician.

The companions spent a chill, sleepless night, penned up in an iron-barred cage on wheels in the Solace Town Square. Three cages were chained to one of the posts driven into the ground around the clearing. The wooden posts were black from flame and heat, the bases scorched and splintered. No living thing grew in the clearing; even the rocks were black and melted.

When day dawned, they could see other prisoners in the other cages. The last slave caravan leaving Solace for Pax Tharkas, it was to be personally led by the Fewmaster himself, Toede having decided to take this opportunity to impress Lord Verminaard who was in residence at Pax Tharkas.

Caramon tried once, during the cover of night, to bend the bars of the cage and had to give up.

A cold mist arose in the early morning hours, hiding the ravaged town from the companions. Tanis glanced over at Goldmoon and Riverwind. Now I understand them, Tanis thought. Now I know the cold emptiness inside that hurts worse than any sword thrust. My home is gone.

He glanced over at Gilthanas, huddled in a corner. The elf had spoken to no one that night, excusing himself by begging that his head hurt and he was tired. But Tanis, who had kept watch all through the night, saw that Gilthanas did not sleep or even make a pretense of sleeping. He gnawed his lower lip and stared out into the darkness. The sight reminded Tanis that he had—if he chose to claim it—another place he could call home: Qualinesti.

No, Tanis thought, leaning against the bars, Qualinesti was never home. It was simply a place I lived. . . .

Fewmaster Toede emerged from the mist, rubbing his fat hands together and grinning widely as he regarded the slave caravan with pride. There may be a promotion here. A fine catch, considering pickings were drying up in this burned-out shell of a town. Lord Verminaard should be pleased, especially with this last batch. That large warrior, particularly—an excellent specimen. He could probably do the work of three men in the mines. The tall barbarian would do nicely, too. Probably have to kill the knight, though, the Solamnics were notoriously uncooperative. But Lord Verminaard will certainly enjoy the two females—very different, but both lovely. Toede himself had always been attracted to the red-haired barmaid, with her alluring green eyes, the low-cut white blouse purposefully revealing just enough of her lightly freckled skin to tantalize a man with thoughts of what lay beyond.

The Fewmaster's reveries were interrupted by the sound of clashing steel and hoarse shouts floating eerily through the mist. The shouts grew louder and louder. Soon almost everyone in the slave caravan was awake and peering through the fog, trying to see.

Toede cast an uneasy glance at the prisoners and wished he'd kept a few more guards handy. The goblins, seeing the prisoners stir, jumped to their

feet and trained their bows and arrows on the wagons.

"What is this?" Toede grumbled aloud. "Can't those fools even take one prisoner without all this turmoil?"

Suddenly a cry bellowed above the noise. It was the cry of a man in torment and pain, but whose rage surpassed all else.

Gilthanas stood up, his face pale.

"I know that voice," he said. "Theros Ironfeld. I feared this. He's been helping elves escape ever since the slaughter. This Lord Verminaard has sworn to exterminate the elves"—Gilthanas watched Tanis's reaction—"or didn't you know?"

"No!" Tanis said, shocked. "I didn't know. How could I?"

Gilthanas fell silent, studying Tanis for long moments. "Forgive me," he said at last. "It appears I have misjudged you. I thought perhaps that was why you had grown the beard."

"Never!" Tanis leaped up. "How dare you accuse me—"

"Tanis," cautioned Sturm.

The half-elf turned to see the goblin guards crowding forward, their arrows trained at his heart. Raising his hands, he stepped back to his place just as a squadron of hobgoblins dragged a tall, powerfully built man into sight.

"I heard Theros had been betrayed," Gilthanas said softly. "I returned to warn him. But for him, I never would have escaped Solace alive. I was supposed to meet him in the Inn last night. When he did not come, I was afraid—"

Fewmaster Toede threw open the door to the companions' cage, yelling and gesturing for the hobgoblins to hurry their prisoner forward. The goblins kept the other prisoners covered while the hobgoblins threw Theros into the cage.

Fewmaster Toede slammed the door shut quickly. "That's it!" he yelled. "Hitch up the beasts. We're moving out."

Fortunately for Flint, Krynn is apparently not a totally horse-driven place.

Squads of goblins drove huge elk† into the clearing and began hitching them to wagons. Their yelling and the confusion registered only in the back of Tanis's mind. For the moment, his shocked attention was on the smith.

Theros Ironfeld lay unconscious on the straw-covered floor of the cage. Where his strong right arm should have been was a mangled stump. His arm had been hacked off, apparently by some blunt weapon, just below the shoulder. Blood poured from the terrible wound and pooled on the floor of the cage.

"Let that be a lesson to all those who help elves!" The Fewmaster peered in the cage, his red pig eyes squinching in their pouches of fat. "He won't be forging anything ever again, unless it be a new arm! I, eh—" A huge elk lumbered into the Fewmaster, forcing him to scramble for his life.

Toede turned on the creature leading the elk. "Sestun! You oaf!" Toede knocked the smaller creature to the ground.

Tasslehoff stared down at the creature, thinking it was a very short goblin. Then he saw it was a gully dwarf dressed in a goblin's armor.†The gully dwarf picked himself up, shoved his oversized helm back, and glared after the Fewmaster, who was waddling up to the front of the caravan. Scowling, the gully dwarf began kicking mud in his direction. This apparently relieved his soul, for he soon quit and returned to prodding the slow elk into line.

This works because a goblin is about the same size as an average gully dwarf.

"My faithful friend," Gilthanas murmured, bending over Theros and taking the smith's strong, black hand in his. "You have paid for your loyalty with your life."

Theros looked at him with vacant eyes, clearly not hearing the elf's voice. Gilthanas tried to stanch the dreadful wound, but blood continued to pump onto the floor of the cart. The smithy's life was emptying before their eyes.

"No," said Goldmoon, coming to kneel beside the smith. "He need not die. I am a healer."

"Lady," Gilthanas said impatiently, "there exists no healer on Krynn who could help this man. He has lost more blood than the dwarf has in his whole body! His lifebeat is so faint I can barely feel it. The kindest thing to do is let him die in peace without any of your barbarian rituals!"

Goldmoon ignored him. Placing her hand upon Theros's forehead, she closed her eyes.

"Mishakal," she prayed, "beloved goddess of healing, grace this man with your blessing. If his

destiny be not fulfilled, heal him, that he may live and serve the cause of truth."

Gilthanas began to remonstrate once more, reaching out to pull Goldmoon away. Then he stopped and stared in amazement. Blood ceased to drain from the smith's wound and, even as the elf watched, the flesh began to close over it. Warmth returned to the smith's dusky black skin, his breathing grew peaceful and easy, and he appeared to drift into a healthful, relaxed sleep. There were gasps and murmurs of astonishment from the other prisoners in the nearby cages. Tanis glanced around fearfully to see if any of the goblins or draconians had noticed, but apparently they were all preoccupied with hitching the recalcitrant elk to the wagons. Gilthanas subsided back into his corner, his eyes on Goldmoon, his expression thoughtful.

"Tasslehoff, pile up some of that straw," Tanis instructed. "Caramon, you and Sturm help me move him to a corner."

"Here." Riverwind offered his cloak. "Take this to cover him from the chill."

Goldmoon made certain Theros was comfortable, then returned to her place beside Riverwind. Her face radiated a peace and calm serenity that made it seem as if the reptilian creatures on the outside of the cage were the true prisoners.

It was nearly noon before the caravan got under way. Goblins came by and threw some food into the cages, hunks of meat and bread. No one, not even Caramon, could eat the rancid, stinking meat and they threw it back out. But they devoured the bread hungrily, having eaten nothing since last nightfall. Soon Toede had everything in order and, riding by on his shaggy pony, gave the orders to move out. The gully dwarf, Sestun, trotted after Toede. Seeing the hunk of meat lying in the mud and filth outside the cage, the gully dwarf stopped, grabbed it eagerly, and crammed it into his mouth.

Each wheeled cage was pulled by four elk. Two hobgoblins sat high on crude wooden platforms, one holding the reins of the elk, the other a whip and a sword. Toede took his place at the front of the line, followed by about fifty draconians dressed in armor and heavily armed. Another

troop of about twice as many hobgoblins fell into line behind the cages.

After a great deal of confusion and swearing, the caravan finally lurched forward. Some of the remaining residents of Solace stared at them as they drove off. If they knew anyone among the prisoners, they made no sound or gesture of farewell. The faces, both inside and outside the cages, were the faces of those who no longer can feel pain. Like Tika, they had vowed never to cry again.

The caravan traveled south from Solace, down the old road through Gateway Pass. The hobgoblins and draconians grumbled about traveling in the heat of the day, but they cheered up and moved faster once they marched into the shade of the Pass's high canyon walls. Although the prisoners were chilled in the canyon, they had their own reasons for being grateful—they no longer had to look upon their ravaged homeland.

It was evening by the time they left the canyon's winding roads and reached Gateway. The prisoners strained against the bars for some glimpse of the thriving market town. But now only two low stone walls, melted and blackened, marked where the town might have once stood. No living creature stirred. The prisoners sank back in misery.

Once more out in the open country, the draconians announced their preference for traveling by night, out of the sun's light. Consequently, the caravan made only brief stops until dawn. Sleep was impossible in the filthy cages jolting and jouncing over every rut in the road. The prisoners suffered from thirst and hunger. Those who managed to gag down the food the draconians tossed them soon vomited it back up. They were given only small cups of water two or three times a day.

Goldmoon remained near the injured smithy. Although Theros Ironfeld was no longer at the point of death, he was still very ill. He developed a high fever and, in his delirium, he raved about the sacking of Solace. Theros spoke of draconians whose bodies, when dead, turned into pools of acid,† burning the flesh of their victims; and of draconians whose bones exploded after death,† destroying everything within a wide radius. Tanis

These are Kapaks, which also have poisonous saliva, and Bozaks respectively.

listened to the smith relive horror after horror until he felt sick. For the first time, Tanis realized the enormity of the situation. How could they hope to fight dragons whose breath could kill, whose magic exceeded that of all but the most powerful magic-users who had ever lived? How could they defeat vast armies of these draconians when even the corpses of the creatures had the power to kill?

All we have, Tanis thought bitterly, are the Disks of Mishakal—and what good are they? He had examined the Disks during their journey from Xak Tsaroth to Solace. He had been able to read little of what was written, however. Although Goldmoon had been able to understand those words that pertained to the healing arts, she could decipher little more.

"All will be made clear to the leader of the people," she said with steadfast faith. "My calling now is to find him."

Tanis wished he could share her faith, but as they traveled through the ravaged countryside, he began to doubt that any leader could defeat the might of this Lord Verminaard.

These doubts merely compounded the half-elf's other problems. Raistlin, bereft of his medicine, coughed until he was nearly in as bad a state as Theros, and Goldmoon had two patients on her hands. Fortunately, Tika helped the Plainswoman tend the mage. Tika, whose father had been a magician of sorts, held anyone who could work magic in awe.

In fact, it had been Tika's father who inadvertently introduced Raistlin to his calling. Raistlin's father took the twin boys and his stepdaughter, Kitiara, to the local Summer's End festival where the children watched the Wonderful Waylan perform his illusions. Eight-year-old† Caramon was soon bored and readily agreed to accompany his teenage half-sister to the event that attracted her—the swordplay. Raistlin, thin and frail even then, had no use for such active sports. He spent the entire day watching Waylan the Illusionist. When the family returned home that evening, Raistlin astounded them by being able to duplicate flawlessly every trick. The next day, his father took the

There are reports that the boys were five at this time; perhaps because Raistlin was so small.

boy to study with one of the great masters of the magic arts.†

I changed this in The Soulforge *to having Kitiara place Raistlin in mage school because we have always represented Kitiara as being the person in the family who had the primary responsibility for the twins. She was the one with the foresight to see that Raistlin would need the magic to help him survive in the world. Raistlin's father—who was extremely worried about money—would not have chosen to enroll his son in an expensive private school.—MW*

Tika had always admired Raistlin and she had been impressed by the stories she heard about his mysterious journey to the fabled Towers of High Sorcery. Now she helped care for the mage out of respect and her own innate need to help those weaker than herself. She also tended him (she admitted privately to herself) because her deeds won a smile of gratitude and approval from Raistlin's handsome twin brother.

Tanis wasn't certain which to worry about most, the worsening condition of the mage or the growing romance between the older, experienced soldier and the young and—Tanis believed, despite gossip to the contrary—inexperienced, vulnerable barmaid.

He had another problem as well. Sturm, humiliated at being taken prisoner and hauled through the countryside like an animal to slaughter, lapsed into a deep depression from which Tanis thought he might never escape. Sturm either sat all day, staring out between the bars, or—perhaps worse—he lapsed into periods of deep sleep from which he could not be wakened.

Finally Tanis had to cope with his own inner turmoil, physically manifested by the elf sitting in the corner of the cage. Every time he looked at Gilthanas, Tanis's memories of his home in Qualinesti haunted him. As they neared his homeland, the memories he had thought long buried and forgotten crept into his mind, their touch every bit as chilling as the touch of the undead in Darken Wood.

Gilthanas, childhood friend—more than friend, brother. Raised in the same household and close to the same age, the two had played and fought and laughed together. When Gilthanas's little sister grew old enough, the boys allowed the captivating blonde child to join them. One of the threesome's greatest delights was teasing the older brother, Porthios, a strong and serious youth who took on the responsibilities and sorrows of his people at an early age. Gilthanas, Laurana,† and Porthios were the children of the Speaker of the Suns, the ruler of the elves of Qualinesti, a position Porthios would inherit at his father's death.

Laurana is, indeed, named after my wife Laura. —TRH

Tanis's troubled background grew out of what seemed, in the beginning, to be relatively basic choices. When the design group came up with the initial "party of adventurers," we wanted a mix of AD&D racial types—humans, dwarves, kender, etc. At some point, in an effort to balance the capabilities of the game personae for play, it was determined we needed a half-elf character. What was a simple choice for the game, however, had large implications for the character. It was not enough simply to say he was half-elf: we had to know why. The result of answering this "why" made Tanis into the central figure of the story—and a complex character with depth. Such large consequences from such a simple game choice.—TRH

Some in the elven kingdom thought it odd that the Speaker would take into his house the bastard son of his dead brother's wife after she had been raped by a human warrior.† She had died of grief only months after the birth of her half-breed child. But the Speaker, who had strong views on responsibility, took in the child without hesitation. It was only in later years, as he watched with growing unease the developing relationship between his beloved daughter and the bastard half-elf, that he began to regret his decision. The situation confused Tanis as well. Being half-human, the young man acquired a maturity the slower developing elfmaid could not understand. Tanis saw the unhappiness their union must bring down upon the family he loved. He also was beset by the inner turmoil that would torment him in later life: the constant battle between the elvish and the human within him. At the age of eighty—about twenty in human years—Tanis left Qualinost. The Speaker was not sorry to see Tanis leave. He tried to hide his feelings from the young half-elf, but both of them knew it.

Gilthanas had not been so tactful. He and Tanis had exchanged bitter words over Laurana. It was years before the sting of those words faded, and Tanis wondered if he had ever truly forgotten or forgiven. Clearly, Gilthanas had done neither.

The journey for these two was very long. Tanis made a few attempts at desultory conversation and became immediately aware that Gilthanas had changed. The young elflord had always been open and honest, fun-loving and light-hearted. He did not envy his older brother the responsibilities inherent in his role as heir to the throne. Gilthanas was a scholar, a dabbler in the magic arts, though he never took them as seriously as Raistlin. He was an excellent warrior, though he disliked fighting, as do all elves. He was deeply devoted to his family, especially his sister. But now he sat silent and moody, an unusual characteristic in elves. The only time he showed any interest in anything was when Caramon had begun plotting an escape. Gilthanas told him sharply to forget it, he would ruin everything. When pressed to elaborate, the elf fell silent, muttering only something about "overwhelming odds."

By sunrise of the third day, the draconian army was flagging from the night's long march and looking forward to a rest. The companions had spent another sleepless night and looked forward to nothing but another chill and dismal day. But the cages suddenly rolled to a stop. Tanis glanced up, puzzled at the change in routine. The other prisoners roused themselves and looked out the cage bars. They saw an old man, dressed in long robes that once might have been white and a battered, pointed hat. He appeared to be talking to a tree.

The mythological prophet—a guardian/ teacher of the characters—returns to our tale.—TRH

"I say, did you hear me?" The old man† shook a worn walking stick at the oak. "I said move and I meant it! I was sitting on that rock"—he pointed to a boulder—"enjoying the rising sun on my old bones when you had the nerve to cast a shadow over it and chill me! Move this instant, I say!"

The tree did not respond. It also did not move.

"I won't take any more of your insolence!" The old man began to beat on the tree with his stick. "Move or I'll, I'll—"

"Someone shut that loony in a cage!" Fewmaster Toede shouted, galloping back from the front of the caravan.

"Get your hands off me!" the old man shrieked at the draconians who ran up and accosted him. He beat on them feebly with his staff until they took it away from him. "Arrest the tree!" he insisted. "Obstructing sunlight! That's the charge!"

The draconians threw the old man roughly into the companions' cage. Tripping over his robes, he fell to the floor.

"Are you all right, Old One?" Riverwind asked as he assisted the old man to a seat.

Goldmoon left Theros's side. "Yes, Old One," she said softly. "Are you hurt? I am a cleric of—"

"Mishakal!" he said, peering at the amulet around her neck. "How very interesting. My, my." He stared at her in astonishment. "You don't look three hundred years old!"

Goldmoon blinked, uncertain how to react. "How did you know? Did you recognize—? I'm not three hundred—" She was growing confused.

"Of course, you're not. I'm sorry, my dear." The old man patted her hand. "Never bring up a lady's age in public. Forgive me. It won't happen again.

Our little secret," he said in a piercing whisper. Tas and Tika started to giggle. The old man looked around. "Kind of you to stop and offer me a lift. The road to Qualinost is long."

"We're not going to Qualinost," Gilthanas said sharply. "We're prisoners, going to the slave mines of Pax Tharkas."

"Oh?" the old man glanced around vaguely. "Is there another group due by here soon, then? I could have sworn this was the one."

"What is your name, Old One?" Tika asked.

"My name?" The old man hesitated, frowning. "Fizban? Yes, that's it. Fizban."†

This crazed old gentleman is one of my dearest friends. He is also one of the most persistent scene-stealers I've ever met. To clear up a question that we are often asked: are Fizban and Zifnab—our crazed wizard from the Deathgate Cycle—the same? The answer is that Fizban is a crazed wizard owned by TSR under copyright, while Zifnab is a completely different crazed wizard owned by Margaret and I. Incidentally, neither Fizban nor Zifnab have any relationship whatever to Zanfib—a crazed wizard from our Starshield series. I hope I have cleared this up once and for all. —TRH

"Fizban!" Tasslehoff repeated as the cage lurched to a start again. "That's not a name!"

"Isn't it?" the old man asked wistfully. "That's too bad. I was rather fond of it."

"I think it's a splendid name," Tika said, glaring at Tas. The kender subsided into a corner, his eyes on the pouches slung over the old man's shoulder.

Suddenly Raistlin began to cough and they all turned their attention to him. His coughing spasms had been growing worse and worse. He was exhausted and in obvious pain; his skin burned to the touch. Goldmoon was unable to help him. Whatever was burning the mage up inside, the cleric could not heal. Caramon knelt beside him, wiping away the bloody saliva that flecked his brother's lips.

"He's got to have that stuff he drinks!" Caramon looked up in anguish. "I've never seen him this bad. If they won't listen to reason"—the big man scowled—"I'll break their heads! I don't care how many there are!"

"We'll talk to them when we stop for the night," Tanis promised, though he could guess the Fewmaster's answer.

"Excuse me," the old man said. "May I?" Fizban sat down beside Raistlin. He laid his hand on the mage's head and sternly spoke a few words.

Caramon, listening closely, heard "Fistandan . . ." and "not the time . . ." Certainly it wasn't a healing prayer, such as Goldmoon had tried, but the big man saw that his brother responded! The response was astonishing, however. Raistlin's eyes fluttered and opened. He looked up at the old man with a wild expression of terror and grasped Fizban's

wrist in his thin, frail hand. For an instant it seemed Raistlin knew the old man, then Fizban passed his hand over the mage's eyes. The look of terror subsided, replaced by confusion.†

"Hullo," Fizban beamed at him. "Name's—uh—Fizban." He shot a stern glance at Tasslehoff, daring the kender to laugh.

"You are . . . magi!" Raistlin whispered. His cough was gone.

"Why, yes, I suppose I am."

"I am magi!" Raistlin said, struggling to sit up.

"No kidding!" Fizban seemed immensely tickled. "Small world,† Krynn. I'll have to teach you a few of my spells. I have one . . . a fireball . . . let's see, how did that go?"

The old man rambled on long past the time the caravan stopped at the rising of the sun.

This passage has caused some confusion. How could Raistlin recognize Paladine (Fizban's alter ego)? The answer is that it is Fistandantilus who recognizes the god and imparts his terror to the young mage.—MW

*I have always forgiven Fizban for his increasingly anachronistic references. After all, in light of future events, he must have really gotten around in time and space. Besides, if Tolkien's hobbits can claim to have invented golf (*The Hobbit*) and appear to have knowledge regarding the sound made by freight trains (*The Fellowship of the Ring*), then my friend Fizban can, too.—TRH*

4

Rescued! Fizban's Magic.

There is a prophecy on Krynn that a hero will arise among the gully dwarves. Don't laugh—it might be Sestun.

Raistlin suffered in body, Sturm suffered in mind, but perhaps the one who experienced the keenest suffering during the companions' four-day imprisonment was Tasslehoff.

The cruelest form of torture one can inflict on a kender is to lock him up. Of course, it is also widely believed that the cruelest form of torture one can inflict on any other species is to lock them up with a kender.† After three days of Tasslehoff's incessant chatter, pranks, and practical jokes, the companions would have willingly traded the kender for a peaceful hour of being stretched on the rack—at least that's what Flint said. Finally, after even Goldmoon lost her temper and nearly slapped him, Tanis sent Tasslehoff to the back of the cart. His legs hanging over the edge, the kender pressed his face against

More of my favorite lines.—MW

One of three conceptual sketches by Larry Elmore used by the DRAGONLANCE team to sell the world to the corporate leaders of TSR. This sketch depicts Goldmoon, Riverwind, and a very serious-looking Tasslehoff.

the iron bars and thought he would die of misery. He had never been so bored in his entire life.

Things got interesting with the discovery of Fizban, but the old man's amusement value wore thin when Tanis made Tas return the old magician's pouches.† And so, driven to the point of desperation, Tasslehoff latched onto a new diversion.

Why didn't the guards take Fizban's pouches—and, perhaps, his pack? —TRH

Sestun, the gully dwarf.

The companions generally regarded Sestun with amused pity. The gully dwarf was the object of Toede's ridicule and mistreatment. He ran the Fewmaster's errands all night long, carrying messages from Toede at the front of the caravan to the hobgoblin captain at the rear, lugging food up to the Fewmaster from the supply cart, feeding and watering the Fewmaster's pony, and any other nasty jobs the Fewmaster could devise. Toede knocked him flat at least three times a day, the draconians tormented him, and the hobgoblins stole his food. Even the elk kicked at him whenever he trotted past. The gully dwarf bore it all with such a grimly defiant spirit that it won him the sympathy of the companions.

Sestun began to stay near the companions when not busy. Tanis, eager for information about Pax Tharkas, asked him about his homeland and how he came to work for the Fewmaster. The story took over a day for Sestun to relate and another day for the companions to piece together, since he started in the middle and plunged headlong into the beginning.

What it amounted to, eventually, wasn't much help. Sestun was among a large group of gully dwarves living in the hills around Pax Tharkas when Lord Verminaard and his draconians captured the iron mines which he needed to make steel weapons for his troops.

"Big fire—all day, all night. Bad smell." Sestun wrinkled his nose. "Pound rock. All day, all night. I get good job in kitchen"—his face brightened a moment—"fix hot soup. Very hot." His face fell. "Spill soup. Hot soup heat up armor real fast. Lord Verminaard sleep on back for week." He sighed. "I go with Fewmaster. Me volunteer."

"Maybe we can shut the mines down," Caramon suggested.

"That's a thought," Tanis mused. "How many draconians does Lord Verminaard have guarding the mines?"

"Two!" Sestun said, holding up ten grubby fingers.

Tanis sighed, remembering where they had heard that before.

Sestun looked at him hopefully. "There be only two dragons, too."

"Two dragons!" Tanis said incredulously.

"Not more than two."

Caramon groaned and settled back. The warrior had been giving dragon fighting serious thought ever since Xak Tsaroth. He and Sturm had reviewed every tale about Huma, the only known dragon fighter the knight could remember. Unfortunately, no one had ever taken the legends of Huma seriously before (except the Solamnic Knights, for which they were ridiculed), so much of Huma's tale had been distorted by time or forgotten.

"A knight of truth and power, who called down the gods themselves and forged the mighty Dragonlance," Caramon murmured now, glancing at Sturm, who lay asleep on the straw-covered floor of their prison.

"Dragonlance?"† muttered Fizban, waking with a snort. "Dragonlance? Who said anything about the Dragonlance?"

One of my more amusing memories about a fight that occurred with the TSR legal department at this point. The word "dragonlance" was trademarked as an adjective. The legal department ruled that therefore "dragonlance" could not be used as a noun or it would weaken the trademark. They insisted that we use the phrase "dragonlance lance" to refer to the weapon. Our editor, Jean Black, said simply, "No."—MW

"My brother," Raistlin whispered, smiling bitterly. "Quoting the Canticle. It seems he and the knight have taken a fancy to children's stories that have come to haunt them."

"Good story, Huma and the Dragonlance," said the old man, stroking his beard.

"Story—that's all it is." Caramon yawned and scratched his chest. "Who knows if it's real or if the Dragonlance was real or if even Huma was real?"

"We know the dragons are real," Raistlin murmured.

"Huma was real," Fizban said softly. "And so was the Dragonlance." The old man's face grew sad.

"Was it?" Caramon sat up. "Can you describe it?"

"Of course!" Fizban sniffed disdainfully.

Everyone was listening now. Fizban was, in fact, a bit disconcerted by his audience for his stories.

"It was a weapon similar to—no, it wasn't. Actually it was—no, it wasn't that either. It was

closer to . . . almost a . . . rather it was, sort of a—lance, that's it! A lance!" He nodded earnestly. "And it was quite good against dragons."

"I'm taking a nap," Caramon grumbled.

Tanis smiled and shook his head. Sitting back against the bars, he wearily closed his eyes. Soon everyone except Raistlin and Tasslehoff fell into a fitful sleep. The kender, wide awake and bored, looked at Raistlin hopefully. Sometimes, if Raistlin was in a good mood, he would tell stories about magic-users of old. But the mage, wrapped in his red robes, was staring curiously at Fizban. The old man sat on a bench, snoring gently, his head bobbing up and down as the cart jounced over the road. Raistlin's golden eyes narrowed to gleaming slits as though he had been struck by a new and disturbing thought. After a moment, he pulled his hood up over his head and leaned back, his face lost in the shadows.

Tasslehoff sighed. Then, glancing around, he saw Sestun walking near the cage. The kender brightened. Here, he knew, was an appreciative audience for his stories.

Tasslehoff, calling him over, began to relate one of his own personal favorites. The two moons sank. The prisoners slept. The hobgoblins trailed along behind, half-asleep, talking about making camp soon. Fewmaster Toede rode up ahead, dreaming about promotion. Behind the Fewmaster, the draconians muttered among themselves in their harsh language, casting baleful glances at Toede when he wasn't looking.

Tasslehoff sat, swinging his legs over the side of the cage, talking to Sestun. The kender noticed without seeming to that Gilthanas was only pretending to sleep. Tas saw the elf's eyes open and glance quickly around when he thought no one was watching. This intrigued Tas immensely. It seemed almost as if Gilthanas was watching or waiting for something. The kender lost the thread of his story.

"And so I . . . uh . . . grabbed a rock from my pouch, threw it and—thunk—hit the wizard right on the head," Tas finished hurriedly. "The demont grabbed the wizard by the foot and dragged him down into the depths of the Abyss."

This is another reference to the first story ever written about Tasslehoff, "A Stone's Throw Away" by Roger Moore.—MW

"But first demon thank you," prompted Sestun who had heard this story—with variations—twice before. "You forgot."

"Did I?" Tas asked, keeping an eye on Gilthanas. "Well, yes, the demon thanked me and took away the magic ring he'd given me. If it wasn't dark, you could see the outline the ring burned on my finger."

"Sun uping. Morning soon. I see then," the gully dwarf said eagerly.

It was still dark, but a faint light in the east hinted that soon the sun would be rising on the fourth day of their journey.

Suddenly Tas heard a bird call in the woods. Several answered it. What odd-sounding birds, Tas thought. Never heard their like before. But then he'd never been this far south before. He knew where they were from one of his many maps. They had passed over the only bridge across the White-rage River and were heading south toward Pax Tharkas, which was marked on the kender's map as the site of the famed Thadarkan† iron mines. The land began to rise, and thick forests of aspens appeared to the west. The draconians and hobgoblins kept eyeing the forests, and their pace picked up. Concealed within these woods was Qualinesti, the ancient elvenhome.

Tas's map had it wrong. It's the Tharkadan mines, not Thadarkan. They're located in the Tharkadan Mountains and are attached to Pax Tharkas.

Another bird called, much nearer now. Then the hair rose on Tasslehoff's neck as the same bird call sounded from right behind him. The kender turned to see Gilthanas on his feet, his fingers to his lips, an eerie whistle splitting the air.

"Tanis!" Tas yelled, but the half-elf was already awake. So was everyone in the cart.

Fizban sat up, yawned, and glanced around. "Oh, good," he said mildly, "the elves are here."

"What elves, where?" Tanis sat up.

There was a sudden whirring sound like a covey of quail taking flight. A cry rang out from the supply wagon in front of them, then there was a splintering sound as the wagon, now driverless, lurched into a rut and tipped over. The driver of their cage wagon pulled sharply on the reins, stopping the elk before they ran into the wrecked supply wagon. The cage tipped precariously, sending the prisoners sprawling. The driver got the elk going again and guided them around the wreckage.

Suddenly the driver of the cage screamed and clutched at his neck where the companions saw the feathered shaft of an arrow silhouetted against the

dimly lit morning sky. The driver's body tumbled from the seat. The other guard stood up, sword raised, then he, too, toppled forward with an arrow in his chest. The elk, feeling the reins go slack, slowed until the cage rolled to a halt. Cries and screams echoed up and down the caravan as arrows whizzed through the air.

The companions fell for cover face first on the floor of the cage.

"What is it? What's going on?" Tanis asked Gilthanas.

But the elf, ignoring him, peered through the dawn gloom into the forest. "Porthios!" he called.

"Tanis, what's happening?" Sturm sat up, speaking his first words in four days.

"Porthios is Gilthanas's brother. I take it this is a rescue," Tanis said. An arrow zipped past and lodged in the wooden side of the cart, narrowly missing the knight.

"It won't be much of a rescue if we end up dead!" Sturm dropped to the floor. "I thought elves were expert marksmen!"

"Keep low." Gilthanas ordered. "The arrows are only to cover our escape. This is a strike-and-run raid. My people are not capable of attacking a large body directly. We must be ready to run for the woods."

"And how do we get out of these cages?" Sturm demanded.

"We cannot do everything for you!" Gilthanas replied coldly. "There are magic-users—"

"I cannot work without my spell components!"† Raistlin hissed from beneath a bench. "Keep down, Old One," he said to Fizban who, head raised, was looking around with interest.

"Perhaps I can help," the old magician said, his eyes brightening. "Now, let me think—"

"What in the name of the Abyss is going on?" roared a voice out of the darkness. Fewmaster Toede appeared, galloping on his pony. "Why have we stopped?"

"We under attack!" Sestun cried, crawling out from under the cage where he'd taken cover.

"Attack? *Blyxtshok!* Get this cart moving!" Toede shouted. An arrow thunked into the Fewmaster's saddle. Toede's red eyes flew open and he stared

AD&D spells have verbal (spoken), somatic (body gestures), and material (chemicals or objects) components that make up the essential parts of magic. Raist is referring to the loss of all his material components, normally kept in pouches. Otherwise, he might have cast a Knock spell on the lock. Actually, though, a Knock spell doesn't require any components.—TRH

fearfully into the woods. "We're under attack! Elves! Trying to free the prisoners!"

"Driver and guard dead!" Sestun shouted, flattening himself against the cage as another arrow just missed him. "What me do?"

An arrow zipped over Toede's head. Ducking, he had to clutch his pony's neck to keep himself from falling off. "I'll get another driver," he said hastily. "You stay here. Guard these prisoners with your life! I'll hold you responsible if they escape."

The Fewmaster stuck his spurs into his pony and the fear-crazed animal leaped forward. "My guard! Hobgoblins! To me!" the Fewmaster yelled as he galloped to the rear of the line. His shouts echoed back. "Hundreds of elves! We're surrounded. Charge to the north! I must report this to Lord Verminaard." Toede reined in at the sight of a draconian captain. "You draconians tend to the prisoners!" He spurred his horse on, still shouting, and one hundred hobgoblins charged after their valiant leader away from the battle. Soon, they were completely out of sight.

"Well, that takes care of the hobgoblins," Sturm said, his face relaxing in a smile. "Now all we have left to worry about is fifty or so draconians. I don't suppose, by the way, that there are hundreds of elves out there?"

Gilthanas shook his head. "More like twenty."

Tika, lying flat on the floor, cautiously raised her head and looked south. In the pale morning light, she could see the hulking forms of the draconians about a mile ahead, leaping into the cover on either side of the road as the elven archers moved down to fire into their ranks. She touched Tanis's arm, pointing.

"We've got to get out of this cage," Tanis said, looking back. "The draconians won't bother taking us to Pax Tharkas now that the Fewmaster's gone. They'll just butcher us in these cages. Caramon?"

"I'll try," the fighter rumbled. He stood and gripped the bars of the cage in his huge hands. Closing his eyes, he took a deep breath and tried to force the bars apart. His face reddened, the muscles in his arms bunched, the knuckles on his big hands turned white. It was useless. Gasping for breath, Caramon flattened himself on the floor.

"Sestun!" Tasslehoff cried. "Your axe! Break the lock!"

The gully dwarf's eyes opened wide. He stared at the companions, then he glanced down the trail the Fewmaster had taken. His face twisted in an agony of indecision.

"Sestun—" Tasslehoff began. An arrow zinged past the kender. The draconians behind them were moving forward, firing into the cages. Tas flattened himself on the floor. "Sestun," he began again, "help free us and you can come with us!"

A look of firm resolve hardened Sestun's features. He reached for his axe, which he wore strapped onto his back. The companions watched in nail-biting frustration as Sestun felt all around his shoulders for the axe, which was located squarely in the middle of his back. Finally, one hand discovered the handle and he pulled the axe out. The blade glinted in the gray light of dawn.

Flint saw it and groaned. "That axe is older than I am! It must date back to the Cataclysm! He probably couldn't cut through a kender's brain, let alone that lock!"

"Hush!" Tanis instructed, although his own hopes sank at the sight of the gully dwarf's weapon. It wasn't even a battle-axe, just a small, battered, rusty wood-cutting axe the gully dwarf had apparently picked up somewhere, thinking it was a weapon. Sestun tucked the axe between his knees and spat on his hands.

Arrows thunked and clattered around the bars of the cage. One struck Caramon's shield. Another pinned Tika's blouse to the side of the cage, grazing her arm. Tika couldn't remember being more terrified in her life—not even the night dragons struck Solace. She wanted to scream, she wanted Caramon to put his arm around her. But Caramon didn't dare move.

Tika caught sight of Goldmoon, shielding the injured Theros with her body, her face pale but calm. Tika pressed her lips together and drew a deep breath. Grimly she yanked the arrow out of the wood and tossed it to the floor, ignoring the stinging pain in her arm. Looking south, she saw that the draconians, momentarily confused by the sudden attack and the disappearance of Toede, were

organized now, on their feet and running toward the cages. Their arrows filled the air. Their chest armor gleamed in the dim gray light of morning, so did the bright steel of their longswords, which they carried clamped in their jaws as they ran.

"Draconians, closing in," she reported to Tanis, trying to keep her voice from shaking.

"Hurry, Sestun!" Tanis shouted.

The gully dwarf gripped the axe, swung it with all his might, and missed the lock, striking the iron bars a blow that nearly jarred the axe from his hands. Shrugging apologetically, he swung again. This time he struck the lock.

"He didn't even dent it," Sturm reported.

"Tanis," Tika quavered, pointing. Several draconians were within ten feet of them, pinned down for a few moments by the elven archers, but all hope of rescue seemed lost.

Sestun struck the lock again.

"He chipped it," Sturm said in exasperation. "At this rate we'll be out in about three days! What are those elves doing, anyway? Why don't they quit skulking about and attack!"

"We don't have enough men to attack a force this size!" Gilthanas returned angrily, crouching next to the knight. "They'll get to us when they can! We are at the front of the line. See, others are escaping."

The elf pointed to the two wagons behind them. The elves had broken the locks and the prisoners were dashing madly for the woods as the elves covered them, darting out from the trees to let fly their deadly barrage of arrows. But once the prisoners were safe, the elves retreated into the trees.

The draconians had no intention of going into the elven woods after them. Their eyes were on the last prison cage and the wagon containing the prisoners' possessions. The companions could hear the shouts of the draconian captains. The meaning was clear: "Kill the prisoners. Divide the spoils."

Everyone could see that the draconians would reach them long before the elves did. Tanis swore in frustration. Everything seemed futile. He felt a stirring at his side. The old magician, Fizban, was getting to his feet.

"No, Old One!" Raistlin grasped at Fizban's robes. "Keep under cover!"

An arrow zipped through the air and stuck in the old man's bent and battered hat. Fizban, muttering to himself, did not seem to notice. He presented a wonderful target in the gray light. Draconian arrows flew around him like wasps, and seemed to have as little effect, although he did appear mildly annoyed when one stuck into a pouch he happened to have his hand in at the moment.

"Get down!" Caramon roared. "You're drawing their fire!"

Fizban did kneel down for a moment, but it was only to talk to Raistlin. "Say there, my boy," he said as an arrow flew past right where he'd been standing. "Have you got a bit of bat guano† on you? I'm out."

Which, interestingly, actually is listed in the AD&D Players Handbook *as a material component of the spell Fizban is about to cast. —TRH*

"No, Old One," Raistlin whispered frantically. "Get down!"

"No? Pity. Well, I guess I'll have to wing it ." The old magician stood up, planted his feet firmly on the floor, and rolled up the sleeves of his robes. He shut his eyes, pointed at the cage door, and began to mumble strange words.

"What spell is he casting?" Tanis asked Raistlin. "Can you understand?"

The young mage listened intently, his brow furrowed. Suddenly Raistlin's eyes opened wide. "NO!" he shrieked, trying to pull on the old magician's robe to break his concentration. But it was too late. Fizban said the final word and pointed his finger at the lock on the back door of the cage.

"Take cover!" Raistlin threw himself beneath a bench. Sestun, seeing the old magician point at the cage door—and at him on the other side of it—fell flat on his face. Three draconians, reaching the cage door, their weapons dripping with their saliva, skidded to a halt, staring up in alarm.

"What is it?" Tanis yelled.

"Fireball!"† Raistlin gasped, and at that moment a gigantic ball of yellow-orange fire shot from the old magician's fingertips and struck the cage door with an explosive boom. Tanis buried his face in his hands as flames billowed and crackled around him. A wave of heat washed over him, searing his lungs. He heard the draconians scream in pain and smelled burning reptile flesh. Then smoke flew down his throat.

This is a rather spectacular third-level spell in AD&D with little finesse but a lot of punch. The highest level spells are ninth level. Fizban is slumming so far as spellcasting is concerned.—TRH

"The floor's on fire!" Caramon yelled.

Tanis opened his eyes and staggered to his feet. He expected to see the old magician nothing but a mound of black ash like the bodies of the draconians lying behind the wagon. But Fizban stood staring at the iron door, stroking his singed beard in dismay. The door was still shut.

"That really should have worked," he said.

"What about the lock?" Tanis yelled, trying to see through the smoke. The iron bars of the cell door already glowed red hot.

"It didn't budge!" Sturm shouted. He tried to approach the cage door to kick it open, but the heat radiating from the bars made it impossible. "The lock may be hot enough to break!" He choked in the smoke.

"Sestun!" Tasslehoff's shrill voice rose above the crackling flames. "Try again! Hurry!"

The gully dwarf staggered to his feet, swung the axe, missed, swung again, and hit the lock. The superheated metal shattered, the lock gave way, and the cage door swung open.

"Tanis, help us!" Goldmoon cried as she and Riverwind struggled to pull the injured Theros from his smoking pallet.

"Sturm, the others!" Tanis yelled, then coughed in the smoke. He staggered to the front of the wagon, as the rest jumped out, Sturm grabbing hold of Fizban, who was still staring sadly at the door.

"Come on, Old One!" he yelled, his gentle actions belying his harsh words as he took Fizban's arm. Caramon, Raistlin, and Tika caught Fizban as he jumped from the flaming wreckage. Tanis and Riverwind lifted Theros by the shoulders and dragged him out, Goldmoon stumbled after them. She and Sturm jumped from the cart just as the ceiling collapsed.

"Caramon! Get our weapons from the supply wagon!" Tanis shouted. "Go with him, Sturm. Flint and Tasslehoff, get the packs. Raistlin—"

"I will, get my pack," the mage said, choking in the smoke. "And my staff. No one else may touch them."

"All right," Tanis said, thinking quickly. "Gilthanas—"

"I am not yours to order around, Tanthalas,"† the elf snapped and ran off into the woods without looking back.

According to some thinking, Tanis was given that name by Eld Ailea, his elven nursemaid after his mother died. She thought it meant "ever-strong" in the human dialect she learned as a child.

Before Tanis could answer, Sturm and Caramon ran back. Caramon's knuckles were split and bleeding. There had been two draconians looting the supply wagon.

"Get moving!" Sturm shouted. "More coming! Where's your elf friend?" he asked Tanis suspiciously.

"He's gone ahead into the woods," Tanis said. "Just remember, he and his people saved us."

"Did they?" Sturm said, his eyes narrow. "It seems that between the elves and the old man, we came closer to getting killed than with just about anything short of the dragon!"

At that moment, six draconians rushed out from the smoke, skidding to a halt at the sight of the warriors.

"Run for the woods!" Tanis yelled, bending down to help Riverwind lift Theros. They carried the smith to cover while Caramon and Sturm stood, side by side, covering their retreat. Both noticed immediately that the creatures they faced were unlike the draconians they had fought before. Their armor and coloring were different, and they carried bows and longswords, the latter dripping with some sort of awful icor. Both men remembered stories about draconians that turned to acid and those whose bones exploded.

Caramon charged forward, bellowing like an enraged animal, his sword slashing in an arc. Two draconians fell before they knew what was attacking. Sturm saluted the other four with his sword and swept off the head of one in the return stroke. He jumped at the others, but they stopped just out of his range, grinning, apparently waiting for something.

Sturm and Caramon watched uneasily, wondering what was going on. Then they knew. The bodies of the slain draconians near them began to melt into the road. The flesh boiled and ran like lard in a skillet. A yellowish vapor formed over them, mixing with the thinning smoke from the smoldering cage. Both men gagged as the yellow vapor rose around them. They grew dizzy and knew they were being poisoned.

"Come on! Get back!" Tanis yelled from the woods.

The two stumbled back, fleeing through a rainstorm of arrows as a force of forty or fifty draconians swept around the cage, screeching in anger. The

draconians started after them, then fell back when a clear voice called out, *"Hai! Ulsain!"* and ten elves, led by Gilthanas, ran from the woods.

"Quen talas uvenelei!"† Gilthanas shouted. Caramon and Sturm staggered past him, the elves covering their retreat, then the elves fell back.

"Follow me," Gilthanas told the companions, switching to High Common. At a sign from Gilthanas, four of the elven warriors picked up Theros and carried him into the woods.

Each language on Krynn strives to have a distinct structure and sound. While a precise grammatical structure may not have been worked out in detail, each has its own internal consistency.—TRH

Tanis looked back at the cage. The draconians had come to a halt, eyeing the woods warily.

"Hurry!" Gilthanas urged. "My men will cover you."

Elven voices rose out of the woods, taunting the approaching draconians, trying to lure them into arrow range. The companions looked at each other hesitantly.

"I do not want to enter Elvenwood," Riverwind said harshly.

"It is all right," Tanis said, putting his hand on Riverwind's arm. "You have my pledge." Riverwind stared at him for a moment, then plunged into the woods, the others walking by his side. Last to come were Caramon and Raistlin, helping Fizban. The old man glanced back at the cage, now nothing more than a pile of ashes and twisted iron.

"Wonderful spell. And did anyone say a word of thanks?" he asked wistfully.

The elves led them swiftly through the wilderness. Without their guidance, the party would have been hopelessly lost. Behind them, the sounds of battle turned half-hearted.

"The draconians know better than to follow us into the woods," Gilthanas said, smiling grimly. Tanis, seeing armed elven warriors hidden among the leaves of the trees, had little fear of pursuit. Soon all sounds of fighting were lost.

A thick carpeting of dead leaves covered the ground. Bare tree limbs creaked in the chill wind of early morning. After spending days riding cramped in the cage, the companions moved slowly and stiffly, glad for the exercise that warmed their blood. Gilthanas led them into a wide glade as the morning sun lit the woods with a pale light.

The glade was crowded with freed prisoners. Tasslehoff glanced eagerly around the group, then shook his head sadly.

"I wonder what happened to Sestun," he said to Tanis. "I thought I saw him run off."

"Don't worry." The half-elf patted him on the shoulder. "He'll be all right. The elves have no love for gully dwarves, but they wouldn't kill him."

Tasslehoff shook his head. It wasn't the elves he was worried about.

Entering the clearing, the companions saw an unusually tall and powerfully built elf speaking to the group of refugees. His voice was cold, his demeanor serious and stern.

"You are free to go, if any are free to go in this land. We have heard rumors that the lands south of Pax Tharkas are not under the control of the Dragon Highlord. I suggest, therefore, that you head southeast. Move as far and as fast as you can this day. We have food and supplies for your journey, all that we can spare. We can do little else for you."

The refugees from Solace, stunned by their sudden freedom, stared around bleakly and helplessly. They had been farmers on the outskirts of Solace, forced to watch while their homes burned and their crops were stolen to feed the Dragon Highlord's army. Most of them had never been farther from Solace than Haven. Dragons and elves were creatures of legend. Now children's stories had come to haunt them.

Goldmoon's clear blue eyes glinted. She knew how they felt. "How can you be so cruel?" she called out angrily to the tall elf. "Look at these people. They have never been out of Solace in their lives and you tell them calmly to walk through a land overrun by enemy forces—"

"What would you have me do, human?" the elf interrupted her. "Lead them south myself? It is enough that we have freed them. My people have their own problems. I cannot be concerned with those of humans." He shifted his eyes to the group of refugees. "I warn you. Time is wasting. Be on your way!"

Goldmoon turned to Tanis, seeking support, but he just shook his head, his face dark and shadowed.

One of the men, giving the elves a haggard glance, stumbled off on the trail that meandered

south through the wilderness. The other men shouldered crude weapons, women caught up their children, and the families straggled off.

Goldmoon strode forward to confront the elf. "How can you care so little for—"

"For humans?" The elf stared at her coldly. "It was humans who brought the Cataclysm upon us. They were the ones who sought the gods, demanding in their pride the power that was granted Huma in humility. It was humans who caused the gods to turn their faces from us—"

"They haven't!" Goldmoon shouted. "The gods are among us!"

Porthios's eyes flared with anger. He started to turn away when Gilthanas stepped up to his brother and spoke to him swiftly in the elven language.

"What do they say?" Riverwind asked Tanis suspiciously.

"Gilthanas is telling how Goldmoon healed Theros," Tanis said slowly. It had been many, many years since he had heard or spoken more than a few words in the elven tongue. He had forgotten how beautiful the language was, so beautiful it seemed to cut his soul and leave him wounded and bleeding inside. He watched as Porthios's eyes widened in disbelief.

Then Gilthanas pointed at Tanis. Both the brothers turned to face him, their expressive elven features hardening. Riverwind flicked a glance at Tanis, saw the half-elf standing pale but composed under this scrutiny.

"You return to the land of your birth, do you not?" Riverwind asked. "It does not seem you are welcome."

"Yes," Tanis said grimly, aware of what the Plainsman was thinking. He knew Riverwind was not prying into personal affairs out of curiosity. In many ways, they were in more danger now than they had been with the Fewmaster.

"They will take us to Qualinost," Tanis said slowly, the words apparently causing him deep pain. "I have not been there for many years. As Flint will tell you, I was not forced out, but few were sorry to see me leave. As you once said to me, Riverwind—to humans I am half-elven.† To elves, I was half-man."

Half-elves were nothing new on Krynn. When human-occupied Ergoth controlled vast areas, humans and elves from the lands Ergoth joined often intermarried, producing half-elves. Eventually, these half-elves had to choose which half to follow in the Kinslayer Wars. Certainly the bitterness has lingered.

"Then let us leave and travel south with the others," Riverwind said.

"You would never get out of here alive," Flint murmured.

Tanis nodded. "Look around," he said.

Riverwind glanced around him and saw the elven warriors moving like shadows among the trees, their brown clothing blending in with the wilderness that was their home. As the two elves ended their conversation, Porthios turned his gaze from Tanis back to Goldmoon.

"I have heard strange tales from my brother that bear investigation. I extend to you, therefore, what the elves have extended to no humans in years—our hospitality. You will be our honored guests. Please follow me."

Porthios gestured. Nearly two dozen elven warriors emerged from the woods, surrounding the companions.

"Honored prisoners is more like it. This is going to be rough on you, my lad," Flint said to Tanis in a low, gentle voice.

"I know, old friend." Tanis rested his hand on the dwarf's shoulder. "I know."

5

The Speaker of the Suns.

"I have never imagined such beauty existed," Goldmoon said softly. The day's march had been difficult, but the reward at the end was beyond their dreams. The companions stood on a high cliff over the fabled city of Qualinost.

Four slender spires rose from the city's corners like glistening spindles, their brilliant white stone marbled with shining silver. Graceful arches, swooping from spire to spire, soared through the air. Crafted by ancient dwarven metalsmiths, they were strong enough to hold the weight of an army, yet they appeared so delicate that a bird lighting on them might overthrow the balance. These glistening arches were the city's only boundaries; there was no wall around Qualinost. The elven city opened its arms lovingly to the wilderness.

The buildings of Qualinost enhanced nature, rather than concealing it. The houses and shops were carved from rose-colored quartz. Tall and slender as aspen trees, they vaulted upward in impossible spirals from quartz-lined avenues. In the center stood a great tower of burnished gold, catching the sunlight and throwing it back in whirling, sparkling patterns that gave the tower life. Looking down upon the city, it seemed that peace and beauty unchanged from ages past must dwell in Qualinost, if it dwelled anywhere in Krynn.

"Rest here," Gilthanas told them, leaving them in a grove of aspen trees. "The journey has been long, and for that I apologize. I know you are weary and you hunger—"

Caramon looked up hopefully.

"But I must beg your indulgence a few moments longer. Please excuse me." Gilthanas bowed, then walked to stand by his brother. Sighing, Caramon began rummaging through his pack for the fifth time, hoping perhaps he had overlooked a morsel. Raistlin read his spellbook, his lips repeating the difficult words, trying to grasp their meaning, to find the correct inflection and phrasing that would make his blood burn and so tell him the spell was his at last.

The others looked around, marveling at the beauty of the city beneath them and the aura of ancient tranquillity that lay over it. Even Riverwind seemed touched; his face softened and he held Goldmoon close. For a brief instant, their cares and their sorrows eased and they found comfort in each other's nearness. Tika sat apart, watching them wistfully. Tasslehoff was trying to map their way from Gateway† into Qualinost, although Tanis had told him four times that the way was secret and the elves would never permit him to carry off a map. The old magician, Fizban, was asleep. Sturm and Flint watched Tanis in concern—Flint because he alone had any idea of what the half-elf was suffering; Sturm because he knew what it was like returning to a home that didn't want you.

Gateway is about one-third of the way between Solace and Qualinost.

The knight laid his hand on Tanis's arm. "Coming home isn't easy, my friend, is it?" he asked.

"No," Tanis answered softly. "I thought I had left this behind long ago, but now I know I never truly left at all. Qualinesti is part of me, no matter how much I want to deny it."

"Hush, Gilthanas," Flint warned.

The elf came over to Tanis. "Runners were sent ahead and now they have returned," he said in elven. "My father has asked to see you—all of you—at once, in the Tower of the Sun. I cannot permit time for refreshment. In this we seem crude and impolite—"

"Gilthanas," Tanis interrupted in Common. "My friends and I have been through unimagined peril. We have traveled roads where—literally—the dead walked. We won't faint from hunger"—he glanced at Caramon—"some of us won't, at any rate."

The warrior, hearing Tanis, sighed and tightened his belt.

"Thank you," Gilthanas said stiffly. "I am glad you understand. Now, please follow as swiftly as you can."

The companions gathered their things hastily and woke Fizban. Rising to his feet, he fell over a tree root. "Big lummox!" he snapped, striking it with his staff. "There—did you see it? Tried to trip me!" he said to Raistlin.

The mage slipped his precious book back into its pouch. "Yes, Old One." Raistlin smiled, assisting Fizban to his feet. The old magician leaned on the young one's shoulder as they walked after the others. Tanis watched them, wondering. The old magician was obviously a dotard. Yet Tanis remembered Raistlin's look of stark terror when he woke and found Fizban leaning over him. What had the mage seen? What did he know about this old man? Tanis reminded himself to ask. Now, however, he had other, more pressing matters on his mind. Walking forward, he caught up with the elf.

"Tell me, Gilthanas," Tanis said in elven, the unfamiliar words haltingly coming back to him. "What's going on? I have a right to know."

"Have you?" Gilthanas asked harshly, glancing at Tanis from the corners of his almond-shaped eyes. "Do you care what happens to elves anymore? You can barely speak our language!"

"Of course, I care," Tanis said angrily. "You are my people, too!"

"Then why do you flaunt your human heritage?" Gilthanas gestured to Tanis's bearded face. "I would think you would be ashamed—" He stopped, biting his lip, his face flushing.

Tanis nodded grimly. "Yes, I was ashamed, and that's why I left. But if I was ashamed—who made me so?"

"Forgive me, Tanthalas," Gilthanas said, shaking his head. "What I said was cruel and, truly, I did not mean it. It's just that . . . if you only understood the danger we face!"

"Tell me!" Tanis practically shouted in his frustration. "I want to understand!"

"We are leaving Qualinesti," Gilthanas said.

Tanis stopped and stared at the elf. "Leaving Qualinesti?" he repeated, switching to Common in his shock. The companions heard him and cast quick glances at each other. The old magician's face darkened as he tugged at his beard.

"You can't mean it!" Tanis said softly. "Leaving Qualinesti! Why? Surely things aren't this bad—"

"They are worse," Gilthanas said sadly. "Look around you, Tanthalas. You see Qualinost in its final days."

They entered the first streets of the city. Tanis, at first glance, saw everything exactly as he had left it fifty years ago. Neither the streets of crushed gleaming rock nor the aspen trees they ran among had changed; the clean streets sparkled brightly in the sunshine; the aspens had grown perhaps, perhaps not. Their leaves glimmered in the late morning light, the gold and silver-inlaid branches rustled and sang. The houses along the streets had not changed. Decorated with quartz, they shimmered in the sunlight, creating small rainbows of color everywhere the eye looked. All seemed as the elves loved it—beautiful, orderly, unchanging. . . .

No, that was wrong, Tanis realized. The song of the trees was now sad and lamenting, not the peaceful, joyful song Tanis remembered. Qualinost *had* changed and the change was change itself. He tried to grasp hold of it, to understand it, even as he felt his soul shrivel with loss. The change was not in the buildings, not in the trees, or the sun shining through the leaves. The change was in the air. It crackled with tension, as before a storm. And, as

Tanis walked the streets of Qualinost, he saw things he had never before seen in his homeland. He saw haste. He saw hurry. He saw indecision. He saw panic, desperation, and despair.

Women, meeting friends, embraced and wept, then parted and hurried on separate ways. Children sat forlorn, not understanding, knowing only that play was out of place. Men gathered in groups, hands on their swords, keeping watchful eyes on their families. Here and there, fires burned as the elves destroyed what they loved and could not carry with them, rather than let the coming darkness consume it.

Tanis had grieved over the destruction of Solace, but the sight of what was happening in Qualinost entered his soul like the blade of a dull knife. He had not realized it meant so much to him. He had known, deep in his heart, that even if he never returned, Qualinesti would always be there. But no, he was losing even that. Qualinesti would perish.

Tanis heard a strange sound and turned around to see the old magician weeping.

"What plans have you made? Where will you go? Can you escape?" Tanis asked Gilthanas bleakly.

"You will find out the answers to those questions and more, too soon, too soon," Gilthanas murmured.

The Tower of the Sun rose high above the other buildings in Qualinost. Sunlight reflecting off the golden surface gave the illusion of whirling movement. The companions entered the Tower in silence, awestruck by the beauty and majesty of the ancient building. Only Raistlin glanced around, unimpressed. To his eyes, there existed no beauty, only death.

Gilthanas led the companions to a small alcove. "This room is just off the main chamber," he said. "My father is meeting with the Heads of Household to plan the evacuation. My brother has gone to tell him of our arrival. When the business is finished, we will be summoned." At his gesture, elves entered, bearing pitchers and basins of cool water. "Please, refresh yourselves as time permits."

The companions drank, then washed the dust of the journey from their faces and hands. Sturm

removed his cloak and carefully polished his armor as best he could with one of Tasslehoff's handkerchiefs. Goldmoon brushed out her shining hair, kept her cloak fastened around her neck. She and Tanis had decided the medallion she wore should remain hidden until the time seemed proper to reveal it; some would recognize it. Fizban tried, without much success, to straighten his bent and shapeless hat. Caramon looked around for something to eat. Gilthanas stood apart from them all, his face pale and drawn.

Within moments, Porthios appeared in the arched doorway. "You are called," he said sternly.

The companions entered the chamber of the Speaker of the Suns. No human had seen the inside of this building for hundreds of years. No kender had ever seen it. The last dwarves who saw it were the ones present at its construction, hundreds of years before.

"Ah, now this is craftsmanship,"† Flint said softly, tears misting his eyes.

The elves feel that architecture that depends on 90-degree angles is the product of an all-too-analytic mind typical of humans. They prefer their buildings to be as varied as nature itself.

The chamber was round and seemed immensely larger than the slender Tower could possibly encompass. Built entirely of white marble, there were no support beams, no columns. The room soared upwards hundreds of feet to form a dome at the very top of the tower where a beautiful mosaic made of inlaid, glittering tile portrayed the blue sky and the sun on one half; the silver moon, the red moon, and the stars on the other half, the halves separated by a rainbow.

There were no lights in the chamber. Cunningly built windows and mirrors focused sunlight into the room, no matter where the sun was located in the sky. The streams of sunlight converged in the center of the chamber illuminating a rostrum.

There were no seats in the Tower. The elves stood—men and women together; only those designated as Heads of Household had the right to be in this meeting.† There were more women present than Tanis ever remembered seeing; many dressed in deep purple, the color of mourning. Elves marry for life and if the spouse dies do not remarry. Thus the widow has the status of Head of Household until her death.

The elven commonfolk look on the court with only vague curiosity, content to let the nobles go about their petty intrigues and amusements as long as it doesn't interfere too much with their day-to-day lives.

The companions were led to the front of the chamber. The elves made room for them in

Therefore they worship only gods of good. Those elves who are actively drawn toward evil are regarded as having "fallen from the light" and are called dark elves.

respectful silence but gave them strange, forbidding looks—particularly the dwarf, the kender, and the two barbarians, who seemed grotesque in their outlandish furs. There were astonished murmurs at the sight of the proud and noble Knight of Solamnia. And there were scattered mutterings over the appearance of Raistlin in his red robes. Elven magic-users wore the white robes of good,† not the red robes proclaiming neutrality. That, the elves believed, was just one step removed from black. As the crowd settled down, the Speaker of the Suns came forward to the rostrum.

It had been many years since Tanis had seen the Speaker, his adopted father, as it were. And here, too, he saw change. The man was still tall, taller even than his son Porthios. He was dressed in the yellow, shimmering robes of his office. His face was stern and unyielding, his manner austere. He was the Speaker of the Suns, called the Speaker; he had been called the Speaker for well over a century. Those who knew his name never pronounced it—including his children. But Tanis saw in his hair touches of silver, which had not been there before, and there were lines of care and sorrow in the face, which had previously seemed untouched by time.

Porthios joined his brother as the companions, led by the elves, entered. The Speaker extended his arms and called them by name. They walked forward into their father's embrace.

"My sons," the Speaker said brokenly, and Tanis was startled at this show of emotion. "I never thought to see either of you in this life again. Tell me of the raid—" he said, turning to Gilthanas.

"In time, Speaker," said Gilthanas. "First, I bid you, greet our guests."

"Yes, I am sorry." The Speaker passed a trembling hand over his face and it seemed to Tanis that he aged even as he stood before them. "Forgive me, guests. I bid you welcome, you who have entered this kingdom no one has entered for many years."

Gilthanas spoke a few words and the Speaker stared shrewdly at Tanis, then beckoned the half-elf forward. His words were cool, his manner polite, if strained. "Is it indeed you, Tanthalas, son of my brother's wife? The years have been long, and all have wondered about your fate. We welcome you

back to your homeland, though I fear you come only to see its final days. My daughter, in particular, will be glad to see you. She has missed her childhood playmate."

Gilthanas stiffened at this, his face darkening as he looked at Tanis. The half-elf felt his own face flush. He bowed low before the Speaker, unable to say a word.

"I welcome the rest of you and hope to learn more of you later. We shall not keep you long, but it is right that you learn in this room what is happening in the world. Then you will be allowed to rest and refresh yourselves. Now, my son—" The Speaker turned to Gilthanas, obviously thankful to end the formalities. "The raid on Pax Tharkas?"

Gilthanas stepped forward, his head bowed. "I have failed, Speaker of the Suns."

A murmur passed among the elves like the wind among the aspens. The Speaker's face bore no expression. He simply sighed and stared unseeing out a tall window. "Tell your story," he said quietly.

Gilthanas swallowed, then spoke, his voice so low many in the back of the room leaned forward to hear.

"I traveled south with my warriors in secrecy, as was planned. All went well. We found a group of human resistance fighters, refugees from Gateway, who joined us, adding to our numbers. Then, by the cruelest mischance, we stumbled into the advance patrols of the dragonarmy. We fought valiantly, elves and humans together, but for naught. I was struck on the head and remember nothing more. When I awoke, I was lying in a ravine, surrounded by the bodies of my comrades. Apparently, the foul dragonmen shoved the wounded over the cliff, leaving us for dead." Gilthanas paused, clearing his throat. "Druids† in the woods tended my injuries. From them, I learned that many of my warriors were still alive and had been taken prisoner. Leaving the druids to bury the dead, I followed the tracks of the dragonarmy and eventually came to Solace."

These priests of nature are rather scarce on Krynn, but anyone who explores forests with only good in their hearts can usually find one or two.

Gilthanas stopped. His face glistened with sweat and his hands twitched nervously. He cleared his throat again, tried to speak and failed. His father watched him with growing concern.

Gilthanas spoke. "Solace is destroyed."

There was a gasp from the audience.

"The mighty vallenwoods have been cut and burned, few now stand."

The elves wailed and cried out in dismay and anger. The Speaker held up his hand for order. "This is grievous news," he said sternly. "We mourn the passing of trees old even to us. But continue—what of our people?"

"I found my men tied to stakes in the center of the town square along with the humans who had helped us," Gilthanas said, his voice breaking. "They were surrounded by draconian guards. I hoped to be able to free them at night. Then—" His voice failed completely and he bowed his head as his older brother came over and laid a hand on his shoulder. Gilthanas straightened. "A red dragon† appeared in the sky—"

Each of the original twelve game modules was designed to feature one of each type of dragon from the original AD&D Monster Manual. *The first module featured a black dragon; this one a red. —TRH*

Sounds of shock and dismay came from the assembled elves. The Speaker shook his head in sorrow.

"Yes, Speaker," Gilthanas said and his voice was loud, unnaturally loud and jarring. "It is true. These monsters have returned to Krynn. The red dragon circled above Solace and all who saw him fled in terror. He flew lower and lower and then landed in the town square. His great gleaming red reptile body filled the clearing, his wings spread destruction, his tail toppled trees. Yellow fangs glistened, green saliva dripped from his massive jaws, his huge talons tore the ground . . . and riding upon his back was a human male.

"Powerfully built, he was dressed in the black robes of a cleric of the Queen of Darkness. A black and gold cape fluttered around him. His face was hidden by a hideous horned mask fashioned in black and gold to resemble the face of a dragon. The dragonmen fell to their knees in worship as the dragon landed. The goblins and hobgoblins and foul humans who fight with the dragonmen cowered in terror; many ran away. Only the example of my people gave me the courage to stay."

Now that he was speaking, Gilthanas seemed eager to tell the story. "Some of the humans tied to stakes went into a frenzy of terror, screaming piteously. But my warriors remained calm and defiant, although all were affected alike by the

dragonfear the monster generates. The dragonrider did not seem to find this pleasing. He glared at them, and then spoke in a voice that came from the depths of the Abyss. His words still burn in my mind.

"'I am Verminaard, Dragon Highlord of the North. I have fought to free this land and these people from the false beliefs spread by those who call themselves Seekers. Many have come to work for me, pleased to further the great cause of the Dragon Highlords. I have shown them mercy and graced them with the blessings my goddess has granted me. Spells of healing I possess, as do no others in this land, and therefore you know that I am the representative of the true gods. But you humans who stand before me now have defied me. You chose to fight me and therefore your punishment will serve as an example to any others who choose folly over wisdom.'

"Then he turned to the elves and said, 'Be it known by this act that I, Verminaard, will destroy your race utterly as decreed by my goddess. Humans can be taught to see the errors of their ways, but elves—never!' The man's voice rose until it raged louder than the winds. 'Let this be your final warning—all who watch! Ember, destroy!'

"And, with that, the great dragon breathed out fire upon all those tied to the stakes. They writhed helplessly, burning to death in terrible agony. . . ."

There was no sound at all in the chamber. The shock and horror were too great for words.

"A madness swept over me," Gilthanas continued, his eyes burning feverishly, almost a reflection of what he had seen. "I started to rush forward, to die with my people, when a great hand grasped me and dragged me backward. It was Theros Ironfeld, 'Now is not the time to die, elf,' he told me. "Now is the time for revenge.' I . . . I collapsed then, and he took me back to his house, in peril of his own life. And he would have paid for his kindness to elves with his life, had not this woman healed him!"

Gilthanas pointed to Goldmoon, who stood at the back of the group, her face shrouded by her fur cape. The Speaker turned to stare at her, as did the other elves in the chamber, their murmurings dark and ominous.

"Theros is the man brought here today, Speaker," Porthios said. "The man with but one arm. Our healers say he will live. But they say it is only by a miracle that his life was spared, so dreadful were his wounds."

"Come forward, woman of the Plains," the Speaker commanded sternly. Goldmoon took a step toward the rostrum, Riverwind at her side. Two elven guards moved swiftly to block him. He glared at them but stood where he was.

The Chieftain's Daughter moved forward, holding her head proudly. As she removed her hood, the sun shone on the silver-gold hair cascading down her back. The elves marveled at her beauty.

"You claim to have healed this man—Theros Ironfeld?" The Speaker asked her with disdain.

"I claim nothing," Goldmoon answered coolly. "Your son saw me heal him. Do you doubt his words?"

"No, but he was overwrought, sick and confused. He may have mistaken witchcraft for healing."

"Look on this," Goldmoon said gently and untied her cape, letting it fall away from her neck. The medallion sparkled in the sunlight.

The Speaker left the rostrum and came forward, his eyes widening in disbelief. Then his face became distorted with rage. "Blasphemy!" he shouted. Reaching out, he started to rip the medallion from Goldmoon's throat.

There was a flash of blue light. The Speaker crumbled to the floor with a cry of pain. As the elves shouted out in alarm, drawing their swords, the companions drew theirs. Elven warriors rushed to surround them.

"Stop this nonsense!" said the old magician in a strong, stern voice. Fizban tottered up to the rostrum, calmly pushing aside the sword blades as if they were slender branches of an aspen tree. The elves stared in astonishment, seemingly unable to stop him. Muttering to himself, Fizban came up to the Speaker, who was lying stunned on the floor. The old man helped the elf to his feet.

"Now then, you asked for that, you know," Fizban scolded, brushing the Speaker's robes as the elf gaped at him.

"Who are you?" the Speaker gasped.

"Mmmm. What was that name?" The old magician glanced around at Tasslehoff.

"Fizban," the kender said helpfully.

"Yes, Fizban. That's who I am." The magician stroked his white beard. "Now, Solostaran, I suggest you call off your guards and tell everyone to settle down. I, for one, would like to hear the story of this young woman's adventures, and you, for one, would do well to listen. It wouldn't hurt you to apologize, either."

As Fizban shook his finger at the Speaker, his battered hat tilted forward, covering his eyes. "Help! I've gone blind!" Raistlin, with a distrustful glance at the elven guards, hurried forward. He took the old man's arm and straightened his hat.

"Ah, thank the true gods," the magician said, blinking and shuffling across the floor. The Speaker watched the old magician, a puzzled expression on his face. Then, as if in a dream, he turned to face Goldmoon.

"I do apologize, lady of the Plains," he said softly. "It has been over three hundred years since the elven clerics vanished, three hundred years since the symbol of Mishakal was seen in this land. My heart bled to see the amulet profaned, as I thought. Forgive me. We have been in despair so long I failed to see the arrival of hope. Please, if you are not weary, tell us your story."

Goldmoon related the story of the medallion, telling of Riverwind and the stoning, the meeting of the companions at the Inn, and their journey to Xak Tsaroth. She told of the destruction of the dragon and of how she received the medallion of Mishakal. But she didn't mention the Disks.

The sun's rays lengthened as she spoke, changing color as twilight approached. When her story ended, the Speaker was silent for long moments.

"I must consider all of this and what it means to us," he said finally. He turned to the companions. "You are exhausted. I see some of you stand by courage alone. Indeed"—he smiled, looking at Fizban who leaned against a pillar, snoring softly—"some of you are asleep on your feet. My daughter, Laurana, will guide you to a place where you can forget your fears. We will hold a banquet in your

honor tonight, for you bring us hope. May the peace of the true gods go with you."

The elves parted, and out of their midst came an elfmaiden who walked forward to stand beside the Speaker. At sight of her, Caramon's mouth sagged open. Riverwind's eyes widened. Even Raistlin stared, his eyes seeing beauty at last, for no hint of decay touched the young elfmaiden. Her hair was honey pouring from a pitcher; it spilled over her arms and down her back, past her waist, touching her wrists as she stood with her arms at her sides. Her skin was smooth and woodland brown. She had the delicate, refined features of the elves,† but these were combined with full, pouting lips and large liquid eyes that changed color like leaves in flickering sunshine.

Qualinesti elves are described in Kindred Spirits *as "all height, no substance." The elves regard as full elves only those with bloodlines that go back to the Kinslayer Wars.*

"On my honor as a knight," Sturm said with a catch in his voice, "I've never seen any woman so lovely."

"Nor will you in this world," Tanis murmured.

All the companions glanced at Tanis sharply as he spoke, but the half-elf did not notice. His eyes were on the elfmaid. Sturm raised his eyebrows, exchanged looks with Caramon who nudged his brother. Flint shook his head and sighed a sigh that seemed to come from his toes.

"Now much is made clear," Goldmoon said to Riverwind.

"It hasn't been made clear to me," Tasslehoff said. "Do you know what's going on, Tika?"

All Tika knew was that, looking at Laurana, she felt suddenly dumpy and half-dressed, freckled and red-headed. She tugged her blouse up higher over her full bosom, wishing it didn't reveal quite so much or that she had less to reveal.

"Tell me what's going on," Tasslehoff whispered, seeing the knowing looks exchanged by the others.

"I don't know!" Tika snapped. "Just that Caramon's making a fool of himself. Look at the big ox. You'd think he'd never seen a woman before."

"She is pretty," Tas said. "Different from you, Tika. She's slender and she walks like a tree bending in the wind and—"

"Oh, shut up!" Tika snapped furiously, giving Tas a shove that nearly knocked him down.

Tasslehoff gave her a wounded glance, then walked over to stand beside Tanis, determined to keep near the half-elf until he figured out what was going on.

"I welcome you to Qualinost, honored guests," Laurana said shyly, in a voice that was like a clear stream rippling among the trees. "Please follow me. The way is not far, and there is food and drink and rest at the end."

Moving with childlike grace, she walked among the companions who parted for her as the elves had done, all of them staring at her admiringly. Laurana lowered her eyes in maidenly modesty and self-consciousness, her cheeks flushing. She looked up only once, and that was as she passed Tanis—a fleeting glance, that only Tanis saw. His face grew troubled, his eyes darkened.

The companions left the Tower of the Sun, waking Fizban as they departed.

6

Tanis and Laurana.

Laurana led them to a sun-dappled grove of aspens in the very center of the city. Here, though surrounded by buildings and streets, they seemed to be in the heart of a forest. Only the murmurings of a nearby brook broke the stillness. Laurana, gesturing toward fruit trees among the aspens, told the companions to pick and eat their fill. Elfmaids brought in baskets of fresh, fragrant bread. The companions washed in the brook, then returned to relax on soft moss beds to revel in the silent peacefulness around them.

All except Tanis. Refusing food, the half-elf wandered around the grove, absorbed in his own thoughts. Tasslehoff watched him closely, eaten alive by curiosity.

Laurana was a perfect, charming hostess. She made certain everyone was seated and comfortable, speaking a few words to each of them.

"Flint Fireforge, isn't it?" she said. The dwarf flushed with pleasure. "I still have some of the wonderful toys you made me. We have missed you, these many years."†

Flint is one of the few outsiders ever let into Qualinesti. Although elves think they are the finest silversmiths and goldsmiths, they value his skill.He befriended the young and lonely Tanis when he came to Qualinesti to carry out some work.

So flustered he couldn't talk, Flint plopped down on the grass and gulped down a huge mug of water.

"You are Tika?" Laurana asked, stopping by the barmaid.

"Tika Waylan," the girl said huskily.

"Tika, what a pretty name. And what beautiful hair you have," Laurana said, reaching out to touch the bouncy red curls admiringly.

"Do you think so?" Tika said, blushing, seeing Caramon's eyes on her.

"Of course! It is the color of flame. You must have a spirit to match. I heard how you saved my brother's life in the Inn, Tika. I am deeply indebted to you."

"Thank you," Tika answered softly. "Your hair is real pretty, too."

Laurana smiled and moved on. Tasslehoff noticed, however, that her eyes constantly strayed to Tanis. When the half-elf suddenly threw down an apple and disappeared into the trees, Laurana excused herself hurriedly and followed.

"Ah, now I'll find out what's going on!" Tas said to himself. Glancing around, he slipped after Tanis.

Tas crept along the winding trail among the trees and suddenly came upon the half-elf standing beside the foaming stream alone, tossing dead leaves into the water. Seeing movement to his left, Tas quickly crouched down into a clump of bushes as Laurana emerged from another trail.

"Tanthalas Quisif nan-Pah!" she called.

As Tanis turned at the sound of his elven name, she flung her arms around his neck, kissing him.† "Ugh," she said teasingly, pulling back. "Shave off that horrible beard. It itches! And you don't look like Tanthalas anymore."

Laurana's character may be old in years, but she is very naive and sheltered in her spoiled outlook. This leaves her much room to grow as a character. —TRH

Tanis put his hands to her waist and gently pushed her away. "Laurana—" he began.

"No, don't be mad about the beard. I'll learn to like it, if you insist," Laurana pleaded, pouting. "Kiss me back. No? Then I'll kiss you until you

cannot help yourself." She kissed him again until finally Tanis broke free of her grip.

"Stop it, Laurana," he said harshly, turning away.

"Why, what's the matter?" she asked, catching hold of his hand. "You've been gone so many years. And now you're back. Don't be cold and gloomy. You are my betrothed, remember? It is proper for a girl to kiss her betrothed."

"That was a long time ago," Tanis said. "We were children, then, playing a game, nothing more. It was romantic, a secret to share. You know what would have happened if your father had found out. Gilthanas did find out, didn't he?"

"Of course! I told him," Laurana said, hanging her head, looking up at Tanis through her long eyelashes. "I tell Gilthanas everything, you know that. I didn't think he'd react like that! I know what he said to you. He told me later. He felt badly."

"I'll bet he did." Tanis gripped her wrists, holding her hands still. "What he said was true, Laurana! I am a bastard half-breed. Your father would have every right to kill me! How could I bring disgrace down on him, after what he did for my mother and me? That was one reason I left—that and to find out who I am and where I belong."

"You are Tanthalas, my beloved, and you belong here!"† Laurana cried. She broke free of his grip and caught his hands in her own. "Look! You wear my ring still. I know why you left. It was because you were afraid to love me, but you don't need to be, not anymore. Everything's changed. Father has so much to worry about, he won't mind. Besides, you're a hero now. Please, let us be married. Isn't that why you came back?"

The basic structure of DRAGONLANCE, as I've mentioned earlier, is a triangle with a fourth concept swinging among the other three. In the case of our characters, Tanis represents the central, swing character. His friends and the world's problems at large represent the chaos pole and Kitiara represents the temptation/evil pole. Laurana is the third pole of this triad, representing the positive/good choice pole.—TRH

"Laurana," Tanis spoke gently but firmly—"my returning was an accident—"

"No!" she cried, pushing him away. "I don't believe you."

"You must have heard Gilthanas's story. If Porthios had not rescued us, we would have been in Pax Tharkas now!"

"He made it up! He didn't want to tell me the truth. You came back because you love me. I won't listen to anything else."

"I didn't want to tell you, but I see that I must," Tanis said, exasperated. "Laurana, I'm in love with

someone else—a human woman. Her name is Kitiara.† That doesn't mean I don't love you, too. I do—" Tanis faltered.

Kitiara, as noted, is the third pole influencing Tanis.—TRH

Laurana stared at him, all color drained from her face.

"I do love you, Laurana. But, you see, I can't marry you, because I love her, too. My heart is divided, just like my blood." He took off the ring of golden ivy leaves and handed it to her. "I release you from any promises you made to me, Laurana. And I ask you to release me."

Laurana took the ring, unable to speak. She looked at Tanis pleadingly, then, seeing only pity in his face, shrieked and flung the ring away from her. It fell at Tas's feet. He picked it up and slipped it into a pouch.

"Laurana," Tanis said sorrowfully, taking her in his arms as she sobbed wildly. "I'm so sorry. I never meant—"

At this point, Tasslehoff slipped out of the brush and made his way back up the trail.

"Well," said the kender to himself, sighing in satisfaction—"now at least I know what's going on."

Tanis awoke suddenly to find Gilthanas standing over him. "Laurana?" he asked, getting to his feet.

"She is all right," Gilthanas said quietly. "Her maidens brought her home. She told me what you said. I just want you to know I understand. It was what I feared all along. The human half of you cries to other humans. I tried to tell her, hoping she wouldn't get hurt. She will listen to me now. Thank you, Tanthalas. I know it cannot have been easy."

"It wasn't," Tanis said, swallowing. "I'm going to be honest, Gilthanas—I love her, I really do. It's just that—"

"Please, say no more. Let us leave it as it is and perhaps, if we cannot be friends, we can at least respect each other." Gilthanas's face was drawn and pale in the setting sun. "You and your friends must prepare yourselves. When the silver moon rises, there will be a feast, and then the High Council meeting. Now is the time when decisions must be made."

He left. Tanis stared after him a moment, then, sighing, went to wake the others.

This is the shortest chapter in the trilogy.

7

Farewell. The companions' decision.

The feast held in Qualinost reminded Goldmoon of her mother's funeral banquet. Like the feast, the funeral was supposed to be a joyous occasion—after all, Tearsong had become a goddess. But the people found it difficult to accept the death of this beautiful woman. And so the Qué-Shu mourned her passing with a grief that approached blasphemy.

Tearsong's funeral banquet was the most elaborate to be given in the memory of the Qué-Shu. Her grieving husband had spared no expense. Like the banquet in Qualinost on this night, there was a great deal of food which few could eat. There were half-hearted attempts at conversation when no one wanted to talk. Occasionally someone, overcome with sorrow, was forced to leave the table.

So vivid was this memory that Goldmoon could eat little; the food was ash in her mouth. Riverwind regarded her with concern. His hand found hers beneath the table and she gripped it hard, smiling as his strength flowed into her body.

The elven feast was held in the courtyard just south of the great golden tower. There were no walls about the platform of crystal and marble which sat atop the highest hill in Qualinost, offering an unobstructed view of the glittering city below, the dark forest beyond, and even the deep purple edge of the Tharkadan Mountains far to the south. But the beauty was lost on those in attendance, or made more poignant by the knowledge that soon it would be gone forever. Goldmoon sat at the right hand of the Speaker. He tried to make polite conversation, but eventually his worries and concerns overwhelmed him and he fell silent.

To the Speaker's left sat his daughter, Laurana. She made no pretense at eating, just sat with her head bowed, her long hair flowing around her face. When she did look up, it was to gaze at Tanis, her heart in her eyes.

The half-elf, very much aware of the heart-broken stare as well as of Gilthanas eyeing him coldly, ate his food without appetite, his eyes fixed on his plate. Sturm, next to him, was drawing up in his mind plans for the defense of Qualinesti.

Flint felt strange and out of place as dwarves always feel among elves. He didn't like elven food anyway and refused everything. Raistlin nibbled at his food absently, his golden eyes studying Fizban. Tika, feeling awkward and out of place among the graceful elven women, couldn't eat a morsel. Caramon decided he knew why elves were so slender: the food consisted of fruits and vegetables, cooked in delicate sauces, served with bread and cheeses and a very light, spicy wine. After starving for four days in the cage, the food did nothing to satisfy the big warrior's hunger.

The only two in the entire city of Qualinost to enjoy the feast were Tasslehoff and Fizban. The old magician carried on a one-sided argument with an aspen, while Tasslehoff simply enjoyed everything, discovering later—to his surprise—that two golden spoons, a silver knife, and a butter dish made of a seashell had wandered into one of his pouches.

The red moon was not visible. Solinari, a slim band of silver in the sky, began to wane. As the first stars appeared, the Speaker of the Suns nodded sadly at his son. Gilthanas rose and moved to stand next to his father's chair.

Gilthanas began to sing. The elven words flowed into a melody delicate and beautiful. As he sang, Gilthanas held a small crystal lamp in both hands, the candlelight within illuminating his marble features. Tanis, listening to the song, closed his eyes; his head sank into his hands.

"What is it? What do the words mean?" Sturm asked softly.

Tanis raised his head. His voice breaking, he whispered:

> The Sun
> The splendid eye
> Of all our heavens
> Dives from the day,
>
> And leaves
> The dozing sky,
> Spangled with fireflies,
> Deepening in gray.

The elves about the table stood quietly now, taking up their own lamps as they joined in the song. Their voices blended, weaving a haunting song of infinite sadness.

> Now Sleep,
> Our oldest friend,
> Lulls in the trees
> And calls
> Us in.
>
> The Leaves
> Give off cold fire,
> They blaze into ash
> At the end of the year.
>
> And birds
> Coast on the winds,

And wheel to the North
When Autumn ends.

The day grows dark,
The seasons bare,
But we
Await the sun's
Green fire upon
The trees.†

Points of flickering lantern light spread from the courtyard like ripples in a still, calm pond, through the streets, into the forests and beyond. And, with each lamp lit, another voice was raised in song, until the surrounding forest itself seemed to sing with despair.

The wind
Dives through the days.
By season, by moon
Great kingdoms arise.

The breath
Of firefly, of bird,
Of trees, of mankind
Fades in a word.

Now Sleep,
Our oldest friend,
Lulls in the trees
And calls
Us in.

The Age,
The thousand lives
Of men and their stories
Go to their graves.

But We,
The people long
In poem and glory
Fade from the song.

Gilthanas's voice died away. With a gentle breath, he blew out the flame of his lamp. One by one, as they had started, the others around the table ended

The trick in writing a rhymed poem with such short lines is to come down easy on the rhymes so they don't draw too much attention to themselves at the expense of other things in the poem. Slant rhymes ("sky" and "gray," "fire" and "year") are one good way to deal with this difficulty—and if you say "those aren't rhymes," read some twentieth-century rhymed poetry and you'll find them all over the place.
—Michael Williams

the song and blew out their candles. All through Qualinost, the voices hushed and the flames were extinguished until it seemed that silence and darkness swept over the land. At the very end, only the distant mountains returned the final chords of the song, like the whispering of leaves falling to the ground.

The Speaker stood.

"And now," he said heavily, "it is time for the meeting of the High Council. It will be held in the Hall of the Sky. Tanthalas, if you will lead your companions there."

The Hall of the Sky, they discovered, was a huge square, lit by torches. The giant dome of the heavens, glittering with stars, arched above it. But it was dark to the north where lightning played on the horizon. The Speaker motioned to Tanis to bring the companions to stand near him, then the entire population of Qualinost gathered around them. There was no need to call for silence. Even the wind hushed as the Speaker began.

I, like Tasslehoff, love both making and reading maps. This map affords us an understanding of the larger events in the world. The original map from this book (shown on page 8) covered only the eastern parts of the Abanasinian peninsula whose contours heavily hinted at the hex grid paper on which I originally drew that map.—TRH

"Here you see our situation." He gestured at something on the ground. The companions saw a gigantic map beneath their feet.† Tasslehoff, standing in the middle of the Plains of Abanasinia, drew in a deep breath. He couldn't remember ever seeing anything so wonderful.

"There's Solace!" he cried in excitement, pointing.

"Yes, Kenderkin," the Speaker replied. "And that is where the dragonarmies mass. In Solace"—he touched the spot on the map with a staff—"and in Haven. Lord Verminaard has made no secret of his plans to invade Qualinesti. He waits only to gather his forces and secure his supply routes. We cannot hope to stand against such a horde."

"Surely Qualinost is easily defended," Sturm spoke up. "There is no direct route overland. We crossed bridges over ravines that no army in existence could get through if the bridges were cut. Why do you not stand up to them?"

"If it were only an army, we could defend Qualinesti," the Speaker answered. "But what can we do against dragons?" The Speaker spread his hands helplessly. "Nothing! According to legends, it was only with the Dragonlance that the mighty Huma

defeated them. There are none now—at least that we know of—who remember the secret of that great weapon."

Fizban started to speak, but Raistlin hushed him.

"No," the Speaker continued, "we must abandon this city and these woods. We plan to go west, into the unknown lands there, hoping to find a new home for our people—or perhaps even return to Silvanesti, the most ancient elvenhome. Until a week ago, our plans were advancing well. It will take three days of forced marching for the Dragon Highlord to move his men into attack position, and spies will inform us when the army leaves Solace. We will have time to escape into the west. But then we learned of a third dragonarmy at Pax Tharkas, less than a day's journey from us. Unless that army is stopped, we are doomed."

"And you know a way to stop that army?" Tanis asked.

"Yes." The Speaker looked at his youngest son. "As you know, men from Gateway and Solace and surrounding communities are being held prisoner in the fortress of Pax Tharkas, working as slaves for the Dragon Highlord. Verminaard is clever. Lest his slaves revolt, he keeps the women and children of these men hostages, ransom for the men's behavior. It is our belief that, were these captives freed, the men would turn on their masters and destroy them. It was to have been Gilthanas's mission to free the hostages and lead the revolt. He would have taken the humans south into the mountains, drawing off this third army in pursuit, allowing us time to escape."

"And what of the humans then?" Riverwind asked harshly. "It seems to me you throw them to the dragonarmies as a desperate man throws hunks of meat to pursuing wolves."

"Lord Verminaard will not keep them alive much longer, we fear. The ore is nearly gone. He is gleaning every last little bit, then the slaves' usefulness to him will end. There are valleys in the mountains, caves where the humans can live and fend off the dragonarmies. They can easily hold the mountain passes against them, especially now that winter is setting in. Admittedly, some may die, but that is a price that must be paid. If you had the choice, man of the Plains, would you rather die in slavery or die fighting?"

Riverwind, not answering, stared down at the map darkly.

"Gilthanas's mission failed," Tanis said, "and now you want us to try and lead the revolt?"

"Yes, Tanthalas," the Speaker replied. "Gilthanas knows a way into Pax Tharkas—the Sla-Mori. He can lead you into the fortress. You not only have a chance to free your own kind, but you offer the elves a chance to escape"†—the Speaker's voice hardened—"a chance to live that many elves were not given when humans brought the Cataclysm down upon us!"

Herein is the objective of the second game module by Douglas Niles: DL-2 Dragons of Flame.

Riverwind glanced up, scowling. Even Sturm's expression darkened. The Speaker drew a deep breath, then sighed. "Please forgive me," he said. "I do not mean to flog you with whips from the past. We are not uncaring about the humans' plight. I send my son, Gilthanas, with you willingly, knowing that—if we part—we may never see each other again. I make this sacrifice, so that my people—and yours—may live."

"We must have time to consider," Tanis said, though he knew what his decision must be. The Speaker nodded and elven warriors cleared a path through the crowd, leading the companions to a grove of trees. Here, they left them alone.

Tanis's friends stood before him, their solemn faces masks of light and shadow beneath the stars. All this time, he thought, I have fought to keep us together. Now I see that we must separate. We cannot risk taking the Disks into Pax Tharkas, and Goldmoon will not leave them behind.

"I will go to Pax Tharkas," Tanis said softly. "But I believe it is time now that we separate, my friends. Before you speak, let me say this. I would send Tika, Goldmoon, Riverwind, Caramon and Raistlin, and you, Fizban, with the elves in hopes that you may carry the Disks to safety. The Disks are too precious to risk on a raid into Pax Tharkas."

"That may be, Half-Elf," Raistlin whispered from the depths of his cowl, "but it is not among the Qualinesti elves that Goldmoon will find the one she seeks."

"How do you know?" Tanis asked, startled.

"He doesn't know anything, Tanis," Sturm interrupted bitterly. "More talk—"

"Raistlin?" Tanis repeated, ignoring Sturm.

"You heard the knight!" the mage hissed. "I know nothing!"

Tanis sighed, letting it go, and glanced around. "You named me your leader—"

"Aye, we did, lad," said Flint suddenly. "But this decision is coming from your head, not your heart. Deep inside, you don't really believe we should split up."

"Well, I'm not staying with these elves," Tika said, folding her arms across her chest. "I'm going with you, Tanis. I plan to become a swordswoman, like Kitiara."

Tanis winced. Hearing Kitiara's name was like a physical blow.

"I will not hide with elves," Riverwind said, "especially if it means leaving my kind behind to fight for me."

"He and I are one," Goldmoon said, putting her hand on his arm. "Besides," she said more softly, "somehow I know that what the mage says is true—the leader is not among the elves. They want to flee the world, not fight for it."

"We're all going, Tanis," Flint said firmly.

The half-elf looked helplessly around at the group, then he smiled and shook his head. "You're right. I didn't truly believe we should separate. It's the sensible, logical thing to do, of course, which is why we won't do it."

"Now maybe we can get some sleep." Fizban yawned.

"Wait a minute, Old One," Tanis said sternly. "You are not one of us. You're definitely going with the elves."

"Am I?" the old mage asked softly as his eyes lost their vague, unfocused look. He stared at Tanis with such a penetrating—almost menacing—gaze that the half-elf involuntarily took a step back, suddenly sensing an almost palpable aura of power surrounding the old man. His voice was soft and intense. "I go where I choose in this world, and I choose to go with you, Tanis Half-Elven."

Raistlin glanced at Tanis as if to say, *Now you understand!* Tanis, irresolute, returned the glance. He regretted putting off discussing this with Raistlin, but wondered how they could confer now, knowing the old man would not leave.

"I speak you this, Raistlin," Tanis said suddenly, using Camptalk, a corrupted form of Common developed among the racially mixed mercenaries of Krynn.† The twins had done a bit of mercenary work in their time, as had most of the companions, in order to eat. Tanis knew Raistlin would understand. He was fairly certain the old man wouldn't.

How convenient! I wonder why Tanis never felt the need to use this language again?—TRH

"We talk if want," Raistlin answered in the same language,. "but little know I."

"You fear. Why?"†

The language structure of Camptalk appears to have its roots with gully dwarf languages.—TRH

Raistlin's strange eyes stared far away as he answered slowly. "I know not, Tanis. But—you right. There power be, within Old One. I feel great power. I fear." His eyes gleamed. "And I hunger!" The mage sighed and seemed to return from wherever it was he had been. "But he right. Try to stop him? Very much danger."

"As if there wasn't enough already," Tanis said bitterly, switching back to Common. "We take our own in with us in the form of a doddering old magician."

"Others there are, as dangerous, perhaps," Raistlin said, with a meaningful look at his brother. The mage returned to Common. "I am weary. I must sleep. Are you staying, brother?"

"Yes," Caramon answered, exchanging glances with Sturm. "We're going to talk with Tanis."

Raistlin nodded and gave his arm to Fizban. The old mage and the young one left, the old mage lashing out at a tree with his staff, accusing it of trying to sneak up on him.†

Fizban and Raistlin began their relationship well—it was not, however, to last.—TRH

"As if one crazed mage wasn't bad enough," Flint muttered. "I'm going to bed."

One by one the others left until Tanis stood with Caramon and Sturm. Wearily, Tanis turned to face them. He had a feeling he knew what this was going to be about. Caramon's face was flushed and he stared at his feet. Sturm stroked his moustaches and regarded Tanis thoughtfully.

"Well?" Tanis asked.

"Gilthanas," Sturm answered.

Tanis frowned and scratched his beard. "That's my business, not yours," he said shortly.

"It is *our* business, Tanis," Sturm persisted, "if he's leading us into Pax Tharkas. We don't want to pry, but it's obvious there's a score to settle between you two. I've seen his eyes when he looks at you,

Tanis, and, if I were you, I wouldn't go anywhere without a friend at my back."

Caramon looked at Tanis earnestly, his brow furrowed. "I know he's an elf and all," the big man said slowly. "But, like Sturm says, he gets a funny look in his eyes sometimes. Don't you know the way to this Sla-Mori? Can't we find it ourselves? I don't trust him. Neither do Sturm and Raist."

"Listen, Tanis," Sturm said, seeing the half-elf's face darken with anger. "If Gilthanas was in such danger in Solace as he claimed, why was he casually sitting in the Inn? And then there's his story about his warriors 'accidentally' running into a whole damn army! Tanis, don't shake your head so quickly. He may not be evil, just misguided. What if Verminaard's got some hold over him? Perhaps the Dragon Highlord convinced him he'd spare his people if—in return—he betrays us! Maybe that's why he was in Solace, waiting for us."

"That's ridiculous!" Tanis snapped. "How would he know we were coming?"

"We didn't exactly keep our journey from Xak Tsaroth to Solace secret," Sturm returned coldly. "We saw draconians all along the way and those that escaped Xak Tsaroth must have realized we came for the Disks. Verminaard probably knows our descriptions better than he knows his own mother."

"No! I don't believe it!" Tanis said angrily, glaring at Sturm and Caramon. "You two are wrong! I'll stake my life on it. I grew up with Gilthanas, I know him! Yes, there *is* a score to settle between us, but we have discussed it and the matter is closed. I'll believe he's turned traitor to his people the day I believe you or Caramon turn traitor. And no, I don't know the way to Pax Tharkas. I've never been there. And one more thing," Tanis shouted, now in a fury, "if there's people I don't trust in this group, it's that brother of yours and that old man!" He stared accusingly at Caramon.

The big man grew pale and lowered his eyes. He began to turn away. Tanis came to his senses, suddenly realizing what he had said. "I'm sorry, Caramon." He put his hand on the warrior's arm. "I didn't mean that. Raistlin's saved our lives more than once on this insane journey. It's just that I can't believe Gilthanas is a traitor!"

"We know, Tanis," Sturm said quietly. "And we trust your judgment. But—it's too dark a night to walk with your eyes closed, as my people say."

Tanis sighed and nodded. He put his other hand on Sturm's arm. The knight clasped him and the three men stood in silence, then they left the grove and walked back to the Hall of the Sky. They could still hear the Speaker talking with his warriors.

"What does Sla-Mori mean?" Caramon asked.

"Secret Way," Tanis answered.

Tanis woke with a start, his hand on the dagger at his belt. A dark shape crouched over him in the night, blotting out the stars overhead. Reaching up quickly, he grabbed hold of and yanked the person down across his body, putting his dagger to the exposed throat.

"Tanthalas!" There was a small scream at the sight of the steel flashing in the starlight.

"Laurana!" Tanis gasped.

Her body pressed against his. He could feel her trembling and, now that he was fully awake, he could see the long hair flowing loosely about her shoulders. She was dressed only in a flimsy night-dress. Her cloak had fallen off in the brief struggle.

Acting on impulse, Laurana had risen from her bed and slipped out into the night, throwing a cloak around her to protect her from the cold. Now she lay across Tanis's chest, too frightened to move. This was a side of Tanis she had never known existed. She realized suddenly that if she had been an enemy, she would be dead now—her throat slit.

"Laurana . . ." Tanis repeated, thrusting the dagger back into his belt with a shaking hand. He pushed her away and sat up, angry at himself for frightening her and angry at her for awakening something deep within him. For an instant, when she lay on top of him, he was acutely conscious only of the smell of her hair, the warmth of her slender body, the play of the muscles in her thighs, the softness of her small breasts. Laurana had been a girl when he left. He returned to find a woman—a very beautiful, desirable woman

"What in the name of the Abyss are you doing here at this time of night?"

"Tanthalas," she said, choking, pulling her cape around her tightly. "I came to ask you to change your mind. Let your friends go to free the humans in Pax Tharkas. You must come with us! Don't throw your life away. My father is desperate. He doesn't believe this will work—I know he doesn't. But he hasn't any choice! He's already mourning Gilthanas as if he were dead. I'm going to lose my brother. I can't lose you, too!" She began to sob. Tanis glanced around hastily. There were almost certainly elven guards around. If the elves caught him in this compromising situation . . .

"Laurana," he said, gripping her shoulders and shaking her. "You're not a child anymore. You've got to grow up and grow up fast.† I wouldn't let my friends face danger without me! I know the risks we're taking; I'm not blind! But if we can free the humans from Verminaard and give you and your people time to escape, it's a chance we have to take! There comes a time, Laurana, when you've got to risk your life for something you believe in—something that means more than life itself. Do you understand?"

Laurana's growth from innocence is her personal journey. Her triad would seem to be Tanis, her own past, and her future. —TRH

She looked up at him through a mass of golden hair. Her sobs stopped and she ceased to tremble. She stared at him very intently.

"Do you understand, Laurana?" he repeated.

"Yes, Tanthalas," she answered softly. "I understand."

"Good!" He sighed. "Now go back to bed. Quickly. You've put me in danger. If Gilthanas saw us like this—"

Laurana stood up and walked swiftly from the grove, flitting along the streets and buildings like the wind among the aspens. Sneaking past the guards to get back inside her father's dwelling was simple—she and Gilthanas had been doing it since childhood. Returning quietly to her room, she stood outside her father's and mother's door for a moment, listening. There was light inside. She could hear parchment rustling, smell an acrid odor. Her father was burning papers. She heard her mother's soft murmur, calling her father to bed. Laurana closed her eyes for a moment in silent agony, then her lips tightened in firm resolve, and she ran down the dark, chill hallway to her bedchamber.

8

Doubts. Ambush!
A new friend.

The elves woke the companions before dawn. Storm clouds lowered on the northern horizon, reaching like grasping fingers toward Qualinesti. Gilthanas arrived after breakfast, dressed in a tunic of blue cloth and a suit of chain mail.

"We have supplies," he said, gesturing toward the warriors who held packs in their hands. "We can also provide weapons or armament, if you have need."

"Tika needs armor and shield and sword," said Caramon.

"We will provide what we can," Gilthanas said, "though I doubt if we have a full set of armor small enough."

"How is Theros Ironfeld this morning?" Goldmoon asked.

"He rests comfortably, cleric of Mishakal." Gilthanas bowed respectfully to Goldmoon. "My people will, of course, take him with them when we leave. You may bid him farewell."

Elves soon returned with armor of every make and description for Tika and a lightweight shortsword, favored by the elven women.† Tika's eyes glowed when she saw the helm and shield. Both were of elvish design, tooled and decorated with jewels.

The Qualinesti women are trained in the use of both the bow and the sword, but only for ceremonial use.

Gilthanas took the helm and shield from the elf. "I have yet to thank you for saving my life in the Inn," he said to Tika. "Accept these. They are my mother's ceremonial armor, dating back to the time of the Kinslayer Wars.† These would have gone to my sister, but Laurana and I both believe you are the proper owner."

Before the first word of the novel was written, we knew when the Kinslayer Wars took place and the basic reasons why. Having a detailed history that the reader catches only in glimpses lends a depth to the backdrop against which the story takes place. It also grounds the characters in the world, giving them a past.—TRH

"How beautiful," Tika murmured, blushing. She accepted the helm, then looked at the rest of the armor in confusion. "I don't know what goes where," she confessed.

"I'll help!" Caramon offered eagerly.

"I'll handle this," Goldmoon said firmly. Picking up the armor, she led Tika into a grove of trees.

"What does she know about armor?" Caramon grumbled.

Riverwind looked at the warrior and smiled, the rare, infrequent smile that softened his stern face. "You forget," he said—"she is Chieftain's Daughter. It was her duty, in her father's absence, to lead the tribe to war. She knows a great deal about armor, warrior—and even more about the heart that beats beneath it."

Caramon flushed. Nervously, he picked up a pack of supplies and glanced inside. "What's this junk?" he asked.

"*Quith-pa,*" said Gilthanas. "Iron rations, in your language. It will last us for many weeks, if need be."

"It looks like dried fruit!" Caramon said in disgust.

"That's what it is," Tanis replied, grinning.

Caramon groaned.

Dawn was just beginning to tinge the wispy storm clouds with a pale, chill light when Gilthanas led the party out of Qualinesti. Tanis kept his eyes straight ahead, refusing to look back. He wished that his final trip here could have been happier. He had not seen Laurana all morning and, though he felt relieved to have avoided a tearful farewell, he secretly wondered why she hadn't come to bid him good-bye.

The trail moved south, descending gradually but constantly. It had been thick and overgrown with brush, but the party of warriors Gilthanas led before had cleared it as they moved, so that walking was relatively easy. Caramon walked beside Tika, resplendent in her mismatched armor, instructing her on the use of her sword. Unfortunately, the teacher was having a bad time of it.

Goldmoon had slit Tika's red barmaid skirt up to her thighs for easier movement. Bits of fluffy white from Tika's fur-trimmed undergarments peeped enticingly through the slits.† Her legs were visible as she walked, and the girl's legs were just as Caramon had always imagined—round and well-formed. Thus Caramon found it rather difficult to concentrate on his lesson. Absorbed in his pupil, he did not notice that his brother had disappeared.

This scene led Michael Williams to write "Caramon's Song," which, for obvious reasons, was never published. "Dragonlance, dragonlance. I see Tika's underpants."

"Where's the young mage?" Gilthanas asked harshly.

"Maybe something's happened to him," Caramon said worriedly, cursing himself for forgetting his brother. The warrior drew his sword and started back along the trail.

"Nonsense!" Gilthanas stopped him. "What could have happened to him? There is no enemy for miles. He must have gone off somewhere—for some purpose."

"What are you saying?" Caramon asked, glowering.

"Maybe he left to—"

"To collect what I need for the making of my magic, elf," Raistlin whispered, emerging from the brush. "And to replenish the herbs that heal my cough."

"Raist!" Caramon nearly hugged him in his relief. "You shouldn't go off by yourself—it's dangerous."

"My spell components are secret," Raistlin whispered irritably, shoving his brother away. Leaning on the Staff of Magius, the mage rejoined Fizban in the line.

Gilthanas cast a sharp glance at Tanis, who shrugged and shook his head. As the group

continued on, the trail became steeper and steeper, leading down from the aspenwoods to the pines of the lowlands. It joined up with a clear brook that soon became a raging stream as they traveled farther south.

When they stopped for a hasty lunch, Fizban came over and hunkered down beside Tanis. "Someone's following us," he said in a penetrating whisper.

"What?" Tanis asked, his head snapping up to stare at the old man incredulously.

"Yes, indeed," the old mage nodded solemnly. "I've seen it—darting in and out among the trees."

Sturm saw Tanis's look of concern. "What's the matter?"

"The Old One says someone's following us."

"Bah!" Gilthanas threw down his last bit of quith-pa in disgust and stood up. "That's insane. Let us go now. The Sla-Mori is still many miles and we must be there by sundown."

"I'll take rear guard," Sturm said to Tanis softly.

They walked through the ragged pines for several more hours. The sun slanted down in the sky, lengthening shadows across the trail, when the group came suddenly to a clearing.

"Hsst!" Tanis warned, falling back in alarm.

Caramon, instantly alert, drew his sword, motioning for Sturm and his brother with his free hand.

"What is it?" piped Tasslehoff. "I can't see!"

"Shhh!" Tanis glared at the kender, and Tas clapped his own hand over his own mouth to save Tanis the trouble.

The clearing was the site of a recent bloody fight. Bodies of men and hobgoblins lay scattered about in the obscene postures of brutal death. The companions looked about fearfully and listened for long minutes but could hear nothing above the roar of the water.

"No enemy for miles!" Sturm glared at Gilthanas and started to step out into the clearing.

"Wait!" Tanis said. "I thought I saw something move!"

"Maybe one of them's still alive," Sturm said coolly and walked forward. The rest followed more slowly. A low moaning sound came from beneath two hobgoblin bodies. The warriors walked toward the carnage, swords level.

"Caramon . . ." Tanis gestured.

The big warrior shoved the bodies to one side. Beneath was a moaning figure.

"Human," Caramon reported. "And covered with blood. Unconscious, I think."

The rest came up to look at the man on the ground. Goldmoon started to kneel down, but Caramon stopped her.

"No, lady," he said gently. "It would be senseless to heal him if we just have to kill him again. Remember—humans fought for the Dragon Highlord in Solace."

The group gathered round to examine the man. He wore chain mail that was of good quality, if rather tarnished. His clothes were rich, though the cloth had worn thin in places. He appeared to be in his late thirties. His hair was thick and black, his chin firm, and his features regular. The stranger opened his eyes and stared up at the companions blearily.

"Thank the gods of the Seekers!" he said hoarsely. "My friends—are they all dead?"

"Worry about yourself first," Sturm said sternly. "Tell us who your friends were—the humans or the hobgoblins?"

"The humans—fighters against the dragonmen." The man broke off, his eyes widening. "Gilthanas?"

"Eben," Gilthanas said in quiet surprise. "How did you survive the battle at the ravine?"

"How did you, for that matter?" The man named Eben tried to stagger to his feet. Caramon reached out a hand to help him when suddenly Eben pointed. "Look out! Drac—"

Caramon whipped around, letting Eben fall back with a groan. The others turned to see twelve draconians standing at the edge of the clearing, weapons drawn.

"All strangers in the land are to be taken to the Dragon Highlord for questioning," one called out. "We charge you to come with us peacefully."

"No one was supposed to know about this path to Sla-Mori," Sturm whispered to Tanis with a meaningful glance at Gilthanas. "According to the elf, that is!"

"We do not take orders from Lord Verminaard!" Tanis yelled, ignoring Sturm.

"You will, soon enough," the draconian said and waved its arm. The creatures surged forward to attack.

Fizban, standing near the edge of the woods, pulled something from his pouch and began to mumble a few words.

"Not Fireball!" Raistlin hissed, grabbing the old mage's arm. "You'll incinerate everyone out there!"

"Oh, really? I suppose you're right." The old mage sighed in disappointment, then brightened. "Wait, I'll think of something else."

"Just stay here, under cover!" Raistlin ordered. "I'm going to my brother."

"Now, what was that web spell?"† The old man pondered.

Tika, her new sword drawn and ready, trembled with fear and excitement. One draconian rushed her and she swung a tremendous blow. The blade missed the draconian by a mile, Caramon's head by inches. Pulling Tika behind him, he knocked the draconian down with the flat of his sword. Before it could rise, he stepped on its throat, breaking its neck.

Another second-level spell. Fizban practices sorcery conservation.—TRH

Probably a good thing. If he'd cast a high-level spell, we'd probably all be dead!—MW

"Get behind me," he said to Tika, then glanced down at the sword she was still waving around wildly. "On second thought," Caramon amended nervously, "run over to those trees with the old man and Goldmoon. There's a good girl."

"I will not!" Tika said indignantly. "I'll show him," she muttered, her sweaty palms slipping on the hilt of the sword. Two more draconians charged Caramon, but his brother was beside him now—the two combining magic and steel to destroy their enemy. Tika knew she would only get in their way, and she feared Raistlin's anger more than she feared draconians. She looked around to see if anyone needed her help. Sturm and Tanis fought side by side. Gilthanas made an unlikely team with Flint, while Tasslehoff, his hoopak planted solidly in the ground, sent a deadly barrage of rocks whizzing onto the field. Goldmoon stood beneath the trees, Riverwind near her. The old magician had pulled out a spellbook and was flipping through its pages.

"Web . . . web . . . how did that go?" he mumbled.

"Aaarrrgghh!" A screech behind Tika nearly caused her to swallow her tongue. Whirling around,

she dropped her sword in alarm as a draconian, laughing horribly, launched itself into the air straight at her. Panic-stricken, Tika gripped her shield in both hands and struck the draconian in its hideous, reptilian face.† The impact nearly jarred the shield from her hands, but it knocked the creature onto its back, unconscious. Tika picked up her sword and, grimacing in disgust, stabbed the creature through the heart. Its body immediately turned to stone, encasing her sword. Tika yanked at it, but it remained stuck fast.

We again see that Skillet-Bashing specialization coming into play.—TRH

"Tika, to your left!" yelled Tasslehoff shrilly.

Tika stumbled around and saw another draconian. Swinging her shield, she blocked its sword thrust. Then, with a strength born of terror, she hit at the creature again and again with her shield, knowing only that she had to kill the thing. She kept bashing until she felt a hand on her arm. Whipping around, her blood-stained shield ready, she saw Caramon.

"It's all right!" the big warrior said soothingly. "It's all over, Tika. They're all dead. You did fine, just fine."

Tika blinked. For a moment she didn't recognize the warrior. Then, with a shudder, she lowered her shield.

"I wasn't very good with the sword," she said, starting to tremble in reaction to her fear and the memory of the horrible creature lunging at her.

Caramon saw her start to shake. He reached out and clasped her in his arms, stroking the sweat-damp red curls.

"You were braver than many men I've seen—experienced warriors," the big man said in a deep voice.†

Tika has great legs, can cook mountains of food with utensils that, in her hands, can be turned instantly into deadly weapons. Caramon's love for her was inevitable. —TRH

Tika looked up into Caramon's eyes. Her terror melted away, replaced by exultation. She pressed against Caramon. The feel of his hard muscles, the smell of sweat mingled with leather, increased her excitement. Tika flung her arms around his neck and kissed him with such violence her teeth bit into his lip. She tasted blood in her mouth.

Caramon, astonished, felt the tingle of pain, an odd contrast to the softness of her lips, and was overwhelmed with desire. He wanted this woman more than any other woman—and there had been

many—in his life. He forgot where he was, who was around him. His brain and his blood were on fire, and he ached with the pain of his passion. Crushing Tika to his chest, he held her and kissed her with bruising intensity.

The pain of his embrace was delicious to Tika. She longed for the pain to grow and envelop her, but at the same time, she felt suddenly cold and afraid. Remembering stories told by the other barmaids of the terrible, wonderful things that happened between men and women, she began to panic.

Caramon completely lost all sense of reality. He caught Tika up in his arms with a wild idea of carrying her into the woods, when he felt a cold, familiar hand on his shoulder.

The big man stared at his brother and regained his senses with a gasp. He gently set Tika on her feet. Dizzy and disoriented, she opened her eyes to see Raistlin standing beside his brother, regarding her with his strange, glittering stare.

Tika's face burned. She backed away, stumbled over the body of the draconian, then picked up her shield and ran.

Caramon swallowed, cleared his throat, and started to say something, but Raistlin simply glanced at him in disgust and walked back to rejoin Fizban. Caramon, trembling like a newborn colt, sighed shakily and walked over to where Sturm, Tanis, and Gilthanas stood, talking to Eben.

"No, I'm fine," the man assured them. "I just felt a little faint when I saw those creatures, that's all. You really have a cleric among you? That's wonderful, but don't waste her healing powers on me. Just a scratch. It's more their blood than mine. My party and I were tracking these draconians through the woods when we were attacked by at least forty hobgoblins."

"And you alone live to tell the tale," Gilthanas said.

"Yes," Eben replied, returning the elf's suspicious gaze. "I am an expert swordsman, as you know. I killed these"—he gestured to the bodies of six hobgoblins who lay around him—"then fell to the overwhelming numbers. The rest must have assumed I was dead and left me. But, enough of my heroics. You fellows are pretty good with swords yourselves. Where are you headed?"

"Some place called the Sla—" began Caramon, but Gilthanas cut him off.

"Our journey is secret," Gilthanas said. Then he added in a tentative voice. "We could use an expert swordsman."

"As long as you're fighting draconians, your fight is my fight," Eben said cheerfully. He pulled his pack out from under the body of a hobgoblin and slung it over his shoulder.

"My name's Eben Shatterstone. I come from Gateway. You've probably heard of my family," he said. "We had one of the most impressive mansions west of—"

"That's it!" cried Fizban. "I remembered!"

Suddenly the air was filled with strands of sticky, floating cobweb.

The sun set just as the group reached an open plain edged by tall mountain peaks. Rivaling the mountains for dominance of the land before it was the gigantic fortress known as Pax Tharkas, which guarded the pass between the mountains. The companions stared at it in awed silence.

Tika's eyes widened at the sight of the massive twin towers soaring into the sky. "I've never seen anything so big! Who built it? They must have been powerful men."

"It was not men," said Flint sadly. The dwarf's beard quivered as he looked at Pax Tharkas with a wistful expression. "It was elves and dwarves working together. Once, long ago, when times were peaceful."

"The dwarf speaks truly," Gilthanas said. "Long ago Kith-Kanan broke his father's heart and left the ancient home of Silvanesti. He and his people came to the beautiful woods given them by the Emperor of Ergoth following the scribing of the Swordsheath Scroll that ended the Kinslayer Wars.† Elves have lived in Qualinesti for long centuries since Kith-Kanan's death. His greatest achievement, however, was the building of Pax Tharkas. Standing between elven and dwarven kingdoms, it was constructed by both in a spirit of friendship since lost on Krynn. It grieves me to see it now, the bastion of a mighty war machine."†

Even as Gilthanas spoke, the companions saw the huge gate that stood at the front of Pax Tharkas

The Swordsheath Scroll, *by Dan Parkinson is part of the Dwarven Nations trilogy, and* The Kinslayer Wars, *by Douglas Niles is part of the Elven Nations trilogy.*

swing open. An army—long rows of draconians, hobgoblins, and goblins—marched out into the plains. The sound of braying horns echoed back from the mountaintops. Watching them from above was a great red dragon. The companions cowered among the scrub brush and trees. Though the dragon was too far away to see them, the dragonfear touched them even from this distance.

I always wonder whenever an adventurer in movies or books comes across ancient ruins why anyone would build these massive structures. Buildings are the evidence of purpose. I was determined to have reason behind our ancient architecture, and our carefully constructed history provided it.—TRH

"They march on Qualinesti," Gilthanas said, his voice breaking. "We must get inside and free the prisoners. Then Verminaard will be forced to call the army back."

"You're going inside Pax Tharkas!" Eben gasped.

"Yes," Gilthanas answered reluctantly, apparently regretting he had said so much.

"Whew!" Eben blew out a deep breath. "You people have guts, I'll give you that. So—how do we get in there? Wait until the army leaves? There will probably be only a couple of guards at the front gate. We could handle them easily, couldn't we, big man?" He nudged Caramon.

"Sure," Caramon grinned.

"That is not the plan," Gilthanas said coldly. The elf pointed to a narrow vale leading into the mountains, just visible in the rapidly fading light. "There is our way. We will cross in the cover of darkness."

He stood up and started off. Tanis hurried forward to catch up with him. "What do you know of this Eben?" the half-elf asked in elven, glancing back to where the man was chatting with Tika.

Gilthanas shrugged. "He was with the band of humans who fought with us at the ravine. Those who survived were taken to Solace and died there. I suppose he could have escaped. I did, after all," Gilthanas said, glancing sideways at Tanis. "He comes from Gateway where his father and father before him were wealthy merchants. The others told me, when he was out of hearing, that his family lost their money and he has since earned his living by his sword."

"I figured as much," Tanis said. "His clothes are rich, but they've seen better days. You made the right decision, bringing him along."

"I dared not leave him behind," Gilthanas answered grimly. "One of us should keep an eye on him."

"Yes." Tanis fell silent.

"And on me, too, you're thinking," Gilthanas said in a tight voice. "I know what the others say—the knight especially. But, I swear to you, Tanis, I'm not a traitor! I want one thing!" The elf's eyes gleamed feverishly in the dying light. "I want to destroy this Verminaard. If you could have seen him as his dragon destroyed my people! I'd gladly sacrifice my life—" Gilthanas stopped abruptly.

"And our lives as well?" Tanis asked.

As Gilthanas turned to face him, his almond-shaped eyes regarding Tanis without emotion. "If you must know, Tanthalas, your life means that—" He snapped his fingers. "But the lives of my people are everything to me. That is all I care for now." He walked on ahead as Sturm caught up with them.

"Tanis," he said. "The old man was right. We are being followed."

9

Suspicions Grow. The Sla-Mori.

The narrow trail climbed steeply up from the plains into a wooded valley in the foothills. Evening's shadows gathered close around them as they followed the stream up into the mountain. They had traveled only a short distance, however, when Gilthanas left the trail and disappeared into the brush. The companions stopped, looking at each other doubtfully.

"This is madness," Eben whispered to Tanis. "Trolls live in this valley—who do you think made that trail?" The dark-haired man took Tanis's arm with a cool familiarity the half-elf found disconcerting. "Admittedly, I'm the new kid in town, so to speak, and the gods know you don't have any reason to trust me, but how much do you know about this Gilthanas?"

"I know—" Tanis began, but Eben ignored him.

"There were some of us who didn't believe that draconian army stumbled onto us by accident, if you take my meaning. My boys and I had been hiding in the hills, fighting the dragonarmies ever since they hit Gateway. Last week, these elves showed up out of nowhere. They told us they were going to raid one of the Dragon Highlord's fortresses and would we like to come along and help? We said, sure, why not—anything to stick a bone in the Dragon High Man's craw.

"As we hiked, we began to get really nervous. There were draconian tracks all over the place! But it didn't bother the elves. Gilthanas said the tracks were old. That night we made camp and posted a watch. It didn't do us a lot of good, just gave us about twenty seconds warning before the draconians hit. And"—Eben glanced around and moved even closer—"while we were trying to wake up, grab our weapons, and fight those foul creatures, I heard the elves calling out, as if someone was lost. And who do you suppose they were calling for?"

Eben regarded Tanis intently. The half-elf frowned and shook his head, irritated at the dramatics.

"Gilthanas!" Eben hissed. "He was gone! They shouted and shouted for him—their leader!" The man shrugged. "Whether he ever showed up or not, I don't know. I was captured. They took us to Solace, where I got away. Anyway, I'd think twice about following that elf. He may have had good reason to be gone when the draconians attacked, but—"

"I've known Gilthanas a long time," Tanis interrupted gruffly, more disturbed than he wanted to admit.

"Sure. Just thought you should know," Eben said, smiling sympathetically. He clapped Tanis on the back and dropped back to stand by Tika.

Tanis didn't have to look around to know Caramon and Sturm had heard every word. Neither said anything, however, and before Tanis could talk to them, Gilthanas appeared suddenly, slipping out from among the trees.

"It is not much farther," the elf said. "The brush thins up ahead and the walking is easier."

"I say we just go in the front gate," Eben said.

"I agree," Caramon said. The big man glanced at his brother who sat limply beneath a tree. Goldmoon was pale with fatigue. Even Tasslehoff's head hung wearily.

"We could camp here tonight and go in by the front gates at dawn," Sturm suggested.

"We stick to the original plan," Tanis said sharply. "We make camp once we reach the Sla-Mori."

Then Flint spoke up. "You can go ring the bell at the gate and ask Lord Verminaard to let you in if you want, Sturm Brightblade. I'm sure he'd oblige. C'mon, Tanis." The dwarf stumped off down the trail.

"At least," Tanis said to Sturm in a low voice, "maybe this will throw off our pursuer."

"Whoever or whatever it is," Sturm answered. "It's woodscrafty, I'll say that for it. Every time I caught a glimpse and started back for a closer look, it vanished. I thought about ambushing it, but there wasn't time."

The group emerged from the brush thankfully, arriving at the base of a gigantic granite cliff. Gilthanas walked along the cliff face for several hundred feet, his hand feeling for something on the rock. Suddenly he stopped.

"We are here," he whispered. Reaching into his tunic, he removed a small gem that began to glow a soft, muted yellow. Running his hand over the rock wall, the elf found what he was searching for, a small niche in the granite. He placed the gem in the niche and began reciting ancient words and tracing unseen symbols in the night air.

"Very impressive," whispered Fizban. "I didn't know he was one of us," he said to Raistlin.

"A dabbler, nothing more," the mage replied. Leaning wearily on his staff, he watched Gilthanas intently, however.

Suddenly and silently, a huge block of stone separated from the cliff face and began moving slowly to one side. The companions backed up as a blast of chill, dank air flowed from the gaping hole in the rock.

"What's in there? " Caramon asked suspiciously.

"I do not know what is in there now," Gilthanas replied. "I have never entered. I know of this place only through the lore of my people."

"All right," Caramon growled. "What *used* to be in there?"

Gilthanas paused, then said. "This was the burial chamber of Kith-Kanan."

"More spooks," Flint grumbled, peering into the darkness. "Send the mage in first, so he can warn them we're coming."

"Throw the dwarf in," Raistlin returned. "They are accustomed to living in dark, dank caves."

"You speak of the mountain dwarves!" Flint said, his beard bristling. "It has been long years since the hill dwarves lived below ground in the kingdom of Thorbardin."

"Only because you were cast out!" Raistlin hissed.

"Stop it, both of you!" Tanis said in exasperation. "Raistlin, what do you sense about this place?"

"Evil. Great evil," the mage replied.

"But I sense great goodness, too," Fizban spoke unexpectedly. "The elves are not truly forgotten within, though evil things have come to rule in their stead."

"This is crazy!" Eben shouted. The noise echoed uncannily among the rocks and the others whirled, startled, staring at him in alarm. "I'm sorry," he said, dropping his voice. "But I can't believe you people are going in there! It doesn't take a magician to tell there's evil inside that hole. *I* can feel it! Go back around to the front," he urged. "Sure, there'll be one or two guards, but that's nothing compared to whatever lurks in that darkness beyond!"

"He's got a point, Tanis," Caramon said. "You can't fight the dead. We learned that in Darken Wood."

"This is the only way!" Gilthanas said angrily. "If you are such cowards—"

"There's a difference between caution and cowardice, Gilthanas," Tanis said, his voice steady and calm. The half-elf thought a moment. "We might be able to take on the guards at the front gate, but not before they could alert others. I say we enter and at least explore this way. Flint, you lead. Raistlin, we'll need your light."

"Shirak," spoke the mage softly, and the crystal on his staff began to glow. He and Flint plunged into the cave, followed closely by the rest. The

tunnel they entered was obviously ancient, but whether it was natural or artifact was impossible to tell.

"What about our pursuer?" Sturm asked in a low voice. "Do we leave the entrance open?"

"A trap," Tanis agreed softly. "Leave it open just a crack, Gilthanas, enough so that whoever's tracking us knows we came in here and can follow, but not enough so that it looks like a trap."

Gilthanas drew forth the gem, placed it in a niche on the inner side of the entrance, and spoke a few words. The stone began to slide silently back into place. At the last moment, when it was about seven or eight inches from closing, Gilthanas swiftly removed the gemstone. The stone shuddered to a halt, and the knight, the elf, and the half-elf joined the companions in the entrance to the Sla-Mori.

"There is a great deal of dust," Raistlin reported, coughing—"but no tracks, at least in this part of the cave."

"About one hundred and twenty feet farther on, there's a crossroads,"† Flint added. "We found footprints there, but we could not make out what they were. They don't look like draconians or hobgoblins and they don't come this direction. The mage says the evil flows from the road to the right."

We're really in dungeon-crawling mode now. As per AD&D custom, most distances will be in ten-foot increments from now on.—TRH

"We will camp here for the night," Tanis said, "near the entry. We'll post double watch—one by the door, one down the corridor. Sturm, you and Caramon first. Gilthanas and I, Eben and Riverwind, Flint and Tasslehoff."

"And me," said Tika stoutly, though she couldn't ever remember being so tired in her life. "I'll take my turn."

Tanis was glad the darkness hid his smile. "Very well," he said. "You watch with Flint and Tasslehoff."

"Good!" Tika replied. Opening her pack, she shook out a blanket and lay down, conscious all the while of Caramon's eyes on her. She noticed Eben watching her, too. She didn't mind that. She was accustomed to men staring at her admiringly and Eben was handsomer even than Caramon. Certainly he was wittier and more charming than the big warrior. Still, just the memory of Caramon's arms around her made her shiver with delightful fear. She

firmly put the memory from her mind and tried to get comfortable. The chain mail was cold and it pinched her through her blouse. Yet she noticed the others didn't take theirs off. Besides, she was tired enough to sleep dressed in a full suit of plate armor. The last thing Tika remembered as she drifted off was telling herself she was thankful she wasn't alone with Caramon.

Goldmoon saw the warrior's eyes linger on Tika. Whispering something to Riverwind—who nodded, smiling—she left him and walked over to Caramon. Touching him on the arm, she drew him away from the others into the shadow of the corridor.

"Tanis tells me you have an older sister," she stated.

"Yes," Caramon answered, startled. "Kitiara. Though she's my half-sister."

Goldmoon smiled and laid her hand gently on Caramon's arm. "I'm going to talk to you like an older sister."

Caramon grinned. "Not like Kitiara,† you won't, Lady of Qué-Shu. Kit taught me the meaning of every swear word I'd ever heard, plus a few I hadn't. She taught me to use a sword and fight with honor in the tournaments, but she also taught me how to kick a man in the groin when the judges weren't watching. No, lady, you're not much like my older sister."

Kitiara is a distant phantom at this point in the tale, a character who is not seen and yet her presence must be felt. Here we have even more of an introduction to this important character who we will not actually meet for quite a while.—TRH

Goldmoon's eyes opened wide, startled by this portrayal of a woman she guessed the half-elf loved. "But I thought she and Tanis, I mean they . . ."

Caramon winked. "They certainly did!" he said.

Goldmoon drew a deep breath. She hadn't meant the conversation to wander off, but it did lead to her subject. "In a way, that's what I wanted to speak to you about. Only this has to do with Tika."

"Tika?" Caramon flushed. "She's a big girl. Begging your pardon, I don't see that what we do is any of your concern."

"She is a *girl*, Caramon," Goldmoon said gently. "Don't you understand?"

Caramon looked blank. He knew Tika was a girl. What did Goldmoon mean? Then he blinked in sudden understanding and groaned. "No, she isn't—"

"Yes." Goldmoon sighed. "She is. She's never been with a man before. She told me, while we were in the grove putting on her armor. She's frightened, Caramon. She's heard a lot of stories. Don't rush her. She desperately wants approval from you, and she might do anything to win it. But don't let her use that as a reason to do something she'll regret later. If you truly love her, time will prove it and enhance the moment's sweetness."

"I guess you know that, huh?" Caramon said, looking at Goldmoon.

"Yes," she said softly her eyes going to Riverwind. "We have waited long, and sometimes the pain is unbearable. But the laws of my people are strict. I don't suppose it would matter now," she spoke in a whisper, more to herself than Caramon, "since we are the only two left. But, in a way, that makes it even more important. When our vows are spoken, we will lie together as man and wife. Not until then."

"I understand. Thanks for telling me about Tika," Caramon said. He patted Goldmoon awkwardly on the shoulder and returned to his post.

The night passed quietly, with no sign of their pursuer. When the watches changed, Tanis discussed Eben's story with Gilthanas and received an unsatisfactory answer. Yes, what the man said was true. Gilthanas had been gone when the draconians attacked. He had been trying to convince the druids to help. He'd returned when he heard the sounds of battle and that's when he'd been struck on the head. He told Tanis all this in a low, bitter voice.

The companions woke when morning's pale light crept through the door. After a quick breakfast, they gathered their things and walked down the corridor into the Sla-Mori.

Arriving at the crossroads, they examined both directions, left and right. Riverwind knelt to study the tracks, then rose, his expression puzzled.

"They are human," he said, "but they are not human. There are animal tracks as well—probably rats. The dwarf was right. I see no sign of draconians or goblins. What is odd, however, is that the animal tracks end right here where the paths cross. They do not go into the right-hand corridor. The other strange tracks do not go to the left."

"Well, which way do *we* go?" Tanis asked.

"I say we don't go either way!" Eben stated. "The entrance is still open. Let's turn back."

"Turning back is no longer an option," Tanis said coldly. "I would give you leave to go yourself, only—"

"Only you don't trust me," Eben finished. "I don't blame you, Tanis Half-Elven. All right, I said I'd help and I meant it. Which way—left or right?"

"The evil comes from the right," Raistlin whispered.

"Gilthanas?" Tanis asked. "Do you have any idea where we are?"

"No, Tanthalas," the elf answered. "Legend says that there were many entrances from Sla-Mori into Pax Tharkas, all secret. Only the elven priests were allowed down here, to honor the dead. One way is as good as another."

"Or as bad," whispered Tasslehoff to Tika. She gulped and crept over to stand near Caramon.

"We'll go left," Tanis said—"since Raistlin feels uneasy about the right."

Walking by the light of the mage's staff, the companions followed the dusty, rock-strewn tunnel for several hundred feet, then reached an ancient stone wall rent by a huge hole through which only darkness was visible. Raistlin's small light showed faintly the distant walls of a great hall.

The warriors entered first, flanking the mage, who held his staff high. The gigantic hall must once have been splendid, but now it had fallen into such decay that its faded splendor seemed pathetic and horrible. Two rows of seven columns ran the length of the hall, though some lay shattered on the floor. Part of the far wall was caved in, evidence of the destructive force of the Cataclysm. At the very back of the room stood two double bronze doors.

As Raistlin advanced, the others spread out, swords drawn. Suddenly Caramon, in the front of the hall, gave a strangled cry. The mage hurried to shine his light where Caramon pointed with a trembling hand.

Before them was a massive throne, ornately carved of granite. Two huge marble statues flanked the throne, their sightless eyes staring forward into the darkness. The throne they guarded was not

empty. Upon it sat the skeletal remains of what had once been a male—of what race, none could say, death being the great equalizer. The figure was dressed in regal robes that, even though faded and decayed, still gave evidence of their richness. A cloak covered the gaunt shoulders. A crown gleamed on the fleshless skull. The bone hands, fingers lying gracefully in death, rested on a sheathed sword.

Gilthanas fell to his knees. "Kith-Kanan," he said in a whisper. "We stand in the Hall of the Ancients, his burial tomb. None have seen this sight since the elven clerics vanished in the Cataclysm."

Tanis stared at the throne until, slowly, overcome by feelings he did not understand, the half-elf sank to his knees. *"Fealan thalos, Im murquanethi. Sai Kith-Kananoth Murtari Larion,"* he murmured in tribute to the greatest of the elven kings.

"What a beautiful sword," Tasslehoff said, his shrill voice breaking the reverent silence. Tanis glared at him sternly. "I'm not going to take it!" the kender protested, looking wounded. "I just mentioned it, as an item of interest."

Tanis rose to his feet. "Don't touch it," he said sternly to the kender, then went to explore other parts of the room.

As Tas walked closer to examine the sword, Raistlin went with him. The mage began to murmur, *"Tsaran korilath ith hakon,"* and moved his thin hand swiftly above the sword in a prescribed pattern. The sword began to give off a faint red glow. Raistlin smiled and said softly, "It is enchanted."†

Detect Magic: basic AD&D first-level spell. —TRH

Tas gasped. "Good enchantment? Or bad?"

"I have no way of knowing," the mage whispered. "But since it has lain undisturbed for so long, I certainly would not venture to touch it!"

He turned away, leaving Tas to wonder if he dared disobey Tanis and risk being turned into something icky.

While the kender was wrestling with temptation, the rest searched the walls for secret entrances. Flint helped by giving them learned and lengthy descriptions of dwarven-built hidden doorways. Gilthanas walked to the far end from Kith-Kanan's throne, where the two huge bronze double doors stood. One, bearing a relief map of Pax Tharkas, was slightly ajar. Calling for light, he and Raistlin studied the map.

Caramon gave the skeletal figure of the long dead king a final backward glance and joined Sturm and Flint in searching the walls for secret doors. Finally Flint called, "Tasslehoff, you worthless kender, this is your specialty. At least you're always bragging about how you found the door that had been lost for one hundred years which led to the great jewel of the something-or-other."

"It was in a place like this, too," Tas said, his interest in the sword forgotten. Skipping over to help, he came to a sudden stop.

"What's that?" he asked, cocking his head.

"What's what?" Flint said absently, slapping the walls.

"A scraping sound," the kender said, puzzled. "It's coming from those doors."

Tanis looked up, having learned, long ago, to respect Tasslehoff's hearing. He walked toward the doors where Gilthanas and Raistlin were intent upon the map. Suddenly Raistlin took a step backward. Foul-smelling air wafted into the room through the open door. Now everyone could hear the scraping sound and a soft, squishing noise.

"Shut the door!" Raistlin whispered urgently.

"Caramon!" Tanis cried. "Sturm!" The two were already running for the door, along with Eben. All of them leaned against it, but they were flung backward as the bronze doors flew open, banging against the walls with a hollow booming sound. A monster slithered into the hall.

"Help us, Mishakal!" Goldmoon breathed the goddess's name as she sank back against the wall. The thing entered the room swiftly despite its great bulk. The scraping sound they had heard was caused by its gigantic, bloated body sliding along the floor.

"A slug!" Tas said, running up to examine it with interest. "But look at the size of that thing! How do you suppose it got so big? I wonder what it eats—"

"Us, you ninny!" Flint shouted, grabbing the kender and flinging him to the ground just as the huge slug spat out a stream of saliva. Its eyes, perched atop slender, rotating stalks on top of its head, were not of much use, nor did it need them. The slug could find and devour rats in the darkness by sense of smell alone. Now it detected much

larger prey, and it shot its paralyzing saliva in the general direction of the living flesh it craved.

The deadly liquid missed as the kender and the dwarf rolled out of the way. Sturm and Caramon charged in, slashing at the monster with their swords. Caramon's sword didn't even penetrate the thick, rubbery hide.† Sturm's two-handed blade bit, causing the slug to rear back in pain. Tanis charged forward as the slug's head swiveled toward the knight.

Oh, by all the gods of Krynn, they would give their kingdom for a bag of salt!—TRH

"Tanthalas!"

The scream pierced Tanis's concentration and he halted, turning back to stare in amazement at the entrance to the hall.

"Laurana!"

At that moment, the slug, sensing the half-elf, spat the corrosive liquid at him. The saliva struck his sword, causing the metal to fizz and smoke, then dissolve in his hand. The burning liquid ran down his arm, searing his flesh. Tanis, screaming in agony, fell to his knees.

"Tanthalas!" Laurana cried again, running to him.

"Stop her!" Tanis gasped, doubled over in pain, clutching a hand and sword-arm suddenly blackened and useless.

The slug, sensing success, slithered forward, dragging its pulsating gray body through the door. Goldmoon cast a fearful glance at the huge monster, then ran to Tanis. Riverwind stood over them, protectively.

"Get away!" Tanis said through clenched teeth.

Goldmoon grasped his injured hand in her own, praying to the goddess. Riverwind fit an arrow to his bow and shot at the slug. The arrow struck the creature in the neck, doing little damage, but distracting its attention from Tanis.

The half-elf saw Goldmoon's hand touch his, but he could feel nothing but pain. Then the pain eased and feeling returned to his hand. Smiling at Goldmoon, he marveled at her healing powers, even as he lifted his head to see what was happening.

The others were attacking the creature with renewed fury, attempting to distract it from Tanis, but they might as well have been plunging their weapons into a thick, rubbery wall.

Tanis rose to his feet shakily. His hand was healed, but his sword lay on the ground, a molten

lump of metal. Weaponless except for his longbow, he fell back, pulling Goldmoon with him as the slug slid into the room.

Raistlin ran to Fizban's side. "Now is the time for the casting of the fireball, Old One," he panted.

"It is?" Fizban's face filled with delight. "Wonderful! How does it go?"

"Don't you remember!" Raistlin practically shrieked, dragging the mage behind a pillar as the slug spat another glob of burning saliva onto the floor.

"I used to . . . let me see." Fizban's brow furrowed in concentration. "Can't you do it?"

"I have not gained the power yet, Old One! That spell is still beyond my strength!"† Raistlin closed his eyes and began to concentrate on those spells he did know.

Fireball, being a third-level AD&D spell, firmly shows that Raistlin is no higher than a fourth-level magic-user. If all this talk about levels is confusing, well, you don't want to know. Bottom line for AD&D: make the rules complex and obscure enough and anything is possible.
—TRH

"Fall back! Get out of here!" Tanis shouted, shielding Laurana and Goldmoon as best he could while he fumbled for his longbow and his arrows.

"It'll just come after us!" Sturm yelled, thrusting his blade home once again. But all he and Caramon accomplished was to enrage the monster further.

Suddenly Raistlin held up his hands. *"Kalith karan, tobanis-kar!"* he cried, and flaming darts sprang from his fingers, striking the creature in the head. The slug reared in silent agony and shook its head, but returned to the hunt. Suddenly it lunged straight forward, sensing victims at the end of the room where Tanis sought to protect Goldmoon and Laurana. Maddened by pain, driven wild by the smell of blood, the slug attacked with unbelievable speed. Tanis's arrow bounced off the leathery hide and the monster dove for him, its mouth gaping open. The half-elf dropped the useless bow and staggered backward, nearly stumbling over the steps leading to the throne of Kith-Kanan.

For anyone who might want to know: A ninth-level magic-user can shape change into anything short of a god or a dragon (apparently quite useful). However, a dragon, as we'll see, is powerful enough to shape change into a human magic-user.

"Behind the throne!" he yelled, preparing to hold the monster's attention while Goldmoon and Laurana ran for cover. His hand reached out, grabbing for a huge rock, anything to hurl at the creature!—when his fingers closed over the metal hilt of a sword.

Tanis nearly dropped the weapon in amazement. The metal was so cold it burned his hand. The blade gleamed brightly in the wavering light of the

mage's staff. There wasn't time to question, however. Tanis drove the point into the slug's gaping maw just as the creature swooped in for the kill.

"Run!" Tanis yelled. Grasping Laurana's hand, he dragged her toward the hole. Pushing her through, he turned around, preparing to help keep the slug at bay while the others escaped. But the slug's appetite had died. Writhing in misery, it slowly turned and slithered back toward its lair. Clear, sticky liquid dribbled from its wounds.

The companions crowded into the tunnel, stopping for a moment to calm their hearts and breathe deeply. Raistlin, wheezing, leaned on his brother. Tanis glanced around. "Where's Tasslehoff?" he asked in frustration. Whirling around to go back into the hall, he nearly fell over the kender.

"I brought you the scabbard," Tas said, holding it up. "For the sword."

"Back down the tunnel," Tanis said firmly, stopping everyone's questions.

Reaching the crossroads and sinking down on the dusty floor to rest, Tanis turned to the elfmaid. "What in the name of the Abyss are you doing here, Laurana? Has something happened in Qualinost?"

"Nothing happened," Laurana said, shaking from the encounter with the slug. "I . . . I . . . just came."

"Then you're going right back!" Gilthanas yelled angrily, grabbing Laurana. She broke away from his grasp.

"I'm not either going back," she said petulantly. "I'm coming with you and Tanis and . . . the rest."

"Laurana, this is madness," Tanis snapped. "We're not going on an outing. This isn't a game. You saw what happened in there—we were nearly killed!"

"I know, Tanthalas," Laurana said pleadingly. Her voice quivered and broke. "You told me that there comes a time when you've got to risk your life for something you believe in. I'm the one who followed you."

"You could have been killed—" Gilthanas began.

"But I wasn't!" Laurana cried defiantly. "I have been trained as a warrior—all elven women are, in memory of the time when we fought beside our men to save our homeland."

"It's not serious training—" Tanis began angrily.

"I followed you, didn't I?" Laurana demanded,

casting a glance at Sturm. "Skillfully?" she asked the knight.

"Yes," he admitted. "Still, that doesn't mean—"

Raistlin interrupted him. "We are losing time," the mage whispered. "And I for one do not want to spend any longer than I must in this dank and musty tunnel." He was wheezing, barely able to breathe. "The girl has made her decision. We can spare no one to return with her, nor do we dare trust her to leave on her own. She might be captured and reveal our plans. We must take her."

Tanis glared at the mage, hating him for his cold, unfeeling logic, and for being right. The half-elf stood up, yanking Laurana to her feet. He came very close to hating her, too, without quite understanding why, knowing simply that she was making a difficult task much harder.

"You are on your own," he told her quietly, as the rest stood up and gathered their things. "I can't hang around, protecting you. Neither can Gilthanas. You have behaved like a spoiled brat. I told you once before—you'd better grow up. Now, if you don't, you're going to die and probably get all the rest of us killed right along with you!"

"I'm sorry, Tanthalas," Laurana said, avoiding his angry gaze. "But I couldn't lose you, not again. I love you." Her lips tightened and she said softly, "I'll make you proud of me."

Tanis turned and walked away. Catching sight of Caramon's grinning face and hearing Tika giggle, he flushed. Ignoring them, he approached Sturm and Gilthanas. "It seems we must take the right-hand corridor after all, whether or not Raistlin's feelings about evil are correct." He buckled on his new sword belt and scabbard, noticing, as he did so, Raistlin's eyes lingering on the weapon.

"What is it now?" he asked irritably.

"The sword is enchanted," Raistlin said softly, coughing. "How did you get it?"

Tanis started. He stared at the blade, moving his hand as though it might turn into a snake. He frowned, trying to remember. "I was near the body of the elven king, searching for something to throw at the slug, when, suddenly, the sword was in my hand. It had been taken out of the sheath and—" Tanis paused, swallowing.

"Yes?" Raistlin pursued, his eyes glittering eagerly.

"*He* gave it to me,"† Tanis said softly. "I remember, his hand touched mine. He pulled it from its sheath."

"Who?" asked Gilthanas. "None of us were near there."

"Kith-Kanan. . . ."

This mighty sword is Wyrmslayer, the weapon of the ancient elven hero Kith-Kanan. It was forged in Silvanesti during the Second Dragon War and remained in the royal house until Kith-Kanan led his people to Qualinesti. After getting out of Sla-Mori, Tanis will not remember how he obtained the sword, nor will he know—until it's almost too late—one of its secrets.

10

The Royal Guard.
The Chain Room.

Perhaps it was just imagination, but the darkness seemed thicker as they walked down the other tunnel and the air grew colder. No one needed the dwarf to tell them that this was not normal in a cave, where the temperature supposedly stayed constant. They reached a branch in the tunnel, but no one felt inclined to go left, which might lead them back to the Hall of the Ancients—and the wounded slug.

"The elf almost got us killed by the slug," Eben said accusingly. "I wonder what's in store for us down here?"

No one answered. By now, everyone was experiencing the sense of growing evil Raistlin had warned of. Their footsteps slowed, and it was only through force of group will that they continued on.

Laurana felt fear convulse her limbs and she clung to the wall for support. She longed for Tanis to comfort her and protect her, as he had done when they were younger and facing imaginary foes, but he walked at the head of the line with her brother. Each had his own fear to contend with. At that moment, Laurana decided that she would die before she asked for their help. It occurred to her, then, that she was really serious when she said she wanted to make Tanis proud of her. Shoving herself away from the side of the crumbling tunnel, she gritted her teeth and moved forward.

The tunnel came to an abrupt end. Crumbled stone and rubble lay beneath a hole in the rock wall. The sense of malevolent evil flowing from the darkness beyond the hole could almost be felt, wafting across the flesh like the touch of unseen fingers. The companions stopped, none of them—not even the nerveless kender—daring to enter.

"It's not that I'm afraid," Tas confided in a whisper to Flint. "Its just that I'd rather be somewhere else."

The silence became oppressive. Each could hear his own heart beat and the breathing of the others. The light jittered and wavered in the mage's shaking hand.

"Well, we can't stay here forever," Eben said hoarsely. "Let the elf go in. He's the one who brought us here!"

"I'll go," Gilthanas answered. "But I'll need light."

"None may touch the staff but I," Raistlin hissed. He paused, then added reluctantly, "I'll go with you."

"Raist—" Caramon began, but his brother stared at him coldly. "I'll go, too," the big man muttered.

"No," Tanis said. "You stay here and guard the others. Gilthanas, Raistlin, and I will go."

Gilthanas entered the hole in the wall, followed by the mage and Tanis, the half-elf assisting Raistlin. The light revealed a narrow chamber, vanishing into darkness beyond the staff's reach. On either side were rows of large stone doors, each held in place by huge iron hinges, spiked directly into the rock wall. Raistlin held the staff high, shining it down the shadowy chamber. Each knew that the evil was centered here.

"There's carving on the doors," Tanis murmured. The staff's light threw the stone figures into high relief.

Gilthanas stared at it. "The Royal Crest!" he said in a strangled voice.

"What does that mean?" Tanis asked, feeling the elf's fear infect him like a plague.

"These are the crypts of the Royal Guard," Gilthanas whispered. "They are pledged to continue their duties, even in death, and guard the king—so the legends speak."

"And so the legends come to life!" Raistlin breathed, gripping Tanis's arm. Tanis heard the sound of huge stone blocks shifting, of rusting iron hinges creaking. Turning his head, he saw each of the stone doors begin to swing wide! The hallway filled with a cold so severe that Tanis felt his fingers go numb. Things moved behind the stone doors.

"The Royal Guard! They made the tracks!" Raistlin whispered frantically. "Human and not human. There is no escape!" he said, grasping Tanis tighter. "Unlike the spectres of Darken Wood, these have but one thought—to destroy all who commit the sacrilege of disturbing the king's rest!"

"We've got to try!" Tanis said, unclenching the mage's biting fingers from his arm. He stumbled backward and reached the entryway, only to find it blocked by two figures.

"Get back!" Tanis gasped. "Run! Who, Fizban? No, you crazy old man! We've got to run! The dead guards—"

"Oh, calm down," the old man muttered. "Young people. Alarmists." He turned around and helped someone else enter. It was Goldmoon, her hair gleaming in the light.

"It's all right, Tanis," she called softly. "Look!" She drew aside her cape: the medallion she wore glowed blue. "Fizban said they would let us pass, Tanis, if they saw the medallion. And when he said that—it began to glow!"

"No!" Tanis started to order her back, but Fizban tapped him on the chest with a long, bony finger.

"You're a good man, Tanis Half-Elven," the old mage said softly, "but you worry too much. Now just relax and let us send these poor souls back to their sleep. Bring the others along, will you?"

Tanis, too startled for words, fell back as Goldmoon and Fizban walked past, Riverwind following. As Tanis watched, they walked slowly between the rows of gaping stone doors. Behind each stone door, movement ceased as she passed. Even at that distance, he could feel the sense of malevolent evil slip away.

As the others came to the crumbling entryway and he helped them through, he answered their whispered questions with a shrug. Laurana didn't say a word to him as she entered; her hand was cold to the touch and he could see, to his astonishment, blood on her lip. Knowing she must have bitten it to keep from screaming, Tanis, remorseful, started to say something to her. But the elfmaid held her head high and refused to look at him.

The others ran after Goldmoon hurriedly, but Tasslehoff, pausing to peek into one of the crypts, saw a tall figure dressed in resplendent armor lying on a stone bier. Skeletal hands grasped the hilt of a longsword lying across the body. Tas looked up at the Royal Crest curiously, sounding out the words.

"Sothi Nuinqua Tsalarioth," said Tanis, coming up behind the kender.

"What does it mean?" Tas asked.

"Faithful beyond Death," Tanis said softly.

At the west end of the crypts, they found a set of bronze double doors. Goldmoon pushed it open easily and led them into a triangular passage that opened into a large hall. Inside this room, the only difficulty they faced was in trying to get the dwarf out of it. The hall was perfectly intact, the only room in the Sla-Mori they had encountered so far that had survived the Cataclysm without damage. And the reason for that, Flint explained to anyone who would listen, was the wonderful dwarven construction—particularly the twenty-three columns supporting the ceiling.

The only way out was two identical bronze doors at the far end of the chamber, leading west. Flint, tearing himself away from the columns, examined each and grumbled that he hadn't any idea what was behind them or where they led. After a brief discussion, Tanis decided to take the door to his right.

The door opened onto a clean, narrow passageway that led them, after about thirty feet, to another

single bronze door. This door, however, was locked. Caramon pushed, tugged, pried—all to no avail.

"It's no use," the big man grunted. "It won't budge."

Flint watched Caramon for several minutes, then finally stumped forward. Examining the door, he snorted and shook his head. "It's a false door!"

"Looks real to me!" Caramon said, staring at the door suspiciously. "It's even got hinges!"

"Of course, it does," Flint snorted. "We don't build false doors to look false—even a gully dwarf knows that."

"So we're at a dead end!" Eben said grimly.

"Stand back," Raistlin whispered, carefully leaning his staff against a wall. He placed both hands on the door, touching it only with the tips of his fingers, then said, *"Khetsaram pakliol!"* There was a flare of orange light, but not from the door—it came from the wall!

"Move!" Raistlin grabbed his brother and jerked him back, just as the entire wall, bronze door and all, began to pivot.

"Quickly, before it shuts," Tanis said, and everyone hurried through the door, Caramon catching his brother as Raistlin staggered.

"Are you all right?" Caramon asked, as the wall slammed shut behind them.

"Yes, the weakness will pass," Raistlin whispered. "That is the first spell I have cast from the spellbook of Fistandantilus. The spell of opening† worked, but I did not believe it would drain me like this."

Raistlin just learned and cast a second-level spell, which makes him a third-level magic-user at the very minimum … oh, never mind. We won't worry about such things after this book.—TRH

The door led them into another passageway that ran straight west for about forty feet, took a sharp turn to the south, then east, then continued south again. Here the way was blocked by another single bronze door.

Raistlin shook his head. "I can only use the spell once. It is gone from my memory."

"A fireball would open the door," said Fizban. "I think I remember that spell now—"

"No, Old One," Tanis said hastily. "It would fry all of us in this narrow passage. Tas—"

Reaching the door, the kender pushed on it. "Drat, it's open," he said, disappointed not to have to pick a lock. He peered inside. "Just another room."

They entered cautiously, Raistlin illuminating the chamber with the staff's light. The room was perfectly round, about one hundred feet in diameter. Directly across from them, to the south, stood a bronze door and in the center of the room—

"A crooked column," Tas said, giggling. "Look, Flint. The dwarves built a crooked column!"

"If they did, they had a good reason," the dwarf snapped, shoving the kender aside to examine the tall, thin column. It definitely slanted.

"Hmmmm," said Flint, puzzled. Then—"It isn't a column at all, you doorknob!" Flint exploded. "It's a great, huge chain! Look, you can see here it's hooked to an iron bracket on the floor."

"Then we are in the Chain Room!" Gilthanas said in excitement. "This is the famed defense mechanism of Pax Tharkas. We must be almost in the fortress."

The companions gathered around, staring at the monstrous chain in wonder. Each link was as long as Caramon was tall and as thick around as the trunk of an oak.

"What does the mechanism do?" asked Tasslehoff, longing to climb up the great chain. "Where does this lead?"

"The chain leads to the mechanism itself," Gilthanas answered. "As to how it works, you must ask the dwarf for I am unfamiliar with engineering. But if this chain is released from its moorings"—he pointed to the iron bracket in the floor—"massive blocks of granite drop down behind the gates of the fortress. Then no force on Krynn can open them."

Leaving the kender to peer up into the shadowy darkness, trying in vain to get a glimpse of the wondrous mechanism, Gilthanas joined the others in searching the room.

"Look at this!" he finally cried, pointing to a faint door-shaped line in the stones on the north wall. "A secret door! This must be the entrance!"

"There's the catch." Tasslehoff, turning from the chain, pointed to a chipped piece of stone at the bottom. "The dwarves slipped up," he said, grinning at Flint. "This is a false door that looks false."

"And therefore not to be trusted," Flint said flatly.

"Bah, dwarves have bad days like everyone else," Eben said, bending down to try the catch.

"Don't open it!" Raistlin said suddenly.

"Why not?" asked Sturm. "Because you want to alert someone before we find the way into Pax Tharkas?"

"If I had wanted to betray you, knight, I could have done so a thousand times before this!" Raistlin hissed, staring at the secret door. "I sense a power behind that door greater than any I have felt since—" He stopped, shuddering.

"Since when?" his brother prompted gently.

"The Towers of High Sorcery!" Raistlin whispered. "I warn you, do not open that door!"

"See where the south door leads," Tanis told the dwarf.

Flint stumped over to the bronze door on the south wall and shoved it open. "Near as I can tell, it leads down another passage exactly like all the others," he reported glumly

"The way to Pax Tharkas is through a secret door," Gilthanas repeated. Before anyone could stop him, he reached down and pulled out the chipped stone. The door shivered and began to swing silently inward.

"You will regret this!" Raistlin choked.

The door slid aside to reveal a large room, nearly filled with yellow, brick-like objects. Through a thick layer of dust, a faint yellowish color was visible.

"A treasure room!" Eben cried. "We've found the treasure of Kith-Kanan!"

"All in gold," Sturm said coldly. "Worthless, these days, since steel's the only thing of any value. . . ." His voice trailed off, his eyes widened in horror.

"What is it?" shouted Caramon, drawing his sword.

"I don't know!" Sturm said, more as a gasp than words.

"I do!" Raistlin breathed as the thing took shape before his eyes. "It is the spirit of a dark elf! I warned you not to open that door."

"Do something!" Eben said, stumbling backward.

"Put up your weapons, fools!" Raistlin said in a piercing whisper. "You cannot fight her! Her touch is death, and if she wails while we are within these walls, we are doomed. Her keening voice alone

kills.† Run, run all of you! Quickly! Through the south door!"

Even as they fell back, the darkness in the treasure room took shape, coalescing into the coldly beautiful, distorted features of a female drow—an evil elf of ages past, whose punishment for crimes unspeakable had been execution. Then the powerful elven magic-users chained her spirit, forcing her to guard forever the king's treasure. At the sight of these living beings, she stretched out her hands, craving the warmth of flesh, and opened her mouth to scream out her grief and her hatred of all living things.

This is a banshee.On Krynn, banshees—the undead spirits of women who harass the living, primarily with an ear-piercing wail—are peculiarly a phenomenon of elves. Thank the gods!

The companions turned and fled, stumbling over each other in their haste to escape through the bronze door. Caramon fell over his brother, knocking the staff from Raistlin's hand. The staff clattered on the floor, its light still glowing, for only dragonfire can destroy the magic crystal. But now its light flared out over the floor, plunging the rest of the room into darkness.

Seeing her prey escaping, the spirit flitted into the Chain Room, her grasping hand brushing Eben's cheek. He screamed at the chilling, burning touch and collapsed. Sturm caught him and dragged him through the door just as Raistlin grabbed his staff and he and Caramon lunged through.

"Is that everyone?" Tanis asked, reluctant to close the door. Then he heard a low, moaning sound, so frightful that he felt his heart stop beating for a moment. Fear seized him. He couldn't breathe. The cry ceased, and his heart gave a great, painful leap. The spirit sucked in its breath to scream again.

"No time to look!" Raistlin gasped. "Shut the door, brother!"

Caramon threw all his weight on the bronze door. It slammed shut with a boom that echoed through the hall.

"That won't stop her!" Eben cried, panic-stricken.

"No," said Raistlin softly. "Her magic is powerful, more powerful than mine. I can cast a spell on the door, but it will weaken me greatly. I suggest you run while you can. If it fails, perhaps I can stall her."

"Riverwind, take the others on ahead," Tanis ordered. "Sturm and I'll stay with Raistlin and Caramon."

The others crept down the dark corridor, looking back to watch in horrible fascination. Raistlin ignored them and handed the staff to his brother. The light from the glowing crystal flashed out at the unfamiliar touch.

The mage put his hands on the door, pressing both palms flat against it. Closing his eyes, he forced himself to forget everything except the magic. *"Kalis-an budrunin—"* His concentration broke as he felt a terrible chill.

The dark elf! She had recognized his spell and was trying to break him! Images of his battle with another dark elf in the Towers of High Sorcery came back to his mind. He struggled to blot out the evil memory of the battle that wrecked his body and came close to destroying his mind, but he felt himself losing control. He had forgotten the words! The door trembled. The elf was coming through!

Then from somewhere inside the mage came a strength he had discovered within himself only twice before—in the Tower and on the altar of the black dragon in Xak Tsaroth. The familiar voice that he could hear clearly in his mind yet never identify, spoke to him, repeating the words of the spell. Raistlin shouted them aloud in a strong, clear voice that was not his own. *"Kalis-an budrunin kara-emarath!"*

From the other side of the door came a wail of disappointment, failure. The door held. The mage collapsed.

Caramon handed the staff to Eben as he picked up his brother in his arms and followed the others as they groped their way along the dark passage. Another secret door opened easily to Flint's hand, leading to a series of short, debris-filled tunnels. Trembling with fear, the companions wearily made their way past these obstacles. Finally they emerged into a large, open room filled from ceiling to floor with stacks of wooden crates. Riverwind lit a torch on the wall. The crates were nailed shut. Some bore the label SOLACE, some GATEWAY.

"This is it. We're inside the fortress." Gilthanas said, grimly victorious. "We stand in the cellar of Pax Tharkas."

"Thank the true gods!" Tanis sighed and sank onto the floor, the others slumping down beside him. It was then they noticed that Fizban and Tasslehoff were missing.

11

Lost. The plan. Betrayed!

Tasslehoff could never afterward clearly recall those last, few, panicked moments in the Chain Room. He remembered saying, "A dark elf? Where?" and standing on his tiptoes, trying desperately to see, when suddenly the glowing staff fell on the floor. He heard Tanis shouting, and—above that—a kind of a moaning sound that made the kender lose all sense of where he was or what he was doing. Then strong hands grabbed him around the waist, lifting him up into the air.

"Climb!" shouted a voice beneath him.

Tasslehoff stretched out his hands, felt the cool metal of the chain, and began to climb. He heard a door boom, far below, and the chilling wail of the dark elf again. It didn't sound deadly this time,

more like a cry of rage and anger. Tas hoped this meant his friends had escaped.

"I wonder how I'll find them again," he asked himself softly, feeling discouraged for a moment. Then he heard Fizban muttering to himself and cheered up. He wasn't alone.

Thick, heavy darkness wrapped around the kender. Climbing by feel alone, he was growing extremely tired when he felt cool air brush his right cheek. He sensed, rather than saw, that he must be coming to the place where the chain and the mechanism linked up (Tas was rather proud of that pun). If only he could see! Then he remembered. He was, after all, with a magician.

"We could use a light," Tas called out.

"A fight? Where?" Fizban nearly lost his grip on the chain.

"Not fight! Light!" Tas said patiently, clinging to a link. "I think we're near the top of this thing and we really ought to have a look around."

"Oh, certainly. Let's see, light . . ."† Tas heard the magician fumbling in his pouches. Apparently he found what he was searching for, because he soon gave a little crow of triumph, spoke a few words, and a small puffball of bluish-yellow flame appeared, hovering near the magician's hat.

Thus, in the tradition of Laurel and Hardy, Abbott and Costello, and Hope and Crosby, is born another great partnership.—TRH

The glowing puffball whizzed up, danced around Tasslehoff as if to inspect the kender, then returned to the proud magician. Tas was enchanted. He had all sorts of questions regarding the wonderful flaming puffball, but his arms were getting shaky and the old magician was nearly done in. He knew they had better find some way to get off this chain.

Looking up, he saw that they were, as he had guessed, at the top part of the fortress. The chain ran up over a huge wooden cogwheel mounted on an iron axle anchored in solid stone. The links of the chain fit over teeth big as tree trunks, then the chain stretched out across the wide shaft, disappearing into a tunnel to the kender's right.

"We can climb onto that gear and crawl along the chain into the tunnel," the kender said, pointing. "Can you send the light up here?"

"Light, to the wheel," Fizban instructed.

This entire scene with Tas and Fizban has always been one of my favorites.
—MW

The light wavered in the air for a moment, then danced back and forth in a decidedly nay-saying manner.†

Fizban frowned. "Light—to the wheel!" he repeated firmly.

The puffball flame darted around to hide behind the magician's hat. Fizban, making a wild grab for it, nearly fell, and flung both arms around the chain. The puffball light danced in the air behind him as if enjoying the game.

"Uh, I guess we've got enough light, after all," Tas said.

"No discipline in the younger generation," Fizban grumbled. "His father—now there was a puffball . . ." The old magician's voice died away as he began to climb again, the puffball flame hovering near the tip of his battered hat.

Tas soon reached the first tooth on the wheel. Discovering the teeth were rough hewn and easy to climb, Tas crawled from one to another until he reached the top. Fizban, his robes hiked up around his thighs, followed with amazing agility.

"Could you ask the light to shine in the tunnel?" Tas asked.

"Light—to the tunnel," Fizban ordered, his bony legs wrapped around a link in the chain.

The puffball appeared to consider the command. Slowly it skittered to the edge of the tunnel, and then stopped.

"Inside the tunnel!" the magician commanded.

The puffball flame refused.

"I think it's afraid of the dark," Fizban said apologetically.

"My goodness, how remarkable!" the kender said in astonishment. "Well," he thought for a moment, "if it will stay where it is, I think I can see enough to make my way across the chain. It looks like it's only about fifteen feet or so to the tunnel." With nothing below but several hundred feet of darkness and air, never mind the stone floor at the bottom, Tas thought.

"Someone should come up here and grease this thing," Fizban said, examining the axle critically. "That's all you get today, shoddy workmanship."

"I'm really rather glad they didn't," Tas said mildly, crawling forward onto the chain. About

halfway across the gap, the kender considered what it would be like to fall from this height, tumbling down and down and down, then hitting the stone floor at the bottom. He wondered what it would feel like to splatter all over the floor. . . .

"Get a move on!" Fizban shouted, crawling out onto the chain after the kender.

Tas crawled forward quickly to the tunnel entrance where the puffball flame waited, then jumped off the chain onto the stone floor about five feet below him. The puffball flame darted in after him, and finally Fizban reached the tunnel entrance, too. At the last moment, he fell, but Tas caught hold of his robes and dragged the old man to safety.

They were sitting on the floor resting when suddenly the old man's head snapped up.

"My staff," he said.

"What about it?" Tas yawned, wondering what time it was.

The old man struggled to his feet. "Left it down below," he mumbled, heading for the chain.

"Wait! You can't go back!" Tasslehoff jumped up in alarm.

"Who says?" asked the old man petulantly, his beard bristling.

"I m-mean . . ." Tas stuttered, "it would be too dangerous. But I know you how feel—my hoopak's down there."

"Hmmmm," Fizban said, sitting back down disconsolately.

"Was it magic?" Tas asked after a moment.

"I was never quite certain," Fizban said wistfully.

"Well," said Tas practically, "maybe after we've finished the adventure we can go back and get it. Now let's try to find some place to rest."

He glanced around the tunnel. It was about seven feet from floor to ceiling. The huge chain ran along the top with numerous smaller chains attached, stretching across the tunnel floor into a vast dark pit beyond. Tas, staring down into it, could vaguely make out the shape of gigantic boulders.

"What time do you suppose it is?" Tas asked.

"Lunch time," said the old man. "And we might as well rest right here. It's as safe a place as any." He plopped back down. Pulling out a handful of quith-pa, he began to chew on it noisily. The puffball flame

wandered over and settled on the brim of the magician's hat.

Tas sat down next to the mage and began to nibble on his own bit of dried fruit. Then he sniffed. There was suddenly a very peculiar smell, like someone burning old socks. Looking up, he sighed and tugged on the magician's robe.

"Uh, Fizban," he said. "Your hat's on fire."

"Flint," Tanis said sternly, "for the last time—I feel as badly as you do about losing Tas, but we cannot go back! He's with Fizban and, knowing those two, they'll both manage to get out of whatever predicament they're in."

"If they don't bring the whole fortress down around our ears," Sturm muttered.

The dwarf wiped his hand across his eyes, glared at Tanis, then whirled on his heel and stumped back to a corner where he hurled himself onto the floor, sulking.

Tanis sat back down. He knew how Flint felt. It seemed odd—there'd been so many times he could happily have strangled the kender, but now that he was gone, Tanis missed him—and for exactly the same reasons. There was an innate, unfailing cheerfulness about Tasslehoff that made him an invaluable companion. No danger ever frightened a kender and, therefore, Tas never gave up. He was never at a loss for something to do in an emergency. It might not always be the right thing, but at least he was ready to act. Tanis smiled sadly. I only hope this emergency doesn't prove to be his last, he thought.

The companions rested for an hour, eating quith-pa and drinking fresh water from a deep well they discovered. Raistlin regained consciousness but could eat nothing. He sipped water, then lay limply back. Caramon broke the news to him about Fizban hesitantly, fearing his brother might take the old mage's disappearance badly. But Raistlin simply shrugged, closed his eyes, and sank into a deep sleep.

After Tanis felt his strength return, he rose and walked toward Gilthanas, noting that the elf was intently studying a map. Passing Laurana, who sat alone, he smiled at her. She refused to acknowledge it. Tanis sighed. Already he regretted speaking

harshly to her back in the Sla-Mori. He had to admit that she had handled herself remarkably well under terrifying circumstances. She had done what she was told to quickly and without question. Tanis supposed he would have to apologize, but first he needed to talk to Gilthanas.

"What's the plan?" he asked, sitting down on a crate.

"Yes, where are we?" Sturm asked. Soon almost everyone was crowded around the map except Raistlin who appeared to sleep, though Tanis thought he saw a slit of gold shining through the mage's supposedly closed eyelids.

Gilthanas spread his map flat.

"Here is the fortress of Pax Tharkas and the surrounding mine area," he said, then he pointed. "We are in the cellars here on the lowest level. Down this hallway, about fifty feet from here, are the rooms where the women are imprisoned. This is a guard room, across from the women, and this"—he tapped the map gently—"is the lair of one of the red dragons, the one Lord Verminaard called Ember. The dragon is so big, of course, that the lair extends up above ground level, communicating with Lord Verminaard's chambers on the first floor, up through the gallery on the second floor, and out into the open sky.

Gilthanas smiled bitterly. "On the first floor, behind Verminaard's chambers, is the prison where the children are kept. The Dragon Highlord is wise. He keeps the hostages separated, knowing that the women would never consider leaving without their children, and the men would not leave without their families. The children are guarded by a second red dragon in this room. The men—about three hundred of them—work in mines out in the mountain caves. There are several hundred gully dwarves working the mines as well."

"You seem to know a lot about Pax Tharkas," Eben said.

Gilthanas glanced up quickly. "What do you insinuate?"

"I'm not insinuating anything," Eben answered. "It's just that you know a lot about this place for never having been here! And wasn't it interesting that we kept running into creatures who damn near killed us back in the Sla-Mori."

"Eben," Tanis spoke very quietly, "we've had enough of your suspicions. I don't believe any of us is a traitor. As Raistlin said, the traitor could have betrayed any of us long before this. What's the point of coming this far?"

"To bring me and the Disks to Lord Verminaard," Goldmoon said softly. "He knows I am here, Tanis. He and I are linked by our faith."

"That's ridiculous!" Sturm snorted.

"No, it isn't," Goldmoon said. "Remember, there are two constellations missing. One was the Queen of Darkness. From what little I have been able to understand in the Disks of Mishakal, the Queen was also one of the ancient gods. The gods of good are matched by the gods of evil, with the gods of neutrality striving to keep the balance.† Verminaard worships the Queen of Darkness as I worship Mishakal: that is what Mishakal meant when she said we were to restore the balance. The promise of good that I bring is the one thing he fears and he is exerting all his will to find me. The longer I stay here . . ." Her voice died.

This is the first statement thus far regarding the triad structure on which all DRAGONLANCE is founded.—TRH

"All the more reason to quit bickering," Tanis stated, switching his gaze to Eben.

The fighter shrugged. "Enough said. I'm with you."

"What is your plan, Gilthanas?" Tanis asked, noticing with irritation that Sturm and Caramon and Eben exchanged quick glances, three humans sticking together against the elves, he caught himself thinking. But perhaps I'm just as bad, believing in Gilthanas because he's an elf.

Gilthanas saw the exchange of glances, too. For a moment he stared at them with an intense, unblinking gaze, then began to speak in a measured tone, considering his words, as if reluctant to reveal any more than was absolutely necessary.

"Every evening, ten to twelve women are allowed to leave their cells and take food to the men in the mines. Thus the Highlord lets the men see that he is keeping his side of the bargain. The women are allowed to visit the children once a day for the same reason. My warriors and I planned to disguise ourselves as women, go out to the men in the mines, tell them of the plan to free the hostages, and alert them to be ready to strike. Beyond that we

had not thought, particularly in regard to freeing the children. Our spies indicated something strange about the dragon guarding the children, but we could not determine what."

"What sp—?" Caramon started to ask, caught Tanis's eye, and thought better of his question. Instead he asked, "When will we strike? And what about the dragon, Ember?"

"We strike tomorrow morning. Lord Verminaard and Ember will most certainly join the army tomorrow as it reaches the outskirts of Qualinesti. He has been preparing for this invasion a long time. I do not believe he will miss it."

The group discussed the plan for several minutes, adding to it, refining it, generally agreeing that it appeared viable. They gathered their things as Caramon woke his brother. Sturm and Eben pushed open the door leading to the hallway. It appeared empty, although they could hear faint sounds of harsh, drunken laughter from a room directly across from them. Draconians. Silently, the companions slipped into the dark and dingy corridor.

Tasslehoff stood in the middle of what he had named the Mechanism Room, staring around the tunnel lighted dimly by the puffball. The kender was beginning to feel discouraged. It was a feeling he didn't get often and likened to the time he'd eaten an entire green tomato pie acquired from a neighbor. To this day, discouragement and green tomato pie both made him want to throw up.

"There's got to be some way out of here," said the kender. "Surely they inspect the mechanism occasionally, or come up to admire it, or give tours, or something!"

He and Fizban had spent an hour walking up and down the tunnel, crawling in and out among the myriad chains. They found nothing. It was cold and barren and covered with dust.

"Speaking of light," said the old magician suddenly, though they hadn't been. "Look there."

Tasslehoff looked. A thin sliver of light was visible through a crack in the bottom of the wall, near the entrance to the narrow tunnel. They could hear voices, and the light grew brighter as if torches were being lit in a room below them.

"Maybe that's a way out," the old man said.

Running lightly down the tunnel, Tas knelt down and peered through the crack. "Come here!"

The two looked down into a large room, furnished with every possible luxury. All that was beautiful, graceful, delicate, or valuable in the lands under Verminaard's control had been brought to decorate the private chambers of the Dragon Highlord. An ornate throne stood at one end of the room. Rare and priceless silver mirrors hung on the walls, arranged so cunningly that no matter where a trembling captive turned, the only image he saw was the grotesque, horned helm of the Dragon Highlord glowering at him.

"That must be him!" Tas whispered to Fizban. "That must be Lord Verminaard!" The kender sucked in his breath in awe. "That must be his dragon—Ember. The one Gilthanas told us about, that killed all the elves in Solace."

The dragons of the typical AD&D world are solitary creatures dedicated to preserving and augmenting their hoard of treasure. Never would they become involved in the affairs of men, as they do on Krynn. In some ways they are the same, however: even small dragons have enormous egos and despise anyone who lacks willpower and confidence.

Ember, or Pyros (his true name being a secret known only to draconians, or to other dragons—never to common mortals) was an ancient and enormous red dragon. Pyros† had been given to Lord Verminaard ostensibly as a reward from the Queen of Darkness to her cleric. In reality, Pyros was sent to keep a watchful eye on Verminaard, who had developed a strange, paranoid fear regarding discovery of the true gods. All the Dragon Highlords on Krynn possessed dragons, however, though perhaps not as strong and intelligent. For Pyros had another, more important mission that was secret even to the Dragon Highlord himself, a mission assigned to him by the Queen of Darkness and known only to her and her evil dragons.

Pyros's mission was to search this part of Ansalon for one man, a man of many names. The Queen of Darkness called him Everman. The dragons called him Green Gemstone Man. His human name was Berem. And it was because of this unceasing search for the human, Berem, that Pyros was present in Verminaard's chamber this afternoon when he would have much preferred to be napping in his lair.

Pyros had received word that Fewmaster Toede was bringing in two prisoners for interrogation. There was always the possibility this Berem might

be one of them. Therefore, the dragon was always present during interrogations, though he often appeared vastly bored. The only time interrogations became interesting—as far as Pyros was concerned—was when Verminaard ordered a prisoner to "feed the dragon."

Pyros was stretched out along one side of the enormous throne room, completely filling it. His huge wings were folded at his sides, his flanks heaved with every breath he took like some great gnomish engine. Dozing, he snorted and shifted slightly. A rare vase toppled to the floor with a crash. Verminaard looked up from his desk where he was studying a map of Qualinesti.

"Transform yourself before you wreck the place," he snarled.

Pyros opened one eye, regarded Verminaard coldly for a moment, then grudgingly rumbled a brief word of magic.

The gigantic red dragon began to shimmer like a mirage, the monstrous dragon shape condensing into the shape† of a human male, slight of build with dark black hair, a thin face, and slanting red eyes. Dressed in crimson robes, Pyros the man walked to a desk near Verminaard's throne. Sitting down, he folded his hands and stared at Verminaard's broad, muscled back with undisguised loathing.

Several of the various kinds of dragon can shapechange, though there is always some small thing that can be perceived as dragonish.

There was a scratch at the door.

"Enter," Verminaard commanded absently.

A draconian guard threw open the door, admitting Fewmaster Toede and his prisoners, then withdrew, swinging the great bronze and gold doors shut. Verminaard kept the Fewmaster waiting several long minutes while he continued to study his battle plan. Then, favoring Toede with a condescending gaze, he walked over and ascended the steps to his throne. It was elaborately carved to resemble the gaping jaws of a dragon.

Verminaard was an imposing figure. Tall and powerfully built, he wore dark night-blue dragonscale armor trimmed in gold. The hideous mask of a Dragon Highlord concealed his face. Moving with a grace remarkable in such a large man, he leaned back comfortably, his leather-encased hand absently caressing a black, gold-trimmed mace by his side.

Verminaard regarded Toede and his two captives irritably, knowing full well that Toede had dredged up these two in an effort to redeem himself from the disastrous loss of the cleric. When Verminaard discovered from his draconians that a woman matching the description of the cleric had been among those prisoners taken from Solace and that she had been allowed to escape, his fury was terrifying. Toede had nearly paid for his mistake with his life, but the hobgoblin was exceptionally skilled at whining and groveling. Knowing this, Verminaard had considered refusing to admit Toede at all today, but he had a strange, nagging sensation that all was not well in his realm.

It's that blasted cleric! Verminaard thought. He could sense her power coming nearer and nearer, making him nervous and uneasy. He intently studied the two prisoners Toede led into the room. Then, seeing that neither of them matched the descriptions of those who had raided Xak Tsaroth, Verminaard scowled behind the mask.

Pyros reacted differently to the sight of the prisoners. The transformed dragon half-rose to his feet while his thin hands clenched the ebony desktop with such ferocity he left the impressions of his fingers in the wood. Shaking with excitement, it took a great effort of will to force himself to sit back down, outwardly calm. Only his eyes, burning with a devouring flame, gave a hint of his inner elation as he stared at the prisoners.

One of the prisoners was a gully dwarf, Sestun, in fact. He was chained hand and foot (Toede was taking no chances) and could barely walk. Stumbling forward, he dropped to his knees before the Dragon Highlord, terror-stricken. The other prisoner—the one Pyros watched—was a human male, dressed in rags, who stood staring at the floor.

"Why have you bothered me with these wretches, Fewmaster?" Verminaard snarled.

Toede, reduced to a quivering mass, gulped and immediately launched into his speech. "This prisoner"—he hobgoblin kicked Sestun—"was the one who freed the slaves from Solace, and this prisoner"—he indicated the man, who lifted his head, a confused and puzzled expression on his face—"was found wandering around Gateway which, as you

know, has been declared off limits to all nonmilitary personnel."

"So why bring them to me?" asked Lord Verminaard irritably. "Throw them into the mines with the rest of the rabble."

Toede stammered. "I thought the human m-m-might b-be a s-spy. . . ."

The Dragon Highlord studied the human intently. He was tall, about fifty human years old. His hair was white and his clean-shaven face brown and weathered, streaked with lines of age. He was dressed like a beggar, which is probably what he was, Verminaard thought in disgust. There was certainly nothing unusual about him, except for his eyes which were bright and young. His hands, too, were those of a man in his prime. Probably elven blood. . . .

"The man is feeble-minded," Verminaard said finally. "Look at him—gaping like a landed fish."

"I b-b-believe he's, uh, deaf and dumb, my lord," Toede said, sweating.

Verminaard wrinkled his nose. Not even the dragonhelm could keep away the foul odor of perspiring hobgoblin.

"So you have captured a gully dwarf and a spy who can neither hear nor speak," Verminaard said caustically. "Well done, Toede. Perhaps now you can go out and pick me a bouquet of flowers."

"If that is your lordship's pleasure," Toede replied solemnly, bowing.

Verminaard began to laugh beneath his helm, amused in spite of himself. Toede was such an entertaining little creature, a pity he couldn't be taught to bathe. Verminaard waved his hand. "Remove them—and yourself."

"What shall I do with the prisoners, my lord?"

"Have the gully dwarf feed Ember tonight. And take your spy to the mines. Keep a watch on him though—he looks deadly!" The Dragon Highlord laughed.

Pyros ground his teeth and cursed Verminaard for a fool.

Toede bowed again. "Come on, you," he snarled, yanking on the manacles, and the man stumbled after him. "You, too!" He prodded Sestun with his foot. It was useless. The gully dwarf, hearing he was to feed the dragon, had fainted. A draconian was called to remove him.

Verminaard left his throne and walked over to his desk. He gathered up his maps in a great roll. "Send the wyvern with dispatches," he ordered Pyros. "We fly tomorrow morning to destroy Qualinesti. Be ready when I call."

When the bronze and golden doors had closed behind the Dragon Highlord, Pyros, still in human form, rose from the desk and began to pace feverishly back and forth across the room. There came a scratching at the door.

"Lord Verminaard has gone to his chambers!" Pyros called out, irritated at the interruption.

The door opened a crack.

"It is you I wish to see, royal one," whispered a draconian.

"Enter," Pyros said. "But be swift."

"The traitor has been successful, royal one," the draconian said softly. "He was able to slip away only for a moment, lest they suspect. But he has brought the cleric—"

"To the Abyss with the cleric!" Pyros snarled. "This news is of interest only to Verminaard. Take it to him. No, wait." The dragon paused.

"As you instructed, I came to you first," the draconian said apologetically, preparing to make a hasty departure.

"Don't go," the dragon ordered, raising a hand. "This news is of value to me after all. Not the cleric. There is much more at stake. . . . I must meet with our treacherous friend. Bring him to me tonight, in my lair. Do not inform Lord Verminaard—not yet. He might meddle." Pyros was thinking rapidly now, his plans coming together. "Verminaard has Qualinesti to keep him occupied."

As the draconian bowed and left the throne room, Pyros began pacing once again, back and forth, back and forth, rubbing his hands together, smiling.

12

The parable of the gem. Traitor revealed. Tas's dilemma.

Stop that, you bold man!" Caramon simpered, slapping Eben's hand as the fighter slyly slid his hand up Caramon's skirt.

The women in the room laughed so heartily at the antics of the two warriors that Tanis glanced nervously at the cell door, afraid of arousing the suspicion of the guards.

Maritta saw his worried gaze. "Don't worry about the guards!" she said with a shrug. "There are only two down here on this level and they're drunk half the time, especially now that the army's moved out." She looked up from her sewing at the women and shook her head. "It does my heart good to hear them laugh, poor things," she said softly. "They've had little enough to laugh about these past days."

Thirty-four women were crowded into one cell—Maritta said there were sixty women living in another nearby—under conditions so shocking that even the hardened campaigners were appalled. Rude straw mats covered the floor. The women had no possessions beyond a few clothes. They were allowed outdoors for a brief exercise period each morning. The rest of the time they were forced to sew draconian uniforms. Though they had been imprisoned only a few weeks, their faces were pale and wan, their bodies thin and gaunt from the lack of nourishing food.

Tanis relaxed. Though he had known Maritta only a few hours, he already relied on her judgment. She was the one who had calmed the terrified women when the companions burst into their cell. She was the one who listened to their plan and agreed that it had possibilities.

"Our menfolk will go along with you," she told Tanis. "It's the Highseekers who'll give you trouble."

"The Council of Highseekers?" Tanis asked in astonishment. "They're here? Prisoners?"

Maritta nodded, frowning. "That was their payment for believing in that black cleric. But they won't want to leave, and why should they? They're not forced to work in the mines—the Dragon Highlord sees to that! But we're with you." She glanced around at the others, who nodded firmly. "On one condition—that you'll not put the children in danger."

"I can't guarantee that," Tanis said. "I don't mean to sound harsh, but we may have to fight a dragon to reach them and—"

"Fight a dragon? Flamestrike?" Maritta looked at him in amazement. "Pah! There's no need to fight the pitiful critter. In fact, were you to hurt her, you'd have half the children ready to tear you apart, they're that fond of her."

"Of a dragon?" Goldmoon asked. "What's she done, cast a spell on them?"

"No. I doubt Flamestrike could cast a spell on anything anymore." Maritta smiled sadly. "The poor critter's more than half-mad. Her own children were killed in some great war or other and now she's got it in her head that our children are *her*

children. I don't know where his lordship dug her up, but it was a sorry thing to do and I hope he pays for it someday!" She snapped a thread viciously.

"T'won't be difficult to free the children," she added, seeing Tanis's worried look. "Flamestrike always sleeps late of a morning. We feed the children their breakfast, take them out for their exercise, and she never stirs. She'll never know they're gone till she wakes, poor thing."

The women, filled with hope for the first time, began modifying old clothes to fit the men. Things went smoothly until it came time to fit them.

"Shave!" Sturm roared in such fury that the women scurried away from the knight in alarm. Sturm had taken a dim view of the disguise idea, anyway, but had agreed to go along with it. It seemed the best way to cross the wide-open courtyard between the fortress and the mines. But, he announced, he would rather die a hundred deaths at the hands of the Dragon Highlord than shave his moustaches. He only calmed down when Tanis suggested covering his face with a scarf.

Just when that was settled, another crisis arose. Riverwind stated flatly that he would not dress up as a woman and no amount of arguing could convince him otherwise. Goldmoon finally took Tanis aside to explain that, in their tribe, any warrior who committed a cowardly act in battle was forced to wear women's clothes until he redeemed himself. Tanis was baffled by this one. But Maritta had wondered how they would manage to outfit the tall man anyway.

After much discussion, it was decided Riverwind would bundle up in a long cloak and walk hunched over, leaning on a staff like an old woman. Things went smoothly after this, for a time at least.

Laurana walked over to a corner of the room where Tanis was wrapping a scarf around his own face.

"Why don't *you* shave?" Laurana asked, staring at Tanis's beard. "Or do you truly enjoy flaunting your human side as Gilthanas says?"

"I don't flaunt it," Tanis replied evenly. "I just got tired of trying to deny it, that's all." He drew a deep breath. "Laurana, I'm sorry I spoke to you as I did back in the Sla-Mori. I had no right—"

"You had every right," Laurana interrupted. "What I did was the act of a lovesick little girl. I foolishly endangered your lives." Her voice faltered, then she regained control. "It will not happen again. I will prove I can be of value to the group."

Exactly how she meant to do this, she wasn't certain. Although she talked glibly about being skilled in fighting, she had never killed so much as a rabbit. She was so frightened now that she was forced to clasp her hands behind her back to keep Tanis from seeing how she trembled. She was afraid that if she let herself, she would give way to her weakness and seek comfort in his arms, so she left him and went over to help Gilthanas with his disguise.

Tanis told himself he was glad Laurana was showing some signs of maturity at last. He steadfastly refused to admit that his soul stood breathless whenever he looked into her large, luminous eyes.

The afternoon passed swiftly and soon it was evening and time for the women to take dinner to the mines. The companions waited for the guards in tense silence, laughter forgotten. There had, after all, been one last crisis. Raistlin, coughing until he was exhausted, said he was too weak to accompany them. When his brother offered to stay behind with him, Raistlin glared at him irritably and told him not to be a fool.

"You do not need me this night," the mage whispered. "Leave me alone. I must sleep."

"I don't like leaving him here—" Gilthanas began, but before he could continue, they heard the sound of clawed feet outside the cell, and another sound of pots rattling. The cell door swung open and two draconian guards, both smelling strongly of stale wine, stepped inside. One of them reeled a bit as it peered, bleary-eyed, at the women.

"Get moving," it said harshly.

As the "women" filed out, they saw six gully dwarves standing in the corridor, lugging large pots of some sort of nameless stew. Caramon sniffed hungrily, then wrinkled his nose in disgust. The draconians slammed the cell door shut behind them. Glancing back, Caramon saw his twin, shrouded in blankets, lying in a dark, shadowy corner.

Fizban clapped his hands. "Well done, my boy!" said the old magician in excitement as part of the wall in the Mechanism Room swung open.

"Thanks," Tas replied modestly. "Actually, *finding* the secret door was more difficult than opening it. I don't know how you managed. I thought I'd looked everywhere."

He started to crawl through the door, then stopped as a thought occurred to him. "Fizban, is there any way you can tell that light of yours to stay behind? At least until we see if anyone's in here? Otherwise, I'm going to make an awfully good target and we're not far from Verminaard's chambers."

"I'm afraid not." Fizban shook his head. "It doesn't like to be left alone in dark places."

Tasslehoff nodded—he had expected the answer. Well, there was no use worrying about it. If the milk's spilled, the cat will drink it, as his mother used to say. Fortunately, the narrow hallway he crawled into appeared empty. The flame hovered near his shoulder. He helped Fizban through, then explored his surroundings. They were in a small hallway that ended abruptly not forty feet away in a flight of stairs descending into darkness. Double bronze doors in the east wall provided the only other exit.

"Now," muttered Tas, "we're above the throne room. Those stairs probably lead down to it. I suppose there's a million draconians guarding it! So that's out." He put his ear to the door. "No sound. Let's look around." Pushing gently, he easily opened the double doors. Pausing to listen, Tas entered cautiously, followed closely by Fizban and the puffball flame.

"Some sort of art gallery," he said, glancing around a giant room where paintings, covered with dust and grime, hung on the walls. High slit windows in the walls gave Tas a glimpse of the stars and the tops of high mountains. With a good idea of where he was now, he drew a crude map in his head.

"If my calculations are correct, the throne room is to the west and the dragon's lair is to the west of that. At least that's where he went when Verminaard left this afternoon. The dragon must have some way to fly out of this building, so the lair should open up into the sky, which means a shaft of some sort, and maybe another crack where we can see what's going on."

So involved was Tas with his plans that he was not paying any attention to Fizban. The old magician was moving purposefully around the room, studying each painting as if searching for one in particular.

"Ah, here it is," Fizban murmured, then turned and whispered, "Tasslehoff!"

The kender lifted his head and saw the painting suddenly begin to glow with a soft light. "Look at that!" Tasslehoff said, entranced. "Why, it's a painting of dragons—red dragons like Ember, attacking Pax Tharkas and . . ."

The kender's voice died. Men—Knights of Solamnia—mounted on other dragons were fighting back! The dragons the Knights rode were beautiful dragons—gold and silver dragons—and the men carried bright weapons that gleamed with a shining radiance. Suddenly Tasslehoff understood! There were *good* dragons in the world, if they could be found, who would help fight the evil dragons, and there was—

"The Dragonlance!" he murmured.

The old magician nodded to himself. "Yes, little one," he whispered. "You understand. You see the answer. And you will remember. But not now. Not now." Reaching out, he ruffled the kender's hair with his gnarled hand.

"Dragons. What was I saying?" Tas couldn't remember. And what was he doing here anyhow, staring at a painting so covered with dust he couldn't make it out. The kender shook his head. Fizban must be rubbing off on him. "Oh, yes. The dragon's lair. If my calculations are correct, it's over here." He walked away.

The old magician shuffled along behind, smiling.

The companions' journey to the mines proved uneventful. They saw only a few draconian guards, and they appeared half-asleep with boredom. No one paid any attention to the women going by. They passed the glowing forge, continually fed by a scrambling mass of exhausted gully dwarves.

Hurrying past that dismal sight quickly, the companions entered the mines where draconian guards locked the men in huge cave rooms at night, then returned to keep an eye on the gully dwarves. Guard duty over the men was a waste of time, anyway, Verminaard figured—the humans weren't going anyplace.

And, for a while, it looked to Tanis as if this might prove horribly true. The men *weren't* going anyplace. They stared at Goldmoon, unconvinced, as she spoke. After all, she was a barbarian, her accent was strange, her dress even stranger. She told what seemed a children's tale of a dragon dying in a blue flame she herself survived. And all she had to show for it was a collection of shining platinum disks.

Hederick, the Solace Theocrat, was loud in his denunciation of the Qué-Shu woman as a witch and a charlatan and a blasphemer. He reminded them of the scene in the Inn, exhibiting his scarred hand as evidence. Not that the men paid a great deal of attention to Hederick. The Seeker gods, after all, had not kept the dragons from Solace.

Many of them, in fact, were interested in the prospect of escape. Nearly all bore some mark of ill-treatment—whip lashes, bruised faces. They were poorly fed, forced to live in conditions of filth and squalor, and everyone knew that when the iron beneath the hills was gone, their usefulness to Lord Verminaard would end. But the Highseekers—still the governing body, even in prison—opposed such a reckless plan.

Arguments started. The men shouted back and forth. Tanis hastily posted Caramon, Flint, Eben, Sturm, and Gilthanas at the doors, fearing the guards would hear the disturbance and return. The half-elf hadn't expected this—the arguing might last for days! Goldmoon sat despondently before the men, looking as though she might cry. She had been so imbued with her newfound convictions, and so eager to bring her knowledge to the world, that she was cast into despair when her beliefs were doubted.

"These humans are fools!" Laurana said softly, coming up to stand beside Tanis.

"No," replied Tanis, sighing. "If they were fools, it would be easier. We promise them nothing tangible and ask them to risk the only thing they have left—

their lives. And for what? To flee into the hills, fighting a running battle all the way. At least here they are alive—for the time being."

"But how can life be worth anything, living like this?" Laurana asked.

"That's a very good question, young woman," said a feeble voice. They turned to see Maritta kneeling beside a man lying on a crude cot in a corner of the cell. Wasted with illness and deprivation, his age was indeterminable. He struggled to sit up, stretching out a thin, pale hand to Tanis and Laurana. His breath rattled in his chest. Maritta tried to hush him, but he stared at her irritably. "I know I'm dying, woman! It doesn't mean I have to be bored to death first. Bring that barbarian woman over to me."

Tanis looked at Maritta questioningly. She rose and came over, drawing him to one side. "He is Elistan," she said as if Tanis should know the name. When Tanis didn't respond, she clarified. "Elistan—one of the Highseekers from Haven. He was much loved and respected by the people, the only one who spoke out against this Lord Verminaard. But no one listened—not wanting to hear, of course."

"You speak of him in the past tense," Tanis said. "He isn't dead yet."

"No, but it won't be long." Maritta wiped away a tear. "I've seen the wasting sickness before. My own father died of it. There's something inside of him, eating him alive. These last few days he has been half mad with the pain, but that's gone now. The end is very near."

"Maybe not." Tanis smiled. "Goldmoon is a cleric. She can heal him."

"Perhaps, perhaps not," Maritta said skeptically. "I wouldn't want to chance it. We shouldn't excite Elistan with false hope. Let him die in peace."

"Goldmoon," Tanis said as the Chieftain's Daughter came near. "This man wants to meet you." Ignoring Maritta, the half-elf led Goldmoon over to Elistan. Goldmoon's face, hard and cold with disappointment and frustration, softened as she saw the man's pitiful condition.

Elistan looked up at her. "Young woman," he said sternly, though his voice was weak, "you claim to bring word from ancient gods. If it truly was we humans who turned from them, not the gods who

turned from us as we've always thought, then why have they waited so long to make their presence known?"

Goldmoon knelt down beside the dying man in silence, thinking how to phrase her answer. Finally, she said, "Imagine you are walking through a wood, carrying your most precious possession—a rare and beautiful gem. Suddenly you are attacked by a vicious beast. You drop the gem and run away. When you realize the gem is lost, you are afraid to go back into the woods and search for it. Then someone comes along with another gem. Deep in your heart, you know it is not as valuable as the one you lost, but you are still too frightened to go back to look for the other. Now, does this mean the gem has left the forest, or is it still lying there, shining brightly beneath the leaves, waiting for you to return?"

Elistan closed his eyes, sighing, his face filled with anguish. "Of course, the gem waits for *our* return. What fools we have been! I wish I had time to learn of your gods," he said, reaching out his hand.

Goldmoon caught her breath, her face drained until she was nearly as pale as the dying man on the cot. "You will be given time," she said softly, taking his hand in hers.

Tanis, absorbed in the drama before him, started in alarm when he felt a touch on his arm. He turned around, his hand on his sword, to find Sturm and Caramon standing behind him.

"What is it?" he asked swiftly. "The guards?"

"Not yet," Sturm said harshly. "But we can expect them any minute. Both Eben and Gilthanas are gone."

Night deepened over Pax Tharkas.

Back in his lair, the red dragon, Pyros, had no room to pace, a habit he had fallen into in his human form. He barely had room to spread his wings in this chamber, though it was the largest in the fortress and had even been expanded to accommodate him. But the ground-floor chamber was so narrow, all the dragon could do was turn his great body around.

Forcing himself to relax, the dragon laid down upon the floor and waited, his eyes on the door. He didn't notice two heads peeking over the railing of a balcony on the third level far above him.

There was a scratch on the door. Pyros raised his head in eager anticipation, then dropped it again with a snarl as two goblins appeared, dragging between them a wretched specimen.

"Gully dwarf!" Pyros sneered, speaking Common to underlings. "Verminaard's taken leave of his senses if he thinks I'd eat gully dwarf. Toss him in a corner and get out!" he snarled at the goblins who hastened to do as instructed. Sestun cowered in the corner, whimpering.

"Shut up!" Pyros ordered irritably. "Perhaps I should just flame you and stop that blubbering—"

There came another sound at the door, a soft knocking the dragon recognized. His eyes burned red. "Enter!"

A figure came into the lair of the dragon. Dressed in a long cloak, a hood covered its face.

"I have come as you commanded, Ember," the figure said softly.

"Yes," Pyros replied, his talons scratching the floor. "Remove the hood. I would see the faces of those I deal with."

The man cast his hood back. Up above the dragon, on the third level, came a strangled, choking gasp. Pyros stared up at the darkened balcony. He considered flying up to investigate, but the figure interrupted his thought.

"I have only limited time, royal one. I must return before they suspect. And I should report to Lord Verminaard—"

"In due course," Pyros snapped irritably. "What are these fools that you accompany plotting?"

"They plan to free the slaves and lead them in revolt, forcing Verminaard to recall the army marching on Qualinesti."

"That's all?"

"Yes, royal one. Now I must warn the Dragon Highlord."

"Bah! What does that matter? It will be I who deal with the slaves if they revolt. Unless they have plans for me?"

"No, royal one. They fear you a great deal, as all must," the figure added. "They will wait until you and Lord Verminaard have flown to Qualinesti. Then they will free the children and escape into the mountains before you return."

"That seems to be a plan equal to their intelligence. Do not worry about Verminaard. I will see he learns of this when I am ready for him to learn of it. Much greater matters are brewing. Much greater. Now listen closely. A prisoner was brought in today by that imbecile Toede—" Pyros paused, his eyes glowing. His voice dropped to a hissing whisper. "It is *he*! The one we seek!"

The figure stared in astonishment. "Are you certain?"

"Of course!" Pyros snarled viciously. "I see this man in my dreams! He is here, within my grasp! When all of Krynn is searching for him, I have found him!"

"You will inform Her Dark Majesty?"

"No. I dare not trust a messenger. I must deliver this man in person, but I cannot leave now. Verminaard cannot deal with Qualinesti alone. Even if the war is just a ruse, we must keep up appearances, and the world will be better for the absence of elves anyway. I will take the Everman to the Queen when time permits."

"So why tell me?" the figure asked, an edge in his voice.

"Because you must keep him safe!" Pyros shifted his great bulk into a more comfortable position. His plans were coming together rapidly now. "It is a measure of Her Dark Majesty's power that the cleric of Mishakal and the man of the green gemstone arrive together within my reach! I will allow Verminaard the pleasure of dealing with the cleric and her friends tomorrow. In fact"—Pyros's eyes gleamed—"this may work out quite well! We can remove the Green Gemstone Man in the confusion and Verminaard will know nothing! When the slaves attack, you must find the Green Gemstone Man. Bring him back here and hide him in the lower chambers. When the humans have all been destroyed, and the army has wiped out Qualinesti, I will deliver him to my Dark Queen."

"I understand." The figure bowed again. "And my reward?"

"Will be all you deserve. Now leave me."

The man cast the hood up over his head and withdrew. Pyros folded his wings and, curling his great body around with the huge tail up over his snout, he lay staring into the darkness. The only sound that could be heard was Sestun's pitiful weeping.

"Are you all right?" Fizban asked Tasslehoff gently as they sat crouched by the balcony, afraid to move. It was pitch dark, Fizban having overturned a vase on the highly indignant puffball flame.

"Yes," Tas said dully. "I'm sorry I choked like that. I couldn't help myself. Even though I expected it—sort of—it's still hard to realize someone you know could betray you. Do you think the dragon heard me?"

"I couldn't say." Fizban sighed. "The question is, what do we do now?"

"I don't know," Tas said miserably. "I'm not supposed to be the one that thinks. I just come along for the fun. We can't warn Tanis and the others, because we don't know where they are. And if we start wandering around looking for them, we might get caught and only make things worse!" He put his chin in his hand. "You know," he said with unusual somberness, "I asked my father once why kenders were little, why we weren't big like humans and elves. I really wanted to be big," he said softly and for a moment he was quiet.

"What did your father say?" asked Fizban gently.

"He said kenders were small because we were meant to do small things. 'If you look at all the big things in the world closely,' he said, 'you'll see that they're really made up of small things all joined together.' That big dragon down there comes to nothing but tiny drops of blood, maybe. It's the small things that make the difference."†

It is this philosophy that makes kender very special people in Krynn.—MW

"Very wise, your father."

"Yes." Tas brushed his hand across his eyes. "I haven't seen him in a long time." The kender's pointed chin jutted forward, his lips tightened. His father, if he had seen him, would not have known this small, resolute person for his son.

"We'll leave the big things to the others," Tas announced finally. "They've got Tanis and Sturm and Goldmoon. They'll manage. We'll do the small thing, even if it doesn't seem very important. We're going to rescue Sestun."

13

Questions. No answers.
Fizban's hat.

Truly, one of the great hats of literature.

"I heard something, Tanis, and I went to investigate," Eben said, his mouth set in a firm line. "I looked outside the cell door I was guarding and I saw a draconian crouched there, listening. I crept out and got it in a choke hold, then a second one jumped me. I knifed it, then took off after the first. I caught it and knocked it out, then decided I'd better get back here."

The companions had returned to the cells to find both Gilthanas and Eben waiting for them. Tanis had Maritta keep the women busy in a far corner while he questioned the two about their absence. Eben's story appeared true—Tanis had seen the bodies of the draconians as he returned to the prison—and Eben had certainly been in a fight. His clothes were torn, blood trickled from a cut on his cheek.

Tika got a relatively clean cloth from one of the women and began washing the cut. "He saved our lives, Tanis," she snapped. "I'd think you'd be grateful, instead of glaring at him as if he'd stabbed your best friend."

"No, Tika," Eben said gently. "Tanis has a right to ask. It did look suspicious, I admit. But I have nothing to hide." Catching hold of her hand, he kissed her fingertips. Tika flushed and dipped the cloth in water, raising it to his cheek again. Caramon, watching, scowled.

"What about you, Gilthanas?" the warrior asked abruptly. "Why did you leave?"

"Do not question me," the elf said sullenly. "You don't want to know."

"Know what?" Tanis said sternly. "Why did you leave?"

"Leave him alone!" Laurana cried, going to her brother's side.

Gilthanas's almond-eyes flashed as he glanced at them; his face was drawn and pale.

"This is important, Laurana," Tanis said. "Where did you go, Gilthanas?"

"Remember—I warned you." Gilthanas's eyes shifted to Raistlin. "I returned to see if our mage was really as exhausted as he said. He must not have been. He was gone."

Caramon stood up, his fists clenched, his face distorted with anger. Sturm grabbed hold of him and shoved him backwards as Riverwind stepped in front of Gilthanas.

"All have a right to speak and all have a right to respond in their own defense," the Plainsman said in his deep voice. "The elf has spoken. Let us hear from your brother."

"Why should I speak?" Raistlin whispered harshly, his voice soft and lethal with hatred. "None of you trusts me, so why should you believe me? I refuse to answer, and you may think as you choose. If you believe I am a traitor—kill me now! I will not stop you—" He began to cough.

"You'll have to kill me, too," Caramon said in a choked voice. He led his brother back to his bed.

Tanis felt sick.

"Double watches all night. No, not you, Eben. Sturm, you and Flint first, Riverwind and I'll take

second." Tanis slumped down on the floor, his head on his arms. We've been betrayed, he thought. One of those three is a traitor and has been all along. The guards might come at any moment. Or perhaps Verminaard was more subtle, some trap to catch us all. . . .

Then Tanis saw it all with sickening clarity. Of course! Verminaard would use the revolt as an excuse to kill the hostages and the cleric. He could always get more slaves, who would have a horrible example before their eyes of what happened to those who disobeyed him. This plan—Gilthanas's plan—played right into his hands!

We should abandon it, Tanis thought wildly, then he forced himself to calm down. No, the people were too excited. Following Elistan's miraculous healing and his announced determination to study these ancient gods, the people had hope. They believed that the gods had truly come back to them. But Tanis had seen the other Highseekers look at Elistan jealously. He knew that, though they made a show of supporting the new leader, given time they would try and subvert him. Perhaps, even now, they were moving among the people, spreading doubt.

If we backed out now, they'd never trust us again, Tanis thought. We must go ahead—no matter how great the risk. Besides, perhaps he was wrong. Maybe there was no traitor. Hoping, he fell into a fitful sleep.

The night passed in silence.

Dawn filtered through the gaping hole in the tower of the fortress. Tas blinked, then sat up, rubbing his eyes, wondering for a moment where he was. I'm in a big room, he thought, staring up at a high ceiling that had a hole cut in it to allow the dragon access to the outside. There are two other doors, besides the one Fizban and I came through last night.

Fizban! The dragon!

Tas groaned, remembering. He hadn't meant to fall asleep! He and Fizban had only been waiting until the dragon slept to rescue Sestun. Now it was morning! Perhaps it was too late! Fearfully the kender crept to the balcony and peered over the edge. No! He sighed in relief. The dragon was asleep. Sestun slept, too, worn out with fear.

Now was their chance! Tasslehoff crawled back to the mage.

"Old One!" he whispered. "Wake up!" He shook him.

"What? Who? Fire?" The mage sat up, peering around blearily. "Where? Run for the exits!"

"No, not a fire." Tas sighed. "It's morning. Here's your hat—" He handed it to the magician who was groping around, searching for it. "What happened to the puffball light?"

"Humpf!" Fizban sniffed. "I sent it back. Kept me awake, shining in my eyes."

"We were supposed to stay awake, remember?" Tas said in exasperation. "Rescue Sestun from the dragon?"

"How were we going to do that?" Fizban asked eagerly.

"You were the one with the plan!"

"I was? Dear, dear." The old magician blinked. "Was it a good one?"

"You didn't tell me!" Tas nearly shouted, then he calmed down. "All you said was that we had to rescue Sestun before breakfast, because gully dwarf might start looking more appetizing to a dragon who hadn't eaten in twelve hours."

"Makes sense," Fizban conceded. "Are you sure I said it?"

"Look," said Tasslehoff patiently, "all we really need is a long rope to throw down to him. Can't you magic that up?"

"Rope!" Fizban glared at him. "As if I'd stoop so low! That is an insult to one of my skill. Help me stand."

Tas helped the mage stand. "I didn't mean to insult you," the kender said, "and I know there's nothing fancy about rope and you are very skilled. . . . It's just that—oh, all right!" Tas gestured toward the balcony. "Go ahead. I just hope we all survive," he muttered under his breath.

"I won't let you down, or Sestun either, for that matter," Fizban promised, beaming. The two peeked over the balcony. Everything was as before. Sestun lay in a corner. The dragon slept soundly. Fizban closed his eyes. Concentrating, he murmured eerie words, then stretched his thin hand

through the railing of the balcony and began to make a lifting motion.

Tasslehoff, watching, felt his heart fly up in his throat. "Stop!" he gurgled. "You've got the wrong one!"

Fizban's eyes flew open to see the red dragon, Pyros, slowly rising off the floor, his body still curled in sleep. "Oh, dear!" the magician gasped and, quickly saying different words, he reversed the spell, lowering the dragon to the ground. "Missed my aim," the mage said. "Now I'm zeroed in. Let's try again."

Tas heard the eerie words again. This time Sestun began to rise off the floor and, breath by breath, came level with the balcony. Fizban's face grew red with exertion.

"He's almost here! Keep going!" Tas said, hopping up and down in excitement. Guided by Fizban's hand, Sestun sailed peacefully over the balcony. He came to rest on the dusty floor, still asleep.

"Sestun!" Tas whispered, putting his hand over the gully dwarf's mouth so that he wouldn't yell. "Sestun! It's me, Tasslehoff. Wake up."

The gully dwarf opened his eyes. His first thought was that Verminaard had decided to feed him to a vicious kender instead of the dragon. Then the gully dwarf recognized his friend and went limp with relief.

"You're safe, but don't say a word," the kender warned. "The dragon can still hear us—" He was interrupted by a loud booming from below. The gully dwarf sat up in alarm.

"Shhh," said Tas, "probably just the door into the dragon's lair." He hurried back to the balcony where Fizban was peering through the railing. "What is it?"

"The Dragon Highlord," Fizban pointed to the second level where Verminaard stood on a ledge overlooking the dragon.

"Ember, awaken!" Verminaard yelled down at the sleeping dragon. "I have received reports of intruders! That cleric is here, inciting the slaves to rebellion!"

Pyros stirred and slowly opened his eyes, awakening from a disturbing dream in which he'd seen a

gully dwarf fly. Shaking his giant head to clear away the sleep, he heard Verminaard ranting about clerics. He yawned. So the Dragon Highlord had found out the cleric was in the fortress. Pyros supposed he'd have to deal with this now, after all.

"Do not trouble yourself, my lord—" Pyros began, then stopped abruptly, staring at something very strange.

"Trouble myself!" Verminaard fumed. "Why I—" He stopped, too. The object at which both stared was drifting down through the air, gently as a feather.

Fizban's hat.

Tanis woke everyone in the darkest hour before dawn.

"Well," said Sturm, "do we go ahead?"

"We have no choice," Tanis said grimly, looking at the group. "If one of you has betrayed us, then he must live with the knowledge that he has brought about the deaths of innocents. Verminaard will kill not only us, but the hostages as well. I pray that there is no traitor, and so I'm going ahead with our plans."

No one said anything, but each glanced sideways at the others, suspicion gnawing at all of them.

When the women were awake, Tanis went over the plan again.

"My friends and I will sneak up to the children's room with Maritta, disguised as the women who usually bring the children breakfast. We'll lead them to the courtyard," Tanis said quietly. "You must go about your business as you do every morning. When you are allowed into the exercise area, get the children and start moving immediately toward the mines. Your menfolk will handle the guards there and you can escape safely into the mountains to the south. Do you understand?"

The women nodded silently as they heard the sound of the guards approaching.

"This is it," Tanis said softly. "Back to your work."

The women scattered. Tanis beckoned to Tika and Laurana. "If we have been betrayed, you will both be in great danger, since you'll be guarding the women—" he began.

"We'll all be in great danger," Laurana amended coldly. She hadn't slept all night. She knew that if she released the tight bands she had wrapped around her soul, fear would overwhelm her.

Tanis saw none of this inner turmoil. He thought she appeared unusually pale and exceptionally beautiful this morning. A long-time campaigner himself, his preoccupation made him forget the terrors of a first battle.

Clearing his throat, he said huskily, "Tika, take my advice. Keep your sword in your scabbard. You're less dangerous that way." Tika giggled and nodded nervously. "Go say good-bye to Caramon," Tanis told her.

Tika blushed crimson and, giving Tanis and Laurana a meaningful look, ran off.

Tanis gazed at Laurana steadily for a moment, and—for the first time—saw that her jaw muscles were clenched so tightly the tendons in her neck were stretched. He reached out to hold her, but she was stiff and cold as a draconian's corpse.

"You don't have to do this," Tanis said, releasing her. "This isn't your fight. Go to the mines with the other women."

Laurana shook her head, waiting to speak until she was certain her voice was under control. "Tika is not trained for fighting. I am. No matter if it was 'ceremonial.' " She smiled bitterly at Tanis's look of discomfiture. "I will do my part, Tanis." His human name came awkwardly to her lips. "Otherwise, you might think I am a traitor."

"Laurana, please believe me!" Tanis sighed. "I don't think Gilthanas is a traitor any more than you do! It's just—damn it, there are so many lives at stake, Laurana! Can't you realize?"

Feeling his hands on her arms shake, she looked up at him and saw the anguish and the fear in his own face, mirroring the fear she felt inside. Only his was not fear for himself, it was fear for others. She drew a deep breath. "I am sorry, Tanis," she said. "You are right. Look. The guards are here. It is time to go."

She turned and walked away without looking back. It didn't occur to her until it was too late that Tanis might have been silently asking for comfort himself.

Maritta and Goldmoon led the companions up a flight of narrow stairs to the first level. The draconian guards didn't accompany them, saying something about "special duty." Tanis asked Maritta if that was usual and she shook her head, her face worried. They had no choice but to go on. Six gully dwarves trailed after them, carrying heavy pots of what smelled like oatmeal. They paid little attention to the women until Caramon stumbled over his skirt climbing the stairs and fell to his knees, uttering a very unladylike oath. The gully dwarves' eyes opened wide.

"Don't even squeak!" Flint said, whirling around to face them, a knife flashing in his hand.

The gully dwarves cowered against the wall, shaking their heads frantically, the pots clattering.

The companions reached the top of the stairs and stopped.

"We cross this hall to the door—" Maritta pointed. "Oh, no!" She grasped Tanis's arm. "There's a guard at the door. It's never guarded!"

"Hush, it could be coincidence," Tanis said reassuringly, although he knew it wasn't. "Just keep on as we planned." Maritta nodded fearfully and walked across the hall.

"Guards!" Tanis turned to Sturm. "Be ready. Remember—quick and deadly. No noise!"

According to Gilthanas's map, the playroom was separated from the children's sleeping quarters by two rooms. The first was a storeroom which Maritta reported was lined with shelves containing toys and clothing and other items. A tunnel ran through this room to the second—the room that housed the dragon, Flamestrike.

"Poor thing," Maritta had said when discussing the plan with Tanis. "She is as much a prisoner as we are. The Dragon Highlord never allows her out. I think they're afraid she'll wander off. They've even built a tunnel through the storeroom, too small for her to fit through. Not that she wants to get out, but I think she might like to watch the children play."

Tanis regarded Maritta dubiously, wondering if they might encounter a dragon very different from the mad, feeble creature she described.

Beyond the dragon's lair was the room where the children slept. This was the room they would have

to enter, to wake the children and lead them outdoors. The playroom connected directly with the courtyard through a huge door locked with a great oaken beam.

"More to keep the dragon in than us," Maritta stated.

It must be just about dawning, Tanis thought, as they emerged from the stairwell and turned toward the playroom. The torchlight cast their shadows ahead of them. Pax Tharkas was quiet, deathly quiet. Too quiet—for a fortress preparing for war. Four draconian guards stood huddled together talking at the doorway to the playroom. Their conversation broke off as they saw the women approach.

Goldmoon and Maritta walked in front, Goldmoon's hood was drawn back, her hair glimmering in the torchlight. Directly behind Goldmoon came Riverwind. Bent over a staff, the Plainsman was practically walking on his knees. Caramon and Raistlin followed, the mage staying close to his brother, then Eben and Gilthanas. All the traitors together, as Raistlin had sarcastically observed. Flint brought up the rear, turning occasionally to glower at the panic-stricken gully dwarves.

"You're early this morning," a draconian growled.

The women clustered like chickens in a half-circle around the guards and stood, waiting patiently to be allowed inside.

"It smells of thunder," Maritta said sharply. "I want the children to have their exercise before the storm hits. And what are you doing here? This door is never guarded. You'll frighten the children."

One of the draconians made some comment in their harsh language and two of the others grinned, showing rows of pointed teeth. The spokesman only snarled.

"Lord Verminaard's command. He and Ember are gone this morning to finish the elves. We're ordered to search you before you enter." The draconian's eyes fastened onto Goldmoon hungrily. "That's going to be a pleasure, I'd say."

"For you maybe," muttered another guard, staring at Sturm in disgust. "I've never seen an uglier female in my life than—ugh—" The creature slumped over, a dagger thrust deep into its ribs. The other three draconians died within seconds. Caramon wrapped his hands around the neck of one. Eben hit his in the stomach and Flint lobbed off its head with an axe as it fell. Tanis stabbed the leader through the heart with his sword. He started to let go of the weapon, expecting it to remain stuck in the creature's stony corpse. To his amazement, his new sword slid out of the stone carcass as easily as if it had been nothing more than goblin flesh.

He had no time to ponder this strange occurrence. The gully dwarves, catching sight of the flash of steel, dropped their pots and ran wildly down the corridor.

"Never mind them!" Tanis snapped at Flint. "Into the playroom. Hurry!" Stepping over the bodies, he flung the door open.

"If anyone finds these bodies, it'll be all over," Caramon said.

"It was over before we began!" Sturm muttered angrily. "We've been betrayed, so it's just a matter of time."

"Keep moving!" Tanis said sharply, shutting the door behind them.

"Be very quiet," Maritta whispered. "Flamestrike generally sleeps soundly. If she does waken, act like women. She'll never recognize you. She's blind in one eye."

The chill dawn light filtered in through tiny windows high above the floor, shining on a grim, cheerless playroom. A few well-used toys lay scattered about. There was no furniture. Caramon walked over to inspect the huge wooden beam barring the double doors that led to the courtyard outside.

"I can manage," he said. The big man appeared to lift the beam effortlessly, then set it against the wall and shoved on the door. "Not locked from the outside," he reported. "I guess they didn't expect us to get this far."

Or perhaps Lord Verminaard wants us out there, Tanis thought. He wondered if what the draconian said was true. Had the Dragon Highlord and the dragon really gone? Or were they—angrily he wrenched his mind back. It doesn't matter, he told himself. We have no choice. We must go on.

"Flint, stay here," he said. "If anyone comes, warn us first, then fight."

Flint nodded and took a position just inside the door leading to the corridor, first opening it a crack to see. The draconian bodies had turned to dust on the floor.

Maritta took a torch from the wall. Lighting it, she led the companions through a dark archway into the tunnel leading to the dragon's lair.

"Fizban! Your hat!" Tas risked whispering. Too late. The old magician made a grab for it but missed.

"Spies!" yelled Verminaard in a rage, pointing up to the balcony. "Capture them, Ember! I want them alive!"

Alive? the dragon repeated to himself. No, that could not be! Pyros recalled the strange sound he had heard last night and he knew without a doubt that these spies had overheard him talking about the Green Gemstone Man! Only a privileged few knew that dread secret, the great secret, the secret that would conquer the world for the Queen of Darkness. These spies must die, and the secret die with them.

Pyros spread his wings and launched himself into the air, using his powerful back legs to propel himself from the floor with tremendous speed.

This is it! thought Tasslehoff. Now we've done it. There's no escape this time.

Just as he resigned himself to being cooked by a dragon, he heard the magician shout a single word of command and a thick, unnatural darkness almost knocked the kender over.

"Run!" panted Fizban, grabbing the kender's hand and dragging Tas to his feet.

"Sestun—"

"I've got him! Run!"

Tasslehoff ran. They flew out the door and into the gallery, then he had no idea where he was going. He just kept hold of the old man and ran. Behind him he could hear the sound of the dragon whooshing up out of his lair and he heard the dragon's voice.

"So you are a magic-user, are you, spy?" Pyros shouted. "We can't have you running around in the dark. You might get lost. Let me light your way!"

Tasslehoff heard a great intake of breath into a giant body, then flames crackled and burned around him. The darkness vanished, driven away by the

fire's flaring light, but, to his amazement, Tas wasn't touched by the flame. He looked at Fizban—hatless—running next to him. They were in the gallery still, heading for the double doors.

The kender twisted his head. Behind him loomed the dragon, more horrible than anything he had imagined, more terrifying than the black dragon in Xak Tsaroth. The dragon breathed on them again and once more Tas was enveloped by flame. The paintings on the walls blazed, furniture burned, curtains flared like torches, smoke filled the room. But none of it touched him and Sestun and Fizban. Tasslehoff looked at the mage in admiration, truly impressed.

"How long can you keep this up?" he shouted to Fizban as they wheeled around a corner, the double bronze doors in sight.

The old man's eyes were wide and staring. "I have no idea!" he gasped. "I didn't know I could do it at all!"

Another blast of flame exploded around them. This time, Tasslehoff felt the heat and glanced at Fizban in alarm. The mage nodded. "I'm losing it!" he cried.

"Hang on," Tasslehoff panted. "We're almost to the door! He can't get through it."

The three pushed through the bronze double doors that led from the gallery back into the hallway just as Fizban's magic spell wore off. Before them was the secret door, still open, that led to the Mechanism Room. Tasslehoff flung the bronze doors shut and stopped a moment to catch his breath.

But just as he was about to say, "We made it!" one of the dragon's huge clawed feet broke through the stone wall, right above the kender's head!

Sestun, giving a shriek, headed for the stairs.

"No!" Tasslehoff grabbed him. "That leads to Verminaard's quarters!"

"Back to the Mechanism Room!" Fizban cried. They dashed through the secret door just as the stone wall gave way with a tremendous crash. But they could not shut the door.

"I have a lot to learn about dragons, apparently," Tas muttered. "I wonder if there are any good books on the subject—"

"So I have run you rats into your hole and now you are trapped," boomed Pyros's voice from outside. "You have nowhere to go and stone walls do not stop me."

There was a terrible grinding and grating sound. The walls of the Mechanism Room trembled, then began to crack.

"It was a nice try," Tas said ruefully. "That last spell was a doozy. Almost worth getting killed by a dragon to see."

"Killed!" Fizban seemed to wake up. "By a dragon? I should say not! I've never been so insulted. There must be a way out—" His eyes began to gleam. "Down the chain!"

"The chain?" repeated Tas, thinking he must have misunderstood, what with the walls cracking around him and the dragon roaring and all.

"We'll crawl down the chain! Come on!" Cackling with delight, the old mage turned and ran down the tunnel.

Sestun looked dubiously at Tasslehoff, but just then the dragon's huge claw appeared through the wall. The kender and the gully dwarf turned and ran after the old magician.

By the time they reached the great wheel, Fizban had already crawled along the chain leading from the tunnel and reached the first tree-trunk tooth of the wheel itself. Tucking his robes up around his thighs,† he dropped down from the tooth onto the first rung of the huge chain. The kender and gully dwarf swung onto the chain after him. Tas was just beginning to think they might get out of this alive after all, especially if the dark elf at the bottom of the chain had taken the day off, when Pyros burst suddenly into the shaft where the great chain hung.

Kitiara finds out the answer to what a magic-user wears under his robes in Legends, when she asks the question of Dalamar.—MW

Sections of the stone tunnel caved in around them, falling to the ground with a hollow booming thud. The walls shuddered, and the chain started to tremble. Above them hovered the dragon. He did not speak but simply stared at them with his red eyes. Then he drew in a huge breath that seemed to suck in the air of the whole valley. Tas started instinctively to close his eyes, then opened them wide. He'd never seen a dragon breathe fire and he wasn't going to miss seeing it now—especially as it would probably be his last chance.

Flames billowed out from the dragon's nose and mouth. The blast from the heat alone nearly knocked Tasslehoff off the chain. But, once again, the fire burned all around him and did not touch him. Fizban cackled with delight.

"Quite clever, old man," said the dragon angrily. "But I, too, am a magic-user and I feel you weakening. I hope your cleverness amuses you—all the way down!"

Flames flared out again, but this time the dragon's fire was not aimed at the trembling figures clinging to the chain. The flames struck the chain itself and the iron links began to glow red hot at the first touch of the dragonfire. Pyros breathed again and the links burned white hot. The dragon breathed a third time. The links melted. The massive chain gave a great shudder and broke, plunging into the darkness below.

Pyros watched it as it plummeted down. Then, satisfied that the spies would not live to tell their tale, he flew back to his lair where he could hear Verminaard shouting for him.

In the darkness left behind by the dragon, the great cogwheel—free of the chain that had held it in place for centuries—gave a groan and began to turn.

14

Matafleur. The magic sword. White feathers.

Light from Maritta's torch illuminated a large, barren windowless room. There was no furniture. The only objects in the chill, stone chamber were a huge basin of water, a bucket filled with what smelled like rotted meat, and a dragon.

Tanis caught his breath. He had thought the black dragon in Xak Tsaroth formidable. He was truly awed at the massive size of this red dragon. Her lair was enormous, probably over one hundred feet in diameter, and the dragon stretched the length of it, the tip of her long tail lying against the far wall. For a moment the companions stood stunned, with ghastly visions of the giant head rising up and searing them with the burning flame breathed by the red dragons, the flames that had destroyed Solace.

Maritta did not appear worried, however. She advanced steadily into the room and, after a moment's hesitation, the companions hurried after her. As they drew closer to the creature, they could see that Maritta had been right—the dragon was clearly in pitiful condition. The great head that lay on the cold stone floor was lined and wrinkled with age, the brilliant red skin grayish and mottled. She breathed noisily through her mouth, her jaws parted to reveal the once sword-sharp teeth, now yellowed and broken. Long scars ran along her sides; her leathery wings were dry and cracked.

Now Tanis could understand Maritta's attitude. Clearly, the dragon had been ill-used, and he caught himself feeling pity, relaxing his guard. He realized how dangerous this was when the dragon—awakened by the torchlight—stirred in her sleep. Her talons were as sharp and her fire as destructive as any other red dragon in Krynn, Tanis reminded himself sharply.

The dragon's eyes opened, slits of glistening red in the torchlight. The companions halted, hands on their weapons.

"Is it time for breakfast already, Maritta?" Matafleur (Flamestrike being her name to common mortals) said in a sleepy, husky voice.

"Yes, we're just a bit early today, dearie," Maritta said soothingly. "But there's a storm brewing and I want the children to have their exercise before it breaks. Go back to sleep. I'll see they don't wake you on their way out."

"I don't mind." The dragon yawned and opened her eyes a bit farther. Now Tanis could see that one of them had a milky covering; she was blind in that eye.

"I hope we don't have to fight her, Tanis," Sturm whispered. "It'd be like fighting someone's grandmother."

Tanis forced his expression to harden. "She's a deadly grandmother, Sturm. Just remember that."

"The little ones had a restful night," the dragon murmured, apparently drifting off to sleep again. "See that they don't get wet if it does storm, Maritta. Especially little Erik. He had a cold last week." Her eyes closed.

Turning, Maritta beckoned the others on, putting her finger to her lips. Sturm and Tanis came last, their weapons and armor muffled by numerous cloaks and skirts. Tanis was about thirty feet from the dragon's head when the noise started.

At first he thought it was his imagination, that his nervousness was making him hear a buzzing sound in his head. But the sound grew louder and louder and Sturm turned, staring at him in alarm. The buzzing sound increased until it was like a thousand swarming locusts. Now the others were looking back, too—all of them staring at him! Tanis looked at his friends helplessly, an almost comic look of confusion on his face.

The dragon snorted and stirred in irritation, shaking her head as though the noise hurt her ears.

Suddenly Raistlin broke from the group and ran back to Tanis. "The sword!" he hissed. He grabbed the half-elf's cloak and threw it back to reveal the blade.

Tanis stared down at the sword in its antique scabbard. The mage was right. The blade hummed as if in the highest state of alarm. Now that Raistlin called his attention to it, the half-elf could actually feel the vibrations.

"Magic," the mage said softly, studying it with interest.

"Can you stop it?" yelled Tanis over the weird noise.

"No," said Raistlin. "I remember now. This is Wyrmslayer,† the famed magical sword of Kith-Kanan. It is reacting to the presence of the dragon."

"This is an abysmal time to remember!" Tanis said in fury.

"Or a very convenient time," snarled Sturm.

The dragon slowly raised her head, her eyes blinking, a thin stream of smoke drifting from a nostril. She focused her bleary red eyes on Tanis, pain and irritation in her gaze.

"Who have you brought, Maritta?" Matafleur's voice was filled with menace. "I hear a sound I have not heard in centuries, I smell the foul smell of steel! These are not the women! These are warriors!"

"Don't hurt her!" Maritta wailed.

"I may not have any choice!" Tanis said viciously, drawing Wyrmslayer from its sheath.

Wyrmslayer's hidden talent: it hums in the presence of a dragon.

For those not familiar with dragonlore, a wyrm is a dragon. The name has nothing to do with "worm."

"Riverwind and Goldmoon, get Maritta out of here!" The blade began to shine with a brilliant white light as the buzzing grew louder and angrier. Matafleur shrank back. The light of the sword pierced her good eye painfully; the terrible sound went through her head like a spear. Whimpering, she huddled away from Tanis.

"Run, get the children!" Tanis yelled, realizing that they didn't need to fight—at least not yet. Holding the shining sword high in the air, he moved forward cautiously, driving the pitiful dragon back against the wall.

Maritta, after one fearful glance at Tanis, led Goldmoon to the children's room. About one hundred children were wide-eyed with alarm over the strange sounds outside their chamber. Their faces relaxed at the sight of Maritta and Goldmoon and a few of the littler ones actually giggled when Caramon came rushing in, his skirts flapping around his armored legs. But at the sight of warriors and their drawn weapons, the children sobered immediately.

"What is it, Maritta?" asked the oldest girl. "What's happening? Is it fighting again?"

"We hope there'll be no fighting, dear one," Maritta said softly. "But I'll not lie to you—it may come to that. Now I want you to gather your things, particularly your warm cloaks, and come with us. The older of you carry the wee ones, as you do when we go outdoors for exercise."

Sturm expected confusion and wailing and demands for explanations. But the children quickly did as they were told, wrapping themselves in warm clothing and helping to dress the younger ones. They were quiet and calm, if a bit pale. These were children of war, Sturm remembered.

"I want you to move very swiftly through the dragon's lair and out into the playroom. When we get there, the big man"—Sturm gestured to Caramon—"will lead you out into the courtyard. Your mothers are waiting for you there. When you get outside, look immediately for your mother and go to her. Does everyone understand?" He glanced dubiously at the smaller children, but the girl at the front of the line nodded.

"We understand, sir," she said.

"All right," Sturm turned. "Caramon?"

The warrior, flushing in embarrassment as one hundred pairs of eyes turned to look at him, led the way back into the dragon's lair. Goldmoon scooped up a toddler in her arms, Maritta picked up another one. The older boys and girls carried little ones on their backs. They hurried out the door in orderly fashion, without saying a word until they saw Tanis, the gleaming sword, and the terrified dragon.

"Hey, you! Don't hurt our dragon!" one little boy yelled. Leaving his place in line, the child ran up to Tanis, his fists raised, his face twisted into a snarl.

"Dougl†!" cried the oldest girl, shocked. "Get back in line this instant!" But some of the children were crying now.

In honor of Doug Niles. —MW

Tanis, the sword still raised—knowing that this was the only thing keeping the dragon at bay—shouted, "Get them out of here!"

"Children, please!" Chieftain's Daughter, her voice stern and commanding, brought order to the chaos. "Tanis will not hurt the dragon if he does not have to. He is a gentle man. You must leave now. Your mothers need you."

There was an edge of fear in Goldmoon's voice, a feeling of urgency that influenced even the youngest child. They got back into line quickly.

"Good-bye, Flamestrike," several of the children called out, wistfully, waving their hands as they followed Caramon. Dougl gave Tanis one final threatening glance, then he returned to line, wiping his eyes with grubby fists.

"No!" shrieked Matafleur in a heartbroken voice. "No! Don't fight my children. Please! It is me you want! Fight me! Don't harm my children!"

Tanis realized the dragon was back in her past, reliving whatever terrible event had deprived her of her children.

Sturm stayed near Tanis. "She's going to kill you when the children are out of danger, you know."

"Yes," said Tanis grimly. Already the dragon's eyes—even the bad eye, were flaring red. Saliva dripped from the great, gaping mouth, and her talons scratched the floor.

"Not my children!" she said with rage.

"I'm with you—" Sturm began, drawing his sword.

"Leave us, knight," Raistlin whispered softly from the shadows. "Your weapon is useless. *I* will stay with Tanis."

The half-elf glanced at the mage in astonishment. Raistlin's strange, golden eyes met his, knowing what he was thinking: do I trust him? Raistlin gave him no help, almost as if he were goading him to refusal.

"Get out," Tanis said to Sturm.

"What?" he yelled. "Are you crazy? You're trusting this—"

"Get out!" Tanis repeated. At that moment, he heard Flint yelling loudly. "Go, Sturm, they need you out there!"

The knight stood a moment, irresolute, but he could not in honor ignore a direct order from one he considered his commander. Casting a baleful glance at Raistlin, Sturm turned on his heel and entered the tunnel.

"There is little magic I can work against a red dragon," Raistlin whispered swiftly.

"Can you buy us time?" Tanis asked.

Raistlin smiled the smile of one who knows death is so near it is past fearing. "I can," he whispered. "Move back near the tunnel. When you hear me start to speak, run."

Tanis began backing up, still holding the sword high. But the dragon no longer feared its magic. She knew only that her children were gone and she must kill those responsible. She lunged directly at the warrior with the sword as he began to run toward the tunnel. Then darkness descended upon her, a darkness so deep Matafleur thought for a horrible moment she had lost the sight of the other eye. She heard whispered words of magic and knew the robed human had cast a spell.

"I'll burn them!" she howled, sniffing the smell of steel through the tunnel. "They will not escape!" But just as she sucked in a great breath, she heard another sound—the sound of her children. "No," she realized in frustration. "I dare not. My children! I might harm my children. . . ." Her head drooped down on the cold stone floor.

Tanis and Raistlin ran down the tunnel, the half-elf dragging the weakened mage with him. Behind them they heard a pitiful, heartbroken moan.

"Not my children! Please, fight me! Don't hurt my children!"

Tanis emerged from the tunnel into the playroom, blinking in the bright light as Caramon swung the huge doors open to the rising sun. The children raced out the door into the courtyard. Through the door, Tanis could see Tika and Laurana, standing with their swords drawn, looking their way anxiously. A draconian lay crumbling on the floor of the playroom, Flint's battle-axe stuck in its back.

"Outside, all of you!" Tanis shouted. Flint, retrieving his battle-axe, joined the half-elf as the last to leave the playroom. As they did so, they heard a terrifying roar, the roar of a dragon, but a very different dragon than the pitiful Matafleur. Pyros had discovered the spies. The stone walls began to tremble—the dragon was rising from his lair.

"Ember!" Tanis swore bitterly. "He hasn't gone!"

The dwarf shook his head. "I'll bet my beard," he said gloomily, "that Tasslehoff 's involved."

The broken chain plummeted to the stone floor of the Chain Room in the Sla-Mori, three little figures falling with it.

Tasslehoff, clinging uselessly to the chain, tumbled through the darkness and thought, this is how it feels to die. It was an interesting sensation and he was sorry he couldn't experience it longer. Above him, he could hear Sestun shrieking in terror. Below, he heard the old mage muttering to himself, probably trying one last spell. Then Fizban raised his voice: *"Pveatherf—"* The word was cut off with a scream. There was the sound of a bone-crushing thud as the old magician crashed to the floor. Tasslehoff grieved, even though he knew he was next. The stone floor was approaching. Within a very few seconds he too would be dead. . . .

Then it was snowing.

At least that was what the kender thought. Then he realized with a shock that he was surrounded by millions and millions of feathers—like an explosion of chickens! He sank into a deep, vast pile of white feathers, Sestun tumbling in after him.

"Poor Fizban," Tas said, blinking tears from his eyes as he floundered in an ocean of white chicken feathers. "His last spell must have been *featherfall* like Raistlin uses. Wouldn't you know it? He just got the feathers."

Above him, the cogwheel turned faster and faster, the freed chain rushing through it as if rejoicing in its release from bondage.

Outdoors in the courtyard chaos reigned.

"Over here!" Tanis yelled, bursting out of the door, knowing they were doomed but refusing to give in. The companions gathered around him, weapons drawn, looking at him anxiously. "Run to the mines! Run for shelter! Verminaard and the red dragon didn't leave. It is a trap. They'll be on us any moment."

The others, their faces grim, nodded. All of them knew it was hopeless—they must cover about two hundred yards of flat, wide-open surface to reach safety.

They tried to herd the women and children along as swiftly as possible, but not very successfully. All the mothers and children needed to be sorted out. Then Tanis, looking over at the mines, swore aloud in added frustration.

The men of the mines, seeing their families free, quickly overpowered the guards and began running toward the courtyard! That wasn't the plan! What was Elistan thinking about? Within moments there would be eight hundred frantic people milling around out in the open without a scrap of shelter! He had to get them to head back south to the mountains.

"Where's Eben?" he called to Sturm.

"Last I saw him, he was running for the mines. I couldn't figure out why—"

The knight and half-elf gasped in sudden realization.

"Of course," said Tanis softly, his voice lost in the commotion. "It all fits."

As Eben ran for the mines, his one thought was to obey Pyros's command. Somehow, in the midst of this furor, he had to find the Green Gemstone Man. He knew what Verminaard and Pyros were going to do to these poor wretches. Eben felt a moment's pity—he was not, after all, cruel and vicious. He had simply seen, long ago, which side

was bound to win, and he determined, for once, to be on a winning side.

When his family's fortune was wiped out, Eben was left with only one thing to sell—himself. He was intelligent, handy with a sword, and as loyal as money could buy. It was on a journey to the north, looking for possible buyers, that Eben met Verminaard. Eben had been impressed with Verminaard's power and had wormed his way into the evil cleric's favor. But more importantly, he had managed to make himself useful to Pyros. The dragon found Eben charming, intelligent, resourceful, and—after a few tests—trustworthy.

Eben was sent home to Gateway just before the dragonarmies struck. He conveniently "escaped" and started his resistance group. Stumbling upon Gilthanas's party of elves the first time they tried to sneak into Pax Tharkas was a stroke of luck that further improved Eben's relationship with both Pyros and Verminaard. When the cleric actually fell into Eben's hands, he couldn't believe his luck. It must go to show how much the Dark Queen favored him, he supposed.

He prayed that the Dark Queen continue to favor him. Finding the Green Gemstone Man in this confusion was going to take divine intervention. Hundreds of men were milling about uncertainly. Eben saw a chance to do Verminaard another favor. "Tanis wants you men to meet in the courtyard," he cried. "Join your families."

"No! That isn't the plan!" Elistan cried, trying to stop them. But he was too late. The men, seeing their families free, surged forward. Several hundred gully dwarves added to the confusion, rushing gleefully out of the mines to join the fun, thinking, perhaps, it was a holiday.

Eben scanned the crowd anxiously for the Green Gemstone Man, then decided to look inside the prison cells. Sure enough, he found the man sitting alone, staring vaguely around the empty cell. Eben swiftly knelt beside him, racking his brain to come up with the man's name. It was something odd, old-fashioned. . . .

"Berem," Eben said after a moment. "Berem?"

The man looked up, interest lighting his face for the first time in many weeks. He was not, as Toede

had assumed, deaf and dumb. He was, instead, a man obsessed, totally absorbed in his own secret quest. He was human, however, and the sound of a human voice speaking his name was inordinately comforting.

"Berem," said Eben again, licking his lips nervously. Now that he had him, he wasn't sure what to do with him. He knew the first thing those poor wretches outside would do when the dragon struck would be to head for the safety of the mines. He had to get Berem out of here before Tanis caught them. But where? He could take the man inside Pax Tharkas as Pyros had ordered, but Eben didn't like that idea. Verminaard would certainly find them and, his suspicions aroused, would ask questions Eben couldn't answer.

No, there was only one place Eben could take him and be safe—outside the walls of Pax Tharkas. They could lie low in the wilderness until the confusion died, then sneak back inside the fortress at night. His decision made, Eben took Berem's arm and helped the man rise to his feet.

"There's going to be fighting," he said. "I'm going to take you away, keep you safe until it is over. I am your friend. Do you understand?"

The man regarded him with a look of penetrating wisdom and intelligence. It was not the ageless look of the elves but of a human who has lived in torment for countless years. Berem gave a small sigh and nodded.

The first Super Endless Quest Adventure Gamebook (before they became AD&D Gamebooks), by Morris Simon, had another hero confronting Verminaard and freeing the Prisoners of Pax Tharkas. The hero's name was Bern Vallenshield, and he, too, came from Solace.

Verminaard† strode from his chamber in a fury, yanking at his leather, armored gloves. A draconian trotted behind, carrying the Highlord's mace, Nightbringer. Other draconians milled around, acting on the orders Verminaard gave as he stepped into the corridor, returning to Pyros's lair.

"No, you fools, don't recall the army! This will take but a moment of my time. Qualinesti will be in flames by nightfall. Ember!" he shouted, throwing open the doors that led to the dragon's lair. He stepped out onto the ledge. Peering upward toward the balcony he could see smoke and flame and, in the distance, hear the dragon's roar.

"Ember!" There was no answer. "How long does it take to capture a handful of spies?" he demanded

furiously. Turning, he nearly fell over a draconian captain.

"Will you be using the dragon saddle, my lord?"

"No, there isn't time. Besides, I use that only for combat and there will be no one to fight out there, simply a few hundred slaves to burn."

"But the slaves have overcome the guards at the mine and are rejoining their families in the courtyard."

"How strong are your forces?"

"Not nearly strong enough, my lord," the draconian captain said, its eyes glinting. The captain had never thought it wise to deplete the garrison. "We are forty or fifty, perhaps, to over three hundred men and an equal number of women. The women will undoubtedly fight alongside the men, your lordship, and if they ever get organized and escape into the mountains—"

"Bah! Ember!" Verminaard called. He heard, in another part of the fortress, a heavy, metallic thud. Then he heard another sound, the great wheel—unused in centuries—creaking with protest at being forced into labor. Verminaard was wondering what these odd sounds portended, when Pyros flew down into his lair.

The Dragon Highlord ran to the ledge as Pyros dropped past him. Verminaard climbed swiftly and skillfully onto the dragon's back. Though separated by mutual distrust, the two fought well together. Their hatred for the petty races they strove to conquer, combined with their desire for power, joined them in a bond much stronger than either cared to admit.

"Fly!" Verminaard roared, and Pyros rose into the air.

"It is useless, my friend," Tanis said quietly to Sturm, laying his hand on the knight's shoulder as Sturm frantically called for order. "You're only wasting your breath. Save it for fighting."

"There'll be no fighting." Sturm coughed, hoarse from shouting. "We'll die, trapped like rats. Why won't these fools listen?"

He and Tanis stood at the northern end of the courtyard, about twenty feet from the front gates of Pax Tharkas. Looking south, they could see the mountains and hope. Behind them were the great gates of the fortress that would, at any moment, open to admit the vast draconian army, and within these walls, somewhere, were Verminaard and the red dragon.

In vain, Elistan sought to calm the people and urge them to move southward. But the men insisted on finding their womenfolk, the women on finding their children. A few families, together again, were starting to move south, but too late and too slowly.

Then, like a blood-red, flaming comet, Pyros soared from the fortress of Pax Tharkas, his wings sleek, held close to his sides. His huge tail trailed behind him. His taloned forefeet were curled close to his body as he gained speed in the air. Upon his back rode the Dragon Highlord, the gilded horns of the hideous dragonmask† glinting in the morning sun. Verminaard held onto the dragon's spiny mane with both hands as they flared into the sunlit sky, bringing night's shadows to the courtyard below.

Throughout these books, the dragonmask worn by the Highlords is described as "hideous," but TSR's artists were unable to make it hideous. It's a fine work of art.See The Art of DRAGONLANCE*.*

The dragonfear spread over the people. Unable to scream or run, they could only cower before the fearful apparition, arms around each other, knowing death was inevitable.

At Verminaard's command, Pyros settled on one of the fortress towers. Verminaard stared out from behind the horned dragonmask, silent, furious.

Tanis, watching in helpless frustration, felt Sturm grip his arm. "Look!" The knight pointed north, toward the gates.

Tanis reluctantly lowered his gaze from the Dragon Highlord and saw two figures running toward the gates of the fortress. "Eben!" he cried in disbelief. "But who's that with him?"

"He won't escape!" Sturm shouted. Before Tanis could stop him, the knight ran after the two. As Tanis followed, he saw a flash of red out of the corner of his eye—Raistlin and his twin.

"I, too, have a score to settle with this man," the mage hissed. The three caught up with Sturm just as the knight gripped Eben by the collar and hurled him to the ground.

"Traitor!" Sturm yelled loudly. "Though I die this day, I'll send you to the Abyss first!" He drew his sword and jerked Eben's head back. Suddenly

Eben's companion whirled around, came back, and caught hold of Sturm's sword-arm.

Sturm gasped. His hand loosened its grip on Eben as the knight stared, amazed at the sight before him.

The man's shirt had been torn open in his wild flight from the mines. Impaled in the man's flesh, in the center of his chest, was a brilliant green jewel! Sunlight flashed on the gem that was as big around as a man's fist, causing it to gleam with a bright and terrible light—an unholy light.

"I have never seen nor heard of magic like this!" Raistlin whispered in awe as he and the others stopped, stunned, beside Sturm.

Seeing their wide eyes focused on his body, Berem instinctively pulled his shirt over his chest. Then, loosening his hold on Sturm's arm, he turned and ran for the gates. Eben scrambled to his feet and stumbled after him.

Sturm leaped forward, but Tanis stopped him.

"No," he said. "It's too late. We have others to think of."

"Tanis, look!" Caramon shouted, pointing above the huge gates.

A section of the stone wall of the fortress above the massive front gates began to open, forming a huge, widening crack. Slowly at first, then with increasing speed, the massive granite boulders began to fall from the crack, smashing to the ground with such force that the flagstone cracked and great clouds of dust rose into the air. Above the roar could be dimly heard the sound of the massive chains releasing the mechanism.

The boulders began to fall just as Eben and Berem arrived at the gates. Eben shrieked in terror, instinctively and pitifully raised his arm to shield his head. The man next to him glanced up and—it seemed—gave a small sigh. Then both were buried under tons of cascading rock as the ancient defense mechanism sealed shut the gates of Pax Tharkas.

"This is your final act of defiance!" Verminaard roared. His speech had been interrupted by the fall of the rocks, an act that only enraged him more. "I offered you a chance to work to further the glory of my Queen. I cared for you and your families. But you are stubborn and foolish. You will pay with

your lives!" The Dragon Highlord raised Nightbringer high in the air. "I will destroy the men. I will destroy the women! I will destroy the children!"

At a touch of the Dragon Highlord's hand, Pyros spread his huge wings and leaped high into the air. The dragon drew in a deep breath, preparing to swoop down upon the mass of people who wailed in terror in the wide-open courtyard and incinerate them with his fiery breath.

But the dragon's deadly dive was stopped.

Sweeping up into the sky from the pile of rubble made when she crashed out of the fortress, Matafleur flew straight at Pyros.

The ancient dragon had sunk deeper into her madness. Once more she relived the nightmare of losing her children. She could see the knights upon the silver and golden dragons, the wicked dragonlances gleaming in the sunshine. In vain she pleaded with her children not to join the hopeless fight, in vain she sought to convince them the war was at an end. They were young and would not listen. They flew off, leaving her weeping in her lair. As she watched in her mind's eye the bloody, final battle, as she saw her children die upon the dragonlances, she heard Verminaard's voice.

"I will destroy the children!"

And, as she had done so many centuries before, Matafleur flew out to defend them.

Pyros, stunned by the unexpected attack, swerved just in time to avoid the broken, yet still lethal teeth of the old dragon aiming for his unprotected flanks. Matafleur hit him a glancing blow, tearing painfully into one of the heavy muscles that drove the giant wings. Rolling in the air, Pyros lashed out at the passing Matafleur with a wicked, taloned forefoot, tearing a gash in the female dragon's soft underbelly.

In her madness, Matafleur did not even feel the pain, but the force of the larger and younger male dragon's blow knocked her backwards in the air.

The rollover maneuver had been an instinctive defensive action on the part of the male dragon. He had been able to gain both altitude and time to plan his attack. He had, however, forgotten his rider. Verminaard—riding without the dragon saddle he used in battle—lost his grip on the dragon's neck

and fell to the courtyard below. It was not a long drop and he landed uninjured, only bruised and momentarily shaken.

Most of the people around him fled in terror when they saw him rise to his feet, but—glancing around swiftly—he noticed that there were four, near the northern end of the courtyard, who did not flee. He turned to face those four.

The appearance of Matafleur and her sudden attack on Pyros jolted the captive people out of their state of panic. This, combined with the fall of Verminaard into their midst, like the fall of some horrifying god, accomplished what Elistan and the others had not. The people were shaken out of their fear, sense returned, and they began fleeing south, toward the safety of the mountains. At this sight, the draconian captain sent his forces pouring into the crowd. He detailed another messenger, a wyvern,† to fly from the fortress to recall the army.

It's surprising that the draconian captain would happen to have a wyvern handy to carry messages. These distant relatives of dragons are more eager to attack than to cooperate with anyone. They have long, thin bodies and curved stinging tails, and none of the cunning of dragons.

The draconians surged into the refugees, but, if they hoped to cause a panic, they failed. The people had suffered enough. They had allowed their freedom to be taken away once, in return for the promise of peace and safety. Now they understood that there could be no peace as long as these monsters roamed Krynn. The people of Solace and Gateway—men, women, and children—fought back using every pitiful weapon they could grab, rocks, stones, their own bare hands, teeth, and nails.

The companions became separated in the crowd. Laurana was cut off from everyone. Gilthanas had tried to stay near her, but he was carried off in the mob. The elfmaiden, more frightened than she believed possible and longing to hide, fell back against the wall of the fortress, her sword in her hand. As she watched the raging battle in horror, a man fell to the ground in front her, clutching his stomach, his fingers red with his own blood. His eyes fixed in death, seeming to stare at her, as his blood formed a pool at her feet. Laurana stared at the blood in horrid fascination, then she heard a sound in front of her. Shaking, she looked up—directly into the hideous, reptilian face of the man's killer.

The draconian, seeing an apparently terror-stricken elven female before him, figured on an easy kill. Licking its blood-stained sword with its long tongue, the creature jumped over the body of his victim and lunged for Laurana.

Clutching her sword, her throat aching with terror, Laurana reacted out of sheer defensive instinct. She stabbed blindly, jabbing upward. The draconian was caught totally off guard. Laurana plunged her weapon into the draconian's body, feeling the sharp elven blade penetrate both armor and flesh, hearing bone splinter and the creature's last gurgling scream. It turned to stone, yanking the sword from her hand. But Laurana, thinking with a cold detachment that amazed her, knew from hearing the warriors talk that if she waited a moment, the stone body would turn to dust, releasing her weapon.

The sounds of battle raged around her, the screams, the death cries, the thuds and groans, the clash of steel—but she heard none of it.

She waited calmly until she saw the body crumble. Then she reached down and, sifting the dust aside with her hand, she grasped the hilt of her sword and lifted it into the air. Sunlight flashed on the blood-stained blade, her enemy lay dead at her feet. She looked around but could not see Tanis. She could not see any of the others. For all she knew, they might be dead. For all she knew, she might herself be dead within the next moment.

Laurana lifted her eyes to the sun-drenched blue sky. The world she might soon be leaving seemed newly made—every object, every stone, every leaf stood out in painful clarity. A warm fragrant southern breeze sprang up, driving back the storm clouds that hung over her homeland to the north. Laurana's spirit, released from its prison of fear, soared higher than the clouds, and her sword flashed in the morning sun.†

This is the epiphany for Laurana's character—that moment when her life is changed forever.—TRH

15

The Dragon Highlord. Matafleur's children.

Verminaard studied the four men as they approached him. These were not slaves, he realized. Then he recognized them as the ones who traveled with the golden-haired cleric. These, then, were the ones who had defeated Onyx in Xak Tsaroth, escaped the slave caravan, and broken into Pax Tharkas. He felt as if he knew them—the knight from that broken land of past glories; a half-elf trying to pass himself off as human; a deformed, sickly magician; and the mage's twin—a human giant whose brain was probably as thick as his arms.

It will be an interesting fight, he thought. He almost welcomed hand-to-hand combat—it had been a long time. He was growing bored with commanding armies from the back of a dragon.

Thinking of Ember, he glanced into the sky, wondering if he might be able to summon aid.

But it appeared that the red dragon was having his own problems. Matafleur had been fighting battles when Pyros was still in the egg; what she lacked in strength, she made up for in guile and cunning. The air crackled with flames, dragon blood dropped down like red rain.

He was named after vermin, by his mother's husband, who was not his father. Though a descendant of Huma, he is seduced into evil by the "Voice," or Takhisis. After he is fully hers, she speaks to him through his mace, Nightbringer. This bitter story is told in Before the Mask, *by Michael and Teri Williams.*

Shrugging, Verminaard† looked back at the four approaching him warily. He could hear the magic-user reminding his companions that Verminaard was a cleric of the Queen of Darkness and—as such—could call upon her aid. Verminaard knew from his spies that this magic-user, though young, was imbued with a strange power and considered very dangerous.

The four did not speak. There was no need for talk among these men, nor was there need for talk between enemies. Respect, grudging as it may be, was apparent on both sides. As for the battle rage, that was unnecessary. This would be fought coolly. The major victor would be death.

And so the four came forward, spreading to outflank him since he had nothing to set his back against. Crouching low, Verminaard swung Nightbringer in an arc, keeping them back, forming his plans. He must even the odds quickly. Gripping Nightbringer in his right hand, the evil cleric sprang forward from his crouched stance with all the strength in his powerful legs. His sudden move took his opponents by surprise. He did not raise his mace. All he needed now was his deadly touch. Landing on his feet in front of Raistlin, he reached out and grasped the magic-user by the shoulder, whispering a swift prayer to his Dark Queen.

Raistlin screamed. His body pierced by unseen, unholy weapons, he sank to the ground in agony. Caramon gave a great, bellowing roar and sprang at Verminaard, but the cleric was prepared. He swung the mace, Nightbringer, and struck the warrior a glancing blow. "Midnight," Verminaard whispered, and Caramon's bellow changed to a shout of panic as the spellbound mace blinded him.

"I can't see! Tanis, help me!" the big warrior cried, stumbling about. Verminaard, laughing

grimly, struck him a solid blow to the head. Caramon went down like a felled ox.

Out of the corner of his eye, Verminaard saw the half-elf leap for him, a two-handed sword of ancient elvish design in his hands. Verminaard whirled, blocking Tanis's sword with Nightbringer's massive, oaken handle. For a moment, the two combatants were locked together, but Verminaard's greater strength won out and he hurled Tanis to the ground.

The Solamnic knight raised his sword in salute—a costly mistake. It gave Verminaard time to remove a small iron needle from a hidden pocket. Raising it, he called once more upon the Queen of Darkness to defend her cleric. Sturm, striding forward, suddenly felt his body grow heavier and heavier until he could walk no more.

Tanis, lying on the ground, felt an unseen hand press down on him. He couldn't move. He couldn't turn his head. His tongue was too thick to speak. He could hear Raistlin's screams choke off in pain. He could hear Verminaard laugh and shout a hymn of praise to the Dark Queen. Tanis could only watch in despair as the Dragon Highlord, mace raised, walked toward Sturm, preparing to end the knight's life.

"Baravais, Kharas!" Verminaard said in Solamnic. He lifted the mace in a gruesome mockery of the knight's salute, then aimed for the knight's head, knowing that this death would be the most torturous possible for a knight—dying at the mercy of the enemy.

Suddenly a hand caught Verminaard's wrist. In astonishment, he stared at the hand, the hand of a female. He felt a power to match his own, a holiness to match his unholiness. At her touch, Verminaard's concentration wavered, his prayers to his Dark Queen faltered.

And then it was that the Dark Queen herself looked up to find a radiant god, dressed in white and shining armor, appear on the horizon of her plans.† She was not ready to fight this god, she had not expected his return, and so she fled to rethink her options and restructure her battle, seeing—for the first time—the possibility of defeat. The Queen of Darkness withdrew and left her cleric to his fate.

This is Paladine, last seen buried under all those feathers.—MW

Sturm felt the spell leave his body, his muscles his own to command once more. He saw Verminaard turn his fury on Goldmoon, striking at her savagely. The knight lunged forward, seeing Tanis rise, the elven sword flashing in the sunlight.

Both men ran toward Goldmoon, but Riverwind was there before them. Thrusting her out of the way, the Plainsman received on his sword arm the blow of the cleric's mace that had been intended to crush Goldmoon's head. Riverwind heard the cleric shout "Midnight!" and his vision was obscured by the same unholy darkness that had overtaken Caramon.

But the Qué-Shu warrior, expecting this, did not panic. Riverwind could still hear his enemy. Resolutely ignoring the pain of his injury, he transferred the sword to his left hand and stabbed in the direction of his enemy's harsh breathing. The blade, turned aside by the Dragon Highlord's powerful armor, was jarred from Riverwind's hand. Riverwind fumbled for his dagger, though he knew it was hopeless, that death was certain.

At that moment, Verminaard realized he was alone, bereft of spiritual help. He felt the cold, skeletal hand of despair clutch at him and he called to his Dark Queen. But she had turned away, absorbed in her own struggle.

Verminaard began to sweat beneath the dragonmask. He cursed it as the helm seemed to stifle him; he couldn't catch his breath. Too late he realized its unsuitableness for hand-to-hand combat—the mask blocked his peripheral vision. He saw the tall Plainsman, blind and wounded, before him—he could kill him at his leisure. But there were two other fighters near. The knight and the half-elf had been freed of the unholy spell he had cast on them and they were coming closer. He could hear them. Catching a glimpse of movement, he turned quickly and saw the half-elf running toward him, the elvish blade glistening. But where was the knight? Verminaard turned and backed up, swinging his mace to keep them at bay, while with his free hand, he struggled to rip the dragonhelm from his head.

Too late. Just as Verminaard's hand closed over the visor, the magic blade of Kith-Kanan pierced his armor and slid into his back. The Dragon Highlord

screamed and whirled in rage, only to see the Solamnic knight appear in his blood-dimmed vision. The ancient blade of Sturm's fathers plunged into his bowels. Verminaard fell to his knees. Still he struggled to remove the helm—he couldn't breathe, he couldn't see. He felt another sword thrust, then darkness overtook him.

High overhead, a dying Matafleur—weakened by loss of blood and many wounds—heard the voices of her children crying to her. She was confused and disoriented: Pyros seemed to be attacking from every direction at once. Then the big red dragon was before her, against the wall of the mountain. Matafleur saw her chance. She would save her children.

Pyros breathed a great blast of flame directly into the face of the ancient red dragon. He watched in satisfaction as the head withered, the eyes melted.

But Matafleur ignored the flames that seared her eyes, forever ending her vision, and flew straight at Pyros.

The big male dragon, his mind clouded by fury and pain and thinking he had finished his enemy, was taken by surprise. Even as he breathed again his deadly fire, he realized with horror the position he was in—he had allowed Matafleur to maneuver him between herself and the sheer face of the mountain. He had nowhere to go, no room to turn.

Matafleur soared into him with all the force of her once-powerful body, striking him like a spear hurled by the gods. Both dragons slammed against the mountain. The peak trembled and split apart as the face of the mountain exploded in flames.†

In later years when the Death of Flamestrike was legend, there were those who claimed to have heard a dragon's voice fade away like smoke on an autumn wind, whispering:

"My children . . . "

Lord Gunthar noted in his war journal (reprinted in Leaves from the Inn of the Last Home*) that Ember, Lord Verminaard's red dragon, was responsible for the downfall of Pax Tharkas, the burning of Solace, and other acts of devastation in and around the lands of Abanasinia. Ember was destroyed by one of his own kind—a female red dragon named Flamestrike, which serves as an example of the way evil always tends to turn upon and destroy itself.*

The Wedding

The last day of autumn dawned clear and bright. The air was warm—touched by the fragrant wind from the south, which had blown steadily ever since the refugees fled Pax Tharkas, taking with them only what they could scrounge from the fortress as they fled the wrath of the dragonarmies.

It had taken long days for the draconian army to scale the walls of Pax Tharkas, its gates blocked by boulders, its towers defended by gully dwarves. Led by Sestun, the gully dwarves stood on top of the walls throwing rocks, dead rats, and occasionally each other down on the frustrated draconians. This allowed the refugees time to escape into the mountains where, although they skirmished with small forces of draconians, they were not seriously threatened.

Flint volunteered to lead a party of men through the mountains, searching for a place where the people could spend the winter. These mountains were familiar to Flint since the hill dwarves' homeland was not far to the south. Flint's party discovered a valley nestled between vast, craggy peaks whose treacherous passes were choked with snow in the winter. The passes could be easily held against the might of the dragonarmies and there were caves where they could hide from the fury of the dragons.

Following a dangerous path, the refugees fled into the mountains and entered the valley. An avalanche soon blocked the route behind them and destroyed all trace of their passing. It would be months before the draconians discovered them.

The valley, far below the mountain peaks, was warm and sheltered from the harsh winter winds and snows. The woods were filled with game. Clear streams flowed from the mountains. The people mourned their dead, rejoiced in their deliverance, built shelters, and celebrated a wedding.

On the last day of autumn, as the sun set behind the mountains, kindling their snow-capped peaks with flame the color of dying dragons, Riverwind and Goldmoon were married.

When the two came to Elistan to ask him to preside over their exchange of vows, he had been deeply honored and had asked them to explain the ways of their people to him. Both of them replied steadily that their people were dead. The Qué-Shu were gone, their ways were no more.

"This will be *our* ceremony," Riverwind said. "The beginning of something new, not the continuation of that which has passed away."

"Though we will honor the memory of our people in our hearts," Goldmoon added softly, "we must look forward, not behind. We will honor the past by taking from it the good and the sorrowful that have made us what we are. But the past shall rule us no longer."

Elistan, therefore, studied the Disks of Mishakal to find what the ancient gods taught about marriage. He asked Goldmoon and Riverwind to write their own vows, searching their hearts for the true meaning of their love—for these vows would be spoken before the gods and last beyond death.†

This is another fundamental belief of my faith.—TRH

One custom of the Qué-Shu the couple kept. This was that the bridegift and the groomgift could not be purchased. This symbol of love must be made by the hand of the beloved. The gifts would be exchanged with the saying of the vows.

As the sun's rays spread across the sky, Elistan took his place on the top of a gentle rise. The people gathered in silence at the foot of the hill. From the east came Tika and Laurana, bearing torches. Behind them walked Goldmoon, Chieftain's Daughter. Her hair fell down around her shoulders in streams of molten gold, mingled with silver. Her head was crowned with autumn leaves. She wore the simple fringed doeskin tunic she had worn through their adventures. The medallion of Mishakal glittered at her throat. She carried her bridegift wrapped in a cloth as fine as cobweb, for the beloved one's eyes must be the first to see it.

Tika walked before her in solemn, misty-eyed wonder, the young girl's heart filled with dreams of her own, beginning to think that this great mystery shared by men and women might not be the terrifying experience she had feared, but something sweet and beautiful.

Laurana, next to Tika, held her torch high, brightening the day's dying light. The people murmured at Goldmoon's beauty; they fell silent when Laurana passed. Goldmoon was human, her beauty the beauty of the trees and mountains and skies. Laurana's beauty was elvish, otherworldly, mysterious.

The two women brought the bride to Elistan, then they turned, looking to the west, waiting for the groom.

A blaze of torches lit Riverwind's way. Tanis and Sturm, their solemn faces wistful and gentle, led. Riverwind came behind, towering over the others, his face stern as always. But a radiant joy, brighter than the torches, lit his eyes. His black hair was crowned with autumn leaves, his groomgift covered by one of Tasslehoff's handkerchiefs.† Behind him walked Flint and the kender. Caramon and Raistlin came last, the mage bearing the lighted-crystal Staff of Magius instead of a torch.

He didn't need to wash them. He never kept one long enough. Tas's handkerchief stealing was an allusion to Oliver Twist, *by Charles Dickens.—MW.*

The men brought the groom to Elistan, then stepped back to join the women. Tika found herself standing next to Caramon. Reaching out timidly, she touched his hand. Smiling down at her gently, he clasped her little hand in his big one.

As Elistan looked at Riverwind and Goldmoon, he thought of the terrible grief and fear and danger they had faced, the harshness of their lives. Did their future hold anything different? For a moment he was overcome and could not speak. The two, seeing Elistan's emotion and, perhaps, understanding his sorrow, reached out to him reassuringly. Elistan drew them close to him, whispering words for them alone.

"It was your love and your faith in each other that brought hope to the world. Each of you was willing to sacrifice your life for this promise of hope, each has saved the life of the other. The sun shines now, but already its rays are dimming and night is ahead. It is the same for you, my friends. You will walk through much darkness before morning. But your love will be as a torch to light the way."

Elistan then stepped back and began to speak to all assembled. His voice, husky to begin with, grew stronger and stronger as he felt the peace of the gods surround him and confirm their blessings on this couple.

"The left hand is the hand of the heart," he said, placing Goldmoon's left hand in Riverwind's left hand and holding his own left hand over them. "We join left hands that the love in the hearts of this man and this woman may combine to form something greater as two streams join together to form a mighty river. The river flows through the land, branching off into tributaries, exploring new ways, yet ever drawn to the eternal sea. Receive their love, Paladine—greatest of the gods; bless it and grant them peace at least in the hearts, if there is no peace in this shattered land."

In the blessed silence, husbands and wives put their arms around each other. Friends drew close, children quieted and crept near their parents. Hearts filled with mourning were comforted. Peace was granted.

"Pledge your vows, one to another," Elistan said, "and exchange the gifts of your hands and hearts."

Goldmoon looked into Riverwind's eyes and began to speak softly.

Wars have settled on the North
and dragons ride the skies,
"Now is the time for wisdom,"
say the wise and the nearly wise.†
"Here in the heart of battle,
the time to be brave is at hand.
Now most things are larger than
the promise of woman to man."

But you and I, through burning plains,
through darkness of the earth,
affirm this world, its people,
the heavens that gave them birth,
the breath that passes between us,
this altar where we stand,
and all those things made larger by
the promise of woman to man.

I remember I was thinking of Mark 13:7—the old King James translation, where it talks about "wars and rumors of wars." Margaret always liked the line about "the wise and the nearly wise."
—Michael Williams

Then Riverwind spoke:

Now in the belly of winter,
when ground and sky are gray,
here in the heart of sleeping snow,
now is the time to say

yes to the sprouting vallenwood
in the green countryside,
for these things are far larger than
a man's word to his bride.

Through these promises we keep,
forged in the yawning night,
proved in the presence of heroes
and the prospect of spring light,
the children will see moons and stars
where now the dragons ride,
and humble things made large by
a man's word to his bride.

When the vows were spoken, they exchanged gifts. Goldmoon shyly handed her present to Riverwind. He unwrapped it with hands that trembled. It was a ring plaited of her own hair, bound with bands of silver and of gold as fine as the hair they surrounded. Goldmoon had given Flint her mother's jewelry; the dwarf's old hands had not lost their touch.

In the wreckage of Solace, Riverwind had found a vallenwood branch spared by the dragon's fire and had carried it in his pack. Now that branch made Riverwind's gift to Goldmoon—a ring, perfectly smooth and plain. When polished, the wood of the tree was a rich gold color, marked by streaks and whorls of softest brown. Goldmoon, holding it, remembered the first night she had seen the great vallenwoods, the night they had stumbled—weary and frightened—into Solace, bearing the blue crystal staff. She began to cry softly and wiped her eyes with Tas's handkerchief.

"Bless the gifts, Paladine," Elistan said, "these symbols of love and sacrifice. Grant that during times of deepest darkness, these two may look upon these gifts and see their path lighted by love. Great and shining god, god of human and elf, god of kender and dwarf, give your blessing to these, your children. May the love they plant in their hearts today be nourished by their souls and grow into a tree of life, providing shelter and protection to all who seek refuge beneath its spreading boughs. With the joining of hands, the exchanging of vows, the giving of gifts, you two, Riverwind,

grandson of Wanderer, and Goldmoon, Chieftain's Daughter—become one—in your hearts, in the sight of men, in the eyes of the gods."

Riverwind took his ring from Goldmoon and placed it upon her slender finger. Goldmoon took her ring from Riverwind. He knelt before her—as would have been the custom of the Qué-Shu. But Goldmoon shook her head.

"Rise, warrior," she said, smiling through her tears.

"Is that a command?" he asked softly.

"It is the last command of Chieftain's Daughter," she whispered.

Riverwind stood up. Goldmoon placed the golden ring on his finger. Then Riverwind took her in his arms. She put her arms around him. Their lips met, their bodies melded together, their spirits joined. The people gave a great shout and torches flared. The sun sank behind the mountains, leaving the sky bathed in a pearl-like hue of purples and soft reds, which soon deepened into the sapphire of night.

The bride and groom were carried down the hill by the cheering throng and feasting and merriment began. Huge tables, carved from the pine trees of the forest, were set up on the grass. The children, freed at last from the awe of the ceremony, ran and shouted, playing at dragon slaying. Tonight care and worry were far from their minds. Men broached the huge casks of ale and wine they had salvaged in Pax Tharkas and began drinking salutes to the bride and groom. Women brought in huge plates of food—game and fruits and vegetables gathered in the forest and taken from the stores in Pax Tharkas.

"Get out of my way, don't crowd me," Caramon grumbled as he sat down at the table. The companions, laughing, moved over to give the big man room. Maritta and two other women came forward and placed a huge platter of deer meat before the big warrior.

"Real food," sighed the warrior.

"Hey," roared Flint, stabbing at a piece of sizzling meat on Caramon's plate with his fork, "you gonna eat that?"

Caramon promptly and silently—without missing a bite—emptied a flagon of ale over the dwarf's head.

Tanis and Sturm sat side by side, talking quietly. Tanis's eyes strayed to Laurana occasionally. She sat at a different table talking animatedly with Elistan. Tanis, thinking how lovely she looked tonight, realized how changed she was from the willful, lovesick girl who had followed him from Qualinesti. He told himself he liked the change in her. But he caught himself wondering just what she and Elistan found so interesting.

Sturm touched his arm. Tanis started. He had lost track of the conversation. Flushing, he began to apologize when he saw the look on Sturm's face.

"What is it?" Tanis said in alarm, half-rising.

"Hush, don't move!" Sturm ordered. "Just look—over there—sitting off to himself."

Tanis looked where Sturm gestured, puzzled, then he saw the man—sitting alone, hunched over his food, eating it absently as if he didn't really taste it. Whenever anyone approached, the man shrank back, eyeing him nervously until he passed. Suddenly, perhaps sensing Tanis's eyes on him, he raised his head and stared directly at them. The half-elf gasped and dropped his fork.

"But that's impossible!" he said in a strangled voice. "We saw him die! With Eben! No one could have survived—"

"Then I was right," Sturm said grimly. "You recognize him, too. I thought I was going mad. Let's go talk to him."

But when they looked again, he was gone. Swiftly, they searched the crowd, but it was impossible to find him now.

As the silver moon and the red rose in the sky, the married couples formed a ring around the bride and groom and began singing wedding songs. Unmarried couples danced in pairs outside the circle while the children leaped and shouted and reveled in staying up past their bedtime. Bonfires burned brightly, voices and music filled the night air, the silver moon and the red rose to light the sky. Goldmoon and Riverwind stood, their arms around each other, their eyes shining brighter than the moons or the blazing fire.

Tanis lingered on the outskirts, watching his friends. Laurana and Gilthanas performed an ancient elvish dance of grace and beauty, singing

together a hymn of joy. Sturm and Elistan fell into conversation about their plans to travel south in search of the legendary seaport city of Tarsis the Beautiful, where they hoped to find ships to carry the people from this war-torn land. Tika, tired of watching Caramon eat, teased Flint until the dwarf finally agreed to dance with her, blushing bright red beneath his beard.

Where was Raistlin? Tanis wondered. The half-elf recalled seeing him at the banquet. The mage ate little and drank his herbal mixture. He had seemed unusually pale and quiet. Tanis decided to go in search of him. The company of the dark-souled, cynical mage seemed more suited to him tonight than music and laughter.

Tanis wandered into the moonlit darkness, knowing somehow he was headed in the right direction. He found Raistlin sitting on the stump of an old tree whose lightning-shattered, blackened remains lay scattered over the ground. The half-elf sat down next to the silent mage.

A small shadow settled among the trees behind the half-elf. Finally, Tas would hear what these two discussed!

Raistlin's strange eyes stared into the southlands, barely visible between a gap in the tall mountains. The wind still blew from the south, but it was beginning to veer again. The temperature was falling. Tanis felt Raistlin's frail body shiver. Looking at him in the moonlight, Tanis was startled to see the mage's resemblance to his half-sister, Kitiara.† It was a fleeting impression and gone almost as soon as it came, but it brought the woman to Tanis's mind, adding to his feelings of unrest and disquiet. He restlessly tossed a piece of bark back and forth, from hand to hand.

When the infant Raistlin arrived unexpectedly (Kitiara's mother not knowing she was expecting twins), Kitiara named him for the strongly willed character in the tales of derring-do she had been told by her real father, Gregory Uth Matar. He had used the name for his hero, who was probably himself.

"What do you see to the south?" Tanis asked abruptly.

Raistlin glanced at him. "What do I ever see with these eyes of mine, Half-Elf?" the mage whispered bitterly. "I see death, death and destruction. I see war." He gestured up above. "The constellations have not returned. The Queen of Darkness is not defeated."

"We may not have won the war," Tanis began, "but surely we have won a major battle—"

Raistlin coughed and shook his head sadly.

"Do you see no hope?"

"Hope is the denial of reality. It is the carrot dangled before the draft horse to keep him plodding along in a vain attempt to reach it."

"Are you saying we should just give up?" Tanis asked, irritably tossing the bark away.

"I'm saying we should remove the carrot and walk forward with our eyes open," Raistlin answered. Coughing, he drew his robes more closely around him. "How will you fight the dragons, Tanis? For there will be more! More than you can imagine! And where now is Huma? Where now is the Dragonlance? No, Half-Elf. Do not talk to me of hope."

Tanis did not answer, nor did the mage speak again. Both sat silently, one continuing to stare south, the other glancing up into the great voids in the glittering, starlit sky.

Tasslehoff sank back into the soft grass beneath the pine trees. "No hope!" the kender repeated bleakly, sorry he had followed the half-elf. "I don't believe it," he said, but his eyes went to Tanis, staring at the stars. Tanis believes it, the kender realized, and the thought filled him with dread.

Ever since the death of the old magician, an unnoticed change had come over the kender. Tasslehoff began to consider that this adventure was in earnest, that it had a purpose for which people gave their lives. He wondered why he was involved and thought perhaps he had given the answer to Fizban—the small things he was meant to do were important, somehow, in the big scheme of things.

But until now it had never occurred to the kender that all this might be for nothing, that it might not make any difference, that they might suffer and lose people they loved like Fizban, and the dragons would still win in the end.

"Still," the kender said softly, "we have to keep trying and hoping. That's what's important, the trying and the hoping. Maybe that's most important of all."

Something floated gently down from the sky, brushing past the kender's nose. Tas reached out and caught it in his hand.

It was a small, white chicken feather.

You've seen Tracy's concept for a trilogy of dragon-based adventures soon grow to one adventure for every color of dragon and the novels that everyone has come to know and love. But there was a very tight point, a juncture on which the entire fate of the proceedings rested.

That was when we presented it to upper management.

A lot of DRAGONLANCE *was the efforts of various individuals up to that point, but was primarily Tracy. Margaret had not yet arrived on the scene. Tracy did the timelines, the map, and the original plot. Harold Johnson encouraged and expanded. During this time, they added me and Carl Smith (the forgotten Beatle of Ansalon) to the mix. They asked that we make a full presentation to the veeps-and-higher management (at this time the Brothers Blume, Kevin and Brian). This is what we would forever after call "The Dog and Pony Show."*

Tracy prepped. We did scripts. We rehearsed. We got Larry Elmore to do four color sketches of the upcoming series (each of the four design members of the team got one after it was all done). We talked about options. We talked about changes. We talked about lead figures and toy tie-ins. And novels.

And then we divvied it up into four pieces, one for every three module adventures. The day came and the meeting was postponed. We prepped for a second meeting. Finally Tracy got up in front of the brass and in his best voice intoned, "Hear now the first tale of DRAGONLANCE*."*

I'd like to say that the initial response was universally positive and excited, and there were *a few of the bosses who thought it was great. And they* did *give the go-ahead to launch into a massive collection of adventures, the largest thing TSR had ever done on a single subject. But they also were worried, so that when Tracy and Margaret got the go-ahead for the novels, they were told to make sure the first one had some type of resolution to it, just in case there wouldn't be a second.*

Not that there need have been any real worry about that, as it turned out.—Jeff Grubb

This elven bard played a major role in keeping the legend of Huma alive with this ever-popular song. He would later write many of the stories and songs about the Heroes that would be performed on the holiday that comes to be called Heroes Meet at the Inn of the Last Home.

The "Song of Huma" was the last, and many consider the greatest, work of the elven bard, Quivalen Soth.† Only fragments of the work remained following the Cataclysm. It is said that those who study it diligently will find hints to the future of the turning world.

SONG OF HUMA

Out of the village, out of the thatched and clutching shires,
Out of the grave and furrow, furrow and grave,
Where his sword first tried
The last cruel dances of childhood, and awoke to the shires
Forever retreating, his greatness a marshfire,
The banked flight of the Kingfisher always above him,
Now Huma walked upon Roses,
In the level Light of the Rose.
And troubled by Dragons, he turned to the end of the land,
To the fringe of all sense and senses,
To the Wilderness, where Paladine bade him to turn,
And there in the loud tunnel of knives
He grew in unblemished violence, in yearning,
Stunned into himself by a deafening gauntlet of voices.

It was there and then that the White Stag found him,
At the end of a journey planned from the shores of Creation,
And all time staggered at the forest edge
Where Huma, haunted and starving,
Drew his bow, thanking the gods for their bounty and keeping,
Then saw, in the ranged wood,
In the first silence, the dazed heart's symbol,
The rack of antlers resplendent.
He lowered the bow and the world resumed.
Then Huma followed the Stag, its tangle of antlers receding
As a memory of young light, as the talons of birds ascending.
The Mountains crouched before them. Nothing would change now,
The three moons stopped in the sky,
And the long night tumbled in shadows.

It was morning when they reached the grove,
The lap of the mountain, where the Stag departed,
Nor did Huma follow, knowing the end of this journey
Was nothing but green and the promise of green that endured
In the eyes of the woman before him.
And holy the days he drew near her, holy the air
That carried his words of endearment, his forgotten songs,
And the rapt moons knelt on the Great Mountain.
Still, she eluded him, bright and retreating as marshfire,
Nameless and lovely, more lovely because she was nameless,
As they learned that the world, the dazzling shelves of the air,
The Wilderness itself
Were plain and diminished things to the heart's thicket.
At the end of the days, she told him her secret.

For she was not of woman, nor was she mortal,
But the daughter and heiress from a line of Dragons.
For Huma the sky turned indifferent, cluttered by moons,
The brief life of the grass mocked him, mocked his fathers,
And the thorned light bristled on the gliding Mountain.
But nameless she tendered a hope not in her keeping,
That Paladine only might answer, that through his enduring wisdom
She might step from forever, and there in her silver arms
The promise of the grove might rise and flourish.
For that wisdom Huma prayed, and the Stag returned,
And east, through the desolate fields, through ash,
Through cinders and blood, the harvest of dragons,
Traveled Huma, cradled by dreams of the Silver Dragon,
The Stag perpetual, a signal before him.

At last the eventual harbor, a temple so far to the east
That it lay where the east was ending.
There Paladine appeared
In a pool of stars and glory, announcing
That of all choices, one most terrible had fallen to Huma.
For Paladine knew that the heart is a nest of yearnings,
That we can travel forever toward light, becoming
What we can never be.
For the bride of Huma could step into the devouring sun,
Together they would return to the thatched shires
And leave behind the secret of the Lance, the world
Unpeopled in darkness, wed to the dragons.
Or Huma could take on the Dragonlance, cleansing all Krynn
Of death and invasion, of the green paths of his love.

The hardest of choices, and Huma remembered
How the Wilderness cloistered and baptized his first thoughts
Beneath the sheltering sun, and now
As the black moon wheeled and pivoted, drawing the air
And the substance from Krynn, from the things of Krynn,
From the grove, from the Mountain, from the abandoned shires,
He would sleep, he would send it all away,
For the choosing was all of the pain, and the choices
Were heat on the hand when the arm has been severed.
But she came to him, weeping and luminous,
In a landscape of dreams, where he saw
The world collapse and renew on the glint of the Lance.
In her farewell lay collapse and renewal.
Through his doomed veins the horizon burst.

He took up the Dragonlance, he took up the story,
The pale heat rushed through his rising arm
And the sun and the three moons, waiting for wonders,
Hung in the sky together.
To the West Huma rode, to the High Clerist's Tower
On the back of the Silver Dragon,
And the path of their flight crossed over a desolate country
Where the dead walked only, mouthing the names of dragons.
And the men in the Tower, surrounded and riddled by dragons,
By the cries of the dying, the roar in the ravenous air,
Awaited the unspeakable silence,
Awaited far worse, in fear that the crash of the senses
Would end in a moment of nothing
Where the mind lies down with its losses and darkness.

But the winding of Huma's horn in the distance
Danced on the battlements. All of Solamnia lifted
Its face to the eastern sky, and the dragons
Wheeled to the highest air, believing
Some terrible change had come.
From out of their tumult of wings, out of the chaos of dragons,
Out of the heart of nothing, the Mother of Night,
Aswirl in a blankness of colors,
Swooped to the East, into the stare of the sun
And the sky collapsed into silver and blankness.
On the ground Huma lay, at his side a woman,
Her silver skin broken, the promise of green
Released from the gifts of her eyes. She whispered her name
As the Queen of Darkness banked in the sky above Huma.

She descended, the Mother of Night,
And from the loft of the battlements, men saw shadows
Boil on the colorless dive of her wings:
A hovel of thatch and rushes, the heart of a Wilderness,
A lost silver light spattered in terrible crimson,
And then from the center of shadows
Came a depth in which darkness itself was aglimmer,
Denying all air, all light, all shadows.
And thrusting his lance into emptiness,
Huma fell to the sweetness of death, into abiding sunlight.
Through the Lance, through the dear might and brotherhood
Of those who must walk to the end of the breath and the senses,
He banished the dragons back to the core of nothing,
And the long lands blossomed in balance and music.

Stunned in new freedom, stunned by the brightness and colors,
By the harped blessing of the holy winds,
The Knights carried Huma, they carried the Dragonlance
To the grove in the lap of the Mountain.
When they returned to the grove in pilgrimage, in homage,
The Lance, the armor, the Dragonbane himself
Had vanished to the day's eye.
But the night of the full moons red and silver
Shines down on the hills, on the forms of a man and a woman
Shimmering steel and silver, silver and steel,
Above the village, over the thatched and nurturing shires.

Every time I've seen Dragons of Autumn Twilight *in a used bookstore, the last page of this last poem has been missing. I'm not sure if it's a binding problem or some kind of divine message that the thing is too long. I lean toward the latter: I wish more of it was of the quality of the first and sixth stanzas.*
—Michael Williams

She descended, the [illegible] of Night
And [illegible] shadows
[illegible] the [illegible] her ways
[illegible] the Wilderness
[illegible]
[illegible] from [illegible]
[illegible]
[illegible]
And [illegible]
[illegible]
Through [illegible] the [illegible] neighborhood
Of those who [illegible] and [illegible]
[illegible] to the care of [illegible]
[illegible]

[illegible] dragon, [illegible]
[illegible]
The [illegible] and the Dragon [illegible]
[illegible] Mountains
[illegible]
The [illegible]
[illegible] the day [illegible]
[illegible] and [illegible]
Some [illegible] the [illegible]
[illegible] and [illegible]
[illegible]

Volume 2

Dragons of Winter Night

DEDICATIONS

My mother and father took me to the library every other week for all the years of my childhood until I left for college. The day I received my first "adult" library card still ranks as a special day in my life. They gave me the greatest gift next to life—reading.—MW

To my parents,
Dr. and Mrs. Harold R. Hickman,
who taught me what true honor is
—Tracy Raye Hickman

To my parents, Frances and George Weis,
who gave me a gift more precious than life—
the love of books
—Margaret Weis

The winter winds raged outside, but within the caverns of the mountain dwarves beneath the Kharolis Mountains, the fury of the storm was not felt. As the Thane called for silence among the assembled dwarves and humans, a dwarven bard stepped forward to do homage to the companions.

Song of the Nine Heroes

From the north came danger, as we knew it would:
In the vanguard of winter, a dragon's dance
Unraveled the land, until out of the forest,
Out of the plains they came, from the mothering earth,
The sky unreckoned before them.
Nine they were, under the three moons,
Under the autumn twilight:
As the world declined, they arose
Into the heart of the story.

One from a garden of stone arising,
From dwarf-halls, from weather and wisdom,
Where the heart and mind ride unquestioned
In the untapped vein of the hand.
In his fathering arms, the spirit gathered.
Nine they were, under the three moons,
Under the autumn twilight:
As the world declined, they arose
Into the heart of the story.

One from a haven of breezes descending,
Light in the handling air,
To the waving meadows, the kender's country,
Where the grain out of smallness arises itself
To grow green and golden and green again.
Nine they were, under the three moons,
Under the autumn twilight:
As the world declined, they arose
Into the heart of the story.

The next from the plains, the long land's keeping,
Nurtured in distance, horizons of nothing.
Bearing a staff she came, and a burden
Of mercy and light converged in her hand:
Bearing the wounds of the world, she came.
Nine they were, under the three moons,
Under the autumn twilight:
As the world declined, they arose
Into the heart of the story.

The next from the plains, in the moon's shadow,
Through custom, through ritual, trailing the moon
Where her phases, her wax and her wane, controlled
The tide of his blood, and his warrior's hand
Ascended through hierarchies of space into light.
Nine they were, under the three moons,
Under the autumn twilight:
As the world declined, they arose
Into the heart of the story.

One within absences, known by departures,
The dark swordswoman at the heart of fire:
Her glories the space between words,
The cradlesong recollected in age,
Recalled at the edge of awakening and thought.
Nine they were, under the three moons,
Under the autumn twilight:
As the world declined, they arose
Into the heart of the story.

One in the heart of honor, formed by the sword,
By the centuries' flight of the kingfisher over the land,
By Solamnia ruined and risen, rising again
When the heart ascends into duty.
As it dances, the sword is forever an heirloom.
Nine they were, under the three moons,
Under the autumn twilight:
As the world declined, they arose
Into the heart of the story.

The next in a simple light a brother to darkness,
Letting the sword hand try all subtleties,
Even the intricate webs of the heart. His thoughts
Are pools disrupted in changing wind—
He cannot see their bottom.
Nine they were, under the three moons,
Under the autumn twilight:
As the world declined, they arose
Into the heart of the story.

The next the leader, half-elven, betrayed
As the twining blood pulls asunder the land,
The forests, the worlds of elves and men.
Called into bravery, but fearing for love,
And fearing that, called into both, he does nothing.
Nine they were, under the three moons,
Under the autumn twilight:
As the world declined, they arose
Into the heart of the story.

The last from the darkness, breathing the night
Where the abstract stars hide a nest of words,
Where the body endures the wound of numbers,
Surrendered to knowledge, until, unable to bless,
His blessing falls on the low, the benighted.
Nine they were, under the three moons,
Under the autumn twilight:
As the world declined, they arose
Into the heart of the story.

Joined by others they were in the telling:
A graceless girl, graced beyond graces;
A princess of seeds and saplings, called to the forest;
An ancient weaver of accidents;
Nor can we say who the story will gather.
Nine they were, under the three moons,
Under the autumn twilight:
As the world declined, they arose
Into the heart of the story.

From the north came danger, as we knew it would:
In encampments of winter, the dragon's sleep
Has settled the land, but out of the forest,
Out of the plains they come, from the mothering earth
Defining the sky before them.
Nine they were, under the three moons,
Under the autumn twilight:
As the world declined, they arose
Into the heart of the story.

Everybody—or at least a lot of devoted DRAGONLANCE *readers—get their shorts in a knot over who is included among the Nine Heroes in this poem. There seems to be a problem with Kitiara's presence here, though it didn't bother Margaret and Tracy at the time, which speaks to the nature of "historical" verse: it's always written from a perspective, with an agenda, and who's to say there wasn't a bard in all of Krynn who would have put Kit on the list?*
—Michael Williams

The Hammer

The end of the first book fell considerably short of where the second book was to have started. We were set to tell the tale of the heroes' journey through Skullcap and their adventures in the Dwarven Kingdom gaining the favor of the Dwarven Thanes by obtaining the Hammer of Kharas—but we ran out of both time and room. This chapter bridges all of those "lost chapters" and brings us to the dwarven Southgate so that our story may once again proceed.—TRH

"The Hammer of Kharas!"

The great Hall of Audience of the King of the Mountain Dwarves echoed with the triumphal announcement. It was followed by wild cheering, the deep booming voices of the dwarves mingling with the slightly higher-pitched shouts of the humans as the huge doors at the rear of the Hall were thrown open and Elistan, cleric of Paladine, entered.

Although the bowl-shaped Hall was large, even by dwarven standards, it was crammed to capacity. Nearly all of the eight hundred refugees from Pax Tharkas lined the walls, while the dwarves packed onto the carved stone benches below.

Elistan appeared at the foot of a long central aisle, the giant warhammer held reverently in his hands. The shouts increased at the sight of the cleric of Paladine in his white robes, the sound booming against the great vault of the ceiling and reverberating through the hall until it seemed that the ground shook with the vibrations.

Tanis winced as the noise made his head throb. He was stifled in the crowd. He didn't like being underground anyway and, although the ceiling was so high that the top soared beyond the blazing torchlight and disappeared into shadow, the half-elf felt enclosed, trapped.†

Elves consider life underground as totally unnatural, and certainly beneath their dignity—pun intended.

"I'll be glad when this is over," he muttered to Sturm, standing next to him.

Sturm, always melancholy, seemed even darker and more brooding than usual. "I don't approve of this, Tanis," he muttered, folding his arms across the bright metal of his antique breastplate.

"I know," said Tanis irritably. "You've said it—not once, but several times. It's too late now. There's nothing to be done but make the best of it."

The end of his sentence was lost in another resounding cheer as Elistan raised the Hammer above his head, showing it to the crowd before beginning the walk down the aisle. Tanis put his hand on his forehead. He was growing dizzy as the cool underground cavern heated up from the mass of bodies.

A thane is both the leader of a dwarven clan and the clan, or tribe, itself.

Elistan started to walk down the aisle. Rising to greet him on a dais in the center of the Hall was Hornfel, Thane† of the Hylar dwarves. Spaced behind the dwarf were seven carved stone thrones, all of them now empty. Hornfel stood before the seventh throne—the most magnificent, the throne for the King of Thorbardin. Long empty, it would be occupied once more, as Hornfel accepted the Hammer of Kharas. The return of this ancient relic was a singular triumph for Hornfel. Since his thanedom was now in possession of the coveted Hammer, he could unite the rival dwarven thanes under his leadership.

The Germanic god Thor had a magical hammer named Mjollner. It, too, was forged by dwarves. "Kharas" means "knight" in Solamnic.

"We fought to recover that Hammer," Sturm said slowly, his eyes upon the gleaming weapon. "The legendary Hammer of Kharas.†Used to forge the dragonlances. Lost for hundreds of years, found again, and lost once more. And now given to the dwarves!" he said in disgust.

"It was given to the dwarves once before," Tanis reminded him wearily, feeling sweat trickle down his forehead. "Have Flint tell you the tale, if you've forgotten. At any rate, it is truly theirs now." Elistan had arrived at the foot of the stone dais where the Thane, dressed in the heavy robes and massive gold chains dwarves loved, awaited him. Elistan knelt at the foot of the dais, a politic gesture, for otherwise the tall, muscular cleric would stand face-to-face with the dwarf, despite the fact that the dais was a good three feet off the ground. The dwarves cheered mightily at this. The humans were, Tanis noticed, more subdued, some muttering among themselves, not liking the sight of their leader abasing himself.

"Accept this gift of our people—" Elistan's words were lost in another cheer from the dwarves.

"Gift!" Sturm snorted. "Ransom is nearer the mark."

"In return for which," Elistan continued when he could be heard, "we thank the dwarves for their generous gift of a place to live within their kingdom."

"For the right to be sealed in a tomb . . ." Sturm muttered.

"And we pledge our support to the dwarves if the war should come upon us!" Elistan shouted.

Cheering resounded throughout the chamber, increasing as Thane Hornfel bent to receive the Hammer. The dwarves stamped and whistled, most climbing up on the stone benches.

Tanis began to feel nauseated.† He glanced around. They would never be missed. Hornfel would speak; so would each of the other six Thanes, not to mention the members of the Highseekers Council. The half-elf touched Sturm on the arm, motioning to the knight to follow him. The two walked silently from the Hall, bending low to get through a narrow archway. Although still underground in the massive dwarven city, at least they were away from the noise, out in the cool night air.

Tanis is claustrophobic.—MW

"Are you all right?" Sturm asked, noticing Tanis's pallor beneath his beard. The half-elf gulped draughts of cool air.

"I am now," Tanis said, flushing in shame at his weakness. "It was the heat . . . and the noise."

"Well, we'll be out of here soon," Sturm said. "Depending, of course, on whether or not the Council of Highseekers votes to let us go to Tarsis."

"Oh, there's no doubt how they'll vote," Tanis said, shrugging. "Elistan is clearly in control, now that he's led the people to a place of safety. None of the Highseekers dares oppose him—at least to his face. No, my friend, within a month's time perhaps, we'll be setting sail in one of the white-winged ships of Tarsis the Beautiful."

"Without the Hammer of Kharas," Sturm added bitterly. Softly, he began to quote. "'*And so it was told that the Knights took the golden Hammer, the Hammer blessed by the great god Paladine and given to the One of the Silver Arm so that he might forge the Dragonlance of Huma, Dragonbane, and gave the Hammer to the dwarf they called Kharas, or Knight, for his extraordinary valor and honor in battle. And he kept Kharas for his name. And the Hammer of Kharas passed into the dwarven kingdom with assurances from the dwarves that it should be brought forth again at need—*"

The Hammer of Kharas

"It *has* been brought forth," Tanis said, struggling to contain his rising anger. He had heard that quotation entirely too many times!

"It has been brought forth and will be left behind!" Sturm bit the words. "We might have

taken it to Solamnia, used it to forge our own dragonlances—"

"And you would be another Huma, riding to glory, the Dragonlance in your hand!" Tanis's control snapped. "Meanwhile you'd let eight hundred people die—"

"No, I would not have let them die!" Sturm shouted in a towering rage. "The first clue we have to the dragonlances and you sell it for—"

Both men stopped arguing abruptly, suddenly aware of a shadow creeping from the darker shadows surrounding them.

"Shirak," whispered a voice, and a bright light flared, gleaming from a crystal ball clutched in the golden, disembodied claw of a dragon atop a plain, wooden staff. The light illuminated the red robes of a magic-user. The young mage walked toward the two, leaning upon his staff, coughing slightly. The light from his staff shone upon a skeletal face, with glistening metallic gold skin drawn tightly over fine bones. His eyes gleamed golden.

"Raistlin," said Tanis, his voice tight. "Is there something you want?"

Raistlin did not seem at all bothered by the angry looks both men cast him, apparently well accustomed to the fact that few felt comfortable in his presence or wanted him around.

He stopped before the two. Stretching forth his frail hand, the mage spoke, *"Akular-alan suh Tagolann Jistrathar,"* and a pale image of a weapon shimmered into being as Tanis and Sturm watched in astonishment.

Although lances were really weapons of cavalry (horse or dragon), the dragonlance was so important that it came in a size that could be carried by infantry—though it must have been easily tripped on. The dragonlance, also called the greater lance, was meant for use on dragonback.

It was a footman's lance,† nearly twelve feet long. The point was made of pure silver, barbed and gleaming, the shaft crafted of polished wood. The tip was steel, designed to be thrust into the ground.

"It's beautiful!" Tanis gasped. "What is it?"

"A dragonlance," Raistlin answered. Holding the lance in his hand, the mage stepped between the two, who stood aside to let him pass as if unwilling to be touched by him. Their eyes were on the lance. Then Raistlin turned and held it out to Sturm.

"There is your dragonlance, knight," Raistlin hissed, "without benefit of the Hammer or the Silver Arm. Will you ride with it into glory, remembering that, for Huma, with glory came death?"

Sturm's eyes flashed. He caught his breath in awe as he reached out to take hold of the dragonlance. To his amazement, his hand passed right through it! The dragonlance vanished, even as he touched it.

"More of your tricks!" he snarled. Spinning on his heel, he stalked away, choking in anger.

"If you meant that as a joke, Raistlin," Tanis said quietly, "it wasn't funny."

"A joke?" the mage whispered. His strange golden eyes followed the knight as Sturm walked into the thick blackness of the dwarven city beneath the mountain. "You should know me better, Tanis."

The mage laughed—the weird laughter Tanis had heard only once before. Then, bowing sardonically to the half-elf, Raistlin disappeared, following the knight into the shadows.

BOOK I

I

White-winged ships.
Hope lies across the Plains of Dust.

Tanis Half-Elven sat in the meeting of the Council of Highseekers and listened, frowning. Though officially the false religion of the Seekers was now dead, the group that made up the political leadership of the eight hundred refugees from Pax Tharkas was still called that.

"It isn't that we're not grateful to the dwarves for allowing us to live here," stated Hederick expansively, waving his scarred hand. "We are all grateful, I'm certain. Just as we're grateful to those whose heroism in recovering the Hammer of Kharas made our move here possible." Hederick bowed to Tanis, who returned the bow with a brief nod of his head. "But we are not dwarves!" This emphatic statement brought murmurs of approval, causing Hederick to warm to his audience.

"We *humans*† were never meant to live underground!" Loud calls of approval and some clapping of hands.

"We are farmers. We cannot grow food on the side of a mountain! We want lands like the ones we were forced to leave behind. And I say that those who forced us to leave our old homeland should provide us with new!"

"Does he mean the Dragon Highlords?" Sturm whispered sarcastically to Tanis. "I'm certain they'd be happy to oblige."

"The fools ought to be thankful they're alive!" Tanis muttered. "Look at them, turning to Elistan—as if it were *his* doing!" The cleric of Paladine—and leader of the refugees—rose to his feet to answer Hederick.

"It is because we need new homes," Elistan said, his strong baritone resounding through the cavern, "that I propose we send a delegation south, to the city of Tarsis the Beautiful."

Tanis had heard Elistan's plan before. His mind wandered over the month since he and his companions had returned from Derkin's Tomb with the sacred Hammer.

The dwarven Thanes, now consolidated under the leadership of Hornfel, were preparing to battle the evil coming from the north. The dwarves did not greatly fear this evil. Their mountain kingdom seemed impregnable. And they had kept the promise they made Tanis in return for the Hammer: the refugees from Pax Tharkas could settle in Southgate, the southernmost part of the mountain kingdom of Thorbardin.

Elistan brought the refugees† to Thorbardin. They began trying to rebuild their lives, but the arrangement was not totally satisfactory.

They were safe, to be sure, but the refugees, mostly farmers, were not happy living underground in the huge dwarven caverns. In the spring they could plant crops on the mountainside, but the rocky soil would produce only a bare living. The people wanted to live in the sunshine and fresh air. They did not want to be dependent on the dwarves.

It was Elistan who recalled the ancient legends of Tarsis the Beautiful and its gull-winged ships. But that's all they were—legends, as Tanis had pointed

Humans don't like the underground any better than elves. The elves would be loath to admit that the two races have anything in common.

The story of a special dwarven sword and the life of the 800 refugees from Pax Tharkas in Thorbardin is told in Stormblade, *by Nancy Varian Berberick.*

Though Northgate and Southgate are supposedly the only entrances into the dwarven kingdom, there may be another: see The Gates of Thorbardin *by Dan Parkinson.*

out when Elistan first mentioned his idea. No one on this part of Ansalon had heard anything about the city of Tarsis since the Cataclysm three hundred years ago. At that time, the dwarves had closed off the mountain kingdom of Thorbardin, effectively shutting off all communication between the south and north, since the only way through the Kharolis Mountains was through Thorbardin.†

Tanis listened gloomily as the Council of Highseekers voted unanimously to approve Elistan's suggestion. They proposed sending a small group of people to Tarsis with instructions to find what ships came into port, where they were bound, and how much it would cost to book passage—or even to buy a ship.

"And who's going to lead this group?" Tanis asked himself silently, though he already knew the answer.

All eyes now turned to him. Before Tanis could speak, Raistlin, who had been listening to all that was said without comment, walked forward to stand before the Council. He stared around at them, his strange eyes glittering golden.

"You are fools," Raistlin said, his whispering voice soft with scorn, "and you are living in a fool's dream. How often must I repeat myself? How often must I remind you of the portent of the stars? What do you say to yourselves when you look into the night sky and see the gaping black holes where the two constellations are missing?"

The Council members shifted in their seats, several exchanging long-suffering glances indicative of boredom.

Raistlin noticed this and continued, his voice growing more and more contemptuous. "Yes, I have heard some of you saying that it is nothing more than a natural phenomenon—a thing that happens, perhaps, like the falling of leaves from the trees."

Several Council members muttered among themselves, nodding. Raistlin watched silently for a moment, his lip curled in derision. Then he spoke once more. "I repeat, you are fools. The constellation known as the Queen of Darkness is missing from the sky because the Queen is present here upon Krynn. The Warrior constellation, which represents the ancient God Paladine, as we are told in

the Disks of Mishakal, has also returned to Krynn to fight her."

Raistlin paused. Elistan, who stood among them, was a prophet of Paladine, and many here were converts to this new religion. He could sense the growing anger at what some considered his blasphemy. The idea that gods would become personally involved in the affairs of men! Shocking! But being considered blasphemous had never bothered Raistlin.

His voice rose to a high pitch. "Mark well my words! With the Queen of Darkness have come her 'shrieking hosts,' as it says in the Canticle. And the shrieking hosts are dragons!" Raistlin drew out the last word into a hiss that, as Flint said, "shivered the skin."

"We know all this," Hederick snapped in impatience. It was past time for the Theocrat's nightly glass of mulled wine, and his thirst gave him courage to speak. He immediately regretted it, however, when Raistlin's hourglass eyes seemed to pierce the Theocrat like black arrows. "W-what are you driving at?"

"That peace no longer exists anywhere on Krynn," the mage whispered. He waved a frail hand. "Find ships, travel where you will. Wherever you go, whenever you look up into the night sky, you will see those gaping black holes. Wherever you go, there will be dragons!" Raistlin began to cough. His body twisted with the spasms, and he seemed likely to fall, but his twin brother, Caramon, ran forward and caught him in his strong arms.

After Caramon led the mage out of the Council meeting, it seemed as if a dark cloud had been lifted. The Council members shook themselves and laughed—if somewhat shakily—and talked of children's tales.† To think that war had spread to all of Krynn was comic. Why, the war was near an end here in Ansalon already. The Dragon Highlord, Verminaard, had been defeated, his draconian armies driven back.

The Council members stood and stretched and left the chamber to head for the alehouse or their homes.

They forgot they had never asked Tanis if he would lead the group to Tarsis. They simply assumed he would.

I much prefer religious ceremony and allegorical writings as a conveyance of ethics and truth to most other means. Children's tales, however, have a staying power that far outlasts any other form. Indeed, the problem with children's tales is that they lose their meaning long before their stories fade. Who of us can actually recount the German political situation as it was immortalized in "The Three Little Pigs"?—TRH

Tanis, exchanging grim glances with Sturm, left the cavern. It was his night to stand watch. Even though the dwarves might consider themselves safe in their mountain fortress, Tanis and Sturm insisted that a watch be kept upon the walls leading into Southgate. They had come to respect the Dragon Highlords too much to sleep in peace without it—even underground.

Tanis leaned against the outer wall of Southgate, his face thoughtful and serious. Before him spread a meadow covered by smooth, powdery snow. The night was calm and still. Behind him was the great mass of the Kharolis Mountains. The gate of Southgate was, in fact, a gigantic plug in the side of the mountains. It was part of the dwarven defenses that had kept the world out for three hundred years following the Cataclysm and the destructive Dwarven Wars.†

This refers to the Dwarfgate Wars some years after the Cataclysm, when the mountain dwarves closed their gates against the human refugees and hill dwarves. The animosity caused by that event has lingered ever since. These new human refugees allowed to live at Southgate were the first humans to reside in Thorbardin since that war.

Sixty feet wide at the base and almost half again as high, the gate was operated by a huge mechanism that forced it in and out of the mountain. At least forty feet thick in its center, the gate was as indestructible as any known on Krynn, except for the one matching it in the north. Once shut, they could not be distinguished from the faces of the mountain, such was the craftsmanship of the ancient dwarven masons.

Yet, since the arrival of the humans at Southgate, torches had been set about the opening, allowing the men, women, and children access to the outside air—a human need that seemed an unaccountable weakness to the subterranean dwarves.

As Tanis stood there, staring into the woods beyond the meadow and finding no peace in their quiet beauty, Sturm, Elistan, and Laurana joined him. The three had been talking—obviously of him—and fell into an uncomfortable silence.

"How solemn you are," Laurana said to Tanis softly, coming near and putting her hand on his arm. "You believe Raistlin is right, don't you, Tanthal—Tanis?" Laurana blushed. His human name still came clumsily to her lips, yet she knew him well enough now to understand that his elven name only brought him pain.

Tanis looked down at the small, slender hand on his arm and gently put his own over it. Only a

few months earlier the touch of that hand would have irritated him, causing confusion and guilt as he wrestled with love for a human woman against what he told himself was a childhood infatuation with this elfmaiden. But now the touch of Laurana's hand filled him with warmth and peace, even as it stirred his blood. He pondered these new, disturbing feelings as he responded to her question.

"I have long found Raistlin's advice sound," he said, knowing how this would upset them. Sure enough, Sturm's face darkened. Elistan frowned. "And I think he is right this time. We have won a battle, but we are a long way from winning the war. We know it is being fought far north, in Solamnia. I think we may safely assume that it is not for the conquest of Abanasinia alone that the forces of darkness are fighting."

"But you are only speculating!" Elistan argued. "Do not let the darkness that hangs around the young mage cloud your thinking. He may be right, but that is no reason to give up hope, to give up trying! Tarsis is a large seaport city—at least according to all we know of it. There we'll find those who can tell us if the war encompasses the world. If so, then surely there still must be havens where we can find peace."

"Listen to Elistan,† Tanis," Laurana said gently. "He is wise. When our people left Qualinesti, they did not flee blindly. They traveled to a peaceful haven. My father had a plan, though he dared not reveal it—"

Laurana broke off, startled to see the effect of her speech. Abruptly Tanis snatched his arm from her touch and turned his gaze on Elistan, his eyes filled with anger.

"Raistlin says hope is the denial of reality," Tanis stated coldly. Then, seeing Elistan's care-worn face regard him with sorrow, the half-elf smiled wearily. "I apologize, Elistan. I am tired, that's all. Forgive me. Your suggestion is good. We'll travel to Tarsis with hope, if nothing else."

Elistan nodded and turned to leave. "Are you coming, Laurana? I know you are tired, my dear, but we have a great deal to do before I can turn the leadership over to the Council in my absence."

Little is told of Elistan in these books, but Michael Dobson, author of D-5 gave him this history:

"Elistan was a cleric of the Seeker faith and a leader of immense charisma, who sought to find true gods to worship. At age forty, Elistan contracted cancer and grew weaker and weaker. Verminaard appeared in Haven and promised divine blessing and temporal power to the Seekers if they gave themselves to his cause, but Elistan refused."

Verminaard captured the High Seekers and took them to Pax Tharkas, where the heroes found him.

I didn't much like Elistan. The character was hopelessly good, which makes for a boring character. He had no flaws. I disliked him so much that I left him out of this section of the book completely. Tracy was reading what I'd written and came to tell me that, according to the plot, Elistan was supposed to be in the elven camp. I'd already written that section. I didn't want to have to go back and add in Elistan.

"Can't we kill him here?" I asked.

"No." Tracy was shocked. "He's the only cleric of Paladine in the world! You can't kill him!"

So I had to go back and write him in. However, I made a deal with Tracy that I would be permitted to kill Elistan in the Legends trilogy. And I did!—MW

"I'll be with you presently, Elistan," Laurana said, flushing. "I—I want to speak a moment with Tanis."

Elistan† gave them both an appraising, understanding look, then walked through the darkened gateway with Sturm. Tanis began dousing the torches, preparatory to the closing of the gate. Laurana stood near the entrance, her expression growing cold as it became obvious Tanis was ignoring her.

"What is the matter with you?" she said finally. "It almost sounds as if you are taking that dark-souled mage's part against Elistan, one of the best and wisest humans I have ever met!"

"Don't judge Raistlin, Laurana," Tanis said harshly, thrusting a torch into a bucket of water. The light vanished with a hiss. "Things aren't always black and white, as you elves are inclined to believe. The mage has saved our lives more than once. I have come to rely upon his thinking—which, I admit, I find easier to rely on than blind faith!"

"*You* elves!" Laurana cried. "How typically human that sounds! There is more elven in you than you care to admit, Tanthalas! You used to say you didn't wear the beard to hide your heritage, and I believed you. But now I'm not so certain. I've lived around humans long enough to know how they feel about elves! But I'm proud of my heritage. You're not! You're ashamed of it. Why? Because of that human woman you're in love with! What's her name, Kitiara?"

"Stop it, Laurana!" Tanis shouted. Hurling down a torch to the ground, he strode to the elven maiden standing in the doorway. "If you want to discuss relationships, what about you and Elistan? He may be a cleric of Paladine, but he's a man, a fact to which you can, no doubt, testify! All I hear from you," he mimicked her voice," is 'Elistan is so wise,' 'Ask Elistan, he'll know what to do,' 'Listen to Elistan, Tanis—' "

This is why, in this book, Elistan has a tendency to poke his head out of a door every now and then and utter some pithy words just so we can see that he's still with us. I did, indeed, make Margaret put him back in on condition that she could kill him in the

"How dare you accuse me of your own failings?" Laurana returned. "I love Elistan. I reverence him. He is the wisest man I have known, and the gentlest. He is self-sacrificing—his entire life is wrapped up in serving others. But there is only one man I love, only one man I have ever loved—

though now I am beginning to ask myself if perhaps I haven't made a mistake! You said, in that awful place, the Sla-Mori, that I was behaving like a little girl and I had better grow up. Well, I have grown, Tanis Half-Elven. In these past few bitter months, I have seen suffering and death. I have been afraid as I never knew fear existed! I have learned to fight, and I have dealt death to my enemies. All of that hurt me inside until I'm so numb I can't feel the pain anymore. But what hurts worse is to see you with clear eyes."

next book—however, I did not know it would take her all three books to do it!
—TRH

"I never claimed to be perfect, Laurana," Tanis said quietly.

The silver moon and the red had risen, neither of them full yet, but shining brightly enough for Tanis to see tears in Laurana's luminous eyes. He reached out his hands to take her in his arms, but she took a step backwards.

"You may never claim it," she said scornfully, "but you certainly enjoy allowing us to think it!"

Ignoring his outstretched hands, she grabbed a torch from the wall and walked into the darkness beyond the gate of Thorbardin. Tanis watched her leave, watched the light shine on her honey-colored hair, watched her walk, as graceful as the slender aspens of their elven homeland of Qualinesti.

Tanis stood for a moment, staring after her, scratching the thick, reddish beard that no elf on Krynn could grow. Pondering Laurana's last statement, he thought, incongruously, of Kitiara. He conjured up pictures in his mind of Kit's cropped, curly black hair, her crooked smile, her fiery, impetuous temper, and her strong, sensual body—the body of a trained swordswoman, but he discovered to his amazement that now the picture dissolved, pierced by the calm, clear gaze of two slightly slanted, luminous, elven eyes.

Thunder rolled out from the mountain. The shaft that moved the huge stone gate began to turn, grinding the door shut. Tanis, watching it shut, decided he would not go in. "Sealed in a tomb." He smiled, recalling Sturm's words, but there was a shiver in his soul as well. He stood for long moments, staring at the door, feeling its weight settle between him and Laurana. The door sealed shut with a dull boom. The face of the mountain was blank, cold, forbidding.

Though the dwarves know that the old land called Kharolis was turned into the Plains of Dust by the Cataclysm, they apparently have not gone far enough down the old road to discover Tarsis.

With a sigh, Tanis pulled his cloak about him and started toward the woods. Even sleeping in the snow was better than sleeping underground. He had better get used to it anyway. The Plains of Dust† they would be traveling through to reach Tarsis would probably be choked with snow, even this early in the winter.

Thinking of the journey as he walked, Tanis looked up into the night sky. It was beautiful, glittering with stars. But two gaping black holes marred the beauty. Raistlin's missing constellations.

Holes in the sky. Holes in himself.

After his fight with Laurana, Tanis was almost glad to start on the journey. All the companions had agreed to go. Tanis knew that none of them felt truly at home among the refugees.

Preparations for the journey gave him plenty to think about. He was able to tell himself he didn't care that Laurana avoided him. And, at the beginning, the journey itself was enjoyable. It seemed as if they were back in the early days of fall instead of the beginning of winter. The sun shone, warming the air. Only Raistlin wore his heaviest cloak.

Conversation as the companions walked through the northern part of the Plains was light-hearted and merry, filled with teasing and bantering and reminding each other of the fun they had shared in earlier, happier days in Solace. No one spoke of the dark and evil things they had seen in the recent past. It was as if, in the contemplation of a brighter future, they willed these things never to have existed.

At night, Elistan explained to them what he was learning of the ancient gods from the Disks of Mishakal, which he carried with him. His stories filled their souls with peace and reinforced their faith. Even Tanis—who had spent a lifetime searching for something to believe in and now that they had found it viewed it with skepticism—felt deep in his soul that he could believe in this if he believed in anything. He wanted to believe in it, but something held him back, and every time he looked at Laurana, he knew what it was. Until he could resolve his own inner turmoil, the raging division between the elven and human inside of him, he would never know peace.

Only Raistlin did not share in the conversations, the merriment, the pranks and jokes, the campfire talks. The mage spent his days studying his spellbook. If interrupted, he would answer with a snarl. After dinner, of which he ate little, he sat by himself, his eyes on the night sky, staring at the two gaping black holes that were mirrored in the mage's black hourglass-shaped pupils.

It was only after several days that spirits began to flag. The sun was obscured by clouds and the wind blew chill from the north. Snow fell so thickly that one day they could not travel at all but were forced to seek shelter in a cave until the blizzard blew itself out. They set double watch at night, though no one could say exactly why, only that they felt a growing sense of threat and menace. Riverwind stared uneasily at the trail they left in the snow behind them. As Flint said, a blind gully dwarf could follow it. The sense of menace grew, the sense of eyes watching and ears listening.

Yet who could it be, out here in the Plains of Dust where nothing and no one had lived for three hundred years?

2

Between Master and Dragon.

Dismal Journey.

The dragon sighed, flexed his huge wings, and lifted his ponderous body from the warm, soothing waters of the hot springs. Emerging from a billowing cloud of vapor, he braced himself to step into the chill air. The clear winter air stung his delicate nostrils and bit into his throat. Swallowing painfully, he firmly resisted the temptation to return to the warm pools and began to climb to the high rocky ledge above him.

The dragon stamped irritably upon rocks slick with ice from the hot springs' vapor, which cooled almost instantly in the freezing air. The stones cracked and broke beneath his clawed feet, bounding and tumbling down into the valley below.

Once he slipped, causing him momentarily to lose his balance. Spreading his great wings, he

recovered easily, but the incident only served to increase his irritation further.

The morning sun lit the mountain peaks, touching the dragon, causing his blue scales to shimmer golden in the clear light but doing little to warm his blood. The dragon shivered again, stamping his feet upon the chill ground. Winter was not for the blue dragons,† nor was traveling this abysmal country. With that thought in mind, as it had been in his mind all the long, bitter night, Skie looked about for his master.

Dragons are, of course, reptiles (well ... rather top-of-the-heap ones) **and** *so, except for white dragons, they don't get along too well in cold climates. Blue dragons thrive primarily in deserts and other dry, barren regions.*

He found the Dragon Highlord standing upon an outcropping of rock, an imposing figure in horned dragonhelm and blue dragon-scale armor. The Highlord, cape whipping in the chill wind, was gazing within tense interest across the great flat plain far below.

"Come, Lord, return to your tent." And let me return to the hot springs, Skie added mentally. "This chill wind cuts to the bone. Why are you out here anyway?"

Skie might have supposed the Highlord† was reconnoitering, planning the disposition of troops, the attacks of the dragonflights. But that was not the case. The occupation of Tarsis had long been planned—planned, in fact, by another Dragon Highlord, for this land was under the command of the red dragons.

The Highlord is Kitiara, as we discover later. We didn't want to give that away this early in the book, however, and so she's not named. It was difficult to write this scene without using pronouns that would identify her to the astute reader.—MW

The blue dragons and their Dragon Highlords controlled the north, yet here I stand, in these frigid southlands, Skie thought irritably. And behind me is an entire flight of blue dragons. He turned his head slightly, looking down upon his fellows beating their wings in the early morning, grateful for the hot springs' warmth which took the chill from their tendons.

Fools, Skie thought scornfully. All they're waiting for is a signal from the Highlord to attack. To light the skies and burn the cities with their deadly bolts of lightning are all they care about. Their faith in the Dragon Highlord is implicit. As well it might be, Skie admitted, their master had led them to victory after victory in the north, and they had not lost one of their number.

They leave it to me to ask the questions—because I am the Highlord's mount, because I am closest to the Highlord. Well, so be it. We understand each other, the Highlord and I.

"We have no reason to be in Tarsis." Skie spoke his feelings plainly. He did not fear the Highlord. Unlike many of the dragons in Krynn, who served their masters with grudging reluctance, knowing themselves to be the true rulers, Skie† served his master out of respect—and love. "The reds don't want us here, that's certain. And we're not needed. That soft city that beckons you so strangely will fall easily. No army. They swallowed the bait and marched off to the frontier."

Though evil dragons are willing to work with people, they apparently hold something back of themselves—their real names. Skie's dragon name is Khellendros.

"We are here because my spies tell me they are here, or will be shortly," was the Highlord's answer. The voice was low but carried even over the biting wind.

"They . . . they . . ." grumbled the dragon, shivering and moving restlessly along the ridge. "We leave the war in the north, waste valuable time, lose a fortune in steel. And for what—a handful of itinerant adventurers."

"The wealth is nothing to me, you know that. I could buy Tarsis if it pleased me." The Dragon Highlord stroked the dragon's neck with an ice-caked leather glove that creaked with the powerful movements."The war in the north is going well. Lord Ariakas did not mind my leaving. Bakaris is a skilled young commander and knows my armies nearly as well as I do. And do not forget, Skie, these are more than vagabonds. These 'itinerant adventurers' killed Verminaard."

"Bah! The man had already dug his own grave. He was obsessed, lost sight of the true purpose." The dragon flicked a glance at his master. "The same might be said of others."

"Obsessed? Yes, Verminaard was obsessed, and there are those who should be taking that obsession more seriously. He was a cleric, he knew what damage the knowledge of the true gods, once spread among the people, can do us," answered the Highlord. "Now, according to reports, the people have a leader in this human called Elistan, who has become a cleric of Paladine. Worshipers of Mishakal bring true healing back to the land. No, Verminaard was farseeing. There is great danger here. We should recognize and move to stop it—not scoff at it."

The dragon snorted derisively. "This priest—Elistan—doesn't lead *the people.* He leads eight hundred wretched humans, former slaves of Verminaard's in Pax Tharkas. Now they're holed up in Southgate with the mountain dwarves." The dragon settled down on the rock, feeling the morning sun finally bringing a modicum of warmth to his scaled skin. "Besides, our spies report they are traveling to Tarsis even as we speak. By tonight, this Elistan will be ours and that will be that. So much for the servant of Paladine!"

"Elistan is of no use to me." The Dragon Highlord shrugged without interest. "He is not the one I seek."

"No?" Skie raised his head, startled. "Who, then?"

"There are three in whom I have particular interest. But I will provide you with descriptions of all of them"—the Dragon Highlord moved closer to Skie—"because it is to capture them that we participate in the destruction of Tarsis tomorrow. Here are those whom we seek. . . ."

Tanis strode across the frozen plains, his booted footsteps punching noisily through the crust of wind-swept snow. The sun rose at his back, bringing a great deal of light but little warmth. He clutched his cloak about him and glanced around to make certain no one was lagging behind. The companions' line stretched out single-file. They trod in each other's tracks, the heavier, stronger people in front clearing the way for the weaker ones behind them.

Tanis led them. Sturm walked beside him, steadfast and faithful as ever, though still upset over leaving behind the Hammer of Kharas, which had taken on an almost mystical quality for the knight. He appeared more careworn and tired than usual, but he never failed to keep step with Tanis. This was not an easy feat, since the knight insisted on traveling in his full, antique battle armor, the weight of which forced Sturm's feet deep into the crusted snow.

Behind Sturm and Tanis came Caramon, trudging through the snow like a great bear, his arsenal of weapons clanking around him, carrying his armor and his share of supplies, as well as those of his twin brother, Raistlin, on his back. Just watching Caramon made Tanis weary, for the big warrior was not only walking through the deep snow with ease but was also managing to widen the trail for the others behind him.

Of all of the companions the one Tanis might have felt closest to, since they had been raised together as brothers, was the next, Gilthanas. But Gilthanas was an elflord, younger son of the Speaker of the Suns, ruler of the Qualinesti elves, while Tanis was a bastard and only half elven, product of a brutal rape by a human warrior. Worse, Tanis had dared to find himself attracted—even if in a childish, immature fashion—to Gilthanas's sister, Laurana. And so, far from being friends, Tanis always had the uneasy impression that Gilthanas might well be pleased to see him dead.

Riverwind and Goldmoon walked together behind the elflord. Cloaked in their furskin capes, the cold was little to the Plainsmen. Certainly the cold was nothing compared to the flame in their hearts.They had been married only a little over a month, and the deep love and compassion each felt for the other, a self-sacrificing love that had led the world to the discovery of the ancient gods, now achieved greater depths as they discovered new ways to express it.

Then came Elistan and Laurana. Elistan and Laurana. Tanis found it odd that, thinking enviously of the happiness of Riverwind and Goldmoon, his eyes should encounter these two. Elistan and Laurana. Always together. Always deeply involved in serious conversation. Elistan, cleric of Paladine, resplendent in white robes that gleamed even against the snow. White-bearded, his hair thinning, he was still an imposing figure. The kind of man who might well attract a young girl. Few men or women could look into Elistan's ice-blue eyes and not feel stirred, awed in the presence of one who had walked the realms of death and found a new and stronger faith.

With him walked his faithful 'assistant,' Laurana. The young elfmaid had run away from her home in Qualinesti to follow Tanis in childish infatuation. She had been forced to grow up rapidly, her eyes opened to the pain and suffering in the world. Knowing that many of the party—Tanis among them—considered her a nuisance, Laurana struggled to prove her

worth. With Elistan she found her chance. Daughter to the Speaker of the Suns of the Qualinesti, she had been born and bred to politics. When Elistan was foundering among the rocks of trying to feed and clothe and control eight hundred men, women, and children, it was Laurana who stepped in and eased his burden. She had become indispensable to him, a fact Tanis found difficult to deal with. The half-elf gritted his teeth, letting his glance flick over Laurana to fall on Tika.

The barmaid turned adventuress walked through the snow with Raistlin, having been asked by his brother to stay near the frail mage, since Caramon was needed up front. Neither Tika nor Raistlin seemed happy with this arrangement.† The red-robed mage walked along sullenly, his head bowed against the wind. He was often forced to stop, coughing until he nearly fell. At these times, Tika would start to put her arm around him hesitantly, her eyes seeing Caramon's worry. But Raistlin always pulled away from her with a snarl.

Raistlin's jealousy over the love affair between Caramon and Tika was fun to work with. I don't think Raistlin was jealous because he wanted Tika for himself. I think he was jealous because suddenly Caramon had found someone else in his life to love and care for besides his brother. A complex part of the love-hate relationship Raistlin has with Caramon.—MW

The ancient dwarf came next, bowling along through the snow; the tip of his helm and the tassel "from the mane of a griffon" were all that were visible above the snow. Tanis had tried to tell him that griffons had no manes, that the tassel was horsehair. But Flint, stoutly maintaining that his hatred of horses stemmed from the fact that they made him sneeze violently, believed none of it. Tanis smiled, shaking his head. Flint had insisted on being at the front of the line. It was only after Caramon had pulled him out of three snow drifts that Flint agreed, grumbling, to walk "rear guard."

Skipping along beside Flint was Tasslehoff Burrfoot, his shrill, piping voice audible to Tanis in the front of the line. Tas was regaling the dwarf with a marvelous tale about the time he found a woolly mammoth†—whatever that was—being held prisoner by two deranged wizards. Tanis sighed. Tas was getting on his nerves. He had already sternly reprimanded the kender for hitting Sturm in the head with a snowball. But he knew it was useless. Kender lived for adventure and new experiences. Tas was enjoying every minute of this dismal journey.

Tas's tale of the woolly mammoth is told fully in Kendermore, *by Mary Kirchoff. Tas rescues the woolly mammoth called Winnie from some gnomes who are raising him to keep in their zoo—which consists of stuffed specimens.*

Yes, they were all there. They were all still following him.

Tanis turned around abruptly, facing south. Why follow me? He asked resentfully. I hardly know where my life is going, yet I'm expected to lead others. I don't have Sturm's driving quest to rid the land of dragons, as did his hero Huma. I don't have Elistan's holy quest to bring knowledge of the true gods to the people. I don't even have Raistlin's burning quest for power.

Sturm nudged him and pointed ahead. A line of small hills stood on the horizon. If the kender's map was correct, the city of Tarsis lay just beyond them. Tarsis, and white-winged ships, and spires of glittering white.

3
Tarsis the Beautiful.

Tanis spread out the kender's map. They had arrived at the foot of the range of barren and treeless hills which, according to the map, must overlook the city of Tarsis.

"We don't dare climb those in daylight," Sturm said, drawing his scarf down from his mouth. "We'd be visible to everything within a hundred miles."

"No," Tanis agreed. "We'll make camp here at the base. I'll climb, though, to get a look at the city."

"I don't like this, not one bit!" Sturm muttered gloomily. "Something's wrong. Do you want me to go with you?"

Tanis, seeing the weariness in the knight's face, shook his head."You get the others organized." Dressed in a winter traveling cloak of white, he prepared to climb the snow-covered, rock-strewn hills.

Ready to start, he felt a cold hand on his arm. He turned and looked into the eyes of the mage.

"I will come with you," Raistlin whispered.

Tanis stared at him in astonishment, then glanced up at the hills. The climb would not be an easy one, and he knew the mage's dislike of extreme physical exertion. Raistlin saw his glance and understood.

"My brother will help me," he said, beckoning to Caramon, who appeared startled but stood up immediately and came over to stand beside his brother. "I would look upon the city of Tarsis the Beautiful."

Tanis regarded him uneasily, but Raistlin's face was as impassive and cold as the metal it resembled.

"Very well," the half-elf said, studying Raistlin. "But you'll show up on the face of that mountain like a blood stain. Cover yourself with a white robe." The half-elf's sardonic smile was an almost perfect imitation of Raistlin's own. "Borrow one from Elistan."

Tanis, standing on the top of the hill overlooking the legendary seaport city of Tarsis the Beautiful, began to swear softly. Wispy clouds of steam floated from his lips with the hot words. Drawing the hood of his heavy cloak over his head, he stared down into the city in bitter disappointment.

Caramon nudged his twin. "Raist," he said. "What's the matter? I don't understand."

Raistlin coughed. "Your brains are in your sword-arm, my brother," the mage whispered caustically. "Look upon Tarsis, legendary seaport city. What do you see?"

"Well . . ." Caramon squinted. "It's one of the biggest cities I've seen. And there are ships—just like we heard—"

"'The white-winged ships of Tarsis the Beautiful,'" Raistlin quoted bitterly. "You look upon the ships, my brother. Do you notice anything peculiar about them?"

"They're not in very good shape. The sails are ragged and—" Caramon blinked. Then he gasped. "There's no water!"

"Most observant."

"But the kender's map—"

"Dated before the Cataclysm," Tanis interrupted. "Damn it, I should have known! I should have

considered this possibility! Tarsis the Beautiful—legendary seaport, now landlocked!"

"And has been for three hundred years, undoubtedly," Raistlin whispered.

"When the fiery mountain fell from the sky, it created seas—as we saw in Xak Tsaroth—but it also destroyed them. What do we do with the refugees now, Half-Elf?"

"I don't know," Tanis snapped irritably. He stared down at the city, then turned away. "It's no good standing around here. The sea isn't going to come back just for our benefit." He turned away and walked slowly down the cliff.

"What *will* we do?" Caramon asked his brother. "We can't go back to Southgate. I know something or someone was dogging our footsteps." He glanced around worriedly. "I feel eyes watching—even now."

Raistlin put his hand through his brother's arm. For a rare instant, the two looked remarkably alike. Light and darkness were not more different than the twins.

"You are wise to trust your feelings, my brother," Raistlin said softly."Great danger and great evil surround us. I have felt it growing on me since the people arrived in Southgate. I tried to warn them—" He broke off in a fit of coughing.

"How do you know?" Caramon asked.

Raistlin shook his head, unable to answer for long moments. Then, when the spasm had passed, he drew a shuddering breath and glanced at his brother irritably. "Haven't you learned yet?" he said bitterly. "I *know!* Put it at that. I paid for my knowledge in the Towers of High Sorcery. I paid for it with my body and very nearly my reason. I paid for it with—" Raistlin stopped, looking at his twin.

Caramon was pale and silent as always whenever the Testing was mentioned. He started to say something, choked, then cleared his throat. "It's just that I don't understand—"

Raistlin sighed and shook his head, withdrawing his arm from his brother's. Then, leaning on his staff, he began to walk down the hill. "Nor will you," he murmured. "Ever."

Three hundred years ago, Tarsis the Beautiful was Lordcity of the lands of Abanasinia. From here set

sail the white-winged ships for all the known lands of Krynn. Here they returned, bearing all manner of objects, precious and curious, hideous and delicate. The Tarsian marketplace was a thing of wonder. Sailors swaggered the streets, their golden earrings flashing as brightly as their knives. The ships brought exotic peoples from distant lands to sell their wares. Some dressed in gaily colored, flowing silks, bedizened with jewels. They sold spices and teas, oranges and pearls, and bright-colored birds in cages. Others, dressed in crude skins, sold luxuriant furs from strange animals as grotesque as those who hunted them.

Of course, there were buyers at the Tarsian market as well; almost as strange and exotic and dangerous as the sellers. Wizards dressed in robes of white, red, or black strode the bazaars, searching for rare spell components to make their magic. Distrusted even then, they walked through the crowds, isolated and alone. Few spoke even to those wearing the white robes, and no one ever cheated them.

Clerics, too, sought ingredients for their healing potions. For there were clerics in Krynn before the Cataclysm. Some worshiped† the gods of good, some the gods of neutrality, some the gods of evil. All had great power. Their prayers, for good or for evil, were answered.

Before the Cataclysm, the people of Krynn worshiped, under various names, seven gods of Good, seven gods of Neutrality, and seven gods of Evil. There's that triad and balance again.

And always, walking among all the strange and exotic peoples gathered in the bazaar of Tarsis the Beautiful, were the Knights of Solamnia: keeping order, guarding the land, living their disciplined lives in strict observance of the Code and the Measure. The Knights were followers of Paladine, and were noted for their pious obedience to the gods.

The walled city of Tarsis had its own army and—so it was said—had never fallen to an invading force. The city was ruled, under the watchful eyes of the Knights—by a Lordfamily and had the good fortune to fall to the care of a family possessing sense, sensitivity, and justice. Tarsis became a center of learning; sages from lands all around came here to share their wisdom. Schools and a great library were established, temples were built to the gods. Young men and women eager for knowledge came to Tarsis to study.

The early dragon wars† had not affected Tarsis. The huge walled city, its formidable army, its fleets of white-winged ships, and its vigilant Knights of Solamnia daunted even the Queen of Darkness. Before she could consolidate her power and strike the Lordcity, Huma drove her dragons from the skies. Thus Tarsis prospered and became, during the Age of Might, one of the wealthiest and proudest cities of Krynn.

The three dragon wars of ancient times began in 3500 PC (Pre-Cataclysm) and ended in 1018 PC. The War of the Lance is, in effect, the Fourth Dragon War.

And, as with so many other cities in Krynn, with its pride grew its conceit. Tarsis began seeking more and more from the gods: wealth, power, glory. The people worshiped the Kingpriest of Istar who, seeing suffering in the land, demanded of the gods in his arrogance what they had granted Huma in humility. Even the Knights of Solamnia—bound by the strict laws of the Measure, encased in a religion that had become all ritual with little depth—fell under the sway of the mighty Kingpriest.

Then came the Cataclysm—a night of terror, when it rained fire. The ground heaved and cracked as the gods in their righteous anger hurled a mountain of rock down upon Krynn, punishing the Kingpriest of Istar and the people for their pride.

The people turned to the Knights of Solamnia. "You who are righteous, help us!" they cried. "Placate the gods!"

But the Knights could do nothing. The fire fell from the heavens, the land split asunder. The seawaters fled,† the ships foundered and toppled, the wall of the city crumbled.

Inspired by events in my youth. My parents used to visit friends at a cabin next to a lake in Yellowstone National Park. I would lie on the dock with the water lapping at my feet. Not long afterward, an earthquake rocked Yellowstone, shifting the lakebed. The next time we returned, the lakeshore had receded out of sight. I still remember that dock standing there, now high and dry—thus, Tarsis. —TRH

When the night of horror ended, Tarsis was landlocked. The white-winged ships lay upon the sand like wounded birds. Dazed and bleeding, the survivors tried to rebuild their city, expecting any moment to see the Knights of Solamnia come marching from their great fortresses in the north, marching from Palanthas, Solanthus, Vingaard Keep, Thelgaard, marching south to Tarsis to help them and protect them once more.

But the Knights did not come. They had their own troubles and could not leave Solamnia. Even if they had been able to march, a new sea split the lands of Abanasinia. The dwarves in their mountain kingdom of Thorbardin shut their gates, refusing admittance to anyone, and so the mountain passes were blocked. The elves withdrew into Qualinesti, nursing their wounds, blaming humans for the catastrophe. Soon, Tarsis lost all contact with the world to the north.

And so, following the Cataclysm, when it became apparent that the city had been abandoned by the Knights, came the Day of Banishment. The lord of the city was placed in an awkward position. He did not truly believe in the corruption of the Knights, but he knew the people needed something or someone to blame. If he sided with the Knights, he would lose control of the city, and so he was forced to close his eyes to angry mobs that attacked the few Knights remaining in Tarsis. They were driven from the city—or murdered.

After a time, order was restored in Tarsis. The lord and his family established a new army. But much was changed. The people believed the ancient gods they had worshiped for so long had turned away from them. They found new gods to worship, even though these new gods rarely answered prayers. All clerical powers that had been present in the land before the Cataclysm were lost. Clerics with false promises and false hopes proliferated. Charlatan healers walked the land, selling their phony cure-alls.

After a time, many of the people drifted away from Tarsis. No longer did sailors walk the marketplace; elves, dwarves, and other races came no more. The people remaining in Tarsis liked it this way. They began to fear and mistrust the outside world. Strangers were not encouraged.

But Tarsis had been a trade center for so long that those people in the outlying countryside who could still reach Tarsis continued to do so. The outer hub of the city was rebuilt. The inner part—the temples, the schools, the great library—was left in ruins. The bazaar was reopened, only now it was a market for farmers and a forum for false clerics preaching new religions. Peace settled over the town like a blanket. Former days of glory were as a dream and might not have even been believed, but for the evidence in the center of town.

Now, of course, Tarsis heard rumors of war, but these were generally discounted, although the lord did send his army out to guard the plains to the

south. If anyone asked why, he said it was a field exercise, nothing more. These rumors, after all, had come out of the north, and all knew the Knights of Solamnia were trying desperately to reestablish their power. It was amazing what lengths the traitorous Knights would go to—even spreading stories of the return of dragons!

This was Tarsis the Beautiful, the city the companions entered that morning, just a short time after sunrise.

Details of this peculiar city can be found in a DRAGONLANCE *mystery:* Murder in Tarsis, *by John Maddox Roberts.*

4

Arrested!
The heroes are separated.
An ominous farewell.

The few sleepy guards upon the city walls that morning woke up at the sight of the sword-bearing, travel-worn group seeking entry. They did not deny them. They did not even question them—much. A red-bearded, soft-spoken half-elf, the like of which had not been seen in Tarsis in decades, said they had traveled far and sought shelter. His companions stood quietly behind him, making no threatening gestures. Yawning, the guards directed them to the Red Dragon Inn.

This might have ended the matter. Tarsis, after all, was beginning to see more and more strange characters as rumors of war spread. But the cloak of one of the humans blew aside as he stepped through the gate, and a guard caught a flash of bright armor in the morning sun. The guard saw the

hated and reviled symbol of the Knights of Solamnia on the antique breastplate. Scowling, the guard melted into the shadows, slinking after the group as it walked through the streets of the waking town.

The guard watched them enter the Red Dragon. He waited outside in the cold until he was sure they must be in their rooms. Then, slipping inside, he spoke a few words to the innkeeper. The guard peeped inside the common room and, seeing the group seated and apparently settled for some time, ran off to make his report.

"This is what comes of trusting a kender's map!" said the dwarf irritably, shoving away his empty plate and wiping his hand across his mouth. "Takes us to a seaport city with no sea!"

"It's not my fault," Tas protested. "I told Tanis when I gave him the map that it dated before the Cataclysm. 'Tas,' Tanis said before we left, 'do you have a map that shows us how to get to Tarsis?' I said I did and I gave him this one. It shows Thorbardin, the dwarven Kingdom under the Mountain, and Southgate, and here it shows Tarsis, and everything else was right where the map said it was supposed to be. I can't help it if something happened to the ocean! I—"

"That's enough, Tas." Tanis sighed. "Nobody's blaming you. It isn't anybody's fault. We just let our hopes get too high."

The kender, his feelings mollified, retrieved his map, rolled it up, and slid it into his mapcase with all his other precious maps of Krynn. Then he put his small chin in his hands and sat staring around the table at his gloomy companions. They began to discuss what to do next, talking half-heartedly.

Tas grew bored. He wanted to explore this city. There were all kinds of unusual sights and sounds—Flint had been forced to practically drag him along as they entered Tarsis. There was a fabulous marketplace with wonderful things just lying around, waiting to be admired. He had even spotted some other kenders, too, and he wanted to talk to them. He was worried about his homeland. Flint kicked him under the table. Sighing, Tas turned his attention back to Tanis.

"We'll spend the night here, rest, and learn what we can, then send word back to Southgate," Tanis

was saying. "Perhaps there is another port city farther south. Some of us might go on and investigate. What do you think, Elistan?"

The cleric pushed away a plate of uneaten food. "I suppose it is our only choice," he said sadly. "But I will return to Southgate. I cannot be away from the people long. You should come with me, too, my dear." He laid his hand over Laurana's. "I cannot dispense with your help."

Laurana smiled at Elistan. Then, her gaze moving to Tanis, the smile vanished as she saw the half-elf scowl.

"Riverwind and I have discussed this already. We will return with Elistan," Goldmoon said. Her silver-gold hair gleamed in the sunlight streaming through the window. "The people need my healing skills."

"Besides which, the bridal couple misses the privacy of their tent," Caramon said in an audible undertone. Goldmoon flushed a dusky rose color as her husband smiled.

Sturm glanced at Caramon in disgust and turned to Tanis. "I will go with you, my friend," he offered.

"Us, too, of course," said Caramon promptly.

Sturm frowned, looking at Raistlin, who sat huddled in his red robes near the fire, drinking the strange herbal concoction that eased his cough.

"I do not think your brother is fit to travel, Caramon—" Sturm began.

"You are suddenly very solicitous of my health, knight," Raistlin whispered sarcastically. "But then, it is not my health that concerns you, is it, Sturm Brightblade? It is my growing power. You fear me—"

"That's enough!" said Tanis as Sturm's face darkened.

"The mage goes back, or I do," Sturm said coldly.

"Sturm—" Tanis began.

Tasslehoff took this opportunity to leave the table very quietly. Everyone was focused on the argument between the knight, the half-elf, and the magic-user. Tasslehoff skipped out the front door of the Red Dragon, a name he thought particularly funny. But Tanis had not laughed.

Tas thought about that as he walked along, looking at the new sights in delight. Tanis didn't laugh at anything anymore. The half-elf was certainly

carrying the weight of the world on his shoulders, it seemed. Tasslehoff suspected he knew what was wrong with Tanis. The kender took a ring out of one of his pouches and studied it. The ring was golden, of elven make, carved in the form of clinging ivy leaves. He had picked it up in Qualinesti. This time, the ring was not something the kender had "acquired." It had been thrown at his feet by a heartbroken Laurana after Tanis had returned it to her.

The kender considered all this and decided that splitting up and going off after new adventure was just what everyone needed. He, of course, would go with Tanis and Flint—the kender firmly believed neither could get along without him. But first, he'd get a glimpse of this interesting city.

Tasslehoff reached the end of the street. Glancing back, he could see the Red Dragon Inn. Good. No one was out looking for him yet. He was just about to ask a passing street peddler how to get to the marketplace when he saw something that promised to make this interesting city a whole lot more interesting. . . .

Tanis settled the argument between Sturm and Raistlin, for the time being at least. The mage decided to stay in Tarsis to hunt for the remains of the old library.† Caramon and Tika offered to stay with him, while Tanis, Sturm, and Flint (and Tas) would push southward, picking up the brothers on their way back. The rest of the group would take the disappointing news back to Southgate.

That being settled, Tanis went to the innkeeper to pay for their night's lodging. He was counting out silver coins when he felt a hand touch his arm.

"I want you to ask to have my room changed to one near Elistan's," Laurana said. Tanis glanced at her sharply.

"Why is that?" he asked, trying to keep the harshness out of his voice.

Laurana sighed. "We're not going to go through this again, are we?"

"I have no idea what you mean," Tanis said coldly, turning away from the grinning innkeeper.

"For the first time in my life, I'm doing something meaningful and useful," Laurana said, catching hold of his arm. "And you want me to quit because of some jealous notion you have about me and Elistan—"

The Tarsis library was, I believe, one of the great libraries of Ansalon prior to the Cataclysm. Tarsis was, in those days, a natural seaport, which served much of the southwestern continent. Like Palanthas in the north, its seaport location made Tarsis a site for the acquisition of books from distant lands as the trade ships carried them. The trade routes had been worked out in some detail prior to our beginning work on the novels and the fact that a library should be found here—indeed, a great library, the Library of Khrystann, at that—should come as no surprise.—TRH

"I am not jealous," Tanis retorted, flushing. "I told you in Qualinesti that what was between us when we were younger is over now. I—" He paused, wondering if that were true. Even as he spoke, his soul trembled at her beauty. Yes, that youthful infatuation was gone, but was it being replaced by something else, something stronger and more enduring? And was he losing it? Had he already lost it, through his own indecisiveness and stubbornness? He was acting typically human, the half-elf thought. Refusing that which was in easy reach, only to cry for it when it was gone. He shook his head in confusion.

"If you're not jealous, then why don't you leave me alone and let me continue my work for Elistan in peace?" Laurana asked coldly "You—"

"Hush!" Tanis held up his hand. Laurana, annoyed, started to talk, but Tanis glared at her so fiercely, she fell silent.

Tanis listened. Yes, he'd been right. He could hear clearly now the shrill, high-pitched, screaming whine of the leather sling on the end of Tas's hoopak staff. It was a peculiar sound, produced by the kender swinging the sling in a circle over his head, and it raised the hair on the back of the neck. It was also a kender signal for danger.

"Trouble," Tanis said softly. "Get the others." Taking one look at his grim face, Laurana obeyed without question. Tanis turned abruptly to face the innkeeper, who was sidling around the desk. "Where are you going?" he asked sharply.

"Just leaving to check your rooms, sir," the innkeeper said smoothly, and he vanished precipitously into the kitchen. Just then, Tasslehoff burst through the door of the inn.

"Guards, Tanis! Guards! Coming this way!"

"Surely they can't be here because of us," Tanis said. He stopped, eyeing the light-fingered kender, struck by a sudden thought. "Tas—"

"It wasn't me, honest!" Tas protested. "I never even reached the marketplace! I just got to the bottom of the street when I saw a whole troop of guards coming this direction."

"What's this about guards?" Sturm asked as he entered from the common room. "Is this one of the kender's stories?"

"No. Listen," Tanis said. Everyone hushed. They could hear the tramp of booted feet coming their direction and glanced at each other in apprehension and concern. "The innkeeper's disappeared. I thought we got into the city a bit too easily. I should have expected trouble." Tanis scratched his beard, well aware that everyone was looking to him for orders.

"Laurana, you and Elistan go upstairs. Sturm, you and Gilthanas remain with me. The rest of you go to your rooms. Riverwind, you're in command. You, Caramon, and Raistlin protect them. Use your magic, Raistlin, if necessary. Flint—"

"I'm staying with you," the dwarf stated firmly.

Tanis smiled and put his hand on Flint's shoulder. "Of course, old friend. I didn't even think you needed telling."

Grinning, Flint pulled his battle-axe out of its holder on his back. "Take this," he said to Caramon. "Better you have it than any scurvy, lice-ridden city guards."

"That's a good idea," Tanis said. Unbuckling his swordbelt, he handed Caramon Wyrmslayer the magical sword given to him by the skeleton of Kith-Kanan, the Elven King.

Gilthanas silently handed over his sword and his elven bow.

"Yours, too, knight," Caramon said, holding out his hand.

Sturm frowned. His antique, two-handed sword and its scabbard were the only legacy he had left of his father, a great Knight of Solamnia, who had vanished after sending his wife and young son into exile. Slowly Sturm unbuckled his swordbelt and handed it to Caramon.

The jovial warrior, seeing the knight's obvious concern, grew serious. "I'll guard it carefully, you know that, Sturm."

"I know," Sturm said, smiling sadly. He glanced up at Raistlin, who was standing on the stairs. "Besides, there is always the great worm, Catyrpelius, to protect it, isn't there, mage?"

Raistlin started at this unexpected reminder of a time in the burned-out city of Solace when he had tricked some hobgoblins into believing Sturm's sword was cursed. It was the closest to an expression of gratitude that the knight had ever made to the mage. Raistlin smiled briefly.

"Yes," he whispered. "There is always the Worm. Do not fear, knight. Your weapon is safe, as are the lives of those you leave in our care . . . if any are safe. . . . Farewell, my friends," he hissed, his strange, hourglass eyes gleaming. "And a long farewell it will be. Some of us are not destined to meet again in this world!" With that, he bowed and, gathering his red robes around him, began to climb the stairs.

Trust Raistlin to exit with a flourish, Tanis thought irritably, hearing booted feet near the door. "Go on!" he ordered. "If he's right, there's nothing we can do about it now."

After a hesitant look at Tanis, the others did as he ordered, climbing the stairs quickly. Only Laurana cast a fearful glance back at Tanis as Elistan took her arm. Caramon, sword drawn, waited behind until the last was past.

"Don't worry," the big warrior said uneasily. "We'll be all right. If you're not back by night-fall—"

"Don't come looking for us!" Tanis said, guessing Caramon's intention. The half-elf was more disturbed than he cared to admit by Raistlin's ominous statement. He had known the mage many years and had seen his power grow, even as the shadows seemed to gather more thickly around him. "If we're not back, get Elistan, Goldmoon, and the others back to Southgate."

Caramon nodded reluctantly, then he walked ponderously up the stairs, his weapons clanking around him.

"It's probably just a routine check," Sturm said hurriedly in a low voice as the guards could be seen through the window now. "They'll ask us a few questions, then release us. But they've undoubtedly got a description of *all* of us!"

"I have a feeling it isn't routine. Not the way everyone's vanished. And they're going to have to settle for some of us," Tanis said softly as the guards entered the door, led by the constable and accompanied by he guard from the wall.

"That's them!" the guard cried, pointing. "There's the knight, like I told you. And the bearded elf, the dwarf, and the kender, and an elflord."

"Right," the constable said briskly. "Now, where

are the others?" At his gesture, his guards leveled their hauberks, pointing them at the companions.

"I don't understand what all this is about," Tanis said mildly. "We are strangers in Tarsis, simply passing through on our way south. Is this how you welcome strangers to your city?"

"We don't welcome strangers to our city," the constable replied. His gaze shifted to Sturm and he sneered. "Especially a Knight of Solamnia. If you're innocent as you say you are, you won't mind answering some questions from the Lord and his council. Where's the rest of your party?"

"My friends are tired and have gone to their rooms to rest. Our journey has been long and tiring. But we do not want to cause trouble. The four of us will come with you and answer your questions. ('Five,' said Tasslehoff indignantly, but everyone ignored him.) There is no need to disturb our companions."

"Go get the others," the constable ordered his men.

Two guards headed for the stairs, which suddenly burst into flame! Smoke billowed into the room, driving the guards back. Everyone ran for the door. Tanis grabbed Tasslehoff, who was staring with wide-eyed interest, and dragged him outside.

The constable was frantically blowing on his whistle, while several of his men prepared to dash off through the streets, raising the alarm. But the flames died as quickly as they had been born.

"Eeep—" The constable choked off his whistle. His face pale, he stepped warily back inside the inn. Tanis, peering over his shoulder, shook his head in awe. There was not a whisper of smoke, not a bit of varnish had so much as peeled. From the top of the stairs, he could hear faintly the sound of Raistlin's voice. As the constable glanced apprehensively up the stairs, the chanting stopped. Tanis swallowed, then drew a deep breath. He knew he must be as pale as the constable, and he glanced at Sturm and Flint. Raistlin's power was growing. . . .

"The magician must be up there," the constable muttered.

"Very good, Birdwhistle, and how long'd it take you to figure that one out—" Tas began in a tone of voice Tanis knew meant trouble. He trod upon the

kender's foot, and Tas subsided into silence with a reproachful glance.

Fortunately, the constable didn't appear to have heard. He glared at Sturm. "You'll come with us peacefully?"

"Yes," answered Sturm. "You have my word of honor," the knight added, "and no matter what you may think of the Knights, you know that my honor is my life."

The constable's eyes went to the dark stairway. "Very well," he said finally. "Two of you guards stay here at the stair. The rest cover the other exits. Check anyone coming in and out. You all have the descriptions of the strangers?" The guards nodded, exchanging uneasy glances. The two slated for guard duty inside the inn gave the staircase a frightened look and stood as far from it as possible. Tanis smiled grimly to himself.

The five companions, the kender grinning with excitement, followed the constable out of the building. As they walked into the street, Tanis caught sight of movement at an upstairs window. Looking up, he saw Laurana watching, her face drawn with fear. She raised her hand, he saw her lips form the words, "I'm sorry," in elven. Raistlin's words came to his mind and he felt chilled. His heart ached. The thought that he might never see her again made the world seem suddenly bleak and empty and desolate. He realized what Laurana had come to mean to him in these last few dark months when even hope had died as he saw the evil armies of the Dragon Highlords overrun the land. Her steadfast faith, her courage, her unfailing, undying hope! How different from Kitiara!

The guard poked Tanis in the back. "Face forward! Quit signaling to those friends of yourn!" he snarled. The half-elf's thoughts returned to Kitiara. No, the warrior woman could never have acted so selflessly. She never could have helped the people as Laurana had helped them. Kit would have grown impatient and angry and left them to live or die as they chose. She detested and despised those weaker than herself.

Tanis thought of Kitiara and he thought of Laurana, but he was interested to note that the old painful thrill didn't knot his soul anymore when he

said Kitiara's name to himself. No, now it was Laurana—the silly little girl who had been no more than a spoiled and irritating child only months before—who made his blood burn and his hands search for excuses to touch her. And now, perhaps, it was too late.

When he reached the end of the street, he glanced back again, hoping to give her some sort of sign. Let her know he understood. Let her know he'd been a fool. Let her know he—

But the curtain was drawn.

5

The riot. Tas disappears. Alhana Starbreeze.

"Foul knight . . ."

A rock struck Sturm on the shoulder. The knight flinched, though the stone could have caused him little pain through his armor. Tanis, looking at his pale face and quivering moustache, knew the pain was deeper than a weapon could inflict.

The crowds grew as the companions were marched through the street and word of their coming spread. Sturm walked with dignity, his head held proudly, ignoring the taunts and jeers. Although their guards shoved the crowd back time and again, they did it half-heartedly and the crowd knew it. More rocks were thrown, as were other objects even less pleasant. Soon all of the companions were cut and bleeding and covered with garbage and filth.

Tanis knew Sturm would never stoop to retaliation, not on this rabble, but the half-elf had to keep a firm grip on Flint. Even then, he was in constant fear the angry dwarf would charge past the guards and start breaking heads. But in watching Flint, Tanis had forgotten Tasslehoff.

Besides being quite casual in respect to other people's property, kenders have another unendearing characteristic known as the "taunt." All kenders possess this talent to a greater or lesser degree.† It is how their diminutive race has managed to thrive and survive in a world of knights and warriors, trolls and hobgoblins. The taunt is the ability to insult an enemy and work him into such a fever pitch of rage that he loses his head and begins fighting wildly and erratically. Tas was a master at the taunt, though he rarely found a need to use it when traveling with his warrior friends. But Tas decided to take full advantage of this opportunity.

This little idea for the kender came out of the game group and forever made life miserable for the people of Krynn. It seemed like an easy idea to implement in the game but turned out to be a long-term challenge for those of us working on stories.—TRH

He began to shout insults back.

Too late Tanis realized what was happening. In vain he tried to shut him up. Tas was at the front of the line, the half-elf at the back, and there was no way to gag the kender.

Such insults as "foul knight" and "elven scum" lacked imagination, Tas felt. He decided to show these people exactly how much range and scope for variety were available in the Common language. Tasslehoff's insults were masterpieces of creativity and ingenuity. Unfortunately, they also tended to be extremely personal and occasionally rather crude, delivered with an air of charming innocence.

"Is that your nose or a disease? Can those fleas crawling on your body do tricks? Was your mother a gully dwarf?" were only the beginning. Matters went rapidly down hill from there.

The guards began eyeing the angry crowd in alarm, while the constable gave the order to hurry the prisoners' march. What he had seen as a victory procession exhibiting trophies of conquest appeared to be disintegrating into a full-scale riot.

"Shut that kender up!" he yelled furiously.

Tanis tried desperately to reach Tasslehoff, but the struggling guards and the surging crowd made it impossible. Gilthanas was knocked off his feet. Sturm bent over the elf, trying to protect him. Flint

was kicking and flailing about in a rage. Tanis had just neared Tasslehoff when he was hit in the face with a tomato and momentarily blinded.

"Hey, constable, you know what you could do with that whistle?You could—"

Tasslehoff never got a chance to tell the constable what he might do with the whistle, because at that instant a large hand plucked him up out of the center of the melee. A hand clapped itself over Tas's mouth, while two more pairs of hands gripped the kender's wildly kicking feet. A sack was popped over his head, and all Tas saw or smelled from that point on was burlap as he felt himself being carried away.

Tanis, wiping tomato from his stinging eyes, heard the sound of booted feet and more shouts and yells. The crowd hooted and jeered, then broke and ran. When he could finally see again, the half-elf glanced around quickly to make certain everyone was all right. Sturm was helping Gilthanas rise, wiping blood from a cut on the elf's forehead. Flint, swearing fluently, plucked cabbage from his beard.

"Where's that blasted kender!" the dwarf roared. "I'll—" He stopped and stared, turning this way and that. "Where *is* that blasted kender? Tas? So help me—"

"Hush!" Tanis ordered, realizing Tas had managed to escape.†

While it is nerve-racking to be in the presence of a kender, it is even more nerve-racking to discover that a kender has gone off on his own.—MW

Flint turned purple. "Why that little bastard!" he swore. "He was the one got us into this and he left us to—"

"Shhh!" Tanis said, glaring at the dwarf. Flint choked and fell silent. The constable hustled his prisoners into the Hall of Justice. It was only when they were safely inside the ugly brick building that he realized one of them was missing.

"Shall we go after him, sir?" asked a guard. The constable thought a moment, then shook his head in anger.

"Don't waste your time," he said bitterly. "Do you know what it's like trying to find a kender who doesn't want to be found? No, let him go. We've still got the important ones. Have them wait here while I inform the Council."

The constable entered a plain wooden door, leaving the companions and their guards standing in a

dark, smelly hallway. A tinker† lay in a corner, snoring noisily, obviously having taken too much wine. The guards wiped pumpkin rind off their uniforms and grimly divested themselves of carrot tops and other garbage that clung to them. Gilthanas dabbed at the blood on his face. Sturm tried to clean his cloak as best he could.

"Tinker" is another name for a gnome. This usually industrious race was originally called tinker gnomes.

The constable returned, beckoning from the doorway.

"Bring them along."

As the guards shoved their prisoners forward, Tanis managed to get near Sturm. "Who's in charge here?" he whispered.

"If we are fortunate, the Lord is still in control of the city," the knight replied softly. "The Tarsian lords always had the reputation for being noble and honorable." He shrugged. "Besides, what charges do they have against us? We've done nothing. At the worst, an armed escort will make us leave the city."

Tanis shook his head dubiously as he entered the courtroom. It took some time for his eyes to adjust to the dimness of the dingy chambers that smelled even worse than the hallway. Two of the Tarsian council members held oranges studded with cloves up to their noses.

The six members of the council were seated at the bench, which stood upon a tall platform, three upon either side of their Lord, whose tall chair sat in the center. The Lord glanced up as they entered. His eyebrows raised slightly at the sight of Sturm, and it seemed to Tanis that his face softened. The Lord even nodded in a gesture of polite greeting to the knight. Tanis's hopes rose. The companions walked forward to stand before the bench. There were no chairs. Supplicants or prisoners before the council stood to present their cases.

"What is the charge against these men?" the Lord asked. The constable gave the companions a baleful glance.

"Inciting a riot, milord," he said.

"Riot!" Flint exploded. "We had nothing to do with any riot! It was that rattle-brained—"

A figure in long robes crept forward from the shadows to whisper in his Lordship's ear. None of the companions had noticed the figure as they entered. They noticed it now.

Flint coughed and fell silent, giving Tanis a meaningful, grim look from beneath his thick, white eyebrows. The dwarf shook his head, his shoulders slumped. Tanis sighed wearily. Gilthanas wiped blood from his cut with a shaking hand, his elven features pale with hatred. Only Sturm stood outwardly calm and unmoved as he looked upon the twisted half-man, half-reptilian face of a draconian.

The companions remaining in the Inn sat together in Elistan's room for at least an hour after the others were taken away by the guards. Caramon remained on guard near the door, his sword drawn. Riverwind kept watch out the window. In the distance, they could hear the sounds of the angry mob and looked at each other with tense, strained faces. Then the noise faded. No one disturbed them. The Inn was deathly quiet.

Because the artists wanted a "babe" to paint, Tika was added to the party from the beginning. Artist Larry Elmore did a racy pen and ink drawing titled "Tika Takes a Bath." It hung on every game designer's cubicle! I wonder what happened to the original? Larry?—MW

The morning wore on without incident. The pale, cold sun climbed in the sky, doing little to warm the winter day. Caramon sheathed his sword and yawned. Tika† dragged a chair over to sit beside him. Riverwind went to stand watchfully near Goldmoon, who was talking quietly to Elistan, making plans for the refugees.

Only Laurana remained standing by the window, though there was nothing to see. The guards had apparently grown tired of marching up and down the street and now huddled in doorways, trying to keep warm. Behind her, she could hear Tika and Caramon laugh softly together. Laurana glanced around at them. Talking too quietly to be heard, Caramon appeared to be describing a battle. Tika listened intently, her eyes gleaming with admiration.

As mentioned at the beginning, the journey to find the Hammer of Kharas occurred between volumes 1 and 2 when no one was looking. By locating the magical hammer in the fortress called Derkin's Tomb (which floats in mid-

The young barmaid had received a great deal of practice in fighting on their journey south to find the Hammer of Kharas† and, though she would never be truly skilled with a sword, she had developed shield-bashing into an art. She wore her armor casually now. It was still mismatched, but she kept adding to it, scrounging pieces left on battlefields. The sunlight glinted on her chain-mail vest, glistened in her red hair. Caramon's face was animated and relaxed as he talked with the young woman. They did not touch—not with the golden eyes of

Caramon's twin on them—but they leaned very near each other.

Laurana sighed and turned away, feeling very lonely and—thinking of Raistlin's words—very frightened.

She heard her sigh echoed, but it was not a sigh of regret. It was a sigh of irritation. Turning slightly, she looked down at Raistlin. The mage had closed the spellbook he was trying to read, and moved into the little bit of sunlight that came through the glass. He had to study his spellbook daily. It is the curse of the magi† that they must commit their spells to memory time and again, for the words of magic flicker and die like sparks from a fire. Each spell cast saps the mage's strength, leaving him physically weakened until he is finally exhausted and cannot work any magic at all without rest.

Raistlin's strength had been growing since the companions' meeting in Solace, as had his power. He had mastered several new spells taught to him by Fizban, the bumbling old magician who had died in Pax Tharkas. As his power grew, so did the misgivings of his companions. No one had any overt cause to mistrust him, indeed, his magic had saved their lives several times. But there was something disquieting about him—secret, silent, self-contained, and solitary as an oyster.†

Absently caressing the night-blue cover of the strange spellbook he had acquired in Xak Tsaroth, Raistlin stared into the street. His golden eyes with their dark, hourglass-shaped pupils glittered coldly.

Although Laurana disliked speaking to the mage, she had to know! What had he meant—a long farewell?

"What do you see when you look far away like that?" she asked softly, sitting down next to him, feeling a sudden weakness of fear sweep over her.

"What do I see?" he repeated softly. There was great pain and sadness in his voice, not the bitterness she was accustomed to hearing. "I see time as it affects all things. Human flesh withers and dies before my eyes. Flowers bloom, only to fade. Trees drop green leaves, never to regain them. In my sight, it is always winter, always night."

air), the heroes were able to reunite the long-separated dwarves.

My eldest son, Curtis, is a professional magician. He mentioned to me how the need of mages to practice their spells in the books very much mirrors his own profession. It is not enough for him simply to learn a magic trick for his act, he must practice it daily in order to maintain the fluid movement of the illusion.

With the complexity of magic spells in Krynn, it is little wonder that the mages must rehearse the spells to themselves each day—especially if we see this learning process as a rehearsal of all the component parts of the mage's spells being used at once.—TRH

This is a fond allusion to one of my favorite stories, A Christmas Carol *by Charles Dickens.—MW*

"And—this was done to you in the Towers of High Sorcery?" Laurana asked, shocked beyond measure. "Why? To what end?"

Raistlin smiled his rare and twisted smile. "To remind me of my own mortality. To teach me compassion." His voice sank. "I was proud and arrogant in my youth. The youngest to take the Test, I was going to show them all!" His frail fist clenched. "Oh, I showed them. They shattered my body and devoured my mind until by the end I was capable of—" He stopped abruptly, his eyes shifting to Caramon.

"Of what?" Laurana asked, fearing to know, yet fascinated.

"Nothing," Raistlin whispered, lowering his eyes. "I am forbidden to speak of it."

Laurana saw his hands tremble. Sweat beaded on his forehead. His breath wheezed and he began to cough. Feeling guilty for having inadvertently caused such anguish, she flushed and shook her head, biting her lip. "I—I'm sorry to have given you pain. I didn't mean to." Confused, she looked down, letting her hair fall forward to hide her face, a girlish habit.

Raistlin leaned forward almost unconsciously, his hand stretching out, trembling, to touch the wondrous hair that seemed possessed of a life of its own, so vibrant and luxuriant was it. Then, seeing before his eyes† his own dying flesh, he withdrew his hand quickly and sank back in his chair, a bitter smile on his lips. For what Laurana did not know, could not know, was that, in looking at her, Raistlin saw the only beauty he would ever see in his lifetime. Young, by elven standards, she was untouched by death or decay, even in the mage's cursed vision.†

When Raistlin was first created by the DRAGONLANCE design group, he was given "hourglass eyes" because we thought they would be "really cool." Little thought was given at the time as to why such a thing would actually occur. It was up to Margaret and I to work out the why. I rather think it worked out to the betterment of Raistlin's character.—TRH

I found this scene rather poignant. Raistlin would see Laurana aging only very gradually and so of all the beautiful women who surround him, he sees beauty only in Laurana. —MW

Laurana saw nothing of this. She was aware only that he moved slightly. She almost got up and left, but she felt drawn to him now, and he still had not answered her question. "I—I meant, can you see the future? Tanis told me your mother was—what do they call it—prescient? I know that Tanis comes to you for advice. . . ."

Raistlin regarded Laurana thoughtfully. "The half-elf comes to me for advice, not because I can see the future. I can't. I am no seer. He comes because I am able to think, which is something most of these other fools seem incapable of doing."

"But what you said. Some of us may not see each other again." Laurana looked up at him earnestly. "You must have foreseen something! What—I must know! Was it . . . Tanis?"

Raistlin pondered. When he spoke, it was more to himself than to Laurana. "I don't know," he whispered. "I don't even know why I said that. It's just that—for an instant—I knew—" He seemed to struggle to remember, then suddenly shrugged.

"Knew what?" Laurana persisted.

"Nothing. My overwrought imagination as the knight would say if he were here. So Tanis told you about my mother," he said, changing the subject abruptly.

Laurana, disappointed but hoping to find out more if she kept talking to him, nodded her head. "He said she had the gift of foresight. She could look into the future and see images of what would come to pass."

"That is true," Raistlin whispered, then smiled sardonically. "Much good it did her. The first man she married was a handsome warrior from the northland. Their passion died within months, and after that they made life miserable for each other. My mother was fragile of health and given to slipping into strange trances from which she might not wake for hours. They were poor, living off what her husband could earn with his sword. Though he was clearly of noble blood, he never spoke of his family. I do not believe he even told her his real name."

Raistlin's eyes narrowed. "He told Kitiara, though. I'm sure of it. That is why she traveled north, to find his family."

"Kitiara . . ." Laurana said in a strained voice. She touched the name as one touches an aching tooth, eager to understand more of this human woman Tanis loved. "Then, that man—the noble warrior—was Kitiara's father?" she said in a husky voice.

Raistlin regarded her with a penetrating gaze. "Yes," he whispered. "She is my elder half-sister. Older than Caramon and I by about eight years. She is very much like her father, I believe. As beautiful as he was handsome. Resolute and impetuous, warlike, strong and fearless. Her father taught her the only thing he knew—the art of warfare.† He began

Kitiara's father Gregor's maxim was "The sword is the truth." How could she have turned out to be anything other than a fighter?

going on longer and longer trips, and one day vanished completely. My mother convinced the Highseekers to declare him legally dead. She then remarried the man who became our father. He was a simple man, a woodcutter by trade. Once again, her farsight did not serve her."

"Why?" Laurana asked gently, caught up in the story, amazed that the usually taciturn mage was so voluble, not knowing that he was drawing more out of her simply by watching her expressive face than he was giving in return.

"The birth of my brother and I for one thing," Raistlin said. Then, overcome by a fit of coughing, he stopped talking and motioned to his brother. "Caramon! It is time for my drink," he said in the hissing whisper that pierced through the loudest talk. "Or have you forgotten me in the pleasure of other company?"

Caramon fell silent in mid-laugh. "No, Raist," he said guiltily, hurriedly rising from his seat to hang a kettle of water over the fire. Tika, subdued, lowered her head, unwilling to meet the mage's gaze.

After staring at her a moment, Raistlin turned back to Laurana, who had watched all this with a cold feeling in the pit of her stomach. He began to speak again as if there had been no interruption. "My mother never really recovered from the childbirth. The midwife gave me up for dead, and I would have died, too, if it hadn't been for Kitiara. Her first battle, she used to say, was against death with me as the prize. She raised us. My mother was incapable of taking care of children, and my father was forced to work day and night simply to keep us fed. He died in an accident when Caramon and I were in our teens. My mother went into one of her trances that day"—Raistlin's voice dropped—"and never came out. She died of starvation."

"How awful!" Laurana murmured, shivering.

Raistlin did not speak for long moments, his strange eyes staring out into the chill, gray winter sky. Then his mouth twisted. "It taught me a valuable lesson—learn to control the power. Never let it control you!"

Laurana did not seem to have heard him. Her hands in her lap twisted nervously. This was the

perfect opportunity to ask the questions she longed to ask, but it would mean giving up a part of her inner self to this man she feared and distrusted. But her curiosity—and her love—were too great. She never realized she was falling into a cunningly baited trap. For Raistlin delighted in discovering the secrets of people's souls, knowing he might find them useful.

"What did you do then?" she asked, swallowing. "Did Kit-Kitiara . . ." Trying to appear natural, she stumbled over the name and flushed in embarrassment.

Raistlin watched Laurana's inner struggle with interest. "Kitiara was gone by then," he answered. "She left home when she was fifteen,† earning her living by her sword. She is an expert—so Caramon tells me—and had no trouble finding mercenary work. Oh, she returned every so often, to see how we were getting along. When we were older, and more skilled, she took us with her. That was where Caramon and I learned to fight together—I using my magic, my brother his sword. Then, after she met Tanis"—Raistlin's eyes glittered at Laurana's discomfiture—"she traveled with us more often."

Or it may have been thirteen, but the twins were still small. One version of the story is told in Dark Heart *by Tina Daniell. Another version can be found in* The Soulforge *by Margaret Weis.*

"Traveled with whom? Where did you go?"

"There was Sturm Brightblade, already dreaming of knighthood, the kender, Tanis, Caramon, and I. We traveled with Flint, before he retired from metalsmithing. The roads grew so dangerous that Flint gave up traveling. And by this time, we had all learned as much as we could from our friends. We were growing restless. It was time to separate, Tanis said."

"And you did as he said? He was your leader, even then?" She looked back to remember him as she had known him before he left Qualinost, beardless and lacking the lines of care and worry she saw now on his face. But even then he was withdrawn and brooding, tormented by his feelings of belonging to both races—and to neither. She hadn't understood him then. Only now, after living in a world of humans, was she beginning to.

"He has the qualities we are told are essential for leadership. He is quick-thinking, intelligent, creative. But most of us possess these—in greater or lesser degree. Why do the others follow Tanis?

Sturm is of noble blood, member of an order whose roots go back to ancient times. Why does he obey a bastard half-elf? And Riverwind? He distrusts all who are not human and half who are. Yet he and Goldmoon both would follow Tanis to the Abyss and back. Why?"

"I *have* wondered," Laurana began, "and I think—"

But Raistlin, ignoring her, answered his own question. "Tanis listens to his feelings. He does not suppress them, as does the knight, or hide them, as does the Plainsman. Tanis realizes that sometimes a leader must think with his heart and not his head." Raistlin glanced at her. "Remember that."

Laurana blinked, confused for a moment, then, sensing a tone of superiority in the mage which irritated her, she said loftily, "I notice you leave out yourself. If you are as intelligent and powerful as you claim, why do you follow Tanis?"

Raistlin's hourglass eyes were dark and hooded. He stopped talking as Caramon brought his twin a cup and carefully poured water from the kettle. The warrior glanced at Laurana, his face dark, embarrassed and uncomfortable as always whenever his brother went on like this.

Raistlin did not seem to notice. Pulling a pouch from his pack, he sprinkled some green leaves† into the hot water. A pungent, acrid smell filled the room. "I do not follow him." The young mage looked up at Laurana. "For the time being, Tanis and I simply happen to be traveling in the same direction."

Tika, presumably having made the tea for him on occasion, was able to put one version of Raistlin's tea in Leaves from the Inn of the Last Home. *It contains at least a half ounce each of mullein, angelica, burdock, and coltsfoot, plus a quarter ounce each of dried lemon peel and dried orange peel. However, he refused ever to let her know his magic ingredient....*

"The Knights of Solamnia are not welcome in our city," the Lord said sternly, his face serious. His dark gaze swept the rest of the company. "Nor are elves, kender, or dwarves, or those who travel in their company. I understand you also have a magic-user with you, one who wears the red robes. You wear armor. Your weapons are blood-stained and come quickly and readily to your hands. Obviously you are skilled warriors."

"Mercenaries, undoubtedly, milord," the constable said.

"We are not mercenaries," Sturm said, coming to stand before the bench, his bearing proud and noble. "We come out of the northern Plains of Abanasinia.

We freed eight hundred men, women, and children from the Dragon Highlord, Verminaard, in Pax Tharkas. Fleeing the wrath of the dragonarmies, we left the people hidden in a valley in the mountains and traveled south, hoping to find ships in the legendary city of Tarsis. We did not know it was landlocked, or we would not have bothered."

The Lord frowned. "You say you came from the north? That is impossible. No one has ever come safely through the mountain kingdom of the dwarves in Thorbardin."

"If you know aught of the Knights of Solamnia, you know we would die sooner than tell a lie—even to our enemies," Sturm said. "We entered the dwarven kingdom and won safe passage by finding and restoring to them the lost Hammer of Kharas."

The Lord shifted uncomfortably, glancing at the draconian who sat behind him. "I do know somewhat of the knights," he said reluctantly."And therefore I must believe your story, though it sounds more a child's bedtime tale than—"

Suddenly the doors banged open and two guards strode in, roughly dragging a prisoner between them. They thrust the companions aside as they flung their prisoner to the floor. The prisoner was a woman. Heavily veiled, she was dressed in long skirts and a heavy cape. She lay for a moment on the floor, as if too tired or defeated to rise. Then, seeming to make a supreme effort of will, she started to push herself up. Obviously no one was going to assist her. The Lord stared at her, his face grim and scowling. The draconian behind him had risen to its feet and was looking down at her with interest. The woman struggled, entangled in her cape and her long, flowing skirts.

Then Sturm was at her side.

The knight had watched in horror, appalled at this callous treatment of a woman. He glanced at Tanis, saw the ever-cautious half-elf shake his head, but the sight of the woman making a gallant effort to rise proved too much for the knight. He took a step forward, and found a hauberk thrust in front of him.

"Kill me if you will," the knight said to the guard, "but I am going to the aid of the lady."

The guard blinked and stepped back, his eyes looking up at the Lord for orders. The Lord shook his head slightly. Tanis, watching closely, held his breath. Then he thought he saw the Lord smile, quickly covering it with his hand.

"My lady, allow me to assist you," Sturm said with the courtly, old-fashioned politeness long lost in the world. His strong hands gently raised her to her feet.

"You had better leave me, sir knight," the woman said, her words barely audible from behind her veil. But at the sound of her voice, Tanis and Gilthanas gasped softly, glancing at each other. "You do not know what you do," she said. "You risk your life—"

"It is my privilege to do so," Sturm said, bowing. Then he stood near her protectively, his eyes on the guards.

"She is Silvanesti elven!"† Gilthanas whispered to Tanis. "Does Sturm know?"

The long years apart have given Silvanesti elves a different accent than the Qualinesti elves. Also, the Silvanesti apparently have finer features.

"Of course not," Tanis said softly. "How could he? I barely recognized her accent myself."

"What could she be doing here? Silvanesti is far away—"

"I—" Tanis began, but one of the guards shoved him in the back. He fell silent just as the Lord started to speak.

"Lady Alhana," he said in a cold voice, "you were warned to leave this city. I was merciful last time you came before me because you were on a diplomatic mission from your people, and protocol is still honored in Tarsis. I told you then, however, you could expect no help from us and gave you twenty-four hours to depart. Now I find you still here." He looked over at the guards. "What is the charge?"

"Trying to buy mercenaries, milord," the constable replied. "She was picked up in an inn along the Old Waterfront, milord." The constable gave Sturm a scathing glance. "It was a good thing she didn't meet up with this lot. Of course, no one in Tarsis would aid an elf."

"Alhana," Tanis muttered to himself. He edged over to Gilthanas. "Why is that name familiar?"

"Have you been gone from your people so long you do not recognize the name?" the elf answered softly in elven. "There was only one among our Silvanesti cousins called Alhana. Alhana Starbreeze, daughter of the Speaker of the Stars,

princess of her people, ruler when her father dies, for she has no brothers."

"Alhana!" Tanis said, memories coming back to him. The elven people were split hundreds of years before, when Kith-Kanan led many of the elves to the land of Qualinesti following the bitter Kinslayer Wars. But the elven leaders still kept in contact in the mysterious manner of the elflords who, it is said, can read messages in the wind and speak the language of the silver moon. Now he remembered Alhana—of all elfmaidens reputed to be the most beautiful, and distant as the silver moon that shone on her birth.

The draconian leaned down to confer with the Lord. Tanis saw the man's face darken, and it seemed as if he was about to disagree, then he bit his lip and, sighing, nodded his head. The draconian melted back into the shadows once more.

"You are under arrest, Lady Alhana," the Lord said heavily. Sturm took a step nearer the woman as the guards closed in around her. Sturm threw back his head and cast them all a warning glance. So confident and noble did he appear, even unarmed, that the guards hesitated. Still, their Lord had given them an order.

"You better do something," Flint growled. "I'm all for chivalry, but there's a time and a place and this isn't either!"

"Have you got any suggestions?" Tanis snapped.

Flint didn't answer. There wasn't a damn thing any of them could do and they knew it. Sturm would die before one of those guards laid a hand on the woman again, even though he had no idea who this woman was. It didn't matter. Feeling himself torn with frustration and admiration for his friend, Tanis gauged the distance between himself and the nearest guard, knowing he could put at least one out of action. He saw Gilthanas close his eyes, his lips moving. The elf was a magic-user, though he rarely treated it seriously. Seeing the look on Tanis's face, Flint heaved a sigh and turned toward another guard, lowering his helmeted head like a battering ram.

Then suddenly the Lord spoke, his voice grating. "Hold, knight!" he said with the authority that had been bred in him for generations. Sturm, recognizing this, relaxed, and Tanis breathed a sigh of relief.

"I will not have blood shed in this Council chamber. The lady has disobeyed a law of the land, laws which, in days gone by, you, sir knight, were sworn to uphold. But I agree, there is no reason to treat her disrespectfully. Guards, you will escort the lady to prison but with the same courtesy you show me. And you, sir knight, will accompany her, since you are so interested in her welfare."

Tanis nudged Gilthanas who came out of his trance with a start. "Truly, as Sturm said, this Lord comes from a noble and honorable line," Tanis whispered.

"I don't see what you're so pleased about, Half-elf." Flint grunted, overhearing them. "First the kender gets us charged with inciting a riot, then he disappears. Now the knight gets us thrown into prison. Next time, remind me to stick with the mage. I *know* he's crazed!"

As the guards started to herd their prisoners away from the bench, Alhana appeared to be hunting for something within the folds of her long skirt.

"I beg a favor, sir knight," she said to Sturm. "I seem to have dropped something. A trifle but precious. Could you look—"

Sturm knelt swiftly and immediately saw the object where it lay, sparkling, on the floor, hidden by the folds of her dress. It was a pin, shaped like a star, glittering with diamonds. He drew in his breath. A trifle! Its value must be incalculable. No wonder she did not want it found by these worthless guards. Quickly he wrapped his fingers around it, then feigned to look about. Finally, still kneeling, he looked up at the woman.

Up to this moment, Alhana's visits to the city have been highly clandestine, and in each previous instance she has entered the city cloaked and with her face veiled or hidden. Thus, though she has been in and out of the city many times, up to this moment human eyes have not gazed on her.—TRH

Sturm caught his breath as the woman removed the hood of her cloak and drew the veil from her face. For the first time, human eyes looked upon the face of Alhana Starbreeze.†

Muralasa, the elves called her, Princess of the Night. Her hair, black and soft as the night wind, was held in place by a net as fine as cobweb, twinkling with tiny jewels like stars. Her skin was the pale hue of the silver moon, her eyes the deep, dark purple of the night sky and her lips the color of the red moon's shadows.

The knight's first thought was to give thanks to Paladine that he was already on his knees. His

second was that death would be a paltry price to pay to serve her, and his third that he must say something, but he seemed to have forgotten the words of any known language.

"Thank you for searching, noble knight," Alhana said softly, staring intently into Sturm's eyes. "As I said, it was a trifle. Please rise. I am very weary and, since it seems we are going to the same place, you could do me a great favor by giving me your assistance."

"I am yours to command," Sturm said fervently, and he rose to his feet, swiftly tucking the jewel inside his belt. He held out his arm, and Alhana put her slender, white hand on his forearm. His arm trembled at her touch.

It seemed to the knight as if a cloud had covered the light of the stars when she veiled her face again. Sturm saw Tanis fall into line behind them, but so enraptured was the knight with the beautiful face burning in his memory that he stared straight at the half-elf without a flicker of recognition.

Tanis had seen Alhana's face and felt his own heart stir with her beauty. But he had seen Sturm's face as well. He had seen that beauty enter the knight's heart, doing more damage than a goblin's poisoned arrowtip. For this love must turn to poison, he knew. The Silvanesti were a proud and haughty race. Fearing contamination and the loss of their way of life, they refused to have even the slightest contact with humans. Thus the Kinslayer Wars had been fought.

No, thought Tanis sadly, the silver moon itself was not higher or farther out of Sturm's reach. The half-elf sighed. This was all they needed.

6

Knights of Solamnia.
Tasslehoff's glasses of true seeing.

As the guards led the prisoners from the Hall of Justice, they passed two figures standing outside in the shadows. Both were so swathed in clothing it was difficult to tell to what race they belonged. Hoods covered their heads, their faces were wrapped in cloth. Long robes shrouded their bodies. Even their hands were wrapped in strips of white, like bandages.† They spoke together in low tones.

Draconians may be everywhere, but they still keep their hands bandaged to try to maintain the illusion that they are "just a bunch of strange humans" as long as possible to the public. —TRH

"See!" one said in great excitement. "There they are. They match the descriptions."

"Not all of them," said the other dubiously.

"But the half-elf, the dwarf, the knight! I tell you, it is them! And I know where the others are," the figure added smugly. "I questioned one of the guards."

The other, taller figure considered, watching the group being led off down the street. "You are right. We should report this to the Highlord at once." The shrouded figure turned, then stopped as it saw the other hesitate. "What are you waiting for?"

"But shouldn't one of us follow? Look at those puny guards. You know the prisoners will try and escape."

The other laughed unpleasantly. "Of course they'll escape. And we know where they'll go—to rejoin their friends." The shrouded figure squinted up at the afternoon sun. "Besides, in a few hours it won't make any difference." The tall figure strode away, the shorter hurrying after.

It was snowing when the companions left the Hall of Justice. This time, the constable knew better than to march his prisoners through the main city streets. He led them into a dark and gloomy alleyway that ran behind the Hall of Justice.

Tanis and Sturm were just exchanging glances, and Gilthanas and Flint were just tensing to attack when the half-elf saw the shadows in the alley begin to move. Three hooded and cloaked figures leaped out in front of the guards, their steel blades gleaming in the bright sunlight.

The constable put his whistle to his lips, but he never made a sound. One of the figures knocked him unconscious with the hilt of his sword, while the other two rushed the guards, who immediately fled. The hooded figures faced the companions.

"Who are you?" Tanis asked, astounded at his sudden freedom. The hooded and cloaked figures reminded him of the hooded draconians they had fought outside of Solace. Sturm pulled Alhana behind him.

"Have we escaped one danger only to find a worse?" Tanis demanded. "Unmask yourselves!"

But one of the hooded men turned to Sturm, his hands raised in the air. *"Oth Tsarthon e Paran,"*† he said.

Sturm gasped. *"Est Tsarthai en Paranaith,"*† he replied, then he turned to Tanis. "Knights of Solamnia," he said, gesturing at the three men.

"Knights?" Tanis asked in astonishment. "Why—"

"There is no time for explanation, Sturm Brightblade," one of the knights said in Common, his

It's been many years since I spoke Solamnic—even then, I found this language old and awkward. Let me see: "Oth:" a state of being, present tense but in this form a question such as "is" or "are?" "Tsarthon:" "meeting/joining. "e:" between. "Paran:" friends/friendship. Thus: "Is our meeting (between us) in friendship?"—TRH

"My companions are (your) friends." That Sturm would also be a friend is implied in his use of Solamnic. It is interesting to note that the root of both sentences—"Tsarthan" and "Tsarthai"—is the basis for the city name of Xak Tsaroth, which literally means, in Solamnic, "Meeting Place." Prior to the Cataclysm, Xak Tsaroth must have been a city of commerce founded by Solamnics.—TRH

accent thick. "The guards will return soon. Come with us."

"Not so fast!" Flint growled, his feet planted firmly in the street, his hands breaking off the handle of a hauberk so that it suited his short stature. "You'll find time for explanations or I'm not going! How'd you know the knight's name and how came you to be waiting for us—"

"Oh, just run him through!" sang a shrill voice out of the shadows. "Leave his body to feed the crows. Not that they'll bother; there's few in this world who can stomach dwarf—"

"Satisfied?" Tanis turned to Flint, who was red-faced with rage.

"Someday," vowed the dwarf, "I'll kill that kender."

Whistles sounded from the street behind them. With no more hesitation, the companions followed the knights through twisting, rat infested alleys. Saying he had business to attend to, Tas disappeared before Tanis could catch hold of him. The half-elf noticed that the knights didn't seem at all surprised by this, nor did they try to stop Tas. They refused, however, to answer any questions, just kept hurrying the group along until they entered the ruins—the old city of Tarsis the Beautiful.

Here the knights stopped. They had brought the companions to a part of the city where no one ever came now. The streets were broken and empty, reminding Tanis strongly of the ancient city of Xak Tsaroth. Taking Sturm by the arm, the knights led him a short distance from his friends and began to confer in Solamnic, leaving the others to rest.

Tanis, leaning against a building, looked around with interest. What remained standing of the buildings on this street was impressive, much more beautiful than the modern city. He saw that Tarsis the Beautiful must have deserved its name before the Cataclysm. Now nothing but huge blocks of granite lay tumbled about. Vast courtyards were choked and overgrown with weeds turned brown by the biting winter winds.

He walked over to sit down on a bench with Gilthanas, who was talking to Alhana. The elflord introduced him.

"Alhana Starbreeze, Tanis Half-Elven," Gilthanas said. "Tanis lived among the Qualinesti for many years. He is the son of my uncle's wife." Alhana drew back the veil from her face and regarded Tanis coldly. *Son of my uncle's wife* was a polite way of saying Tanis was illegitimate, otherwise Gilthanas would have introduced him as the "son of my uncle." The half-elf flushed, the old pain returning forcibly, hurting as much now as it had fifty years before. He wondered if he would ever be free of it.

Scratching his beard, Tanis said harshly, "My mother was raped by human warriors during years of darkness following the Cataclysm. The Speaker kindly took me in following her death and raised me as his own."

Alhana's dark eyes grew darker until they were pools of night. She raised her eyebrows. "Do you see a need to apologize for your heritage?" she asked in a chill voice.

"N-no . . ." Tanis stammered, his face burning. "I—"

"Then do not," she said, and she turned away from him to Gilthanas. "You asked why I came to Tarsis? I came seeking aid. I must return to Silvanesti to search for my father."

"Return to Silvanesti?" Gilthanas repeated. "We—my people did not know the Silvanesti elves had left their ancient homeland. No wonder we lost contact—"

"Yes," Alhana's voice grew sad. "The evil that forced you, our cousins, to leave Qualinesti came to us as well." She bowed her head, then looked up, her own voice soft and low. "Long we fought this evil. But in the end we were forced to flee or perish utterly. My father sent the people, under my leadership, to Southern Ergoth. He stayed in Silvanesti to fight the evil alone. I opposed this decision, but he said he had the power to prevent the evil from destroying our homeland.With a heavy heart, I led my people to safety and there they remain.But I came back to seek my father, for the days have been long and we have heard no word of him."

"But had you no warriors, lady, to accompany you on such a dangerous journey?" Tanis asked.

Alhana, turning, glanced at Tanis as if amazed that he had intruded upon their conversation. At first she seemed about to refuse to answer him, then—looking longer at his face—she changed her mind.

"There were many warriors who offered to escort me," she said proudly. "But when I said I led my people to safety, I spoke rashly. Safety no longer exists in this world. The warriors stayed behind to guard the people. I came to Tarsis hoping to find warriors to travel into Silvanesti with me. I presented myself to the Lord and the Council, as protocol demands—"

Tanis shook his head, frowning darkly. "That was stupid," he said bluntly. "You should have known how they feel about elves, even before the draconians came! You were damn lucky they only ordered you tossed out of the city."

Alhana's pale face became—if possible—paler. Her dark eyes glittered. "I did as protocol demands," she replied, too well bred to show her anger beyond the cool tones of her voice. "To do otherwise would have been to come as a barbarian. When the Lord refused to aid me, I told him I intended to seek help on my own. To do less would have not been honorable."

Flint, who had been able to follow only bits and pieces of the conversation in elven, nudged Tanis. "She and the knight will get on perfectly." He snorted. "Unless their honor gets them killed first." Before Tanis could reply, Sturm rejoined the group.

"Tanis," Sturm said in excitement, "the knights have found the ancient library! That's why they're here. They discovered records in Palanthas saying that in ancient times knowledge of dragons was kept in the library here, at Tarsis. The Knights Council sent them to see if the library still survived."

Sturm gestured for the knights to come forward. "This is Brian Donner, Knight of the Sword," he said. "Aran Tallbow, Knight of the Crown, and Derek Crowngaurd, Knight of the Rose."† The knights bowed.

The categories of Knighthood are again a threesome, in typical DRAGONLANCE fashion.

"And this is Tanis Half-Elven, our leader," Sturm said. The half-elf saw Alhana start and look at him in wonder, glancing at Sturm to see if she had heard correctly.

Sturm introduced Gilthanas and Flint, then he turned to Alhana. "Lady Alhana," he began, then

stopped, embarrassed, realizing he knew nothing more about her.

"Alhana Starbreeze," Gilthanas finished. "Daughter of the Speaker of the Stars. Princess of the Silvanesti elves."

The knights bowed again, lower this time.

"Accept my heartfelt gratitude for rescuing me," Alhana said coolly. Her gaze encompassed all the group but lingered longest on Sturm. Then she turned to Derek, whom she knew from his Order of the Rose to be the leader. "Have you discovered the records the Council sent you to find?"

As she spoke, Tanis examined the knights, now unhooded, with interest. He, too, knew enough to know that the Knights Council—the ruling body of the Solamnic knights—had sent the best. In particular he studied Derek, the elder and the highest in rank. Few knights attained the Order of the Rose. The tests were dangerous and difficult, and only knights of pure bloodline could belong.

"We have found a book, my lady," Derek said, "written in an ancient language we could not understand. There were pictures of dragons, however, so we were planning to copy it and return to Sancrist where, we hoped, scholars would be able to translate it. But instead we have found one who can read it. The kender—"

"Tasslehoff!" Flint exploded.

Tanis's mouth gaped open. "Tasslehoff?" he repeated incredulously. "He can barely read Common. He doesn't know any ancient languages. The only one among us who might possibly be able to translate an ancient language is Raistlin."

Derek shrugged. "The kender has a pair of glasses he says are 'magical glasses of true seeing.' He put them on and he has been able to read the book. It says—"

"I can imagine what it says!" Tanis snapped. "Stories about automatons and magic rings of teleporting and plants that live off air. Where is he? I'm going to have a little talk with Tasslehoff Burrfoot."

"Magical glasses of true seeing," Flint grumbled. "And I'm a gully dwarf!"

The companions entered a shattered building. Climbing over rubble, they followed Derek's lead through a low archway. The smell of must and

mildew was strong. The darkness was intense after the brightness of the afternoon sun outside and for a moment, everyone was blinded.Then Derek lit a torch, and they saw narrow, winding stairs leading down into more darkness.

"The library was built below ground," Derek explained. "Probably the only reason it survived the Cataclysm so well."

The companions descended the stairs rapidly and soon found themselves inside a huge room. Tanis caught his breath and even Alhana's eyes widened in the flickering torchlight. The gigantic room was filled from ceiling to floor with tall, wooden shelves, stretching as far as the eye could see. On the shelves were books. Books of all kinds. Books with leather bindings, books bound in wood, books bound in what looked like leaves from some exotic tree. Many were not bound at all but were simply sheaves of parchment, held together with black ribbons. Several shelves had toppled over, spilling the books to the floor until it was ankle-deep in parchment.†

The greatest crimes, for me, involve the loss of libraries and knowledge. I still am upset about the Library in Alexandria. Before we become too smug about our vast electronic knowledge, we should note that it is even more fragile than Alexandria. In any case, a find such as Tas has stumbled upon is one of my personal fantasies. —TRH

"There must be thousands!" Tanis said in awe. "How did you ever find one among these?"

Derek shook his head. "It was not easy," he said. "Long days we have spent down here, searching. When we discovered it at last, we felt more despair than triumph, for it was obvious that the book cannot be moved. Even as we touched the pages, they crumbled to dust. We feared we would spend long, weary hours copying it. But the kender—"

"Right, the kender," Tanis said grimly. "Where is he?"

"Over here!" piped a shrill voice.

Tanis peered through the dimly lit room to see a candle burning on a table. Tasslehoff, seated on a high wooden chair, was bent over a thick book. As the companions neared him, they could see a pair of small glasses perched on his nose.

"All right, Tas," Tanis said. "Where did you get them?"

"Get what?" the kender asked innocently. He saw Tanis's eyes narrow and put his hand to the small wire-rimmed glasses. "Oh, uh, these? I had them in a pouch . . . and, well, if you must know, I found them in the dwarven kingdom—"†

Flint groaned and put his hand over his face.

"They were just lying on a table!" Tas protested, seeing Tanis scowl. "Honest! There was no one around. I thought perhaps someone misplaced them. I only took them for safekeeping. Good thing, too. Some thief might have come along and stolen them, and they're very valuable! I meant to return them, but after that we were so busy, what with fighting dark dwarves and draconians and finding the Hammer, and I—sort of—forgot I had them. When I remembered them, we were miles away from the dwarves, on our way to Tarsis, and I didn't think you'd want me to go back, just to return them, so—"

Tas claims he found the magical glasses in the dwarven kingdom, but some people insist he could only have found them in the Library of Khrystann in Tarsis, where he wasn't supposed to be. He did disappear for a while. . . .

"What do they do?" Tanis interrupted the kender, knowing they'd be here until the day after tomorrow if he didn't.

"They're wonderful," Tas said hastily, relieved that Tanis wasn't going to yell at him. "I left them lying on a map one day." Tas patted his mapcase. "I looked down and what do you suppose? I could read the writing on the map through the glasses! Now, that doesn't sound very wonderful," Tas said hurriedly, seeing Tanis start to frown again, "but this was a map written in a language I'd never been able to understand before. So I tried them on all my maps and I could read them, Tanis! Every one! Even the real, real old ones!"

"And you never mentioned this to us?" Sturm glared at Tas.

"Well, the subject just never came up," Tas said apologetically. "Now, if you had asked me directly—'Tasslehoff, do you have a pair of magical seeing glasses?—' I would have told you the truth† straight off. But you never did, Sturm Brightblade, so don't look at me like that. Anyway, I can read this old book. Let me tell you what I—"

The kender believe in truth-telling just as we do . . . it's ownership that is a bit of a foggy concept to them.—TRH

"How do you know they're magic and not just some mechanical device of the dwarves?" Tanis asked, sensing that Tas was hiding something.

Tas gulped. He had been hoping Tanis wouldn't ask him *that* question.

"Uh," Tas stammered, "I—I guess I did sort of, happened to, uh, mention them to Raistlin one night when you were all busy doing something else. He told me they might be magic. To find out, he said one of those weird spells of his and they—uh—

began to glow. That meant they were enchanted. He asked me what they did and I demonstrated and he said they were 'glasses of true seeing.' The dwarven magic-users of old made them to read books written in other languages and—" Tas stopped.

"And?" Tanis pursued.

"And—uh—magic spellbooks." Tas's voice was a whisper.

"And what else did Raistlin say?"

"That if I touched his spellbooks or even looked at them sideways, he'd turn me into a cricket and s-swallow m-me whole," Tasslehoff stammered. He looked up at Tanis with wide eyes. "I believed him, too."

Tanis shook his head. Trust Raistlin to come up with a threat awful enough to quench the curiosity of a kender. "Anything else?" he asked.

"No, Tanis," Tas said innocently. Actually Raistlin *had* mentioned something else about the glasses, but Tas hadn't been able to understand it very well. Something about the glasses seeing things too truly, which didn't make any sense, so he figured it probably wasn't worth bringing up. Besides, Tanis was mad enough already.

"Well, what have you discovered?" Tanis asked grudgingly.

"Oh, Tanis, it's so interesting!" Tas said, thankful the ordeal was over. He carefully turned a page and, even as he did so, it split and cracked beneath his small fingers. He shook his head sadly. "That happens almost every time. But you can see here"—the others leaned around to stare beneath the kender's finger—"pictures of dragons. Blue dragons, red dragons, black dragons, green dragons. I didn't know there were so many. Now, see this thing?" He turned another page. "Oops. Well, you can't see it now, but it was a huge ball of glass. And—so the book says—if you have one of these glass balls, you can gain control over the dragons and they'll do what you say!"

"Glass ball!" Flint sniffed, then sneezed. "Don't believe him, Tanis. I think the only thing those glasses have done is magnify his tall stories."

"I am *so* telling the truth!" Tas said indignantly. "They're called dragon orbs, and you can ask Raistlin about them! He must know because,

according to this, they were made by the great wizards, long ago."

"I believe you," Tanis said gravely, seeing that Tasslehoff was really upset. "But I'm afraid it won't do us much good. They were probably all destroyed in the Cataclysm and we wouldn't know where to look anyway—"

"Yes, we do," Tas said excitedly. "There's a list here, of where they were kept. See—" He stopped, cocking his head. "Shhhh," he said, listening. The others fell silent. For a moment they heard nothing, then their ears caught what the kender's quicker hearing had already detected.

Tanis felt his hands grow cold; the dry, bitter taste of fear filled his mouth. Now he could hear, in the distance, the sound of hundreds of horns braying, horns all of them had heard before. The bellowing, brass horns that heralded the approach of the draconian armies—and the approach of the dragons.

The horns of death.

7

"—Not destined to meet again in this world."

The companions had just reached the marketplace when the first flight of dragons struck Tarsis.

The group had separated from the knights, not a pleasant parting. The knights had tried to convince them to escape with them into the hills. When the companions refused, Derek demanded that Tasslehoff accompany them, since the kender alone knew the location of the dragon orbs. Tanis knew Tas would only run away from the knights and was forced to refuse again.

"Bring the kender, Sturm, and come with us," Derek commanded, ignoring Tanis.

"I cannot, sir," Sturm replied, laying his hand on Tanis's arm. "He is my leader, and my first loyalty is to my friends."

Derek's voice was cold with anger. "If that is your decision," he answered, "I cannot stop you. But this is a black mark against you, Sturm Brightblade. Remember that you are not a knight. Not yet. Pray that I am not there when the question of your knighthood comes before the Council."

Sturm became as pale as death. He cast a sideways glance at Tanis, who tried to hide his astonishment at this startling news. But there was no time to think about it. The sound of the horns, screaming discordantly on the chill air, was coming closer and closer each second.The knights and the companions parted; the knights heading for their camp in the hills, the companions returning to town.

They found the townspeople outside their houses, speculating on the strange horn calls, which they had never heard before and did not understand. One Tarsian alone heard and understood. The Lord in the council chamber rose to his feet at the sound. Whirling, he turned upon the smug-looking draconian seated in the shadows behind him.

"You said we would be spared!" the Lord said through clenched teeth. "We're still negotiating—"

"The Dragon Highlord grew weary of negotiation," the draconian said, stifling a yawn. "And the city *will* be spared—after it has been taught a lesson, of course."

The Lord's head sank into his hands. The other council members, not fully comprehending what was happening, stared at each other in horrified awareness as they saw tears trickle through the Lord's fingers.

Outside, the red dragons were visible in the skies, hundreds of them. Flying in regimented groups of three to five, their wings glistened flame red in the setting sun. The people of Tarsis knew one thing and one thing only: death flew overhead.

As the dragons swooped low, making their first passes over the town, the dragonfear flowed from them, spreading panic more deadly than fire. The people had one thought in their minds as the shadows of the wings blotted out the dying light of day—escape.

But there was no escape.

The essence of a red dragon is fire. These are the biggest dragons on Krynn, and apparently the Dark Queen's right-hand dragons.

I studied World War II films of the bombing of London in order to make this fantasy battle as realistic as possible.—MW

After the first pass, knowing now that they would meet no resistance, the dragons struck. One after the other, they circled, then dropped from the sky like red-hot shot, their fiery breath engulfing building after building with flame.† The spreading fires created their own windstorms. Choking smoke filled the street, turning twilight into midnight. Ash poured down like black rain. Screams of terror changed to screams of agony as people died in the blazing abyss that was Tarsis.†

And as the dragons struck, a sea of fear-crazed humanity surged through the flame-lit streets. Few had any clear idea of where they were going. Some shouted they would be safe in the hills, others ran down by the old waterfront, still others tried to reach the city gates. Above them flew the dragons, burning at their discretion, killing at their leisure.

The human sea broke over Tanis and the companions, crushing them into the street, swirling them apart, smashing them up against buildings. The smoke choked them and stung their eyes, tears blinded them as they fought to control the dragon fear that threatened to destroy their reason.

The heat was so intense that whole buildings blew apart. Tanis caught Gilthanas as the elf was hurled into the side of a building. Holding onto him, the half-elf could only watch helplessly as the rest of his friends were swept away by the mob.

"Back to the Inn!" Tanis shouted. "Meet at the Inn!" But whether they heard him or not, he could not say. He could only trust that they would all try to head in that direction.

Sturm caught hold of Alhana in his strong arms, half-carrying, half dragging her through the death-filled streets. Peering through the ash, he tried to see the others, but it was hopeless. And then began the most desperate battle he had ever fought, striving to keep his feet and support Alhana as time and again the dreadful waves of humanity broke over them.

Then Alhana was ripped from his arms by the shrieking mob, whose booted feet trampled all that lived. Sturm flung himself into the crowd, shoving and bashing with his armored arms and body, and caught Alhana's wrists. Deathly pale, she was shaking with fright. She hung onto his hands with all her strength, and finally he was able to pull her close. A

shadow swept over them. A dragon, screaming cruelly, bore down upon the street that heaved and surged with men, women, and children. Sturm ducked into a doorway, dragging Alhana with him, and shielded her with his body as the dragon swooped low overhead. Flame filled the street; the screams of the dying were heart-rending.

"Don't look!" Sturm whispered to Alhana, pressing her against him, tears streaming down his own face. The dragon passed, and suddenly the streets were horribly, unbearably still. Nothing moved.

"Let's go, while we can," Sturm said, his voice shaking. Clinging to each other, the two stumbled out of the doorway, their senses numbed, moving only by instinct. Finally, sickened and dizzy from the smell of charred flesh and smoke, they were forced to seek shelter in another doorway.

For a moment, they could do nothing but hold onto each other, thankful for the brief respite, yet haunted by the knowledge that in seconds they must return to the deadly streets.

Alhana rested her head against Sturm's chest. The ancient, old fashioned armor felt cool against her skin. Its hard metal surface was reassuring, and beneath it she could feel his heart beat, rapid, steady, and soothing. The arms that held her were strong, hard, well-muscled. His hand stroked her black hair.

Alhana, chaste maiden of a stern and rigid people, had long known when, where, and whom she would marry. He was an elflord, and it was a mark of their understanding that, in all the years since this had been arranged they had never touched. He had stayed behind with the people, while Alhana returned to find her father. She had strayed into this world of humans, and her senses reeled from the shock. She detested them, yet was fascinated by them. They were so powerful, their emotions raw and untamed. And just when she thought she would hate and despise them forever, one stepped apart from the others.

Alhana looked up into Sturm's grieved face and saw etched there pride, nobility, strict inflexible discipline, constant striving for perfection—perfection unattainable. And thus the deep sorrow in his eyes. Alhana felt herself drawn to this man, this human. Yielding to his strength, comforted by his presence, she felt a sweet, searing warmth steal over her, and suddenly she realized she was in more danger from this fire than from the fire of a thousand dragons.

"We'd better go," Sturm whispered gently, but to his amazement Alhana pushed herself away from him.

"Here we part," she said, her voice cold as the night wind. "I must return to my lodging. Thank you for escorting me."

"What?" Sturm said. "Go by yourself? That's madness." He reached out and gripped her arm. "I cannot allow—" The wrong thing to do, he realized, feeling her stiffen. She did not move but simply stared at him imperiously until he released her.

"I have friends of my own," she said, "as you do. Your loyalty is to them. My loyalty is to mine. We must go our separate ways." Her voice faltered at the look of intense pain on Sturm's face, still wet with tears. For a moment Alhana could not bear it and wondered if she would have the strength to continue. Then she thought of her people—depending on her. She found the strength. "I thank you for your kindness and your help, but now I must go, while the streets are empty."

Sturm stared at her, hurt and puzzled. Then his face hardened. "I was happy to be of service, Lady Alhana. But you are still in danger. Allow me to take you to your lodgings, then I will trouble you no more."

"That is quite impossible," Alhana said, gritting her teeth to keep her jaw set firmly. "My lodgings are not far, and my friends wait for me. We have a way out of the city. Forgive me for not taking you, but I am never certain about trusting humans."

Sturm's brown eyes flashed. Alhana, standing close, could feel his body tremble. Once more she nearly lost her resolve.

"I know where you are staying," she said, swallowing. "The Red Dragon Inn. Perhaps, if I find my friends—we could offer you help—"

"Do not concern yourself." Sturm's voice echoed her coldness. "And do not thank me. I did nothing more than my Code required of me. Farewell," he said, and started to walk away.

Then, remembering, he turned back. Drawing the sparkling diamond pin from his belt, he placed

it in Alhana's hand. "Here," he said. Looking into her dark eyes, he suddenly saw the pain she tried to hide. His voice softened, though he could not understand. "I am pleased you trusted me with this gem," he said gently, "even for a few moments."

The elfmaid stared at the jewel for an instant, then she began to shake. Her eyes lifted to Sturm's eyes and she saw in them not scorn, as she expected, but compassion. Once more, she wondered at humans. Alhana dropped her head, unable to meet his gaze, and took his hand in hers. Then she laid the jewel in his palm and closed his fingers over it.

"Keep this," she said softly. "When you look at it, think of Alhana Starbreeze and know that, somewhere, she thinks of you."

Sudden tears flooded the knight's eyes. He bowed his head, unable to speak. Then, kissing the gem, he placed it carefully back into his belt and he reached out his hands, but Alhana drew back into the doorway, her pale face averted.

"Please go," she said. Sturm stood for a moment, irresolute, but he could not—in honor—refuse to obey her request. The knight turned and plunged back into the nightmarish street. Alhana watched him from the doorway for a moment, a protective shell hardening around her. "Forgive me, Sturm," she whispered to herself. Then she stopped. "No, do not forgive me," she said harshly. "Thank me."

Closing her eyes, she conjured up an image in her mind and sent a message† speeding to the outskirts of the city where her friends waited to carry her from this world of humans. Receiving their telepathic answer in reply, Alhana sighed and began anxiously to scan the smoke-filled skies, waiting.

Telepathy was an ancient art known among the Silvanesti Elves and, prior to the Cataclysm, was practiced primarily only by the royal household and their staff for purposes of administering royal edicts across the rather large expanse of Silvanesti. After the Cataclysm, telepathic use dwindled even further until, by the time of the War of the Lance, it was known only among the royal household itself. It fell into complete disuse soon thereafter. —TRH

"Ah," said Raistlin calmly as the first horn calls shattered the stillness of the afternoon, "I told you so."

Riverwind cast an irritated glance at the mage, even as he tried to think what to do. It was all very well for Tanis to say protect the group from the town guards, but to protect them from armies of draconians, from dragons! Riverwind's dark eyes went over the group. Tika rose to her feet, her hand on her sword. The young girl was brave and steady, but

unskilled. The Plainsman could still see the scars on her hand where she had cut herself.

"What is it?" Elistan asked, looking bewildered.

"The Dragon Highlord, attacking the city," Riverwind answered harshly, trying to think.

He heard a clanking sound. Caramon was getting up, the big warrior appearing calm and unperturbed. Thank goodness for that. Even though Riverwind detested Raistlin, he had to admit that the mage and his warrior brother combined steel and magic effectively. Laurana, too, he saw, appeared cool and resolute, but then she was an elf—Riverwind had never really learned to trust elves.†

It's doubtful that Riverwind had ever seen an elf before coming to Solace, but he picked up on the human prejudice immediately.

"Get out of the city, if we don't return," Tanis had told him. But Tanis hadn't foreseen this! They would get out of the city only to meet the armies of the Dragon Highlords on the Plains. Riverwind now had an excellent idea who had been watching them as they traveled to this doomed place. He swore to himself in his own language, then—even as the first dragons swept down over the city—he felt Goldmoon's arm around him. Looking down, he saw her smile—the smile of Chieftain's Daughter—and he saw the faith in her eyes. Faith in the gods, and faith in him. He relaxed, his brief moment of panic gone.

A shock wave hit the building. They could hear the screams in the streets below, the roaring whoosh of the fires.

"We've got to get off this floor, back to ground level," Riverwind said. "Caramon, bring the knight's sword and the other weapons. If Tanis and the others are—" He stopped. He had been about to say "still alive," then saw Laurana's face. "If Tanis and the others escape, they'll return here. We'll wait for them."

"Excellent decision!" hissed the mage caustically, "especially as we have nowhere else to go!"

Riverwind ignored him. "Elistan, take the others downstairs. Caramon and Raistlin, stay with me a moment." After they were gone, he said swiftly, "Our best chance, the way I see it, is to stay inside, barricade ourselves in the Inn. The streets will be deadly."

"How long do you think we can hold out?" Caramon asked.

Riverwind shook his head. "Hours, maybe," he said briefly.

The brothers looked at him, each of them thinking about the tortured bodies they had seen in the village of Qué-Shu, of what they had heard about the destruction of Solace.

"We cannot be taken alive," Raistlin whispered.

Riverwind took a deep breath. "We'll hold out as long as we can," he said, his voice shaking slightly, "but when we know we can last no longer—"

He stopped, unable to continue, his hand on his knife, thinking of what he must do.

"There will be no need for that," Raistlin said softly. "I have herbs. A tiny bit in a glass of wine. Very quick, painless."

"Are you certain?" Riverwind asked.

"Trust me," Raistlin replied. "I am skilled in the art. The art of herblore," he amended smoothly, seeing the Plainsman shudder.

"If I am alive," Riverwind said softly, "I will give her, them—the drink myself. If not—"

"I understand. You may trust me," the mage repeated.

"What about Laurana?" Caramon asked. "You know elves. She won't—"

"Leave it to me," Raistlin repeated softly.

The Plainsman stared at the mage, feeling horror creep over him. Raistlin stood before him coolly, his arms folded in the sleeves of his robe, his hood pulled up over his head. Riverwind looked at his dagger, considering the alternative. No, he couldn't do it. Not that way.

"Very well," he said, swallowing. He paused, dreading to go downstairs and face the others. But the sounds of death in the street were growing louder. Riverwind turned abruptly and left the brothers alone.

"I will die fighting," Caramon said to Raistlin, trying to speak in a matter-of-fact tone. After the first few words, though, the big warrior's voice broke. "Promise me, Raist, you'll take this stuff if I'm . . . not there. . . ."

"There will be no need," Raistlin said simply. "I have not the strength to survive a battle of this magnitude. I will die within my magic."

Tanis and Gilthanas fought their way through the crowd, the stronger half-elf holding onto the elf as they shoved and clawed and pushed through the panicked masses. Time and again, they ducked for shelter from the dragons. Gilthanas wrenched his knee, fell into a doorway, and was forced to limp in agony, leaning on Tanis's shoulder.

The half-elf breathed a prayer of thankfulness when he saw the Red Dragon Inn, a prayer that changed to a curse when he saw the black reptilian forms surging around the front. He dragged Gilthanas, who had been stumbling along blindly, exhausted by pain, back into a recessed doorway.

"Gilthanas!" Tanis shouted. "The Inn! It's under attack!"

Gilthanas raised glassy eyes and stared uncomprehendingly. Then, apparently understanding, he sighed and shook his head. "Laurana," he gasped, and he pushed himself forward, trying to stagger out of the doorway. "We've got to reach them." He collapsed in Tanis's arms.

"Stay here," the half-elf said, helping him sit down. "You're not capable of moving. I'll try and get through. I'll go around the block and come in from the back."

Tanis ran forward, darting in and out of doorways, hiding in the wreckage. He was about a block from the Inn when he heard a hoarse shout. Turning to look, he saw Flint gesturing wildly. Tanis dashed across the street.

"What is it?" he asked.

"Why aren't you with the others—" The half-elf stopped. "Oh, no," he whispered.

The dwarf, his face smudged with ash and streaked with tears, knelt beside Tasslehoff. The kender was pinned beneath a beam that had fallen in the street. Tas's face, looking like the face of a wise child, was ashen, his skin clammy.

"Blasted, rattle-brained kender," Flint moaned. "Had to go and let a house fall on him." The dwarf's hands were torn and bleeding from trying to lift a beam that would take three men or one Caramon to get off the kender. Tanis put his hand to Tas's neck. The lifebeat was very weak.

"Stay with him!" Tanis said unnecessarily. "I'm going to the Inn. I'll bring Caramon!"

Flint looked up at him grimly, then glanced over at the Inn. Both could hear the yells of the draconians, see their weapons flash in the glare of the firelight. Occasionally an unnatural light flared from the Inn—Raistlin's magic. The dwarf shook his head. He knew Tanis was about as capable of returning with Caramon as he was of flying.

But Flint managed to smile. "Sure, lad, I'll stay with him. Farewell, Tanis."

Tanis swallowed, tried to answer, then gave up and ran on down the street.

Raistlin, coughing until he could barely stand, wiped blood from his lips and drew a small, black leather pouch from the innermost pockets of his robes. He had just one spell left and barely energy enough to cast it. Now, his hands shaking with fatigue, he tried to scatter the contents of the little pouch into a pitcher of wine he had ordered Caramon to bring him before the battle started. But his hand trembled violently, and his coughing spasms doubled him over.

Then he felt another hand grasp his own. Looking up, he saw Laurana. She took the pouch from his frail fingers. Her own hand was stained with the dark green† draconian blood.

Draconian blood is green primarily because the creatures' blood is copper based.—TRH

"What's this?" she asked.

"Ingredients for a spell." The mage choked. "Pour it into the wine." Laurana nodded and poured in the mixture as instructed. It vanished instantly.

"Don't drink it," the mage warned when the coughing spasm passed. Laurana looked at him. "What is it?"

"A sleeping potion," Raistlin whispered, his eyes glittering.

Laurana smiled wryly. "You don't think we're going to be able to get to sleep tonight?"

"Not that kind," Raistlin answered, staring at her intently. "This one feigns death. The heartbeat slows to almost nothing, the breathing nearly stops, the skin grows cold and pale, the limbs stiffen."

Laurana's eyes opened wide. "Why—" she began.

"To be used as a last resort. The enemy thinks you are dead, leaves you on the field—if you are lucky. If not—"

"If not?" she prompted, her face pale.

"Well, a few have been known to waken on their

own funeral pyres," Raistlin said coolly. "I don't believe that is likely to happen to us, however."

Breathing more easily, he sat down, ducking involuntarily as a spent arrow fluttered overhead and fell to the floor behind him. He saw Laurana's hand tremble then and realized she was not as calm as she was forcing herself to appear.

"Are you intending that we take this?" she asked.

"It will save us from being tortured by draconians."

"How do you know that?"

"Trust me," the mage said with a slight smile.

Laurana glanced at him and shivered. Absently, she wiped blood-stained fingers on her leather armor. The blood did not come off, but she didn't notice. An arrow thudded next to her. She didn't even start, just stared at it dully.

Caramon appeared, stumbling out of the smoke of the burning common room. He was bleeding from an arrow wound in the shoulder, his own red blood mingling oddly with the green blood of his enemy.

"They're breaking down the front door," he said, breathing heavily."Riverwind ordered us back here."

"Listen!" Raistlin warned. "That's not the only place they're breaking in!" There was a splintering crash at the door leading from the kitchen to the back alley.

Ready to defend themselves, Caramon and Laurana whirled just as the door shattered. A tall, dark figure entered.

"Tanis!" Laurana cried. Sheathing her weapon, she ran toward him.

"Laurana!" he breathed. Catching her in his arms, he held her close, nearly sobbing in his relief. Then Caramon flung his huge arms around both of them.

"How is everyone?" Tanis asked, when he could talk.

"So far, so good," Caramon said, peering behind Tanis. His face fell when he saw he was alone. "Where's—"

"Sturm's lost," Tanis said wearily. "Flint and Tas are across the street. The kender's pinned under a beam. Gilthanas is about two blocks away. He's hurt," Tanis told Laurana, "not badly, but he couldn't make it any farther."

"Welcome, Tanis," Raistlin whispered, coughing. "You have come in time to die with us."

Tanis looked at the pitcher, saw the black pouch lying near it, and stared at Raistlin in sudden shock.

"No," he said firmly. "We're not going to die. At least not like th—" he broke off abruptly. "Get everyone together."

Caramon lumbered off, yelling at the top of his lungs. Riverwind ran in from the common room where he had been firing the enemy's arrows back at them, his own having run out long ago. The others followed him, smiling hopefully at Tanis.

The sight of their faith in him infuriated the half-elf. Someday, he thought, I'm going to fail them. Maybe I already have. He shook his head angrily.

"Listen!" he shouted, trying to make himself heard over the noise of the draconians outside. "We can try and escape out the back! Only a small force is attacking the Inn. The main part of the army isn't in the city yet."

"Somebody's after *us,*" Raistlin murmured.

Tanis nodded. "So it would appear. We haven't much time. If we can make it into the hills—"

He suddenly fell silent, raising his head. They all fell silent, listening, recognizing the shrill scream, the creak of giant leather wings, coming nearer and nearer.

"Take cover!" Riverwind yelled. But it was too late.

There was a screaming whine and a boom. The Inn, three stories tall and built of stone and wood, shook as if it were made of sand and sticks. The air exploded with dust and debris. Flames erupted outside. Above them, they could hear the sound of wood splitting and breaking, the thud of falling timber. The building began to collapse in on itself.

The companions watched in stunned fascination, paralyzed by the sight of the gigantic ceiling beams shuddering beneath the strain as the roof caved in onto the upper floors.

"Get out!" Tanis shouted. "The whole place is—"

The beam directly above the half-elf gave a great groan, then split and cracked. Gripping Laurana around the waist, Tanis flung her as far from him as he could and saw Elistan, standing near the front of the Inn, catch her in his arms.

As the huge beam above Tanis gave way with a shuddering snap, he heard the mage shriek strange words. Then he was falling, falling into blackness—and it seemed that the world fell on top of him.

Sturm rounded a corner to see the Inn of the Red Dragon collapse in a cloud of flame and smoke as a dragon soared in the sky above it. The knight's heart beat wildly with grief and fear.

He ducked into a doorway, hiding in the shadows as some draconians passed him—laughing and talking in their cold, guttural language. Apparently they assumed this job was finished and were seeking other amusement. Three others, he noticed—dressed in blue uniforms, not red—appeared extremely upset at the Inn's destruction, shaking their fist at the red dragon overhead.

Sturm felt the weakness of despair sweep over him. He sagged against the door, watching the draconians dully, wondering what to do next. Were they all still in there? Perhaps they had escaped. Then his heart gave a painful bound. He saw a flash of white.

"Elistan!" he cried, watching the cleric emerge from the rubble, dragging someone with him. The draconians, swords drawn, ran toward the cleric, calling out in Common for him to surrender. Sturm yelled the challenge of a Solamnic knight to an enemy and ran out from his doorway. The draconians whirled about, considerably disconcerted to see the knight.

Sturm became dimly aware that another figure was running with him. Glancing to his side, he saw the flash of firelight off a metal helm and heard the dwarf roaring. Then, from a doorway, he heard words of magic.†

Gilthanas, unable to stand without help, had crawled out and was pointing at the draconians, reciting his spell. Flaming darts leaped from his hands. One of the creatures fell over, clutching its burning chest. Flint leaped on another, beating it over the head with a rock, while Sturm felled the other draconian with a blow from his fists. Sturm caught Elistan in his arms as the man staggered forward. The cleric was carrying a woman.

Elven magic and human magic is all the same magic. There may be some cultural differences in their approaches but the same Towers of High Sorcery lord over both. —TRH

"Laurana!" Gilthanas cried from the doorway.

Dazed and sick from the smoke, the elfmaid

lifted her glazed eyes. "Gilthanas?" she murmured. Then, looking up, she saw the knight.

"Sturm," she said confusedly, pointing behind her vaguely. "Your sword, it's here. I saw it—"

Sure enough, Sturm saw a flash of silver, barely visible beneath the rubble. His sword, and next to it was Tanis's sword, the elven blade of Kith-Kanan. Moving aside piles of stone, Sturm reverently lifted the swords that lay like artifacts within a hideous, gigantic cairn. The knight listened for movement, calls, cries. There was only a dreadful silence.

"We've got to get out of here," he said slowly, without moving. He looked at Elistan, who was staring back at the wreckage, his face deathly pale. "The others?"

"They were all in there," Elistan said in a trembling voice. "And the half-elf . . ."

"Tanis?"

"Yes. He came through the back door, just before the dragon hit the Inn. They were all together, in the very center. I was standing beneath a doorway. Tanis saw the beam breaking. He threw Laurana. I caught her, then the ceiling collapsed on top of them. There's no way they could have—"

"I don't believe it!" Flint said fiercely, leaping into the rubble. Sturm grasped hold of him, yanked him back.

"Where's Tas?" the knight asked the dwarf sternly.

The dwarf's face fell. "Pinned under a beam," he said, his face gray with grief and sorrow. He clutched at his hair wildly, knocking off his helm. "I've got to go back to him. But I can't leave them—Caramon—" The dwarf began to cry, tears streaming into his beard. "That big, dumb ox! I need him. He can't do this to me! And Tanis, too!" The dwarf swore. "Damn it, I need them!"

Sturm put his hand on Flint's shoulder. "Go back to Tas. He needs you now. There are draconians roaming the streets. We'll be all—"

Laurana screamed, a terrifying, pitiful sound that pierced Sturm like a spear. Turning, he caught hold of her just as she started to rush into the debris.

"Laurana!" he cried. "Look at that! Look at it!" He shook her in his own anguish. "Nothing could be alive in there!"

"You don't know that!" she screamed at him in fury, tearing away from his grasp. Falling onto her hands and knees, she tried to lift one of the blackened stones. "Tanis!" she cried. The stone was so heavy, she could only move it a few inches.

Sturm watched, heartsick, uncertain what to do. Then he had his answer. Horns! Nearer and nearer. Hundreds, thousands of horns. The armies were invading. He looked at Elistan, who nodded in sorrowful understanding. Both men hurried over to Laurana.

"My dear," Elistan began gently, "there is nothing you can do for them. The living need you. Your brother is hurt, so is the kender. The draconians are invading. We must either escape now, and keep fighting these horrible monsters, or waste our lives in useless grief. Tanis gave his life for you, Laurana. Don't let it be a needless sacrifice."

Laurana stared up at him, her face black with soot and filth, streaked with tears and blood. She heard the horns, she heard Gilthanas calling, she heard Flint shouting something about Tasslehoff dying, she heard Elistan's words. And then the rain began, dripping from the skies as the heat of the dragonfire melted the snow, changing it to water.

The rain ran down her face, cooling her feverish skin.

"Help me, Sturm," she whispered through lips almost too numb to shape the words. He put his arm around her. She stood up, dizzy and sick with shock.

"Laurana!" her brother called. Elistan was right. The living needed her. She must go to him. Though she would rather lie down on this pile of rocks and die, she must go on. That was what Tanis would do. They needed her. She must go on.

"Farewell, Tanthalas," she whispered.

The rain increased, pouring down gently, as if the gods themselves wept for Tarsis the Beautiful.

Water dripped on his head. It was irritating, cold. Raistlin tried to roll over, out of the way of the water. But he couldn't move. There was a heavy weight pressing down on top of him. Panicking, he tried desperately to escape. As fear surged through his body, he came fully to consciousness. With

knowledge, panic vanished. Raistlin was in control once more and, as he had been taught, he forced himself to relax and study the situation.

He could see nothing. It was intensely dark, so he was forced to rely on his other senses. First, he had to get this weight off. He was being smothered and crushed. Cautiously he moved his arms. There was no pain, nothing appeared broken. Reaching up, he touched a body. Caramon, by the armor—and the smell. He sighed. He might have known. Using all his strength, Raistlin shoved his brother aside and crawled out from under him.

The mage breathed more easily, wiping water from his face. He located his brother's neck in the darkness and felt for the lifebeat. It was strong, the man's flesh was warm, his breathing regular. Raistlin lay back down on the floor in relief. At least, wherever he was, he wasn't alone.

Where was he? Raistlin reconstructed those last few terrifying moments. He remembered the beam splitting and Tanis throwing Laurana out from under it. He remembered casting a spell, the last one he had strength enough to manage. The magic coursed through his body, creating around him and those near him a force capable of shielding them from physical objects. He remembered Caramon hurling himself on top of him, the building collapsing around them, and a falling sensation.

Falling . . .

Ah, Raistlin understood. We must have crashed through the floor into the Inn's cellar. Groping around the stone floor, the mage suddenly realized he was soaked through. Finally, however, he found what he had been searching for—the Staff of Magius.† Its crystal was unbroken; only dragonfire could damage the Staff given him by Par-Salian in the Towers of High Sorcery.

"Shirak," whispered Raistlin, and the Staff flared into light. Sitting up, he glanced around. Yes, he was right. They were in the cellar of the Inn. Broken bottles of wine spilled their contents onto the floor. Casks of ale were split in two. It wasn't all water he had been lying in.

The mage flashed the light around the floor. There were Tanis, Riverwind, Goldmoon, and Tika, all huddled near Caramon. They seemed all right,

Raistlin's Staff of Magius was created long before it came down to its most famous owner, Magius, a Red-Robed wizard who was Huma Dragonbane's friend and follower. When the wizards at the Tower of High Sorcery tell the tale of Huma, they make Magius the hero and Huma a nice chap, all brawn and heart, relying on Magius to shape the course of the battle. The Knights of Solamnia, who generally distrust magic, tell the tale the other way around.

he thought, giving them a quick inspection. Around them lay scattered debris. Half of the beam slanted down through the rubble to rest on the stone floor. Raistlin smiled. A nice bit of work, that spell. Once more they were in his debt.

If we don't perish from the cold, he reminded himself bitterly. His body was shaking so he could barely hold the staff. He began to cough.This would be the death of him. They had to get out.

"Tanis," he called, reaching out to shake the half-elf.

Tanis lay crumpled at the very edge of Raistlin's magic, protective circle. He murmured and stirred. Raistlin shook him again. The half-elf cried out, reflexively covering his head with his arm.

"Tanis, you're safe," Raistlin whispered, coughing. "Wake up."

"What?" Tanis sat bolt upright, staring around him. "Where—" Then he remembered. "Laurana?"

"Gone." Raistlin shrugged. "You threw her out of danger—"

"Yes . . ." Tanis said, sinking back down. "And I heard you say words, magic—"

"That's why we're not crushed." Raistlin clutched his sopping wet robes around him, shivering, and drew nearer Tanis, who was staring around as if he'd fallen onto a moon.

"Where in the name of the Abyss—"

"We're in the cellar of the Inn," the mage said. "The floor gave way and dropped us down here." Tanis looked up. "By all the gods," he whispered in awe.

"Yes," Raistlin said, his gaze following Tanis's. "We're buried alive."

Beneath the ruins of the Red Dragon Inn, the companions took stock of their situation. It did not look hopeful. Goldmoon treated their injuries, which were not serious, thanks to Raistlin's spell. But they had no idea how long they had been unconscious or what was happening above them. Worse still, they had no idea how they could escape.

Caramon tried cautiously to move some of the rocks above their heads, but the whole structure creaked and groaned. Raistlin reminded him sharply that he had no energy to cast more spells,

and Tanis wearily told the big man to forget it. They sat in the water that was growing deeper all the time.

As Riverwind stated, it seemed to be a matter of what killed them first: lack of air, freezing to death, the Inn falling down on top of them, or drowning.

"We could shout for help," suggested Tika, trying to keep her voice steady.

"Add draconians to the list, then," Raistlin snapped. "They're the only creatures up there liable to hear you."

Tika's face flushed, and she brushed her hand quickly across her eyes. Caramon cast a reproachful glance at his brother, then put his arm around Tika and held her close. Raistlin gave them both a look of disgust.

"I haven't heard a sound up there," Tanis said, puzzled. "You'd think the dragons and the armies—" He stopped, his glance meeting Caramon's, both soldiers nodding slowly in sudden grim understanding.

"What?" asked Goldmoon, looking at them.

"We're behind enemy lines," Caramon said. "The armies of draconians occupy the town. And probably the land for miles and miles around. There's no way out, and nowhere to go if there were a way out."

As if to emphasize his words, the companions heard sounds above them. Guttural draconian voices that they had come to know all too well drifted down through to them.

"I tell you, this is a waste of time," whined another voice, goblin by the sound, speaking in Common. "There's no one alive in this mess."

"Tell that to the Dragon Highlord, you miserable dog-eaters," snarled the draconian. "I'm sure his lordship'll be interested in your opinion. Or rather, his dragon'll be interested. You have your orders. Now dig, all of you."

There were sounds of scraping, sounds of stones being dragged aside. Rivulets of dirt and dust started to sift down through the cracks. The big beam shivered slightly but held.

The companions stared at each other, almost holding their breaths, each remembering the strange draconians who had attacked the Inn. "Somebody's after us," Raistlin had said.

Caramon tells Tas in Time of the Twins *that he was once captured by goblins. Probably where he learned the language.—MW*

"What are we looking for in this rubble?" croaked a goblin in the goblin tongue. "Silver? Jewels?"

Tanis and Caramon, who spoke a little goblin,† strained to hear.

"Naw," said the first goblin, who had grumbled about orders. "Spies or some such wanted personally by the Dragon Highlord for questioning."

"In here?" the goblin asked in amazement.

"That's what *I* said," snarled his companion. "You saw how far I got. The lizardmen say they had them trapped in the Inn when the dragon hit it. Said none of them escaped, and so the Highlord figures they must still be here. If you ask me—the dracos screwed up and now we've got to pay for their mistakes."

The sounds of digging and of rock moving grew louder, as did the sound of goblin voices, occasionally punctuated by a sharp order in the guttural voice of the draconians. There must be fifty of them up there! Tanis thought, stunned.

Riverwind quietly lifted his sword out of the water and began wiping it dry. Caramon, his usually cheerful face somber, released Tika and found his sword. Tanis didn't have a sword, Riverwind tossed him his dagger. Tika started to draw her sword, but Tanis shook his head. They would be fighting in close quarters, and Tika needed lots of room.† The half-elf looked questioningly at Raistlin.

Of course, Tanis could have used Tika's sword if she was not going to use it, but it must not have occurred to him at the time. Besides, they are in the rubble of a collapsed Inn. There must be a frying pan Tika can swing around here somewhere with, apparently, much greater effect.—TRH

The mage shook his head. "I will try, Tanis," he whispered. "But I am very tired. Very tired. And I can't think, I can't concentrate." He bowed his head, shivering violently in his wet robes. He was exerting all his effort not to cough and give them away, muffling his choking in his sleeve.

One spell will finish him, if he gets that off, Tanis realized. Still, he may be luckier than the rest of us. At least he won't be taken alive.

The sounds above them grew louder and louder. Goblins are strong, tireless workers. They wanted to finish this job quickly, then get back to looting Tarsis. The companions waited in grim silence below. An almost steady stream of dirt and crushed rock dropped down upon them, along with fresh rainwater. They gripped their weapons. It was only a matter of minutes, maybe, before they were discovered.

Then, suddenly, there were new sounds. They heard the goblins yell in fear, the draconians shout to them, ordering them back to work. But they could hear the sounds of shovels and picks being dropped down onto the rocks above them, then the cursing of the draconians as they tried to stop what was apparently a full-scale goblin revolt.

And above the noise of the shrieking goblins rose a loud, clear, high pitched call, which was answered by another call farther away. It was like the call of an eagle, soaring above the plains at sunset. But this call was right above them.

There was a scream—a draconian. Then a rending sound—as if the body of the creature were being ripped apart. More screams, the clash of steel being drawn, another call and another answer—this one much nearer.

"What is that?" Caramon asked, his eyes wide. "It isn't a dragon. It sounds like—like some gigantic bird of prey!"

"Whatever it is, it's tearing the draconians to shreds!" Goldmoon said in awe as they listened. The screaming sounds stopped abruptly, leaving a silence behind that was almost worse. What new evil replaced the old?

Then came the sound of rocks and stones, mortar and timber being lifted and sent crashing to the streets. Whatever was up there was intent on reaching them!

"It's eaten all the draconians," whispered Caramon gruffly, "and now it's after us!"

Tika turned deathly white, clutching at Caramon's arm. Goldmoon gasped softly and even Riverwind appeared to lose some of his stoic composure, staring intently upward.

"Caramon," Raistlin said, shivering, "shut up!"

Tanis felt inclined to agree with the mage. "We're all scaring ourselves over noth—" he began. Suddenly there was a rending crash. Stone and rubble, mortar and timber clattered down around them. They scrambled for cover as a huge, clawed foot plunged through the debris, its talons gleaming in the light of Raistlin's staff.

Helplessly seeking shelter beneath broken beams or under the casks of ale, the companions watched in wonder as the gigantic claw extricated itself from

the rubble and withdrew, leaving behind it a wide, gaping hole.

All was silent. For a few moments, none of the companions dared move. But the silence remained unbroken.

"This is our chance," Tanis whispered loudly. "Caramon, see what's up there."

But the big warrior was already creeping out of his hiding place, moving across the rubble-strewn floor as best he could. Riverwind followed behind, his sword drawn.

"Nothing," said Caramon, puzzled, peering up.

Tanis, feeling naked without his sword, came over to stand beneath the hole, gazing upward. Then, to his amazement, a dark figure appeared above them, silhouetted against the burning sky. Behind the figure towered a large beast. They could just make out the head of a gigantic eagle, its eyes glittering in the firelight, its wickedly curved beak gleaming in the flames.

The companions shrank back, but it was too late. Obviously the figure had seen them. It stepped nearer. Riverwind thought—too late—of his bow. Caramon pulled Tika close with one hand, holding his sword in his other.

The figure, however, simply knelt down near the edge of the hole, being careful of its footing among the loose stones, and removed the hood covering its head.

"We meet again, Tanis Half-Elven," said a voice as cool and pure and distant as the stars.

8

Escape from Tarsis.
The story of the dragon orbs.

Dragons flew on their leathery wings above the gutted city of Tarsis as the draconian armies swarmed in to take possession. The task of the dragons was completed. Soon the Dragon Highlord would call them back, holding them in readiness for the next strike. But for now they could relax, drifting on the super-heated air currents rising from the burning town, picking off the occasional human foolish enough to come out of hiding. The red dragons floated in the sky, keeping in their well-organized flights, gliding and dipping in a wheeling dance of death.

No power on Krynn existed now that could stop them. They knew this and exulted in their victory. But occasionally something would occur to interrupt their dance. One flight leader, for example,

received a report of fighting near the wreckage of an inn. A young male red dragon, he led his flight to the site, muttering to himself about the inefficiency of the troop commanders. What could you expect, though, when the Dragon Highlord was a bloated hobgoblin who hadn't even courage enough to watch the takeover of a soft town like Tarsis?

The male red sighed, recalling the days of glory when Verminaard had led them personally, sitting astride the back of Pyros. He had been a Dragon Highlord! The red shook his head disconsolately. Ah, there was the battle. He could see it clearly now. Ordering his flight to stay airborne, he swooped in low for a better look.

"I command you! Stop!"

The red halted in his flight, staring upward in astonishment. The voice was strong and clear, and it came from the figure of a Dragon Highlord. But the Dragon Highlord was certainly not Toede! This Dragon Highlord, although heavily cloaked and dressed in the shining mask and dragon-scale armor of the Highlords, was human, to judge by the voice, not hobgoblin. But where had this Highlord come from? And why? For, to the red dragon's amazement, he saw that the Highlord rode upon a huge blue dragon and was attended by several flights of blues.

"What is your bidding, Highlord?" the red asked sternly. "And by what right do you stop us, you who have no business in this part of Krynn?"

"The fate of mankind is my business,† whether it be in this part of Krynn or another," the Dragon Highlord returned. "And the might of my sword-arm gives me all the right I need to command you, gallant red. As for my bidding, I ask that you capture these pitiful humans, do not kill them. They are wanted for questioning. Bring them to me. You will be well rewarded."

Another allusion to A Christmas Carol *by Charles Dickens. This one turns the quote from meaning good to meaning harm.—MW*

"Look!" called a young female red. "Griffons!"

The Dragon Highlord gave an exclamation of astonishment and displeasure. The dragons looked down to see three griffons sweeping up out of the smoke. Not quite half the size of a red dragon, griffons were noted for their ferocity. Draconian troops scattered like ashes in the wind before the creatures, whose sharp talons and ripping beaks were tearing

the heads from those reptile-men unlucky enough to have been caught in their path.

The red snarled in hatred and prepared to dive, his flight with him, but the Dragon Highlord swooped down in front of him, causing him to pull up.

"I tell you, they must not be killed!" the Dragon Highlord said sternly.

"But they're escaping!" the red hissed furiously.

"Let them," the Highlord said coldly. "They will not go far. I relieve you of your duty in this. Return to the main body. And if that idiot Toede mentions this, tell him that the secret of how he lost the blue crystal staff did not die with Lord Verminaard. The memory of Fewmaster Toede lives on—in *my* mind—and will become known to others if he dares to challenge me!"

The Dragon Highlord saluted, then wheeled the large blue dragon in the air to fly swiftly after the griffons, whose tremendous speed had allowed them to escape with their riders well past the city gates. The red watched the blues disappear through the night skies in pursuit.

"Shouldn't we give chase as well?" asked the female red.

"No," the red male replied thoughtfully, his fiery eyes on the figure of the Dragon Highlord dwindling in the distance. "I will not cross *that* one!"

"Your thanks are not necessary, or even wanted," Alhana Starbreeze cut off Tanis's halting, exhausted words in midsentence. The companions rode through the slashing rain on the backs of three griffons, clutching their feathered necks with their hands, peering apprehensively down at the dying city falling rapidly away beneath them.

"And you may not wish to extend them after you hear me out," Alhana stated coldly, glancing at Tanis, riding behind her. "I rescued you for my own purposes. I need warriors to help me find my father. We fly to Silvanesti."

"But that's impossible!" Tanis gasped. "We must meet our friends! Fly to the hills. We *can't* go to Silvanesti, Alhana. There's too much at stake! If we can find these dragon orbs, we have a chance to destroy these foul creatures and end this war. *Then* we can go to Silvanesti—"

"*Now* we are going to Silvanesti," Alhana retorted. "You have no choice in the matter,† Half-Elven. My griffons obey my command and mine alone. They would tear you apart, as they did those dragonmen, if I gave the order."

High-handed of our elven princess, to be sure, but she did do both Margaret and me a large favor—she helped us break up our over-large group of heroes into two far more manageable groups. From this point on, the story in the novels was the driving force behind DRAGONLANCE *as opposed to the storyline the game modules were following, and I believe both improved tremendously in the bargain.—TRH*

"Someday the elves will wake up and find they are members of a vast family," Tanis said, his voice shaking with anger. "No longer can they be treated as the spoiled elder child who is given everything while the rest of us wait for the crumbs."

"What gifts we received from the gods we earned. You humans and *half*-humans"—the scorn in her voice cut like a dagger—"had these same gifts and threw them away in your greed for more. We are capable of fighting for our own survival without your help. As to your survival, that matters little to us."

"You seem willing enough to accept our help now!"

"For which you will be well-rewarded," Alhana returned.

"There is not steel nor jewels enough in Silvanesti to pay us—"

"You seek the dragon orbs," Alhana interrupted. "I know where one is located. It is in Silvanesti."

Tanis blinked. For a moment, he could think of nothing to say, but the mention of the dragon orb brought back thoughts of his friend. "Where's Sturm?" he asked Alhana. "The last I saw him, he was with you."

"I don't know," she replied. "We parted. He was going to the Inn, to find you. I called my griffons to me."

"Why didn't you let him take you to Silvanesti if you needed warriors?"

"That is none of your concern." Alhana turned her back to Tanis, who sat wordlessly, too tired to think clearly. Then he heard a voice shouting at him, barely distinguishable through the feathery rustle† of the griffon's mighty wings.

A griffon will probably never take you by surprise. In order to keep its powerful body in the air, it must beat its gigantic wings hard and loud.

It was Caramon. The warrior was shouting and pointing behind them. What now? Tanis thought wearily.

They had left behind the smoke and the storm clouds that covered Tarsis, flying out into the clear night sky. The stars gleamed above them, their

sparkling lights shining as cold as diamonds, emphasizing the gaping black holes in the night sky where the two constellations had wheeled in their track above the world. The moons, silver and red, had set, but Tanis did not need their light to recognize the dark shapes blotting out the shining stars.

"Dragons," he said to Alhana. "Following us."

Tanis could never afterward clearly remember the nightmare flight from Tarsis. It was hours of chill, biting wind that made even death by a dragon's flaming breath seem appealing. It was hours of panic, staring behind to see the dark shapes gaining on them, staring until his eyes watered and the tears froze on his cheeks, yet unable to turn away. It was stopping at dusk, worn out from fear and fatigue, to sleep in a cave on a high rock cliff. It was waking at dawn only to see—as they soared through the air again, the dark, winged shapes still behind them.

Few living creatures can outfly the eagle-winged griffon. But the dragons—blue dragons, the first they had ever seen—were always on the horizon, always pursuing, allowing no rest during the day, forcing the companions into hiding at night when the exhausted griffons must sleep. There was little food, only quith-pa, a dried-fruit type of iron ration that sustains the body, but does little to ease hunger—which Alhana carried and shared. But even Caramon was too weary and dispirited to eat much.

The only thing Tanis remembered vividly occurred on the second night of their journey. He was telling the small group huddled around a fire in a damp and cheerless cave about the kender's discovery in the library at Tarsis.†At the mention of the dragon orbs, Raistlin's eyes glittered, his thin face lit from within by an eager, intense glow.

The fact that Tas seems to remember picking up the glasses in two separate locations should come as no surprise to anyone who has dealt with kenders.

They are wonderful creatures at locating interesting objects but never remember where they picked the darn things up. This explains why things they have "borrowed" never seem to make it back to their original owners.—TRH

"Dragon orbs?" he repeated softly.

"I thought you might know of them," Tanis said. "What are they?"

Raistlin did not answer immediately. Wrapped in both his own and his brother's cloak, he lay as near the fire as possible, and still his frail body shook with the chill. The mage's golden eyes stared at Alhana, who sat somewhat apart from the group, deigning to share the cave but not the conversation.

Now, however, it seemed she half-turned her head, listening.

"You said there is a dragon orb in Silvanesti," the mage whispered, glancing at Tanis. "Surely I am not the one to ask."

"I know little about it," Alhana said, turning her pale face to the firelight. "We keep it as a relic of bygone days, more a curiosity than anything else. Who believed humans† would once again wake this evil and bring the dragons back to Krynn?"

The elves have always blamed the humans for the ills of the world and often with good cause.—TRH

Before Raistlin could answer, Riverwind spoke angrily. "You have no proof it was humans!"

Alhana swept the Plainsman an imperious glance. She did not reply, considering it beneath her to argue with a barbarian.

Tanis sighed. The Plainsman had little use for elves. It had taken long days before he had come to trust Tanis, longer for Gilthanas and Laurana. Now, just as Riverwind seemed to be able to overcome his inherited prejudices, Alhana with her equal prejudices had inflicted new wounds.

"Very well, Raistlin," Tanis said quietly, "tell us what you know of the dragon orbs."

"Bring my drink, Caramon," the mage ordered. Bringing the cup of hot water as commanded, Caramon set it before his brother. Raistlin propped himself up on one elbow and mixed herbs into the water. The strange, acrid odor filled the air. Raistlin, grimacing, sipped the bitter mixture as he talked.

"During the Age of Dreams, when those of my order were respected and revered upon Krynn, there were five Towers of High Sorcery."The mage's voice sank, as if recalling painful memories. His brother sat staring at the rock floor of the cave, his face grave. Tanis, seeing the shadow fall across both twins, wondered again what had happened within the Tower of High Sorcery to change their lives so drastically. It was useless to ask, he knew. Both had been forbidden to discuss it.†

But we aren't. You can read the story in Margaret's novel The Soulforge.

Raistlin paused a moment before he continued, then drew a deep breath. "When the Second Dragon Wars came, the highest of my order met together in the greatest of the Towers—the Tower of Palanthas—and created the dragon orbs."

Raistlin's eyes grew unfocused, his whispering voice ceased a moment. When he spoke next, it was

as if recounting a moment he was reliving in his mind. Even his voice changed, becoming stronger, deeper, clearer. He no longer coughed. Caramon looked at him in astonishment.

"Those of the White Robes entered the chamber at the top of the Tower first, as the silver moon, Solinari, rose. Then Lunitari appeared in the sky, dripping with blood, and those of the Red Robes entered. Finally the black disk, Nuitari,† a hole of darkness among the stars, could be seen by those who sought it, and the Black Robes walked into the chamber.

"It was a strange moment in history, when all enmity between the Robes was suppressed. It would come but one more time in the world, when the wizards joined together in the Lost Battles, but that time could not be foreseen. It was enough to know that, for now, the great evil must be destroyed. For at last we had seen that evil was intent on destroying *all* the magic of the world, so that only its own would survive! Some there were among the Black Robes, who might have tried to ally with this great power"—Tanis saw Raistlin's eyes burn—"but soon realized they would not be masters of it, only its slaves. And so the dragon orbs were born, on a night when all three moons were full in the sky."

"*Three* moons?"† Tanis asked softly, but Raistlin did not hear him and continued to speak in the voice not his own.

"Great and powerful magic was worked that night—so powerful that few could withstand it and they collapsed, their physical and mental strength drained. But that morning, five dragon orbs stood upon pedestals, glistening with light, dark with shadows. All but one were taken from Palanthas and carried, in great peril, to each of the other four Towers. Here they helped rid the world of the Queen of Darkness."

The feverish gleam faded from Raistlin's eyes. His shoulders slumped, his voice sank, and he began to cough, violently. The others stared at him in breathless silence.

Finally Tanis cleared his throat. "What do you mean, three moons?"

Raistlin looked up dully. "Three moons?" he whispered. "I know nothing of three moons.† What were we discussing?"

This is the first time in the Chronicles that Nuitari, the third moon, has been mentioned. Most people on Krynn do not even know the third moon exists.

The three moons may be the residences of the three gods, called the Three Brothers by wizards, or they may be the gods themselves. Lunitari is the daughter of Gilean. Solinari is the son of Paladine. Nuitari is the son of Takhisis and Sargonnas. Although the gods obviously have children, gender per se may not have much meaning for gods. Solinari, the white moon, influences good magic on Krynn. Lunitari influences neutral magic, and Nuitari reigns over dark magic.

If Sturm were here, he would know about the three moons, for they are mentioned in "The Song of Huma." As it is, Raistlin is obviously lying. He would not have come so far in magic and not have known about them.

"Dragon orbs. You told us how they were created. How did you—" Tanis stopped, seeing Raistlin sink onto his pallet.

"I have told you nothing," Raistlin said irritably. "What are you talking about?"

Tanis glanced at the others. Riverwind shook his head. Caramon bit his lip and looked away, his face drawn with worry.

"We were speaking of the dragon orbs," Goldmoon said. "You were going to tell us what you knew of them."

Raistlin wiped blood from his mouth. "I do not know much," he said wearily, shrugging. "The dragon orbs were created by the high mages. Only the most powerful of my order could use them. It was said that great evil would come to those not strong in magic who tried to command the orbs. Beyond that, I know nothing. All knowledge of the dragon orbs perished during the Lost Battles. Two, it was said, were destroyed in the Fall of the Towers of High Sorcery, destroyed rather than let the rabble have them. Knowledge of the other three died with their wizards." His voice died. Sinking back onto his pallet, exhausted, he fell asleep.

"The Lost Battles, three moons, Raistlin talking with a strange voice. None of this makes sense," Tanis muttered.

"I don't believe any of it!" Riverwind said coldly. He shook out their furs, preparing to sleep.

Tanis was starting to follow his example when he saw Alhana creep from the shadows of the cave and come to stand next to Raistlin. Staring down at the sleeping mage, her hands twisted together.

"Strong in magic!" she whispered in a voice filled with fear. "My father!"

Tanis looked at her in sudden understanding.

"You don't think your father tried to use the orb?"

"I am afraid," Alhana whispered, wringing her hands. "He said he alone could fight the evil and keep it from our land. He must have meant—" Swiftly she bent down near Raistlin. "Wake him!" she commanded, her black eyes flaring. "I must know! Wake him and make him tell me what the danger is!"

Caramon pulled her back, gently but firmly. Alhana glared at him, her beautiful face twisted in

fear and rage, and it seemed for a moment as if she might strike him, but Tanis reached her side and caught hold of her hand.

"Lady Alhana," he said calmly, "it would do no good to wake him. He has told us everything *he* knows. As for that other voice, he obviously remembers nothing about what it said."

"I've seen it happen to Raist before," Caramon said in low tones, "as if he becomes someone else.† But it always leaves him exhausted and he never remembers."

This is, of course, Fistandantilus speaking.—MW

Alhana jerked her hand away from Tanis's, her face resuming its cold, pure, marble stillness. She whirled and walked to the front of the cave. Catching hold of the blanket Riverwind had hung to hide the fire's light, she nearly tore it down as she flung it aside and stalked outdoors.

"I'll stand first watch," Tanis told Caramon. "You get some sleep."

"I'll stay up with Raist awhile," the big man said, spreading out his pallet next to his frail twin's. Tanis followed Alhana outside.

The griffons slept soundly, their heads buried on the soft feathers of their necks, taloned front feet clutching the cliff edge securely. For a moment he could not find Alhana in the darkness, then he saw her, leaning against a huge boulder, weeping bitterly, her head buried in her arms.

The proud Silvanesti woman would never forgive him if he saw her weak and vulnerable. Tanis ducked back behind the blanket.

"I'll stand watch!" he called out loudly before he walked outside again. Lifting the blanket, he saw, without seeming to, Alhana start up and wipe her hands hurriedly across her face. She turned her back to him, and he walked slowly toward her, giving her time to pull herself together.

"The cave was stifling," she said in a low voice. "I could not bear it. I had to come out for a breath of air."

"I have first watch," Tanis said. He paused, then added, "You seem afraid your father might have tried to use this dragon orb. Surely he would know its history. If I remember what I know of your people, he was a magic-user."

"He knew where the orb came from," Alhana said, her voice quivering before she could regain

control. "The young mage was right when he spoke of the Lost Battles and the destruction of the Towers. But he was wrong when he said the other three orbs were lost. One was brought to Silvanesti by my father for safe-keeping."

"What *were* the Lost Battles?" Tanis asked, leaning on the rocks next to Alhana.

"Is no lore at all kept in Qualinost?" she returned, regarding Tanis with scorn. "What barbarians you have become since mingling with humans!"

"Say the fault is my own," Tanis said, "that I did not pay enough heed to the Loremaster."†

"Loremaster" is more usually a term that the dwarves use for their bards who retain the clan lore, but apparently Tanis's teacher in Qualinesti was also referred to as the Loremaster. It's also a name sometimes given to Astinus.

Alhana glanced at him, suspecting him of being sarcastic. Seeing his serious face and not particularly wanting him to leave her alone, she decided to answer his question. "As Istar rose during the Age of Might to greater and greater glories, the Kingpriest of Istar and his clerics became increasingly jealous of the magic-users' power. The clerics no longer saw the need for magic in the world, fearing it—of course—as something they could not control. Magic-users themselves, although respected, were never widely trusted, even those wearing the white robes. It was a simple matter for the priests to stir the people against the wizards. As times grew more and more evil, the priests placed the blame upon the magic-users. The Towers of High Sorcery, where the magicians must pass their final, grueling tests, were where the powers of the mages rested. The Towers became natural targets. Mobs attacked them, and it was as your young friend said: for only the second time in their history, the Robes came together to defend their last bastions of strength."

"But how could they be defeated?" Tanis said incredulously.

"Can you ask that, knowing what you do of your mage friend? Powerful he is, but he must have rest. Even the strongest must have time to renew their spells, recommit them to memory. Even the eldest of the order—wizards whose might has not been seen on Krynn since—had to sleep and spend hours reading their spellbooks. And then, too, as now, the number of magic-users was small. There are few who dare take the tests in the Towers of High Sorcery, knowing that to fail is to die."

"Failure means death?" Tanis said softly.

"Yes," Alhana replied. "Your friend is very brave, to have taken the Test so young. Very brave, or very ambitious. Didn't he ever tell you?"

"No," Tanis murmured. "He never speaks of it. But go on."

Alhana shrugged. "When it became clear that the battle was hopeless, the wizards themselves destroyed two of the Towers. The blasts devastated the countryside for miles around.† Only three remained—the Tower of Istar, the Tower of Palanthas, and the Tower of Wayreth. But the terrible destruction of the other two Towers scared the Kingpriest. He granted the wizards in the Towers of Istar and Palanthas safe passage from these cities if they left the Towers undamaged, for the wizards could have destroyed the two cities, as the Kingpriest well knew.

Actually, before the mages at the Tower at Daltigoth were ready, a mob arrived and set fire to it, casting it into ruin. They succeeded with the other, perhaps all too well—the location now is known only as the Ruins, and kender are the only ones who go there (they use the stone for building).

"And so the mages traveled to the one Tower which was never threatened—the Tower of Wayreth in the Kharolis Mountains. To Wayreth they came to nurse their wounds and to nurture the small spark of magic still left in the world. Those spellbooks they could not take with them—for the number of books was vast and many were bound with spells of protection—were given to the great library at Palanthas, and there they still remain, according to the lore of my people."

The silver moon had risen, its moonbeams graced their daughter with a beauty that took Tanis's breath away, even as its coldness pierced his heart.

"What do you know of a third moon?" he asked, staring into the night sky, shivering. "A black moon . . ."

"Little," Alhana replied. "The magic-user draws power from the moons: the White Robes from Solinari, the Red Robes from Lunitari. There is, according to lore, a moon that gives the Black Robes† their power, but only they know its name or how to find it in the sky."

It was Tracy and particularly Margaret who pulled all the pieces of Raistlin's evolution together and made him one of the most beloved figures, both in the initial trilogy and particularly in the second trilogy. Margaret always had a thing for men in black (she had an autographed picture of Darth Vader on her desk when I first met her), and Raistlin is among her personal favorites of the group.
—Jeff Grubb

Raistlin knew its name, Tanis thought, or at least that other voice knew it. But he did not speak this aloud.

"How did your father get the dragon orb?"

"My father, Lorac, was an apprentice," Alhana replied softly, turning her face to the silver moon. "He traveled to the Tower of High Sorcery at Istar for the Tests, which he took and survived. It was

there he first saw the dragon orb." She fell silent for a moment. "I am going to tell you what I have never told anyone, and what he has never told, except to me. I tell you only because you have a right to know what—what to expect.

"During the Tests, the dragon orb . . ."—Alhana hesitated, seeming to search for the right words—"*spoke* to him, to his mind. It feared some terrible calamity was approaching. 'You must not leave me here in Istar,' it told him. 'If so, I will perish and the world will be lost.' My father—I suppose you could say he stole the dragon orb, although he saw himself as rescuing it.

"The Tower of Istar was abandoned. The Kingpriest moved in and used it for his own purposes. Finally the mages left the Tower of Palanthas." Alhana shivered. "Its story is a terrible one. The Regent of Palanthas, a disciple of the Kingpriest, arrived at the Tower to seal the gates shut—so he said. But all could see his eyes lingering on the beautiful Tower greedily, for legends of the wonders within—both fair and evil—had spread throughout the land.

"The Wizard of the White closed the Tower's slender gates of gold and locked them with a silver key. The Regent stretched out his hand, eager for the key, when one of the Black Robes appeared in a window in one of the upper stories.

"'The gates will remain closed and the halls empty until the day when the master of both the past and the present returns with power,' he cried. Then the evil mage leaped out, hurling himself down at the gates. As the barbs pierced the black robes, he cast a curse upon the Tower. His blood poured down on the ground, the silver and golden gates withered and twisted and turned to black. The shimmering tower of white and red faded to ice-gray stone, its black minarets crumbling to dust.

"The Regent and the people fled in terror. To this day, no one has dared enter the Tower of Palanthas—or even approach its gates. It was after the cursing of the Tower that my father brought the dragon orb to Silvanesti."

"But surely your father knew something about the orb before he took it," Tanis persisted. "How to use it—"

"If so, he did not speak of it," Alhana said wearily, "for that is all I know. I must rest now. Good-night," she said to Tanis without looking at him.

"Good-night, Lady Alhana," Tanis said gently. "Rest easily this night. And don't worry. Your father is wise and has lived through much. I'm certain everything is all right."

Alhana started to sweep past without a word, then, hearing the sympathy in his voice, she hesitated.

"Though he passed the Test," she said so softly Tanis had to step closer to hear, "he was not as powerful in his magic as your young friend is now. And if he thought the dragon orb was our only hope, I fear—" Her voice broke.

"The dwarves have a saying." Sensing for a moment that the barriers between them had been lowered, Tanis put his arm around Alhana's slender shoulders and drew her close. "'Trouble borrowed will be paid back with interest compounded on sorrow.' Don't worry. We're with you."

Alhana did not answer. She let herself be comforted for just an instant, then, slipping free of his grasp, walked to the entrance of the cave. There she stopped and looked back.

"You are worried about your friends," she said. "Do not be. They escaped the city and are safe. Though the kender was close to death for a time, he survived, and now they travel to Ice Wall in search of a dragon orb."

"How do you know this?" Tanis gasped.

"I have told you all I can." Alhana shook her head.

"Alhana! How do you know?" Tanis asked sternly.

Her pale cheeks stained with pink, Alhana murmured, "I—I gave the knight a Starjewel. He does not know its power, of course, nor how to use it. I don't know why I gave it to him, even, except—"

"Except what?" Tanis asked, amazed beyond belief.

"He was so gallant, so brave. He risked his life to help me, and he didn't even know who I was. He helped me because I was in trouble. And—" Her eyes glimmered. "And he wept, when the dragons killed the people. I've never seen an adult weep before. Even when the dragons came and drove us from our home, we did not weep. I think, perhaps, we've forgotten how."

Then, as if realizing she had said too much, she hastily pulled aside the blanket and entered the cave.

"In the name of the gods!" Tanis breathed. A Star-jewel!† What a rare and priceless gift! A gift exchanged by elven lovers forced to part, the jewel creates a bond between souls. Thus linked, they share the innermost emotions of the loved one and can grant strength to each other in times of need. But never before in Tanis's long life, had the half-elf heard of a Starjewel being given to a human. What would it do to a human? What kind of effect would it have? And Alhana—she could never love a human, never return love. This must be some sort of blind infatuation. She had been frightened, alone. No, this could only end in sorrow, unless something changed drastically among the elves or within Alhana herself.

Even as Tanis's heart expanded with relief to know Laurana and the others were safe, it contracted with fear and grief for Sturm.

I originally created the Star-jewel for my galactic fantasy series, The Star of the Guardians. *That series was not yet sold to a publisher, so like many other artists before me, I robbed myself.—MW*

9

Silvanesti. Entering the dream.

The third day, they continued their journey, flying into the sunrise. They had lost the dragons, apparently, although Tika, keeping watch behind, thought she could see black dots upon the horizon. And that afternoon, as the sun was sinking behind them, they neared the river known as Thon-Thalas—Lord's River—which divided the outside world from Silvanesti.

All of his life, Tanis had heard of the wonder and beauty of the ancient Elven Home, though the elves of Qualinesti spoke of it without regret. They did not miss the lost wonders of Silvanesti, for the wonders themselves became a symbol of the differences that had developed between the elven kin.

The elves in Qualinesti lived in harmony with nature, developing and enhancing its beauty. They

built their homes among the aspens, magically gilding the trunks with silver and gold. They built their dwellings of shimmering rose quartz, and invited nature to come dwell with them.

The Silvanesti, however, loved uniqueness and diversity in all objects. Not seeing this uniqueness existing naturally, they reshaped nature to conform to their ideal. They had patience and they had time, for what were centuries to elves whose life spans measured in the hundreds of years? And so they reformed entire forests, pruning and digging, forcing the trees and flowers into fantastic gardens of incredible beauty.

They did not 'build' dwellings, but carved and molded the marble rock that existed naturally in their land into such strange and wondrous shapes that—in the years before the races were estranged—dwarven craftsmen traveled thousands of miles to view them, and then could do nothing but weep at the rare beauty. And, it was said, a human who wandered into the gardens of Silvanesti could not leave, but stayed forever, enraptured, caught in a beautiful dream.

All this was known to Tanis only through legend, of course, for none of the Qualinesti had set foot in their ancient home since the Kinslayer wars. No human, it was believed, had been allowed in Silvanesti since a hundred years before that.†

Tanis is primarily working from the limited knowledge that he has of Silvanost and the lands of Silvanesti when he says this. In all likelihood,there were many others who entered the land in the centuries since the Kinslayer Wars, but none of them were welcome guests and many of those never were known outside the borders of Silvanesti again.—TRH

"What about the stories," Tanis asked Alhana as they flew above the aspens on the backs of the griffons, "the stories of humans trapped by the beauty of Silvanesti, unable to leave? Do my friends dare go to this land?"

Alhana glanced back at him.

"I knew humans were weak," she said coldly, "but I did not think they were *that* weak. It is true humans do not come to Silvanesti, but that is because we keep them out. We certainly wouldn't want to keep any in. If I thought there was danger of that, I would not allow you into my homeland."

"Not even Sturm?" he couldn't help asking wryly, nettled by her stinging tone.

But he was not prepared for the answer. Alhana twisted to face him, whipping around so fast her long black hair flailed his skin. Her face was so pale

with anger, it seemed translucent and he could see the veins pulse beneath her skin. Her dark eyes seemed to swallow him in their black depths.

"Never speak of that to me!" she said through clenched teeth and white lips. "Never speak of him!"

"But last night—" Tanis faltered, astonished, putting his hand to his burning cheek.

"Last night never happened," Alhana said. "I was weak, tired, frightened. As I was when . . . when I met Sturm, the knight. I regret speaking of him to you. I regret telling you of the Starjewel."

"Do you regret giving it to him?" Tanis asked.

"I regret the day I set foot in Tarsis," Alhana said in a low, passionate voice. "I wish I had never gone there! Never!" She turned away abruptly, leaving Tanis to dark thoughts.

The companions had just reached the river, within sight of the tall Tower of the Stars, shining like a strand of pearls twisting into the sun, when the griffons suddenly halted their flight. Tanis, glancing ahead, could see no sign of danger. But their griffons continued to descend rapidly.

Indeed, it seemed hard to believe that Silvanesti had been under attack. There were no thin columns of campfire smoke rising into the air, as there would be if the draconians occupied the country. The land was not blackened and ruined. He could see, below him, the green of the aspens gleaming in the sunlight. Here and there, the marble buildings dotted the forest with their white splendor.

"No!" Alhana spoke to the griffons in elven. "I command you! Keep going! I must reach the Tower!"

But the griffons circled lower and lower, ignoring her.

"What is it?" Tanis asked. "Why are we stopping? We're in sight of the Tower. What's the matter?" He looked all around. "I see nothing to be concerned over."

"They refuse to go on," Alhana said, her face drawn with worry. "They won't tell me why, only that we must travel on our own from here. I don't understand this."

Tanis didn't like it. Griffons were known as fierce, independent creatures, but once their loyalty was gained, they served their masters with undying

Elven royalty have flown on griffons since time immemorial. Royal griffons are bonded to their riders, and no more loyal creatures exist on Krynn. There are tales of riders dying and their griffons following them into death out of sheer grief.

devotion. The elven royalty of Silvanesti have always tamed griffons for their use. Though smaller than dragons, the griffons' lightning speed, sharp talons, tearing beak, and lion-clawed hind feet made them enemies to be respected. There was little they feared on Krynn, so Tanis had heard. These griffons† he remembered, had flown into Tarsis through swarms of dragons without apparent fear.

Yet now the griffons were obviously afraid. They landed on the banks of the river, refusing all of Alhana's angry, imperious commands to fly farther. Instead, they moodily preened themselves and steadfastly refused to obey.

Finally there was nothing for the companions to do but climb off the griffons' backs and unload their supplies. Then the bird-lion creatures, with fierce, apologetic dignity, spread their wings and soared away.

"Well, that is that," said Alhana sharply, ignoring the angry glances she felt cast at her. "We shall simply have to walk, that's all. The way is not far."

The companions stood stranded upon the riverbank, staring across the sparkling water into the forest beyond. None of them spoke. All of them were tense, alert, searching for trouble. But all they saw were the aspen trees glistening in the last, lingering rays of sunset. The river murmured as it lapped on the shore. Though the aspens were green still, the silence of winter blanketed the land.

"I thought you said your people fled because they were under siege?" Tanis said to Alhana finally.

"If this land is under control of dragons, I'm a gully dwarf!" Caramon snorted.

"We were!" Alhana answered, her eyes scanning the sunlit forest."Dragons filled the skies, as in Tarsis! The dragonmen entered our beloved woods, burning, destroying—" Her voice died.

Caramon leaned near Riverwind and muttered, "Wild goose chase!"

The Plainsman scowled. "If it's nothing more than that, we'll be fortunate," he said, his eyes on the elfmaid. "Why did she bring us here? Perhaps it's a trap."

Caramon considered this a moment, then glanced uneasily at his brother, who had not spoken or moved or taken his strange eyes from the forest

since the griffons left. The big warrior loosened his sword in its scabbard and moved a step nearer Tika. Almost accidentally, it seemed, their two hands clasped. Tika cast a fearful look at Raistlin but held onto Caramon tightly.

The mage just stared fixedly into the wilderness.

"Tanis!" Alhana said suddenly, forgetting herself in her joy and putting her hand on his arm. "Maybe it worked! Maybe my father defeated them, and we can come home! Oh, Tanis—" She trembled with excitement. "We've got to cross the river and find out! Come! The ferry landing's down around the bend—"

"Alhana, wait!" Tanis called, but she was already running along the smooth, grassy bank, her long full skirts fluttering around her ankles. "Alhana! Damn it. Caramon and Riverwind, go after her. Goldmoon, try to talk some sense into her."

Riverwind and Caramon exchanged uneasy glances, but they did as Tanis ordered, running along the riverbank after Alhana. Goldmoon and Tika followed more slowly.

"Who knows what's in these woods?" Tanis muttered. "Raistlin—"

The mage did not seem to hear. Tanis moved closer. "Raistlin?" he repeated, seeing the mage's abstracted stare.

Raistlin stared at him blankly, as if waking from a dream. Then the mage became aware of someone speaking to him. He lowered his eyes.

"What is it, Raistlin?" Tanis asked. "What do you sense?"

"Nothing, Tanis," the mage replied.

Tanis blinked. "Nothing?" he repeated.

"It is like an impenetrable fog, a blank wall," Raistlin whispered. "I see nothing, sense nothing."

Tanis stared at him intently, and suddenly he knew Raistlin was lying. But why? The mage returned the half-elf's gaze with equanimity, even a small, twisted smile on his thin lips, as if he knew Tanis didn't believe him but really didn't care.

"Raistlin," Tanis said softly, "suppose Lorac, the elfking, tried to use the dragon orb—what would happen?"

The mage lifted his eyes to stare into the forest. "Do you think that is possible?" he asked.

"Yes," Tanis said, "from what little Alhana told me, during the Tests in the Tower of High Sorcery at Istar, a dragon orb spoke to Lorac, asking him to rescue it from the impending disaster."

"And he obeyed it?" Raistlin asked, his voice as soft as the murmuring water of the ancient river.

"Yes. He brought it to Silvanesti."

"So this is the dragon orb of Istar," Raistlin whispered. His eyes narrowed, and then he sighed, a sigh of longing. "I know nothing about the dragon orbs," he remarked, coolly, "except what I told you. But I know this, Half-Elf—none of us will come out of Silvanesti unscathed, if we come out at all."

"What do you mean? What danger is there?"

"What does it matter what danger I see?" Raistlin asked, folding his hands in the sleeves of his red robes. "We must enter Silvanesti. You know it as well as I. Or will you forego the chance to find a dragon orb?"

"But if you see danger, tell us! We could at least enter prepared—"Tanis began angrily.

"Then prepare," Raistlin whispered softly, and he turned away and began to walk slowly along the sandy beach after his brother.

The companions crossed the river just as the last rays of the sun flickered among the leaves of the aspens on the opposite bank. And then the fabled forest of Silvanesti was gradually swamped by darkness. The shadows of night flowed among the feet of the trees like the dark water flowing beneath the keel of the ferry boat.

Their journey was slow. The ferry—an ornately carved, flat-bottomed boat connected to both shores by an elaborate system of ropes and pulleys, seemed at first to be in good condition. But once they set foot on board and began to cross the ancient river, they discovered that the ropes were rotting. The boat began to decay before their eyes. The river itself seemed to change. Reddish-brown water seeped through the hull, tainted with the faint smell of blood.

They had just stepped out of the boat on the opposite bank and were unloading their supplies, when the frayed ropes sagged and gave way.

The river swept the ferry boat downstream in an instant. Twilight vanished at the same moment, and

night swallowed them. Although the sky was clear, without a cloud to mar its dark surface, there were no stars visible. Neither the red nor the silver moon rose. The only light came from the river, which seemed to gleam with an unwholesome brilliance, like a ghoul.

"Raistlin, your staff," Tanis said. His voice echoed too loudly through the silent forest. Even Caramon cringed.

"Shirak." Raistlin spoke the word of command and the crystal globe clutched in the disembodied dragon's claw flared into light. But it was a cold, pale light. The only thing it seemed to illuminate were the mage's strange, hourglass eyes.

"We must enter the woods," Raistlin said in a shaking voice. Turning, he stumbled toward the dark wilderness.

No one else spoke or moved. They stood on the bank, fear overtaking them. There was no reason for it, and it was all the more frightening because it was illogical. Fear crept up on them from the ground. Fear flowed through their limbs, turning the bowels to water, sapping the strength of heart and muscle, eating into the brain.

Fear of what? There was nothing, nothing there! Nothing to be afraid of, yet all of them were more terrified of this nothing than they had been of anything before in their lives.

"Raistlin's right. We've—got to—get into the woods—find shelter . . ." Tanis spoke with an effort, his teeth chattering. "F-follow Raistlin."

Shaking, he staggered forward, not knowing if anyone followed, not caring. Behind him, he could hear Tika whimper and Goldmoon trying to pray through lips that would not form words. He heard Caramon shout for his brother to stop and Riverwind cry out in terror, but it didn't matter. He had to run, get away from here! His only guidance was the light of Raistlin's staff.

Desperately, he stumbled after the mage into the woods. But when Tanis reached the trees, he found his strength was gone. He was too scared to move. Trembling, he sank down on his knees, then pitched forward, his hands clutching at the ground.

"Raistlin!" His throat was torn by a ragged scream.

But the mage could not help. The last thing Tanis saw was the light from Raistlin's staff falling slowly to the ground, slowly, and more slowly, released by the young mage's limp, seemingly lifeless hand.

The trees. The beautiful trees of Silvanesti. Trees fashioned and coaxed through centuries into groves of wonder and enchantment. All around Tanis were the trees. But these trees now turned upon their masters, becoming living groves of horror. A noxious green light filtered through the shivering leaves.

Tanis stared about in horror. Many strange and terrible sights he had seen in his life, but nothing like this. This, he thought, might drive him insane. He turned this way and that, frantically, but there was no escape. All around were the trees—the trees of Silvanesti. Hideously changed.

The soul of every tree around him appeared† trapped in torment, imprisoned within the trunk. The twisted branches of the tree were the limbs of its spirit, contorted in agony. The grasping roots clawed the ground in hopeless attempts to flee. The sap of the living trees flowed from huge gashes in the trunk. The rustling of its leaves were cries of pain and terror. The trees of Silvanesti wept blood.

I have always been fascinated by truth vs. apparent truth. While I am not fond of violent films, I like themes like those presented in Total Recall. *Perhaps that is why I find stage magicians so interesting.—TRH*

Tanis had no idea where he was or how long he had been here. He remembered he had begun walking toward the Tower of the Stars that he could see rising above the branches of the aspens. He had walked and walked, and nothing had stopped him. Then he'd heard the kender shriek in terror, like the scream of some small animal being tortured. Turning, he saw Tasslehoff pointing at the trees. Tanis, staring horrified at the trees, only eventually comprehended that Tasslehoff wasn't supposed to be here. And there was Sturm, ashen with fear, and Laurana, weeping in despair, and Flint, his eyes wide and staring.

Tanis embraced Laurana, and his arms encompassed flesh and blood, but still he knew she *was not there*—even as he held her, and the knowledge was terrifying.

Then, as he stood there in the grove that was like a prison of the damned, the horror increased.

Animals bounded out from among the tormented trees and fell upon the companions.

Tanis drew his sword to strike back, but the weapon shook in his trembling hand, and he was forced to avert his eyes for the living animals had themselves been twisted and misshapen into hideous aspects of undying death.

Riding among the misshapen beasts were legions of elven warriors, their skull-like features hideous to behold. No eyes glittered in the hollow sockets of their faces, no flesh covered the delicate bones of their hands. They rode among the companions with brightly burning swords that drew living blood. But when any weapon struck them, they disappeared into nothing.

The wounds they inflicted, however, were real. Caramon, battling a wolf with snakes growing out of its body, looked up to see one of the elven warriors bearing down on him, a shining spear in his fleshless hand. He screamed to his brother for help.

Raistlin spoke, *"Ast kiranann kair Soth-aran/Suh kali Jalaran."* A ball of flame flashed from the mage's hands to burst directly upon the elf—without effect. Its spear, driven by incredible force, pierced Caramon's armor, entering his body, nailing him to the tree behind.

The elven warrior yanked his weapon free from the big man's shoulder. Caramon slumped to the ground, his life's blood mingling with the tree's blood. Raistlin, with a fury that surprised him, drew the silver dagger from the leather thong he wore hidden on his arm and flung it at the elf. The blade pricked its undead spirit and the elven warrior, horse and all, vanished into air. Yet Caramon lay upon the ground, his arm hanging from his body by only a thin strip of flesh.

Goldmoon knelt to heal him, but she stumbled over her prayers, her faith failing her amid the horror.

"Help me, Mishakal," Goldmoon prayed. "Help me to help my friend."

The dreadful wound closed. Though blood still seeped from it, trickling down Caramon's arm, death loosed its grip on the warrior. Raistlin knelt beside his brother and started to speak to him. Then suddenly the mage fell silent. He stared past

Caramon into the trees, his strange eyes widening with disbelief.

"You!" Raistlin whispered.

"Who is it?" Caramon asked weakly, hearing a thrill of horror and fear in Raistlin's voice. The big man peered into the green light but could see nothing. "Who do you mean?"

But Raistlin, intent upon another conversation, did not answer.

"I need your aid," the mage said sternly. "Now, as before."

Caramon saw his brother stretch out his hand, as though reaching across a great gap, and was consumed with fear without knowing why.

"No, Raist!" he cried, clutching at his brother in panic. Raistlin's hand dropped.

"Our bargain remains. What? You ask for more?" Raistlin was silent a moment, then he sighed. "Name it!"

For long moments, the mage listened, absorbing. Caramon, watching him with loving anxiety, saw his brother's thin metallic-tinged face grow deathly pale. Raistlin closed his eyes, swallowing as though drinking his bitter herbal brew. Finally he bowed his head.

"I accept."

Caramon cried out in horror as he saw Raistlin's robes, the red robes that marked his neutrality in the world, begin to deepen to crimson, then darken to a blood red, and then darken more—to black.†

The color of a mage's robe on Krynn are more than just an ornamentation or sign of fealty to a particular order of magic. The color of a wizard's robes reflects an entire attitude and philosophy of magic—a magical way of life, if you will. The change in Raistlin's robe color from red—the offices of neutrality—to black—the markings of dark or evil magic in Krynn—foreshadow Raistlin's own future choices and the dark destiny that lies before him.—TRH

"I accept this,"Raistlin repeated more calmly, "with the understanding that the future can be changed. What must we do?"

He listened. Caramon clutched his arm, moaning in agony.

"How do we get through to the Tower alive?" Raistlin asked his unseen instructor. Once more he attended carefully, then nodded. "And I will be given what I need? Very well. Farewell then, if such a thing is possible for you on your dark journey."

Raistlin rose to his feet, his black robes rustling around him. Ignoring Caramon's sobs and Goldmoon's terrified gasp as she saw him, the mage went in search of Tanis. He found the half-elf, back against a tree, battling a host of elven warriors.

Calmly, Raistlin reached into his pouch and drew forth a bit of rabbit fur and a small amber rod. Rubbing these together in his left palm, he held forth his right hand and spoke. *"Ast kiranann kair Gadurm Sotharn/Suh kali Jalaran."*

Bolts of lightning shot from his fingertips, streaking through the green-tinted air, striking the elven warriors. As before, they vanished. Tanis stumbled backward, exhausted.

Raistlin stood in the center of a clearing of the distorted, tormented trees.

"Come around me!" the mage commanded his companions.

Tanis hesitated. Elven warriors hovered on the fringes of the clearing. They surged forward to attack, but Raistlin raised his hand, and they stopped as though crashing against an unseen wall.

"Come to stand near me." The companions were astonished to hear Raistlin speak—for the first time since his Tests—in a normal voice."Hurry," he added, "they will not attack now. They fear me. But I cannot hold them back long."

Tanis came forward, his face pale beneath the red beard, blood dribbling from a wound on his head. Goldmoon helped Caramon stagger forward. He clutched his bleeding arm as his face was twisted in pain. Slowly, one by one, the other companions crept forward. Finally, only Sturm stood outside the circle.

"I always knew it would come to this," the knight said slowly. "I will die before I place myself under your protection, Raistlin."

And with that, the knight turned and walked deeper into the forest. Tanis saw the leader of the elven undead make a gesture, detailing some of his ghastly band to follow. The half-elf started after, then stopped as he felt a surprisingly strong hand grip his arm.

"Let him go," the mage said sternly, "or we are all lost. I have information to impart and my time is limited. We must make our way through this forest to the Tower of the Stars. We must walk the way of death, for every hideous creature ever conceived in the twisted, tortured dreams of mortals will arise to stop us. But know this—we walk in a *dream,* Lorac's nightmare. And our own nightmares as well.

Visions of the future can arise to help us, or hinder. Remember, that though our bodies are awake, our minds sleep. Death exists only in our minds—unless we believe otherwise."

"Then why can't we wake up?" Tanis demanded angrily.

"Because Lorac's belief in the dream is too strong and your belief too weak. When you are firmly convinced, beyond doubt, that this is a dream, you will return to reality."

"If this is true," Tanis said, "and you're convinced it is a dream, why don't you awaken?"

"Perhaps," Raistlin said, smiling, "I choose not to."

"I don't understand!" Tanis cried in bitter frustration.

"You will," Raistlin predicted grimly, "or you will die. In which case, it won't matter."

10

Waking Dreams. Future Visions.

Ignoring the horrified stares of his companions, Raistlin walked to his brother, who stood clutching his bleeding arm.

"I will take care of him," Raistlin said to Goldmoon, putting his own black-robed arm around his twin.

"No," Caramon gasped, "you're not strong en—" His voice died as he felt his brother's arm support him.

"I am strong enough now, Caramon," Raistlin said gently, his very gentleness sending a shiver through the warrior's body. "Lean on me, my brother."

Weak from pain and fear, for the first time in his life Caramon leaned on Raistlin. The mage supported him as, together, they starting walking through the hideous forest.

"What's happening, Raist?" Caramon asked, choking. "Why do you wear the Black Robes? And your voice—"

"Save your breath, my brother," Raistlin advised softly.

The two traveled deeper into the forest, and the undead elven warriors stared menacingly at them from the trees. They could see the hatred the dead bear the living, see it flicker in the hollow eye sockets of the undead warriors. But none dared attack the black-robed mage. Caramon felt his life's blood well thick and warm from between his fingers. As he watched it drip upon the dead, slime-coated leaves beneath his feet, he grew weaker and weaker. He had the fevered impression that the black shadow of himself gained in strength even as he lost it.

Tanis hurried through the forest, searching for Sturm. He found him fighting off a group of shimmering elven warriors.

"It's a dream," Tanis shouted to Sturm, who stabbed and slashed at the undead creatures. Every time he struck one, it vanished, only to reappear once more. The half-elf drew his sword, running to fight at Sturm's side.

"Bah!" the knight grunted, then gasped in pain as an arrow thudded into his arm. The wound was not deep, because the chain mail protected him, but it bled freely. "Is this dreaming?" Sturm said, yanking out the blood-stained shaft.

Tanis jumped in front of the knight, keeping their foes back until Sturm could stanch the flow of blood.

"Raistlin told us—" Tanis began.

"Raistlin! Hah! Look at his robes, Tanis!"

"But you're here! In Silvanesti!" Tanis protested in confusion. He had the strangest feeling he was arguing with himself. "Alhana said you were in Ice Wall!"†

Ice Wall is the glacial world south of the Plains of Dust. The glacier is gradually encroaching on the Plains.

The knight shrugged. "Perhaps I was sent to help you."

All right. It's a dream, Tanis told himself. I *will* wake up.

But there was no change. The elves were still there, still fighting. Sturm must be right. Raistlin *had*

lied. Just as he had lied before they entered the forest. But why? To what purpose?

Then Tanis knew. The dragon orb!

"We've got to reach the Tower before Raistlin!" Tanis cried to Sturm. "I know what the mage is after!"

The knight could do nothing more than nod. It seemed to Tanis that from then on they did nothing but fight for every inch of ground they gained. Time and again, the two warriors forced the elven undead back, only to be attacked in ever-increasing numbers. Time passed, they knew, but they had no conception of its passing. One moment the sun shone through the stifling green haze. Then night's shadows hovered over the land like the wings of dragons.

Then, just as the darkness deepened, Sturm and Tanis saw the Tower. Built of marble, the tall Tower glistened white. It stood alone in a clearing, reaching up to the heavens like a skeletal finger clawing up from the grave.

At sight of the Tower, both men began to run. Though weak and exhausted, neither wanted to be in these deadly woods after nightfall. The elven warriors—seeing their prey escaping—screamed in rage and charged after them.

Tanis ran until it seemed his lungs would burst with pain. Sturm ran ahead of him, slashing at the undead who appeared before them, trying to block their path. Just as Tanis neared the Tower, he felt a tree root twist itself around his boot. He pitched headlong onto the ground.

Frantically Tanis fought to free himself, but the root held him fast. Tanis struggled helplessly as an undead elf, his face twisted grotesquely, raised a spear to drive it through Tanis's body. Suddenly the elf's eyes widened, the spear fell from nerveless fingers as a sword punctured its transparent body. The elf vanished with a shriek.

Tanis looked up to see who had saved his life. It was a strange warrior, strange—yet familiar. The warrior removed his helm, and Tanis stared into bright brown eyes!

"Kitiara!" he gasped in shock. "You're here! How? Why?"

"I heard you needed some help," Kit said, her crooked smile as charming as ever. "Seems I was

right." She reached out her hand. He grasped it, doubting as she pulled him to his feet. But she was flesh and blood. "Who's that ahead? Sturm? Wonderful! Like old times! Shall we go to the Tower?" she asked Tanis, laughing at the surprise on his face.

Riverwind fought alone, battling legions of undead elven warriors. He knew he could not take much more. Then he heard a clear call. Raising his eyes, he saw Qué-Shu tribesmen! He cried out joyfully. But, to his horror, he saw them turning their arrows upon him.

"No!" he shouted in Qué-Shu. "Don't you recognize me? I—"

The Qué-Shu warriors answered only with their bowstrings. Riverwind felt shaft after feathered shaft sink into his body.

"You brought the blue crystal staff among us!" they cried. "Your fault! The destruction of our village was your fault!"

"I didn't mean to," he whispered as he slumped to the ground. "I didn't know. Forgive me."

Tika hacked and slashed her way through elven warriors only to see them turn suddenly into draconians! Their reptile eyes gleamed red, their tongues licked their swords. Fear chilled the barmaid. Stumbling, she bumped into Sturm. Angrily the knight whirled, ordering her out of his way. She staggered back and jostled Flint. The dwarf impatiently shoved her aside.

Blinded by tears, panic-stricken at the sight of the draconians, who sprang back into battle full-grown from their own dead bodies, Tika lost control. In her fear, she stabbed wildly at anything that moved.

Only when she looked up and saw Raistlin standing before her in his black robes did she come to her senses. The mage said nothing, he simply pointed downward. Flint lay dead at her feet, pierced by her own sword.

I led them here, Flint thought. This is my responsibility. I'm the eldest. I'll get them out.

The dwarf hefted his battle-axe and yelled a challenge to the elven warriors before him. But they just laughed.

Angrily, Flint strode forward—only to find himself walking stiffly. His knee joints were swollen and hurt abominably. His gnarled fingers trembled with a palsy that made him lose his grip on the battle-axe. His breath came short. And then Flint knew why the elves weren't attacking: they were letting old age finish him.

Even as he realized this, Flint felt his mind begin to wander. His vision blurred. Patting his vest pocket, he wondered where he had put those confounded spectacles. A shape loomed before him, a familiar shape. Was it Tika? Without his glasses, he couldn't see—

Goldmoon ran among the twisted, tortured trees. Lost and alone, she searched desperately for her friends. Far away, she heard Riverwind calling for her above the ringing clash of swords. Then she heard his call cut off in a bubble of agony. Frantically she dashed forward, fighting her way through the brambles until her hands and face were bleeding. At last she found Riverwind. The warrior lay upon the ground, pierced by many arrows—arrows she recognized!

Running to him, she knelt beside him. "Heal him, Mishakal," she prayed, as she had prayed so often.

But nothing happened. The color did not return to Riverwind's ashen face. His eyes remained locked, staring fixedly into the green tinged sky.

"Why don't you answer? Heal him!" Goldmoon cried to the gods. And then she knew. "No!" she screamed. "Punish *me*! I am the one who has doubted. *I* am the one who has questioned! I saw Tarsis destroyed, children dying in agony! How could you allow that? I try to have faith, but I cannot help doubting when I see such horrors! Do not punish him." Weeping, she bent over the lifeless body of her husband. She did not see the elven warriors closing in around her.

Tasslehoff, fascinated by the horrible wonders around him, wandered off the path, and then discovered that—somehow—his friends had managed to lose him. The undead did not bother him. They who fed off fear felt no fear in his small body.

Finally, after roaming here and there for nearly a day, the kender reached the doors to the Tower of the Stars. Here his lighthearted journey came to a sudden halt, for he had found his friends—one of them at least.

Backed up against the closed doors, Tika fought for her life against a host of misshapen, nightmare-begotten foes. Tas saw that if she could get inside the Tower, she would be safe. Dashing forward, his small body flitting easily through the melee, he reached the door and began to examine the lock while Tika held the elves back with her wildly swinging sword.

"Hurry, Tas!" she cried breathlessly.

It was an easy lock to open; with such a simplistic trap to protect it, Tas was surprised that the elves even bothered.

"I should have this lock picked in seconds," he announced. Just as he set to work, however, something bumped him from behind, causing him to fumble.

"Hey!" he shouted at Tika irritably, turning around. "Be a little more careful—" He stopped short, horrified. Tika lay at his feet, blood flowing into her red curls.

"No, not Tika!" Tas whispered. Maybe she was only wounded! Maybe if he got her inside the Tower, someone could help her. Tears dimmed his vision, his hands shook.

I've got to hurry, Tas thought frantically. Why won't this open? It's so simple! Furious, he tore at the lock.

He felt a small prick in his finger just as the lock clicked. The door to the Tower began to swing open. But Tasslehoff just stared at his finger where a tiny spot of blood glistened. He looked back at the lock where a small, golden needle sparkled. A simple lock, a simple trap. He'd sprung them both. And, as the first effects of the poison surged with a terrible warmness through his body, he looked down to see he was too late. Tika was dead.

Raistlin and his brother made their way through the forest without injury. Caramon watched in growing amazement as Raistlin drove back the evil creatures that assailed them; sometimes with feats of incredible magic, sometimes through the sheer force of his will.

Raistlin was kind and gentle and solicitous. Caramon was forced to stop frequently as the day waned. By twilight, it was all Caramon could do to drag one foot in front of the other, even leaning upon his brother for support. And as Caramon grew ever weaker, Raistlin grew stronger.

Finally, when night's shadows fell, bringing a merciful end to the tortured green day, the twins reached the Tower. Here they stopped. Caramon was feverish and in pain.

"I've got to rest, Raist," he gasped. "Put me down."

"Certainly, my brother," Raistlin said gently. He helped Caramon lean against the pearl wall of the Tower, then regarded his brother with cool, glittering eyes.

"Farewell, Caramon," he said.

Caramon looked at his twin in disbelief. Within the shadows of the trees, the warrior could see the undead elves, who had followed them at a respectful distance, creep closer as they realized the mage who had warded them off was leaving.

"Raist," Caramon said slowly, "you can't leave me here! I can't fight them. I don't have the strength! I need you!"

"Perhaps, but you see, my brother, I no longer need you. I have gained your strength. Now, finally, I am as I was meant to be but for nature's cruel trick—one whole person."

As Caramon stared, uncomprehending, Raistlin turned to leave.

"Raist!"

Caramon's agonized cry halted him. Raistlin stopped and gazed back at his twin, his golden eyes all that were visible from within the depths of his black hood.

"How does it feel to be weak and afraid, my brother?" he asked softly. Turning, Raistlin walked to the Tower entrance where Tika and Tas lay dead. Raistlin stepped over the kender's body and vanished into the darkness.

Sturm and Tanis and Kitiara, reaching the Tower, saw a body lying on the grass at its base. Phantom shapes of undead elves were starting to surround it, shrieking and yelling, hacking at it with their cold swords.

"Caramon!" Tanis cried, heartsick.

"And where's his brother?" Sturm asked with a sidelong glance at Kitiara. "Left him to die, no doubt."

Tanis shook his head as they ran forward to aid the warrior. Wielding their swords, Sturm and Kitiara kept the elves at bay while Tanis knelt beside the mortally wounded warrior.

Caramon lifted his glazed eyes and met Tanis's, barely recognizing him through the bloody haze that dimmed his vision. He tried desperately to talk.

"Protect Raistlin, Tanis—" Caramon choked on his own blood—"since I won't be there now. Watch over him."

"Watch over *Raistlin?"* Tanis repeated furiously. "He left you here, to die!" Tanis held Caramon in his arms.

An allusion to Shakespeare's Othello.*—MW*

Caramon closed his eyes wearily. "No, you're wrong, Tanis. I sent him away. . . ." †The warrior's head slumped forward.

Night's shadows closed over them. The elves had disappeared. Sturm and Kit came to stand beside the dead warrior.

"What did I tell you?" Sturm asked harshly.

"Poor Caramon," Kitiara whispered, bending down near him. "Somehow I always guessed it would end this way." She was silent for a moment, then spoke softly. "So my little Raistlin has become truly powerful," she mused, almost to herself.

"At the cost of your brother's life!"

Kitiara looked at Tanis as if perplexed at his meaning. Then, shrugging, she glanced down at Caramon, who lay in a pool of his own blood. "Poor kid," she said softly.

Sturm covered Caramon's body with his cloak, then they sought the entrance to the Tower.

"Tanis—" Sturm said, pointing.

"Oh, no. Not Tas," Tanis murmured. "And Tika."

The kender's body lay just inside the doorway, his small limbs twisted by convulsions from the poison. Near him lay the barmaid, her red curls matted with blood. Tanis knelt beside them. One of the kender's packs had opened in his death throes, its contents scattered. Tanis caught sight of a glint of gold. Reaching down, he picked up the ring of elven make, carved in the shape of ivy leaves. His vision

blurred, tears filled his eyes as he covered his face with his hands.

"There's nothing we can do, Tanis." Sturm put his hand on his friend's shoulder. "We've got to keep going and put an end to this. If I do nothing else, I'll live to kill Raistlin."

Death is in the mind. This is a dream, Tanis repeated. But it was Raistlin's words he was remembering, and he'd seen what the mage had become.

I will wake up, he thought, bending the full force of his will to believing it was a dream. But when he opened his eyes, the kender's body still lay on the floor.

Clasping the ring in his hand, Tanis followed Kit and Sturm into a dank, slime-covered, marble hallway. Paintings hung in golden frames upon marble walls. Tall, stained-glass windows let in a lurid, ghastly light. The hallway might have been beautiful once, but now even the paintings on the walls appeared distorted, portraying horrifying visions of death. Gradually, as the three walked, they became aware of a brilliant green light† emanating from a room at the end of the corridor.

They could feel a malevolence radiate from that green light, beating upon their faces with the warmth of a perverted sun.

"The center of the evil," Tanis said. Anger filled his heart—anger, grief, and a burning desire for revenge. He started to run forward, but the green-tainted air seemed to press upon him, holding him back until each step was an effort.

Next to him, Kitiara staggered. Tanis put his arm around her, though he could barely find the strength to move himself. Kit's face was drenched with sweat, the dark hair curled around her damp forehead. Her eyes were wide with fear—the first time Tanis ever saw her afraid. Sturm's breath came in gasps as the knight struggled forward, weighted down by his armor.

At first, they seemed to make no progress at all. Then slowly, they realized they were inching forward, drawing nearer and nearer the green-lit room. Its bright light was now painful to their eyes, and movement exacted a terrible toll. Exhaustion claimed them, muscles ached, lungs burned.

It has been pointed out to me that green in our books is almost always a sign of evil. I don't recall ever being attacked by a lawn in my youth but I must admit that I find more evil in green than I do in blue or even red. I have no clue why.—TRH

Just as Tanis realized he could not take another step, he heard a voice call his name. Lifting his aching head, he saw Laurana standing in front of him, her elven sword in her hand. The heaviness seemingly had no effect on her at all, for she ran to him with a glad cry.

"Tanthalas! You're all right! I've been waiting—"

She broke off, her eyes on the woman clasped in Tanis's arm.

"Who—" Laurana started to ask, then suddenly, somehow she knew. This was the human woman, Kitiara. The woman Tanis loved. Laurana's face went white, then red.

"Laurana—" Tanis began, feeling confusion and guilt sweep over him, hating himself for causing her pain.

"Tanis! Sturm!" Kitiara cried, pointing.

Startled by the fear in her voice, all of them turned, staring down the green-lit marble corridor.

"Drakus Tsaro, deghnyah!"† Sturm intoned in Solamnic.

Solamnic, literally for,"Great Dragon, well met!"—TRH

At the end of the corridor loomed a gigantic green dragon. His name was Cyan Bloodbane, and he was one of the largest dragons on Krynn. Only the Great Red herself was larger. Snaking his head through a doorway, he blotted out the blinding green light with his hulking body. Cyan smelled steel and human flesh and elven blood. He peered with fiery eyes at the group.

They could not move. Overcome with the dragon fear, they could only stand and stare as the dragon crashed through the doorway, shattering the marble wall as easily as if it had been baked mud. His mouth gaping wide, Cyan moved down the corridor.

There was nothing they could do. Their weapons dangled from hands gone nerveless. Their thoughts were of death. But, even as the dragon neared, a dark shadowy figure crept from the deeper shadows of an unseen doorway and came to stand before them, facing them.

"Raistlin!" Sturm said quietly. "By all the gods, you will pay for your brother's life!"

Forgetting the dragon, remembering only Caramon's lifeless body, the knight sprang toward the mage, his sword raised. Raistlin just stared at him coldly.

"Kill me, knight, and you doom yourself and the others to death, for through my magic—and my magic alone—will you be able to defeat Cyan Bloodbane!"

"Hold, Sturm!" Though his soul was filled with loathing, Tanis knew the mage was right. He could feel Raistlin's power radiate through the black robes. "We need his help."

"No," Sturm said, shaking his head and backing away as Raistlin neared the group. "I said before—I will not rely on his protection. Not now. Farewell, Tanis."

Before any of them could stop him, Sturm walked past Raistlin toward Cyan Bloodbane.†The great dragon's head wove back and forth in eager anticipation of this first challenge to his power since he had conquered Silvanesti.

Those familiar with the future history of Krynn—and Raistlin in particular—will note that the dealings between Cyan Bloodbane and Raistlin do not end with this tale. —TRH

Tanis clutched Raistlin. "Do something!"

"The knight is in my way. Whatever spell I cast will destroy him, too," Raistlin answered.

"Sturm!" Tanis shouted, his voice echoing mournfully.

The knight hesitated. He was listening, but not to Tanis's voice. What he heard was the clear, clarion call of a trumpet, its music cold as the air from the snow-covered mountains of his homeland. Pure and crisp, the trumpet call rose bravely above the darkness and death and despair to pierce his heart.

Sturm answered the trumpet's call with a glad battle cry. He raised his sword—the sword of his father, its antique blade twined with the kingfisher and the rose. Silver moonlight streaming through a broken window caught the sword in a pure-white radiance that shredded the noxious green air.

Again the trumpet sounded, and again Sturm answered, but this time his voice faltered, for the trumpet call he heard had changed tone. No longer sweet and pure, it was braying and harsh and shrill.

No! thought Sturm in horror as he neared the dragon. Those were the horns of the enemy! He had been lured into a trap! Around him now he could see draconian soldiers, creeping from behind the dragon, laughing cruelly at his gullibility.

Sturm stopped, gripping his sword in a hand that was sweating inside its glove. The dragon loomed above him, a creature undefeatable, surrounded by masses of its troops, slavering and licking its jowls with its curled tongue.

Fear knotted Sturm's stomach; his skin grew cold and clammy. The horn call sounded a third time, terrible and evil. It was all over. It had all been for nothing. Death, ignominious defeat awaited him. Despair descending, he looked around fearfully. Where was Tanis? He needed Tanis, but he could not find him. Desperately he repeated the code of the knights, *My Honor Is My Life*, but the words sounded hollow and meaningless in his ears. He was not a knight. What did the Code mean to him?† He had been living a lie! Sturm's sword arm wavered, then dropped; his sword fell from his hand and he sank to his knees, shivering and weeping like a child, hiding his head from the terror before him.

Sturm's first traumatic encounter with the Solamnic Code is shown in Michael Williams's novel The Oath and the Measure.

With one swipe of his shining talons, Cyan Bloodbane ended Sturm's life, impaling the knight's body upon a bloodstained claw. Disdainfully, Cyan shook the wretched human to the floor while the draconians swept shrieking toward the knight's still-living body, intent upon hacking it to pieces.

But they found their way blocked. A bright figure, shining silver in the moonlight, ran to the knight's body. Reaching down swiftly, Laurana lifted Sturm's sword. Then, straightening, she faced the draconians.

"Touch him and you will die," she said through her tears.

"Laurana!" Tanis screamed and tried to run forward to help her. But draconians sprang at him. He slashed at them desperately, trying to reach the elfmaid. Just when he had won through, he heard Kitiara call his name. Whirling, he saw her being beaten back by four draconians. The half-elf stopped in agony, hesitating, and at that moment Laurana fell across Sturm's body, her own body pierced by draconian swords.

"No! Laurana!" Tanis shouted. Starting to go to her, he heard Kitiara cry out again. He stopped, turning. Clutching at his head, he stood irresolute and helpless, forced to watch as Kitiara fell beneath the enemy.

The half-elf sobbed in frenzy, feeling himself begin to sink into madness, longing for death to

end this pain. He clutched the magic sword of Kith-Kanan and rushed toward the dragon, his one thought to kill and be killed.

But Raistlin blocked his path, standing in front of the dragon like a black obelisk.

Tanis fell to the floor, knowing his death was fixed. Clasping the small golden ring firmly in his hand, he waited to die.

Then he heard the mage chanting strange and powerful words. He heard the dragon roar in rage. The two were battling, but Tanis didn't care. With eyes closed fast, he blotted out the sounds around him, blotted out life. Only one thing remained real. The golden ring he held tightly in his hand.

Suddenly Tanis became acutely conscious of the ring pressing into his palm: the metal was cool, its edges rough. He could feel the golden twisted ivy leaves bite into his flesh.

Tanis closed his hand, squeezing the ring. The gold bit into his flesh, bit deeply. Pain . . . real pain . . .

I am dreaming!

Tanis opened his eyes. Solinari's silver moonlight flooded the Tower, mingled with the red beams of Lunitari. He was lying on a cold, marble floor. His hand was clasped tightly, so tightly that pain had wakened him. Pain! The ring. The dream! Remembering the dream, Tanis sat up in terror and looked around. But the hall was empty except for one other person. Raistlin slumped against a wall, coughing.

The half-elf staggered to his feet and walked shakily toward Raistlin. As he drew nearer, he could see blood on the mage's lips. The blood gleamed red in Lunitari's light—as red as the robes that covered Raistlin's frail, shivering body.

The dream.

Tanis opened his hand. It was empty.

11

The dream ends.
The nightmare begins.

The half-elf stared around the hallway. It was as empty as his hand. The bodies of his friends were gone. The dragon was gone. Wind blew through a shattered wall, fluttering Raistlin's red robes about him, scattering dead aspen leaves along the floor. The half-elf walked over to Raistlin, catching the young mage in his arms as he collapsed.

"Where are they?" Tanis asked, shaking Raistlin. "Laurana? Sturm? And the others, your brother? Are they dead?" He glanced around. "And the dragon—"

"The dragon is gone. The orb sent the dragon away when it realized it could not defeat me." Pushing himself from Tanis's grasp, Raistlin stood alone, huddled against the marble wall. "It could

not defeat me as I was. A child could defeat me now," he said bitterly. "As for the others"—he shrugged—"I do not know." He turned his strange eyes on Tanis. "You lived, half-elf, because your love was strong. I lived because of my ambition. We clung to reality in the midst of the nightmare. Who can say with the others?"

"Caramon's alive, then," Tanis said. "Because of his love. With his last breath, he begged me to spare your life. Tell me, mage, was this future you say we saw irreversible?"

"Why ask?" Raistlin said wearily. "Would you kill me, Tanis? Now?"

"I don't know," Tanis said softly, thinking of Caramon's dying words. "Perhaps."

Raistlin smiled bitterly. "Save your energy," he said. "The future changes as we stand here, else we are the game pieces of the gods,† not their heirs, as we have been promised. But"—the mage pushed himself away from the wall—"this is far from over. We must find Lorac, and the dragon orb."

Game pieces? But ones with wills of their own. See Dragons of Summer Flame.

Raistlin shuffled down the hall, leaning heavily upon the Staff of Magius, its crystal lighting the darkness now that the green light had died.

Green light. Tanis stood in the hallway, lost in confusion, trying to wake up, trying to separate the dream from reality—for the dream seemed much more real than any of this did now. He stared at the shattered wall. Surely there had been a dragon? And a blinding green light at the end of the corridor? But the hallway was dark. Night had fallen. It had been morning when they started. The moons had not been up, yet now they were full. How many nights had passed? How many days?

Then Tanis heard a booming voice at other end of the corridor, near the doorway.

"Raist!"

The mage stopped, his shoulder slumped. Then he turned slowly. "My brother," he whispered.

Caramon—alive and apparently uninjured—stood in the doorway, outlined against the starry night. He stared at his twin.

Then Tanis heard Raistlin sigh softly.

"I am tired, Caramon." The mage coughed, then drew a wheezing breath. "And there is still much to be done before this nightmare is ended, before the three moons set." Raistlin extended his thin arm. "I need your help, brother."

Tanis heard Caramon heave a shuddering sob. The big man ran into the room, his sword clanking at his thigh. Reaching his brother, he put his arm around him.

Raistlin leaned on Caramon's strong arm. Together, the twins walked down the cold hallway and through the shattered wall toward the room where Tanis had seen the green light and the dragon. His heart heavy with foreboding, Tanis followed them.

The three entered the audience room of the Tower of the Stars. Tanis looked at it curiously. He had heard of its beauty all his life. The Tower of the Sun in Qualinost had been built in remembrance of this Tower—the Tower of the Stars. The two were alike, yet not alike. One was filled with light, one filled with darkness. He stared around. The Tower soared above him in marble spirals that shimmered with a pearly radiance. It had been built to collect moonlight, as the Tower of the Sun collected sunlight. Windows carved into the Tower were faceted with gems that caught and magnified the light of the two moons, Solinari and Lunitari, making red and silver moonbeams dance in the chamber. But now the gems were broken. The moonlight that filtered in was distorted, the silver turning to the pale white of a corpse, the red to blood.

Tanis, shivering, looked straight up to the top. In Qualinost, there were murals on the ceiling, portraying the sun, the constellations, and the two moons. But here there was nothing but a carved hole in the top of the Tower. Through the hole, he could see only empty blackness.† The stars did not shine. It was as if a perfectly round, black sphere had appeared in the starry darkness. Before he could ponder what this portended, he heard Raistlin speak softly, and he turned.

The open top rooms of the Tower of the Stars had been created to encourage contemplation and meditation.

There, in the shadows at the front of the audience chamber was Alhana's father, Lorac, the elfking. His shrunken and cadaverous body almost disappeared in a huge stone throne, fancifully carved with birds and animals. It must once have been beautiful, but now the animals' heads were skulls.

Lorac sat motionless, his head thrown back, his mouth wide in a silent scream. His hand rested upon a round crystal globe.†

Artist Clyde Caldwell painted a wonderful picture of this scene, which I used as reference when I wrote it. The painting can be found in The Art of the Dragonlance Saga, *page 100.—MW*

"Is he alive?" Tanis asked in horror.

"Yes," Raistlin answered, "undoubtedly to his sorrow."

"What's wrong with him?"

"He is living a nightmare," Raistlin answered, pointing to Lorac's hand. "There is the dragon orb. Apparently he tried to take control of it. He was not strong enough, so the orb seized control of him. The orb called Cyan Bloodbane here to guard Silvanesti, and the dragon decided to destroy it by whispering nightmares into Lorac's ear. Lorac's belief in the nightmare was so strong, his empathy with his land so great, that the nightmare became reality. Thus, it was his dream we were living when we entered. His dream—and our own. For we too came under the dragon's control when we stepped into Silvanesti."

"You knew we faced this!" Tanis accused, grabbing Raistlin by the shoulder and spinning him around. "You knew what we were walking into, there on the shores of the river—"

"Tanis," Caramon said warningly, removing the half-elf's hand. "Leave him alone."

"Perhaps," Raistlin said, rubbing his shoulder, his eyes narrow. "Perhaps not. I need not reveal my knowledge or its source to you!"

Before he could reply, Tanis heard a moan. It sounded as if it came from the base of the throne. Casting Raistlin an angry glance, Tanis turned quickly from him and stared into the shadows. Warily he approached, his sword drawn.

"Alhana!" The elfmaid crouched at her father's feet, her head in his lap, weeping. She did not seem to hear Tanis. He went to her. "Alhana," he said gently.

She looked up at him without recognition.

"Alhana," he said again.

She blinked, then shuddered, and grabbed hold of his hand as if clutching at reality.

"Half—Elven!" she whispered.

"How did you get here? What happened?"

"I heard the mage say it was a dream," Alhana answered, shivering at the memory, "and I—I refused to believe in the dream. I woke, but only to

find the nightmare was real! My beautiful land filled with horrors!" She hid her face in her hands. Tanis knelt beside her and held her close.

"I made my way here. It took—days. Through the nightmare." She gripped Tanis tightly. "When I entered the Tower, the dragon caught me. He brought me here, to my father, thinking to make Lorac murder me. But not even in his nightmare could my father harm his own child. So Cyan tortured him with visions, of what he would do to me."

"And you? You saw them, too?" Tanis whispered, stroking the woman's long, dark hair with a soothing hand.

After a moment, Alhana spoke. "It wasn't so bad. I knew it was nothing but a dream. But to my poor father it was reality—" She began to sob.

The half-elf motioned to Caramon. "Take Alhana to a room where she can lie down. We'll do what we can for her father."

"I will be all right, my brother," Raistlin said in answer to Caramon's look of concern. "Do as Tanis says."

"Come, Alhana," Tanis urged her, helping her stand. She staggered with weariness. "Is there a place you can rest? You'll need your strength."

At first she started to argue, then she realized how weak she was. "Take me to my father's room," she said. "I'll show you the way." Caramon put his arm around her, and slowly they began to walk from the chamber.

Tanis turned back to Lorac. Raistlin stood before the elf king. Tanis heard the mage speaking softly to himself.

"What is it?" the half-elf said quietly. "Is he dead?"

"Who?" Raistlin started, blinking. He saw Tanis looking at Lorac. "Oh, Lorac? No, I do not believe so. Not yet."

Tanis realized the mage had been staring at the dragon orb.

"Is the orb still in control?" Tanis asked nervously, his eyes on the object they had gone through so much to find.

The dragon orb was a huge globe of crystal, at least twenty-four inches across. It sat upon a stand of gold that had been carved in hideous, twisted designs, mirroring the twisted, tormented life of

Silvanesti. Though the orb must have been the source of the brilliant green light, there was now only a faint, iridescent, pulsing glow at its heart.

Raistlin's hands hovered over the globe, but, Tanis noted, he was careful not to touch it as he chanted the spidery words of magic. A faint aura of red began to surround the globe. Tanis backed away.

"Do not fear," Raistlin whispered, watching as the aura died. "It is my spell. The globe is enchanted—still. Its magic has not died with the passing of the dragon, as I thought possible. It is still in control, however."

"Control of Lorac?"

"Control of itself. It has released Lorac."

"Did you do this?" Tanis murmured. "Did you defeat it?"

"The orb is not defeated!" Raistlin said sharply. "With help, I was able to defeat the dragon. Realizing Cyan Bloodbane was losing, the orb sent him away.† It let go of Lorac because it could no longer use him. But the orb is still very powerful."

"Raistlin, tell me—"

"I have no more to say, Tanis." The young mage coughed. "I must conserve my energy."

Whose help had Raistlin received? What else did he know of this orb? Tanis opened his mouth to pursue the subject, then he saw Raistlin's golden eyes flicker. The half-elf fell silent.

"We can free Lorac now," Raistlin added. Walking to the elf king, he gently removed Lorac's hand from the dragon orb, then put his slender fingers to Lorac's neck. "He lives. For the time being. The lifebeat is weak. You may come closer."

But Tanis, his eyes on the dragon orb, held back. Raistlin glanced at the half-elf, amused, then beckoned.

Reluctantly, Tanis approached. "Tell me one more thing—can the orb still be of use to us?"

For long moments, Raistlin was silent. Then, faintly, he replied, "Yes, if we dare."

Lorac drew a shivering breath, then screamed, a thin, wailing scream horrible to hear. His hands—little more than living skeletal claws—twisted and writhed. His eyes were tightly closed. In vain, Tanis tried to calm him. Lorac screamed until he was out of breath, and then he screamed silently.

This actually seems to be in contradiction to what I remember about the Orbs of Dragonkind. The orbs themselves were to attract dragons—not repel them.

Nevertheless, the orbs were powerful devices which, over time, seemed to grow their own mind about things. Sending Cyan away certainly would be well within the orb's power, although I think Raistlin is misspoken here. In my mind, the orb did not so much send the dragon away as it simply became overwhelmingly repellent to the dragon.—TRH

"Father!" Tanis heard Alhana cry. She reappeared in the doorway of the audience chamber and pushed Caramon aside. Running to her father, she grasped his bony hands in hers. Kissing his hands, she wept, pleading for him to be silent.

"Rest, Father," she repeated over and over. "The nightmare is ended. The dragon is gone. You can sleep, Father!"

But the man's screaming continued.

"In the name of the gods!" Caramon said as he came up to them, his face pale. "I can't take much of this."

"Father!" Alhana pleaded, calling to him again and again. Slowly her beloved voice penetrated the twisted dreams that lingered on in Lorac's tortured mind. Slowly his screams died to little more than horrified whimpers. Then, as if fearing what he might see, he opened his eyes.

"Alhana, my child. Alive!" He lifted a shaking hand to touch her cheek. "It cannot be! I saw you die, Alhana. I saw you die a hundred times, each time more horrifying than the last. He killed you, Alhana. He wanted *me* to kill you. But I could not. Though I know not why, as I have killed so many." Then he caught sight of Tanis. His eyes flared open, shining with hatred.

"You!" Lorac snarled, rising from his chair, his gnarled hands clutching the sides of the throne. "You, half-elf! I killed you—or tried to. I must protect Silvanesti! I killed you! I killed those with you." Then his eyes went to Raistlin. The look of hatred was replaced by one of fear. Trembling, he shrank away from the mage. "But you, you I could not kill!"

Lorac's look of terror changed to confusion. "No," he cried. "You are not he! Your robes are not black! Who are you?" His eyes went back to Tanis. "And you? You are not a threat? What have I done?" He moaned.

"Don't, Father," Alhana pleaded, soothing him, stroking his fevered face. "You must rest now. The nightmare is ended. Silvanesti is safe."

Caramon lifted Lorac in his strong arms and carried him to his chambers. Alhana walked next to him, her father's hand held fast in her own.

Safe, Tanis thought, glancing out the windows at the tormented trees. Although the undead elven

warriors no longer stalked the woods, the tortured shapes Lorac had created in his nightmare still lived. The trees, contorted in agony, still wept blood. Who will live here now? Tanis wondered sadly. The elves will not return. Evil things will enter this dark forest and Lorac's nightmare will become reality.

Thinking of the nightmarish forest, Tanis suddenly wondered where his other friends were. Were they all right? What if they had believed the nightmare—as Raistlin said? Would they have truly died? His heart sinking, he knew he would have to go back into that demented forest and search for them.

Just as the half-elf began to try and force his weary body to action, his friends entered the Tower room.

"I killed him!" Tika cried, catching sight of Tanis. Her eyes were wide with grief and terror. "No! Don't touch me, Tanis. You don't know what I've done. I killed Flint! I didn't mean to, Tanis, I swear!"

As Caramon entered the room, Tika turned to him, sobbing. "I killed Flint, Caramon. Don't come near me!"

"Hush," Caramon said, gently enfolding her in his big arms. "It was a dream, Tika. That's what Raist says. The dwarf was never here. Shhh." Stroking Tika's red curls, he kissed her. Tika clung to him, Caramon clung to her, each finding comfort with the other. Gradually Tika's sobs lessened.

"My friend," Goldmoon said, reaching out to embrace Tanis.

Seeing the grave, somber expression on her face, the half-elf held her tightly, glancing questioningly at Riverwind. What had each of them dreamed? But the Plainsman only shook his head, his own face pale and grieved.

Then it occurred to Tanis that each must have lived through his or her own dream, and he suddenly remembered Kitiara! How real she had been! And Laurana, dying. Closing his eyes, Tanis laid his head against Goldmoon's. He felt Riverwind's strong arms surround them both. Their love blessed him. The horror of the dream began to recede.

And then Tanis had a terrifying thought. Lorac's dream became reality! *Would theirs?*

Behind him, Tanis heard Raistlin begin to cough. Clutching his chest, the mage sank down onto the steps leading up to Lorac's throne. Tanis saw Caramon, still holding Tika, glance at his brother in concern. But Raistlin ignored his brother. Gathering his robes around him, the mage lay down on the cold floor and closed his eyes in exhaustion.

Sighing, Caramon pressed Tika closer. Tanis watched her small shadow become part of Caramon's larger one as they stood together, their bodies outlined in the distorted silver and red beams of the fractured moonlight.

We all must sleep, Tanis thought, feeling his own eyes burn. Yet how can we? How can we ever sleep again?

It was all figured out in advance, so we'd know just what the people of Krynn were seeing in the night sky at any particular time. But, of course, only the truly evil can perceive Nuitari.—TRH

I could never keep the phases of the moon straight. At last I decided that they would be up if I needed them up and down if I didn't!—MW

Moon Tracking Chart

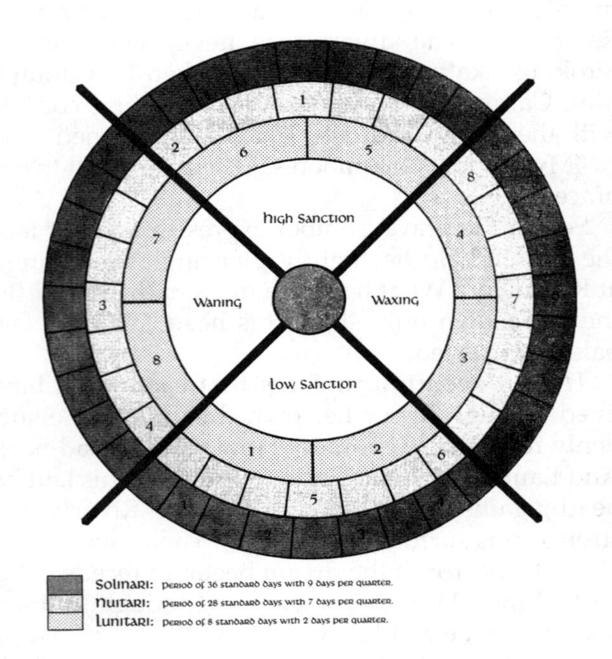

12

Visions shared.
The death of Lorac.

Yet finally they slept. Huddled on the stone floor of the Tower of the Stars, they kept as near each other as possible. While, as they slept, others in lands cold and hostile, lands far from Silvanesti, wakened.

Laurana woke first. Starting up from a deep sleep with a cry, at first she had no idea where she was. She spoke one word—"Silvanesti!"

Flint, trembling, woke to find that his fingers still moved, the pains in his legs were no worse than usual.

Sturm woke in panic. Shaking with terror, for long moments he could only crouch beneath his blankets, shuddering. Then he heard something outside his tent. Starting up, hand on his sword, he crept forward and threw open the tent flap.

"Oh!" Laurana gasped at the sight of his haggard face.

"I'm sorry," Sturm said. "I didn't mean—" Then he saw she was shaking so she could scarcely hold her candle. "What is it?" he asked, alarmed, drawing her out of the cold.

"I—I know this sounds silly," Laurana said, flushing, "but I had the most frightening dream and I couldn't sleep."

Shivering, she allowed Sturm to lead her inside the tent. The flame of her candle cast leaping shadows around the tent. Sturm, afraid she might drop it, took it from her.

"I didn't mean to wake you, but I heard you call out. And my dream was so real! You were in it—I saw you—"

"What is Silvanesti like?" Sturm interrupted abruptly.

Laurana stared at him. "But that's where I dreamed we were! Why did you ask? Unless . . . you dreamed of Silvanesti, too!"

Sturm wrapped his cloak around him, nodding. "I—" he began, then heard another noise outside the tent. This time, he just opened the tent flap. "Come in, Flint," he said wearily.

The dwarf stumped inside, his face flushed. He seemed embarrassed to find Laurana there, however, and stammered and stamped until Laurana smiled at him.

"We know," she said. "You had a dream. Silvanesti?"

Flint coughed, clearing his throat and wiping his face with his hand. "Apparently I'm not the only one?" he asked, staring narrowly at the other two from beneath his bushy eyebrows. "I suppose you—you want me to tell you what I dreamed?"

"No!" Sturm said hurriedly, his face pale. "No, I do not want to talk about it—ever!"

"Nor I," Laurana said softly.

Hesitantly, Flint patted her shoulder. "I'm glad," he said gruffly. "I couldn't talk about mine either. I just wanted to see if it was a dream. It seemed so real I expected to find you both—"

The dwarf stopped. There was a rustling sound outside, then Tasslehoff burst excitedly through the tent flap.

"Did I hear you talking about a dream? I *never* dream, at least not that I remember. Kender don't, much.† Oh, I suppose we do. Even animals dream, but—" He caught Flint's eye and came hurriedly back to the original subject. "Well! I had the most fantastic dream! Trees crying blood. Horrible dead elves going around killing people! Raistlin wearing black robes! It was the most incredible thing! And you were there, Sturm. Laurana and Flint. And everyone died! Well, almost everyone. Raistlin didn't. And there was a green dragon—"

Kender dreams—and they do dream—are not much different from their waking lives … usually.

Tasslehoff stopped. What was wrong with his friends? Their faces were deathly pale, their eyes wide. "G-green dragon," he stammered. "Raistlin, dressed in black. Did I mention that? Q-quite becoming, actually. Red always makes him look kind of jaundiced, if you know what I mean. You don't. Well, I g-guess I'll go back to bed. If you don't want to hear anymore?" He looked around hopefully. No one answered.

"Well, g-night," he mumbled. Backing out of the tent precipitously, he returned to his bed, shaking his head, puzzled. What was the matter with everyone? It was only a dream—

For long moments, no one spoke. Then Flint sighed.

"I don't mind having a nightmare," the dwarf said dourly. "But I object to sharing it with a kender. How do you suppose we all came to have the same dream? And what does it mean?"

"A strange land—Silvanesti," Laurana said. Taking her candle, she started to leave. Then she looked back. "Do you—do you think it was real? Did they die, as we saw?" Was Tanis with that human woman? she thought, but didn't ask aloud.

"We're here," said Sturm. "We didn't die. We can only trust the others didn't either. And"—he paused—"this seems funny, but somehow I k*now* they're all right."

Laurana looked at the knight intently for a moment, saw his grave face calm after the initial shock and horror had worn off. She felt herself relax. Reaching out, she took Sturm's strong lean hand in her own and pressed it silently. Then she turned and left, slipping back into the starlit night.

The dwarf rose to his feet. "Well, so much for sleep. I'll take my turn at watch now."

"I'll join you," said Sturm, standing and buckling on his swordbelt.

"I suppose we'll never know," Flint said, "why or how we all dreamed the same dream."

"I suppose not," Sturm agreed.

The dwarf walked out of the tent. Sturm started to follow, then stopped as his eyes caught a glimpse of light. Thinking perhaps that a bit of wick had fallen from Laurana's candle, he bent down to put it out, only to find instead that the jewel Alhana had given him had slipped from his belt and lay upon the ground. Picking it up, he noticed it was gleaming with its own inner light, something he'd never seen it do before.

"I suppose not," Sturm repeated thoughtfully, turning the jewel over and over in his hand.

Morning dawned in Silvanesti for the first time in many long, horrifying months. But only one saw it. Lorac, watching from his bedchamber window, saw the sun rise above the glistening aspens. The others, worn out, slept soundly.

Alhana had not left her father's side all night. But exhaustion had overwhelmed her, and she fell asleep sitting in her chair. Lorac saw the pale sunlight light her face. Her long black hair fell across her face like cracks in white marble. Her skin was torn by thorns, caked with dried blood. He saw beauty, but that beauty was marred by arrogance. She was the epitome of her people. Turning back, he looked outside into Silvanesti, but found no comfort there. A green, noxious mist still hung over Silvanesti, as though the ground itself was rotting.

"This is my doing," he said to himself, his eyes lingering on the twisted, tortured trees, the pitiful misshapen beasts that roamed the land, seeking an end to their torment.

For over four hundred years, Lorac had lived in this land. He had watched it take shape and flower beneath his hands and the hands of his people.

There had been times of trouble, too. Lorac was one of the few still living on Krynn to remember the Cataclysm. But the Silvanesti elves had survived it far better than others in the world—being estranged

from other races. They knew why the ancient gods left Krynn—they saw the evil in humankind—although they could not explain why the elven clerics vanished as well.

The elves of Silvanesti heard, of course, via the winds and birds and other mysterious ways, of the sufferings of their cousins, the Qualinesti, following the Cataclysm. And, though grieved at the tales of rapine and murder, the Silvanesti asked themselves what could one expect, living among humans? They withdrew into their forest, renouncing the outside world and caring little that the outside world renounced them.

Thus Lorac had found it impossible to understand this new evil sweeping out of the north, threatening his homeland. Why should they bother the Silvanesti? He met with the Dragon Highlords, explaining to them that the Silvanesti would give them no trouble. The elves believed everyone had the right to live upon Krynn, each in his own unique fashion, evil and good. He talked and they listened and, at first, all seemed well. Then the day came when Lorac realized he had been deceived—the day the skies erupted with dragons.

The elves were not, after all, caught unprepared. Lorac had lived too long for that. Ships waited to take the people to safety. Lorac ordered them to depart under his daughter's command. Then, when he was alone, he descended to the chambers beneath the Tower of the Stars where he had secreted the dragon orb.

Only his daughter and the long-lost elven clerics knew of the orb's existence. All others in the world believed it destroyed in the Cataclysm. Lorac sat beside it, staring at it for long days. He recalled the warnings of the High Mages,† bringing to mind everything he could remember about the orb. Finally, though fully aware that he had no idea how it worked, Lorac decided he had to use it to try and save his land.

† The wizards in charge of the remaining Towers of High Sorcery, to whom Lorac, as a mage, would have gone for advice.

He remembered the globe vividly, remembered it burning with a swirling, fascinating green light that pulsed and strengthened as he looked at it. And he remembered knowing, almost from the first seconds he had rested his fingers on the globe, that he had made a terrible mistake. He had neither the strength nor the control to command the magic. But by then, it was too late. The orb had captured him and held him enthralled, and it had been the most hideous part of his nightmare to be constantly reminded that he *was* dreaming, yet unable to break free.

And now the nightmare had become waking reality. Lorac bowed his head, tasting bitter tears in his mouth. Then he felt gentle hands upon his shoulders.

"Father, I cannot bear to see you weep. Come away from the window. Come to bed. The land will be beautiful once more in time. You will help to shape it—"

But Alhana could not look out the window without a shudder. Lorac felt her tremble and he smiled sadly.

"Will our people return, Alhana?" He stared out into the green that was not the vibrant green of life but that of death and decay.

"Of course," Alhana said quickly.

Lorac patted her hand. "A lie, my child? Since when have the elves lied to each other?"

"I think perhaps we may have always lied to ourselves," Alhana murmured, recalling what she had learned of Goldmoon's teaching. "The ancient gods did not abandon Krynn, Father. A cleric of Mishakal the Healer traveled with us and told us of what she had learned. I—I did not want to believe, Father. I was jealous. She is a human, after all, and why should the gods come to the humans with this hope? But I see now, the gods are wise.†They came to humans because we elves would not accept them. Through our grief, living in this place of desolation, we will learn—as you and I have learned—that we can no longer live within the world and live apart *from* the world. The elves will work to rebuild not only this land, but all lands ravaged by the evil."

Nice to know that not all Silvanesti elves are too arrogant to learn something about themselves.

Lorac listened. His eyes turned from the tortured landscape to his daughter's face, pale and radiant as the silver moon, and he reached out his hand to touch her.

"You will bring them back? Our people?"

"Yes, Father," she promised, taking his cold, fleshless hand in her own and holding it fast. "We will work and toil. We will ask forgiveness of the

gods. We will go out among the peoples of Krynn and—" Tears flooded her eyes and choked her voice, for she saw Lorac could no longer hear her. His eyes dimmed, and he began to sink back in the chair.

"I give myself to the land," he whispered. "Bury my body in the soil, daughter. As my life brought this curse upon it, so, perhaps, my death will bring its blessing."

Lorac's hand slipped from his daughter's grasp. His lifeless eyes stared out into the tormented land of Silvanesti. But the look of horror on his face faded away, leaving it filled with peace.

And Alhana could not grieve.

That night, the companions prepared to leave Silvanesti. They were to travel under the cover of darkness for much of their journey north, since by now they knew the dragonarmies controlled the lands they must pass through. They had no maps to guide them. They feared trusting ancient maps anymore, after their experience with the landlocked seaport city, Tarsis. But the only maps that could be found in Silvanesti dated back thousands of years. The companions decided to travel north from Silvanesti blindly, with some hope of discovering a seaport where they could find passage to Sancrist.†

Sancrist is an island off the west coasts of Northern and Southern Ergoth. It was one of the few places unchanged by the Cataclysm, except for the number of people who moved there. The Council of Whitestone had been formed on Sancrist some months before in an attempt to unite the races of Krynn to fight the war.

They traveled lightly, so they could travel swiftly. Besides, there was little to take; the elves had stripped their country bare of food and supplies when they left.

The mage took possession of the dragon orb—a charge no one disputed him. Tanis at first despaired of how they could carry the massive crystal with them—it was nearly two feet in diameter and extraordinarily heavy. But the evening before they left—Alhana came to Raistlin, a small sack in her hand.

"My father carried the orb in this sack. I always thought it odd, considering the orb's size, but he said the sack was given to him in the Tower of High Sorcery. Perhaps this will help you."

The mage reached out his thin hand to grasp it eagerly.

"Jistrah tagopar Ast moirparann Kini," he murmured and watched in satisfaction as the nondescript bag began to glow with a pale pink light.

"Yes, it is enchanted," he whispered. Then he lifted his gaze to Caramon. "Go and bring me the orb."

Caramon's eyes opened wide in horror. "Not for any treasure in this world!" the big man said with an oath.

"Bring me the orb!" Raistlin ordered, staring angrily at his brother, who still shook his head.

"Oh, don't be a fool, Caramon!" Raistlin snapped in exasperation."The orb cannot hurt those who do not attempt to use it. Believe me, my dear brother, you do not have the power to control a cockroach, let alone a dragon orb!"

"But it might trap me," Caramon protested.

"Bah! It seeks those with—" Raistlin stopped suddenly.

"Yes?" Tanis said quietly. "Go on. Who does it seek?"

"People with intelligence," Raistlin snarled. "Therefore I believe the members of *this* party are safe. Bring me the orb, Caramon, or perhaps you want to carry it yourself? Or you, Half-Elf? Or you, cleric of Mishakal?"

Caramon glanced uncomfortably at Tanis, and the half-elf realized that the big man was seeking *his* approval. It was an odd move for the twin, who had always done what Raistlin commanded without question.

Tanis saw that he wasn't the only one who noticed Caramon's mute appeal. Raistlin's eyes glittered in rage.

Now more than ever, Tanis felt wary of the mage, distrusting Raistlin's strange and growing power. It's illogical, he argued with himself. A reaction to a nightmare, nothing more. But that didn't solve his problem. What should he do about the dragon orb? Actually, he realized ruefully, he had little choice.

"Raistlin's the only one with the knowledge and the skill and—let's face it—the guts to handle that thing," Tanis said grudgingly. "I say he should take it, unless one of you wants the responsibility?"

No one spoke, though Riverwind shook his head, frowning darkly. Tanis knew the Plainsman would leave the orb—and Raistlin as well—here in Silvanesti if he had the choice.

"Go ahead, Caramon," Tanis said. "You're the only one strong enough to lift it."

Reluctantly, Caramon went to fetch the orb from its golden stand. His hands shook as he reached out to touch it, but, when he laid his hands upon it, nothing happened. The globe did not change in appearance. Sighing in relief, Caramon lifted the orb, grunting from the weight, and carried it back to his brother, who held the sack open.

"Drop it in the bag," Raistlin ordered.

"What?" Caramon's jaw sagged as he stared from the giant orb to the small bag in the mage's frail hands. "I can't, Raist! It won't fit in there! It'll smash!"

The big man fell silent as Raistlin's eyes flared golden in the dying light of day.

"No! Caramon, wait!" Tanis leaped forward, but this time Caramon did as Raistlin commanded. Slowly, his eyes held fast by his brother's intense gaze, Caramon dropped the dragon orb.

The orb vanished!

"What? Where—" Tanis glared at Raistlin suspiciously.

"In the sack," the mage replied calmly, holding forth the small bag. "See for yourself, if you do not trust me."

Tanis peered into the bag. The orb was inside and it was the true dragon orb, all right. He had no doubt. He could see the swirling mist of green, as though some faint life stirred within. It must have shrunk, he thought in awe, but the orb appeared to be the same size as always, giving Tanis the fearful impression that it was *he* who had grown.

Shuddering, Tanis stepped back. Raistlin gave the drawstring on the top of the bag a quick jerk, snapping it shut. Then, glancing at them distrustfully, he slipped the bag within his robes, secreting it in one of his numerous hidden pockets, and began to turn away. But Tanis stopped him.

"Things can never again be the same between us, can they?" the half-elf asked quietly.

Raistlin looked at him for a moment, and Tanis saw a brief flicker of regret in the young mage's eyes, a longing for trust and friendship and a return to the days of youth.

"No," Raistlin whispered. "But such was the price I paid." He began to cough.

"Price? To whom? For what?"

"Do not question, Half-Elf." The mage's thin shoulders bent with coughing. Caramon put his strong arm around his brother and Raistlin leaned weakly against his twin. When he recovered from the spasm, he lifted his golden eyes. "I cannot tell you the answer, Tanis, because I do not know it myself."

Then, bowing his head, he let Caramon lead him away to find what rest he could before their journey.

"I wish you would reconsider and let us assist you in the funeral rites for your father," Tanis said to Alhana as she stood in the door of the Tower of the Stars to bid them farewell. "A day will not make a difference to us."

"Yes, let us," Goldmoon entreated earnestly. "I know much about this from our people, for our burial customs are similar to yours, if Tanis has told me correctly. I was priestess in my tribe, and I presided over the wrapping of the body in the spiced cloths that will preserve it—"

"No, my friends," Alhana said firmly, her face pale. "It was my father's wish that I—I do this alone."

This was not quite true, but Alhana knew how shocked these people would be at the sight of her father's body being consigned to the ground—a custom practiced only by goblins and other evil creatures. The thought appalled her.† Involuntarily, her gaze was drawn to the tortured and twisted tree that was to mark his grave, standing over it like some fearful carrion bird. Quickly she looked away, her voice faltered.

The elves normally inter their dead in stone sarcophagi that are kept above ground.

"His tomb is—is long prepared and I have some experience of these things myself. Do not worry about me, please."

Tanis saw the agony in her face, but he could not refuse to honor her request.

"We understand," Goldmoon said. Then, on impulse, the Qué-Shu Plainswoman put her arms around the elven princess and held her as she might have held a lost and frightened child. Alhana stiffened at first, then relaxed in Goldmoon's compassionate embrace.

"Be at peace," Goldmoon whispered, stroking back Alhana's dark hair from her face. Then the Plainswoman left.

"After you bury your father, what then?" Tanis asked as he and Alhana stood alone together on the steps of the Tower.

"I will return to my people," Alhana replied gravely. "The griffons will come to me, now that the evil in this land is gone, and they will take me to Ergoth. We will do what we can to help defeat this evil, then we will come home."

Tanis glanced around Silvanesti. Horrifying as it was in the daytime, its terrors at night were beyond description.

"I know," Alhana said in answer to his unspoken thoughts. "This will be our penance."

Tanis raised his eyebrows skeptically, knowing the fight she had ahead of her to get her people to return. Then he saw the conviction on Alhana's face. He gave her even odds.

Smiling, he changed the subject. "And will you find time to go to Sancrist?" he asked. "The knights would be honored by your presence. Particularly one of them."

Alhana's pale face flushed. "Perhaps," she said, barely speaking above a whisper. "I cannot say yet. I have learned many things about myself. But it will take me a long time to make these things a part of me." She shook her head, sighing. "It may be I can never truly be comfortable with them."

"Like learning to love a human?"

Alhana lifted her head, her clear eyes looked into Tanis's. "Would he be happy, Tanis? Away from his homeland, for I must return to Silvanesti? And could I be happy, knowing that I must watch him age and die while I am still in my youth?"

"I asked myself these same questions, Alhana," Tanis said, thinking with pain of the decision he had reached concerning Kitiara. "If we deny love that is given to us, if we refuse to give love because we fear the pain of loss, then our lives will be empty, our loss greater."

"I wondered, when first we met, why these people follow you, Tanis Half-Elven," Alhana said softly. "Now I understand. I will consider your words. Farewell, until your life's journey's end."

"Farewell, Alhana," Tanis answered, taking the hand she extended to him. He could find nothing more to say, and so turned and left her.

But he could not help wondering, as he did, that if he was so damn wise, why was his life in such a mess?

Tanis joined the companions at the edge of the forest. For a moment they stood there, reluctant to enter the woods of Silvanesti. Although they knew the evil was gone, the thought of traveling for days among the twisted, tortured forest was a somber one. But they had no choice. Already they felt the sense of urgency that had driven them this far. Time was sifting through the hourglass, and they knew they could not let the sands run out, although they had no idea why.

"Come, my brother," said Raistlin finally. The mage led the way into the woods, the Staff of Magius shedding its pale light as he walked. Caramon followed, with a sigh. One by one the others trailed after. Tanis alone turned to look back.

They would not see the moons tonight. The land was covered with a heavy darkness as if it too mourned Lorac's death. Alhana stood in the doorway to the Tower of the Stars, her body framed by the Tower, which glimmered in the light of moon rays captured ages ago. Only Alhana's face was visible in the shadows, like the ghost of the silver moon. Tanis caught a glimpse of movement. She raised her hand and there was a brief, clear flash of pure white light—the Starjewel. And then she was gone.

BOOK 2

The story of the companions' journey to Ice Wall Castle and their defeat of the evil Dragon Highlord, Feal-thas, became legend among the Ice Barbarians who inhabit that desolate land. It is still told by the village cleric on long winter nights when heroic deeds are remembered and songs are sung.

Song of the Ice Reaver

I am the one who brought them back.
I am Raggart I am telling you this.
Snow upon snow cancels the signals of ice
Over the snow the sun bleeds whiteness
In cold light forever unbearable.
And if I do not tell you this
The snow descends on the deeds of heroes
And their strength in my singing
Lies down in a core of frost rising no more
No more as the lost breath crumbles.

Seven they were from the hot lands
(I am the one who brought them back)
Four swordsmen sworn in the North
The elf-woman Laurana
The dwarf from the floes of stone
The kender small-boned as a hawk.
Riding three blades they came to the tunnel
To the throat of the only castle.

The ice reaver

Down among Thanoi the old guardians
Where their swordsmen carved hot air
Finding tendon finding bone
As the tunnels melted red.
Down upon minotaur upon ice bear
And the swords whistled again
Bright on the corner of madness
The tunnel knee-high in arms
In claws in unspeakable things
As the swordsmen descended
Bright steam freezing behind them.

Then to the chambers at the castle heart
Where Feal-thas awaited lord of dragons and wolves
Armored in white that is nothing
That covers the ice as the sun bleeds whiteness.
And he called on the wolves the baby-stealers
Who suckled on murder in the lairs of ancestors.
Around the heroes a circle of knives of craving
As the wolves stalked in their master's eye.

And Aran the first to break the circle
Hot wind at the throat of Feal-thas
Brought down and unraveled
In the reel of the hunt perfected.
Brian the next when the sword of the wolf lord
Sent him seeking the warm lands.
All stood frozen in the wheel of razors
All stood frozen except for Laurana.
Blind in a hot light flashing the crown of the mind
Where death melts in a diving sun
She takes up the Ice Reaver
And over the boil of wolves over the slaughter
Bearing a blade of ice bearing darkness
She opened the throat of the wolf lord
And the wolves fell silent as the head collapsed.

Just sort of playing around with Anglo-Saxon prosody, not as much adopting it as letting its music influence the rhythms of the poem. When you do things like that, you take on other baggage: once the meter was set, the story could be no other than a bleak Anglo-Saxon folktale. I like Raggart, the speaker of the poem, who emerges as a character himself: it's a "bring back" the hero when the heroic deeds are sung.—Michael Williams

The rest is short in the telling.
Destroying the eggs the violent get of the dragons
A tunnel of scales and ordure
Followed into the terrible larder
Followed further followed to treasure.
There the orb danced blue danced white
Swelled like a heart in its endless beating
(They let me hold it I brought them back).
Out from the tunnel blood on blood under the ice
Bearing their own incredible burden
The young knights silent and tattered
They came five now only
The kender last small pockets bulging.
I am Raggart I am telling you this.
I am the one who brought them back.

I
The Flight from Ice Wall.

The old dwarf lay dying.

His limbs would no longer support him. His bowels and stomach twisted together like snakes. Waves of nausea broke over him. He could not even raise his head from his bunk. He stared above him at an oil lamp swinging slowly overhead. The lamp's light seemed to be getting dimmer. This is it, thought the dwarf. The end. The darkness is creeping over my eyes. . . .

He heard a noise near him, a creaking of wooden planks as if someone were very quietly stealing up on him. Feebly, Flint managed to turn his head.

"Who is it?" he croaked.

"Tasslehoff," whispered a solicitous voice. Flint sighed and reached out a gnarled hand. Tas's hand closed over his own.

"Ah, lad. I'm glad you've come in time to say farewell," said the dwarf weakly. "I'm dying, lad. I'm going to Reorx—"

"What?" asked Tas, leaning closer.

"Reorx," repeated the dwarf irritably. "I'm going to the arms of Reorx."

"No, we're not," said Tas. "We're going to Sancrist. Unless you mean an inn. I'll ask Sturm. The Reorx Arms. Hmmm—"

"Reorx, the God of the Dwarves, you doorknob!" Flint roared.

"Oh," said Tas after a moment. "*That* Reorx."

"Listen, lad," Flint said more calmly, determined to leave no hard feelings behind. "I want you to have my helm. The one you brought me in Xak Tsaroth, with the griffon's mane."

"Do you really?" Tas asked, impressed. "That's awfully nice of you, Flint, but what will you do for a helm?"

"Ah, lad, I won't need a helm where I'm going."

"You might in Sancrist," Tas said dubiously. "Derek thinks the Dragon Highlords are preparing to launch a full-scaled attack, and I think a helm could come in handy—"

"I'm not talking about Sancrist!" Flint snarled, struggling to sit up. "I won't need a helm because I'm dying!"

"I nearly died once," Tas said solemnly. Setting a steaming bowl on a table, he settled back comfortably in a chair to relate his story. "It was that time in Tarsis when the dragon knocked the building down on top of me. Elistan said I was nearly a goner. Actually those weren't his exact words, but he said it was only through the inter . . . interces . . . oh well, inter-something-or-other of the gods that I'm here today."

Flint gave a mighty groan and fell back limply on his bunk. "Is it too much to ask," he said to the lamp swinging above his head, "that I be allowed to die in peace? Not surrounded by kenders!" This last was practically a shriek.

"Oh, come now. You're not dying, you know," Tas said. "You're only seasick."

"I'm dying," the dwarf said stubbornly. "I've been infected with a serious disease and now I'm dying. And on your heads be it. You dragged me onto this confounded boat—"

"Ship," interrupted Tas.

"Boat!" repeated Flint furiously. "You dragged me onto this confounded boat, then left me to perish of some terrible disease in a rat infested bedroom—"

The story of events in Ice Wall was related by Mary Kirchoff—well, actually, it is related by Raggart of the Ice Folk—in "Finding the Faith" in The Magic of Krynn.

"We could have left you back in Ice Wall,† you know, with the walrus-men and—" Tasslehoff stopped.

Flint was once again struggling to sit up, but this time there was a wild look in his eyes. The kender rose to his feet and began edging his way toward the door. "Uh, I guess I better be going. I just came down here to—uh—see if you wanted anything to eat. The ship's cook made something he calls green pea soup—"

Laurana, huddled out of the wind on the foredeck, started as she heard the most frightful roaring sound come from below decks, followed by the cracking of smashed crockery. She glanced at Sturm, who was standing near her. The knight smiled.

"Flint," he said.

"Yes," Laurana said, worried. "Perhaps I should—"

She was interrupted by the appearance of Tasslehoff dripping with green pea soup.

"I think Flint's feeling better," Tasslehoff said solemnly. "But he's not quite ready to eat anything yet."

When DRAGONLANCE *was first being created, the Highlords were, indeed, called Dragonlords. However, we discovered that another company was doing a product that used "Dragonlords," so we had to come up with another name for our commanders. The result was Dragon Highlords. It looks here as if one of those pesky Dragonlords snuck in here.—TRH*

The journey from Ice Wall had been swift. Their small ship fairly flew through the sea waters, carried north by the currents and the strong, cold prevailing winds.

The companions had traveled to Ice Wall where, according to Tasslehoff, a dragon orb was kept in Ice Wall Castle. They found the orb and defeated its evil guardian, Feal-thas—a powerful Dragonlord.† Escaping the destruction of the castle with the help of the Ice Barbarians, they were now on a ship bound for Sancrist. Although the precious dragon orb was stowed safely in a chest below decks, the horrors of their journey to Ice Wall still tormented their dreams at night.

But the nightmares of Ice Wall were nothing compared to that strange and vivid dream they had

experienced well over a month ago. None of them referred to it, but Laurana occasionally saw a look of fear and loneliness, unusual to Sturm, that made her think he might be recalling the dream as well.

Other than that, the party was in good spirits—except the dwarf, who had been hauled on the ship bodily and was promptly seasick. The journey to Ice Wall had been an undoubted victory. Along with the dragon orb, they carried away with them the broken shaft of an ancient weapon, believed to be a dragonlance. And they carried something more important, though they did not realize it at the time they found it. . . .

The companions, accompanied by Derek Crownguard and the other two young knights† who had joined them at Tarsis, had been searching Ice Wall castle for the dragon orb. The search had not gone well. Time and again they had fought off the evil walrus-men, winter wolves, and bears. The companions began to think they may have come here for nothing, but Tas swore that the book he read in Tarsis said there was an orb located here. So they kept looking.

One of whom is Aran Tallbow, mentioned in "Song of the Ice Reaver"

It was during their search that they came upon a startling sight—a huge dragon, over forty feet long, its skin a shimmering silver, completely encased in a wall of ice. The dragon's wings were spread, poised for flight. The dragon's expression was fierce, but his head was noble, and he did not inspire them with the fear and loathing they remembered experiencing around the red dragons. Instead, they felt a great, overwhelming sorrow for this magnificent creature.

But strangest to them was the fact that this dragon had a rider! They had seen the Dragon Highlords ride their dragons, but this man appeared by his ancient armor to have been a Knight of Solamnia! Held tightly in his gloved hand was the broken shaft of what must have been a large lance.

"Why would a Knight of Solamnia be riding a dragon?" Laurana asked, thinking of the Dragon Highlords.

"There have been knights who turned to evil," Lord Derek Crownguard said harshly. "Though it shames me to admit it."

"I get no feeling of evil here," Elistan said. "Only a great sorrow. I wonder how they died. I see no wounds—"

"This seems familiar," Tasslehoff interrupted, frowning. "Like a picture. A knight riding a silver dragon. I've seen—"

"Bah!" Flint snorted. "You've seen furry elephant—"

"I'm serious," Tas protested.

"Where was it, Tas?" Laurana asked gently, seeing a hurt expression on the kender's face. "Can you remember?"

"I think . . ." Tasslehoff's eyes lost their focus. "It puts me in mind of Pax Tharkas and Fizban. . . ."

"Fizban!" Flint exploded. "That old mage was crazier than Raistlin, if that's possible."

"I don't know what Tas is talking about," Sturm said, gazing up at the dragon and its rider thoughtfully. "But I remember my mother telling me that Huma rode upon a Silver Dragon, carrying the Dragonlance, in his final battle."

"And I remember my mother telling me to leave sweetcakes for the white-robed Old One who came to our castle at Yuletime,"† scoffed Derek. "No, this is undoubtedly some renegade Knight, enslaved by evil."

If you're wondering why people who don't have Christmas celebrate Yule, I see Yule as more of the pagan celebration, a mid-winter festival.—MW

Derek and the other two young knights turned to go, but the rest lingered, staring up at the figure on the dragon.

"You're right, Sturm. That's a dragonlance," Tas said wistfully. "I don't know how I know, but I'm sure of it."

"Did you see it in the book in Tarsis?" Sturm asked, exchanging glances with Laurana, each of them thinking that the kender's seriousness was unusual, even frightening.

Tas shrugged. "I don't know," he said in a small voice. "I'm sorry."

"Maybe we should take it with us," Laurana suggested uneasily. "It couldn't hurt."

"Come along, Brightblade!" Derek's voice came back to them, echoing sternly. "The Thanoi may have lost us for the moment, but they'll discover our trail before long."

"How can we get it?" Sturm asked, ignoring Derek's order. "It's encased in ice at least three feet thick!"

"I can," Gilthanas said.

Jumping up onto the huge cliff of ice that had formed around the dragon and its rider, the elf found a handhold and began to inch his way up the monument. From the dragon's frozen wing, he was able to crawl along on his hands and knees until he came to the lance, clutched in the rider's hand. Gilthanas pressed his hand against the ice wall covering the lance and spoke the strange, spidery language of magic.

A red glow spread from the elf's hand to the ice, melting it away rapidly. Within moments, he was able to reach his hand through the hole to grasp the lance. But it was held fast in the dead knight's hand.

Gilthanas tugged and even tried to pry the frozen fingers of the hand loose. Finally he could stand the cold of the ice no longer and dropped, shivering, back down to the ground. "There's no way," he said. "He's got it gripped tight."

"Break the fingers—" suggested Tas helpfully.

Sturm silenced the kender with a furious look. "I will not have his body desecrated," he snapped. "Maybe we can slide the lance out of his hand. I'll try—"

"No good," Gilthanas told his sister as they watched Sturm climb up the side of the ice. "It's as if the lance has become part of the hand. I—" The elf stopped.

As Sturm put his hand through the hole in the ice and took hold of the lance, the ice-bound figure of the knight seemed to move suddenly, just slightly. Its stiff and frozen hand relaxed its grip on the shattered lance. Sturm nearly fell in his amazement, and, letting go of the weapon hurriedly, he backed away along the dragon's ice-coated wing.

"He's giving it to you," cried Laurana. "Go ahead, Sturm! Take it! Don't you see, he's giving it to another knight."

"Which I'm not," Sturm said bitterly. "But perhaps that's indicative, perhaps it is evil—" Hesitantly, he slid back to the hole and grasped the lance once more. The stiff hand of the dead knight released its grip. Taking hold of the broken weapon, Sturm carefully brought it out of the ice. He jumped back to the ground and stood staring at the ancient shaft.

"That was wonderful!" Tas said in awe. "Flint, did you see the corpse come alive?"

"No!" snapped the dwarf. "And neither did you. Let's get out of here," he added, shivering.

Then Derek appeared. "I gave you an order, Sturm Brightblade! What's the delay?" Derek's face darkened with anger as he saw the lance.

"I asked him to get it for me," Laurana said, her voice as cool as the wall of ice behind her. Taking the lance, she began to wrap it swiftly in a fur cloak from her pack.

Derek regarded her angrily for a moment, then bowed stiffly and turned on his heel.

"Dead knights, live knights, I don't know who's worse," Flint grumbled, grabbing Tas and dragging him along after Derek.

"What if it is a weapon of evil?" Sturm asked Laurana in a low voice as they traveled the icy corridors of the castle.

Laurana looked back one final time at the dead knight mounted on the dragon. The cold pale sun of the southland was setting, its light casting watery shadows across the corpses, giving them a sinister aspect. Even as she watched, she thought she saw the body slump lifelessly.

"Do you believe the story of Huma?" Laurana asked softly.

"I don't know what to believe anymore," Sturm said, bitterness hardening his voice. "Everything used to be black and white for me, all things clear-cut and well-defined. I believed in the story of Huma. My mother taught it to me as the truth. Then I went to Solamnia."† He paused, as if unwilling to continue. Finally, seeing Laurana's face filled with interest and compassion, he swallowed and went on. "I never told anyone this, not even Tanis. When I returned to my homeland, I found that the Knighthood was not the order of honorable, self-sacrificing men my mother had described. It was rife with political intrigue. The best of the men were like Derek, honorable, but strict and unbending, with little use for those they consider beneath them. The worst—" He shook his head. "When I spoke of Huma, they laughed. An itinerant knight, they called him. According to their story, he was cast out of the order for disobeying its

After traveling briefly with Kitiara five years before, Sturm went to Castle Brightblade in Solamnia, where he found his father's sword and armor. However, it took Kitiara's return to rescue him from possible death. The story is in Darkness and Light *by Paul B. Thompson and Tonya R. Carter.*

laws. Huma roamed the countryside, they said, endearing himself to peasants, who thus began to create legends about him."

"But did he really exist?" Laurana persisted, saddened by the sorrow in Sturm's face.

"Oh, yes. Of that there can be no doubt. The records that survived the Cataclysm list his name among the lower orders of the knights. But the story of the Silver Dragon, the Final Battle, even the Dragonlance itself—no one believes anymore. Like Derek says, there is no proof. The tomb of Huma, according to the legend, was a towering structure—one of the wonders of the world. But you can find no one who has ever seen it. All we have are children's stories, as Raistlin would say." Sturm put his hand to his face, covering his eyes, and gave a deep, shuddering sigh.

"Do you know," he said softly, "I never thought I'd say it, but I miss Raistlin. I miss all of them. I feel as if a part of me's been cut off, and that's how I felt when I was in Solamnia. That's why I came back, instead of waiting and completing the tests for my knighthood. These people—my friends—were doing more to combat evil in the world than all the Knights lined up in a row. Even Raistlin, in some way I can't understand. *He* could tell us what all this means." He jerked his thumb back at the ice-encased knight. "At least he would believe in it. If he were here. If Tanis were here—" Sturm could not go on.

"Yes," Laurana said quietly. "If Tanis were here—"

Remembering her great sorrow, so much greater than his own, Sturm put his arm around Laurana and held her close. The two stood for a moment, each comforted for their losses by the other's presence. Then Derek's voice came sharply back to them, reprimanding them for lagging behind.

And now, the broken lance, wrapped in Laurana's fur cloak, lay in the chest with the dragon orb and Wyrmslayer, Tanis's sword, which Laurana and Sturm had carried with them from Tarsis. Beside the chest lay the bodies of the two young knights, who had given their lives in defense of the group, and who were being carried back to be buried in their homeland.

The strong southern wind, blowing swift and cold from the glaciers, propelled the ship across the Sirrion Sea. The captain said that, if the winds held, they might make Sancrist in two days.

"That way lies Southern Ergoth." The captain told Elistan, pointing off to starboard. "We'll be just coming up on the south end of it. This nightfall, you'll see the Isle of Cristyne.† Then, with a fair wind, we'll be in Sancrist. Strange thing about Southern Ergoth," the captain added, glancing at Laurana, "it's filled with elves, they say, though I haven't been there to know if that's true."

I believe that Cristyne—with some spelling revision—was named after Doug Niles's wife.—TRH

"Elves!" said Laurana eagerly, coming forward to stand beside the captain, the early morning wind whipping her cloak.

"Fled their homeland, so I heard," the captain continued. "Driven off by the dragonarmies."

Cristyne is a small island that separates from Southern Ergoth in the Cataclysm. It has an ancient citadel abandoned long ago by a wizard named Magus. Years after the War of the Lance, when other troubles loom on Krynn, it will be necessary for the elves to move there.

"Perhaps it's our people!" Laurana said, clutching at Gilthanas, who stood next to her. She gazed out over the bow of the ship intently, as if she could will the land to appear.

"Most likely the Silvanesti," Gilthanas said. "In fact, I think Lady Alhana may have mentioned something about Ergoth. Do you remember, Sturm?"

"No," the knight answered abruptly. Turning and walking over to the port side of the ship, he leaned against the railing, staring out across the pink-tinged sea. Laurana saw him pull something from his belt and run his fingers over it lovingly. There was a bright flash, as it caught the sun's rays, then he slipped it back into his belt. His head bowed. Laurana started to go to him when suddenly she stopped, catching a glimpse of movement.

"What kind of strange cloud is that to the south?"

The captain turned immediately, whipping his spyglass out of the pocket of his fur parka and placing it to his eye. "Send a man aloft," he snapped to his first mate.

Within moments, a sailor was scampering up the rigging. Clinging to the dizzying heights of the mast with one arm, he peered south through the spyglass.

"Can you make it out?" the captain called aloft.

"No, capt'n," the man bellowed. "If it's a cloud, it's like none I've seen afore."

"I'll look!" volunteered Tasslehoff eagerly. The kender began to climb the ropes as skillfully as the sailor. Reaching the mast, he clung to the rigging near the man and stared south.

It certainly seemed to be a cloud. It was huge and white and appeared to be floating above the water. But it was moving much more rapidly than any other cloud in the sky and—

Tasslehoff gasped. "Let me borrow that," he asked, holding out his hand for the watch's spyglass. Reluctantly, the man gave it to him. Tas put it to his eye, then he groaned softly. "Oh, dear," he muttered. Lowering the spyglass, he shut it up with a snap and absently stuffed it into his tunic. The sailor caught him by the collar as he was about to slide down.

"What?" Tas said, startled. "Oh! Is that yours? Sorry." Giving the spyglass a wistful pat, he handed it back to the sailor. Tas slid skillfully down the ropes, landed lightly on the deck, and came running over to Sturm.

"It's a dragon," he reported breathlessly.

2

The White Dragon. Captured!

The dragon's name was Sleet. She was a white dragon, a species of dragon smaller than other dragons dwelling in Krynn. Born and bred in the arctic regions, these dragons were able to withstand extreme cold, and controlled the ice-bound southern regions of Ansalon.

Because of their smaller size, the white dragons† were the swiftest flyers of all dragonkind. The Dragon Highlords often used them for scouting missions. Thus Sleet had been away from her lair in Ice Wall when the companions entered it in search of the dragon orb. The Dark Queen had received a report that Silvanesti had been invaded by a group of adventurers. They had managed, somehow, to defeat Cyan Bloodbane and were reportedly in possession of a dragon orb.

White dragons are, of course, evil. They rejoice in being loners, quite willing to isolate themselves in the wastes of the icy lands. Their breath weapon is a death-dealing blast of frigid air.

The Dark Queen guessed they might be traveling across the Plains of Dust, along the Kings Road, which was the most direct overland route to Sancrist where the Knights of Solamnia were reportedly trying to regroup. The Dark Queen ordered Sleet† and her flight of white dragons to speed north to the Plains of Dust, now lying under a thick, heavy blanket of packed snow, to find the orb.

Sleet's dragon name, which undoubtedly the Dark Queen knows, is Terrisleetix.

Seeing the snow glistening beneath her, Sleet doubted very much if even humans would be foolhardy enough to attempt to cross the wasteland. But she had her orders and she followed them. Scattering her flight, Sleet scoured every inch of land from the borders of Silvanesti on the east to the Kharolis Mountains on the west. A few of her dragons even flew as far north as New Coast, which was held by the blues.

The dragons met to report that they had seen no sign of any living being on the Plains when Sleet received word that danger had marched in the back door while she was out scouting the front.

Furious, Sleet flew back but arrived too late. Fealthas was dead, the dragon orb missing. But her walrus-men allies, the Thanoi,† were able to describe the group who had committed this heinous act. They even pointed out the direction their ship had sailed, although there was only one direction any ship could sail from Ice Wall—north.

The Thanoi used to be regarded as one of the "lost races" of Krynn, but apparently the Dark Queen moved a few evolutionary stragglers to the wastes of Ice Wall, where they have thrived—under her command.

Sleet reported the loss of the dragon orb to her Dark Queen, who was intensely angry and frightened. Now there were two orbs missing! Although secure in the knowledge that her force for evil was the strongest in Krynn, the Dark Queen knew with a nagging certainty that the forces of good still walked the land. One of these might prove strong and wise enough to figure out the secret of the orb.

Sleet, therefore, was ordered to find the orb and bring it not back to Ice Wall, but to the Queen herself. Under no circumstances was the dragon to lose it or allow it to be lost. The orbs were intelligent and imbued with a strong sense of survival. Thus they had lived this long when even those who created them were dead.

Sleet sped out over the Sirrion Sea, her strong white wings soon carrying her swiftly to within sight of the ship. But now Sleet was presented with

an interesting intellectual problem, and she was not prepared to handle it.

Perhaps because of the inbreeding necessary to create a reptile that can tolerate cold weather, white dragons are the lowest in intelligence among dragonkind. Sleet had never needed to think much on her own. Feal-thas† always told her what to do. Consequently, she was considerably perplexed over her current problem as she circled the ship: how could she get the orb?

The Dragon Highlord of the White Wing, Feal-thas was a dark elf who sold out his race in return for power.

At first she had just planned to freeze the ship with her icy breath. Then she realized this would simply enclose the orb in a frozen block of wood, making it extremely difficult to remove. There was also every probability the ship would sink before she could tear it apart. And if she did manage to take the ship apart, the orb might sink. The ship was too heavy to lift in her claws and fly to land. Sleet circled the ship and pondered, while down below she could see the pitiful humans racing around like scared mice.

The white dragon considered sending another telepathic message to her Queen, asking for help. But Sleet hesitated to remind the vengeful queen of either her presence or her ignorance. The dragon followed the ship all day, hanging just above it, pondering. Floating easily on the wind currents, she let her dragon fear stir the humans into a frenzy of panic. Then, just as the sun was setting, Sleet had an idea. Without stopping to think, she acted upon it at once.

Tasslehoff's report of the white dragon following the vessel sent waves of terror through the crew. They armed themselves with cutlasses and grimly prepared to fight the beast as long as they could, though all knew how such a contest must end. Gilthanas and Laurana, both skillful archers, fit arrows to their bows. Sturm and Derek held shield and sword. Tasslehoff grabbed his hoopak. Flint tried to get out of bed, but he couldn't even stand up. Elistan was calm, praying to Paladine.

"I have more faith in my sword than that old man and his god," Derek said to Sturm.

"The Knights have always honored Paladine," Sturm said in rebuke.

"I honor him—his memory," Derek said. "I find this talk of Paladine's 'return' disturbing, Brightblade. And so will the Council, when they hear of it. You would do well to consider that when the question of your knighthood arises."

Sturm bit his lip, swallowing his angry retort like bitter medicine.

Long minutes passed. Everyone's eyes were on the white-winged creature flying above them. But they could do nothing, and so they waited.

And waited. And waited. The dragon did not attack.

She circled above them endlessly, her shadow crossing and crisscrossing the deck with monotonous, chilling regularity. The sailors, who had been prepared to fight without question, soon began to mutter among themselves as the waiting grew unbearable. To make matters worse, the dragon seemed to be sucking up the wind, for the sails fluttered and drooped lifelessly. The ship lost its graceful forward momentum and began to flounder in the water. Storm clouds gathered on the northern horizon and slowly drifted over the water, casting a pall across the bright sea.

Laurana finally lowered her bow and rubbed her aching back and shoulder muscles. Her eyes, dazzled from staring into the sun, were blurred and watery.

"Put 'em in a lifeboat and cast 'em adrift," she overheard one old grizzled sailor suggest to a companion in a voice meant to carry. "Perhaps yon great beast will let us go. It's them she's after, not us."

It's not even us she's after, Laurana thought uneasily. It's probably the dragon orb. That's why she hasn't attacked. But Laurana couldn't tell this, even to the captain. The dragon orb must be kept secret.

The afternoon crept on, and still the dragon circled like a horrible seabird. The captain was growing more and more irritable. Not only did he have a dragon to contend with, but the likelihood of mutiny as well. Near dinnertime, he ordered the companions below decks.

Derek and Sturm both refused, and it appeared things might get out of hand when, "Land ho, off the starboard bow!"

"Southern Ergoth," the captain said grimly. "The current's carrying us toward the rocks." He glanced

up at the circling dragon. "If a wind doesn't come soon, we'll smash up on them."

At that moment, the dragon quit circling. She hovered a moment, then soared upward. The sailors cheered, thinking she was flying away. But Laurana knew better, remembering Tarsis.

"She's going to dive!" she cried. "She's going to attack!"

"Get below!" Sturm shouted, and the sailors, after one hesitant look skyward, began to scramble for the hatches. The captain ran to the wheel.

"Get below," he ordered the helmsman, taking over.

"You can't stay up here!" Sturm shouted. Leaving the hatch, he ran back to the captain. "She'll kill you!"

"We'll founder if I don't," the captain cried angrily.

"We'll founder if you're dead!" Sturm said. Clenching his fist, he hit the captain in the jaw and dragged him below.

Laurana stumbled down the stairs with Gilthanas behind her. The elflord waited until Sturm brought the unconscious captain down, then he pulled the hatch cover shut.

At that moment, the dragon hit the ship with a blast that nearly sent the vessel under. The ship listed precariously. Everyone, even the most hardened sailor, lost his feet and went skidding into each other in the crowded quarters below deck. Flint rolled onto the floor with a curse.

"Now's the time to pray to your god," Derek said to Elistan.

"I am," Elistan replied coolly, helping the dwarf up.

Laurana, clinging to a post, waited fearfully for the flaring orange light, the heat, the flames. Instead, there was a sudden sharp and biting cold that took her breath away and chilled her blood. She could hear, above her, rigging snap and crack, the flapping of the sails cease. Then, as she stared upward, she saw white frost begin to sift down between the cracks in the wooden deck.

"The white dragons don't breathe flame!" Laurana said in awe. "They breathe ice! Elistan! Your prayers were answered!"

"Bah! It might as well be flame," the captain said, shaking his head and rubbing his jaw. "Ice'll freeze us up solid."

"A dragon breathing ice!" Tas said wistfully. "I wish I could see!"

"What will happen?" Laurana asked, as the ship slowly righted itself, creaking and groaning.

"We're helpless," the captain snarled. "The riggin'll snap beneath the weight of the ice, dragging the sails down. The mast'll break like a tree in an ice storm. With no steerage, the current will smash her upon the rocks, and that'll be an end of her. There's not a damn thing we can do!"

"We could try to shoot her as she flies past," Gilthanas said. But Sturm shook his head, pushing on the hatch.

"There must be a foot of ice on top of this," the knight reported. "We're sealed in."

This is how the dragon will get the orb, Laurana thought miserably. She'll drive the ship aground, kill us, then recover the orb where there's no danger of it sinking into the ocean.

"Another blast like that will send us to the bottom," the captain predicted, but there was not another blast like the first. The next blast was more gentle, and all of them realized the dragon was using her breath to blow them to shore.

It was an excellent plan, and one of which Sleet was rather proud. She skimmed after the ship, letting the current and the tide carry it to shore, giving it a little puff now and then. It was only when she saw the jagged rocks sticking up out of the moonlit water that the dragon suddenly saw the flaw in her scheme. Then the moon's light was gone, swept away by the storm clouds, and the dragon could see nothing. It was darker than her Queen's soul.

The dragon cursed the storm clouds, so well suited to the purposes of the Dragon Highlords in the north. But the clouds worked against her as they blotted out the two moons. Sleet could hear the rending and cracking sounds of splintering wood as the ship struck the rocks. She could even hear the cries and shouts of the sailors—but she couldn't see! Diving low over the water, she hoped to encase the miserable creatures in ice until daylight. Then she heard another, more frightening sound in the darkness—the twanging of bow strings.

An arrow whistled past her head. Another tore through the fragile membrane of her wing. Shrieking in pain, Sleet pulled up from her steep dive. There must be elves down there, she realized in a fury! More arrows zinged past her. Cursed, night-seeing elves! With their elvensight, they would find her an easy target, especially crippled in one wing.

Feeling her strength ebb, the dragon decided to return to Ice Wall. She was tired from flying all day, and the arrow wound hurt abominably. True, she would have to report another failure to the Dark Queen, but—as she came to think of it—it wasn't such a failure after all. She had kept the dragon orb from reaching Sancrist, and she had demolished the ship. She knew the location of the orb. The Queen, with her vast network of spies on Ergoth, could easily recover it.

Mollified, the white dragon fluttered south, traveling slowly. By morning she had reached her vast glacier home. Following her report, which was moderately well-received, Sleet was able to slip into her cavern of ice and nurse her injured wing back to health.

"She's gone!" said Gilthanas in astonishment.

"Of course," said Derek wearily as he helped salvage what supplies they could from the wrecked ship. "Her vision cannot match your elfsight. Besides, you hit her once."

"Laurana's shot, not mine," Gilthanas said, smiling at his sister, who stood on shore, her bow in her hand.

Derek sniffed doubtfully. Carefully setting down the box he carried, the knight started back out into the water. A figure looming out of the darkness stopped him.

"No use, Derek," Sturm said. "The ship sank."

Sturm carried Flint on his back. Seeing Sturm stagger with weariness, Laurana ran back into the water to help him. Between them, they got the dwarf to shore and stretched him on the sand. Out to sea, the sounds of cracking timber had ceased, replaced now by the endless breaking of the waves.

Then there was a splashing sound, Tasslehoff waded ashore after them, his teeth chattering, but

his grin as wide as ever. He was followed by the captain, being helped by Elistan.

"What about the bodies of my men?" Derek demanded the moment he saw the captain. "Where are they?"

"We had more important things to carry," Elistan said sternly. "Things needed for the living, such as food and weapons."

"Many another good man has found his final home beneath the waves. Yours won't be the first—nor the last—I suppose, more's the pity," the captain added.

Derek seemed about to speak, but the captain, grief and exhaustion in his eyes, said, "I've left six of my own men there this night, sir. Unlike yours, they were alive when we started this voyage. To say nothing of the fact that my ship and my livelihood lies down there, too. I wouldn't consider adding anything further, if you take my meaning. Sir."

"I am sorry for your loss, captain," Derek answered stiffly. "And I commend you and your crew for all you tried to do."

The captain muttered something and stood looking aimlessly around the beach, as if lost.

"We sent your men north along the shore, captain," Laurana said, pointing. "There's shelter there, within those trees."

As if to verify her words, a bright light flared, the light of a huge bonfire.

"Fools!" Derek swore bitterly. "They'll have the dragon back on us."

"It's either that or catch our deaths of cold," the captain said bitterly over his shoulder. "Take your choice, sir knight. It matters little to me." He disappeared into the darkness.

Sturm stretched and groaned, trying to ease chilled, cramped muscles. Flint lay huddled in misery, shaking so the buckles on his armor jangled. Laurana, leaning down to tuck her cloak around him, realized suddenly how cold she was.

In the excitement of trying to escape the ship and fighting the dragon, she had forgotten the chill. She couldn't even remember, in fact, any details of her escape. She remembered reaching the beach, seeing the dragon diving on them. She remembered fumbling for her bow with numb, shaking fingers. She

wondered how anyone had presence of mind to save anything—

"The dragon orb!" she said fearfully.

"Here, in this chest," Derek answered. "Along with the lance and that elvish sword you call Wyrmslayer. And now, I suppose, we should take advantage of the fire—"

"I think not." A strange voice spoke out of the darkness as lighted torches flared around them, blinding them.

The companions started and immediately drew their weapons, gathering around the helpless dwarf. But Laurana, after an instant's fright, peered into the faces in the torchlight.

"Hold!" she cried. "These are our people! These are elves!"

"Silvanesti!" Gilthanas said heartily. Dropping his bow to the ground, he walked forward toward the elf who had spoken. "We have journeyed long through darkness," he said in elven, his hands outstretched. "Well met, my broth—"

He never finished his ancient greeting. The leader of the elven party stepped forward and slammed the end of his staff across Gilthanas's face, knocking him to the sand, unconscious.

Sturm and Derek immediately raised their swords, standing back to back. Steel flashed among the elves.

"Stop!" Laurana shouted in elven. Kneeling by her brother, she threw back the hood of her cloak so that the light fell upon her face."We are your cousins. Qualinesti! These humans are Knights of Solamnia!"

"We know well enough who you are!" The elven leader spit the words, "Qualinesti spies! And we do not find it unusual that you travel in the company of humans. Your blood has long been polluted. Take them," he said, motioning to his men. "If they don't come peacefully, do what you must. And find out what they mean by this dragon orb they mentioned."

The elves stepped forward.

"No!" Derek cried, jumping to stand before the chest. "Sturm, they must not have the orb!"

Sturm had already given the Knight's salute to an enemy and was advancing, sword drawn.

"It appears they will fight. So be it," the leader of the elves said, raising his weapon.

"I tell you, this is madness!" Laurana cried angrily. She threw herself between the flashing swordblades. The elves halted uncertainly. Sturm grabbed hold of her to drag her back, but she jerked free of his restraining hand.

"Goblins and draconians, in all their hideous evil, do not sink to fighting among themselves"—her voice shook with rage—"while we elves, the ancient embodiment of good, try to kill each other! Look!"She lifted the lid of the chest with one hand and threw it open. "In here we have the hope of the world! A dragon orb, taken at great peril from Ice Wall. Our ship lies wrecked in the waters out there. We drove away the dragon that sought to recover this orb. And, after all this, we find our greatest peril among our own people! If this is true, if we have sunk so low, then kill us now, and I swear, not one person in this group will try to stop you."

Sturm, not understanding elven, watched for a moment, then saw the elves lower their weapons. "Well, whatever she said, it seems to have worked." Reluctantly, he sheathed his weapon. Derek, after a moment's hesitation, lowered his sword, but he did not put it back in its scabbard.

"We will consider your story," the elven leader began, speaking haltingly in Common. Then he stopped as shouts and cries were heard from down the beach. The companions saw dark shadows converge on the campfire. The elf glanced that direction, waited a moment until all had quieted, then turned back to the group. He looked particularly at Laurana, who was bending over her brother. "We may have acted in haste, but when you have lived here long, you will come to understand."

"I will never understand this!" Laurana said, tears choking her voice.

An elf appeared out of the darkness. "Humans, sir." Laurana heard him report in elven. "Sailors by their appearance. They say their ship was attacked by a dragon and wrecked on the rocks."

"Verification?"

"We found bits of wreckage floating ashore. We can search in the morning. The humans are wet and

miserable and half-drowned. They offered no resistance. I don't think they've lied."

The elven leader turned to Laurana. "Your story appears to be true," he said, speaking once more in Common. "My men report that the humans they captured are sailors. Do not worry about them. We will take them prisoner, of course. We cannot have humans wandering around this island with all our other problems. But we will care for them well. We are not goblins," he added bitterly. "I regret striking your friend—"

"Brother," Laurana replied. "And younger son of the Speaker of the Suns. I am Lauralanthalasa, and this is Gilthanas. We are of the royal house of Qualinesti."

It seemed to her that the elf paled at this news, but he regained his composure immediately. "Your brother will be well tended. I will send for a healer—"

"We do not need your healer!" Laurana said. "This man"—she gestured toward Elistan—"is a cleric of Paladine. He will aid my brother—"

"A human?" the elf asked sternly.

"Yes, human!" Laurana cried impatiently. "Elves struck my brother down! I turn to humans to heal him. Elistan—"

The cleric started forward, but, at a sign from their leader, several elves quickly grabbed him and pinned his arms behind him. Sturm started to go to his aid, but Elistan stopped him with a look, glancing at Laurana meaningfully. Sturm fell back, understanding Elistan's silent warning. Their lives depended on her.

"Let him go!" Laurana demanded. "Let him treat my brother!"

"I find this news of a cleric of Paladine impossible to believe, Lady Laurana," the elf leader said. "All know the clerics vanished from Krynn when the gods turned their faces from us. I do not know who this charlatan is, or how he has tricked you into believing him, but we will not allow him to lay his human hands upon an elf!"

"Even an elf who is an enemy?" she cried furiously.

"Even if the elf had killed my own father," the elf said grimly. "And now, Lady Laurana, I must speak

to you privately and try to explain what is transpiring on Southern Ergoth."

Seeing Laurana hesitate, Elistan spoke, "Go on, my dear. You are the only one who can save us now. I will stay near Gilthanas."

"Very well," Laurana said, rising to her feet. Her face pale, she walked apart with the elven leader.

"I don't like this," Derek said, scowling. "She told them of the dragon orb, which she should not have done."

"They heard us talking about it," Sturm said wearily.

"Yes, but she told them where it was! I don't trust her, or her people. Who knows what kind of deals they are making?" Derek added.

"That does it!" grated a voice.

Both men turned in astonishment to see Flint staggering to his feet. His teeth still chattered, but a cold light glinted in his eyes as he looked at Derek. "I—I've had a-about enough of y-you, S-Sir High and M-Mighty." The dwarf gritted his teeth to stop shivering long enough to speak.

Sturm started to intervene, but the dwarf shoved him aside to confront Derek. It was a ludicrous sight, and one Sturm often remembered with a smile, storing it up to share with Tanis. The dwarf, his long white beard wet and scraggly, water dripping from his clothes to form puddles at his feet, stood nearly level with Derek's belt buckle, scolding the tall, proud Solamnic knight as he might have scolded Tasslehoff.

"You knights have lived encased in metal so long it's shaken your brains to mush!" The dwarf snorted. "If you ever had any brains to begin with, which I doubt. I've seen that girl grow from a wee bit of a thing to the beautiful woman she is now. And I tell you there isn't a more courageous, nobler person on Krynn. What's got you is that she just saved your hide. And you can't handle that!"

Derek's face flushed dark in the torchlight.

"I need neither dwarves nor elves defending me—" Derek began angrily when Laurana came running back, her eyes glittering.

"As if there is not evil enough," she muttered through tight lips, "I find it brewing among my own kindred!"

"What's going on?" asked Sturm.

"The situation stands thus: There are now three races of elves† living in Southern Ergoth—"

All elves together, in the days before they split, were called Colinesti, meaning "people of the morning." They have always regarded themselves as the first race to be created by the gods and the most favored of the gods of Good in particular.

"Three races?" interrupted Tasslehoff, staring at Laurana with interest. "What's the third race? Where'd they come from? Can I see them? I never heard—"

Laurana had had enough. "Tas," she said, her voice taut. "Go stay with Gilthanas. And ask Elistan to come here."

"But—"

Sturm gave the kender a shove. "Go!" he ordered.

Wounded, Tasslehoff trailed off disconsolately to where Gilthanas still lay. The kender slumped down in the sand, pouting. Elistan patted him kindly as he went to join the others.

"The Kaganesti, known as Wilder Elves in the Common tongue, are the third race," Laurana continued. "They fought with us during the Kinslayer wars. In return for their loyalty, Kith-Kanan gave them the mountains of Ergoth—this was before Qualinesti and Ergoth were split apart by the Cataclysm. I am not surprised you have never heard of the Wilder Elves. They are a secretive people and keep to themselves. Once called the Border Elves, they are ferocious fighters and served Kith-Kanan well, but they have no love for cities. They mingled with Druids and learned their lore. They brought back the ways of the ancient elves. My people consider them barbarians—just as your people consider the Plainsmen barbaric.

"Some months ago, when the Silvanesti were driven from their ancient homeland, they fled here,† seeking permission of the Kaganesti to dwell in Ergoth temporarily. Then came my people, the Qualinesti, from across the sea. And so they met, at last, kindred who had been separated for hundreds of years."

The elves took over the southwestern portion of the island, separated from the east by mountains and a parallel region known as the Wasted Lands for good reason.

"I fail to see the relevance—" Derek interrupted.

"You will," she said, drawing a deep breath. "For your lives depend upon understanding what is happening on this sad isle." Her voice broke. Elistan moved near her and put his arm around her comfortingly.

"All started out peacefully enough. After all, the two exiled cousins had much in common—both

driven from their beloved homelands by the evil in the world. They established homes upon the Isle—the Silvanesti upon the western shore, the Qualinesti upon the eastern, separated by a strait known as Thon-Tsalarian, which means the 'River of the Dead' in Kaganesti. The Kaganesti† live in the hill country north of the river.

"For a time, there was even some attempt to establish friendships between the Silvanesti and the Qualinesti. And that is where the trouble began. For these elves could not meet, even after hundreds of years, without the old hatreds and misunderstandings beginning to surface." Laurana closed her eyes a moment. "The River of the Dead could very well be known as Thon-Tsalaroth—'River of Death.' "

This difference between "Kagonesti" (as became the accepted spelling in later years) and "Kaganesti" is primarily a problem with phonetic translation. Elves from southern Qualinesti have a tendency to speak the word with the Kagonesti sound, while more northern elves speak it with an accent that sounds more like Kaganesti. We apologize for the translation problem. —TRH

"There now, lass," Flint said, touching her hand. "The dwarves have known it, too. You saw the way I was treated in Thorbardin—a hill dwarf among mountain dwarves. Of all the hatreds, the ones between families are the cruelest."

"There has been no killing yet, but so shocked were the elders at the thought of what might happen—elves killing their own kindred—that they decreed no one may cross the straits on penalty of arrest," Laurana continued. "And this is where we stand. Neither side trusts the other. There have even been charges of selling out to the Dragon Highlords! Spies have been captured on both sides."

"That explains why they attacked us," Elistan murmured.

"What about the Kag—Kag—" Sturm stammered over the unfamiliar elven word.

"Kaganesti." Laurana sighed wearily. "They, who allowed us to share their homeland, have been treated worst of all. The Kaganesti have always been poor in material wealth. Poor, by our standards, though not by theirs. They live in the forests and mountains, taking what they need from the land. They are gatherers, hunters. They raise no crops, they forge no metal. When we arrived, our people appeared rich to them with our golden jewelry and steel weapons. Many of their young people came to the Qualinesti and the Silvanesti, seeking to learn the secrets of making shining gold and silver—and steel."

Laurana bit her lip, her face hardened. "I say it to my shame, that my people have taken advantage of the Wilder Elves' poverty. The Kaganesti work as slaves† among us. And, because of that, the Kaganesti elders grow more savage and warlike as they see their young people taken away and their old way of life threatened."

The Qualinesti regard the Kagonesti elves as slaves. The Silvanesti, on the other hand, regard them as just more members of House Servitor, which is the lowest class. They also tend to put all foreigners in the same category.

"Laurana!" called Tasslehoff.

She turned. "Look," she said to Elistan softly. "There is one of them now." The cleric followed her gaze to see a lithe young woman—at least he supposed it was a young woman by the long hair; she was dressed in male clothing—kneel down beside Gilthanas and stroke his forehead. The elflord stirred at her touch, groaning in pain. The Kaganesti reached into a pouch at her side and began busily to mix something in a small clay cup.

"What is she doing?" Elistan asked.

"She is apparently the 'healer' they sent for," Laurana said, watching the girl closely. "The Kaganesti are noted for their Druidic skills."

Wilder elf was a suitable name, Elistan decided, studying the girl intently. He had certainly never seen any intelligent being on Krynn quite so wild-looking. She was dressed in leather breeches tucked into leather boots. A shirt, obviously cast off by some elflord, hung from her shoulders. She was pale and too thin, undernourished. Her matted hair was so filthy it was impossible to distinguish its color. But the hand that touched Gilthanas was slender and shapely. Concern and compassion for him was apparent in her gentle face.

"Well," Sturm said, "what are we to do in the midst of all this?"

"The Silvanesti have agreed to escort us to my people," Laurana said, her face flushing. Evidently this had been a point of bitter contention. "At first they insisted that we go to their elders, but I said I would go nowhere without first bidding my father greeting and discussing the matter with him. There wasn't much they could say to that." Laurana smiled slightly, though there was a touch of bitterness in her voice. "Among all the kindred, a daughter is bound to her father's house until she comes of age. Keeping me here, against my will, would be viewed as kidnapping and would cause open hostility. Neither side is ready for that."

"They are letting us go, though they know we have the dragon orb?" Derek asked in astonishment.

"They are *not* letting us go," Laurana said sharply. "I said they are escorting us to my people."

"But there is a Solamnic outpost to the north," Derek argued. "We could get a ship there to take us to Sancrist—"

"You would never live to reach those trees if you tried to escape," Flint said, sneezing violently.

"He is right," Laurana said. "We must go to the Qualinesti and convince my father to help us get the orb to Sancrist." A small dark line appeared between her eyebrows which warned Sturm she didn't believe that was going to be as easy as it sounded. "And now, we've been talking long enough. They gave me leave to explain things to you, but they're getting restless to go. I must see to Gilthanas. Are we agreed?"

Laurana regarded each knight with a look that was not so much seeking approbation as simply waiting for an acknowledgement of her leadership. For a moment, she appeared so like Tanis in the firm set of her jaw and the calm, steady deliberation in her eyes that Sturm smiled. But Derek was not smiling. He was infuriated and frustrated, the more so because he knew there wasn't a thing he could do.

Finally, however, he snarled a muttered reply that he supposed they must make the best of it and angrily stalked over to pick up the chest. Flint and Sturm followed, the dwarf sneezing until he nearly sneezed himself off his feet.

Laurana walked back to her brother, moving quietly along the sand in her soft leather boots. But the Wilder elf heard her approach. Raising her head, she gave Laurana a fearful look and crept backward as an animal cringes at the sight of man. But Tas, who had been chatting with her in an odd mixture of Common and elven, gently caught hold of the Wilder elf's arm.

"Don't leave," said the kender cheerfully. "This is the elflord's sister. Look, Laurana. Gilthanas is coming around. It must be that mud stuff she stuck on his forehead. I could have sworn he'd be out for days." Tas stood up. "Laurana, this is my friend—what did you say your name was?"

The girl, her eyes on the ground, trembled violently. Her hands picked up bits of sand, then

dropped them again. She murmured something none of them could hear.

"What was it, child?" Laurana asked in such a sweet and gentle voice that the girl raised her eyes shyly.

"Silvart," she said in a low voice.

"That means 'silver-haired' in the Kaganesti language, does it not?" Laurana asked. Kneeling down beside Gilthanas, she helped him sit up. Dizzily, he put his hand to his face where the girl had plastered a thick paste over his bleeding cheek.

"Don't touch," Silvart warned, clasping her hand over Gilthanas's hand quickly. "It will make you well." She spoke Common, not crudely, but clearly and concisely.

Gilthanas groaned in pain, shutting his eyes and letting his hand fall. Silvart gazed at him in deep concern. She started to stroke his face, then—glancing swiftly at Laurana—hurriedly withdrew her hand and started to rise.

"Wait," Laurana said. "Wait, Silvart."

The girl froze like a rabbit, staring at Laurana with such fear in her large eyes that Laurana was overcome with shame.

"Don't be frightened. I want to thank you for caring for my brother. Tasslehoff is right. I thought his injury was grave indeed, but you have aided him. Please stay with him, if you would."

Silvart stared at the ground. "I will stay with him, mistress, if such is your command."

"It is not my command, Silvart," Laurana said. "It is my wish. And my name is Laurana."

Silvart lifted her eyes. "Then I will stay with him gladly, mis—Laurana, if that is your wish." She lowered her head, and they could barely hear her words. "My true name, Silvara, means silver-haired. Silvart is what *they* call me." She glanced at the Silvanesti warriors, then her eyes went back to Laurana. "Please, I want you to call me Silvara."

The Silvanesti elves brought over a makeshift litter they had constructed of a blanket and tree limbs. They lifted the elflord—not ungently—onto the litter. Silvara walked beside it. Tasslehoff walked near her, still chattering, pleased to find someone who had not yet heard his stories. Laurana and Elistan walked on the other side of Gilthanas.

Laurana held his hand in hers, watching over him tenderly. Behind them came Derek, his face dark and shadowed, the chest with the dragon orb on his shoulder. Behind them marched a guard of Silvanesti elves.

Day was just beginning to dawn, gray and dismal, when they reached the line of trees along the shore. Flint shivered. Twisting his head, he gazed out to sea. "What was that Derek said about a—a ship to Sancrist?"

"I am afraid so," Sturm replied. "It is also an island."

"And we've *got* to go there?"

"Yes."

"To use the dragon orb? We don't know anything about it!"

"The Knights will learn," Sturm said softly. "The future of the world rests on this."

"Humpf!" The dwarf sneezed. Casting a terrified glance at the night-dark waters, he shook his head gloomily. "All I know is I've been drowned twice, stricken with a deadly disease—"

"You were seasick."

"Stricken with a deadly disease," Flint repeated loudly, "and sunk. Mark my words, Sturm Brightblade—boats are bad luck to us. We've had nothing but trouble since we set foot in that blasted boat on Crystalmir Lake. That was where the crazed magician first saw the constellations had disappeared, and our luck's gone straight downhill from there. As long as we keep relying on boats, it's going to go from bad to worse."

Sturm smiled as he watched the dwarf squish through the sand. But his smile turned to a sigh. I wish it were all that simple, the knight thought.

3

The Speaker of the Suns.
Laurana's decision.

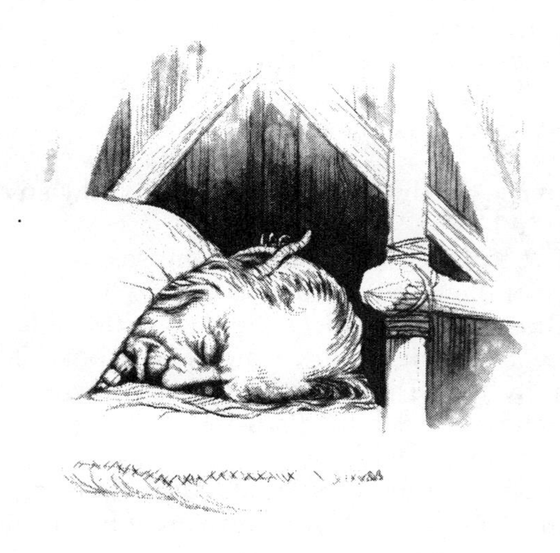

The Speaker of the Suns, leader of the Qualinesti elves, sat in the crude shelter of wood and mud the Kaganesti elves had built for his domicile. He considered it crude, the Kaganesti considered it a marvelously large and well-crafted dwelling, suitable for five or six families. They had, in fact, intended it as such and were shocked when the Speaker declared it barely adequate for his needs and moved in with his wife—alone.

Of course, what the Kaganesti could not know was that the Speaker's home in exile became the central headquarters for all the business of the Qualinesti. The ceremonial guards assumed exactly the same positions as they had in the sculptured halls of the palace in Qualinost. The Speaker held audience at the same time and in the same courtly manner,

save that his ceiling was a mud-covered dome of thatched grass instead of glittering mosaic, his walls wood instead of crystal quartz.

The Speaker sat in state every day, his wife's sister's daughter by his side acting as his scribe. He wore the same robes, conducted business with the same cold aplomb. But there were differences. The Speaker had changed dramatically in the past few months. There were none in the Qualinesti who marveled at this, however. The Speaker had sent his younger son on a mission that most considered suicidal. Worse, his beloved daughter had run away to chase after her half-elven lover. The Speaker expected never to see either of these children again.

He could have accepted the loss of his son, Gilthanas. It was, after all, a heroic, noble act. The young man had led a group of adventurers into the mines of Pax Tharkas to free the humans imprisoned there and draw off the dragonarmies threatening Qualinesti. This plan had been a success—an unexpected success. The dragonarmies had been recalled to Pax Tharkas, giving the elves time to escape to the western shores of their land, and from there across the sea to Southern Ergoth.

The Speaker could not, however, accept his daughter's loss—or her dishonor.

It was the Speaker's elder son, Porthios,† who had coldly explained the matter to him after Laurana had been discovered missing. She had run off after her childhood friend—Tanis Half-Elven. The Speaker was heartsick, consumed with grief. How could she do this? How could she bring disgrace upon their household? A princess of her people chasing after a bastard half-breed!

Tanis is between Porthios and Gilthanas in age.

Laurana's flight quenched the light of the sun for her father. Fortunately, the need to lead his people gave him the strength to carry on. But there were times when the Speaker asked what was the use? He could retire, turn the throne over to his eldest son. Porthios ran almost everything anyway, deferring to his father in all that was proper, but making most decisions himself. The young elflord, serious beyond his years, was proving an excellent leader, although some considered him too harsh in his dealings with the Silvanesti and the Kaganesti.

The Speaker was among these, which was the main reason he did *not* turn things over to Porthios. Occasionally he tried to point out to his elder son that moderation and patience won more victories than threats and sword-rattling. But Porthios believed his father to be soft and sentimental. The Silvanesti, with their rigid caste structure,† considered the Qualinesti barely part of the elven race and the Kaganesti no part of the elven race at all, viewing them as a subrace of elves, much as gully dwarves were seen as a subrace of the dwarves.Porthios firmly believed, although he did not tell his father, that it must end in bloodshed.

The Silvanesti had 3,000 years of peace in isolation, with no outside influences. Their caste system grew up during that time. And woe to anyone who tried to change things.

His views were matched on the other side of the Thon-Tsalarian by a stiff-necked, cold-blooded lord named Quinath, who, it was rumored, was the betrothed of the Princess Alhana Starbreeze. Lord Quinath was now leader of the Silvanesti in her unexplained absence, and it was he and Porthios who divided the isle between the two warring nations of elves, disregarding the third race entirely.

The borderlines were patronizingly communicated to the Kaganesti, as one might communicate to a dog that it is not to enter the kitchen. The Kaganesti, notable for their volatile tempers, were outraged to find their land being divided up and parceled out. Already the hunting was growing bad. The animals the Wilder elves depended on for their survival were being wiped out in great numbers to feed the refugees. As Laurana had said, the River of the Dead could, at any moment, run red with blood, and its name change tragically.

And so the Speaker found himself living in an armed camp. But if he grieved over this fact at all, it was lost in such a multitude of griefs that eventually he grew numb. Nothing touched him. He withdrew into his mud home and allowed Porthios to handle more and more.

The Speaker was up early the morning the companions arrived in what was now called Qualin-Mori. He always rose early. Not so much because he had a great deal to do, but because he had already spent most of the night staring at the ceiling. He was jotting down notes for the day's meetings with the Heads of Household—an unsatisfactory task, since the Heads of Household could do nothing but

complain—when he heard a tumult outside his dwelling.

The Speaker's heart sank. What now? he wondered fearfully. It seemed these alarms came once or twice every day. Porthios had probably caught some hot-blooded Qualinesti and Silvanesti youths raiding or fighting. He kept writing, expecting the tumult to die down. But instead it increased, coming nearer and nearer. The Speaker could only suppose something more serious had happened. And not for the first time, he wondered what he would do if the elves went to war again.

Dropping the quill pen, he wrapped himself in his robes of state and waited with dread. Outside, he heard the guards snap to attention. He heard Porthios's voice perform the traditional rights of seeking entry, since it was before hours. The Speaker glanced fearfully at the door that led to his private chambers, fearing his wife might be disturbed. She had been in ill health since their departure from Qualinesti. Trembling, he rose to his feet, assuming the stern and cold look he had become accustomed to putting on as one might put on an article of clothing, and bade them come inside.

One of the guards opened the door, obviously intending to announce someone. But words failed him and, before he could speak, a tall, slender figure dressed in a heavy, hooded fur cloak, pushed past the guard and ran toward the Speaker. Startled, seeing only that the figure was armed with sword and bow, the Speaker shrank back in alarm.

The figure threw back the hood of her cloak. The Speaker saw honey-colored hair flow down around a woman's face—a face remarkable even among the elves for its delicate beauty.

"Father!" she cried, then Laurana was in his arms.

The return of Gilthanas, long mourned as dead by his people, was the occasion of the greatest celebration to be held by the Qualinesti since the night the companions had been feasted before setting off for the Sla-Mori.

Gilthanas had recovered sufficiently from his wounds to be able to attend the festivities, a small scar on his cheekbone the only sign of his injury. Laurana and her friends wondered at this, for they

had seen the terrible blow inflicted upon him by the Silvanesti elf. But when Laurana mentioned it to her father, the Speaker only shrugged and said that the Kaganesti had befriended druids† living in the forests; they had probably learned much in the way of healing arts from them.

Druids, who worship the god Habbakuk, have been scarce since the Cataclysm, but they will regain ground in years to come.

This frustrated Laurana, who knew the rarity of true healing powers on Krynn. She longed to discuss it with Elistan, but the cleric was closeted for hours with her father, who was very soon impressed by the man's true clerical powers.

Laurana was pleased to see her father accept Elistan—remembering how the Speaker had treated Goldmoon when she first came to Qualinesti wearing the medallion of Mishakal, Goddess of Healing. But Laurana missed her wise mentor. Though overjoyed at being home, Laurana was beginning to realize that for her, home had changed and would never be the same again.

Everyone appeared very glad to see her, but they treated her with the same courtesy they gave Derek and Sturm, Flint and Tas. She was an outsider. Even her parents' manner was cool and distant after their initial emotional welcome. She might not have wondered at this, if they hadn't been so doting over Gilthanas. Why the difference? Laurana couldn't understand. It remained to her elder brother, Porthios, to open her eyes.

The incident began at the feast.

"You will find our lives much different from our lives in Qualinesti," her father told her brother that night as they sat at the banquet held indoors in a great log hall built by the Kaganesti. "But you will soon become accustomed to it." Turning to Laurana, he spoke formally. "I would be glad to have you back in your old place as my scribe,† but I know you will be busy with other things around our household."

Jeff Grubb once told me that no matter how old we get, we will always be twelve years old to our fathers. I think, to a great extent—elven tradition aside—this is part of the Speaker's problem as he considers Laurana.—TRH

Laurana was startled. She had not intended to stay, of course, but she resented being replaced in what was a daughter's traditional role in the royal household. She also resented the fact that, though she had talked to her father about taking the orb to Sancrist, he had apparently ignored her.

"Speaker," she said slowly, trying to keep the irritation from her voice, "I have told you. We cannot

stay. Haven't you been listening to me and to Elistan? We have discovered the dragon orb! Now we have the means to control dragons and bring an end to this war! We must take the orb to Sancrist—"

"Stop, Laurana!" her father said sharply, exchanging looks with Porthios. Her brother regarded her sternly. "You know nothing of what you speak, Laurana. The dragon orb is truly a great prize, and so should not be discussed here. As for taking it to Sancrist, that is out of the question."

"I beg your pardon, sir," Derek said, rising and bowing, "but you have no say in the matter. The dragon orb is not yours. I was sent by the Knights Council to recover a dragon orb, if possible. I have succeeded and I intend to take it back as I was ordered. You have no right to stop me."

"Haven't I?" the Speaker's eyes glittered angrily. "My son, Gilthanas, brought it into this land which we, the Qualinesti, declare to be our homeland in exile. That makes it ours by right."

"I never claimed that, Father,"† Gilthanas said, flushing as he felt the companions' eyes turn to him. "It is not mine. It belongs to all of us—"

Porthios shot his younger brother a furious glance. Gilthanas stammered, then fell silent.

"If it is anyone's to claim, it is Laurana's," Flint Fireforge spoke up, not at all intimidated by the elves' glaring stares. "For it was she who killed Fealthas, the evil elven magic-user."

"If it be hers," the Speaker said in a voice older than his hundreds of years, "then it is mine by right. For she is not of age, what is hers is mine, since I am her father. That is elven law and dwarven law, too, if I'm not mistaken."

Flint's face flushed. He opened his mouth to reply, but Tasslehoff beat him to it.

"Isn't that odd?" remarked the kender cheerfully, having missed the serious portent of the conversation. "According to kender law, if there is a kender law, everybody sort of owns everything." (This was quite true. The kenders' casual attitude toward the possessions of others extended to their own. Nothing in a kender house remained there long, unless it was nailed to the floor. Some neighbor was certain to wander in, admire it, and absentmindedly walk off with it. A family heirloom among kenders was

Gilthanas appears to be suffering the same conflict as Laurana at this feast. There comes a time in all sons' lives when they confront their fathers in a very primal challenge for supremacy of the tribe that has been enacted since the dawn of thought. In the best circumstances, the battlefield is that of thought, ideology, and argument, with the results of mutual respect and independence. In the worst, the battlefield may be physical or the results wounds that go beyond scars to those which never heal. Whatever the arena, the struggle of sons to become wholly men in their own right seems forever to be with us.
—TRH

defined as anything remaining in a house longer than three weeks.)

No one spoke after that. Flint kicked Tas under the table, and the kender subsided in hurt silence which lasted until he discovered his neighbor, an elvenlord, had been called from the table, leaving his purse behind. Rummaging through the elflord's possessions kept the kender happily occupied throughout the rest of the meal.

Flint, who ordinarily would have kept an eye on Tas, did not notice this in his other worries. It was obvious there was going to be trouble. Derek was furious. Only the rigid code of the Knights kept him seated at the table. Laurana sat in silence, not eating. Her face was pale beneath her tanned skin, and she was punching small holes in the finely woven table cloth with her fork. Flint nudged Sturm.

"We thought getting the dragon orb out of Ice Wall was tough," the dwarf said in an undertone. "There we only had to escape a crazed wizard and a few walrus-men. Now we're surrounded by three nations of elves!"

"We'll have to reason with them," Sturm said softly.

"Reason!" The dwarf snorted. "Two stones would have a better chance of reasoning with each other!"

That proved to be the case. By the Speaker's request, the companions remained seated after the other elves left, following dinner. Gilthanas and his sister sat side by side, their faces drawn and worried as Derek stood up before the Speaker to "reason" with him.

"The orb is ours," Derek stated coldly. "You have no right to it at all. It certainly does not belong to your daughter or to your son. They traveled with me only by my courtesy, after I rescued them from the destruction of Tarsis. I am happy to have been able to escort them back to their homeland, and I thank you for your hospitality. But I leave tomorrow for Sancrist, taking the orb with me."

Porthios stood up to face Derek. "The kender may say the dragon orb is his. It doesn't matter." The elflord spoke in a smooth, polite voice that slid through the night air like a knife. "The orb is in elven hands now, and here it will stay. Do you think

we are foolish enough to let this prize be taken by humans to cause more trouble in this world?"

"More trouble!" Derek's face flushed deep red. "Do you realize the trouble this world is in now? The dragons drove you from your homeland. They are approaching our homeland now! Unlike you, we do not intend to run. We will stand and fight! This orb could be our only hope—"

"You have my leave to go back to your homeland and be burned to a crisp for all I care," Porthios returned. "It was you humans who stirred up this ancient evil. It is fitting that you fight it. The Dragon Highlords have what they want from us. They will undoubtedly leave us in peace. Here, on Ergoth, the orb will be kept safe."

"Fool!" Derek slammed his fist on the table. "The Dragon Highlords have only one thought and that is to conquer all of Ansalon! That includes this miserable isle! You may be safe here for a time, but if we fall, you will fall, too!"

"You know he speaks truly, Father," Laurana said, greatly daring. Elven women did not attend war meetings, much less speak. Laurana was present only because of her unique involvement. Rising to her feet, she faced her brother, who glowered at her disapprovingly. "Porthios, our father told us in Qualinesti that the Dragon Highlord wanted not only our lands but also the extermination of our race! Have you forgotten?"

"Bah! That was one Dragon Highlord, Verminaard. He is dead—"

"Yes, because of us," Laurana shouted angrily, "not you!"

"Laurana!" The Speaker of the Suns rose to his full height, taller even than his oldest son. His presence towered over them all. "You forget yourself, young woman. You have no right to speak to your elder brother like that. We faced perils of our own in our journey. *He* remembered his duty and his responsibility, as did Gilthanas. They did not go running off after a half-elven bastard like a brazen, human wh—" The Speaker stopped abruptly.

Laurana went white to the lips. She swayed, clutching the table for support. Gilthanas rose swiftly, coming to her side, but she pushed him

away. "Father," she said in a voice she did not recognize as her own, "what were you about to say?"

"Come away, Laurana," Gilthanas begged. "He didn't mean it. We'll talk in the morning."

The Speaker said nothing, his face, gray and cold.

"You were about to say 'human whore!' " Laurana said softly, her words falling like pins on nerves stretched taut.

"Go to your lodgings, Laurana," the Speaker ordered in a tight voice.

"So that is what you think of me," Laurana whispered, her throat constricting. "That is why everyone stares and stops talking when I come near them. Human whore."

"Sister, do as your father commands," Porthios said. "As for what we think of you—remember, you brought this on yourself. What do you expect? Look at you, Laurana! You are dressed like a man. You proudly wear a sword stained with blood. You talk glibly of your 'adventures!' Traveling with men such as these, humans and dwarves! Spending the nights with them. Spending the nights with your half-breed lover. Where is he? Did he tire of you and—"

The firelight flared before Laurana's eyes. Its heat swept over her body, to be replaced by a terrible cold. She could see nothing and remembered only a horrifying sensation of falling without being able to catch herself. Voices came at her from a great distance, distorted faces bent over her.

"Laurana, my daughter . . ."

Then nothing.

"Mistress . . ."

"What? Where am I? Who are you? I—I can't see! Help me!"

"There, mistress. Take my hand. Shhhh. I am here. I am Silvara. Remember?"

Laurana felt gentle hands take her own as she sat up.

"Can you drink this, mistress?"

A cup was placed to her lips. Laurana sipped at it, tasting clear, cold water. She grasped it and drank eagerly, feeling it cool her fevered blood. Strength returned, she found she could see again. A small

candle burned beside her bed. She was in her room, in her father's house. Her clothes lay on a crude wooden bench, her swordbelt and scabbard stood near, her pack was on the floor. At a table, across from her bed, sat a nursemaid, her head cradled in her arms, fast asleep.

Laurana turned to Silvara, who, seeing the question in her eyes, put her finger to her lips.

"Speak softly," the Wilder elf replied. "Oh, not for that one"—Silvara glanced at the nurse—"she will sleep peacefully for many, many hours before the potion wears off. But there are others in the house who may be wakeful. Do you feel better?"

"Yes," Laurana answered, confused. "I don't remember . . ."

"You fainted," Silvara answered. "I heard them talking about it when they carried you back here. Your father is truly grieved. He never meant to say those things. It is just that you hurt him so terribly—"

"How did you hear?"

"I was hiding, in the shadows in the corner there. An easy thing for my people to do. The old nurse said you were fine, you just needed rest, and they left. When she went to fetch a blanket, I put the sleep juice in her tea."

"Why?" Laurana asked. Looking at the girl closely, Laurana saw that the Wilder elf must be a beautiful woman—or would be if the layers of grime and filth were washed from her.

Silvara, aware of Laurana's scrutiny, flushed in embarrassment."I—I ran away from the Silvanesti, mistress, when they brought you across the river."

"Laurana. Please, child, call me Laurana."

"Laurana," Silvara corrected, blushing. "I—I came to ask you to take you with me when you leave."

"Leave?" Laurana said. "I'm not goi—" She stopped.

"Aren't you?" Silvara asked gently.

"I . . . I don't know," Laurana said in confusion.

"I can help," Silvara said eagerly. "I know the way through the mountains to reach the Knights' outpost where the ships with birds' wings sail. I will help you get away."

"Why would you do this for us?" Laurana asked. "I'm sorry, Silvara. I don't mean to be suspicious—

but you don't know us, and what you're doing is very dangerous. Surely you could escape more easily on your own."

"I know you carry the dragon orb," Silvara whispered.

"How do you know about the orb?" Laurana asked, astounded.

"I heard the Silvanesti talking, after they left you at the river."

"And you knew what it was? How?"

"My . . . people have stories . . . about it," Silvara said, her hands twisting. "I—I know it is important to end this war. Your people and the Silvan elves will go back to their homes and let the Kaganesti live in peace. There is that reason and—" Silvara was silent for a moment, then she spoke so softly Laurana could barely hear her. "You are the first person who ever knew the meaning of my name."

Silvara in an early artist's sketch

Laurana looked at her, puzzled. The girl seemed sincere. But Laurana didn't believe her. Why would she risk her life to help them? Perhaps she was a Silvanesti spy, sent to get the orb? It seemed unlikely, but stranger things—

Laurana put her head in her hands, trying to think. Could they trust Silvara, at least enough to get them out of here? They apparently had no choice. If they were going into the mountains, they would have to pass through Kaganesti lands. Silvara's help would be invaluable.

"I must talk to Elistan," Laurana said. "Can you bring him here?"

"No need, Laurana," Silvara answered. "He has been waiting outside for you to awaken."

"And the others? Where are the rest of my friends?"

"Lord Gilthanas is within the house of your father, of course—" Was it Laurana's imagination, or did Silvara's pale cheek flush when she said that name? "The others have been given 'guest quarters.'"

"Yes," said Laurana grimly, "I can imagine."

Silvara left her side. Creeping quietly across the floor of the room, she went to the door, opened it, and beckoned.

"Laurana?"

"Elistan!" She flung her arms around the cleric. Laying her head on his chest, Laurana shut her

In depictions of the characters that followed this early color Elmore sketch, Sturm's face grew fuller, Lorac became more insane, Tika got sexier, and the Highlord's horns shrank.

eyes, feeling his strong arms embrace her tenderly. Everything will be fine now, she knew. Elistan will take charge. He'll know what to do.

"Are you feeling better?" the cleric asked. "Your father—"

"Yes, I know," Laurana interrupted him. She felt a dull ache in her heart whenever her father was mentioned. "You must decide what we are to do, Elistan. Silvara has offered to help us escape. We could take the orb and leave tonight."

"If that is what you must do, my dear, then you should waste no more time," Elistan said, sitting by her in a chair.

Laurana blinked. Reaching out, she grabbed hold of his arm. "Elistan, what do you mean? You must come with us—"

"No, Laurana," Elistan said, grasping her hand tightly in his own. "If you do this, you will have to leave on your own. I have sought help from Paladine, and I must stay here, with the elves. I believe if I stay, I will be able to convince your father that I am a cleric of the true gods. If I leave, he would always believe I am a charlatan, as your brother brands me."

"What about the dragon orb?"

"That is up to you, Laurana. The elves are wrong in this. Hopefully, in time, they will come to see it. But we do not have centuries to talk this over. I think you should take the orb to Sancrist."

"Me?" Laurana gasped. "I can't!"

"My dear," Elistan said firmly, "you must realize that if you make this decision, the burden of leadership will be upon you. Sturm and Derek are too caught up in their own quarrel and, besides, they are human. You will be dealing with elves, your own people and the Kaganesti. Gilthanas sides with your father. You are the only one who has a chance to succeed."

"But I'm not capable—"

"You are more capable than you give yourself credit for, Laurana. Perhaps everything you have been through up to now has been preparing you for this. You must waste no more time. Farewell, my dear." Elistan rose to his feet and laid his hand on her head. "May Paladine's blessing—and my own—go with you."

"Elistan!" Laurana whispered, but the cleric was gone. Silvara quietly shut the door.

Laurana sank back into her bed, trying to think. Elistan is right, of course. The dragon orb cannot stay here. And if we are going to escape, it must be tonight. But it's all happening so fast! And it's all up to me! Can I trust Silvara? But why ask? She's the only one who can guide us. Then all I have to do is get the orb and the lance and free my friends. I know how to get to the orb and the lance. But my friends—

Laurana knew, suddenly, what she would do. She realized she had been planning it in the back of her mind even as she talked to Elistan.

This commits me, she thought. There will be no turning back. Stealing the dragon orb, fleeing into the night, into strange and hostile country. And then, there is Gilthanas. We've been through too much together for me to leave him behind. But he will be appalled at the idea of stealing the orb and running away. And if he chooses not to go with me, would he betray us?

Laurana closed her eyes for a moment. She laid her head down wearily on her knees. Tanis, she thought, where are you? What should I do? Why is it up to me? I didn't want this.

And then, as she sat there, Laurana remembered seeing weariness and sorrow on Tanis's face that mirrored her own. Maybe he asked himself these same things. All the times I thought he was so strong, perhaps he really felt as lost and frightened† as I do. Certainly he felt abandoned by his people. And we depended on him, whether he wanted us to or not. But he accepted it. He did what he believed was right.

She is finally beginning to feel inside the heart of someone else.

And so must I.

Briskly, refusing to allow herself to think any further, Laurana lifted her head and beckoned for Silvara to come near.

Sturm paced the length of the crude cabin that had been given to them, unable to sleep. The dwarf lay stretched out on a bed, snoring loudly. Across the room, Tasslehoff lay curled in a ball of misery, chained by his foot to the bedpost. Sturm sighed. How much more trouble could they get into?

The evening had gone from bad to worse. After Laurana had fainted, it had been all Sturm could

do to hold back the enraged dwarf. Flint vowed to tear Porthios limb from limb. Derek stated that he considered himself to be a prisoner held by the enemy and, as such, it was his duty to try and escape; then he would bring the Knights down to recover the dragon orb by force. Derek was immediately escorted away by the guards. Just when Sturm got Flint calmed down, an elflord appeared out of nowhere and accused Tasslehoff of stealing his purse.

Now they were being held under double guard, "guests" of the Speaker of the Suns.

"Must you pace about like that?" Derek asked coldly.

"Why? Am I keeping you awake?" snapped Sturm.

"Of course not. Only fools could sleep under these circumstances. You're breaking my concen—"

"Hsst!" Sturm said, raising his hand warningly.

Derek instantly fell silent. Sturm gestured. The older knight joined Sturm in the center of the room where he was staring up at the ceiling. The log house was rectangular, with one door, two windows, and a firepit in the center of the floor. A hole cut in the roof provided ventilation.

It was through this hole Sturm heard the odd sound that caught his attention. It was a shuffling, scraping sound. The wooden beams in the ceiling creaked as though something heavy was crawling over it.

"A wild beast of some sort," Derek muttered. "And we're weaponless!"

"No," Sturm said, listening closely. "It's not growling. It's moving too silently, as if it didn't want to be heard or seen. What are those guards doing out there?"

Derek went to the window and peered out. "Sitting around a fire. Two are asleep. They're not overly concerned about us, are they?" he asked bitterly.

"Why should they be?" Sturm said, keeping his eyes on the ceiling."There's a couple of thousand elves within the sound of a whisper. What the—"

Sturm fell back in alarm as the stars he had been watching through the hole were suddenly blotted out by a dark, shapeless mass. Sturm reached down

swiftly and grabbed a log from the smoldering fire, holding it by the end like a club.

"Sturm! Sturm Brightblade!" said the shapeless mass.

Sturm stared, trying to remember the voice. It was familiar. Thoughts of Solace flooded his mind. "Theros!" he gasped. "Theros Ironfeld! What are you doing here? The last I saw you, you were lying near death in the elven kingdom!"

The huge blacksmith of Solace struggled down through the opening in the ceiling, bringing part of the roof with him. He landed heavily, waking the dwarf, who sat up and peered, bleary-eyed, at the apparition in the center of the cabin.

"What—" the dwarf started up, fumbling for his battle-axe which was no longer by his side.

"Hush!" the smith commanded. "No time for questions. The Lady Laurana sent me to free you. We're to meet her in the woods beyond the camp. Make haste! We have only a few hours before dawn and we must be across the river by then." Theros strode over to look at Tasslehoff, who was trying without success to free himself. "Well, master thief, I see someone caught you at last."

"I'm not a thief!" Tas said indignantly. "You know me better than that, Theros. That purse was planted on me—"

The smith chuckled. Taking hold of the chain in his hands, he gave a sudden heave and it split apart. Tasslehoff, however, did not even notice. He was staring at the smith's arms. One arm, the left, was a dusky black, the color of the smith's skin. But the other arm, the right, was bright, shining silver!

"Theros," Tas said in a strangled voice. "Your arm—"

"Questions later, little thief," the smith said sternly. "Now we move swift and now we move silent."

"Across the river," Flint moaned, shaking his head. "More boats. More boats . . ."

"I want to see the Speaker," Laurana told the guard at the door to her father's suite of rooms.

"It is late," the guard said. "The Speaker is sleeping."

Laurana drew back her hood. The guard bowed. "Forgive me, Princess. I did not recognize you."

He glanced at Silvara suspiciously. "Who is that with you?"

"My maid. I would not travel at night by myself."

"No, of course not," the guard said hurriedly as he opened the door. "Go ahead. His sleeping room is the third one down the hall on your right."

"Thank you,"Laurana answered and brushed past the guard. Silvara, muffled in a voluminous cape, swept softly after her.

"The chest is in his room, at the foot of his bed," Laurana whispered to Silvara. "Are you sure you can carry the dragon orb? It is big and very heavy."

"It's not that big," Silvara murmured, staring perplexed at Laurana."Only about so—" She made a gesture with her hands roughly the shape of a child's ball.

"No," Laurana said, frowning. "You have not seen it. It is nearly two feet in diameter. That's why I had you wear that long cape."

Silvara stared at her in wonder. Laurana shrugged. "Well, we can't stand here arguing. We'll figure something out when the time comes."

The two crept down the hallway, silently as kender, until they came to the bedroom.

Holding her breath, fearing that even her heartbeat was too loud, Laurana pressed on the door. It opened with a creaking sound that made her grit her teeth. Next to her, Silvara shivered in fear. A figure in the bed stirred and turned over—her mother. Laurana saw her father, even in his sleep, put out his hand to pat her reassuringly. Tears dimmed Laurana's eyes. Tightening her lips resolutely, she gripped Silvara's hand and slipped inside the room.

The chest stood at the end of her father's bed. It was locked, but the companions all carried a copy of the small silver key. Swiftly Laurana unlocked the chest and lifted the lid. Then she nearly dropped it in her amazement. The dragon orb was there, still glowing with the soft white and blue light. But it wasn't the same orb! Or if it was, it had shrunk! As Silvara said, it was now no more than the size of a child's playing ball! Laurana reached in to take it. It was still heavy, but she could lift it easily. Gingerly grasping it, her hand shaking, she raised it from the box and handed it to Silvara. The Wilder elf immediately hid it beneath her cloak. Laurana picked up the wood shaft of the broken dragonlance, wondering, as she did so, why she bothered taking the broken old weapon.

I'll take it because the knight handed it to Sturm, she thought. He wanted him to have it.

At the bottom of the chest lay Tanis's sword, Wyrmslayer, given him by Kith-Kanan. Laurana looked from the sword to the dragonlance. I can't carry both, she thought, and started to put the lance back.† But Silvara grabbed her.

Later, in Dragons of Spring Dawning, *Laurana must again choose between duty and love. Then she will choose love. Now she chooses duty.—MW*

"What are you doing?" Her mouth formed the words, her eyes flashed. "Take it! Take it, too!"

Laurana stared at the girl in amazement. Then, hastily, she retrieved the lance, concealed it beneath her cloak, and carefully shut the chest, leaving the sword inside. Just as the lid left her cold fingers, her father rolled over in his bed, half-sitting up.

"What? Who is there?" he asked, starting to shake off his sleep in his alarm.

Laurana felt Silvara trembling and clutched the girl's hand reassuringly, warning her to be silent.

"It is I, Father," she said in a faint voice. "Laurana. I—I wanted to—to tell you I am sorry, Father. And I ask you to forgive me."

"Ah, Laurana." The Speaker lay back down on his pillows, closing his eyes. "I forgive you, my daughter. Now return to your bed. We'll talk in the morning."

Laurana waited until his breathing became quiet and regular. Then she led Silvara from the room, gripping the dragonlance firmly beneath her cloak.

"Who goes there?" softly called a human voice in elven.

"Who asks?" replied a clear elven voice.

"Gilthanas? Is that you?"

"Theros! My friend!" The young elflord stepped swiftly from the shadows to embrace the human blacksmith. For a moment Gilthanas was so overcome he could not speak. Then, startled, he pushed back from the smith's bearlike hug. "Theros! You have two arms! But the draconians in Solace cut off your right arm! You would have died, if Goldmoon hadn't healed you."

"Do you remember what that pig of a Fewmaster told me?" Theros asked in his rich, deep voice, whispering softly. " 'The only way you'll get a new arm, smith, is to forge it yourself!' Well, I did just that! The story of my adventures to find the Silver Arm† I wear now is a long one—"

"And not for telling now," grumbled another voice behind him. "Unless you want to ask a couple of thousand elves to hear it with us."

Theros wears the magical Silver Arm of Ergoth, which was forged, not by Theros but by good dragons and men of various races during an early dragon war. At that time, the Arm was required, along with the Hammer of Kharas, to forge dragonlances.

"So you managed to escape, Gilthanas," said Derek's voice out of the shadows. "Did you bring the dragon orb?"

"I did not *escape,*" Gilthanas returned coldly. "I left my father's house to accompany my sister and Silvara, her maid, through the darkness. Taking the orb is my sister's idea, not mine. There is still time to reconsider this madness, Laurana." Gilthanas turned to her. "Return the orb. Don't let Porthios's hasty words drive away your common sense. If we keep the orb here, we can use it to defend our people. We can find out how it works, we have magic-users among us."

"Let's just turn ourselves over to the guards now! Then we can get some sleep where it's warm!" Flint's words came out in explosive puffs of frost.

"Either sound the alarm now, elf, or let us go. At least give us time before you betray us," Derek said.

"I have no intention of betraying you," Gilthanas stated angrily. Ignoring the others, he turned once more to his sister. "Laurana?"

"I am determined on this course of action," she answered slowly. "I have thought about it and I believe we are doing the right thing. So does Elistan. Silvara will guide us through the mountains—"

"I, too, know the mountains," Theros spoke up. "I have had little to do here but wander them. And you'll need me to get you past the guards."

"Then we are resolved."

"Very well." Gilthanas sighed. "I am coming with you. If I stayed behind, Porthios would always suspect me of complicity."

"Fine," snapped Flint. "Can we escape now? Or do we need to wake up anyone else?"

"This way," Theros said. "The guards are accustomed to my late night rambles. Stay in the shadows, and let *me* do the talking." Reaching down, he caught hold of Tasslehoff by the collar of his heavy fur coat and lifted the kender off the ground to look him right in the eye."That means you, little thief," the big smith said sternly.

"Yes, Theros," the kender replied meekly, squirming in the man's silver hand until the smith set him down. Somewhat shaken, Tas readjusted his pouches and tried to regain his injured dignity.

The companions followed the tall, dark-skinned smith along the outskirts of the silent elven encampment, moving as quietly as possible for two armor-clad knights and a dwarf. To Laurana, they sounded as loud as a wedding party. She bit her lip to keep silent as the knights clanked and rattled in the darkness, while Flint fell over every tree root and splashed through every puddle.

But the elves lay wrapped in their complacency like a soft, fleecy blanket. They had safely fled the danger. None believed it would find them again. And so they slept as the companions escaped into the night.

Silvara, carrying the dragon orb, felt the cold crystal grow warm as she held it near her body, felt it stir and pulse with life.

"What am I to do?" she whispered to herself distractedly in Kaganesti, stumbling almost blindly through the darkness. "This came to *me*! Why? I don't understand? What am I to do?"

4

River of the Dead.
The Legend of the Silver Dragon.

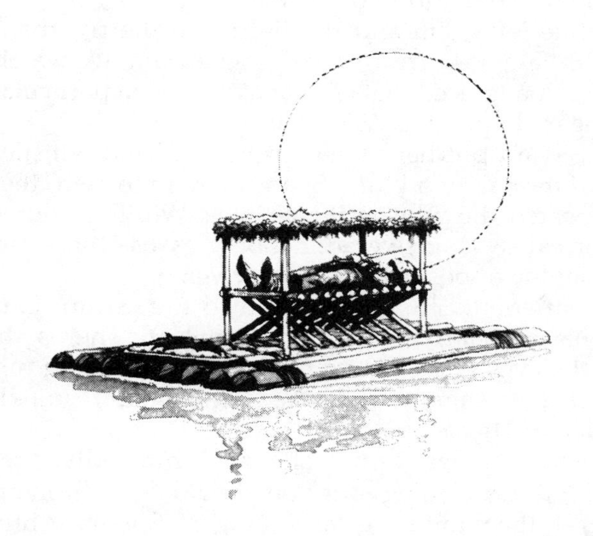

The night was still and cold. Storm clouds blotted out the light of the moons and stars. There was no rain, no wind, just an oppressive sense of waiting. Laurana felt that all of nature was alert, wary, fearful. And behind her, the elves slept, cocooned in a web of their own petty fears and hatreds. What horrible winged creature would burst from that cocoon, she wondered.

The companions had little trouble slipping past the elven guards. Recognizing Theros, the guards stood and chatted amiably with him, while the others crept through the woods around them. They reached the river in the first chill light of dawn.

"And how are we to get across?" the dwarf asked, staring out at the water gloomily. "I don't think much of boats, but they beat swimming."

"That should not be a problem." Theros turned to Laurana and said, "Ask your little friend," nodding at Silvara.

Startled, Laurana looked at the Wilder elf, as did the others. Silvara, embarrassed at so many eyes upon her, flushed deeply, bowing he head. "Kargai Sargaron is right," she murmured. "Wait here, within the shadows of the trees."

She left them and ran lightly to the riverbank with a wild, free grace, enchanting to watch. Laurana noticed that Gilthanas's gaze, in particular, lingered upon the Wilder elf.

Silvara put her fingers to her lips and whistled like the call of a bird.† She waited a moment, then repeated the whistle three times. Within minutes, her call was answered, echoing across the water from the opposite bank of the river.

The Kagonesti language itself has been described as sounding like the calls of wild birds.

Satisfied, Silvara returned to the group. Laurana saw that, though Silvara spoke to Theros, the girl's eyes were drawn to Gilthanas. Finding him staring at her, she blushed and looked quickly back at Theros.

"Kargai Sargaron," she said hurriedly, "my people are coming, but you should be with me to meet them and explain things." Silvara's blue eyes—Laurana could see them clearly in the morning light—went to Sturm and Derek. The Wilder elf shook her head slightly. "They will not be happy about bringing these humans to our land, nor these elves either, I am afraid," she said, with an apologetic glance at Laurana and Gilthanas.

"I will talk to them," Theros said. Gazing across the lake, he gestured. "Here they come now."

Laurana saw two black shapes sliding across the sky-gray river. The Kaganesti must keep watch there constantly, she realized. They recognized Silvara's call. Odd—for a slave to have such freedom. If escape was this easy, why did Silvara stay among the Silvanesti? It didn't make any sense . . . unless escape was not her purpose.

"What does 'Kargai Sargaron' mean?" she asked Theros abruptly.

"He of the Silver Arm," Theros answered, smiling.

"They seem to trust you."

"Yes. I told you I spend a good part of my time wandering. That is not quite true. I spend much

time among Silvara's people." The smith's dusky face creased in a scowl. "Meaning no disrespect, elflady, but you have no idea what hardships your people are causing these wild ones: shooting the game or driving it away, enslaving the young with gold and silver and steel." Theros heaved an angry sigh. "I have done what I could. I showed them how to forge hunting weapons and tools. But the winter will be long and hard, I fear. Already, game is becoming scarce. If it comes to starving or killing their elven kin—"

"Maybe if I stayed," Laurana murmured, "I could help—" Then she realized that was ridiculous. What could she do? She wasn't even accepted by her own people!

"You can't be in all places at the same time," Sturm said. "The elves must solve their problems, Laurana. You are doing the right thing."

"I know," she said, sighing. She turned her head, looking behind her, toward the Qualinesti camp. "I was just like them, Sturm," she said, shivering. "My beautiful tiny world had revolved around me for so long that I thought I was the center of the universe. I ran after Tanis because I was certain I could make him love me. Why shouldn't he? Everyone else did. And then I discovered the world didn't revolve around me. It didn't even care about me! I saw suffering and death. I was forced to kill"—she stared down at her hands—"or be killed. I saw real love. Love like Riverwind's and Goldmoon's, love that was willing to sacrifice everything—even life itself. I felt very petty and very small. And now that's how my people seem to me. Petty and small. I used to think they were perfect, but now I understand how Tanis felt—and why he left."

The boats of the Kaganesti had reached the shore. Silvara and Theros walked down to talk to the elves who paddled them. At a gesture from Theros, the companions stepped out of the shadows of the trees and stood upon the bank—hands well away from their weapons—so the Kaganesti could see them. At first, it seemed hopeless. The elves chattered in their strange, uncouth version of elven which Laurana had difficulty following. Apparently they refused outright to have anything to do with the group.

Then horn calls sounded from the woods behind them. Gilthanas and Laurana looked at each other in alarm. Theros, glancing back, stabbed his silver finger at the group urgently, then thumped himself on the chest—apparently pledging his word to answer for the companions. The horns sounded again. Silvara added her own pleas. Finally, the Kaganesti agreed, although with a marked lack of enthusiasm.

The companions hurried down to the water, all of them aware now that their absence had been discovered and that pursuit had started. One by one, they all stepped carefully into the boats that were no more than hollowed-out trunks of trees. All, that is, except Flint, who groaned and cast himself down on the ground, shaking his head and muttering in dwarven. Sturm eyed him in concern, fearing a repetition of the incident at Crystalmir when the dwarf had flatly refused to set foot in a boat. It was Tasslehoff, however, who tugged and pulled and finally dragged the grumbling dwarf to his feet.

"We'll make a sailor of you yet," the kender said cheerfully, prodding Flint in the back with his hoopak.

"You will not! And quit sticking me with that thing!" the dwarf snarled. Reaching the edge of the water, he stopped, nervously fumbling with a piece of wood. Tas hopped into a boat and stood waiting expectantly, his hand outstretched.

"Confound it, Flint, get in the boat!" Theros ordered.

"Just tell me one thing," the dwarf said, swallowing. "Why do they call it the 'River of the Dead'?"

"You'll see, soon enough," Theros grunted. Reaching out his strong black hand, he plucked the dwarf off the bank and plopped him like a sack of potatoes on to the seat. "Shove off," the smith told the Wilder elves, who needed no bidding. Their wooden oars were already biting deep into the water.

The log boat caught the current and floated swiftly downstream, heading west. The tree-shrouded banks fairly flew past, and the companions huddled down into the boats as the cold wind stung their faces and took away their breath. They saw no signs of life along the southern shore where

the Qualinesti made their home. But Laurana caught glimpses of shadowy, darting figures ducking in and out of the trees on the northern shore. She realized then that the Kaganesti† were not as naive as they seemed—they were keeping close watch upon their cousins. She wondered how many of the Kaganesti living as slaves were, in reality, spies. Her eyes went to Silvara.

The history of the Wilder elves is told in Douglas Niles's book, The Kagonesti. *Their legendary hero was a pathfinder named Kagonos—another reason for the name change.*

The current carried them swiftly to a fork in the river where two streams joined together. One flowed from the north, the other—the stream they traveled—flowed into it from the east. Both merged into one wide river, flowing south into the sea. Suddenly Theros pointed.

"There, dwarf, is your answer," he said solemnly.

Drifting down the branch of the river that flowed from the north was another boat. At first, they thought it had slipped its moorings, for they could see no one inside. Then they saw that it rode too low in the water to be empty. The Wilder elves slowed their own boats, steering them into the shallow water, and held them steady, heads bowed in silent respect.

And then Laurana knew.

"A funeral boat," she murmured.

"Aye," said Theros, watching with sad eyes. The boat drifted past, carried near them by the current. Inside they could see the body of a young Wilder elf, a warrior to judge by his crude leather armor. His hands, folded across his chest, clasped an iron sword in cold fingers. A bow and quiver of arrows lay at his side. His eyes were closed in the peaceful sleep from which he would never waken.

"Now you know why it is called *Thon-Tsalarian*, the River of the Dead," Silvara said in her low, musical voice. "For centuries, my people have returned the dead to the sea where we were born. This ancient custom† of my people has become a bitter point of contention between the Kaganesti and our cousins." Her eyes went to Gilthanas. "Your people consider this a desecration of the river. They try to force us to stop."

The Vikings and the ancient Egyptians as well as other cultures placed their important dead in funeral boats.

"Someday the body that floats down the river will be Qualinesti, or Silvanesti, with a Kaganesti arrow in his chest," Theros predicted. "And then there will be war."

"I think all the elves will have a much more deadly enemy to face," Sturm said, shaking his head. "Look!" He pointed.

At the feet of the dead warrior lay a shield, the shield of the enemy he had died fighting. Recognizing the foul symbol traced on the battered shield, Laurana drew in her breath.

"Draconian!"

The journey up the Thon-Tsalarian was long and arduous, for the river ran swift and strong. Even Tas was given an oar to help paddle, but he promptly lost it overboard, then nearly went in headfirst trying to retrieve it. Catching hold of Tas by his belt, Derek dragged him back as the Kaganesti indicated by sign language that if he caused any more trouble, they'd throw him out.

Tasslehoff soon grew bored and sat peering over the side, hoping to see a fish.

"Why, how odd!" the kender said suddenly. Reaching down, he put his small hand into the water. "Look," he said in excitement. His hand was coated in fine silver and sparkled in the early morning light. "The water glitters! Look, Flint," he called to the dwarf in the other boat."Look into the water—"

"I will *not,*" said the dwarf through chattering teeth. Flint rowed grimly, though there was some question as to his effectiveness. He steadfastly refused to look into the water and consequently was out of time with everyone else.

"You are right, Kenderken," Silvara said, smiling. "In fact, the Silvanesti named the river *Thon-Sargon,* which means 'Silver Road.' It is too bad you have come here in such dismal weather. When the silver moon rises in its fullness, the river turns to molten silver and is truly beautiful."

"Why? What causes it?" the kender asked, studying his shimmering hand with delight.

"No one knows, though there is a legend among my people—" Silvara fell silent abruptly, her face flushed.

"What legend?" Gilthanas asked. The elflord sat facing Silvara, who was in the prow of the boat. His paddling was not much better than Flint's, Gilthanas being much more interested in Silvara's face than his work. Every time Silvara looked up,

she found he was staring at her. She became more confused and flustered as the hours passed.

"Surely you are not interested," she said, gazing out across the silver-gray water, trying to avoid Gilthanas's gaze. "It is a child's tale about Huma—"

"Huma!" Sturm said from where he sat behind Gilthanas, his swift, strong oar strokes making up for the ineptness of both elf and dwarf."Tell us your legend of Huma, Wilder elf."

"Yes, tell us your legend,"† Gilthanas repeated smiling.

"Very well," she said, flushing. Clearing her throat, she began. "According to the Kaganesti, in the last days of the terrible dragon wars, Huma traveled through the land, seeking to help the people. But he realized, to his sorrow, that he was powerless to stop the desolation and destruction of the dragons. He prayed to the gods for an answer." Silvara glanced at Sturm, who nodded his head solemnly.

Legends grew naturally out of the extensive background we created for the DRAGONLANCE world—and with intention. Legends such as this add depth to the world and our characters, giving them a sense of coming from somewhere with deep roots.—TRH

"True," the knight said. "And Paladine answered his prayer, sending the White Stag. But where it led him, none know."

"My people know," Silvara said softly, "because the Stag led Huma, after many trials and dangers, to a quiet grove, here, in the land of Ergoth. In the grove he met a woman, beautiful and virtuous, who eased his pain. Huma fell in love with her and she with him. But she refused his pledges of love for many months. Finally, unable to deny the burning fire within her, the woman returned Huma's love. Their happiness was like the silver moonlight in a night of terrible darkness."

Silvara fell silent a moment, her eyes staring far away. Absently she reached down to touch the coarse fabric of the cloak covering the dragon orb which lay at her feet.

"Go on," Gilthanas urged. The elflord had given up all pretext of paddling and sat still, enchanted by Silvara's beautiful eyes, her musical voice.

Silvara sighed. Dropping the fabric from her hands, she stared out over the water into the shadowy woods. "Their joy was brief," she said softly. "For the woman had a terrible secret—she was not born of woman, but of dragon. Only by her magic did she keep the shape of womankind. But she could no longer lie to Huma. She loved him too much. Fearfully she revealed to Huma what she was, appearing before him one night in her true shape—that of a silver dragon. She hoped he would hate her, even destroy her, for her pain was so great she did not want to live. But, looking at the radiant, magnificent creature before him, the knight saw within her eyes the noble spirit of the woman he loved. Her magic returned her to the shape of woman, and she prayed to Paladine that he give her woman's shape forever. She would give up her magic and the long life span of the dragons to live in the world with Huma."

Silvara closed her eyes, her face drawn with pain. Gilthanas, watching her, wondered why she was so affected by this legend. Reaching out, he touched her hand. She started like a wild animal, drawing back so suddenly the boat rocked.

"I'm sorry," Gilthanas said. "I didn't mean to scare you. What happened? What was Paladine's answer?"

Silvara drew a deep breath. "Paladine granted her wish, with a terrible condition. He showed them both the future. If she remained a dragon, she and Huma would be given the Dragonlance and the power to defeat the evil dragons. If she became mortal, she and Huma would live together as man and wife, but the evil dragons would remain in the land forever. Huma vowed he would give up everything—his knighthood, his honor—to remain with her. But she saw the light die in his eyes as he spoke, and, weeping, she knew the answer she must give. The evil dragons must not be allowed to stay in the world. And the silver river, it is said, was formed from the tears shed by the dragon when Huma left her to find the Dragonlance."

"Nice story. Kind of sad," said Tasslehoff, yawning. "Did old Huma come back? Does the story have a happy ending?"

"Huma's story does not end happily," Sturm said, frowning at the kender. "But he died most gloriously in battle,† defeating the leader of the dragons, though he himself had sustained a mortal wound. I have heard, though," the knight added thoughtfully, "that he rode to battle upon a Silver Dragon."

See the short story "Silver and Steel" by Kevin Randle in Love and War.

"And we saw a knight on a silver dragon in Ice Wall," Tas said brightly. "He gave Sturm the—"

The knight gave the kender a swift poke in the back. Too late, Tas remembered that was supposed to be secret.

"I don't know about a Silver Dragon," Silvara said, shrugging. "My people know little about Huma. He was, after all, a human. I think they tell this legend only because it is about the river they love, the river who takes their dead."

At this point, one of the Kaganesti pointed at Gilthanas and said something sharply to Silvara. Gilthanas looked at her, not understanding. The elf-maid smiled. "He asks if you are too grand an elflord to paddle, because—if you are—he will allow your lordship to swim."

Gilthanas grinned at her, his face flushing. Quickly he picked up his paddle and set to work.

Despite all their efforts—and by the end of the day even Tasslehoff was paddling again—the journey upstream was slow and taxing. By the time they made landfall, their muscles ached with the strain, their hands were bloody and blistered. It was all they could do to drag the boats ashore and help hide them.

"Do you think we've thrown off the pursuit?" Laurana asked Theros wearily.

"Does that answer your question?" He pointed downstream.

In the deepening dusk, Laurana could barely make out several dark shapes upon the water. They were still far down river, but it was clear to Laurana that there would be little rest for the companions tonight. One of the Kaganesti, however, spoke to Theros, gesturing downstream. The big smith nodded.

"Do not worry. We are safe until morning. He says they will have to make landfall as well. None dare travel the river at night. Not even the Kaganesti, and they know every bend and every snag. He says he will make camp here, near the river. Strange creatures walk the forest at night—men with the heads of lizards. Tomorrow we will travel by water as far as we can, but soon we will have to leave the river and take to land."

"Ask him if his people will stop the Qualinesti from pursuing us if we enter his land," Sturm told Theros.

Theros turned to the Kaganesti elf, speaking the elven tongue clumsily but well enough to be understood. The Kaganesti elf shook his head. He was a wild, savage-looking creature. Laurana could see how her people thought them only one step removed from animals. His face revealed traces of distant human ancestry. Though he had no beard—the elven blood ran too purely in the veins of the Kaganesti to allow that—the elf reminded Laurana vividly of Tanis with his quick, decisive way of speaking, his strong, muscular build, and his emphatic gestures. Overcome with memories, she turned away.

Theros translated. "He says that the Qualinesti must follow protocol and ask permission from the elders to enter Kaganesti lands in search of you. The elders will likely grant permission, maybe even offer to help. They don't want humans in Southern Ergoth any more than their cousins. In fact," Theros added slowly, "he's made it plain that the only reason he and his friends are helping us now is to return favors I've done in the past and to help Silvara."

Laurana's gaze went to the girl. Silvara stood on the riverbank, talking to Gilthanas.

Theros saw Laurana's face harden. Looking at the Wilder elf and the elflord, he guessed her thoughts.

"Odd to see jealousy† in the face of one who—according to rumor—ran away to become the lover of my friend, Tanis, the half-elf," Theros remarked. "I thought you were different from your people, Laurana."

Two steps forward, one step back.

"It's not that!" she said sharply, feeling her skin burn. "I'm not Tanis's lover. Not that it makes any difference. I simply don't trust the girl. She's—well—too eager to help us, if that makes any sense."

"Your brother might have something to do with that."

"He's an elflord—" Laurana began angrily. Then, realizing what she had been about to say, she broke off. "What do you know of Silvara?"she asked instead.

"Little," Theros answered, regarding Laurana with a disappointed look that made her unreasonably angry. "I know she is highly respected and

much loved by her people, especially for her healing skills."

"And her spying skills?" Laurana asked coolly.

"These people are fighting for their own survival. They do what they must," Theros said sternly. "That was a fine talk you made back on the beach, Laurana. I almost believed it."

The blacksmith went to help the Kaganesti hide the boats. Laurana, angry and ashamed, bit her lip in frustration. Was Theros right? Was she jealous of Gilthanas's attention? Did she consider Silvara unworthy of him? It was how Gilthanas had always considered Tanis, certainly. Was this different?

Listen to your feelings, Raistlin had told her. That was all very well, but first she had to understand her feelings! Hadn't her love for Tanis taught her anything?

Yes, Laurana decided finally, her mind clearing. She'd meant what she'd said to Theros. If there was something about Silvara she didn't trust, it had nothing to do with the fact that Gilthanas was attracted to the girl. It was something indefinable. Laurana was sorry Theros had misunderstood her, but she would take Raistlin's advice and trust her instincts.

She would keep an eye on Silvara.

5

Silvara.

Although every muscle in Gilthanas's body cried for rest and he thought he couldn't crawl into his bedroll soon enough, the elflord found himself wide awake, staring into the sky. Storm clouds still hung thickly overhead, but a breeze tinged with salt air was blowing from the west, breaking them up. Occasionally he caught a glimpse of stars, and once the red moon flickered in the sky like a candle flame, then was snuffed out by the clouds.

The elf tried to get comfortable, turning and twisting until his bedroll was a shambles, then he had to sit up and untangle himself. Finally he gave up, deciding it was impossible to sleep on the hard, frozen ground.

None of the rest of his companions seemed to be having any problems, he noticed bitterly. Laurana

lay sleeping soundly, her cheek resting on her hand as was her habit from childhood. How strangely she'd been acting lately, Gilthanas thought. But then, he supposed he could hardly blame her. She had given up everything to do what she believed right and take the orb to Sancrist. Their father might have accepted her back into the family once, but now she was an outcast forever.

Gilthanas sighed. What about himself? He'd wanted to keep the orb in Qualin-Mori. He believed his father was right. . . . Or did he?

Apparently not, since I'm here, Gilthanas told himself. By the gods, his values were getting as muddled as Laurana's! First, his hatred for Tanis—a hatred he'd nurtured righteously for years—was starting to dwindle away, replaced by admiration, even affection. Next, he'd felt his hatred of other races beginning to die. He'd known few elves as noble or self-sacrificing as the human, Sturm Brightblade. And, though he didn't like Raistlin, he envied the young mage's skill. It was something Gilthanas, a dabbler in magic, had never had the patience or the courage to acquire. Finally, he had to admit he even liked the kender and the grumpy old dwarf. But he had never thought he would fall in love with a Wilder elf.

"There!" Gilthanas said aloud. "I've admitted it. I love her!" But was it love, he wondered, or simply physical attraction. At that, he grinned, thinking of Silvara with her dirt-streaked face, her filthy hair, her tattered clothes. My soul's eye must be seeing more clearly than my head, he thought, glancing fondly over at her bedroll.

To his astonishment, he saw it was empty! Startled, Gilthanas looked quickly around the camp. They had not dared light a fire—not only were the Qualinesti after them, but Theros had talked of groups of draconians roaming the land.

Thinking of this, Gilthanas rose to his feet quickly and began to search for Silvara. He moved silently, hoping to avoid the questions of Sturm and Derek, who were standing watch. A sudden chilling thought crossed his mind. Hurriedly, he looked for the dragon orb. But it was still where Silvara had put it. Beside it lay the broken shaft of the dragonlance.

Gilthanas breathed more easily. Then his quick ears caught the sound of water splashing. Listening carefully, he determined it wasn't a fish or a night-bird diving for its catch in the river. The elflord glanced at Derek and Sturm. The two stood apart from one another on a rock outcropping overlooking the camp. Gilthanas could hear them arguing with each other in fierce whispers. The elflord crept away from camp, heading toward the sound of softly splashing water.

Gilthanas walked through the dark forest with no more noise than the shadows of night itself would make. Occasionally he caught a glimpse of the river glistening faintly through the trees. Then he came to a place where the water, flowing among the rocks, had become trapped in a small pool. Here Gilthanas stopped, and here his heart almost stopped beating. He had found Silvara.

A dark circle of trees stood starkly outlined against the racing clouds. The silence of the night was broken only by the gentle murmurs of the silver river, which fell over rock steps into the pool, and by the splashing sounds that had caught Gilthanas's attention. Now he knew what they were.

Silvara was bathing. Oblivious to the chill in the air, the elfmaid was submerged in the water. Her clothes lay scattered on the bank next to a frayed blanket. Only her shoulders and arms were visible to Gilthanas's elvensight. Her head was thrown back as she washed the long hair that trailed out behind her, floating like a dark cobweb on the darker pool. The elflord held his breath, watching her. He knew he should leave, but he was held fast, entranced.

And then, the clouds parted. Solinari, the silver moon, though only half-full, burned in the night sky with a cold brilliance. The water in the pool turned to molten silver. Silvara rose up out of the pool. The silver water glistened on her skin, gleamed in her silver hair, ran in shining rivulets down her body that was painted in silver moonlight. Her beauty struck Gilthanas's heart with such intense pain that he gasped.

Silvara started, looking around her terrified. Her wild, abandoned grace added so much to her loveliness that Gilthanas, though he longed to speak to her reassuringly, couldn't force the words past the pain in his chest.

Silvara ran from the water to the bank where her clothes lay. But she did not touch them. Instead, she reached into a pocket. Grabbing a knife, she turned, ready to defend herself.

Gilthanas could see her body quivering in the silvery moonlight, and he was reminded vividly of a doe he had cornered after a long hunt. The creature's eyes sparkled with the same fear he now saw in Silvara's luminous eyes. The Wilder elf stared around, terrified. Why doesn't she see me? Gilthanas wondered briefly, feeling her eyes pass over him several times. With the elven sight, he should stand out to her like a—

Suddenly Silvara turned, starting to flee from the danger she could feel, yet could not see.

Gilthanas felt his voice freed. "No! Wait, Silvara! Don't be frightened. It's me, Gilthanas." He spoke in firm, yet hushed tones—as he had spoken to the cornered doe. "You shouldn't be out alone, it's dangerous. . . ."

Silvara paused, standing half in silver light, half in protecting shadows, her muscles tense, ready to spring. Gilthanas followed his huntsman's instinct, walking slowly, continuing to talk, holding her with his steady voice and his eyes.

"You shouldn't be out here alone. I'll stay with you. I want to talk to you anyway. I want you to listen to me for a moment. I need to talk to you, Silvara. I don't want to be here alone, either. Don't leave me, Silvara. So much has left me in this world. Don't leave. . . ."

Talking softly, continuously, Gilthanas moved with smooth, deliberate steps toward Silvara until he saw her take a step backward. Raising his hands, he sat down quickly on a boulder at the pool's edge, keeping the water between them. Silvara stopped, watching him. She made no move to clothe herself, apparently deciding that defense was more important than modesty. She still held the knife poised in her hand.

Gilthanas admired her determination, although he was ashamed for her nakedness. Any well-bred elven woman would have fainted dead away by now. He knew he should avert his eyes, but he was too awed by her beauty. His blood burned. With an effort, he kept talking, not even knowing what he was saying. Only gradually did he become aware that he was speaking the innermost thoughts of his heart.

"Silvara, what am I doing here? My father needs me, my people need me. Yet here I am, breaking the law of my lord. My people are in exile. I find the one thing that might help them—a dragon orb—but now I risk my life taking it from my people to give to humans to aid them in their war! It's not even my war, it's not my people's war." Gilthanas leaned toward her earnestly, noticing that she had not taken her eyes from him. "Why, Silvara? Why have I brought this dishonor on myself? Why have I done this to my people?"

He held his breath. Silvara glanced into the darkness and the safety of the woods, then looked back at him. She will flee, he thought, his heart pounding. Then, slowly, Silvara lowered her knife. There was such sadness and sorrow in her eyes that, finally, Gilthanas looked away, ashamed of himself.

"Silvara," he began, choking, "forgive me. I didn't mean to involve you in my trouble. I don't understand what it is that I must do. I only know . . ."

" . . . that you must do it," Silvara finished for him.

Gilthanas looked up. Silvara had covered herself with the frayed blanket. This modest effort served only to fan the flames of his desire. Her silver hair, hanging down past her waist, gleamed in the moonlight. The blanket eclipsed her silver skin.

Gilthanas rose slowly and began to walk along the shore toward her. She still stood at the edge of the forest's safety. He could still sense her coiled fear. But she had dropped the knife.

"Silvara," he said, "what I have done is against all elven custom. When my sister told me of her plot to steal the orb, I should have gone directly to my father. I should have sounded the alarm. I should have taken the orb myself—"

Silvara took a step toward him, still clutching the blanket around her. "Why didn't you?" she asked in a low voice.

Gilthanas was nearing the rock steps at the north end of the pond. The water flowing over them made a silver curtain in the moonlight."Because I know that my people are wrong. Laurana is right. Sturm

is right. Taking the orb to the humans is right! We must fight this war. My people are wrong, their laws, their customs are wrong. I know this—in my heart! But I can't make my head believe it. It torments me—"

Silvara walked slowly along the pool's edge. She, too, was nearing the silver curtain of water from the opposite side.

"I understand," she said softly. "My own . . . people do not understand what I do or why I do it. But I understand. I know what is right and I believe in it."

"I envy you, Silvara," Gilthanas whispered.

Gilthanas stepped to the largest rock, a flat island in the glittering, cascading water. Silvara, her wet hair falling over her like a silver gown, stood but a few feet from him now.

"Silvara," Gilthanas said, his voice shaking, "there was another reason I left my people. You know what it is."

He extended his hand, palm up, toward her.

Silvara drew back, shaking her head. Her breath came faster.

Gilthanas took another step nearer. "Silvara, I love you," he said softly. "You seem so alone, as alone as I am. Please, Silvara, you will never be alone again. I swear it. . . ."

Hesitantly, Silvara lifted her hand toward his. With a sudden move, Gilthanas grabbed her arm and pulled her across the water. Catching her as she stumbled, he lifted her onto the rock beside him.

Too late the wild doe realized she was trapped. Not by the man's arms, she could easily have broken free of his embrace. It was her own love for this man that had ensnared her. That his love for her was deep and tender sealed their fate. He was trapped as well.†

I was making a hash of the love scene. I wanted to get on with the war! Tracy wrote this scene, one of the best, I think.—MW

Gilthanas could feel her body trembling, but he knew now—as he looked into her eyes—that she trembled with passion, not fear. Cupping her face in his hands, he kissed her tenderly. Silvara still held the blanket clasped around her body with one hand, but he felt her other hand close around his. Her lips were soft and eager. Then, Gilthanas tasted a salty tear on his lips. He drew back, amazed to see her crying.

"Silvara, don't. I'm sorry— " He released her.

"No!" she whispered, her voice husky. "My tears are not because I am frightened of your love. They are only for myself. You cannot understand."

Reaching out, she shyly put one hand around his neck and drew him near. And then, as he kissed her, he felt her other hand, the hand that had been clasping the blanket around her body, move up to caress his face.

Silvara's blanket slipped unnoticed into the stream and was borne away by the silver water.†

Margaret often used to say, when we were asked about how we write together, that she wrote all the big blood-and-guts battle scenes and that the hottest love scene we ever wrote was penned by me. So much for stereotypes. She also used to say that my wife Laura and I were the last of the true Romantics. Since this chapter was written, however, Margaret and Don Perrin found each other and have had their own classic romance. I doubt that Margaret would find writing this scene now as difficult as she found it then.—TRH

6

Pursuit. A desperate plan.

At noon the next day, the companions were forced to abandon the boats, having reached the river's headwaters, where it flowed down out of the mountains. Here the water was shallow and frothy white from the tumbling rapids ahead. Many Kaganesti boats were drawn up on the bank. Dragging their boats ashore, the companions were met by a group of Kaganesti elves coming out of the woods. They carried with them the bodies of two young elven warriors. Some drew weapons and would have attacked had not Theros Ironfeld and Silvara hurried to talk with them.

The two spoke long with the Kaganesti, while the companions kept an uneasy watch downriver. Though they had been awake before dawn, starting as early as the Kaganesti felt was safe to travel

through the swift water, they had, more than once, caught glimpses of the black boats pursuing them.

When Theros returned, his dark face was somber. Silvara's was flushed with anger.

"My people will do nothing to help us," Silvara reported. "They have been attacked by lizardmen twice in the last two days. They blame the coming of this new evil on humans who, they say, brought them here in a white-winged ship—"

"That's ridiculous!" Laurana snapped. "Theros, didn't you tell them about these draconians?"

"I tried," the blacksmith stated. "But I am afraid the evidence is against you. The Kaganesti saw the white dragon above the ship, but they did not, apparently, see you drive her off. At any rate, they have finally agreed to let us pass through their lands, but they will give us no aid. Silvara and I both pledged our lives for your good conduct."

"What are the draconians doing here?" Laurana asked, memories haunting her. "Is it an army? Is Southern Ergoth being invaded? If so, perhaps we should go back—"

"No, I think not," Theros said thoughtfully. "If the armies of the Dragon Highlords were ready to take this isle, they would do so with flights of dragons and thousands of troops. These appear to be small patrols sent out to make this bad situation deteriorate further. The Highlords probably hope the elves will save them the trouble of a war by destroying each other first."

"The Dragon High Command is not ready to attack Ergoth," Derek said. "They haven't got a firm hold on the north yet. But it is only a matter of time. That is why it is imperative we get the dragon orb to Sancrist and call a meeting of the Council of Whitestone to determine what to do with it."

Gathering their supplies, the companions set out for the high country. Silvara led them along a trail beside the splashing silver river that ran from the hills. They could feel the unfriendly eyes of the Kaganesti follow them out of sight.

The land began rising almost immediately. Theros soon told them they had traveled into regions where he had never been before; it was up to Silvara to guide them. Laurana was not altogether pleased with this situation. She guessed something

had happened between her brother and the girl when she saw them share a sweet, secret smile.

Silvara had found time, among her people, to change her clothing. She was now dressed as a Kaganesti woman, in a long leather tunic over leather breeches, covered by a heavy fur cloak. With her hair washed and combed, all of them could see how she had come by her name. Her hair, a strange, metallic silver color, flowed from a peak on her forehead to fall about her shoulders in radiant beauty.

Silvara turned out to be an exceptionally good guide, pushing them along at a rapid pace. She and Gilthanas walked side by side, talking together in elven. Shortly before sundown, they came to a cave.

"Here we can spend the night," Silvara said. "We should have left the pursuit behind us. Few know these mountains as well as I do. But we dare not light a fire. Dinner will be cold, I'm afraid."

Exhausted by the day's climb, they ate a cheerless meal, then made their beds in the cave. The companions, huddled in their blankets and every piece of clothing they owned, slept fitfully. They set the watch, Laurana and Silvara both insisting on taking turns. The night passed quietly, the only sound they heard was the wind howling among the rocks.

But the next morning Tasslehoff, squeezing out through a crack in the cave's hidden entrance to take a look around, suddenly hurried back inside. Putting his finger to his lips, Tas motioned them to follow him outdoors. Theros pushed aside the huge boulder they had rolled across the mouth of the cave, and the companions crept after Tas. He led them to a stop not twenty feet from the cave and pointed grimly at the white snow.

On it were footprints, fresh enough that the blowing, drifting snow had not quite covered them. The light, delicate tracks had not sunk deeply into the snow. No one spoke. There was no need. Everyone recognized the crisp, clear outline of elven boots.

"They must have passed by us in the night," Silvara said. "But we dare not stay here any longer. Soon they will discover they have lost the trail and will backtrack. We must be gone."

"I don't see that it will make much difference," Flint grumbled in disgust. He pointed at their own, highly visible tracks. Then he looked up at the clear, blue sky. "We might as well just sit and wait for them. Save them time and save us bother. There's no way we can hide our trail!"

"Maybe we cannot hide our trail," said Theros, "but we can gain some miles on them, perhaps."

"Perhaps," Derek repeated grimly. Reaching down, he loosened his sword in its scabbard, then he walked back to the cave.

Laurana caught hold of Sturm. "It must not come to bloodshed!" she whispered frantically, alarmed by Derek's action.

The knight shook his head as they followed the others. "We cannot allow your people to stop us from taking the orb to Sancrist."†

Sancrist Isle was known throughout Ansalon as the last remaining stronghold of the Solamnic Knights—and the only possible organized force with any hope of stopping the Dragon Highlords. Laurana, as a member of the royal elven court in Qualinost, would have known this. So, too, would Elistan as a former High Theocrat. Their choice to take the orb to Sancrist is a good one.—TRH

"I know!" Laurana said softly. Bowing her head, she entered the cave in silent misery.

The rest were ready within moments. Then Derek stood, fuming in the doorway, watching Laurana impatiently.

"Go ahead," she told him, unwilling to let him see her cry. "I'll be along."

Derek left immediately. Theros, Sturm, and the others trudged out more slowly, glancing uneasily at Laurana.

"Go ahead." She gestured. She needed a moment to be by herself. But all she could think of was Derek's hand on his sword. "No!" she told herself sternly. "I will not fight my people. The day that happens is the day the dragons have won. I will lay down my own sword first—"

She heard movement behind her. Whirling around, her hand going reflexively to her sword, Laurana stopped.

"Silvara?" she said in astonishment, seeing the girl in the shadows. "I thought you had gone. What are you doing?"

Laurana walked swiftly to where Silvara had been kneeling in the darkness, her hands busy with something on the cavern floor. The Wilder elf rose quickly to her feet.

"N-nothing," Silvara murmured. "Just gathering my things."

Behind Silvara, on the cold floor of the cave, Laurana thought she saw the dragon orb, its crystal surface shining with a strange swirling light. But before she could look more closely, Silvara swiftly dropped

her cloak over the orb. As she did so, Laurana noticed she kept standing in front of whatever it was she had been handling on the floor.

"Come, Laurana," Silvara said, "we must hurry. I am sorry if I was slow—"

"In a moment," Laurana said sternly. She started to walk past the Wilder elf. Silvara's hand clutched at her.

"We must hurry!" she said, and there was an edge of steel in her low voice. Her grip on Laurana's arm was painful, even through the thick fur of Laurana's heavy cloak.

"Let go of me," Laurana said coldly, staring at the girl, her green eyes showing neither fear nor anger. Silvara let fall her hand, lowering her eyes.

Laurana walked to the back of the shallow cave. Looking down, however, she could see nothing that made any sense. There was a tangle of twigs and bark and charred wood, some stones, but that was all. If it was a sign, it was a clumsy one. Laurana kicked at it with her booted foot, scattering the stones and sticks. Then she turned and took Silvara's arm.

"There," Laurana said, speaking in even, quiet tones. "Whatever message you left for your friends will be difficult to read."

Laurana was prepared for almost any reaction from the girl—anger, shame at being discovered. She even half-expected her to attack. But Silvara began to tremble. Her eyes—as she stared at Laurana—were pleading, almost sorrowful. For a moment, Silvara tried to speak, but she couldn't. Shaking her head, she jerked away from Laurana's grasp and ran outside.

"Hurry up, Laurana!" Theros called gruffly.

"I'm coming!" she answered, glancing back at the debris on the cave floor. She thought of taking a moment longer to investigate further, but she knew she dare not take the time.

Perhaps I *am* being too suspicious of the girl, and for no reason,Laurana thought with a sigh as she hurried out of the cave. Then about half-way up the trail, she stopped so abruptly that Theros, walking rear-guard, slammed into her. He caught her arm, steadying her.

"You all right?" he asked.

"Y-yes," Laurana answered, only half-hearing him.

"You look pale. Did you see something?"

"No. I'm fine," Laurana said hurriedly, and she started up the rocky cliff again, slipping in the snow. What a fool she'd been!

What fools they'd all been! Once again, she could see clearly in her mind's eye Silvara rising to her feet, dropping her cloak over the dragon orb. The dragon orb that was shining with a strange light!

She started to ask Silvara about the orb when suddenly her thoughts were scattered. An arrow zinged through the air and thudded into a tree near Derek's head.

"Elves! Brightblade, attack!" the knight cried, drawing his sword.

"No!" Laurana ran forward, grabbing his sword arm. "We will not fight! There will be no killing!"

"You're mad!" Derek shouted. Angrily breaking loose of Laurana's grip, he shoved her backward into Sturm.

Another arrow flew by.

"She's right!" Silvara pleaded, hurrying back. "We cannot fight them. We must reach the pass! There we can stop them."

Another arrow, nearly spent, struck the chain-mail vest Derek wore over his leather tunic. He brushed it away irritably.

"They're not aiming to kill," Laurana added. "If they were, you would be dead by now. We must run for it. We can't fight here, anyhow." She gestured at the thick woods. "We can defend the pass better."

"Put your sword away, Derek," Sturm said, drawing his blade. "Or you'll fight me first."

"You're a coward, Brightblade!" Derek shouted, his voice shaking with fury. "You're running from the enemy!"

"No," Sturm answered coolly, "I'm running from my friends." The knight kept his sword drawn. "Get moving, Crownguard, or the elves will find they have arrived too late to take you prisoner."

Another arrow flew past, lodging in a tree near Derek. The knight, his face splotched with fury, sheathed his sword and, turning, plunged ahead up the trail. But not before he had cast Sturm a look of such intense enmity that Laurana shuddered.

"Sturm—" she began, but he only grabbed her by the elbow and hustled her forward too fast to talk. They climbed rapidly. Behind her, she could hear Theros crashing through the snow, occasionally stopping to send a boulder bouncing down after them. Soon it sounded like the entire side of the mountain was sliding down the steep trail, and the arrows ceased.

"But it's only temporary," the smith puffed, catching up with Sturm and Laurana. "That won't stop them for long."

Laurana couldn't answer. Her lungs were on fire. Blue and gold stars burst before her eyes. She was not the only one suffering. Sturm's breath rasped in his throat. His grasp on her arm was weak and his hand shook. Even the strong smith was blowing like a winded horse. Rounding a boulder, they found the dwarf on his knees, Tasslehoff trying vainly to lift him.

"Must . . . rest . . ." Laurana said, her throat aching. She started to sit down, but strong hands grabbed her.

"No!" Silvara said urgently. "Not here! Just a few more feet! Come on! Keep going!"

The Wilder elf dragged Laurana forward. Dimly she was aware of Sturm helping Flint to his feet, the dwarf groaning and swearing. Between them, Theros and Sturm dragged the dwarf up the trail. Tasslehoff stumbled behind, too tired even to talk.

Finally they came to the top of the pass. Laurana slumped into the snow, past caring what happened to her. The rest sank down beside her, all except Silvara who was staring below them.

Where does she get the strength? Laurana thought through a bleak haze of pain. But she was too exhausted to question. At the moment, she was too tired to care whether the elves found her or not. Silvara turned to face them.

"We must split up," she said decisively.

Laurana stared at her, uncomprehending.

"No," Gilthanas began, trying without success to get to his feet.

"Listen to me!" Silvara said urgently, kneeling down. "The elves are too close. They will catch us for certain, then we must either fight or surrender."

"Fight," Derek muttered savagely.

"There is a better way," Silvara hissed. "You, knight, must take the dragon orb to Sancrist alone! We will draw off the pursuit."

For a moment no one spoke. Everyone stared silently at Silvara, considering this new possibility. Derek lifted his head, his eyes gleaming. Laurana flashed a look of alarm at Sturm.

"I do not think one person should be charged with such a grave responsibility," Sturm said, his breath coming haltingly. "Two of us should go—at least."

"Meaning yourself, Brightblade?" Derek asked angrily.

"Yes, of course, Sturm should go," Laurana said, "if anyone."

"I can draw a map through the mountains," Silvara said eagerly. "The way is not difficult. The outpost of the knights is only a two-day journey from here."

"But we can't fly," Sturm protested. "What about our tracks? Surely the elves will see we've split up."

"An avalanche," Silvara suggested. "Theros throwing the boulders down behind us gave me the idea." She glanced up. They followed her gaze. Snow-covered peaks towered above them, the snow hanging over the edges.

"I can cause an avalanche with my magic," Gilthanas said slowly. "It will obliterate everyone's tracks."

"Not entirely," cautioned Silvara. "We must allow ours to be found once again—though not too obviously. After all, we want them to follow us."

"But where will we go?" asked Laurana. "I don't intend to wander aimlessly through the wilderness."

"I—I know a place."Silvara faltered, her gaze dropping to the ground. "It is secret, known only to my people. I will take you there."She clasped her hands together. "Please, we must hurry. There isn't much time!"

"I will take the orb to Sancrist," Derek said, "and I will go alone. Sturm should go with your group. You'll need a fighter."

"We have fighters," Laurana said. "Theros, my brother, the dwarf. I, myself, have seen my share of battle—"

"And me," piped Tasslehoff.

"And the kender," Laurana added grimly. "Besides, it will not come to bloodshed." Her eyes saw Sturm's troubled face and wondered what he was thinking. Her voice softened. "The decision is up to Sturm, of course. He must do as he believes best, but I think he should accompany Derek."

"I agree," muttered Flint. "After all, we're not the ones who are going to be in danger. We'll be safer without the dragon orb. It's the orb the elves want."

"Yes," agreed Silvara, her voice soft. "We'll be safer without the orb. It is you who will be in danger."

"Then my way is clear," Sturm said. "I will go with Derek."

"And if I order you to stay behind?" Derek demanded.

"You have no authority over me," Sturm said, his brown eyes dark."Have you forgotten? I am not a knight."

There was a painful, profound silence. Derek stared at Sturm intently.

"No," he said, "and if I have my way, you never will be!"

Sturm flinched, as if Derek had struck him a physical blow. Then he stood up, sighing heavily.

Derek had already begun to gather his gear. Sturm moved more slowly, picking up his bedroll with thoughtful deliberation. Laurana pulled herself to her feet and went to Sturm.

"Here," she said, reaching into her pack. "You'll need food—"

"You could come with us," Sturm said in low tones as she divided up their supplies. "Tanis knows we were going to Sancrist. He will come there, too, if possible."

"You're right," Laurana said, her eyes brightening. "Perhaps that would be a good idea—" Then her eyes went to Silvara. The Wilder elf held the dragon orb, still shrouded in its cloak. Silvara's eyes were closed, almost as if she were communing with some unseen spirit. Sighing, Laurana shook her head. "No, I've got to stay with her, Sturm," she said softly. "Something's not right. I don't understand—" she broke off, unable to articulate her thoughts. "What about Derek?" she asked instead. "Why is he so insistent on going alone? The dwarf's right about the danger. If the elves capture you, without us, they won't hesitate to kill you."

Sturm's face was drawn, bitter. "Can you ask? Lord Derek Crownguard returns alone out of horrifying dangers, bearing with him the coveted dragon orb—" Sturm shrugged.

"But there's so much at stake," Laurana protested.

"You're right, Laurana," Sturm said harshly. "There's a lot at stake. More than you know—the leadership of the Knights of Solamnia.† I can't explain it now. . . ."

"Come along, Brightblade, if you're coming!" Derek snarled.

The Knights of Solamnia, such as they are, are involved in a bitter struggle for leadership, although what of remains a question.

Apparently, of the sixty-three known knights still remaining at this time, all sixty-three want power.

Sturm took the food, stowing it in his pack. "Farewell, Laurana," he said, bowing to her with the quiet gallantry that marked all his actions.

"Farewell, Sturm, my friend," she whispered, putting her arms around the knight.

He held her closely, then kissed her gently on the forehead.

"We will give the orb to the wise men to study. The Council of Whitestone will meet soon," he said. "The elves will be invited to attend, since they are advisory members. You must come to Sancrist as soon as possible, Laurana. Your presence will be needed."

"I'll be there, the gods willing," Laurana said, her eyes going to Silvara, who was handing Derek the dragon orb. An expression of inexpressible relief flitted over Silvara's face when Derek turned to go.

Sturm said good-bye, then he plunged into the snow after Derek.The companions saw a flash of light as his shield caught the sun.

Suddenly Laurana took a step forward. "Wait!" she cried. "I've got to stop them. They should take the dragonlance, too."

"No!" Silvara shouted, running to block Laurana's path.

Angrily, Laurana reached out to shove the girl aside, then she saw Silvara's face and her hand stopped.

"What are you doing, Silvara?" Laurana asked. "Why did you send them off? Why were you so eager to split us up? Why give them the orb and not the lance—"

Silvara didn't answer. She simply shrugged and stared at Laurana with eyes bluer than midnight.

Laurana felt her will being drained by those blue, blue eyes. She was reminded terrifyingly of Raistlin.

Gilthanas, too, stared at Silvara with a perplexed and worried expression. Theros stood grim and stern, glancing at Laurana as if beginning to share her doubts. But they were not able to move. They were completely under Silvara's control—yet what had she done to them? They could only stand and stare at the Wilder elf as she walked calmly over to where Laurana had wearily let fall her pack. Bending down, Silvara unwrapped the broken piece of splintered wood. Then she raised it in the air.

Sunlight flashed on Silvara's silver hair, mimicking the flash from Sturm's shield.

"The dragonlance stays with me," Silvara said. Glancing swiftly around the spellbound group, she added, "As do you."

7

Dark Journey.

Though he can magically set off an avalanche, Gilthanas has never taken the Test because it would have required more commitment to magic than he is willing to give.

Behind them, the snow rumbled and toppled over the side of the mountain. Cascading down in white sheets, blocking and choking the pass, it obliterated their presence. The echoes of Gilthanas's magical thunder† still resounded in the air, or perhaps it was the booming of the rocks as they bounded down the slopes. They could not be certain.

The companions, led by Silvara, traveled the trails east slowly and cautiously, walking where it was rocky, avoiding the snowy patches if at all possible. They walked through each other's footsteps so that the pursuing elves would never know for certain how many were in their party. They were so careful, in fact, that Laurana grew worried.

"Remember, we want them to find *us*," she said to Silvara as they crept across the top of a rocky defile.

"Do not be upset. They will have no trouble finding us," answered Silvara.

"What makes you so certain?" Laurana started to ask, then she slipped and fell to her hands and knees. Gilthanas helped her stand. Grimacing with pain, she stared at Silvara in silence. None of them, including Theros, trusted the sudden change that had come over the Wilder elf since their parting with the knights. But they had no choice except to follow her.

"Because they know our destination," Silvara answered. "You were clever to think I left a sign to them in the cave. I did. Fortunately, you did not find it. Below those sticks you so kindly scattered for me I had drawn a crude map. When they find it, they will think I drew it to show you our destination. You made it look most realistic, Laurana."Her voice was defiant until she met Gilthanas's eyes.

The elflord turned away from her, his face grave. Silvara faltered. Her voice became pleading. "I did it for a reason, a good reason. I knew then, when I saw the tracks, we would have to split up. You must believe me!"

"What about the dragon orb? What were you doing with it?" Laurana demanded.

"N-nothing," Silvara stammered. "You must trust me!"

"I don't see why," Laurana returned coldly.

"I have done you no harm—" Silvara began.

"Unless you have sent the knights and the dragon orb into a deathtrap!" Laurana cried.

"No!" Silvara wrung her hands. "I haven't! Believe me. They will be safe. That has been my plan all along. Nothing must happen to the dragon orb. Above all, it must not fall into the hands of the elves. That is why I sent it away. That is why I helped you escape!" She glanced around, seeming to sniff the air like an animal. "Come! We have lingered too long."

"If we go with you at all!" Gilthanas said harshly. "What do you know about the dragon orb?"

"Don't ask me!" Silvara's voice was suddenly deep and filled with sadness. Her blue eyes stared into Gilthanas's with such love that he could not

bear to face her. He shook his head, avoiding her gaze. Silvara caught hold of his arm. "Please, *shalori,* beloved, trust me! Remember what we talked about, at the pool. You said you had to do these things—defy your people, become an outcast, because of what you believed in your heart. I said that I understood, that I had to do the same. Didn't you believe me?"

Gilthanas stood a moment, his head bowed. "I believed you," he said softly. Reaching out, he pulled her to him, kissing her silver hair. "We'll go with you. Come on, Laurana." Arms around each other, the two trudged off through the snow.

Laurana looked blankly at the others. They avoided her eyes. Then Theros came up to her.

Don Perrin tells the story of the amazing smith and his life before the Silver Arm in the novel Theros Ironfeld.

"I've lived in this world nearly fifty years,† young woman," he said gently. "Not long to you elves, I know. But we humans live those years, we don't just let them drift by. And I'll tell you this—that girl loves your brother as truly as I've ever seen woman love man. And he loves her. Such love cannot come to evil. For the sake of their love alone, I'd follow them into a dragon's den."

The smith walked after the two.

"For the sake of my cold feet, I'd follow them into a dragon's den, if he'd warm my toes!" Flint stamped on the ground. "Come on, let's go." Grabbing the kender, he dragged Tas along after the blacksmith.

Laurana remained standing, alone. That she would follow was settled. She had no choice. She wanted to trust Theros's words. One time, she would have believed the world ran that way. But now she knew much she had believed in was false. Why not love?

All she could see in her mind were the swirling colors of the dragon orb.

The companions traveled east, into the gloom of gathering night. Descending from the high mountain pass, they found the air easier to breathe. The frozen rocks gave way to scraggly pines, then the forests closed in around them once more. Silvara confidently led them at last into a fog-shrouded valley.

The Wilder elf no longer seemed to care about covering their tracks. All that concerned her now

was speed. She pushed the group on, as if racing the sun across the sky. When night fell, they sank into the tree-rimmed darkness, too tired even to eat. But Silvara allowed them only a few hours of restless, aching sleep. When the moons rose, the silver and the red, nearing their fullness now, she urged the companions on.

When anyone questioned, wearily, why they hurried, she only answered, "They are near. They are very near."

Each assumed she meant the elves, though Laurana had long ago lost the feeling of dark shapes trailing them.

Dawn broke, but the light was filtered through fog so thick Tasslehoff thought he might grab a handful and store it in one of his pouches. The companions walked close together, even holding hands to avoid being separated. The air grew warmer. They shed their wet and heavy cloaks as they stumbled along a trail that seemed to materialize beneath their feet, out of the fog.† Silvara walked before them. The faint light shining from her silver hair was their only guide.

The source of the fog is a hot spring that was exposed to the air when the land moved during the Cataclysm.

Finally the ground grew level at their feet, the trees cleared, and they walked on smooth grass, brown with winter. Although none of them could see more than a few feet in the gray fog, they had the impression they were in a wide clearing.

"This is Foghaven Vale," Silvara replied in answer to their questions. "Long years ago, before the Cataclysm, it was one of the most beautiful places upon Krynn . . . so my people say."

"It might still be beautiful," Flint grumbled, "if we could see it through this confounded mist."

"No," said Silvara sadly. "Like much else in this world, the beauty of Foghaven has vanished. Once the fortress of Foghaven floated above the mist as if floating on a cloud. The rising sun colored the mists pink in the morning, burned them off at midday so that the soaring spires of the fortress could be seen for miles. In the evening, the fog returned to cover the fortress like a blanket. By night, the silver and the red moons shone on the mists with a shimmering light. Pilgrims came, from all parts of Krynn—" Silvara stopped abruptly. "We will make camp here tonight."

"What pilgrims?" Laurana asked, letting her pack fall.

Silvara shrugged. "I do not know," she said, averting her face. "It is only a legend of my people. Perhaps it is not even true. Certainly no one comes here now."

She's lying, thought Laurana, but she said nothing. She was too tired to care. And even Silvara's low, gentle voice seemed unnaturally loud and jarring in the eerie stillness. The companions spread their blankets in silence. They ate in silence, too, nibbling without appetite on the dried fruit in their packs. Even the kender was subdued. The fog was oppressive, weighing them down. The only thing they could hear was a steady drip, drip, drip of water plopping onto the mat of dead leaves on the forest floor below.

"Sleep now," said Silvara softly, spreading her blanket near Gilthanas's, "for when the silver moon has neared its zenith, we must leave."

"What difference will that make?" The kender yawned. "We can't see it anyway."

"Nonetheless, we must go. I will wake you."

"When we return from Sancrist—after the Council of Whitestone—we can be married," Gilthanas said softly to Silvara as they lay together, wrapped in his blanket.

The girl stirred in his arms. He felt her soft hair rub against his cheek. But she did not answer.

"Don't worry about my father," Gilthanas said, smiling, stroking the beautiful hair that shone even in the darkness. "He'll be stern and grim for a while, but I am the younger brother, no one cares what becomes of me. Porthios will rant and rave and carry on. But we'll ignore him. We don't have to live with my people. I'm not sure how I'd fit in with yours, but I could learn. I'm a good shot with a bow. And I'd like our children to grow up in the wilderness, free and happy . . . what . . . Silvara, why—you're crying!"

Gilthanas held her close as she buried her face in his shoulder, sobbing bitterly. "There, there," he whispered soothingly, smiling in the darkness. Women were such funny creatures. He wondered what he'd said. "Hush, Silvara," he murmured. "It will be all right." And Gilthanas fell asleep,

dreaming of silver-haired children running in the green woods.

"It is time. We must leave."

Laurana felt a hand on her shoulder, shaking her. Startled, she woke from a vague, frightening dream that she could not remember to find the Wilder elf kneeling above her.

"I'll wake the others," Silvara said, and disappeared.

Feeling more tired than if she hadn't slept, Laurana packed her things by reflex and stood waiting, shivering, in the darkness. Next to her, she heard the dwarf groan. The damp air was making his joints ache painfully. This journey had been hard on Flint, Laurana realized. He was, after all, what—almost one hundred and fifty years old? A respectable age for a dwarf. His face had lost some of its color during his illness on the voyage. His lips, barely visible beneath the beard, had a bluish tinge, and occasionally he pressed his hand against his chest.† But he always stoutly insisted he was fine and kept up with them on the trail.

His father died of a weak heart when Flint was young. He had a hereditary heart condition that plagues the Fireforge family. Flint has always managed to ignore it … until now.

"All set!" cried Tas. His shrill voice echoed weirdly in the fog, and he had the distinct feeling he'd disturbed something. "I'm sorry," he said, cringing. "Gee," he muttered to Flint, "it's like being in a temple."

"Just shut up and start moving!" the dwarf snapped.

A torch flared. The companions started at the sudden, blinding light that Silvara held.

"We must have light," she said before any could protest. "Do not fear. The vale we are in is sealed shut. Long ago, there were two entrances: one led to human lands where the knights had their outpost, the other led east into the lands of the ogres. Both passes were lost during the Cataclysm. We need have no fear. I have led you by a way known only to myself."

"And to your people," Laurana reminded her sharply.

"Yes—my people . . ." Silvara said, and Laurana was surprised to see the girl grow pale.

"Where are you taking us?" Laurana insisted.

"You will see. We will be there within the hour."

The companions glanced at each other, then all of them looked at Laurana.

Damn them! she thought. "Don't look to me for answers!" she said angrily. "What do you want to do? Stay out here, lost in the fog—"

"I won't betray you!" Silvara murmured despondently. "Please, just trust me a little further."

"Go ahead," said Laurana tiredly. "We'll follow."

The fog seemed to close around them more thickly, until all that kept the darkness at bay was the light of Silvara's torch.

No one had any idea of the direction they traveled. The landscape did not change. They walked through tall grass. There were no trees.

Occasionally a large boulder loomed out of the darkness, but that was all. Of night birds or animals, there was no sign. There was a sense of urgency that increased as they walked until all of them felt it, and they hurried their steps, keeping ever within the light of the torch.

Then, suddenly, without warning, Silvara stopped.

"We are here," she said, and she held the torch aloft. The torch's light pierced the fog. They could all see a shadowy something beyond. At first, it was so ghostly materializing out of the fog that the companions could not recognize it.

Silvara drew closer. They followed her, curious, fearful.

Then the silence of the night was broken by bubbling sounds like water boiling in a giant kettle. The fog grew denser, the air was warm and stifling.

"Hot springs!" said Theros in sudden understanding. "Of course, that explains the constant fog. And this dark shape—"

"The bridge which leads across them," Silvara replied, shining the torchlight upon what they could see was a glistening stone bridge spanning the water boiling in the streams below them, filling the night air with its warm, billowing fog.

"We're supposed to cross that!" Flint exclaimed, staring at the black, boiling water in horror. "We're supposed to cross—"

"It is called the Bridge of Passage," said Silvara.

The dwarf's only answer was a strangled gulp.

The Bridge of Passage was a long, smooth arch of pure white marble. Along its sides—carved in vivid

relief—long columns of knights walked symbolically across the bubbling streams. The span was so high that they could not see the top through the swirling mists. And it was old, so old that Flint, reverently touching the worn rock with his hand, could not recognize the craftsmanship. It was not dwarven, not elven, not human. Who† had done such marvelous work?

This bridge was actually constructed by gnomes who were attempting the first stone boat but allowed the design to get out of hand....

Sorry, I couldn't resist. Actually I believe that this span was constructed by the Irda—the pure race from which the Ogres fell—in homage to Huma. —TRH

Then he noticed there were no hand-rails, nothing but the marble span itself, slick and glistening with the mist rising constantly from the bubbling springs beneath.

"We cannot cross that," said Laurana, her voice trembling. "And now we are trapped—"

"We *can* cross," Silvara said. "For we have been summoned."

"Summoned?" Laurana repeated in exasperation. "By what? Where?"

"Wait," commanded Silvara.

They waited. There was nothing left for them to do. Each stood staring around in the torchlight, but they saw only the mist rising from the streams, heard only the gurgling water.

"It is the time of Solinari," Silvara said suddenly, and—swinging her arm—she hurled her torch into the water.†

Bound in the magic of this place, those who seek it have difficulty finding it. Those who give themselves over to the place find their way more easily. By dowsing the light, Silvara is looking for the way in her soul, as she knows she must.—TRH

Darkness swallowed them. Involuntarily, they crept closer together. Silvara seemed to have vanished with the light. Gilthanas called for her, but she did not answer.

Then the mist turned to shimmering silver. They could see once more, and now they could see Silvara, a dark, shadowy outline against the silvery mist. She stood at the foot of the bridge, staring up into the sky. Slowly she raised her hands, and slowly the mists parted. Looking up, the companions saw the mists separate like long, graceful fingers to reveal the silver moon, full and brilliant in the starry sky.

Silvara spoke strange words, and the moonlight poured down upon her, bathing her in its light. The moon's light shone upon the bubbling waters, making them come alive, dancing with silver. It shone upon the marble bridge, giving life to the knights who spent eternity crossing the stream.

But it was not these beautiful sights that caused the companions to clasp each other with shaking hands or to hold each other closely. The moon's light on the water did not cause Flint to repeat the name of Reorx in the most reverent prayer he ever uttered, or cause Laurana to lean her head against her brother's shoulder, her eyes dimmed with sudden tears, or cause Gilthanas to hold her tightly, overwhelmed by a feeling of fear and awe and reverence.

Soaring high above them, so tall its head might have torn a moon from the sky, was the figure of a dragon, carved out of a mountain of rock, shining silver in the moonlight.

"Where are we?" Laurana asked in a hushed voice. "What is this place?"

"When you cross the Bridge of Passage, you will stand before the Monument of the Silver Dragon," answered Silvara softly. "It guards the Tomb of Huma, Knight of Solamnia."

8

The Tomb of Huma.

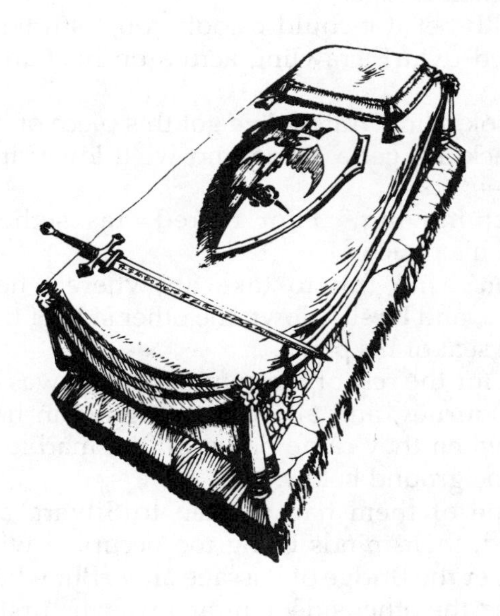

In Solinari's light, the Bridge of Passage across the bubbling streams of Foghaven Vale gleamed like bright pearls threaded on a silver chain.

"Do not fear," Silvara said again. "The crossing is difficult only for those who seek to enter the Tomb for evil purposes."

But the companions remained unconvinced. Fearfully they climbed the few stairs leading them up to bridge itself. Then, hesitantly, they stepped upon the marble arch that rose before them, glistening wet with the steam from the springs. Silvara crossed first, walking lightly and with ease. The rest followed her more cautiously, keeping to the very center of the marble span.

Across from them, on the other side of the bridge, loomed the Monument of the Dragon. Even though

The springs are so hot because they flow in the heat given off by volcanic activity just below the ground, though it's not known whether volcanoes have actually erupted in the area.

they knew they must watch their footing, their eyes seemed constantly drawn up to it. Many times, they were forced to stop and stare in awe, while below them the hot springs boiled and steamed.†

"Why—I bet that water's so hot you could cook meat in it!" Tasslehoff said. Lying flat on his stomach, he peered over the edge of the highest part of the arched bridge.

"I'll b-bet it c-could c-cook you," stuttered the terrified dwarf, crawling across on his hands and knees.

"Look, Flint! Watch. I've got this piece of meat in my pack. I'll get a string and we'll lower it in the water—"

"Get moving!" Flint roared. Tas sighed and closed his pouch.

"You're no fun to take anywhere," he complained, and he slid down the other side of the span on the seat of his pants.

But for the rest of the companions, it was a terrifying journey, and all of them sighed in heartfelt relief when they came down off the marble bridge onto the ground below.

None of them had spoken to Silvara as they crossed, their minds being too occupied with getting over the Bridge of Passage alive. But when they reached the other side, Laurana was the first to ask questions.

"Why have you brought us here?"

"Do you not trust me yet?" Silvara asked sadly.

Laurana hesitated. Her gaze went once again to the huge stone dragon, whose head was crowned with stars. The stone mouth was open in a silent cry, and the stone eyes stared fiercely. The stone wings were carved out of the sides of the mountain. A stone claw stretched forth, as massive as the trunks of a hundred vallenwood trees.

"You send the dragon orb away, then bring us to a monument dedicated to a dragon!" Laurana said after a moment, her voice quivering."What am I to think? And you bring us to this place you *call* Huma's Tomb. We do not even know if Huma lived, or if he was legend. What is to prove this is his resting place? Is his body within?"

"N-no," Silvara faltered. "His body disappeared, as did—"

"As did what?"

"As did the lance he carried, the Dragonlance he used to destroy the Dragon of All Colors and of None." Silvara sighed and lowered her head. "Come inside," she begged, "and rest for the night. In the morning, all will be made clear, I promise."

"I don't think—" Laurana began.

"We're going inside!" Gilthanas said firmly. "You're behaving like a spoiled child, Laurana! Why would Silvara lead us into danger? Surely, if there was a dragon living here, everyone on Ergoth would know it! It could have destroyed everyone on the island long ago. I sense no evil about this place, only a great and ancient peace. And it's a perfect hiding place! Soon the elves will receive word that the orb has reached Sancrist safely. They'll quit searching, and we can leave. Isn't that right, Silvara? Isn't that why you brought us here?"

"Yes," Silvara said softly. "Th-that was my plan. Now, come, come quickly, while the silver moon still shines. For only then can we enter."

Gilthanas, his hand holding Silvara's hand, walked into the shimmering silver fog. Tas skipped ahead of them, his pouches bouncing. Flint and Theros followed more slowly, Laurana more slowly still. Her fears were not eased by Gilthanas's glib explanation, nor by Silvara's reluctant agreement. But there was no place else to go and—as she admitted—she was intensely curious.

The grass on the other side of the bridge was smooth and flat with the steamy clouds of moisture, but the ground began to rise as they approached the body of the dragon carved out of the cliff. Suddenly Tasslehoff's voice floated back to them from the mist where he had run far ahead of the group.

"Raistlin!" they heard him cry in a strangled voice. "He's turned into a giant!"

"The kender's gone mad," Flint said with gloomy satisfaction. "I always knew it—"

Running forward, the companions found Tas jumping up and down and pointing. They stood by his side, panting for breath.

"By the beard of Reorx," gasped Flint in awe. "It *is* Raistlin!"

Looming† out of the swirling mist, rising nine feet in the air, stood a stone statue carved in a perfect

I always laugh inside whenever I see this word. Once, when I was writing the original Ravenloft module with my wife, the editor on the project noted that everything in the gothic horror game was either "heavy" or it "loomed." Heavy fog, heavy beams, heavy footsteps were interspersed with looming gates or buildings that loomed overhead. At one point the editor found something that "loomed heavily" in my text and came directly to my office cubicle to strangle me. In those days, I was called the "Captain of Purple Prose."—TRH

likeness of the young mage. Accurate in every detail, it even captured his cynical, bitter expression and the carven eyes with their hourglass pupils.

"And there's Caramon!" Tas cried.

A few feet away stood another statue, this time shaped like the mage's warrior twin.

"And Tanis . . . " Laurana whispered fearfully. "What evil magic is this?"

"Not evil," Silvara said, "unless you bring evil to this place. In that case, you would see the faces of your worst enemies within the stone statues.† The horror and fear they generate would not allow you to pass. But you see only your friends, and so you may pass safely."

Although I had no qualms about making up spells by this time in the writing process, this one is a permanent Illusion spell from AD&D.—MW

"I wouldn't exactly count Raistlin among my friends," muttered Flint.

"Nor I," Laurana said. Shivering, she walked hesitantly past the cold image of the mage. The mage's obsidian robes gleamed black in the moons' light. Laurana remembered vividly the nightmare of Silvanesti, and she shuddered as she entered what she saw now was a ring of stone statues—each of them bearing a striking, almost frightening resemblance to her friends. Within that silent ring of stone stood a small temple.

The simple rectangular building thrust up into the fog from an octagonal base of shining steps. It, too, was made of obsidian, and the black structure glistened wet with the perpetual fog. Each feature stood as if it had been carved only days before; no sign of wear marred the sharp, clean lines of the carving. Its knights, each bearing the dragonlance, still charged huge monsters. Dragons screamed silently in frozen death, pierced by the long, delicate shafts.

"Inside this temple, they placed Huma's body," Silvara said softly as she led them up the stairs.

Cold bronze doors swung open on silent hinges to Silvara's touch. The companions stood uncertainly on the stairs that encircled the columned temple. But, as Gilthanas had said, they could sense no evil coming from this place. Laurana remembered vividly the Tomb of the Royal Guard in the Sla-Mori and the terror generated by the undead guards left to keep eternal watch over their dead king, Kith-Kanan. In this temple, however, she felt

only sorrow and loss, tempered by the knowledge of a great victory—a battle won at terrible cost, but bringing with it eternal peace and sweet restfulness.

Laurana felt her burden ease, her heart become lighter. Her own sorrow and loss seemed diminished here. She was reminded of her own victories and triumphs. One by one, all the companions entered the tomb. The bronze doors swung shut behind them, leaving them in total darkness.

Then light flared. Silvara held a torch in her hand, apparently taken from the wall. Laurana wondered briefly how she had managed to light it. But the trivial question left her mind as she stood gazing around the tomb in awe.

It was empty except for a bier carved out of obsidian,† which stood in the center of the room. Chiseled images of knights supported the bier, but the body of the knight that was supposed to have rested upon it was gone. An ancient shield lay at the foot, and a sword, similar to Sturm's, lay near the shield. The companions gazed at these artifacts in silence. It seemed a desecration to the sorrowful serenity of the place to speak, and none touched them, not even Tasslehoff.

Obsidian is such a wonderful material for use in literature. Black, smooth glass formed as ejecta matter from volcanoes, obsidian in its natural form has convoluted, smooth flowing lines that abruptly end in razor-sharp edges where the obsidian has broken. Not only does it embody the violent forces of nature in a placid state and has the mystery of its blackness, but it also is a wonderful sounding word, rolling sweetly off the tongue. Obsidian, as a symbol of harnessed powers of darkness, is a fantasy writer's friend. —TRH

"I wish Sturm could be here," murmured Laurana, looking around, tears coming to her eyes. "This *must* be Huma's resting place . . . yet—"

She couldn't explain the growing sense of uneasiness that was creeping over her. Not fear, it was more like the sensation she had felt upon entering the vale—a sense of urgency.

Silvara lit more torches along the wall, and the companions walked past the bier, gazing around the tomb curiously. It was not large. The bier stood in the center and stone benches lined the walls, presumably for the mourners to rest upon while paying their respects. At the far end stood a small stone altar. Carved in its surface were the symbols of the orders of the Knights, the crown, the rose, the kingfisher. Dried rose petals and herbs lay scattered on the top, their fragrance still lingering sweetly in the air after hundreds of years. Below the altar, sunk into the stone floor, was a large iron plate.

As Laurana stared curiously at this plate, Theros came over to stand beside her.

"What do you suppose this is?" she wondered. "A well?"

"Let's see," grunted the smith. Bending over, he lifted the ring on top of the plate in his huge, silver hand and pulled. At first nothing happened. Theros placed both hands on the ring and heaved with all his strength. The iron plate gave a great groan and slid across the floor with a scraping, squeaking sound that set their teeth on edge.

"What have you done?" Silvara, who had been standing near the tomb regarding it sadly, whirled to face them.

Theros stood up in astonishment at the shrill sound of her voice. Laurana involuntarily backed away from the gaping hole in the floor. Both of them stared at Silvara.

"Do not go near that!" Silvara warned, her voice shaking. "Stand clear! It is dangerous!"

"How do you know?" Laurana said coolly, recovering herself. "No one's come here for hundreds of years. Or have they?"

"No!" Silvara said, biting her lip. "I—I know from the . . . legends of my people . . ."

Ignoring the girl, Laurana stepped to the edge of the hole and peered inside. It was dark. Even holding the torch Flint brought her from the wall, she could see nothing down there. A faint musty odor drifted from the hole, but that was all.

"I don't think it's a well," said Tas, crowding to see.

"Stay away from it! Please!" Silvara begged.

"She's right, little thief!" Theros grabbed Tas and pulled him away from the hole. "If you fell in there, you might tumble through to the other side of the world."

"Really?" asked Tasslehoff breathlessly. "Would I really fall through to the other side, Theros? I wonder what it would be like? Would there be people there? Like us?"

"Not like kenders hopefully!" Flint grumbled. "Or they'd all be dead of idiocy by now. Besides, everyone knows that the world rests on the Anvil of Reorx. Those falling to the other side are caught between his hammer blows and the world still being forged. People on the other side indeed!" He snorted as he watched Theros unsuccessfully try to

replace the plate. Tasslehoff was still staring at it curiously. Finally Theros was forced to give up, but he glared at the kender until Tas heaved a sigh and wandered away to the stone bier to stare with longing eyes at the shield and sword.

Flint tugged Laurana's sleeve.

"What is it?" she asked absently, her thoughts elsewhere.

"I know stonework," the dwarf said softly, "and there's something strange about all this." He paused, glancing to see if Laurana might laugh. But she was paying serious attention to him. "The tomb and the statues built outside are the work of men. It is old. . . ."

"Old enough to be Huma's tomb?" Laurana interrupted.

"Every bit of it." The dwarf nodded emphatically. "But yon great beast outside"—he gestured in the direction of the huge stone dragon—"was never built by the hands of man or elf or dwarf."†

The Silver Dragon monument was constructed in ancient times as an honored burial ground for Huma, a knight of Solamnia and source in legend of the dragonlance. In this era, the monument was designed by Jeff Grubb. —TRH

Laurana blinked, uncomprehending.

"And it is older still," the dwarf said, his voice growing husky. "So old it makes this"—he waved his hand at the tomb—"modern."

Laurana began to understand. Flint, seeing her eyes widen, nodded slowly and solemnly.

"No hand of any being that walks upon Krynn with two legs carved the side out of that cliff," he said.

"It must have been a creature with awesome strength," Laurana murmured. "A huge creature—"

"With wings—"

"With wings," Laurana murmured.

Suddenly she stopped talking, her blood chilled in fear as she heard words being chanted, words she recognized as the strange, spidery language of magic.

"No!" Turning, she lifted her hand instinctively to ward off the spell, knowing as she did so that it was futile.

Silvara stood beside the altar, crumbling rose petals in her hand, chanting softly.

Laurana fought the enchanted drowsiness that crept over her. She fell to her knees, cursing herself for a fool, clinging to the stone bench for support. But it did no good. Lifting her sleep-glazed eyes, she saw Theros topple over and Gilthanas slump to the ground. Beside her, the dwarf was snoring even before his head hit the bench.

Laurana heard a clattering sound, the sound of a shield crashing to the floor, then the air was filled with the fragrance of roses.

The Stone Dragon represents an important milestone in the development of DRAGONLANCE, *though not one that most fans know. Since the game modules and the novels were written concurrently, Tracy and Margaret would often be writing to catch up and fit with already created game material and background, and had to tap dance mightily to make what works in terms of a game adventure be exciting in terms of a novel.*

At the Stone Dragon, Margaret and Tracy caught up. I was the designer of module DL7, Dragons of Light, *and that was the point where Margaret and Tracy's writing for the novels caught up with game material. Before that, the novels had to take into account material that was already "in the pipeline." After the Stone Dragon, the games followed and designers had to double-check against the book material.—Jeff Grubb*

9

The kender's startling discovery.

Tasslehoff heard Silvara chanting. Recognizing the words of a magic spell, he reacted instinctively, grabbed hold of the shield that lay on the bier, and pulled. The heavy shield fell on top of him, striking the floor with a ringing clang, flattening the kender. The shield covered Tas completely.†

The Sleep spell is somewhat directional in nature. Tas may have pulled the shield over himself for protection, but it would not have stopped the effects of the spell had Silvara wished it.—TRH

He lay still beneath it until he heard Silvara finish her chant. Even then, he waited a few moments to see if he was going to turn into a frog or go up in flames or something interesting like that. He didn't—rather to his disappointment. He couldn't even hear Silvara. Finally, growing bored lying in the darkness on the cold stone floor, Tas crept out from beneath the heavy shield with the silence of a falling feather.†

Astute readers will see in this a foreshadowing of the arrival of that master of Featherfall—Fizban! —MW

All his friends were asleep! So that was the spell she cast. But where was Silvara? Gone somewhere to get a horrible monster to come back and devour them?

Cautiously, Tas raised his head and peered over the bier. To his astonishment, he saw Silvara crouched on the floor, near the tomb entrance. As Tas watched, she rocked back and forth, making small, moaning sounds.

"How can I go through with it?" Tas heard her say to herself. "I've brought them here. Isn't that enough? No!" She shook her head in misery. "No, I've sent the orb away. They don't know how to use it. I must break the oath. It is as you said, sister—the choice is mine. But it is hard! I love him—"

Sobbing, muttering to herself like one possessed, Silvara buried her face in her knees. The tender-hearted kender had never seen such sorrow, and he longed to go comfort her. Then he realized what she was talking about didn't sound good. "Choice is a hard one, break the oath . . ."

No, Tas thought, I better find a way out of here before she realizes her spell didn't work on me.

But Silvara blocked the entrance to the tomb. He might try to sneak past her. . . . Tas shook his head. Too risky.

The hole! He brightened. He'd wanted to examine it more carefully anyway. He just hoped the lid was still off.

The kender tiptoed around the bier until he came to the altar. There was the hole, still gaping open. Theros lay beside it, sound asleep, his head pillowed upon his silver arm. Glancing back at Silvara, Tas sneaked silently to the edge.

It would certainly be a better place to hide than where he was now.† There were no stairs, but he could see handholds on the wall. A deft kender—such as himself—should have no trouble at all climbing down. Perhaps it led outside. Suddenly Tas heard a noise behind him. Silvara sighing and stirring. . . .

Any excuse to do something he wanted to do anyway will serve.

Without another thought, Tas lowered himself silently into the hole and began his descent. The walls were slick with moisture and moss, the handholds were spaced far apart. Built for humans, he thought irritably. No one ever considered little people!

He was so preoccupied that he didn't notice the gems until he was practically on top of them.

"Reorx's beard!" he swore. (He was fond of this oath, having borrowed it from Flint.) Six beautiful jewels—each as big around as his hand—were spaced in a horizontal ring around the walls of the shaft. They were covered with moss, but Tas could tell at a glance how valuable they were.

"Now why would anyone put such wonderful jewels down here?" he asked aloud. "I'll bet it was some thief. If I can pry them loose, I'll return them to their rightful owner." His hand closed over a jewel.

A tremendous blast of wind filled the shaft, pulling the kender off the wall as easily as a winter gale rips a leaf off a tree. Falling, Tas looked back up, watching the light at the top of the shaft grow smaller and smaller. He wondered briefly just how big the Hammer of Reorx was, and then he stopped falling.

For a moment, the wind tumbled him end over end. Then it switched directions, blowing him sideways. I'm not going to the other side of the world after all, he thought sadly. Sighing, he sailed along through another tunnel. Then he suddenly felt himself start to rise! A great wind was wafting him up the shaft! It was an unusual sensation, quite exhilarating. Instinctively, he spread his arms to see if he could touch the sides of whatever it was he was in. As he spread his arms, he noticed that he rose faster, borne gently upward on swift currents of air.†

Tas is, of course, in a rather complex system of air shafts designed specifically to transport things and, occasionally, people to the various levels of the vast monument. This system was also designed, I believe, by our DRAGONLANCE engineer Jeff Grubb.—TRH

Perhaps I'm dead, Tas thought. I'm dead and now I'm lighter than air. How can I tell? Putting his arms down, he felt frantically for his pouches. He wasn't certain; the kender had very vague ideas as to the afterlife—but he had a feeling they wouldn't let him take his things with him. No, everything was there. Tas breathed a sigh of relief that turned into a gulp when he discovered himself slowing down and even starting to fall!

What? he thought wildly, then realized he had pulled both his arms in close to his body. Hurriedly he thrust his arms out again and, sure enough, he began to rise. Convinced that he wasn't dead, he gave himself up to enjoying the flight.

Fluttering his hands, the kender rolled over on his back in midair, and stared up to see where he was going.

Ah, there was a light far above him, growing brighter and brighter. Now he could see that he was in a shaft, but it was much longer than the shaft he had tumbled down.

"Wait until Flint hears about this!" he said wistfully. Then he caught a glimpse of six jewels, like the ones he'd seen in the other shaft. The rushing wind began to lessen.

Just as he decided that he could really enjoy taking up flying as a way of life, Tas reached the top of the shaft. The air currents held him even with the stone floor of a torch-lit chamber. Tas waited a moment to see if he might start flying again, and he even flapped his arms a bit to help, but nothing happened. Apparently his flight had ended.

I might as well explore while I'm up here, the kender thought with a sigh. Jumping out of the air currents, he landed lightly on the stone floor, then began to look around.

Several torches flared on the walls, illuminating the chamber with a bright white radiance. This room was certainly much larger than the tomb! He was standing at the bottom of a great curving staircase. The huge flagstones of each step—as well as all the other stones in the room—were pure white, much different from the black stone of the tomb. The staircase curved to the right, leading up to what appeared to be another level of the chamber. Above him, he could see a railing overlooking the stairs, apparently there was some sort of balcony up there. Nearly breaking his neck trying to see, Tas thought he could make out swirls and splotches of bright colors shining in the torchlight from the opposite wall.

Who lit the torches, he wondered? What is this place? Part of Huma's tomb? Or did I fly up into the Dragon Mountain? Who lives here? Those torches didn't light themselves!

At that thought—just to be safe—Tas reached into his tunic and drew out his little knife. Holding it in his hand, he climbed the grand stairs and came out onto the balcony. It was a huge chamber, but he could see little of it in the flickering torch-

light. Gigantic pillars supported the massive ceiling overhead. Another great staircase rose from this balcony level to yet another floor. Tas turned around, leaning against the railing to look at the walls behind him.

"Reorx's beard!" he said softly. "Look at *that!*"

That was a painting. A mural, to be more precise. It began opposite where Tas was standing, at the head of the stairs, and extended on around the balcony in foot after foot of shimmering color. The kender was not much interested in artwork, but he couldn't recall ever seeing anything quite so beautiful. Or had he? Somehow, it seemed familiar. Yes, the more he looked at it, the more he thought he'd seen it before.

Tas studied the painting, trying to remember. On the wall directly across from him was pictured a horrible scene of dragons of every color and description descending upon the land. Towns blazed in flames—like Tarsis—buildings crumbled, people were fleeing. It was a terrible sight, and the kender hurried past it.

He continued walking along the balcony, his eyes on the painting. He had just reached the central portion of the mural when he gasped.

"The Dragon Mountain! That's it—there, on the wall!" he whispered to himself and was startled to hear his whisper come echoing back to him. Glancing around hastily, he crept closer to the other edge of the balcony. Leaning over the rail, he stared closely at the painting. It indeed showed the Dragon Mountain, where he was now. Only this showed a view of the mountain as if some giant sword had chopped it completely in half vertically!

"How wonderful!" The map-loving kender sighed. "Of course," he said. "It *is* a map! And that's where I am! I've gone up into the mountain." He looked around the room in sudden realization. "I'm in the throat of the dragon. That's why this room is such a funny shape." He turned back to the map. "There's the painting on the wall and there's the balcony I'm standing on. And the pillars . . ." He turned completely around. "Yes, there's the grand staircase." He turned back. "It leads up into the head! And there's how I came up. Some sort of wind chamber. But who built this . . . and why?"

Tasslehoff continued on around the balcony, hoping to find a clue in the painting. On the right-hand side of the gallery, another battle was portrayed. But this one didn't fill him with horror. There were red dragons, and black, and blue, and white—breathing fire and ice—but fighting them were other dragons, dragons of silver and of gold. . . .

"I remember!" shouted Tasslehoff.

The kender begin jumping up and down, yelling like a wild thing. "I remember! I remember! It was in Pax Tharkas. Fizban showed me. There are *good* dragons in the world. They'll help us fight the evil ones! We just have to find them. And there are the dragonlances!"

"Confound it!" snarled a voice below the kender. "Can't a person get some sleep? What is all this racket? You're making noise enough to wake the dead!"

Tasslehoff whirled around in alarm, his knife in his hand. He could have sworn he was alone up here. But no. Rising up off a stone bench that stood in a shadowy area out of the torchlight was a dark, robed figure. It shook itself, stretched, then got up and began to climb the stairs, moving swiftly toward the kender. Tas could not have gotten away, even if he had wanted to, and the kender found himself intensely curious about who was up here. He opened his mouth to ask this strange creature what it was and why it had chosen the throat of a Dragon Mountain to nap in, when the figure emerged into the light. It was an old man. It was—

Tasslehoff's knife clattered to the floor. The kender sagged back against the railing. For the first, last, and only time in his life, Tasslehoff Burrfoot was struck speechless.

"F-F-F . . ." Nothing came out of his throat, only a croak.

"Well, what is it? Speak up!" snapped the old man, looming over him. "You were making enough noise a minute ago. What's the matter? Something go down the wrong way?"

"F-F-F . . ." stuttered Tas weakly.

"Ah, poor boy. Afflicted, eh? Speech impediment. Sad, sad. Here—"The old man fumbled in his robes, opening numerous pouches while Tasslehoff stood trembling before him.

"There," the figure said. Drawing forth a coin, he put it in the kender's numb palm and closed his small, lifeless fingers over it. "Now, run along. Find a cleric . . ."

"Fizban!"† Tasslehoff was finally able to gasp.

"Where?" The old man whirled around. Raising his staff, he peered fearfully into the darkness. Then something seemed to occur to him.Turning back around, he asked Tas in a loud whisper, "I say, are you sure you saw this Fizban? Isn't he dead?"

"I know *I* thought so . . . " Tas said miserably.

"Then he shouldn't be wandering around, scaring people!" the old man declared angrily. "I'll have a talk with him. Hey, you!" he began to shout.

Tas reached out a trembling hand and tugged at the old man's robe."I—I'm not sure, b-but I think *you're* Fizban."

"No, really?" the old man said, taken aback. "I was feeling a bit under the weather this morning, but I had no idea it was as bad as all that." His shoulders sagged. "So I'm dead. Done for. Bought the farm. Kicked the bucket." He staggered to a bench and plopped down. "Was it a nice funeral?" he asked. "Did lots of people come? Was there a twenty-one gun salute? I always wanted a twenty-one gun salute."†

"I—uh," Tas stammered, wondering what a gun was. "Well, it was . . . more of a . . . memorial service you might say. You see, we—uh—couldn't find your—how shall I put this?"

"Remains?" the old man said helpfully.

"Uh . . . remains." Tas flushed. "We looked, but there were all these chicken feathers . . . and a dark elf . . . and Tanis said we were lucky to have escaped alive. . . ."

"Chicken feathers!" said the old man indignantly. "What have chicken feathers got to do with my funeral?"

"We—uh—you and me and Sestun. Do you remember Sestun, the gully dwarf? Well, there was that great, huge chain in Pax Tharkas. And that big red dragon. We were hanging onto the chain and the dragon breathed fire on it and the chain broke and we were falling"—Tas was warming up to his story; it had become one of his favorites—"and I knew it was all over. We were going to die. There must have

At last, our wise wizard has returned! As the guardian character in our drama, Fizban is an important element in the story. There is considerable precedent in literature, of course. Gandalf, too, came back to keep troubling Frodo's life. It's hard to keep a good wizard down—especially when he provides such a crucial element to the story.—TRH

Fizban, being in reality a god, can look forward to the future wherein gnomes will invent gunpowder. By accident. They were working on incense. —MW

been a seventy-foot drop" (this increased every time Tas told the tale) "and you were beneath me and I heard you chanting a spell—"

"Yes, I'm quite a good magician, you know."

"Uh, right," Tas stammered, then continued hurriedly. "You chanted this spell, Featherfall or something like that. Anyway, you only said the first word, 'feather' and suddenly"—the kender spread his hands, a look of awe on his face as he remembered what happened then—"there were millions and millions and millions of chicken feathers. . . ."

"So what happened next?" the old man demanded, poking Tas.

"Oh, uh, that's where it gets a bit—uh—muddled," Tas said. "I heard a scream and a thump. Well, it was more like a splatter actually, and I f-f-figured the splatter was you."

"Me?" the old man shouted. "Splatter!" He glared at the kender furiously. "I never in my life *splattered!*"

"Then Sestun and I tumbled down into the chicken feathers, along with the chain. I looked—I really did." Tas's eyes filled with tears as he remembered his heartbroken search for the old man's body. "But there were too many feathers . . . and there was this terrible commotion outside where the dragons were fighting. Sestun and I made it to the door, and then we found Tanis, and I wanted to go back to look for you some more, but Tanis said no . . ."

"So you left me buried under a mound of chicken feathers?"

"It was an *awfully* nice memorial service," Tas faltered. "Goldmoon spoke, and Elistan. You didn't meet Elistan, but you remember Goldmoon, don't you? And Tanis?"

"Goldmoon . . ." the old man murmured. "Ah, yes. Pretty girl. Big, stern-looking chap in love with her."

"Riverwind!" said Tas in excitement. "And Raistlin?"

"Skinny fellow. Damn good magician," the old man said solemnly, "but he'll never amount to anything if he doesn't do something about that cough."

"You *are* Fizban!" Tas said. Jumping up gleefully, he threw his arms around the old man and hugged him tight.

"There, there," Fizban said, embarrassed, patting Tas on the back."That's quite enough. You'll crumple my robes. Don't sniffle. Can't abide it. Need a hankie?"

"No, I've got one—"

"Now, that's better. Oh, I say, I believe that handkerchief's mine. Those are my initials, "

"Is it? You must have dropped it."

"I remember you now!" the old man said loudly. "You're Tassle—Tassle-something-or-other."

"Tasslehoff. Tasslehoff Burrfoot," the kender replied.

"And I'm—" The old man stopped. "What did you say the name was?"

"Fizban."

"Fizban. Yes . . ." The old man pondered a moment, then he shook his head. "I sure thought he was dead. . . ."

10

Silvara's secret.

How *did* you survive?" Tas asked, pulling some dried fruit from a pouch to share with Fizban.

The old man appeared wistful. "I really didn't think I did," he said apologetically. "I'm afraid I haven't the vaguest notion. But, come to think of it, I haven't been able to eat a chicken since. Now"—he stared at the kender shrewdly—"what are you doing here?"

"I came with some of my friends. The rest are wandering around somewhere, if they're still alive." He sniffed again.

"They are. Don't worry." Fizban patted him on the back.

"Do you think so?" Tas brightened. "Well, anyway, we're here with Silvara—"

"Silvara!" The old man leaped to his feet, his white hair flying out wildly. The vague look faded from his face.

"Where is she?" the old man demanded sternly. "And your friends, where are they?"

"D-downstairs," stammered Tas, startled at the old man's transformation. "Silvara cast a spell on them!"

"Ah, she did, did she?" the old man muttered. "We'll see about that. Come on." He started off along the balcony, walking so rapidly, Tas had to run to keep up.

"Where'd you say they were?" the old man asked, stopping near the stairs. "Be specific," he snapped.

"Uh—the tomb! Huma's tomb! I think it's Huma's tomb. That's what Silvara said."

"Humpf. Well, at least we don't have to walk."

Descending the stairs to the hole in the floor Tas had come up through, the old man stepped out into its center. Tas, gulping a little, joined him, clutching at the old man's robes.† They hung suspended over nothing but darkness, feeling cool air waft up around them.

How many people could accompany the old wizard on his spell? The answer, of course, is—as many as believably necessary to in order to move the plot forward. This same answer, of course, applies equally to time-machine capabilities and spaceship transporters. In this case, of course, it's only one small kender.—TRH

"Down," the old man stated.

They began to rise, drifting toward the ceiling of the upper gallery. Tas felt the hair stand up on his head.

"I said *down!*" the old man shouted furiously, waving his staff menacingly at the hole below him.

There was a slurping sound and both of them were sucked into the hole so rapidly that Fizban's hat flew off. It's just like the hat he lost in the red dragon's lair, Tas thought. It was bent and shapeless, and apparently possessed of a mind of its own. Fizban made a wild grab for it, but missed. The hat, however, floated down after them, about fifty feet above.

Tasslehoff peered down, fascinated, and started to ask a question, but Fizban shushed him. Gripping his staff, the old mage began whispering to himself, making an odd sign in the air.

Laurana opened her eyes. She was lying on a cold stone bench, staring at a black, glistening ceiling.

She had no idea where she was. Then memory returned. Silvara!

Sitting up swiftly, she flashed a glance around the room. Flint was groaning and rubbing his neck. Theros blinked and looked around, puzzled. Gilthanas, already on his feet, stood at the end of Huma's tomb, gazing down at something by the door. As Laurana walked over to him, he turned around. Putting his finger to his lips, he nodded in the direction of the doorway.

Silvara sat there, her head in her arms, sobbing bitterly.

Laurana hesitated, the angry words on her lips dying. This certainly wasn't what she had expected. What had she expected? she asked herself. Never to wake again, most likely. There had to be an explanation. She started forward.

"Silvara—" she began.

The girl leaped up, her tear-stained face white with fear.

"What are you doing awake? How did you free yourself from my spell?" she gasped, falling back against the wall.

"Never mind that!" Laurana answered, though she hadn't any idea how she had wakened. "Tell us—"

"It was *my* doing!" announced a deep voice. Laurana and the rest turned around to see a white-bearded old man in mouse-colored robes rise up solemnly out of the hole in the floor.

"Fizban!" whispered Laurana in disbelief.

There was a clunk and a thud. Flint toppled over in a dead faint. No one even looked at him. They simply stared at the old mage in awe. Then, with a shrill shriek, Silvara flung herself flat on the cold stone floor, shivering and whimpering softly.

Ignoring the stares of the others, Fizban walked across the floor of the tomb, past the bier, past the comatose dwarf, to come to Silvara. Behind him, Tasslehoff scrambled up out of the hole.

"Look who *I* found," the kender said proudly. "Fizban! And I flew, Laurana. I jumped into the hole and just flew straight up into the air. And there's a painting up there with gold dragons, and then Fizban sat up and yelled at me and—I must admit I felt really queer there for a while. My voice was gone and . . . what happened to Flint?"

"Hush, Tas," Laurana said weakly, her eyes on Fizban. Kneeling down, he shook the Wilder elfmaid.

"Silvara, what have you done?" Fizban asked sternly. Laurana thought then that perhaps she had made a mistake—this must be some other old man dressed in the old magician's clothes. This stern-faced, powerful man was certainly not the befuddled old mage she remembered. But no, she'd recognize that face anywhere, to say nothing of the hat!

Watching the two of them—Silvara and Fizban—before her, Laurana felt great and awesome power like silent thunder surging between the two. She had a terrible longing to run out of this place and keep running until she dropped with exhaustion. But she couldn't move. She could only stare.

"What have you done, Silvara?" Fizban demanded. "You have broken your oath!"

"No!" The girl moaned, writhing on the ground at the old mage's feet. "No, I haven't. Not yet—"

"You have walked the world in another body, meddling in the affairs of men. That alone would be sufficient. But you brought them here!"

Silvara's tear-stained face was twisted in anguish. Laurana felt her own tears sliding unchecked down her cheeks.

"All right then!" Silvara cried defiantly. "I broke my oath, or at least I intended to. I brought them here. I had to! I've seen the misery and the suffering. Besides"—her voice fell, her eyes stared far away—"they had an orb . . ."

"Yes," said Fizban softly. "A dragon orb. Taken from Ice Wall Castle. It fell into your possession. What have you done with it, Silvara? Where is it now?"

"I sent it away . . ." Silvara said almost inaudibly.

Fizban seemed to age. His face grew weary. Sighing deeply, he leaned heavily upon his staff. "Where did you send it, Silvara? Where is the dragon orb now?"

"St-Sturm has it," Laurana interrupted fearfully. "He took it to Sancrist. What does this mean? Is Sturm in danger?"

"Who?" Fizban peered around over his shoulder. "Oh, hullo there, my dear." He beamed at her. "So nice to see you again. How's your father?"

"My father—" Laurana shook her head, confused. "Look, old man, never mind my father! Who—"

"And your brother." Fizban extended a hand to Gilthanas. "Good to see you, son. And you, sir." He bowed to an astonished Theros. "Silver arm? My, my"—he stole a look back at Silvara—"what a coincidence. Theros Ironfeld, isn't it? Heard a lot about you. And my name is . . ." The old magician paused, his brow furrowed.

"My name is . . ."

"Fizban," supplied Tasslehoff helpfully.

"Fizban." The old man nodded, smiling.

Laurana thought she saw the old magician cast a warning glance at Silvara. The girl lowered her head as if to acknowledge some silent, secret signal passed between them.

But before Laurana could sort out her whirling thoughts, Fizban turned back to her again. "And now, Laurana, you wonder who Silvara is? It is up to Silvara to tell you. For I must leave you now. I have a long journey ahead of me."

"Must I tell them?" Silvara asked softly. She was still on her knees and, as she spoke, her eyes went to Gilthanas. Fizban followed her gaze. Seeing the elflord's stricken face, his own face softened. Then he shook his head sadly.

Silvara raised her hands to him in a pleading gesture. Fizban walked over to her. Taking her hands, he raised her to her feet. She threw her arms around him, and he held her close.

"No, Silvara," he said, his voice kind and gentle, "you do not have to tell them. The choice is yours that was your sister's. You can make them forget they were ever here."

Suddenly the only color left in Silvara's face was the deep blue of her eyes. "But, that will mean—"

"Yes, Silvara," he said. "It is up to you." He kissed the girl on the forehead. "Farewell, Silvara."

Turning, he looked back at the rest. "Good-bye, good-bye. Nice seeing you again. I'm a bit miffed about the chicken feathers, but—no hard feelings." He waited impatiently a minute, glaring at Tasslehoff. "Are you coming? I haven't got all night!"

"Coming? With you?" Tas cried, dropping Flint's head back onto the stone floor with a thunk. The kender stood up. "Of course, let me get my pack . . ." Then he stopped, glancing down at the unconscious dwarf. "Flint—"

"He'll be fine," Fizban promised. "You won't be parted from your friends long. We'll see them"—he frowned, muttering to himself—"seven days, add three, carry the one, what's seven times four? Oh well, around Famine Time.† That's when they'll hold the Council meeting. Now, come along. I've got work to do. Your friends are in good hands. Silvara will take care of them, won't you, my dear?" He turned to the Wilder elf.

Famine Time commemorates the terrible period after the Cataclysm when so many people died of starvation, but only the goblins actually give a month—January—the name "Famine."

"I will tell them," she promised sadly, eyes on Gilthanas.

The elflord was staring at her and at Fizban, his face pale, fear spreading through his soul.

Silvara sighed. "You are right. I broke the oath long ago. I must finish what I set out to do."

"As you think best." Fizban laid his hand upon Silvara's head, stroking her silver hair. Then he turned away.

"Will I be punished?" she asked, just as the old man stepped into the shadows.

Fizban stopped. Shaking his head, he looked back over his shoulder "Some would say you are being punished right now, Silvara," he said softly. "But what you do, you do out of love. As the choice was up to you, so is your punishment."

The old man stepped into the darkness. Tasslehoff ran after him, his pouches bouncing behind him. "Good-bye, Laurana! Good-bye, Theros! Take care of Flint!" In the silence that followed, Laurana could hear the old man's voice.

"What was that name again? Fizbut, Furball—"

"Fizban!" said Tas shrilly.

"Fizban . . . Fizban . . ." muttered the old man.†

Tasslehoff's adventure with Fizban is recounted in the short story "The Story that Tasslehoff Promised He Would Never, Ever, Ever Tell" by Margaret Weis and Tracy Hickman in The War of the Lance.

All eyes turned to Silvara.

She was calm now, at peace with herself. Although her face was filled with sorrow, it was not the tormented, bitter sorrow they had seen earlier. This was the sorrow of loss, the quiet, accepting sorrow of one who has nothing to regret. Silvara walked toward Gilthanas. She took hold of his

hands and looked up into his face with so much love that Gilthanas felt blessed, even as he knew she was going to tell him good-bye.

"I am losing you, Silvara," he murmured in broken tones. "I see it in your eyes. But I don't know why! You love me—"

"I love you, elflord," Silvara said softly. "I loved you when I saw you lying injured upon the sand. When you looked up and smiled at me, I knew that the fate which had befallen my sister was to be mine, too." She sighed. "But it is a risk we take when we choose this form. For though we bring our strength into it, the form inflicts its weaknesses upon us. Or is it a weakness? To love . . ."

"Silvara, I don't understand!" Gilthanas cried.

"You will," she promised, her voice soft. Her head bowed.

Gilthanas took her in his arms, holding her. She buried her face in his chest. He kissed her beautiful silver hair, then clasped her with a sob.

Laurana turned away. This grief seemed too sacred for her eyes to intrude upon. Swallowing her own tears, she looked around and then remembered the dwarf. She took some water from his waterskin and sprinkled it on Flint's face.

His eyes fluttered, then opened. The dwarf stared up at Laurana for a moment and reached out a trembling hand.

"Fizban!" the dwarf whispered hoarsely.

"I know," Laurana said, wondering how the dwarf would take the news about Tas's leaving.

"Fizban's *dead!*" Flint gasped. "Tas said so! In a pile of chicken feathers!" The dwarf struggled to sit up. "Where is that rattle-brained kender?"

"He's gone, Flint," Laurana said. "He went with Fizban."

"Gone?" The dwarf looked around blankly. "You let him go? With that old man?"

"I'm afraid so—"

"You let him go with a dead old man?"

"I really didn't have much choice." Laurana smiled. "It was his decision. He'll be fine—"

"Where'd they go?" Flint stood and shouldered his pack.

"You can't go after them," Laurana said. "Please, Flint." She put her arm around the dwarf's

shoulders. "I need you. You're Tanis's oldest friend, my advisor—"

"But he's gone without me," Flint said plaintively. "How could he leave? I didn't see him go."

"You fainted—"

"I did no such thing!" the dwarf roared.

"You—you were out cold," Laurana stammered.

"I never faint!" stated the dwarf indignantly. "It must have been a recurrence of that deadly disease I caught on board that boat—" Flint dropped his pack and slumped down beside it. "Idiot kender. Running off with a dead old man."

Theros came over to Laurana, drawing her to one side. "Who was that old man?" he asked curiously.

"It's a long story." Laurana sighed. "And I'm not certain I could answer that question anyway."

"He seems familiar." Theros frowned and shook his head. "But I can't remember where I've seen him before, though he puts me in mind of Solace and the Inn of the Last Home. And he knew me . . ."The blacksmith stared at his silver hand. "I felt a shock go through me when he looked at me, like lightning striking a tree." The big blacksmith shivered, then he glanced over at Silvara and Gilthanas. "And what of this?"

"I think we're finally about to find out," Laurana said.

"You were right," Theros said. "You didn't trust her—"

"But not for the right reasons," Laurana admitted guiltily.

With a small sigh, Silvara pushed herself away from Gilthanas's embrace. The elflord let her go reluctantly.

"Gilthanas," she said, drawing a shuddering breath, "take a torch off the wall and hold it up before me."

Gilthanas hesitated. Then, almost angrily, he followed her directions.

"Hold the torch there . . ." she instructed, guiding his hand so that the light blazed right before her. "Now—look at my shadow on the wall behind me," she said in trembling tones.

The tomb was silent, only the sputtering of the flaming torch made any sound. Silvara's shadow sprang into life on the cold stone wall behind her.

Silvara's casting a dragon's shadow is one of those things that a shape-changing dragon can't do anything about.—TRH

The companions stared at it and—for an instant—none of them could say a word.

The shadow Silvara cast upon the wall was not the shadow of a young elfmaid.

It was the shadow of a dragon.†

"*You're* a dragon!" Laurana said in shocked disbelief. She laid her hand on her sword, but Theros stopped her.

"No!" he said suddenly. "I remember. That old man—" He looked at his arm. "Now I remember. He used to come into the Inn of the Last Home! He was dressed differently. He wasn't a mage, but it was him! I'll swear it! He told stories to the children. Stories about good dragons. Gold dragons and—"

"Silver dragons," Silvara said, looking at Theros. "I am a silver dragon. My sister was the Silver Dragon who loved Huma and fought the final great battle with him—"

"No!" Gilthanas flung the torch to the ground. It lay flickering for a moment at his feet, then he stamped on it angrily, putting out its light. Silvara, watching him with sad eyes, reached out her hand to comfort him.

Gilthanas shrank from her touch, staring at her in horror.

Silvara lowered her hand slowly. Sighing gently, she nodded. "I understand," she murmured. "I'm sorry."

Gilthanas began to shake, then doubled over in agony. Putting his strong arms around him, Theros led Gilthanas to a bench and covered him with his cloak.

"I'll be all right," Gilthanas mumbled. "Just leave me alone, let me think. This is madness! It's all a nightmare. A dragon!" He closed his eyes tightly as if he could blot out their sight forever. "A dragon . . ." he whispered brokenly. Theros patted him gently, then returned to the others.

In addition to silver and gold, the good (metallic) dragons include bronze, brass, and copper.

"Where are the rest of the good dragons?" Theros asked. "The old man said there were many. Silver dragons, gold dragons—"

"There are many† of us," Silvara answered reluctantly.

"Like the silver dragon we saw in Ice Wall!" Laurana said. "It was a good dragon. If there are many

of you, band together! Help us fight the evil dragons!"

"No!" Silvara cried fiercely. Her blue eyes flared, and Laurana fell back a pace before her anger.

"Why not?"

"I cannot tell you." Silvara's hands clenched nervously.

"It has something to do with that oath!" Laurana persisted. "Doesn't it? The oath you've broken. And the punishment you asked Fizban about—"

"I cannot tell you!" Silvara spoke in a low, passionate voice. "What I have done is bad enough. But I had to do something! I could no longer live in this world and see the suffering of innocent people! I thought perhaps I could help, so I took elven form, and I did what I could. I worked long, trying to get the elves to join together. I kept them from war, but matters were growing worse. Then you came, and I saw that we were in great peril, greater than any of us had ever imagined. For you brought with you—" Her voice faltered.

"The dragon orb!" Laurana said suddenly.

"Yes." Silvara's fists clenched in misery. "I knew then I had to make a decision. You had the orb, but you also had the lance. The lance and the orb coming to me! Both, together! It was a sign, I thought, but I didn't know what to do. I decided to bring the orb here and keep it safe forever. Then, as we traveled, I realized the knights would never allow it to remain here. There would be trouble. So, when I saw my chance, I sent it away." Her shoulders sagged. "That was apparently the wrong decision. But how was I to know?"

"Why?" Theros asked severely. "What does the orb do? Is it evil? Have you sent those knights to their doom?"

"Great evil," Silvara murmured. "Great good. Who can say? Even *I* do not understand the dragon orbs. They were forged long ago by the most powerful of magic-users."

"But the book Tas read said they could be used to control dragons!"Flint stated. "He read it with some kind of glasses. Glasses of true seeing, he called 'em. He said they don't lie—"

"No," said Silvara sadly. "That is true. It is too true, as I fear you friends may discover to their bitter regret."

That last battle was about a thousand years before the Cataclysm. Huma and his love, the silver dragon—known as Heart—succeeded in forcing Takhisis and her evil dragons to retire from Krynn. As a human, Heart was known as Gwyneth. See the story in The Legend of Huma *by Richard A. Knaak, the first* DRAGONLANCE *book that did not deal with the companions.*

The companions, fear closing around them, sat together in silence broken only by Gilthanas's choking sobs. The torches sent shadows dodging and dancing around the quiet tomb like undead spirits. Laurana remembered Huma and the Silver Dragon. She thought of that final, terrible battle—† the skies filled with dragons, the land erupting in flame and in blood.

"Why have you brought us here, then?" Laurana asked Silvara quietly. "Why not just let us all take the orb away?"

"Can I tell them? Do I have the strength?" Silvara whispered to an unseen spirit.

She sat quietly for a long time, her face expressionless, her hands twisting in her lap. Her eyes closed, her head bowed, her lips moved. She covered her face with her hands and sat quite still. Then, shuddering, she made her decision.

Rising to her feet, Silvara walked over to Laurana's pack. Kneeling down, she slowly and carefully unwrapped the broken shaft of wood that the companions had carried such a long and weary distance. Silvara stood, her face once more filled with peace. But now there was also pride and strength. For the first time, Laurana began to believe this girl was something as powerful and magnificent as a dragon. Walking proudly, her silver hair glistening in the torchlight, Silvara walked over to stand before Theros Ironfeld.

"To Theros of the Silver Arm," she said, "I give the power to forge the dragonlance."

BOOK 3

I

The Red Wizard and His Wonderful Illusions!

Shadows crept across the dusty tables of the Pig and Whistle tavern. The sea breeze off the Bay of Balifor made a shrill whistling sound as it blew through the ill-fitting front windows, that distinctive whistle giving the inn the last part of its name. Any guesses as to how the tavern got the first part ended on sight of the innkeeper. A jovial, kind-hearted man, William Sweetwater had been cursed at birth (so town legend went) when a wandering pig overturned the baby's cradle, so frightening young William that the mark of the pig was forever imprinted on his face.

This unfortunate resemblance had certainly not impaired William's temper, however. A sailor by trade until he had retired to fulfill a lifelong ambition of keeping an inn, there was not a more

respected or well-liked man in Port Balifor than William Sweetwater. No one laughed more heartily at pig jokes than did William. He could even grunt quite realistically and often did pig imitations for the amusement of his customers. (But no one ever—after the untimely death of Peg-Leg Al—called William by the name "Piggy.")

William rarely grunted for his customers these days. The atmosphere of the Pig and Whistle was dark and gloomy. The few old customers that came sat huddled together, talking in low voices. For Port Balifor was an occupied town—overrun by the armies of the highlords, whose ships had recently sailed into the Bay, disgorging troops of the hideous dragonmen.

The people of Port Balifor—mostly humans—felt extremely sorry for themselves. They had no knowledge of what was going on in the outside world, of course, or they would have counted their blessings. No dragons came to burn their town. The draconians generally left the citizens alone. The Dragon Highlords were not particularly interested in the eastern part of the Ansalon continent. The land was sparsely populated: a few poor, scattered communities of humans and Kendermore,† the homeland of the kenders. A flight of dragons could have leveled the countryside, but the Dragon Highlords were concentrating their strength in the north and the west. As long as the ports remained opened, the Highlords had no need to devastate the lands of Balifor and Goodlund.

This is a region on Northern Ergoth. Hylo is the capital. Apparently there's a good deal of traffic between Kenderhome and Kendermore, which is the capital of Goodlund, located on the Blood Sea east of Flotsam. Tas once spent considerable time in Kendermore and was forced by circumstances (a minor matter of a forgotten marriage oath) when the companions parted. (The marriage oath business is covered in Kendermore *by Mary Kirchoff.)*

Although not many old customers came to the Pig and Whistle, business had improved for William Sweetwater. The draconian and goblin troops of the Highlord were well paid, and their one weakness was strong drink. But William had not opened his tavern for money. He loved the companionship of old friends and new. He did *not* enjoy the companionship of the Highlord's troops. When they came in, his old customers left. Therefore, William promptly raised his prices for draconians to three times higher than in any other inn in town. He also watered the ale. Consequently, his bar was nearly deserted except for a few old friends. This arrangement suited William fine.

He was talking to a few of these friends—sailors mostly, with brown, weathered skin and no teeth—on the evening that the strangers entered his tavern. William glared at them suspiciously for a moment, as did his friends. But, seeing road-weary travelers and not the Highlord's soldiers, he greeted them cordially and showed them to a table in the corner.

The strangers ordered ale all around—except for a red-robed man who ordered nothing but hot water. Then, after a subdued discussion centering around a worn leather purse and the number of coins therein, they asked William to bring them bread and cheese.

"They're not from these parts," William said to his friends in a low voice as he drew the ale from a special keg he kept beneath the bar (not the keg for draconians). "And poor as a sailor after a week ashore, if I make my guess."

"Refugees," said his friend, eyeing them speculatively.

"Odd mixture, though," added the other sailor. "Yon red-bearded fellow's a half-elf, if ever I saw one. And the big one's got weapons enough to take on the Highlord's whole army."

"I'll wager he's stuck a few of them with that sword, too," William grunted. "They're on the run from something, I'll bet. Look at the way that bearded fellow keeps his eyes on the door. Well, we can't help them fight the Highlord, but I'll see they don't want for anything." He went to serve them.

"Put your money away," William said gruffly, plunking down not only bread and cheese but also a tray full of cold meats as well. He shoved the coins away. "You're in trouble of some kind, that's plain as this pig's snout upon my face."

One of the women smiled at him. She was the most beautiful woman William had ever seen. Her silver-gold hair gleamed from beneath a fur hood, her blue eyes were like the ocean on a calm day. When she smiled at him, William felt the warmth of fine brandy run through his body. But a stern-faced, dark-haired man next to her shoved the coins back to the innkeeper.

"We'll not accept charity," the tall, fur-cloaked man said.

"We won't?" asked the big man wistfully, staring at the smoked meat with longing eyes.

"Riverwind," the woman remonstrated, putting a gentle hand on his arm. The half-elf, too, seemed about to interpose when the red-robed man, who had ordered the hot water, reached out and picked up a coin from the table.

Balancing the coin on the back of his bony, metallic-colored hand, the man suddenly and effortlessly sent it dancing along his knuckles. William's eyes opened wide. His two friends at the bar came closer to see better. The coin flickered in and out of the red-robed man's fingers, spinning and jumping. It vanished high in the air, only to reappear above the mage's head in the form of six coins, spinning around his hood. With a gesture, he sent them to spin around William's head. The sailors watched in open-mouthed wonder.

"Take one for your trouble," said the mage in a whisper.

Hesitantly, William tried to grab the coins that whirled past his eyes, but his hand went right through them! Suddenly all six coins disappeared. One only remained now, resting in the palm of the red-robed mage.

"I give you this in payment," the mage said with a sly smile, "but be careful. It may burn a hole in your pocket."

William accepted the coin gingerly. Holding it between two fingers, he gazed at it suspiciously. Then the coin burst into flame! With a startled yelp, William dropped it to the floor, stomping on it with his foot. His two friends burst out laughing. Picking up the coin, William discovered it to be perfectly cold and undamaged.

"That's worth the meat!" the innkeeper said, grinning.

"And a night's lodgings," added his friend, the sailor, slapping down a handful of coins.

"I believe," said Raistlin softly, glancing around at the others, "that we have solved our problems."

Thus was born The Red Wizard and His Wonderful Illusions, a traveling road show that is still talked of today as far south as Port Balifor and as far north as the Ruins.†

When the Cataclysm decimated the land of Balifor, turning it into a desert waste, the kender left their homeland to barbaric desert nomads and migrated north. They founded a small forest city on the edge of a human ruin, now called simply "the Ruins" by the kender who explore it. Some kender believe the Ruins are the remains of one of the missing Towers of High Sorcery.

The very next night the red-robed mage began to perform his tricks to an admiring audience of William's friends. The word spread rapidly. After the mage had performed in the Pig and Whistle for about a week, Riverwind—at first opposed to the whole idea—was forced to admit that Raistlin's act seemed likely to solve not only their financial problems but other, more pressing problems as well.

The shortage of money was the most urgent. The companions might have been able to live off the land—even in the winter, both Riverwind and Tanis being skilled hunters. But they needed money to buy passage on a ship to take them to Sancrist. Once they had the money, they needed to be able to travel freely through enemy-occupied lands.

In his youth, Raistlin had often used his considerable talents at sleight of hand to earn bread for himself and his brother. Although this was frowned on by his master, who threatened to expel the young mage from his school, Raistlin had become quite successful. Now his growing powers in magic gave him a range not possible before. He literally kept his audiences spellbound with tricks and phantasms.

At Raistlin's command, white-winged ships sailed up and down the bar at the Pig and Whistle, birds flew out of soup tureens, while dragons peered through the windows, breathing fire upon the startled guests. In the grand finale, the mage—resplendent in red robes sewn by Tika—appeared to be totally consumed in raging flames, only to walk in through the front door moments later (to tumultuous applause) and calmly drink a glass of white wine to the health of the guests.

Within a week, the Pig and Whistle did more business than William had done in a year. Better still—as far as he was concerned—his friends were able to forget their troubles. Soon, however, unwanted guests began to arrive. At first, he had been angered by the appearance of draconians and goblins in the crowd, but Tanis placated him, and William grudgingly permitted them to watch.†

Now that draconians are around and the war has come home to roost, William Sweetwater sometimes has strange dreams; see "Dreams of Darkness, Dreams of Light" by Warren B. Smith in The Magic of Krynn.

Tanis was, in fact, pleased to see them. It worked out well from the half-elf's point of view and solved their second problem. If the Highlord's troops enjoyed the show and spread the word, the companions could travel the countryside unmolested.

It was their plan—after consulting with William—to make for Flotsam, a city north of Port Balifor, located on the Blood Sea of Istar. Here they hoped to find a ship. No one in Port Balifor would give them passage, William explained. All the local shipowners were in the employ of (or their vessels had been confiscated by) the Dragon Highlords. But Flotsam was a known haven for those more interested in money than politics.

The companions stayed at the Pig and Whistle for a month. William provided free room and board and even allowed them to keep all the money they made. Though Riverwind protested this generosity, William stated firmly that all he cared about was seeing his old customers come back.

During this time, Raistlin refined and enlarged his act which, at first consisted only of his illusions.† But the mage tired rapidly, so Tika offered to dance and give him time to rest between acts. Raistlin was dubious, but Tika sewed a costume for herself that was so alluring Caramon was—at first—totally opposed to the scheme. But Tika only laughed at him. Her dancing was a success and increased the money they collected dramatically. Raistlin added her immediately to the act.

I've always been impressed by illusions and stage magic. My eldest son, Curtis, is quite an accomplished magician and not long ago I—like Raistlin here—stood amazed at this ancient craft. I've been to many conventions in my time but none so amazing as the World Magic Seminar.—TRH

Finding the crowds enjoyed this diversion, the mage thought of others. Caramon—blushing furiously—was persuaded to perform feats of strength, the highlight coming when he lifted stout William over his head with one hand. Tanis amazed the crowd with his elven ability to "see" in the dark. But Raistlin was startled one day when Goldmoon came to him as he was counting the money from the previous night's performance.

"I would like to sing in the show tonight," she said.

Raistlin looked up at her incredulously. His eyes flicked to Riverwind. The tall Plainsman nodded reluctantly.

"You have a powerful voice," Raistlin said, sliding the money into a pouch and drawing the string tightly. "I remember quite well. The last song I heard you sing in the Inn of the Last Home touched off a riot that nearly got us killed."

Goldmoon flushed, remembering the fateful song that had introduced her to the group. Scowling, Riverwind laid his hand on her shoulder.

"Come away!" he said harshly, glaring at Raistlin. "I warned you—"

But Goldmoon shook her head stubbornly, lifting her chin in a familiar, imperious gesture. "I will sing," she said coolly, "and Riverwind will accompany me. I have written a song."

"Very well," the mage snapped, slipping the money pouch into his robes. "We will try it this evening."

The Pig and Whistle was crowded that night. It was a diverse audience—small children and their parents, sailors, draconians, goblins, and several kender, who caused everyone to keep an eye on his belongings. William and two helpers bustled about, serving drinks and food. Then the show began.

The crowd applauded Raistlin's spinning coins, laughed when an illusory pig danced upon the bar, and scrambled out of their chairs in terror when a giant troll thundered in through a window. Bowing, the mage left to rest. Tika came on.

The crowd, particularly the draconians, cheered Tika's dancing, banging their mugs on the table.

Then Goldmoon appeared before them, dressed in a gown of pale blue. Her silver-gold hair flowed over her shoulders like water shimmering in the moonlight. The crowd hushed instantly. Saying nothing, she sat down in a chair on the raised platform William had hastily constructed. So beautiful was she that not a murmur escaped the crowd. All waited expectantly.

Riverwind sat upon the floor at her feet. Putting a hand-carved flute to his lips, he began to play and, after a few moments, Goldmoon's voice blended with the flute. Her song was simple, the melody sweet and harmonious, yet haunting. But it was the words that caught Tanis's attention, causing him to exchange worried glances with Caramon. Raistlin, sitting next to him, grasped hold of Tanis's arm.

"I feared as much!" the mage hissed. "Another riot!"

"Perhaps not," Tanis said, watching. "Look at the audience."

Women leaned their heads onto their husband's shoulders, children were quiet and attentive. The draconians seemed spellbound, as a wild animal will sometimes be held by music. Only the goblins

shuffled their flapping feet, seemingly bored but so in awe of the draconians that they dared not protest.

Goldmoon's song was of the ancient gods.† She told how the gods had sent the Cataclysm to punish the Kingpriest of Istar and the people of Krynn for their pride. She sang of the terrors of that night and those that followed. She reminded them of how the people, believing themselves abandoned, had prayed to false gods. Then she gave them a message of hope: the gods had not abandoned them. The true gods were here, waiting only for someone to listen to them.

Although many songs of Krynn have come to us, this song of Goldmoon did not. Perhaps because one can hear it only with the heart.—MW

After her song ended, and the plaintive wailing of the flute died, most in the crowd shook their heads, seeming to wake from a pleasant dream. When asked what the song had been about, they couldn't say. The draconians shrugged and called for more ale. The goblins shouted for Tika to dance again. But, here and there, Tanis noticed a face still holding the wonder it had worn during the song. And he was not surprised to see a young, dark-skinned woman approach Goldmoon shyly.

"I ask your pardon for disturbing you, my lady," Tanis overheard the woman say, "but your song touched me deeply. I—I want to learn of the ancient gods, to learn their ways."

Goldmoon smiled. "Come to me tomorrow," she said, "and I shall teach you what I know."

And thus, slowly, word of the ancient gods began to spread. By the time they left Port Balifor, the dark-skinned woman, a soft-voiced young man, and several other people wore the blue medallion of Mishakal, Goddess of Healing. Secretly they went forth, bringing hope to the dark and troubled land.

By the end of the month, the companions were able to buy a wagon, horses to pull it, horses to ride, and supplies. What was left went toward purchase of ship's passage to Sancrist. They planned to add to their money by performing in the small farming communities between Port Balifor and Flotsam.

When the Red Wizard left Port Balifor shortly before the Yuletide season, his wagon was seen on its way by enthusiastic crowds. Packed with their costumes, supplies for two months, and a keg of ale (provided by William), the wagon was big enough

for Raistlin to sleep and travel inside. It also held the multi-colored, striped tents in which the others would live.

Tanis glanced around at the strange sight they made, shaking his head. It seemed that—in the midst of everything else that had happened to them—this was the most bizarre. He looked at Raistlin sitting beside his brother, who drove the wagon. The mage's red-sequined robes blazed like flame in the bright winter sunlight. Shoulders hunched against the wind, Raistlin stared straight ahead, wrapped in a show of mystery that delighted the crowd. Caramon, dressed in a bearskin suit (a present of William's), had pulled the head of the bear over his own, making it look as though a bear drove the wagon. The children cheered as he growled at them in mock ferocity.

They were nearly out of town when a draconian commander stopped them. Tanis, his heart caught in his throat, rode forward, his hand pressed against his sword. But the commander only wanted to make certain they passed through Bloodwatch where draconian troops were located. The draconian had mentioned the show to a friend. The troops were looking forward to seeing it. Tanis, inwardly vowing not to set foot near the place, promised faithfully that they would certainly appear.

Finally they reached the city gates. Climbing down from their mounts, they bid farewell to their friend. William gave them each a hug, starting with Tika and ending with Tika. He was going to hug Raistlin, but the mage's golden eyes widened so alarmingly when William approached that the innkeeper backed away precipitously.

The companions climbed back onto their horses. Raistlin and Caramon returned to the wagon. The crowd cheered and urged them to return for the spring Harrowing celebration†. The guards opened the gates, bidding them a safe journey, and the companions rode through. The gates shut behind them.

Harrowing celebrations vary depending on the part of Krynn you're in, though they always have to do with spring. Among the kender, it involves goatsucker birds and

The wind blew chill. Gray clouds above them began to spit snow fitfully. The road, which they were assured was well traveled, stretched before them, bleak and empty. Raistlin began to shiver and cough. After awhile, he said he would ride inside

the wagon. The rest pulled their hoods up over their heads and clutched their fur cloaks more closely about them.

Caramon, guiding the horses along the rutted, muddy road, appeared unusually thoughtful.

"You know, Tanis," he said solemnly above the jingling of the bells Tika had tied to the horses' manes, "I'm more thankful than I can tell that none of our friends saw this. Can you hear what Flint would say? That grumbling old dwarf would never let me live this down. And can you imagine Sturm!" The big man shook his head, the thought being beyond words.

Yes, Tanis sighed. I can imagine Sturm. Dear friend, I never realized how much I depended on you—your courage, your noble spirit. Are you alive, my friend? Did you reach Sancrist safely? Are you now the knight in body that you have always been in spirit? Will we meet again, or have we parted never to meet in this life—as Raistlin predicted?

The group rode on. The day grew darker, the storm wilder. Riverwind dropped back to ride beside Goldmoon. Tika tied her horse behind the wagon and crawled up to sit near Caramon. Inside the wagon, Raistlin slept.

Tanis rode alone, his head bowed, his thoughts far away.

young children with good aim at throwing eggs. Among the Plainspeople, it's a more solemn fertility celebration. Here in Port Balifor, it's a straightforward fun day to celebrate the end of winter.

2

The Knights Trials.

"And—finally," said Derek in a low and measured voice, "I accuse Sturm Brightblade of cowardice in the face of the enemy."

A low murmur ran through the assemblage of knights gathered in the castle of Lord Gunthar. Three knights, seated at the massive black oak table in front of the assembly, leaned their heads together to confer in low tones.

Long ago, the three seated at this Knights Trials—as prescribed by the Measure—would have been the Grand Master, the High Clerist, and the High Justice. But at this time there was no Grand Master.There had not been a High Clerist since the time of the Cataclysm. And while the High Justice—Lord Alfred MarKenin—was present, his hold on that position was tenuous at best.

Whoever became the new Grand Master had leave to replace him.

Despite these vacancies in the Head of the Order, the business of the Knights must continue. Though not strong enough to claim the coveted position of Grand Master, Lord Gunthar Uth Wistan was strong enough to act in that role. And so he sat here today, at the beginning of the Yuletide season, in judgment on this young squire, Sturm Brightblade. To his right sat Lord Alfred, to his left, young Lord Michael Jeoffrey, filling in as High Clerist.

Facing them, in the Great Hall of Castle Uth† Wistan, were twenty other Knights of Solamnia who had been hastily gathered from all parts of Sancrist to sit as witnesses to this Knights Trials—as prescribed by the Measure. These now muttered and shook their heads as their leaders conferred.

From a table directly in front of the three Knights Seated in Judgment, Lord Derek rose and bowed to Lord Gunthar. His testimony had reached its end. There remained now only the Knight's Answer and the Judgment itself. Derek returned to his place among the other knights, laughing and talking with them.

Only one person in the hall was silent. Sturm Brightblade sat unmoving throughout all of Lord Derek Crownguard's damning accusations. He had heard charges of insubordination, failure to obey orders, masquerading as a knight—and not a word or murmur had escaped him. His face was carefully expressionless, his hands were clasped on the top of the table.

Lord Gunthar's eyes were on Sturm now, as they had been throughout the Trials. He began to wonder if the man was even still alive, so fixed and white was his face, so rigid his posture. Gunthar had seen Sturm flinch only once. At the charge of cowardice, a shudder convulsed the man's body. The look on his face . . . well, Gunthar recalled seeing that same look once previously—on a man who had just been run through by a spear. But Sturm quickly regained his composure.

Gunthar was so interested in watching Brightblade that he nearly lost track of the conversation of the two knights next to him. He caught only the end of Lord Alfred's sentence.

The "Uth" in Solamnic names has caused some confusion over the years. Unlike the French "de," which primarily denotes place, it is a linking form taken from ancient Welsh forms of "Ap" (son of) and "Verch" (daughter of) that denote patronymics. This is best shown by example. Madoc ap Maredydd (Madoc son of Maredydd) was the son of Maredydd ap Bleddyn (father) and Hunydd verch Eunydd (mother). Maredydd ap Bleddyn was the son of Bleddyn ap Cynwyn and Haer verch Cynyllyn. While these names may not roll off the tongue, the important thing to remember here is that the son's last name is his father's first name. Therefore, Gunthar Uth Wistan would read "Gunthar, son of Wistan." If Gunthar had a son that was named traditionally, his name might be Semore Uth Gunthar although I would hope not. And Kitiara just uses her father's name—Uth Matar.—TRH

" . . . not allow Knight's Answer."

"Why not?" Lord Gunthar asked sharply, though keeping his voice low. "It is his right according to the Measure."

"We have never had a case like this," Lord Alfred, Knight of the Sword, stated flatly. "Always before, when a squire has been brought up before the Council of the Order to attain his knighthood, there have been witnesses, many witnesses. He is given an opportunity to explain his reasons for his actions. No one ever questions that he committed the acts. But Brightblade's only defense—"

"Is to tell us that Derek lies," finished Lord Michael Jeoffrey, Knight of the Crown. "And that is unthinkable. To take the word of a squire over a Knight of the Rose."

The Measure actually consists of thirty-seven 300-page volumes. These days, hardly anyone has read it or studied it in detail. The Measure is mostly known by tradition.

"Nonetheless, the young man will have his say," Lord Gunthar said, glancing sternly at each of the men. "That is the Law according to the Measure.† Do either of you question it?"

"No . . ."

"No, of course not. But—"

"Very well." Gunthar smoothed his moustaches and, leaning forward, tapped gently on the wooden table with the hilt of the sword—Sturm's sword—that lay upon it. The other two knights exchanged looks behind his back, one raising his eyebrows, the other shrugging slightly. Gunthar was aware of this, as he was aware of all the covert scheming and plotting now pervasive in the Knighthood. He chose to ignore it.

Not yet strong enough to claim the vacant position of Grand Master, but still the strongest and most powerful of the knights currently seated on the Council, Gunthar had been forced to ignore a great deal of what he would have—in another day and age—quashed without hesitation. He expected this disloyalty of Alfred MarKenin—the knight had long been in Derek's camp—but he was surprised at Michael, whom he had thought loyal to him. Apparently Derek had gotten to him, too.

Gunthar watched Derek Crownguard as the knights returned to their places. Derek was the only rival with the money and backing capable of claiming the rank of Grand Master. Hoping to earn additional votes, Derek had eagerly volunteered to

undertake the perilous quest in search of the legendary dragon orbs. Gunthar was given little choice but to agree. If he had refused, he would appear frightened of Derek's growing power. Derek was undeniably the most qualified—if one strictly followed the Measure. But Gunthar, who had known Derek a long time, would have prevented his going if he could have—not because he feared the knight but because he truly did not trust him. The man was vainglorious and power-hungry, and—when it came down to it—Derek's first loyalties lay to Derek.†

Derek Crownguard's story is told in "Glory Descending" by Chris Pierson in The Dragons at War.

And now it appeared that Derek's successful return with a dragon orb had won the day. It had brought many knights into his camp who had been heading that direction anyway and actually enticed away some in Gunthar's own faction. The only ones who opposed him still were the younger knights in the lowest order of the Knighthood—Knights of the Crown.

These young men had little use for the strict and rigid interpretation of the Measure that was life's blood to the older knights. They pushed for change—and had been severely chastened by Lord Derek Crownguard.† Some came close to losing their knighthood. These young knights were firmly behind Lord Gunthar. Unfortunately, they were few in number and, for the most part, had more loyalty than money. The young knights had, however, adopted Sturm's cause as their own.

Sturm himself has said, "The Measure and the Oath were never meant to be easy burdens to bear; by carrying their ponderous weight on his back, a knight becomes strong and upright."

But this was Derek Crownguard's master stroke, Gunthar thought bitterly. With one slice of his sword, Derek was going to get rid of a man he hated and his chief rival as well.

Lord Gunthar was a well-known friend of the Brightblade family, a friendship that traced back generations. It was Gunthar† who had advanced Sturm's claim when the young man appeared out of nowhere five years before to seek his father and his inheritance. Sturm had been able, with letters from his mother, to prove his right to the Brightblade name. A few insinuated this had been accomplished on the wrong side of the sheets, but Gunthar quickly squelched those rumors. The young man was obviously the son of his old friend—that much could be seen in Sturm's face. By backing Sturm, however, the lord was risking a great deal.

The castle where the Knights are meeting is Gunthar's ancient family home, where Sturm's father, Angriff Brightblade, often dined. After being sent into exile, Sturm first met Lord Gunthar when he, Sturm, was only seventeen. The tale is told in The Oath and Measure *by Michael Williams.*

Gunthar's gaze went to Derek, walking among the knights, smiling and shaking hands. Yes, this trial was making him—Lord Gunthar Uth Wistan—appear a fool.

Worse still, Gunthar thought sadly, his eyes returning to Sturm, it was probably going to destroy the career of what he believed to be a very fine man, a man worthy of walking his father's path.

"Sturm Brightblade," Lord Gunthar said when silence descended on the hall, "you have heard the accusations made against you?"

"I have, my lord," Sturm answered. His deep voice echoed eerily in the hall. Suddenly a log in the huge fireplace behind Gunthar split, sending a flare of heat and a shower of sparks up the chimney. Gunthar paused while the servants hustled in efficiently to add more wood. When the servants were gone, he continued the ritual questioning.

"Do you, Sturm Brightblade, understand the charges made against you, and do you further understand that these are grievous charges and could cause this Council to find you unfit for the knighthood?"

"I do," Sturm started to reply. His voice broke. Coughing, he repeated more firmly, "I do, my lord."

Gunthar smoothed his moustaches, trying to think how to lead into this, knowing that anything the young man said against Derek was going to reflect badly upon Sturm himself.

"How old are you, Brightblade?" Gunthar asked.

Sturm blinked at this unexpected question.

"Over thirty, I believe?" Gunthar continued, musing.

"Yes, my lord," Sturm answered.

"And, from what Derek tells us about your exploits in Ice Wall Castle, a skilled warrior—"

"I never denied that, my lord," Derek said, rising to his feet once again. His voice was tinged with impatience.

"Yet you accuse him of cowardice," Gunthar snapped. "If my memory serves me correctly, you stated that when the elves attacked, he refused to obey your order to fight."

Derek's face was flushed. "May I remind your lordship that *I* am not on trial—"

"You charge Brightblade with cowardice in the face of the enemy," Gunthar interrupted. "It has been many years since the elves were our enemies."

Derek hesitated. The other knights appeared uncomfortable. The elves were members of the Council of Whitestone, but they were not allowed a vote. Because of the discovery of the dragon orb, the elves would be attending the upcoming Council, and it would never do to have word get back to them that the knights considered them enemies.

"Perhaps 'enemy' *is* too strong a word, my lord." Derek recovered smoothly. "If I am at fault, it is simply that I am being forced to go by what is written in the Measure. At the time I speak of, the elves—though not our enemies in point of fact—were doing everything in their power to prevent us from bringing the dragon orb to Sancrist. Since this was my mission—and the elves opposed it—I therefore am forced to define them as 'enemies'—according to the Measure."

Slick bastard, Gunthar thought grudgingly.

With a bow to apologize for speaking out of turn, Derek sat down again. Many of the older knights nodded in approval.

"It also says in the Measure," Sturm said slowly, "that we are not to take life needlessly, that we fight only in defense—either our own or the defense of others. The elves did not threaten our lives. At no time were we in actual physical danger."

"They were shooting arrows at you, man!" Lord Alfred struck the table with his gloved hand.

"True, my lord," Sturm replied, "but all know the elves are expert marksmen. If they had wanted to kill us, they would not have been hitting trees!"

"What do you believe would have happened if you had attacked the elves?" Gunthar questioned.

"The results would have been tragic in my view, my lord," Sturm said, his voice soft and low. "For the first time in generations, elves and humans would be killing each other. I think the Dragon Highlords would have laughed."

Several of the young knights applauded.

Lord Alfred glared at them, angry at this serious breach of the Measure's rules of conduct. "Lord Gunthar, may I remind you that Lord Derek Crownguard is not on trial here. He has proven his valor time and again upon the field of battle. I think we may safely take his word for what is an enemy action and what isn't. Sturm Brightblade, do you say that the charges made against you by Lord Derek Crowngard are false?"

"My lord," Sturm began, licking his lips which were cracked and dry, "I do not say the knight has lied. I say, however, that he has misrepresented me."

"To what purpose?" Lord Michael asked.

Sturm hesitated. "I would prefer not to answer that, my lord," he said so quietly that many knights in the back row could not hear and called for Gunthar to repeat the question. He did so and received the same reply—this time louder.

"On what grounds do you refuse to answer that question, Brightblade?" Lord Gunthar asked sternly.

"Because—according to the Measure—it impinges on the honor of the Knighthood," Sturm replied.

Lord Gunthar's face was grave. "That is a serious charge. Making it, you realize you have no one to stand with you in evidence?"

"I do, my lord," Sturm answered, "and that is why I prefer not to respond."

"If I command you to speak?"

"That, of course, would be different."

"Then speak, Sturm Brightblade. This is an unusual situation, and I do not see how we can make a fair judgment without hearing everything. Why do you believe Lord Derek Crowngard misrepresents you?"

Sturm's face flushed. Clasping and unclasping his hands, he raised his eyes and looked directly at the three knights who sat in judgment on him. His case was lost, he knew that. He would never be a knight, never attain what had been dearer to him than life itself. To have lost it through fault of his own would have been bitter enough, but to lose it like this was a festering wound. And so he spoke the words that he knew would make Derek his bitter enemy for the rest of his days.

"I believe Lord Derek Crowngard misrepresents me in an effort to further his own ambition, my lord."

Tumult broke out. Derek was on his feet. His friends restrained him forcibly, or he would have

attacked Sturm in the Council Hall. Gunthar banged the sword hilt for order and eventually the assembly quieted down, but not before Derek had challenged Sturm to test his honor in the field.

Gunthar stared at the knight coldly.

"You know, Lord Derek, that in this—a declared time of war—the contests of honor are forbidden! Come to order or I'll have you expelled from this assembly."

Breathing heavily, his face splotched with red, Derek relapsed back into his seat.

Gunthar gave the Assembly a few more moments to settle down, then resumed. "Have you anything more to say in your defense, Sturm Brightblade?"

"No, my lord," Sturm said.

"Then you may withdraw while this matter is considered."

Sturm rose and bowed to the lords. Turning, he bowed to the Assembly. Then he left the room, escorted by two knights who led him to an antechamber. Here, the two knights, not unkindly, left Sturm to himself. They stood near the closed door, talking softly of matters unrelated to the trial.

Sturm sat on a bench at the far end of the chamber. He appeared composed and calm, but it was all an act. He was determined not to let these knights see the tumult in his soul. It was hopeless, he knew. Gunthar's grieved expression told him that much. But what would the judgment be? Exile, being stripped of lands and wealth? Sturm smiled bitterly. He had nothing they could take from him. He had lived outside of Solamnia so long, exile would be meaningless. Death? He would almost welcome that. Anything was better than this hopeless existence, this dull throbbing pain.

Hours passed. The murmur of three voices rose and fell from within the corridors around the Hall, sometimes angrily. Most of the other knights had gone out, since only the three as Heads of the Council could pass judgment. The other knights were split into differing factions.

The young knights spoke openly of Sturm's noble bearing, his acts of courage, which even Derek could not suppress. Sturm was right in not fighting the elves. The Knights of Solamnia needed all the friends they could get these days. Why attack needlessly, and

so forth. The older knights had only one answer—the Measure. Derek had given Sturm an order. He had refused to obey. The Measure said this was inexcusable. Arguments raged most of the afternoon.

Then, near evening, a small silver bell rang.

"Brightblade," said one of the knights.

Sturm raised his head. "Is it time?"

The knight nodded.

Sturm bowed his head for a moment, asking Paladine for courage. Then he rose to his feet. He and his guards waited for the other knights to reenter and be seated. He knew that they were learning the verdict as soon as they entered.

Finally, the two knights detailed as escort opened the door and motioned for Sturm to enter. He walked into the Hall, the knights following behind. Sturm's gaze went at once to the table before Lord Gunthar.

The sword of his father—a sword that legend said was passed down from Berthel Brightblade himself, a sword that would break only if its master broke—lay on the table. Sturm's eyes went to the sword. His head dropped to hide the burning tears in his eyes.

Wreathed around the blade was the ancient symbol of guilt, black roses.

"Bring the man, Sturm Brightblade, forward," called Lord Gunthar.

The man, Sturm Brightblade, not *the knight!* thought Sturm in despair. Then he remembered Derek. His head came up swiftly, proudly, as he blinked away his tears. Just as he would have hidden his pain from his enemy on the field of battle, so he was determined to hide it now from Derek. Throwing back his head defiantly, his eyes on Lord Gunthar and on no one else, the disgraced squire walked forward to stand before the three officers of the Order to await his fate.

"Sturm Brightblade, we have found you guilty. We are prepared to render judgment. Are you prepared to receive it?"

"Yes, my lord," Sturm said tightly.

Gunthar tugged his moustaches, a sign that the men who had served with him recognized. Lord Gunthar always tugged his moustaches just before riding into battle.

"Sturm Brightblade, it is our judgment that you henceforth cease wearing any of the trappings or accoutrements of a Knight of Solamnia."

"Yes, my lord," Sturm said softly, swallowing.

"And, henceforth, you will not draw pay from the coffers of the Knights, nor obtain any property or gift from them. . . ."

The knights in the hall shifted restlessly. This was ridiculous! No one had drawn pay in the service of the Order since the Cataclysm. Something was up. They smelled thunder before the storm.

"Finally—" Lord Gunthar paused. He leaned forward, his hands toying with the black roses that graced the antique sword. His shrewd eyes swept the Assembly, gathering up his audience, allowing the tension to build. By the time he spoke, even the fire behind him had ceased to crackle.

"Sturm Brightblade. Assembled Knights. Never before has a case such as this come before the Council. And that, perhaps, is not as odd as it may seem, for these are dark and unusual days. We have a young squire—and I remind you that Sturm Brightblade is young by all standards of the Order—a young squire noted for his skill and valor in battle. Even his accuser admits that. A young squire charged with disobeying orders and cowardice in the face of the enemy. The young squire does not deny this charge, but states that he has been misrepresented.

"Now, by the Measure, we are bound to accept the word of a tried and tested knight such as Derek Crowngaurd over the word of a man who has not yet won his shield. But the Measure also states that this man shall be able to call witnesses in his own behalf. Due to the unusual circumstances occasioned by these dark times, Sturm Brightblade is not able to call witnesses. Nor, for that matter, was Derek Crownguard able to produce witnesses to support his own cause. Therefore, we have agreed on the following, slightly irregular, procedure."

Sturm stood before Gunthar, confused and troubled. What was happening? He glanced at the other two knights. Lord Alfred was not bothering to conceal his anger. It was obvious, therefore, that this "agreement" of Gunthar's had been hard won.

"It is the judgment of this Council," Lord Gunthar continued, "that the young man, Sturm Brightblade, be accepted into the lowest order of the knights—the Order of the Crown—*on my honor . . .*"

There was a universal gasp of astonishment.

"And that, furthermore, he be placed as third in command of the army that is due to set sail shortly for Palanthas. As prescribed by the Measure, the High Command must have a representative from each of the Orders.† Therefore, Derek Crownguard will be High Commander, representing the Order of the Rose. Lord Alfred MarKenin will represent the Order of the Sword, and Sturm Brightblade will act—on my honor—as commander for the Order of the Crown."

The Knighthood was inspired by Paladine, Kiri-Jolith, and Habbakuk—three gods of Good. Thus the three orders of Crown, Sword, and Rose, each with a different emphasis.

Amid the stunned silence, Sturm felt tears course down his cheeks, but now he need hide them no longer. Behind him, he heard the sound of someone rising, of a sword rattling in anger. Derek stalked furiously out of the Hall, the other knights of his faction following him. There were scattered cheers, too. Sturm saw through his tears that about half the knights in the room—particularly the younger knights, the knights he would command—were applauding. Sturm felt swift pain well deep from inside his soul. Though he had won his victory, he was appalled by what the knighthood had become, divided into factions by power-hungry men. It was nothing more than a corrupt shell of a once-honored brotherhood.

"Congratulations, Brightblade," Lord Alfred said stiffly. "I hope you realize what Lord Gunthar has done for you."

"I do, my lord," Sturm said, bowing, "and I swear by my father's sword"—he laid his hand upon it—"that I will be worthy of his trust."

"See to it, young man," Lord Alfred replied and left. The younger lord, Michael, accompanied him without a word to Sturm.

But the other young knights came forward then, offering their enthusiastic congratulations. They pledged his health in wine and would have stayed for an all-out drinking bout if Gunthar had not sent them on their way.

When the two of them were alone in the Hall, Lord Gunthar smiled expansively at Sturm and shook his hand. The young knight returned the handshake warmly, if not the smile. The pain was too fresh.

Then, slowly and carefully, Sturm took the black roses from his sword. Laying them on the table, he slid the blade back in the scabbard at his side. He started to brush the roses aside, but paused, then picked up one and thrust it into his belt.

"I must thank you, my lord," Sturm began, his voice quivering.

"You have nothing to thank me for, son," Lord Gunthar said. Glancing around the room, he shivered. "Let's get out of this place and go somewhere warm. Mulled wine?"

The two knights walked down the stone corridors of Gunthar's ancient castle, the sounds of the young knights leaving drifting up from below—horses's hooves clattering on the cobblestone, voices shouting, some even raising in a military song.

"I must thank you, my lord," Sturm said firmly. "The risk you take is very great. I hope I will prove worthy—"

"Risk! Nonsense, my boy." Rubbing his hands to restore the circulation, Gunthar led Sturm into a small room decorated for the approaching Yule celebration—red winter roses, grown indoors, kingfisher feathers,† and tiny, delicate golden crowns. A fire blazed brightly. At Gunthar's command, servants brought in two mugs of steaming liquid that gave off a warm, spicy odor. "Many were the times your father threw his shield in front of me and stood over me, protecting me when I was down."

They used the deep blue long feathers from the crest of this big bird of prey.

"And you did the same for him," Sturm said. "You owe him nothing. Pledging your honor for me means that, if I fail, you will suffer. You will be stripped of your rank, your title, your lands. Derek would see to that," he added gloomily.

As Gunthar took a deep drink of his wine, he studied the young man before him. Sturm merely sipped at his wine out of politeness, holding the mug with a hand that trembled visibly. Gunthar laid his hand kindly on Sturm's shoulder, pushing the young man down gently into a chair.

"Have you failed in the past, Sturm?" Gunthar asked.

Sturm looked up, his brown eyes flashing. "No, my lord," he answered. "I have not. I swear it!"

"Then I have no fear for the future," Lord Gunthar said, smiling. He raised his mug. "I pledge your good fortune in battle, Sturm Brightblade."

Sturm shut his eyes. The strain had been too much. Dropping his head on his arm, he wept—his body shaking with painful sobs. Gunthar gripped his shoulder.

"I understand . . ." he said, his eyes looking back to a time in Solamnia when this young man's father had broken down and cried that same way—the night Lord Brightblade had sent his young wife and infant son on a journey into exile—a journey from which he would never see them return.

Exhausted, Sturm finally fell asleep, his head lying on the table. Gunthar sat with him, sipping the hot wine, lost in memories of the past, until he, too, drifted into slumber.

The few days left before the army sailed to Palanthas passed swiftly for Sturm. He had to find armor—used; he couldn't afford new. He packed his father's carefully, intending to carry it since he had been forbidden to wear it. Then there were meetings to attend, battle dispositions to study, information on the enemy to assimilate.

The battle for Palanthas would be a bitter one, determining control of the entire northern part of Solamnia. The leaders were agreed upon their strategy. They would fortify the city walls with the city's army. The knights themselves would occupy the High Clerist's Tower that stood blocking the pass through the Vingaard Mountains. But that was all they agreed upon. Meetings between the three leaders were tense, the air chill.

Finally the day came for the ships to sail. The knights gathered on board. Their families stood quietly on the shore. Though faces were pale, there were few tears, the women standing as tight-lipped and stern as their men. Some wives wore swords buckled around their own waists. All knew that, if the battle in the north was lost, the enemy would come across the sea.

Gunthar stood upon the pier, dressed in his bright armor, talking with the knights, bidding farewell to his sons. He and Derek exchanged a few ritual words as prescribed by the Measure. He and

Lord Alfred embraced perfunctorily. At last, Gunthar sought out Sturm.The young knight, clad in plain, shabby armor, stood apart from the crowd.

"Brightblade," Gunthar said in a low voice as he came near him, "I have been meaning to ask this but never found a moment in these last few days. You mentioned that these friends of yours would be coming to Sancrist. Are there any who could serve as witnesses before the Council?"

Sturm paused. For a wild moment the only person he could think of was Tanis. His thoughts had been with his friend during these last trying days. He'd even had a surge of hope that Tanis might arrive in Sancrist. But the hope had died. Wherever Tanis was, he had his own problems, he faced his own dangers. There was another person, too, whom he had hoped against hope he might see. Without conscious thought, Sturm placed his hand over the Starjewel that hung around his neck against his breast. He could almost feel its warmth, and he knew—without knowing how—that though far away, Alhana was with him. Then—

"Laurana!" he said.

"A woman?" Gunthar frowned.

"Yes, but daughter of the Speaker of the Suns, a member of the royal household of the Qualinesti. And there is her brother, Gilthanas. Both would testify for me."

"The royal household . . ." Gunthar mused. His face brightened. "That would be perfect, especially since we have received word that the Speaker himself will attend the High Council to discuss the dragon orb. If that happens, my boy, somehow I'll get word to you, and you can put that armor back on! You'll be vindicated! Free to wear it without shame!"

"And you will be free of your pledge," Sturm said, shaking hands with the knight gratefully.

"Bah! Don't give that a thought." Gunthar laid his hand on Sturm's head, as he had laid his hand on the heads of his own sons. Sturm knelt before him reverently. "Receive my blessing, Sturm Brightblade, a father's blessing I give in the absence of your own father. Do your duty, young man, and remain your father's son. May Lord Huma's spirit be with you."

"Thank you, my lord," Sturm said, rising to his feet. "Farewell."

"Farewell, Sturm," Gunthar said. Embracing the young knight swiftly, he turned and walked away.

The knights boarded the ships. It was dawn, but no sun shone in the winter sky. Gray clouds hung over a lead-gray sea. There were no cheers, the only sounds were the shouted commands of the captain and the responses of his crew, the creaking of the winches, and the flapping of the sails in the wind.

Slowly the white-winged ships weighed anchor and sailed north. Soon the last sail was out of sight, but still no one left the pier, not even when a sudden rain squall struck, pelting them with sleet and icy drops, drawing a fine gray curtain across the chill waters.

3

The Dragon Orb.
Caramon's Pledge.

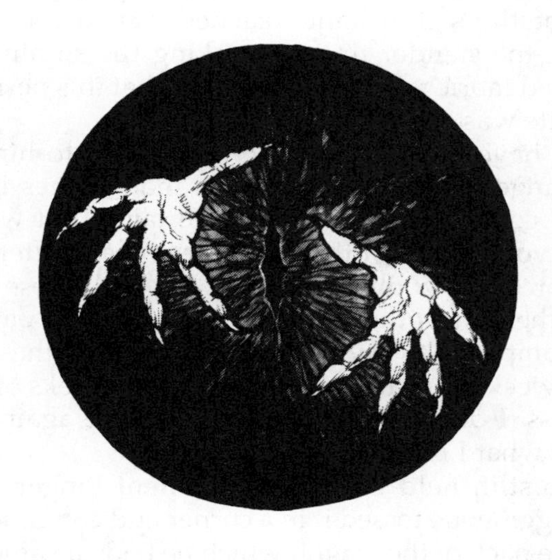

Raistlin stood in the small doorway of the wagon, his golden eyes peering into the sunlit woods. All was quiet. It was past Yuletide. The countryside was held fast in the grip of winter. Nothing stirred in the snow-blanketed land. His companions were gone, busy about various tasks. Raistlin nodded grimly. Good. Turning, he went back inside the wagon and shut the wooden doors firmly.

The companions had been camped here for several days, on the outskirts of Kendermore. Their journey was nearing an end. It had been unbelievably successful. Tonight they would leave, traveling to Flotsam under the cover of darkness. They had money enough to hire a ship, plus some left over for supplies and payment for a week's

lodging in Flotsam. This afternoon had been their final performance.

The young mage made his way through the clutter to the back of the wagon. His gaze lingered on the shimmering red robe that hung on a nail. Tika had started to pack it away, but Raistlin had snarled at her viciously. Shrugging, she let it remain, going outside to walk in the woods, knowing Caramon—as usual—would find her.

Raistlin's thin hand reached out to touch the robe, the slender fingers stroking the shining, sequined fabric wistfully, regretting that this period in his life was over.

"I have been happy," he murmured to himself. "Strange. There have not been many times in my life I could make that claim. Certainly not when I was young, nor in these past few years, after they tortured my body and cursed me with these eyes. But then I never expected happiness. How paltry it is, compared to my magic! Still . . . still, these last few weeks have been weeks of peace. Weeks of happiness. I don't suppose any will come again. Not after what I must do—"

Raistlin held the robe a moment longer, then, shrugging, he tossed it in a corner and continued on to the back of the wagon which he had curtained off for his own private use. Once inside, he pulled the curtains securely together.

Excellent. He would have privacy for several hours, until nightfall, in fact. Tanis and Riverwind had gone hunting. Caramon had, too, supposedly, though everyone knew this was just an excuse for him to find time alone with Tika. Goldmoon was preparing food for their journey. No one would bother him. The mage nodded to himself in satisfaction.

Sitting down at the small drop-leaf table Caramon had constructed for him, Raistlin carefully withdrew from the very innermost pocket of his robes an ordinary-looking sack, the sack that contained the dragon orb. His skeletal fingers trembled as he tugged on the drawstring. The bag opened. Reaching in, Raistlin grasped the dragon orb and brought it forth. He held it easily in his palm, inspecting it closely to see if there had been any change.

No. A faint green color still swirled within. It still felt as cold to the touch as if he held a hailstone. Smiling, Raistlin clasped the orb tightly in one hand while he fumbled through the props beneath the table. He finally found what he sought—a crudely carved, three-legged wooden stand. Lifting it up, Raistlin set it on the table. It wasn't much to look at—Flint would have scoffed. Raistlin had neither the love nor the skill needed to work wood. He had carved it laboriously, in secret, shut up inside the jouncing wagon during the long days on the road. No, it was not much to look at, but he didn't care. It would suit his purpose.

Placing the stand upon the table, he set the dragon orb on it. The marble-sized† orb looked ludicrous, but Raistlin sat back, waiting patiently. As he had expected, soon the orb began to grow. Or did it? Perhaps *he* was shrinking. Raistlin couldn't tell. He knew only that suddenly the orb was the right size. If anything was different, it was he that was too small, too insignificant to even be in the same room with the orb.

Apparently children in Krynn also play with marbles, which, if we understand correctly, are about the same size as our own. It is difficult to imagine Raistlin pondering a shot with a cleary or cat's eye.—TRH

The mage shook his head. He must stay in control, he knew, and he was immediately aware of the subtle tricks the orb was playing to undermine that control. Soon these tricks would not be subtle. Raistlin felt his throat tighten. He coughed, cursing his weak lungs. Drawing a shuddering breath, he forced himself to breathe deeply and easily.

Relax, he thought. I must relax. I do not fear. I am strong. Look what I have done! Silently he called upon the orb: Look at the power I have attained! Witness what I did in Darken Wood. Witness what I did in Silvanesti. I am strong. I do not fear.

The orb's colors swirled softly. It did not answer.

The mage closed his eyes for a moment, blotting the orb from sight. Regaining control, he opened them again, regarding the orb with a sigh. The moment approached.

The dragon orb was now back to its original size. He could almost see Lorac's wizened hands grasping it. The young mage shuddered involuntarily. No! Stop it! he told himself firmly, and immediately banished the vision from his mind.

Once more he relaxed, breathing regularly, his hourglass eyes focused on the orb. Then—slowly—

he stretched forth his slender, metallic-colored fingers. After a moment's final hesitation, Raistlin placed his hands upon the cold crystal of the dragon orb and spoke the ancient words.

"Ast bilak moiparalan/Suh akvlar tantangusar." How did he know what to say? How did he know what ancient words would cause the orb to understand him, to be aware of his presence? Raistlin did not know. He knew only that—somehow, somewhere—inside of him, he *did* know the words! The voice that had spoken to him in Silvanesti? Perhaps. It didn't matter. Again he said the words aloud.

"Ast bilak moiparalan/Suh akvlar tantangusar!" Slowly the drifting green color was submerged in a myriad of swirling, gliding colors that made him dizzy to watch. The crystal was so cold beneath his palms that it was painful to touch. Raistlin had a terrifying vision of pulling away his hands and leaving the flesh behind, frozen to the orb. Gritting his teeth, he ignored the pain and whispered the words again.

The colors ceased to swirl. A light glowed in the center, a light neither white nor black, all colors, yet none. Raistlin swallowed, fighting the choking phlegm that rose in his throat.

Out of the light came two hands! He had a desperate urge to withdraw his own, but before he could move, the two hands grasped his in a grip both strong and firm. The orb vanished! The room vanished! Raistlin saw nothing around him. No light. No darkness. Nothing! Nothing . . . but two hands, holding his. Out of sheer terror, Raistlin concentrated on those hands.

Human? Elven? Old? Young? He could not tell. The fingers were long and slender, but their grip was the grip of death. Let go and he would fall into the void to drift until merciful darkness consumed him. Even as he clung to those hands with strength lent him by fear, Raistlin realized the hands were slowly drawing him nearer, drawing him into . . . into . . .

Raistlin came to himself suddenly, as if someone had dashed cold water in his face. No! he told the mind that he sensed controlled the hands. I will not go! Though he feared losing that saving grip, he feared even more being dragged where he did not want to go. He would not let loose. I *will* maintain

control, he told the mind of the hands savagely. Tightening his own grip, the mage summoned all of his strength, all of his will, and pulled the hands toward him!

The hands stopped. For a moment, the two wills vied together, locked in a life-or-death contest. Raistlin felt the strength ebb from his body, his hands weakened, the palms began to sweat. He felt the hands of the orb begin to pull him again, ever so slightly. In agony, Raistlin summoned every drop of blood, focused every nerve, sacrificed every muscle in his frail body to regain control.

Slowly . . . slowly . . . just when he thought his pounding heart would burst from his chest or his brain explode in fire—Raistlin felt the hands cease their tug. They still maintained their firm grip on him—as he maintained his firm grip on them. But the two were no longer in contest. His hands and the hands of the dragon orb remained locked together, each conceding respect, neither seeking dominance.

The ecstasy of the victory, the ecstasy of the magic flowed through Raistlin and burst forth, wrapping him in a warm, golden light. His body relaxed. Trembling, he felt the hands hold him gently, support him, lend him strength.

What are you? he questioned silently. Are you good? Evil?

I am neither. I am nothing. I am everything. The essence of dragons captured long ago is what I am.

How do you work? Raistlin asked. How do you control the dragons?

At your command, I will call them to me. They cannot resist my call. They will obey.

Will they turn upon their masters? Will they fall under my command?

That depends on the strength of the master and the bond between the two. In some instances, this is so strong that the master can maintain control of the dragon. But most will do what you ask of them. They cannot help themselves.

I must study this, Raistlin murmured, feeling himself growing weaker. I do not understand. . . .

Be easy. I will aid you. Now that we have joined, you may seek my help often. I know of many secrets long forgotten. They can be yours.

What secrets? . . . Raistlin felt himself losing

consciousness. The strain had been too much. He struggled to keep his hold on the hands, but he felt his grip slipping.

The hands held onto him gently, as a mother holds a child.

Relax, I will not let you fall. Sleep. You are weary.

Tell me! I must know! Raistlin cried silently.

This only I will tell you, then you must rest. In the library of Astinus of Palanthas are books, hundreds of books, taken there by the mages of old in the days of the Lost Battle.† To all who look at these books, they seem nothing more than encyclopedias of magic, dull histories of mages who died in the caverns of time.

The Lost Battle is the time about twenty years before the Cataclysm when public anger—urged on by the Kingpriest—forced the wizards to shut down two of the five Towers of High Sorcery and destroy them.

Raistlin saw darkness creeping toward him. He clutched at the hands.

What do the books really contain? he whispered.

Then he knew, and with the knowledge, darkness crashed over him like the wave of an ocean.

In a cave near the wagon, hidden by shadows, warmed by the heat of their passion, Tika and Caramon lay in each other's arms. Tika's red hair clung around her face and forehead in tight curls, her eyes were closed, her full lips parted. Her soft body clad in her gaily-colored skirt and puffy-sleeved white blouse pressed against Caramon. Her legs twined around his, her hand caressed his face, her lips brushed his.

"Please, Caramon," she whispered. "This is torture. We want each other. I'm not afraid. Please love me!"

Caramon closed his eyes. His face shone with sweat. The pain of his love seemed impossible to bear. He could end it, end it all in sweet ecstasy. For a moment he hesitated. Tika's fragrant hair was in his nostrils, her soft lips on his neck. It would be so easy . . . so wonderful. . . .

Caramon sighed. Firmly he closed his strong hands around Tika's wrists. Firmly he drew them away from his face and pushed the girl from him.

"No," he said, his passion choking him. Rolling over, he stood up."No," he repeated. "I'm sorry. I didn't mean to . . . to let things get this far."

"Well, I did!" Tika cried. "I'm *not* frightened! Not anymore."

No, he thought, pressing his hands against his pounding head. I feel you trembling in my hands

like a snared rabbit. Tika began to tie the string on her white blouse. Unable to see it through her tears, she jerked at the drawstring so viciously it snapped.

"Now! See there!" She hurled the broken silken twine across the cave. "I've ruined my blouse! I'll have to mend it. They'll all know what happened, of course! Or think they know! I—I . . . Oh, what's the use!" Weeping in frustration, Tika covered her face with her hands, rocking back and forth.

"I don't care what they think!" Caramon said, his voice echoing in the cave. He did not comfort her. He knew if he touched her again, he would yield to his passion. "Besides, they don't think anything at all. They are our friends. They care for us—"

"I know!" Tika cried brokenly. "It's Raistlin, isn't it? He doesn't approve of me. He *hates* me!"

"Don't say that, Tika." Caramon's voice was firm. "If he did and if he were stronger, it wouldn't matter. I wouldn't care what anyone said or thought. The others want us to be happy. They don't understand why we—we don't become—er—lovers. Tanis even told me to my face I was a fool—"

"He's right." Tika's voice was muffled by tear-damp hair.

"Maybe. Maybe not."

Something in Caramon's voice made the girl quit crying. She looked up at him as Caramon turned around to face her.

"You don't know what happened to Raist in the Towers of High Sorcery. None of you know. None of you ever will. But *I* know. I was there. I saw. They *made* me see!" Caramon shuddered, putting his hands over his face. Tika held very still. Then, looking at her again, he drew a deep breath. "They said, 'His strength will save the world.' What strength? Inner strength? I'm his outer strength! I—I don't understand, but Raist said to me in the dream that we were one whole person, cursed by the gods and put into two bodies. We need each other—right now at least." The big man's face darkened. "Maybe someday that will change. Maybe some day he'll find the outer strength—"

Caramon fell silent. Tika swallowed and wiped her hand across her face. "I—" she began, but Caramon cut her off.

"Wait a minute," he said. "Let me finish. I love you, Tika, as truly as any man loves any woman in this world. I want to make love to you. If we weren't involved in this stupid war, I'd make you mine today. This minute. But I can't. Because if I did, it would be a commitment to you that I would dedicate my life to keeping. You must come first in all my thoughts. You deserve no less than that. But I can't make that commitment, Tika. My first commitment is to my brother." Tika's tears flowed again—this time not for herself, but for him. "I must leave you free to find someone† who can—"

Caramon is a selfless individual—someone capable of loving another person completely and at his own expense. It is this quality that both makes him great and makes him vulnerable. Raistlin represents the bad side of a codependent relationship. This particular scene is ironic considering that it will soon be Raistlin who will abandon Caramon.
—TRH

"Caramon!" A call split the afternoon's sweet silence. "Caramon, come quickly!" It was Tanis.

"Raistlin!" said the big man, and without another word, ran out of the cave.

Tika stood a moment, watching after him. Then, sighing, she tried to comb her damp hair into place.

"What is it?" Caramon burst into the wagon. "Raist?"

Tanis nodded, his face grave.

"I found him like this." The half-elf drew back the curtain to the mage's small apartment. Caramon shoved him aside.

Raistlin lay on the floor, his skin white, his breathing shallow. Blood trickled from his mouth. Kneeling down, Caramon lifted him in his arms.

"Raistlin?" he whispered. "What happened?"

"*That's* what happened," Tanis said grimly, pointing.

Caramon glanced up, his gaze coming to rest on the dragon orb—now grown to the size Caramon had seen in Silvanesti. It stood on the stand Raistlin had made for it, its swirling colors shifting endlessly as he watched. Caramon sucked in his breath in horror. Terrible visions of Lorac flooded his mind. Lorac insane, dying . . .

"Raist!" he moaned, clutching his brother tightly.

Raistlin's head moved feebly. His eyelids fluttered, and he opened his mouth.

"What?" Caramon bent low, his brother's breath cold upon his skin."What?"

"Mine . . ." Raistlin whispered. "Spells . . . of the ancients . . . mine . . . Mine . . ." The mage's head lolled, his words died. But his face was calm, placid, relaxed. His breathing grew regular.

Raistlin's thin lips parted in a smile.

4

Yuletide Guests.

It took Lord Gunthar several days of hard riding to reach his home in time for Yule following the departure of the knights for Palanthas. The roads were knee-deep in mud. His horse foundered more than once, and Gunthar, who loved his horse nearly as well as his sons, walked whenever necessary. By the time he returned to his castle,† therefore, he was exhausted, drenched, and shivering. The stableman came out to take charge of the horse personally.

"Rub him down well," Gunthar said, dismounting stiffly. "Hot oats and—" He proceeded with his instructions, the stableman nodding patiently, as if he'd never cared for a horse before in his life. Gunthar was, in fact, on the point of

Gunthar's castle is located in western Sancrist, in the region called Gunthar. Whitestone Glade lies between the castle and Mount Nevermind.The castle is the center of life on Sancrist.

walking his horse to the stables himself when his ancient retainer came out in search of him.

"My lord." Wills drew Gunthar to one side in the entryway. "You have visitors. They arrived just a few hours ago."

"Who?" Gunthar asked without much interest, visitors being nothing new, especially during Yule. "Lord Michael? He could not travel with us, but I asked him to stop on his way home—"

"An old man, my lord," Wills interrupted, "and a kender."

"A kender?" Gunthar repeated in some alarm.

"I'm afraid so, my lord. But don't worry," the retainer added hastily. "I've locked the silver in a drawer, and your lady wife has taken her jewelry to the cellar."

"You'd think we were under siege!" Gunthar snorted. He did, however, go through the courtyard faster than usual.

"You can't be too careful around those critters, my lord," Wills mumbled, trotting along behind.

"What are these two, then? Beggars? Why did you let them in?" Gunthar demanded, beginning to get irritated. All he wanted was his mulled wine, warm clothes, and one of his wife's backrubs. "Give them some food and money, and send them on their way. Search the kender first, of course."

"I was going to, my lord," Wills said stubbornly. "But there's something about them—the old man in particular. He's crackers, if you ask me, but he's a smart crackers, for all that. Knows something, and it may be more than's good for him—or us either."

"What do you mean?"

The two had just opened the huge, wooden doors leading into the living quarters of the castle proper. Gunthar stopped and stared at Wills, knowing and respecting his retainer's keen power of observation. Wills glanced around, then leaned close.

"The old man said I was to tell you he had urgent news regarding the dragon orb, my lord!"

"The dragon orb!" Gunthar murmured. The orb was secret, or he presumed it was. The Knights knew of it, of course. Had Derek told anyone else? Was this one of his maneuvers?

"You acted wisely, Wills, as always," Gunthar said finally. "Where are they?"

"I put them in your war room, my lord, figuring they could cause little mischief there."

"I'll change clothes before I catch my death, then see them directly. Have you made them comfortable?"

"Yes, my lord," Wills replied, hurrying after Gunthar, who was on the move again. "Hot wine, a bit of bread and meat. Though I trust the kender's lifted the plates by now—"

Gunthar and Wills stood outside the door of the war room for a moment, eavesdropping on the visitors' conversation.

"Put that back!" ordered a stern voice.

"I won't! It's mine! Look, it was in my pouch."

"Bah! I saw you put it there not five minutes ago!"

"Well, you're wrong," protested the other voice in wounded tones. "It's mine! See, there's my name engraved—"

" 'To Gunthar, my beloved husband on the Day of Life-Gift,' " said the first voice.

There was a moment's silence in the room. Wills turned pale. Then the shrill voice spoke, more subdued this time.

"I guess it must have fallen into my pack,† Fizban. That's it! See, my pack was sitting under that table. Wasn't that lucky? It would have broken if it had hit the floor—"

Even in his sleep, Tas can be heard murmuring, "I guess you must have dropped it."

His face grim, Lord Gunthar flung open the door.

"Merry Yuletide to you, sirs," he said. Wills popped in after him, his eyes darting quickly around the room.

The two strangers whirled around, the old man holding a crockery mug in his hand. Wills made a leap for the mug, whisking it away. With an indignant glance at the kender, he placed it upon the mantlepiece, high above the kender's reach.

"Will there be anything else, my lord?" Wills asked, glaring meaningfully at the kender. "Shall I stay and keep an eye on things?"

Gunthar opened his mouth to reply, but the old man waved a negligent hand.

"Yes, thank you, my good man. Bring up some more ale. And don't bring any of that rotgut stuff from the servants' barrels, either!" The old man looked at Wills sternly. "Tap the barrel that's in the dark corner by the cellar stairs. You know—the one that's all cobwebby."

Wills stared at him, open-mouthed.

"Well, go on. Don't stand there gaping like a landed fish! A bit dim-witted, is he?" the old man asked Gunthar.

"N-no," Gunthar stammered. "That's all right, Wills. I—I believe I'll have a mug, too—of—of the ale from the cask by the—uh—stairs. How did *you* know?" He demanded of the old man suspiciously.

"Oh, he's a magic-user," the kender said, shrugging and sitting down without being invited.

"A magic-user?" The old man peered around. "Where?"

Tas whispered something, poking the old man.

"Really? Me?" he said. "You don't say! How remarkable. Now you know, come to think of it, I do seem to remember a spell . . . Fireball. How did it go?"

The old mage began to speak the strange words. Alarmed, the kender leaped out of his seat and grabbed the old man.

"No, Old One!" he said, tugging him back into a chair. "Not now!"

"I suppose not," the old man said wistfully. "Wonderful spell, though . . ."

"I'm certain," murmured Gunthar, absolutely mystified. Then he shook his head, regaining his sternness. "Now, explain yourselves. Who are you? Why are you here? Wills said something about a dragon orb—"

"I'm—" The mage stopped, blinking.

"Fizban," said the kender with a sigh. Standing, he extended his small hand politely to Gunthar. "And I am Tasslehoff Burrfoot." He started to sit down. "Oh," he said, popping up again. "A Merry Yuletide to you, too, sir knight."

"Yes, yes," Gunthar shook hands, nodding absently. "Now about the dragon orb?"

"Ah, yes, the dragon orb!" The befuddled look left Fizban's face. He stared at Gunthar with shrewd, cunning eyes. "Where is it? We've come a long way in search of it."

"I'm afraid I can't tell you," Gunthar said coolly. "If, indeed, such a thing were ever here—"

"Oh, it was here," Fizban replied. "Brought to you by a Knight of the Rose, one Derek Crownguard. And Sturm Brightblade was with him."

"They're friends of mine," explained Tasslehoff, seeing Gunthar's jaw go slack. "I helped get the orb, in fact," the kender added modestly. "We took it away from an evil wizard in a palace made of ice. It's the most wonderful story—" He sat forward eagerly. "Do you want to hear it?"

"No," said Gunthar, staring at them both in amazement. "And if I believed this swimming bird tale†—wait—" He sank back in his chair. "Sturm did say something about a kender. Who were the others in your party?"

"Flint the dwarf, Theros the blacksmith, Gilthanas and Laurana—"

"It must be!" Gunthar exclaimed, then he frowned. "But he never mentioned a magic-user. . . ."

"Oh, that's because I'm dead," Fizban stated, propping his feet upon the table.

Gunthar's eyes opened wide, but before he could reply, Wills came in. Glaring at Tasslehoff, the retainer set mugs down on the table in front of his lordship.

"Three mugs, here, my lord. And one on the mantle makes four. And there better be *four* when I come back!"

He walked out, shutting the door with a thud.

"I'll keep an eye on them," Tas promised solemnly. "Do you have a problem with people stealing mugs?" he asked Gunthar.

"I—no. . . . Dead?" Gunthar felt he was rapidly losing his grip on the situation.

"It's a long story," said Fizban, downing the liquid in one swallow. He wiped the foam from his lips with the tip of his beard. "Ah, excellent. Now, where was I?"

"Dead," said Tas helpfully.

"Ah, yes. A long story. Too long for now. Must get the orb. Where is it?"

Gunthar stood up angrily, intending to order this strange old man and this kender from his chamber and his castle. He was going to call his guards to extract them. But, instead, he found himself caught by the old man's intense gaze.

The Knights of Solamnia have always feared magic. Though they had not taken part in the destruction of the Towers of High Sorcery—that would have been against the Measure—they had

Gunthar refers to a child's story common among humans of the period regarding a small boy who had broken a wizard's favorite jar while washing it in a large pool at the center of the wizard's home. When the wizard demanded of his apprentice what had happened to the jar, the boy at first replied that a fish had knocked it out of his hands as he carefully washed it. When the wizard pointed out that there were no fish in his pond. The boy, rather than admit the truth, told the wizard that it was a bird who had flown over the wall that had caused the accident. When the wizard asked how the bird had disturbed a jar already under water, the apprentice replied that it had been a swimming bird. The boy's punishment was all the greater for the greater lie. From this tale, then, came the swimming bird phrase, which forever after to humans of all ages stands for a lie that is growing by the minute—and the punishment that grows with it.—TRH

not been sorry to see magic-users driven from Palanthas.

"Why do you want to know?" Gunthar faltered, feeling a cold fear seep into his blood as he felt the old man's strange power engulf him. Slowly, reluctantly, Gunthar sat back down.

Fizban's eyes glittered. "I keep my own counsel," he said softly. "Let it be enough for you to know that *I* have come seeking the orb. It was made by magic-users, long ago! I know of it. I know a great deal about it."

Gunthar hesitated, wrestling with himself. After all, there were knights guarding the orb, and if this old man really did know something about it, what harm could there be in telling him where it was? Besides, he really didn't feel like he had any choice in the matter.

Fizban absently picked up his empty mug again and started to drink. He peered inside it mournfully as Gunthar answered.

"The dragon orb is with the gnomes."

Fizban dropped his mug with a crash. It broke into a hundred pieces that went skittering across the wooden floor.

"There, what'd I tell you?" Tas said sadly, eyeing the shattered mug.

The gnomes had lived in Mount Nevermind for as long as they could remember—and since they were the only ones who cared, they were the only ones who counted. Certainly they were there when the first knights arrived in Sancrist, traveling from the newly created kingdom of Solamnia to build their keeps and fortress along the westernmost part of their border.

Gnomes generally avoid living where humans are (preferring Mount Nevermind, of course), but occasionally one will get adventuresome. Roger Moore tells the story of Gilbenstock, a gnome living in Palanthas who becomes very involved with humans, in "A Dragon to the Core" in The Dragons of Krynn.

Always suspicious of outsiders, the gnomes were alarmed to see a ship arriving upon their shores, bearing hordes of tall, stern-faced, warlike humans.† Determined to keep what they considered a mountain paradise secret from the humans, the gnomes launched into action. Being the most technologically minded of the races on Krynn (they are noted for having invented the steam-powered engine and the coiled spring), the gnomes first thought of hiding within their mountain caverns, but then had a better idea. Hide the mountain itself!

After several months of unending toil by their greatest mechanical geniuses, the gnomes were prepared. Their plan? They were going to make their mountain disappear!

It was at this juncture that one of the members of the gnomish Philosopher's Guild asked if it wasn't likely that the knights would have already noticed the mountain, the tallest on the island. Might not the sudden disappearance of the mountain create a certain amount of curiosity in the humans?

This question threw the gnomes into turmoil. Days were spent in discussion. The question soon divided the Philosopher gnomes into two factions: those who believed that if a tree fell in a forest and no one heard it, it still made a crashing sound; and those who believed it didn't. Just what this had to do with the original question was brought up on the seventh day, but was promptly referred to committee.

Meanwhile, the Mechanical Engineers, in a huff, decided to set off the device anyhow.

And thus occurred the day that is still remembered in the annals of Sancrist (when almost everything else was lost during the Cataclysm) as the Day of Rotten Eggs.

On that day an ancestor of Lord Gunthar woke up wondering sleepily if his son had fallen through the roof of the hen house again. This had happened only a few weeks before. The boy had been chasing a rooster.

"You take him down to the pond," Gunthar's ancestor told his wife sleepily, rolling over in bed and drawing the covers up over his head.

"I can't!" she said drowsily. "The chimney's smoking!"

It was then that both fully woke up, realizing that the smoke filling the house was not coming from the chimney and that the ungodly odor was not coming from the hen house.

Along with every other resident of the new colony, the two rushed outside, choking and gagging with the smell that grew worse by the minute. They could see nothing, however. The land was covered with a thick yellow smoke, redolent of eggs that had been sitting in the sun for three days.

Within hours, everyone in the colony was deathly sick from the smell. Packing up blankets and clothes, they headed for the beaches. Breathing the fresh salt breezes thankfully, they wondered if they could ever go back to their homes.

While discussing this and watching anxiously to see if the yellow cloud on the horizon might lift, the colonists were considerably startled to see what appeared to be an army of short, brown creatures stagger out of the smoke to fall almost lifeless at their feet.

The kindly people of Solamnia immediately went to the aid of the poor gnomes, and thus did the two races of people living on Sancrist meet.

The meeting of the gnomes and the knights turned out to be a friendly one. The Solamnic people had a high regard for four things: individual honor, the Code, the Measure, and technology. They were vastly impressed with the labor-saving devices the gnomes had invented at this time, which included the pulley, the shaft, the screw, and the gear.

It was during this first meeting that Mount Nevermind got its name as well.

The knights soon discovered that, while gnomes appeared to be related to the dwarves—being short and stocky—all similarity ended there. The gnomes were a skinny people with brown skin and pale white hair, highly nervous and hot-tempered. They spoke so rapidly that the knights at first thought they were speaking a foreign language. Instead, it turned out to be Common spoken at an accelerated pace. The reason for this became obvious when an elder made the mistake of asking the gnomes the name of their mountain.

Roughly translated, it went something like this: A Great, Huge, Tall Mound Made of Several Different Strata of Rock of Which We Have Identified Granite, Obsidian, Quartz With Traces of Other Rock We Are Still Working On, That Has Its Own Internal Heating System Which We Are Studying In Order to Copy Someday That Heats the Rock Up to Temperatures That Convert It Into Both Liquid and Gaseous States Which Occasionally Come to the Surface and Flow Down the Side of the Great, Huge, Tall Mound—

"Nevermind," the elder said hastily.

Nevermind! The gnomes were impressed. To think that these humans could reduce something

so gigantic and marvelous into something so simple was wonderful beyond belief. And so, the mountain was called Mount Nevermind from that day forth, to the vast relief of the gnomish Map-Makers Guild.

The knights on Sancrist and the gnomes lived in harmony after that, the knights bringing the gnomes any questions of a technological nature that needed solving, the gnomes providing a steady flood of new inventions.

When the dragon orb arrived, the knights needed to know how the thing worked. They gave it into the keeping of the gnomes, sending along two young knights to guard it. The thought that the orb might be magic did not occur to them.

One of the goals of DRAGONLANCE was to do different things with what were then established D&D concepts. No orcs or lycanthropes. Minotaurs as an intelligent race. Kender as more than just Tolkien-clone halflings.

And then there were the gnomes.

I'll take the blame for the last one.

Gnomes, up to that point, were the poor-relation player-characters of AD&D. They were late arrivals. They were one more little-people race in the game, joining the doughty dwarves and happy halflings. They had one cool ability—they could become illusionists, which were already a DM's nightmare. And they could talk to burrowing animals. Yeah, there's a reason to play a gnome—I want to chat with a woodchuck. Gnomes were not the most desirable characters in the bag, but we had to take them into account in the game.

So we were casting about for what role the gnomes would play (if any) in DRAGONLANCE, and I started on a riff about my previous occupation—engineering. Most of my brief engineering career had consisted of making repairs for things that other engineers had designed and later discovered were impossible to accomplish. I pitched the idea of gnomes as the ultimate inventors, but that most of their inventions were made in order to fix their previous inventions.

Tracy thought that was hilarious, and soon the gnomeflingers and all the other devices of Mt. Nevermind appeared. The gnomes themselves took on a new lease on life and eventually escaped to space (and possibly to other people's campaigns). In AD&D campaigns, both DMs and players learned to fear when a fast-talking, curious, helpful gnome appeared.

And it's all because I made fun of engineers.—Jeff Grubb

5

GNOMEFLINGERS.

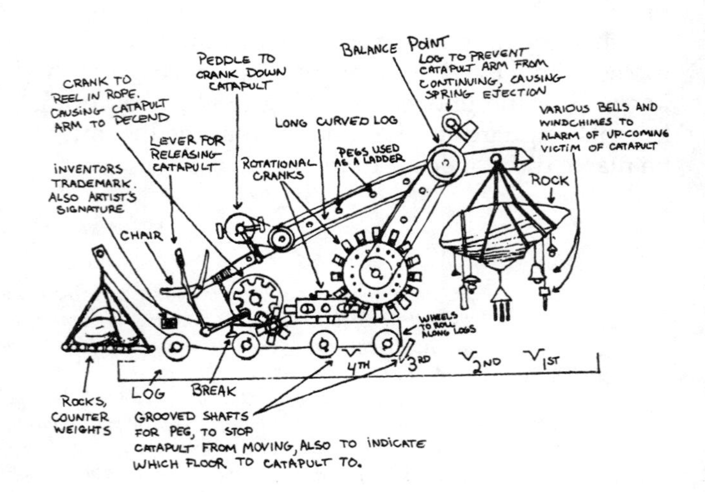

The story of the Graygem is recounted in Dragonlance Adventures. *Reorx was tricked into creating the gem, which created magical havoc in the world. A human named Gargath caught the gem and took it to his fortress. The gnomes, who had been pursuing the gem for years, laid siege to the castle. The gnomes built many siege engines, one of which sort of worked. The gnomes entered the castle, where the power of the Graygem caused them to start fighting with each other. The gnomes who wanted the stone out of greed were changed to dwarves. The gnomes who wanted the stone out of curiosity were changed to kender. (The dwarves dispute this version of history!)—MW*

Now remember. No gnome living or dead ever in his life completed a sentence. The only way you get anywhere is to interrupt them. Don't worry about being rude. They expect it."

The old mage himself was interrupted by the appearance of a gnome dressed in long brown robes, who came up to them and bowed respectfully.

Tasslehoff studied the gnome with excited curiosity, the kender had never seen a gnome before, although old legends concerning the Graygem of Gargath† indicated that the two races were distantly connected. Certainly there was something kenderish in the young gnome, his slender hands, eager expression, and sharp, bright eyes intent on observing everything. But here the resemblance ended. There was nothing

of the kender's easy-going manner. The gnome was nervous, serious, and businesslike.

"Tasslehoff Burrfoot," said the kender politely, extending his hand. The gnome took Tas's hand, peered at it intently, then, finding nothing of interest—shook it limply. "And this—" Tas started to introduce Fizban, but stopped when the gnome reached out and calmly took hold of the kender's hoopak.

"Ah . . ." the gnome said, his eyes shining as he grasped the weapon. "Sendforamemberofthe WeaponsGuild—"

The guard at the ground-level entrance to the great mountain did not wait for the gnome to finish. Reaching up, he pulled a lever and a shriek sounded. Certain that a dragon had landed behind him, Tas whirled around, ready to defend himself.

"Whistle," said Fizban. "Better get used to it."

"Whistle?" repeated Tas, intrigued. "I never heard one like that before. Smoke comes out of it! How does it wor—Hey! Come back! Bring back my hoopak!" he cried as his staff went speeding down the corridor, carried by three eager gnomes.

"Examinationroom," said the gnome, "upon-Skimbosh—"

"What?"

"Examination Room," Fizban translated. "I missed the rest. You really must speak slower," he said, shaking his staff at the gnome.

The gnome nodded, but his bright eyes were fixed on Fizban's staff. Then, seeing it was just plain, slightly battered wood, the gnome returned his attention to the mage and kender.

"Outsiders," he said. "I'lltryand'member . . . I will try and remember, so do not worry because"—he now spoke slowly and distinctly—"your weapon will not be harmed since we are merely going to render a drawing—"

"Really," interrupted Tas, rather flattered. "I could give you a demonstration of how it works, if you like."

The gnome's eyes brightened. "Thatwouldbe-much—"

"And now," interrupted the kender again, feeling pleased that he was learning to communicate, "what is your name?"

An early sketch of Tasslehoff and the hoopak that fascinates the gnomes

Fizban made a quick gesture, but too late.

"Gnoshoshallamarionininillisyylphanitdisdis-slishxdie—"

He paused to draw a breath.

"Is that your *name*?" Tas asked, astounded.

The gnome let his breath out. "Yes," he snapped, a bit disconcerted."It's my first name, and now if you'll let me proceed—"

"Wait!" cried Fizban. "What do your friends call you?"

The gnome sucked in a breath again. "Gnoshosh-allamarioninillis—"

"What do the knights call you?"

"Oh"—the gnome seemed downcast—"Gnosh, if you—

"Thank you," snapped Fizban. "Now, Gnosh, we're in rather a hurry. War going on and all that. As Lord Gunthar stated in his communique, we must see this dragon orb."

Gnosh's small, dark eyes glittered. His hands twisted nervously. "Of course, you may see the dragon orb since Lord Gunthar has requested it, but, if I might ask, what is your interest in the orb besides normalcuri—?"

"I am a magic-user—" Fizban began.

"Magicuser!" the gnome stated, forgetting, in his excitement, to speak slowly. "Comethiswayimme-diatelytothe Examinationroomsincethedragon-orbwasmadebymagicuser—"

Both Tas and Fizban blinked uncomprehendingly.

"Oh, just come—" the gnome said impatiently.

Before they quite knew what was happening, the gnome, still talking, hustled them through the mountain's entrance, setting off an inordinate number of bells and whistles.

"Examination Room?" Tas said in an undertone to Fizban as they hurried after Gnosh. "What does that mean? They wouldn't have hurt it, would they?"

"I don't think so," Fizban muttered, his bushy white eyebrows coming together in an ominous V-shape over his nose. "Gunthar sent knights to guard it, remember."

"Then what are you worried about?" Tas asked.

"The dragon orbs are strange things. Very powerful. My fear," said Fizban more to himself than to Tas, "is that they may try to *use* it!"

"But the book I read in Tarsis said the orb could control dragons!" Tas whispered. "Isn't that good? I mean, the orbs aren't evil, are they?"

"Evil? Oh, no! Not evil." Fizban shook his head. "That's the danger. They're not good, not evil. They're not *anything!* Or perhaps I should say, they're *everything.*"

Tas saw he would probably never get a straight answer out of Fizban, whose mind was far away. In need of diversion, the kender turned his attention to their host.

"What does your name mean?" Tas asked.

Gnosh smiled happily. "In The Beginning, The Gods Created the Gnomes, and One of the First They Created Was Named Gnosh I and these are the Notable Events Which Occurred in His Life: He Married Marioninillis . . ."

Tas had a sinking feeling. "Wait—" he interrupted. "How long is your name?"

"It fills a book this big in the library," Gnosh said proudly, holding his hands out, "because we are a very old family as you will see when I contin—"

"That's all right," Tas said quickly. Not watching where he was going, he stumbled over a rope. Gnosh helped him to his feet. Looking up, Tas saw the rope led up into a nest of ropes connected to each other, snaking out in all directions. He wondered where they led. "Perhaps another time."

"But there are some very good parts," Gnosh said as they walked toward a huge steel door, "and I could skip to those, if you like, such as the part where great-great-great-grandmother Gnosh invented boiling water—"

"I'd love to hear it." Tas gulped. "But, no time—"

"Yes, I suppose so," Gnosh said, "and anyway, here we are at the entrance to the main chamber, so if you'll excuse me—"

Still talking, he reached up and pulled a cord. A whistle blew. Two bells and a gong rang out.† Then, with a tremendous blast of steam that nearly parboiled all of them, two huge steel doors located in the interior of the mountain began to slide open. Almost immediately, the doors stuck, and within minutes the place was swarming with gnomes, yelling and pointing and arguing about whose fault it was.

There is a saying on Krynn that says that everything gnomish makes five times the noise it needs to.

Tasslehoff Burrfoot had been making plans in the back of his mind as to what he would do after this adventure had ended and all the dragons were slain (the kender tried to maintain a positive outlook).The first thing he had planned to do was to go and spend a few months with his friend, Sestun, the gully dwarf in Pax Tharkas. The gully dwarves led interesting lives, and Tas knew he could settle there quite happily, as long as he didn't have to eat their cooking.

But the moment Tas entered Mount Nevermind, he decided the first thing he would do was come back and live with the gnomes. The kender had never seen anything quite so wonderful in his entire life. He stopped dead in his tracks.

Gnosh glanced at him. "Impressive, isn't it?" he asked.

"Not quite the word *I'd* use," Fizban muttered. They stood in the central portion of the gnome city. Built within an old shaft of a volcano,† it was hundreds of yards across and miles high.The city was constructed in levels around the shaft. Tas stared up . . . and up . . . and up. . . .

"How many levels are there?" the kender asked, nearly falling over backward trying to see.

"Thirty-five and—"

"Thirty-five!" Tas repeated in awe. "I'd hate to live on that thirty-fifth level. How many stairs do you have to climb?"

Gnosh sniffed. "Primitive devices we improved upon long ago and now"—he gestured—"view someofthemarvelsoftechnologywehaveinoperat—"

"I can see," said Tas, lowering his eyes to ground level. "You must be preparing for a great battle. I never saw so many catapults in my life . . ."

The kender's voice died. Even as he watched, a whistle sounded, a catapult went off with a twang, and a gnome went sailing through the air. Tas wasn't looking at machines of war, he was looking at the devices that had replaced stairs!

The bottom floor of the chamber was filled with catapults, every type of catapult ever conceived by gnomes. There were sling catapults, cross-bow catapults, willow-sprung catapults, steam-driven catapults (still experimental—they were working on adjusting the water temperature).

In an early draft of the story, we explained the gnomish efforts to invent a lighting system for the long tunnel that connected the exterior of the volcano to its large open interior. Concerned that the human knights of Solamnia could not see in the dark as the gnomes could, they built the following:

Action: They placed long steel rods running the length of the corridor, the ends of which were lowered down into the molten magma of the volcano far below.

Result: The hall was lit but the heat roasted anything that attempted to pass through Krynn's first toaster oven.

Action: Plumbing of ice-cold water down from the mountain glacier lake at the top of Mt. Nevermind to cool the space between the rods.

Result: The pipes leaked. This made the corridor both hot and cold at the same time and

Surrounding the catapults, over the catapults, under the catapults, and through the catapults were strung miles and miles of rope which operated a crazed assortment of gears and wheels and pulleys, all turning and squeaking and cranking. Out of the floor, out of the machines themselves, and thrusting out from the sides of the walls were huge levers which scores of gnomes were either pushing or pulling or sometimes both at once.

"I don't suppose," Fizban asked in a hopeless tone, "that the Examination Room would be on the ground level?"

Gnosh shook his head. "Examination Room on level fifteen—"

The old mage heaved a heart-rending sigh.

Suddenly there was a horrible grinding sound that set Tas's teeth on edge.

"Ah, they're ready for us. Come along, " Gnosh said.

Tas leaped after him gleefully as they approached a giant catapult. A gnome gestured at them irritably, pointing to a long line of gnomes waiting their turn. Tas jumped into the seat of the huge sling catapult, staring eagerly up into the shaft. Above him, he could see gnomes peering down at him from various balconies, all of them surrounded by great machines, whistles, ropes, and huge, shapeless things hanging from the sides of the wall like bats. Gnosh stood beside him, scolding.

"Elders first, young man, so get outoftherethisinstantandlet"—he dragged Tasslehoff out of the seat with remarkable strength—"themagicusergofirst—"

"Uh, that's quite all right," Fizban protested, stumbling backward into a pile of rope. "I—I seem to recall a spell of mine that will take me right to the top. Levitate. How did that g-go? Just give me a moment."

"*You* were the one in a hurry—" Gnosh said severely, glaring at Fizban. The gnomes standing in line began to shout rudely, pushing and shoving and jostling.

"Oh, very well," the old mage snarled, and he climbed into the seat,with Gnosh's help.

The gnome operating the lever that launched the catapult yelled something at Gnosh which sounded like "whalevel?"

filled the corridor with an impenetrable fog.

Action: A gigantic mechanical fan was set at one end of the tunnel to blow out the fog.

Result: The tunnel was freezing cold, burning hot, impossible to see in, and filled with a roaring wind that made it impossible to hear—but, by Paladine, that corridor was LIT!

The gnomes were the contribution of rebel-engineer-turned-storyteller Jeff Grubb. As a failed tinkerer myself, I find that I identify with the gnomes quite a bit. —TRH

Gnosh pointed up, yelling back. *"Skimbosh!"*

The chief walked over to stand in front of the first of a series of five levers. An inordinate number of ropes stretched upward into infinity. Fizban sat miserably in the seat of the catapult, still trying to recall his spell.

"Now," yelled Gnosh, drawing Tas closer so he could have the advantage of an excellent view, "in just a moment, the chief will give the signal—yes, there it is—"

The chief pulled on one of the ropes.

"What does that do?" Tas interrupted.

"The rope rings a bell on *Skimbosh,* er, level fifteen, telling them to expect an arrival—"

"What if the bell doesn't ring?" Fizban demanded loudly.

"Then a second bell rings telling them that the first bell didn't—"

"What happens down here if the bell didn't ring?"

"Nothing. It's Skimbosh'sproblemnotyours—"

"It's my problem if they don't know I'm coming!" Fizban shouted."Or do I just drop in and surprise them!"

"Ah," Gnosh said proudly, "you see—"

"I'm getting out . . ." stated Fizban.

"No, wait," Gnosh said, talking faster and faster in his anguish, "they're ready—"

"Who's ready?" Fizban demanded irritably.

"Skimbosh! With the net tocatchyou,yousee—"

"Net!" Fizban turned pale. "That does it!" He flung a foot over the edge.

But before he could move, the chief reached out and pulled on the first lever. The grinding sound started again as the catapult began pivoting in its mooring. The sudden motion threw Fizban back, knocking his hat over his eyes.

"What's happening?" Tas shouted.

"They're getting him in position," Gnosh yelled. "The longitude and latitude have been precalculated and the catapult set to come into the correct location to send the passenger—"

"What about the net?" Tas yelled.

"The magician flies up to Skimbosh—oh, quite safely, I assure you—we've done studies, in fact, proving that flying is safer than walking—and just

when he's at the height of his trajectory, beginning to drop a bit, Skimbosh throws a net out underneath him, catching him just like this"—Gnosh demonstrated with his hand, making a snapping motion like catching a fly—"and hauls him—"

"What incredible timing that must take!"

"The timing is ingenious since it all depends on a certain hook we've developed, though"—Gnosh pursed his lips, his eyebrows drawing together—"something is throwing the timing off a bit, but there's a committee—"†

There are at least fifty gnomish guilds, and each guild has a variable—but innumerable—number of committees. Rarely does the right hand let the left guild know what it is doing.

The gnome pulled down on the lever and Fizban—with a shriek—went sailing through the air.

"Oh dear," said Gnosh, staring, "it appears—"

"What? What?" Tas yelled, trying to see.

"The net's opened too soon again"—Gnosh shook his head—"and that's the second time today that's happened on Skimbosh alone andthisdefinitelywillbebroughtupatthe nextmeetingoftheNet Guild—"

Tas stared, open-mouthed, at the sight of Fizban whizzing through the air, propelled from below by the tremendous force of the catapult, and suddenly the kender saw what Gnosh was talking about. The net on level fifteen—instead of opening *after* the mage had flown past and then catching him as he started to fall—opened *before* the mage reached level fifteen. Fizban hit the net and was flattened like a squashed spider. For a moment he clung there precariously—arms and legs akimbo, then he fell.

Instantly bells and gongs rang out.

"Don't tell me," Tas guessed miserably. "That's the alarm which means the net failed."

"Quite, but don't be alarmed (small joke)," Gnosh chuckled, "because the alarms trip a device to open the net on level thirteen, just in time, oops—a bit late, well, there's still level twelve—"

"Do something!" Tas shrieked.

"Don't get so worked up!" Gnosh said angrily. "And I'll finishwhatIwasabouttosayaboutthefinal emergencybackupsystem andthatis, oh, hereitgoes—"

Tas watched in amazement as the bottoms dropped out of six huge barrels hanging from the walls on level three, sending thousands of sponges tumbling down onto the floor in the center of the chamber.This was done—apparently—in case all the nets on every level failed. Fortunately, the net on level nine actually worked, spreading out beneath the mage just in time. Then it folded up around him and whisked him over to the balcony where the gnomes, hearing the mage cursing and swearing inside, appeared reluctant to let him out.

"Sonoweverything'sfineandit'syourturn," said Gnosh.

"Just one last question!" Tas yelled at Gnosh as he sat down in the seat. "What happens if the emergency backup system with the sponges fails?"

"Ingenious—" said Gnosh happily, "because you see if the sponges come down a little too late, the alarm goes off, releasing a huge barrel of water into the center, and, since the sponges are there already, its easy to clean up the mess—"

The chief pulled the lever.

Tas had been expecting all sorts of fascinating things in the Examination Room, but he found it—to his surprise—nearly empty. It was lighted by a hole drilled through the face of the mountain which admitted the sunlight. (This simple but ingenious device had been suggested to the gnomes by a visiting dwarf who called it a 'window;' the gnomes were quite proud of it.) There were three tables, but little else. On the central table, surrounded by gnomes, rested the dragon orb and his hoopak.†

Tas is in luck, because gnomish philosophy is: If it's fixed, break it.—MW

It was back to its original size, Tas noted with interest. It looked the same—still a round piece of crystal, with a kind of milky colored mist swirling around inside. A young Knight of Solamnia with an intensely bored expression on his face stood near the orb, guarding it. His bored expression changed sharply at the approach of strangers.

"Quiteallright," Gnosh told the knight reassuringly, "these are the two Lord Gunthar sent word about—" Still talking, Gnosh hustled them over to the central table. The gnome's eyes were bright as he regarded the orb. "A dragon orb," he murmured happily, "after all these years—"

"What years?" Fizban snapped, stopping at some distance from the table.

"You see," Gnosh explained, "each gnome has a Life Quest assigned to him at birth, and from then

on his only ambition in life is to fulfill that Life Quest, and it was my Life Quest to study the dragon orb since—"

"But the dragon orbs have been missing for hundreds of years!" Tas said incredulously. "No one knew about them! How could it be your Life Quest?"

"Oh, we knew about them," Gnosh answered, "because it was my grandfather's Life Quest, and then my father's Life Quest. Both of them died without ever seeing a dragon orb. I feared I might, too, but now finally, one has appeared, and I can establish our family's place in the afterlife—"

"You mean you can't get to the—er—afterlife until you complete the Life Quest?" Tas asked. "But your grandfather and your father—"

"Probably most uncomfortable," Gnosh said, looking sad, "wherever they are—My goodness!"

A remarkable change had come over the dragon orb. It began to swirl and shimmer with many different colors—as if in agitation.

Muttering strange words, Fizban walked to the orb and set his hand upon it. Instantly, it went black. Fizban cast a glance around the room, his expression so severe and frightening that even Tas fell back before him. The knight sprang forward.

"Get out!" the mage thundered. "All of you!"

"I was ordered not to leave and I'm not—" The knight reached for his sword, but Fizban whispered a few words. The knight slumped to the floor.

The gnomes vanished from the room instantly, leaving only Gnosh, wringing his hands, his face twisted in agony.

"Come on, Gnosh!" Tas urged. "I've never seen him like this. We better do as he says. If we don't, he's liable to turn us into gully dwarves or something icky like that!"

Whimpering, Gnosh allowed Tas to lead him out of the room. As he stared back at the dragon orb, the door slammed shut.

"My Life Quest . . ." the gnome moaned.

"I'm sure it will be all right," Tas said, although he wasn't sure, not in the least. He hadn't liked the look on Fizban's face. In fact, it hadn't even seemed to be Fizban's face at all—or anyone Tas wanted to know!

Tas felt chilled and there was a tight knot in the pit of his stomach. The gnomes muttered among

themselves and cast baleful glances at him. Tas swallowed, trying to get a bitter taste out of his mouth. Then he drew Gnosh to one side.

"Gnosh, did you discover anything about the orb when you studied it?" Tas asked in a low voice.

"Well," Gnosh appeared thoughtful, "I did find out that there's something inside of it, or seems to be, because I'd stare at it and stare at it without seeing anything for the longest time then, right when I was ready to quit, I'd see words swirling about in the mist—"

"Words?" Tas interrupted eagerly. "What did they say?"

Gnosh shook his head. "I don't know," he said solemnly, "because I couldn't read them; no one could, not even a member of the Foreign Language Guild—"

"Magic, probably," Tas muttered to himself.

"Yes," Gnosh said miserably, "that's what I decided—"

The door blew open, as if something had exploded.

Gnosh whirled around, terrified. Fizban stood in the doorway, holding a small black bag in one hand, his staff and Tasslehoff's hoopak in the other. Gnosh sprang past him.

"The orb!" he screeched, so upset he actually completed a sentence. "You've got it!"

"Yes, Gnosh," said Fizban.

The mage's voice sounded tired, and Tas, looking at him closely, saw that he was on the verge of exhaustion. His skin was gray, his eyelids drooped. He leaned heavily on his staff. "Come with me, my boy," he said to the gnome. "And do not worry. Your Life Quest will be fulfilled. But now the orb must be taken before the Council of Whitestone."

"Come with you," Gnosh repeated in astonishment, "to the Council"—he clasped his hands together in excitement—"where perhaps I'll be asked to make a report, do you think—"

"I wouldn't doubt it in the least," Fizban answered.

"Right away, just give me time to pack, where's my papers—"

Gnosh dashed off. Fizban whipped around to face the other gnomes who had been sneaking up

behind him, reaching out eagerly for his staff. He scowled so alarmingly that they stumbled backward and vanished into the Examination Room.

"What did you find out?" Tas asked, hesitantly approaching Fizban. The old mage seemed surrounded by darkness. "The gnomes didn't do anything to it, did they?"

"No, no." Fizban sighed. "Fortunately for them. For it is still active and very powerful. Much will depend on the decisions a few make—perhaps the fate of the world."

"What do you mean? Won't the Council make the decisions?"

"You don't understand, my boy," Fizban said gently. "Stop a moment, I must rest." The mage sat down, leaning against a wall. Shaking his head, he continued. "I concentrated my will on the orb, Tas. Oh, not to control dragons," he added, seeing the kender's eyes widen. "I looked into the future."

"What did you see?" Tas asked hesitantly, not certain from the mage's somber expression that he wanted to know.

"I saw two roads stretching before us. If we take the easiest, it will appear the best at the beginning, but darkness will fall at the end, never to be lifted. If we take the other road, it will be hard and difficult to travel. It could cost the lives of some we love, dear boy. Worse, it might cost others their very souls. But only through these great sacrifices will we find hope." Fizban closed his eyes.

"And this involves the orb?" Tas asked, shivering.

"Yes."

"Do you know what must be done to . . . to take the d-dark road?"Tas dreaded the answer.

"I do," Fizban replied in a low voice. "But the decisions have not been left in my hands. That will be up to others."

"I see," Tas sighed. "Important people, I suppose. People like kings and elflords and knights." Then Fizban's words echoed in his mind. *The lives of some we love . . .*

Suddenly a lump formed in Tas's throat, choking him. His head dropped into his hands. This adventure was turning out all wrong! Where was Tanis? And dear old Caramon? And pretty Tika? He had tried not to think about them, particularly after that dream.

And Flint—I shouldn't have gone without him, Tas thought miserably. He might die, he might be dead right now! *The lives of some you love!* I never thought about any of us dying—not really. I always figured that if we were together we could beat anything! But now, we've gotten scattered somehow. And things are going all wrong!

Tas felt Fizban's hand stroke his topknot, his one great vanity. And for the first time in his life, the kender felt very lost and alone and frightened. The mage's grip tightened around him affectionately. Burying his face in Fizban's sleeve, Tas began to cry.

Fizban patted him gently. "Yes," the mage repeated, "important people."

6

The Council of Whitestone. An important person.

The Council of Whitestone met upon the twenty-eighth day of December, a day known as Famine Day† in Solamnia, for it commemorated the suffering of the people during the first winter following the Cataclysm. Lord Gunthar thought it fitting to hold the Council meeting on this day, which was marked by fasting and meditation.

Famine Day in Solamnia is apparently more specific a commemoration than the generalized Famine Time remembered elsewhere on Krynn.

It had been over a month since the armies sailed for Palanthas. The news Gunthar received from that city was not good. A report had arrived early on the morning of the twenty-eighth, in fact. Reading it twice over, he sighed heavily, frowned, and tucked the paper into his belt.

The Council of Whitestone had met once before within the recent past, a meeting precipitated by the arrival of the refugee elves in Southern Ergoth and the appearance of the dragonarmies in northern Solamnia. This Council meeting was several months in the planning, and so all members—either seated or advisory—were represented. Seated members, those who could vote, included the Knights of Solamnia, the gnomes, the hill dwarves, the dark-skinned, sea-faring people of Northern Ergoth,† and a representative of the Solamnic exiles living on Sancrist. Advisory members were the elves, the mountain dwarves, and the kender. These members were invited to express their opinions, but they could not vote.

These dark-skinned humans share the island of Northern Ergoth with the kender who remain in Kenderhome (AKA: Hylo).

The first Council meeting, however, had not gone well. Some of the old feuds and animosities between the races represented burst into flame. Arman Kharas, representative of the mountain dwarves, and Duncan Hammerrock, of the hill dwarves, had to be physically restrained at one point, or blood from that ancient feud might have flowed again. Alhana Starbreeze, representative of the Silvanesti in her father's absence, refused to speak a word during the entire session. Alhana had come only because Porthios of the Qualinesti was there. She feared an alliance between the Qualinesti and the humans and was determined to prevent it.

Alhana need not have worried. Such was the distrust between humans and elves, that they spoke to each other only out of politeness. Not even Lord Gunthar's impassioned speech in which he had declared, "Our unity begins peace; our division ends hope!" made an impression.

Porthios's answer to this had been to blame the dragons' reappearance on the humans. The humans, therefore, could extricate themselves from this disaster. Shortly after Porthios made his position clear, Alhana rose haughtily and left, leaving no one with any doubts about the position of the Silvanesti.

The mountain dwarf, Arman Kharas, had declared that his people would be willing to help, but that until the Hammer of Kharas was found, the mountain dwarves could not be united. No one knew at the time that the companions would soon return the Hammer, so Gunthar was forced to discount the aid of the dwarves. The only person, in

fact, who offered help was Kronin Thistleknott, chief of the kender. Since the last thing any sane country wanted was the "aid" of an army of kenders, this gesture was received with polite smiles, while the members exchanged horrified looks behind Kronin's back.

The first Council disbanded, therefore, without accomplishing much of anything.†

Gunthar had higher hopes for this second Council meeting. The discovery of the dragon orb, of course, put everything in a much brighter light. Representatives from both elven factions had arrived. These included the Speaker of the Suns, who brought with him a human claiming to be a cleric of Paladine. Gunthar had heard a great deal about Elistan from Sturm, and he looked forward to meeting him. Just who would represent the Silvanesti, Gunthar wasn't certain. He assumed it was the lord who had been declared regent following Alhana Starbreeze's mysterious disappearance.

Although it may have existed at some time in the past, during this era, the Council of Whitestone was formed and held its first meeting between Dragons of Autumn Twilight *and* Dragons of Winter Night.

The elves had arrived on Sancrist two days ago. Their tents stood out in the fields, gaily colored silk flags fluttering in brilliant contrast to the gray, stormy sky. They were the only other race to attend. There had not been time to send a message to the mountain dwarves, and the hill dwarves were reported to be fighting for their lives against the dragonarmies; no messenger could reach them.

Gunthar hoped this meeting would unite the humans and the elves in the great fight to drive the dragonarmies from Ansalon. But his hopes were dashed before the meeting began.

After scanning the report from the armies in Palanthas, Gunthar left his tent, preparing to make a final tour of the Glade of the Whitestone to see that everything was in order. Wills, his retainer, came dashing after him.

"My lord," the old man puffed, "return immediately."

"What is it?" Gunthar asked. But the old retainer was too much out of breath to reply.

Sighing, the Solamnic lord went back to his tent where he found Lord Michael, dressed in full armor, pacing nervously.

"What's the matter?" Gunthar said, his heart sinking as he saw the grave expression on the young lord's face.

Michael advanced quickly, seizing Gunthar by the arm. "My lord, we have received word that the elves will demand the return of the dragon orb. If we won't return it, they are prepared to go to war to recover it!"

"What?" Gunthar demanded incredulously. "War! Against us! That's ludicrous! They can't—Are you certain? How reliable is this information?"

"Very reliable, I'm afraid, Lord Gunthar."

"My lord, I present Elistan, cleric of Paladine," Michael said. "I beg pardon for not introducing him earlier, but my mind has been in a turmoil since he first brought me this news."

"I have heard a great deal about you, sir," Lord Gunthar said, extending his hand to the man.

The knight's eyes studied Elistan curiously. Gunthar hardly knew what he had expected to see in a purported cleric of Paladine, perhaps a weak-eyed aesthetic, pale and lean from study. Gunthar was not prepared for this tall, well-built man who might have ridden to battle with the best of the knights. The ancient symbol of Paladine—a platinum medallion engraved with a dragon—hung about his neck.

Gunthar reviewed all he had heard from Sturm concerning Elistan, including the cleric's intention to try and convince the elves to unite with the humans. Elistan smiled wearily, as if aware of every thought passing through Gunthar's mind. They were the thoughts he answered.

"Yes, I have failed," Elistan admitted. "It was all I could do to persuade them to attend the Council meeting, and they have come here only, I fear, to give you an ultimatum: return the orb to the elves or fight to retain it."

Gunthar sank into a chair, gesturing weakly with his hand for the others to be seated. Before him, on a table, were spread maps of the lands of Ansalon, showing in shades of darkness, the insidious advance of the dragonarmies. Gunthar's gaze rested on the maps, then suddenly he swept them to the floor.

"We might as well give up right now!" he snarled. "Send a message to the Dragon Highlords: 'Don't bother to come and wipe us out. We're managing quite nicely on our own.' "

Angrily, he hurled on the table the message he had received."There! That's from Palanthas. The

people have insisted the knights leave the city. The Palanthians are negotiating with the Dragon Highlords, and the presence of the knights 'seriously compromises their position.' They refuse to give us any aid. And so an army of a thousand Palanthians sits idle!"

"What is Lord Derek doing, my lord?" Michael asked.

"He and the knights and a thousand footmen, refugees from the occupied lands in Throtyl, are fortifying the High Clerist's tower, south of Palanthas," Gunthar said wearily. "It guards the only pass through the Vingaard Mountains. We'll protect Palanthas for a time, but if the dragonarmies get through . . ." He fell silent. "Damn it," he whispered, beating his fist gently upon the table, "we could hold that pass with two thousand men! The fools! And now this!" He waved his hand in the direction of the elven tents.

Gunthar sighed, letting his head fall into his hands. "Well, what do you counsel, cleric?"

Elistan was quiet for a moment, before he answered. "It is written in the Disks of Mishakal that evil, by its very nature, will always turn in upon itself. Thus it becomes self-defeating." He laid his hand upon Gunthar's shoulder. "I do not know what may come of this meeting. My gods have kept this secret from me. It could be they themselves do not know; that the future of the world stands in balance, and what we decide here will determine it. I do know this: Do not enter with defeat in your heart, for that will be the first victory of evil."

So saying, Elistan rose and left the tent quietly.

Gunthar sat in silence after the cleric had gone. It seemed that the whole world was silent, in fact, he thought. The wind had died during the night. The storm clouds hung low and heavy, muffling sound so that even the clarion trumpet's call marking day's dawning seemed flat. A rustling broke his concentration. Michael was slowly gathering up the spilled maps.

Gunthar raised his head, rubbing his eyes.

"What do you think?"

"Of what? The elves?"

"That cleric," Gunthar said, staring out the tent opening.

"Certainly not what I would have expected," Michael answered, his gaze following Gunthar's. "More like the stories we've heard of the clerics of old, the ones that guided the Knights in the days before the Cataclysm. He's not much like these charlatans we've got now. Elistan is a man who would stand beside you on the field of battle, calling down Paladine's blessing with one hand while wielding his mace with the other. He wears the medallion that none have seen since the gods abandoned us. But is he a true cleric?" Michael shrugged. "It will take a lot more than a medallion to convince me."

"I agree." Gunthar rose to his feet and began to walk toward the tent flap. "Well, it is nearly time. Stay here, Michael, in case any more reports come in." Starting to leave, he paused at the entrance to the tent. "How odd it is, Michael," he murmured, his eyes following Elistan, now no more than a speck of white in the distance. "We have always been a people who looked to the gods for our hope, a people of faith, who distrusted magic. Yet now we look to magic for that hope, and when a chance comes to renew our faith, we question it."

Lord Michael made no answer. Gunthar shook his head and, still pondering, made his way to the Glade of the Whitestone.

As Gunthar said, the Solamnic people had always been faithful followers of the gods. Long ago, in the days before the Cataclysm, the Glade of the Whitestone had been one of the holy centers of worship.† The phenomenon of the white rock had attracted the attention of the curious longer than anyone remembered. The Kingpriest of Istar himself had blessed the huge white rock that sat in the middle of a perpetually green glade, declaring it sacred to the gods and forbidding any mortal being to touch it.

Whitestone Glade has always been an important religious site to the Solamnics because it was here that Vinas Solamnus received the order of the Knighthood from the three gods Paladine, Kiri-Jolith, and Habbakuk.

Even after the Cataclysm, when belief in the old gods died, the Glade remained a sacred place. Perhaps that was because not even the Cataclysm had affected it. Legend held that when the fiery mountain fell from the sky, the ground around the Whitestone cracked and split apart, but the Whitestone remained intact.

So awesome was the sight of the huge white rock that even now none dared either approach or touch it. What strange powers it possessed, none could say. All they knew was that the air around the Whitestone was always springlike and warm. No matter how bitter the winter, the grass in Whitestone Glade was always green.

Though his heart was heavy, Gunthar relaxed as he stepped inside the glade and breathed the warm, sweet air. For a moment, he felt once again the touch of Elistan's hand upon his shoulder, imparting a feeling of inner peace.

Glancing around quickly, he saw all in readiness. Massive wooden chairs with ornately carved backs had been placed on the green grass. Five for the voting members of the Council stood to the left side of the Whitestone, three for the advisory members stood on the right. Polished benches for the witnesses to the proceedings as demanded by the Measure, sat facing the Whitestone and the Council members.

Some of the witnesses had already begun arriving, Gunthar noticed. Most of the elven party traveling with the Speaker and the Silvanesti lord were taking their seats. The two estranged elven races sat near each other, apart from the humans who were filing in as well. Everyone sat quietly, some in remembrance of Famine Day; others, like the gnomes, who did not celebrate that holiday, in awe of their surroundings. Seats in the front row were reserved for honored guests or for those with leave to speak before the Council.

Gunthar saw the Speaker's stern-faced son, Porthios, enter with a retinue of elven warriors. They took their seats in the front. Gunthar wondered where Elistan was. He'd intended to ask him to speak. He had been impressed with the man's words (even if he was a charlatan) and hoped he would repeat them.

As he searched in vain for Elistan, he saw three strange figures enter and seat themselves in the front row: it was the old mage in his bent and shapeless hat, his kender friend, and a gnome they had brought back with them from Mount Nevermind. The three had arrived back from their journey only last night.

Gunthar was forced to turn his attention back to the Whitestone. The advisory Council members were entering. There were only two, Lord Quinath of the Silvanesti, and the Speaker of the Suns.† Gunthar looked at the Speaker curiously, knowing he was one of the few beings on Krynn to still remember the horrors of the Cataclysm.

The correct form of address is Speaker of Suns. The fact that the address form is plural seems to indicate an ancient knowledge by the elves that there are 'other suns.' although there is no real foundation for this beliefe other than my own opinion. As to the reference here to 'Speaker of the Suns,' I can only hope that Lord Gunthar realizes that this is a slight breach of etiquette and does not use this form again, even though it was heard frequently in Qualinost.—TRH

The Speaker was so stooped that he seemed almost crippled. His hair was gray, his face haggard. But as he took his seat and turned his gaze to the witnesses, Gunthar saw the elf's eyes were bright and arresting. Lord Quinath, seated next to him, was known to Gunthar, who considered him as arrogant and proud as Porthios of the Qualinesti, but lacking in the intelligence Porthios possessed.

As for Porthios, Gunthar thought he could probably come to like the Speaker's eldest son quite well. Porthios had every characteristic the knights admired, with one exception, his quick temper.

Gunthar's observations were interrupted, for now it was time for the voting Council members to enter and Gunthar had to take his place. First came Mir Kar-thon of Northern Ergoth, a dark complexioned man with iron-gray hair and the arms of a giant. Next came Serdin MarThasal, representing the Exiles on Sancrist, and finally Lord Gunthar, Knight of Solamnia.

Once seated, Gunthar glanced around a final time. The huge Whitestone glistened behind him, casting its own strange radiance, for the sun would not shine today. On the other side of the Whitestone sat the Speaker, next to him Lord Quinath. Across from them, facing the Council, sat the witnesses upon their benches. The kender was sitting subdued, swinging his short legs on his tall bench. The gnome shuffled through what looked like a ream of paper; Gunthar shuddered, wishing there'd been time to ask for a condensed report. The old magician yawned and scratched his head, peering around vaguely.

All was ready. At Gunthar's signal, two knights entered, bearing a golden stand and a wooden chest. A silence that was almost deathlike descended on the crowd as they watched the entrance of the dragon orb.

The knights came to a halt, standing directly in front of the Whitestone. Here, one of the knights

placed the golden stand upon the ground. The other set down the chest, unlocked it, and carefully brought forth the orb that was back to its original size, over two feet in diameter.

A murmur went through the crowd. The Speaker of the Suns shifted uncomfortably, scowling. His son, Porthios, turned to say something to an elflord near him. All of the elves, Gunthar noted, were armed. Not a good sign, from what little he knew of elven protocol.

He had no choice but to proceed. Calling the meeting to order, Lord Gunthar Uth Wistan announced, "Let the Council of Whitestone begin."

After about two minutes, it was obvious to Tasslehoff that things were in a real mess. Before Lord Gunthar had even concluded his speech of welcome, the Speaker of the Suns rose.

"My talk will be brief," the elven leader stated in a voice that matched the steely gray of the storm clouds above him. "The Silvanesti, the Qualinesti, and the Kaganesti met in council shortly after the orb was removed from our camp. It is the first time the members of the three communities have met since the Kinslayer wars." He paused, laying a heavy emphasis on those last words. Then he continued.

"We have decided to set aside our own differences in our perfect agreement that the dragon orb belongs in the hands of the elves, not in the hands of humans or any other race upon Krynn. Therefore, we come before the Council of Whitestone and ask that the dragon orb be given over to us forthwith. In return, we guarantee that we will take it to our lands and keep it safe until such time—if ever—it be needed."

The Speaker sat down, his dark eyes sweeping over the crowd, its silence broken now by a murmur of soft voices. The other Council members, sitting next to Lord Gunthar, shook their heads, their faces grim. The dark-skinned leader of the Northern Ergoth people whispered to Lord Gunthar in a harsh voice, clenching his fist to emphasize his words.

Lord Gunthar, after listening and nodding for several minutes, rose to his feet to respond. His speech was cool, calm, complimentary to the elves.

But it said—between the lines—that the Knights would see the elves in the Abyss before they gave them the dragon orb.

The Speaker, understanding perfectly the message of steel couched in the pretty phrases, rose to reply. He spoke only one sentence, but it brought the crowd of witnesses to their feet.

"Then, Lord Gunthar," the Speaker said, "the elves declare that, from this time on—we are at war!"

Humans and elves both headed for the dragon orb that sat upon its golden stand, its milky white insides swirling gently within the crystal. Gunthar shouted for order time and again, banging the hilt of his sword upon the table. The Speaker spoke a few words sharply in elven, staring hard at his son, Porthios, and finally order was restored.

But the atmosphere snapped like the air before a storm. Gunthar talked. The Speaker answered. The Speaker talked. Gunthar answered. The dark-skinned mariner lost his temper and made a few cutting remarks about elves. The lord of the Silvanesti reduced him to quivering anger with his sarcastic rejoinders. Several of the knights left, only to return armed to the teeth. They came to stand near Gunthar, their hands on their weapons. The elves, led by Porthios, rose to surround their own leaders.

Gnosh, his report held fast in his hand, began to realize he wasn't going to be asked to give it.

Tasslehoff looked around despairingly for Elistan. He kept hoping desperately the cleric would come. Elistan could calm these people down. Or maybe Laurana. Where was she? There'd been no word of his friends, the elves had told the kender coldly. She and her brother had apparently vanished in the wilderness. I shouldn't have left them, Tas thought. I shouldn't be here. Why, why did this crazy old mage bring me? I'm useless! Maybe Fizban could do something? Tas looked at the mage hopefully, but Fizban was sound asleep!

"Please, wake up!" Tas begged, shaking him. "Somebody's got to do something!"

At that moment, he heard Lord Gunthar yell, "The dragon orb is *not* yours by right! Lady Laurana and the others were bringing it to *us* when they were shipwrecked! You tried to keep it on Ergoth by force, and your own daughter—"

"Mention not my daughter!" the Speaker said in a deep, harsh voice. "I do not have a daughter."

Something broke within Tasslehoff. Confused memories of Laurana fighting desperately against the evil wizard who guarded the orb, Laurana battling draconians, Laurana firing her bow at the white dragon, Laurana ministering to him so tenderly when he'd been near death. To be cast off by her own people when she was working so desperately to save them, when she had sacrificed so much. . . .

"Stop this!" Tasslehoff heard himself yelling at the top of his voice. "Stop this right now and listen to me!"

Suddenly he saw, to his astonishment, that everyone *had* stopped talking and was staring at him.

Now that he had his audience, Tas realized he didn't have any idea what to say to all of these important people. But he knew he had to say something. After all, he thought, this is my fault—I read about these damn orbs. Gulping, he slid off his bench and walked toward the Whitestone and the two hostile groups clustered around it. He thought he saw—out of the corner of his eye—Fizban grinning from under his hat.

"I—I . . ." The kender stammered, wondering what to say. He was saved by a sudden inspiration.

"I demand the right to represent my people," Tasslehoff said proudly, "and take my place on the advisory council."

Flipping his tassle of brown hair over his shoulder, the kender came to stand right in front of the dragon orb. Looking up, he could see the Whitestone towering over it and over him. Tas stared at the stone, shivering, then quickly turned his gaze from the rock to Gunthar and the Speaker of the Suns.

And then Tasslehoff knew what he had to do. He began to shake with fear. He—Tasslehoff Burrfoot—who'd never been afraid of anything in his life! He'd faced dragons without trembling, but the knowledge of what he was going to do now appalled him. His hands felt as if he'd been making snowballs without gloves on. His tongue seemed to belong in some larger person's mouth. But Tas was resolute. He just had to keep them talking, keep them from guessing what he planned.

"You've never taken us kenders very seriously, you know," Tas began, his voice sounding too loud and shrill in his own ears, "and I can't say I blame you much. We don't have a strong sense of responsibility, I guess, and we are probably too curious for own good—but, I ask you, how are you going to find out anything if you're not curious?"

Tas could see the Speaker's face turn to steel, even Lord Gunthar was scowling. The kender edged nearer the dragon orb.

"We cause lots of trouble, I suppose, without meaning to, and occasionally some of us do happen to acquire certain things which aren't ours. But one thing the kender know is—"

Tasslehoff broke into a run. Quick and lithe as a mouse, he slipped easily through the hands that tried to catch him, reaching the dragon orb within a matter of seconds. Faces blurred around him, mouths opened, shrieking and yelling at him. But they were too late.

In one swift, smooth movement, Tasslehoff hurled the dragon orb at the huge, gleaming Whitestone.

The round, gleaming crystal—its insides swirling in agitation—hung suspended in the air for long, long seconds. Tas wondered if the orb had the power to halt its flight. But it was just a fevered impression in the kender's mind.

The dragon orb struck the rock and shattered, bursting into a thousand sparkling pieces. For an instant, a ball of milky white smoke hung in the air, as if trying desperately to hold itself together. Then the warm, springlike breeze of the glade caught it and swept it apart.

There was intense, awful silence.

The kender stood, looking calmly down at the shattered dragon orb.

"We know," he said in a small voice that dropped into the dreadful silence like a tiny drop of rain, "we should be fighting dragons. Not each other."

No one moved. No one spoke. Then there was a thump.

Gnosh had fainted.

The silence broke—almost as shattering as the breaking of the orb. Lord Gunthar and the Speaker both lunged at Tas. One caught hold of the kender's left shoulder, one his right.

"What have you done?" Lord Gunthar's face was livid, his eyes wild as he gripped the kender with trembling hands.

"You have brought death upon us all!" The Speaker's fingers bit into Tas's flesh like the claws of a predatory bird. "You have destroyed our only hope!"

"And for that, he himself will be the first to die!"

Porthios—tall, grim-faced elflord—loomed above the cowering kender, his sword glistening in his hand. The kender stood his ground between the elven king and the knight, his small face pale, his expression defiant. He had known when he committed his crime that death would be the penalty.

Tanis will be unhappy over what I've done, Tas thought sadly. But at least he'll hear that I died bravely.

"Now, now, now . . ." said a sleepy voice. "No one's going to die! At least not at this moment. Quit waving that sword around, Porthios! Someone'll get hurt."

Tas peered out from under a heaving sea of arms and shining armor to see Fizban, yawning, step over the inert body of the gnome and totter toward them. Elves and humans made way for him to pass, as if compelled to do so by an unseen force.

Porthios whirled to face Fizban, so angry that saliva bubbled on his lips and his speech was nearly incoherent.

"Beware, old man, or you will share in the punishment!"

"I said quit waving that sword around," Fizban snapped irritably, wiggling a finger at the sword.

Porthios dropped his weapon with a wild cry. Clutching his stinging, burning hand, he stared down at the sword in astonishment—the hilt had grown thorns! Fizban came to stand next to the elflord and regarded him angrily.

"You're a fine young man, but you should have been taught some respect for your elders. I said to put that sword down and I meant it! Maybe you'll believe me next time!" Fizban's baleful gaze switched to the Speaker. "And you, Solostaran, were a good man about two hundred years ago. Managed to raise three fine children—*three* fine children, I said. Don't give me any of this nonsense about not having a daughter. You have one, and a fine girl she is. More sense than her father. Must take after her mother's side. Where was I? Oh, yes. You brought up Tanis Half-Elven, too. You know, Solostaran, between the four of these young people, we might save this world yet.

"Now I want everyone to take his seat. Yes, you, too, Lord Gunthar. Come along, Solostaran, I'll help. We old men have to stick together. Too bad you're such a damn fool."

Muttering into his beard, Fizban led the astounded Speaker to his chair. Porthios, his face twisted in pain, stumbled back to his seat with the help of his warriors.

Slowly the assembled elves and knights sat down, murmuring among themselves—all casting dark looks at the shattered dragon orb that lay beneath the Whitestone.

Fizban settled the Speaker in his seat, glowered at Lord Quinath, who thought he had something to say but quickly decided he didn't. Satisfied, the old mage came back to the front of the Whitestone where Tas stood, shaken and confused.

"You," Fizban looked at the kender as if he'd never seen him before, "go and attend to that poor chap." He waved a hand at the gnome, who was still out cold.

Feeling his knees tremble, Tasslehoff walked slowly over to Gnosh and knelt down beside him, glad to look at something other than the angry, fear-filled faces.

"Gnosh," he whispered miserably, patting the gnome on the cheek, "I'm sorry. I truly am. I mean about your Life Quest and your father's soul and everything. But there just didn't seem to be anything else to do."

Fizban turned around slowly and faced the assembled group, pushing his hat back on his head. "Yes, I'm going to lecture you. You deserve it, every one of you—so don't sit there looking self-righteous. That kender"—he pointed at Tasslehoff, who cringed—"has more brains beneath that ridiculous topknot of his than the lot of you have put together.† Do you know what would have happened to you if the kender hadn't had the guts to do what he did? Do you? Well, I'll tell you. Just let me find a

Dragon orbs cannot be harmed by magic. Only something as ruthless as Tas's breaking it could have had any effect.

seat here. . . ." Fizban peered around vaguely. "Ah, yes, there . . ." Nodding in satisfaction, the old mage toddled over and sat down on the ground, leaning his back against the sacred Whitestone!

The assembled knights gasped in horror. Gunthar leaped to his feet, appalled at this sacrilege.

"No mortal can touch the Whitestone!" he yelled, striding forward.

Fizban slowly turned his head to regard the furious knight. "One more word," the old mage said solemnly, "and I'll make your moustaches fall off. Now sit down and shut up!"

Sputtering, Gunthar was brought up short by an imperious gesture from the old man. The knight could do nothing but return to his seat.

"Where was I before I was interrupted?" Fizban scowled. Glancing around, his gaze fell on the broken pieces of the orb. "Oh, yes. I was about to tell you a story. One of you would have won the orb, of course. And you would have taken it—either to keep it 'safe' or to 'save the world.' And, yes, it is capable of saving the world, but only if you know how to use it. Who of you has this knowledge? Who has the strength? The orb was created by the greatest, most powerful mages of old. *All* the most powerful—do you understand? It was created by those of the White Robes and those of the Black Robes. It has the essence of both evil and good. The Red Robes brought both essences together and bound them with their force. Few there are now with the power and strength to understand the orb, to fathom its secrets, and to gain mastery over it. Few indeed"—Fizban's eyes gleamed—"and none who sit here!"

Silence had fallen now, a profound silence as they listened to the old mage, whose voice was strong and carried above the rising wind that was blowing the storm clouds from the sky.

"One of you would have taken the orb and used it, and you would have found that you had hurled yourself upon disaster. You would have been broken as surely as the kender broke the orb. As for hope being shattered, I tell you that hope was lost for a time, but now it has been new born—"

A sudden gust of wind caught the old mage's hat, blowing it off his head and tossing it playfully away from him. Snarling in irritation, Fizban crawled forward to pick it up.

Just as the mage leaned over, the sun broke through the clouds.There was a blazing flash of silver, followed by a splintering, deafening crack as though the land itself had split apart.

Half-blinded by the flaring light, people blinked and gazed in fear and awe at the terrifying sight before their eyes.

The Whitestone had been split asunder.

The old magician lay sprawled at its base, his hat clutched in his hand, his other arm flung over his head in terror. Above him, piercing the rock where he had been sitting, was a long weapon made of gleaming silver. It had been thrown by the silver arm of a black man, who walked over to stand beside it. Accompanying him were three people: an elven woman dressed in leather armor, an old, white-bearded dwarf, and Elistan.

Amid the stunned silence of the crowd, the black man reached out and lifted the weapon from the splintered remains of the rock. He held it high above his head, and the silver barbed point glittered brightly in the rays of the midday sun.

"I am Theros Ironfeld," the man called out in a deep voice, "and for the last month I have been forging these!" He shook the weapon in his hand. "I have taken molten silver from the well hidden deep within the heart of the Monument of the Silver Dragon. With the silver arm given me by the gods, I have forged the weapon as legend foretold. And this I bring to you—to all the people of Krynn—that we may join together and defeat the great evil that threatens to engulf us in darkness forever.

"I bring you—the Dragonlance!"

With that, Theros thrust the weapon deep into the ground. It stood, straight and shining, amid the broken pieces of the dragon orb.

7

An unexpected journey.

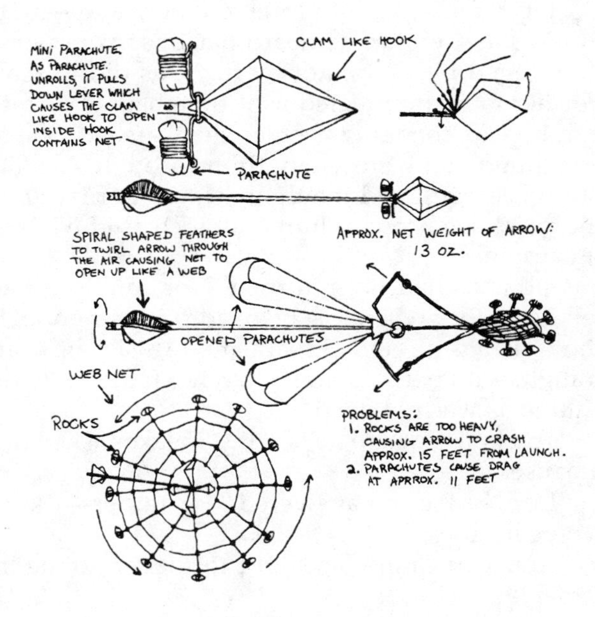
MINI PARACHUTE
AS PARACHUTE
UNROLLS, IT PULLS
DOWN LEVER WHICH
CAUSES THE CLAM
LIKE HOOK TO OPEN
INSIDE HOOK
CONTAINS NET
CLAM LIKE HOOK
PARACHUTE
SPIRAL SHAPED FEATHERS
TO TWIRL ARROW THROUGH
THE AIR CAUSING NET TO
OPEN UP LIKE A WEB
APPROX. NET WEIGHT OF ARROW:
13 OZ.
OPENED PARACHUTES
WEB NET
ROCKS
PROBLEMS:
1. ROCKS ARE TOO HEAVY,
CAUSING ARROW TO CRASH
APPROX. 15 FEET FROM LAUNCH.
2. PARACHUTES CAUSE DRAG
AT APPROX. 11 FEET

"And now my task is finished," Laurana said. "I am free to leave."

"Yes," Elistan said slowly, "and I know why you leave"—Laurana flushed and lowered her eyes—"but where will you go?"

"Silvanesti," she replied. "The last place I saw him."

"Only in a dream—"

"No, that was more than a dream," Laurana replied, shuddering. "It was real. He was there. He is alive and I must find him."

"Surely, my dear, you should stay here, then," Elistan suggested. "You say that in the dream he had found a dragon orb. If he has it, he will come to Sancrist."

Laurana did not answer. Unhappy and irresolute, she stared out the window of Lord Gunthar's castle where she, Elistan, Flint, and Tasslehoff were staying as his guests.

She should have been with the elves. Before they left Whitestone Glade, her father had asked her to come back with them to Southern Ergoth. But Laurana refused. Although she did not say it, she knew she would never live among her people again.

Her father had not pressed her, and—in his eyes—she saw that he heard her unspoken words. Elves aged by years, not by days, as did humans. For her father, it seemed as if time had accelerated and he was changing even as she watched. She felt as though she were seeing him through Raistlin's hourglass eyes, and the thought was terrifying. Yet the news she brought him only increased his bitter unhappiness.

Gilthanas had not returned. Nor could Laurana tell her father where his beloved son had gone, for the journey he and Silvara made was dark and fraught with peril. Laurana told her father only that Gilthanas was not dead.

"You know where he is?" the Speaker asked after a pause.

"I do," Laurana answered, "or rather—I know where he goes."

"And you cannot speak of this, even to me, his father?"

Laurana shook her head steadfastly. "No, Speaker, I cannot. Forgive me, but we agreed when the decision was made to undertake this desperate action that those of us who knew would tell no one. No one," she repeated.

"So you do not trust me—"

Laurana sighed. Her eyes went to the shattered Whitestone. "Father," she said, "you nearly went to war . . . with the only people who can help save us. . . ."

Her father had not replied, but—in his cool farewell and in the way he leaned upon the arm of his elder child†—he made it clear to Laurana that he now had only *one* child.

Little does the Speaker know that it will be Porthios, his eldest child, who becomes the next Speaker of the Suns who will attempt to unify the elven nations.

Theros went with the elves. Following his dramatic presentation of the dragonlance, the Council of Whitestone had voted unanimously to make more of these weapons and unite all races in the fight against the dragonarmies.

"At present," Theros announced, "we have only those few lances I was able to forge by myself within a month's time, and I bring several ancient lances the silver dragons hid at the time the dragons were banished from the world. But we'll need more, many more. I need men to help me!"

The elves agreed to provide men to help make the dragonlances, but whether or not they would help fight—

"That remains a matter we must discuss," the Speaker said.

"Don't discuss it too long," Flint Fireforge snapped, "or you might find yourself discussing it with a Dragon Highlord."

"The elves keep their own counsel and ask for no advice from dwarves," the Speaker replied coldly. "Besides, we do not even know if these lances work! The legend said they were to be forged by one of the Silver Arm, that is certain. But it also says that the Hammer of Kharas was needed in the forging. Where is the Hammer now?" he asked Theros.

"The Hammer could not be brought here in time, even if it could be kept from the dragonarmies. The Hammer of Kharas was required in days of old, because man's skill was not sufficient by itself to produce the lances. Mine is," he added proudly. "You saw what the lance did to that rock."

"We shall see what it does to dragons," the Speaker said, and the Second Council of Whitestone drew to a close. Gunthar proposed at the last that the lances Theros had brought with him be sent to the knights in Palanthas.

These thoughts passed through Laurana's mind as she stared out across the bleak winter landscape. It would be snowing in the valley soon, Lord Gunthar said.

I cannot stay here, Laurana thought, pressing her face against the chill glass. I shall go mad.

"I've studied Gunthar's maps," she murmured, almost speaking to herself, "and I've seen the location of the dragonarmies. Tanis will never reach Sancrist. And if he does have the orb, he may not know the danger it poses. I must warn him."

"My dear, you're not talking sensibly," Elistan said mildly. "If Tanis cannot reach Sancrist safely, how will you reach him? Think logically, Laurana—"

"I don't want to think logically!" Laurana cried, stomping her foot and glaring angrily at the cleric. "I'm sick of being sensible! I'm tired of this whole war. I've done my part—more than my part. I just want to find Tanis!"

Seeing Elistan's sympathetic face, Laurana sighed. "I'm sorry, my dear friend. I know what you say is true," she said, ashamed. "But I can't stay here and do nothing!"

Though Laurana didn't mention it, she had another concern. That human woman, that Kitiara. Where was she? Were they together as she had seen in the dream? Laurana realized now, suddenly, that the remembered image of Kitiara standing with Tanis's arm around her was more disturbing than the image she had seen of her own death.

At that moment, Lord Gunthar suddenly entered the room.

"Oh!" he said, startled, seeing Elistan and Laurana. "I'm sorry, I hope I am not disturbing—"

"Please, no, come in," Laurana said quickly.

"Thank you," Gunthar said, stepping inside and carefully shutting the door, first glancing down the hallway to make certain no one was near. He joined them at the window. "Actually I needed to talk to you both, anyway. I sent Wills looking for you. This is best, however. No one knows we're speaking."

More intrigue, Laurana thought wearily. Throughout their journey to Gunthar's castle, she had heard about nothing but the political infighting that was destroying the Knighthood.

Shocked and outraged at Gunthar's story of Sturm's trial, Laurana had gone before a Council of Knights to speak in Sturm's defense. Although the appearance of a woman at a Council was unheard of, the knights were impressed by this vibrant, beautiful young woman's eloquent speech on Sturm's behalf. The fact that Laurana was a member of the royal elven household, and that she had brought the dragonlances, also spoke highly in her favor.

Even Derek's faction—those that remained—were hard-pressed to fault her. But the knights had been unable to reach a decision. The man appointed to stand in Lord Alfred's place was strongly in

Derek's tent—as the phrase went—and Lord Michael had vacillated to such a degree that Gunthar had been forced to throw the matter to an open vote. The knights demanded a period of reflection and the meeting was adjourned. They had reconvened this afternoon. Apparently, Gunthar had just come from this meeting.

Laurana knew, from the look on Gunthar's face, that things had gone favorably. But if so, why the maneuvering?

"Sturm's been pardoned?" she asked.

Gunthar grinned and rubbed his hands together. "Not pardoned, my dear. That would have implied his guilt. No. He has been completely vindicated! I pushed for that. Pardon would not have suited us at all. His knighthood is granted. He has his command officially bestowed upon him. And Derek is in serious trouble!"

"I am happy, for Sturm's sake," Laurana said coolly, exchanging worried looks with Elistan. Although she liked what she had seen of Lord Gunthar, she had been brought up in a royal household and knew Sturm was being made a game piece.

Gunthar caught the edge of ice in her voice, and his face became grave. "Lady Laurana," he said, speaking more somberly, "I know what you are thinking—that I am dangling Sturm from puppet strings. Let us be brutally frank, lady. The Knights are divided, split into two factions—Derek's and my own. And we both know what happens to a tree split in two: both sides wither and die. This battle between us must end, or it will have tragic consequences. Now, lady and Elistan, for I have come to trust and rely on your judgment, I leave this in your hands. You have met me and you have met Lord Derek Crownguard. Who would you choose to head the Knights?"

"You, of course, Lord Gunthar," Elistan said sincerely.

Laurana nodded her head. "I agree. This feud is ruinous to the Knighthood. I saw that myself, in the Council meeting. And—from what I've heard of the reports coming from Palanthas—it is hurting our cause there as well. My first concern must be for my friend, however."

"I quite understand, and I am glad to hear you say so," Gunthar said approvingly, "because it makes the very great favor I am about to ask of you easier." Gunthar took Laurana's arm. "I want you to go to Palanthas."

"What? Why? I don't understand!"

"Of course not. Let me explain. Please sit down. You, too, Elistan. I'll pour some wine—"

"I think not," Laurana said, sitting near the window.

"Very well." Gunthar's face became grave. He laid his hand over Laurana's. "We know politics, you and I, lady. So I am going to arrange all my game pieces before you. Ostensibly you will be traveling to Palanthas to teach the knights to use the dragonlances. It is a legitimate reason. Without Theros, you and the dwarf are the only ones who understand their usage. And—let's face it—the dwarf is too short to handle one."

Gunthar cleared his throat. "You will take the lances to Palanthas. But more importantly, you will carry with you a Writ of Vindication from the Council fully restoring Sturm's honor. That will strike the death's blow to Derek's ambition. The moment Sturm puts on his armor, all will know I have the Council's full support. I shouldn't wonder if *Derek* won't go on trial when he returns."

"But why me?" Laurana asked bluntly. "I can teach anyone—Lord Michael, for example—to use a dragonlance. He can take them to Palanthas. He can carry the Writ to Sturm—"

"Lady"—Lord Gunthar gripped her hand hard, drawing near and speaking barely above a whisper—"you still do not understand! I cannot trust Lord Michael! I cannot—I dare not trust any one of the knights with this! Derek has been knocked from his horse—so to speak—but he hasn't lost the tourney yet. I need someone I can trust implicitly! Someone who knows Derek for what he is, who has Sturm's best interests at heart!"

"I *do* have Sturm's interests at heart," Laurana said coldly. "I put them above the interests of the Knighthood."

"Ah, but remember, Lady Laurana," Gunthar said, rising to his feet and bowing as he kissed her hand, "Sturm's *only* interest is the Knighthood.

What would happen to him, do you think, if the Knighthood should fall? What will happen to him if Derek seizes control?"

In the end, of course, Laurana agreed to go to Palanthas, as Gunthar had known she must. As the time of her departure drew nearer, she began to dream almost nightly of Tanis arriving on the island just hours after she left. More than once she was on the verge of refusing to go, but then she thought of facing Tanis, of having to tell him she had refused to go to Sturm to warn him of this peril. This kept her from changing her mind. This—and her regard for Sturm.

It was during the lonely nights, when her heart and her arms ached for Tanis and she had visions of him holding that human woman with the dark, curly hair, flashing brown eyes, and the charming, crooked smile, that her soul was in turmoil.

Her friends could give her little comfort. One of them, Elistan, left when a messenger arrived from the elves, requesting the cleric's presence, and asking that an emissary from the knights accompany him.There was little time for farewells. Within a day of the arrival of the elven messenger, Elistan and Lord Alfred's son, a solemn, serious young man named Douglas, began their journey back to Southern Ergoth. Laurana had never felt so alone as she bid her mentor good-bye.

Tasslehoff faced a sad parting as well.

In the midst of the excitement over the dragonlance, everyone forgot poor Gnosh and his Life Quest, which lay in a thousand sparkling pieces on the grass. Everyone but Fizban. The old magician rose from where he lay cowering on the ground before the shattered Whitestone and went to the stricken gnome, who was staring woefully at the shattered dragon orb.

"There, there, my boy," said Fizban, "this isn't the end of everything!"

"It isn't?" asked Gnosh, so miserable he finished a sentence.

"No, of course not! You've got to look at this from the proper perspective. Why, now you've got a chance to study a dragon orb from the inside out!"

Gnosh's eyes brightened. "You're right," he said after a short pause, "and, in fact, I bet I could glue—"

"Yes, yes," Fizban said hurriedly, but Gnosh lunged forward, his speech growing faster and faster.

To the gnomes there is no such thing as disaster—merely opportunity.

"We could tag the pieces,† don'tyousee,andthen-drawadiagramofwhereeachpiece waslyingonthe-ground,which—"

"Quite, quite," Fizban muttered.

"Step aside, step aside," Gnosh said importantly, shooing people away from the orb. "Mind where you walk, Lord Gunthar, and, yes, we're going to study it from the inside out now, and I should have a report in a matter of weeks—"

Gnosh and Fizban cordoned off the area and set to work. For the next two days, Fizban stood on the broken Whitestone making diagrams, supposedly marking the exact location of each piece before it was picked up. (One of Fizban's diagrams accidentally ended up in the kender's pouch. Tas discovered later that it was actually a game known as "x's and zeroes" which the mage had been playing against himself and apparently—lost.)

Gnosh, meanwhile, crawled happily around on the grass, sticking bits of parchment adorned with numbers on pieces of glass smaller than the bits of parchment. He and Fizban finally collected the 2,687 pieces of dragon orb in a basket and transported them back to Mount Nevermind.

Tasslehoff had been offered the choice of staying with Fizban or going to Palanthas with Laurana and Flint. The choice was simple. The kender knew two such innocents as the elfmaid and the dwarf could not survive without him. But it was hard leaving his old friend. Two days before the ship sailed, he paid a final visit to the gnomes and to Fizban.

After an exhilarating ride in the catapult, he found Gnosh in the Examination Room. The pieces of the broken dragon orb—tagged and numbered—were spread out across two tables.

"Absolutelyfascinating," Gnosh spoke so fast he stuttered, "because wehaveanalyzedtheglass, curiousmaterial, unlikenothingwe'veeverseen, greatest-discovery, thiscentury—"

"So your Life Quest is over?" Tas interrupted. "Your father's soul—"

"Restingcomfortably!" Gnosh beamed, then returned to his work."Andsogladyoucouldstopby andifyou'reeverintheneighborhoodcomebyandseeusagain—"

"I will," Tas said, smiling.

Tas found Fizban two levels down. (A fascinating journey—he simply yelled out the name of his level, then leaped into the void. Nets flapped and fluttered, bells went off, gongs sounded and whistles blew. Tas was finally caught one level above the ground, just as the area was being inundated with sponges.)†

An outsider ventured into Mt. Nevermind and ended up exploring—via the gnomeflinger—almost every level of the gnomes' volcanic city. See Gnomes–100, Dragons–0, *by James M. Ward and Jean Blashfield.*

Fizban was in Weapons Development, surrounded by gnomes, all gazing at him with unabashed admiration.

"Ah, my boy!" he said, peering vaguely at Tasslehoff. "You're just in time to see the testing of our new weapon. Revolutionize warfare. Make the dragonlance obsolete."

"Really?" Tas asked in excitement.

"A fact!" Fizban confirmed. "Now, you stand over here—" He motioned to a gnome who leaped to do his bidding, running to stand in the middle of the cluttered room.

Fizban picked up what looked, to the kender's confused mind, like a crossbow that had been attacked by an enraged fisherman. It was a crossbow all right. But instead of an arrow, a huge net dangled from a hook on the end. Fizban, grumbling and muttering, ordered the gnomes to stand behind him and give him room.

"Now, you are the enemy," Fizban told the gnome in the center of the room. The gnome immediately assumed a fierce, warlike expression. The other gnomes nodded appreciatively.

Fizban aimed, then let fly. The net sailed out into the air, got snagged on the hook at the end of crossbow, and snapped back like a collapsing sail to engulf the magician.

"Confounded hook!" Fizban muttered.

Between the gnomes and Tas, they got him disentangled.

"I guess this is good-bye," Tas said, slowly extending his small hand.

"It is?" Fizban looked amazed. "Am I going somewhere? No one told me! I'm not packed—"

"I'm going somewhere," Tas said patiently, "with Laurana. We're taking the lances and—oh, I don't think I'm supposed to be telling anyone," he added, embarrassed.

"Don't worry. Mum's the word," Fizban said in a hoarse whisper that carried clearly through the crowded room. "You'll love Palanthas. Beautiful city. Give Sturm my regards. Oh, and Tasslehoff"—the old magician looked at him shrewdly—"you did the right thing, my boy!"

"I did?" Tas said hopefully. "I'm glad." He hesitated. "I wondered . . . about what you said—the dark path. Did I—?"

Fizban's face grew grave as he gripped Tas firmly on the shoulder "I'm afraid so. But you have the courage to walk it."

"I hope so," Tas said with a small sigh. "Well, good-bye. I'll be back. Just as soon as the war's over."

"Oh, I probably won't be here," Fizban said, shaking his head so violently his hat slid off. "Soon as the new weapon's perfected, I'll be leaving for—" he paused. "Where was that I was supposed to go? I can't seem to recall. But don't worry. We'll meet again. At least you're not leaving me buried under a pile of chicken feathers!" he muttered, searching for his hat.

Tas picked it up and handed it to him.

"Good-bye," the kender said, a choke in his voice.

"Good-bye, good-bye!" Fizban waved cheerfully. Then—giving the gnomes a hunted glance—he pulled Tas over to him. "Uh, I seem to have forgotten something. What was my name again?"

Someone else said good-bye to the old magician, too, although not under quite the same circumstances.

Elistan was pacing the shore of Sancrist, waiting for the boat that would take him back to Southern Ergoth. The young man, Douglas, walked along beside him. The two were deep in conversation, Elistan explaining the ways of the ancient gods to a rapt and attentive listener.

Suddenly Elistan looked up to see the old, befuddled magician he had seen at the Council meeting. Elistan had tried for days to meet the old mage, but Fizban always avoided him. Thus it was with

astonishment Elistan saw the old man come walking toward them now along the shoreline. His head was bowed, he was muttering to himself. For a moment, Elistan thought he would pass by without noticing them, when suddenly the old mage raised his head.

"Oh, I say! Haven't we met?" he asked, blinking.

For a moment Elistan could not speak. The cleric's face turned deathly white beneath its weathered tan. He was finally able to answer the old mage, his voice was husky. "Indeed we have, sir. I did not realize it before now. And though we were but lately introduced, I feel that I have known you a long, long time."

"Indeed?" The old man scowled suspiciously. "You're not making some sort of comment on my age, are you?"

"No, certainly not!" Elistan smiled.

The old man's face cleared.

"Well, have a pleasant journey. And a safe one. Farewell."

Leaning on a bent and battered staff, the old man toddled on past them. Suddenly he stopped and turned around. "Oh, by the way, the name's Fizban."

"I'll remember," Elistan said gravely, bowing. "Fizban."

Pleased, the old magician nodded and continued on his way along the shoreline while Elistan, suddenly thoughtful and quiet, resumed his walk with a sigh.

8

The Perechon

Memories of long ago.

"This is crazy, I hope you realize that!" Caramon hissed.

"We wouldn't be here if we were sane, would we?" Tanis responded, gritting his teeth.

"No," Caramon muttered. "I suppose you're right."

The two men stood in the shadows of a dark alleyway, in a town where generally the only things ever found in alleyways were rats, drunks, and dead bodies.

The name of the wretched town was Flotsam, and it was well named, for it lay upon the shores of the Blood Sea of Istar like the wreckage of a broken vessel tossed upon the rocks. Peopled by the dregs of most of the races of Krynn, Flotsam was, in addition, an occupied town now, overrun

with draconians, goblins, and mercenaries of all races, attracted to the Highlords by high wages and the spoils of war.

And so, "like the other scum," as Raistlin observed, the companions floated along upon the tides of war and were deposited in Flotsam.† Here they hoped to find a ship that would take them on the long, treacherous journey around the northern part of Ansalon to Sancrist—or wherever—

There is a saying that "when the pot boils, the scum floats to the top." After the Cataclysm, Flotsam collected the scum, both physically—from the debris that floated to the surface of the Blood Sea from the destroyed city of Istar—and personality wise.

Where they were going was a point that had been much in contention lately—ever since Raistlin's recovery from his illness. The companions had anxiously watched him following his use of the dragon orb, their concern not completely centered on his health. What had happened when he used the orb? What harm might he have brought upon them?

"You need not fear," Raistlin told them in his whispering voice. "I am not weak and foolish like the elven king. I gained control of the orb. It did not gain control of me."

"Then what does it do? How can we use it?" Tanis asked, alarmed by the frozen expression on the mage's metallic face.

"It took all my strength to gain control of the orb," Raistlin replied, his eyes on the ceiling above his bed. "It will require much more study before I learn how to use it."

"Study . . ." Tanis repeated. "Study of the orb?"

Raistlin flicked him a glance, then resumed staring at the ceiling. "No," he replied. "The study of books, written by the ancient ones who created the orb. We must go to Palanthas, to the library of one Astinus, who resides there."

Tanis was silent for a moment. He could hear the mage's breath rattle in his lungs as he struggled to draw breath.

What keeps him clinging to this life? Tanis wondered silently.

It had snowed that morning, but now the snow had changed to rain. Tanis could hear it drumming on the wooden roof of the wagon. Heavy clouds drifted across the sky. Perhaps it was the gloom of the day, but as he looked at Raistlin, Tanis felt a chill creep through his body until the cold seemed to freeze his heart.

"Was this what you meant, when you spoke of ancient spells?" Tanis asked.

"Of course. What else?" Raistlin paused, coughing, then asked,"When did I speak of . . . ancient spells?"

"When we first found you," Tanis answered, watching the mage closely. He noticed a crease in Raistlin's forehead and heard tension in his shattered voice.

"What did I say?"

"Nothing much," Tanis replied warily. "Just something about ancient spells, spells that would soon be yours."

"That was all?"

Tanis did not reply immediately. Raistlin's strange, hourglass eyes focused on him coldly. The half-elf shivered and nodded. Raistlin turned his head away. His eyes closed. "I will sleep now," he said softly. "Remember, Tanis. Palanthas."

Tanis was forced to admit he wanted to go to Sancrist for purely selfish reasons. He hoped against hope that Laurana and Sturm and the others would be there. And it was where he had promised he would take the dragon orb. But against this, he had to weigh Raistlin's steady insistence that they must go to the library of this Astinus to discover how to use the orb.

His mind was still in a quandary when they reached Flotsam. Finally, he decided they would set about getting passage on a ship going north first and decide where to land later.

But when they reached Flotsam, they had a nasty shock. There were more draconians in that city than they had seen on their entire journey from Port Balifor north. The streets were crawling with heavily armed patrols, taking an intense interest in strangers. Fortunately, the companions had sold their wagon before entering the town, so they were able to mingle with the crowds on the streets. But they hadn't been inside the city gates five minutes before they saw a draconian patrol arrest a human for "questioning."

This alarmed them, so they took rooms in the first inn they came to—a run-down place at the edge of town.

"How are we going to even get to the harbor, much less buy passage on a ship?" Caramon asked as they settled into their shabby rooms. "What's going on?"

"The innkeeper says a Dragon Highlord is in town. The draconians are searching for spies or something," Tanis muttered uncomfortably. The companions exchanged glances.

"Maybe they're searching for *us,*" Caramon said.

"That's ridiculous!" Tanis answered quickly—too quickly. "We're getting spooked. How could anyone know we're here? Or know what we carry?"

"I wonder . . ." Riverwind said grimly, glancing at Raistlin.

The mage returned his glance coolly, not deigning to answer. "Hot water for my drink," he instructed Caramon.

"There's only one way I can think of," Tanis said, as Caramon brought his brother the water as ordered. "Caramon and I will go out tonight and waylay two of the dragonarmy soldiers. We'll steal their uniforms. Not the draconians—" he said hastily, as Caramon's brow wrinkled in disgust. "The human mercenaries. Then we can move around Flotsam freely."

After some discussion, everyone agreed it was the only plan that seemed likely to work. The companions ate dinner without much appetite—dining in their rooms rather than risk going into the common room.

"You'll be all right?" Caramon asked Raistlin uneasily when the two were alone in the room they shared.

"I am quite capable of taking care of myself," Raistlin replied. Rising to his feet, he had picked up a spellbook to study, when a fit of coughing doubled him over.

Caramon reached out his hand, but Raistlin flinched away.

"Be gone!" the mage gasped. "Leave me be!"

Caramon hesitated, then he sighed. "Sure, Raist," he said, and left the room, shutting the door gently behind him.

Raistlin stood for a moment, trying to catch his breath. Then he moved slowly across the room, setting down the spellbook. With a trembling hand, he picked up one of the many sacks that Caramon had placed on the table beside his bed. Opening it, Raistlin carefully withdrew the dragon orb.

Tanis and Caramon—the half-elf keeping his hood pulled low over his face and ears—walked the streets of Flotsam, watching for two guards whose uniforms might fit them. This would have been relatively easy for Tanis, but finding a guard whose armor fit the giant Caramon was more difficult.

They both knew they had better find something quickly. More than once, draconians looked them over suspiciously. Two draconians even stopped them, insisting roughly on knowing their business. Caramon replied in the crude mercenary dialect that they were seeking employment in the Dragon Highlord's army, and the draconians let them go. But both men knew it was only a matter of time before a patrol caught them.

"I wonder what's going on?" Tanis muttered worriedly.

"Maybe the war's heating up for the Highlords," Caramon began."There, look, Tanis. Going into that bar—"

"I see. Yeah, he's about your size. Duck into that alley. We'll wait until they come out, then—" The half-elf made a motion of wringing a neck. Caramon nodded. The two slipped through the filthy streets and vanished into the alley, hiding where they could keep on eye on the front door of the bar.

It was nearly midnight. The moons would not rise tonight. The rain had ceased, but clouds still obscured the sky. The two men crouched in the alley were soon shivering, despite their heavy cloaks. Rats skittered across their feet, making them cringe in the darkness. A drunken hobgoblin took a wrong turn and lurched past them, falling headfirst into a pile of garbage. The hobgoblin did not get back up again and the stench nearly made Tanis and Caramon sick, but they dared not leave their vantage point.

Then they heard welcome sounds—drunken laughter and human voices speaking Common. The two guards they had been waiting for lurched out of the bar and staggered toward them.

A tall iron brazier stood on the sidewalk, lighting the night. The mercenaries lurched into its light, giving Tanis a close look at them. Both were officers in the dragonarmy, he saw. Newly promoted, he guessed, which may have been what they were celebrating. Their armor was shining new, relatively

clean, and undented. It was good armor, too, he saw with satisfaction. Made of blue steel, it was fashioned after the style of the Highlords' own dragon-scale armor.

"Ready?" Caramon whispered. Tanis nodded.

Caramon drew his sword. "Elven scum!" he roared in his deep, barrel-chested bass. "I've found you out, and now you'll come with me to the Dragon Highlord, spy!"

"You'll never take me alive!" Tanis drew his own sword.

At the sound of their voices, the two officers staggered to a stop, peering bleary-eyed into the dark alley.

The officers watched with growing interest as Caramon and Tanis made a few passes at each other, maneuvering themselves into position. When Caramon's back was to the officers and Tanis was facing them, the half-elf made a sudden move. Disarming Caramon, he sent the warrior's sword flying.

"Quick! Help me take him!" Caramon bellowed. "There's a reward out for him—dead or alive!"

The officers never hesitated. Fumbling drunkenly for their weapons, they headed for Tanis, their faces twisted into expressions of cruel pleasure.

"That's it! Nail 'im!" Caramon urged, waiting until they were past him. Then—just as they raised their swords—Caramon's huge hands encircled their necks. He slammed their heads together, and the bodies slumped to the ground.

"Hurry!" Tanis grunted. He dragged one body by the feet away from the light. Caramon followed with the other. Quickly they began to strip off the armor.

"Phew! This one must have been half-troll," Caramon said, waving his hand to clear the air of the foul smell.

"Quit complaining!" Tanis snapped, trying to figure out how the complex system of buckles and straps worked. "At least you're used to wearing this stuff. Give me a hand with this, will you?"

"Sure." Caramon, grinning, helped to buckle Tanis into the armor. "An elf in plate armor. What's the world coming to?"

"Sad times," Tanis muttered. "When are we supposed to meet that ship captain William told you about?"

"He said we could find her on board around daybreak."

"The name's Maquesta Kar-thon," said the woman, her expression cool and businesslike. "And—let me guess—you're *not* officers in the dragonarmy. Not unless they're hiring elves these days."

Tanis flushed, slowly drawing off the helm of the officer. "Is it that obvious?"

The woman shrugged. "Probably not to anyone else. The beard is very good—perhaps I should say half-elf, of course. And the helm hides your ears. But unless you get a mask, those pretty, almond shaped eyes of yours are a dead give-away. But then, not many draconians are apt to look into your pretty eyes, are they?" Leaning back in her chair, she put a booted foot on a table, and regarded him coolly.

Tanis heard Caramon chuckle, and felt his skin burn.

They were on board the *Perechon,* sitting in the captain's cabin, across from the captain herself. Maquesta Kar-thon was one of the dark-skinned race living in Northern Ergoth. Her people† had been sailors for centuries and, it was popularly believed, could speak the languages of seabirds and dolphins. Tanis found himself thinking of Theros Ironfeld as he looked at Maquesta. The woman's skin was shining black, her hair tightly curled and bound with a gold band around her forehead. Her eyes were brown and shining as her skin. But there was the glint of steel from the dagger at her belt, and the glint of steel in her eyes.

That's her father's people—her mother was an elf. It's unlikely, though, that Maquesta would ever have fit into elf society.

"We're here to discuss business, Captain Maque—" Tanis stumbled over the strange name.

"Sure you are," the woman said. "And call me Maq. Easier for both of us. It's well you have this letter from Pig-faced William, or I wouldn't have even talked to you. But he says you're square and your money's good, so I'll listen. Now, where're you bound?"

Tanis exchanged glances with Caramon. That was the question. Besides, he wasn't certain he wanted either of their destinations known. Palanthas was the capital city of Solamnia, while Sancrist was a well-known haven of the Knights.

"Oh, for the love of—" Maq snapped, seeing them hesitate. Her eyes flared. Removing her foot from the table, she stared at them grimly. "You either trust me or you don't!"

"Should we?" Tanis asked bluntly.

Maq raised an eyebrow. "How much money do you have?"

"Enough," Tanis said. "Let's just say that we want to go north, around the Cape of Nordmaar. If, at that point, we still find each other's company agreeable, we'll go on. If not, we'll pay you off, and you put us in a safe harbor."

"Kalaman," said Maq, settling back. She seemed amused. "That's a safe harbor. As safe as any these days. Half your money now. Half at Kalaman. Any farther is negotiable."

"*Safe* delivery to Kalaman," Tanis amended.

"Who can promise?" Maq shrugged. "It's a rough time of year to travel by sea." She rose languidly, stretching like a cat. Caramon, standing up quickly, stared at her admiringly.

"It's a deal," she said. "Come on. I'll show you the ship."

Maq led them onto the deck. The ship seemed fit and trim as far as Tanis, who knew nothing about ships, could tell. Her voice and manner had been cold when they first talked to her, but when she showed them around her ship, she seemed to warm up. Tanis had seen the same expression, heard the same warm tones Maq used in talking about her ship that Tika used when talking about Caramon. The *Perechon* was obviously Maq's only love.†

At eighteen, Maquesta had acquired Perechon in a tale told in Maquesta Kar-Thon *by Tina Daniell.*

The ship was quiet, empty. Her crew was ashore, along with her first mate, Maq explained. The only other person Tanis saw on board was a man sitting by himself, mending a sail. The man looked up as they passed, and Tanis saw his eyes widen in alarm at the sight of the dragon armor.

"*Nocesta,* Berem," Maq said to him soothingly as they passed. She made a slashing motion with her hand, gesturing to Tanis and Caramon. "*Nocesta.* Customers. Money."

The man nodded and went back to his work.

"Who is he?" Tanis asked Maq in a low voice as they walked toward her cabin once more to conclude their business.

"Who? Berem?" she asked, glancing around. "He's the helmsman. Don't know much about him. He came around a few months back, looking for work. Took him on as a deckswab. Then my helmsman was killed in a small altercation with—well, never mind. But this fellow turned out to be a damn good hand at the wheel, better than the first, in fact. He's an odd one, though. A mute. Never speaks. Never goes ashore, if he can help it. Wrote his name down for me in the ship's book, or I wouldn't have known that much about him. Why?" she asked, noticing Tanis studying the man intently.

Berem was tall, well-built. At first sight, one might guess him to be middle-aged, by human terms. His hair was gray; his face was clean shaven, deeply tanned, and weathered from months spent on board ship. But his eyes were youthful, clear, and bright. The hands that held the needle were smooth and strong, the hands of a young man. Elven blood, perhaps, Tanis thought, but if so it wasn't apparent in any of his features.

"I've seen him somewhere," Tanis murmured. "How about you, Caramon? Do you remember him?"

"Ah, come on," said the big warrior. "We've seen hundreds of people this past month, Tanis. He was probably in the audience at one of our shows.

"No." Tanis shook his head. "When I first saw him, I thought of Pax Tharkas and Sturm. . . ."

"Hey, I got a lot of work to do, half-elf," Maquesta said. "You coming, or you gonna gawk at a guy stitching a sail?"

She climbed down the hatch. Caramon followed clumsily, his sword and armor clanking. Reluctantly, Tanis went after them. But he turned for one final look at the man, and caught the man regarding him with a strange, penetrating gaze.

"All right, you go back to the inn with the others. I'll buy the supplies. We sail when the ship's ready. Maquesta says about four days."

"I wish it was sooner," muttered Caramon.

"So do I," said Tanis grimly. "There's too damn many draconians around here. But we've got to wait for the tide or some such thing. Go back to the inn and keep everyone inside. Tell your brother to

lay in a store of that herb stuff he drinks—we'll be at sea a long time. I'll be back in a few hours, after I get the supplies."

Tanis walked down the crowded streets of Flotsam, no one giving him a second glance in his dragon armor. He would be glad to take it off. It was hot, heavy and itchy. And he had trouble remembering to return the salutes of draconians and goblins. It was beginning to occur to him—as he saw the respect his uniform commanded—that the humans they stole the uniforms from must have held a high rank. The thought was not comforting. Any moment now, someone might recognize his armor.

But he couldn't do without it, he knew. There were more draconians in the streets than ever today. The air of tension in Flotsam was high. Most of the town's citizens were staying home, and most of the shops were closed—with the exception of the taverns. In fact, as he passed one closed shop after another, Tanis began to worry about where he was going to buy supplies for the long ocean voyage.

Tanis was musing on this problem as he stared into a closed shop window, when a hand suddenly wrapped around his boot and yanked him to the ground.

The fall knocked the breath from the half-elf's body. He struck his head heavily on the cobblestones and—for a moment—was groggy with pain. Instinctively he kicked out at whatever had him by the feet, but the hands that grasped him were strong. He felt himself being dragged into a dark alley.

Shaking his head to clear it, he strained to look at his captor. It was an elf! His clothes filthy and torn, his elven features distorted by grief and hatred, the elf stood above him, a spear in his hand.

"Dragon man!" the elf snarled in Common. "Your foul kind slaughtered my family—my wife and my children! Murdered them in their beds, ignoring their pleas for mercy. This is for them!" The elf raised his spear.

"Shak! It mo dracosali!" Tanis cried desperately in elven, struggling to pull off his helmet. But the elf, driven insane by grief, was beyond hearing or understanding. His spear plunged downward. Suddenly the elf's eyes grew wide, riveted in shock. The spear fell from his nerveless fingers as a sword

punctured him from behind. The dying elf fell with a shriek, landing heavily upon the pavement.

Tanis looked up in astonishment to see who had saved his life. A Dragon Highlord stood over the elf's body.

"I heard you shouting and saw one of my officers in trouble. I guessed you needed some help," said the Highlord, reaching out a gloved hand to help Tanis up.

Confused, dizzy with pain and knowing only that he mustn't give himself away, Tanis accepted the Highlord's hand and struggled to his feet. Ducking his face, thankful for the dark shadows in the alley, Tanis mumbled words of thanks in a harsh voice. Then he saw the Highlord's eyes behind the mask widen.

"Tanis?"

The half-elf felt a shudder run through his body, a pain as swift and sharp as the elven spear. He could not speak, he could only stare as the Highlord swiftly removed the blue and gold dragonmask.

"Tanis! It *is* you!" the Highlord cried, grasping him by the arms. Tanis saw bright brown eyes, a crooked, charming smile.

"Kitiara . . ."

9

Tanis captured.

"So, Tanis! An officer, and in my own command. I should review my troops more often!" Kitiara laughed, sliding her arm through his. "You're shaking. You took a nasty fall. Come on. My rooms aren't far from here. We'll have a drink, patch up that wound, then . . . talk."

Dazed—but not from the head wound—Tanis let Kitiara lead him out of the alley onto the sidewalk. Too much had happened too fast. One minute he had been buying supplies and now he was walking arm in arm with a Dragon Highlord who had just saved his life and who was also the woman he had loved for so many years. He could not help but stare at her, and Kitiara—knowing his eyes were on her—returned his gaze from beneath her long, sooty-black eyelashes.

The gleaming, night-blue dragon-scale armor of the Highlords suited her well, Tanis caught himself thinking. It was tight-fitting, emphasizing the curves of her long legs.

Draconians swarmed around them, hoping for even a brief nod from the Highlord. But Kitiara ignored them, chatting breezily with Tanis as if it were only an afternoon since they had parted, instead of five years. He could not absorb her words, his brain was still fumbling to make sense of this, while his body was reacting—once again—to her nearness.

The mask had left her hair somewhat damp, the curls clung to her face and forehead. Casually she ran her gloved hand through her hair, shaking it out. It was an old habit of hers and that small gesture brought back memories—

Tanis shook his head, struggling desperately to pull his shattered world together and attend to her words. The lives of his friends depended on what he did now.

"It's hot beneath that dragon helm!" she was saying. "I don't need the frightful thing to keep my men in line. Do I?" she asked, winking.

"N-no," Tanis stammered, feeling himself flush.

"Same old Tanis," she murmured, pressing her body against his."You still blush like a schoolboy. But you were never like the others, never. . ." she added softly. Pulling him close, she put her arms around him. Closing her eyes, her moist lips brushed his. . . .

"Kit—" Tanis said in a strangled voice, wrenching backward. "Not here! Not in the street," he added lamely.

For a moment Kitiara regarded him angrily, then—shrugging, she dropped her hand down to clasp his arm again. Together they continued along the street, the draconians leering and joking.

"Same Tanis," she said again, this time with a little, breathless sigh."I don't know why I let you get away with it. Any other man who refused me like that would have died on my sword. Ah, here we are."

She entered the best inn in Flotsam, the Saltbreeze. Built high on a cliff, it overlooked the Blood Sea of Istar, whose waves broke on the rocks below. The innkeeper hurried forward.

"Is my room made up?" Kit asked coolly.

"Yes, Highlord," the innkeeper said, bowing again and again. As they ascended the stairs, the innkeeper hustled ahead of them to make certain that all was in order.

Kit glanced around. Finding everything satisfactory, she casually tossed the dragonhelm on a table and began pulling off her gloves. Sitting down in a chair, she raised her leg with sensual and deliberate abandon.

"My boots," she said to Tanis, smiling.

Swallowing, giving her a weak smile in return, Tanis gripped her leg in his hands. This had been an old game of theirs, him taking off her boots. It had always led to—Tanis tried to keep himself from thinking about that!

"Bring us a bottle of your finest wine," Kitiara told the hovering innkeeper, "and two glasses." She raised her other leg, her brown eyes on Tanis. "Then leave us alone."

"But—my lord—" the innkeeper said hesitantly, "there have been messages from Dragon Highlord Ariakas. . . ."

"If you show your face in this room—*after* you bring the wine—I'll cut off your ears," Kitiara said pleasantly. But, as she spoke, she drew a gleaming dagger from her belt.

The innkeeper turned pale, nodded, and left hurriedly.

Kit laughed. "There!" she said, wiggling her toes in their blue silken hose. "Now, I'll take off your boots—"

"I—I really must go," Tanis said, sweating beneath his armor. "My c-company commander will be missing me . . ."

"But *I'm* commander of your company!" Kit said gaily. "And tomorrow *you'll* be commander of your company. Or higher, if you like. Now, sit down."

Tanis could do nothing but obey, knowing, however, that in his heart he *wanted* to do nothing but obey.

"It's so good to see you," Kit said, kneeling before him and tugging at his boot. "I'm sorry I missed the reunion in Solace. How is everyone? How is Sturm? Probably fighting with the Knights, I suppose. I'm not surprised you two separated. That was one friendship I never could understand—"

Kitiara talked on, but Tanis ceased to listen. He could only look at her. He had forgotten how lovely she was, how sensual, inviting. Desperately he concentrated on his own danger. But all he could think of were nights of bliss† spent with Kitiara.

At that moment, Kit looked up into his eyes. Caught and held by the passion she saw in them, she let his boot slip from her hands. Involuntarily, Tanis reached out and drew her near. Kitiara slid her hand around his neck and pressed her lips against his.

At her touch, the desires and longings that had tormented Tanis for five years surged through his body. Her fragrance, warm and womanly—mingled with the smell of leather and steel. Her kiss was like flame. The pain was unbearable. Tanis knew only one way to end it.

When the innkeeper knocked on the door, he received no answer. Shaking his head in admiration—this was the third man in as many days—he set the wine upon the floor and left.†

I often have referred to this type of scene as a "boot scene." A "boot scene" is when you are watching Captain Kirk fall into the arms of a magnificent alien goddess, the music swells—then we cut away to McCoy and Spock batting some plot point back and forth between them and by the time we cut back—well, Kirk is putting on his boots.

Now there's nothing particularly suggestive about Kirk's boots per se, but we all know what actually happened (even if, being an alien goddess, we aren't exactly sure how it happened—but we'll let that pass). The point is that I believe sex is best conveyed in a story or film through such a "boot scene." The actual details of who put what hand where and whether

"And now," Kitiara murmured sleepily, lying in Tanis's arms. "Tell me about my little brothers. Are they with you? The last I saw them, you were escaping from Tarsis with that elf woman."

"That was you!" Tanis said, remembering the blue dragons.

"Of course!" Kit cuddled nearer. "I like the beard," she said, stroking his face. "It hides those weak elvish features. How did you get into the army?"

How indeed? thought Tanis frantically.

"We . . . were captured in Silvanesti. One of the officers convinced me I was a fool to fight the D-Dark Queen."

"And my little brothers?"

"We—we were separated," Tanis said weakly.

"A pity," Kit said with a sigh. "I'd like to see them again. Caramon must be a giant by now. And Raistlin—I hear he is quite a skilled mage. Still wearing the Red Robes?"

"I—I guess," Tanis muttered. "I haven't seen him—"

"That won't last long," Kit said complacently. "He's like me. Raist always craved power . . ."

"What about you?" Tanis interrupted quickly. "What are you doing here, so far from the action? The fighting's north—"

"Why, I'm here for the same reason you are," Kit answered, opening her eyes wide. "Searching for the Green Gemstone Man, of course."

"That's where I've seen him before!" Tanis said, memories flooding his mind. The man on the *Perechon*! The man in Pax Tharkas, escaping with poor Eben. The man with the green gemstone embedded in the center of his chest.

"You've found him!" Kitiara said, sitting up eagerly. "Where, Tanis? Where?" Her brown eyes glittered.

"I'm not sure," Tanis said, faltering. "I'm not sure it was him. I—we were just given a rough description. . . ."

"He looks about fifty in human years," Kit said in excitement, "but he has strange, young eyes, and his hands are young. And in the flesh of his chest is a green gemstone. We had reports he was sighted in Flotsam. That's why the Dark Queen sent me here. He's the key, Tanis! Find him—and no force on Krynn can stop us!"

"Why?" Tanis made himself ask calmly. "What's he got that's so essential to—uh—our side winning this war?"

"Who knows?" Shrugging her slender shoulders, Kit lay back in Tanis's arms. "You're shivering. Here, this will warm you." She kissed his neck, running her hands over his body. "We were just told the most important thing we could do to end this war in one swift stroke is to find this man."

Tanis swallowed, feeling himself warming to her touch.

"Just think," Kitiara whispered in his ear, her breath hot and moist against his skin, "if we found him—you and I—we would have all of Krynn at our feet! The Dark Queen would reward us beyond anything we ever dreamed! You and I, together always, Tanis. Let's go now!"

Her words echoed in his mind. The two of them, together, forever. Ending the war. Ruling Krynn. No, he thought, feeling his throat constrict. This is madness! Insanity! My people, my friends. . . . Yet,

anything "pulsed" or "throbbed" does not add anything to the story nor give us any particularly deeper understanding of the characters. Besides, sex is one of those things that loses almost everything when it is reduced to words on a page or pictures on the screen. For sex in stories, give me a good "boot scene" every time.—TRH

haven't I done enough? What do I owe any of them, humans or elves? Nothing! They are the ones who have hurt me, derided me! All these years, a cast-out. Why think about them? *Me!* It's time I thought about *me* for a change! This is the woman I've dreamed of for so long. And she can be mine! Kitiara . . . so beautiful, so desirable . . .

"No!" Tanis said harshly, then, "No," he said more gently. Reaching out his hand, he pulled her back near him. "Tomorrow will do. If it was him, he isn't going anywhere. I know. . . ."

Kitiara smiled and, with a sigh, lay back down. Tanis, bending over her, kissed her passionately. Far away, he could hear the waves of the Blood Sea of Istar crashing on the shore.

10

The High Clerist's Tower.
The Knighting.

By morning, the storm over Solamnia had blown itself out. The sun rose, a disk of pale gold that warmed nothing. The knights who stood watch upon the battlements of the Tower of the High Clerist went thankfully to their beds, talking of the wonders they had seen during the awful night, for such a storm as this had not been known in the lands of Solamnia since the days after the Cataclysm. Those who took over the watch from their fellow knights were nearly as weary; no one had slept.

Now they looked out upon a plain covered with snow and ice. Here and there the landscape was dotted with flickering flames where trees, blasted by the jagged lightning that had streaked out of the sky during the blizzard, burned eerily. But it was

not to those strange flames the eyes of the knights turned as they ascended the battlements. It was to the flames that burned upon the horizon—hundreds and hundreds of flames, filling the clear, cold air with their foul smoke.

The campfires of war. The campfires of the dragonarmies.

One thing stood between the Dragon Highlord and victory in Solamnia. That "thing" (as the Highlord often referred to it) was the Tower of the High Clerist.† Built long ago by Vinas Solamnus, founder of the Knights, in the only pass through the snow-capped, cloud-shrouded Vingaard Mountains, the Tower protected Palanthas, capital city of Solamnia, and the harbor known as the Gates of Paladine. Let the Tower fall, and Palanthas would belong to the dragonarmies. It was a soft city—a city of wealth and beauty, a city that had turned its back upon the world to gaze with admiring eyes into its own mirror.

This tower has none of the beauty or enchantment of the Towers of High Sorcery or the elf towers. It's a massive fortress of strange design set in a valley where no one can get through toward Palanthas. Even at this time, when there are so few Knights of Solamnia, the tower is held by the Knights.

With Palanthas in her hands and the harbor under her control, the Highlord could easily starve the rest of Solamnia into submission and then wipe out the troublesome Knights.

The Dragon Highlord, called the Dark Lady by her troops, was not in camp this day. She was gone on secret business to the east. But she had left loyal and able commanders behind her, commanders who would do anything to win her favor.

Of all the Dragon Highlords, the Dark Lady was known to sit highest in the regard of her Dark Queen. And so the troops of draconians, goblins, hobgoblins, ogres, and humans sat around their campfires, staring at the Tower with hungry eyes, longing to attack and earn her commendation.

The Tower was defended by a large garrison of Knights of Solamnia who had marched out from Palanthas only a few weeks ago. Legend recalled that the Tower had never fallen while men of faith held it, dedicated as it was to the High Clerist—that position which, second only to the Grand Master, was most revered in the Knighthood.

The clerics of Paladine had lived in the High Clerist's Tower during the Age of Dreams.† Here young knights had come for their religious training

During the period of the ancient Dragon Wars.

and indoctrination. There were still many traces of the clerics' presence left behind.

It wasn't only fear of the legend that forced the dragonarmies to sit idle. It didn't take a legend to tell their commanders that taking this tower was going to be costly.

"Time is in our favor," stated the Dark Lady before she left. "Our spies tell us the knights have received little help from Palanthas. We've cut off their supplies from Vingaard Keep to the east. Let them sit in their tower and starve. Sooner or later their impatience and their stomachs will cause them to make a mistake. When they do, we will be ready."

"We could take it with a flight of dragons," muttered a young commander. His name was Bakaris,† and his bravery in battle and his handsome face had done much to advance him in the Dark Lady's favor. She eyed him speculatively, however, as she prepared to mount her blue dragon, Skie.

Originally from Estwilde, Bakaris is the Blue Dragon Lieutenant, second in command to Kitiara—and undoubtedly a participant in a "boot scene."

"Perhaps not," she said coolly. "You've heard the reports of the discovery of the ancient weapon—the dragonlance?"

"Bah! Children's stories!" The young commander laughed as he assisted her onto Skie's back. The blue dragon stood glaring at the handsome commander with fierce, fiery eyes.

"Never discount children's stories," the Dark Lady said, "for these were the same tales that were told of dragons." She shrugged. "Do not worry, my pet. If my mission to capture the Green Gemstone Man is successful, we will not need to attack the Tower, for its destruction will be assured. If not, perhaps I will bring you that flight of dragons you ask for."

With that, the giant blue lifted his wings and sailed off toward the east, heading for a small and wretched town called Flotsam on the Blood Sea of Istar.

And so the dragonarmies waited, warm and comfortable around their fires, while—as the Dark Lady had predicted—the knights in their Tower starved. But far worse than the lack of food was the bitter dissension within their own ranks.

The young knights under Sturm Brightblade's command had grown to revere their disgraced leader during the hard months that followed their departure from Sancrist. Although melancholy and

often aloof, Sturm's honesty and integrity won him his men's respect and admiration. It was a costly victory, causing Sturm a great deal of suffering at Derek's hands. A less noble man might have turned a blind eye to Derek's political maneuvers, or at least kept his mouth shut (as did Lord Alfred), but Sturm spoke out against Derek constantly—even though he knew it worsened his own cause with the powerful knight.

It was Derek who had completely alienated the people of Palanthas. Already distrustful, filled with old hatreds and bitterness, the people of the beautiful, quiet city were alarmed and angered by Derek's threats when they refused to allow the Knights to garrison the city. It was only through Sturm's patient negotiations that the knights received any supplies at all.

The situation did not improve when the knights reached the High Clerist's Tower. The disruption among the knights lowered the morale of the footmen,† already suffering from a lack of food. Soon the Tower itself became an armed camp—the majority of knights who favored Derek were now openly opposed by those siding with Lord Gunthar, led by Sturm. It was only because of the knights' strict obedience to the Measure that fights within the Tower itself had not yet broken out. But the demoralizing sight of the dragonarmies camped nearby, as well as the lack of food, led to frayed tempers and taut nerves.

Footmen are a conscripted army under the direction of the knights but not part of the knighthood itself.
—TRH

Too late, Lord Alfred realized their danger. He bitterly regretted his own folly in supporting Derek, for he could see clearly now that Derek Crownguard was going insane.

The madness grew on him daily; Derek's lust for power ate away at him and deprived him of his reason. But Lord Alfred was powerless to act. So locked into their rigid structure were the knights that it would take—according to the Measure—months of Knights Councils to strip Derek of his rank.

News of Sturm's vindication struck this dry and crackling forest like a bolt of lightning. As Gunthar had foreseen, this completely shattered Derek's hopes. What Gunthar had not foreseen was that this would sever Derek's tenuous hold on sanity.

On the morning following the storm, the eyes of the guards turned for a moment from their vigilance over the dragonarmies to look down into the courtyard of the Tower of the High Clerist. The sun filled the gray sky with a chill, pale light that was reflected in the coldly gleaming armor of the Knights of Solamnia as they assembled in the solemn ceremony awarding knighthood.

Above them, the flags with the Knight's Crest seemed frozen upon the battlements, hanging lifeless in the still, cold air. Then a trumpet's pure notes split the air, stirring the blood. At that clarion call, the knights lifted their heads proudly and marched into the courtyard.

Lord Alfred stood in the center of a circle of knights. Dressed in his battle armor, his red cape fluttering from his shoulders, he held an antique sword in an old, battered scabbard. The kingfisher,† the rose, and the crown—ancient symbols of the Knighthood—were entwined upon the scabbard. The lord cast a swift, hopeful gaze around the assembly, but then lowered his eyes, shaking his head.

Caramon, in his Bestiary, *later wrote: "I still have no clue what the Knights of Solamnia find so appealing about this bird. It isn't a great warrior, it doesn't do anything special or have any prophetic markings. Why do they make such a fuss over it?" To this, Bertrem the Aesthetic adds: "Whatever else can be said about a kingfisher, it is a protective parent. It guards its nest zealously, refusing to leave even in the face of death itself. Several books on natural science report that kingfishers do anything to feed their young, including tearing off strips of their own flesh. I believe that this boundless sense of responsibility and honor that parallels the Solamnic Measure gives the kingfisher a place of honor within the Knighthood."*

Lord Alfred's worst fears were realized. He had hoped bleakly that this ceremony might reunite the knights. But it was having the opposite effect. There were great gaps in the Sacred Circle, gaps that the knights in attendance stared at uncomfortably. Derek and his entire command were absent.

The trumpet call sounded twice more, then silence fell upon the assembled knights. Sturm Brightblade, dressed in long, white robes, stepped out of the Chapel of the High Clerist where he had spent the night in solemn prayer and meditation as prescribed by the Measure. Accompanying him was an unusual Guard of Honor.

Beside Sturm walked an elven woman, her beauty shining in the bleakness of the day like the sun dawning in the spring. Behind her walked an old dwarf, the sunlight bright on his white hair and beard. Next to the dwarf came a kender dressed in bright blue leggings.

The circle of knights opened to admit Sturm and his escorts. They came to a halt before Lord Alfred. Laurana, holding his helm in her hands, stood on his right. Flint, carrying his shield, stood on his left, and

after a poke in the ribs from the dwarf—Tasslehoff hurried forward with the knight's spurs.

Sturm bowed his head. His long hair, already streaked with gray though he was only in his early thirties, fell about his shoulders. He stood a moment in silent prayer, then, at a sign from Lord Alfred, fell reverently to his knees.

"Sturm Brightblade," Lord Alfred declared solemnly, opening a sheet of paper, "the Knights Council, on hearing testimony given by Lauralanthalasa of the royal family of Qualinesti and further testimony by Flint Fireforge, hill dwarf of Solace township, has granted you Vindication from the charges brought against you. In recognition of your deeds of bravery and courage as related by these witnesses, you are hereby declared a Knight of Solamnia." Lord Alfred's voices softened as he looked down upon the knight. Tears streamed unchecked down Sturm's gaunt cheeks. "You have spent the night in prayer, Sturm Brightblade," Alfred said quietly. "Do you consider yourself worthy of this great honor?"

"No, my lord," Sturm answered, according to ancient ritual, "but I most humbly accept it and vow that I shall devote my life to making myself worthy." The knight lifted his eyes to the sky. "With Paladine's help," he said softly, "I shall do so."

Lord Alfred had been through many such ceremonies, but he could not recall such fervent dedication in a man's face.

"I wish Tanis were here," Flint muttered gruffly to Laurana, who only nodded briefly.

She stood tall and straight, wearing armor specially made for her in Palanthas at Lord Gunthar's command. Her honey-colored hair streamed from beneath a silver helm. Intricate gold designs glinted on her breastplate, her soft black leather skirt—slit up the side to allow freedom of movement—brushed the tips of her boots. Her face was pale and grim, for the situation in Palanthas and in the Tower itself was dark and seemingly without hope.

She could have returned to Sancrist. She had been ordered to, in fact. Lord Gunthar had received a secret communique from Lord Alfred relating the desperate straits the knights were in, and he had sent Laurana orders to cut short her stay.

But she had chosen to remain, at least for a while. The people of Palanthas had received her politely—she was, after all, of royal blood and they were charmed with her beauty. They were also quite interested in the dragonlance and asked for one to exhibit in their museum. But when Laurana mentioned the dragonarmies, they only shrugged and smiled.

Then Laurana found out from a messenger what was happening in the High Clerist's Tower. The knights were under siege. A dragonarmy numbering in the thousands waited upon the field. The knights needed the dragonlances, Laurana decided, and there was no one but her to take the lances to the knights and teach them their use. She ignored Lord Gunthar's command to return to Sancrist.

The journey from Palanthas to the Tower was nightmarish. Laurana started out accompanying two wagons filled with meager supplies and the precious dragonlances. The first wagon bogged down in snow only a few miles outside of the city. Its contents were redistributed between the few knights riding escort, Laurana and her party, and the second wagon. It, too, foundered. Time and again they dug it out of the snow drifts until, finally, it was mired fast. Loading the food and the lances onto their horses, the knights and Laurana, Flint, and Tas walked the rest of the way. Theirs was the last group to make it through. After the storm of last night, Laurana knew, as did everyone in the Tower, no more supplies would be coming. The road to Palanthas was now impassable.

Even by strictest rationing, the knights and their footmen had food enough for only a few days. The dragonarmies seemed prepared to wait for the rest of the winter.

The dragonlances were taken from the weary horses who had borne them and, by Derek's orders, were stacked in the courtyard. A few of the knights looked at them curiously, then ignored them. The lances seemed clumsy, unwieldy weapons.†

The dragonlances were much longer than a normal footman's lance and heavier. They were designed almost exclusively to be used mounted on the saddles designed for the backs of good dragons and were used primarily as an air-to-air weapon.—TRH

When Laurana timidly offered to instruct the knights in the use of the lances, Derek snorted in derision. Lord Alfred stared out the window at the campfires burning on the horizon. Laurana turned to Sturm to see her fears confirmed.

"Laurana," he said gently, taking her cold hand in his, "I don't think the Highlord will even bother to send dragons. If we cannot reopen the supply lines, the Tower will fall because there will be only the dead left to defend it."

So the dragonlances lay in the courtyard, unused, forgotten, their bright silver buried beneath the snow.

II

A kender's curiosity. The Knights ride forth.

Sturm and Flint walked the battlements the night of Sturm's knighting, reminiscing.

"A well of pure silver—shining like a jewel—within the heart of the Dragon Mountain," Flint said, awe his voice. "And it was from that silver Theros forged the dragonlances."

"I should have liked—above all things—to have seen Huma's Tomb," Sturm said quietly. Staring out at the campfires on the horizon, he stopped, resting his hand on the ancient stone wall. Torchlight from a nearby window shone on his thin face.

"You will," said the dwarf. "When this is finished, we'll go back. Tas drew a map, not that it's likely to be any good—"

As he grumbled on about Tas, Flint studied his other old friend with concern. The knight's face was grave and melancholy—not unusual for Sturm. But there was something new, a calmness about him that came not from serenity, but from despair.

"We'll go there together," he continued, trying to forget about his hunger. "You and Tanis and I. And the kender, too, I suppose, plus Caramon and Raistlin. I never thought I'd miss that skinny mage, but a magic-user might be handy now. It's just as well Caramon's not here. Can you imagine the belly-aching we'd hear about missing a couple of meals?"

Sturm smiled absently, his thoughts far away. When he spoke, it was obvious he hadn't heard a word the dwarf said.

"Flint," he began, his voice soft and subdued, "we need only one day of warm weather to open the road. When that day comes, take Laurana and Tas and leave. Promise me."

"We should all leave if you ask me!" the dwarf snapped. "Pull the knights back to Palanthas. We could hold that town against even dragons, I'll wager. Its buildings are good solid stone. Not like this place!"† The dwarf glanced around the human-built Tower with scorn. "Palanthas could be defended."

Apparently the humans did a good enough job; the Tower of the High Clerist has stood for thousands of years.

Sturm shook his head. "The people won't allow it. They care only for their beautiful city. As long as they think it can be saved, they won't fight. No, we must make our stand here."

"You don't have a chance," Flint argued.

"Yes, we do," Sturm replied, "if we can just hold out until the supply lines can be firmly established. We've got enough manpower. That's why the drag-onarmies haven't attacked—"

"There's another way," came a voice.

Sturm and Flint turned. The torchlight fell on a gaunt face, and Sturm's expression hardened.

"What way is that, Lord Derek?" Sturm asked with deliberate politeness.

"You and Gunthar believe you have defeated me," Derek said, ignoring the question. His voice was soft and shaking with hatred as he stared at Sturm. "But you haven't! By one heroic act, I will have the Knights in my palm"—Derek held out his mailed hand, the armor flashing in the firelight—

"and you and Gunthar will be finished!" Slowly, he clenched his fist.

"I was under the impression our war was out there, with the dragonarmies," Sturm said.

"Don't give me that self-righteous twaddle!" Derek snarled. "Enjoy your knighthood, Brightblade. You paid enough for it. What did you promise the elfwoman in return for her lies? Marriage? Make a respectable woman of her?"

"I cannot fight you—according to the Measure—but I do not have to listen to you insult a woman who is as good as she is courageous," Sturm said, turning upon his heel to leave.

"Don't you ever walk away from me!" Derek cried. Leaping forward, he grabbed Sturm's shoulder. Sturm whirled in anger, his hand on his sword. Derek reached for his weapon as well, and it seemed for a moment that the Measure might be forgotten. But Flint laid a restraining hand on his friend. Sturm drew a deep breath and lifted his hand away from the hilt.

"Say what you have to say, Derek!" Sturm's voice quivered.

"You're finished, Brightblade. Tomorrow I'm leading the knights onto the field. No more skulking in this miserable rock prison. By tomorrow night, my name will be legend!"

Flint looked up at Sturm in alarm. The knight's face had drained of blood. "Derek," Sturm said softly, "you're mad! There are thousands of them! They'll cut you to ribbons!"

"Yes, that's what you'd like to see, isn't it?" Derek sneered. "Be ready at dawn, Brightblade."

That night, Tasslehoff—cold, hungry, and bored—decided that the best way to take his mind off his stomach was to explore his surroundings. There are plenty of places to hide things here, thought Tas. This is one of the strangest buildings I've ever seen.

The Tower of the High Clerist sat solidly against the west side of the Westgate Pass, the only canyon pass that crossed the Habbakuk Range of mountains separating eastern Solamnia from Palanthas. As the Dragon Highlord knew, anyone trying to reach Palanthas other than by this route would have to

The Gates of Paladine is the cliff-edged entrance to the long fjord called the Bay of Branchala leading to Palanthas. Branchala is a god of Good.

travel hundreds of miles around the mountains, or through the desert, or by sea. And ships entering the Gates of Paladine† were easy targets for the gnomes' fire-throwing catapults.

The High Clerist's Tower had been built during the Age of Might. Flint knew a lot about the architecture of this period—the dwarves having been instrumental in designing and building most of it. But they had not built or designed this Tower. In fact, Flint wondered who had—figuring the person must have been either drunk or insane.

An outer curtain wall of stone formed an octagon as the Tower's base. Each point of the octagonal wall was surmounted by a turret. Battlements ran along the top of the curtain wall between turrets. An inner octagonal wall formed the base of a series of towers and buttresses that swept gracefully upward to the central Tower itself.

Considering that the coinage of Krynn is based on steel, these doors would be incredibly valuable.

This was fairly standard design, but what puzzled the dwarf was the lack of internal defense points. Three great steel† doors breached the outer wall, instead of one door—as would seem most reasonable, since three doors took an incredible number of men to defend. Each door opened into a narrow courtyard at the far end of which stood a portcullis leading directly into a huge hallway. Each of these three hallways met in the heart of the Tower itself!

"Might as well invite the enemy inside for tea!" the dwarf had grumbled. "Stupidest way to build a fortress I ever saw."

No one entered the Tower. To the knights, it was inviolate. The only one who could enter the Tower was the High Clerist himself, and since there was no High Clerist, the knights would defend the Tower walls with their lives, but not one of them could set foot in its sacred halls.

Originally the Tower had merely guarded the pass, not blocked it. But the Palanthians had later built an addition to the main structure that sealed off the pass. It was in this addition that the knights and the footmen were living. No one even thought of entering the Tower itself.

No one except Tasslehoff.

Driven by his insatiable curiosity and his gnawing hunger, the kender made his way along the top

of the outer wall. The knights on guard duty eyed him warily, gripping their swords in one hand, their purses in the other. But they relaxed as soon as he passed, and Tas was able to slip down the steps and into the central courtyard.†

It's handy to have a kender around when danger might lurk because kender will notice anything, no matter how miniscule, in a scene that might indicate trouble ahead. Of course, they might go explore it first, forgetting to warn you about it. So, off Tas goes.

Only shadows walked down here. No torches burned, no guard was posted. Broad steps led up to the steel portcullis. Tas padded up the stairs toward the great, yawning archway and peered eagerly through the bars. Nothing. He sighed. The darkness beyond was so intense he might have been staring into the Abyss itself.

Frustrated, he pushed up on the portcullis, more out of habit than hope, for only Caramon or ten knights would have the strength necessary to raise it.

To the kender's astonishment, the portcullis began to rise, making the most god-awful screeching! Grabbing for it, Tas dragged it slowly to a halt. The kender looked fearfully up at the battlements, expecting to see the entire garrison thundering down to capture him. But apparently the knights were listening only to the growlings of their empty stomachs.

Tas turned back to the portcullis. There was a small space open between the sharp iron spikes and the stone work, a space just big enough for a kender. Tas didn't waste any time or stop to consider the consequences. Flattening himself, he wriggled beneath the spikes.

He found himself in a large, wide hall, nearly fifty feet across. He could see just a short distance. There were old torches on the wall, however. After a few jumps, Tas reached one and lit it from Flint's tinder box he found in his pouch.

Now Tas could see the gigantic hall clearly. It ran straight ahead, right into the heart of the Tower. Strange columns ranged along either side, like jagged teeth. Peering behind one, he saw nothing but an alcove.

The hall itself was empty. Disappointed, Tas continued walking down it, hoping to find something interesting. He came to a second portcullis, already raised, much to his chagrin. "Anything easy is more trouble than it's worth," was an old kender saying.† Tas walked beneath that portcullis into a second

There's also "Curiosity killed the kender."

hallway, narrower than the first—only about ten feet wide—but with the same strange, toothlike columns on either side.

Why build a tower so easy to enter? Tas wondered. The outer wall was formidable, but once past that, five drunken dwarves could take this place. Tas peered up. And why so huge? The main hall was thirty feet high!

Perhaps the knights back in those days had been giants, the kender speculated with interest as he crept down the hall, peering into open doors and poking into corners.

At the end of the second hallway, he found a third portcullis. This one was different from the other two, and as strange as the rest of the Tower. This portcullis had two halves, which slid together to join in the center. Oddest of all, there was a large hole cut right through the middle of the doors!

Crawling through this hole, Tas found himself in a smaller room. Across from him stood two huge steel doors. Pushing on them casually, he was startled to find them locked. None of the portcullises had been locked. There was nothing to protect.

Well, at least here was something to keep him occupied and make him forget about his empty stomach. Climbing onto a stone bench, Tas stuck his torch into a wall sconce, then began to fumble through his pouches. He finally discovered the set of lock-picking devices that are a kender's birthright—"Why insult the door's purpose by locking it?" is a favorite kender expression.

Quickly Tas selected the proper tool and set to work. The lock was simple. There was a slight click, and Tas pocketed his tools with satisfaction as the door swung inward. The kender stood a moment, listening carefully. He could hear nothing. Peering inside, he could see nothing. Climbing up on the bench again, he retrieved his torch and crept carefully through the steel doors.

Holding his torch aloft, he found himself in a great, wide, circular room. Tas sighed. The great room was empty except for a dust-covered object that resembled an ancient fountain standing squarely in the center. This was the end of the corridor, too, for though there were two more sets of double doors leading out of the room, it was

obvious to the kender that they only led back up the other two giant hallways. This was the heart of the Tower. This was the sacred place.† This was what all the fuss was about.

Nothing.

Tas walked around a bit, shining his torchlight here and there. Finally the disgruntled kender went to examine the fountain in the center of the room before leaving.

As Tas drew closer, he saw it wasn't a fountain at all, but the dust was so thick, he couldn't figure it out. It was about as tall as the kender, standing four feet off the ground. The round top was supported on a slender three-legged stand.

Tas inspected the object closely, then he took a deep breath and blew as hard as he could. Dust flew up his nose and he sneezed violently, nearly dropping the torch. For a moment he couldn't see a thing. Then the dust settled and he could see the object. His heart leaped into his throat.

"Oh, no!" Tas groaned. Diving into another pouch, he pulled out a handkerchief and rubbed the object. The dust came off easily, and he knew now what it was. "Drat!" he said in despair. "I was right. Now what do I do?"

The original design for the High Clerist's Tower was a gargantuan structure of immense complexity and detail. Every consideration was given to its defense—particularly against dragons. Indeed, the interior structure was designed specifically to combat dragons.

As my wife and I envisioned it in the game design, the tower itself was haunted by spectral revelers whose souls were trapped in an eternal celebration of death. The knights never seem to penetrate too far into the interior of the tower in the book—it's probably just as well for them that they did not.—TRH

The sun rose red the next morning, glimmering through a haze of smoke hovering above the dragonarmies. In the courtyard of the Tower of the High Clerist, the shadows of night had not yet lifted before activity began. One hundred knights mounted their horses, adjusted the girths, called for shields, or buckled on armor, while a thousand footmen milled around, searching for their proper places in line.

Sturm, Laurana, and Lord Alfred stood in a dark doorway, watching in silence as Lord Derek, laughing and calling out jokes to his men, rode into the courtyard. The knight was resplendent in his armor, the rose glistening on his breastplate in the first rays of the sun. His men were in good spirits, the thought of battle making them forget their hunger.

"You've got to stop this, my lord," Sturm said quietly.

"I can't!" Lord Alfred said, pulling on his gloves. His face was haggard in the morning light. He had not slept since Sturm awakened him in the waning

hours of the night. "The Measure gives him the right to make this decision."

In vain had Alfred argued with Derek, trying to convince him to wait just a few more days! Already the wind was starting to shift, bringing warm breezes from the north.

But Derek had been adamant. He would ride out and challenge the dragonarmies on the field. As for being outnumbered, he laughed in scorn. Since when do goblins fight like Knights of Solamnia? The Knights had been outnumbered fifty to one in the Goblin and Ogre wars† of the Vingaard Keep one hundred years ago, and they'd routed the creatures with ease!

The Goblin and Ogre War is, perhaps, the least chronicled of the conflicts in Krynn—primarily due to the fact that the human historians' primary interest in the war was not so much related to who won but how effective both sides were in killing off the other. The outcome was something of a stalemate, but it did manage to keep peace in the human communities for quite some time.—TRH

"But you'll be fighting draconians," Sturm warned. "They are not like goblins. They are intelligent and skilled. They have magic-users among their ranks, and their weapons are the finest in Krynn. Even in death they have the power to kill—"

"I believe we can deal with them, Brightblade," Derek interrupted harshly. "And now I suggest you wake your men and tell them to make ready."

"I'm not going," Sturm said steadily. "And I'm not ordering my men to go, either."

Derek paled with fury. For a moment he could not speak, he was so angry. Even Lord Alfred appeared shocked.

"Sturm," Alfred began slowly, "do you know what you are doing?"

"Yes, my lord," Sturm answered. "We are the only thing standing between the dragonarmies and Palanthas. We dare not leave this garrison unmanned. I'm keeping my command here."

"Disobeying a direct order," Derek said, breathing heavily. "You are a witness, Lord Alfred. I'll have his *head* this time!" He stalked out. Lord Alfred, his face grim, followed, leaving Sturm alone.

In the end, Sturm had given his men a choice. They could stay with him at no risk to themselves—since they were simply obeying the orders of their commanding officer—or they could accompany Derek. It was, he mentioned, the same choice Vinas Solamnus had given his men long ago, when the Knights rebelled against the corrupt Emperor of Ergoth. The men did not need to be reminded of this legend. They saw it as a sign and, as with So-

lamnus, most of them chose to stay with the commander they had come to respect and admire.

Now they stood watching, their faces grim, as their friends prepared to ride out. It was the first open break in the long history of the Knighthood, and the moment was grievous.

"Reconsider, Sturm," Lord Alfred said as the knight helped him mount his horse. "Lord Derek is right. The dragonarmies have not been trained, not like the Knights. There's every probability we'll route them with barely a blow being struck."

"I pray that is true, my lord," Sturm said steadily.

Alfred regarded him sadly. "If it *is* true, Brightblade, Derek will see you tried and executed for this. There'll be nothing Gunthar can do to stop him."

"I would willingly die that death, my lord, if it would stop what I fear will happen," Sturm replied.

"Damn it, man!" Lord Alfred exploded. "If we are defeated, what will you gain by staying here? You couldn't hold off an army of gully dwarves with your small contingent of men! Suppose the roads do open up? You won't be able to hold the Tower long enough for Palanthas to send reinforcements."

"At the least we can buy Palanthas time to evacuate her citizens, if—"

Lord Derek Crownguard edged his horse between those of his men. Glaring down at Sturm, his eyes glittering from behind the slits in his helm, Lord Derek raised his hand for silence.

"According to the Measure, Sturm Brightblade," Derek began formally, "I hereby charge you with conspiracy and—"

"To the Abyss with the Measure!" Sturm snarled, his patience snapping. "Where has the Measure gotten us? Divided, jealous, crazed! Even our own people prefer to treat with the armies of our enemies! The Measure has failed!"

A deathly hush settled over the knights in the courtyard, broken only by the restless pawing of a horse or the jingle of armor as here and there a man shifted in his saddle.

"Pray for my death, Sturm Brightblade," Derek said softly, "or by the gods I'll slit your throat at your execution myself!" Without another word, he wheeled his horse around and cantered to the head of the column.

"Open the gates!" he called.

The morning sun climbed above the smoke, rising into the blue sky. The winds blew from the north, fluttering the flag flying bravely from the top of the Tower. Armor flashed. There was a clatter of swords against shields and the sound of a trumpet call as men rushed to open the thick wooden gates.

Derek raised his sword high in the air. Lifting his voice in the Knight's salute to the enemy, he galloped forward. The knights behind him picked up his ringing challenge and rode forth out onto the fields where—long ago—Huma had ridden to glorious victory. The footmen marched, their footsteps beating a tattoo upon the stone pavement. For a moment, Lord Alfred seemed about to speak to Sturm and the young knights who stood watching. But he only shook his head and rode away.

The gates swung shut behind him. The heavy iron bar was dropped down to lock them securely. The men in Sturm's command ran to the battlements to watch.

Sturm stood silently in the center of the courtyard, his gaunt face expressionless.

The young and handsome commander of the dragonarmies in the Dark Lady's absence was just waking to breakfast and the start of another boring day when a scout galloped into camp.

Commander Bakaris glared at the scout in disgust. The man was riding through camp wildly, his horse scattering cooking pots and goblins. Draconian guards leaped to their feet, shaking their fists and cursing. But the scout ignored them.

"The Highlord!" he called, sliding off his horse in front of the tent. "I must see the Highlord."

"The Highlord's gone," said the commander's aide.

"I'm in charge," snapped Bakaris. "What's your business?"

The ranger looked around quickly, not wanting to make a mistake. But there was no sign of the dread Dark Lady or the big blue dragon she rode.

"The Knights have taken the field!"

"What?" The commander's jaw sagged. "Are you certain?"

"Yes!" The scout was practically incoherent. "Saw them! Hundreds on horseback! Javelins, swords. A thousand foot."

"She was right!" Bakaris swore softly to himself in admiration. "The fools have made their mistake!"

Calling for his servants, he hurried back to his tent. "Sound the alarm," he ordered, rattling off instructions. "Have the captains here in five minutes for final orders." His hands shook in eagerness as he strapped on his armor. "And send the wyvern to Flotsam with word for the Highlord."

Goblin servants ran off in all directions, and soon blaring horn calls were echoing throughout the camp. The commander cast one last, quick glance at the map on his table, then left to meet with his officers.

"Too bad," he reflected coolly as he walked away. "The fight will probably be over by the time she gets the news. A pity. She would have wanted to be present at the fall of the High Clerist's Tower. Still," he reflected, "perhaps tomorrow night we'll sleep in Palanthas, she and I."

12

Death on the plains.
Tasslehoff's discovery.

The sun climbed high in the sky. The knights stood upon the battlements of the Tower, staring out across the plains until their eyes ached. All they could see was a great tide of black, crawling figures swarming over the fields, ready to engulf the slender spear of gleaming silver that advanced steadily to meet it.

The armies met. The knights strained to see, but a misty gray veil crept across the land. The air became tainted with a foul smell, like hot iron. The mist grew thicker, almost totally obscuring the sun.

Now they could see nothing. The Tower seemed afloat on a sea of fog. The heavy mist even deadened sound, for at first they heard the clash of weapons and the cries of the dying. But even that faded, and all was silent.

The day wore on. Laurana, pacing restlessly in her darkening chamber, lit candles that sputtered and flickered in the foul air. The kender sat with her. Looking down from her tower window, Laurana could see Sturm and Flint, standing on the battlements below her, reflected in ghostly torchlight.

A servant brought her the bit of maggoty bread and dried meat that was her ration for the day. It must be only midafternoon, she realized. Then movement down on the battlements caught her attention. She saw a man dressed in mud-splattered leather approach Sturm. A messenger, she thought. Hurriedly, she began to strap on her armor.

"Coming?" she asked Tas, thinking suddenly that the kender had been awfully quiet. "A messenger's arrived from Palanthas!"

"I guess," Tas said without interest.

Laurana frowned, hoping he wasn't growing weak from lack of food. But Tas shook his head at her concern.

"I'm all right," he mumbled. "Just this stupid gray air."

Laurana forgot about him as she hurried down the stairs.

"News?" she asked Sturm, who peered over the walls in a vain effort to see out onto the field of battle. "I saw the messenger—"

"Oh, yes." He smiled wearily. "Good news, I suppose. The road to Palanthas is open. The snow melted enough to get through. I have a rider standing by to take a message to Palanthas in case we are def—" He stopped abruptly, then drew a deep breath. "I want you to be ready to go back to Palanthas with him."

Laurana had been expecting this and her answer was prepared. But now that the time had come for her speech, she could not give it. The bitter air dried her mouth, her tongue seemed swollen. No, that wasn't it, she chided herself. She was frightened. Admit it. She *wanted* to go back to Palanthas! She wanted to get out of this grim place where death lurked in the shadows. Clenching her fist, she beat her gloved hand nervously on the stone, gathering her courage.

"I'm staying here, Sturm," she said. After pausing to get her voice under control, she continued, "I know what you're going to say, so listen to me first. You're going to need all the skilled fighters you can get. You know my worth."

Sturm nodded. What she said was true. There were few in his command more accurate with a bow. She was a trained swordsman, as well. She was battle-tested—something he couldn't say about many of the young knights under his command. So he nodded in agreement. He meant to send her away anyhow.

"I am the only one trained to use the dragon-lance—"

"Flint's been trained," Sturm interrupted quietly.

Laurana fixed the dwarf with a penetrating stare.

Caught between two people he loved and admired, Flint flushed and cleared his throat. "That's true," he said huskily, "but—uh—I—must admit—er, Sturm, that I *am* a bit short."

"We've seen no sign of dragons, anyhow," Sturm said as Laurana flashed him a triumphant glance. "The reports say they're south of us, fighting for control of Thelgaard."†

Located straight south of the High Clerist's Tower, Thelgaard is unusual for Krynn in having an inner-city castle, Thelgaard Keep.

"But you believe the dragons are on the way, don't you?" Laurana returned.

Sturm appeared uncomfortable. "Perhaps," he muttered.

"You can't lie, Sturm, so don't start now. I'm staying. It's what Tanis would do—"

"Damn it, Laurana!" Sturm said, his face flushed. "Live your own life! *You* can't be Tanis! *I* can't be Tanis! He isn't here! We've got to face that!" The knight turned away suddenly. "He isn't here," he repeated harshly.

Flint sighed, glancing sorrowfully at Laurana. No one noticed Tasslehoff, who sat huddled miserably in a corner.

Laurana put her arm around Sturm. "I know I'm not the friend Tanis is to you, Sturm. I can never take his place. But I'll do my best to help you. That's what I meant. You don't have to treat me any differently from your knights—"

"I know, Laurana," Sturm said. Putting his arm around her, he held her close. "I'm sorry I snapped at you." Sturm sighed. "And you know why I must send you away. Tanis would never forgive me if anything happened to you."

"Yes, he would," Laurana answered softly. "He would understand. He told me once that there comes a time when you've got to risk your life for something that means more than life itself. Don't you see, Sturm? If I fled to safety, leaving my friends behind, he would say he understood. But, deep inside, he wouldn't. Because it is so far from what he would do himself. Besides"—she smiled—"even if there were no Tanis in this world, I still could not leave my friends."

Sturm looked into her eyes and saw that no words of his would make any difference. Silently, he held her close. His other arm went around Flint's shoulder and drew the dwarf near.

Tasslehoff, bursting into tears, stood up and flung himself on them, sobbing wildly. They stared at him in astonishment.

"Tas, what is it?" Laurana asked, alarmed.

"It's all my fault! I broke one! Am I doomed to go around the world breaking these things?" Tas wailed incoherently.

"Calm down," Sturm said, his voice stern. He gave the kender a shake. "What are you talking about?"

"I found another one," Tas blubbered. "Down below, in a big empty chamber."

"Another what, you doorknob?" Flint said in exasperation.

"Another dragon orb!" Tas wailed.

Night settled over the Tower like a thicker, heavier fog. The knights lighted torches, but the flame only peopled the darkness with ghosts.The knights kept silent watch from the battlements, straining to hear or see something, anything. . . .

Then, when it was nearly midnight, they were startled to hear, not the victorious shouts of their comrades or the flat, blaring horns of the enemy, but the jingle of harness, the soft whinny of horses approaching the fortress.

Rushing to the edge of the battlements, the knights shone torches down into the fog. They heard the hoofbeats slowly come to a halt. Sturm stood above the gate.

"Who rides to the Tower of the High Clerist?" he called.

A single torch flared below. Laurana, staring down into the misty darkness, felt her knees grow weak and grabbed the stone wall to support herself. The knights cried out in horror.

The rider who held the flaming torch was dressed in the shining armor of an officer in the dragonarmy. He was blonde, his features handsome, cold, and cruel. He led a second horse across which were thrown two bodies—one of them headless, both bloody, mutilated.

"I have brought back your officers," the man said, his voice harsh and blaring. "One is quite dead, as you can see. The other, I believe, still lives. Or he did when I started on my journey. I hope he is still living, so that he can recount for you what took place upon the field of battle today. If you could even call it a battle."

Bathed in the glare of his own torch, the officer dismounted. He began to untie the bodies, using one hand to strip away the ropes binding them to the saddle. Then he glanced up.

"Yes, you could kill me now. I am a fine target, even in this fog. But you won't. You're Knights of Solamnia"—his sarcasm was sharp—"and your honor is your life. You wouldn't shoot an unarmed man returning the bodies of your leaders." He gave the ropes a yank. The headless body slid to the ground. The officer dragged the other body off the saddle. He tossed the torch down into the snow next to the bodies. It sizzled, then went out, and the darkness swallowed him.

"You have a surfeit of honor out there on the field," he called. The knights could hear the leather creak, his armor clang as he remounted his horse. "I'll give you until morning to surrender. When the sun rises, lower your flag. The Dragon Highlord will deal with you mercifully—"

Suddenly there was the twang of a bow, the thunk of an arrow striking into flesh, and the sound of startled swearing from below them. The knights turned around to stare in astonishment at a lone figure standing on the wall, a bow in its hand.

"I am not a knight," Laurana called out, lowering her bow. "I am Lauralanthalasa, daughter of the Qualinesti. We elves have our own code of honor and, as I'm sure you know, I can see you quite well

in this darkness. I could have killed you. As it is, I believe you will have some difficulty using that arm for a long time. In fact, you may never hold a sword again."

"Take that as our answer to your Highlord," Sturm said harshly. "We will lie cold in death before we lower our flag!"

"Indeed you will!" the officer said through teeth clenched in pain. The sound of galloping hooves was lost in the darkness.

"Bring in the bodies," Sturm ordered.

Cautiously, the knights opened the gates. Several rushed out to cover the others who gently lifted the bodies and bore them inside. Then the guard retreated back into the fortress and bolted the gates behind them.

Sturm knelt in the snow beside the body of the headless knight. Lifting the man's hand, he removed a ring from the stiff, cold fingers. The knight's armor was battered and black with blood. Dropping the lifeless hand back into the snow, Sturm bowed his head. "Lord Alfred," he said tonelessly.

"Sir," said one of the young knights, "the other is Lord Derek. The foul dragon officer was right—he is still alive."

Sturm rose and walked over to where Derek lay on the cold stone. The lord's face was white, his eyes wide and glittering feverishly. Blood caked his lips, his skin was clammy. One of the young knights supporting him, held a cup of water to his lips, but Derek could not drink.

Sick with horror, Sturm saw Derek's hand was pressed over his stomach, where his life's blood was welling out, but not fast enough to end the agonizing pain. Giving a ghastly smile, Derek clutched Sturm's arm with a bloody hand.

"Victory!" he croaked. "They ran before us and we pursued! It was glorious, glorious! And I—I will be Grand Master!" He choked and blood spewed from his mouth as he fell back into the arms of the young knight, who looked up at Sturm, his youthful face hopeful.

"Do you suppose he's right, sir? Maybe that was a ruse—" His voice died at the sight of Sturm's grim face, and he looked back at Derek with pity. "He's mad, isn't he, sir?"

"He's dying—bravely—like a true knight," Sturm said.

"Victory!" Derek whispered, then his eyes fixed in his head and he gazed sightlessly into the fog.

"No, you mustn't break it," said Laurana.

"But Fizban said—"

"I know what he said," Laurana replied impatiently. "It isn't evil, it isn't good, it's not anything, it's everything. That"—she muttered—"is so like Fizban!"

She and Tas stood in front of the dragon orb. The orb rested on its stand in the center of the round room, still covered with dust except for the spot Tas had rubbed clean. The room was dark and eerily silent, so quiet, in fact, that Tas and Laurana felt compelled to whisper.

Laurana stared at the orb, her brow creased in thought. Tas stared at Laurana unhappily, afraid he knew what she was thinking.

"These orbs have to work, Tas!" Laurana said finally. "They were created by powerful magic-users! People like Raistlin who do not tolerate failure. If only we knew how—"

"I know how," Tas said in a broken whisper.

"What?" Laurana asked. "You know! Why didn't you—"

"I didn't know I knew—so to speak," Tas stammered. "It just came to me. Gnosh—the gnome—told me that he discovered writing inside the orb, letters that swirled around in the mist. He couldn't read them, he said, because they were written in some sort of strange language—"

"The language of magic."

"Yes, that's what I said and—"

"But that won't help us! We can't either of us speak it. If only Raistlin—"

"We don't need Raistlin," Tas interrupted. "I can't speak it, but I can read it. You see, I have these glasses—glasses of true seeing, Raistlin called them. They let me read languages—even the language of magic. I know because he said if he caught me reading any of his scrolls he'd turn me into a cricket and swallow me whole."

"And you think you can read the orb?"

"I can try," Tas hedged, "but, Laurana, Sturm said there probably wouldn't be any dragons. Why should we risk even bothering with the orb? Fizban said only the most powerful magic-users dared use it."

"Listen to me, Tasslehoff Burrfoot," Laurana said softly, kneeling down beside the kender and staring him straight in the eye. "If they bring even one dragon here, we're finished. That's why they gave us time to surrender instead of just storming the place. They're using the extra time to bring in dragons. We must take this chance!"

A dark path and a light path. Tasslehoff remembered Fizban's words and hung his head. *Death of those you love, but you have the courage.*

Slowly Tas reached into the pocket of his fleecy vest, pulled out the glasses, and fit the wire frames over his pointed ears.

13

The sun rises. Darkness descends.

The fog lifted with the coming of morning. The day dawned bright and clear—so clear that Sturm, walking the battlements, could see the snow-covered grasslands of his birthplace near Vingaard Keep—† lands now completely controlled by the dragonarmies. The sun's first rays struck the flag of the Knights—kingfisher beneath a golden crown, holding a sword decorated with a rose in his claws. The golden emblem glittered in the morning light. Then Sturm heard the harsh, blaring horns.

Vingaard Keep is the now-abandoned castle once owned by the Brightblades. It lies straight across the Plains of Solamnia from the Tower of the High Clerist.

The dragonarmies marched upon the Tower at dawn.

The young knights—the hundred or so that were left—stood silently on the battlements watching as the vast army crawled across the land with the inexorability of devouring insects.

At first Sturm had wondered about the knight's dying words. "They ran before us!" Why had the dragonarmy run? Then it became clear to him—the dragonmen had used the knights' own vainglory against them in an ancient, yet simple, maneuver. Fall back before your enemy . . . not too fast, just let the front lines show enough fear and terror to be believable. Let them seem to break in panic. Then let your enemy charge after you, overextending his lines. And let your armies close in, surround him, and cut him to shreds.

It didn't need the sight of the bodies—barely visible in the distant trampled, bloody snow—to tell Sturm he had judged correctly. They lay where they had tried desperately to regroup for a final stand. Not that it mattered how they died. He wondered who would look on his body when it was all over.

Flint peered out from a crack in the wall. "At least I'll die on dry land," the dwarf muttered.

Sturm smiled slightly, stroking his moustaches. His eyes went to the east. As he thought about dying, he looked upon the land where he'd been born—a home he had barely known, a father he barely remembered, a country that had driven his family into exile. He was about to give his life to defend that country. Why? Why didn't he just leave and go back to Palanthas?

All of his life he had followed the Code and the Measure. The Code: *Est Sularus oth Mithas*—My Honor Is My Life. The Code was all he had left. The Measure was gone. It had failed. Rigid, inflexible, the Measure had encased the Knights in steel heavier than their armor. The Knights, isolated, fighting to survive, had clung to the Measure in despair—not realizing that it was an anchor, weighing them down.

Why was I different? Sturm wondered. But he knew the answer, even as he listened to the dwarf grumble. It was because of the dwarf, the kender, the mage, the half-elf. . . . They had taught him to see the world through other eyes: slanted eyes, smaller eyes, even hourglass eyes. Knights like Derek saw the world in stark black and white. Sturm had seen the world in all its radiant colors, in all its bleak grayness.

"It's time," he said to Flint. The two descended from the high lookout point just as the first of the

enemy's poison-tipped arrows arched over the walls.

With shrieks and yells, the blaring of horns, and clashing of shield and sword, the dragonarmies struck the Tower of the High Clerist as the sun's brittle light filled the sky.

By nightfall, the flag still flew. The Tower stood.

But half its defenders were dead.

The living had no time during the day to shut the staring eyes or compose the contorted, agonized limbs. The living had all they could do to stay alive. Peace came at last with the night, as the dragonarmies withdrew to rest and wait for the morrow.

Sturm paced the battlements, his body aching with weariness. Yet every time he tried to rest, taut muscles twitched and danced, his brain seemed on fire. And so he was driven to pace again—back and forth, back and forth with slow, measured tread. He could not know that his steady pace drove the day's horrors from the thoughts of the young knights who listened. Knights in the courtyard, laying out the bodies of friends and comrades, thinking that tomorrow someone might be doing this for them, heard Sturm's steady pacing and felt their fears for tomorrow eased.

The ringing sound of the knight's footfalls brought comfort to everyone, in fact, except to the knight himself. Sturm's thoughts were dark and tormented: thoughts of defeat; thoughts of dying ignobly, without honor; tortured memories of the dream, seeing his body hacked and mutilated by the foul creatures camped beyond. Would the dream come true? he wondered, shivering. Would he falter at the end, unable to conquer fear? Would the Code fail him, as had the Measure?

Step . . . step . . . step . . . step . . .

Stop this! Sturm told himself angrily. You'll soon be mad as poor Derek. Spinning abruptly on his heel to break his stride, the knight turned to find Laurana behind him. His eyes met hers, and the black thoughts were brightened by her light. As long as such peace and beauty as hers existed in this world there was hope. He smiled at her and she smiled back—a strained smile—but it erased lines of fatigue and worry in her face.

"Rest," he told her. "You look exhausted."

"I tried to sleep," she murmured, "but I had terrible dreams—hands encased in crystal, huge dragons flying through stone hallways." She shook her head, then sat down, exhausted, in a corner sheltered from the chill wind.

Sturm's gaze moved to Tasslehoff, who lay beside her. The kender was fast asleep, curled into a ball. Sturm looked at him with a smile. Nothing bothered Tas. The kender'd had a truly glorious day, one that would live in his memory forever.

"I've never been at a siege before," Sturm had heard Tas confide to Flint just seconds before the dwarf's battle-axe swept off a goblin's head.

"You know we're all going to die," Flint growled, wiping black blood from his axe blade.

"That's what you said when we faced that black dragon in Xak Tsaroth," Tas replied. "Then you said the same thing in Thorbardin, and then there was the boat—"

"This time we're going to die!" Flint roared in a rage. "If I have to kill you myself!"

But they hadn't died—at least not today. There's always tomorrow, Sturm thought, his gaze resting on the dwarf who leaned against a stone wall, carving at a block of wood.†

Flint always needs to keep his hands busy. He uses a single-edged blade to whittle on, picking up any interesting piece of wood he sees to shape. When not whittling, he keeps the knife handy in his boot.

Flint looked up. "When will it start?" he asked.

Sturm sighed, his gaze shifting out to the eastern sky. "Dawn," he replied. "A few hours yet."

The dwarf nodded. "Can we hold?" His voice was matter-of-fact, the hand that held the wood firm and steady.

"We must," Sturm replied. "The messenger will reach Palanthas tonight. If they act at once, it's still a two-day march to reach us. We must give them two days—"

"If they act at once!" Flint grunted.

"I know . . ." Sturm said softly, sighing. "You should leave," he turned to Laurana, who came out of her reverie with a start. "Go to Palanthas. Convince them of the danger."

"Your messenger must do that," Laurana said tiredly. "If not, no words of mine will sway them."

"Laurana," he began.

"Do you need me?" she asked abruptly. "Am I of use here?"

"You know you are," Sturm answered. He had marveled at the elfmaid's unflagging strength, her courage, and her skill with the bow.'

"Then I'm staying," Laurana said simply. Drawing the blanket up more closely around her, she closed her eyes. "I can't sleep," she whispered. But within a few moments, her breathing became soft and regular as the slumbering kender's.

Sturm shook his head, swallowing a choking thickness in his throat. His glance met Flint's. The dwarf sighed and went back to his carving. Neither spoke, both men thinking the same thing. Their deaths would be bad if the draconians overran the Tower. Laurana's death could be a thing of nightmares.

The eastern sky was brightening, foretelling the sun's approach, when the knights were roused from their fitful slumber by the blaring of horns. Hastily they rose, grabbed their weapons, and stood to the walls, peering out across the dark land.

The campfires of the dragonarmies burned low, allowed to go out as daylight neared. They could hear the sounds of life returning to the horrible body. The knights gripped their weapons, waiting. Then they turned to each other, bewildered.

The dragonarmies were retreating! Although only dimly seen in the faint half-light, it was obvious that the black tide was slowly withdrawing. Sturm watched, puzzled. The armies moved back, just over the horizon. But they were still out there, Sturm knew. He sensed them.

Some of the younger knights began to cheer.

"Keep quiet!" Sturm commanded harshly. Their shouts grated on his raw nerves. Laurana came to stand beside him and glanced at him in astonishment. His face was gray and haggard in the flickering torchlight. His gloved fists, resting atop the battlements, clenched and unclenched nervously His eyes narrowed as he leaned forward, staring eastward.

Laurana, sensing the rising fear within him, felt her own body grow chill. She remembered what she had told Tas.

"Is it what we feared?" she asked, her hand on his arm.

"Pray we are wrong!" he spoke softly, in a broken voice.

Minutes passed. Nothing happened. Flint came to join them, clambering up on a huge slab of broken stone to see over the edge of the wall. Tas woke, yawning.

"When's breakfast?" the kender inquired cheerfully, but no one paid any attention to him.

Still they watched and waited. Now all the knights, each of them feeling the same rising fear, lined the walls, staring eastward without any clear idea why.

"What is it?" Tas whispered. Climbing up to stand beside Flint, he saw the small red sliver of sun burning on the horizon, its orange fire turning the night sky purple, dimming the stars.

"What are we looking at?" Tas whispered, nudging Flint.

"Nothing," Flint grumbled.

"Then why are we looking—" The kender caught his breath with a sharp gulp. "Sturm—" he quavered.

"What is it?" the knight demanded, turning in alarm.

Tas kept staring. The rest followed his gaze, but their eyes were no match for the kender's.

"Dragons . . ." Tasslehoff replied. "Blue dragons."

"I thought as much," Sturm said softly. "The dragonfear. That's why they pulled the armies back. The humans† fighting among them could not withstand it. How many dragons?"

Dragonfear seems to be peculiarly human oriented. Other races have some resistance to dragonfear—not enough for them to ignore it completely, but at least enough to continue functioning.

"Three," answered Laurana. "I can see them now."

"Three," Sturm repeated, his voice empty, expressionless.

"Listen, Sturm—" Laurana dragged him back away from the wall. "I—we—weren't going to say anything. It might not have mattered, but it does now. Tasslehoff and I know how to use the dragon orb!"

"Dragon orb?" Sturm muttered, not really listening.

"The orb here, Sturm!" Laurana persisted, her hands clutching him eagerly. "The one below the Tower, in the very center. Tas showed it to me. Three long, wide hallways lead to it and—and—" Her voice died. Suddenly she saw vividly, as her

subconscious had seen during the night, dragons flying down stone halls. . . .

"Sturm!" she shouted, shaking him in her excitement. "I know how the orb works! I know how to kill the dragons! Now, if we just have the time—"

Sturm caught hold of her, his strong hands grasping her by the shoulders. In all the months he had known her, he could not recall seeing her more beautiful. Her face, pale with weariness, was alight with excitement.

"Tell me, quickly," he ordered. Laurana explained, her words falling over themselves as she painted the picture for him that became clearer to her as she talked. Flint and Tas watched from behind Sturm, the dwarf's face aghast, the kender's face filled with consternation.

"Who'll use the orb?" Sturm asked slowly.

"I will," Laurana replied.

"But, Laurana," Tasslehoff cried, "Fizban said—"

"Tas, shut up!" Laurana said through clenched teeth. "Please, Sturm!" she urged. "It's our only hope. We have the dragonlances—and the dragon orb!"

The knight looked at her, then toward the dragons speeding out of the ever-brightening east.

"Very well," he said finally. "Flint, you and Tas go down and gather the men together in the center courtyard. Hurry!"

Tasslehoff, giving Laurana a last, troubled glance, jumped down from the rock where he and the dwarf had been standing. Flint came after him more slowly, his face somber and thoughtful. Reaching the ground, he walked up to Sturm.

Must you? Flint asked Sturm silently, as their eyes met.

Sturm nodded once. Glancing at Laurana, he smiled sadly. "I'll tell her," he said softly. "Take care of the kender. Good-bye, my friend."

Flint swallowed, shaking his old head. Then, his face a mask of sorrow, the dwarf brushed his gnarled hand across his eyes and gave Tas a shove in the back.

"Get moving!" the dwarf snapped.

Tas turned to look at him in astonishment, then shrugged and ran skipping along the top of the battlements, his shrill voice shouting out to the startled knights.

Laurana's face glowed. "You come, too, Sturm!" she said, tugging at him like a child eager to show a parent a new toy. "I'll explain this to the men if you want. Then you can give the orders and arrange the battle disposition—"

"You're in command, Laurana," Sturm said.

"What?" Laurana stopped, fear replacing the hope in her heart so suddenly the pain made her gasp.

"You said you needed time," Sturm said, adjusting his swordbelt, avoiding her eyes. "You're right. You must get the men in position. You must have time to use the orb. I will gain you that time." He picked up a bow and a quiver of arrows.

"No! Sturm!" Laurana shivered with terror. "You can't mean this! I can't command! I need you! Sturm, don't do this to yourself!" Her voice died to a whisper. "Don't do this to me!"

"You can command, Laurana," Sturm said, taking her head in his hands. Leaning forward, he kissed her gently. "Farewell, elfmaid," he said softly. "Your light will shine in this world. It is time for mine to darken. Don't grieve, dear one. Don't cry." He held her close. "The Forestmaster said to us, in Darken Wood, that we should not mourn those who have fulfilled their destiny. Mine is fulfilled. Now, hurry, Laurana. You'll need every second."

"At least take the dragonlance with you," she begged.

Sturm shook his head, his hand on the antique sword of his father. "I don't know how to use it. Good-bye, Laurana. Tell Tanis—" He stopped, then he sighed. "No," he said with a slight smile. "He will know what was in my heart."

"Sturm . . ." Laurana's tears choked her into silence. She could only stare at him in mute appeal.

"Go," he said.

Stumbling blindly, Laurana turned around and somehow made her way down the stairs to the courtyard below. Here she felt a strong hand grasp hers.

"Flint," she began, sobbing painfully, "he, Sturm . . ."

"I know, Laurana," the dwarf replied. "I saw it in his face. I think I've seen it there for as long as I can remember. It's up to you now. You can't fail him."

Laurana drew a deep breath, then wiped her eyes with her hands, cleaning her tear-streaked face as best she could. Taking another breath, she lifted her head.

"There," she said, keeping her voice firm and steady. "I'm ready. Where's Tas?"

"Here," said a small voice.

"Go on down. You read the words in the orb once before. Read them again. Make absolutely certain you've got it right."

"Yes, Laurana." Tas gulped and ran off.

"The knights are assembled," Flint said. "Waiting your command."

"Waiting my command," Laurana repeated absently.

Hesitating, she looked up. The red rays of the sun flashed on Sturm's bright armor as the knight climbed the narrow stairs that led to a high wall near the central Tower. Sighing, she lowered her gaze to the courtyard where the knights waited.

Laurana drew another deep breath, then walked toward them, the red crest fluttering from her helmet, her golden hair flaming in the morning light.

†The cold and brittle sun stained the sky blood red, deepening into the velvet blue-blackness of receding night. The Tower stood in shadow still, though the sun's rays sparkled off the golden threads in the fluttering flag.

When working on the Chronicles story, I came across a Norse legend about a clan/king who stood upon the battlements of his fortress. He saw an arrow flying toward him and, in an instant, saw a vision of his destiny. The arrow would kill him, but his death would inspire his own warriors to crush their enemies in his name. His death would be the stuff of ballads for generations and his future in Valhalla assured.

Even as the vision glowed within him, his

Sturm reached the top of the wall. The Tower soared above him. The parapet Sturm stood upon extended a hundred feet or more to his left. Its stone surface was smooth, providing no shelter, no cover.

Looking east, Sturm saw the dragons.

They were blue dragons, and on the back of the lead dragon in the formation sat a Dragon Highlord, the blue-black dragon-scale armor gleaming in the sunlight. He could see the hideous horned mask, the black cape fluttering behind. Two other blue dragons with riders followed the Dragon Highlord. Sturm gave them a brief, perfunctory glance. They did not concern him. His battle was with the leader, the Highlord.

The knight looked into the courtyard far below him. Sunlight was just climbing the walls. Sturm

saw it flicker red off the tips of the silver dragonlances that each man held now in his hand. He saw it burn on Laurana's golden hair. He saw the men look up at him. Grasping his sword, he raised it into the air. Sunlight flashed from the ornately carved blade.

Smiling up at him, though she could barely see him through her tears, Laurana raised her dragonlance into the air in answer—in good-bye.

Comforted by her smile, Sturm turned back to face his enemy.

Walking to the center of the wall, he seemed a small figure poised halfway between land and sky. The dragons could fly past him, or circle around him, but that wasn't what he wanted. They must see him as a threat. They must take time to fight him.

Sheathing his sword, Sturm fit an arrow to his bow and took careful aim at the lead dragon. Patiently he waited, holding his breath. I cannot waste this, he thought. Wait . . . wait . . .

The dragon was in range. Sturm's arrow sped through the morning brilliance. His aim was true. The arrow struck the blue dragon in the neck. It did little damage, bouncing off the dragon's blue scales, but the dragon reared its head in pain and irritation, slowing its flight. Quickly Sturm fired again, this time at the dragon flying directly behind the leader.

The arrow tore into a wing, and the dragon shrieked in rage. Sturm fired once more. This time the lead dragon's rider steered it clear. But the knight had accomplished what he set out to do: capture their attention, prove he was a threat, force them to fight him. He could hear the sound of running footsteps in the courtyard and the shrill squeak of the winches raising the portcullises.

Now Sturm could see the Dragon Highlord rise to his feet in the saddle. Built like a chariot, the saddle could accommodate its rider in a standing position for battle. The Highlord carried a spear in his gloved hand. Sturm dropped his bow. Picking up his shield and drawing his sword, he stood upon the wall, watching as the dragon flew closer and closer, its red eyes flaring, its white teeth gleaming.

Then—far away—Sturm heard the clear, clarion call of a trumpet, its music cold as the air from the snow-covered mountains of his homeland in the

wife threw herself in the arrow's path—shot by the arrow meant for her husband and, in the Norse legend, robbed her husband of his destiny. While I did not like the ancient sexism inherent in the tale, the idea of sacrificing one's life at the apex of destiny stayed with me in Sturm. Sturm's death was no whim—it was his destiny in the story and his greatest act of sacrifice. Sturm became the catalyst for the Knights to finally be forged as one. Destined or not, you should know that Margaret and I both cried when he died, even as we typed the words. —TRH

distance. Pure and crisp, the trumpet call pierced his heart, rising bravely above the darkness and death and despair that surrounded him.

Sturm answered the call with a wild battle-cry, raising his sword to meet his enemy. The sunlight flashed red on his blade. The dragon swooped in low.

Again the trumpet sounded, and again Sturm answered, his voice rising in a shout. But this time his voice faltered, for suddenly Sturm realized he had heard this trumpet before.

The dream!

Sturm stopped, gripping his sword in a hand that was sweating inside its glove. The dragon loomed above him. Astride the dragon was the Highlord, the horns of his mask flickering blood-red, his spear poised and ready.

Fear knotted Sturm's stomach, his skin grew cold. The horn call sounded a third time. It had sounded three times in the dream, and after the third call he had fallen. The dragon fear was overwhelming him. Escape! his brain screamed.

Escape! The dragons would swoop into the courtyard. The knights could not be ready yet, they would die, Laurana, Flint, and Tas. . . .The Tower would fall.

No! Sturm got hold of himself. Everything else was gone: his ideals, his hopes, his dreams. The Knighthood was collapsing. The Measure had been found wanting. Everything in his life was meaningless. His death must not be so. He would buy Laurana time, buy it with his life, since that was all he had to give. And he would die according to the Code, since that was all he had to cling to.

Raising his sword in the air, he gave the knight's salute to an enemy. To his surprise, it was returned with grave dignity by the Dragon Highlord. Then the dragon dove, its jaws open, prepared to slash the knight apart with its razor-sharp teeth. Sturm swung his sword in a vicious arc, forcing the dragon to rear its head back or risk decapitation. Sturm hoped to disrupt its flight. But the creature's wings held it steady, its rider guiding it with a sure hand while holding the gleaming-tipped spear in the other.

Sturm faced east. Half-blinded by the sun's brilliance, Sturm saw the dragon as a thing of

blackness. He saw the creature dip in its flight, diving below the level of the wall, and he realized the blue was going to come up from beneath, giving its rider the room needed to attack. The other two dragon riders held back, watching, waiting to see if their lord required help finishing this insolent knight.

For a moment the sun-drenched sky was empty, then the dragon burst up over the edge of the wall, its horrifying scream splitting Sturm's eardrums, filling his head with pain. The breath from its gaping mouth gagged him. He staggered dizzily but managed to keep his feet as he slashed out with his sword. The ancient blade struck the dragon's left nostril. Black blood spurted into the air. The dragon roared in fury.

But the blow was costly. Sturm had no time to recover.

The Dragon Highlord raised his spear, its tip flaming in the sun. Leaning down, he thrust it deep, piercing through armor, flesh, and bone.

Sturm's sun shattered.†

We had no idea that Sturm's death would cause such an uproar among the fans.

We received tons of letters from fans who were shocked that we would actually kill off a hero, despite the fact that we had foreshadowed his death through two books.

A fan once accosted me at Gen Con, accusing me of "not caring" about Sturm.

"He's just a character to you!" the fan told me.

In fact, Sturm was not just a character. Characters become a part of you. You get to know them better than family and friends sometimes.

It was terribly hard for me to write this death scene. I was crying so by the end that I had trouble seeing the computer screen. And I cried again when I had to write the funeral.—MW

14

Dragon orb. Dragonlance.

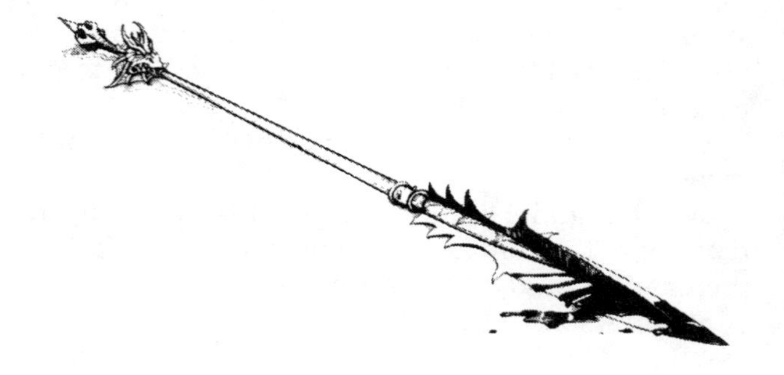

The knights surged past Laurana into the High Clerist's Tower, taking their places where she had told them. Although at first skeptical, hope dawned as Laurana explained her plan.

The courtyard was empty after the knights' departure. Laurana knew she should hurry. Already she should be with Tas, preparing herself to use the dragon orb. But Laurana could not leave that gleaming, solitary figure standing alone—waiting—upon the wall.

Then, silhouetted in the rising sun, she saw the dragons.

Sword and spear flashed in the brilliant sunlight.

Laurana's world stopped turning. Time slowed to a dream. The sword drew blood. The dragon

screamed. The spear held poised for an eternity. The sun stood still.

The spear struck.

A glittering object fell slowly from the top of the wall into the courtyard. The object was Sturm's sword, dropped from his lifeless hand, and it was—to Laurana—the only movement in a static world. The knight's body stood still, impaled upon the spear of the Dragon Highlord. The dragon hovered above, its wings poised. Nothing moved, everything held perfectly still.

Then the Highlord jerked the spear free and Sturm's body crumpled where he stood, a dark mass against the sun. The dragon roared in outrage and a bolt of lightning streaked from the blue's blood-frothed mouth and struck the High Clerist's Tower. With a booming explosion, the stone burst apart. Flames flared, brighter than the sun. The other two dragons dove for the courtyard as Sturm's sword clattered to the pavement with a ringing sound.

Time began.

Laurana saw the dragons diving at her. The ground around her shook as stone and rock rained down upon her and smoke and dust filled the air. Still Laurana could not move. To move would make the tragedy real. Some inane voice kept whispering in her brain—if you stand perfectly still, this will not have happened.

But there lay the sword, only a few feet from her. And as she watched, she saw the Dragon Highlord wave the spear, signaling to the dragonarmies that waited out upon the plains, telling them to attack. Laurana heard the blaring of the horns. In her mind's eye, she could see the dragonarmies surging across the snow-covered land.

Again the ground shook beneath her feet. Laurana hesitated one instant more, bidding a silent farewell to the spirit of the knight. Then she ran forward, stumbling as the ground heaved and the air crackled with terrifying lightning blasts. Reaching down, she grabbed Sturm's sword and raised it defiantly in the air.

"*Soliasi Arath!!*" she cried in elven, her voice ringing above the sounds of destruction in challenge to the attacking dragons.

The dragon riders laughed, shouting their scornful challenges in return. The dragons shrieked in cruel enjoyment of the kill. Two dragons who had accompanied the Highlord plummeted after Laurana into the courtyard.

The High Clerist Tower's main level was designed to draw dragons down its large corridors and into its interior spaces where the dragon would be increasingly constricted in its movements. Easy for the dragon to enter but difficult to withdraw, the corridor provided for side access through which knights could attack the dragon at close quarters—thereby bringing the knights' most effective weapons to bear on the dragon's hide while simultaneously robbing the beast of its two greatest strengths—flight and its breath of destruction.—TRH

Laurana ran toward the huge, gaping portcullis, the entryway into the Tower† that made so little sense. The stone walls were a blur as she fled past them. Behind her she could hear a dragon swooping after her. She could hear its stertorous breathing, the rush of air past its wings. She heard the dragon rider's command that stopped the dragon from following her right into the Tower. Good! Laurana smiled grimly to herself.

Running through the wide hallway, she sped swiftly past the second portcullis. Knights stood there, poised and ready to drop it.

"Keep it open!" she gasped breathlessly. "Remember!"

They nodded. She sped on. Now she was in the dark, narrower chamber where the oddly shaped, toothlike pillars slanted toward her with razor sharpness. Behind the pillars, she saw white faces beneath gleaming helms. Here and there, light sparkled on a dragonlance. The knights peered at her as she ran past.

"Get back!" she shouted. "Stay behind the pillars."

"Sturm?" one asked.

Laurana shook her head, too exhausted to talk. She ran through the third portcullis—the strange one, the one with a hole in the center. Here stood four knights, along with Flint. This was the key position. Laurana wanted someone here she could depend on. She had no time for more than an exchange of glances with the dwarf, but that was enough. Flint read the story of his friend in her face. The dwarf's head bowed for a moment, his hand covering his eyes.

Laurana ran on. Through this small room, beneath double doors made of solid steel and then into the chamber of the dragon orb.

Tasslehoff had dusted the orb with his handkerchief. Laurana could see inside it now, a faint red mist swirling with a myriad colors. The kender stood before it, staring into it, his magical glasses perched upon his small nose.

"What do I do?" Laurana gasped, out of breath.

"Laurana," Tas begged, "don't do this! I've read—if you fail to control the essence of the dragons within the orb, the dragons will come, Laurana, and take control of you!"

"Tell me what I need to do!" Laurana said firmly.

"Put your hands on the orb," Tas faltered, "and—no—wait, Laurana!"

It was too late. Laurana had already placed both slender hands upon the chill crystal globe. There was a flash of color from inside the orb, so bright Tas had to avert his eyes.

"Laurana!" he cried in his shrill voice. "Listen! You must concentrate, clear your mind of everything except bending the orb to your will! Laurana . . ."

If she heard him, she made no response, and Tas realized she was already caught up in the battle for control of the orb. Fearfully he remembered Fizban's warning, death for those you love, worse—the loss of the soul. Only dimly did he understand the dire words written in the flaming colors of the orb, but he knew enough to realize that Laurana's soul was at balance here.

In agony he watched her, longing to help—yet knowing that he did not dare do anything. Laurana stood for long moments without moving, her hands upon the orb, her face slowly draining of all life. Her eyes stared deep into the spinning, swirling colors. The kender grew dizzy looking at it and turned away, feeling sick. There was another explosion outside. Dust drifted down from the ceiling. Tas stirred uneasily. But Laurana never moved.

Her eyes closed, her head bent forward. She clutched the orb, her hands whitening from the pressure she exerted. Then she began to whimper and shake her head. "No," she moaned, and it seemed as if she were trying desperately to pull her hands away. But the orb held them fast.

Tas wondered bleakly what he should do. He longed to run up and pull her away. He wished he had broken this orb, but there was nothing he could do now. He could only stand and watch helplessly.

Laurana's body gave a convulsive shudder. Tas saw her drop to her knees, her hands still holding fast to the orb. Then Laurana shook her head angrily. Muttering unfamiliar words in elven, she fought to stand, using the orb to drag herself up. Her hands turned white with the strain and sweat trickled down her face. She was exerting every ounce of strength she possessed. With agonizing slowness, Laurana stood.

The orb flared a final time, the colors swirled together, becoming many colors and none. Then a bright, beaming, pure white light poured from the orb. Laurana stood tall and straight before it. Her face relaxed. She smiled.

And then she collapsed, unconscious, to the floor.

In the courtyard of the High Clerist's Tower, the dragons were systematically reducing the stone walls to rubble. The army was nearing the Tower, draconians in the forefront, preparing to enter through the breached walls and kill anything left alive inside. The Dragon Highlord circled above the chaos, his blue dragon's nostril black with dried blood. The Highlord supervised the destruction of the Tower. All was proceeding well when the bright daylight was pierced by a pure white light beaming out from the three huge, gaping entryways into the Tower.

The dragon riders glanced at these light beams, wondering casually what they portended. Their dragons, however, reacted differently. Lifting their heads, their eyes lost all focus. The dragons heard the call.

Captured by ancient magic-users, brought under control by an elfmaiden, the essence of the dragons held within the orb did as it was bound to do when commanded. It sent forth its irresistible call. And the dragons had no choice but to answer that call and try desperately to reach its source.

In vain the startled dragon riders tried to turn their mounts. But the dragons no longer heard the riders' commanding voices, they heard only a single voice, that of the orb. Both dragons swooped toward the inviting portcullises while their riders shouted and kicked wildly.

The white light spread beyond the Tower, touching the front ranks of the dragonarmies, and the human commanders stared as their army went mad.

The orb's call sounded clearly to dragons. But draconians, who were only part dragon, heard the

call as a deafening voice shouting garbled commands. Each one heard the voice differently, each one received a different call.

Some draconians fell to their knees, clutching their heads in agony.† Others turned and fled an unseen horror lurking in the Tower. Still others dropped their weapons and ran wildly, straight *toward* the Tower. Within moments an organized, well-planned attack had turned into mass confusion as a thousand draconians dashed off shrieking in a thousand directions. Seeing the major part of their force break and run, the goblins promptly fled the battlefield, while the humans stood bewildered amidst the chaos, waiting for orders that were not forthcoming.

Draconians have been described as the darkling spawn of the betrayal of the mighty by the mighty. Something is mightier.

The Dragon Highlord's own mount was barely kept in control by the Highlord's powerful force of will. But there was no stopping the other two dragons or the madness of the army. The Highlord could only fume in impotent fury, trying to determine what this white light was and where it was coming from. And—if possible—try to eradicate it.

The first blue dragon reached the first portcullis and sped inside the huge entryway, its rider ducking just in time to avoid having his head taken off by the wall. Obeying the call of the orb, the blue dragon flew easily through the wide stone halls, the tips of her wings just barely brushing the sides.

Through the second portcullis she darted, entering the chamber with the strange, toothlike pillars. Here in this second chamber she smelled human flesh and steel, but she was so in thrall to the orb she paid no attention to them. This chamber was smaller, so she was forced to pull her wings close to her body, letting momentum carry her forward.

Flint watched her coming. In all his one hundred forty-some years, he had never seen a sight like this . . . and he hoped he never would again. The dragonfear broke over the men confined in the room like a stupifying wave. The young knights, lances clutched in their shaking hands, fell back against the walls, hiding their eyes as the monstrous, blue-scaled body thundered past them.

The dwarf staggered back against the wall, his nerveless hand resting feebly on the mechanism that would slide shut the portcullis. He had never been so terrified in his life. Death would be welcome if it would end this horror. But the dragon sped on, seeking only one thing—to reach the orb. Her head glided under the strange portcullis.

Acting instinctively, knowing only that the dragon must not reach the orb, Flint released the mechanism. The portcullis closed around the dragon's neck, holding it fast. The dragon's head was now trapped within the small chamber. Her struggling body lay helpless, wings pressed against her sides, in the chamber where the knights stood, dragonlances ready.

Too late, the dragon realized she was trapped. She howled in such fury the rocks shuddered and cracked as she opened her mouth to blast the dragon orb with her lightning breath. Tasslehoff, trying frantically to revive Laurana, found himself staring into two flaming eyes. He saw the dragon's jaws part, he heard the dragon suck in her breath.

Lightning crackled from the dragon's throat, the concussion knocking the kender flat. Rock exploded into the room and the dragon orb shuddered on its stand. Tas lay on the floor, stunned by the blast. He could not move, did not even want to move, in fact. He just lay there, waiting for the next bolt which he knew would kill Laurana—if she wasn't already dead—and him, too. At this point, he really didn't much care.

But the blast never came.

The mechanism finally activated. The double steel door slammed shut in front of the dragon's snout, sealing the creature's head inside the small room.

At first it was deathly silent. Then the most horrible scream imaginable reverberated through the chamber. It was high-pitched, shrill, wailing, bubbling in agony, as the knights lunged out of their hiding places behind the tooth-like pillars and drove the silver dragonlances into the blue, writhing body of the trapped dragon.

Tas covered his ears with his hands, trying to block out the awful sound. Over and over he pictured the terrible destruction he had seen the dragons wreak on towns, the innocent people they had slaughtered. The dragon would have killed

him, too, he knew—killed him without mercy. It had probably already killed Sturm. He kept reminding himself of that, trying to harden his heart.

But the kender buried his head in his hands and wept.

Then he felt a gentle hand touch him.

"Tas," whispered a voice.

"Laurana!" He raised his head. "Laurana! I'm sorry. I shouldn't care what they do to the dragon, but I can't stand it, Laurana! Why must there be killing? I can't stand it!" Tears streaked his face.

"I know," Laurana murmured, vivid memories of Sturm's death mingling with the shrieks of the dying dragon. "Don't be ashamed, Tas. Be thankful you can feel pity and horror at the death of an enemy. The day we cease to care, even for our enemies, is the day we have lost this battle."

The fearful wailing grew even louder. Tas held out his arms and Laurana gathered him close. The two clung to each other, trying to blot out the screams of the dying dragon. Then they heard another sound—the knights calling out a warning. A second dragon had entered the other chamber, slamming its rider into the wall as it struggled to enter the smaller entryway in response to the beaming call of the dragon orb. The knights were sounding the alarm.

At that moment, the Tower itself shuddered from top to foundation, shaken by the violent flailings of the tortured dragon.

"Come on!" Laurana cried. "We've got to get out of here!" Dragging Tas to his feet, she ran stumbling toward a small door in the wall that would lead them out into the courtyard. Laurana yanked open the door, just as the dragon's head burst into the room with the orb. Tas could not help stopping, just a moment, to watch. The sight was so fascinating. He could see the dragon's flaring eyes—mad with rage at the sounds of his dying mate, knowing—too late—that he had flown into the same trap. The dragon's mouth twisted into a vicious snarl, he sucked in his breath. The double steel doors dropped in front of the dragon—but only halfway.

"Laurana, the door's stuck!" Tas shouted. "The dragon orb—"

"Come on!"Laurana yanked at the kender's hand. Lightning flashed, and Tas turned and fled, hearing the room behind him explode into flame. Rock and stone filled the chamber. The white light of the dragon orb was buried in the debris as the Tower of the High Clerist collapsed on top of it.

The shock threw Laurana and Tas off balance, sending them slamming against the wall. Tas helped Laurana to her feet, and the two of them kept going, heading for the bright daylight.

Then the ground was still. The thunder of falling rock ceased. There was only a sharp crack now and again or a low rumble. Pausing a moment to catch their breath, Tas and Laurana looked behind them. The end of the passage was completely blocked, choked by the huge boulders of the Tower.

"What about the dragon orb?" Tas gasped.

"It is better destroyed."

Now that Tas could see Laurana more clearly in the daylight, he was stunned at the sight. Her face was deathly white, even her lips drained of blood. The only color was in her green eyes, and they seemed disturbingly large, shadowed by purple smudges.

"I could not use it again," she whispered, more to herself than to him. "I nearly gave up. Hands . . . I can't talk about it!" Shivering, she covered her eyes.

"Then I remembered Sturm, standing upon the wall, facing his death alone. If I gave in, his death would be meaningless. I couldn't let that happen. I couldn't let him down." She shook her head, trembling. "I forced the orb to obey my command, but I knew I could do it only once. And I can never, never go through that again!"

"Sturm's dead?" Tas's voice quavered.

Laurana looked at him, her eyes softened. "I'm sorry, Tas," she said "I didn't realize you didn't know. He—he died fighting a Dragon Highlord."

"Was it—was it . . ." Tas choked.

"Yes, it was quick," Laurana said gently. "He did not suffer long."

Tas bowed his head, then raised it again quickly as another explosion shook what was left of the fortress.

"The dragonarmies . . ." Laurana murmured. "Our fight is not ended." Her hand went to the hilt

of Sturm's sword, which she had buckled around her slender waist. "Go find Flint."

Laurana emerged from the tunnel into the courtyard, blinking in the bright light, almost surprised to see it was still day. So much had happened, it seemed to her years might have passed. But the sun was just lifting over the courtyard wall.

The tall Tower of the High Clerist was gone, fallen in upon itself, a heap of stone rubble in the center of the courtyard. The entryways and halls leading to the dragon orb were not damaged, except where the dragons had smashed into them. The walls of the outer fortress still stood, although breached in places, their stone blackened by the dragons' lightning bolts.

But no armies poured through the breaches. It was quiet, Laurana realized. In the tunnels behind her, she could hear the dying screams of the second dragon, the hoarse shouts of the knights finishing the kill.

What had happened to the army? Laurana wondered, looking around in confusion. They must be coming over the walls. Fearfully she looked up at the battlements, expecting to see the fierce creatures pouring over them.

And then she saw the flash of sunlight shining on armor. She saw the shapeless mass lying on the top of the wall.

Sturm. She remembered the dream, remembered the bloody hands of the draconians hacking at Sturm's body.

It must not happen! she thought grimly. Drawing Sturm's sword, she ran across the courtyard and immediately realized the ancient weapon would be too heavy for her to wield. But what else was there? She glanced around hurriedly. The dragonlances! Dropping the sword, she grabbed one. Then, carrying the lightweight footman's lance easily, she climbed the stairs.

Laurana reached the top of the battlements and stared out across the plain, expecting to see the black tide of the army surging forward. But the plain was empty. There were only a few groups of humans standing, staring vaguely around.

What could it mean? Laurana had no idea, and she was too exhausted to think. Her wild elation died.

Weariness descended on her now, as did her grief. Dragging the lance behind her, she stumbled over to Sturm's body lying in the blood-stained snow.

Laurana knelt beside the knight. Putting her hand out, she brushed back the wind-blown hair to look once more upon the face of her friend. For the first time since she had met him, Laurana saw peace in Sturm's lifeless eyes.

Lifting his cold hand, she pressed it to her cheek. "Sleep, dear friend," she murmured, "and let not your sleep be troubled by dragons." Then, as she lay the cold white hand upon the shattered armor, she saw a bright sparkle in the blood-stained snow. She picked up an object so covered with blood she could not see what it was. Carefully Laurana brushed the snow and blood away. It was a piece of jewelry. Laurana stared at it in astonishment.

But before she could wonder how it came to be here, a dark shadow fell over her. Laurana heard the creak of huge wings, the intake of breath into a gigantic body. Fearfully she leaped to her feet and whirled around.

A blue dragon landed upon the wall behind her. Stone gave way as the great claws scrabbled for a hold. The creature's great wings beat the air. From the saddle upon the dragon's back, a Dragon Highlord gazed at Laurana with cold, stern eyes from behind the hideous mask.

Laurana took a step backward as the dragonfear overcame her. The dragonlance slipped from her nerveless hand, and she dropped the jewel into the snow. Turning, she tried to flee, but she could not see where she was going. She slipped and fell into the snow to lie trembling beside Sturm's body.

In her paralyzing fear, all she could think of was the dream! Here she had died—as Sturm had died. Laurana's vision was filled with blue scales as the creature's great neck reared above her.

The dragonlance! Scrambling for it in the blood-wet snow, Laurana's fingers closed over its wooden shaft. She started to rise, intending to plunge it into the dragon's neck.

But a black boot slammed down upon the lance, narrowly missing her hand. Laurana stared at the shining black boot, decorated with gold work that gleamed in the sun. She stared at the black boot

standing in Sturm's blood, and she drew a deep breath.

"Touch his body, and you will die," Laurana said softly. "Your dragon will not be able to save you. This knight was my friend, and I will not let his killer defile his body."

"I have no intention of defiling the body," the Dragon Highlord said. Moving with elaborate slowness, the Highlord reached down and gently shut the knight's eyes, which were fixed upon the sun he would see no more.

The Dragon Highlord stood up, facing the elfmaid who knelt in the snow, and removed the booted foot from the dragonlance. "You see, he was my friend, too. I knew—the moment I killed him."

Laurana stared up at the Highlord. "I don't believe you," she said tiredly. "How could that be?"

Calmly, the Dragon Highlord removed the hideous horned dragon mask. "I think you might have heard of me, Lauralanthalasa. That is your name, isn't it?"

Laurana nodded dumbly, rising to her feet.

The Dragon Highlord smiled, a charming, crooked smile. "And my name is—"

"Kitiara."

"How did you know?"

"A dream . . ." Laurana murmured.

"Oh, yes—the dream." Kitiara ran her gloved hand through her dark, curly hair. "Tanis told me about the dream. I guess you all must have shared it. He thought his friends might have." The human woman glanced down at the body of Sturm, lying at her feet. "Odd, isn't it—the way Sturm's death came true? And Tanis said the dream came true for him as well: the part where I saved his life."

Laurana began to tremble. Her face, which had already been white with exhaustion, was so drained of blood it seemed transparent. "Tanis? . . . You've seen Tanis?"

"Just two days ago," Kitiara said. "I left him in Flotsam, to look after matters while I was gone."

Kitiara's cold, calm words drove through Laurana's soul like the Highlord's spear had driven through Sturm's flesh. Laurana felt the stones start to shift from under her. The sky and ground mixed, the pain cleaved her in two. She's lying, Laurana thought desperately. But she knew with despairing certainty that, though Kitiara might lie when she chose—she was not lying now.

Laurana staggered and nearly fell. Only the grim determination not to reveal any weakness before this human woman kept the elfmaiden on her feet.

Kitiara had not noticed. Stooping down, she picked up the weapon Laurana had dropped and studied it with interest.

"So this is the famed dragonlance?" Kitiara remarked.

Laurana swallowed her grief, forcing herself to speak in a steady voice. "Yes," she replied. "If you want to see what it's capable of, go look within the walls of the fortress at what's left of your dragons."

Kitiara glanced down into the courtyard briefly, without a great deal of interest. "It was not these that lured my dragons into your trap," she said, her brown eyes appraising Laurana coolly, "nor scattered my army to the four winds."

Once more Laurana glanced across the empty plains.

"Yes," Kitiara said, seeing the dawning comprehension on Laurana's face. "You have won—today. Savor your victory now, Elf, for it will be short-lived." The Dragon Highlord dexterously flipped the lance in her hand and held it aimed at Laurana's heart. The elfmaid stood unmoving before her, the delicate face empty of expression.

Kitiara smiled. With a quick motion, she reversed the killing stroke "Thank you for this weapon,"she said, standing the lance in the snow. "We've received reports of these. Now we can find out if it as formidable a weapon as you claim."

Kitiara made Laurana a slight bow from the waist. Then, replacing the dragonmask over her head, she grasped the dragonlance and turned to go. As she did, her gaze went once more to the body of the knight.

"See that he is given a knight's funeral," Kitiara said. "It will take at least three days to rebuild the army. I give you that time to prepare a ceremony befitting him."

"We will bury our own dead," Laurana said proudly. "We ask you for nothing!"

The memory of Sturm's death, the sight of the

knight's body, brought Laurana back to reality like cold water poured on the face of a dreamer. Moving to stand protectively between Sturm's body and the Dragon Highlord, Laurana looked into the brown eyes, glittering behind the dragonmask.

"What will you tell Tanis?" she asked abruptly.

"Nothing," Kit said simply. "Nothing at all." Turning, she walked away.

Laurana watched the Dragon Highlord's slow, graceful walk, the black cape fluttering in the warm breeze blowing from the north. The sun glinted off the prize Kitiara held in her hand. Laurana knew she should get the lance away. There was an army of knights below. She had only to call.

But Laurana's weary brain and her body refused to act. It was an effort just to remain standing. Pride alone kept her from falling to the cold stones.

Take the dragonlance, Laurana told Kitiara silently. Much good it will do you.

Kitiara walked to the giant blue dragon. Down below, the knights had come into the courtyard, dragging with them the head of one of her blue dragons. Skie tossed his own head angrily at the sight, a savage growl rumbling deep within his chest. The knights turned their amazed faces toward the wall where they saw the dragon, the Dragon Highlord, and Laurana. More than one drew his weapon, but Laurana raised her hand to stop them. It was the last gesture she had strength to make.

Kitiara gave the knights a disdainful look and laid her hand upon Skie's neck, stroking him, reassuring him. She took her time, letting them see she was not afraid of them.

Reluctantly, the knights lowered their weapons.

Laughing scornfully, Kitiara swung herself onto the dragon.

"Farewell, Lauralanthalasa," she called.

Lifting the dragonlance in the air, Kitiara commanded Skie to fly. The huge blue dragon spread his wings, rising effortlessly into the air. Guiding him skillfully, Kitiara flew just above Laurana.

The elfmaid looked up into the dragon's fiery red eyes. She saw the wounded, bloodied nostril, the gaping mouth twisted in a vicious snarl. On his back, sitting between the giant wings, was Kitiara, the dragon-scale armor glistening, the sun glinting off the horned mask. Sunlight flashed from the point of the dragonlance.

Then, glittering as it turned over and over, the dragonlance fell from the Dragon Highlord's gloved hand. Clattering on the stones, it landed at Laurana's feet.

"Keep it," Kitiara called to her in a ringing voice. "You're going to need it!"

The blue dragon lifted his wings, caught the air currents, and soared into the sky to vanish into the sun.

The Funeral

Winter's night was dark and starless. The wind had become a gale, bringing driving sleet and snow that pierced armor with the sharpness of arrows, freezing blood and spirit. No watch was set. A man standing upon the battlements of the High Clerist's Tower would have frozen to death at his post.

There was no need for the watch. All day, as long as the sun shone, the knights had stared across the plains, but there was no sign of the dragonarmies' return. Even after darkness fell, the knights could see few campfires on the horizon.

On this winter's night, as the wind howled among the ruins of the crumbled Tower like the shrieks of the slaughtered dragons, the Knights of Solamnia buried their dead.

The bodies were carried into a cavelike sepulcher beneath the Tower. Long ago, it had been used for the dead of the Knighthood. But that had been in ages past, when Huma rode to glorious death upon the fields beyond. The sepulcher might have remained forgotten but for the curiosity of a kender. Once it must have been guarded and well kept, but time had touched even the dead, who are thought to be beyond time. The stone coffins were covered with a fine sifting of thick dust. When it was brushed away, nothing could be read of the writings carved into the stone.

Called the Chamber of Paladine,† the sepulcher was a large rectangular room, built far below the ground where the destruction of the Tower did not affect it. A long, narrow staircase led down to it from two huge iron doors marked with the symbol of Paladine—the platinum dragon, ancient symbol of death and rebirth. The knights brought torches to light the chamber, fitting them into rusted iron sconces upon the crumbling stone walls.

In years to come, people looking for heroes and inspiration will visit the Chamber of Paladine and pray before Sturm's body. It remains in a state of perfect preservation, perhaps because of the Starjewel that lies on his breast.

The stone coffins of the ancient dead lined the walls of the room. Above each one was an iron plaque giving the name of the dead knight, his family, and the date of his death. A center aisle led between the rows of coffins toward a marble altar at

the head of the room. In this central aisle of the Chamber of Paladine, the knights lay their dead.

There was no time to build coffins. All knew the dragonarmies would return. The knights must spend their time fortifying the ruined walls of the fortress, not building homes for those who no longer cared. They carried the bodies of their comrades down to the Chamber of Paladine and laid them in long rows upon the cold stone floor. The bodies were draped with ancient winding sheets which had been meant for the ceremonial wrapping. There was no time for that either. Each dead knight's sword was laid upon his breast, while some token of the enemy—an arrow perhaps, a battered shield, or the claws of a dragon—were laid at his feet.

When the bodies had been carried to the torch-lit chamber, the knights assembled. They stood among their dead, each man standing beside the body of a friend, a comrade, a brother. Then, amid a silence so profound each man could hear his own heart beating, the last three bodies were brought inside. Carried upon stretchers, they were attended by a solemn Guard of Honor.

This should have been a state funeral, resplendent with the trappings detailed by the Measure. At the altar should have stood the Grand Master, arrayed in ceremonial armor. Beside him should have been the High Clerist, clad in armor covered with the white robes of a cleric of Paladine. Here should have stood the High Justice, his armor covered by the judicial robes of black. The altar itself should have been banked with roses. Golden emblems of the kingfisher, the crown, and the sword should have been placed upon it.

But here at the altar stood only an elfmaiden, clad in armor that was dented and stained with blood. Beside her stood an old dwarf, his head bowed in grief, and a kender, his impish face ravaged by sorrow. The only rose upon the altar was a black one, found in Sturm's belt; the only ornament was a silver dragonlance, black with clotted blood.

The Guard carried the bodies to the front of the chamber and reverently laid them before the three friends.

On the right lay the body of Lord Alfred MarKenin, his mutilated, headless corpse mercifully

shrouded in white linen. On the left lay Lord Derek Crownguard, his body covered with white cloth to hide the hideous grin death had frozen upon his face. In the center lay the body of Sturm Brightblade. He was not covered by a white sheet. He lay in the armor he had worn at his death: his father's armor. His father's antique sword was clasped in cold hands upon his breast. One other ornament lay upon his shattered breast, a token none of the knights recognized.

It was the Starjewel,† which Laurana had found in a pool of the knight's own blood. The jewel was dark, its brilliance fading even as Laurana had held it in her hand. Many things became clear to her later, as she studied the Starjewel. This, then, was how they shared the dream in Silvanesti. Had Sturm realized its power? Did he know of the link that had been forged between himself and Alhana? No, Laurana thought sadly, he had probably not known. Nor could he realize the love it represented. No human could. Carefully she had placed it upon his breast as she thought with sorrow of the dark-haired elven woman, who must know the heart upon which the glittering Starjewel rested was stilled forever.

This has come to be regarded on Krynn as the Starjewel. However, starjewels in general, while rare, have been known to the elves since ancient times. Among the Silvanesti Elves, gift of a Starjewel is considered the greatest possible honor and a statement of eternal love.

The Honor Guard stepped back, waiting. The assembled knights stood with heads bowed for a moment, then lifted them to face Laurana.

This should have been the time for proud speeches, for recitals of the dead knights' heroic deeds. But for a moment, all that could be heard was the wheezing sobs of the old dwarf and Tasslehoff's quiet snuffle. Laurana looked down into Sturm's peaceful face, and she could not speak.

For a moment she envied Sturm, envied him fiercely. He was beyond pain, beyond suffering, beyond loneliness. His war had been fought. He was victorious.

You left me! Laurana cried in agony. Left me to cope with this by myself! First Tanis, then Elistan, now you. I can't! I'm not strong enough! I can't let you go, Sturm. Your death was senseless, meaningless! A fraud and a sham! I won't let you go. Not quietly! Not without anger!

Laurana lifted her head, her eyes blazing in the torchlight.

"You expect a noble speech," she said, her voice cold as the air of the sepulcher. "A noble speech honoring the heroic deeds of these men who have died. Well, you won't get it. Not from me!"

The knights glanced at each other, faces dark.

"These men, who should have been united in a brotherhood forged when Krynn was young, died in bitter discord, brought about by pride, ambition, and greed. Your eyes turn to Derek Crownguard, but he was not totally to blame. You are. All of you! All of you who took sides in this reckless bid for power."

A few knights lowered their heads, some paled with shame and anger. Laurana choked with her tears. Then she felt Flint's hand slip into hers, squeezing it comfortingly. Swallowing, she drew a deep breath.

"Only one man was above this. Only one man here among you lived the Code every day of his life. And for most of those days, he was not a knight. Or rather, he was a knight where it meant the most—in spirit, in heart, not in some official list."

Reaching behind her, Laurana took the blood-stained dragonlance from the altar and raised it high over her head. And as she lifted the lance, her spirit was lifted. The wings of darkness that had hovered around her were banished. When she raised her voice, the knights stared at her in wonder. Her beauty blessed them like the beauty of a dawning spring day.†

This forecasts her role in the next book, Dragons of Spring Dawning.—MW

"Tomorrow I will leave this place," Laurana said softly, her luminous eyes on the dragonlance. "I will go to Palanthas. I will take with me the story of this day! I will take this lance and the head of a dragon. I will dump that sinister, bloody head upon the steps of their magnificent palace. I will stand upon the dragon's head and make them listen to me! And Palanthas will listen! They will see their danger! And then I will go to Sancrist and to Ergoth and to every other place in this world where people refuse to lay down their petty hatreds and join together. For until we conquer the evils within ourselves—as this man did—we can never conquer the great evil that threatens to engulf us!"

Laurana raised her hands and her eyes to heaven. "Paladine!" she called out, her voice ringing like the

trumpet's call. "We come to you, Paladine, escorting the souls of these noble knights who died in the High Clerist's Tower. Give us who are left behind in this war-torn world the same nobility of spirit that graces this man's death!"

Laurana closed her eyes as tears spilled unheeded and unchecked down her cheeks. No longer did she grieve for Sturm. Her sorrow was for herself, for missing his presence, for having to tell Tanis of his friend's death, for having to live in this world without this noble friend by her side.

Slowly she laid the lance upon the altar. Then she knelt before it a moment, feeling Flint's arm around her shoulder and Tasslehoff's gentle touch on her hand.

As if in answer to her prayer, she heard the knights' voices rising behind her, carrying their own prayers to the great and ancient god, Paladine.

Return this man to Huma's breast:
Let him be lost in sunlight,
In the chorus of air where breath is translated;
At the sky's border receive him.

Beyond the wild, impartial skies
Have you set your lodgings,
In cantonments of stars, where the sword aspires
In an arc of yearning, where we join in singing.

Grant to him a warrior's rest.
Above our singing, above song itself,
May the ages of peace converge in a day,
May he dwell in the heart of Paladine.

And set the last spark of his eyes
In a fixed and holy place
Above words and the borrowed land too loved
As we recount the ages.

Free from the smothering clouds of war
As he once rose in infancy,
The long world possible and bright before him,
Lord Huma, deliver him.

Upon the torches of the stars
Was mapped the immaculate glory of childhood;

From that wronged and nestling country,
Lord Huma, deliver him.

Let the last surge of his breath
Perpetuate wine, the attar of flowers;
From the vanguard of love, the last to surrender,
Lord Huma, deliver him.

Take refuge in the cradling air
From the heart of the sword descending,
From the weight of battle on battle;
Lord Huma, deliver him.

Above the dreams of ravens where
His dreams first tried a rest beyond changing,
From the yearning for war and the war's ending,
Lord Huma, deliver him.

Only the hawk remembers death
In a late country; from the dusk,
From the fade of the senses, we are thankful that you,
Lord Huma, deliver him.

Then let his shade to Huma rise
Out of the body of death, of the husk unraveling;
From the lodging of mind upon nothing,
we are thankful that you,
Lord Huma, deliver him.

Beyond the wild, impartial skies
Have you set your lodgings,
In cantonments of stars, where the sword aspires
In an arc of yearning, where we join in singing.

Return this man to Huma's breast
Beyond the wild, impartial skies;
Grant to him a warrior's rest
And set the last spark of his eyes
Free from the smothering clouds of wars
Upon the torches of the stars.
Let the last surge of his breath
Take refuge in the cradling air
Above the dreams of ravens where
Only the hawk remembers death.
Then let his shade to Huma rise
Beyond the wild, impartial skies.

The chant ended. Slowly, solemnly, the knights walked forward one by one to pay homage to the dead, each kneeling for a moment before the altar. Then the Knights of Solamnia left the Chamber of Paladine, returning to their cold beds to try and find some rest before the next day's dawning.

Laurana, Flint, and Tasslehoff stood alone beside their friend, their arms around each other, their hearts full. A chill wind whistled through the open door of the sepulcher where the Honor Guard stood, ready to seal the chamber.

"Kharan bea Reorx," said Flint in dwarven, wiping his gnarled and shaking hand across his eyes. "Friends meet in Reorx." Fumbling in his pouch, he took out a bit of wood, beautifully carved into the shape of a rose. Gently he laid it upon Sturm's breast, beside Alhana's Starjewel.

"Good-bye, Sturm," Tas said awkwardly. "I only have one gift that, that you would approve of. I—I don't think you'll understand. But then again, maybe you do now. Maybe you understand better than I do." Tasslehoff placed a small white feather in the knight's cold hand.

"Quisalan elevas," Laurana whispered in elven. "Our loves-bond eternal." She paused, unable to leave him in this darkness.

"Come, Laurana," Flint said gently. "We've said our good-byes. We must let him go. Reorx waits for him."

Laurana drew back. Silently, without looking back, the three friends climbed the narrow stairs leading from the sepulcher and walked steadfastly into the chill, stinging sleet of the bitter winter's night.

Far away from the frozen land of Solamnia, one other person said good-bye to Sturm Brightblade.

Silvanesti had not changed with the passing months. Though Lorac's nightmare was ended, and his body lay beneath the soil of his beloved country, the land still remembered Lorac's terrible dreams. The air smelled of death and decay. The trees bent and twisted in unending agony. Misshapen beasts roamed the woods, seeking an end to their tortured existence.

In vain Alhana watched from her room in the Tower of the Stars for some sign of change.

The griffons had come back—as she had known they would once the dragon was gone. She had fully intended to leave Silvanesti and return to her people on Ergoth. But the griffons carried disturbing news: war between the elves and humans.

It was a mark of the change in Alhana, a mark of her suffering these past months, that she found this news distressing. Before she met Tanis and the others, she would have accepted war between elves and humans, perhaps even welcomed it. But now she saw that this was only the work of the evil forces in the world.

She should return to her people, she knew. Perhaps she could end this insanity. But she told herself the weather was unsafe for traveling. In reality, she shrank from facing the shock and the disbelief of her people when she told them of the destruction of their land and her promise to her dying father that the elves would return and rebuild—after they had helped the humans fight the Dark Queen and her minions.

Oh, she would win. She had no doubt. But she dreaded leaving the solitude of her self-imposed exile to face the tumult of the world beyond Silvanesti.

And she dreaded—even as she longed—to see the human she loved. The knight, whose proud and noble face came to her in her dreams, whose very soul she shared through the Starjewel. Unknown to him, she stood beside him in his fight to save his honor. Unknown to him, she shared his agony and came to learn the depths of his noble spirit. Her love for him grew daily, as did her fear of loving him.

And so Alhana continually put off her departure. I will leave, she told herself, when I see some sign I may give my people, a sign of hope. Otherwise they will not come back. They will give up in despair. Day after day, she looked from her window.

But no sign came.

The winter nights grew longer. The darkness deepened. One evening Alhana walked upon the battlements of the Tower of the Stars. It was afternoon in Solamnia then, and—on another Tower—Sturm Brightblade faced a sky-blue dragon and a

Dragon Highlord called the Dark Lady. Suddenly Alhana felt a strange and terrifying sensation—as though the world had ceased to turn. A shattering pain pierced her body, driving her to the stone below. Sobbing in fear and grief, she clutched the Starjewel she wore around her neck and watched in agony as its light flickered and died.

"So this is my sign!" she screamed bitterly, holding the darkened jewel in her hand and shaking it at the heavens. "There is no hope! There is nothing but death and despair!"

Holding the jewel so tightly that the sharp points bit into her flesh, Alhana stumbled unseeing through the darkness to her room in the Tower. From there she looked out once more upon her dying land. Then, with a shuddering sob, she closed and locked the wooden shutters of her window.

Let the world do what it will, she told herself bitterly. Let my people meet their end in their own way. Evil will prevail. There is nothing we can do to stop it. I will die here, with my father.

That night she made one final journey out into the land. Carelessly she threw a thin cape over her shoulders and headed for a grave lying beneath a twisted, tortured tree. In her hand, she held the Starjewel.

Throwing herself down upon the ground, Alhana began to dig frantically with her bare hands, scratching at the frozen ground of her father's grave with fingers that were soon raw and bleeding. She didn't care. She welcomed the pain that was so much easier to bear than the pain in her heart.

Finally, she had dug a small hole. The red moon, Lunitari, crept into the night sky, tinging the silver moon's light with blood. Alhana stared at the Starjewel until she could no longer see it through her tears, then she cast it into the hole she had dug. She forced herself to quit crying. Wiping the tears from her face, she started to fill in the hole.

Then she stopped.

Her hands trembled. Hesitantly, she reached down and brushed the dirt from the Starjewel, wondering if her grief had driven her mad. No, from it came a tiny glimmer of light that grew even stronger as she watched. Alhana lifted the shimmering jewel from the grave.

"But he's dead," she said softly, staring at the jewel that sparkled in Solinari's silver light.

"I know death has claimed him. Nothing can change that. Yet, why this light—"

Trilogies come to us in fantasy primarily because we are the children of J. R. R. Tolkien. His Lord of the Rings was the godfather of us all.

However, trilogies are not necessarily made "just because that's the way it has always been done." Since ancient time, the idea of three acts making up a complete story has come down to us. In stories of tremendous scope, three books representing three acts are a logical extension of the stage form. Generally speaking, second acts are the hardest to write and the most difficult to convey with interest. Dragons of Winter Night, *however, is not only a strong book on its own but a powerful narrative that takes us from the smaller world of the first novel into the larger world issues that must be confronted at the end of our tale.*

For these reasons, I find it to be my favorite book of the three Chronicles.
—TRH

A sudden rustling sound startled her. Alhana fell back, fearing that the hideously deformed tree above Lorac's grave might be reaching to grasp her in its creaking branches. But as she watched she saw the limbs of the tree cease their tortured writhing. They hung motionless for an instant, then—with a sigh—turned toward the heavens. The trunk straightened and the bark became smooth and began to glisten in the silver moonlight. Blood ceased to drip from the tree. The leaves felt living sap flow once more through their veins.

Alhana gasped. Rising unsteadily to her feet, she looked around the land. But nothing else had changed. None of the other trees were different—only this one, above Lorac's grave.

I am going mad, she thought. Fearfully she turned back to look at the tree upon her father's grave. No, it was changed. Even as she watched, it grew more beautiful.

Carefully, Alhana hung the Starjewel back in its place over her heart. Then she turned and walked back toward the Tower. There was much to be done before she left for Ergoth.

The next morning, as the sun shed its pale light over the unhappy land of Silvanesti, Alhana looked out over the forest. Nothing had changed. A noxious green mist still hung low over the suffering trees. Nothing would change, she knew, until the elves came back and worked to make it change. Nothing had changed except the tree above Lorac's grave.

"Farewell, Lorac," Alhana called, "until we return."

Summoning her griffon, she climbed onto its strong back and spoke a firm word of command. The griffon spread its feathery wings and soared into the air, rising in swift spirals above the stricken land of Silvanesti. At a word from Alhana, it turned its head west and began the long flight to Ergoth.

Far below, in Silvanesti, one tree's beautiful green leaves stood out in splendid contrast to the black desolation of the forest around it. It swayed in the winter wind, singing soft music as it spread its limbs to shelter Lorac's grave from the winter's darkness, waiting for spring.

I agree with Tracy. This book's my favorite of the three.—MW

Volume 3

Dragons of Spring Dawning

DEDICATIONS

We were the outsiders. We weren't hippies, we weren't sorority or fraternity. None of us dated much. We were too busy playing bridge. We were addicted to the game. We played every spare moment, to the detriment of class work and a social life—although I do remember taking time out to write poetry, with the Beatles and Aretha and the Four Tops blaring on the juke box in the background. I still remember the devastating day I heard that Bob had been killed in Viet Nam. I have been to the Wall to find his name. I left a copy of this book for him. I did not find John's name. I hope this means that somewhere, he's still playing bridge!—MW

To Angel, Curtis, and Tasha, my children,
my hope, and my life
—Tracy Raye Hickman

To the Commons Bridge Group,
University of Missouri, 1966-1970:
Nancy Olson, Bill Fisher, Nancy Burnett,
Ken Randolph, Ed Bristol, Herb the fry
cook, and in memory of Bob Campbell and
John Steele, who died in Viet Nam, and to
the rest of that wonderful group of
mismatched friends—
this book about friends is fondly dedicated
—Margaret Weis

Kitiara, of all the days these days
are rocked in dark and waiting, in regret.
The clouds obscure the city as I write this,
delaying thought and sunlight, as the streets
hang between day and darkness. I have waited
past all decision, past the heart in shadows
to tell you this.
In absences you grew
more beautiful, more poisonous, you were
an attar of orchids in the swimming night,
where passion, like a shark drawn down a bloodstream,
murders four senses, only taste preserving,
buckling into itself, finding the blood its own,
a small wound first, but as the shark unravels
the belly tatters in the long throat's tunnel.
And knowing this, the night still seems a richness,
a gauntlet of desires ending in peace,
I would still be part of these allurements,
and to my arms I would take in the darkness,
blessed and renamed by pleasure;
but the light,
the light, my Kitiara, when the sun
spangles the rain-gorged sidewalks, and the oil
from doused lamps rises in the sunstruck water,
splintering the light to rainbows! I arise,
and though the storm resettles on the city,
I think of Sturm, Laurana, and the others,
but Sturm the foremost, who can see the sun
straight through the fog and cloudrack. How could I
abandon these?
And so into the shadow,
and not your shadow but the eager grayness
expecting light, I ride the storm away.

Tanis's farewell pirates a whole lot of phrases and lines from a shorter,much happier love poem I wrote to an old girlfriend about seven years earlier.
I question a lot about this poem now: most basically that it doesn't capture Tanis's tune—too nervous and shifting, which was not how I came to understand the character.
—Michael Williams

Michael is too harsh on himself. This has become my favorite of all the DL poems.—MW

The Everman

hy, look, Berem. Here 's a path. . . . How strange. All the times we've been hunting in these woods and we've never seen it."

"It's not so strange. The fire burned off some of the brush, that's all. Probably just an animal trail."

"Let's follow it. If it is an animal trail, maybe we'll find a deer. We've been hunting all day with nothing to show for it. I hate to go home empty-handed."

Without waiting for my reply, she turns onto the trail.† Shrugging, I follow her. It is pleasant being outdoors today, the first warm day after the bitter chill of winter. The sun is warm on my neck and shoulders. Walking through the fire-ravaged woods is easy. No vines to snag you. No brush to tear at your clothing. Lightning, probably that thunderstorm which struck late last fall.

Long ago, the brother and sister came from what was still the village of Neraka and were out exploring in the Khalkist Mountains near their home. Gargath (which is where the old tower associated with the Graygem is located) is "just up the road a piece."

But we walk for a long time and finally I begin to grow weary. She is wrong—this is no animal trail. It is a man-made path and an old one at that. We're not likely to find any game. Just the same as it's been all day. The fire, then the hard winter: The animals dead or gone. There'll be no fresh meat tonight.

More walking. The sun is high in the sky. I'm tired, hungry. There's been no sign of any living creature.

"Let's turn back, sister. There's nothing here. . . ."

She stops, sighing. She is hot and tired and discouraged, I can tell. And too thin. She works too hard, doing women's work and men's as well. Out hunting when she should be home, receiving the pledges of suitors. She's pretty, I think. People say we look alike, but I know they are wrong. It is only that we are so close—closer than other brothers and their sisters. But we've had to be close. Our life has been so hard. . . .

"I suppose you're right, Berem. I've seen no sign . . . Wait, brother. . . Look ahead. What's that?"

I see a bright and shining glitter, a myriad colors dancing in the sunlight—as if all the jewels on Krynn were heaped together in a basket.

Her eyes widen. "Perhaps it's the gates of the rainbow!"

Ha! Stupid girlish notion. I laugh, but I find myself running forward. It is hard to catch up with her. Though I am bigger and stronger, she is fleet as a deer.

We come to a clearing in the forest. If lightning did strike this forest, this must have been where the bolt hit. The land around is scorched and blasted. There was a building here once, I notice. Ruined, broken columns jut up from the blackened ground like broken bones sticking through decaying flesh. An oppressive feeling hangs over the place. Nothing grows here, nor has anything grown here for many springs. I want to leave, but I cannot. . . .

Before me is the most beautiful, wonderful sight I have ever seen in my life, in my dreams. . . . A piece of a stone column, encrusted with jewels! I know nothing about gemstones, but I can tell these are valuable beyond belief! My body begins to shake. Hurrying forward, I kneel down beside the fire-blasted stone and brush away the dirt and filth.

She kneels beside me.

"Berem! How wonderful! Did you ever see anything like it? Such beautiful jewels in such a horrible place." She looks around and I feel her shivering. "I wonder what this used to be? There's such a solemn feeling about it, a holy feeling. But an evil feeling, too. It must have been a temple before the Cataclysm. A temple to the evil gods . . . Berem! What are you doing?"

I have taken out my hunting knife and I begin to chip away the stone around one of the jewels—a radiant green gemstone. It is as big as my fist and sparkles more brilliantly than the sun shining on green leaves. The rock around it comes away easily beneath my knife blade. "Stop it, Berem!" Her voice is shrill. "It—it's desecration! This place is sacred to some god! I know it!"

I can feel the gemstone's cold crystal, yet it burns with an inner green fire! I ignore her protests.

"Bah! You said before it was the rainbow's gates! You're right! We've found our fortune, as the old story† *says. If this place was sacred to the gods, they must have abandoned it years ago. Look round, it's nothing but rubble! If they wanted it, they should have taken care of it. The gods won't mind if I take a few of these jewels. . . ."*

"Berem!"

An edge of fear in her voice! She's really frightened! Foolish girl. She's beginning to irritate me. The gemstone is almost free. I can wiggle it.

"Look, Jasla." I am shaking with excitement. I can barely talk. "We've nothing to live on, now—what with the fire and the hard winter. These jewels will bring money enough in the market at Gargath for us to move

I added this about rainbows because of something that happened to me when I was first coming to work for TSR. I had been offered the job of book editor for TSR in Lake Geneva, Wisconsin. I currently lived with my two children in Missouri, so that meant a move. I had just come through a bad divorce. I had to borrow money from my parents to even make the trip. I came up to Lake Geneva to try to find a place to rent that would accept two kids and three cats. I searched and searched.

I had only one day, and I couldn't find anything.

I finally went back to my motel room and lay down and the bed and cried.

I was so exhausted. I couldn't move up here without a place to live. After a while, I got up and looked out the window. There was the most gorgeous rainbow I had ever seen in my life. It lifted my spirits and gave me hope. Sure enough, the very next phone call brought me a place to rent. So this is the "old story" about rainbows.—MW

away from this wretched place. We'll go to a city, maybe Palanthas! You know you've wanted to see the wonders there. . . ."

"No! Berem, I forbid it! You are committing sacrilege!"

Her voice is stern. I have never seen her like this! For a moment I hesitate. I draw back, away from the broken stone column with its rainbow of jewels. I, too, am beginning to feel something frightening and evil about this place. But the jewels are so beautiful! Even as I stare at them, they glitter and sparkle in the sunshine. No god is here. No god cares about them. No god will miss them. Embedded in some old column that is crumbling and broken.

I reach down to pry the jewel out of stone with my knife. It is such a rich green, shining as brilliantly as the spring sun shines through the new leaves of the trees. . . .

"Berem! Stop!"

Her hand grasps my arm, her nails dig into my flesh. It hurts . . . I grow angry, and, as sometimes happens when I grow angry a haze dims my vision and I feel a suffocating swelling inside of me. My head pounds until it seems my eyes must burst from their sockets.

"Leave me be!" I hear a roaring voice—my own!

I shove her. . .

She falls . . .

It all happens so slowly. She is falling forever. I didn't mean to . . . I want to catch her. . . But I cannot move.

She falls against the broken column.

Blood . . . blood . . .

"Jas!" I whisper, lifting her in my arms.

But she doesn't answer me. Blood covers the jewels. They don't sparkle anymore. Just like her eyes. The light is gone. . . .

And then the ground splits apart! Columns rise from the blackened, blasted soil, spiraling into the air! A great darkness comes forth and I feel a horrible, burning pain in my chest. . . .

"Berem!"

Maquesta stood on the foredeck, glaring at her helmsman.

"Berem, I told you. A gale's brewing. I want the ship battened down. What are you doing? Standing there, staring out to sea. What are you practicing to be—a monument? Get moving, you lubber! I don't pay good wages to statues!"

Berem started. His face paled and he cringed before Maquesta's irritation in such a pitiful manner that the captain of the *Perechon* felt as if she were taking out her anger on a helpless child.

That's all he is, she reminded herself wearily. Even though he must be fifty or sixty years old, even though he was one of the best helmsmen she had ever sailed with, mentally, he was still a child.

"I'm sorry, Berem," Maq said, sighing. "I didn't mean to yell at you. It's just the storm . . . it makes me nervous. There, there. Don't look at me like that. How I wish you could talk! I wish I knew what was going on in that head of yours—if there is anything! Well, never mind. Attend to your duties, then go below. Better get used to lying in your berth for a few days until the gale blows itself out."

Berem smiled at her—the simple, guileless smile of a child.

Maquesta smiled back, shaking her head. Then she hurried away, her thoughts busy with getting her beloved ship prepared to ride out the gale. Out of the corner of her eye, she saw Berem shuffle below, then promptly forgot about him when her first mate came aboard to report that he had found most of the crew and only about one-third of them were so drunk as to be useless. . . .

Berem lay in the hammock slung in the crew's quarters of the *Perechon.* The hammock swung back and forth violently as the first winds of the gale struck the *Perechon* as it rode at anchor in the harbor of Flotsam on the Blood Sea of Istar. Putting his hands—the hands that looked too young on the body of a fifty-year-old human—beneath his head, Berem stared up at the lamp swinging from the wooden planks above him.

"Why, look, Berem. Here's a path. . . . How strange. All the times we've been hunting in these woods and we've never seen it."

"It's not so strange. The fire burned off some of the brush, that's all. Probably just an animal trail."

"Let's follow it. If it is an animal trail, maybe we'll find a deer. We've been hunting all day with nothing to show for it. I hate to go home empty-handed."

Without waiting for my reply, she turns onto the trail. Shrugging, I follow her. It is pleasant being outdoors today—the first warm day after the bitter chill of winter. The sun is warm on my neck and shoulders. Walking through the fire-ravaged woods is easy. No vines to snag you. No brush to tear at your clothing. Lightning, probably that thunderstorm which struck late last fall. . . .

It was a weird bit of synergy, and an odd chunk of serendipity that brought Mishakal, Gilean, and the rest of the gods of Krynn into the DRAGONLANCE *Chronicles. They came from my original campaign from college (circa mid-seventies, when the D&D game was new). That original scratchbuilt campaign was built with a "fighter's god," a "monk's god," a "knowledge god," a "healing god," and several "wizard gods" (one for each alignment—good, neutral, and evil). And in the pantheon were the two most powerful figures of the game at that time—the Platinum Dragon, Bahamut, and the Chromatic Dragon, Tiamat.*

When DRAGONLANCE *was aborning, I threw my collection of gods and their origins at Tracy, who picked them up and moved them into the new world. Bahamut became Paladine and Tiamat beame Takhisis. Most of the rest kept their original names—Gilead became Gilean, and Mishakal went from being a male figure to a female. The three "spheres of magic" gods became the moons of Krynn, and the rest of the gods became represented by constellations.*

The names came from a variety of sources, from pure inventions (Kiri-Jolith the bison-headed minotaur and Reorx the Forge just sounded right) to modifications on biblical names (Gilead from the phrase "There is a Balm in Gilead" and Mishakal from the fiery furnace (Meshach, Shadrach, and Abednego). Again, as a shared concept, the gods have gone in a number of interesting directions as they developed, but they were originally a twenty-one-god pantheon for my home campaign.

And the kicker is: The name of that original campaign was Toril, which we eventually used as the name for the FORGOTTEN REALMS' *planet. So you can say the gods of Krynn were originally Torillian gods and be correct. That's part of the nature of shared worlds.*

—Jeff Grubb

BOOK I

I

Flight from darkness into darkness.

The dragonarmy officer slowly descended the stairs from the second floor of the Saltbreeze Inn. It was past midnight. Most of the inn's patrons had long since gone to bed. The only sound the officer could hear was the crashing of waves of Blood Bay on the rocks below.

The officer paused a moment on the landing, casting a quick, sharp glance around the common room that lay spread out below him. It was empty, except for a draconian sprawled across a table, snoring loudly in a drunken stupor. The dragonman's wings shivered with each snort. The wooden table creaked and swayed beneath it.

The officer smiled bitterly, then continued down the stairs. He was dressed in the steel dragon-scale armor copied from the real dragonscale armor of

the Dragon Highlords. His helm covered his head and face, making it difficult to see his features. All that was visible beneath the shadow cast by the helm was a reddish brown beard that marked him—racially—as human.

At the bottom of the stairs, the officer came to a sudden halt, apparently nonplussed at the sight of the innkeeper, still awake and yawning over his account books. After a slight nod, the dragon officer seemed about to go on out of the inn without speaking, but the innkeeper stopped him with a question.

"You expecting the Highlord tonight?"

The officer halted and half turned. Keeping his face averted, he pulled out a pair of gloves and began putting them on. The weather was bitterly chill. The sea city of Flotsam† was in the grip of a winter storm the like of which it had not experienced in its three hundred years of existence on the shores of Blood Bay.

Flotsam came into existence after the Cataclysm only because its location happened to be where the odd currents in the newly created Blood Sea dumped debris ashore. Ever since, it has continued to be the magnet for Krynn's living debris. A prize example of the kind of flotsam that this city on the Blood Sea collected is the fact that a nearby thirty-foot bluff was the site of Fewmaster Toede's manor.

"In this weather?" The dragonarmy officer snorted. "Not likely! Not even dragons can outfly these gale winds!"

"True. It's not a fit night out for man or beast," the innkeeper agreed. He eyed the dragon officer shrewdly. "What business do you have, then, that takes you out in this storm?"

The dragonarmy officer regarded the innkeeper coldly. "I don't see that it's any of your business where I go or what I do."

"No offense," the innkeeper said quickly, raising his hands as if to ward off a blow. "It's just that if the Highlord comes back and happens to miss you, I'd be glad to tell her where you could be found."

"That won't be necessary," the officer muttered. "I—I've left her a—note . . . explaining my absence. Besides, I'll be back before morning. I—I just need a breath of air. That's all."

"I don't doubt that!" The innkeeper sniggered. "You haven't left her room for three days! Or should I say three nights! Now, don't get mad"—this on seeing the officer flush angrily beneath the helm, "I admire the man can keep *her* satisfied that long! Where was she bound for?"

"The Highlord was called to deal with a problem in the west, somewhere near Solamnia," the officer

replied, scowling. "I wouldn't inquire any further into her affairs if I were you."

"No, no," replied the innkeeper hastily. "Certainly not. Well, I bid you good evening. What was your name? She introduced us, but I failed to catch it."

"Tanis," the officer said, his voice muffled. "Tanis Half-Elven. And a good evening to you."

Nodding coldly, the officer gave his gloves a final sharp tug, then, pulling his cloak around him, he opened the door to the inn and stepped out into the storm. The bitter wind swept into the room, blowing out candles and swirling the innkeeper's papers around. For a moment, the officer struggled with the heavy door while the innkeeper cursed fluently and grabbed for his scattered accounts. Finally the officer succeeded in slamming the door shut behind him, leaving the inn peaceful, quiet, and warm once more.

Staring out after him, the innkeeper saw the officer walk past the front window, his head bent down against the wind, his cloak billowing out behind him.

Though occasionally a draconian is referred to as "he," there are no female draconians. Rumor has it that there were female draconian eggs, but that these were not allowed to hatch because the human commanders feared that if allowed to breed, the draconians would grow too strong. See The Doom Brigade *and* Draconian Measures *by Margaret Weis and Don Perrin.—MW*

One other figure watched the officer as well. The instant the door shut, the drunken draconian raised its† head, its black, reptilian eyes glittering. Stealthily it rose from the table, its steps quick and certain. Padding lightly on its clawed feet, it crept to the window and peered outside. For a few moments, the draconian waited, then it too flung open the door and disappeared into the storm.

Through the window, the innkeeper saw the draconian head in the same direction as the dragonarmy officer. Walking over, the innkeeper peered out through the glass. It was wild and dark outside, the tall iron braziers of flaming pitch that lit the night streets sputtering and flickering in the wind and the driving rain. But the innkeeper thought he saw the dragonarmy officer turn down a street leading to the main part of town. Creeping along behind him, keeping to the shadows, came the draconian.

Shaking his head, the innkeeper woke the night clerk, who was dozing in a chair behind the desk. "I've a feeling the Highlord will be in tonight, storm or no storm," the innkeeper told the sleepy clerk. "Wake me if she comes."

Shivering, he glanced outside into the night once more, seeing in his mind's eye the dragonarmy officer walking the empty streets of Flotsam, the shadowy figure of the draconian slinking after him.

"On second thought," the innkeeper muttered, "let me sleep."

The storm shut down Flotsam tonight. The bars that normally stayed open until the dawn straggled through their grimy windows were locked up and shuttered against the gale. The streets were deserted, no one venturing out into the winds that could knock a man down and pierce even the warmest clothing with biting cold.

Tanis walked swiftly, his head bowed, keeping near the darkened buildings that broke the full force of the gale. His beard was soon rimed with ice. Sleet stung his face painfully. The half-elf shook with the cold, cursing the dragonarmor's cold metal against his skin. Glancing behind him occasionally, he watched to see if anyone had taken an unusual interest in his leaving the inn. But the visibility was reduced to almost nothing. Sleet and rain swirled around him so that he could barely see tall buildings looming up in the darkness, much less anything else. After a while, he realized he had better concentrate on finding his way through town. Soon he was so numb with cold that he didn't much care if anyone was following him or not.

He hadn't been in the town of Flotsam long—only four days to be precise. And most of those days had been spent with her.

Tanis blocked the thought from his mind as he stared through the rain at the street signs. He knew only vaguely where he was going. His friends were in an inn somewhere on the edge of town, away from the wharf, away from the bars and brothels. For a moment he wondered in despair what he would do if he got lost. He dared not ask about them. . . .

And then he found it. Stumbling through the deserted streets, slipping on the ice, he almost sobbed in relief when he saw the sign swinging wildly in the wind. He hadn't even been able to remember the name, but now he recognized it—the Jetties.

Stupid name for an inn, he thought, shaking so with the cold he could barely grasp the door handle.

Pulling the door open, he was blown inside by the force of the wind, and it was with an effort that he managed to shove the door shut behind him.

There was no night clerk on duty, not at this shabby place. By the light of a smoking fire in the filthy grate, Tanis saw a stub of a candle sitting on the desk, apparently for the convenience of guests who staggered in after hours. His hands shook so he could barely strike the flint. After a moment he forced his cold-stiffened fingers to work, lit the candle, and made his way upstairs by its feeble light.

If he had turned around and glanced out the window, he would have seen a shadowy figure huddle in a doorway across the street. But Tanis did not look out the window behind him, his eyes were on the stairs.

"Caramon!"

The big warrior instantly sat bolt upright, his hand reaching reflexively for his sword, even before he turned to look questioningly at his brother.

"I heard a noise outside," Raistlin whispered. "The sound of a scabbard clanking against armor."

Caramon shook his head, trying to clear the sleep away, and climbed out of bed, sword in hand. He crept toward the door until he, too, could hear the noise that had wakened his light-sleeping brother. A man dressed in armor was walking stealthily down the hall outside their rooms. Then Caramon could see the faint glow of candlelight beneath the door. The sound of clanking armor came to a halt, right outside their room.

Gripping his sword, Caramon motioned to his brother. Raistlin nodded and melted back into the shadows. His eyes were abstracted. He was calling to mind a magic spell. The twin brothers worked well together, effectively combining magic and steel to defeat their foes.†

Raistlin and Caramon learned that they could work well together during their mercenary years (told in Brothers in Arms*). The two had planned this career for themselves ever since they were young. Raistlin has common sense enough to realize that he needs his stronger brother's protection in a fight.* *—MW*

The candlelight beneath the door wavered. The man must be shifting the candle to his other hand, freeing his sword hand. Reaching out, Caramon slowly and silently slid the bolt on the door. He waited a moment. Nothing happened. The man was hesitating, perhaps wondering if this was the right room. He'll find out soon enough, Caramon thought to himself.

Caramon flung open the door with a sudden jerk. Lunging around it, he grasped hold of the dark figure and dragged him inside. With all the strength of his brawny arms, the warrior flung the armor-clad man to the floor. The candle dropped, its flame extinguishing in melted wax. Raistlin began to chant a magic spell† that would entrap their victim in a sticky web-like substance.

Haven't seen a Web spell for a while.

"Hold! Raistlin, stop!" the man shouted. Recognizing the voice, Caramon grabbed hold of his brother, shaking him to break the concentration of his spellcasting.

"Raist! It's Tanis!"

Shuddering, Raistlin came out of his trance, arms dropped limply to his sides. Then he began to cough, clutching his chest.

Caramon cast an anxious glance at his twin, but Raistlin warded him away with a wave of the hand. Turning, Caramon reached down to help the half-elf to his feet.

"Tanis!" he cried, nearly squeezing the breath out of him with an enthusiastic embrace. "Where have you been? We were sick with worry. By all the gods, you're freezing! Here, I'll poke up the fire. Raist"—Caramon turned to his brother—"are you sure you're all right?"

"Don't concern yourself with me!" Raistlin whispered. The mage sank back down on his bed, gasping for breath. His eyes glittered gold in the flaring firelight as he stared at the half-elf, who huddled thankfully beside the blaze. "You'd better get the others."

"Right." Caramon started out the door.

"I'd put some clothes on first," Raistlin remarked caustically.

Blushing, Caramon hurried back to his bed and grabbed a pair of leather breeches. Pulling these on, he slipped a shirt over his head, then went out into the hallway, softly closing the door behind him. Tanis and Raistlin could hear him knocking gently on the Plainsmen's door. They could hear Riverwind's stern reply and Caramon's hurried, excited explanation.

Tanis glanced at Raistlin, saw the mage's strange hourglass eyes focused on him with a piercing stare, and turned uncomfortably back to gaze into the fire.

"Where *have* you been, Half-Elf?" Raistlin asked in his soft, whispering voice.

Tanis swallowed nervously. "I was captured by a Dragon Highlord," he said, reciting the answer he had prepared. "The Highlord thought I was one of his officers, naturally, and asked me to escort him to his troops, who are stationed outside of town. Of course, I had to do as he asked or make him suspicious. Finally, tonight, I was able to get away."

"Interesting." Raistlin coughed the word.

Tanis glanced at him sharply. "What's interesting?"

"I've never heard you lie before, Half-Elf," Raistlin said softly. "I find it . . . quite . . . fascinating."

Tanis opened his mouth, but, before he could reply, Caramon returned, followed by Riverwind and Goldmoon and Tika, yawning sleepily.

Hurrying to him, Goldmoon embraced Tanis swiftly. "My friend!" she said brokenly, holding onto him tightly. "We've been so worried—"

Riverwind clasped Tanis by the hand, his usually stern face relaxed in a smile. Gently he took hold of his wife and removed her from Tanis's embrace, but it was only to take her place.

"My brother!" Riverwind said in Qué-Shu, the dialect of the Plains people, hugging the half-elf tightly. "We feared you were captured! Dead! We didn't know—"

"What happened? Where were you?" Tika asked eagerly, coming forward to hug Tanis.

Tanis looked over at Raistlin, but he was lying back on his hard pillow, his strange eyes fixed on the ceiling, seemingly uninterested in anything being said.

Clearing his throat self-consciously, intensely aware of Raistlin listening, Tanis repeated his story. The others followed it with expressions of interest and sympathy. Occasionally they asked questions. Who was this Highlord? How big was the army? Where was it located? What were the draconians doing in Flotsam? Were they really searching for them? How had Tanis escaped?

Tanis answered all their questions glibly. As for the Highlord, he hadn't seen much of him. He didn't know who he was. The army was not large. It was located outside of town. The draconians were searching for someone, but it was not them. They

were looking for a human named Berem or something strange like that.

At this Tanis shot a quick look at Caramon, but the big man's face registered no recognition. Tanis breathed easier. Good, Caramon didn't remember the man they had seen patching the sail on the *Perechon.* He didn't remember or he hadn't caught the man's name. Either way was fine.

The others nodded, absorbed in his story. Tanis sighed in relief. As for Raistlin . . . well, it didn't really matter what the mage thought or said. The others would believe Tanis over Raistlin even if the half-elf claimed day was night. Undoubtedly Raistlin knew this, which was why he didn't cast any doubts on Tanis's story. Feeling wretched, hoping no one would ask him anything else and force him to mire himself deeper and deeper in lies, Tanis yawned and groaned as if exhausted past endurance.

Goldmoon immediately rose to her feet, her face soft with concern. "I'm sorry, Tanis," she said gently. "We've been selfish. You are cold and weary and we've kept you up talking. And we must be up early in the morning to board the ship."

"Damn it, Goldmoon! Don't be a fool! We won't board any ship in this gale!" Tanis snarled.†

Tanis snarling?! Especially at Goldmoon! I loved this moment! It provided us with the first signs of Tanis losing the sheen on his armor. —MW

Everyone stared at him in astonishment, even Raistlin sat up. Goldmoon's eyes were dark with pain, her face set in rigid lines, reminding the half-elf that no one spoke to her in that tone. Riverwind stood beside her, a troubled look on his face.

The silence grew uncomfortable. Finally Caramon cleared his throat with a rumble. "If we can't leave tomorrow, we'll try the next day," he said comfortably. "Don't worry about it, Tanis. The draconians won't be out in this weather. We're safe—"

"I know. I'm sorry," he muttered. "I didn't mean to snap at you, Goldmoon. It's been—nerve-racking these last few days. I'm so tired I can't think straight. I'll go to my room."

"The innkeeper gave it to someone else," Caramon said, then added hurriedly, "but you can sleep here, Tanis. Take my bed—"

"No, I'll just lie down on the floor." Avoiding Goldmoon's gaze, Tanis began unbuckling the dragonarmor, his eyes fixed firmly on his shaking fingers.

"Sleep well, my friend," Goldmoon said softly.

Hearing the concern in her voice, he could imagine her exchanging compassionate glances with Riverwind. There was the Plainsman's hand on his shoulder, giving him a sympathetic pat. Then they were gone. Tika left, too, closing the door behind her after a murmured goodnight.

"Here, let me help you," Caramon offered, knowing that Tanis, unaccustomed to wearing plate armor, found the intricate buckles and straps difficult to manage. "Can I get you something to eat? Drink? Some mulled wine?"

"No," Tanis said wearily, divesting himself thankfully of the armor, trying not to remember that in a few hours he would have to put it on again. "I just need sleep."

"Here—at least take my blanket," Caramon insisted, seeing that the half-elf was shivering with the cold.

Tanis accepted the blanket gratefully, although he was not certain whether he was shaking with the chill or the violence of his turbulent emotions. Lying down, he wrapped himself in both the blanket and his cloak. Then he closed his eyes and concentrated on making his breathing even and regular, knowing that the mother-hen, Caramon, would never sleep until he was certain Tanis was resting comfortably. Soon he heard Caramon get into bed. The fire burned low, darkness fell. After a moment, he heard Caramon's rumbling snore. In the other bed, he could hear Raistlin's fitful cough.

When he was certain both the twins were asleep, Tanis stretched out, putting his hands beneath his head. He lay awake, staring into the darkness.

It was near morning when the Dragon Highlord arrived back at the Saltbreeze Inn. The night clerk could see immediately that the Highlord was in a foul temper. Flinging open the door with more force than the gale winds, she glared angrily into the inn, as if its warmth and comfort were offensive. Indeed, she seemed to be at one with the storm outside. It was she who caused the candles to flicker, rather than the howling wind. It was she who brought the darkness indoors. The clerk stumbled fearfully to his feet, but the Highlord's

eyes were not on him. Kitiara was staring at a draconian, who sat at a table and who signaled, by an almost imperceptible flicker in the dark reptilian eyes, that something was awry.

Behind the hideous dragonmask, the Highlord's eyes narrowed alarmingly, their expression grew cold. For a moment she stood in the doorway, ignoring the chill wind that blew through the inn, whipping her cloak around her.

"Come upstairs," she said finally, ungraciously, to the draconian.

The creature nodded and followed after her, its clawed feet clicking on the wooden floors.

"Is there anything—" the night clerk began, cringing as the door blew shut with a shattering crash.

"No!" Kitiara snarled. Hand on the hilt of her sword, she stalked past the quivering man without a glance and climbed the stairs to her suite of rooms, leaving the man to sink back, shaken, into his chair.

Fumbling with her key, Kitiara threw open the door. She gave the room a quick sweeping glance.

It was empty.

The draconian waited behind her, standing patiently and in silence.

Furious, Kitiara tugged viciously at the hinges on the dragonmask and yanked it off. Tossing it on the bed, she spoke over her shoulder.

"Come inside and shut the door!"

The draconian did as it was commanded, closing the door softly.

Kitiara did not turn to face the creature. Hands on her hips, she stared grimly at the rumpled bed.

"So, he's gone." It was a statement, not a question.

"Yes, Highlord," lisped the draconian in its hissing voice.

"You followed him, as I ordered?"

"Of course, Highlord." The draconian bowed.

"Where did he go?"

Kitiara ran a hand through her dark, curly hair. She still had not turned around. The draconian could not see her face and he had no idea what emotions, if any, she was keeping hidden.

"An inn, Highlord. Near the edge of town. Called the Jetties."

Even Dragon Highlord Kitiara can have a lot of emotional energy tied up in a man, and Tanis has played a role in her life for a decade or more. Kitiara and Tanis's early relationship is told in Steel and Stone *by Ellen Porath.*

"Another woman?" The Highlord's voice was tense.†

"I think not, Highlord." The draconian concealed a smile. "I believe he has friends there. We had reports of strangers staying in the inn, but since they did not match the description of the Green Gemstone Man, we did not investigate them."

"Someone is there now, watching him?"

"Certainly, Highlord. You will be informed immediately if he—or any inside—leaves the building."

The Highlord stood in silence for a moment, then she turned around. Her face was cold and calm, although extremely pale. But there were a number of factors which could have accounted for her pallor, the draconian thought. It was a long flight from the High Clerist's Tower, rumor had it her armies had been badly defeated there, the legendary Dragonlance had reappeared, along with the dragon orbs. Then there was her failure to find the Green Gemstone Man, so desperately sought by the Queen of Darkness, and who was reported to have been seen in Flotsam. The Highlord had a great many things to worry about, the draconian thought with amusement. Why concern herself over one man? She had lovers aplenty, most of them much more charming, much more eager to please than that moody half-elf. Bakaris, for example . . .

"You have done well," Kitiara said finally, breaking in on the draconian's musings. Stripping off her armor with a careless lack of modesty, she waved a negligent hand. She almost seemed herself again. "You will be rewarded. Now leave me."

The draconian bowed again and left, eyes staring at the floor. The creature was not fooled. As it left, the dragonman saw the Highlord's gaze fall upon a scrap of parchment resting on the table. The draconian had seen that parchment upon entering. It was, the creature noted, covered with writing in a delicate elvish script. As the draconian shut the door, there came a crashing sound, the sound of a piece of dragonarmor being hurled full force against a wall.

2

Pursuit.

The gale blew itself out toward morning. The sound of water dripping monotonously from the eaves thudded in Tanis's aching head, almost making him wish for a return of the shrieking wind. The sky was gray and lowering. Its leaden weight pressed down upon the half-elf.

"The seas will be running high," Caramon said sagely. Having listened eagerly to the sea stories told them by William, the innkeeper of the Pig and Whistle in Port Balifor, Caramon considered himself somewhat of an expert on nautical matters. None of the others disputed him, knowing nothing about the sea themselves. Only Raistlin regarded Caramon with a sneering smile when his brother, who had been on small boats only a few times in his life, began talking like an old seadog.

Tanis is running away—away from his shame, away from Kitiara, away from his wrongful lust, and, in a very real sense, away from himself. He cannot leave quickly enough—he will never be able to run far enough. —TRH

"Maybe we shouldn't even risk going out—" Tika began.

"We're going. Today," Tanis said grimly. "If we have to swim, we're leaving Flotsam."†

The others glanced at each other, then looked back at Tanis. Standing, staring out the window, he did not see their raised eyebrows or their shrugging shoulders, though he was aware of them all the same.

The companions were gathered in the brothers' room. It would not be dawn for another hour, but Tanis had awakened them as soon as he heard the wind cease its savage howl.

He drew a deep breath, then turned to face them. "I'm sorry. I know I sound arbitrary," he said, "but there are dangers I know about that I can't explain right now. There isn't time. All I can tell you is this—we have never in our lives been in more dire peril than we are at this moment in this town. We must leave and we must leave now!" He heard an hysterical note creep into his voice and broke off.

There was silence, then, "Sure, Tanis," Caramon said uneasily.

"We're all packed," Goldmoon added. "We can leave whenever you're ready."

"Let's go then," Tanis said.

"I've got to get my things," Tika faltered.

"Go on. Be quick," Tanis told her.

"I—I'll help her," Caramon offered in a low voice.

The big man, dressed, like Tanis, in the stolen armor of a dragonarmy officer, and Tika left quickly, probably hoping to snatch time enough for a last few minutes alone, Tanis thought, fuming in impatience. Goldmoon and Riverwind left to gather their things as well. Raistlin remained in the room, not moving. He had all he needed to carry with him—his pouches with his precious spell components, the Staff of Magius, and the precious marble of the dragon orb, tucked away inside its nondescript bag.

He can get a very hard look on his face that Flint refers to as his "infernal mulish elven look."

Tanis could feel Raistlin's strange eyes boring into him.† It was as if Raistlin could penetrate the darkness of the half-elf's soul with the glittering light from those golden eyes. But still the mage said nothing. Why? Tanis thought angrily. He would almost have welcomed Raistlin's questioning, his accusations. He would almost welcome a chance to

unburden himself and tell the truth, even though he knew what consequences would result.

But Raistlin was silent, except for his incessant cough.

Within a few minutes, the others came back inside the room.

"We're ready, Tanis," Goldmoon said in a subdued voice.

For a moment, Tanis couldn't speak. I'll tell them, he resolved. Taking a deep breath, he turned around. He saw their faces, he saw trust; a belief in him. They were following him without question. He couldn't let them down. He couldn't shake this faith. It was all they had to cling to. Sighing, he swallowed the words he had been about to speak.

"Right," he said gruffly and started toward the door.

Maquesta Kar-Thon was awakened from a sound sleep by a banging on her cabin door. Accustomed to having her sleep interrupted at all hours, she was almost immediately awake and reaching for her boots.

"What is it?" she called out.

Before the answer came, she was already getting the feel of the ship, assessing the situation. A glance through the porthole showed her the gale winds had died, but she could tell from the motion of the ship itself that the seas were running high.

"The passengers are here,"called out a voice she recognized as that of her first mate.

Landlubbers, she thought bitterly, sighing and dropping the boot she had been dragging on.

"Send 'em back," she ordered, lying down again. "We're not sailing today."

There seemed to be some sort of altercation going on outside, for she heard her first mate's voice raised in anger and another voice shouting back. Wearily Maquesta struggled to her feet. Her first mate,† Bas Ohn-Koraf, was a minotaur, a race not noted for its easy-going temper. He was exceptionally strong and was known to kill without provocation—one reason he had taken to the sea. On a ship like the *Perechon*, no one asked questions about the past.

Throwing open the door to her cabin, Maq hurried up onto deck.

The only person Maquesta comes close to trusting. They met when Maq was being held prisoner by minotaurs for encroaching on their territory. Koraf was also a prisoner on the Isle of Mithas, under a sentence of death. Koraf saved Maq's life and helped her escape. The story is told in Maquesta Kar-Thon *by Tina Daniell and Jean Rabe.*

"What's going on?" she demanded in her sternest voice as her eyes went from the bestial head of her first mate to the bearded face of what appeared to be a dragonarmy officer. But she recognized the slightly slanted brown eyes of the bearded man and fixed him with a cold stare. "I said we're not sailing today, Half-Elf, and I meant—"

"Maquesta," Tanis said quickly, "I've got to talk to you!" He started to push his way past the minotaur to reach her, but Koraf grabbed hold of him and yanked him backward. Behind Tanis, a larger dragonarmy officer growled and took a step forward. The minotaur's eyes glistened eagerly as he deftly slipped a dirk from the wide, bright-colored sash around his waist.

The crew above decks gathered around immediately, hoping for a fight.

"Caramon—" Tanis warned, holding out his hand restrainingly.

"Kof—!" Maquesta snapped with an angry look meant to remind her first mate that these were paying customers and were not to be handled roughly, at least while in sight of land.

The minotaur scowled, but the dirk disappeared as quickly as it had flashed into the open. Koraf turned and walked away disdainfully, the crew muttering in disappointment, but still cheerful. It promised already to be an interesting voyage.

Maquesta helped Tanis to his feet, studying the half-elf with the same intense scrutiny she fixed on a man wanting to sign on as a crew member. She saw at once that the half-elf had changed drastically since she had seen him only four days before, when he and the big man behind him closed the bargain for passage aboard the *Perechon.*

He looks like he's been through the Abyss and back. Probably in some sort of trouble, she decided ruefully. Well, I'm not getting him out of it! Not at the risk of my ship. Still, he and his friends had paid for half their passage. And she needed the money. It was hard these days for a pirate to compete with the Highlords. . . .

"Come to my cabin," Maq said ungraciously, leading the way below.

"Stay with the others, Caramon," the half-elf told his companion. The big man nodded. Glancing

darkly at the minotaur, Caramon went back over to stand with the rest of the companions, who stood silently, huddled around their meager belongings.

Tanis followed Maq down to her cabin and squeezed inside. Even two people in the small cabin were a tight fit. The *Perechon* was a trim vessel, designed for swift sailing and quick maneuvers. Ideal for Maquesta's trade,† for which it was necessary to slip in and out of harbors quickly, unloading or picking up cargo that wasn't necessarily hers either to pick up or deliver. On occasion, she might enhance her income by catching a fat merchant ship sailing out of Palanthas or Tarsis and slip up on it before it knew what was happening. Then board it quickly, loot it, and make good her escape.

Maquesta's major inheritance from her father was his admonition never to trust anyone and to do whatever she had to in order to make money—wealth being the only thing worthwhile in this world. The pirate's story is told in Maquesta Kar-Thon, *by Tina Daniell and Jean Rabe.*

She was adept at outrunning the massive ships of the Dragon Highlords, too, although she made it a point to leave them strictly alone. Too often now, though, the Highlords' ships were seen "escorting" the merchant vessels. Maquesta had lost money on her last two voyages, one reason why she had deigned to carry passengers—something she would never do under normal circumstances.

Removing his helm, the half-elf sat down at the table, or rather fell down, since he was unaccustomed to the motion of the rocking ship. Maquesta remained standing, balancing easily.

"Well, what is it you want?" she demanded, yawning. "I told you we can't sail. The seas are—"

"We have to," Tanis said abruptly.

"Look," Maquesta said patiently (reminding herself he was a paying customer), "if you're in some kind of trouble, it's not my concern! I'm not risking my ship or my crew—"

"Not me," Tanis interrupted, looking at Maquesta intently, "you."

"Me?" Maquesta said, drawing back, amazed.

Tanis folded his hands on the table and gazed down at them. The pitching and tossing of the vessel at anchor, combined with his exhaustion from the past few days, made him nauseous. Seeing the faint green tinge of his skin beneath his beard and the dark shadows under his hollow eyes, Maquesta thought she'd seen corpses that looked better than this half-elf.

"What do you mean?" she asked tightly.

"I—I was captured by a Dragon Highlord . . . three days ago," Tanis began, speaking in a low voice, staring at his hands. "No, I guess 'captured' is the wrong word. H-He saw me dressed like this and assumed I was one of his men. I had to accompany h-him back to his camp. I've been there, in camp, the last few days, and I—I found out something. I know why the Highlord and the draconians are searching Flotsam. I know what—who—they're looking for."

"Yes?" Maquesta prompted, feeling his fear creep over her like a contagious disease. "Not the *Perechon*—"

"Your helmsman." Tanis finally looked up at her. "Berem."

"Berem!" Maquesta repeated, stunned. "What for? The man's a mute! A half-wit! A good helmsman, maybe, but nothing more. What could he have done that the Dragon Highlords are looking for him?"

"I don't know," Tanis said wearily, fighting his nausea. "I wasn't able to find out. I'm not sure they know! But they're under orders to find him at all costs and bring him alive to"—he closed his eyes to shut out the swaying lamps—"the Dark Queen. . . ."

The breaking light of dawn threw slanted red beams across the sea's rough surface. For an instant it shone on Maq's glistening black skin, a flash like fire came from her golden earrings that dangled nearly to her shoulders. Nervously she ran her fingers through her closely cropped black hair.

Maquesta felt her throat close. "We'll get rid of him!" she muttered tightly, pushing herself up from the table. "We'll put him ashore. I can find another helmsman—"

"Listen!" Catching hold of Maquesta's arm, Tanis gripped her tightly, forcing her to stop. "They may already know he's here! Even if they don't and they catch him, it won't make any difference. Once they find out he was here, on this vessel, and they *will* find out, believe me; there are ways of making even a mute talk—they'll arrest you and everyone on this ship. Arrest you or get rid of you."

He dropped his hand from her arm, realizing he hadn't the strength to hold her. "It's what they've done in the past. I know. The Highlord told me. Whole villages destroyed. People tortured, murdered.

Anyone this man comes in contact with is doomed. They fear whatever deadly secret he carries will be passed on, and they can't allow that."

Maquesta sat down. "Berem?" she whispered softly, unbelievingly.

"They couldn't do anything because of the storm," Tanis said wearily, "and the Highlord was called away to Solamnia, some battle there. But sh—the Highlord will be back today. And then, " He couldn't go on. His head sank into his hands as a shudder racked his body.

Maquesta eyed him warily. Could this be true? Or was he making all this up to force her to take him away from some danger? Watching him slump miserably over the table, Maquesta swore softly. The ship's captain was a shrewd judge of men. She needed to be, in order to control her rough-and-ready crew. And she knew the half-elf wasn't lying. At least, not much. She suspected there were things he wasn't telling, but this story about Berem, as strange as it seemed, had the ring of truth.

It all made sense, she thought uneasily, cursing herself. She prided herself on her judgment, her good sense. Yet she had turned a blind eye to Berem's strangeness. Why? Her lip curled in derision. She liked him—admit it. He was like a child, cheerful, guileless. And so she had overlooked his unwillingness to go ashore, his fear of strangers, his eagerness to work for a pirate when he refused to share in the loot they captured. Maquesta sat a moment, getting the feel of her ship. Glancing outside, she watched the golden sun glint off the white caps, then the sun vanished, swallowed by the lowering gray clouds. It would be dangerous, taking the ship out, but if the wind was right . . .

"I'd rather be out on the open sea," she murmured, more to herself than to Tanis, "than trapped like a rat on shore."

Making up her mind, Maq rose quickly and started for the door. Then she heard Tanis groan. Turning around, she regarded him pityingly.

"Come on, Half-Elf," Maquesta said, not unkindly. She put her arms around him and helped him stand. "You'll feel better above deck in the fresh air. Besides, you'll need to tell your friends that this isn't going to be what you might call a

'relaxing ocean voyage.' Do you know the risk you're taking?"

Tanis nodded. Leaning heavily on Maquesta, he walked across the heaving deck.

"You're not telling me everything, that's for certain," Maquesta said under her breath as she kicked open the cabin door and helped Tanis struggle up the stairs to the main deck. "I'll wager Berem's not the only one the Highlord's looking for. But I have a feeling this isn't the first bad weather you and your crew have ridden out. I just hope your luck holds!"

The *Perechon* wallowed in the high seas. Riding under short sail, the ship seemed to make little headway, fighting for every inch it gained. Fortunately, the wind backed. Blowing steadily from the southwest, it was taking them straight into the Blood Sea of Istar. Since they were heading for Kalaman, northwest of Flotsam, around the cape of Nordmaar, this was a little out of their way. But Maquesta didn't mind. She wanted to avoid land as much as possible.

There was even the possibility, she told Tanis, that they could sail northeast and arrive in Mithras, homeland of the minotaurs. Although a few minotaurs fought in the armies of the Highlords, the minotaurs in general had not yet sworn allegiance to the Dark Queen. According to Koraf, the minotaurs wanted control of eastern Ansalon in return for their services. And control of the east had just been handed over to a new Dragon Highlord, a hobgoblin called Toede.† The minotaurs had no love for humans or elves, but, at this point in time, neither had they any use for the Highlords. Maq and her crew had sheltered in Mithras before. They would be safe there again, at least for a little while.

Tanis was not happy at this delay, but his fate was no longer in his hands. Thinking of this, the half-elf glanced over at the man who stood alone at the center of a whirlwind of blood and flame. Berem was at the helm, guiding the wheel with firm, sure hands, his vacant face unconcerned, unworried.

Tanis, staring hard at the helmsman's shirt front, thought perhaps he could detect a faint glimmer of green. What dark secret beat in the chest where, months ago at Pax Tharkas, he had seen the green

I don't remember creating Fewmaster Toede, though he sounds like something I would do—short name, silly idea, humorous delivery. I think I'll blame Tracy for this one, anyway.

In the midst of the serious, epic nature of DRAGONLANCE, *Toede was a necessity—a weak villain whom the heroes could defeat early on. However, once created, he just wouldn't go away. If anything, he rose in power and prestige over his long career. His first appearance is as the slaver who captured the heroes. Then he comes back as Verminaard's flunky. Then he's back again running the town of Flotsam. By the end of the war he had his own dragon wing under his command (though a temporary, brevet command, as later revealed). If anyone ever fell upward through the chain of command it was Toede.*

Here's an example: Many years after the publication of the original Chronicles, Pat McGilligan, editor fantastic, called me on the phone.

"Jeff," said he, "we're doing a series on the villains of the lance. Would you like to do a book on Lord Toede?"

I said I was interested and would do some homework and get back to him. When I did get back to him, I said, "Did you know he's dead?"

glowing jewel embedded in the man's flesh? Why were hundreds of draconians wasting their time, searching for this one man when the war still hung in balance? Why was Kitiara so desperate to find Berem that she had given up command of her forces in Solamnia to supervise the search of Flotsam on just a rumor that he had been seen there?

"He is the key!" Tanis remembered Kitiara's words. "If we capture him, Krynn will fall to the might of the Dark Queen. There will be no force in the land able to defeat us then!"

Shivering, his stomach heaving, Tanis stared at the man in awe. Berem seemed so, so apart from everything, beyond everything, as if the problems of the world affected him not at all. Was he half-witted, as Maquesta said? Tanis wondered. He remembered Berem as he had seen him for those few brief seconds in the midst of the horror of Pax Tharkas. He remembered the look on the man's face as he allowed the traitor Eben to lead him away in a desperate attempt to escape. The look on his face had not been fearful or dull or uncaring. It had been, what? Resigned! That was it! As if he knew the fate that awaited him and went ahead anyway. Sure enough, just as Berem and Eben reached the gates, hundreds of tons of rocks had cascaded down from the gate-blocking mechanism, burying them beneath boulders it would take a dragon to lift. Both bodies were lost, of course.

Or at least Eben's body was lost. Only weeks later, during the celebration of the wedding of Goldmoon and Riverwind, Tanis and Sturm had seen Berem again—alive! Before they could catch him, the man had vanished into the crowd. And they had not seen him again. Not until Tanis found him three, no, four, days ago, calmly sewing a sail on this ship.

Berem steered the ship on its course, his face filled with peace. Tanis leaned over the ship's side and retched.

Maquesta said nothing to the crew about Berem. In explanation of their sudden departure, she said only that she had received word that the Dragon Highlord was a bit too interested in their ship, it would be wise to head for the open seas. None of the crew questioned her. They had no love for the

"He's dead?" repeated Pat.

"Yeah, Harold Bakst killed him off in 'Lord Toede's Disastrous Hunt.' "

There was a pause on the phone, then Pat said, "Well, can you work with it?"

And that's sort of Lord Toede in a nutshell—not even clear and obvious death can stop him (the resulting novel, Lord Toede, *almost killed Margaret's husband Don, though—he read it after an operation and almost pulled his stitches laughing). I really worry that if the gods of Krynn ever return, Toede will be there, with malice on his mind and a bouncy, evil song in his heart.*
—Jeff Grubb

Highlords, and most had been in Flotsam long enough to lose all their money anyway.

Nor did Tanis reveal to his friends the reason for their haste. The companions had all heard the story of the man with the green gemstone and, though they were too polite to say so (with the exception of Caramon), Tanis knew they thought he and Sturm had drunk one too many toasts at the wedding. They did not ask for reasons why they were risking their lives in the rough seas. Their faith in him was complete.

Suffering from bouts of seasickness and torn by gnawing guilt, Tanis hunched miserably upon the deck, staring out to sea. Goldmoon's healing powers had helped him recover somewhat, though there was apparently little even clerics could do for the turmoil in his stomach. But the turmoil in his soul was beyond her help.

He sat upon the deck, staring out to sea, fearing always to see the sails of a ship on the horizon. The others, perhaps because they were better rested, were little affected by the erratic motion of the ship as it swooped through the choppy water, except that all were wet to the skin from an occasional high wave breaking over the side.

Even Raistlin, Caramon was astonished to see, appeared quite comfortable. The mage sat apart from the others, crouched beneath a sail one of the sailors had rigged to help keep the passengers as dry as possible. The mage was not sick. He did not even cough much. He just seemed lost in thought, his golden eyes glittering brighter than the morning sun that flickered in and out of view behind the racing storm clouds.

Maquesta shrugged when Tanis mentioned his fears of pursuit. The *Perechon* was faster than the Highlords' massive ships. They'd been able to sneak out of the harbor safely, the only other ships aware of their going were pirate ships like themselves. In that brotherhood, no one asked questions.

The seas grew calmer, flattening out beneath the steady breeze. All day, the storm clouds lowered threateningly, only to be finally blown to shreds by the freshening wind. The night was clear and starlit. Maquesta was able to add more sail. The ship flew over the water. By morning, the companions

awakened to one of the most dreadful sights in all of Krynn.

They were on the outer edge of the Blood Sea of Istar.

The sun was a huge, golden ball balanced upon the eastern horizon when the *Perechon* first sailed into the water that was red as the robes the mage wore, red as the blood that flecked his lips when he coughed.

The Blood Sea is also called the Nightmare Sea, for good reason.

"It is well-named,"† Tanis said to Riverwind as they stood on deck, staring out into the red, murky water. They could not see far ahead. A perpetual storm hung from the sky, shrouding the water in a curtain of leaden gray.

"I did not believe it," Riverwind said solemnly, shaking his head. "I heard William tell of it and I listened as I listened to his tales of sea dragons that swallow ships and women with the tails of fish instead of legs. But this—" The barbarian Plainsman shook his head, eyeing the blood-colored water uneasily.

"Do you suppose it's true that this is the blood of all those who died in Istar when the fiery mountain struck the Kingpriest's temple?" Goldmoon asked softly, coming to stand beside her husband.

"What nonsense!" Maquesta snorted. Walking across the deck to join them, her eyes flicked constantly around to make certain that she was getting the most out of her ship and her crew.

"You've been listening to Pig-faced William again!" She laughed. "He loves to frighten lubbers. The water gets its color from soil washed up from the bottom. Remember, this is not sand we're sailing over, like the bottom of the ocean. This used to be dry land—the capital city of Istar and the rich countryside around it. When the fiery mountain fell, it split the land apart. The waters from the ocean rushed in, creating a new sea. Now the wealth of Istar lies far beneath the waves."

Maquesta stared over the railing with dreamy eyes, as if she could penetrate the choppy water and see the rumored wealth of the glittering lost city below. She sighed longingly. Goldmoon glanced at the swarthy ship's captain in disgust, her own eyes filled with sadness and horror at the thought of the terrible destruction and loss of life.

"What keeps the soil stirred up?" Riverwind asked, frowning down at the blood-red water. "Even with the motion of the waves and the tides, the heavy soil should settle more than it appears to have."

"Truly spoken, barbarian." Maquesta looked at the tall, handsome Plainsman with admiration. "But then, your people are farmers, or so I've heard, and know a lot about soil. If you put your hand into the water, you can feel the grit of the dirt. Supposedly there is a maelstrom† in the center of the Blood Sea that whirls with such force it drags the soil up from the bottom. But whether that is true or another one of Pigface's stories, I cannot say. *I* have never seen it, nor have any I've sailed with and I've sailed these waters since I was a child, learning my craft from my father. No one I ever knew was foolish enough to sail into the storm that hangs over the center of the sea."

About 100 miles in diameter, the Maelstrom churns in a clockwise direction, but the winds blow in the opposite direction, thus the perpetual storms.

"How do we get to Mithras, then?" Tanis growled. "It lies on the other side of the Blood Sea, if your charts are correct."

"We can reach Mithras† by sailing south, if we are pursued. If not, we can circle the western edge of the sea and sail up the coast north to Nordmaar. Don't worry, Half-Elven." Maq waved her hand grandly. "At least you can say you've seen the Blood Sea. One of the wonders of Krynn."

Both "Mithas" and "Mithras" refer to the same place. The two different spellings are, again, the result of phonetic translation errors of a word uttered by minotaurs and rendered differently between two different human tongues.—TRH

In talking to minotaurs for his book Land of the Minotaurs, *Richard A. Knaak opted for "Mithas."*

Turning to walk aft, Maquesta was hailed from the crow's nest.

"Deck ho! Sail to the west!" the lookout called.

Instantly Maquesta and Koraf both pulled out spyglasses and trained them upon the western horizon. The companions exchanged worried glances and drew together. Even Raistlin left his place beneath the shielding sail and walked across the deck, peering westward with his golden eyes.

"A ship?" Maquesta muttered to Koraf.

"No," the minotaur grunted in his corrupt form of Common. "A cloud, mebbe. But it go fast, very fast. Faster any cloud I ever see."

Now they all could make out the specks of darkness on the horizon, specks that grew larger even as they watched.

Then Tanis felt a wrenching pain inside of him, as if he'd been pierced by a sword. The pain was so swift and so real he gasped, clutching hold of Caramon to keep from falling. The rest stared at him in concern, Caramon wrapping his big arm around his friend to support him.

Tanis knew what flew toward them.

And he knew who led them.

3

Gathering Darkness.

A flight of dragons," said Raistlin, coming to stand beside his brother. "Five, I believe."

"Dragons!" Maquesta breathed. For a moment, she clutched the rail with trembling hands, then she whirled around. "Set all sail!" she commanded.

The crew stared westward, their eyes and minds locked onto the approaching terror. Maquesta raised her voice and shouted her order again, her only thoughts on her beloved ship. The strength and calmness in her voice penetrated the first faint feelings of dragonfear creeping over the crew. Instinctively a few sprang to carry out their orders, then more followed. Koraf with his whip helped as well, striking briskly at any man who didn't move quickly enough to suit him. Within moments, the

great sails billowed out. Lines creaked ominously, the rigging sang a whining tune.

"Keep her near the edge of the storm!" Maq yelled to Berem. The man nodded slowly, but it was hard to tell from the vacant expression on his face if he heard or not.

Apparently he did, for the *Perechon* hovered close to the perpetual storm that shrouded the Blood Sea, skimming along on the surface of the waves, propelled by the storm's fog-gray wind.

It was reckless sailing, and Maq knew it. Let a spar be blown away, a sail split, a line break, and they would be helpless. But she had to take the risk.

"Useless," Raistlin remarked coolly. "You cannot outsail dragons. Look, see how fast they gain on us. You were followed, Half-Elf." He turned to Tanis. "You were followed when you left the camp . . . either that"—the mage's voice hissed—"or you led them to us!"

"No! I swear—" Tanis stopped.

The drunken draconian! . . . Tanis shut his eyes, cursing himself. Of course, Kit would have had him watched! She didn't trust him any more than she trusted the other men who shared her bed. What a damn egotistical fool he was! Believing he was something special to her, believing she loved him! She loved no one. She was incapable of loving—

"I was followed!" Tanis said through clenched teeth. "You must believe me. I—I may have been a fool. I didn't think they'd follow me in that storm. But I didn't betray you! I swear!"

"We believe you, Tanis," Goldmoon said, coming to stand beside him, glancing at Raistlin angrily out of the corner of her eyes.

Raistlin said nothing, but his lip curled in a sneer. Tanis avoided his gaze, turning instead to watch the dragons. They could see the creatures clearly now. They could see the enormous wingspans, the long tails snaking out behind, the cruel taloned feet hanging beneath the huge blue bodies.

"One has a rider," Maquesta reported grimly, the spyglass to her eye. "A rider with a horned mask."†

"A Dragon Highlord," Caramon stated unnecessarily, all of them knowing well enough what that description meant. The big man turned a somber gaze to Tanis. "You better tell us what's

An early sketch of a Dragon Highlord's mask

Even his own friends consider Caramon a "lunkhead" fighter, but he is smarter than even he knows, as evidenced by this astute observation. He will come into his own in DRAGONLANCE *Legends.*
—MW

going on, Tanis. If this Highlord thought you were a soldier under his own command, why has he taken the trouble to have you followed and come out after you?"†

Tanis started to speak, but his faltering words were submerged in an agonized, inarticulate roar; a roar of mingled fear and terror and rage that was so beastlike, it wrenched everyone's thoughts from the dragons. It came from near the ship's helm. Hands on their weapons, the companions turned. The crew members halted their frantic labors, Koraf came to a dead stop, his bestial face twisted in amazement as the roaring sound grew louder and more fearful.

Only Maq kept her senses. "Berem," she called, starting to run across the deck, her fear giving her sudden horrifying insight into his mind. She leaped across the deck, but it was too late.

A look of insane terror on his face, Berem fell silent, staring at the approaching dragons. Then he roared again, a garbled howl of fear that chilled even the minotaur's blood. Above him, the sails were tight in the wind, the rigging stretched taut. The ship, under all the sail it could bear, seemed to leap over the waves, leaving a trail of white foam behind. But still the dragons gained.

Maq had nearly reached him when, shaking his head like a wounded animal, Berem spun the wheel.

"No! Berem!" Maquesta shrieked.

Berem's sudden move brought the small ship around so fast he nearly sent it under. The mizzenmast snapped with the strain as the ship heeled. Rigging, shrouds, sails, and men plummeted to the deck or fell into the Blood Sea.

Grabbing hold of Maq, Koraf dragged her clear of the falling mast. Caramon caught his brother in his arms and hurled him to the deck, covering Raistlin's frail body with his own as the tangle of rope and splintered wood crashed over them. Sailors tumbled to the deck or slammed up against the bulkheads. From down below, they could hear the sound of cargo breaking free. The companions clung to the ropes or whatever they could grab, hanging on desperately as it seemed Berem would run the ship under. Sails flapped horribly, like dead bird's wings, the rigging went slack, the ship floundered helplessly.

But the skilled helmsman, though seemingly mad with panic, was a sailor still. Instinctively, he held the wheel in a firm grip when it would have spun free. Slowly, he nursed the ship back into the wind with the care of a mother hovering over a deathly sick child. Slowly the *Perechon* righted herself. Sails that had been limp and lifeless caught the wind and filled. The *Perechon* came about and headed on her new course.

It was only then that everyone on board realized that sinking into the sea might have been a quicker and easier death as a gray shroud of wind-swept mist engulfed the ship.

"He's mad! He's steering us into the storm over the Blood Sea!" Maquesta said in a cracked, nearly inaudible voice as she pulled herself to her feet. Koraf started toward Berem, his face twisted in a snarl, a belaying pin in his hand.

"No! Koraf!" Maquesta gasped, grabbing hold of him. "Maybe Berem's right! This could be our only chance! The dragons won't dare follow us into the storm. Berem got us into this, he's the only helmsman we've got with a chance of getting us out! If we can just keep on the outskirts—"

A jagged flash of lightning tore through the gray curtain. The mists parted, revealing a gruesome sight. Black clouds swirled in the roaring wind, green lightning cracked, charging the air with the acrid smell of sulphur. The red water heaved and tossed. Whitecaps bubbled on the surface, like froth on the mouth of a dying man. No one could move for an instant. They could only stare, feeling petty and small against the awesome forces of nature. Then the wind hit them. The ship pitched and tossed, dragged over by the trailing, broken mast. Sudden rain slashed down, hail clattered on the wooden deck, the gray curtain closed around them once more.

Under Maquesta's orders, men scrambled aloft to reef the remaining sails. Another party worked desperately to clear the broken mast that was swinging around wildly. The sailors attacked it with axes, cutting away the ropes, letting it fall into the blood-red water. Free of the mast's dragging weight, the ship slowly righted itself. Though still tossed by the wind, under shortened sail, the

Perechon seemed capable of riding out the storm, even with one mast gone.

The immediate peril had nearly driven all thoughts of dragons from their minds. Now that it seemed they might live a few moments longer, the companions turned to stare through the driving, leaden gray rain.

"Do you think we've lost them?" Caramon asked. The big warrior was bleeding from a savage cut on his head. His eyes showed the pain. But his concern was all for his brother. Raistlin staggered beside him, uninjured, but coughing so he could barely stand.

Tanis shook his head grimly. Glancing around quickly to see if anyone was hurt, he motioned the group to keep together. One by one, they stumbled through the rain, clinging to the ropes until they were gathered around the half-elf. All of them stared back out over the tossing seas.

At first they saw nothing; it was hard to see the bow of the ship through the rain and wind-tossed seas. Some of the sailors even raised a ragged cheer, thinking they had lost them.

But Tanis, his eyes looking to the west, knew that nothing short of death itself would stop the Highlord's pursuit. Sure enough, the sailor's cheers changed to cries of shock when the head of a blue dragon suddenly cleaved the gray clouds, its fiery eyes blazing red with hatred, its fanged mouth gaping open.

The dragon flew closer still, its great wings holding steady even though buffeted by gusts of wind and rain and hail. A Dragon Highlord sat upon the blue dragon's back. The Highlord held no weapon, Tanis saw bitterly. She needed no weapon. She would take Berem, then her dragon would destroy the rest of them. Tanis bowed his head, sick with the knowledge of what would come, sick with the knowledge that *he* was responsible.

Then he looked up. There was a chance, he thought frantically. Maybe she won't recognize Berem . . . and she wouldn't dare destroy them all for fear of harming him. Turning to look at the helmsman, Tanis's wild hope died at birth. It seemed the gods were conspiring against them.

The wind had blown Berem's shirt open. Even through the gray curtain of rain, Tanis could see the

green jewel embedded in the man's chest glow more brilliantly than the green lightning, a terrible beacon shining through the storm. Berem did not notice. He did not even see the dragon. His eyes stared with fixed intensity into the storm as he steered the ship farther and farther into the Blood Sea of Istar.

Only two people saw that glittering jewel. Everyone else was held in thrall by the dragonfear, unable to look away from the huge blue creature soaring above them. Tanis saw the gemstone, as he had seen it before, months ago. And the Dragon Highlord saw it. The eyes behind the metal mask were drawn to the glowing jewel, then the Highlord's eyes met Tanis's eyes as the half-elf stood upon the storm-tossed deck.

A sudden gust of wind caught the blue dragon. It veered slightly, but the Highlord's gaze never wavered. Tanis saw the horrifying future in those brown eyes. The dragon would swoop down upon them and snatch Berem up in its claws. The Highlord would exult in her victory for a long agonizing moment, then she would order the dragon to destroy them all. . . .

Tanis saw this in her eyes as clearly as he had seen the passion in them only days before when he held her in his arms.

Never taking her eyes from him, the Dragon Highlord raised a gloved hand. It might have been a signal to the dragon to dive down upon them; it might have been a farewell to Tanis. He never knew, because at that moment a shattered voice shouted above the roar of the storm with unbelievable power.

"Kitiara!" Raistlin cried.

Shoving Caramon aside, the mage ran toward the dragon. Slipping on the wet deck, his red robes whipped about him in the wind that was blowing stronger every moment. A sudden gust tore the hood from his head. Rain glistened on his metallic-colored skin, his hourglass eyes gleamed golden through the gathering darkness of the storm.

The Dragon Highlord grabbed her mount by the spiky mane along his blue neck, pulling the dragon up so sharply that Skie roared in protest. She stiffened in shock, her brown eyes grew wide behind the dragonhelm as she stared down at the frail

half-brother she had raised from a baby. Her gaze shifted slightly as Caramon came to stand beside his twin.

"Kitiara?" Caramon whispered in a strangled voice, his face pale with horror as he watched the dragon hovering above them, riding the winds of the storm.

The Highlord turned the masked head once more to look at Tanis, then her eyes went to Berem. Tanis caught his breath. He saw the turmoil in her soul reflected in those eyes.

To get Berem, she would have to kill the little brother who had learned all of what he knew about swordsmanship from her. She would have to kill his frail twin. She would have to kill a man she had, once—loved. Then Tanis saw her eyes grow cold, and he shook his head in despair. It didn't matter. She would kill her brothers, she would kill him. Tanis remembered her words: "Capture Berem and we will have all Krynn at our feet. The Dark Queen will reward us beyond anything we ever dreamed!"

Kitiara pointed at Berem and loosed her hold upon the dragon. With a cruel shriek, Skie prepared to dive. But Kitiara's moment of hesitation proved disastrous. Steadfastly ignoring her, Berem had steered the ship deeper and deeper into the heart of the storm. The wind howled, snapping the rigging. Waves crashed over the bows. The rain slashed down like knives, and hailstones began to pile up on the deck, coating it with ice.

Suddenly the dragon was in trouble. A gust of wind hit him, then another. Skie's wings beat frantically as gust after gust pummeled him. The hail drummed upon his head and threatened to tear through the leathery wings. Only the supreme will of his master kept Skie† from fleeing this perilous storm and flying to the safety of calmer skies.

Unusual, because Kitiara and Skie are one. Kitiara's rise in the Dark Queen's hierachy has been helped by her alliance with Skie, the blue dragon. On occasion, Skie has polymorphed into a human to spy for Kitiara. But mostly their alliance depends on Skie's ability to anticipate Kitiara's actions.

Tanis saw Kitiara gesture furiously toward Berem. He saw Skie make a valiant effort to fly closer to the helmsman.

Then a gust of wind hit the ship. A wave broke over them. Water cascaded around them, foaming white, knocking men off their feet and sending them skidding across the deck. The ship listed. Everyone grabbed what they could—ropes, netting, anything—to keep from being washed overboard.

Berem fought the wheel, which was like a living thing, leaping in his hands. Sails split in two, men disappeared into the Blood Sea with terrifying screams. Then, slowly, the ship righted itself again, the wood creaking with the strain. Tanis looked up quickly.

The dragon—and Kitiara—were gone.

Freed from the dragonfear, Maquesta sprang into action, determined once more to save her dying ship. Shouting orders, she ran forward and stumbled into Tika.

"Get below, you lubbers!"† Maquesta shouted furiously to Tanis above the storm wind. "Take your friends and get below! You're in our way! Use my cabin."

The correct term is "land-lubber," a sailor's derogatory term for those who are not sailors. Comes from "land-leaper," a term that meant "vagabond"—one who "leaps" about the land.

Numbly, Tanis nodded. Acting by instinct, feeling as if he were in a senseless dream filled with howling darkness, he led everyone below.

The haunted look in Caramon's eyes pierced his heart as the big man staggered past him, carrying his brother. Raistlin's golden eyes swept over him like flame, burning his soul. Then they were past him, stumbling with the others into the small cabin that shivered and rocked, tossing them about like rag dolls.

Tanis waited until everyone was safely inside the tiny cabin, then he slumped against the wooden door, unable to turn around, unable to face them. He had seen the haunted look in Caramon's eyes as the big man staggered past, he had seen the exultant gleam in Raistlin's eyes. He heard Goldmoon weeping quietly and he wished he might die on this spot before he had to face her.

But that was not to be. Slowly he turned around. Riverwind stood next to Goldmoon, his face dark and brooding as he braced himself between ceiling and deck. Tika bit her lip, tears sliding down her cheeks. Tanis stayed by the door, his back against it, staring at his friends mutely. For long moments, no one said a word. All that could be heard was the storm, the waves crashing onto the deck. Water trickled down on them. They were wet and cold and shaking with fear and sorrow and shock.

"I—I'm sorry," Tanis began, licking his salt-coated lips. His throat hurt, he could barely speak. "I—I wanted to tell you—"

"So *that's* where you were these four days," Caramon said in a soft, low voice. "With our *sister.* Our sister, the Dragon Highlord!"

Tanis hung his head. The ship listed beneath his feet, sending him staggering into Maquesta's desk, which was bolted to the floor. He caught himself and slowly pushed himself back to face them. The half-elf had endured much pain in his life, pain of prejudice, pain of loss, pain of knives, arrows, swords. But he did not think he could endure this pain. The look of betrayal in their eyes ran straight through his soul.

"Please, you must believe me . . ." What a stupid thing to say! he thought savagely. Why *should* they believe me! I've done nothing but lie to them ever since I returned. "All right," he began again, "I know you don't have any reason to believe me, but at least listen to me! I was walking through Flotsam when an elf attacked me. Seeing me in this get-up"—Tanis gestured at his dragonarmor—"he thought I was a dragon officer. Kitiara saved my life, then she recognized me. She thought I had joined the dragonarmy!† What could I say? She"—Tanis swallowed and wiped his hand across his face, "she took me back to the inn and . . . and . . ." He choked, unable to continue.

Kit had long hoped that she could persuade her brothers to join her in the Dark Queen's army

"And you spent four days and nights in the loving embrace of a Dragon Highlord!" Caramon said, his voice rising in fury. Lurching to his feet, he stabbed an accusing finger at Tanis. "Then after four days, you needed a little rest! So you remembered us and you came calling to make certain we were still waiting for you! And we were! Just like the bunch of trusting lame-brains—"

"All right, so I was with Kitiara!" Tanis shouted, suddenly angry. "Yes, I loved her! I don't expect you to understand, any of you! But I never betrayed you! I swear by the gods! When she left for Solamnia, it was the first chance I had to escape and I took it. A draconian followed me, apparently under Kit's orders. I may be a fool. But I'm not a traitor!"

"Pah!" Raistlin spit on the floor.

"Listen, mage!" Tanis snarled. "If I had betrayed you, why was she so shocked to see you two, her brothers! If I had betrayed you, why didn't I just send a few draconians to the inn to pick you up? I

could have, any time. I could have sent them to pick up Berem, too. *He's* the one she wants. *He's* the one the draconians are searching for in Flotsam! I knew he was on this ship. Kitiara offered me the rulership of Krynn if I'd tell her. That's how important he is. All I would've had to do was lead Kit to him and the Queen of Darkness herself would have rewarded me!"

"Don't tell us you didn't consider it!" Raistlin hissed.

No hero is ever perfect. Perfect heroes are boring and without interest. They have nothing to which we can relate. Imperfection, however, is almost certainly the defining trait of humanity—and as such, gives Tanis a quality to which all of us can relate.—TRH

Tanis opened his mouth, then fell silent. He knew his guilt† was as plain on his face as the beard no true elf could grow. He choked, then put his hand over his eyes to block out their faces. "I—I loved her," he said brokenly. "All these years. I refused to see what she was. And even when I knew, couldn't help myself. You love"—his eyes went to Riverwind—"and you"—turning to Caramon. The boat pitched again. Tanis gripped the side of the desk as he felt the deck cant away beneath his feet. "What would you have done? For five years, she's been in my dreams!" He stopped. They were quiet. Caramon's face was unusually thoughtful. Riverwind's eyes were on Goldmoon.

"When she was gone," Tanis continued, his voice soft and filled with pain, "I lay in her bed and I *hated* myself. You may hate me now, but you cannot hate me as much as I loathe and despise what I have become! I thought of Laurana and—"

Tanis fell silent, raising his head. Even as he talked, he had become aware of the motion of the ship changing. The rest glanced around, too. It did not take an experienced seaman to notice that they were no longer pitching around wildly. Now they were running in a smooth forward motion, a motion somehow more ominous because it was so unnatural. Before anyone could wonder what it meant, a crashing knock nearly split the cabin door.

"Maquesta she say get up here!" shouted Koraf hoarsely.

Tanis cast one swift glance around at his friends. Riverwind's face was dark; his eyes met Tanis's and held them, but there was no light in them. The Plainsman had long distrusted all who were not human. Only after weeks of danger faced together had he come to love and trust Tanis as a brother.

Had all that been shattered? Tanis looked at him steadily. Riverwind lowered his gaze and, without a word, started to walk past Tanis, then he stopped.

"You are right, my friend," he said, glancing at Goldmoon who was rising to her feet. "I have loved." Without another word, he turned abruptly and went up on deck.

Goldmoon gazed mutely as Tanis as she followed her husband, and he saw compassion and understanding in that silent look. He wished he understood, that he could be so forgiving.

Caramon hesitated, then walked past him without speaking or looking at him. Raistlin followed silently, his head turning, keeping his golden eyes on Tanis every step of the way. Was there a hint of glee in those golden eyes? Long mistrusted by the others, was Raistlin happy to have company in ignominy at last? The half-elf had no idea what the mage might be thinking. Then Tika went past him, giving him a gentle pat on the arm. She knew what it was to love. . . .

Tanis stood a moment alone in the cabin, lost in his own darkness. Then, with a sigh, he followed his friends.

As soon as he set foot on the deck, Tanis realized what had happened. The others were staring over the side, their faces pale and strained. Maquesta paced the foredeck, shaking her head and swearing fluently in her own language.

Hearing Tanis approach, she looked up, hatred in her black flashing eyes.

"You have destroyed us," she said venomously. "You and the god-cursed helmsman!"

Maquesta's words seemed redundant, a repetition of words resounding in his own mind. Tanis began to wonder if she had even spoken, or if it was himself he was hearing.

"We are caught in the maelstrom."

4

"My brother ..."

The *Perechon* hurtled forward, skimming along on top of the water as lightly as a bird. But it was a bird with its wings clipped, riding the swirling tide of a watery cyclone into a blood-red darkness.

The terrible force pulled the sea waters smooth, until they looked like painted glass. A hollow, eternal roar swelled from the black depths. Even the storm clouds circled endlessly above it, as if all nature were caught in the maelstrom,† hurtling to its own destruction.

The maelstrom is divided into regions that reflect its danger: Outer Reach, Tightening Ring, Nightmare Sea, and finally, Heart of Darkness.

Tanis gripped the rail with hands that ached from the tension. Staring into the dark heart of the whirlpool, he felt no fear, no terror, only a strange numb sensation. It didn't matter anymore. Death would be swift and welcome.

Everyone on board the doomed ship stood silently, their eyes wide with the horror of what they saw. They were still some distance from the center; the whirlpool was miles and miles in diameter. Smoothly and swiftly, the water flowed. Above them and around them the winds still howled, the rain still beat upon their faces. But it didn't matter. They didn't notice it anymore. All they saw was that they were being carried relentlessly into the center of the darkness.

This fearsome sight was enough to wake Berem from his lethargy. After the first shock, Maquesta began shouting frantic orders. Dazedly, the men carried them out, but their efforts were useless. Sails rigged against the whirling wind tore apart; ropes snapped, flinging men screaming into the water. Try as he might, Berem could not turn the ship or break it free of the water's fearsome grip. Koraf added his strength to the handling of the wheel, but they might as well have been trying to stop the world from revolving.

Then Berem quit. His shoulders sagged. He stood staring out into the swirling depths, ignoring Maquesta, ignoring Koraf. His face was calm, Tanis saw; the same calm Tanis remembered seeing on Berem's face at Pax Tharkas when he took Eben's hand and ran with him into that deadly wall of cascading boulders. The green jewel in his chest glowed with an eerie light, reflecting the blood red of the water.

Tanis felt a strong hand clutch his shoulder, shaking him out of his rapt horror.

"Tanis! Where's Raistlin?"

Tanis turned. For a moment he stared at Caramon without recognition, then he shrugged.

"What does it matter?" he muttered bitterly. "Let him die where he chooses—"

"Tanis!" Caramon took him by the shoulders and shook him. "Tanis! The dragon orb! His magic! Maybe it can help—"

Tanis came awake. "By all the gods! You're right, Caramon!"

The half-elf looked around swiftly, but he saw no sign of the mage. A cold chill crept over him. Raistlin was capable either of helping them or of helping himself! Dimly Tanis remembered the elven princess,

Alhana, saying the dragon orbs had been imbued by their magical creators with a strong sense of self-preservation.

"Below!" Tanis yelled. Leaping for the hatch, he heard Caramon pounding along behind.

"What is it?" called Riverwind from the rail.

Tanis shouted over his shoulder. "Raistlin. The dragon orb. Don't come. Let Caramon and I handle this. You stay here, with them."

"Caramon—" Tika yelled, starting to run after until Riverwind caught her and held her. Giving the warrior an anguished look, she fell silent, slumping back against the rail.

Caramon did not notice. He plunged ahead of Tanis, his huge body moving remarkably fast. Tumbling down the stairway below decks after him, Tanis saw the door to Maquesta's cabin open, swinging on its hinges with the motion of the ship. The half-elf dashed in and came to a sudden stop, just inside the door, as if he had run headlong into a wall.

Raistlin stood in the center of the small cabin. He had lit a candle in a lamp clamped to the bulkhead. The flame made the mage's face glisten like a metal mask, his eyes flared with golden fire. In his hands, Raistlin held the dragon orb, their prize from Silvanesti. It had grown, Tanis saw. It was now the size of child's ball. A myriad colors swirled within it. Tanis grew dizzy watching and wrenched his gaze away.

In front of Raistlin stood Caramon, the big warrior's face as white as Tanis had seen his corpse in the Silvanesti dream when the warrior lay dead at his feet.

Raistlin coughed, clutching at his chest with one hand. Tanis started forward, but the mage looked up quickly.

"Don't come near me, Tanis!" Raistlin gasped through blood-stained lips.

"What are you doing?"

"I am fleeing certain death, Half-Elf!" The mage laughed unpleasantly, the strange laughter Tanis had heard only twice before. "What do you think I am doing?"

"How?" Tanis asked, feeling a strange fear creep over him as he looked into the mage's

golden eyes and saw them reflect the swirling light of the orb.

I believe that Fistandantilus has been "persuading" Raistlin to use the dragon orb, although at this point, Raistlin doesn't know the voice he hears whispering in his soul.—MW

"Using my magic. And the magic of the dragon orb.† It is quite simple, though probably beyond your weak mind. I now have the power to harness the energy of my corporeal body and the energy of my spirit into one. I will become pure energy—light, if you want to think of it that way. And, becoming light, I can travel through the heavens like the rays of the sun, returning to this physical world whenever and wherever I choose!"

Tanis shook his head. Raistlin was right—the thought was beyond him. He could not grasp it, but hope sprang into his heart.

"Can the orb do this for all of us?" he demanded.

"Possibly," Raistlin answered, coughing, "but I am not certain. I will not chance it. I know I can escape. The others are not my concern. You led *them* into this blood-red death, Half-Elf. You get them out!"

Anger surged through Tanis, replacing his fear. "At least, your brother—" he began hotly.

"No one," Raistlin said, his eyes narrowing. "Stand back."

Insane, desperate rage twisted Tanis's mind. Somehow he'd make Raistlin listen to reason! Somehow they would all use this strange magic to escape! Tanis knew enough about magic to realize that Raistlin dared not cast a spell now. He would need all his strength to control the dragon orb. Tanis started forward, then saw silver flash in the mage's hand. From nowhere, seemingly, had come a small silver dagger,† long concealed on the mage's wrist by a cunningly designed leather thong. Tanis stopped, his eyes meeting Raistlin's.

Huma ordered that all mages should be allowed to carry one, small, bladed weapon as a defense in memory of the murder of his faithful friend, Magius. But Huma probably did not intend one to be used like this.

"All right," Tanis said, breathing heavily. "You'd kill me without a second thought. But you won't harm your brother. Caramon, stop him!"

Caramon took a step toward his twin. Raistlin raised the silver dagger warningly.

"Don't do it, my brother," he said softly. "Come no closer."

Caramon hesitated.

"Go ahead, Caramon!" Tanis said firmly. "He won't hurt you."

"Tell him, Caramon," Raistlin whispered. The mage's eyes never left his brother's. Their hourglass pupils dilated, the golden light flickered dangerously. "Tell Tanis what I am capable of doing. You remember. So do I. It is in our thoughts every time we look at one another, isn't it, my dear brother?"

"What's he talking about?" Tanis demanded, only half listening. If he could distract Raistlin . . . jump him . . .

Caramon blanched. "The Towers of High Sorcery . . ." he faltered. "But we are forbidden to speak of it! Par-Salian said—"

"That doesn't matter now," Raistlin interrupted in his shattered voice. "There is nothing Par-Salian can do to me. Once I have what has been promised me, not even the great Par-Salian will have the power to face me! But that's none of your concern. This is."

Raistlin drew a deep breath, then began to speak, his strange eyes still on his twin. Only half-listening, Tanis crept closer, his heart pounding in his throat. One swift movement and the frail mage would crumble. . . . Then Tanis found himself caught and held by Raistlin's voice, compelled to stop for a moment and listen, almost as if Raistlin was weaving a spell around him.

"The last test in the Tower of High Sorcery, Tanis, was against myself. And I failed. I killed him, Tanis. I killed my brother"—Raistlin's voice was calm—"or at least I thought it was Caramon." The mage shrugged. "As it turned out, it was an illusion created to teach me the depths of my hatred and jealousy. Thus they thought to purge my soul of darkness. What I truly learned was that I lacked self-control. Still, since it was not part of the true Test, my failure did not count against me—except with one person."

"I watched him kill me!" Caramon cried wretchedly. "They made me watch so that I would understand him!" The big man's head dropped in his hands, his body convulsed with a shudder. "I do understand!" he sobbed. "I understood then! I'm sorry! Just don't go without me, Raist! You're so weak! You need me—"

"No longer, Caramon," Raistlin whispered with a soft sigh. "I need you no longer!"

Tanis stared at them both, sick with horror. He couldn't believe this! Not even of Raistlin! "Caramon, go ahead!" he commanded hoarsely.

"Don't make him come near me, Tanis," Raistlin said, his voice gentle, as if he read the half-elf's thoughts. "I assure you, I am capable of this. What I have sought all my life is within my grasp. I will let nothing stop me. Look at Caramon's face, Tanis. He knows! I killed him once. I can do it again. Farewell, my brother."

The mage put both hands upon the dragon orb and held it up to the light of the flaming candle. The colors swirled madly in the orb, flaring brilliantly. A powerful magical aura surrounded the mage.

Fighting his fear, Tanis tensed his body to make a last desperate attempt to stop Raistlin. But he could not move. He heard Raistlin chanting strange words. The glaring, whirling light grew so bright it pierced his head. He covered his eyes with his hands, but the light burned right through his flesh, searing his brain. The pain was intolerable. He stumbled back against the door frame, hearing Caramon cry out in agony beside him. He heard the big man's body fall to the floor with a thud.

Then all was still, the cabin plunged into darkness. Trembling, Tanis opened his eyes. For a moment he could see nothing but the afterimage of a giant red globe imprinted on his brain. Then his eyes became accustomed to the chill dark. The candle guttered, hot wax dripping onto the wooden floor of the cabin to form a white puddle near where Caramon lay, cold and unmoving. The warrior's eyes were wide open, staring blankly into nothingness.

Raistlin was gone.

Tika Waylan stood on the deck of the *Perechon* staring into the blood-red sea and trying very hard to keep from crying. You must be brave, she told herself over and over. You've learned to fight bravely in battle. Caramon said so. Now you must be brave about this. We'll be together, at least, at the end. He mustn't see me cry.

But the last four days had been unnerving for all of them. Fearful of discovery by the draconians swarming over Flotsam, the companions had

remained hidden in the filthy inn. Tanis's strange disappearance had been terrifying. They were helpless, they dared do nothing, not even inquire about him. So for long days they had been forced to stay in their rooms and Tika had been forced to be around Caramon. The tension of their strong attraction to each other, an attraction they were not able to express, was torture. She wanted to put her arms around Caramon, to feel his arms around her, his strong, muscular body pressed against hers.

Caramon wanted the same thing, she was certain. He looked at her, sometimes, with so much tenderness in his eyes that she longed to nestle close to him and share the love that she knew was in the big man's heart.

It could never be, not as long as Raistlin hovered near his twin brother, clinging to Caramon like a frail shadow. Over and over she repeated Caramon's words, spoken to her before they reached Flotsam.

"My commitment is to my brother. They told me, in the Tower of High Sorcery, that his strength would help save the world. I am his strength, his physical strength. He needs me. My first duty is to him, and until that changes, I can't make any other commitments. You deserve someone who puts you first, Tika. And so I'll leave you free to find someone like that."

But I don't *want* anyone else, Tika thought sadly. And then the tears did start to fall. Turning quickly, she tried to hide them from Goldmoon and Riverwind. They would misunderstand, think she was crying from fear. No, fear of dying was something she had conquered long ago. Her biggest fear was fear of dying *alone.*

What are they doing? she wondered frantically, wiping her eyes with the back of her hand. The ship was being carried closer and closer into that dreadful dark eye. Where was Caramon? I'll go find them, she decided. Tanis or no Tanis.

Then she saw Tanis come slowly up out of the hatchway, half-dragging, half-supporting Caramon. One look at the big warrior's pale face and Tika's heart stopped beating.

She tried to call out, but she couldn't speak. At her inarticulate scream, however, Goldmoon and Riverwind both turned around from where they had

been watching the awesome maelstrom. Seeing Tanis stagger beneath his burden, Riverwind ran forward to help. Caramon walked like a man in drunken stupor, his eyes glazed and sightless. Riverwind caught hold of Caramon just as Tanis's legs gave way completely.

"I'm all right," Tanis said softly in answer to Riverwind's look of concern. "Goldmoon, Caramon needs your help."

"What is it, Tanis?" Tika's fear gave her a voice. "What's the matter? Where's Raistlin? Is he—" She stopped. The half-elf's eyes were dark with the memory of what he had seen and heard below.

"Raistlin's gone," Tanis said briefly.

"Gone? Where?" Tika asked, staring wildly around as if expecting to see his body in the swirling blood-colored water.

"He lied to us," Tanis answered, helping Riverwind ease Caramon down onto a mass of coiled rope. The big warrior said nothing. He didn't seem to see them, or anything for that matter; he just stared sightlessly out over the blood-red sea. "Remember how he kept insisting we had to go to Palanthas, to *learn how* to use the dragon orb? He *knows how* to use the orb already. And now he's gone—to Palanthas, perhaps. I don't suppose it matters." Looking at Caramon, he shook his head in sorrow, then turned away abruptly and walked to the rail.

Goldmoon laid her gentle hands upon the big man, murmuring his name so softly the others could not hear it above the rush of the wind. At her touch, however, Caramon shivered, then began to shake violently. Tika knelt beside him, holding his hand in hers. Still staring straight ahead, Caramon began to cry silently, tears spilling down his cheeks from wide open, staring eyes. Goldmoon's eyes glimmered with her own tears, but she stroked his forehead and kept calling to him as a mother calls a lost child.

Riverwind, his face stern and dark with anger, joined Tanis.

"What happened?" the Plainsman asked grimly.

"Raistlin said he—I can't talk about it. Not now!" Tanis shook his head, shuddering. Leaning over the rail, he stared into the murky water below.

Swearing softly in elven—a language the half-elf rarely used—† he clutched his head with his hands.

The elven language has been described by humans, especially Dark Knights, as "slimy elf words."

Saddened by his friend's anguish, Riverwind laid his hand comfortingly on the half-elf's slumped shoulders.

"So at the end it comes to this," the Plainsman said. "As we foresaw in the dream, the mage has gone, leaving his brother to die."

"And as we saw in the dream, I have failed you," Tanis mumbled, his voice low and trembling. "What have I done? This is my fault! I have brought this horror upon us!"

"My friend," Riverwind said, moved by the sight of Tanis's suffering. "It is not ours to question the ways of the gods—"

"Damn the gods!" Tanis cried viciously. Lifting his head to stare at his friend, he struck his clenched fist on the ship's rail. "It was *me! My choosing!* How often during those nights when she and I were together and I held her in my arms, how often did I tell myself it would be so easy to stay there, with her, forever! I can't condemn Raistlin! We're very much alike, he and I. Both destroyed by an all-consuming passion!"

"You *haven't* been destroyed, Tanis," Riverwind said. Gripping the half-elf's shoulders in his strong hands, the stern-faced Plainsman forced Tanis to face him. "You did not fall victim to your passion, as did the mage.† If you had, you would have stayed with Kitiara. You left her, Tanis—"

To a great extent, Raistlin and Tanis both are victims of their passions, although ultimately we see each of these characters handle the problem differently. Tanis will come to accept it, understand it and harness his passions. Raistlin, in many ways, will become its slave.—TRH

"I left her," Tanis said bitterly. "I sneaked out like a thief! I should have confronted her. I should have told her the truth about myself! She would have killed me then, but you would have been safe. You and the others could have escaped. How much easier my death would have been—But I didn't have the courage. Now I've brought us to this," the half-elf said, wrenching himself free of Riverwind's grip. "I have failed—not only myself, but all of you."

He glanced around the deck. Berem still stood at the helm, gripping the useless wheel in his hands, that strange look of resignation on his face. Maquesta still fought to save her ship, shrieking commands above the wind's howl and the deep-throated roaring that issued from the depths of the maelstrom. But her crew, stunned by terror, no longer obeyed.

Some wept. Some cursed. Most made no sound but stared in horrid fascination at the gigantic swirl that was pulling them inexorably into the vast darkness of the deep. Tanis felt Riverwind's hand once again touch his shoulder. Almost angrily, he tried to withdraw, but the Plainsman was firm.

"Tanis, my brother, you made your choice to walk this road in the Inn of the Last Home in Solace, when you came to Goldmoon's aid. In my pride, I would have refused your help, and both she and I would have died. Because you could not turn from us in our need, we brought the knowledge of the ancient gods into the world. We brought healing. We brought hope. Remember what the Forestmaster told us? We do not grieve for those who fulfill their purpose in life.† We *have* fulfilled our purpose, my friend. Who knows how many lives we have touched? Who knows but that this hope will lead to a great victory? For us, it seems, the battle has ended. So be it. We lay down our swords, only that others may pick them up and fight on."

A recurring theme in the Chronicles is the value of a life whose purpose has been fulfilled. Sturm's death in Winter Night *exemplifies this issue. Here we see echoes of that theme—which will be reiterated far more forcefully soon enough. —TRH*

"Your words are pretty, Plainsman," Tanis snapped, "but tell me truthfully. Can you look on death and not feel bitterness? You have everything to live for, Goldmoon, the children not yet born to you—"

A swift spasm of pain crossed Riverwind's face. He turned his head to hide it, but Tanis, watching him closely, saw the pain and suddenly understood. So he was destroying that, too! The half-elf shut his eyes in despair.

"Goldmoon and I weren't going to tell you. You had enough to worry about." Riverwind sighed. "Our baby would have been born in the autumn," he murmured, "in the time when the leaves on the vallenwoods turn red and golden as they were when Goldmoon and I came into Solace that day, carrying the blue crystal staff. That day the knight, Sturm Brightblade, found us and brought us to the Inn of the Last Home—"

Tanis began to sob, deep racking sobs that tore through his body like knives. Riverwind put his arms around his friend and held him tightly.

"The vallenwoods we know are dead now, Tanis," he continued in a hushed voice. "We could have shown the child only burned and rotted

stumps. But now the child will see the vallenwoods as the gods meant them to be, in a land where the trees live forever. Do not grieve, my friend, my brother. You helped bring knowledge of the gods back to the people. You must have faith in those gods."

Gently Tanis pushed Riverwind away. He could not meet the Plainsman's eyes. Looking into his own soul, Tanis saw it twist and writhe like the tortured trees of Silvanesti. Faith? He had no faith. What were the gods to him? *He* had made the decisions. *He* had thrown away everything he ever had of value in his life—his elven homeland, Laurana's love. He had come close to throwing away friendship, too. Only Riverwind's strong loyalty—a loyalty that was badly misplaced—kept the Plainsman from denouncing him.

Suicide† is forbidden to the elves. They consider it blasphemy, the gift of life being the most precious of all gifts. But Tanis stared into the blood-red sea with anticipation and longing.

Let death come swiftly, he prayed. Let these blood-stained waters close over my head. Let me hide in their depths. And if there *are* gods, if you *are* listening to me, I ask only one thing: keep the knowledge of my shame from Laurana. I have brought pain to too many. . . .

But even as his soul breathed this prayer he hoped would be his last upon Krynn, a shadow darker than the storm clouds fell across him. Tanis heard Riverwind cry out and Goldmoon scream, but their voices were lost in the roar of the water as the ship began to sink into the heart of the maelstrom. Dully, Tanis looked up to see the fiery red eyes of a blue dragon shining through the black swirling clouds. Upon the dragon's back was Kitiara.

Unwilling to give up the prize that would win them glorious victory, Kit and Skie had fought their way through the storm, and now the dragon, wicked talons extended, dove straight for Berem. The man's feet might have been nailed to the deck. In dreamlike helplessness he stared at the diving dragon.

Jolted to action, Tanis flung himself across the heaving deck as the blood-red water swirled around him. He hit Berem full in the stomach, knocking the man backward just as a wave broke over them. Tanis

Life is a gift—both here and on Krynn. Though seemingly common, it is the most precious of commodities. To me, to deny one's own life is to squander all opportunity of making life better for oneself and others. Life has value—to turn one's back on that is a foolish waste.—TRH

grabbed hold of something, he wasn't sure what, and clung to the deck as it canted away beneath him. Then the ship righted itself. When he looked up, Berem was gone. Above him, he heard the dragon shriek in anger.

And then Kitiara was shouting above the storm, pointing at Tanis. Skie's fiery gaze turned on him. Raising his arm as if he could ward off the dragon, Tanis looked up into the enraged eyes of the beast who was fighting madly to control his flight in the whipping winds.

This is life, the half-elf found himself thinking, seeing the dragon's claws above him. This is life! To live, to be carried out of this horror! For an instant Tanis felt himself suspended in mid-air as the bottom dropped out of his world. He was conscious only of shaking his head wildly, screaming incoherently. The dragon and the water hit him at the same time. All he could see was blood. . . .

Tika crouched beside Caramon, her fear of death lost in her concern for him. But Caramon wasn't even aware of her presence. He stared out into the darkness, tears coursing down his face, his hands clenched into fists, repeating two words over and over in a silent litany.

In agonizing dreamlike slowness, the ship balanced on the edge of the swirling water, as if the very wood of the vessel itself hesitated in fear. Maquesta joined her frail ship in its final desperate struggle for life, lending her own inner strength, trying to change the laws of nature by force of will alone. But it was useless. With a final, heart-breaking shudder, the *Perechon* slipped over the edge into the swirling, roaring darkness.

Timber cracked. Masts fell. Men were flung, screaming, from the listing decks as the blood-red blackness sucked the *Perechon* down into its gaping maw.

After all was gone, two words lingered like a benediction.

"My brother . . ."

5

The Chronicler and the Mage.

Astinus of Palanthas sat in his study. His hand guided the quill pen he held in firm, even strokes. The bold, crisp writing flowing from that pen could be read clearly, even at a distance. Astinus† filled a sheet of parchment quickly, rarely pausing to think. Watching him, one had the impression that his thoughts flowed from his head straight into the pen and out onto the paper, so rapidly did he write. The flow was interrupted only when he dipped the quill in ink, but this, too, had become such an automatic motion to Astinus that it interrupted him as little as the dotting of an "i" or the crossing of a "t."

Astinus is also called the Lorekeeper of Krynn and the Deathless One.

The door to his study creaked opened. Astinus did not look up from his writing, though the door did not often open while he was engaged in his work. The historian could count the number of times on his fingers. One of those times had been during the Cataclysm. That had disturbed his writing, he recalled, remembering with disgust the spilled ink that had ruined a page.

Each of the hours in the Palanthian day were named. The two noted in the text here are "Afterwatch Hour" and "Restful Hour," respectively. The hour itself was then divided into two sets of thirty minutes: "Falling," referring to the minutes from the top of the hour down to the bottom half hour and "Climbing," referring to the minutes from the bottom half hour to the top of the hour. Unlike our own system, however, the hour was considered to start at the bottom of the clock. It is not as difficult as it first sounds, however, since it has a direct Earth equivalent. Restful Hour was around nine o'clock p.m. This being the case, "Restful Hour climbing 29" would be equal to saying "Twenty-nine minutes before the hour of nine." "Afterwatch Hour falling 30," on the other hand, would be equal to saying "Thirty minutes past the hour of eight."
—TRH

The door opened and a shadow fell across his desk. But there came no sound, though the body belonging to the shadow drew in a breath as though about to speak. The shadow wavered, the sheer enormity of its offense causing the body to tremble.

It is Bertrem, Astinus noted, as he noted everything, filing the information for future reference in one of the many compartments of his mind.

This day, as above Afterwatch Hour† *falling 29, Bertrem entered my study.*

The pen continued its steady advance over the paper. Reaching the end of a page, Astinus lifted it smoothly and placed it on top of similar pieces of parchment stacked neatly at the end of his desk. Later that night, when the historian had finished his work and retired, the Aesthetics would enter the study reverently, as clerics enter a shrine, and gather up the stacks of paper. Carefully they would take them into the great library. Here the pieces of parchment covered with the bold, firm handwriting, were sorted, categorized, and filed in the giant books labeled *Chronicles, A History of Krynn* by Astinus of Palanthas.

"Master . . ." spoke Bertrem in a shivering voice.

This day, as above Afterwatch Hour falling 30, Bertrem spoke, Astinus noted in the text.

"I regret disturbing you, Master," said Bertrem faintly, "but a young man is dying on your doorstep."

This day, as above Restful Hour climbing 29, a young man died on our doorstep.

"Get his name," Astinus said without looking up or pausing in his writing, "so that I may record it. Be certain as to the spelling. And find out where he's from and his age, if he's not too far gone."

"I have his name, Master," Bertrem replied. "It is Raistlin. He comes from Solace township in the land of Abanasinia."

This day, as above Restful Hour climbing 28, Raistlin of Solace died—

Astinus stopped writing. He looked up.

"Raistlin . . . of Solace?"

"Yes, Master," Bertrem replied, bowing at this great honor. It was the first time Astinus had ever looked directly at him, though Bertrem had been with the Order of Aesthetics who lived in the great library for over a decade. "Do you know him, Master? That was why I took the liberty of disturbing your work. He has asked to see you."

"Raistlin . . ."

A drop of ink fell from Astinus's pen onto the paper.

"Where is he?"

"On the steps, Master, where we found him. We thought, perhaps, one of these new healers we have heard about, the ones who worship the Goddess Mishakal, might aid him. . . ."

The historian glared at the blot of ink in annoyance. Taking a pinch of fine, white sand, he carefully sprinkled it over the ink to dry it so that it would not stain other sheets that would later be set upon it. Then, lowering his gaze, Astinus returned to his work.

"No healer can cure this young man's malady," the historian remarked in a voice that might have come from the depths of time. "But bring him inside. Give him a room."

"Bring him inside the library?" Bertrem repeated in profound astonishment. "Master, no one has ever been admitted except those of our order—"

"I will see him, if I have time at the end of the day," Astinus continued as if he had not heard the Aesthetic's words. "If he is still alive, that is."

The pen moved rapidly across the paper.

"Yes, Master," Bertrem murmured and backed out of the room.

Shutting the door to the study, the Aesthetic hurried through the cool and silent marble halls of the ancient library, his eyes wide with the wonder of this occurrence. His thick, heavy robes swept the floor behind him, his shaved head glistened with sweat as he ran, unaccustomed to such strenuous exertion. The others of his order gazed at him in astonishment as he swept into the library's front entryway. Glancing quickly through the glass pane set in the door, he could see the young man's body upon the stairs.

While Astinus captured the overall tapestry of Krynnish history, his Aesthetics penned treatises providing deeper details on the people, places, and incidents described therein. Astinus demanded fairness and neutrality in all things from his followers, telling the Aesthetics that their purpose was to preserve so accurate a record that people of future generations could read it and then decide the truth of the matter on their own. Astinus would tell the Aesthetics, "Tell the readers what to see and what to hear, but never tell them what to think."
—TRH

"We are commanded to bring him inside," Bertrem told the others. "Astinus will see the young man tonight, if the mage is still alive."

One by one, the Aesthetics† regarded each other in shocked silence, wondering what doom this portended.

I am dying.

The knowledge was bitter to the mage. Lying in the bed in the cold, white cell where the Aesthetics had placed him, Raistlin cursed his frail and fragile body, he cursed the Tests that shattered it, he cursed the gods who had inflicted it upon him. He cursed until he had no more words to hurl, until he was too exhausted even to think. And then he lay beneath the white linen sheets that were like winding cloths and felt his heart flutter inside his breast like a trapped bird.

For the second time in his life, Raistlin was alone and frightened. He had been alone only once before, and that had been during those three torturous days of Testing in the Tower of High Sorcery. Even then, had he been alone? He didn't think so, although he couldn't remember clearly. The voice . . . the voice that spoke to him sometimes, the voice he could never identify, yet seemed to know . . . He always connected the voice with the Tower. It had helped him there, as it had helped him since. Because of that voice he had survived the ordeal.

But he wouldn't survive this, he knew. The magical transformation he had undergone had placed too great a strain on his frail body. He had succeeded, but at what a cost!

The Aesthetics found him huddled in his red robes, vomiting blood upon their stairs. He managed to gasp out the name of Astinus and his own name when they asked. Then he lost consciousness. When he awoke, he was here, in this cold, narrow monk's cell. And with waking came the knowledge that he was dying. He had asked more of his body than it was capable of giving. The dragon orb might save him, but he had no more strength to work his magic. The words to draw upon its enchantment were gone from his mind.

I am too weak to control its tremendous power anyway, he realized. Let it once know I have lost my strength and it would devour me.

No, there was only one chance remaining to him, the books inside the great library. The dragon orb had promised him that these books held the secrets of the ancient ones, great and powerful mages whose like would never be seen again on Krynn. Perhaps there he could find the means to extend his life. He had to talk to Astinus! He had to gain admittance to the great library, he had shrieked at the complacent Aesthetics. But they only nodded.

"Astinus will see you," they said, "this evening, if he has time."

If *he* has time! Raistlin swore viciously. If *I* have time! He could feel the sands of his life running through his fingers and, grasp at them as he might, he could not stop them.

Gazing at him with pitying eyes, not knowing what to do for him, the Aesthetics brought Raistlin food, but he could not eat. He could not even swallow the bitter herbal medicine that eased his cough. Furious, he sent the idiots away from him. Then he lay back on his hard pillow, watching the sun's light creep across his cell. Exerting all his effort to cling to life, Raistlin forced himself to relax, knowing that this feverish anger would burn him up. His thoughts went to his brother.

Closing his eyes wearily, Raistlin imagined Caramon sitting beside him. He could almost feel Caramon's arms around him, lifting him up so that he could breathe more easily. He could smell his brother's familiar scent of sweat and leather and steel. Caramon would take care of him. Caramon would not let him die. . . .

No, Raistlin thought dreamily. Caramon is dead now. They are all dead, the fools. I must look after myself. Suddenly he realized he was losing consciousness again. Desperately he fought, but it was a losing battle. Making a final, supreme effort, he thrust his shaking hand into a pocket in his robe. His fingers closed around the dragon orb, shrunk to the size of a child's marble, even as he sank into darkness.

He woke to the sound of voices and the knowledge that someone was in the cell with him.

Fighting through layers of blackness, Raistlin struggled to the surface of his consciousness and opened his eyes.

It was evening. Lunitari's red light glanced through his window, a shimmering blood-stain upon the wall. A candle burned beside his bed and, by its light, he saw two men standing over him. One he recognized as the Aesthetic who had discovered him. The other? He seemed familiar. . . .

"He wakes, Master," said the Aesthetic.

"So he does," remarked the man imperturbably. Bending down, he studied the young mage's face, then smiled and nodded to himself, almost as if someone he had long expected had finally arrived. It was a peculiar look, and it did not go unnoticed by either Raistlin or the Aesthetic.

"I am Astinus," the man spoke. "You are Raistlin of Solace."

"I am." Raistlin's mouth formed the words, his voice was little more than a croak. Gazing up at Astinus, Raistlin's anger returned as he remembered the man's callous remark that he would see him *if he had time.* As Raistlin stared at the man, he felt suddenly chilled. He had never seen a face so cold and unfeeling, totally devoid of human emotion and human passion. A face untouched by time—

Raistlin gasped. Struggling to sit up—with the Aesthetic's help—he stared at Astinus.

Noticing Raistlin's reaction, Astinus remarked, "You look at me strangely, young mage. What do you see with those hourglass eyes of yours?"

Some have claimed that Astinus is actually one of the gods of Krynn.
I will not dispute it.
—TRH

"I see . . . a man . . . who is *not* dying. . . ." Raistlin could speak only through painful struggles to draw breath.

"Of course, what did you expect?" the Aesthetic chided, gently propping the dying man against the pillows of his bed. "The Master was here to chronicle the birth of the first upon Krynn and so he will be here to chronicle the death of the last. So we are taught by Gilean, God of the Book."†

The constellation Gilean

"Is that true?" Raistlin whispered.

Astinus shrugged slightly.

"My personal history is of no consequence compared to the history of the world. Now speak, Raistlin of Solace. What do you want of me? Whole

volumes are passing as I waste my time in idle talk with you."

"I ask . . . I beg . . . a favor!" The words were torn from Raistlin's chest and came out stained with blood. "My life . . . is measured . . . in hours. Let me . . . spend them . . . in study . . . in the great library!"

Bertrem's tongue clicked against the roof of his mouth in shock at this young mage's temerity. Glancing at Astinus fearfully, the Aesthetic waited for the scathing refusal which, he felt certain, must flail this rash young man's skin from his bones.

Long moments of silenced passed, broken only by Raistlin's labored breathing. The expression on Astinus's face did not change. Finally he answered coldly. "Do what you will."

Ignoring Bertrem's shocked look, Astinus turned and began to walk toward the door.

"Wait!" Raistlin's voice rasped. The mage reached out a trembling hand as Astinus slowly came to a halt. "You asked me what I saw when I looked at you. Now I ask you the same thing. I saw that look upon your face when you bent over me. You recognized me! You know me! Who am I? What do you see?"

Astinus looked back, his face cold, blank, and impenetrable as marble.

"You said you saw a man who was not dying," the historian told the mage softly. Hesitating a moment, he shrugged and once again turned away. "I see a man who is."

And, with that, he walked out the door.

It is assumed that You who hold this Book in your Hands have successfully passed the Tests in one of the Towers of High Sorcery and that You have demonstrated Your Ability to exert Control over a Dragon Orb or some other approved Magical Artifact (see Appendix C) and, further that You have demonstrated Proven Ability in casting the Spells—

"Yes, yes," muttered Raistlin, hurriedly scanning the runes that crawled like spiders across the page. Reading impatiently through the list of spells, he finally reached the conclusion.

Having completed these Requirements to the Satisfaction of Your Masters, We give into Your Hands this Spellbook. Thus, with the Key, You unlock Our Mysteries.

With a shriek of inarticulate rage, Raistlin shoved the spellbook with its night-blue binding and silver runes aside. His hand shaking, he reached for the next night-blue bound book in the huge pile he had amassed at his side. A fit of coughing forced him to stop. Fighting for breath, he feared for a moment that he could not go on.

The pain was unbearable. Sometimes he longed to sink into oblivion, end this torture he must live with daily. Weak and dizzy, he let his head sink to the desk, cradled in his arms. Rest, sweet, painless rest. An image of his brother came to his mind. There was Caramon in the afterlife, waiting for his little brother. Raistlin could see his twin's sad, dog-like eyes, he could feel his pity. . . .

Raistlin drew a breath with a gasp, then forced himself to sit up. Meeting Caramon! I'm getting light-headed, he sneered at himself. What nonsense!

Moistening his blood-caked lips with water, Raistlin took hold of the next night-blue spellbook and pulled it over to him. Its silver runes flashed in the candlelight, its cover—icy cold to the touch—was the same as the covers of all the other spellbooks stacked around him. Its cover was the same as the spellbook in his possession already, the spellbook he knew by heart and by soul, the spellbook of the greatest mage who ever lived, Fistandantilus.

With trembling hands, Raistlin opened the cover. His feverish eyes devoured the page, reading the same requirements—only mages high in the Order had the skill and control necessary to study the spells recorded inside. Those without it who tried to read the spells saw nothing on the pages but gibberish.

Raistlin fulfilled all the requirements. He was probably the only White or Red-Robed mage on Krynn, with the possible exception of the great Par-Salian himself, who could say that. Yet, when Raistlin looked at the writing inside the book, it was nothing more than a meaningless scrawl.

Thus, with the Key, You unlock our Mysteries—

Raistlin screamed, a thin, wailing sound cut off by a choking sob. In bitter anger and frustration, he flung himself upon the table, scattering the books to the floor. Frantically his hands clawed the air and he

screamed again. The magic that he had been too weak to summon came now in his anger.

The Aesthetics, passing outside the doors of the great library, exchanged fearful glances as they heard those terrible cries. Then they heard another sound. A crackling sound followed by a booming explosion of thunder. They stared at the door in alarm. One put his hand upon the handle and turned it, but the door was locked fast. Then one pointed and they all backed up as a ghastly light flared beneath the closed door. The smell of sulphur drifted out of the library, only to be blown away by a great gust of wind that hit the door with such force it seemed it might split in two. Again the Aesthetics heard that bubbling wail of rage, and then they fled down the marble hallway, calling wildly for Astinus.

The historian arrived to find the door to the great library held spellbound. He was not much surprised. With a sigh of resignation, he took a small book from the pocket of his robes and then sat down in a chair, beginning to write in his quick, flowing script.† The Aesthetics huddled together near him, alarmed at the strange sounds emanating from within the locked room.

Do things happen if they are not recorded? I once asked Astinus this question. He replied that everything is recorded—just not always in his books.—TRH

Thunder boomed and rolled, shaking the library's very foundation. Light flared around the closed door so constantly it might have been day within the room instead of the darkest hour of the night. The howling and shrieking of a windstorm blended with the mage's shrill screams. There were thuds and thumps, the rustling sounds of sheaves of paper swirling about in a storm. Tongues of flame flicked from beneath the door.

"Master!" one of the Aesthetics cried in terror, pointing to the flames. "He is destroying the books!"

Astinus shook his head and did not cease his writing.

Then, suddenly, all was silent. The light seen beneath the library door went out as if swallowed by darkness. Hesitantly the Aesthetics approached the door, cocking their heads to listen. Nothing could be heard from within, except a faint rustling sound. Bertrem placed his hand upon the door. It yielded to his gentle pressure.

"The door opens, Master," he said.

Astinus stood up. "Return to your studies," he commanded the Aesthetics. "There is nothing you can do here."

Bowing silently, the monks gave the door a final, scared glance, then walked hurriedly down the echoing corridor, leaving Astinus alone. He waited a few moments to make certain they were gone, then the historian slowly opened the door to the great library.

Silver and red moonlight streamed through the small windows. The orderly rows of shelves that held thousands of bound books stretched into the darkness. Recessed holes containing thousands of scrolls lined the walls. The moonlight shone upon a table, buried under a pile of paper. A guttered candle stood in the center of the table, a night-blue spellbook lay open beside it, the moonlight shining on its bone-white pages. Other spellbooks lay scattered on the floor.

Did we know about Raistlin and Fistandantilus at this point in the story? Margaret and I maintain that the period when the original DRAGONLANCE was being created was, indeed, a magical time for us both. There were moments when we felt we were not so much creating a story as simply reporting a history of events that took place somewhere in story form. While we may not have understood at the time the depth of the relationship between Fistandantilus and Raistlin—there is no denying that the foundations for all of that appear here.—TRH

Looking around, Astinus frowned. Black streaks marked the walls. The smell of sulphur and of fire was strong inside the room. Sheets of paper swirled in the still air, falling like leaves after an autumn storm upon a body lying on the floor.

Entering the room, Astinus carefully shut and locked the door behind him. Then he approached the body, wading through the mass of parchment scattered on the floor. He said nothing, nor did he bend down to help the young mage. Standing beside Raistlin, he regarded him thoughtfully.

But, as he drew near, Astinus's robes brushed the metallic-colored, outstretched hand. At that touch, the mage lifted his head. Raistlin stared at Astinus with eyes already darkening with the shadows of death.

"You did not find what you sought?" Astinus asked, staring down at the young man with cold eyes.

"The Key!" Raistlin gasped through white lips flecked with blood. "Lost . . . in time! . . . Fools!" His clawlike hand clenched, anger the only fire that burned in him. "So simple! Everyone knew it. . . no one recorded it! The Key . . . all I need . . . lost!"

"So this ends your journey, my old friend," Astinus said without compassion.

Raistlin raised his head, his golden eyes glittering feverishly. "You *do* know me! *Who am I?*"† he demanded.

"It is no longer important," Astinus said. Turning, he started to walk out of the library.

There was a piercing shriek behind him, a hand grasped his robe, dragging him to a halt.

"Don't turn your back on me as you have turned it on the world!" Raistlin snarled.

"Turn my back on the world . . ." the historian repeated softly and slowly, his head moving to face the mage. "Turn my back on the world!" Emotion rarely marred the surface of Astinus's cold voice, but now anger struck the placid calm of his soul like a rock hurled into still water.

"I? Turn my back on the world?" Astinus's voice rolled around the library as the thunder had rolled previously. "I *am* the world, as you well know, old friend! Countless times I have been born! Countless deaths I have died! Every tear shed—mine have flowed! Every drop of blood spilled—mine has drained! Every agony, every joy ever felt has been mine to share!

"I sit with my hand on the Sphere of Time, the sphere *you* made for me, old friend, and I travel† the length and breadth of this world chronicling its history. I have committed the blackest deeds! I have made the noblest sacrifices. I am human, elf, and ogre. I am male and female. I have borne children. I have murdered children. I saw you as you were. I see you as you are. If I seem cold and unfeeling, it is because that is how I survive without losing my sanity! My passion goes into my words. Those who read my books *know* what it is to have lived in any time, in any body that ever walked this world!"

Astinus is a very accomplished man in magical and miraculous arts. One of his traits is an ability to be everywhere at once and experience all that is happening in the world simultaneously. This is the quality that allows him to record every event taking place across the globe of Krynn. Astinus holds the godly trait of being omnipresent.—TRH

Raistlin's hand loosed its grip on the historian's robes and he fell weakly to the floor. His strength was fading fast. But the mage clung to Astinus's words, even as he felt the coldness of death clutch his heart. I must live, just a moment longer. Lunitari, give me just a moment more, he prayed, calling upon the spirit of the moon from which Red-Robed mages draw their magic. Some word was coming, he knew. Some word that would save him. If only he could hold on!

Astinus's eyes flared as he gazed upon the dying man. The words he hurled at him had been pent up inside the chronicler for countless centuries.

"On the last, perfect day," Astinus said, his voice shaking, "the three gods will come together: Paladine in his Radiance, Queen Takhisis in her Darkness, and lastly Gilean, Lord of Neutrality. In their hands, each bears the Key of Knowledge. They will place these Keys upon the great Altar, and upon the Altar will also be placed my books—the story of every being who has lived upon Krynn throughout time! And then, at last, the world will be complete —"

Astinus stopped, appalled, realizing what he had said, what he had done.

But Raistlin's eyes no longer saw him. The hourglass pupils were dilated, the golden color surrounding them gleamed like flame.

"The Key . . ." Raistlin whispered in exultation. "The Key! I know . . . I know!"†

The one question the readers always ask about this chapter, is this: What is the Key that Raistlin uses to discover the truth about Fistandantilus? That answer is provided inadvertently by Astinus (who realizes that he's given it away) in the sentence: "On the last, perfect day, the three gods will come together … In their hands, each bears the Key of Knowledge. . . ." The answer is Knowledge. Raistlin gains knowledge of himself at that moment. He accepts both the dark and the light, and when he does so, he remembers the Test. He remembers the bargain he made with Fistandantilus.—MW

So weak he could scarcely move, Raistlin reached into the small, nondescript pouch that hung from his belt and brought forth the marble-sized dragon orb. Holding it in his trembling hand, the mage stared into it with eyes that were fast growing dim.

"I know who you are," Raistlin murmured with his dying breath. "I know you now and I beseech you—come to my aid as you came to my aid in the Tower and in Silvanesti! Our bargain is struck! Save me, and you save yourself!"

The mage collapsed. His head with its sparse white wispy hair lolled back onto the floor, his eyes with their cursed vision closed. The hand that held the orb went limp, but its fingers did not relax. It held the orb fast in a grip stronger than death.

Little more than a heap of bones garbed in blood-red robes, Raistlin lay unmoving amid the papers that littered the spell-blasted library.

Astinus stared at the body for long moments, bathed in the garish purplish light of the two moons. Then, his head bowed, the historian left the silent library, closing and locking the door behind him with hands that shook.

Returning to his study, the historian sat for hours, gazing unseeing into the darkness.

6

Palanthas.

I tell you, it was Raistlin!"

"And I tell you, one more of your furry-elephant, teleporting-ring, plants-living-off-air stories and I'll twist that hoopak around your neck!" Flint snapped angrily.

"It was *too* Raistlin," Tasslehoff retorted, but he said it under his breath as the two walked along the wide, gleaming streets of the beautiful city of Palanthas. The kender knew by long association just how far he could push the dwarf, and Flint's threshold for irritation was very low these days.

"And don't go bothering Laurana with your wild tales, either," Flint ordered, correctly guessing Tas's intentions. "She has enough problems."

"But—"

The dwarf stopped and gazed grimly at the kender from beneath bushy white eyebrows.

"Promise?"

Tas sighed. "Oh, all right."

It wouldn't have been so bad if he didn't feel quite certain he had seen Raistlin! He and Flint were walking past the steps of the great library of Palanthas when the kender's sharp eyes caught sight of a group of monks clustered around something lying on the steps. When Flint stopped for a moment to admire some particularly fine piece of dwarven-crafted stonework in a building opposite, Tas took advantage of the opportunity to creep silently up the stairs to see what was going on.

To his amazement, he saw a man that looked just like Raistlin, golden-colored metallic skin, red robes, and all, being lifted up off the stairs and carried inside the library. But by the time the excited kender ran across the street, grabbed Flint, and hauled the grumbling dwarf back again, the group was gone.

Tasslehoff even ran up to the door, banging on it and demanding entrance. But the Aesthetic who answered appeared so horrified at the thought of a kender coming into the great library that the scandalized dwarf hustled Tas off before the monk could open his mouth.

Promises being very nebulous things to kenders, Tas considered telling Laurana anyway, but then he thought of the elfmaid's face as it had appeared lately, wan and drawn from grief, worry, and lack of sleep, and the soft-hearted kender decided maybe Flint was right. If it was Raistlin, he was probably here on some secret business of his own and wouldn't thank them for dropping in on him uninvited. Still . . .

Essentially the last thousand years pre-Cataclysm, when humans became the dominant beings on Krynn.

Heaving a sigh, the kender walked on, kicking stones with his feet and looking around the city once more. Palanthas was well worth the look. The city had been fabled even during the Age of Might† for its beauty and grace. There was no other city on Krynn that could compare to it, at least to human thought. Built on a circular pattern like a wheel, the center was, literally, the hub of the city. All the major official buildings were located here, and the great sweeping staircases and graceful columns were

breathtaking in their grandeur. From this central circle, wide avenues led off in the directions of the eight major compass points. Paved with fitted stone (dwarven work, of course) and lined with trees whose leaves were like golden lace year-round, these avenues led to the seaport on the north and to the seven gates of the Old City† Wall.

Even these gates were masterpieces of architecture, each one guarded by twin minarets whose graceful towers rose over three hundred feet into the air. The Old Wall itself was carved with intricate designs, telling the story of Palanthas during the Age of Dreams. Beyond Old City Wall lay New City. Carefully planned to conform to the original design, New City extended from Old City Wall in the same circular pattern with the same wide, tree-lined avenues. There were, however, no walls around New City. The Palanthians didn't particularly like walls (walls ruined the over-all design), and nothing in either Old or New City was ever built these days without first consulting the overall design, both within and without. Palanthas's silhouette upon the horizon in the evening was as lovely to the eye as the city itself, with one exception.

The Old City is the town that built up around the Tower of High Sorcery thousands of years ago. Originally called Bright Horizon, the town was claimed by Vinas Solamnus for the Knights of Solamnia. Supposedly the gods told Vinas that the city of Bright Horizon lay on sacred ground, the exact spot on which Paladine first stepped foot on Krynn. He then renamed Bright Horizon in Paladine's honor and began its expansion.

Tas's thoughts were rudely interrupted by a poke in the back from Flint.

"What is the matter with you?" the kender demanded, facing the dwarf.

"Where are we?" Flint asked surlily, hands on his hips.

"Well, we're . . ." Tas looked around. "Uh . . . that is, I think we're . . . then again, perhaps we're not." He fixed Flint with a cold stare. "How did you get us lost?"

"ME!" The dwarf exploded. "*You're* the guide! *You're* the map reader. *You're* the kender who knows this city like he knows his own house!"

"But *I* was thinking," Tas said loftily.

"What with?" Flint roared.

"I was thinking deep thoughts," Tas said in wounded tones.

"I—oh, never mind," Flint grumbled and began to peer up and down the street. He didn't quite like the looks of things.

"This certainly does seem strange," Tas said cheerfully, echoing the dwarf's thoughts. "It's so

empty, not at all like the other streets of Palanthas." He stared longingly down the rows of silent empty buildings. "I wonder—"

"No," said Flint.

"Absolutely not. We're going back the way we came—"

"Oh, come on!" Tas said, heading down the deserted street. "Just a little way, to see what's down here. You know Laurana told us to look around, inspect the forti—forta—the whatch-ma-call-its."

"Fortifications," muttered Flint, stumping reluctantly along after the kender. "And there aren't any around here, you doorknob. This is the center of the city! She meant the walls around the outside of the city."

"There aren't any walls around the outside of the city," Tas said triumphantly. "Not around New City, anyway. And if it's the center, why is it deserted? I think we should find out."

Flint snorted. The kender was beginning to make sense, a fact that caused the dwarf to shake his head and wonder if maybe he shouldn't lie down somewhere out of the sun.

The two walked for several minutes in silence, traveling deeper and deeper into the heart of the city. To one side, only a few blocks away, rose the palatial mansion of the Lord of Palanthas. They could see its towering spires from here. But ahead of them, nothing was visible. It was all lost in shadow. . . .

Tas glanced into windows and stuck his nose into doorways of the buildings they passed. He and Flint proceeded clear to the end of the block before the kender spoke.

"You know, Flint," Tas said uneasily, "these buildings are all empty."

"Abandoned," said Flint in hushed tones. The dwarf laid his hand on his battle-axe, starting nervously at the sound of Tas's shrill voice.

"There's a queer feeling about this place," Tas said, edging closer to the dwarf. "I'm not afraid, mind you—"

"I am," said Flint emphatically. "Let's get out of here!"

Tas looked up at the tall buildings on either side of them. They were well-kept. Apparently the

Palanthians were so proud of their city that they even spent money keeping up vacant buildings. There were shops and dwellings of all kinds, obviously structurally sound. The streets were clean and free from litter and garbage. But it was all deserted. This had once been a prosperous area, the kender thought. Right in the heart of the city. Why wasn't it now? Why had everyone left? It gave him an "eerie" feeling and there were not many things in Krynn that gave kender "eerie" feelings.

"There aren't even any rats!" Flint muttered. Taking hold of Tas's arm, he tugged at the kender. "We've seen enough."

"Oh, come on," Tas said. Pulling his arm away, he fought down the strange eerie sensation and, straightening his small shoulders, started off down the sidewalk once more. He hadn't gone three feet when he realized he was alone. Stopping in exasperation, he looked back. The dwarf was standing on the sidewalk, glowering at him.

"I only want to go as far as that grove of trees at the end of the street," Tas said, pointing. "Look—it's just an ordinary grove of ordinary oak trees. Probably a park or something. Maybe we could have lunch—"

"I don't like this place!" Flint said stubbornly. "It reminds me of . . . of . . . Darken Wood—that place where Raistlin spoke to the spooks."

"Oh, you're the only spook here!" Tas said irritably, determined to ignore the fact that it reminded him of the same thing. "It's broad daylight. We're in the center of a city, for the love of Reorx—"

"Then why is it freezing cold?"

"It's winter!" the kender shouted, waving his arms. He hushed immediately, staring around in alarm at the weird way his words echoed through the silent streets. "Are you coming?" he asked in a loud whisper.

Flint drew a deep breath. Scowling, he gripped his battle-axe and marched down the street toward the kender, casting a wary eye at the buildings as though at any moment a spectre might leap out at him.

"'Tisn't winter," the dwarf muttered out of the corner of his mouth. "Except around here."

"It won't be spring for weeks," Tas returned, glad to have something to argue about and keep his mind

off the strange things his stomach was doing—twisting into knots and the like.

But Flint refused to quarrel—a bad sign. Silently, the two crept down the empty street until they reached the end of the block. Here the buildings ended abruptly in a grove of trees. As Tas had said, it seemed just an ordinary grove of oak trees, although they were certainly the tallest oaks either the dwarf or the kender had seen in long years of exploring Krynn.

But as the two approached, they felt the strange chilling sensation become stronger until it was worse than any cold they had ever experienced, even the cold of the glacier in Ice Wall. It was worse because it came from within and it made no sense! Why should it be so cold in just this part of the city? The sun was shining. There wasn't a cloud in the sky. But soon their fingers were numb and stiff. Flint could no longer hold his battle-axe and was forced to put it back in its holder with shaking hands. Tas's teeth chattered, he had lost all feeling in his pointed ears, and he shivered violently.

"L-let's g-get out-t of h-here . . ." stammered the dwarf through blue lips.

"W-we're j-just s-standing in a sh-shadow of a building." Tas nearly bit his tongue. "W-when we g-get in the s-s-sunshine, it'll war-warm up."

"No f-fire on K-K-Krynn will w-warm th-this!" Flint snapped viciously, stomping on the ground to get the circulation started in his feet.

"J-just a f-few m-more f-feet . . ." Tas kept going along gamely, even though his knees knocked together. But he went alone. Turning around, he saw that Flint seemed paralyzed, unable to move. His head was bowed, his beard quivered.

I should go back, Tas thought, but he couldn't. The curiosity that did more than anything in the world to reduce the kender population kept drawing him forward.

Tas came to the edge of the grove of oak trees and—here—his heart almost failed him. Kender are normally immune to the sensation of fear, so only a kender could have come even this far. But now Tas found himself a prey to the most unreasoning terror he had ever experienced. And whatever was causing it was located within that grove of oak trees.

They're ordinary trees, Tas said to himself, shivering. I've talked to spectres in Darken Wood. I've faced three or four dragons. I broke a dragon orb. Just an ordinary grove of trees. I was prisoner in a wizard's castle. I saw a demon from the Abyss.† Just a grove of ordinary trees.

That event happened to Tas in "A Stone's Throw Away."

Slowly, talking to himself, Tasslehoff inched his way through the oak trees. He didn't go far, not even past the row of trees that formed the outer perimeter of the grove. Because now he could see into the heart of the grove.

Tasslehoff gulped, turned, and ran.

At the sight of the kender running back toward him, Flint knew it was All Over. Something Awful was going to crash out of that grove of trees. The dwarf whirled so rapidly he tripped over his feet and fell sprawling to the pavement. Running up to him, Tas grabbed Flint's belt and pulled him up. Then the two dashed madly down the street, the dwarf running for his very life. He could almost hear gigantic footsteps thudding along behind him. He did not dare turn around. Visions of a slobbering monster drove him on until his heart seemed about to burst from his body. Finally they reached the end of the street.

It was warm. The sun shone.

They could hear the voices of real live people drifting from the crowded streets beyond. Flint stopped, exhausted, gasping for breath. Glancing fearfully back down the street, he was surprised to see it was still empty.

"What was it?" he managed to ask when he could speak past the thudding of his heart.

The kender's face was pale as death. "A-a t-tower . . ." Tas gulped, puffing.

Flint's eyes opened wide. "A tower?" the dwarf repeated. "I *ran* all that way, nearly killing myself, and I was running from a *tower!* I don't suppose"—Flint's bushy eyebrows came together alarmingly—"that the tower was chasing you?"

"N-no," Tas admitted. "It, it just stood there. But it was the most horrible thing I've ever seen in my life," the kender avowed solemnly, shuddering.

"That would be the Tower of High Sorcery," the Lord of Palanthas told Laurana that evening as they

Each of the Towers of High Sorcery was given a different guardian forest to keep away people who might not appreciate the mages who lived and worked inside. The Shoikan Grove around the Palanthas Tower casts a continuous Fear spell.

entered the map room of the beautiful palace on the hill overlooking the city. "No wonder your little friend was terrified. I'm surprised he got as far as the Shoikan Oak Grove."†

"He's a kender," Laurana replied, smiling.

"Ah, yes. Well, that explains it. Now that's something I hadn't considered, you know. Hiring kender to do the work around the Tower. We have to pay the most outrageous prices to get men to go into those buildings once a year and keep them in good repair. But then"—the Lord appeared downcast—"I don't suppose the townspeople would be at all pleased to see a sizeable number of kender in the city."

Amothus, Lord of Palanthas, padded across the polished marble floor of the map room, his hands clasped behind his robes of state. Laurana walked next to him, trying to keep from tripping over the hem of the long, flowing gown the Palanthians had insisted she wear. They had been quite charming about the dress, offering it as a gift. But she knew they were horrified to see a Princess of the Qualinesti parading around in blood-stained, battle-scarred armor. Laurana had no choice but to accept it; she could not afford to offend the Palanthians whom she was counting on for help. But she felt naked and fragile and defenseless without her sword at her side and the steel around her body.

And she knew that the generals of the Palanthian army, the temporary commanders of the Solamnic Knights, and the other nobles, advisors from the City Senate, were the ones making her feel fragile and defenseless. All of them reminded her with every look that she was, to them, a woman playing at being a soldier. All right, she had done well. She had fought her little war and she had won. Now, back to the kitchen. . . .

"What *is* the Tower of High Sorcery?" Laurana asked abruptly. She had learned after a week of negotiating with the Lord of Palanthas that, although an intelligent man, his thoughts tended to wander into unexplored regions and he needed constant guidance to keep to the central topic.

"Oh, yes. Well, you can see it from the window here, if you really want to . . ." The Lord seemed reluctant.

"I would like to see it," Laurana said coolly.

Shrugging, Lord Amothus veered from his course and led Laurana to a window she had already noticed because it was covered with thick curtains. The curtains over the other windows of the room were open, revealing a breathtaking view of the city in whatever direction one looked.

"Yes, this is the reason I keep these shut," the Lord said with a sigh in answer to Laurana's question. "A pity, too. This was once the most magnificent view in the city, according to the old records. But that was before the Tower was cursed—"

The Lord† drew the curtains aside with a trembling hand, his face dark with sorrow. Startled at such emotion, Laurana looked out curiously, then drew in a breath. The sun was sinking behind the snow-capped mountains, streaking the sky with red and purple. The vibrant colors shimmered on the pure white buildings of Palanthas as the rare, translucent marble from which they were built caught the dying light. Laurana had never imagined such beauty could exist in the world of humans. It rivaled her beloved homeland of Qualinesti.

The family of Amothus Palanthus has ruled the city of Palanthas for hundreds of years. Rulership of Palanthas was always passed on to the eldest son, while the younger sons generally served in the Knights of Solamnia. Also, each ruler had the choice of spelling the name "-thus" or "-thas." All the inhabitants of Krynn make their own choice.

Then her eyes were drawn to a darkness within the shimmering pearl radiance. A single tower rose up to the sky. It was tall; even though the palace was perched on a hill, the top of the Tower was only slightly below her line of sight. Made of black marble, it stood out in distinct contrast to the white marble of the city around it. Minarets must have once graced its gleaming surface, she saw, though these were now crumbling and broken. Dark windows, like empty eyesockets, stared sightlessly into the world. A fence surrounded it. The fence, too, was black and, on the gate of the fence, Laurana saw something fluttering. For a moment she thought it was a huge bird, trapped there, for it seemed alive. But just as she was about to call the Lord's attention to it, he shut the curtains with a shiver.

"I'm sorry," he apologized. "I can't stand it. Shocking. And to think we've lived with that for centuries. . . ."

"I don't think it's so terrible," Laurana said earnestly, her mind's eye remembering the view of the Tower and the city around it. "The Tower . . . seems right somehow. Your city is very beautiful,

but sometimes it's such a cold, perfect beauty that I don't notice it anymore." Looking out the other windows, Laurana was once more as enchanted with the view as she had been when she first entered Palanthas. "But after seeing that, that flaw in your city, it makes the beauty stand out in my mind . . . if you understand. . . ."

It was obvious from the bemused expression on the Lord's face that he did not understand. Laurana sighed, though she caught herself glancing at the drawn curtains with a strange fascination. "How did the Tower come to be cursed?" she asked instead.

"It was during the—oh, I say, here's someone who can tell the story far better than I," Lord Amothus said, looking up in relief as the door opened. "It isn't a story I enjoy relating, to be perfectly honest."

"Astinus of the Library of Palanthas," announced the herald.

To Laurana's astonishment, every man in the room rose respectfully to his feet, even the great generals and noblemen. All this, she thought, for a librarian? Then, to her even greater astonishment, the Lord of Palanthas and all his generals and all the nobles bowed as the historian entered. Laurana bowed, too, out of confused courtesy. As a member of the royal house of Qualinesti, she was not supposed to bow before anyone on Krynn unless it be her own father, Speaker of the Suns. But when she straightened and studied this man, she felt suddenly that bowing to him had been most fitting and proper.

He may have many interesting ways to travel throughout Krynn, but in this case he apparently just walked across the courtyard.

Astinus† entered with an ease and assurance that led her to believe he would stand unabashed in the presence of all the royalty on Krynn and the heavens as well. He seemed middle-aged, but there was an ageless quality about him. His face might have been chiseled out of the marble of Palanthas itself and, at first, Laurana was repelled by the cold, passionless quality of that face. Then she saw that the man's dark eyes literally blazed with life, as though lit from within by the fire of a thousand souls.

"You are late, Astinus," Lord Amothus said pleasantly, though with a marked respect. He and his generals all remained standing until the historian had seated himself, Laurana noticed, as did

even the Knights of Solamnia. Almost overcome with an unaccustomed awe, she sank into her seat at the huge, round table covered with maps which stood in the center of the great room.

"I had business to attend to," Astinus replied in a voice that might have sounded from a bottomless well.

"I heard you were troubled by a strange occurrence." The Lord of Palanthas flushed in embarrassment. "I really must apologize. We have no idea how the young man came to be found in such an appalling condition upon your stairs. If only you had let us know! We could have removed the body without fuss—"

"It was no trouble," Astinus said abruptly, glancing at Laurana. "The matter has been properly dealt with. All is now at an end."

"But . . . uh . . . what about the. . . uh . . . remains?" Lord Amothus asked hesitantly. "I know how painful this must be, but there are certain health proclamations that the Senate has passed and I'd like to be sure all has been attended to. . . ."

"Perhaps I should leave," Laurana said coldly, rising to her feet, "until this conversation has ended."

"What? Leave?" The Lord of Palanthas stared at her vaguely. "You've only just come—"

"I believe our conversation is distressing to the elven princess," Astinus remarked. "The elves, as you remember, my lord, have a great reverence for life. Death is not discussed in this callous fashion among them."

"Oh, my heavens!" Lord Amothus flushed deeply, rising and taking her hand. "I do beg your pardon, my dear. Absolutely abominable of me. Please forgive me and be seated again. Some wine for the princess—" Amothus hailed a servant, who filled Laurana's glass.

"You were discussing the Towers of High Sorcery as I entered. What do you know of the Towers?" Astinus asked, his eyes staring into Laurana's soul.

Shivering at that penetrating gaze, she gulped a sip of wine, sorry now that she had mentioned it. "Really," she said faintly, "perhaps we should turn to business. I'm certain the generals are anxious to return to their troops and I—"

"What do you know of the Towers?" Astinus repeated.

"I—uh—not much," Laurana faltered, feeling as if she were back in school being confronted by her tutor. "I had a friend, that is, an acquaintance, who took the Tests at the Tower of High Sorcery in Wayreth, but he is—"

"Raistlin of Solace, I believe," Astinus said imperturbably.

"Why, yes!" Laurana answered, startled. "How—"

"I am a historian, young woman. It is my business to know," Astinus replied. "I will tell you the history of the Tower of Palanthas. Do not consider it a waste of time, Lauralanthalasa, for its history is bound up in your destiny." Ignoring her shocked look, he gestured to one of the generals. "You, there, open that curtain. You are shutting out the best view in the city, as I believe the princess remarked before I entered. This, then, is the story of the Tower of High Sorcery of Palanthas.

"My tale must begin with what became known, in hindsight, as the Lost Battles. During the Age of Might, when the Kingpriest of Istar began jumping at shadows, he gave his fears a name—magic-users! He feared them, he feared their vast power. He did not understand it, and so it became a threat to him.

"It was easy to arouse the populace against the magic-users. Although widely respected, they were never trusted, primarily because they allowed among their ranks representatives of all three powers in the universe, the White Robes of Good, the Red Robes of Neutrality, and the Black Robes of Evil. For they understood—as the Kingpriest† did not—that the universe swings in balance among these three and that to disturb the balance is to invite destruction.

"And so the people rose against the magic-users. The five Towers of High Sorcery were prime targets, naturally, for it was in these Towers that the powers of the Order were most concentrated. And it was in these Towers that the young mages came to take the Tests—those who dared. For the Trials are arduous and, worse, hazardous. Indeed, failure means one thing: death!"

"Death?" repeated Laurana, incredulously. "Then Raistlin—"

The Kingpriest and his folly, of course, became one of the foundations of the DRAGONLANCE Legends trilogy. As noted before, DRAGONLANCE was built upon a triangular structure with each point striving for balance around a central figure or concept. Balance among all these conflicting elements is the ideal attainment, but occasionally someone comes along disturbing that balance. It does not seem to matter what the initial motivations of the character are: selflessness, selfishness, domination, power or the enforcement

"Risked his life to take the Test. And he nearly paid the price. That is neither here nor there, however. Because of this deadly penalty for failure, dark rumors were spread about the Towers of High Sorcery. In vain the magic-users sought to explain that these were only centers of learning and that each young mage risking his life did so willingly, understanding the purpose behind it. Here, too, in the Towers, the mages kept their spellbooks and their scrolls, their implements of magic. But no one believed them. Stories of strange rites and rituals and sacrifices spread among the people, fostered by the Kingpriest and his clerics for their own ends.

of religious ideals. The Kingpriest wanted to enforce good—force his personal view of morality on the entire world. As such, his efforts counter to the will of heaven met with every bit as much failure as those of Takhisis in her struggle to enforce her will on Krynn.—TRH

"And the day came when the populace rose against the magic-users. And for only the second time in the history of the Order, the Robes came together. The first time was during the creation of the dragon orbs which contained the essences of good and evil, bound together by neutrality. After that, they went their separate ways. Now, allied by a common threat, they came together once more to protect their own.

"The magicians themselves destroyed two of the Towers, rather than let the mobs invade them and meddle with that which was beyond their understanding. The destruction of these two Towers† laid waste to the countryside around them and frightened the Kingpriest, for there was a Tower of High Sorcery located in Istar and one in Palanthas. As for the third, in the Forest of Wayreth, few cared what became of it, for it was far from any center of civilization.

† The Tower at Daltigoth and the one at the Ruins, which went down in history without its own name.

"And so the Kingpriest approached the magic-users with a show of piety. If they would leave the two Towers standing, he would let them withdraw in peace, removing their books and scrolls and magical implements to the Tower of High Sorcery in Wayreth. Sorrowfully the magic-users accepted his offer."

"But why didn't they fight?" Laurana interrupted. "I've seen Raistlin and . . . and Fizban when they're angry! I can't imagine what truly powerful wizards must be like!"

"Ah, but stop and consider this, Laurana. Your young friend, Raistlin, grew exhausted casting even a few relatively minor spells. And once a spell is cast, it is gone from his memory forever unless he reads his spellbook and studies it once more. This is true of even the highest level mages. It is how the gods protect us from those who might otherwise become too powerful and aspire to godhood itself. Wizards must sleep, they must be able to concentrate, they must spend time in daily study. How could they withstand besieging mobs? And, too, how could they destroy their own people?

"No, they felt they had to accept the Kingpriest's offer. Even the Black Robes, who cared little for the populace, saw that they must be defeated and that magic itself might be lost from the world. They withdrew from the Tower of High Sorcery at Istar, and almost immediately the Kingpriest moved in to occupy it. Then they abandoned the Tower here, in Palanthas. And the story of this Tower is a terrible one."

Astinus, who had been relating this without expression in his voice, suddenly grew solemn, his face darkening.

"Well I remember that day," he said, speaking more to himself than to those around the table. "They brought their books and scrolls to me, to be kept in my library. For there were many, many books and scrolls in the Tower, more than the magic-users could carry to Wayreth. They knew I would guard them and treasure them. Many of the spellbooks were ancient and could no longer be read, since they had been bound with spells of protection, spells to which the Key . . . had been lost. The Key . . ."

Astinus fell silent, pondering. Then, with a sigh, as if brushing away dark thoughts, he continued.

"The people of Palanthas gathered around the Tower as the highest of the Order—the Wizard of the White Robes—closed the Tower's slender gates of gold and locked them with a silver key. The Lord of Palanthas watched him eagerly. All knew the Lord intended to move into the Tower, as his mentor, the Kingpriest of Istar, had done. His eyes lingered greedily on the Tower, for legends of the wonders within, both fair and evil, had spread throughout the land."

"Of all the beautiful buildings in Palanthas," murmured Lord Amothus, "the Tower of High

Sorcery was said to be the most splendid. And now . . ."

"What happened?" asked Laurana, feeling chilled as the darkness of night crept through the room, wishing someone would summon the servants to light the candles.

"The Wizard started to hand the silver key to the Lord," continued Astinus in a deep, sad voice. "Suddenly, one of the Black Robes appeared in a window in the upper stories. As the people stared at him in horror, he shouted, 'The gates will remain closed and the halls empty until the day comes when the master of both the past and the present returns with power!' Then the evil mage† leaped out, hurling himself down upon the gates. And as the barbs of silver and of gold pierced the black robes, he cast a curse upon the Tower. His blood stained the ground, the silver and golden gates withered and twisted and turned to black. The shimmering tower of white and red faded to ice-gray stone, its black minarets crumbled.

Mary Kirchoff, in The Medusa Plague, *identified this black-robed mage as a faithful wizard of Evil named Rannoch. He went insane at the attack on his beloved magic.*

"The Lord and the people fled in terror and, to this day, no one dares approach the Tower of Palanthas. Not even kender"—Astinus smiled briefly—"who fear nothing in this world. The curse is so powerful it keeps away *all* mortals—"

"Until the master of past and present returns," Laurana murmured.

"Bah! The man was mad." Lord Amothus sniffed. "No man is master of past and present, unless it be you, Astinus."

"I am not master!" Astinus said in such hollow, ringing tones that everyone in the room stared at him. "I remember the past, I record the present. I do not seek to dominate either!"

"Mad, like I said." The Lord shrugged. "And now we are forced to endure an eyesore like the Tower because no one can stand to live around it or get close enough to tear it down."

"I think to tear it down would be a shame," Laurana said softly, gazing at the Tower through the window. "It belongs here. . . ."

"Indeed it does, young woman," Astinus replied, regarding her strangely.

Night's shadows had deepened as Astinus talked. Soon the Tower was shrouded in darkness while

lights sparkled in the rest of the city. Palanthas seemed to be trying to out-glitter the stars, thought Laurana, but a round patch of blackness will remain always in its center.

"How sad and how tragic," she murmured, feeling that she must say something, since Astinus was staring straight at her. "And that, that dark thing I saw fluttering, pinned to the fence. . . ." She stopped in horror.

"Mad, mad," repeated Lord Amothus gloomily. "Yes, that is what's left of the body, so we suppose. No one has been able to get close enough to find out."

Laurana shuddered. Putting her hands to her aching head, she knew that this grim story would haunt her for nights, and she wished she'd never heard it. *Bound up in her destiny!* Angrily she put the thought out of her mind. It didn't matter. She didn't have time for this. Her destiny looked bleak enough without adding nightmarish nursery tales.

As if reading her thoughts, Astinus suddenly rose to his feet and called for more light.

"For," he said coldly, staring at Laurana, "the past is lost. Your future is your own. And we have a great deal of work to do before morning."

7

Commander of the Knights of Solamnia.

"First, I must read a communique I received from Lord Gunthar only a few hours ago." The Lord of Palanthas withdrew a scroll from the folds of his finely woven, woolen robes and spread it on the table, smoothing it carefully with his hands. Leaning his head back, he peered at it, obviously trying to bring it into focus.

Laurana, feeling certain that this must be in reply to a message of her own she had prompted Lord Amothus to send to Lord Gunthar two days earlier, bit her lip in impatience.

"It's creased," Lord Amothus said in apology. "The griffons the elven lords have so kindly loaned us"—he bowed to Laurana, who bowed back, suppressing the urge to rip the message from his hand—"cannot be taught to carry these scrolls without

rumpling them. Ah, now I can make it out. 'Lord Gunthar to Amothus, Lord of Palanthas. Greetings.' Charming man, Lord Gunthar." The Lord looked up. "He was here only last year, during Spring Dawning festival,† which, by the way, takes place in three weeks, my dear. Perhaps you would grace our festivities—"

The festival obviously welcomes in spring, but only the elves call the entire month that follows Spring Dawning.

"I would be pleased to, lord, *if* any of us are here in three weeks," Laurana said, clenching her hands tightly beneath the table in an effort to remain calm.

Lord Amothus blinked, then smiled indulgently. "Certainly. The dragonarmies. Well, to continue reading. 'I am truly grieved to hear of the loss of so many of our Knighthood. Let us find comfort in the knowledge that they died victorious, fighting this great evil that darkens our lands. I feel an even greater personal grief in the loss of three of our finest leaders: Derek Crownguard, Knight of the Rose, Alfred MarKenin, Knight of the Sword, and Sturm Brightblade, Knight of the Crown.' " The Lord turned to Laurana. "Brightblade. He was your close friend, I believe, my dear?"

"Yes, my lord," Laurana murmured, lowering her head, letting her golden hair fall forward to hide the anguish in her eyes. It had been only a short time since they had buried Sturm in the Chamber of Paladine beneath the ruins of the High Clerist's Tower. The pain of his loss still ached.

"Continue reading, Amothus," Astinus commanded coldly. "I cannot afford to take too much time from my studies."

"Certainly, Astinus," the Lord said, flushing. He began to read again hurriedly. " 'This tragedy leaves the Knights in unusual circumstances. First, the Knighthood is now made up of, as I understand, primarily Knights of the Crown, the lowest order of Knights. This means that, while all have passed their tests and won their shields, they are, however, young and inexperienced. For most, this was their first battle. It also leaves us without any suitable commanders since—according to the Measure—there must be a representative from each of the three Orders of Knights in command.' "

Laurana could hear the faint jingle of armor and the rattle of swords as the knights present shifted uncomfortably. They were temporary leaders until

this question of command could be settled. Closing her eyes, Laurana sighed. Please, Gunthar, she thought, let your choice be a wise one. So many have died because of political manuevering. Let this be an end to it!

" 'Therefore I appoint to fill the position of leadership of the Knights of Solamnia, Lauralanthalasa of the royal house of Qualinesti . . .' " The Lord paused a moment, as if uncertain he had read correctly. Laurana's eyes opened wide as she stared at him in shocked disbelief. But she was not more shocked than the knights themselves.

Lord Amothus peered vaguely at the scroll, rereading it. Then, hearing a murmur of impatience from Astinus, he hurried on, " 'who is the most experienced person currently in the field and the only one with knowledge of how to use the dragonlances. I attest to the validity of this Writ by my seal. Lord Gunthar Uth Wistan, Grand Master of the Knights of Solamnia, and so forth.' " The Lord looked up. "Congratulations, my dear, or perhaps I should say 'general.' "

Laurana sat very still. For a moment she was so filled with anger she thought she might stalk out of the room. Visions swam before her eyes, Lord Alfred's headless corpse, poor Derek dying in his madness, Sturm's peace-filled, lifeless eyes, the bodies of the knights who had died in the Tower laid out in a row. . . .

And now *she* was in command. An elfmaid from the royal household. Not even old enough, by elven standards, to be free of her father's house. A spoiled little girl who had run away from her home to "chase after" her childhood sweetheart, Tanis Half-Elven. That spoiled little girl had grown up. Fear, pain, great loss, great sorrow, she knew that, in some ways, she was older than her father now.

Turning her head, she saw Sir Markham and Sir Patrick exchange glances. Of all the Knights of the Crown, these two had served longest. She knew both men to be valiant soldiers and honorable men. They had both fought bravely at the High Clerist's Tower. Why hadn't Gunthar picked one of them, as she herself had recommended?

Sir Patrick stood up, his face dark. "I cannot accept this," he said in a low voice. "Lady Laurana

is a valiant warrior, certainly, but she has never commanded men in the field."

"Have you, young knight?" Astinus asked imperturbably.

Patrick flushed. "No, but that's different. She's a wom—"

"Oh, really, Patrick!" Sir Markham laughed. He was a carefree, easy-going young man, a startling contrast to the stern and serious Patrick. "Hair on your chest doesn't make you a general. Relax! It's politics. Gunthar has made a wise move."

Laurana flushed, knowing he was right. She was a safe choice until Gunthar had time to rebuild the Knighthood and entrench himself firmly as leader.

"But there is no precedent for this!" Patrick continued to argue, avoiding Laurana's eyes.

"I'm certain that, according to the Measure, women are not permitted in the Knighthood—"

"You are wrong," Astinus stated flatly. "And there is precedent. In the Third Dragonwar,† a young woman was accepted into the Knighthood following the deaths of her father and her brothers. She rose to Knight of the Sword and died honorably in battle, mourned by her brethren."†

When Huma Dragonbane fought the Dark Queen's dragons.

That story deserves telling—it's still being researched.

No one spoke. Lord Amothus appeared extremely embarrassed, he had almost sunk beneath the table at Sir Markham's reference to hairy chests. Astinus stared coldly at Sir Patrick. Sir Markham toyed with his wine glass, glancing once at Laurana and smiling. After a brief, internal struggle, visible in his face, Sir Patrick sat back down, scowling.

Sir Markham raised his glass. "To our commander."

Laurana did not respond. She was in command. Command of what? she asked herself bitterly. The tattered remnants of the Knights of Solamnia who had been sent to Palanthas; of the hundreds that had sailed, no more than fifty survived. They had won a victory . . . but at what terrible cost? A dragon orb destroyed, the High Clerist's Tower in ruins. . . .

"Yes, Laurana," said Astinus, "they have left you to pick up the pieces."

She looked up startled, frightened of this strange man who spoke her thoughts.

"I didn't want this," she murmured through lips that felt numb.

"I don't believe any of us were sitting around praying for a war," Astinus remarked caustically. "But war has come, and now you must do what you can to win it." He rose to his feet. The Lord of Palanthas, the generals, and the Knights stood up respectfully.

Laurana remained seated, her eyes on her hands. She felt Astinus staring at her, and she stubbornly refused to look at him.

"Must you go, Astinus?" Lord Amothus asked plaintively.

"I must. My studies wait. Already I have been gone too long. You have a great deal to do now, much of it mundane and boring. You do not need me. You have your leader." He made a motion with his hand.

"What?" Laurana said, catching his gesture out of the corner of her eye. Now she looked at him, then her eyes went to the Lord of Palanthas. "Me? You can't mean that! I'm only in command of the Knights—"

"Which makes you commander of the armies of the city of Palanthas, if we so choose," the Lord said. "And if Astinus recommends you—"

"I don't," Astinus said bluntly. "I cannot recommend anyone. I do not shape history, "† He stopped suddenly, and Laurana was surprised to see the mask slip from his face, revealing grief and sorrow. "That is, I have endeavored not to shape history. Sometimes, even I fail. . . ." He sighed, then regained control of himself, replacing the mask. "I have done what I came to do, given you a knowledge of the past. It may or may not be relevant to your future."

Astinus endeavors to observe history without affecting it. Such is the purest form of history, but it is an impossible goal, especially for Astinus. His very presence in the world changes it from moment to moment, a fact of which he is keenly aware. Indeed, this very conversation with Laurana changes the future.—TRH

He turned to leave.

"Wait!" Laurana cried, rising. She started to take a step toward him, then faltered as the cold, stern eyes met hers, forbidding as solid stone. "You—you see—everything that is happening, as it occurs?"

"I do."

"Then you could tell us, where the dragonarmies are, what they are doing—"

"Bah! You know that as well as I do." Astinus turned away again.

Laurana cast a quick glance around the room. She saw the lord and the generals watching her with amusement. She knew she was acting like that

spoiled little girl again, but she must have answers! Astinus was near the door, the servants were opening it. Casting a defiant look at the others, Laurana left the table and walked quickly across the polished marble floor, stumbling over the hem of her dress in her haste. Astinus, hearing her, stopped within the doorway.

"I have two questions," she said softly, coming near him.

"Yes," he answered, staring into her green eyes, "one in your head and one in your heart. Ask the first."

"Is there a dragon orb still in existence?"

Astinus was silent a moment. Once more Laurana saw pain in his eyes as his ageless face appeared suddenly old. "Yes," he said finally. "I can tell you that much. One still exists. But it is beyond your ability to use or to find. Put it out of your thoughts."

"Tanis had it," Laurana persisted. "Does this mean he has lost it? Where"—she hesitated, this was the question in her heart—"where is he?"

"Put it out of your thoughts."

"What do you mean?" Laurana felt chilled by the man's frost-rimed voice.

"I do not predict the future. I see only the present as it becomes the past. Thus I have seen it since time began. I have seen love that, through its willingness to sacrifice everything, brought hope to the world. I have seen love that tried to overcome pride and a lust for power, but failed. The world is darker for its failure, but it is only as a cloud dims the sun. The sun—the love, still remains. Finally I have seen love lost in darkness. Love misplaced, misunderstood, because the lover did not know his—or her—own heart."

"You speak in riddles," Laurana said angrily.

"Do I?" Astinus asked. He bowed. "Farewell, Lauralanthalasa. My advice to you is: concentrate on your duty."

The historian walked out the door.

Laurana stood staring after him, repeating his words: "love lost in darkness." Was it a riddle or did she know the answer and simply refuse to admit it to herself, as Astinus implied?

" 'I left Tanis in Flotsam to handle matters in my absence.'" Kitiara had said those words. Kitiara,

the Dragon Highlord. Kitiara, the human woman Tanis loved.

Suddenly the pain in Laurana's heart, the pain that had been there since she heard Kitiara speak those words, vanished, leaving a cold emptiness, a void of darkness like the missing constellations in the night sky. "Love lost in darkness." Tanis was lost. That is what Astinus was trying to tell her. Concentrate on your duties. Yes, she would concentrate on her duties, since that was all she had left.

Turning around to face the Lord of Palanthas and his generals, Laurana threw back her head, her golden hair glinting in the light of the candles. "I will take the leadership of the armies," she said in a voice nearly as cold as the void in her soul.

"Now *this* is stonework!" stated Flint in satisfaction, stamping on the battlements of the Old City Wall beneath his feet. "Dwarves built this, no doubt about it. Look how each stone is cut with careful precision to fit perfectly within the wall, no two quite alike."

"Fascinating," said Tasslehoff, yawning. "Did dwarves build that Tower we—"

"Don't remind me!" Flint snapped. "And dwarves did *not* build the Towers of High Sorcery. They were built by the wizards themselves, who created them from the very bones of the world, raising the rocks up out of the soil with their magic."

"That's wonderful!" breathed Tas, waking up. "I wish I could have been there. How—"

"It's nothing," continued the dwarf loudly, glaring at Tas, "compared to the work of the dwarven rockmasons, who spent centuries perfecting their art. Now look at this stone. See the texture of the chisel marks—"

"Here comes Laurana," Tas said thankfully, glad to end his lesson in dwarven architecture.

Flint quit peering at the rock wall to watch Laurana walk toward them from a great dark hallway which opened onto the battlement. She was dressed once more in the armor she had worn at the High Clerist's Tower; the blood had been cleaned off the gold-decorated steel breastplate, the dents repaired. Her long, honey-colored hair flowed from beneath her red-plumed helm, gleaming in Solinari's light.

She walked slowly, her eyes on the eastern horizon where the mountains were dark shadows against the starry sky. The moonlight touched her face as well. Looking at her, Flint sighed.

"She's changed," he said to Tasslehoff softly. "And elves never change. Do you remember when we met her in Qualinesti? In the fall, only six months ago. Yet it could be years—"

"She's still not over Sturm's death. It's only been a week," Tas said, his impish kender face unusually serious and thoughtful.

"It's not just that." The old dwarf shook his head. "It had something to do with that meeting she had with Kitiara, up on the wall of the High Clerist's Tower. It was something Kitiara did or said. Blast her!" the dwarf snapped viciously. "I never did trust her! Even in the old days. It didn't surprise me to see her in the get-up of a Dragon Highlord! I'd give a mountain of steel coins to know what she said to Laurana that snuffed the light right out of her. She was like a ghost when we brought her down from the wall, after Kitiara and her blue dragon left. I'll bet my beard," muttered the dwarf, "that it had something to do with Tanis."

"I can't believe Kitiara's a Dragon Highlord. She was always . . . always . . ." Tas groped for words. "Well, fun!"

"Fun?" said Flint, his brows contracting. "Maybe. But cold and selfish, too. Oh, she was charming enough when she wanted to be." Flint's voice sank to a whisper. Laurana was getting close enough to hear. "Tanis never did see it. He always believed there was more to Kitiara beneath the surface. He thought he alone knew her, that she covered herself with a hard shell to conceal her tender heart. Hah! She had as much heart as these stones."

"What's the news, Laurana?" Tas asked cheerfully as the elfmaid came up to them.

Laurana smiled down at her old friends, but, as Flint said, it was no longer the innocent, gay smile of the elfmaid who had walked beneath the aspen trees of Qualinesti. Now her smile was like the bleakness of the sun in a cold winter sky. It gave light but no warmth, perhaps because there was no matching warmth in her eyes.

"I am commander of the armies," she said flatly.

"Congratu—" began Tas, but his voice died at the sight of her face.

"There is nothing to congratulate me about," Laurana said bitterly. "What do I command? A handful of knights, stuck in a ruined bastion miles away in the Vingaard Mountains, and a thousand men who stand upon the walls of this city." She clenched her gloved fist, her eyes on the eastern sky that was beginning to show the faintest glimmer of morning light. "We should be out there! Now! While the dragonarmy is still scattered and trying to regroup! We could defeat them easily. But, no, we dare not go out onto the Plains, not even with the dragonlances. For what good are they against dragons in flight? If we had a dragon orb—"

She fell silent for a moment, then drew a deep breath. Her face hardened. "Well, we don't. It's no use thinking about it. So we'll stand here, on the battlements of Palanthas, and wait for death."

"Now, Laurana," Flint remonstrated, clearing his throat gruffly, "perhaps things aren't that dark. There are good solid walls around this city. A thousand men can hold it easily. The gnomes with their catapults guard the harbor.† The knights guard the only pass through the Vingaard Mountains and we've sent men to reinforce them. And we do have the dragonlances, a few at any rate, and Gunthar sent word more are on the way. So we can't attack dragons in flight? They'll think twice about flying over the walls—"

Gnomish catapults and their makers are guarding the Gates of Paladine at the entrance to the Bay of Branchala on which Palanthas sits. Each catapult is powerful enough to propel a mammoth rock toward any ship attempting to enter the bay. Unfortunately for the gnomes and Palanthas, the catapults are not powerful enough for the rocks to reach the center of the bay, and, of course, every captain knows it.

"That isn't enough, Flint!" Laurana sighed. "Oh, sure, we may hold the dragonarmies off for a week or two weeks or maybe even a month. But then what? What happens to us when they control the land around us? All we can do against the dragons is shut ourselves up in safe little havens. Soon this world will be nothing but tiny islands of light surrounded by vast oceans of darkness. And then, one by one, the darkness will engulf us all."

Laurana laid her head down upon her hand, resting against the wall.

"How long has it been since you've slept?" Flint asked sternly.

"I don't know," she answered. "My waking and sleeping seem mixed together. I'm walking in a

dream half the time, and sleeping through reality the other half."

"Get some sleep now," the dwarf said in what Tas referred to as his Grandfather Voice. "We're turning in. Our watch is almost up."

"I can't," Laurana said, rubbing her eyes. The thought of sleep suddenly made her realize how exhausted she was. "I came to tell you, we received reports that dragons were seen, flying westward over the city of Kalaman."

"They're heading this direction then," Tas said, visualizing a map in his head.

"Whose reports?" asked the dwarf suspiciously.

"The griffons. Now don't scowl like that." Laurana smiled slightly at the sight of the dwarf's disgust. "The griffons have been a vast help to us. If the elves contribute nothing more to this war than their griffons, they will have already done a great deal."

"Griffons are dumb animals," Flint stated. "And I trust them about as far as I trust kender. Besides," the dwarf continued, ignoring Tas's indignant glare, "it doesn't make sense. The Highlords don't send dragons to attack without the armies backing them up. . . ."

"Maybe the armies aren't as disorganized as we heard." Laurana sighed wearily. "Or maybe the dragons are simply being sent to wreak what havoc they can. Demoralize the city, lay waste to the surrounding countryside. I don't know. Look, word's spread."

Flint glanced around. Those soldiers that were off duty were still in their places, staring eastward at the mountains whose snow-capped peaks were turning a delicate pink in the brightening dawn. Talking in low voices they were joined by others, just waking and hearing the news.

"I feared as much." Laurana sighed. "This will start a panic! I warned Lord Amothus to keep the news quiet, but the Palanthians aren't used to keeping anything quiet! There, what did I tell you?"

Looking down from the wall, the friends could see the streets starting to fill with people—half-dressed, sleepy, frightened. Watching them run from house to house, Laurana could imagine the rumors being spread.

She bit her lip, her green eyes flared in anger. "Now I'll have to pull men off the walls to get these people back into their homes. I can't have them in the streets when the dragons attack! You men, come with me!" Gesturing to a group of soldiers standing nearby, Laurana hurried away. Flint and Tas watched her disappear down the stairs, heading for the Lord's palace. Soon they saw armed patrols fanning out into the streets, trying to herd people back into their homes and quell the rising tide of panic.

"Fine lot of good that's doing!" Flint snorted. The streets were getting more crowded by the moment.

But Tas, standing on a block of stone staring out over the wall, shook his head. "It doesn't matter!" he whispered in despair "Flint, look—"

The dwarf climbed hurriedly up to stand beside his friend. Already men were pointing and shouting, grabbing bows and spears. Here and there, the barbed silver point of a dragonlance could be seen, glinting in the torchlight.

"How many?" Flint asked, squinting.

"Ten," Tas answered slowly. "Two flights. Big dragons, too. Maybe the red ones, like we saw in Tarsis. I can't see their color against the dawn's light, but I can see riders on them. Maybe a Highlord. Maybe Kitiara . . . Gee," Tas said, struck by a sudden thought, "I hope I get to talk to her this time. It must be interesting being a Highlord—"

His words were lost in the sound of bells ringing from towers all over the city. The people in the streets stared up at the walls where the soldiers were pointing and exclaiming. Far below them, Tas could see Laurana emerge from the Lord's palace, followed by the Lord himself and two of his generals. The kender could tell from the set of her shoulders that Laurana was furious. She gestured at the bells, apparently wanting them silenced. But it was too late. The people of Palanthas went wild with terror. And most of the inexperienced soldiers were in nearly as bad a state as the civilians. The sound of shrieks and wails and hoarse calls rose up into the air. Grim memories of Tarsis came back to Tas, people trampled to death in the streets, houses exploding in flames.

The kender turned slowly around. "I guess I don't want to talk to Kitiara," he said softly, brushing his hand across his eyes as he watched the dragons fly closer and closer. "I don't want to know what it's like being a Highlord, because it must be sad and dark and horrible. . . . Wait—"

Tas stared eastward. He couldn't believe his eyes, so he leaned far out, perilously close to falling over the edge of the wall.

"Flint!" he shouted, waving his arms.

"What is it?" Flint snapped. Catching hold of Tas by the belt of his blue leggings, the dwarf hauled the excited kender back in with jerk.

"It's like in Pax Tharkas!" Tas babbled incoherently. "Like Huma's Tomb. Like Fizban said! They're here! They've come!"

"Who's here!" Flint roared in exasperation.

Jumping up and down in excitement, his pouches bouncing around wildly, Tas turned without answering and dashed off, leaving the dwarf fuming on the stairs, calling out, "Who's here, you rattlebrain?"

"Laurana!" shouted Tas's shrill voice, splitting the early morning air like a slightly off-key trumpet. "Laurana, they've come! They're here! Like Fizban said! Laurana!"

Cursing the kender beneath his breath, Flint stared back out to the east. Then, glancing around swiftly, the dwarf slipped a hand inside a vest pocket. Hurriedly he drew out a pair of glasses and, looking around again to make certain no one was watching him, he slipped them on.

At last we come to the moment I envisioned so many years ago —and what I ultimately wanted to see in DRAGONLANCE: dragons and their riders doing battle in the skies. I was a sailplane pilot at seventeen and a power pilot at nineteen. Flying has been a dream of mine as long as I can remember. This, for me, was a great moment in the story.
—TRH

Now he could make out what had been nothing more than a haze of pink light broken by the darker, pointed masses of the mountain range. The dwarf drew a deep, trembling breath. His eyes dimmed with tears. Quickly he snatched the glasses off his nose and put them back into their case, slipping them back into his pocket. But he'd worn the glasses just long enough to see the dawn touch the wings of dragons with a pink light, pink glinting off silver.

"Put your weapons down, lads," Flint said to the men around him, mopping his eyes with one of the kender's handkerchiefs. "Praise be to Reorx. Now we have a chance. Now we have a chance. . . ."

8

The Oath of the Dragons.

As the silver dragons settled to the ground on the outskirts of the great city of Palanthas, their wings filled the morning sky with a blinding radiance. The people crowded the walls to stare out uneasily at the beautiful, magnificent creatures.

At first the people had been so terrified of the huge beasts that they were intent on driving them away, even when Laurana assured them that these dragons were not evil.† Finally Astinus himself emerged from his library and coldly informed Lord Amothus that these dragons would not harm them. Reluctantly the people of Palanthas laid down their weapons.

The dragons of good are the metallic dragons—silver, gold, bronze, copper, and brass.

Laurana knew, however, that the people would have believed Astinus if he told them the sun

would rise at midnight. They did *not* believe in the dragons.

It wasn't until Laurana herself walked out of the city gates and straight into the arms of a man who had been riding one of the beautiful silver dragons that the people begin to think there might be something to this children's story after all.

"Who is that man? Who has brought the dragons to us? Why have the dragons come?"

Jostling and shoving, the people leaned over the wall, asking questions and listening to the wrong answers. Out in the valley, the dragons slowly fanned their wings to keep their circulation going in the chill morning.

As Laurana embraced the man, another person climbed down off one of the dragons, a woman whose hair gleamed as silver as the dragon's wings. Laurana embraced this woman, too. Then, to the wonder of the people, Astinus led the three of them to the great library, where they were admitted by the Aesthetics. The huge doors shut behind them.

The people were left to mill about, buzzing with questions and casting dubious glances at the dragons sitting before their city walls.

Then the bells rang out once more. Lord Amothus was calling a meeting. Hurriedly the people left the walls to fill the city square before the Lord's palace as he came out onto a balcony to answer their questions.

"These are silver dragons," he shouted, "good dragons who have joined us in our battle against the evil dragons as in the legend of Huma. The dragons have been brought to our city by—"

Whatever else the Lord intended to say was lost in cheering. The bells rang out again, this time in celebration. People flooded the streets, singing and dancing. Finally, after a futile attempt to continue, the Lord simply declared the day a holiday and returned to his palace.

The following is an excerpt from the Chronicles, A History of Krynn, *as recorded by Astinus of Palanthas. It can be found under the heading: "The Oath of the Dragons."*

As I, Astinus, write these words, I look on the face of the elflord, Gilthanas, younger son of

Solostaran, Speaker of the Suns, lord of the Qualinesti. Gilthanas's face is very much like his sister Laurana's face, and not just in family resemblance. Both have the delicate features and ageless quality of all elves. But these two are different. Both faces are marked with a sorrow not to be seen on the faces of elves living on Krynn. Although I fear that before this war is ended, many elves will have this same look. And perhaps this is not a bad thing, for it seems that, finally, the elves are learning that they are part of this world, not above it.

To one side of Gilthanas sits his sister. To the other sits one of the most beautiful women I have seen walk on Krynn. She appears to be an elfmaid, a Wilder elf. But she does not deceive my eyes with her magic arts. She was never born of woman, elf or no. She is a dragon, a silver dragon, sister of the Silver Dragon who was beloved of Huma, Knight of Solamnia. It has been Silvara's fate to fall in love with a mortal, as did her sister. But, unlike Huma, this mortal, Gilthanas, cannot accept his fate. He looks at her . . . she looks at him. Instead of love, I see a smoldering anger within him that is slowly poisoning both their souls.

Silvara speaks. Her voice is sweet and musical. The light of my candle gleams in her beautiful silver hair and in her deep night-blue eyes.

"After I gave Theros Ironfeld the power to forge the dragonlances within the heart of the Monument of the Silver Dragon," Silvara tells me, "I spent much time with the companions before they took the lances to the Council of Whitestone. I showed them through the Monument, I showed them the paintings of the Dragon War, which picture good dragons, silver and gold and bronze, fighting the evil dragons.†

" 'Where are your people?' the companions asked me. 'Where are the good dragons? Why aren't they helping us in our time of need?'

"I held out against their questions, as long as I could. . . ."

Here Silvara stops speaking and looks at Gilthanas with her heart in her eyes. He does not meet her gaze but stares at the floor. Silvara sighs and resumes her story.

One story that tells of the creation of good and evil dragons back at the dawn of Krynn is "Aurora's Eggs" by Douglas Niles, in The Dragons at War.

"Finally, I could resist his—their—pressure no longer. I told them about the Oath.

"When Takhisis, the Queen of Darkness, and her evil dragons were banished, the good dragons left the land to maintain the balance between good and evil. Made of the world, we returned to the world, sleeping an ageless sleep.† We would have remained asleep, in a world of dreams, but then came the Cataclysm and Takhisis found her way back into the world again.

Roger Moore reports that when the dragons disappeared from Krynn, they went into dragonsleep, which is a mystical merging of a dragon with the very earth and rock of Krynn. A dragon essentially remains in suspended animation until wakened from dragonsleep. Most of the good dragons sank into dragonsleep at Paladine's bidding. It is said that only Takhisis and Paladine can awaken dragons from dragonsleep.

"Long had she planned for this return, should fate give it to her, and she was prepared. Before Paladine was aware of her, Takhisis woke the evil dragons from their sleep and ordered them to slip into the deep and secret places of the world and steal the eggs of the good dragons, who slept on, unaware. . . .

"The evil dragons brought the eggs of their brethren to the city of Sanction where the dragonarmies were forming. Here, in the volcanoes known as the Lords of Doom, the eggs of the good dragons were hidden.

"Great was the grief of the good dragons when Paladine woke them from their sleep and they discovered what had occurred. They went to Takhisis to find out what price they would have to pay for the return of their unborn children. It was a terrible price. Takhisis demanded an oath. Each of the good dragons must swear that they would not participate in the war she was about to wage on Krynn. It was the good dragons who had helped bring about her defeat in the last war. This time she meant to insure that they would not become involved."

Here Silvara looks at me pleadingly, as if I were to judge them. I shake my head sternly. Far be it from me to judge anyone. I am a historian.

She continues:

"What could we do? Takhisis told us they would murder our children as they slept in their eggs unless we took the Oath. Paladine could not help us. The choice was ours. . . ."

Silvara's head droops, her hair hiding her face. I can hear tears choke her voice. Her words are barely audible to me.

"We took the Oath."

She cannot continue, that is obvious. After staring at her for a moment, Gilthanas clears his throat and begins to speak, his voice harsh.

"I, that is, Theros and my sister and I, finally persuaded Silvara that this Oath was wrong. There must be a way, we said, to rescue the eggs of the good dragons. Perhaps a small force of men might be able to steal the eggs back. Silvara was not convinced that I was right, but she did agree, after much talking, to take me to Sanction so that I could see for myself if such a plan might work.

"Our journey was long and difficult. Someday I may relate the dangers we faced, but I cannot now. I am too weary and we do not have time. The dragonarmies are reorganizing. We can catch them off-guard, if we attack soon. I can see Laurana burning with impatience, eager to pursue them, even as we are speaking. So I will make our tale short.

"Silvara, in her 'elven form' as you see her now"—the bitterness in the elflord's voice cannot be expressed—"and I were captured outside of Sanction and made prisoners of the Dragon Highlord, Ariakas."

Gilthanas's fist clenches, his face is pale with anger and fear.

"Lord Verminaard was nothing, nothing compared to Lord Ariakas. This man's evil power is immense! And he is as intelligent as he is cruel, for it is his strategy that controls the dragonarmies and has led them to victory after victory.

"The suffering we endured at his hands, I cannot describe. I do not believe I can ever relate what they did to us!"

The young elflord trembles violently. Silvara starts to reach out a hand to comfort him, but he draws away from her and continues his story.

"Finally, with help, we escaped. We were in Sanction itself, a hideous town, built in the valley formed by the volcanoes, the Lords of Doom.† These mountains tower over all, their foul smoke corrupts the air. The buildings are all new and modern, constructed with the blood of slaves. Built into the sides of the mountains is a temple to Takhisis, the Dark Queen. The dragon eggs are held deep within the heart of the volcanoes. It was here, into the temple of the Dark Queen, that Silvara and I made our way.

Now it can be told. I was working on the ninth DRAGONLANCE *game module,* Dragons of Deceit, *which took place in the city of Sanction, a place of fire and gloom, lava and doom. Indeed,the active volcanoes surrounding the city were known as the Lords of Doom. As part of the story design, I had to come up with names for the three volcanoes. I called the mountains Huerzyd, Duerghast, and Luerkhisis, which I hope seem like sinister and appropriate names. I don't believe that I've ever told anyone the inspiration for those names. I had just seen the splendid science fiction movie,* Silent Running, *in which Bruce Dern plays a lonely astronaut accompanied on his ship only by three small robots. He dubbed those robots Huey, Dewey, and Louie, after the Disney cartoon characters. With a secret chuckle, I adapted those monikers to name the three nastiest mountains in all Krynn.*
—Doug Niles

"Can I describe the temple, except to say it is a building of darkness and of flame? Tall pillars, carved out of the burning rock, soar into the sulphurous caverns. By secret ways known only to the priests of Takhisis themselves, we traveled, descending lower and lower. You ask who helped us? I cannot say, for her life would be forfeit. I will add only that some god must have been watching over us."

Here Silvara interrupts to murmur, "Paladine," but Gilthanas brushes that aside with a gesture.

"We came to the very bottom chambers and here we found the eggs of the good dragons. At first it seemed all was well. I had . . . a plan. It matters little now, but I saw how we might have been able to rescue the eggs. As I said, it matters little. Chamber after chamber we passed, and the shining eggs, the eggs tinged with silver, gold, and bronze lay gleaming in the fire's light. And then . . ."

The elflord pauses. His face, already paler than death, grows more pallid still. Fearing he might faint, I beckon to one of the Aesthetics to bring him wine. On taking a sip, he rallies and keeps on talking. But I can tell by the far-off look in his eyes that he sees the remembered horror of what he witnessed. As for Silvara, I will write of her in its place.

Gilthanas continues:

"We came to a chamber and found there . . . not eggs . . . nothing but the shells . . . shattered, broken. Silvara cried out in anger, and I feared we might be discovered. Neither of us knew what this portended, but we both felt a chill in our blood that not even the heat of the volcano could warm."

Gilthanas pauses. Silvara begins to sob, very softly. He looks at her and I see, for the first time, love and compassion in his eyes.

"Take her out," he tells one of the Aesthetics. "She must rest."

The Aesthetics lead her gently from the room. Gilthanas licks lips that are cracked and dry, then speaks softly.

"What happened next will haunt me, even after death. Nightly I dream of it. I have not slept since but that I waken, screaming.

"Silvara and I stood before the chamber with the shattered eggs, staring at it, wondering . . . when we

heard the sound of chanting coming from the flame-lit corridor.

" 'The words of magic!' Silvara said.

"Cautiously we crept nearer, both of us frightened, yet drawn by some horrid fascination. Closer and closer we came, and then we could see . . . "

He shuts his eyes, he sobs. Laurana lays her hand on his arm, her eyes soft with mute sympathy. Gilthanas regains control and goes on.

"Inside a cavern room, at the bottom of the volcano, stands an altar to Takhisis. What it may have been carved to represent, I could not tell, for it was so covered with green blood and black slime that it seemed a horrid growth springing from the rock. Around the altar were robed figures—dark clerics of Takhisis and magic-users wearing the Black Robes. Silvara and I watched in awe as a dark-robed cleric brought forth a shining golden dragon egg and placed it upon that foul altar. Joining hands, the Black Robed magic-users and the dark clerics began a chant. The words burned the mind. Silvara and I clung to each other, fearing we would be driven mad by the evil we could feel but could not understand.

"And then . . . then the golden egg upon the altar began to darken. As we watched, it turned to a hideous green and then to black. Silvara began to tremble.

"The blackened egg upon the altar cracked open . . . and a larva-like creature emerged from the shell. It was loathsome and corrupt to look upon, and I retched at the sight. My only thought was to flee this horror, but Silvara realized what was happening and she refused to leave. Together we watched as the larva split its slime-covered skin and from its body came the evil forms of . . . draconians."

There is a gasp of shock at this statement. Gilthanas's head sinks into his hands. He cannot continue. Laurana puts her arms around him, comforting him, and he holds onto her hands. Finally he draws a shuddering breath.

"Silvara and I . . . were nearly discovered. We escaped Sanction, with help once again, and, more dead than alive, we traveled paths unknown to man or elf to the ancient haven of the good dragons."†

Douglas Niles let readers write their own story of Gilthanas and Silvara's journey into the volcanoes in a gamebook, The Lords of Doom.

Gilthanas sighs. A look of peace comes to his face.

"Compared to the horrors we had endured, this was like sweet rest after a night of feverish nightmares. It was difficult to imagine, amid the beauty of the place, that what we had seen really occurred. And when Silvara told the dragons what was happening to their eggs, they refused at first to believe it. Some even accused Silvara of making it up to try to win their aid. But, deep within their hearts, all knew she spoke truly, and so, at last, they admitted that they had been deceived and that the Oath was no longer binding.

"The good dragons have come to aid us now. They are flying to all parts of the land, offering their help. They have returned to the Monument of the Dragon, to aid in forging the dragonlances just as they came to Huma's aid long ago. And they have brought with them the Greater Lances that can be mounted on the dragons themselves, as we saw in the paintings. Now we may ride the dragons into battle and challenge the Dragon Highlords in the sky."

Gilthanas adds more, a few minor details that I need not record here. Then his sister leads him from the library to the palace, where he and Silvara may find what rest they can. I fear it will be long before the terror fades for them, if it ever does. Like so much that is beautiful in the world, it may be that their love will fall beneath the darkness that spreads its foul wings over Krynn.

Thus ends the writing of Astinus of Palanthas on the Oath of the Dragons. A footnote reveals that further details of the journey of Gilthanas and Silvara into Sanction, their adventures there, and the tragic history of their love were recorded by Astinus at a later date and may be found in subsequent volumes of his Chronicles.

Laurana sat late at night, writing up her orders for the morrow. Only a day had passed since the arrival of Gilthanas and the silver dragons, but already her plans† for pressing the beleaguered enemy were taking shape. Within a few days more, she would lead flights of dragons with mounted riders, wielding the new dragonlances, into battle.

The Knights of Solamnia have finally allied with the the good dragons, and this mighty army sweeps eastward from the mountains, driving the dragonarmies back from a great swath of northern Ansalon in the period of little more than a month. But how could an army have advanced so far against such powerful opposition in such a short time? The opportunity to answer this question created, for me, a

She hoped to secure Vingaard Keep first, freeing the prisoners and slaves held there. Then she planned to push on south and east, driving the dragonarmies before her. Finally she would catch them between the hammer of her troops and the anvil of the Dargaard Mountains that divided Solamnia from Estwilde. If she could retake Kalaman and its harbor, she could cut the supply lines the dragonarmy depended on for its survival on this part of the continent.

So intent was Laurana on her plans that she ignored the ringing challenge of the guard outside her door, nor did she hear the answer. The door opened, but, assuming it was one of her aides, she did not look up from her work until she had completed detailing her orders.

Only when the person who entered took the liberty of sitting down in a chair across from her did Laurana glance up, startled.

"Oh," she said, flushing, "Gilthanas, forgive me. I was so involved. . . . I thought you were . . . but, never mind. How are you feeling? I was worried—"

"I'm all right, Laurana," Gilthanas said abruptly. "I was just more tired than I realized and I—I haven't slept very well since Sanction." Falling silent, he sat staring at the maps she had spread on her table. Absently he picked up a freshly sharpened quill pen and began to smooth the feather with his fingers.

"What is it, Gilthanas?" Laurana asked softly.

Her brother looked up at her and smiled sadly. "You know me too well," he said. "I never could hide anything from you, not even when we were children."

"Is it Father?" Laurana asked fearfully. "Have you heard something—"

"No, I've heard nothing about our people," Gilthanas said, "except what I told you, that they have allied with the humans and are working together to drive the dragonarmies from the Ergoth Isles and from Sancrist."

"It was all because of Alhana," Laurana murmured. "She convinced them that they could no longer live apart from the world. She even convinced Porthios. . . ."

"I gather she has convinced him of more than that?" Gilthanas asked without looking at his sister.

fascinating chance to tell a tale of fantasy tactics and dramatic battlefield success. As a basis for Laurana's campaign, I used the model of WW2 aircraft carrier combat in the Pacific Ocean. In this story, the dragons represent the air wings of the opposing navies, while the ground armies marching and countermarching across the plains are like the surface ships. Most of the battles are fought by the dragons, but there were several key confrontations in which the ground armies (the "battleships") came up against each other and fought it out on the plains. In a series of engagements, the knights and their beautiful commander defeated some of the enemy forces in piecemeal fashion, before finally facing a vast and evil horde in the climactic battle of Margaard Ford.—Doug Niles

He began to poke holes in the parchment with the point of the quill.

"There has been talk of a marriage," Laurana said slowly. "If so, I am certain it would be a marriage of convenience only, to unite our people. I cannot imagine Porthios has it in his heart to love anyone, even a woman as beautiful as Alhana. As for the elven princess herself—"

Gilthanas sighed. "Her heart is buried in the High Clerist's Tower with Sturm."

"How did you know?" Laurana looked at him, astonished.

"I saw them together in Tarsis," Gilthanas said. "I saw his face, and I saw hers. I knew about the Starjewel, too. Since he obviously wanted to keep it secret, I did not betray him. He was a fine man," Gilthanas added gently. "I am proud to have known him, and I never thought I would say that of a human."

Laurana swallowed, brushing her hand across her eyes. "Yes," she whispered huskily, "but that wasn't what you came to tell me."

"No," Gilthanas said, "although perhaps it leads into it." For a moment he sat in silence, as if making up his mind. Then he drew a breath. "Laurana, something happened in Sanction that I did not tell Astinus. I won't tell anyone else, ever, if you ask me not to—"

"Why me?" Laurana said, turning pale. Her hand trembling, she laid down her pen.

Gilthanas seemed not to have heard her. He stared fixedly at the map as he spoke. "When—when we were escaping from Sanction, we had to go back to the palace of Lord Ariakas. I cannot tell you more than that, for to do so would betray the one who saved our lives many times and who lives in danger there still, doing what she can to save as many of her people as possible.

"The night we were there, in hiding, waiting to escape, we overheard a conversation between Lord Ariakas and one of his Highlords. It was a woman, Laurana"—Gilthanas looked up at her now—"a human woman named Kitiara."

Laurana said nothing. Her face was deathly white, her eyes large and colorless in the lamplight.

Gilthanas sighed, then leaned near her and placed his hand on hers. Her flesh was so cold, she

might have been a corpse, and he saw, then, that she knew what he was about to say.

"I remembered what you told me before we left Qualinesti, that this was the human woman Tanis Half-Elven loved, sister to Caramon and Raistlin. I recognized her from what I had heard the brothers say about her. I would have recognized her anyway, she and Raistlin, particularly, bear a family resemblance. She, she was talking of Tanis, Laurana." Gilthanas stopped, wondering whether or not he could go on. Laurana sat perfectly still, her face a mask of ice.

"Forgive me for causing you pain, Laurana, but you must know," Gilthanas said at last. "Kitiara laughed about Tanis with this Lord Ariakas and said"—Gilthanas flushed—"I cannot repeat what she said. But they are lovers, Laurana, that much I can tell you. She made it graphically clear. She asked Ariakas's permission to have Tanis promoted to the rank of general in the dragonarmy . . . in return for some sort of information he was going to provide, something about a Green Gemstone Man—"

"Stop," Laurana said without a voice.

"I'm sorry, Laurana!" Gilthanas squeezed her hand, his face filled with sorrow. "I know how much you love him. I—I understand now what it is like to, to love someone that much." He closed his eyes, his head bowed. "I understand what it is like to have that love betrayed. . . ."

"Leave me, Gilthanas," Laurana whispered.

Patting her hand in silent sympathy, the elflord rose and walked softly from the room, shutting the door behind him.

Laurana sat without moving for long moments. Then, pressing her lips firmly together, she picked up her pen and continued writing where she had left off when her brother entered.

9

Victory.

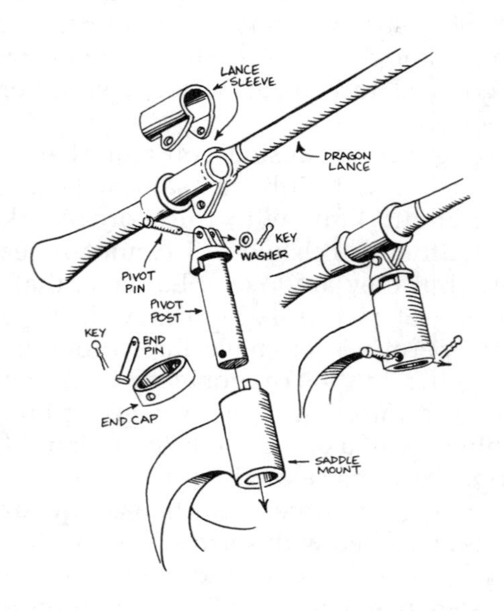

"Let me give you a boost," Tas said helpfully.

"I . . . no! Wait!" Flint yelled. But it did no good. The energetic kender had already grabbed hold of the dwarf's boot and heaved, propelling Flint head first right into the hard-muscled body of the young bronze dragon. Hands flailing wildly, Flint caught hold of the harness on the dragon's neck and hung on for dear life, revolving slowly in the air like a sack on a hook.

"What are you doing?" Tas asked in disgust, gazing up at Flint. "This is no time to play! Here, let me help—"

"Stop it! Let go!" roared Flint, kicking at Tasslehoff's hands. "Get back! Get back, I say!"

"Get up yourself, then," Tas said, hurt, backing up.

Puffing and red-faced, the dwarf dropped to the ground. "I'll get on in my own good time!" he said, glaring at the kender. "Without help from you!"

"Well, you'd better do it quickly!" Tas shouted, waving his arms. "Because the others are already mounted!"

The dwarf cast a glance back at the big bronze dragon and folded his arms across his chest stubbornly. "I've got to give this some thought—"

"Oh, come on, Flint!" Tas begged. "You're only stalling. I want to *fly!* Please, Flint, hurry!" The kender brightened. "I could go by myself. . . ."

"You'll do no such thing!" The dwarf snorted. "The war's finally turning in our favor. Send a kender up on a dragon and that'd be the end. We could just hand the Highlord the keys to the city. Laurana said the only way you'd fly is with me—"

"Then get on!" Tas yelled shrilly. "Or the war will be over! I'll be a grandfather before you move from that spot!"

"You a grandfather," Flint grumbled, glancing once more at the dragon, who was staring at him with a very unfriendly eye, or so the dwarf imagined. "Why, the day you're a grandfather is the day my beard will fall out—"

Khirsah,† the dragon, gazed down at the two with amused impatience. A young dragon, as dragons count their time on Krynn, Khirsah agreed with the kender: it was time to fly, time to fight. He had been one of the first to answer the Call that went out to all the gold and silver, bronze and brass dragons. The fire of battle burned hot within him.

Khirsah the bronze dragon later became known as "Tasslehoff's Dragon." He is the only dragon ever known to allow a dwarf or a kender to ride upon his back. Tas claimed that Khirsah has accompanied him on certain adventures following the war. If so, that would certainly be remarkable for the usually serious-minded dragons.

Yet, young as he was, the bronze dragon held a great reverence and respect for the elders of the world. Though vastly older than the dwarf in years, Khirsah saw in Flint one who had led a long, full, rich life; one worthy of respect. But, Khirsah thought with a sigh, if I don't do something, the kender's right—the battle *will* be over!

"Pardon me, Respected Sire," Khirsah interrupted, using a term of high respect among dwarves, "may I be of assistance?"

Startled, Flint whirled around to see who spoke.

The dragon bowed its great head. "Honored and Respected Sire," Khirsah said again, in dwarven.

Amazed, Flint stumbled backward, tripping over Tasslehoff and sending the kender tumbling to the ground in a heap.

The dragon snaked forth his huge head and, gently taking hold of the kender's fur vest in his great teeth, lifted him to his feet like a newborn kitten.

"Well, I—I don't know," stammered Flint, flushing in pleased embarrassment at being thus addressed by a dragon. "You might . . . and then again you might not." Recovering his dignity, the dwarf was determined not to act overawed. "I've done this a lot, mind you. Riding dragons is nothing new to me. It's just, well, just that I've—"

"You've never ridden a dragon before in your life!" Tasslehoff said indignantly. "And—ouch!"

"Just that I've had more important things on my mind lately," Flint said loudly, punching Tas in the ribs, "and it may take me a while to get the hang of it again."

"Certainly, Sire," Khirsah said without the ghost of a smile. "May I call you Flint?"

"You may," said the dwarf gruffly.

"And I'm Tasslehoff Burrfoot," said the kender, extending his small hand. "Flint never goes anywhere without me. Oh, I guess you haven't any hand to shake with. Never mind. What's your name?"

"My name to mortals is Fireflash." The dragon gracefully bowed his head. "And now, Sir Flint, if you will instruct your squire,† the kender—"

We'll just hope Tas doesn't know that a good squire can aspire to become a Knight of the Crown and begin to work his way up through the ranks of the Knights of Solamnia.

"Squire!" Tas repeated, shocked. But the dragon ignored him.

"Instruct your squire to come up here; I will help him prepare the saddle and the lance for you."

Flint stroked his beard thoughtfully. Then, he made a grand gesture.

"You, squire," he said to Tas, who was staring at him with his mouth open, "get up there and do as you're told."

"I—you—we—" Tas stuttered. But the kender never finished what he had been about to say because the dragon had lifted him off the ground again. Teeth clamped firmly in the kender's fur vest, Khirsah raised him up and plopped him back onto the saddle that was strapped to the dragon's bronze body.

So enchanted was Tas with the idea of actually being atop a dragon that he hushed up, which is just what Khirsah had intended.

"Now, Tasslehoff Burrfoot," said the dragon, "you were trying to boost your master up into the saddle backward. The correct position† is the one you are in now. The metal lance mounting must be on the front right side of the rider, sitting squarely forward of my right wing joint and above my right fore-shoulder. Do you see?"

"Yes, I see!" called Tas in high excitement.

"The shield, which you see on the ground, will protect you from most forms of dragonbreath—"

"Whoah!" shouted the dwarf, crossing his arms and looking stubborn once more. "What do you mean *most* forms? And how am I supposed to fly and hold a lance and a shield all at the same time? Not to mention the fact that the blasted shield's bigger than me and the kender put together—"

"I thought you had done this before, *Sir Flint!*" Tas yelled.

The dwarf's face went red with rage and he let out a bellow, but Khirsah cut in smoothly.

"Sir Flint probably isn't accustomed to this newer model, Squire Burrfoot. The shield fits over the lance. The lance itself fits through that hole and the shield rests on the saddle and slides from side to side on the track. When attacked, you simply duck behind it."

"Hand me the shield, Sir Flint!" the kender yelled.

Grumbling, the dwarf stumped over to where the huge shield lay on the ground. Groaning with the weight, he managed to lift it up and haul it over to the dragon's side. With the dragon's help, the dwarf and the kender between them managed to get the shield mounted. Then Flint went back for the dragonlance. Lugging it back, he thrust the tip of the lance up to Tas, who caught hold of it and, after nearly losing his balance and tumbling overboard, pushed the lance through the hole in the shield. When the pivot locked into position, the lance was counterbalanced and swung lightly and easily, guided by the kender's small hand.

"This is great!" Tas said, experimenting. "Wham! There goes one dragon! Wham! There goes another.

The TSR artists had to work out the mechanics of using a dragonlance mounted on a dragonsaddle.

I—oh!" Tas stood up on the dragon's back, balanced lightly as the lance itself. "Flint! Hurry! They're getting ready to leave. I can see Laurana! She's riding that big silver dragon and she's flying this way, checking the line. They're going to be signaling in a minute! Hurry, Flint!" Tas began jumping up and down in excitement.

"First, Sir Flint," said Khirsah, "you must put on the padded vest. There . . . that's right. Put the strap through that buckle. No, not that one. The other—there, you have it."

"You look like a woolly mammoth I saw once." Tas giggled. "Did I ever tell you that story? I—"

"Confound it!" Flint roared, barely able to walk, engulfed in the heavy, fur-lined vest. "This is no time for any of your hare-brained stories." The dwarf came nose-tip to nose-tip with the dragon. "Very well, beast! How do I get up? And mind you, don't you dare lay a tooth on me!"

"Certainly not, Sire," Khirsah said in deep respect. Bowing his head, the dragon extended one bronze wing full length upon the ground.

"Well, that's more like it!" Flint said. Smoothing his beard with pride, he shot a smug glance at the stunned kender. Then, solemnly mounting the dragon's wing, Flint ascended, regally taking his place at the front of the saddle.

"There's the signal!" Tas shrieked, leaping back into the saddle behind Flint. Kicking his heels against the dragon's flanks, he yelled, "Let's go! Let's go!"

"Not so fast," said Flint, coolly testing the workings of the dragonlance. "Hey! How do I steer?"

"You indicate which direction you want me to turn by pulling on the reins," Khirsah said, watching for the signal. There it was.

"Ah, I see," said Flint, reaching down. "After all, I am in charge—ulp!"

"Certainly, Sire!" Khirsah leaped into the air, spreading his great wings to catch the rising currents of air that floated up the face of the small cliff they stood upon.

"Wait, the reins—" Flint cried, grasping at them as they slid out of his reach.

Smiling to himself, Khirsah pretended not to hear.

Larry Elmore sketched the earliest portrayal of Caramon and Raistlin. Note the flying citadel's flat, geometrically precise base, as if sawed, not ripped from the ground. The twins, on the other hand, changed relatively little in later pictures.

The good dragons and the knights who rode them were gathered on the rolling foothills east of the Vingaard Mountains. Here, the chill winter winds had given way to warm breezes from the north, melting the frost from the ground. The rich smell of growth and renewal perfumed the air as the dragons rose in flashing arcs to take their places in formation.

It was a sight that took the breath away. Tasslehoff knew he would remember it forever—and maybe even beyond that. Bronze and silver, brass and copper wings flared in the morning light. The Greater Dragonlances,† mounted on the saddles, glittered in the sun. The knights' armor shone brilliantly. The Kingfisher flag with its golden thread sparkled against the blue sky.

Greater Lances are those that are most commonly identified as being Dragonlances. These are mounted lances affixed to special saddles via an ingenious swivel mechanism. This not only allows the rider to position the lance for greatest effect but also puts the full weight of the dragon behind the thrust as well without unseating the rider. Larry Elmore, during the development of DRAGONLANCE *at TSR, created an exploded schematic drawing of the lance and its dragon mounting on his own time at home. Part of this fascinating drawing became an illustration at the beginning of chapter 9. —TRH*

The past few weeks had been glorious. As Flint said, it seemed the tide of war was finally flowing in their direction.

The Golden General, as Laurana came to be called by her troops, had forged an army seemingly out of nothing. The Palanthians, caught up in the excitement, rallied to her cause. She won the respect of the Knights of Solamnia with her bold ideas and firm, decisive actions. Laurana's ground forces surged out of Palanthas, flowing across the plain, pressing the unorganized armies of the Dragon Highlord, known as the Dark Lady, into panic-stricken flight.

Now, with victory after victory behind them and the dragonarmies fleeing before them, the men considered the war as good as won.

But Laurana knew better. They had yet to fight the dragons of the Highlord. Where these were and why they had not fought before was something Laurana and her officers couldn't figure out. Day after day, she held the knights and their mounts in readiness, prepared to take to the air.

And now that day had come. The dragons had been sighted—flights of blues and reds reportedly heading westward to stop the insolent general and her rag-tag army.

In a shimmering chain of silver and bronze, the Dragons of Whitestone, as they were called, soared across the Solamnic Plain. Although all the dragon-mounted knights had been trained in flight as much as time allowed (with the exception of the dwarf who steadfastly refused), this world of wispy, low-hanging clouds and rushing air was still new and foreign to them.

Their banners whipped about wildly. The foot soldiers beneath them seemed no more than bugs crawling across the grasslands. To some of the knights, flying was an exhilarating experience. To others, it was a test of every bit of courage they possessed.

But always before them, leading them in spirit and by example, flew Laurana upon the great silver dragon her brother had ridden from the Dragon Isles.† The sunlight itself was not more golden than the hair that streamed out from beneath her helm. She had become a symbol to them like the dragonlance itself—slender and delicate, fair and deadly. They would have followed her to the Gates of the Abyss itself.

The Dragon Isles are a group of largely unknown islands approximately at Krynn's equator. Legends say they shift in shape and position when human ships approach. Many a captain has reported pursuing one of the isles out to sea only to be closed upon by night. Apparently the metallic dragons took up residence in the City of Gold on Misty Isle. Other beings and people reside on the seven other islands. See The Dragon Isles *by Stephen D. Sullivan.*

Tasslehoff, peering over Flint's shoulder, could see Laurana ahead of them. She rode at the head of the line, sometimes looking back to make certain everyone was keeping up, sometimes bending down to consult with her silver mount. She seemed to have things well under control, so Tas decided he could relax and enjoy the ride. It was truly one of the most wondrous experiences of his life. Tears streaked his wind-blown face as he stared down in absolute joy.

The map-loving kender had found the perfect map.

Below him was spread, in tiny, perfect detail, rivers and trees, hills and valleys, towns and farms. More than anything in the world, Tas wished he could capture the sight and keep it forever.

Why not? he wondered suddenly. Clinging to the saddle with his knees and thighs, the kender let go of Flint and began rummaging around in his pouches. Dragging out a sheet of parchment, he rested it firmly against the dwarf's back and began to draw on it with a piece of charcoal.

"Quit wiggling!" he shouted at Flint, who was still trying to grab the reins.

"What're you doing, you doorknob?" the dwarf yelled, pawing frantically at Tas behind his back like an itch he couldn't scratch.

"I'm making a map!" Tas yelled in ecstasy. "The *perfect* map! I'll be famous. Look! There are our own

troops, like little ants. And there's Vingaard Keep! Stop moving! You made me mess up."

Groaning, Flint gave up trying to either grasp the reins or brush away the kender. He decided he had better concentrate on keeping a firm grip on both the dragon and his breakfast. He had made the mistake of looking down. Now he stared straight ahead, shivering, his body rigid. The hair from the mane of a griffon that decorated his helm whipped about his face wildly in the rushing wind. Birds wheeled in the skies *beneath* him. Flint decided then and there that dragons were going on his list with boats and horses as Things to Avoid at All Costs.†

Other items on his list: kender, boats, gnomes, gully dwarves, horses, kender, string beans, bad ale, wizards, kender, oatmeal, kender, kender, kender ...—MW

"Oh!" Tas gasped in excitement. "There are the dragonarmies! It's a battle! And I can see the whole thing!" The kender leaned over in the saddle, peering down. Now and again, through the rushing eddies of air, he thought he could hear the clash of armor and cries and shouts. "Say, could we fly a bit closer? I—whoops! Oh, no! My map!"

Khirsah had made a sudden, swooping dive. The force ripped the parchment from Tas's hands. Forlornly he watched it flutter away from him like a leaf. But he hadn't time to feel sad, for suddenly he felt Flint's body go even more rigid than before.

"What? What is it?" Tas yelled.

Flint was shouting something and pointing. Tas tried desperately to see and hear, but at that moment they flew into a low-hanging cloud and the kender couldn't see his nose in front of his face, as the gully dwarves said.

Then Khirsah emerged from the cloud bank and Tas saw.

"Oh my!" said the kender in awe. Below them, bearing down on the small antlike troops of men, flew line after line of dragons. Their red and blue leathery wings spread like evil banners as they dove down upon the helpless armies of the Golden General.

Tasslehoff could see the solid lines of men waver and break as the terrible dragonfear swept over them. But there was nowhere to run, nowhere to hide on the broad grasslands. This is why the dragons had waited, Tas realized, sick with the thought of the fire and lightning breath exploding among the unprotected troops.

"We've got to stop them—oof!"

Khirsah wheeled so suddenly that Tas nearly swallowed his tongue. The sky flipped over on its side and for an instant the kender had the most interesting sensation of falling *up*. More by instinct than conscious thought, Tas grabbed hold of Flint's belt, remembering suddenly that he was supposed to have strapped himself in as Flint had done. Well, he would do so next time.

If there was a next time. The wind roared around him, the ground spun below him as the dragon spiraled downward. Kenders were fond of new experiences, and this was certainly one of the most exciting, but Tas *did* wish the ground wasn't rushing up to meet them quite so *fast!*

"I didn't mean we had to stop them *right now!*" Tas shouted to Flint. Glancing up—or was it down?—he could see the other dragons far above them, no, below them. Things were getting all muddled. Now the dragons were *behind* them! They were out here in front! Alone! What was Flint doing?

"Not so fast! Slow this thing down!" he yelled at Flint. "You've gotten ahead of everybody! Even Laurana!"

The dwarf would have liked nothing better than to slow the dragon down. That last swoop had tossed the reins within his reach and now he was tugging with all his might, shouting "Whoah, beast, whoah!" which he dimly remembered was supposed to work with horses. But it wasn't working with the dragon.

It was no comfort to the terrified dwarf to notice that he wasn't the only one having trouble managing the dragons. Behind him, the delicate line of bronze and silver broke as if by some silent signal, as the dragons veered off into small groups—flights—of twos and threes.

Frantically the knights jerked on the reins, endeavoring to pull the dragons back into straight and orderly cavalry rows. But the dragons knew better, the sky was their domain. Fighting in the air was far different from fighting on the ground. They would show these horse riders how to fight on dragonback.

Spinning gracefully, Khirsah dove into another cloud, and Tas instantly lost all sense of up or

down as the thick fog enveloped him. Then the sunlit sky exploded before his eyes as the dragon burst out. Now he knew which way was up and which was down. *Down* was, in fact, getting uncomfortably close!

Then Flint roared. Startled, Tas looked up and saw that they were heading straight into a flight of blue dragons who, intent upon pursuing a group of panic-stricken foot soldiers, hadn't seen them yet.

"The lance! The lance!" Tas shouted.

Flint grappled with the lance, but he didn't have time to adjust it or set it properly against his shoulder. Not that it mattered. The blue dragons still hadn't seen them. Gliding out of the cloud, Khirsah fell in behind them. Then, like a bronze flame, the young dragon flashed over the group of blues, aiming for their leader, a big blue dragon with a blue-helmed rider. Diving swiftly and silently, Khirsah struck the lead dragon with all four murderously sharp talons.

The force of the impact threw Flint forward in his harness. Tas landed on top of him, flattening the dwarf. Frantically, Flint struggled to sit up, but Tas had one arm wrapped around him tightly. Beating the dwarf on the helm with the other, Tas was shouting encouragement to the dragon.

"That was great! Hit him again!" shrieked the kender, wild with excitement, pounding Flint on the head.

Swearing loudly in dwarven, Flint flung Tas off him. At that moment, Khirsah soared upward, darting into another cloud before the flight of blues could react to his attack.

Khirsah waited for an instant, perhaps to give his shaken riders time to pull themselves together. Flint sat up and Tas clasped his arms around the dwarf tightly. He thought Flint looked strange, sort of gray-colored and oddly preoccupied. But then this certainly wasn't a normal experience, Tas reminded himself. Before he could ask Flint if he felt all right, Khirsah dove out of the cloud once more.

Tas could see the blue dragons below them. The lead dragon had pulled up in mid-air, hovering on his great wings. The blue was shaken and wounded slightly; there was blood on the rear flanks where Khirsah's sharp talons had punctured the dragon's

tough, scaly hide. The dragon and his blue-helmed rider were both scanning the skies, searching for their attacker. Suddenly the rider pointed.

Risking a quick glance behind him, Tas caught his breath. The sight was magnificent. Bronze and silver flashed in the sun as the Whitestone Dragons broke out of the cloud cover and descended screaming upon the flight of blues. Instantly the flight broke as the blues fought to gain altitude and keep their pursuers from attacking them from behind. Here and there battles broke out. Lightning cracked and flared, nearly blinding the kender, as a great bronze dragon to his right screamed in pain and fell from the air, its head blackened and burning. Tas saw its rider helplessly grasping the reins, his mouth opened in a scream the kender could see but not hear as dragon and rider plunged to the ground below.

Tas stared at the ground rushing closer and closer and wondered in a dreamlike haze what it would be like to smash into the grass. But he didn't have time to wonder long, because suddenly Khirsah let out a roar.

The blue leader spotted Khirsah and heard his ringing challenge. Ignoring the other dragons fighting in the skies around him, the blue leader and his rider flew up to continue their duel with the bronze.

"Now it is your turn, dwarf! Set the lance!" Khirsah yelled. Lifting his great wings, the bronze soared up and up, gaining altitude for maneuvering and also giving the dwarf time to prepare.

"I'll hold the reins!" Tas shouted.

But the kender couldn't tell if Flint heard him or not. The dwarf's face was rigid and he was moving slowly and mechanically. Wild with impatience, Tas could do nothing but hang onto the reins and watch while Flint fumbled with gray fingers until he finally managed to fix the hilt of the lance beneath his shoulder and brace it as he had been taught. Then he just stared straight ahead, his face empty of all expression.

Khirsah continued rising, then leveled off, and Tas looked around, wondering where their enemies were. He had completely lost sight of the blue and its rider. Then Khirsah suddenly leaped

upward and Tas gasped. *There* was their enemy, right ahead of them!

He saw the blue open his hideous fanged mouth. Remembering the lightning, Tas ducked behind the shield. Then he saw that Flint was still sitting straight-backed, staring grimly out over the shield at the approaching dragon! Reaching around Flint's waist, Tas grabbed hold of the dwarf's beard and yanked his head downward, behind the shield.

Lightning flared and crackled around them. The instant booming thunder nearly knocked both kender and dwarf senseless. Khirsah roared in pain but held true upon his course.

The dragons struck, head-on, and the dragonlance speared its victim.

For an instant all Tas could see were blurs of blue and red. The world spun round and round. Once a dragon's hideous, fiery eyes stared at him balefully. Claws flashed. Khirsah shrieked, the blue screamed. Wings beat upon the air. The ground spiraled round and round as the struggling dragons fell.

Why doesn't Fireflash let go? Tas thought frantically. Then he could see,

We're locked together! Tasslehoff realized numbly.

The dragonlance had missed its mark. Striking the wingbone joint of the blue dragon, the lance had bent into his shoulder and was now lodged tight. Desperately the blue fought to free himself, but Khirsah, now filled with battle rage, lashed out at the blue with his sharp fangs and ripping taloned front feet.

Intent upon their own battle, both dragons had completely forgotten their riders. Tas had forgotten the other rider, too, until, glancing up helplessly, he saw the blue-helmed dragon officer clinging precariously to his saddle only a few feet away.

Then sky and ground became a blur once more as the dragons whirled and fought. Tas watched in a haze as the blue helm of the officer fell from his head, and the officer's blonde hair whipped in the wind. His eyes were cold and bright and not the least afraid. He stared straight into Tasslehoff's eyes.

He looks familiar, thought Tas with an odd sort of detachment, as if this were happening to some other kender while he watched. Where could I have seen him before? Thoughts of Sturm came to his mind.

The dragon officer freed himself from his harness and stood up in the stirrups. One arm—his right arm—hung limply at his side, but his other hand was reaching forward—

Everything became very clear to Tas suddenly. He knew exactly what the officer intended to do. It was as if the man spoke to him, telling him his plans.

"Flint!" cried Tas frantically. "Release the lance! Release it!"

But the dwarf held onto the lance fast, that strange faraway look on his face. The dragons fought and clawed and bit in mid-air; the blue twisting, trying to free himself from the lance as well as fend off its attacker. Tas saw the blue's rider shout something, and the blue broke off its attack for an instant, holding himself steady in the air.

With remarkable agility, the officer leaped from one dragon to the other. Grasping Khirsah around the neck with his good arm, the dragon officer pulled himself upright, his strong legs and thighs clamping themselves firmly onto the struggling dragon's neck.

Khirsah paid the human no attention. His thoughts were fixed totally on his enemy.

The officer cast one quick glance back at the kender and the dwarf behind him and saw that neither was likely to be a threat, strapped, as they must be, into place. Coolly the officer drew his longsword and, leaning down, began to slash at the bronze dragon's harness straps where they crossed across the beast's chest, ahead of the great wings.

"Flint!" pleaded Tas. "Release the lance! Look!" The kender shook the dwarf. "If that officer cuts through the harness, our saddle will fall off! The lance will fall off! *We'll* fall off!"

Flint turned his head slowly, suddenly understanding. Still moving with agonizing slowness, his shaking hand fumbled at the mechanism that would release the lance and free the dragons from their deadly embrace. But would it be in time?

Tas saw the longsword flash in the air. He saw one of the harness straps sag and flutter free. There wasn't time to think or plan. While Flint grappled with the release, Tas, rising up precariously, wrapped the reins around his waist. Then, hanging onto the edge of the saddle, the kender crawled

around the dwarf until he was in front of him. Here he lay down flat along the dragon's neck and, wrapping his legs around the dragon's spiny mane, he wormed his way forward and came up silently behind the officer.

The man wasn't paying any attention to the riders behind him, assuming both were safely locked in their harnesses. Intent upon his work—the harness was nearly free—he never knew what hit him.

Rising up, Tasslehoff leaped onto the officer's back. Startled, scrabbling wildly to keep himself balanced, the officer let his sword fall as he clung desperately to the dragon's neck.

Snarling in rage, the officer tried to see what had struck him when suddenly everything went dark! Small arms wrapped themselves around his head, blinding him. Frantically the officer let go of his hold on the dragon in an effort to free himself of what seemed to his enraged mind to be a creature with six legs and arms, all of them clinging to him with a buglike tenacity. But he felt himself start to slide off the dragon and was forced to grab hold of the mane.

"Flint! Release the lance! Flint . . ." Tas didn't even know what he was saying anymore. The ground was rushing up to meet him as the weakened dragons toppled from the skies. He couldn't think. White flashes of light burst in his head as he clung with all his strength to the officer, who was still struggling beneath him.

Then a great metallic bang sounded.

The lance released. The dragons were freed.

Spreading his wings, Khirsah pulled out of his spinning dive and leveled off. The sky and ground resumed their proper, correct positions. Tears streamed down Tas's cheeks. He hadn't been frightened,† he told himself, sobbing. But nothing had ever looked so beautiful as that blue, blue sky, back up where it should be!

We see that Tas's fear is not for himself, but for others.—MW

"Are you all right, Fireflash?" Tas yelled.

The bronze nodded wearily.

"I've got a prisoner," Tas called, suddenly realizing that fact himself. Slowly he let go of the man, who shook his head dizzily, half-choked.

"I guess you're not going anywhere," Tas muttered. Sliding off the man's back, the kender crawled down the mane toward the dragon's

shoulders. Tas saw the officer look up into the skies, and clench his fist in bitter rage as he watched his dragons being slowly driven from the skies by Laurana and her forces. In particular, the officer's gaze fixed on Laurana, and suddenly Tas knew where he had seen him before.

The kender caught his breath. "You better take us down to the ground, Fireflash!" he cried, his hands shaking. "Hurry!"

The dragon arched his head to look around at his riders, and Tas saw that one eye was swollen shut. There were scorch and burn marks all along one side of the bronze head, and blood dripped from a torn nostril. Tas glanced around for the blue. He was nowhere to be seen.

Looking back at the officer, Tas suddenly felt wonderful. It occurred to him what he had done.

"Hey!" he yelled in elation, turning around to Flint. "We *did* it! We fought a dragon and *I* captured a prisoner! Single-handed!"

Flint nodded slowly. Turning back, Tas watched as the ground rose up to meet him, and the kender thought it had never looked so . . . so wonderfully groundlike before!

Khirsah landed. The foot-soldiers gathered around them, yelling and cheering. Someone led the officer away, Tas was not sorry to see him go, noticing that the officer gave him a sharp, penetrating look before he was led off. But then the kender forgot him as he glanced up at Flint.

The dwarf was slumped over the saddle, his face old and tired-looking, his lips blue.

"What's the matter?"

"Nothing."

"But you're holding your chest. Are you wounded?"

"No, I'm not."

"Then why are you holding your chest?"

Flint scowled. "I suppose I'll have no peace until I answer you. Well, if you must know, it's that confounded lance! And whoever designed this stupid vest was a bigger ninny than you are! The shaft of the lance drove right into my collarbone. I'll be black and blue for a week. And as for your prisoner, it's a wonder you weren't both killed, you rattlebrain! Captured, humpf! More like an accident, if

you ask me. And I'll tell you something else! I'm never getting on another one of those great beasts as long as I live!"

Flint shut his lips with an angry snap, glaring at the kender so fiercely that Tas turned around and walked quickly away, knowing that when Flint was in *that* kind of mood, it was best to leave him alone to cool off. He'd feel better after lunch.

It wasn't until that night, when Tasslehoff was curled up next to Khirsah, resting comfortably against the dragon's great bronze flank, that he remembered Flint had been clutching the left side of his chest.

The lance had been on the old dwarf's right.

BOOK 2

I

Spring Dawning.

Kalaman is on the northern coast of Solamnia, between Palanthas and Nordmaar. It is where the Dark Queen's flying citadels were first seen. Its recapture by the Golden General marked the beginning of the end for the dragonarmies—or so people said.

As the day dawned, pink and golden light spreading across the land, the citizens of Kalaman woke to the sound of bells. Leaping out of bed, children invaded parental bedrooms, demanding that mother and father arise so that this special day could get underway. Though some grumbled and feigned to pull the blankets over their heads, most parents laughingly climbed out of bed, not less eager than their children.

Today was a memorable day in the history of Kalaman.† Not only was it the annual Spring Dawning festival, it was also a victory celebration for the armies of the Knights of Solamnia. Camped on the plains outside the walled city, the army, led by its now-legendary general, an elfwoman, would be making a triumphal entry into the city at noon.

As the sun peeped over the walls, the sky above Kalaman was filled with the smoke of cooking fires, and soon smells of sizzling ham and warm muffins, frying bacon and exotic coffees rousted even the sleepiest from warm beds. They would have been roused soon enough anyway, for almost immediately the streets were filled with children. All discipline was relaxed on the occasion of Spring Dawning. After a long winter of being cooped up indoors, children were allowed to "run wild" for a day. By nightfall there would be bruised heads, skinned knees, and stomach aches from too many sweets. But all would remember it as a glorious day.

By mid-morning the festival was in full swing. Vendors hawked their wares in gaily colored booths. The gullible lost their money on games of chance. Dancing bears capered in the streets, and illusionists drew gasps of amazement from young and old.

Then at noon the bells rang out again. The streets cleared. People lined the sidewalks. The city gates were flung open, and the Knights of Solamnia prepared to enter Kalaman.

An expectant hush came over the crowd. Peering ahead eagerly, they jostled to get a good view of the Knights, particularly the elfwoman† of whom they had heard so many stories. She rode in first, alone, mounted on a pure white horse. The crowd, prepared to cheer, found themselves unable to speak, so awed were they by the woman's beauty and majesty. Dressed in flashing silver armor decorated with beaten gold work, Laurana guided her steed through the city gates and into the streets. A delegation of children had been carefully rehearsed to strew flowers in Laurana's path, but so overcome were the children at the sight of the lovely woman in the glittering armor that they clutched their flowers and never threw a single one.

When did Laurana stop being an "elfmaid" and became an "elfwoman"?

The change is simply a recognition of her improving social status in the eyes of the world.
—TRH

Behind the golden-haired elfmaiden rode two who caused not a few in the crowd to point in wonder—a kender and a dwarf, mounted together on a shaggy pony with a back as broad as a barrel. The kender seemed to be having a wonderful time, yelling and waving to the crowds. But the dwarf, sitting behind him, grasping him around the waist with a deathlike grip, was sneezing so badly he

seemed likely to sneeze himself right off the back of the animal.

Following the dwarf and kender rode an elflord, so like the elfmaiden that no one in the crowd needed his neighbor to tell him they were brother and sister. Beside the elflord rode another elfmaid with strange silver hair and deep blue eyes, who seemed shy and nervous among the crowd. Then came the the Knights of Solamnia, perhaps seventy-five strong, resplendent in gleaming armor. The crowd began to cheer, waving flags in the air.

A few of the Knights exchanged grim glances at this, all of them thinking that if they had ridden into Kalaman only a month before, they would have received a far different reception. But now they were heroes. Three hundred years of hatred and bitterness and unjust accusations were wiped from the minds of the public as they cheered those who had saved them from the terrors of the dragonarmies.

Marching after the Knights were several thousand footmen. And then, to the great delight of the crowd, the sky above the city filled with dragons—not the dreaded flights of red and blue the people had feared all winter. Instead, the sun flashed off wings of silver and bronze and gold as the awesome creatures circled and dove and pivoted in their well-organized flights. Knights sat in the dragonsaddles, the barbed blades of the dragonlances sparkling in the morning light.

After the parade, the citizens gathered to hear their Lord speak a few words in honor of the heroes. Laurana blushed to hear it told that she alone was responsible for the discovery of the dragonlances, the return of the good dragons, and the tremendous victories of the armies. Stammering, she tried to deny this, gesturing to her brother and to the Knights. But the yells and cheers of the crowd drowned her out. Helplessly Laurana looked at Lord Michael, Grand Master Gunthar Uth Wistan's representative, who had lately arrived from Sancrist. Michael only grinned.

"Let them have their hero," he said to her above the shouting. "Or heroine, I should say. They deserve it. All winter they lived in fear, waiting for the day the dragons would appear in the skies. Now

they have a beautiful heroine who rides out of children's tales to save them."

"But it's not true!" Laurana protested, edging nearer Michael to make herself heard. Her arms were filled with winter roses. Their fragrance was cloying, but she dared not offend anyone by setting them aside. "I didn't ride out of a children's story. I rode out of fire and darkness and blood. Putting me in command was a political stratagem of Lord Gunthar's, we both know that. And if my brother and Silvara hadn't risked their lives to bring the good dragons, we'd be parading down these streets in chains behind the Dark Lady."

"Bah! This is good for them. Good for us, too," Michael added, glancing at Laurana out of the corner of his eye as he waved to the crowd. "A few weeks ago we couldn't have begged the Lord to give us a crust of stale bread. Now, because of the Golden General, he's agreed to garrison the army in the town, provide us with supplies, horses, anything we want. Young men are flocking to join up. Our ranks will be swelled by a thousand or more before we leave for Dargaard. And you've lifted the morale of our own troops. You saw the Knights as they were in the High Clerist's Tower—look at them now."

Yes, thought Laurana bitterly. I saw them. Split by dissension among their own ranks, fallen into dishonor, bickering and plotting among themselves. It took the death of a fine and noble man to bring them to their senses. Laurana closed her eyes. The noise, the smell of the roses, which always brought Sturm to her mind, the exhaustion of battle, the heat of the noonday sun, all crashed over her in a stifling wave. She grew dizzy and feared she might faint. The thought was mildly amusing. How would that look—for the Golden General to keel over like a wilted flower?

Then she felt a strong arm around her.

"Steady, Laurana," said Gilthanas, supporting her. Silvara was beside her, taking the roses from her arms. Sighing, Laurana opened her eyes and smiled weakly at the Lord, who was just concluding his second speech of the morning to thunderous applause.

I'm trapped, Laurana realized. She would have to sit here the rest of the afternoon, smiling and waving and enduring speech after speech praising her heroism when all she wanted was to lie down in some dark, cool place and sleep. And it was all a lie, all a sham. If only they knew the truth. What if she stood up and told them she was so frightened during the battles that she could remember details only in her nightmares? Told them that she was nothing but a game piece for the Knights? Told them that she was here only because she had run away from her home, a spoiled little girl chasing after a half-elven man who didn't love her. What would they say?

"And now"—the Lord of Kalaman's voice rang out above the noise of the crowd—"it is my honor and my very great privilege to present to you the woman who has turned the tide of this war, the woman who has sent the dragonarmies fleeing for their lives over the plains, the woman who has driven the evil dragons from the sky, the woman whose armies captured the evil Bakaris, commander of the Dragon Highlord's armies, the woman whose name is even now being coupled with the great Huma's as the most valiant warrior on Krynn. Within a week, she will be riding to Dargaard Keep to demand the surrender of the Dragon Highlord known as the Dark Lady. . . ."

The Lord's voice was drowned in cheering. He paused dramatically, then, reaching behind him, caught hold of Laurana and nearly dragged her forward.

"Lauralanthalasa of the Royal House of Qualinesti!"

The noise was deafening. It reverberated off the tall stone buildings. Laurana looked out over the sea of open mouths and wildly waving flags. They don't want to hear about my fear, she realized wearily. They've fears enough of their own. They don't want to hear about darkness and death. They want children's tales about love and rebirth and silver dragons.

Don't we all.

With a sigh, Laurana turned to Silvara. Taking the roses back, she held them up into the air, waving to the jubilant crowd. Then she began her speech.

Tasslehoff Burrfoot was having a splendid time. It had been an easy task to evade Flint's watchful

gaze and slip off the platform where he had been told to stand with the rest of the dignitaries. Melting into the crowd, he was now free to explore this interesting city again. Long ago, he'd come to Kalaman with his parents and he cherished fond memories of the open-air bazaar, the seaport where the white-winged ships lay at anchor, and a hundred other wonders.

Idly he wandered among the festive crowd, his keen eyes seeing everything, his hands busy stuffing objects into his pouches. Really, Tas thought, the people of Kalaman were extremely careless! Purses had the most uncanny habit of falling from people's belts into Tas's hands. The streets might be paved with jewels the way he discovered rings and other fascinating trinkets.

Then the kender was transported into realms of delight when he came across a cartographer's stall. And, as fortune would have it, the cartographer had gone to watch the parade. The stall was locked and shuttered, with a large "CLOSED" sign hanging on a hook.

"What a pity," thought Tas. "But I'm sure he wouldn't mind if I just looked at his maps." Reaching out, he gave the lock an expert twitch, then smiled happily. A few more "twitches" and it would open easily. "He mustn't really mean for people to keep out if he puts on such a simple-minded lock. I'll just pop in and copy a few of his maps to update my collection."

Suddenly Tas felt a hand on his shoulder. Irritated that someone should bother him at a time like this, the kender glanced around to see a strange figure that seemed vaguely familiar. It was dressed in heavy cloaks and robes, though the spring day was warming rapidly. Even its hands were wrapped in cloth, like bandages. Bother—a cleric, thought the kender, annoyed and preoccupied.

"I beg your pardon," said Tas to the cleric who had hold of him, "I don't mean to be rude, but I was just—"

"Burrfoot?" interrupted the cleric in a cold, lisping voice. "The kender who rides with the Golden General?"

"Why, yes," Tas said, flattered that someone had recognized him. "That's me. I've ridden with Laura—

the, er—Golden General—for a long time now. Let's see, I think it was in the late fall. Yes, we met her in Qualinesti right after we escaped from the hobgoblins' prison wagons which was a short time after we killed a black dragon in Xak Tsaroth. That's the most wonderful story—" Tas forgot about the maps. "You see we were in this old, old city that had fallen into a cavern and it was filled with gully dwarves. We met one named Bupu, who had been charmed by Raistlin—"

"Shut up!" The cleric's wrapped hand went from Tasslehoff's shoulder to the collar of his shirt. Gripping it expertly, the cleric twisted it with a sudden jerk of its hand and lifted the kender off his feet. Although kender are generally immune to the emotion of fear, Tas found that being unable to breathe was an extremely uncomfortable sensation.

"Listen to me carefully," the cleric hissed, shaking the frantically struggling kender as a wolf shakes a bird to break its neck. "That's right. Hold still and it hurts less. I've got a message for the Golden General." Its voice was soft and lethal. "It's here—" Tas felt a rough hand stuffing something into his vest pocket. "See that you deliver it some time tonight when she's alone. Understand?"

Choked by the cleric's hand, Tas couldn't speak or even nod, but he blinked his eyes twice. The cloaked head nodded, dropped the kender back to the ground, and walked rapidly off down the street.

Gasping for breath, the shaken kender stared at the figure as it walked away, its long robes fluttering in the wind. Tas absently patted the scroll that had been thrust into his pocket. The sound of that voice brought back very unpleasant memories: the ambush on the road from Solace, heavily cloaked figures like clerics . . . only they weren't clerics! Tas shuddered. A draconian! Here! In Kalaman!

Shaking his head, Tas turned back to the cartographer's stall. But the pleasure had gone out of the day. He couldn't even feel excited when the lock fell open into his small hand.

"Hey, you!" shrieked a voice. "Kender! Get away from there!"

A man was running up to him, puffing and red in the face. Probably the cartographer himself.

"You shouldn't have run," Tas said listlessly. "You needn't bother opening up for me."

"Opening!" The man's jaw sagged. "Why, you little thief! I got here just in time—"

"Thanks all the same." Tas dropped the lock into the man's hand and walked off, absent-mindedly evading the enraged cartographer's effort to grab him. "I'll be going now. I'm not feeling very well. Oh, by the way, did you know that lock's broken? Worthless. You should be more careful. You never know who could sneak in. No, don't thank me. I haven't got time. Good-bye."

Tasslehoff wandered off. Cries of "Thief! Thief!" rang out behind him. A town guardsman appeared, forcing Tas to duck into a butcher's shop to avoid being run over. Shaking his head over the corruption of the world, the kender glanced about, hoping for a glimpse of the culprit. Seeing no one interesting in sight, he kept going, and suddenly wondered irritably how Flint had managed to lose him again.

Laurana shut the door, turned the key in the lock, and leaned thankfully against it, reveling in the peace and quiet and welcome solitude of her room. Tossing the key on a table, she walked wearily over to her bed, not even bothering to light a candle. The rays of the silver moon streamed in through the leaded glass panes of the long, narrow window.

Downstairs, in the lower rooms of the castle, she could still hear the sounds of merrymaking she had just left. It was nearly midnight. She had been trying for two hours to escape. It finally took Lord Michael's intercession on her behalf, pleading her exhaustion from the battles, that induced the lords and ladies of the city of Kalaman to part with her.

Her head ached from the stuffy atmosphere, the smell of strong perfume, and too much wine. She shouldn't have drunk so much, she knew. She had a weak head for wine and, anyway, she didn't really like it. But the pain in her head was easier to bear than the pain in her heart.

Throwing herself down on the bed, she thought hazily about getting up and closing the shutters, but the moon's light was comforting. Laurana detested lying in the darkness. Things lurked in the shadows, ready to spring out at her. I should get undressed,

Probably from the Lord of Kalaman's wife.

she thought, I'll wrinkle this dress . . . and it's borrowed. . . .†

There was a knock at her door.

Laurana woke with a start, trembling. Then she remembered where she was. Sighing, she lay very still, closing her eyes again. Surely they'd realize she was asleep and go away.

There was another knock, more insistent than the first.

"Laurana . . ."

"Tell me in the morning, Tas," Laurana said, trying to keep the irritation from her voice.

"It's important, Laurana," Tas called. "Flint's with me."

Laurana heard a scuffling sound outside the door.

"Come on, tell her—"

"I will not! This was your doing!"

"But he said it was important and I—"

"All right, I'm coming!" Laurana sighed. Stumbling out of bed, she fumbled for the key on the table, unlocked the door, and flung it open.

"Hi, Laurana!" Tas said brightly, walking inside. "Wasn't that a wonderful party? I've never eaten roast peacock before—"

"What is it, Tas?" Laurana sighed, shutting the door behind them.

Seeing her pale, drawn face, Flint poked the kender in the back. Giving the dwarf a reproachful look, Tas reached into the pocket of his fleecy vest and drew forth a rolled scroll of parchment, tied with a blue ribbon.

"A-a cleric—sort of—said to give this to you, Laurana," Tas said.

"Is that all?" Laurana asked impatiently, snatching the scroll from the kender's hand. "It's probably a marriage proposal. I've had twenty in the last week. Not to mention proposals of a more unique nature."

"Oh, no," said Tas, suddenly serious. "It's not anything like that, Laurana. It's from . . ." He stopped.

"How do you know who it's from?" Laurana fixed the kender with a piercing gaze.

"I—uh—guess I—sort of—glanced at it—" Tas admitted. Then he brightened. "But it was only because I didn't want to bother you with anything that wasn't important."

Flint snorted.

"Thank you," Laurana said. Unrolling the scroll, she walked over to stand by the window where the moonlight was bright enough to read by.

"We'll leave you alone," Flint said gruffly, herding the protesting kender toward the door.

"No! Wait!" Laurana choked. Flint turned, staring at her in alarm.

"Are you all right?" he said, hurrying over to her as she sank down into a nearby chair. "Tas—get Silvara!"

"No, no. Don't bring anyone. I'm . . . all right. Do you know what this says?" she asked in a whisper.

"I tried to tell him," Tasslehoff said in an injured voice, "but he wouldn't let me."

Her hand shaking, Laurana handed the scroll to Flint.

The dwarf opened it and read aloud.

"Tanis Half-Elven received a wound in the battle of Vingaard Keep. Although at first he believed it was slight, it has worsened so that he is past even the help of the dark clerics. I ordered that he be brought to Dargaard Keep,† where I could care for him. Tanis knows the gravity of his injury. He asks that he be allowed to be with you when he dies, that he may explain matters to you and so rest with an easy spirit.

Dargaard Keep is where the death knight Lord Soth lives, currently with Kitiara in residence.

"I make you this offer. You have as your captive my officer, Bakaris, who was captured near Vingaard Keep. I will exchange Tanis Half-Elven for Bakaris. The exchange will take place at dawn tomorrow in a grove of trees beyond the city walls. Bring Bakaris with you. If you are mistrustful, you may also bring Tanis's friends, Flint Fireforge and Tasslehoff Burrfoot. But no one else! The bearer of this note waits outside the city gate. Meet him tomorrow at sunrise. If he deems all is well, he will escort you to the half-elf. If not, you will never see Tanis alive.

"I do this only because we are two women who understand each other.

"Kitiara"

There was an uneasy silence, then, "Humpf," Flint snorted, and rolled up the scroll.

"How can you be so calm!" Laurana gasped, snatching the scroll from the dwarf's hand. "And

you"—her gaze switched angrily to Tasslehoff—"why didn't you tell me before now? How long have you known? You *read* he was dying, and you're so— so—"

Laurana put her head in her hands.

Tas stared at her, his mouth open. "Laurana," he said after a moment, "surely you don't think Tanis—"

Laurana's head snapped up. Her dark, stricken eyes went to Flint, then to Tas. "You don't believe this message is real, do you?" she asked incredulously.

"Of course not!" Flint said.

"No," scoffed Tas. "It's a trick! A *draconian* gave it to me! Besides Kitiara's a Dragon Highlord now. What would Tanis be doing with her—"

Laurana turned her face away abruptly. Tasslehoff stopped and glanced at Flint, whose own face suddenly seemed to age.

"So that's it," the dwarf said softly. "We saw you talking to Kitiara on the wall of the High Clerist's Tower. You were discussing more than Sturm's death, weren't you?"

Laurana nodded, wordlessly, staring at her hands in her lap.

"I never told you," she murmured in a voice barely audible, "I couldn't . . . I kept hoping. . . . Kitiara said . . . said she'd left Tanis in—some place called Flotsam . . . to look after things while she was gone."

"Liar!" said Tas promptly.

"No." Laurana shook her head. "When she says we are two women who understand each other, she's right. She wasn't lying. She was telling the truth, I know. And at the Tower she mentioned the dream." Laurana lifted her head. "Do you remember the dream?"

Flint nodded uncomfortably. Tasslehoff shuffled his feet.

"Only Tanis could have told her about the dream we all shared," Laurana continued, swallowing a choking feeling in her throat. "I saw him with her in the dream, just as I saw Sturm's death. The dream's coming true. . . ."

"Now wait a minute," Flint said gruffly, grabbing hold of reality as a drowning man grabs a piece of

wood. "You said yourself you saw your own death in the dream, right after Sturm's. And you didn't die. And nothing hacked up Sturm's body, either."

"I haven't died yet, like I did in the dream," Tas said helpfully. "And I've picked lots of locks, well, not lots, but a few here and there, and none were poisoned. Besides, Laurana, Tanis wouldn't —"

Flint shot Tas a warning glance. The kender lapsed into silence. But Laurana had seen the glance and understood. Her lips tightened.

"Yes, he would. You both know it. He loves her." Laurana was quiet a moment, then, "I'm going. I'll exchange Bakaris."

Flint heaved a sigh. He had seen this coming. "Laurana—"

"Wait a minute, Flint," she interrupted. "If Tanis received a message saying you were dying, what would he do?"

"That's not the point," Flint mumbled.

"If he had to go into the Abyss itself, past a thousand dragons, he'd come to you—"

"Perhaps and perhaps not," said Flint gruffly. "Not if he was leader of an army. Not if he had responsibilities, people depending on him. He'd know I'd understand—"

Laurana's face might have been carved of marble, so impassive and pure and cold was her expression. "I never asked for these responsibilities. I never wanted them. We can make it look as if Bakaris escaped—"

"Don't do it, Laurana!" Tas begged. "He's the officer who brought back Derek and Lord Alfred's body at the High Clerist's Tower, the officer you shot in the arm with the arrow. He hates you, Laurana! I—I saw the way he looked at you the day we captured him!"

Flint's brows drew together. "The lords and your brother are still below. We'll discuss the best way to handle this—"

"I'm not discussing anything," Laurana stated, lifting her chin in the old imperious gesture the dwarf knew so well. "*I'm* the general. It's my decision."

"Maybe you should ask someone's advice—"

Laurana regarded the dwarf with bitter amusement. "Whose?" she asked. "Gilthanas's? What would I say? That Kitiara and I want to exchange lovers? No, we'll tell no one. What would the knights have done with Bakaris anyway? Execute him according to knightly ritual. They owe me something for all I've done. I'll take Bakaris as payment."

"Laurana"—Flint tried desperately to think of some way to penetrate her frozen mask—"there is a protocol that must be followed in prisoner exchange. You're right. You are the general, and you must know how important this is! You were in your father's court long enough—" *That* was a mistake. The dwarf knew it as soon as he opened his mouth and he groaned inwardly.

"I am no longer in my father's court!" Laurana flashed. "And to the Abyss with protocol!" Rising to her feet, she regarded Flint coldly, as if he were someone she had just met. The dwarf was, in fact, strongly reminded of her as he had seen her in Qualinesti, the evening she had run away from her home to follow after Tanis in childish infatuation.

"Thank you for bringing this message. I have a great deal to do before morning. If you have any regard for Tanis, please return to your rooms and say nothing to anyone."†

This scene precipitated the first disagreement between Tracy and I while writing these books. The plot had been designed from the beginning to have Laurana give up her generalship to go chasing after Tanis. By the time we came to write this part, I did not believe that Laurana as I knew her would give up her generalship—in effect, leave her troops in the lurch—to go save her fickle lover. Tracy the romantic maintained that love conquers all and that she would. Because she had to do this in order for the plot to work, I gave in. But it was difficult writing this scene and providing her with a convincing motivation that didn't make her sound like a love-sick ninny. By the way, Tracy has since come to agree with me!—MW

Tasslehoff cast Flint an alarmed glance. Flushing, the dwarf tried hastily to undo the damage.

"Now, Laurana," he said gruffly, "don't take my words to heart. If you've made your decision, I'll support you. I'm just being an old crotchety grandfather, that's all. I worry about you, even if you are a general. And you should take me with you—like the note says—"

"Me, too!" cried Tas indignantly.

Flint glared at him, but Laurana didn't notice. Her expression softened. "Thank you, Flint. You too, Tas," she said wearily. "I'm sorry I snapped at you. But I really believe I should go alone."

"No," Flint said stubbornly. "I care about Tanis as much as you. If there's any chance he is dy—" The dwarf choked and wiped his hand across his eyes. Then he swallowed the lump in his throat. "I want to be with him."

"Me, too," mumbled Tas, subdued.

"Very well." Laurana smiled sadly. "I can't blame you. And I'm sure he'd want you to be there."

She sounded so certain, so positive she would see Tanis.† The dwarf saw it in her eyes. He made one final effort. "Laurana, what if it's a trap? An ambush—"

Laurana's expression froze again. Her eyes narrowed angrily. Flint's protest was lost in his beard. He glanced at Tas. The kender shook his head.

The old dwarf sighed.

Yes, Laurana is acting as a love-sick ninny here. Indeed, I do agree with Margaret now. As I look back, my initial understanding of the character and her motivations were centered around rather adolescent images rather than mature ones. In the book as it stands, Laurana's motivations are questionable and irrational. While I remain an incurable romantic, I believe that Laurana's choice here makes her more of a victim than a leader—and women shouldn't be victims. Love may conquer a good many things—but abusive relationships are not among them.—TRH

2

The penalty of failure.

"There it is, sir," said the dragon, a huge red monster with glistening black eyes and a wing span that was like the shadows of night. "Dargaard Keep. Wait, you can see it clearly in the moonlight . . . when the clouds part."

"I see it," replied a deep voice. The dragon, hearing the dagger-edged anger in the man's tone, began his descent swiftly, spiraling round and round as he tested the shifting air currents among the mountains. Nervously eyeing the keep surrounded by the rocky crags of the jagged mountains, the dragon looked for a place to make a smooth and easy landing. It would never do to jounce Lord Ariakas.

At the far northern end of the Dargaard Mountains stood their destination—Dargaard Keep, as

dark and dismal as its legends. Once—when the world was young—Dargaard Keep had graced the mountain peaks, its rose-colored walls rising in graceful sweeping beauty up from the rock in the very likeness of a rose itself. But now, thought Ariakas grimly, the rose has died. The Highlord was not a poetic man, nor was he much given to flights of fancy. But the fire-blackened, crumbling castle atop the rock looked so much like a decayed rose upon a withering bush that the image struck him forcibly. Black latticework, stretching from broken tower to broken tower, no longer formed the petals of the rose. Instead, mused Ariakas, it is the web of the insect whose poison had killed it.

The great red dragon wheeled a final time. The southern wall surrounding the courtyard had fallen a thousand feet to the base of the cliff during the Cataclysm, leaving a clear passage to the gates of the keep itself. Breathing a heartfelt sigh of relief, the red saw smooth tiled pavement beyond, broken only here and there by rents in the stonework, suitable for a smooth landing. Even dragons—who feared few things on Krynn—found it healthier to avoid Lord Ariakas's displeasure.

In the courtyard below, there was a sudden fever of activity, looking like an anthill disturbed by the approach of a wasp. Draconians shrieked and pointed. The captain of the night watch came hurrying to the battlements, looking over the edge into the courtyard. The draconians were right. A flight of red dragons were indeed landing in the courtyard, one of them bearing an officer, too, by the armor. The captain watched uneasily as the man leaped from the dragon-saddle before his mount had come to halt. The dragon's wings beat furiously to avoid striking the officer, sending dust billowing about him in moonlit clouds as he strode purposefully across the stones of the courtyard toward the door. His black boots rang on the pavement, sounding like a death knell.

And, with that thought, the captain gasped, suddenly recognizing the officer. Turning, nearly stumbling over the draconian in his haste, he cursed the soldier and ran through the keep in search of Acting Commander Garibanus.

Lord Ariakas's mailed fist fell upon the wooden door with a thunderous blow that sent splinters

flying. Draconians scrambled to open it, then shrank back abjectly as the Dragon Highlord stalked inside, accompanied by a blast of cold wind that extinguished the candles and caused torch flames to waver.

Casting a swift glance from behind the gleaming mask of the dragonhelm as he entered, Ariakas saw a large circular hallway spanned by a vaulted, domed ceiling. Two giant curved staircases rose from either side of the entryway, leading up to a balcony on the second level. As Ariakas looked around, ignoring the groveling draconians, he saw Garibanus emerge from a doorway near the top of the stairs, hastily buttoning his trousers and pulling a shirt over his head. The captain of the watch stood, quaking, next to Garibanus, pointing down at the Dragon Highlord.

Ariakas guessed in a moment whose company the acting commander had been enjoying. Apparently he was filling in for the missing Bakaris in more ways than one!

"So *that's* where she is!" Lord Ariakas thought in satisfaction. He strode across the hallway and up the stairs, taking them two at a time. Draconians scuttled out of his path like rats. The captain of the guard disappeared. Ariakas was fully halfway up the stairs before Garibanus had collected himself enough to address him.

"L-Lord Ariakas," he stammered, stuffing his shirt into his pants and hurrying down the stairs. "This is an—er—unexpected honor."

"Not *unexpected,* I believe?" Arkiakas said smoothly, his voice sounding strangely metallic coming from the depths of the dragonhelm.

"Well, perhaps not," Garibanus said with a weak laugh.

Ariakas continued climbing, his eyes fixed on a doorway above him. Realizing the Lord's intended destination, Garibanus interposed himself between Ariakas and the door.

"My lord," he began apologetically, "Kitiara is dressing. She—"

Without a word, without even pausing in his stride, Lord Ariakas swung his gloved hand. The blow caught Garibanus in the ribcage. There was a whooshing sound, like a bellows deflating, and the

sound of bones cracking, then a wet soggy splatter as the force of the blow sent the young man's body into the wall opposite the stairs some ten yards distant. The limp body slid to the floor below, but Ariakas never noticed. Without a backward glance, he resumed his climb, his eyes on the door at the top of the stairs.

Lord Ariakas,† commander-in-chief of the dragonarmies, reporting directly to the Dark Queen herself, was a brilliant man, a military genius. Ariakas had nearly held the rulership of the Ansalon continent in his grasp. Already he was styling himself "Emperor." His Queen was truly pleased with him, his rewards from her were many and lavish.

According to the novel Emperor of Ansalon, *Duulket Ariakas was an early convert (initially by force) to the Dark Queen's side. The novel relates his conversion to mercenary to cleric/warrior and thus to Highlord. He let it be known—and author Doug Niles picked up the story—that his father had been killed by ogres instead of by Ariakas himself—a lie that just endears him further to Takhisis.*

But now he saw his beautiful dream slipping through his fingers like smoke from autumn fires. He had received reports of his troops fleeing wildly across the Solamnic plains, falling back from Palanthas, withdrawing from Vingaard Keep, abandoning plans for the siege of Kalaman. The elves had allied with human forces in Northern and Southern Ergoth. The mountain dwarves had emerged from their subterranean home of Thorbardin and, it was reported, allied with their ancient enemies, the hill dwarves and a group of human refugees in an attempt to drive the dragonarmies from Abanasinia. Silvanesti had been freed. A Dragon Highlord had been killed in Ice Wall. And, if rumor was to be believed, a group of gully dwarves held Pax Tharkas!

Thinking of this as he swept up the stairs, Ariakas worked himself into a fury. Few survived Lord Ariakas's displeasure. None survived his furies.

Ariakas inherited his position of authority from his father, who had been a cleric in high standing with the Queen of Darkness. Although only forty, Ariakas had held his position almost twenty years—his father having met an untimely death at the hands of his own son. When Ariakas was two, he had watched his father brutally murder his mother, who had been attempting to flee with her little son before the child became as perverted with evil as his father.

Though Ariakas always treated his father with outward shows of respect, he never forgot his mother's murder. He worked hard and excelled in his studies, making his father inordinately proud.

Many wondered whether that pride was with the father as he felt the first thrusts of the knife-blade his nineteen-year-old son plunged into his body in revenge for his mother's death—and with an eye to the throne of Dragon Highlord.

Certainly it was no great tragedy to the Queen of Darkness, who quickly found young Ariakas more than made up for the loss of her favorite cleric. The young man had no clerical talents himself, but his considerable skills as a magic-user won him the Black Robes and the commendations of the evil wizards who instructed him. Although he passed the dreadful Tests in the Tower of High Sorcery, magic was not his love. He practiced it infrequently, and never wore the Black Robes that marked his standing as a wizard of evil powers.†

In the game, Ariakas is a cleric, not a magic-user. However, since we had dealt with an evil cleric in Verminaard, we decided to make Ariakas in the book a black-robed mage.—MW

Ariakas's true passion was war. It was he who had devised the strategy that had enabled the Dragon Highlords and their armies to subjugate almost all of the continent of Ansalon. It was he who had insured that they met with almost no resistance, for it had been Ariakas's brilliant strategy to move swiftly, striking the divided human, elf, and dwarven races before they had time to unite, and snap them up piecemeal. By summer, Ariakas's plan called for him to rule Ansalon unchallenged. Other Dragon Highlords on other continents of Krynn were looking to him with undisguised envy, and fear. For one continent could never satisfy Ariakas. Already his eyes were turning westward, across the Sirrion Sea.†

Probably toward Ergoth and Sancrist

But now—disaster.

Reaching the door of Kitiara's bedchamber, Ariakas found it locked. Coldly he spoke one word in the language of magic and the heavy wooden door blew apart. Ariakas strode through the shower of sparks and blue flame that engulfed the door into Kitiara's chamber, his hand on his sword.

Kit was in bed. At the sight of Ariakas she rose, her hand clutching a silken dressing gown around her lithe body. Even through his raging fury, Ariakas was still forced to admire the woman who, of all his commanders, he had come to rely on most. Though his arrival must have caught her offguard, though she must know she had forfeited her life by allowing herself to be defeated, she faced him coolly

and calmly. Not a spark of fear lit her brown eyes, not a murmur escaped her lips.

This only served to enrage Ariakas further, reminding him of his extreme disappointment in her. Without speaking, he yanked off the dragonhelm and hurled it across the room where it slammed into an ornately carved wooden chest, shattering it like glass.

At the sight of Ariakas's face, Kitiara momentarily lost control and shrank back in her bed, her hand nervously clasping the ribbons of her gown.

Few there were who could look up Ariakas's face without blenching. It was a face devoid of any human emotion. Even his anger showed only in the twitching of a muscle along his jaw. Long black hair swept down around his pallid features. A day's growth of beard appeared blue on his smooth-shaven skin. His eyes were black and cold as an ice-bound lake.

Ariakas reached the side of the bed in a bound. Ripping down the curtains that hung around it, he reached out and grabbed hold of Kitiara's short, curly hair. Dragging her from her bed, he hurled her to the stone floor.

Kitiara fell heavily, an exclamation of pain escaping her. But she recovered quickly, and was already starting to twist to her feet like a cat when Ariakas's voice froze her.

"Stay on your knees, Kitiara," he said. Slowly and deliberately he removed his long, shining sword from its scabbard. "Stay on your knees and bow your head, as the condemned do when they come to the block. For I am your executioner, Kitiara. Thus do my commanders pay for their failure!"

Kitiara remained kneeling, but she looked up at him. Seeing the flame of hatred in her brown eyes, Ariakas felt a moment's thankfulness that he held his sword in his hand. Once more he was compelled to admire her. Even facing imminent death, there was no fear in her eyes. Only defiance.

He raised his blade, but the blow did not fall.

Bone-cold fingers wrapped around the wrist of his swordarm.

"I believe you should hear the Highlord's explanation," said a hollow voice.

Lord Ariakas was a strong man. He could hurl a spear with force enough to drive it completely

through the body of a horse. He could break a man's neck with one twist of his hand. Yet he found he could not wrench himself loose from the chill grasp that was slowly crushing his wrist. Finally, in agony, Ariakas dropped the sword. It fell to the floor with a clatter.

Somewhat shaken, Kitiara rose to her feet. Making a gesture, she commanded her minion to release Ariakas. The Lord whirled around, raising a hand to call forth the magic that would reduce this creature to cinders.

Then he stopped. Sucking in his breath, Ariakas stumbled backward, the magic spell he had been prepared to cast slipping from his mind.

Before him stood a figure no taller than himself, clad in armor so old it predated the Cataclysm. The armor was that of a Knight of Solamnia. The symbol of the Order of the Rose was traced upon the front, barely visible and worn with age. The armored figure wore no helm, it carried no weapon. Yet Ariakas—staring at it—fell back another step. For the figure he stared at was not the figure of a living man.

The being's face was transparent. Ariakas could see right through it to the wall beyond. A pale light flickered in the cavernous eyes. It stared straight ahead, as if it, too, could see right through Ariakas.

"A death knight!"† he whispered in awe.

The Lord rubbed his aching wrist, numb with the cold of those who dwell in realms far removed from the warmth of living flesh. More frightened than he dared admit, Ariakas bent down to retrieve his sword, muttering a charm to ward off the aftereffects of such a deadly touch. Rising, he cast a bitter glance at Kitiara, who was regarding him with a crooked smile.

"This—this creature serves you?" he asked hoarsely.

Kitiara shrugged. "Let us say, we agree to serve each other."

Ariakas regarded her in grudging admiration. Casting a sidelong glance at the death knight, he sheathed his sword.

"Does he always frequent your bedroom?" he sneered. His wrist ached abominably.

"He comes and goes as he chooses," Kitiara replied. She gathered the folds of the gown

The death knight as an AD&D character was first featured in the Fiend Folio. *When I was doing research into the types of creatures and foes we might include in the world of Krynn, I happened across the death knight as one possible monster type with great dramatic possibilities. It was not long before Soth became one of our favorite creations with a background that was both dark and rich. The biggest problem with Soth is that he is so cool and so powerful that whenever he shows up in the books he completely dominates and takes over the story. He is*

casually around her body, reacting apparently more from the chill in the early spring air than out of a desire for modesty. Shivering, she ran her hand through her curly hair and shrugged. "It's *his* castle, after all."

Ariakas paused, a faraway look in his eyes, his mind running back over ancient legends.

"Lord Soth!" he said suddenly, turning to the figure. "Knight of the Black Rose."

The knight bowed in acknowledgment.

"I had forgotten the ancient story of Dargaard Keep," Ariakas murmured, regarding Kitiara thoughtfully. "You have more nerve than even *I* gave you credit for, lady, taking up residence in this accursed dwelling! According to legend, Lord Soth commands a troop of skeletal warriors—"

"An effective force in a battle," Kitiara replied, yawning. Walking over to a small table near a fireplace, she picked up a cut-glass carafe. "Their touch alone"—she regarded Ariakas with smile—"well, you know what their touch is like to those who lack the magic skills to defend against it. Some wine?"

"Very well," Ariakas replied, his eyes still on the transparent face of Lord Soth. "What about the dark elves, the banshee women who reputedly follow him?"

"They're here . . . somewhere." Kit shivered again, then lifted her wine glass. "You'll probably hear them before long. Lord Soth doesn't sleep, of course. The ladies help him pass the long hours in the night."

For an instant, Kitiara paled, holding the wine glass to her lips. Then she set it down untouched, her hand shaking slightly. "It is not pleasant," she said briefly. Glancing around, she asked, "What have you done with Garibanus?"

Tossing off the glass of wine, Ariakas gestured negligently. "I left him . . . at the bottom of the stairs."

"Dead?" Kitiara questioned, pouring the Highlord another glass.

Ariakas scowled. "Perhaps. He got in my way. Does it matter?"

"I found him . . . entertaining," Kitiara said. "He filled Bakaris's place in more than one respect."

a dangerous character both in Krynn and in the writing of the novels as well. To my knowledge, there are no other death knights on Krynn—undoubtedly a good thing.—TRH

"Bakaris, yes." Lord Ariakas drank another glass. "So your commander managed to get himself captured as your armies went down to defeat!"

"He was an imbecile," Kitiara said coldly. "He tried riding dragonback, even though he is still crippled."

"I heard. What happened to his arm?"

"The elfwoman shot him with an arrow at the High Clerist's Tower. It was his own fault, and he now has paid for it. I had removed him from command, making him my bodyguard. But he insisted on trying to redeem himself."

"You don't appear to be mourning his loss," Ariakas said, eyeing Kitiara. The dressing gown, tied together only by two ribbons at the neck, did little to cover her lithe body.

Kit smiled. "No, Garibanus is . . . quite a good replacement. I hope you haven't killed him. It will be a bother getting someone else to go to Kalaman tomorrow."

"What are you doing at Kalaman—preparing to surrender to the elfwoman and the knights?" Lord Ariakas asked bitterly, his anger returning with the wine.

"No," Kitiara said. Sitting down in a chair opposite Ariakas, she regarded him coolly. "I'm preparing to accept *their* surrender."

"Ha!" Ariakas snorted. "They're not insane. They know they're winning. And they're right!" His face flushed. Picking up the carafe, he emptied it into his glass.

"You owe your death knight your life, Kitiara. Tonight at least. But he won't be around you forever."

"My plans are succeeding much better than I had hoped," Kitiara replied smoothly, not in the least disconcerted by Ariakas's flickering eyes. "If I fooled you, my lord, I have no doubt that I have fooled the enemy."

"And how have you fooled me, Kitiara?" Ariakas asked with lethal calm. "Do you mean to say that you are *not* losing on all fronts? That you are *not* being driven from Solamnia? That the dragonlances and the good dragons have *not* brought about ignominious defeat?" His voice rose with each word.

"They have not!" Kitiara snapped, her brown eyes flashing. Leaning across the table, she caught hold of Ariakas's hand as he was about to raise the wine glass to his lips. "As for the good dragons, my lord, my spies tell me their return was due to an elflord and a silver dragon breaking into the temple at Sanction where they discovered what was happening to the good dragon eggs. Whose fault was that? Who slipped up there? Guarding that temple was *your* responsibility—"

Furiously, Ariakas wrenched his hand free of Kitiara's grip. Hurling the wine glass across the room, he stood and faced her.

"By the gods, you go too far!" he shouted, breathing heavily.

"Quit posturing," Kitiara said. Coolly rising to her feet, she turned and walked across the room. "Follow me to my war room, and I will explain my plans."

Ariakas stared down at the map of northern Ansalon. "It might work," he admitted.

"Of course, it will work," Kit said, yawning and stretching languidly. "My troops have run before them like frightened rabbits. Too bad the knights weren't astute enough to notice that we always drifted southward, and they never wondered why my forces just seemed to melt away and vanish. Even as we speak, my armies are gathering in a sheltered valley south of these mountains. Within a week, an army several thousand strong will be ready to march on Kalaman. The loss of their 'Golden General' will destroy their morale. The city will probably capitulate without a fight. From there, I regain all the land we appear to have lost. Give me command of that fool Toede's armies to the south, send the flying citadels I've asked for, and Solamnia will think it's been hit by another Cataclysm!"

"But the elfwoman—"

"Need not concern us," Kitiara said.

Ariakas shook his head. "This seems the weak link in your plans, Kitiara. What about Half-Elven? Can you be certain he won't interfere?"

"It doesn't matter about him. *She* is the one who counts and she is a woman in love." Kitiara shrugged. "She trusts me, Ariakas. You scoff, but it's

true. She trusts me too much and Tanis Half-Elven too little. But that's always the way of lovers. The ones we love most are those we trust least. It proved quite fortunate Bakaris fell into their hands."

Hearing a change in her voice, Ariakas glanced at Kitiara sharply, but she had turned from him, keeping her face averted. Immediately he realized she was not as confident as she seemed, and then he knew she had lied to him. The half-elf! What about him? Where *was* he, for that matter. Ariakas had heard a great deal about him, but had never met him. The Dragon Highlord considered pressing her on this point, then abruptly changed his mind. Much better to have in his possession the knowledge that she had lied. It gave him a power over this dangerous woman. Let her relax in her supposed complacency.

Yawning elaborately, Ariakas feigned indifference. "What will you do with the elfwoman?" he asked as she would expect him to ask. Ariakas's passion for delicate blonde women was well-known.

Kitiara raised her eyebrows, giving him a playful look. "Too bad, my lord," she said mockingly, "but Her Dark Highness has asked for the lady. Perhaps you could have her when the Dark Queen is finished."

Ariakas shivered. "Bah, she'll be of no use to me then. Give her to your friend, Lord Soth. He liked elfwomen once upon a time, if I remember correctly."

"You do," murmured Kitiara. Her eyes narrowed. She held up her hand. "Listen," she said softly.

Ariakas fell silent. At first he heard nothing, then he gradually became aware of a strange sound—a wailing keen, as if a hundred women† mourned their dead. As he listened, it grew louder and louder, piercing the stillness of the night.

These are banshees, undead spirits who, appearing to Soth as elfmaids, were murdered by him but brought about his downfall. They may have been sent by Paladine to remind Soth eternally of his crime—which they do, quite vocally.

The Dragon Highlord set down his wine glass, startled to see his hand trembling. Looking at Kitiara, he saw her face pale beneath its tan. Her large eyes were wide. Feeling his eyes upon her, Kitiara swallowed and licked her dry lips.

"Awful, isn't it?" she asked, her voice cracking.

"I faced horrors in the Towers of High Sorcery," said Ariakas softly, "but that was nothing compared to this. What is it?"

"Come," Kit said, standing up.

"If you have the nerve, I'll show you."

Together, the two left the war room, Kitiara leading Ariakas through the winding corridors of the castle until they came back to Kit's bedroom above the circular entryway with the vaulted ceiling.

"Stay in the shadows," Kitiara warned.

An unnecessary warning, Ariakas thought as they crept softly out onto the balcony overlooking the circular room. Looking down over the edge of the balcony, Ariakas was overcome with sheer horror at the sight below him. Sweating, he drew back swiftly in the shadows of Kitiara's bedroom.

"How can you stand that?" he asked her as she entered and shut the door softly behind her. "Does that go on every night?"

"Yes," she said, trembling. She drew a deep breath and closed her eyes. Within a moment she was back in control. "Sometimes I think I'm used to it, then I make the mistake of looking down there. The song isn't so bad. . . ."

"It's ghastly!" Ariakas muttered, wiping cold sweat from his face. "So Lord Soth sits down there on his throne every night, surrounded by his skeletal warriors, and the dark hags sing that horrible lullaby!"

"And it is the same song, always," Kitiara murmured. Shivering, she absently picked up the empty wine carafe, then set it back down on the table. "Though the past tortures him, he cannot escape it. Always he ponders, wondering what he might have done to avoid the fate that dooms him to walk forever upon the land without rest. The dark elven women, who were part of his downfall, are forced to relive his story with him. Nightly they must repeat it. Nightly he must hear it."

"What are the words?"

"I know them, now, almost as well as he does." Kitiara laughed, then shuddered. "Call for another carafe of wine and I'll tell you his tale, if you have the time."

"I have time," Ariakas said, settling back in his chair. "Though I must leave in the morning if I am to send the citadels."

Kitiara smiled at him, the charming, crooked smile that so many had found so captivating.

"Thank you, my lord," she said. "I will not fail you again."

"No," said Ariakas coolly, ringing a small silver bell, "I can promise you that, Kitiara. If you do, you will find *his* fate"—he motioned downstairs where the wailing had reached a shivering pitch—"a pleasant one compared to your own."

The Knight of the Black Rose

As you know," began Kitiara, "Lord Soth was a true and noble knight of Solamnia. But he was an intensely passionate man, lacking in self-discipline, and this was his downfall.

"Soth fell in love with a beautiful elfmaid, a disciple of the Kingpriest of Istar. He was married at the time, but thoughts of his wife vanished at the sight of the elfmaid's beauty. Forsaking both his sacred marriage vows and his knightly vows, Soth gave in to his passion. Lying to the girl, he seduced her and brought her to live at Dargaard Keep, promising to marry her. His wife disappeared under sinister circumstances."

Kitiara shrugged, then continued:

"According to what I've heard of the song, the elfmaid remained true to the knight, even after she discovered his terrible misdeeds. She prayed to the Goddess Mishakal that the knight be allowed to redeem himself and, apparently, her prayers were answered. Lord Soth was given the power to prevent the Cataclysm, though it would mean sacrificing his own life.

"Strengthened by the love of the girl he had wronged, Lord Soth left for Istar, fully intending to stop the Kingpriest and restore his shattered honor.

"But the knight was halted in his journey by elven women, disciples of the Kingpriest, who knew of Lord Soth's crime and threatened to ruin him. To weaken the effects of the elfmaid's love, they intimated that she had been unfaithful to him in his absence.

"Soth's passions took hold of him, destroying his reason. In a jealous rage he rode back to Dargaard Keep. Entering his door, he accused the innocent girl of betraying him. Then the Cataclysm struck. The great chandelier in the entryway fell to the floor, consuming the elfmaid and her child in flames. As she died, she called down a curse upon the knight, condeming him to eternal, dreadful life. Soth and his followers perished in the fire, only to be reborn in hideous form."

"So this is what he hears," Ariakas murmured, listening.

And in the climate of dreams
When you recall her, when the world of the dream
expands, wavers in light,
when you stand at the edge of blessedness and sun,

Then we shall make you remember,
shall make you live again
through the long denial of body

For you were first dark in the light's hollow,
expanding like a stain, a cancer

For you were the shark in the slowed water
beginning to move

For you were the notched head of a snake,
sensing forever warmth and form

For you were inexplicable death in the crib,
the long house in betrayal

And you were more terrible than this
in a loud alley of visions,
for you passed through unharmed, unchanging

As the women screamed, unraveling silence,
halving the door of the world,
bringing forth monsters

As a child opened in parabolas of fire
There at the borders
of two lands burning

As the world split, wanting to swallow you back
willing to give up everything
to lose you in darkness.

You passed through these unharmed, unchanging,
but now you see them
strung on our words, on your own conceiving
as you pass from night, to awareness of night
to know that hatred is the calm of philosophers
that its price is forever

that it draws you through meteors
through winter's transfixion
through the blasted rose
through the sharks' water
through the black compression of oceans
through rock, through magma
to yourself, to an abscess of nothing
that you will recognize as nothing
that you will know is coming again and again
under the same rules.

This is, in part, an imitation of the British poet Ted Hughes. It has some of his violence and melodrama, and stringing together of isolated images. For the life of me, I can't recall what "hatred is the calm of philosophers" was supposed to mean.
—Michael Williams

3
The trap . . .

Bakaris slept fitfully in his jail cell. Though haughty and insolent during the day, his nights were tortured by erotic dreams of Kitiara and fearful dreams of his execution at the hands of the Knights of Solamnia. Or perhaps it was his execution at Kitiara's hands. He was never certain, when he woke in a cold sweat, which it had been. Lying in his cold cell in the still hours of the night when he could not sleep, Bakaris cursed the elven woman who had been the cause of his downfall. Over and over he plotted his revenge upon her—if only she would fall into his hands.

Bakaris was thinking of this, hovering between sleep and wakefulness, when the sound of a key in the lock of his cell door brought him to his feet. It

was near dawn, near the hour of execution! Perhaps the knights were coming for him!

"Who is it?" Bakaris called harshly.

"Hush!" commanded a voice. "You are in no danger, if you keep quiet and do as you are told."

Bakaris sat back down on his bed in astonishment. He recognized the voice. How not? Night after night it had spoken in his vengeful thoughts. The elfwoman! And the commander could see two other figures in the shadows, small figures. The dwarf and the kender, most likely. They always hung around the elfwoman.

The cell door opened. The elfwoman glided inside. She was heavily cloaked and carried another cloak in her hand.

"Hurry," she ordered coldly. "Put this on."

"Not until I know what this is about," Bakaris said suspiciously, though his soul sang for joy.

"We are exchanging you for . . . for another prisoner," Laurana replied.

Bakaris frowned. He mustn't seem too eager.

"I don't believe you," he stated, lying back down on his bed. "It's a trap—"

"I don't care what you believe!" Laurana snapped impatiently. "You're coming if I have to knock you senseless! It won't matter whether you are conscious or not, just so long as I'm able to exhibit you to Kiti—the one wants you!"

Kitiara! So that was it. What was she up to? What game was she playing? Bakaris† hesitated. He didn't trust Kit any more than she trusted him. She was quite capable of using him to further her own ends, which is undoubtedly what she was doing now. But perhaps he could use her in return. If only he knew what was going on! But looking at Laurana's pale, rigid face, Bakaris knew that she was quite prepared to carry out her threat. He would have to bide his time.

"It seems I have no choice," he said. Moonlight filtered through a barred window into the filthy cell, shining on Bakaris's face. He'd been in prison for weeks. How long he didn't know, he'd lost count. As he reached for the cloak, he caught Laurana's cold green eyes, which were fixed on him intently, narrow slightly in disgust.

Self-consciously, Bakaris raised his good hand and scratched the new growth of beard.

Bakaris originally came from an area of Estwilde where his wild spirit and fearsome temper caused problems for him. The darkness of his heart and his constant lust for pleasure are his greatest weaknesses. He rose in the ranks of the dragonarmy, continually brought along by Kitiara.

He is more devoted to her than to the army, but he also knows she could betray him at any time.

"Pardon, your ladyship," he said sarcastically, "but the servants in your establishment have not thought fit to bring me a razor. I know how the sight of facial hair disgusts you elves!"

To his surprise, Bakaris saw his words draw blood. Laurana's face turned pale, her lips chalk-white. Only by a supreme effort did she control herself. "Move!" she said in a strangled voice.

At the sound, the dwarf entered the room, hand on his battle-axe. "You heard the general," Flint snarled. "Get going. Why your miserable carcass is worth trading for Tanis—"

"Flint!" said Laurana tersely.

Suddenly Bakaris understood!

Kitiara's plan began to take shape in his mind.

"So—Tanis! He's the one I'm being exchanged for." He watched Laurana's face closely. No reaction. He might have been speaking of a stranger instead of a man Kitiara had told him was this woman's lover. He tried again, testing his theory. "I wouldn't call him a prisoner, however, unless you speak of a prisoner of love. Kit must have tired of him. Ah, well. Poor man. I'll miss him. He and I have much in common—"

Now there was a reaction. He saw the delicate jaws clench, the shoulders tremble beneath the cloak. Without a word, Laurana turned and stalked out of the cell. So he was right. This had something to do with the bearded half-elf. But what? Tanis had left Kit in Flotsam. Had she found him again? Had he returned to her? Bakaris fell silent, wrapping the cloak around him. Not that it mattered, not to him. He would be able to use this new information for his own revenge. Recalling Laurana's strained and rigid face in the moonlight, Bakaris thanked the Dark Queen for her favors as the dwarf shoved him out the cell door.

The sun had not risen yet, although a faint pink line on the eastern horizon foretold that dawn was an hour or so away. It was still dark in the city of Kalaman—dark and silent as the town slept soundly following its day and night of revelry. Even the guards yawned at their posts or, in some cases, snored as they slept soundly. It was an easy task for the four heavily cloaked figures to flit silently

through the streets until they came to a small locked door in the city wall.

"This used to lead to some stairs that led up to the top of the wall, across it, then back down to the other side," whispered Tasslehoff, fumbling in one of his pouches until he found his lock-picking tools.

"How do you know?" Flint muttered, peering around nervously.

"I used to come to Kalaman when I was little," Tas said. Finding the slender piece of wire, his small, skilled hands slipped it inside the lock. "My parents brought me. We always came in and out this way."†

Although the senior Burrfoots called Kendermore home, they apparently traveled a great deal, even with their children. No wonder Tas left home on his own wanderlust at about age sixteen.

"Why didn't you use the front gate, or would that have been too simple?" Flint growled.

"Hurry up!" ordered Laurana impatiently.

"We would have used the front gate," Tas said, manipulating the wire. "Ah, there." Removing the wire, he put it carefully back into his pouch, then quietly swung the old door open. "Where was I? Oh, yes. We would have used the front gate, but kender weren't allowed in the city."

"And your parents came in anyway!" Flint snorted, following Tas through the door and up a narrow flight of stone stairs. The dwarf was only half-listening to the kender. He kept his eye on Bakaris, who was, in Flint's view, behaving himself just a bit too well. Laurana had withdrawn completely within herself. Her only words were sharp commands to hurry.

"Well, of course," Tas said, prattling away cheerfully. "They always considered it an oversight. I mean, why should we be on the same list as goblins? Someone must have put us there accidentally. But my parents didn't consider it polite to argue, so we just came in and out by the side door. Easier for everyone all around. Here we are. Open that door—it's not usually locked. Oops, careful. There's a guard. Wait until he's gone."

Pressing themselves against the wall, they hid in the shadows until the guard had stumbled wearily past, nearly asleep on his feet. Then they silently crossed the wall, entered another door, ran down another flight of stairs, and were outside the city walls.

They were alone. Flint, looking around, could see no sign of anybody or anything in the half-light

before dawn. Shivering, he huddled in his cloak, feeling apprehension creep over him. What if Kitiara was telling the truth? What if Tanis was with her? What if he was dying?

Angrily Flint forced himself to stop thinking about that. He almost hoped it was a trap! Suddenly his mind was wrenched from its dark thoughts by a harsh voice, speaking so near that he started in terror.

"Is that you, Bakaris?"

"Yes. Good to see you again, Gakhan."

Shaking, Flint turned to see a dark figure emerge from the shadows of the wall. It was heavily cloaked and swathed in cloth. He remembered Tas's description of the draconian.

"Are they carrying any other weapons?" Gakhan demanded, his eyes on Flint's battle-axe.

"No," Laurana answered sharply.

"Search them," Gakhan ordered Bakaris.

"You have my word of honor," Laurana said angrily. "I am a princess of the Qualinesti—"

Bakaris took a step toward her. "Elves have their own code of honor," he sneered. "Or so you said the night you shot me with your cursed arrow."

Laurana's face flushed, but she made no answer nor did she fall back before his advance.

Coming to stand in front of her, Bakaris lifted his right arm with his left hand, then let it fall. "You destroyed my career, my life."

Laurana, holding herself rigid, watched him without moving. "I said I carry no weapons."

"You can search me, if you like," offered Tasslehoff, interposing himself—accidentally—between Bakaris and Laurana. "Here!" He dumped the contents of a pouch onto Bakaris's foot.

"Damn you!" Bakaris swore, cuffing the kender on the side of the head.

"Flint!" Laurana cautioned warningly through clenched teeth. She could see the dwarf's face red with rage. At her command, the dwarf choked back his anger.

"I'm s-sorry, truly!" Tas snuffled, fumbling around the ground after his things.

"If you delay much longer, we won't have to alert the guard," Laurana said coldly, determined not to tremble at the man's foul touch. "The sun will be up and they will see us clearly."

"The elfwoman is right, Bakaris," Gakhan said, an edge in his reptilian voice. "Take the dwarf's battle-axe and let's get out of here."

Looking at the brightening horizon—and at the cloaked and hooded draconian—Bakaris gave Laurana a vicious glance, then snatched the battle-axe away from the dwarf.

"He's no threat! What's an old man like him going to do, anyway?" Bakaris muttered.

"Get moving," Gakhan ordered Laurana, ignoring Bakaris. "Head for that grove of trees. Keep hidden and don't try alerting the guard. I am a magic-user and my spells are deadly. The Dark Lady said to bring you safely, 'general.' I have no instructions regarding your two friends."

They followed Gakhan across the flat, open ground outside the city gates to a large grove of trees, keeping in the shadows as much as possible. Bakaris walked beside Laurana. Holding her head high, she resolutely refused to even acknowledge his existence. Reaching the trees, Gakhan pointed.

"Here are our mounts," he said.

"We're not going anywhere!" Laurana said angrily, staring at the creatures in alarm.

At first Flint thought they were small dragons, but as he drew nearer, the dwarf caught his breath.

"Wyvern!" he breathed.

Distantly related to dragons, wyvern are smaller and lighter and were often used by the Highlords to relay messages, as the griffons were used by the elven lords. Not nearly as intelligent as dragons, the wyvern are noted for their cruel and chaotic† natures. The animals in the grove peered at the companions with red eyes, their scorpionlike tails curled menacingly. Tipped with poison, the tail could sting an enemy to death within seconds.

Wyvern must not be too chaotic in nature or they wouldn't deliver the messages where they are intended.

"Where is Tanis?" Laurana demanded.

"He grew worse," Gakhan answered. "If you want to see him, you must come to Dargaard Keep."

"No," Laurana drew back, only to feel Bakaris's hand close over her arm in a firm grip.

"Don't call for help," he said pleasantly, "or one of your friends will die. Well, it seems we're taking a little trip to Dargaard Keep. Tanis is a *dear* friend. I'd hate for him to miss seeing you." Bakaris turned to the draconian. "Gakhan, go back to Kalaman. Let us know the reaction of the people when they discover their 'general' missing."

Gakhan hesitated, his dark reptilian eyes regarding Bakaris warily. Kitiara had warned him something like this might occur. He guessed what Bakaris had in mind—his own private revenge. Gakhan could stop Bakaris, that was no problem. But there was the chance that—during the unpleasantness—one of the prisoners might escape and go for help. They were too near the city walls for comfort. Blast Bakaris anyway! Gakhan scowled, then realized there was nothing he could do but hope Kitiara had provided for this contingency. Shrugging, Gakhan comforted himself with the thought of Bakaris's fate when he returned to the Dark Lady.

"Certainly, Commander," the draconian replied smoothly. Bowing, Gakhan faded back into the shadows. They could see his cloaked figure darting from tree to tree, heading for Kalaman. Bakaris's face grew eager, the cruel lines around the bearded mouth deepened.

"Come on, General." Bakaris shoved Laurana toward the wyvern.

But instead of advancing, Laurana whirled to face the man.

"Tell me one thing," she said through pale lips. "Is it true? Is Tanis with . . . with Kitiara? Th-the note said he was wounded at Vingaard Keep . . . dying!"

Seeing the anguish in her eyes—anguish not for herself, but for the half-elf—Bakaris smiled. He had never dreamed revenge could be so satisfying. "How should I know? I've been locked in your stinking prison. But I find it difficult to believe he'd be wounded. Kit never allowed him near a fight! The only battles he wages are those of love. . . ."

Laurana's head drooped. Bakaris laid a hand on her arm in mocking sympathy. Angrily Laurana shook free, turning to keep her face hidden.

"I don't believe you!" Flint growled. "Tanis would never allow Kitiara to do this—"

"Oh, you're right there, dwarf," Bakaris said, realizing quickly just how far his lies would be believed. "He knows nothing of this. The Dark Lady sent him to Neraka weeks ago, to prepare for our audience with the Queen."

"You know, Flint," Tas said solemnly. "Tanis was really fond of Kitiara. Do you remember that party at the Inn of the Last Home? It was Tanis's Day of Life Gift party. He'd just 'come of age' by elven standards† and, boy! Was that some party! Do you remember? Caramon got a tankard of ale dumped over his head when he grabbed Dezra. And Raistlin drank too much wine and one of his spells misfired and burned up Otik's apron, and Kit and Tanis were together in that corner next to the firepit, and they were—"

Young people of Qualinesti nobility go through a three-day ceremony of adulthood called Kentommen, which means "coming of age." It takes place on their ninety-ninth birthday. Tanis was forced to leave long before he would have been eligible, and it's doubtful that the Speaker would have allowed him to go through the ceremony anyway. The companions must have celebrated Tanis's coming of age a bit early—he would have been only ninety-six—perhaps because they were separating for five years.

Bakaris glanced at Tas in annoyance. The commander disliked being reminded of how close Kitiara really was to the half-elf. "Tell the kender to keep quiet, General," Bakaris growled, "or I'll let the wyvern have him. Two hostages would suit the Dark Lady just as well as three."

"So it is a trap," Laurana said softly, looking around in a daze. "Tanis isn't dying . . . he's not even there! I've been a fool—"

"We're not going anywhere with you!" Flint stated, planting his feet on the ground firmly.

Bakaris regarded him coolly. "Have you ever seen a wyvern sting anyone to death?"

"No," said Tas with interest, "but I saw a scorpion once. Is it like that? Not that I'd want to try it, mind you," the kender faltered, seeing Bakaris's face darken.

"The guards on the walls of the city might well hear your screams," Bakaris said to Laurana, who stared at him as if he were speaking a language she didn't comprehend. "But, by then, it would be too late."

"I've been a fool," Laurana repeated softly.

"Say the word, Laurana!" Flint said stubbornly. "We'll fight—"

"No," she said in a small voice, like a child's. "No. I won't risk your lives, not you and Tas. It was my folly. I will pay. Bakaris, take me. Let my friends go—"

"Enough of this!" Bakaris said impatiently. "I'm not letting anyone go!" Climbing onto the back of a wyvern, he extended his hand to Laurana. "There's only two, so we'll have to double up."

Her face expressionless, Laurana accepted Bakaris's help and climbed onto the wyvern. Putting

his good arm around her, he held her close, grinning.

At his touch, Laurana's face regained some of its color. Angrily, she tried to free herself from his grip.

"You are much safer this way, General," Bakaris said harshly in her ear. "I would not want you to fall."

Laurana bit her lip and stared straight ahead, forcing herself not to cry.

Wyvern are dumb and stubborn, which makes training them to carry people a frustrating process. But if successful, they make energetic, steady mounts. They have no forelegs, so all their muscles are dedicated to flight.

"Do these creatures *always* smell so awful," Tas said, regarding the wyvern† with disgust as he helped Flint mount. "I think you should convince them to bathe—"

"Watch the tail," Bakaris said coldly. "The wyvern will generally not kill unless I give them the command, but they are high-strung. Little things upset them."

"Oh." Tas gulped. "I'm sure I didn't mean to be insulting. Actually, I suppose one could get used to the smell, after a bit—"

At a signal from Bakaris, the wyvern spread their leathery wings and soared into the air, flying slowly under the unaccustomed burden. Flint gripped Tasslehoff tightly and kept his eyes on Laurana, flying ahead of them with Bakaris. Occasionally the dwarf saw Bakaris lean close to Laurana and he saw Laurana pull away from him. The dwarf's face grew grim.

"That Bakaris is up to no good!" the dwarf muttered to Tas.

"What?" said Tas, turning around.

"I said that Bakaris is up to no good!" the dwarf shouted. "And I'll wager he's acting on his own and not following orders, either. That Gakhan-character wasn't at all pleased about being ordered off."

"What?" Tas yelled. "I can't hear! All this wind—"

"Oh, never mind!" The dwarf felt dizzy all of a sudden. He was finding it hard to breathe. Trying to take his mind off himself, he stared gloomily down at the tree tops emerging from the shadows as the sun began to rise.

After flying for about an hour, Bakaris made a motion with his hand and the wyvern began slowly circling, searching for a clear place to land on the heavily forested mountainside. Pointing at a small clearing just barely visible among the trees, Bakaris

shouted instructions to the lead beast. The wyvern landed as ordered and Bakaris climbed down.

Flint glanced around, his fears growing. There was no sign of any fortress. No sign of life of any kind. They were in a small cleared area, surrounded by tall pine trees whose ancient limbs were so thick and tangled that they effectively shut out most of the sun's light. Around them, the forest was dark and filled with moving shadows. At one end of the clearing Flint saw a small cave, carved out of the cliff face.

"Where are we?" Laurana asked sternly. "This can't possibly be Dargaard Keep. Why are we stopping?"

"Astute observation, General," Bakaris said pleasantly. "Dargaard Keep is about a mile farther up the mountain. They're not expecting us yet. The Dark Lady probably hasn't even had her breakfast. We wouldn't want to be impolite and disturb her, would we?" He glanced over at Tas and Flint. "You two—stay put," he instructed as the kender seemed about to jump down. Tas froze.

Moving to stand near Laurana, Bakaris placed his hand on the neck of the wyvern. The beast's lidless eyes followed his every move as expectantly as a dog waiting to be fed.

"You get down, Lady Laurana," Bakaris said with lethal softness, coming quite near her as she sat upon the wyvern's back, regarding him scornfully. "We've time for a little . . . breakfast ourselves. . . ."

Laurana's eyes flashed. Her hand moved to her sword with such conviction she almost convinced herself it was there. "Stand away from me!" she commanded with such presence that, for a moment, Bakaris halted. Then, grinning, he reached up and grabbed hold of her wrist.

"No, lady. I wouldn't struggle. Remember the wyvern—and your friends over there. One word from me, and they will die very nasty deaths!"

Cringing, Laurana looked over to see the wyvern's scorpion tail poised above Flint's back. The beast quivered with anticipation of the kill.

"No! Laurana, " Flint began in agony, but she cast a sharp glance at him, reminding him that she was still the general. Her face drained of life, she allowed Bakaris to help her down.

"There, I thought you looked hungry," Bakaris said, grinning.

"Let them go!" Laurana demanded. "It's me you want—"

"You're right there," Bakaris said, grabbing hold of her around her waist. "But their presence seems to insure your good behavior."

"Don't you worry about us, Laurana!" Flint roared.

"Shut up, dwarf!" Bakaris cried in a rage. Shoving Laurana back against the body of the wyvern, he turned to stare at the dwarf and the kender. Flint's blood chilled as he saw the wild madness in the man's eyes.

"I—I think we'd better do as he says, Flint," Tas said, swallowing. "He'll hurt Laurana—"

"Hurt her? Oh, not much," Bakaris said, laughing. "She will still be useful to Kitiara for whatever purpose she may have in mind. But don't move, dwarf. I may forget myself!" Bakaris warned, hearing Flint choke in anger. He turned back to Laurana. "As it is, Kitiara won't mind if I have a little fun with the lady first. No, don't faint—"

I think people get the wrong idea about this "fainting" technique. The objective is not to lose consciousness but, rather, to allow yourself to go completely limp. A person standing with the muscles tense is relatively easy to move about compared to a hundred-plus pounds of limp noodle. The technique is to make yourself as cumbersome as possible to your opponent, force him to make a mistake, and then take instant advantage of it—as Laurana demonstrates so forcefully here.—TRH

It was an old elven self-defense technique.† Flint had seen it done often and he tensed, ready to act as Laurana's eyes rolled up, her body sagged, and her knees seemed to give way.

Instinctively, Bakaris reached to catch her.

"No, you don't ! I like my women lively—oof!"

Laurana's fist slammed into his stomach, knocking the breath from his body. Doubling over in pain, he fell forward. Bringing her knee up, Laurana caught him directly under the chin. As Bakaris pitched into the dirt, Flint grabbed the startled kender and slid off the wyvern.

"Run, Flint! Quickly!" Laurana gasped, leaping away from the wyvern and the man groaning on the ground. "Get into the woods!"

But Bakaris, his face twisted with rage, reached out his hand and grabbed Laurana's ankle. She stumbled and fell flat, kicking frantically at him. Wielding a tree limb, Flint leaped at Bakaris as the commander was struggling to his feet. Hearing Flint's roar, Bakaris spun around and struck the dwarf in the face with the back of his hand. In the same motion, he caught hold of Laurana's arm and

dragged her to her feet. Then, turning, he glared at Tas, who had run up beside the unconscious dwarf.

"The lady and I are going into the cave . . . " Bakaris said, breathing heavily. He gave Laurana's arm a wrench, causing her to cry out in pain. "Make one move, kender, and I'll break her arm. Once we get into the cave, I don't want to be disturbed. There's a dagger in my belt. I'll be holding it to the lady's throat. Do you understand, little fool?"

"Yes, s-sir," stammered Tasslehoff. "I—I wouldn't dream of interfering. I—I'll just stay here with—with Flint."

"Don't go into the woods." Bakaris began to drag Laurana toward the cave. "Draconians guard the forest."

"N-no, sir," stuttered Tas, kneeling down beside Flint, his eyes wide.

Satisfied, Bakaris glared once more at the cowering kender, then shoved Laurana toward the entrance to the cave.

Blinded by tears, Laurana stumbled forward. As if to remind her she was trapped, Bakaris twisted her arm again. The pain was excruciating. There was no way to break free of the man's powerful grip. Cursing herself for falling into this trap, Laurana tried to battle her fear and think clearly. It was hard, the man's hand was strong, and his smell—the human smell—reminded her of Tanis in a horrifying way.

As if guessing her thoughts, Bakaris clutched her close to him, rubbing his bearded face against her smooth cheek.

"You will be one more woman the half-elf and I have shared—" he whispered hoarsely, then his voice broke off in a bubble of agony.

For an instant, Bakaris's grip on Laurana's arm tightened almost past endurance. Then it loosened. His hand slipped from her arm. Laurana tore free of his grip, then spun around to face him.

Blood oozed between Bakaris's fingers as he clutched at his side where Tasslehoff's little knife† still protruded from the wound. Drawing his own dagger, the man lunged at the defiant kender.

Rabbitslayer—Caramon was very wrong when he said earlier that it would only be useful in killing rabbits!

Something snapped in Laurana, letting loose a wild fury and hatred she had not guessed lurked inside her. No longer feeling any fear, no longer caring if she lived or died, Laurana had one thought in mind—she would kill this human male.

With a savage shriek, she flung herself at him, knocking him to the ground. He gave a grunt, then lay still beneath her. Desperately Laurana fought, trying to grab his knife. Then she realized his body was not moving. Slowly she rose to her feet, shaking in reaction.

For a moment she could see nothing through the red mist before her eyes. When it cleared, she saw Tasslehoff roll the body over. Bakaris lay dead. His eyes stared up at the sky, a look of profound shock and surprise on his face. His hand still clutched the dagger he had driven into his own gut.

"What happened?" Laurana whispered, quivering with anger and revulsion.

"You knocked him down and he fell on his knife," Tas said calmly.

"But before that—"

"Oh, I stuck him," Tas said. Plucking his knife from the man's side, he looked at it proudly. "And Caramon told me it wouldn't be of any use unless I met a vicious rabbit! Wait until I tell him!

"You know, Laurana," he continued, somewhat sadly, "everyone always underestimates us kender. Bakaris really should have searched my pouches. Say, that was a neat fainting trick you pulled. Did you—"

"How's Flint?" Laurana interrupted, not wanting to remember those last few horrible moments. Without quite knowing what she was doing or why, she pulled her cape from her shoulders and threw it down over the bearded face. "We've got to get out of here."

"He'll be all right," Tas said, glancing over at the dwarf, who was groaning and shaking his head. "What about the wyvern? Do you think they'll attack us?"

"I don't know," Laurana said, eyeing the animals. The wyvern stared around uneasily, uncertain as to what had happened to their master. "I've heard they're not very smart. They generally won't act on their own. Maybe—if we don't make any sudden moves—we can escape into the forest before they figure out what's happened. Help Flint."

"Come on, Flint," Tas said urgently, tugging at the dwarf. "We've got to esc—"

The kender's voice was cut off by a wild cry, a cry of such fear and terror that it made Tas's hair stand on end. Looking up, he saw Laurana staring at a figure that had—apparently—emerged from the cave. At the sight of the figure, Tasslehoff felt the most terrible sensation sweep over his body. His heart raced, his hands went cold, he couldn't breathe.

"Flint!" he managed to gasp before his throat closed completely.

The dwarf, hearing a tone in the kender's voice he'd never heard before, struggled to sit up. "What—"

Tas could only point.

Flint focused his bleary vision in the direction Tas indicated.

"In the name of Reorx," the dwarf said, his voice breaking, "what is that?"

The figure moved relentlessly toward Laurana, who—held spellbound at its command—could do nothing but stare at it. Dressed in antique armor, it might have been a Knight of Solamnia. But the armor was blackened as if it had been burned by fire. An orange light flared beneath its helm, while the helm itself seemed perched on empty air.

The figure† reached out an armored arm. Flint choked in horror. The armored arm did not end in a hand. The knight seemingly grasped hold of Laurana with nothing but air. But she screamed in pain, falling to her knees in front of the ghastly vision. Her head slumped forward, she collapsed, senseless from the chill touch. The knight released his grip, letting the inert body slip to the ground. Bending down, the knight lifted her in his arms.

Years later, Caramon wrote of Lord Soth: "Dozens of bards sing songs about Soth. Mostly, they describe the former Solamnic as the monster it is. A few, though, say that it should be pitied and that it suffers greater than any being. These bards preach that we should look to Soth as an example of the fact that 'things could always be worse.' I usually throw these bards out on their ears."

Tas started to move, but the knight turned his flaring orange gaze upon him and the kender was held fast, gazing into the orange flame of the creature's eyes. Neither he nor Flint could look away, though the horror was so great that the dwarf feared he might lose his reason. Only his love and concern for Laurana kept him clinging to consciousness. Over and over he told himself he must do something, he must save her. But he couldn't make his trembling body obey. The knight's flickering gaze swept over the two.

"Go back to Kalaman," said a hollow voice. "Tell them we have the elfwoman. The Dark Lady will arrive tomorrow at noon, to discuss terms of surrender."

Turning, the knight walked over Bakaris's body, the figure's shimmering armor passing right through the corpse as if it no longer existed. Then the knight vanished into the dark shadows of the woods, carrying Laurana in his arms.

With the knight's departure, the spell was lifted. Tas, feeling weak and sick, began to shiver uncontrollably. Flint struggled to his feet.

"I'm going after it—" the dwarf muttered, though his hands shook so he could barely lift his helm from the dirt.

"N-no," stammered Tasslehoff, his face strained and white as he stared after the knight. "Whatever that thing was, we can't fight it. I—I was scared,† Flint!" The kender shook his head in misery. "I—I'm sorry, but I can't face that, that thing again! We've got to go back to Kalaman. Maybe we can get help—"

Tasslehoff? Scared? Obviously, kender DO occasionally find fear (after much effort), but they forget about the experience so quickly that each time is like the first for them.—TRH

Tas started off into the woods at a run. For a moment Flint stood angry and irresolute, staring after Laurana. Then his face crumpled in agony. "He's right," he mumbled. "I can't go after that thing either. Whatever it was, it wasn't of this world."

Turning away, Flint caught a glimpse of Bakaris, lying beneath Laurana's cloak. Swift pain cramped the dwarf's heart. Ignoring it, Flint said to himself with sudden certainty, "He was lying about Tanis. And so was Kitiara. He's not with her, I know it!" The dwarf clenched his fist. "I don't know where Tanis is, but someday I'll have to face him and I'll have to tell him . . . I let him down. He trusted me to keep her safe, and I failed!" The dwarf closed his eyes. Then he heard Tas shout. Sighing, he stumbled blindly after the kender, rubbing his left arm as he ran. "How will I ever tell him?" he moaned. "How?"

4

A peaceful interlude.

All right," said Tanis, glaring at the man who sat so calmly in front of him. "I want answers. You deliberately took us into the maelstrom! Why? Did you know this place was here? Where are we? Where are the others?"

Berem sat before Tanis in a wooden chair. It was ornately carved with figures of birds and animals in a style popular among the elves. In fact, it reminded Tanis strongly of Lorac's throne in the doomed elven kingdom of Silvanesti. The likeness did nothing to calm Tanis's spirits, and Berem flinched under the half-elf's angry stare. The hands that were too young for the middle-aged man's body plucked at his shabby trousers. He shifted his gaze to glance nervously around their strange surroundings.

"Damn it! Answer me!" Tanis raved. Flinging himself at Berem, he gripped the man's shirt and yanked him up from his chair. Then his clenching hands moved to the man's throat.

"Tanis!" Swiftly Goldmoon rose and laid a restraining hand on Tanis's arm. But the half-elf was beyond reason. His face was so twisted with fear and anger that she didn't recognize him. Frantically she tore at the hands that gripped Berem. "Riverwind, make him stop!"

The big Plainsman grasped Tanis by the wrists and wrenched him away from Berem, holding the half-elf in his strong arms.

"Leave him alone, Tanis!"

For a moment, Tanis struggled, then went limp, drawing a deep, shuddering breath.

"He's a mute," Riverwind said sternly. "Even if he wanted to tell you, he couldn't. He can't talk—"

"Yes, I can."

The three stopped, startled, staring at Berem.

"I can talk," he said calmly, speaking Common. Absently he rubbed his throat where the marks of Tanis's fingers stood out red against his tan skin.

"Then why pretend you can't?" Tanis asked, breathing heavily.

Berem rubbed his neck, his eyes on Tanis. "People don't ask questions of a man who can't talk. . . ."

Tanis forced himself to calm down, to think about this a moment. Glancing at Riverwind and Goldmoon, he saw Riverwind scowl and shake his head. Goldmoon shrugged slightly. Finally Tanis dragged another wooden chair over to sit in front of Berem. Noticing that the back of the chair was split and cracked, he sat down carefully. "Berem," Tanis spoke slowly, curbing his impatience, "you're talking to us. Does that mean you'll answer our questions?"

Berem stared at Tanis, then nodded his head, once.

"Why?" Tanis asked.

Berem licked his lips, glancing around. "I—You must help me—get out of here—I—I can't stay here—"

Tanis felt chilled, despite the warm stuffiness of the room. "Are you in danger? Are we in danger? What is this place?"

"I don't know!" Berem looked around helplessly. "I don't know where we are. I only know I cannot stay here. I must get back!"

"Why? The Dragon Highlords are hunting for you. One of th-the Highlords—" Tanis coughed, then spoke huskily. "One of them told me that you were the key to complete victory for the Dark Queen. Why, Berem? What do you have that they want?"

"I don't know!" Berem cried, clenching his fist. "I only know that they have been chasing me . . . I have been fleeing them for, for years! No peace . . . no rest!"

"How long, Berem?" Tanis asked softly. "How long have they been chasing you?"

"Years!" Berem said in a strangled voice. "Years . . . I don't know how long." Sighing, he seemed to sink back into his calm complacency. "I am three hundred and twenty-two years old. Twenty-three? Twenty-four?" He shrugged. "For most of those years, the Queen has been seeking me."

"Three hundred and twenty-two!" Goldmoon said in astonishment. "But—but you're human! That's not possible!"

"Yes, I am human," Berem said, his blue eyes focusing on Goldmoon. "I know it is impossible. I have died. Many times." His gaze switched to Tanis. "You saw me die. It was in Pax Tharkas. I recognized you when you first came on the ship."

"You *did* die when the rocks fell on you!" Tanis exclaimed. "But we saw you *alive* at the wedding feast, Sturm and I—"

"Yes. I saw you, too. That's why I fled. I knew . . . there would be more questions." Berem shook his head. "How could I explain my survival to you? I do not know myself how I survive! All I know is that I die and then I'm alive again. Again and again." His head sank into his hands. "All I want is peace!"

Tanis was completely mystified. Scratching his beard, he stared at the man. That he was lying was almost certain. Oh, not about dying and coming back to life. Tanis had seen that himself. But he knew for a fact that the Queen of Darkness was exerting almost all the forces she could spare from the war to search for this man. Surely he must know why!

"Berem, how did the green gemstone get, uh, into your flesh?"

"I don't know," Berem answered in such a low voice they could barely hear him. Self-consciously, his hand clutched his breast as if it pained him. "It is part of my body, like my bones and my blood. I—I think it is what brings me back to life."

"Can you remove it?" Goldmoon asked gently, sinking down onto a cushion next to Berem, her hand on his arm.

Berem shook his head violently, his gray hair falling over his eyes. "I've tried!" he muttered, "Many times I've tried to rip it out! I might as well try to tear out my own heart!"

Tanis shivered, then sighed in exasperation. This was no help! He still had no idea where they were. He'd hoped Berem could tell them. . . .

Once more, Tanis looked around their strange surroundings. They were in a room of an obviously ancient building, lit with a soft eerie light that seemed to come from the moss that covered the walls like tapestry. The furniture was as old as the building and in battered, shabby condition, though it must have been rich once. There were no windows. Nothing could be heard outside. They had no idea how long they'd been here. Time had grown confused, broken only by eating some of the strange plants and sleeping fitfully.

Tanis and Riverwind had explored the building but could find no exit and no other signs of life. Tanis wondered, in fact, if some magical spell had not been laid over the whole thing, a spell designed to keep them inside. For every time they ventured forth, the narrow, dimly lit hallways always led them inexplicably back to this room.

They remembered little about what happened after the ship sank into the maelstrom. Tanis recalled hearing the wooden planks shattering. He remembered seeing the mast fall, the sails rip. He heard screams. He saw Caramon washed overboard by a gigantic wave. He remembered seeing Tika's red curls swirling in the water, then she, too, was gone. There had been the dragon . . . and Kitiara . . . The scratches of the dragon's talons remained on his arm. Then there was another wave . . . he remembered holding his breath until he knew he would die from the pain in his lungs. He remembered thinking that death would be easy and

welcome, even as he fought to grab hold of a piece of wood. He remembered surfacing in the rushing water, only to be sucked down again and knowing it was the end. . . .

And then he had awakened in this strange place, his clothes wet with sea water, to find Riverwind and Goldmoon and Berem here with him.

At first Berem had seemed terrified of them, crouching in a corner, refusing to let them come near. Patiently Goldmoon spoke to him and brought him food. Gradually, her gentle ministrations won him over. That and—Tanis recognized now—his intense desire to leave this place.

Tanis had supposed, when he first began to question Berem, that the man had steered the ship into the maelstrom because he knew this place existed, that he had brought them here on purpose.

But now the half-elf wasn't so certain. It was apparent from the confused and frightened look on Berem's face that he had no idea where they were either. The mere fact that he was even talking to them gave an indication that what he said was true. He was desperate. He wanted out of here. Why?

"Berem . . ." Tanis began, getting up and pacing about the room. He felt Berem's gaze follow him. "If you are running from the Queen of Darkness, this seems like it might be an ideal place to hide—"

"No!" Berem shouted, half-rising.

Tanis spun around. "Why not? Why are you so determined to get out of here? Why do you want to go back to where she will find you?"

Berem cringed, huddling back down in his chair. "I—I don't know anything about this place! I swear it! I—I m—must get back. . . . There's someplace I must go . . . I'm hunting for something. . . . Until I find it, there'll be no rest."

"Find it! Find what?" Tanis shouted. He felt Goldmoon's hand on his arm and he knew he was raving like a maniac, but it was so frustrating! To have what the Queen of Darkness would give the world to acquire and not know why!

"I can't tell you!" Berem whimpered.

Tanis sucked in his breath, closing his eyes, trying to calm himself. His head throbbed. He felt as if he might fly into a thousand pieces. Goldmoon rose to her feet. Putting both her hands on his shoulders, she whispered soothing words he could not comprehend, except for the name of Mishakal. Slowly the terrible feeling passed, leaving him drained and exhausted.

"All right, Berem." Tanis sighed. "It's all right. I'm sorry. We won't talk about it anymore. Tell me about yourself. Where are you from?"

Berem hesitated a moment, his eyes narrowed and he grew tense. Tanis was struck by Berem's peculiar manner. "I'm from Solace. Where are you from?" he repeated casually.

Berem regarded him warily. "You, you would never have heard of it. A—A small village outside of . . . outside of . . ." He swallowed, then cleared his throat. "Neraka."

"Neraka?" Tanis looked at Riverwind.

The Plainsman shook his head. "He's right. I have never heard of it."

"Nor I," Tanis muttered. "Too bad Tasslehoff and his maps aren't here. . . . Berem, why—"

"Tanis!" Goldmoon cried.

The half-elf rose at the sound of her voice, his hand going reflexively to the sword that wasn't there. Dimly he remembered struggling with it in the water, its weight dragging him down. Cursing himself for not setting Riverwind to guard the door, he could do nothing now but stare at the red-robed man who stood framed in its opening.

"Hello," the man said pleasantly, speaking Common.

The red robes brought Raistlin's image back to Tanis with such force that the half-elf's vision blurred. For a moment he thought it was Raistlin. Then he saw clearly. This mage was older, much older, and his face was kind.

"Where are we?" Tanis demanded harshly. "Who are you? Why were we brought here?"

"KreeaQUEKH," the man said in disgust. Turning, he walked away.

"Damn!" Tanis jumped forward, intent on grabbing the man and dragging him back. But he felt a firm hand on his shoulder.

"Wait," Riverwind counseled. "Calm down, Tanis. He's a magic-user. You couldn't fight him even if you had a sword. We'll follow him, see where he goes. If he laid a spell on this place, perhaps he'll have to lift it to get out himself."

Tanis drew a deep breath. "You're right, of course." He gasped for air. "I'm sorry. I don't know what's wrong with me. I feel tight and stretched, like the skin over a drum. We'll follow him. Goldmoon, you stay here with Berem—"

"No!" Berem shouted. Throwing himself out of the chair, he clutched at Tanis with such force he nearly knocked him down. "Don't leave me here! Don't!"

"We're not going to leave you!" Tanis said, trying to extricate himself from Berem's deathlike grip. "Oh, all right. Maybe we'd all better stay together anyway."

Hurrying out into the narrow corridor, they started down the bleak, deserted hallway.

"There he goes!" Riverwind pointed.

In the dim light, they could just see a bit of red robe whisking around a corner. Walking softly, they followed after it. The hallway led down another hallway with other rooms branching off it.

"This was never here before!" Riverwind exclaimed. "There was always solid wall."

"Solid illusion," Tanis muttered.

Stepping into the hallway, they looked around curiously. Rooms filled with the same ancient, mismatched furniture as in their room opened from the empty corridor. These rooms, too, were empty, but all lit with the same strange glowing lights. Perhaps it was an inn. If so, they appeared to be its only customers and might have been its only customers for a hundred years.

They made their way through broken corridors and vast pillared halls. There wasn't time to investigate their surroundings, not while trailing the red-robed man, who was proving remarkably quick and elusive. Twice they thought they had lost him, only to catch a glimpse of the red robes floating down a circular stairway beneath them, or flitting through an adjacent hallway.

It was at one such juncture that they stood for a moment, glancing down two divergent hallways, feeling lost and frustrated.

"Split up," Tanis said after a moment. "But don't go far. We'll meet back here. If you see any sign of him, Riverwind, whistle once. I'll do the same."

Nodding, the Plainsman and Goldmoon slipped down one hallway while Tanis—with Berem practically tripping on his heels—searched the other one.

He found nothing. The hallway led to a large room, eerily lit as was everything else in this strange place. Should he look in it or turn back? After hesitating a moment, Tanis decided to take a quick glance inside. The room was empty, except for a huge round table. And on the table, he saw as he drew closer, was a remarkable map!

Tanis bent quickly over the map, hoping for a clue as to where and what this mysterious place was. The map was a miniature replica of the city! Protected by a dome of clear crystal, it was so exact in detail that Tanis had the strange feeling the city beneath the crystal was more real than the one where he stood.

"Too bad Tas isn't here," he thought to himself wistfully, picturing the kender's delight.

Istar had been around for thousands of years before the gods blew it off the map.

The buildings were constructed in the ancient style;† delicate spires rose into the crystal sky, light sparkled off the white domes. Stone archways spanned garden boulevards. The streets were laid out like a great spider web, leading directly into the heart of the city itself.

Tanis felt Berem pluck nervously at his sleeve, gesturing that they should leave. Even though he could talk, it was obvious that the man had grown accustomed to, and perhaps even preferred, silence.

"Yes, just a moment," Tanis said, reluctant to go. He had heard nothing from Riverwind and there was every possibility this map might lead them out of this place.

Bending over the glass, he stared at the miniature more closely. Around the center of the city stood great pavilions and columned palaces. Domes made of glass cradled summer flowers amid the winter snows. In the exact center of the city itself rose a building that seemed familiar to Tanis, though he knew he had never been in this city in his life. Still, he recognized it. Even as he studied it, searching his memory, the hair prickled on the back of his neck.

Bard Quivalen Soth, in his "Five Hymns," describes "The splendid and featureless Ice and marble of doomed and imperial Istar."

It seemed to be a temple to the gods. And it was the most beautiful structure† he had ever seen, more beautiful than the Towers of the Sun and the Stars in the elven kingdoms. Seven towers rose to

the heavens as if praising the gods for their creation. The center tower soared into the skies far above the rest, as if it did not praise the gods, but rivaled them. Confused memories of his elven teachers came back to him, telling him stories of the Cataclysm, stories of the Kingpriest—

Tanis drew back from the miniature, his breath catching in his throat. Berem stared at him in alarm, the man's face going white.

"What is it?" he croaked in fear, clutching at Tanis.

The half-elf shook his head. He could not speak. The terrible implications of where they were and what was going on were breaking over him like red waters of the Blood Sea.

In confusion, Berem looked at the center of the map. The man's eyes widened, then he shrieked, a scream unlike any Tanis had heard before. Suddenly Berem threw himself bodily upon the crystal dome, beating at it as if he would tear it apart.

"The City of Damnation!" Berem moaned. "The City of Damnation."

Tanis started forward to calm him, then he heard Riverwind's shrill whistle. Grabbing Berem, Tanis hauled him away from the crystal. "I know," he said. "Come on, we've got to get out of here."

But how? How did you get out of a city that was supposed to have been blasted off the face of Krynn? How did you get out of a city that must lie at the very bottom of the Blood Sea? How did you get out of—

As he shoved Berem through the door of the map room, Tanis glanced above the doorway. Words were carved in its crumbling marble. Words that had once spoken of one of the wonders of the world. Words whose letters were now cracked and covered with moss. But he could read them.

Welcome, O noble visitor, to our beautiful city.
Welcome to the city beloved of the gods.
Welcome, honored guest, to
Istar.

Many different views of the last days of Istar and the Cataclysm are told in two short story collections: The Cataclysm *and* The Reign of Istar.

5

"I killed him once . . ."

I've seen what you're doing to him! You're trying to murder him!" Caramon shouted at Par-Salian. Head of the Tower of High Sorcery, the last Tower of High Sorcery located in the weird, alien forests of Wayreth, Par-Salian was the highest ranking in the Order of magic-users currently living on Krynn.

To the twenty-year-old warrior, the withered old man in the snowy white robes was a thing he might have broken with his bare hands. The young warrior had put up with a good deal the last two days, but now his patience had run out.

"We are not in the business of murder," Par-Salian said in his soft voice. "Your brother knew what he faced when he agreed to undergo these Trials. He knew death was the penalty for failure."

"He didn't, not really," Caramon mumbled, brushing his hand across his eyes. "Or if he did, he didn't care. Sometimes his . . . his love for his magic clouds his thinking."

"Love? No." Par-Salian smiled sadly. "I do not think we could call it love."

"Well, whatever," Caramon muttered. "He didn't realize what you were going to do to him! It's all so damn serious—"

"Of course," Par-Salian said mildly "What would happen to you, warrior, if you went into battle without knowing how to use your sword?"

Caramon scowled. "Don't try to weasel out—"

"What would happen?" Par-Salian persisted.

"I'd be killed," Caramon said with the elaborate patience one uses when speaking to an elderly person who is growing a bit childish. "Now—"

"Not only would you die," Par-Salian continued, "but your comrades, those who depend on you, might they also die because of your incompetence?"

"Yes," Caramon said impatiently, starting to continue his tirade. Then, pausing, he fell silent.

"You see my point," Par-Salian said gently. "We do not require this Test of all who would use magic. There are many with the gift who go through life content with using the first elementary spells taught by the schools. These are enough to help them in their day-to-day lives, and that is all they want. But sometimes there comes a person like your brother. To him, the gift is more than a tool to help him through life. To him, the gift is life. He aspires higher. He seeks knowledge and power that can be dangerous, not only to the user but to those around him as well. Therefore we force all magic-users who would enter into those realms where true power can be attained to take the Test, to submit themselves to the Trials. Thus we weed out the incompetent. . . ."

"You've done your best to weed out Raistlin!" Caramon snarled. "He's not incompetent, but he's frail and now he's hurt, maybe dying!"

"No, he isn't incompetent. Quite the contrary. Your brother has done very well, warrior. He has defeated all of his enemies. He has handled himself like a true professional. Almost too professional." Par-Salian appeared thoughtful. "I wonder if someone hasn't taken an interest in your brother."

"I wouldn't know." Caramon's voice hardened with resolve. "And I don't care. All I know is that I am putting a stop to it. Right now."

We are again reminded here of the Test of the Tower of High Sorcery for a good reason. Raistlin relinquished his body to the power of magic, and it was not enough. The magic demands everything from him. For Raistlin, the Test of the Tower of High Sorcery never ends.
—TRH

"You cannot. You will not be permitted. He isn't dying—"

"You can't stop me!" Caramon stated coldly. "Magic! Tricks to keep kids amused! True power! Bah! It's not worth getting killed over—"

"Your brother believes it is," Par-Salian said softly. "Shall I show you how much he believes in his magic? Shall I show you true power?"

Ignoring Par-Salian, Caramon took a step forward, determined to end his brother's suffering. That step was his last, at least for some time. He found himself immobilized, frozen in place as surely as if his feet were encased in ice. Fear gripped Caramon. It was the first time he had ever been spellbound, and the helpless feeling of being totally under another's control was more terrifying than facing six axe-wielding goblins.

"Watch." Par-Salian† *began to chant strange words. "I am going to show you a vision of what might have been. . . ."*

It was Par-Salian who made the important decision to allow the young mage, Raistlin Majere, to take the Test at an age earlier than most; some wizards believed that it was because of this decision that Fistandantilus was able to seal a bargain with Raistlin and thus lead him into paths of Evil. Par-Salian saw Raistlin as a major weapon in the forthcoming war against Evil.

Suddenly Caramon saw himself entering the Tower of High Sorcery! He blinked in astonishment. He was walking through the doors and down the eerie corridors! The image was so real that Caramon looked down at his own body in alarm, half-afraid he might find he wasn't really there. But he was. He seemed to be in two places at the same time. True power: The warrior began to sweat, then shivered with a chill.

Caramon—the Caramon in the Tower—was searching for his brother. Up and down empty corridors he wandered, calling Raistlin's name. And finally he found him.

The young mage lay on the cold stone floor. Blood trickled from his mouth. Near him was the body of a dark elf, dead, by Raistlin's magic. But the cost had been terrible. The young mage himself seemed near death.

Caramon ran to his brother and lifted the frail body in his strong arms. Ignoring Raistlin's frantic pleas to leave him alone, the warrior began to carry his twin from this evil Tower. He would take Raistlin from this place if it was the last thing he did.

But, just as they came near the door that led out of the Tower, a wraith appeared before them. Another test, Caramon thought grimly. Well, this will be one test Raistlin won't have to handle. Gently laying his brother down, the warrior turned to meet this final challenge.

What happened then made no sense. The watching Caramon blinked in astonishment. He saw himself cast a

magic spell! Dropping his sword, he held strange objects in his hands and began to speak words he didn't understand! Lightning bolts shot from his hands! The wraith† vanished with a shriek.

The real Caramon looked wildly at Par-Salian, but the mage only shook his head and—wordlessly—pointed back to the image that wavered before Caramon's eyes. Frightened and confused, Caramon turned back to watch.

He saw Raistlin rise slowly

"How did you do that?" Raistlin asked, propping himself up against the wall.

Caramon didn't know. How could he do something that took his brother years of study! But the warrior saw himself rattling off a glib explanation. Caramon also saw the look of pain and anguish on his brother's face.

"No, Raistlin!" the real Caramon cried. "It's a trick! A trick of this old man's! I can't do that! I'd never steal your magic from you! Never!"

But the image Caramon, swaggering and brash, went over to "rescue" his "little" brother, to save him from himself.

Raising his hands, Raistlin held them out toward his brother. But not to embrace him. No. The young mage, sick and injured and totally consumed with jealousy, began to speak the words of the one spell, the last spell he had strength to cast.

Flames flared from Raistlin's hands. The magical fire billowed forth, and engulfed his brother.

Caramon watched in horror, too stunned to speak, as his own image was consumed in fire. . . . He watched as his brother collapsed onto the cold stone floor.

"No! Raist—"

Cool, gentle hands touched his face. He could hear voices, but their words were meaningless. He could understand, if he chose. But he didn't want to understand. His eyes were closed. He could open them, but he refused. Opening his eyes, hearing those words, would only make the pain real.

"I must rest," Caramon heard himself say, and he sank back into darkness.

He was approaching another Tower, a different Tower. The Tower of the Stars in Silvanesti. Once more Raistlin was with him, only now his brother wore the Black Robes. And now it was Raistlin's turn to help Caramon. The big warrior was wounded. Blood pulsed steadily

A wraith is a black cloud made of pure Evil that was once a living being. It is vaguely manlike in shape but cannot speak. No way short of magic can allow you to know which Evil soul has returned to continue wreaking havoc on the peoples' lives. No matter what its goals during life, a wraith exists only to create terror and pain. It usually haunts an area surrounding the place where its body is buried.

from a spear-wound that had nearly taken off his arm.

"I must rest," Caramon said again.

Gently Raistlin laid him down, making him comfortable, his back propped up against the cold stone of the Tower. And then Raistlin started to leave.

"Raist! Don't," Caramon cried. "You can't leave me here!"

Looking around, the injured, defenseless warrior saw hordes of the undead elves who had attacked them in Silvanesti waiting to leap upon him. Only one thing held them back, his brother's magical power.

"Raist! Don't leave me!" he screamed.

"How does it feel to be weak and alone?" Raistlin asked him softly.

"Raist! My brother . . ."

"I killed him once, Tanis. I can do it again!"

"Raist! No! Raist!"

"Caramon, please . . ." Another voice. This one gentle. Soft hands touched him.

"Caramon, please! Wake up! Come back, Caramon. Come back to me. I need you."

No! Caramon pushed away that voice. He pushed away the soft hands. No, I don't want to come back. I won't. I'm tired. I hurt. I want to rest.

But the hands, the voice, wouldn't let him rest. They grabbed him, pulling him from the depths where he longed to sink.

And now he was falling, falling into a horrible red darkness. Skeletal fingers clutched at him, eyeless heads whirled past him, their mouths gaping in silent cries. He drew a breath, then sank into blood. Struggling, smothering, he finally fought his way back to the surface and gasped for air once more. Raistlin! But no, he's gone. His friends. Tanis. Gone, too. He saw him swept away. The ship. Gone. Cracked in half. Sailors cut apart, their blood mingling with the blood-red sea.

Tika! She was near him. He pulled her close. She was gasping for air. But he could not hold onto her. The swirling water tore her from his arms and swept him under. This time he could not find the surface. His lungs were on fire, bursting. Death . . . rest . . . sweet, warm. . . .

But always those hands! Dragging him back to the gruesome surface. Making him breathe the burning air. No, let me go!

And then other hands, rising up from the blood-red water. Firm hands, they took him down from the surface.

He fell down . . . down . . . into merciful darkness. Whispered words of magic soothed him, he breathed. . . breathed water. . . and his eyes closed . . . the water was warm and comforting . . . He was a child once more.

But not complete. His twin was missing.

No! Waking was agony Let him float in that dark dream forever. Better than the sharp, bitter pain.

But the hands tugged at him. The voice called to him.

"Caramon, I need you . . ."

Tika.

"I'm no cleric, but I believe he'll be all right now. Let him sleep awhile."

Tika brushed away her tears quickly, trying to appear strong and in control.

"What . . . what was wrong?" she made herself ask calmly, though she was unable to restrain a shudder. "Was he hurt when the ship . . . went into th-the whirlpool? He's been like this for days! Ever since you found us."

"No, I don't think so. If he had been injured, the sea elves would have healed him. This was something within himself. Who is this 'Raist' he talks about?"

"His twin brother," Tika said hesitantly.

"What happened? Did he die?"

"No—no. I—I'm not quite sure what happened. Caramon loved his brother very much and he . . . Raistlin betrayed him."

"I see." The man nodded solemnly. "It happens, up there. And you wonder why I choose to live down here."

"You saved his life!" Tika said. "And I don't know you . . . your name."

"Zebulah," the man answered, smiling. "And I didn't save his life. He came back for love of you."

Tika lowered her head, her red curls hid her face. "I hope so," she whispered. "I love him so much. I would die myself, if it would save him."

Now that she was certain Caramon would be all right, Tika focused her attention on this strange man. She saw he was middle-aged, clean-shaven, his eyes as wide and frank as his smile. Human, he was dressed in red robes. Pouches dangled from his belt.

"You're a magic-user," Tika said suddenly. "Like Raistlin!"

"Ah, that explains it." Zebulah smiled. "Seeing me, in his semiconscious state, made this young man think of his brother."

"But what are you doing here?" Tika glanced around at her strange surroundings, seeing them for the first time.

She had seen them, of course, when the man brought her here, but she hadn't noticed them in her worry. Now she realized she was in a chamber of a ruined, crumbling building. The air was warm and stifling. Plants grew lushly in the moist air.

There was some furniture, but it was as ancient and ruined as the room in which it was haphazardly placed. Caramon lay on a three-legged bed, the fourth corner being held up by a stack of old, moss-covered books. Thin rivulets of water, like small, glistening snakes, trickled down a stone wall that gleamed with moisture. Everything gleamed with moisture, in fact, reflecting the pale, eerie, green light that glowed from the moss growing on the wall. The moss was everywhere, of every different color and variety. Deep green, golden yellow, coral red, it climbed the walls and crawled across the domed ceiling.

"What am *I* doing here?" she murmured. "And where *is* here?"

"Here is—Well, I suppose you could say *here*," Zebulah answered pleasantly. "The sea elves saved you from drowning and I brought you here."

"Sea elves? I never heard of sea elves," Tika said, glancing around curiously, as if she might see one hiding in a closet. "And I don't remember elves saving me. All I remember is some sort of huge, gentle fish. . . ."

"Oh, you needn't look around for the sea elves. You won't see them. They fear and distrust *KreeaQUEKH*—'air-breathers' in their language. And those fish were the sea elves, in the only shape they let *KreeaQUEKH* see them. Dolphins, you call them."

Caramon stirred and moaned in his sleep. Laying her hand upon his forehead, Tika brushed back his damp hair, soothing him.

"Why did they save our lives, then?" she asked.

"Do you know any elves, land elves?" Zebulah asked.

"Yes," Tika answered softly, thinking of Laurana.
"Then you know that to all elves, life is sacred."
"I understand." Tika nodded. "And like the land elves, they renounce the world rather than help it."
"They are doing what they can to help," Zebulah rebuked her severely. "Do not criticize what you do not understand, young woman."
"I'm sorry," Tika said, flushing. She changed the subject. "But you, you're human. Why—"
"Why am I here? I have neither the time nor the inclination to relate my story to you, for it is obvious you would not understand me either. None of the others do."
Tika caught her breath. "There are others? Have you seen any more from our ship . . . our friends?"
Zebulah shrugged. "There are *always* others down here. The ruins are vast, and many hold small pockets of air. We take those we rescue to the nearest dwellings. As for your friends, I couldn't say. If they were on the ship with you, they were most likely lost. The sea elves have given the dead the proper rituals and sent their souls upon their way." Zebulah stood up. "I'm glad your young man survived. There's lots of food around here. Most of the plants you see are edible. Wander about the ruins if you like. I've laid a magic spell on them so you can't get into the sea and drown. Fix the place up. You'll find more furniture—"
"But wait!" Tika cried. "We can't stay here! We must return to the surface. Surely there must be some way out?"
"They all ask me that," Zebulah said with a touch of impatience. "And, frankly, I agree. There *must* be some way out. People seem to find it on occasion. Then, there are those who simply decide that—like me—they don't want to leave. I have several old friends who have been around for years. But, see for yourself. Look around. Just be careful you stay in the parts of the ruins we've arranged." He turned toward the door.
"Wait! Don't go!" Jumping up, tipping over the rickety chair she sat upon, Tika ran after the red-robed magic-user. "You might see my friends. You could tell them—"
"Oh, I doubt it," Zebulah replied. "To tell you the truth—and no offense, young woman—I'm fed up

with your conversation. The longer I live here, the more *KreeaQUEKH* like you irritate me. Always in a hurry. Never satisfied to stay in one place. You and your young man would be much happier down here in this world than up there in that one. But no, you'll kill yourselves trying to find your way back. And what do you face up there? Betrayal!" He glanced back at Caramon.

"There is a war up there!" Tika cried passionately. "People are suffering. Don't you care about that?"

"People are always suffering up there," Zebulah said. "Nothing I can do about it. No, I don't care. After all, where does caring get you? Where did it get him?" With a angry gesture at Caramon, Zebulah turned and left, slamming the ramshackle door behind him.

Tika stared after the man uncertainly, wondering if she shouldn't run out and and grab him and hang onto him. He was apparently their only link to the world *up there.* Wherever *down here* was . . .

"Tika . . ."

"Caramon!" Forgetting Zebulah, Tika ran to the warrior, who was struggling to sit up.

"Where in the name of the Abyss are we?" he asked, looking around with wide eyes. "What happened? The ship—"

"I'm—I'm not sure," Tika faltered. "Do you feel well enough to sit? Perhaps you should lie down. . . ."

"I'm all right," Caramon snapped. Then, feeling her flinch at his harshness, he reached out and pulled her in his arms. "I'm sorry, Tika. Forgive me. It's just . . . I . . ." He shook his head.

"I understand," Tika said softly. Resting her head on his chest, she told him about Zebulah and the sea elves. Caramon listened, blinking in confusion as he slowly absorbed all he heard. Scowling, he looked at the door.

"I wish I'd been conscious," he muttered. "That Zebulah character knows the way out, more than likely. I'd have made him show us."

"I'm not so sure," Tika said dubiously. "He's a magic-user like—" She broke off hurriedly. Seeing the pain in Caramon's face, she nestled closer to him, reaching up to stroke his face.

"Do you know, Caramon," she said softly, "he's right in a way. We *could* be happy here. Do you

realize, this is the first time we've ever been alone? I mean really and truly alone together? And it's so still and peaceful and beautiful in a way. The glowing light from the moss is so soft and eerie, not harsh and glaring like sunlight. And listen to the water murmuring, it's singing to us. Then there's this old, old furniture, and this funny bed . . ."

Tika stopped talking. She felt Caramon's arms tighten around her. His lips brushed her hair. Her love for him surged through her, making her heart stand still with pain and longing. Swiftly she put her arms around him, holding him close, feeling his heart beat against hers.

"Oh, Caramon!" she whispered breathlessly. "Let's be happy! Please! I—I know that—that sometime we'll have to leave. We'll have to find the others and return to the world above. But for now, let's be alone, together!"

"Tika!" Caramon clasped her, crushing her to him as if he would mold their bodies into one, single, living being. "Tika, I love you! I—I told you once that I couldn't make you mine until I could commit myself to you completely. I can't do that—not yet."

"Yes, you can!" Tika said fiercely. Pushing away from him, she looked into his eyes. "Raistlin's gone, Caramon! You can make your own life!"

Caramon shook his head gently. "Raistlin's still a part of me. He always will be, just as I'll always be a part of him. Can you understand?"

No, she couldn't, but she nodded anyway, her head drooping.

Smiling, Caramon drew a quivering breath. Then he put his hand beneath her chin and raised her head. Her eyes were beautiful, he thought. Green with flecks of brown. They shimmered now with tears. Her skin was tan from living outdoors and more freckled than ever. Those freckles embarrassed her. Tika would have given seven years of her life for creamy skin like Laurana's. But Caramon loved every freckle, he loved the crisp, curling red hair that clung to his hands.

Tika saw the love in his eyes. She caught her breath. He drew her near. His heart beating faster, he whispered, "I'll give you what I can of myself, Tika, if you'll settle for that. I wish, for your sake, it was more."

"I love you!" was all she said, clasping him around the neck.

He wanted to be certain she understood. "Tika— " he began.

"Hush, Caramon . . ."

6

Apoletta.

After a long chase through the streets of a city whose crumbling beauty seemed a horror to Tanis, they entered one of the lovely palaces in the center. Running through a dead garden and into a hall, they rounded a corner and came to a halt. The redrobed man was nowhere to be seen.

"Stairs!" Riverwind said suddenly. His own eyes growing accustomed to the strange light, Tanis saw they were standing at the top of a flight of marble stairs that descended so steeply they had lost sight of their quarry. Hurrying to the landing, they could once more see the red robes fluttering down them.

"Keep in the shadows near the wall," Riverwind cautioned, motioning them to the side of the stairway that was big enough for fifty men to walk down it abreast.

Faded and cracked murals on the walls were still so exquisite and life-like that Tanis had the fevered impression the people portrayed there were more alive than he was. Perhaps some of them had been standing in this very spot when the fiery mountain struck the Temple of the Kingpriest†. . . . Putting the thought out of his mind, Tanis kept going.

The actual Temple of the Kingpriest is no longer in the sunken city of Istar. The Dark Queen sent it into the Abyss to try to figure out how to use it as her new entree into the world. Where the Temple was located is now the Pit of Istar, a gate into the Abyss, but the companions do not discover that.

After running down about twenty steps, they came to a broad landing, decorated with life-size statues of silver and gold. From here, the stairs continued down, leading to another landing, leading to more steps, and so on until they were all exhausted and breathless. Still the red robes fluttered ahead of them.

Suddenly Tanis noticed a change in the air. It was becoming more humid, the smell of the sea was strong. Listening, he could hear the faint sounds of water lapping against stone. He felt Riverwind touch his arm, pulling him back into the shadows. They were near the bottom of the steps. The red-robed man was in front of them, standing at the very bottom, peering into a pool of dark water that stretched out before him into a vast, shadowy cavern.

The red-robed man knelt by the side of the water. And then Tanis was aware of another figure; this one in the water! He could see hair shining in the torchlight—it had a faint greenish cast. Two slender white arms rested on the stone steps, the rest of the figure was submerged. The figure's head lay cradled on its arms, in a state of complete relaxation. The red-robed man reached out a hand and gently touched the figure in the water. The figure raised its head.

"I have been waiting," a woman's voice said, sounding reproachful.

Tanis gasped. The woman spoke elven! Now he could see her face, the large, luminous eyes, pointed ears, delicate features. . . .

A sea elf!

Confused tales from his childhood came back to Tanis as he tried to follow the conversation of the red-robed man and the elven woman, who was smiling at him fondly.

"I'm sorry, beloved," the red-robed man said soothingly, in elven, sitting down beside her. "I

went to see how the young man you were concerned about was doing. He'll be all right, now. It was a close one, though. You were correct. He was certainly intent on dying. Something about his brother— a magic-user—betraying him."

"Caramon!" Tanis murmured. Riverwind looked at him questioningly. The Plainsman could not, of course, follow the elven conversation. Tanis shook his head, not wanting to miss what else was said.

"QueaKI' ICHKeecx," said the woman in scorn. Tanis was puzzled, that word was certainly not elven!

"Yes!" The man frowned. "After I made sure those two were safe, I went to see some of the others. One of them, a bearded fellow, a half-elf, leaped at me as if he would swallow me whole! The others we managed to save are doing well."

"We laid out the dead with ceremony," said the woman, and Tanis could hear the ages-old sorrow in her voice, the sorrow of the elves† for the loss of life.

"I would have liked to ask them what they were doing in the Blood Sea of Istar. I've never known a ship's captain foolish enough to dare the maelstrom. The girl told me there's war going on above. Maybe they had no choice."

The sea elves were created by the Graygem in one of its moments of creative havoc. If the land elves are standoffish, the sea elves are doubly so. The two groups of sea elves don't even communicate unless they have to. The Dargonesti are deep-sea elves, and the Dimernesti are shoal-living elves.

The elven woman playfully splashed water on the red-robed man. "There's *always* war going on above! You are too curious, my beloved. Sometimes I think you might leave me and return to your world. Especially after you talk with these *KreeaQUEKH."*

Tanis heard a note of true concern in the woman's voice, though she was still playfully splashing the man.

The red-robed man leaned down and kissed her on the wet, greenish hair shining in the light of the sputtering torch on the wall above them. "No, Apoletta. Let them have their wars and their brothers who betray brothers. Let them have their impetuous half-elves and their foolish sea captains. As long as my magic serves me, I will live below the waves—"

"Speaking of impetuous half-elves," Tanis interrupted in elven as he strode rapidly down the stairs. Riverwind, Goldmoon, and Berem followed, though they had no idea what was being said.

The man turned his head in alarm. The elven woman disappeared into the water so swiftly that

Tanis wondered for a moment if he might have imagined her existence. Not a ripple on the dark surface betrayed where she had been. Reaching the bottom of the steps, Tanis caught hold of the magic-user's hand just as he was about to follow the sea elf into the water.

"Wait! I'm *not* going to swallow you!" Tanis pleaded. "I'm sorry I acted the way I did back there. I know this looks bad, sneaking around after you like this. But we had no choice! I know I can't stop you if you're going to cast a spell or something. I know you could engulf me in flames or put me to sleep or wrap me in cobweb or a hundred other things. I've been around magic-users. But won't you please listen to us? Please help us. I heard you talking about two of our friends—a big man and a pretty red-haired girl. You said the man nearly died—his brother betrayed him. We want to find them. Won't you tell us where they are?"

The man hesitated.

Tanis went on hurriedly, losing coherence in his efforts to keep hold of this man who might be able to help them. "I saw the woman here with you. I heard her speak. I know who she is. A sea elf, isn't she? You are right. I am half-elven. But I was raised among the elves, and I've heard their legends. I thought that's all they were, legends. But then I thought dragons were legends, too. There *is* a war being fought in the world above. And you're right. There always seems to be a war being fought somewhere. But this war won't stay up above. If the Queen of Darkness conquers, you can be certain she'll find out the sea elves are down here. I don't know if there are dragons below the ocean, but—"

"There are sea dragons,† half-elf," said a voice, and the elven woman reappeared in the water once more. Moving with a flash of silver and green, she glided through the dark sea until she reached the stone steps. Then, resting her arms on them, she gazed up at him with brilliant green eyes. "And we have heard rumors of their return. We did not believe them, though. We did not know the dragons had awakened. Whose fault was that?"

"Does it matter?" asked Tanis wearily. "They have destroyed the ancient homeland. Silvanesti is

Sea dragons (which look more like giant turtles than air-breathing dragons) joined the Dark Queen's army, forming their own aquatic wing to attack enemy shipping. They may have played a role in preventing the sea elves from contacting the land elves, until the sea elves have no desire to know them.

a land of nightmares now. The Qualinesti were driven from their homes. The dragons are killing, burning. Nothing, no one is safe. The Dark Queen has one purpose—to gain dominance over every living being. Will you be safe? Even down here? For I presume we are below the sea?"

"You are right, half-elf," said the red-robed man, sighing. "You are below the sea, in the ruins of the city of Istar. The sea elves saved you and brought you here, as they bring all those whose ships are wrecked. I know where your friends are and I can take you there. Beyond that, I don't see what more I can do for you."

"Get us out of here," Riverwind said flatly, understanding the conversation for the first time. Zebulah had spoken in Common. "Who is this woman, Tanis? She looks elven."

"She is a sea elf. Her name is . . ." Tanis stopped.

"Apoletta," said the elven woman, smiling. "Forgive me for not extending a formal greeting, but we do not clothe our bodies as do you KreeaQUEKH. Even after all these years, I cannot persuade my husband to quit covering his body in those ridiculous robes when he goes onto the land. Modesty, he calls it. So I will not embarrass either you or him by getting out of the water to greet you as is proper."

Flushing, Tanis translated the elven woman's words to his friends. Goldmoon's eyes widened. Berem did not seem to hear, he was lost in some sort of inner dream, only vaguely aware of what was happening around him. Riverwind's expression did not change. Apparently nothing he heard about elves could surprise him anymore.

"Anyway, the sea elves are the ones who rescued us," Tanis went on. "Like all elves, they consider life sacred and will help anyone lost at sea or drowning. This man, her husband—"

"Zebulah," he said, extending his hand.

"I am Tanis Half-Elven, Riverwind and Goldmoon of the Qué-Shu tribe, and Berem, uh—" Tanis faltered and fell silent, not quite knowing where to go from here.

Apoletta smiled politely, but her smile quickly faded. "Zebulah," she said, "find the friends the half-elf speaks of and bring them back here."

"We should go with you," Tanis offered. "If you thought I was going to swallow you, there's no telling what Caramon might do—"

"No," said Apoletta, shaking her head. The water glistened on her hair and sparkled on her smooth green-tinged skin. "Send the barbarians, half-elf. You stay here. I would talk with you and learn more of this war you say could endanger us. It saddens me to hear the dragons have awakened. If that is true, I fear you might be right. Our world will no longer be safe."

"I will be back soon, beloved," Zebulah said.

Apoletta reached out her hand to her husband. Taking it, he raised it to his lips, kissing it gently. Then he left. Tanis quickly translated for Riverwind and Goldmoon, who readily agreed to go in search of Caramon and Tika.

As they followed Zebulah back through the eerie, broken streets, he told them tales of the fall of Istar, pointing out various landmarks as they went along.

"You see," he explained, "when the gods hurled the fiery mountain onto Krynn, it struck Istar, forming a giant crater in the land. The sea water rushed in to fill up the void, creating what came to be known as the Blood Sea. Many of the buildings in Istar were destroyed, but some survived and, here and there, retained small pockets of air. The sea elves discovered that this was an excellent place to bring mariners they rescued from capsized ships. Most of them soon feel quite at home."

The mage spoke with a hint of pride which Goldmoon found amusing, though she kindly did not allow her amusement to show. It was the pride of ownership, as if the ruins belonged to Zebulah and he had arranged to display them for the public's enjoyment.

"But you are human. You are not a sea elf. How did you come to live here?" Goldmoon asked.

The magic-user smiled, his eyes looking back across the years. "I was young and greedy," he said softly, "always in hopes of finding a quick way to make my fortune. My magic arts took me down into the depths of the ocean, searching for the lost wealth of Istar. I found riches all right, but not gold or silver.

"One evening I saw Apoletta, swimming among the sea forests. I saw her before she saw me, before she could change her shape. I fell in love with her . . . and long I worked to make her mine. She could not live up above and, after I had existed so long in the peace and tranquil beauty down here, I knew I no longer had a life in the world above either. But I enjoy talking to your kind occasionally, so I wander among the ruins now and then, to see who the elves have brought in."

Goldmoon looked around the ruins as Zebulah paused to catch his breath between stories.

"Where is the fabled temple of the Kingpriest?" she asked.

A shadow passed over the mage's face. The look of pleasure he had worn was replaced by an expression of deep sorrow tinged with anger.

"I'm sorry," Goldmoon said quickly. "I did not mean to cause you pain. . . ."

"No, it's all right," Zebulah said with a brief, sad smile. "In fact, it is good for me to remember the darkness of that dreadful time. I tend to forget—in my daily ramblings here—that this used to be a city of laughing, crying, living, and breathing beings. Children played in these streets—they were playing that terrible evening when the gods cast the fiery mountain down."

He was silent for a moment then, with a sigh, continued.

"You ask where the temple stands. It stands no longer. In the place where the Kingpriest stood, shouting his arrogant demands to the gods, there is a dark pit. Although it is filled with sea water, nothing lives within it. None know its depth, for the sea elves will not venture near it. I have looked into its dark, still waters as long as I could bear the terror, and I do not believe there is an end to its darkness. It is as deep as the heart of evil itself."

Apparently the sea elves have been out of touch for so long they don't know about the disappearance of the old gods. They just accepted as a gift from those gods the fact that Istar descended into their realm, though obviously Zebulah learned the story.

Zebulah stopped in one of the sea-dark streets and peered at Goldmoon intently. "The guilty were punished. But why the innocent? Why did they have to suffer? You wear the medallion of Mishakal† the Healer. Do you understand? Did the goddess explain it to you?"

Goldmoon hesitated, startled by the question, searching within her soul for the answer. Riverwind

stood beside her, stern and silent as always, his thoughts hidden.

"Often I myself have questioned," Goldmoon faltered. Moving nearer Riverwind, she touched his arm with her hand as though to reassure herself he was near. "In a dream, once, I was punished for my questioning, for my lack of faith. Punished by losing the one I love." Riverwind put his strong arm around her and held her close. "But whenever I feel ashamed of my questioning, I am reminded that it was my questioning that led me to find the ancient gods."

She was silent a moment. Riverwind stroked her silver-gold hair and she glanced up at him with a smile. "No," she said softly to Zebulah, "I do not have the answer to this great riddle. I still question. I still burn with anger when I see the innocent suffer and the guilty rewarded. But I know now that my anger can be as a forging fire. In its heat, the raw lump of iron that is my spirit is tempered and shaped to form the shining rod of steel that is my faith. That rod supports my weak flesh."

Zebulah studied Goldmoon silently as she stood amid the ruins of Istar, her silver-golden hair shining like the sunlight that would never touch the crushed buildings. The classic beauty of her face was marked by the effects of the dark roads she had traveled. Far from marring that beauty, the lines of suffering and despair had refined it. There was wisdom in her eyes, enhanced now by the great joy that came from the knowledge of the new life she carried within her body.

The mage's gaze went to the man who held the woman so tenderly. His face, too, bore the marks of the long, tortuous path he had walked.

Although stern and stoic that face would always be, his deep love for this woman showed clearly in the man's dark eyes and the gentleness of his touch.

Perhaps I have made a mistake staying beneath the waters so long, Zebulah thought, suddenly feeling very old and sad. Perhaps I could have helped, if I had stayed above and used my anger as these two used theirs, to help them find answers. Instead, I let my anger gnaw at my soul until it seemed easiest to hide it down here.

"We should delay no longer," said Riverwind abruptly. "Caramon will soon get it into his head to come looking for us, if he has not already."

"Yes," said Zebulah, clearing his throat. "We should go, although I do not think the young man and woman will have left. He was very weak—"

"Was he injured?" Goldmoon asked in concern.

"Not in body," Zebulah replied as they entered a tumble-down building on a crumbling side-street. "But he has been injured in his soul. I could see that even before the girl told me about his twin brother."

A dark line appeared between Goldmoon's finely drawn brows, her lips tightened.

"Pardon me, Lady of the Plains," Zebulah said with a slight smile, "but I see that the forging fire you spoke of blazes in your eyes."

Goldmoon flushed. "I told you I was still weak. I should be able to accept Raistlin and what he did to his brother without questioning. I should have faith that it is all part of the greater good I cannot envision. But I'm afraid I can't. All I can do is pray that the gods keep him out of my path."

"Not me," said Riverwind suddenly, his voice harsh. "Not me," he repeated grimly.

Caramon lay staring into the darkness. Tika, cradled in his arms, was fast asleep. He could feel her heart beating, he could hear her soft breathing. He started to run his hand through the tangle of red curls that lay upon his shoulder, but Tika stirred at his touch and he stopped, fearful of waking her. She should rest. The gods alone knew how long she had been awake, watching over him. She would never tell him, he knew that. When he had asked, she had only laughed and teased him about his snoring.

But there had been a tremor in her laughter, and she had been unable to look into his eyes.

Caramon patted her shoulder reassuringly and she nestled close. He felt comforted as he realized she slept soundly, and then he sighed. Only a few weeks ago, he had vowed to Tika that he would never take her love unless he could commit himself to her body and soul. He could still hear his words, "My first commitment is to my brother. I am his strength."

Now Raistlin was gone, he had found his own strength. As he had told Caramon, "I need you no longer."

I should be glad, Caramon told himself, staring into the darkness. I love Tika and I have her love in return. And now we are free to express that love. I can make that commitment to her. She can come first in all my thoughts now. She is loving, giving. She deserves to be loved.

Raistlin never did. At least that's what they all believe. How often have I heard Tanis ask Sturm when he thought I couldn't hear why I put up with the sarcasm, the bitter recriminations, the imperious commands. I've seen them look at me with pity. I know they think I'm slow-thinking sometimes and I am—compared to Raistlin. I am the ox, lumbering along, bearing the burden without complaint. That's what they think of me.

They don't understand. They don't *need* me. Even Tika doesn't *need* me, not like Raist needed me. They never heard him wake screaming in the night when he was little. We were left alone so much, he and I. There was no one there in the darkness to hear him and comfort him but me. He could never remember those dreams, but they were awful. His thin body shook with fear. His eyes were wild with the sight of terrors only he could see. He clutched at me, sobbing. And I'd tell him stories or make funny shadow-pictures on the wall to drive away the horror.

"Look, Raist," I'd say, "bunnies . . ."† and I'd hold up two fingers and wiggle them like a rabbit's ears.

After a while, he'd stop trembling. He wouldn't smile or laugh. He never did either, much, even when he was little. But he would relax.

"I must sleep. I am so tired," he'd whisper, holding my hand fast. "But you stay awake, Caramon. Guard my sleep. Keep them away. Don't let them get me."

"I'll stay awake. I won't let anything hurt you, Raist!" I'd promise.

Then he would smile—almost—and, exhausted, his eyes would close. I kept my promise. I would stay awake while he slept. And it was funny. Maybe I did keep them away, because as long as I

This came about due to Michael Williams. Tracy and Michael and I were sitting around in one of the small cubicles trying to plot out the ending for the first book—an ending that was never used, by the way, because the book had gone over length. We had come to the big climax. The heroes are in the dwarven kingdom. They're standing on a platform over a lake of fire. Verminaard and his henchmen enter. The heroes have been betrayed.

They're going to die. Fire dragons spring up out of the lake. Flames shoot high into the air.

"What are the heroes doing?" Tracy asks.

was awake and watching, the nightmares never came to him.

Even when he was older, sometimes he'd still cry out in the night and reach out to me. And I'd be there. But what will he do now? What will he do without me when he's alone, lost, and frightened in the darkness?

What will I do without him?

Caramon shut his eyes and, softly, fearful of waking Tika, he began to cry.

"I know what Caramon's doing," Michael answers. He holds up his hand in the shape of a shadow puppet. "Look, Raistlin! Bunnies!"

We collapsed into laughter and did no more constructive work that day. I just had to commemorate that moment.—MW

Trust Margaret to take Michael's joke and turn it back on him in one of the most moving passages in our books.—TRH

7

Berem. Unexpected help.

And that's our story," said Tanis simply.

Apoletta had listened attentively to him, her green eyes intent upon his face. She had not interrupted. When he was finished, she remained silent. Resting her arms on the side of the steps leading into the still water, she seemed lost in thought. Tanis did not disturb her. The feeling of peace and serenity present beneath the sea soothed and comforted him. The thought of returning to the harsh, glaring world of sunlight and blaring noise seemed suddenly frightening. How easy it would be to ignore everything and stay here, beneath the sea, hidden forever in this silent world.

"What about him?" she asked finally, nodding her head at Berem.

Tanis came back to reality with a sigh.

"I don't know," he said, shrugging, glancing at Berem. The man was staring into the darkness of the cavern. His lips were moving, as if repeating a chant over and over.

"He is the key, according to the Queen of Darkness. Find him, she said, and victory is hers."

"Well," Apoletta said abruptly, "you've got him. Does that make victory yours?"

Tanis blinked. The question caught him by surprise. Scratching his beard, he pondered. It was something that had not occurred to him.

"True . . . we have got him," he murmured, "but what do we do with him? What is there about him that grants victory—to either side?"

"Doesn't he know?"

"He claims he doesn't."

Apoletta regarded Berem, frowning. "I would say he was lying," she said after a moment, "but then he is human, and I know little of the strange workings of the human mind. There is a way you can find out, however. Journey to the Temple of the Dark Queen at Neraka."

"Neraka!" repeated Tanis, startled. "But that's . . ." He was interrupted by a cry of such wild fear and terror that he nearly leaped into the water. His hand went to his empty scabbard. With a curse, he whirled around expecting nothing less than a horde of dragons.

There was only Berem, staring at him with wide eyes.

"What is it, Berem?" Tanis asked irritably. "Did you see something?"

"He didn't see anything, Half-Elf," Apoletta said, studying Berem with interest. "He reacted that way when I said Neraka—"

"Neraka!" Berem repeated, shaking his head wildly. "Evil! Great evil! No . . . no . . ."

"That's where you came from," Tanis told him, stepping nearer.

Berem shook his head firmly.

"But you told me—"

"A mistake!" Berem muttered. "I didn't mean Neraka. I m-meant . . . Takar . . . Takar! That's what I meant . . ."

"You meant Neraka. You know the Dark Queen has her great Temple there, in Neraka!" Apoletta said sternly.

"Does she?" Berem looked directly at her, his blue eyes wide and innocent. "The Dark Queen, a Temple in Neraka? No, there's nothing there but a small village. My village . . ." Suddenly he grasped his stomach and doubled over, as if in pain. "I don't feel good. Leave me alone," he mumbled like a child and slumped to the marble floor near the edge of the water. Sitting there, clutching his stomach, he stared into the darkness.

"Berem!" said Tanis in exasperation.

"Don't feel good . . ." Berem muttered sullenly.

"How old did you say he was?" Apoletta asked.

"Over three hundred years, or so he claims," Tanis said in disgust. "If you believe only half of what he says, that cuts it down to one hundred and fifty, which doesn't seem too plausible either, not for a human."

The Dark Queen's Temple at Neraka is the perverted form of the Temple of the Kingpriest, which had gone to the Abyss.

"You know," replied Apoletta thoughtfully, "the Queen's Temple† at Neraka is a mystery to us. It appeared suddenly, after the Cataclysm, so far as we have been able to determine. Now we find this man who would trace his own history to that same time and place."

"It is strange . . ." said Tanis, glancing again at Berem.

"Yes. It may be nothing more than coincidence, but follow coincidence far enough and you'll find it tied to fate, so my husband says." Apoletta smiled.

"Coincidence or not, I don't see myself walking into the Temple of the Queen of Darkness and asking why she's searching the world for a man with a green gemstone buried in his chest," Tanis said wryly, sitting down near the water's edge again.

"I suppose not," Apoletta admitted. "It's hard to believe, though from what you say, that she has grown so powerful. What have the good dragons been doing all this time?"

"Good dragons!" Tanis repeated, astounded. "What good dragons?"

Now it was Apoletta's turn to look amazed. "Why, the good dragons. The silver dragons and gold dragons. Bronze dragons. And the dragonlances. Surely the silver dragons gave you those that were in their keeping. . . ."

"I never heard of silver dragons," Tanis replied, "except in some old song about Huma. The same

with dragonlances. We've been searching for them so long without a trace, I was beginning to believe they didn't exist except in children's stories."

"I don't like this." Apoletta rested her chin on her hands, her face drawn and pale. Something's wrong. Where are the good dragons? Why aren't they fighting? At first I discounted rumors of the sea dragons' return, for I knew the good dragons would never permit it. But if the good dragons have disappeared, as I must believe from talking with you, Half-Elf, then I fear my people truly are in danger." She lifted her head, listening. "Ah, good, here comes my husband with the rest of your friends." She pushed away from the edge. "He and I can go back to my people and discuss what we must do—"

"Wait!" Tanis said, hearing footsteps coming down the marble stairs. "You've got to show us the way out! We can't stay here!"

"But I don't know the way out," Apoletta said, her hands making circles in the water as she kept herself afloat. "Neither does Zebulah. It was never our concern."

"We could wander through these ruins for weeks!" Tanis cried. "Or maybe forever! You're not certain people do escape from this place, are you? Maybe they just die!"

"As I said," Apoletta repeated coldly, "it was never our concern."

"Well, make it your concern!" Tanis shouted. His voice echoed back eerily across the water. Berem looked up at him and shrank away in alarm. Apoletta's eyes narrowed in anger. Tanis drew in a deep breath, then bit his lip, suddenly ashamed.

"I'm sorry, " he began, but then Goldmoon came up to him, placing her hand on his arm.

"Tanis? What is it?" she asked.

"Nothing that can be helped." Sighing, he glanced past her. "Did you find Caramon and Tika? Are they all right?"

"Yes, we found them," Goldmoon answered, her gaze following Tanis's. Together they watched the two come slowly down the stairs behind Riverwind and Zebulah. Tika was staring around in wonder. Caramon, Tanis noticed, kept his eyes focused straight ahead. Seeing the man's face, Tanis looked back at Goldmoon.

"You didn't answer my second question?" he said softly.

"Tika's all right," Goldmoon answered. "As for Caramon, " She shook her head.

Tanis looked back at Caramon and could barely restrain an exclamation of dismay. He would not have recognized the jovial, good-natured warrior in this man with the grim, tear-streaked face, the haunted, shadowed eyes.

Seeing Tanis's shocked look, Tika drew near Caramon and slipped her hand through his arm. At her touch, the warrior seemed to awaken from his dark thoughts. He smiled down at her. But there was something in Caramon's smile—a gentleness, a sorrow—that had never been there before.

Tanis sighed again. More problems. If the ancient gods had returned, what were they trying to do to them? See how heavy the burden could get before they collapsed beneath it? Did they find this amusing? Trapped beneath the sea . . . Why not just give up? Why not just stay down here? Why bother searching for a way out? Stay down here and forget everything. Forget the dragons . . . forget Raistlin . . . forget Laurana . . . Kitiara. . . .

"Tanis . . ." Goldmoon shook him gently.

They were all standing around him now. Waiting for him to tell them what to do.

Clearing his throat, he started to speak. His voice cracked and he coughed. "You needn't look at me!" he said finally, harshly. "I don't have any answers. We're trapped, apparently. There's no way out."

Still they watched him, with no dimming of the faith and trust in their eyes. Tanis glared at them angrily. "Quit looking at me to lead you! I *betrayed* you! Don't you realize that! It's my fault. Everything's my fault!† Find someone else—"

Tanis seems to want to corner the market on guilt. —*TRH*

Turning to hide tears he could not stop, Tanis stared out across the dark water, wrestling with himself to regain control. He did not realize, until she spoke, that Apoletta had been watching him.

"Perhaps I can help you, after all," the sea elf said slowly.

"Apoletta, what are you saying?" Zebulah said fearfully, hurrying to the edge of the water. "Consider—"

"I have considered," Apoletta replied. "The half-elf said we should be concerned about what happens in the world. He is right. The same thing could happen to us that happened to our Silvanesti cousins. They renounced the world and allowed dark and evil things to creep into their land. We have been warned in time. We can still fight the evil. Your coming here may have saved us, Half-Elf," she said earnestly. "We owe you something in return."

"Help us get back to our world," Tanis said.

Apoletta nodded gravely. "I will do so. Where would you go?"

Sighing, Tanis shook his head. He couldn't think. "I suppose one place is as good as another," he said wearily.

"Palanthas," Caramon said suddenly. His deep voice echoed across the still water.

The others glanced at him in uncomfortable silence. Riverwind frowned darkly.

"No," said Apoletta, swimming to the edge once more, "I cannot take you to Palanthas. Our borders extend only as far as Kalaman. Beyond that, we dare not venture. Especially if what you say is true, for beyond Kalaman lies the ancient home of the sea dragons."

Tanis wiped his eyes and nose, then turned back to face his friends. "Well? Any more suggestions?"

They were silent, watching him. Then Goldmoon stepped forward.

"Shall I tell you a story, Half-Elf?" she said, resting her gentle hand upon his arm. "A story of a woman and man, lost and alone and frightened. Bearing a great burden, they came to an inn. The woman sang a song, a blue crystal staff performed a miracle, a mob attacked them. One man stood up. One man took charge. One man—a stranger—said, 'We'll go out through the kitchen.' " She smiled. "Do you remember, Tanis?"

"I remember," he whispered, caught and held by her beautiful, sweet expression.

"We're waiting, Tanis," she said simply.

Tears dimmed his vision again. Tanis blinked rapidly, then glanced around. Riverwind's stern face was relaxed. Smiling a half-smile, he laid his hand on Tanis's arm. Caramon hesitated a moment,

then—striding forward—embraced Tanis in one of his bearlike hugs.

"Take us to Kalaman," Tanis told Apoletta when he could breathe again. "It's where we were headed anyway."

The companions slept at the edge of the water, getting what rest they could before the journey, which Apoletta told them would be long and strenuous.

"How will we travel? By boat?" Tanis asked, watching as Zebulah stripped off his red robes and dove into the water.

Apoletta glanced at her husband, treading water easily beside her. "You will swim," she said. "Didn't you wonder how we brought you down here? Our magic arts, and those of my husband, will give you the ability to breathe water as easily as you now breathe air."

"You're going to turn us into fish?" Caramon asked, horrified.

"I suppose you could look at it that way," Apoletta replied. "We will come for you at the ebb tide."

Tika clasped Caramon's hand. He held onto her tightly, and Tanis, seeing them share a secret look between them, suddenly felt his burden lighten. Whatever turmoil surged in Caramon's soul, he had found a strong anchor to keep him from being swept out into dark waters.

"We'll never forget this beautiful place," Tika said softly.

Apoletta only smiled.

8

Dark tidings.

Papa! Papa!"

"What is it, Little Rogar?"† The fisherman, accustomed to the excited cries of his small son, who was just big enough to begin discovering the wonders of the world, did not raise his head from his work. Expecting to hear about anything from a starfish stranded on the bank to a lost shoe found stuck in the sand, the fisherman kept on re-stringing his net as the little boy dashed up to him.

Note that the little boy's name is "Rogar." That is a reference to Roger Moore, who was at the time the editor of Dragon *magazine. Roger played a barbarian character named Rogar of Mooria.—MW*

"Papa," said the tow-haired child, eagerly grabbing his father's knee and getting himself entangled in the net in the process, "a pretty lady. Drown dead."

"Eh?" the fisherman asked absently.

"A pretty lady. Drown dead," the little boy said solemnly, pointing with a chubby finger behind him.

The fisherman stopped his work now to stare at his son. This was something new.

"A pretty lady? Drowned?"

The child nodded and pointed again, down the beach.

The fisherman squinted his eyes against the blazing noon sun and peered down the shoreline. Then he looked back at his son and his brows came together in a stern expression.

"Is this more of Little Rogar's stories?" he asked severely. "Because if it is, you'll be taking yer dinner standing up."

The child shook his head, his eyes wide. "No," he said, rubbing his small bottom in memory. "I promised."

The fisherman frowned, looking out to sea. There'd been a storm last night, but he hadn't heard anything that sounded like a ship smashing up on the rocks. Perhaps some of the town's people with their fool pleasure boats had been out yesterday and been stranded after dark. Or worse, murder. This wouldn't be the first body washed up ashore with a knife in its heart.

Hailing his oldest son, who was sluicing out the bottom of the dingy, the fisherman put his work aside and stood up. He started to send the small boy in to his mother, then remembered he needed the child to guide them.

"Take us to the pretty lady," the fisherman said in a heavy voice, giving his other son a meaningful glance.

Tugging his father along eagerly, Little Rogar headed back down the beach while his parent and his older brother followed more slowly, fearing what they might find.

They had gone only a short distance before the fisherman saw a sight that caused him to break into a run, his older son pounding along behind.

"A shipwreck. No doubt!" the fisherman puffed. "Blasted landlubbers! Got no business going out in those eggshell boats."

There was not just one pretty lady lying on the beach, but two. Near them were four men. All were dressed in fine clothes. Broken timbers lay scattered around, obviously the remains of a small pleasure craft.

"Drown dead,"† said the little boy, bending to pat one of the pretty ladies.

Rogar says the pretty lady is "drown dead." This is an allusion to David Copperfield.*—MW*

"No, they're not!" grunted the fisherman, feeling for the lifebeat in the woman's neck. One of the men was already beginning to stir—an older man, seemingly about fifty, he sat up and stared around in confusion. Seeing the fisherman, he started in terror and crawled over on his hands and knees to shake one of his unconscious companions.

"Tanis, Tanis!" the man cried, rousing a bearded man, who sat up suddenly.

"Don't be afraid," the fisherman said, seeing the bearded man's alarm. "We're going to help, if we can. Davey, run back and get yer ma. Tell her to bring blankets and that bottle of brandy I saved from Yuletide. Here, mistress," he said gently, helping one of the women to sit up. "Take it easy. You'll be all right. Strange sort of business," the fisherman muttered to himself, holding the woman in his arms and patting her soothingly. "For being near drowned, none of them seems to have swallowed any water. . . ."

Wrapped in blankets, the castaways were escorted back to the fisherman's small house near the beach. Here they were given doses of brandy and every other remedy the fisherman's wife could think of for drowning. Little Rogar regarded them all with pride, knowing that his "catch" would be the talk of the village for the next week.

"Thank you again for your help," Tanis said gratefully.

"Glad to be there," the man said gruffly. "Just be wary. Next time you go out in one of them small boats, head for shore the first sign of a storm."

"Er, yes, I'll—we'll do that," Tanis said in some confusion. "Now, if you could just tell us where we are. . . ."

"Yer north of the city," the fisherman said, waving a hand. "About two-three miles. Davey can give ye a lift in the cart."

"That's very kind of you," Tanis said, hesitating and glancing at the others. They returned his look, Caramon shrugging. "Uh, I know this sounds strange, but we—we were blown off course. What city are we north of?"

"Why, Kalaman, to be sure," the fisherman said, eyeing them suspiciously.

"Oh!" said Tanis. Laughing weakly, he turned to Caramon. "What did I tell you? We—uh—weren't blown as far off course as you thought."

"We weren't?" Caramon said, his eyes open wide. "Oh, we weren't," he amended hastily as Tika dug her elbow into his ribs. "Yeah, I guess I was wrong, as usual. You know me, Tanis, never could get my bearings—"

"Don't overdo it!" Riverwind muttered, and Caramon fell silent.

The fisherman gave them all a dark look. "Yer a strange bunch, no doubt," he said. "You can't remember how you came to smash up. Now you don't even know where you are. I reckon you was all drunk, but that's not my concern. If you'll take my advice, you'll none of you set foot in a boat again, drunk or sober. Davey, bring round the cart."

Giving them a final, disgusted glance, the fisherman lifted his small son on his shoulder and went back to work. His older son disappeared, presumably going to fetch the cart.

Tanis sighed, looking around at his friends.

"Do any of you know how we got here?" he asked quietly. "Or why we're dressed like this?"

One by one, they all shook their heads.

"I remember the Blood Sea and the maelstrom," Goldmoon said. "But then the rest seems like something I dreamed."

"I remember Raist . . ." Caramon said softly, his face grave. Then, feeling Tika's hand slip through his, he looked down at her. His expression softened. "And I remember—"

"Hush," Tika said, blushing, laying her cheek against his arm. Caramon kissed her red curls. "It wasn't a dream,"† she murmured.

Caramon's love for Tika must be stronger than the Forget spell the sea elves cast.

"I remember a few things, too," Tanis said grimly, looking at Berem. "But it's disjointed, fragmented. None of it seems to go together right in my mind. Well, it's no good looking back. We've got to look forward. We'll go to Kalaman and find out what's been happening. I don't even know what day it is! Or month for that matter. Then—"

"Palanthas," Caramon said. "We'll go to Palanthas."

"We'll see," Tanis said, sighing. Davey was returning with the cart, drawn by a bony horse. The

half-elf looked at Caramon. "Are you really certain you want to find that brother of yours?" he asked quietly.

Caramon did not answer.

The companions arrived in Kalaman about mid-morning.

"What's going on?" Tanis asked Davey as the young man drove the cart through the city streets. "Is there a festival?"

The streets were crowded with people. Most of the shops were closed and shuttered. Everyone stood around in small clumps, talking together in excited tones.

"It looks more like a funeral," Caramon said. "Someone important must have died."

"That, or war," Tanis muttered. Women were weeping, men looked sorrowful or angry, children stood about, staring fearfully at their parents.

"Can't be war, sir," Davey said, "and Spring Dawning festival was two days ago. Don't know what's the matter. Just a minute. I can find out if you want," he said, pulling the horse to a stop.

"Go ahead," Tanis said. "Just a minute, though. Why can't it be war?"

"Why, we've won the war!" Davey said, staring at Tanis in astonishment. "By the gods, sir, you musta been drunk if you don't remember. The Golden General and the good dragons—"

"Oh, yes," Tanis said hastily.

"I'll stop in here, at the fish market," Davey said, hopping down. "They'll know."

"We'll come with you." Tanis motioned the others.

"What's the news?" Davey called, running up to a knot of men and women standing before a shop redolent with the odor of fresh fish.

Several men turned immediately, all speaking at once. Coming up behind the boy, Tanis caught only parts of the excited conversation. "Golden General captured! . . . City doomed . . . people fleeing . . . evil dragons . . ."

Try as they might, the companions could make nothing out of this. The people seemed reluctant to talk around strangers—giving them dark, mistrustful glances, especially seeing their rich clothing.

The companions thanked Davey once more for the ride into town, then left him among his friends. After a brief discussion, they decided to head for the marketplace, hoping to find out more details of what had happened. The crowds grew denser as they walked until they practically had to fight their way through the packed streets. People ran here and there, asking for the latest rumors, shaking their heads in despair. Occasionally they saw some citizens, their belongings hastily packed in bundles, heading for the city gates.

"We should buy weapons," Caramon said grimly. "The news doesn't sound good. Who do you suppose this 'Golden General' is, anyway? The people seem to think a lot of him if his disappearance throws them into this much turmoil."

"Probably some Knight of Solamnia," Tanis said. "And you're right, we should buy weapons." He put his hand to his belt. "Damn! I had a purse of funny-looking old gold coins, but it's gone now! As if we didn't have enough trouble. . . ."

"Wait a minute!" Caramon grunted, feeling his belt. "Why! What the— My purse was here a second ago!" Whirling around, the big warrior caught a glimpse of small figure disappearing among the crush of people, a worn leather pouch in its hand. "Hey! You! That's mine!" Caramon roared. Scattering people like straws in the wind, he leaped after the small thief. Reaching out a huge hand, he caught hold of a fleecy vest and plucked the squirming figure up off the street. "Now give me back—" The big warrior gasped. "Tasslehoff!"

"Caramon!" Tasslehoff cried.

Caramon dropped him in astonishment. Tasslehoff stared around wildly.

"Tanis!" he shouted, seeing the half-elf coming through the crowd. "Oh, Tanis!" Running forward, Tas threw his arms around his friend. Burying his face in Tanis's belt, the kender burst into tears.

The people of Kalaman lined the walls of their city. Just a few days before they had done the same thing, only then their mood had been festive as they watched the triumphant procession of knights and silver and golden dragons. Now they were quiet, grim with despair. They looked out over the plain

as the sun rose to its zenith in the sky. Nearly noon. They waited silently.

Tanis stood next to Flint, his hand on the dwarf's shoulder. The old dwarf had nearly broken down at the sight of his friend.

It was a sad reunion. In hushed and broken voices, Flint and Tasslehoff took turns telling their friends what had happened since they were parted in Tarsis months ago. One would talk until overcome, then the other would carry on the story. Thus the companions heard of the discovery of the dragonlances, the destruction of the dragon orb, and Sturm's death.

Tanis bowed his head, overwhelmed with sorrow at this news. For a moment, he couldn't imagine the world without this noble friend.† Seeing Tanis's grief, Flint's gruff voice went on to tell of Sturm's great victory and the peace he had found in death.

Tanis and Sturm's friendship deepened forever in the desperate adventure described in "Snowsong" in Kender, Gully Dwarves, and Gnomes.

"He is a hero in Solamnia now," Flint said. "Already they're telling stories of him, like they do of Huma. His great sacrifice saved the Knighthood, or so it is said. He would have asked for nothing more, Tanis."

The half-elf nodded wordlessly. Then, trying to smile, "Go on," he said. "Tell me what Laurana did when she arrived in Palanthas. And is she still there? If so, we were thinking about going—"

Flint and Tas exchanged glances. The dwarf's head bowed. The kender looked away, snuffling and wiping his small nose with a handkerchief.

"What is it?" Tanis asked in a voice he didn't recognize as his own. "Tell me."

Slowly, Flint related the story. "I'm sorry, Tanis," the dwarf said, wheezing. "I let her down—"

The old dwarf began to sob so pitifully that Tanis's heart ached with sorrow. Clasping his friend in his arms, he held him tightly.

"It wasn't your fault, Flint," he said, his voice harsh with tears. "It's mine, if anyone's. It was for me she risked death and worse."

"Start placing blame and you will end cursing the gods," said Riverwind, laying his hand on Tanis's shoulder. "Thus do my people say."

Tanis was not comforted.

"What time is the—the Dark Lady to come?"

"Noon," said Tas softly.

Now it was nearly noon and Tanis stood with the rest of the citizens of Kalaman, waiting for the arrival of the Dark Lady. Gilthanas stood some distance from Tanis, pointedly ignoring him. The half-elf couldn't blame him. Gilthanas knew why Laurana had left, he knew what bait Kitiara had used to snare his sister. When he asked Tanis coldly if it was true that he had been with the Dragon Highlord, Kitiara, Tanis could not deny it.

"Then I hold you responsible for whatever happens to Laurana," Gilthanas said, his voice shaking in rage. "And I will pray to the gods nightly that whatever cruel fate befalls her, you will meet the same thing—only a hundred times worse!"

"Don't you think I'd accept that if it would bring her back!" Tanis cried in anguish. But Gilthanas only turned away.

Now the people began to point and murmur. A dark shadow was visible in the sky—a blue dragon.

"That's her dragon," Tasslehoff said solemnly. "I saw it at the High Clerist's Tower."

The blue dragon circled lazily above the city in slow spirals, then landed leisurely within bow-shot of the city walls. A deathly hush fell upon the city as the dragon's rider stood up in the stirrups. Removing her helm, the Dark Lady began to speak, her voice ringing through the clear air.

"By now you have heard that I have captured the elfwoman you call the 'Golden General!'" Kitiara shouted. "In case you need proof, I have this to show you." She raised her hand. Tanis saw the flash of sunlight on a beautifully crafted silver helm. "In my other hand, though you cannot see it from where you stand, I have a lock of golden hair. I will leave both these here, on the plain, when I depart, that you may have something to remember your 'general' by."

There was a harsh murmur from the people lining the walls. Kitiara stopped speaking a moment, regarding them coldly. Watching her, Tanis dug his nails into his flesh to force himself to remain calm. He had caught himself contemplating a mad scheme to leap from the wall and attack her where she stood.

Goldmoon, seeing the wild, desperate look on his face, moved near and laid her hand on his arm. She

felt his body shaking, then he stiffened at her touch, bringing himself under control. Looking down at his clenched hands, she was horrified to see blood trickling down his wrists.

"The elfmaid, Lauralanthalasa, has been taken to the Queen of Darkness at Neraka. She will remain as hostage with the Queen until the following conditions are met. First, the Queen demands that a human called Berem, the Everman, be turned over to her immediately. Second, she demands that the good dragons return to Sanction, where they will give themselves up to Lord Ariakas. Finally, the elflord Gilthanas will call for the Knights of Solamnia and the elves of both the Qualinesti and Silvanesti tribes to lay down their arms. The dwarf, Flint Fireforge will require of his people that they do the same."

"This is madness!" Gilthanas called out in answer, stepping forward to the edge of the wall and staring down at the Dark Lady. "We cannot agree to these demands! We have no idea who this Berem is, or where to find him. I cannot answer for my people, nor can I answer for the good dragons. These demands are totally unreasonable!"

"The Queen is not unreasonable," Kitiara replied smoothly. "Her Dark Majesty has foreseen that these demands will need time to be acted upon. You have three weeks. If, within that time, you have not found the man Berem, whom we believe to be in the area around Flotsam, and if you have not sent away the good dragons, I will return and, this time, you will find more than a lock of your general's hair before the gates of Kalaman."

Kitiara paused.

"You will find her head."

With that, she tossed the helm down onto the ground at her dragon's feet, then, at a word, Skie lifted his wings and rose into the air.

For long moments, no one spoke or moved. The people stared down at the helm lying before the wall. The red ribbons† fluttering bravely from the top of the silver helm seemed the only movement, the only color. Then someone cried out in terror, pointing.

She wore red so that her troops could see her in battle—an indication of her bravery, for when she shows up for her forces, she is also visible to the enemy.—MW

Upon the horizon appeared an incredible sight. So awful was it that no one believed it at first, each thinking privately he must be going mad. But the object drifted closer and all were forced to admit its reality, though that did not diminish the horror.

Thus it was that the people of Krynn had their first glimpse of Lord Ariakas's most ingenious war machine, the flying citadels.

Working in the depths of the temples of Sanction, the black-robed magic-users and dark clerics ripped a castle from its foundations and set it in the skies. Now, floating upon dark gray storm clouds, lit by jagged barbs of white lightning, surrounded by a hundred flights of red and black dragons, the citadel loomed over Kalaman, blotting out the noon sun, casting its dreadful shadow over the city.

The people fled the walls in terror. Dragonfear worked its horrible spell, causing panic and despair to fall upon all who dwelt in Kalaman. But the citadel's dragons did not attack. Three weeks, their Dark Queen had ordered. They would give these wretched humans three weeks. And they would keep watch to see that, during this time, the Knights and the good dragons did not take the field.

Tanis turned to the rest of the companions who stood huddled upon the walls, staring bleakly at the citadel. Accustomed to the effects of dragonfear, they had been able to withstand it and were not fleeing in panic as were the rest of the citizens of Kalaman. Consequently they stood alone together upon the walls.

"Three weeks," Tanis said clearly, and his friends turned to him,

For the first time since they had left Flotsam, they saw that his face was free of its self-condemning madness. There was peace in his eyes, much as Flint had seen peace in Sturm's eyes after the knight's death.

"Three weeks," Tanis repeated in a calm voice that sent shivers up Flint's spine, "we have three weeks. That should be time enough. I'm going to Neraka, to the Dark Queen." His eyes went to Berem, who stood silently nearby. "You're coming with me."

Berem's eyes opened wide in stark terror. "No!" he whimpered, shrinking backward. Seeing the man about to run, Caramon's huge hand reached out and caught hold of him.

"You will go with me to Neraka," Tanis said in a soft voice, "or I will take you right now and give you to Gilthanas. The elflord loves his sister dearly. He would not hesitate to hand you over to the Queen of Darkness if he thought that would buy Laurana's freedom. You and I know differently. We know that giving you up wouldn't change matters a bit. But he doesn't. He is an elf, and he would believe she would keep her bargain."

Berem stared at Tanis warily. "You won't give me up?"

"I'm going to find out what's going on," Tanis stated coldly, avoiding the question. "At any rate, I'll need a guide, someone who knows the area. . . ."

Wrenching himself free of Caramon's grip, Berem regarded them with a hunted expression. "I'll go," he whimpered. "Don't give me to the elf . . ."

"All right," Tanis said coldly. "Quit sniveling. I'll be leaving before dark and I've got a lot to do—"

Turning abruptly, he was not surprised to feel a strong hand grip his arm. "I know what you're going to say, Caramon." Tanis did not turn around. "And the answer is no. Berem and I are going alone."

"Then you'll go to your deaths alone," Caramon said quietly, holding onto Tanis firmly.

"If so, then that's what I'll do!" Tanis tried without success to break free of the big man. "I'm not taking any of you with me."

"And you'll fail," Caramon said. "Is that what you want? Are you going just to find a way to die that will end your guilt? If so, I can offer you my sword right now. But if you truly want to free Laurana, then you're going to need help."

"The gods have reunited us," Goldmoon said gently. "They have brought us together again in our time of greatest need. It is a sign from the gods, Tanis. Don't deny it."

The half-elf bowed his head. He could not cry, there were no tears left. Tasslehoff's small hand slipped into his.

"Besides," said the kender cheerfully, "think how much trouble you'd get into without me!"

9
A Single Candle.

The city of Kalaman was deathly silent the night after the Dark Lady issued her ultimatum. Lord Calof declared a State of War, which meant all taverns were closed, the city gates were locked and barred, no one allowed to leave. The only people permitted to enter were families from the small farming and fishing villages near Kalaman. These refugees began arriving near sundown, telling fearful tales of draconians swarming over their land, looting and burning.

Although some of the noblemen of Kalaman had been opposed to such a drastic measure as a declared State of War, Tanis and Gilthanas—united for once—had forced the Lord to make this decision. Both of them painted vivid and horrifying pictures of the burning of the city of Tarsis. These proved

extremely convincing. Lord Calof made his declaration, but then stared at the two men helplessly. It was obvious he had no idea what to do in regard to the defense of the city. The horrifying shadow of the floating citadel† hovering above had completely unnerved the lord, and most of his military leaders were in little better shape. After listening to some of their wilder ideas, Tanis rose to his feet.

These flying citadels were actually part of the game design way back at the end of the first Chronicles novel but were cut for lack of time and space. However, I loved the idea of castles flying in the sky—possibly from my childhood confusion when I watched the B17s—literally "Flying Fortresses"—on television.—TRH

"I have a suggestion, my lord," he said respectfully. "You have a person here, well-qualified to take over the defense of this city—"

"You, Half-Elf?" interrupted Gilthanas with a bitter smile.

"No," said Tanis gently. "You, Gilthanas."

"An elf?" said Lord Calof in amazement.

"He was in Tarsis. He has had experience fighting the draconians and the dragons. The good dragons trust him and will follow his judgment."

"That's true!" Calof said. A look of vast relief crossed his face as he turned to Gilthanas. "We know how elves feel about humans, my lord, and—I must admit—most humans feel the same about elves. But we would be eternally grateful if you could help us in this time of peril."

Gilthanas stared at Tanis, puzzled for a moment. He could read nothing in the half-elf's bearded face. It was almost, he thought, the face of a dead man. Lord Calof repeated his question, adding something about "reward," apparently thinking Gilthanas's hesitation was due to a reluctance to accept the responsibility.

"No, my lord!" Gilthanas came out of his reverie with a start. "No reward is necessary or even wanted. If I can help save the people of this city, that will be reward enough. As for being of different races"—Gilthanas looked once more at Tanis—"perhaps I have learned enough to know that doesn't make any difference. It never did."

"Tell us what to do," Calof said eagerly.

"First, I would like a word with Tanis," Gilthanas said, seeing the half-elf preparing to depart.

"Certainly. There is a small room through the door to your right where you may talk in private." The Lord gestured.

Once inside the small, luxuriously appointed room, both men stood in uncomfortable silence for

long moments, neither looking at the other directly. Gilthanas was the first to break the silence.

"I have always despised humans," the elflord said slowly, "and now I find myself preparing to take on the responsibility of protecting them." He smiled. "It is a good feeling," he added softly, looking directly at Tanis for the first time.

Tanis's eyes met Gilthanas's and his grim face relaxed for a moment, though he did not return the elflord's smile. Then his gaze fell, his grave expression returned.

"You're going to Neraka, aren't you?" Gilthanas said after another long pause.

Tanis nodded, wordlessly.

"Your friends? They're going with you?"

"Some of them," Tanis replied. "They all want to go, but—" He found he could not continue, remembering their devotion. He shook his head.

Gilthanas stared down at an ornately carved table, absently running his hand over the gleaming wood.

"I must leave," Tanis said heavily, starting for the door. "I have a lot yet to do. We plan to leave at midnight, after Solinari's set—"

"Wait." Gilthanas put his hand on the half-elf's arm. "I—I want to tell you I'm sorry . . . about what I said this morning. No, Tanis, don't leave. Hear me out. This isn't easy for me." Gilthanas paused a moment. "I've learned a great deal, Tanis—about myself. The lessons have been hard ones. I forgot them . . . when I heard about Laurana. I was angry and frightened and I wanted to hit someone. You were the closest target. What Laurana did, she did out of love for you. I'm learning about love, too, Tanis. Or I'm trying to learn." His voice was bitter. "Mostly I'm learning about pain. But that's my problem."

Tanis was watching him now. Gilthanas's hand was still on his shoulder.

"I know now, after I've had time to think," Gilthanas continued softly, "that what Laurana did was right. She *had* to go, or her love would have been meaningless. She had faith in you, believed in you enough to go to you when she heard you were dying, even though it meant going to that evil place—"

Tanis's head bowed. Gilthanas gripped him tightly, both hands on his shoulders.

"Theros Ironfeld said once that—in all the years he had lived—he had never seen anything done out of love come to evil. We have to believe that, Tanis. What Laurana did, she did out of love. What you do now, you do out of love. Surely the gods will bless that."

"Did they bless Sturm?" Tanis asked harshly. "He loved!"

"Didn't they? How do you know?"

Tanis's hand closed over Gilthanas's. He shook his head. He wanted to believe. It sounded wonderful, beautiful . . . just like tales of dragons. As a child, he'd wanted to believe in dragons, too. . . .

Sighing, he walked away from the elflord. His hand was on the doorknob when Gilthanas spoke again.

"Farewell . . . brother."

The companions met by the wall, at the secret door Tasslehoff had found that led up and over the walls, out into the plains beyond. Gilthanas could, of course, have given them permission to leave by the front gates, but the fewer people who knew of this dark journey the better as far as Tanis was concerned.

Now they were gathered inside the small room at the top of the stairs. Solinari was just sinking behind the distant mountains. Tanis, standing apart from the others, watched the moon as its last silvery rays touched the battlements of the horrible citadel hovering above them. He could see lights in the floating castle. Dark shapes moved around. Who lived in that dreadful thing? Draconians? The black-robed mages and dark clerics whose power had torn it from the soil and now kept it drifting among masses of thick gray clouds?

Behind him, he heard the others talking in soft voices—all except for Berem. The Everman—watched over closely by Caramon—stood apart, his eyes wide and fearful.

For long moments Tanis watched them, then he sighed. He faced another parting, and this one grieved him so that he wondered if he had the strength to make it. Turning slightly, he saw the last

beaming rays of Solinari's fading light touch Goldmoon's beautiful silver-gold hair. He saw her face, peaceful and serene, even though she contemplated a journey into darkness and danger. And he knew he had the strength.

With a sigh, he walked away from the window to rejoin his friends.

"Is it time?" Tasslehoff asked eagerly.

Tanis smiled, his hand reaching out fondly to stroke Tas's ridiculous topknot of hair. In a changing world, kenders remained constant.

"Yes," Tanis said, "it is time." His eyes went to Riverwind. "For *some* of us."

As the Plainsman met the half-elf's steady, unwavering gaze, the thoughts in his mind were reflected in his face, as clear to Tanis as clouds flitting across the night sky. First Riverwind was uncomprehending, perhaps he had not even heard Tanis's words. Then the Plainsman realized what had been said. Now he understood, and his stern, rigid face flushed, the brown eyes flared. Tanis said nothing. He simply shifted his gaze to Goldmoon.

Riverwind looked at his wife, who stood in a pool of silvery moonlight, waiting, her own thoughts far away. There was a sweet smile on her lips. A smile Tanis had seen only recently. Perhaps she was seeing her child playing in the sun.

Tanis looked back at Riverwind. He saw the Plainsman's inner struggle, and Tanis knew that the Qué-Shu warrior would offer, no, he would insist, on accompanying them, even though it meant leaving Goldmoon behind.

Walking to him, Tanis put his hands on the tall man's shoulders, looking into the Plainsman's dark eyes.

"Your work is done, my friend," Tanis said. "You have walked winter's path far enough. Here our roads separate. Ours leads into a bleak desert. Yours wends its way through green and blossoming trees. You have a responsibility to the son or daughter you are bringing into the world." He put his hand on Goldmoon's shoulder now, drawing her near, seeing her about to protest.

We're happy to announce that Riverwind and Goldmoon have a son first, and later twin girls, both with silver-gold hair.

"The baby will be born† in the autumn," Tanis said softly, "when the vallenwoods are red and golden. Don't cry, my dear." He gathered Goldmoon

into his arms. "The vallenwoods will grow again. And you will take the young warrior or the young maiden into Solace, and you will tell them a story of two people who loved each other so much they brought hope into a world of dragons."

He kissed her beautiful hair. Then Tika, weeping softly, took his place, bidding Goldmoon farewell. Tanis turned to Riverwind. The Plainsman's stern mask was gone, his face showed plainly the marks of his grief. Tanis himself could barely see through his tears.

"Gilthanas will need help, planning the defense of the city." Tanis cleared his throat. "I wish to the gods this was truly the end of your dark winter, but I'm afraid it must last a little longer."

"The gods are with us, my friend, my brother," Riverwind said brokenly, embracing the half-elf. "May they be with you, as well. We will wait here for your return."

Solinari dipped behind the mountains. The only lights in the night sky were the cold and glittering stars and the hideous gleam of windows in the citadel, watching them with yellow eyes. One by one, the companions bid the Plainsmen good-bye. Then, following Tasslehoff, they silently crossed the wall, entered another door, and crept down another staircase. Tas shoved open the door at the bottom. Moving cautiously, hands on their weapons, the companions stepped out onto the plain.

For a moment, they stood huddled together, staring out across the plain where, even in the deep darkness, it seemed to them they would be visible to thousands of eyes watching from the citadel above.

Standing next to Berem, Tanis could feel the man shivering with fear and he felt glad he had assigned Caramon to watch him. Ever since Tanis had stated they were going to Neraka, the half-elf had seen a frantic, haunted look in the man's blue eyes, much like the look of a trapped animal. Tanis caught himself pitying the man, then hardened his heart. Too much was at stake. Berem was the key, the answer lay within him and within Neraka. Just how they were going to go about discovering the answer, Tanis hadn't decided yet, although the beginnings of a plan stirred in his brain.

Far away, the blaring noise of horns split the night air. An orange light flared on the horizon. Draconians, burning a village. Tanis gripped his cloak around him. Though Spring Dawning had come and past, the chill of winter was still in the air.

"Move out," he said softly.

In later years, Khirsah, the bronze dragon, claims to be the only dragon to let a kender ride him. He's fudging a bit, because Tas is accompanying the remaining companions on these brass dragons.

One by one, he watched them run across the strip of open grassland, racing to reach the shelter of the grove of trees beyond. Here small, fast-flying brass dragons† waited to carry them into the mountains.

This might all end tonight, Tanis though nervously, watching Tasslehoff scamper into the darkness like a mouse. If the dragons were discovered, if the watching eyes in the citadel saw them, it would be all over. Berem would fall into the hands of the Queen. Darkness would cover the land.

Tika followed Tas, running lightly and surely. Flint ran close behind, wheezing. The dwarf looked older. The thought that he was unwell crossed Tanis's mind, but he knew Flint would never agree to stay behind. Now Caramon ran through the darkness, his armor clanking. One hand was fixed firmly on Berem, tugging him along beside him.

My turn, Tanis realized, seeing the others safely sheltered within the grove. This is it. For good or for evil, the story is drawing near its end. Glancing up, he saw Goldmoon and Riverwind watching them from the small window in the tower room.

For good or for evil.

What if it does end in darkness, Tanis wondered for the first time. What will become of the world? What will become of those I'm leaving behind?

Steadily he looked up at these two people who were as dear to him as the family he'd never known. And, as he watched, he saw Goldmoon light a candle. For a brief instant the flame illuminated her face and Riverwind's. They raised their hands in parting, then extinguished the flame lest unfriendly eyes see it.

Taking a deep breath, Tanis turned and tensed himself to run.

The darkness might conquer, but it could never extinguish hope. And though one candle, or many, might flicker and die, new candles would be lit from the old.

Thus hope's flame always burns, lighting the darkness until the coming of day.

BOOK 3

I

An Old Man and a Golden Dragon.

He was an ancient gold dragon, the oldest of his kind. In his day, he had been a fierce warrior. The scars of his victories were visible on his wrinkled golden skin. His name had once been as shining as his glories, but he had forgotten it long ago. A few of the younger, irreverent gold dragons referred to him affectionately as Pyrite, Fool's Gold, due to his not infrequent habit of mentally fading out of the present and reliving his past.†

Gold dragons may easily live at least five hundred years. Pyrite, however, must already be over a thousand years old. Of course, naps do help.

Most of his teeth were gone. It had been eons since he had munched up a nice bit of deer meat or torn apart a goblin. He was able to gum a rabbit now and then, but mostly he lived on oatmeal.

When Pyrite lived in the present, he was an intelligent, if irrascible, companion. His vision was dimming, though he refused to admit it, and he

was as deaf as a doorknob. His mind was quick. His conversation was still sharp as a tooth, so the saying went among dragons. It was just that he rarely discussed the same topic as anyone else in his company.

But when he was back in his past, the other golds took to their caves. For when he remembered them, he could still throw spells remarkably well, and his breath weapons were as effective as ever.

On this day, however, Pyrite was neither in past nor in present. He lay on the Plains of Estwilde,† napping in the warm spring sunshine. Next to him sat an old man doing the same thing, his head pillowed on the dragon's flank.

Estwilde is the flat area south of Kalaman.

A battered and shapeless pointed hat rested over the old man's face to shield his eyes from the sun. A long white beard flowed out from under the hat. Booted feet stuck out from beneath long, mouse-colored robes.

Both slept soundly. The gold dragon's flanks heaved and thrummed with his wheezing breath. The old man's mouth was wide open, and he sometimes woke himself with a prodigious snore. When this happened, he would sit bolt upright—sending his hat rolling onto the ground (which did not help its appearance)—and look around in alarm. Seeing nothing, he would grunt to himself in annoyance, replace his hat (after he found it), poke the dragon irritably in the ribs, then go back to his nap.

A casual passerby might have wondered what in the name of the Abyss these two were doing calmly sleeping on the Plains of Estwilde, even though it was a fine, warm spring day. The passerby might have supposed the two were waiting for someone, for the old man† would occasionally awaken, remove his hat, and peer solemnly up into the empty sky.

One gets the feeling that Fizban goes off for long breaks somewhere between appearances to the Heroes of the Lance in the book. Truth is that Fizban is active all the time, for though the story revolves around our central characters, the world does not and Fizban has many other tasks to perform. Those stories are told elsewhere.—TRH

A passerby might have wondered, had there been any passersby. There were not. At least no friendly ones. The Plains of Estwilde were crawling with draconian and goblin troops. If the two knew they were napping in a dangerous place, they did not seem to mind.

Awakening from a particularly violent snore, the old man was just about to scold his companion sternly for making such terrible noises when a shadow fell across them.

"Ha!" the old man said angrily, staring up. "Dragonriders! A whole passel of 'em. Up to no good, too, I suppose." The old man's white eyebrows came together in a V-shape above his nose. "I've had about enough of this. Now they have the nerve to come and cut off my sunshine. Wake up!" he shouted, poking at Pyrite with a weather-beaten old wooden staff.

The gold dragon grumbled, opened one golden eye, stared at the old man (seeing only a mouse-colored blur), and calmly shut his eye again.

The shadows continued to pass over, four dragons with riders.

"Wake up, I say, you lazy lout!" the old man yelled. Snoring blissfully, the gold rolled over on his back, his clawed feet in the air, his stomach turned to the warm sun.

The old man glared at the dragon for a moment, then, in sudden inspiration, ran around to the great head. "War!" he shouted gleefully, directly into one of the dragon's ears. "It's war! We're under attack—"

The effect was startling. Pyrite's eyes flared open. Rolling over onto his stomach, his feet dug into the ground so deeply he nearly mired himself. His head reared up fiercely, his golden wings spread and began to beat, sending clouds of dust and sand a mile high.

"War!" he trumpeted. "War! We're called. Gather the flights! Mount the attack!"†

Pyrite was dedicated—heart and soul—to Huma, so even now, all it takes is the warning of attack, and the senile old beast is up and away.

The old man appeared rather taken aback by this sudden transformation, and he was also rendered momentarily speechless by the accidental inhalation of a mouthful of dust. Seeing the dragon start to leap into the air, however, he ran forward, waving his hat.

"Wait!" he yelled, coughing and choking. "Wait for me!"

"Who are you that I should wait?" Pyrite roared. The dragon stared through the billowing sand. "Are you my wizard?"

"Yes, yes," the old man called hastily. "I'm—uh—your wizard. Drop your wing a bit so I can climb on. Thanks, there's a good fellow. Now I . . . oh! Whoah! I'm not strapped in! . . . Look out! My hat! Confound it, I didn't tell you to take off yet!"

"We've got to reach the battle in time," Pyrite cried fiercely. "Huma's fighting alone!"

"Huma!" The old man snorted. "Well, you're not going to arrive in time for *that* battle! Few hundred years late. But that's not the battle I had in mind. It's those four dragons there, to the east. Evil creatures! We've got to stop them—"

"Dragons! Ah, yes! I see them!" roared Pyrite, swooping up in hot pursuit of two extremely startled and highly insulted eagles.

"No! No!" yelled the old man, kicking the dragon in the flanks. "East, you ninny! Fly two more points to the east!"

"Are you sure you're my wizard?" Pyrite asked in a deep voice. "My wizard never spoke to me in that tone."

"I'm—uh, sorry, old fellow," the old man said quickly, "just a bit nervous. Upcoming conflict and all that."

"By the gods, there are four dragons!" Pyrite said in astonishment, having just caught a blurred glimpse of them.

"Take me in close so I can get a good shot at them," the old man shouted. "I have a really wonderful spell—Fireball. Now," he muttered, "if I can just remember how it goes."

Two dragonarmy officers rode among the flight of four brass dragons. One rode at the front. A bearded man, his helm seemed slightly large for him and was worn pulled well down over his face, shadowing his eyes. The other officer rode behind the group. He was a huge man, nearly splitting out of his black armor. He wore no helm—there probably wasn't one large enough—but his face was grim and watchful, particularly over the prisoners who rode the dragons in the center of the flight.

It was an odd assortment of prisoners, a woman dressed in mismatched armor, a dwarf, a kender, and a middle-aged man with long, unkempt gray hair.

The same passerby who had observed the old man and his dragon might have noticed that the officers and their prisoners went out of their way to avoid detection by any ground troops of the Dragon Highlord. Indeed, when one group of draconians spotted them and began to shout, trying to attract their attention, the dragonarmy officers studiously ignored them. A truly sharp observer might also have wondered what brass dragons were doing in the Dragon Highlord's service.

Unfortunately, neither the old man nor his decrepit golden dragon was a sharp observer.

Keeping in the clouds, they sneaked up on the unsuspecting group.

"Whiz down out of here at my command," the old man said, cackling to himself in high glee over the prospect of a fight. "We'll attack 'em from the rear."

"Where's Sir Huma?" the gold asked, peering blearily through the cloud.

"Dead," muttered the old man, concentrating on his spell.

"Dead!" roared the dragon in dismay. "Then we're too late?"

"Oh, never mind!" snapped the old man irritably. "Ready?"

"Dead," repeated the dragon sadly. Then his eyes blazed. "But we'll avenge him!"

"Yes, quite," said the old man. "Now . . . at my signal, No! Not yet! You—"

The old man's words were lost in a rush of wind as the gold dove out of the cloud, plummeting down on the four smaller dragons beneath him like a spear shooting from the sky.

The big dragonarmy officer in the back caught a glimpse of movement above him and glanced up. His eyes widened.

"Tanis!" he yelled in alarm at the officer in the front.

The half-elf turned. Alerted by the sound of Caramon's voice, he was ready for trouble, but at first he couldn't see anything. Then Caramon pointed.

Tanis looked up.

"What in the name of the gods—" he breathed.

Streaking down out of the sky, diving straight for them, was a golden dragon. Riding on the dragon was an old man, his white hair flying out behind him (he'd lost his hat†), his long white beard blowing back over his shoulders. The dragon's mouth was bared in a snarl that would have been vicious if it hadn't been toothless.

Fizban's hat seems to have a mind of its own. Its appearance changes at will, and it has a tendency to come back to its master whenever it is lost.
—TRH

"I think we're under attack," Caramon said in awe.

Tanis had come to the same conclusion. "Scatter!" he yelled, swearing under his breath. Down below them, an entire division of draconians watched the aerial battle with intense interest. The last thing he had wanted to do was call attention to the group, now some crazy old man was ruining everything.

The four dragons, hearing Tanis's command, broke instantly from formation, but not soon enough. A brilliant fireball burst right in their midst, sending the dragons reeling in the sky.

Momentarily blinded by the brilliant light, Tanis dropped the reins and threw his arms around the creature's neck as it went rolling about out of control.

Then he heard a familiar voice.

"That got 'em! Wonderful spell, Fireball—"

"Fizban!" Tanis groaned.

Blinking his eyes, he fought desperately to bring his dragon under control. But it seemed the beast knew how to handle himself better than the inexperienced rider, for the brass soon righted himself. Now that Tanis could see, he flashed a glance around at the others. They appeared unhurt, but they were scattered all over the sky. The old man and his dragon were pursuing Caramon—the old man had his hand outstretched, apparently all set to cast another devastating spell. Caramon was yelling and gesturing—he, too, had recognized the befuddled old mage.

Racing toward Fizban from behind came Flint and Tasslehoff, the kender shrieking in glee and waving his hands, Flint hanging on for dear life. The dwarf looked positively green.

But Fizban was intent upon his prey. Tanis heard the old man shout several words and extend his hand. Lightning shot from his fingertips. Fortunately his aim was off. The lightning streaked past Caramon's head, forcing the big man to duck but otherwise not injuring him.

Tanis swore an oath so vile he startled himself. Kicking his dragon in the flanks, he pointed at the old man.

"Attack!" he commanded the dragon. "Don't hurt him, just drive him out of here."

To his amazement, the brass refused. Shaking his head, the dragon began to circle, and it suddenly occurred to Tanis that the creature intended to land!

"What? Are you mad?" Tanis swore at the dragon. "You're taking us down into the dragonarmies!"

The dragon seemed deaf, and now Tanis saw that all the other brass dragons were circling, preparing to land.

In vain Tanis pleaded with his dragon. Berem, sitting behind Tika, clutched the woman so desperately she could barely breathe. The Everman's eyes were on the draconians, who were swarming over the plains toward where the dragons were going to land. Caramon was flailing about wildly, trying to avoid the lightning bolts that zapped all around him. Flint had even come to life, tugging frantically at his dragon's reins, roaring in anger, while Tas was still yelling wildly at Fizban. The old man followed after them all, herding the brass dragons before him like sheep.

They landed near the foothills of the Khalkist Mountains. Looking quickly across the plains, Tanis could see draconians swarming toward them.

We might bluff our way out of this, Tanis thought feverishly, though their disguises had been intended only to get them into Kalaman, not to deceive a party of suspicious draconians. However, it was worth a shot. If only Berem would remember to stay in the background and keep quiet.

But before Tanis could say a word, Berem leaped from the back of his dragon and took off, running frantically into the foothills. Tanis could see the draconians pointing at him, yelling.

So much for keeping in the background. Tanis swore again. The bluff might still work. . . . They could always claim a prisoner was trying to escape. No, he realized in despair, the draconians would simply chase after Berem and catch him. According to what Kitiara had told him, all the draconians in Krynn had descriptions of Berem.

"In the name of the Abyss!" Tanis forced himself to calm down and think logically, but the situation was fast getting out of control. "Caramon! Go after Berem. Flint, you— No, Tasslehoff, get back here! Damn it! Tika, go after Tas. No, on second thought, stay with me. You, too, Flint—"

"But Tasslehoff's gone after that crazy old—"

"And if we're lucky, the ground will open and swallow them both!" Tanis glanced back over his shoulder and swore savagely. Berem—driven by fear—was clambering over rocks and scrub bushes with the lightness of a mountain goat, while Caramon—hampered by the dragonarmor and his own arsenal of weapons—slipped down two feet for every foot he gained.

Looking back across the Plains, Tanis could see the draconians clearly. Sunlight gleamed off their armor and their swords and spears. Perhaps there was still a chance, if the brass dragons would attack,

But just as he started to order them into battle, the old man came running up from where he had landed his ancient gold dragon. "Shoo!" said the old man to the brass dragons. "Shoo—get away! Go back to wherever you came from!"

"No! Wait!" Tanis nearly tore out his beard in frustration, watching as the old man ran among the brass dragons, waving his arms like a farmer's wife driving her chickens to shelter. Then the half-elf stopped swearing for—to his astonishment—the brass dragons prostrated themselves flat on the ground before the old man in his mouse-colored robes. Then, lifting their wings, they soared gracefully into the air

In a rage, forgetting he was dressed in captured dragonarmy armor, Tanis ran across the trampled grass toward the old man, following Tas. Hearing them coming, Fizban turned around to face them.

"I've a good mind to wash your mouth out with soap," the old mage snapped, glowering at Tanis. "You're my prisoners now, so just come along quietly or you'll taste my magic—"

"Fizban!" cried Tasslehoff, throwing his arms around the old man.

The old mage peered down at the kender hugging him, then staggered backward in amazement.

"It's Tassle—Tassle—" he stammered.

"Burrfoot," Tas said, backing off and bowing politely. "Tasslehoff Burrfoot."

"Great Huma's ghost!" Fizban exclaimed.

"This is Tanis Half-Elven. And that is Flint Fireforge. You remember him?" Tasslehoff continued, waving a small hand at the dwarf.

"Uh, yes, quite," Fizban muttered, his face flushing.

"And Tika . . . and that's Caramon up there . . . oh, well, you can't see him now. Then there's Berem. We picked him up in Kalaman and, oh—Fizban!—he's got a green gem—ugh, ouch, Tanis, that hurt!"

Clearing his throat, Fizban cast a bleak look around.

"You're—uh—*not* with the—er—uh—dragonarmies?"

"No," said Tanis grimly, "we're not! Or at least we weren't." He gestured behind them. "That's likely to change any moment now, though."

"Not with the dragonarmies at all?" Fizban pursued hopefully. "You're sure you haven't converted? Been tortured? Brainwashed?"

"No, damn it!" Tanis yanked off his helm. "I'm Tanis Half-Elven, remember—"

Fizban beamed. "Tanis Half-Elven! So pleased to see you again, sir." Grabbing Tanis's hand, he shook it heartily.

"Confound it!" Tanis snapped in exasperation, snatching his hand out of the old man's grip.

"But you were riding dragons!"

"Those were *good* dragons!" Tanis shouted. "They've come back!"

"No one told me!" The old man gasped indignantly.

"Do you know what you've done?" Tanis continued, ignoring the interruption. "You've blown us out of the skies! Sent back our only means to get to Neraka—"

"Oh, I know what I've done," Fizban mumbled. He glanced back over his shoulder. "My, my. Those fellows seem to be gaining. Mustn't be caught by them. Well, what are we doing standing around?" He glared at Tanis. "Some leader you are! I suppose I'll have to take charge. . . . Where's my hat?"

"About five miles back," stated Pyrite with a great yawn.

"You still here?" Fizban said, glaring at the gold dragon in annoyance.

"Where else would I be?" the dragon asked gloomily.

"I told you to go with the others!"

"I didn't want to." Pyrite snorted. A bit of fire flared from his nose, making it twitch. This was followed by a tremendous sneeze. Sniffing, the dragon

continued peevishly. "No respect for age, those brass dragons. They talk constantly! And giggle. Gets on my nerves, that silly giggle. . . ."

"Well, you'll just have to go back by yourself then!" Fizban stalked up to stare the dragon in its bleary eye. "We're going on a long journey into dangerous country—"

"*We're* going?" Tanis cried. "Look, old man, Fizban, whatever your name is, why don't you *and* your—uh—friend here go back. You're right. It's going to be a long, dangerous journey. Longer, now, that we've lost our dragons and—"

"Tanis . . . "said Tika warningly, her eyes on the draconians.

"Into the hills quick," Tanis said, drawing a deep breath, trying to control his fear and his anger. "Go on, Tika. You and Flint. Tas—" He grabbed the kender.

"No, Tanis! We can't leave him here!" Tas wailed.

"Tas" Tanis said in a voice that warned the kender the half-elf had plainly had enough and wasn't going to stand for anything further. Apparently the old man understood the same thing.

"I've got to go with these folks," he said to the dragon. "They need me. You can't go back on your own. You'll just have to sallyforth—"

"Polymorph!" the dragon said indignantly. "The word is 'polymorph!' You never get that right—"

"Whatever!" the old man yelled. "Quickly! We'll take you with us."

"Very well," the dragon said. "I *could* use the rest."

"I don't think, " Tanis began, wondering what they would do with a large gold dragon, but it was too late.

While Tas watched, fascinated, and Tanis fumed in impatience, the dragon spoke a few words in the strange language of magic. There was a bright flash and then, suddenly, the dragon vanished.†

Most dragons can polymorph into any of a variety of interesting shapes. Pyrite appears to still have that spell well in hand at his age.

"What? Where?" Tasslehoff looked all around.

Fizban leaned over to pick up something out of the grass.

"Get moving! Now!" Tanis hustled Tas and the old man into the foothills, following after Tika and Flint.

"Here," Fizban said to Tas as they ran. "Hold out your hand."

Tas did as instructed. Then the kender caught his breath in awe. He would have come to a dead stop to examine it, except Tanis caught him by the arm and dragged him forward.

In the palm of Tas's hand gleamed a tiny golden figure of a dragon, carved in exquisite detail. Tas imagined he could even see the scars on the wings. Two small red jewels glittered in the eyes, then—as Tas watched—the jewels winked out as golden eyelids closed over them.

"Oh, Fizban, it—it's—beautiful! Can I truly keep it?" Tas yelled over his shoulder to the old man, who was puffing along behind.

"Sure, my boy!" Fizban beamed. "At least until this adventure's ended."

"Or it ends us," Tanis muttered, climbing rapidly over the rocks. The draconians were drawing nearer and nearer.

2

The Golden Span.

p and up into the hills† they climbed, the draconians in pursuit of the group, who now appeared to them to be spies.

They are going into the Khalkist Mountains. Sanction is also in the Khalkists, but the region they are heading into—Neraka—is not volcanic.

The group had lost the trail Caramon used chasing after Berem, but could not take time to search for it. They were considerably startled, therefore, when they suddenly came across Caramon, sitting calmly on a boulder, Berem—unconscious—stretched out beside him.

"What happened?" Tanis asked, breathing heavily, exhausted after the long climb.

"I caught up with him, finally." Caramon shook his head. "And he put up a fight. He's strong for an old guy, Tanis. I had to clunk him. I'm afraid I was a bit too hard, though," he added, staring down at the comatose figure remorsefully.

"Great!" Tanis was too tired even to swear.

"I'll handle this," Tika said, reaching into a leather pouch.

"The draconians are coming up past that last big rock," Flint reported as he stumbled into view. The dwarf seemed about done in. He collapsed onto a rock, mopping his sweating face with the end of his beard.

"Tika—" Tanis began.

"Found it!" she said triumphantly, pulling out a small vial. Kneeling down beside Berem, she took the stopper from the vial and waved it under his nose. The unconscious man drew a breath, then immediately began to cough.

Tika slapped him on the cheeks. "On your feet!" she said in her barmaid voice. "Unless you want the draconians to catch you."

Berem's eyes flew open in alarm. Clutching his head, he sat up dizzily. Caramon helped him stand.

"That's wonderful, Tika!" Tas said in excitement. "Let me—" Before she could stop him, Tas grabbed the vial and held it up to his own nose, inhaling deeply.

"Eeee Ahhhh!" The kender gagged, staggering back into Fizban, who had come up the path after Flint. "Ugh! Tika! That's . . . awful!" He could barely speak. "What is it?"

"Some concoction of Otik's," Tika said, grinning. "All of us barmaids carried it. Came in handy in lots of instances, if you take my meaning." Her smile slipped. "Poor Otik," she said softly. "I wonder what's become of him. And the Inn—"

"No time for that now, Tika," Tanis said impatiently. "We've got to go. On your feet, old man!" This to Fizban, who was just sitting down comfortably.

"I've got a spell," Fizban protested as Tas tugged and prodded him up. "Take care of those pests instantly. Poof!"

"No!" Tanis said. "Absolutely not. With my luck, you'd turn them all into trolls."

"I wonder if I could . . ." Fizban's face brightened.

The afternoon sun was just beginning to slide down the rim of the sky when the trail they had been following ever higher into the mountains suddenly branched off into two different directions. One led into the mountain peaks, the other seemed

to wind around the side. There might be a pass among the peaks, Tanis thought; a pass they could defend, if necessary.

But before he could say a word, Fizban started off on the trail that wound around the mountain. "This way," the old mage announced, leaning on his staff as he tottered forward.

"But—" Tanis started to protest.

"Come on, come on. This way!" said Fizban insistently, turning around and glaring at them from beneath his bushy white eyebrows. "That way leads to a dead end—in more ways than one. I know. I've been here before. This leads around the side of a mountain to a great gorge. Bridge over the gorge. We can get across, then fight the draconians when they try to come after us."

Tanis scowled, unwilling to trust the crazy old mage.

"It is a good plan, Tanis," Caramon said slowly. "It's obvious we're going to have to fight them sometime." He pointed to the draconians climbing up the mountain trails after them.

Tanis glanced around. They were all exhausted. Tika's face was pale, her eyes glazed. She leaned on Caramon, who had even left his spears back on the trail to lighten his burden.

Tasslehoff grinned at Tanis cheerfully. But the kender was panting like a small dog and he was limping on one foot.

Berem looked the same as always, sullen and frightened. It was Flint that worried Tanis most. The dwarf had not said a word during their flight. He had kept up with them without faltering, but his lips were blue and his breath came in short gasps. Every once in a while—when he thought no one was looking—Tanis had seen him put his hand over his chest or rub his left arm as if it pained him.

"Very well." The half-elf decided. "Go on, old mage. Though I'm probably going to regret this," he added, under his breath as the rest hurried along after Fizban.

Near sundown, the companions came to a halt. They stood on a small rocky ledge about three-quarters of the way up the side of the mountain. Before them was a deep, narrow gorge. Far below they could see a river winding its way through the bottom of the gorge like a glistening snake.

It must be a four-hundred-foot drop, Tanis calculated. The trail they stood on hugged the side of the mountain, with a sheer cliff on one side and nothing but air on the other. There was only one way across the gorge.

"And that bridge," said Flint—the first words he had spoken in hours, "is older than I am . . . and in worse shape."

"That bridge has stood for years!" Fizban said indignantly. "Why, it survived the Cataclysm!"

"I believe it," Caramon said sincerely.

"At least it's not too long," Tika tried to sound hopeful, though her voice faltered.

The bridge across the narrow gorge was of a unique construction. Huge vallenwood limbs were driven into the sides of the mountain on either side of the gorge. These limbs formed an X-shape that supported the wooden plank platform. Long ago, the structure must have been an architectural marvel. But now the wooden planks were rotted and splitting. If there had been a railing, it had long since fallen down into the chasm below. Even as they watched, the timbers creaked and shuddered in the chill wind of evening.

Then, behind them, they heard the sound of guttural voices and the clash of steel on rock.

"So much for going back," Caramon muttered. "We should cross over one by one."

"No time," Tanis said, rising to his feet. "We can only hope the gods are with us. And—I hate to admit it—but Fizban's right. Once we get across, we can stop the draconians easily. They'll be excellent targets, stuck out there on that bridge. I'll go first. Keep behind me, single-file. Caramon, you're rear guard. Berem, stay behind me."

Moving as swiftly as he dared, Tanis set foot on the bridge. He could feel the planks quiver and shake. Far below, the river flowed swiftly between the canyon walls; sharp rocks jutted up from its white, foaming surface. Tanis caught his breath and looked away quickly.

"Don't look down," he said to the others, feeling a chill emptiness where his stomach had been. For an instant he couldn't move, then, getting a grip on

himself, he edged his way forward. Berem came right behind him, fear of the dragonmen completely obliterating any other terrors the Everman might have experienced.

After Berem came Tasslehoff, walking lightly with kender skill, peering over the edge in wonder. Then the terrified Flint, supported by Fizban. Finally Tika and Caramon set foot on the shivering planks, keeping nervous watch behind them.

Tanis was nearly halfway across when part of the platform gave way, the rotten wood splintering beneath his feet.

Acting instinctively, in a paroxysm of terror, he clutched desperately at the planking and caught hold of the edge. But the rotten wood crumbled in his grasp. His fingers slipped and—

—a hand closed over his wrist.

"Berem!" Tanis gasped.

"Hold on!" He forced himself to hang limply, knowing that any movement on his part would only make Berem's hold on him harder to maintain.

"Pull him up!" he heard Caramon roar, then, "Don't anybody move! The whole thing's liable to give way!"

His face tight with the strain, sweat beading on his forehead, Berem pulled. Tanis saw the muscles on the man's arm bulge, the veins nearly burst from the skin. With what seemed like agonizing slowness, Berem dragged the half-elf up over the edge of the broken bridge. Here Tanis collapsed. Shaking with fright, he lay clinging to the wood, shivering.

Then he heard Tika cry out. Raising his head, he realized with grim amusement that he had probably just gained his life only to lose it. About thirty draconians appeared on the trail behind them. Tanis turned to look across the gaping hole in the center of the bridge. The other side of the platform was still standing. He might jump across the huge hole to safety, and so might Berem and Caramon—but not Tas, not Flint, not Tika, or the old mage.

"Excellent targets, you said," Caramon murmured, drawing his sword.

"Cast a spell, Old One!" Tasslehoff said suddenly.

"What?" Fizban blinked.

"A spell!" Tas cried, pointing at the draconians, who—seeing the companions trapped on the bridge—hurried up to finish them off.

"Tas, we're in enough trouble," Tanis began, the bridge creaking beneath his feet. Moving warily, Caramon stationed himself squarely in front of them, facing the draconians.

Fitting an arrow to his bowstring, Tanis fired. A draconian clutched its chest and fell, shrieking, off the cliff. The half-elf fired again and hit again. The draconians in the center of the line hesitated, milling about in confusion. There was no cover, no way to escape the half-elf's deadly barrage. The draconians in the front of the line surged forward toward the bridge.

At that moment, Fizban began to cast his spell.

Hearing the old mage chant, Tanis felt his heart sink. Then he reminded himself bitterly that they really couldn't be in a worse position. Berem, next to him, was watching the draconians with a stoic composure that Tanis found startling until he remembered that Berem didn't fear death; he would always return to life. Tanis fired again and another draconian howled in pain. So intent was he on his targets, that he forgot Fizban until he heard Berem gasp in astonishment. Glancing up, Tanis saw Berem staring into the sky. Following Berem's gaze, the half-elf was so astonished he nearly dropped his bow.

Descending from the clouds, glittering brightly in the dying rays of the sun, was a long golden bridge span. Guided by motions of the old mage's hand, the golden span dropped down out of the heavens to close the gap in the bridge.

Tanis came to his senses. Looking around, he saw that—for the moment—the draconians were also transfixed, staring at the golden span with glittering reptilian eyes.

"Hurry!" Tanis yelled. Gripping Berem by the arm, he dragged the Everman after him and jumped up onto the span as it hovered just about a foot above the gap. Berem followed, stumbling up clumsily. Even as they stood on it, the span kept dropping, slowing a bit under Fizban's guidance.

The span was still about eight inches above the platform when Tasslehoff, shrieking wildly, leaped onto it, pulling the awestruck dwarf up after him.

The draconians—suddenly realizing their prey was going to escape—howled in rage and surged onto the wooden bridge. Tanis stood on the golden span, near its end, firing his arrows at the lead draconians. Caramon remained behind, driving them back with his sword.

"Get on across!" Tanis ordered Tika as she hopped onto the span beside him. "Stay beside Berem. Keep an eye on him. You, too, Flint, go with her. Go on!" he snarled viciously.

"I'll stay with you, Tanis," Tasslehoff offered.

Casting a backward glance at Caramon, Tika reluctantly obeyed orders, grabbing hold of Berem and shoving him along before her. Seeing the draconians coming, he needed little urging. Together they dashed across the span onto the remaining half of the wooden bridge. It creaked alarmingly beneath their weight. Tanis only hoped it would hold, but he couldn't spare a glance. Apparently it was, for he heard Flint's thick boots clumping across it.

"We made it!" Tika yelled from the side of the canyon.

"Caramon!" Tanis shouted, firing another arrow, trying to keep his footing on the golden span.

"Go ahead!" Fizban snapped at Caramon irritably. "I'm concentrating. I have to set the span down in the right place. A few more centimeters to the left, I think—"

"Tasslehoff, go on across!" Tanis ordered.

"I'm not leaving Fizban!" said the kender stubbornly as Caramon stepped up onto the golden span. The draconians, seeing the big warrior leaving, surged forward again. Tanis fired arrows as fast as he could; one draconian lay on the bridge in a pool of green blood, another toppled over the edge. But the half-elf was growing tired. Worse, he was running out of arrows. And the draconians kept coming. Caramon came to a stop beside Tanis on the span.

"Hurry, Fizban!" pleaded Tasslehoff, wringing his hands.

"There!" Fizban said in satisfaction. "Perfect fit. And the gnomes said I was no engineer."

Just as he spoke, the golden span carrying Tanis, Caramon, and Tasslehoff dropped firmly into place between the two sections of the broken bridge.

And at that moment, the other half of the wooden bridge—the half still standing, the half that led to safety on the other side of the canyon—creaked, crumbled, and fell into the canyon.

"In the name of the gods!" Caramon gulped in fear, catching hold of Tanis and dragging him back just as the half-elf had been about to set foot on the wooden planking.

"Trapped!" Tanis said hoarsely, watching the logs tumble end over end into the ravine, his soul seeming to plummet with them. On the other side, he could hear Tika scream, her cries blending with the exultant shouts of the draconians.

There was a rending, snapping sound. The draconian's cries of exultation changed at once to horror and fear.

"Look! Tanis!" Tasslehoff cried in wild excitement. "Look!"

Tanis glanced back in time to see the other part of the wooden bridge tumble into the ravine, carrying with it most of the draconians. He felt the golden span shudder.

"We'll fall, too!" Caramon roared. "There's nothing to support—"

Caramon's tongue froze to the roof of his mouth. With a strangled gulp, he looked slowly from side to side.

"I don't believe it," he muttered.

"Somehow, I do. . . ." Tanis drew a shuddering breath.

In the center of the canyon, suspended in midair, hung the magical golden span, glittering in the light of the setting sun as the wooden bridge on either side of it plunged into the ravine. Upon the span stood four figures, staring down at the ruins beneath them—and across the great gaps between them and the sides of the gorge.

For long moments, there was complete, absolute, deathly silence. Then Fizban turned triumphantly to Tanis.

"Wonderful spell," said the mage with pride. "Got a rope?"

It was well after dark by the time the companions finally got off the golden span. Flinging a rope to Tika, they waited while she and the dwarf fastened

it securely to a tree. Then—one by one—Tanis, Caramon, Tas, and Fizban swung off the span and were hauled up the side of the cliff by Berem. When they were all across, they collapsed, exhausted from fatigue. So tired were they that they didn't even bother to find shelter, but spread their blankets in a grove of scrubby pine trees and set the watch. Those not on duty fell instantly asleep.

The next morning, Tanis woke, stiff and aching. The first thing he saw was the sun shining brightly off the sides of the golden span, still suspended solidly in mid-air.

"I don't suppose you can get rid of that thing?" he asked Fizban as the old mage helped Tas hand out a breakfast of quith-pa.

"I'm afraid not," the old man said, eyeing the span wistfully.

"He tried a few spells this morning," Tas said, nodding in the direction of a pine tree completely covered with cobwebs and another that was burned to a crisp. "I figured he better quit before he turned us all into crickets or something."

"Good idea," muttered Tanis, staring gloomily out at the gleaming span. "Well, we couldn't leave a clearer trail if we painted an arrow on the side of the cliff." Shaking his head, he sat down beside Caramon and Tika.

"They'll be after us, too, you can bet," Caramon said, munching half-heartedly on quith-pa.† "Have dragons bring 'em across." Sighing, he stuck most of the dried fruit back in his pouch.

"Caramon?" said Tika. "You didn't eat much. . . ."

"I'm not hungry," he mumbled as he stood up. "Guess I'll scout ahead a ways." Shouldering his pack and his weapons, he started off down the trail.

Her face averted, Tika began busily packing away her things, avoiding Tanis's gaze.

"Raistlin?" Tanis asked.

Tika stopped. Her hands dropped into her lap.

"Will he always be like this, Tanis?" she asked helplessly, looking fondly after him. "I don't understand!"

"I don't either," Tanis said quietly, watching the big man disappear into the wilderness. "But, then, I never had a brother or a sister."

"*I* understand!" said Berem. His soft voice quivered with a passion that caught Tanis's attention.

"Quith-pa" may be a generic term for a nutritious, easy-to-carry meal, kind of like K rations, because some elves bake it as a bread, and others dry fruit.

"What do you mean?"

But—at his question—the eager, hungry look on the Everman's face vanished.

"Nothing," he mumbled, his face a blank mask.

"Wait!" Tanis rose quickly. "Why do you understand Caramon?" He put his hand on Berem's arm.

"Leave me alone!" Berem shouted fiercely, flinging Tanis backward.

"Hey, Berem," Tasslehoff said, looking up and smiling as if he hadn't heard a thing. "I was sorting through my maps and I found one that has the most interesting story—"

Giving Tanis a hunted glance, Berem shuffled over to where Tasslehoff sat cross-legged on the ground, his sheaf of maps spread out all around him. Hunching down over the maps, the Everman soon appeared lost in wonder listening to one of Tas's tales.

"Better leave him alone, Tanis," Flint advised. "If you ask me, the only reason he understands Caramon is that he's as crazy as Raistlin."

"I didn't ask you, but that's all right," Tanis said, sitting down beside the dwarf to eat his own ration of quith-pa. "We're going to have to be going soon. With luck, Tas will find a map—"

Flint snorted. "Humpf! A lot of good *that* will do us. The last map of his we followed took us to a seaport without a sea!"

Tanis hid his smile. "Maybe this will be different," he said. "At least it's better than following Fizban's directions."

"Well, you're right there," the dwarf admitted grumpily. Giving Fizban a sideways glance, Flint leaned over near Tanis. "Didn't you ever wonder how he managed to live through that fall at Pax Tharkas?" he asked in a loud whisper.

"I wonder about a lot of things," Tanis said quietly. "Like—how are you feeling?"

The dwarf blinked, completely taken aback by the unexpected question. "Fine!" he snapped, his face flushing.

"It's just, sometimes I've seen you rub your left arm," Tanis continued.

"Rheumatism," the dwarf growled. "You know it always bothers me in the spring. And sleeping on the ground doesn't help. I thought you said we

should be moving along." The dwarf busied himself with packing.

"Right." Tanis turned away with a sigh. "Found anything, Tas?"

"Yes, I think so," the kender said eagerly. Rolling up his maps, he stashed them in his map case, then slipped the case into a pouch, taking a quick peek at his golden dragon while he was at it. Although seemingly made of metal, the figurine changed position in the oddest way. Right now, it was curled around a golden ring—Tanis's ring, the one Laurana had given him and he had returned to her, when he told her he was in love with Kitiara. Tasslehoff became so absorbed in staring at the dragon and the ring that he nearly forgot Tanis was waiting.

"Oh," he said, hearing Tanis cough impatiently. "Map. Right. Yes, you see, once when I was just a little kender, my parents and I traveled through the Khalkist Mountains—that's where we are now—on our way to Kalaman. Usually, you know, we took the northern, longer route. There was a fair, every year, at Taman Busuk, where they sold the most marvelous things, and my father never missed it. But one year—I think it was the year after he'd been arrested and put in the stocks over a misunderstanding with a jeweler—we decided to go through the mountains. My mother'd always wanted to see Godshome, so we—"

"The map?" interrupted Tanis.

"Yes, the map." Tas sighed. "Here. It was my father's, I think. Here's where we are, as near as Fizban and I can figure. And here's Godshome."

"What's that?"

"An old city. It's in ruins, abandoned during the Cataclysm—"

"And probably crawling with draconians," Tanis finished.

"No, not *that* Godshome," Tas continued, moving his small finger over into the mountains near the dot that marked the city. "*This* place is also called Godshome. In fact, it was called that long before there was a city, according to Fizban."

Tanis glanced at the old mage, who nodded.

"Long ago, people believed the gods lived there," he said solemnly. "It is a very holy place."

"And it's hidden," added Tas, "in a bowl in the center of these mountains. See? No one ever goes

there, according to Fizban. No one knows about the trail except him. And there is a trail marked on my map, at least into the mountains. . . ."

"No one ever goes there?" Tanis asked Fizban.

The old mage's eyes narrowed in irritation. "No."

"No one except you?" Tanis pursued.

"I've been lots of places, Half-Elven!" The mage snorted. "Got a year? I'll tell you about them!" He shook a finger at Tanis. "You don't appreciate me, young man! Always suspicious! And after everything I've done for you—"

"Uh, I wouldn't remind him about *that!*" Tas said hurriedly, seeing Tanis's face darken. "Come along, Old One."

The two hurried off down the trail, Fizban stomping along angrily, his beard bristling.

"Did the gods really live in this place we're going to?" Tas asked him to keep him from bothering Tanis.

"How should I know?" Fizban demanded irritably. "Do I look like a god?"

"But—"

"Did anyone ever tell you that you talk entirely too much?"

"Almost everyone," Tas said cheerfully. "Did I ever tell you about the time I found a woolly mammoth?

Tanis heard Fizban groan. Tika hurried past him, to catch up with Caramon.

"Coming, Flint?" Tanis called.

"Yes," the dwarf answered, sitting down suddenly on a rock. "Give me a moment. I've dropped my pack. You go on ahead."

Occupied in studying the kender's map as he walked, Tanis did not see Flint collapse. He did not hear the odd note in the dwarf's voice, or see the spasm of pain that briefly contracted the dwarf's face.

"Well, hurry up," Tanis said absently. "We don't want to leave you behind."

"Aye, lad," Flint said softly, sitting on the rock—waiting for the pain to subside, as it always did.

Flint watched his friend walk down the trail, still moving somewhat clumsily in the dragonarmor. *We don't want to leave you behind.*

"Aye, lad," Flint repeated to himself. Brushing his gnarled hand quickly across his eyes, the dwarf stood up and followed his friends.

3

Godshome.

It was a long and weary day spent wandering through the mountains, aimlessly, as near as the impatient half-elf could tell.

The only thing that kept him from throttling Fizban—after they had walked into the second box canyon in less than four hours—was the undeniable fact that the old man kept them headed in the right direction. No matter how lost and turned around they seemed to get, no matter how often Tanis could have sworn they'd passed the same boulder three times, whenever he caught a glimpse of the sun they were still traveling unerringly to the southeast.

But as the day wore on, he saw the sun less and less frequently. Winter's bitter chill had gone from the air and there was even the faint smell of green and growing things borne on the wind. But soon the sky darkened with lead-gray clouds and it began to rain, a dull, drumming drizzle that penetrated the heaviest cloak.

By mid-afternoon, the group was cheerless and dispirited—even Tasslehoff, who had argued violently with Fizban over directions to Godshome. This was all the more frustrating to Tanis since it was obvious that neither of them knew where they were. (Fizban, in fact, was caught holding the map upside down.) The fight resulted in Tasslehoff stuffing his maps back in his pouch and refusing to get them out again while Fizban threatened to cast a spell that would turn Tasslehoff's topknot into a horse's tail.

Fed up with both of them, Tanis sent Tas to the back of the line to cool off, mollified Fizban, and nursed secret thoughts of sealing them both up in a cave.

The calmness that the half-elf had felt in Kalaman was slowly vanishing on this dismal journey. It had been a calmness, he realized now, brought about by activity, the need to make decisions, the comforting thought that he was finally doing something tangible to help Laurana. These thoughts kept him afloat in the dark waters that surrounded him, much as the sea elves had aided him in the Blood Sea of Istar. But now he felt the dark waters begin to close over his head once more.

Tanis's thoughts were constantly with Laurana. Over and over, he heard Gilthanas's accusing words—*She did this for you!* And though Gilthanas had, perhaps, forgiven him, Tanis knew he could never forgive himself. What was happening to Laurana in the Dark Queen's Temple? Was she still alive? Tanis's soul shrank from that thought. Of course she was alive! The Dark Queen would not kill her, not as long as she wanted Berem.

Tanis's eyes focused on the man walking ahead of him, near Caramon. I will do anything to save Laurana, he swore beneath his breath, clenching his fist. Anything! If it means sacrificing myself or . . .

He stopped. Would he really give up Berem? Would he really trade the Everman to the Dark Queen, perhaps plunge the world into a darkness so vast it would never see light again?

No, Tanis told himself firmly. Laurana would die before she would be part of such a bargain. Then—after he'd walked a few more steps—he'd change his mind. Let the world take care of itself, he thought gloomily. We're doomed. We can't win, no matter what happens. Laurana's life, that's the only thing that counts . . . the only thing . . .

Tanis was not the only gloomy member of the group. Tika walked beside Caramon, her red curls a bright spot of warmth and light in the gray day. But the light was only in the vibrant red of her hair, it had gone out of her eyes. Although Caramon was unfailingly kind to her, he had not held her since that wonderful, brief moment beneath the sea when his love had been hers. This made her angry in the long nights—he had used her, she decided, simply to ease his own pain. She vowed she would leave him when this was over. There was a wealthy young nobleman in Kalaman who had not been able to take his eyes off her. . . . But those were night thoughts. During the day, when Tika glanced at Caramon, and saw him plodding along next to her, his head bowed, her heart melted. Gently she touched him. Looking up at her quickly, he smiled. Tika sighed. So much for wealthy young noblemen.

Flint stumped along, rarely speaking, never complaining. If Tanis had not been wrapped up in his own inner turmoil, he would have noted this as a bad sign.

As for Berem—no one knew what he was thinking, if anything. He seemed to grow more nervous and wary the farther they traveled. The blue eyes that were too young for his face darted here and there like those of a trapped animal.

It was on the second day in the mountains that Berem vanished.

Everyone had been more cheerful in the morning, when Fizban announced that they should arrive in Godshome soon. But gloom quickly followed. The rain grew heavier. Three times in one hour the old mage led them plunging through the brush with excited cries of "This is it! Here we are!" only to find themselves in a swamp, a gorge, and—finally—staring at a rock wall.

It was this last time, the dead end, that Tanis felt his soul start to rip from his body. Even Tasslehoff

fell back in alarm at the sight of the half-elf's rage-distorted face. Desperately Tanis fought to hold himself together, and it was then he noticed.

"Where's Berem?" he asked, a sudden chill freezing his anger.

Caramon blinked, seemingly coming back from some distant world. The big warrior looked around hastily, then turned to face Tanis, his face flushed with shame. "I—I dunno, Tanis. I—I thought he was next to me."

"He's our only way into Neraka," the half-elf said through clenched teeth, "and he's the only reason they're keeping Laurana alive. If they catch him—"

Tanis stopped, sudden tears choking him. Desperately he tried to think, despite the blood pounding in his head.

"Don't worry, lad," Flint said gruffly, patting the half-elf on the arm. "We'll find him."

"I'm sorry, Tanis," Caramon mumbled. "I was thinking about—about Raist. I—I know I shouldn't —"

"How in the name of the Abyss does that blasted brother of yours work mischief when he's not even here!" Tanis shouted. Then he caught himself. "I'm sorry, Caramon," he said, drawing a deep breath. "Don't blame yourself. I should have been watching, too. We all should have. We've got to backtrack anyway, unless Fizban can take us through solid rock . . . no, don't even consider it, old man. . . . Berem can't have gone far and his trail should be easy to pick up. He's not skilled in woodlore."

Tanis was right. After an hour tracing back their own footsteps, they discovered a small animal trail none of them had noticed in passing. It was Flint who saw the man's tracks in the mud. Calling excitedly to the others, the dwarf plunged into the brush, following the clearly marked trail easily. The rest hurried after him, but the dwarf seemed to have experienced an unusual surge of energy. Like a hunting hound who knows the prey is just ahead of him, Flint trampled over tangleshoot vines and hacked his way through the undergrowth without pause. He quickly outdistanced them.

"Flint!" Tanis shouted more than once. "Wait up!"

But the group fell farther and farther behind the excited dwarf until they lost sight of him altogether. Flint's trail proved even clearer than Berem's, however. They had little difficulty following the print of the dwarf's heavy boots, not to mention the broken tree limbs and uprooted vines that marked his passing.

Then suddenly they were brought to a halt.

They had reached another rock cliff, but this time there was a way through—a hole in the rock formed a narrow tunnel-like opening. The dwarf had entered easily—they could see his tracks—but it was so narrow that Tanis stared at it in dismay.

"Berem got through it," Caramon said grimly, pointing at a smear of fresh blood on the rock.

"Maybe," Tanis said dubiously. "See what's on the other side, Tas," he ordered, reluctant to enter until he was certain he was not being led a merry chase.

The advantage of a kender in the group—they'll charge ahead where no man has gone before.

Tasslehoff crawled through with ease,† and soon they heard his shrill voice exclaiming in wonder over something, but it echoed so they had trouble understanding his words.

Suddenly Fizban's face brightened. "This is it!" cried the old mage in high glee. "We've found it! Godshome! The way in, through this passageway!"

"There's no other way?" Caramon asked, staring at the narrow opening gloomily.

Fizban appeared thoughtful. "Well, I seem to recall—"

Then, "Tanis! Hurry!" came through quite clearly from the other side.

"No more dead ends. We'll get through this way," Tanis muttered, "somehow."

Crawling on hands and knees, the companions crept into the narrow opening. The way did not become easier; sometimes they were forced to flatten themselves and slither through the mud like snakes. Broad-shouldered Caramon had the worst time, and for a while Tanis thought perhaps they might have to leave the big man behind. Tasslehoff waited for them on the other side, peering in at them anxiously as they crawled.

"I heard something, Tanis," he kept saying. "Flint shouting. Up ahead. And wait until you see this place, Tanis! You won't believe it!"

But Tanis couldn't take time to listen or look around, not until everyone was safely through the tunnel. It took all of them, pulling and tugging, to drag Caramon through and when he finally emerged, the skin on his arms and back was cut and bleeding.

"This is it!" Fizban stated. "We're here."

The half-elf turned around to see the place called Godshome.†

There was once a village named Godshome in Taman Busuk, farther east (which showed on Tas's map), but that place now lies in ruins. This Godshome in the Khalkists is a mystical place, findable only by people of magic.

In ancient times there was a wonderful temple built here. It was destroyed at the time of the Cataclysm. It is at Godshome that Huma's dragonlance was purified and given power over the Dark Queen.

"Not exactly the place *I'd* choose to live if I were a god," Tasslehoff remarked in a subdued voice.

Tanis was forced to agree.

They stood at the edge of a circular depression in the center of a mountain. The first thing that struck Tanis when he looked upon Godshome was the overwhelming desolation and emptiness of the place. All along the path up into the mountains, the companions had seen signs of new life: trees budding, grass greening, wild flowers pushing their way through the mud and remnants of snow. But here there was nothing. The bottom of the bowl was perfectly smooth and flat, totally barren, gray and lifeless. The towering peaks of the mountain surrounding the bowl soared above them. The jagged rock of the peaks seemed to loom inward, giving the observer the impression of being pressed down into the crumbling rock beneath his feet. The sky above them was azure, clear, and cold, devoid of sun or bird or cloud, though it had been raining when they entered the tunnel. It was like an eye staring down from gray, unblinking rims. Shivering, Tanis quickly withdrew his gaze from the sky to look once more within the bowl.

Below that staring eye, within the center of the bowl itself, stood a circle of huge, tall, shapeless boulders. It was a perfect circle made up of imperfect rocks. Yet they matched so nearly and stood so close together that when Tanis tried to look between them, he could not make out from where he was standing what the strange stones guarded so solemnly. These boulders were all that was visible in the rock-strewn and silent place.

"It makes me feel so terribly sad," Tika whispered. "I'm not frightened—it doesn't seem evil, just so sorrowful! If the gods do come here, it must be to weep over the troubles of the world."

Fizban turned to regard Tika with a penetrating look and seemed about to speak, but before he could comment, Tasslehoff shouted. "There, Tanis!"

"I see!" The half-elf broke into a run.

On the other side of the bowl, he could see the vague outline of what appeared to be two figures—one short and the other tall—struggling.

"It's Berem!" screamed Tas. The two were plainly visible to his keen kender eyes. "And he's doing something to Flint! Hurry, Tanis!"

Bitterly cursing himself for letting this happen, for not keeping a closer watch on Berem, for not forcing the man to reveal those secrets he was so obviously holding back, Tanis ran across the stony ground with a speed born of fear. He could hear the others calling to him, but he paid no attention. His eyes were on the two in front of him and now he could see them clearly. Even as he watched, he saw the dwarf fall to the ground. Berem stood over him.

"Flint!" Tanis screamed.

His heart was pounding so that blood dimmed his vision. His lungs ached, there didn't seem air enough to breathe. Still he ran faster, and now he could see Berem turn to look at him. He seemed to be trying to say something, Tanis could see the man's lips moving, but the half-elf couldn't hear through the surge of blood beating in his ears. At Berem's feet lay Flint. The dwarf's eyes were closed, his head lolled over to one side, his face was ashen gray.

"What have you done?" Tanis shrieked at Berem. "You've killed him!" Grief, guilt, despair, and rage exploded within Tanis like one of the old mage's fireballs, flooding his head with unbearable pain. He could not see, a red tide blurred his sight.

His sword was in his hand, he had no idea how. He felt the cold steel of the hilt. Berem's face swam within a blood-red sea; the man's eyes filled—not with terror—but with deep sorrow. Then Tanis saw the eyes widen with pain, and it was only then he knew he had plunged the sword† into Berem's unresisting body, plunged it so deeply that he felt it cleave through flesh and bone and scrape the rock upon which the Everman was leaning.

Tanis is still answering every question with either the edge or the point of his sword.—TRH

Warm blood washed over Tanis's hands. A horrible scream burst in his head, then a heavy weight fell on him, nearly knocking him down.

Berem's body slumped over him, but Tanis didn't notice. Frantically he struggled to free his weapon and stab again. He felt strong hands grab him. But in his madness, the half-elf fought them off. Finally pulling his sword free, he watched Berem fall to the ground, blood streaming from the horrible wound just below the green gemstone that glittered with an unholy life in the man's chest.

Behind him, he heard a deep, booming voice and a woman's sobbing pleas and a shrill wail of grief. Furious, Tanis spun around to face those who had tried to thwart him. He saw a big man with a griefstricken face, a red-haired girl with tears streaming down her cheeks. He recognized neither of them. And then there appeared before him an old, old man. His face was calm, his ageless eyes filled with sorrow. The old man smiled gently at Tanis and, reaching out, laid his hand on the half-elf's shoulder.

His touch was like cool water to a fevered man. Tanis felt reason return. The bloody haze cleared from his vision. He dropped the blood-stained sword from his red hands and collapsed, sobbing, at Fizban's feet. The old man leaned down and gently patted him.

"Be strong, Tanis," he said softly, "for you must say good-bye to one who has a long journey before him.

Tanis remembered. "Flint!" he gasped.

Fizban nodded sadly, glancing at Berem's body. "Come along. There's nothing more you can do here."

Swallowing his tears, Tanis staggered to his feet. Shoving aside the mage, he stumbled over to where Flint lay on the rocky ground, his head resting on Tasslehoff's lap.

The dwarf smiled as he saw the half-elf approach. Tanis dropped down on his knees beside his oldest friend. Taking Flint's gnarled hand in his, the half-elf held it fast.

"I almost lost him, Tanis," Flint said. With his other hand he tapped his chest. "Berem was just about to slip out through that other hole in the rocks over there when this old heart of mine finally burst. He—he heard me cry out, I guess, because the next thing I knew he had me in his arms and was laying me down on the rocks."

"Then he didn't—he didn't—harm you . . ." Tanis could barely speak.

Flint managed a snort. "Harm me! He couldn't harm a mouse, Tanis. He's as gentle as Tika." The dwarf smiled up at the girl, who also knelt beside him. "You take care of that big oaf, Caramon, you hear?" he said to her. "See he comes in out of the rain."

"I will, Flint." Tika wept.

"At least you won't be trying to drown me anymore," the dwarf grumbled, his eyes resting fondly on Caramon. "And if you see that brother of yours, give him a kick in the robes for me."

Caramon could not speak. He only shook his head. "I—I'll go look after Berem," the big man mumbled. Taking hold of Tika, he gently helped her stand and led her away.

"No, Flint!† You can't go off adventuring without me!" Tas wailed. "You'll get into no end of trouble, you know you will!"

Flint's death, unlike Sturm's, was not determined early. But by the time we came to this book, we wanted to show that someone who had lived a heroic life should be honored as much as one who had died a heroic death.—MW

"It'll be the first moment of peace I've had since we met," the dwarf said gruffly. "I want you to have my helm, the one with the *griffon's* mane." He glared at Tanis sternly, then turned his gaze back to the sobbing kender. Sighing, he patted Tas's hand. "There, there, lad, don't take on so. I've had a happy life, blessed with faithful friends. I've seen evil things, but I've seen a lot of good things, too. And now hope has come into the world. I hate to leave you"—his rapidly dimming vision focused on Tanis—"just when you need me. But I've taught you all I know, lad. Everything will be fine. I know . . . fine . . ."

His voice sank, he closed his eyes, breathing heavily. Tanis held tightly to his hand. Tasslehoff buried his face in Flint's shoulder. Then Fizban appeared, standing at Flint's feet.

The dwarf opened his eyes. "I know you, now," he said softly, his eyes bright as he looked at Fizban. "You'll come with me, won't you? At least at the beginning of the journey . . . so I won't be alone? I've walked with friends so long, I feel . . . kind of funny . . . going off like this . . . by myself."

"I'll come with you," Fizban promised gently. "Close your eyes and rest now, Flint. The troubles of this world are yours no longer. You have earned the right to sleep."

"Sleep," the dwarf said, smiling. "Yes, that's what I need. Wake me when you're ready. . . wake me when it's time to leave . . ." Flint's eyes closed. He drew in a smooth easy breath, then let it out. . . .†

Most death in the world is quiet—which sometimes blankets the fact that it is the consistency of a person's life that brings meaning to our existence. Not everyone dies defending their country or saving children from burning buildings. Some of the greatest heroes I have ever known lived strong, supportive, and truly great lives in small communities. Their names may not have been heard beyond a hundred-mile radius, yet they are no less heroes.—TRH

Tanis pressed the dwarf's hand to his lips. "Farewell, old friend," the half-elf whispered, and he placed the hand on the dwarf's still chest.

"No! Flint! No!" Screaming wildly, Tasslehoff flung himself across the dwarf's body. Gently Tanis lifted the sobbing kender in his arms. Tas kicked and fought, but Tanis held him firmly, like a child, and finally Tas subsided—exhausted. Clinging to Tanis, he wept bitterly.

Tanis stroked the kender's topknot, then—glancing up—stopped.

"Wait! What are you doing, old man?" he cried.

Setting Tas back down on the ground, Tanis rose quickly to his feet. The frail old mage had lifted Flint's body in his arms and, as Tanis watched in shock, began walking toward the strange circle of stones.

"Stop!" Tanis ordered. "We must give him a proper ceremony, build a cairn."

Fizban turned to face Tanis. The old man's face was stern. He held the heavy dwarf gently and with ease.

"I promised him he would not travel alone," Fizban said simply.

Then, turning, he continued to walk toward the stones. Tanis, after a moment's hesitation, ran after him. The rest stood as if transfixed, staring at Fizban's retreating figure.

It had seemed an easy thing to Tanis to catch up with an old man bearing such a burden. But Fizban moved incredibly fast, almost as if he and the dwarf were as light as the air. Suddenly aware of the weight of his own body, Tanis felt as if he were trying to catch a wisp of smoke soaring heavenward. Still he stumbled after them, reaching them just as the old mage entered the ring of boulders, carrying the dwarf's body in his arms.

Tanis squeezed through the circle of rocks without thinking, knowing only that he must stop this crazed old mage and recover his friend's body.

Then he stopped within the circle. Before him spread what he first took to be a pool of water, so

still that nothing marred its smooth surface. Then he saw that it wasn't water, it was a pool of glassy black rock! The deep black surface was polished to a gleaming brilliance. It stretched before Tanis with the darkness of night and, indeed, looking down into its black depths, Tanis was startled to see stars!† So clear were they that he looked up, half-expecting to see night had fallen, though he knew it was only mid-afternoon. The sky above him was azure, cold and clear, no stars, no sun. Shaken and weak, Tanis dropped to his knees beside the pool and stared once more into its polished surface. He saw the stars, he saw the moons, he saw three moons, and his soul trembled, for the black moon visible only to those powerful mages of the Black Robes was now visible to him, like a dark circle cut out of blackness. He could even see the gaping holes where the constellations of the Queen of Darkness and the Valiant Warrior had once wheeled in the sky.

This is, indeed, a heat-blasted bed of obsidian, which has a highly polished surface. This reflects the stars of the night sky. Fizban uses this place as a metaphor for the heroes signifying Flint's passage into another phase of existence.—TRH

Tanis recalled Raistlin's words, "Both gone. She has come to Krynn, Tanis, and he has come to fight her. . . ."

Looking up, Tanis saw Fizban step onto the black rock pool, Flint's body in his arms.

The half-elf tried desperately to follow, but he could no more force himself to crawl out upon that cold rock surface than he could have made himself leap into the Abyss. He could only watch as the old mage, walking softly as if unwilling to waken a sleeping child in his arms, moved out into the center of glistening black surface.

"Fizban!" Tanis called.

The old man did not stop or turn but walked on among the glittering stars. Tanis felt Tasslehoff creep up next to him. Reaching out, Tanis took his hand and held it fast, as he had held Flint's.

The old mage reached the center of the rock pool . . . and then disappeared.

Tanis gasped. Tasslehoff leaped past him, starting to run out onto the mirrorlike surface. But Tanis caught him.

"No, Tas," the half-elf said gently. "You can't go on this adventure with him. Not yet. You must stay with me awhile. *I* need you now."

Tasslehoff fell back, unusually obedient, and as he did so, he pointed.

"Look, Tanis!" he whispered, his voice quivering. "The constellation! It's come back!"

As Tanis stared into the surface of the black pool, he saw the stars of the constellation of the Valiant Warrior return. They flickered, then burst into light, filling the dark pool with their blue-white radiance. Swiftly Tanis looked upward—but the sky above was dark and still and empty.

Valiant Warrior

The image in the mirror of the Valiant Warrior constellation returning to the sky is, again, an illusionary part of the metaphor-lesson that Fizban is giving to the heroes. It is a symbol of who Fizban really is—but note that when Tanis looks up, the stars are still missing.—TRH

4

Everman's story.

Tanis!" called Caramon's voice.

"Berem!" Suddenly remembering what he had done, Tanis turned and stumbled over the rock-strewn ground toward Caramon and Tika, who were staring in horror at the blood-smeared rock where Berem's body lay. As they watched, Berem began to stir, groaning—not in pain, but as if with remembered pain. His shaking hand clutching his chest, Berem rose slowly to his feet. The only sign of his hideous injury was traces of blood upon his skin, and these vanished as Tanis watched.

"He is called the Everman, remember?" Tanis said to the ashen-faced Caramon. "Sturm and I saw him die in Pax Tharkas, buried under a ton of rock. He's died countless deaths, only to rise again. And he claims he doesn't know why." Tanis came forward to stand very close to Berem, staring at the man, who watched him approach with sullen, wary eyes.

"But you do know, don't you, Berem?" Tanis said. The half-elf's voice was soft, his manner calm. "You know," he repeated, "and you're going to tell us. The lives of more may hang in balance."

Berem's gaze lowered. "I'm sorry . . . about your friend," he mumbled. "I—I tried to help, but there was nothing—"

"I know." Tanis swallowed. "I'm sorry . . . about what I did, too. I—I couldn't see . . . I didn't understand—"

But as he said the words, Tanis realized he was lying. He had seen, but he had seen only what he wanted to see. How much of what happened in his life was like that? How much of what he saw was distorted by his own mind? He hadn't understood Berem because he didn't *want* to understand Berem! Berem had come to represent for Tanis those dark and secret things† within himself he hated. He had killed Berem, the half-elf knew; but in reality, he had driven that sword through himself.

When Tanis was growing up, the Speaker of the Sun refers to him as, "... half of two things and all of nothing." Small wonder that he carried "dark and secret things" in him.

And now it was as if that sword wound had spewed out the foul, gangrenous poison corrupting his soul. Now the wound could heal. The grief and sorrow of Flint's death was like a soothing balm poured inside, reminding him of goodness, of higher values. Tanis felt himself freed at last of the dark shadows of his guilt. Whatever happened, he had done his best to try and help, to try and make things right. He had made mistakes, but he could forgive himself now and go on.

Perhaps Berem saw this in Tanis's eyes. Certainly he saw grief, he saw compassion. Then, "I am tired, Tanis," Berem said suddenly, his eyes on the half-elf's tear-reddened eyes. "I am so very tired." His glance went to the black pool of rock. "I—I envy your friend. He is at rest now. He has found peace. Am I never to have that?" Berem's fist clenched, then he shuddered and his head sank into his hands. "But I am afraid! I see the end, it is very close. And I am frightened!"

"We're all frightened." Tanis sighed, rubbing his burning eyes. "You're right—the end is near, and it seems fraught with darkness. You hold the answer, Berem."

"I'll—I'll tell you, what I can—" Berem said haltingly, as if the words were being dragged out of him. "But you've got to help me!" His hand clutched Tanis's. "You must promise to help me!"

"I cannot promise," Tanis said grimly, "not until I know the truth."

Berem sat down, leaning his back against the blood-stained rock. The others settled around him, drawing their cloaks close as the wind rose, whistling down the sides of the mountains, howling among the strange boulders. They listened to Berem's tale without interruption, though Tas was occasionally seized by a fit of weeping, and he snuffled quietly, his head resting on Tika's shoulder.

At first Berem's voice was low, his words spoken reluctantly. Sometimes they could see him wrestling with himself, then he would blurt forth the story as if it hurt. But gradually he began speaking faster and faster, the relief of finally telling the truth after all these years flooding his soul.

"When—when I said I understood how you"—he nodded at Caramon—"felt about, about losing your brother, I spoke the truth. I—I had a sister. We—we weren't twins, but we were probably as close as twins. She was just a year younger. We lived on a small farm, outside of Neraka. It was isolated. No neighbors. My mother taught us to read and write at home, enough to get by. Mostly we worked on the farm. My sister was my only companion, my only friend. And I was hers.

"She worked hard—too hard. After the Cataclysm, it was all we could to do to keep food on the table. Our parents were old and sick. We nearly starved that first winter. No matter what you have heard about the Famine Times, you cannot imagine." His voice died, his eyes dimmed. "Ravenous packs of wild beasts and wilder men roamed the land. Being isolated, we were luckier than some. But many nights we stayed awake, clubs in our hands, as the wolves prowled around the outside of the house—waiting. . . . I watched my sister—who was a pretty little thing—grow old before she was twenty. Her hair was gray as mine is now, her face pinched and wrinkled. But she never complained.

"That spring, things didn't improve much. But at least we had hope, my sister said. We could plant seeds and watch them grow. We could hunt the game that returned with the spring. There would be food on the table. She loved hunting. She was a good shot with a bow, and she enjoyed being outdoors. We often went together. That day—"

Berem stopped. Closing his eyes, he began to shake as if chilled. But, gritting his teeth, he continued.

"That day, we'd walked farther than usual. A lightning fire had burned away the brush and we found a trail we'd never seen before. It had been a bad day's hunting and we followed the trail, hoping to find game. But after a while, I saw it wasn't an animal trail. It was an old, old path made by human feet; it hadn't been used in years. I wanted to turn back, but my sister kept going, curious to see where it led."

Berem's face grew strained and tense. For a moment Tanis feared he might stop speaking, but Berem continued feverishly, as if driven.

"It led to a—a strange place. My sister said it must have been a temple once, a temple to evil gods. I don't know. All I know is that there were broken columns lying tumbled about, overgrown with dead weeds. She was right. It *did* have an evil feel to it and we should have left. We should have left the evil place. . . ." Berem repeated this to himself several times, like a chant. Then he fell silent.

No one moved or spoke and, after a moment, he began speaking so softly the others were forced to lean close to hear. And they realized, slowly, that he had forgotten they were there or even where he was. He had gone back to that time.

"But there is one beautiful, beautiful object in the ruins: the base of a broken column, encrusted with jewels!" Berem's voice was soft with awe. "I have never seen such beauty! Or such wealth! How can I leave it? Just one jewel! Just one will make us rich! We can move to the city! My sister will have suitors, as she deserves. I—I fall to my knees and I take out my knife. There is one jewel—a green gemstone—that glitters brightly in the sunlight! It is lovely beyond anything I have ever seen! I will take it. Thrusting the knife blade"—here Berem made a swift motion with his hand—"into the stone beneath the jewel, I begin to pry it out.

"My sister is horrified. She cries to me, she commands me to stop.

" 'This place is holy,' she pleads. 'The jewels belong to some god. This is sacrilege, Berem!'"

Berem shook his head, his face dark with remembered anger.

"I ignore her, though I feel a chill in my heart even as I pry at the jewel. But I tell her—'If it belonged to the gods, they have abandoned it, as they have abandoned us!' But she won't listen."

Berem's eyes flared open, they were cold and frightening to see. His voice came from far away.

"She grabs me! Her fingernails dig into my arm! It hurts!

" 'Stop, Berem!' she commands me—me, her older brother! 'I will not let you desecrate what belongs to the gods!'

"How dare she talk to me like that? I'm doing this for her! For our family! She should not cross me! She knows what can happen when I get mad. Something breaks in my head, flooding my brain. I can't think or see. I yell at her—'Leave me be!'—but her hand grabs my knife hand, jarring the blade, scratching the jewel.

Berem's eyes flashed with a crazed light. Surreptitiously Caramon laid his hand on his dagger as the man's hands clenched to fists and his voice rose to an almost hysterical pitch.

"I—I shove her . . . not that hard . . . I never meant to shove her that hard! She's falling! I've got to catch her, but I can't. I'm moving too slowly, too slowly. Her head . . . hits the column. A sharp rock pierces her here"—Berem touched his temple—"blood covers her face, spills over the jewels. They don't shine anymore. Her eyes don't shine either. They stare at me, but they don't see me. And then . . . and then . . ."

His body shuddered convulsively.

"It is a horrible sight, one I see in my sleep every time I close my eyes! It is like the Cataclysm, only during that, all was destroyed! This is a creation, but what a ghastly, unholy creation! The ground splits open! Huge columns begin to reform before my eyes. A temple springs up from a hideous darkness below the ground. But it isn't a beautiful temple—it is horrible and deformed. I see Darkness rise up

before me, Darkness with five heads, all of them twisting and writhing in my sight. The heads speak to me in a voice colder than a tomb.

" 'Long ago was I banished from this world, and only through a piece of the world may I enter again. The jeweled column was—for me—a locked door, keeping me prisoner. You have freed me, mortal, and therefore I give you what you seek—the green gemstone is yours! '

"There is terrible, mocking laughter. I feel a great pain in my chest. Looking down, I see the green gemstone embedded in my flesh, even as you see it now. Terrified by the hideous evil before me, stunned by my wicked act, I can do nothing but stare as the dark, shadowy shape begins to grow clearer and clearer. It is a dragon! I can see it now—a five-headed dragon† such as I had heard nightmarish tales about when I was a child!

The five-headed chromatic dragon (each head different) is Takhisis, one of the forms the Dark Queen takes, and, indeed, it is the form of her constellation. Lord Toede sometimes swears by saying, "By the five-headed bitch-dragon!"

In the Legends trilogy, the five-headed dragon is visible at portals into the Abyss.

"And I know then that once the dragon enters the world, we are doomed. For at last I understand what I have done. This is the Queen of Darkness the clerics teach us about. Banished long ago by the great Huma, she has long sought to return. Now—by my folly—she will be able again to walk the land. One of the huge heads snakes toward me, and I know I am going to die, for she must not allow any to witness her return. I see the slashing teeth. I cannot move. I don't care.

"And then, suddenly, my sister stands in front of me! She is alive, but when I try to reach out to her, my hands touch nothing. I scream her name, 'Jasla! '

" 'Run, Berem!' she calls. 'Run! She cannot get past me,† not yet! Run!'

Jasla is the other half of Berem. She represents love. Berem is confused in his state, but Jasla is not and knows that she is the only thing standing in the way of the Dark Queen. —TRH

"I stand staring for a moment. My sister hovers between me and the Dark Queen. Horrified, I see the five heads rear back in anger, their screams split the air. But they cannot pass my sister. And, even as I watch, the Queen's shape begins to waver and dim. She is still there, a shadowy figure of evil, but nothing more. But her power is great. She lunges for my sister. . . .

"And then I turn and run. I run and run, the green gemstone burning a hole in my chest. I run until everything goes black."

Berem stopped speaking. Sweat trickled down his face as if he had truly been running for days. None of the companions spoke. The dark tale might have turned them to stone like the boulders around the black pool.

Finally Berem drew a shuddering breath. His eyes focused and he saw them once more.

"There follows a long span of my life of which I know nothing. When I came to myself, I had aged, even as you see me now. At first I told myself it was a nightmare, a horrible dream. But then I felt the green gemstone burning in my flesh, and I knew it was real. I had no idea where I was. Perhaps I had traveled the length and breadth of Krynn in my wanderings. I longed desperately to return to Neraka. Yet that was the one place I knew I couldn't go. I didn't have the courage.

"Long years more I wandered, unable to find peace, unable to rest, dying only to live again. Everywhere I went I heard stories of evil things abroad in the land and I knew it was my fault. And then came the dragons and the dragonmen. I alone knew what they meant. I alone knew the Queen had reached the summit of her power and was trying to conquer the world. The one thing she lacks is me. Why? I'm not certain. Except that I feel like someone who is trying to shut a door another is trying to force open. And I am tired . . ."

Berem's voice faltered. "So tired," he said, his head dropping into his hands. "I want it to end!"

The companions sat silently for long moments, trying to make sense of a story that seemed like something an old nursemaid might have told in the dark hours of the night.

"What must you do to shut this door?" Tanis asked Berem.

"I don't know," Berem said, his voice muffled. "I only know that I feel drawn to Neraka, yet it's the one place on the face of Krynn I *dare* not enter! That's—that's why I ran away."

"But you're going to enter it," Tanis said slowly and firmly. "You're going to enter it with us. We'll be with you. You won't be alone."

Berem shivered and shook his head, whimpering. Then suddenly he stopped and looked up, his

face flushed. "Yes!" he cried. "I cannot stand it anymore! I will go with you! You'll protect me—"

"We'll do our best," Tanis muttered, seeing Caramon roll his eyes, then look away. "We'd better find the way out."

"I found it." Berem sighed. "I was nearly through, when I heard the dwarf cry out. This way." He pointed to another narrow cleft between the rocks. Caramon sighed, glancing ruefully at the scratches on his arms. One by one, the companions entered the cleft.

Tanis was the last. Turning, he looked back once more upon the barren place. Darkness was falling swiftly, the azure blue sky deepening to purple and finally to black. The strange boulders were shrouded in the gathering gloom. He could no longer see the dark pool of rock where Fizban had vanished.

It seemed odd to think of Flint being gone. There was a great emptiness inside of him. He kept expecting to hear the dwarf's grumbling voice complain about his various aches and pains or argue with the kender.

For a moment Tanis struggled with himself, holding onto his friend as long as he could. Then, silently, he let Flint go. Turning, he crept through the narrow cleft in the rocks, leaving Godshome, never to see it again.

Once back on the trail, they followed it until they came to a small cave. Here they huddled together, not daring to build a fire this near to Neraka, the center of the might of the dragonarmies. For a while, no one spoke, then they began to talk about Flint—letting him go—as Tanis had done. Their memories were good ones, recalling Flint's rich, adventurous life.

They laughed heartily when Caramon recounted the tale of the disastrous camping trip, how he had overturned the boat, trying to catch a fish by hand, knocking Flint into the water. Tanis recalled how Tas and the dwarf had met when Tas "accidentally" walked off with a bracelet Flint had made and was trying to sell at a fair. Tika remembered the wonderful toys he had made for her. She recalled his kindness when her father disappeared, how he had taken the young girl into his own home until Otik had given her a place to live and work.†

Tika's father was Waylan the Magician, an itinerant illusionist and petty thief. He disappeared from Solace and, it is is presumed, came to no good end. In the meantime, Flint and Otik raised her.—MW

All these and more memories they recalled until, by the end of the evening, the bitter sting had gone out of their grief, leaving only the ache of loss.

That is—for most of them.

Late, late in the dark watches of the night, Tasslehoff sat outside the cave entrance, staring up into the stars. Flint's helm was clutched in his small hands, tears streamed unchecked down his face.

KENDER MOURNING SONG

Always before, the spring returned.
The bright world in its cycle spun
In air and flowers, grass and fern,
Assured and cradled by the sun.

Always before, you could explain
The turning darkness of the earth,
And how that dark embraced the rain,
And gave the ferns and flowers birth.

Already I forget those things,
And how a vein of gold survives
The mining of a thousand springs,
The seasons of a thousand lives.

Now winter is my memory,
Now autumn, now the summer light—
So every spring from now will be
Another season into night.

5

Neraka.

As it turned out, the companions discovered it was going to be easy getting into Neraka.

Deadly easy.

"What in the name of the gods is happening?" Caramon muttered as he and Tanis, still dressed in their stolen dragonarmor, stared down onto the plains from their hidden vantage point in the mountains west of Neraka.

Writhing black lines snaked across the barren plain toward the only building within a hundred miles, the Temple of the Queen of Darkness. It looked as though hundreds of vipers were slithering down from the mountains, but these were not vipers. These were the dragonarmies, thousands strong. The two men watching saw here and there the flash of sun off spear and shield. Flags of black

and red and blue fluttered from tall poles that bore the emblems of the Dragon Highlords. Flying high above them, dragons filled the air with a hideous rainbow of colors—reds, blues, greens, and blacks. Two gigantic flying citadels† hovered over the walled Temple compound; the shadows they cast made it perpetual night down below.

The citadels were originally land-bound fortresses, but the black-robed magic users and dark clerics of Sanction mastered the secret of ripping a castle from its foundations and setting it in the skies.

Previously, only the forces of Good were known to possess this skill, having lifted the Floating Tomb of Derkin and the now-vanished Floating Palace of Foghaven Vale.A flying citadel can be visited in the Legends trilogy.

"You know," said Caramon slowly, "it's a good thing that old man attacked us back there. We would have been massacred if we'd ridden our brass dragons into this mob."

"Yes," Tanis agreed absently. He'd been thinking about that "old man," adding a few things together, remembering what he himself had seen and what Tas had told him. The more he thought about Fizban, the closer he came to realizing the truth. His skin "shivered," as Flint would have said.

Recalling Flint, a sudden swift aching in his heart made him put thoughts of the dwarf—and the old man—from his mind. He had enough to worry about now, and there would be no old mages to help him out of this one.

"I don't know what's happening," Tanis said quietly, "but it's working for us now, not against us. Remember what Elistan said once? It is written in the Disks of Mishakal that evil turns upon itself. The Dark Queen is gathering her forces, for whatever reason. Probably preparing to deal Krynn a final death blow. But we can slip in easily among the confusion. No one will notice two guards bringing in a group of prisoners."

"You hope," Caramon added gloomily.

"I pray," Tanis said softly.

The captain of the guard at the gates of Neraka was a sorely harrassed man. The Dark Queen had called a Council of War and, for only the second time since the war began, the Dragon Highlords on the continent of Ansalon were gathering together. Four days ago, they began arriving in Neraka and, since then, the captain's life had been a waking nightmare.

The Highlords were supposed to enter the city by order of rank. Thus Lord Ariakas entered first with his personal retinue, his troops, his bodyguards, his dragons; then Kitiara, the Dark Lady, with her

There were rumors that Lucien was the White Dragon Highlord after Feal-thas's death, but he arrived in Neraka as the Green Highlord.

personal retinue, her troops, her bodyguards, her dragons; then Lucien of Takar† with his personal retinue, his troops and so forth through all the Highlords down to Dragon Highlord Toede, of the eastern front.

The system was designed to do more than simply honor the higher-ups. It was intended to move large numbers of troops and dragons, as well as all their supplies, into and out of a complex that had never been intended to hold large concentrations of troops. Nor, as distrustful as the Highlords were of each other, could any Highlord be persuaded to enter with a single draconian less than any other Highlord. It was a good system and it should have worked. Unfortunately, there was trouble from the very outset when Lord Ariakas arrived two days late.

Had he done this purposefully to create the confusion he knew must result? The captain did not know and he dared not ask, but he had his own ideas. This meant, of course, that those Highlords who arrived before Ariakas were forced to camp on the plains outside the Temple compound until the Lord made his entry. This provoked trouble. The draconians, goblins, and human mercenaries wanted the pleasures of the camp city that had been hastily erected in the Temple square. They had marched long distances and were justifiably angry when this was denied them.

Many sneaked over the walls at night, drawn to the taverns as flies to honey. Brawls broke out—each Highlord's troops being loyal to that particular Highlord and no other. The dungeons below the Temple were filled to overflowing. The captain finally ordered his forces to haul the drunks out of the city in wheelbarrows every morning and dump them on the plains where they were retrieved by their irate commanders.

Quarrels started among the dragons, too, as each lead dragon sought to establish dominance over the others. A big green, Cyan Bloodbane, had actually killed a red in a fight over a deer. Unfortunately for Cyan, the red had been a pet of the Dark Queen's. The big green was now imprisoned in a cave beneath Neraka, where his howls and violent taillashings caused many up above to think an earthquake had struck.

The captain had not slept well in two nights. When word reached him early in the morning of the third day that Ariakas had arrived, the captain very nearly gave thanks on his knees. Hurriedly marshaling his staff, he gave orders for the grand entrance to begin. Everything proceeded smoothly until several hundred of Toede's draconians saw Ariakas's troops entering the Temple square. Drunk and completely out of the control of their ineffectual leaders, they attempted to crowd in as well. Angry at the disruption, Ariakas's captains ordered their men to fight back. Chaos erupted.

Furious, the Dark Queen sent out her own troops, armed with whips, steel-link chains, and maces. Black-robed magic-users walked among them, as well as dark clerics. Between the whippings, head-bashings, and spellcasting, order was eventually restored. Lord Ariakas and his troops finally entered the Temple compound with dignity—if not grace.

It might have been mid-afternoon—by now the captain had completely lost track of time (those blasted citadels cut off the sunlight)—when one of the guards appeared, requesting his presence at the front gates.

"What is it?" the captain snarled impatiently, fixing the guard with a piercing gaze from his one good eye (the other had been lost in a battle with the elves in Silvanesti). "Another fight? Knock 'em both over the head and haul 'em to prison. I'm sick—"

"N-not a fight, sir," stuttered the guard, a young goblin terrified of his human captain. "The watch at the g-gate sent m-me. T-Two officers with p-prisoners want p-permission to enter."

The captain swore in frustration. What next? He almost told the goblin to go back and let them enter. The place was crawling with slaves and prisoners already. A few more wouldn't matter. Highlord Kitiara's troops were gathering outside, ready to come in. He had to be on hand to extend official greetings.

"What kind of prisoners?" he asked irritably, trying hastily to catch up on reams of paperwork before leaving to attend the ceremony. "Drunken draconians? Just take them—"

"I—I think you should c-come, s-sir." The goblin was sweating, and sweating goblins are not pleasant

to be around. "Th-There's a couple of h-humans, and a k-kender."

The captain wrinkled his nose. "I said," He stopped. "A kender?" he said, looking up with considerable interest. "There wasn't, by any chance, a dwarf?"

"Not as I know of, sir," answered the poor goblin. "But I might have missed one in the c-crowd, sir."

"I'll come," the captain said. Hastily strapping on his sword, he followed the goblin down to the front gate.

Here, for the moment, peace reigned. Ariakas's troops were all within the tent city now. Kitiara's were jostling and fighting, forming ranks to march inside. It was nearly time for the ceremony to begin. The captain cast a swift glance over the group standing before him, just inside the front gates.

Two dragonarmy officers of high rank stood guard over a group of sullen prisoners. The captain studied the prisoners carefully, remembering orders he had received only two days ago. He was to watch, in particular, for a dwarf traveling with a kender. There might possibly be an elflord with them and an elfwoman with long, silver hair—in reality, a silver dragon. These had been the companions of the elfwoman they were holding prisoner, and the Dark Queen expected any or all of them to attempt to rescue her.

Here was a kender, all right. But the woman had curly red hair, not silver, and if she was a dragon, the captain would eat his plate-mail. The stooped old man with the long scraggly beard was certainly human, not a dwarf or an elflord. All in all, he couldn't imagine why two dragonarmy officers had bothered taking the motley group prisoner.

"Just slit their throats and be done with it instead of bothering us," the captain said sourly. "We're short of prison space as it is. Take them away."

"But what a waste!" said one of the officers—a giant of a man with arms like tree-trunks. Grabbing the red-headed girl, he dragged her forward. "I've heard they're paying good money in the slave markets for her kind!"

"You're right there," the captain muttered, running his good eye over the girl's voluptuous body, which was enhanced, to his mind, by her chain-mail

armor. "But I don't know what you think you'll get for this lot!" He poked the kender, who gave an indignant cry, and was instantly shushed by the other dragonarmy guard. "Kill 'em—"

The big dragonarmy officer seemed confounded by this argument, blinking in obvious confusion. Before he could reply, however, the other officer—who had been quiet and hidden in the background—stepped forward.

"The human's a magic-user," the officer said. "And we believe the kender is a spy. We caught him near Dargaard Keep."

"Well, why didn't you say so in the first place," the captain snapped, "instead of wasting my time. Yeah, go ahead and haul 'em inside," he spoke hurriedly as horns blared. It was time for the ceremony, the massive iron gates were shivering, beginning to swing open. "I'll sign your papers. Hand them over."

"We don't have—" began the big officer.

"What papers do you mean?" the bearded officer cut in, fumbling in a pouch. "Identification—"

"Naw!" said the captain, fuming in impatience. "Your leave of absence from your commander to bring in prisoners."

"We weren't given that, sir," said the bearded officer coolly. "Is that a new order?"

"No, it isn't," said the captain, eyeing them suspiciously. "How'd you get through the lines without it? And how do you expect to get back? Or were you going back? Thinking of taking a little trip with the money you'd make from these, were you?"

"Naw!" The big officer flushed angrily, his eyes flaring. "Our commander just forgot, maybe, that's all. He's got a lot on his mind, and there's not much mind there to handle it, if you take my meaning." He glared at the captain menacingly.

The gates swung open. Horns blared loudly. The captain sighed in frustration. Right now he was supposed to be standing in the center, prepared to greet the Lord Kitiara. He beckoned to some of the Dark Queen's guards who were standing nearby.

"Take 'em below," he said, twitching his uniform into place. "We'll show them what we do to deserters!"

As he hurried off, he saw with pleasure that the Queen's guards were carrying out their assignments, quickly and efficiently grabbing the two dragonarmy officers and divesting them of their weapons.

Caramon cast an alarmed glance at Tanis as the draconians grasped him by the arms and unbuckled his sword belt. Tika's eyes were wide with fear, this certainly wasn't the way things were supposed to be going. Berem, his face nearly hidden by his false whiskers, looked as if he might cry or run or both. Even Tasslehoff seemed a bit stunned by the sudden change in plans. Tanis could see the kender's eyes dart around, seeking escape.

Tanis thought frantically. He believed he had considered every possible occurrence when he had formed this plan for entering Neraka, but he'd obviously missed one. Certainly being arrested as a deserter from the dragonarmies had never crossed his mind!

If the guards took them into the dungeons, it would be all over. The moment they took off his helmet, they'd recognize him as half-elven. Then they'd examine the others more closely . . . they'd discover Berem. . . .

He was the danger. Without him Caramon and the others might still pull it off. Without him . . .

There was a blaring of trumpets and wild cheering from the crowd as a huge blue dragon bearing a Dragon Highlord entered the Temple gates. Seeing the Highlord, Tanis's heart constricted with pain and, suddenly, a wild elation. The crowd surged forward roaring Kitiara's name and, for the moment, the guards were distracted as they looked to see if the Highlord might be in danger. Tanis leaned as near Tasslehoff as he could.

"Tas!" he said swiftly, under the cover of the noise, hoping Tas remembered enough elven to understand him. "Tell Caramon to keep up the act. No matter what I do, he must trust me! Everything depends on that. No matter what I do. Understand?"

Tas stared at Tanis in astonishment, then nodded hesitantly. It had been a long time since he'd been forced to translate elven.

Tanis could only hope he understood. Caramon spoke no elven at all, and Tanis didn't dare risk speaking Common, even if his voice was swallowed by the noise of the crowd. As it was, one of the guards wrenched his arm painfully, ordering him to be silent.

The noise died down, the crowd was bullied and shoved back into place. Seeing things under control, the guards turned to lead their prisoners away.

Suddenly Tanis stumbled and fell, tripping his guard, who sprawled headlong into the dust.

"Get up, slime!" Cursing, the other guard cuffed Tanis with the handle of a whip, striking him across the face. The half-elf lunged for the guard, grabbing the whip handle and the hand that held it. Tanis yanked with all his strength, and his sudden move sent the guard head over heels. For a split second, he was free.

Hurling himself forward, aware of the guards behind him, aware also of Caramon's astonished face, Tanis threw himself toward the regal figure riding the blue dragon.

"Kitiara!" he yelled, just as the guards caught hold of him. "Kitiara!" he screamed, a hoarse, ragged shout that seemed torn from his chest. Fighting the guards, he managed to free one hand. With it, he gripped his helmet and tore it off his head, hurling it to the ground.

The Highlord in the night-blue, dragon-scale armor turned upon hearing her name. Tanis could see her brown eyes widen in astonishment beneath the hideous dragonmask she wore. He could see the fiery eyes of the male blue dragon turn to gaze at him as well.

"Kitiara!" Tanis shouted. Shaking off his captors with a strength born of desperation, he dove forward again. But draconians in the crowd flung themselves on him, knocking him to the ground, where they held him pinned by his arms. Still Tanis struggled, twisting to look into the eyes of the Highlord.

"Halt, Skie," Kitiara said, placing a gloved hand commandingly on the dragon's neck. Skie stopped obediently, his clawed feet slipping slightly on the cobblestones of the street. But the dragon's eyes, as they glared at Tanis, were filled with jealousy and hatred.

Tanis held his breath. His heart beat painfully. His head ached and blood dribbled into one eye, but he didn't notice. He waited for the shout that would tell him Tasslehoff hadn't understood, that his friends had tried to come to his aid. He waited for Kitiara to look behind him and see Caramon—her half-brother—and recognize him. He didn't dare turn around to see what had happened to his friends. He could only hope Caramon had sense enough—and faith enough in him—to keep out of sight.

And now here came the captain, his cruel one-eyed face distorted in rage. Raising a booted foot, the captain aimed a kick for Tanis's head, preparing to render this meddlesome troublemaker unconscious.

"Stop," said a voice.

The captain halted so suddenly that he staggered off-balance.

"Let him go." The same voice.

Reluctantly, the guards released Tanis and fell back away from him at an imperious gesture from the Dark Lady.

"What is so important, commander, that you disrupt my entrance?" she asked in cool tones, her voice sounding deep and distorted behind the dragonhelm.

Stumbling to his feet, weak with relief, his head swimming from his struggles with the guards, Tanis made his way forward to stand beside her. As he drew nearer, he saw a flicker of amusement in Kitiara's brown eyes. She was enjoying this; a new game with an old toy. Clearing his throat, Tanis spoke boldly.

"These idiots arrested me for desertion," he stated, "all because that imbecile Bakaris forgot to give me the proper papers."

"I'll see he pays the penalty for having caused you trouble, good Tanthalasa," replied Kitiara. Tanis could hear the laughter in her voice. "How dare you?" she added, whirling to glower at the captain, who cringed as the helmed visage turned toward him.

"I—I was j-just following or-orders, my lord," he stuttered, shaking like a goblin.

"Be off with you, or you'll feed my dragon," Kitiara commanded peremptorily, waving her

hand. Then, in the same graceful gesture, she held out her gloved hand to Tanis. "May I offer you a ride, commander? To make amends, of course."†

Asked if Kitiara has a sense of humor, Margaret answered, "I think Kit has a very wry and sardonic sense of humor. Cynical, existentialist."

"Thank you, Lord," Tanis said.

Casting a dark glance at the captain, Tanis accepted Kitiara's hand and swung himself up beside her on the back of the blue dragon. His eyes quickly scanned the crowd as Kitiara ordered Skie forward once more. For a moment, his agonized search could detect nothing, then he sighed in relief as he saw Caramon and the others being led away by the guards. The big man glanced up at him as they passed, a hurt and puzzled expression on his face. But he kept moving. Either Tas had passed along the message or the big man had sense enough to keep up the act. Or perhaps Caramon trusted him anyway. Tanis didn't know. His friends were safe now—at least safer than they were with him.

This might be the last time I ever see them, he thought suddenly, with pain. Then he shook his head. He could not let himself dwell on that. Turning away, he discovered Kitiara's brown eyes regarding him with an odd mixture of cunning and undisguised admiration.

Tasslehoff stood on his tiptoes, trying to see what became of Tanis. He heard shouts and yells, then a moment of silence. Then he saw the half-elf climb onto the dragon and sit beside Kitiara. The procession started up again. The kender thought he saw Tanis look his way, but—if so—it was without recognition. The guards shoved their remaining prisoners through the jostling crowd, and Tas lost sight of his friend.

One of the guards prodded Caramon in his ribs with a short sword.

"So your buddy gets a lift from the Highlord and you rot in prison," the draconian said, chuckling.

"He won't forget me," Caramon muttered.

The draconian grinned and nudged its partner, who was dragging Tasslehoff along, one clawed hand on the kender's collar. "Sure, he'll come back for you—if he can manage to find his way out of her bed!"

Caramon flushed, scowling. Tasslehoff shot the big warrior an alarmed glance. The kender hadn't had a chance to give Caramon Tanis's last message, and he was terrified the big man would ruin everything, although Tas wasn't really certain what there was left to ruin. Still . . .

But Caramon only tossed his head in injured dignity. "I'll be out before nightfall," he rumbled in his deep baritone. "We've been through too much together. He wouldn't let me down."†

The others have all doubted Tanis at various times, but Caramon is faithful to his trust in his friend.

Catching a wistful note in Caramon's voice, Tas wriggled in anxiety, longing to get close enough to Caramon to explain. But at that moment Tika cried out in anger. Twisting his head, Tas saw the guard rip her blouse; there were already bloody gashes made by its clawing hands on her neck. Caramon shouted, but too late. Tika struck the guard with a backhand on the side of its reptilian face in the best barroom tradition.

Furious, the draconian hurled Tika to the street and raised its whip. Tas heard Caramon suck in his breath and the kender cringed, preparing himself for the end.

"Hey! Don't damage her!" Caramon roared. "Unless you want to be held accountable. Lord Kitiara told us to get six silver pieces for her, and we won't do it if she's marked up!"

The draconian hesitated. Caramon was a prisoner, that was true. But the guards had all seen the welcome reception his friend had received from the Dark Lady. Did they dare take a chance on offending another man who might stand high in her favor? Apparently they decided not. Roughly dragging Tika to her feet, they shoved her forward.

Tasslehoff breathed a sigh of relief, then stole a worried peek back at Berem, thinking that the man had been very quiet. He was right. The Everman might have been in a different world. His eyes, wide open, were fixed in a strange stare. His mouth gaped, he almost appeared half-witted. At least he didn't look like he was about to cause trouble. It seemed that Caramon was going to continue playing his role and that Tika would be all right. For the time being, no one needed him. Sighing in relief, Tas began to look with interest around the Temple compound, at least as well as he could with the draconian hanging onto his collar.

He was sorry he did. Neraka looked exactly like what it was—a small, ancient impoverished village built to serve those who inhabited the Temple, now overrun by the tent city that had sprouted up around it like fungus.

At the far end of the compound the Temple itself loomed over the city like a carrion bird of prey—its twisted, deformed, obscene structure seeming to dominate even the mountains on the horizon behind. Once anyone set foot in Neraka, his eyes went first to the Temple. After that, no matter where else he looked or what other business occupied him, the Temple was always there, even at night, even in his dreams.

Tas took one look, then hurriedly glanced away, feeling a cold sickness creep over him. But the sights before him were almost worse. The tent city was filled with troops; draconians and human mercenaries, goblins and hobgoblins spilled out of the hastily constructed bars and brothels onto the filthy streets. Slaves of every race had been brought in to serve their captors and provide for their unholy pleasures. Gully dwarves swarmed underfoot like rats, living off the refuse. The stench was overpowering, the sights were like something from the Abyss. Although it was midday, the square was dark and chill as night. Glancing up, Tas saw the huge flying citadels, floating above the Temple in terrible majesty, their dragons circling them in unceasing watchfulness.

When they had first started down the crowded streets, Tas had hoped he might have a chance to break free. He was an expert in melting in with a crowd. He saw Caramon's eyes flick about, too; the big man was thinking the same thing. But after walking only a few blocks, after seeing the citadels keeping their dreadful watch above, Tas realized it was hopeless. Apparently Caramon reached the same conclusion, for the kender saw the warrior's shoulders slump.

Appalled and horrified, Tas suddenly thought of Laurana, being held prisoner here. The kender's buoyant spirit seemed finally crushed by the weight of the darkness and evil all around him, darkness and evil he had never dreamed existed.†

Kender are the true innocents of the world. Thus, if we consider a kender as being childlike, he would have about the same concept of evil as a child. He may know it exists, but it always exists someplace else.—MW

Their guards hurried them along, pushing and shoving their way through the drunken, brawling soldiers, down the clogged and narrow streets. Try as he might, Tas couldn't figure out any way of relaying Tanis's message to Caramon. Then they were forced to come to a halt as a contingent of Her Dark Majesty's troops, lined up shoulder to shoulder, came marching through the streets. Those who did not get out of their way were hurled bodily to the sidewalk by the draconian officers or were simply knocked down and trampled. The companions' guards hastily shoved them up against a crumbling wall and ordered them to stand still until the soldiers had passed.

Tasslehoff found himself flattened between Caramon on one side and a draconian on the other. The guard had loosened its clawed grip on Tas's shirt, evidently figuring that not even a kender would be foolish enough to try to escape in this mob. Though Tas could feel the reptile's black eyes on him, he was able to squirm near enough to Caramon to talk. He hoped he wasn't overheard, and didn't expect to be, with all the head-bashing and boot-thumping going on around him.

"Caramon!" Tas whispered. "I've got a message. Can you hear me?"

Caramon did not turn, but kept staring straight ahead, his face set rock-hard. But Tas saw one eyelid flutter.

"Tanis said to trust him!" Tas whispered swiftly. "No matter what. And . . . and to . . . keep up the act . . . I think that's what he said."

Tas saw Caramon frown.

"He spoke in elven," Tas added huffily. "And it was hard to hear."

Caramon's expression did not change. If anything, it grew darker.

Tas swallowed. Edging closer, he pressed up against the wall right behind the big warrior's broad back. "That . . . that Dragon Highlord," the kender said hesitantly. "That . . . was Kitiara, wasn't it?"

Caramon did not answer. But Tas saw the muscles in the man's jaw tighten, he saw a nerve begin to twitch in Caramon's neck.

Tas sighed. Forgetting where he was, he raised his voice. "You do trust him, don't you, Caramon? Because—"

Without warning, Tas's draconian guard turned and bashed the kender across the mouth, slamming him into the wall. Dazed with pain, Tasslehoff sank down to the ground. A dark shadow bent over him. His vision fuzzy, Tas couldn't see who it was and he braced himself for another blow. Then he felt strong, gentle hands lift him by his fleecy vest.

"I told you not to damage them," growled Caramon.

"Bah! A kender!" The draconian spat.

The troops had nearly all passed by now. Caramon set Tas on his feet. The kender tried to stand up, but for some reason the sidewalk kept sliding out from underneath him.

"I—I'm sorry . . ." he heard himself mumble. "Legs acting funny . . ." Finally he felt himself hoisted in the air and, with a protesting squeak, was flung over Caramon's broad shoulder like a meal sack.

"He's got information," Caramon said in his deep voice. "I hope you haven't addled his brain so that he's lost it. The Dark Lady won't be pleased."

"What brain?" snarled the draconian, but Tas, from his upside-down position on Caramon's back, thought the creature appeared a bit shaken.

They began walking again. Tas's head hurt horribly, his cheek stung. Putting his hand to it, he felt sticky blood where the draconian's claws had dug into his skin. There was a sound in his ears like a hundred bees had taken up residence in his brain. The world seemed to be slowly circling around him, making his stomach queasy, and being jounced around on Caramon's armor-plated back wasn't helping.

"How much farther is it?" He could feel Caramon's voice vibrate in the big man's chest. "The little bastard's heavy."

In answer, the draconian pointed a long, bony claw.

With a great effort, trying to take his mind off his pain and dizziness, Tas twisted his head to see. He could manage only a glance, but it was enough. The

building had been growing larger and larger as they approached until it filled, not only the vision, but the mind as well.

Tas slumped back. His sight was growing dim and he wondered drowsily why it was getting so foggy. The last thing he remembered was hearing the words, "To the dungeons . . . beneath the Temple of Her Majesty, Takhisis, Queen of Darkness."

6

Tanis bargains. Gakhan investigates.

"Wine?"

"No."

Kitiara shrugged. Taking the pitcher from the bowl of snow in which it rested to keep cool, she slowly poured some for herself, idly watching the blood-red liquid run out of the crystal carafe and into her glass. Then she carefully set the crystal carafe back into the snow and sat down opposite Tanis, regarding him coolly.

She had taken off the dragon helm, but she wore her armor still, the night-blue armor, gilded with gold, that fit over her lithe body like scaled skin. The light from the many candles in the room gleamed in the polished surfaces and glinted off the sharp metal edges until Kitiara seemed ablaze in flame. Her dark hair, damp with perspiration, curled around her face. Her brown eyes were bright as fire, shadowed by long, dark lashes.

"Why are you here, Tanis?" she asked softly, running her finger along the rim of her glass as she gazed steadily at him.

"You know why," he answered briefly.

"Laurana, of course," Kitiara said.

Tanis shrugged, careful to keep his face a mask, yet fearing that this woman—who sometimes knew him better than he knew himself—could read every thought.

"You came alone?" Kitiara asked, sipping at the wine.

"Yes," Tanis replied, returning her gaze without faltering.

Kitiara raised an eyebrow in obvious disbelief.

"Flint's dead," he added, his voice breaking. Even in his fear, he still could not think of his friend without pain. "And Tasslehoff wandered off somewhere. I couldn't find him. I . . . I didn't really want to bring him anyway."

"I can understand," Kit said wryly. "So Flint is dead."

"Like Sturm," Tanis could not help but add through clenched teeth.

Kit glanced at him sharply. "The fortunes of war, my dear," she said. "We were both soldiers, he and I. He understands. His spirit bears me no malice."

Tanis choked angrily, swallowing his words. What she said was true. Sturm *would* understand.

Kitiara was silent as she watched Tanis's face a few moments. Then she set the glass down with a clink.

"What about my brothers?" she asked. "Where—"

"Why don't you just take me to the dungeons and interrogate me?" Tanis snarled. Rising out of his chair, he began to pace the luxurious room.

Kitiara smiled, an introspective, thoughtful smile. "Yes," she said, "I could interrogate you there. And you would talk, dear Tanis. You would tell me all I wanted to hear, and then you would beg to tell me more. Not only do we have those who are skilled in the art of torture, but they are passionately dedicated to their profession." Rising languorously, Kitiara walked over to stand in front of Tanis. Her wine glass in one hand, she placed her other hand

on his chest and slowly ran her palm up over his shoulder. "But this is not an interrogation. Say, rather, it is a sister, concerned about her family. Where are my brothers?"

"I don't know," Tanis said. Catching her wrist firmly in his hand, he held her hand away from him. "They were both lost in the Blood Sea. . . ."

"With the Green Gemstone Man?"

"With the Green Gemstone Man."

"And how did you survive?"

"Sea elves rescued me."

"Then they might have rescued the others?"

"Perhaps. Perhaps not. I am elven, after all. The others were human."

Kitiara stared at Tanis long moments. He still held her wrist in his hand. Unconsciously, under her penetrating gaze, his fingers closed around it.

"You're hurting me . . ." Kit whispered softly. "Why did you come, Tanis? To rescue Laurana . . . alone? Even you were never that foolish—"

"No," Tanis said, tightening his grasp on Kitiara's arm. "I came to make a trade. Take me. Let her go."

Kitiara's eye opened wide. Then, suddenly, she threw back her head and laughed. With a quick, easy move, she broke free of Tanis's grip and, turning, walked over to the table to refill her wine glass.

She grinned at him over her shoulder. "Why, Tanis," she said, laughing again, "what are you to me that I should make this trade?"

Tanis felt his face flush. Still grinning, Kitiara continued.

"I have captured their Golden General, Tanis. I have taken their good-luck charm, their beautiful elven warrior. She wasn't a bad general, either, for that matter. She brought them the dragonlances and taught them to fight. Her brother brought back the good dragons, but everyone credits her. She kept the Knights together, when they should have split apart long before this. And you want me to exchange her for"—Kitiara gestured contemptuously—"a half-elf who's been wandering the countryside in the company of kender, barbarians, and dwarves!"

Kitiara began to laugh again, laughing so hard she was forced to sit down and wipe tears from her eyes. "Really, Tanis, you have a high opinion of yourself. What did you think I'd take you back for? Love?"

There was a subtle change in Kit's voice, her laugh seemed forced. Frowning suddenly, she twisted the wineglass in her hand.

Tanis did not respond. He could only stand before her, his skin burning at her ridicule. Kitiara stared at him, then lowered her gaze.

"Suppose I said yes?" she asked in a cold voice, her eyes on the glass in her hand. "What could you give me in return for what I would lose?"

Tanis drew a deep breath. "The commander of your forces is dead," he said, keeping his voice even. "I know. Tas told me he killed him. I'll take his place."

"You'd serve under . . . in the dragonarmies?" Kit's eyes widened in genuine astonishment.

"Yes." Tanis gritted his teeth. His voice was bitter. "We've lost anyway. I've seen your floating citadels. We can't win, even if the good dragons stayed. And they won't—the people will send them back. The people never trusted them anyway, not really. I care for only one thing—let Laurana go free, unharmed."

"I truly believe you would do this," Kitiara said softly, marveling. For long moments she stared at him. "I'll have to consider . . ."

Then, as if arguing with herself, she shook her head. Putting the glass to her lips, she swallowed the wine, set the glass down, and rose to her feet.

"I'll consider," she repeated. "But now I must leave you, Tanis. There is a meeting of the Dragon Highlords tonight. They have come from all over Ansalon to attend. You are right, of course. You *have* lost the war. Tonight we make plans to clench the fist of iron. You will attend me. I will present you to Her Dark Majesty."

"And Laurana?" Tanis persisted.

"I said I would consider it!" A dark line marred the smooth skin between Kitiara's feathery eyebrows. Her voice was sharp. "Ceremonial armor will be brought to you. Be dressed and ready to accompany me within the hour." She started to go, then turned to face Tanis once more. "My decision may depend on how you conduct yourself this evening," she said softly. "Remember, Half-Elven, from this moment you serve *me!*"

The brown eyes glittered clear and cold as they held Tanis in their thrall. Slowly he felt the will of this woman press upon him until it was like a strong hand forcing him down onto the polished marble floor. The might of the dragonarmies was behind her, the shadow of the Dark Queen hovered around her, imbuing her with a power Tanis had noticed before.

Suddenly Tanis felt the great distance between them. She was supremely, superbly human. For only the humans were endowed with the lust for power so strong that the raw passion of their nature could be easily corrupted.† The humans' brief lives were as flames that could burn with a pure light like Goldmoon's candle, like Sturm's shattered sun. Or the flame could destroy, a searing fire that consumed all in its path. He had warmed his cold, sluggish elven blood by that fire; he had nurtured the flame in his heart. Now he saw himself as he would become—as he had seen the bodies of those who died in the flames of Tarsis—a mass of charred flesh, the heart black and still.

The other races of Krynn seemingly think that because humans are so short-lived, they use power as a substitute. Perhaps this is why most of the Dark Queen's Highlords are humans.

It was his due, the price he must pay. He would lay his soul upon this woman's altar as another might lay a handful of silver upon a pillow. He owed Laurana that much. She had suffered enough because of him. His death would not free her but his life might.

Slowly, Tanis placed his hand over his heart and bowed.

"My lord," he said.

Kitiara walked into her private chamber, her mind in a turmoil. She felt her blood pulse through her veins. Excitement, desire, the glorious elation of victory made her more drunk than the wine. Yet beneath was a nagging doubt, all the more irritating because it turned the elation flat and stale. Angrily she tried to banish it from her mind, but it was brought sharply into focus as she opened the door to her room.

The servants had not expected her so soon. The torches had not been lit; the fire was laid, but not burning. Irritably she reached for the bell rope that would send them scurrying in to be berated for their laxness, when suddenly a cold and fleshless hand closed over her wrist.

The touch of that hand sent a burning sensation of cold through her bones and blood until it nearly froze her heart. Kitiara gasped with the pain and started to pull free, but the hand held her fast.

"You have not forgotten our bargain?"

"No, of course not!" Kitiara said. Trying to keep the quiver of fear from her voice, she commanded sternly, "Let me go!"

Soth lets go, not because she ordered him to, but because he doesn't want to hurt her. Already we see that the death knight is becoming enamored of her.—MW

The hand slowly released its grip.† Kitiara hurriedly snatched her arm away, rubbing the flesh that, even in that short span of time, had turned bluish white.

"The elfwoman will be yours when the Queen has finished with her, of course."

"Of course. I would not want her otherwise. A living woman is of no use to me, not like a living man is of use to you. . . ." The dark figure's voice lingered unpleasantly over the words.

Kitiara cast a scornful glance at the pallid face, the flickering eyes that floated—disembodied—above the black armor of the knight.

"Don't be a fool, Soth," she said, pulling the bell rope hastily. She felt a need for light. "I am able to separate the pleasures of the flesh from the pleasures of business—something you were unable to do, from what I know of your life."

"Then what are your plans for the half-elf?" Lord Soth asked, his voice seeming, as usual, to come from far below ground.

"He will be mine, utterly and completely," Kitiara said, gently rubbing her injured wrist.

Servants hurried in with hesitant, sideways glances at the Dark Lady, fearing her notorious explosions of wrath. But Kitiara, preoccupied with her thoughts, ignored them. Lord Soth faded back into the shadows as always when the candles were lit.

"The only way to possess the half-elf is to make him watch as I destroy Laurana," Kitiara continued.

"That is hardly the way to win his love," Lord Soth sneered.

"I don't want his love." Pulling off her gloves and unbuckling her armor, Kitiara laughed shortly. "I want *him!* As long as she lives, his thoughts will be of her and of the noble sacrifice he has made. No, the only way he will be mine—totally—is to be ground beneath the heel of my boot until he is

nothing more than a shapeless mass. Then, he will be of use to me."

"Not for long," Lord Soth remarked caustically. "Death will free him."

Kitiara shrugged. The servants had completed their tasks and vanished quickly. The Dark Lady stood in the light, silent and thoughtful, her armor half-on and half-off, her dragon helm dangling from her hand.

"He has lied to me," she said softly, after a moment. Then, flinging the helm down on a table, where it struck and shattered a dusty, porcelain vase, Kit began to pace back and forth. "He has lied. My brothers did not die in the Blood Sea—at least one of them lives, I know. And so does he—the Everman!" Peremptorily, Kitiara flung open the door. "Gakhan!" she shouted.

A draconian hurried into the room.

"What news? Have they found that captain yet?"

"No, lord," the draconian replied. He was the same one who had followed Tanis from the inn in Flotsam, the same who had helped trap Laurana. "He is off-duty, lord," the creature added as if that explained everything.

Kitiara understood. "Search every beer tent and brothel until he is found. Then bring him here. Lock him in irons if you have to. I'll question him when I return from the Highlords' Assembly. No, wait . . ." Kitiara paused, then added, "*You* question him. Find out if the half-elf was truly alone—as he said—or if there were others with him. If so—"

The draconian bowed. "You will be informed at once, my lord."

Kitiara dismissed him with a gesture, and the draconian, bowing again, left, shutting the door behind him. After standing thoughtfully for a moment, Kitiara irritably ran her hand through her curly hair, then began yanking at the straps of her armor once again.

"You will attend me, tonight," she said to Lord Soth, without looking at the apparition of the death knight which, she assumed, was still in its same place behind her.

"Be watchful. Lord Ariakas will not be pleased with what I intend to do."

Tossing the last piece of armor to the floor, Kitiara pulled off the leather tunic and the blue silken hose.

Then, stretching in luxurious freedom, she glanced over her shoulder to see Lord Soth's reaction to her words. He was not there. Startled, she glanced quickly around the room.

The spectral knight stood beside the dragonhelm that lay on the table amidst pieces of the broken vase. With a wave of his fleshless hand, Lord Soth caused the shattered remains of the vase to rise into the air and hover before him. Holding them by the force of his magic, the death knight turned to regard Kitiara with his flaming orange eyes as she stood naked before him. The firelight turned her tanned skin golden, made her dark hair shine with warmth.

"You are a woman still, Kitiara," Lord Soth said slowly. "You love . . ."

The knight did not move or speak, but the pieces of the vase fell to the floor. His pallid boot trod upon them as he passed, leaving no trace of his passing.

"And you hurt," he said softly to Kitiara as he drew near her. "Do not deceive yourself, Dark Lady. Crush him as you will, the half-elf will always be your master—even in death."

Lord Soth melded with the shadows of the room. Kitiara stood for long moments, staring into the blazing fire, seeking, perhaps, to read her fortune in the flames.

Gakhan walked rapidly down the corridor of the Queen's palace, his clawed feet clicking on the marble floors. The draconian's thoughts kept pace with his stride. It had suddenly occurred to him where the captain might be found. Seeing two draconians attached to Kitiara's command lounging at the end of the corridor, Gakhan motioned them to fall in behind him. They obeyed immediately. Though Gakhan held no rank in the dragonarmy—not any more—he was known officially as the Dark Lady's military aide. Unofficially he was known as her personal assassin.

The Dark Queen would have kept a close eye on the blue crystal staff in the temple at Xak Tsaroth just because it is a very powerful and holy artifact of good.—MW

Gakhan had been in Kitiara's service a long time. When word of the discovery of the blue crystal staff† had reached the Queen of Darkness and her minions, few of the Dragon Highlords attached much importance to its disappearance. Deeply involved in the war that was slowly stamping the life out of the northern lands of Ansalon, something as

trivial as a staff with healing powers did not merit their attention. It would take a great deal of healing to heal the world, Ariakas had stated, laughing, at a Council of War.

But two Highlords did take the disappearance of the staff seriously: one who ruled that part of Ansalon where the staff had been discovered, and one who had been born and raised in the area. One was a dark cleric, the other a skilled swordswoman. Both knew how dangerous proof of the return of the ancient gods could be to their cause.

They reacted differently, perhaps because of location. Lord Verminaard sent out swarms of draconians, goblins, and hobgoblins with full descriptions of the blue crystal staff and its powers. Kitiara sent Gakhan.

It was Gakhan† who traced Riverwind and the blue crystal staff to the village of Qué-Shu, and it was Gakhan who ordered the raid on the village, systematically murdering most of the inhabitants in a search for the staff.

Like her blue dragon, Skie, Gakhan has aligned his career with the Blue Lady—and they both love her.

But he left Qué-Shu suddenly, having heard reports of the staff in Solace. The draconian traveled to that town, only to find that he had missed it by a matter of weeks. But there he discovered that the barbarians who carried the staff had been joined by a group of adventurers, purportedly from Solace, according to the locals he "interviewed."

Gakhan was faced with a decision at this point. He could try and pick up their trail, which had undoubtedly grown cold during the intervening weeks, or he could return to Kitiara with descriptions of these adventurers to see if she knew them. If so, she might be able to provide him with information that would allow him to plot their movements in advance.

He decided to return to Kitiara, who was fighting in the north. Lord Verminaard's thousands were much more likely to find the staff than Gakhan. He brought complete descriptions of the adventurers to Kitiara, who was startled to learn that they were her two half-brothers, her old comrades-in-arms, and her former lover. Immediately Kitiara saw the workings of a great power here, for she knew that this group of mismatched wanderers could be forged into a dynamic force for either good or evil.

She immediately took her misgivings to the Queen of Darkness, who was already disturbed by the portent of the missing constellation of the Valiant Warrior. At once the Queen knew she had been correct, Paladine had returned to fight her. But by the time she realized the danger, the damage had been done.

Kitiara set Gakhan back on the trail. Step by step, the clever draconian traced the companions from Pax Tharkas to the dwarven kingdom. It was he who followed them in Tarsis, and there he and the Dark Lady would have captured them had it not been for Alhana Starbreeze and her griffons.

Patiently Gakhan kept on their trail. He knew of the group's separation, hearing reports of them from Silvanesti, where they drove off the great green dragon, Cyan Bloodbane, and then from Ice Wall, where Laurana killed the dark elven magic-user, Feal-Thas. He knew of the discovery of the dragon orbs—the destruction of one, the frail mage's acquisition of the other.

It was Gakhan who followed Tanis in Flotsam, and who was able to direct the Dark Lady to them aboard the *Perechon.* But here again, as before, Gakhan moved his game piece only to find an opponent's piece blocking a final move. The draconian did not despair. Gakhan knew his opponent, he knew the great power opposing him. He was playing for high stakes, very high stakes indeed.

Also called the Grand Council

Thinking of all this as he left the Dark Majesty's Temple, where even now the Dragon Highlords were gathering for High Conclave,† Gakhan entered the streets of Neraka. It was light now, just at the end of day. As the sun slid down from the sky, its last rays were freed from the shadow of the citadels. It burned now above the mountains, gilding the still snow-capped peaks blood red.

It is the fate of evil to never trust any other evil.—MW

Gakhan's reptilian gaze did not linger on the sunset. Instead it flicked among the streets of the tent town, now almost completely empty since most of the draconians were required to be in attendance upon their lords this evening. The Highlords had a notable lack of trust in each other and in their Queen.† Murder had been done before in her chambers, and would, most likely, be done again.

That did not concern Gakhan, however. In fact, it made his job easier. Quickly he led the other draconians through the foul-smelling, refuse-littered streets. He could have sent them on this mission without him, but Gakhan had come to know his great opponent very well and he had a distinct feeling of urgency. The wind of momentous events was starting to swirl into a huge vortex. He stood in the eye now, but he knew it would soon sweep him up. Gakhan wanted to be able to ride those winds, not be hurled upon the rocks.

"This is the place," he said, standing outside of a beer tent. A sign tacked to a post read in Common—The Dragon's Eye—while a placard propped in front stated in crudely lettered Common: *Dracos and goblins not allowed.* Peering through the filthy tent flap, Gakhan saw his quarry. Motioning to his escorts, he thrust aside the flap and stepped inside.

An uproar greeted his entrance as the humans in the bar turned their bleary eyes on the newcomers and—seeing three draconians—immediately began to shout and jeer. The shouts and jeers died almost instantly, however, when Gakhan removed the hood that covered his reptilian face. Everyone recognized Lord Kitiara's henchman. A pall settled over the crowd thicker than the rank smoke and foul odors that filled the bar. Casting fearful glances at the draconians, the humans hunched their shoulders over their drinks and huddled down, trying to become inconspicuous.

Gakhan's glittering black gaze swept over the crowd.

"There," he said in draconian, motioning to a human slouched over the bar. His escorts acted instantly, seizing the one-eyed human soldier, who stared at them in drunken terror.

"Take him outside, in back," Gakhan ordered.

Ignoring the bewildered captain's protests and pleadings, as well as the baleful looks and muttered threats from the crowd, the draconians dragged their captive out into the back. Gakhan followed more slowly.

It took only a few moments for the skilled draconians to sober their prisoner up enough to talk—the man's hoarse screams caused many of the bar's patrons to lose their taste for their liquor—but eventually he was able to respond to Gakhan's questioning.

"Do you remember arresting a dragonarmy officer this afternoon on charges of desertion?"

The captain remembered questioning many officers today . . . he was a busy man . . . they all looked alike. Gakhan gestured to the draconians, who responded promptly and efficiently.

The captain screamed in agony. Yes, yes! He remembered! But it wasn't just one officer. There had been two of them.

"Two?" Gakhan's eyes glittered. "Describe the other officer."

"A big human, really big. Bulging out of his uniform. And there had been prisoners. . . ."

"Prisoners!" Gakhan's reptilian tongue flicked in and out of his mouth. "Describe them!"

The captain was only too happy to describe. "A human woman, red curls, breasts the size of . . ."

"Get on with it," Gakhan snarled. His clawed hands trembled. He glanced at his escorts and the draconians tightened their grip.

Sobbing, the captain gave hurried descriptions of the other two prisoners, his words falling over themselves.

"A kender," Gakhan repeated, growing more and more excited. "Go on! An old man, white beard—" He paused, puzzled. The old magic-user? Surely they would not have allowed that decrepit old fool to accompany them on a mission so important and fraught with peril. If not, then who? Someone else they had picked up?

"Tell me more about the old man," Gakhan ordered.

The captain cast desperately about in his liquor-soaked and pain-stupefied brain. The old man . . . white beard . . .

"Stooped?"

No . . . tall, broad shoulders. . . blue eyes. Queer eyes— The captain was on the verge of passing out. Gakhan clutched the man in his clawed hand, squeezing his neck.

"What about the eyes?"

Fearfully the captain stared at the draconian who was slowly choking the life from him. He babbled something.

"Young . . . too young!" Gakhan repeated in exultation. Now he knew!"Where are they?"

The captain gasped out a word, then Gakhan hurled him to the floor with a crash.

The whirlwind was rising. Gakhan felt himself being swept upward. One thought beat in his brain like the wings of a dragon as he and his escorts left the tent, racing for the dungeons below the palace.

The Everman . . . the Everman . . . the Everman!

7
The Temple of the Queen of Darkness.

Tas!"

"Hurt . . . lemme 'lone . . ."

"I know, Tas. I'm sorry, but you've got to wake up. Please, Tas!"

An edge of fear and urgency in the voice pierced the pain-laden mists in the kender's mind. Part of him was jumping up and down, yelling at him to wake up. But another part was all for drifting back into the darkness that, while unpleasant, was better than facing the pain he knew was lying in wait for him, ready to spring—

"Tas . . . Tas . . ." A hand patted his cheek. The whispered voice was tense, tight with terror kept under control. The kender knew suddenly that he had no choice. He had to wake up. Besides, the jumping-up-and-down part of his brain shouted, you might be missing something!

"Thank the gods!" Tika breathed as Tasslehoff's eyes opened wide and stared up at her. "How do you feel?"

"Awful," Tas said thickly, struggling to sit up. As he had foreseen, pain leaped out of a corner and pounced on him. Groaning, he clutched his head.

"I know . . . I'm sorry," Tika said again, stroking back his hair with a gentle hand.

"I'm sure you mean well, Tika," Tas said miserably, "but would you mind not doing that? It feels like dwarf hammers pounding on me."

Tika drew back her hand hurriedly. The kender peered around as best he could through one good eye. The other had nearly swollen shut. "Where are we?"

"In the dungeons below the Temple," Tika said softly. Tas, sitting next to her, could feel her shiver with fear and cold. Looking around, he could see why. The sight made him shudder, too. Wistfully he remembered the good old days when he hadn't known the meaning of the word of fear. He should have felt a thrill of excitement. He was, after all, someplace he'd never been before and there were probably lots of fascinating things to investigate.

But there was death here, Tas knew; death and suffering. He'd seen too many die, too many suffer. His thoughts went to Flint, to Sturm, to Laurana. . . . Something had changed inside Tas.† He would never again be like other kender. Through grief, he had come to know fear; fear not for himself but for others. He decided right now that he would rather die himself than lose anyone else he loved.

Tas may not have learned fear, but he has become more compassionate. He's "lost his innocence."—MW

You have chosen the dark path, but you have the courage to walk it, Fizban had said.

Did he? Tas wondered. Sighing, he hid his face in his hands.

"No, Tas!" Tika said, shaking him. "Don't do this to us! We need you!"

Painfully Tas raised his head. "I'm all right," he said dully. "Where's Caramon and Berem?"

"Over there," Tika gestured toward the far end of the cell. "The guards are holding all of us together until they can find someone to decide what to do with us. Caramon's being splendid," she added with a proud smile and a fond glance at the big man, who was slouched, apparently sulking, in a

far corner, as far from his 'prisoners' as he could get. Then Tika's face grew fearful. She drew Tas nearer. "But I'm worried about Berem! I think he's going crazy!"

Tasslehoff looked up quickly at Berem. The man was sitting on the cold, filthy stone floor of the cell, his gaze abstracted, his head cocked as though listening. The fake white beard Tika had made out of goat hair was torn and bedraggled. It wouldn't take much for it to fall off completely, Tas realized in alarm, glancing quickly out the cell door.

The dungeons were a maze of corridors tunneled out of the solid rock beneath the Temple. They appeared to branch off in all directions from a central guardroom, a small, round, open-ended room at the bottom of a narrow winding staircase that bored straight down from the ground floor of the Temple. In the guardroom, a large hobgoblin sat at a battered table beneath a torch, calmly munching on bread and swilling it down with a jug of something. A ring of keys hanging on a nail above his head proclaimed him the head jailor. He ignored the companions; he probably couldn't see them clearly in the dim light anyway, Tas realized, since the cell they were in was about a hundred paces away, down a dark and dismal corridor.

Creeping over to the cell door, Tas peered down the corridor in the opposite direction. Wetting a finger, he held it up in the air. That way was north, he determined. Smoking, foul-smelling torches flickered in the dank air. A large cell farther down was filled with draconians and goblins sleeping off drunken revels. At the far end of the corridor beyond their cell stood a massive iron door, slightly ajar. Listening carefully, Tas thought he could hear sounds from beyond the door: voices, low moaning. That's another section of the dungeon, Tas decided, basing his decision on past experience. The jailor probably left the door ajar so he could make his rounds and listen for disturbances.

"You're right, Tika," Tas whispered. "We're locked in some kind of holding cell, probably awaiting orders." Tika nodded. Caramon's act, if not completely fooling the guards, was at least forcing them to think twice before doing anything rash.

"I'm going over to talk to Berem," Tas said.

"No, Tas"—Tika glanced at the man uneasily—"I don't think—"

But Tas didn't listen. Taking one last look at the jailor, Tas ignored Tika's soft remonstrations and crawled toward Berem with the idea of sticking the man's false beard back on his face. He had just neared him and was reaching out his small hand when suddenly the Everman roared and leaped straight at the kender.

Startled, Tas fell backward with a shriek. But Berem didn't even see him. Yelling incoherently, he sprang over Tasslehoff and flung himself bodily against the cell door.

Caramon was on his feet now—as was the hobgoblin.

Trying to appear irritated at having his rest disturbed, Caramon darted a stern glance at Tasslehoff on the floor.

"What did you do to him?" the big man growled out of the side of his mouth.

"N-nothing, Caramon, honest!" Tas gasped. "He—he's crazy!"

Berem did indeed seem to have gone mad. Oblivious to pain, he flung himself at the iron bars, trying to break them open. When this didn't work, he grasped the bars in his hands and started to wrench them apart.

"I'm coming, Jasla!" he screamed. "Don't leave! Forgive—"

The jailor, his pig eyes wide in alarm, ran over to the stairs and began shouting up them.

"He's calling the guards!" Caramon grunted. "We've got to get Berem calmed down. Tika—"

But the girl was already by Berem's side. Holding onto his shoulder, she pleaded with him to stop. At first the berserk man paid no attention to her, roughly shaking her off him. But Tika petted and stroked and soothed until eventually it seemed Berem might listen. He quit attempting to force the cell door open and stood still, his hands clenching the bars. The beard had fallen to the floor, his face was covered with sweat, and he was bleeding from a cut where he had rammed the bars with his head.

There was a rattling sound near the front of the dungeon as two draconians came dashing down the stairs at the jailor's call. Their curved swords drawn and ready, they advanced down the narrow corridor, the jailor at their heels. Swiftly Tas grabbed the beard and stuffed it into one of his pouches, hoping they wouldn't remember that Berem had come in with whiskers.

Tika, still stroking Berem soothingly, babbled about anything that came into her head. Berem did not appear to be listening, but at least he appeared quiet once more. Breathing heavily, he stared with glazed eyes into the empty cell across from them. Tas could see muscles in the man's arm twitch spasmodically.

"What is the meaning of this?" Caramon shouted as the draconians came up to the cell door. "You've locked me in here with a raving beast! He tried to kill me! I demand you get me out of here!"

Tasslehoff, watching Caramon closely, saw the big warrior's right hand make a small quick gesture toward the guard. Recognizing the signal, Tas tensed, ready for action. He saw Tika tense, too. One hobgoblin and two guards. . . . They'd faced worse odds.

The draconians looked at the jailor, who hesitated. Tas could guess what was going through the creature's thick mind. If this big officer was a personal friend of the Dark Lady, she would certainly not look kindly on a jailor who allowed one of her close friends to be murdered in his prison cell.

"I'll get the keys," the jailor muttered, waddling back down the corridor.

The draconians began to talk together in their own language, apparently exchanging rude comments about the hobgoblin. Caramon flashed a look at Tika and Tas, making a quick gesture of heads banging together. Tas, fumbling in one of his pouches, closed his hand over his little knife. (They had searched his pouches, but—in an effort to be helpful—Tas kept switching his pouches around until the confused guards, after their fourth search of the same pouch, gave up. Caramon had insisted the kender be allowed to keep his pouches, since there were items the Dark Lady wanted to examine. Unless, of course, the guards wanted to be responsible . . .) Tika kept patting Berem, her hypnotic voice bringing a measure of peace back to his fevered, staring blue eyes.

The jailor had just grabbed the keys from the wall and was starting to walk back down the corridor again when a voice from the bottom of the stairs stopped him.

"What do you want?" the jailor snarled, irritated and startled at the sight of the cloaked figure appearing suddenly, without warning.

"I am Gakhan," said the voice.

Hushing immediately at the sight of the newcomer, the draconians drew themselves up in respect, while the hobgoblin turned a sickly green color, the keys clinking together in his flabby hand. Two more guards clattered down the stairs. At a gesture from the cloaked figure, they came to stand beside him.

Walking past the quaking hobgoblin, the figure drew closer to the cell door. Now Tas could see the figure clearly. It was another draconian, dressed in armor with a dark cape thrown over its face. The kender bit his lip in frustration. Well, the odds still weren't *that* bad—not for Caramon.

The hooded draconian, ignoring the stammering jailor who was trotting along behind him like a fat dog, grabbed a torch from the wall and came over to stand directly in front of the companions' jail cell.

"Get me out of this place!" Caramon shouted, elbowing Berem to one side.

But the draconian, ignoring Caramon, reached through the bars of the cell and laid a clawed hand on Berem's shirt front. Tas darted a frantic look at Caramon. The big man's face was deathly pale. He made a desperate lunge at the draconian, but it was too late.

With a twist of its clawed hand, the draconian ripped Berem's shirt to shreds. Green light flared into the jail cell as the torchlight illuminated the gemstone embedded in Berem's flesh.

"It is he," Gakhan said quietly. "Unlock the cell."

The jailor put the key in the cell door with hands that shook visibly. Snatching it away from the hobgoblin, one of the draconian guards opened the cell door, then they surged inside. One guard struck Caramon a vicious blow on the side of the head with the hilt of its sword, felling the warrior like an ox, while another grabbed Tika.

Gakhan entered the cell.

"Kill him"—the draconian motioned at Caramon—"and the girl and the kender." Gakhan laid his clawed hand on Berem's shoulder. "I will take this one to Her Dark Majesty." The draconian flashed a triumphant glance around at the others.

"This night, victory is ours," he said softly.

Sweating in the dragon-scale armor, Tanis stood beside Kitiara in one of the vast antechambers leading into the Great Hall of Audience. Surrounding the half-elf were Kitiara's troops, including the hideous skeletal warriors under the command of the death knight, Lord Soth. These stood in the shadows just behind Kitiara. Though the antechamber was crowded—Kitiara's draconian troops were packed in spear to spear—there was, nevertheless, a vast empty space around the undead warriors. None came near them, none spoke to them, they spoke to no one. And though the room was stifling hot with the crushing press of many bodies, a chill flowed from these that nearly stopped the heart if one ventured too near.

Feeling Lord Soth's flickering eyes upon him, Tanis could not repress a shudder. Kitiara glanced up at him and smiled, the crooked smile he had once found so irresistible. She stood close to him, their bodies touching.

"You'll get used to them," she said coolly. Then her gaze returned to the proceedings in the vast Hall. The dark line appeared between her brows, her hand tapped irritably upon her sword hilt. "Get moving, Ariakas," she muttered.

Tanis looked over her head, staring through the ornate doorway they would enter when it was their turn, watching in an awe he could not hide as the spectacle unfolded before his eyes.

The Hall of Audience of Takhisis, Queen of Darkness, first impressed the viewer with a sense of his own inferiority. This was the black heart which kept the dark blood flowing and—as such—its appearance was fitting. The antechamber in which they stood opened onto a huge circular room with a floor of polished black granite. The floor continued up to form the walls, rising in tortured curves like dark waves frozen in time. Any moment, it seemed, they could crash down and engulf all those within the

Hall in blackness. It was only Her Dark Majesty's power that held them in check. And so the black waves swept upward to a high domed ceiling, now hidden from view by a wispy wall of shifting, eddying smoke—the breath of dragons.

The floor of the vast Hall was empty now, but it would soon be filling rapidly as the troops marched in to take up their positions beneath the thrones of their Highlords. These thrones—four of them—stood about ten feet above the gleaming granite floor. Squat gates opened from the concave walls onto black tongues of rock that licked outward from the walls. Upon these four huge platforms—two to each side—sat the Highlords—and only the Highlords. No one else—not even bodyguards—was allowed beyond the top step of the sacred platforms. Bodyguards and high-ranking officers stood upon stairs that extended up to the thrones from the floor like the ribs of some giant prehistoric beast.

From the center of the Hall rose another, slightly larger platform, curling upward from the floor like a giant, hooded snake—which is exactly what it had been carved to represent. One slender bridge of rock ran from the snake's 'head' to another gate in the side of the Hall. The head faced Ariakas—and the darkness-shrouded alcove above Ariakas.

The "Emperor," as Ariakas styled himself, sat upon a slightly larger platform at the front of the great Hall, about ten feet above those around it.

Tanis felt his gaze drawn irresistibly to an alcove carved into the rock above Ariakas's throne. It was larger than the rest of the alcoves and—within it—lurked a darkness that was almost alive. It breathed and pulsed and was so intense that Tanis looked quickly away. Although he could see nothing, he guessed who would soon sit within those shadows.

Shuddering, Tanis turned back to the darkness within the Hall. There was not much left to see. All around the domed ceiling, in alcoves similar though smaller than the Highlords' alcoves, perched the dragons. Almost invisible, obscured by their own smoking breath, these creatures sat opposite their respective Highlords' alcoves, keeping vigilant watch—so the Highlords supposed—upon their "masters." Actually only one dragon in the assemblage was truly concerned over his master's welfare.

This was Skie, Kitiara's dragon, who—even now—sat in his place, his fiery red eyes staring at the throne of Ariakas with much the same intensity and far more visible hatred than Tanis had seen in the eyes of Skie's master.

A gong rang. Masses of troops poured into the Hall, all of them wearing the red dragon colors of Ariakas's troops. Hundreds of clawed and booted feet scraped the floor as the draconians and human guard of honor entered and took their places beneath Ariakas's throne. No officers ascended the stairs, no bodyguards took their places in front of their lord.

Then the man himself entered through the gate behind his throne. He walked alone, his purple robes of state sweeping majestically from his shoulders, dark armor gleaming in the torchlight. Upon his head glistened a crown, studded with jewels the hue of blood.

"The Crown of Power," Kitiara murmured, and now Tanis saw emotion in her eyes—longing, such longing as he had rarely seen in human eyes before.

" 'Whoever wears the Crown, rules,' " came a voice behind her. "So it is written."

Lord Soth. Tanis stiffened to keep from trembling, feeling the man's presence like a cold skeletal hand upon the back of his neck.

Ariakas's troops cheered him long and loudly, thumping their spears upon the floor, clashing their swords against their shields. Kitiara snarled in impatience. Finally Ariakas extended his hands for silence. Turning, he knelt in reverence before the shadowy alcove above him, then, with a wave of his gloved hand, the head of the Dragon Highlords made a patronizing gesture to Kitiara.

Glancing at her, Tanis saw such hatred and contempt on her face that he barely recognized her. "Yes, lord," whispered Kitiara, her eyes now dark and gleaming. " 'Whoever wears the Crown, rules. So it is written . . . written in blood!'" Half turning her head, she beckoned to Lord Soth. "Fetch the elfwoman."

Lord Soth bowed and flowed from the antechamber like a malevolent fog, his skeletal warriors drifting after him. Draconians stumbled over themselves in frantic efforts to get out of his deadly path.

Tanis gripped Kitiara's arm. "You promised!" he said in a strangled voice.

Staring at him coldly, Kitiara snatched her arm free, easily breaking the half-elf's strong grasp. But her brown eyes held him, drained him, sucking the life from him until he felt like nothing more than a dried shell.

"Listen to me, Half-Elven," Kitiara said, her voice cold and thin and sharp. "I am after one thing and one thing only—the Crown of Power Ariakas wears. That is the reason I captured Laurana, that is all she means to me. I will present the elfwoman to Her Majesty, as I have promised. The Queen will reward me—with the Crown, of course—then she will order the elf taken to the Death Chambers far below the Temple. I care nothing for what happens to the elf after that, and so I give her to you. At my gesture, step forward. I will present you to the Queen. Beg of her a favor. Ask that you be allowed to escort the elfwoman to her death. If she approves of you, she will grant it. You may then take the elfwoman to the city gates or wherever you choose, and there you may set her free. But I want your word of honor,† Tanis Half-Elven, that you will return to me."

She knows that Tanis will keep his word. She pretends that this is a weakness, but in truth, she admires him for this quality, which she knows is lacking in herself. —MW

"I give it," Tanis said, his eyes meeting Kitiara's without wavering.

Kitiara smiled. Her face relaxed. It was so beautiful once more, that Tanis, startled by the sudden transformation, almost wondered if he had seen that other cruel face at all. Putting her hand on Tanis's cheek, she stroked his beard.

"I have your word of honor. That might not mean much to other men, but I know you will keep it! One final warning, Tanis," she whispered swiftly, "you *must* convince the Queen that you are her loyal servant. She is powerful, Tanis! She is a goddess, remember that! She can see into your heart, your soul. You must convince her beyond doubt that you are hers. One gesture, one word that rings false, and she will destroy you. There will be nothing I can do. If you die, so does your Lauralanthalasa!"

"I understand," Tanis said, feeling his body chill beneath the cold armor.

There was a blaring trumpet call.

"There, that is our signal," Kitiara said. Pulling her gloves on, she drew the dragonhelm over her

head. "Go forward, Tanis. Lead my troops. I will enter last."

Resplendent in her glittering night-blue dragon-scale armor, Kitiara stepped haughtily to one side as Tanis walked through the ornate doorway into the Hall of Audience.

The crowd began to cheer at the sight of the blue banner. Perched above the audience with the other dragons, Skie bellowed in triumph. Aware of thousands of glittering eyes upon him, Tanis firmly put everything out of his mind except what he must do. He kept his eyes fixed on his destination—the platform in the Hall next to Lord Ariakas's, the platform decorated with the blue banner. Behind him, he could hear the rhythmic stamp of clawed feet as Kit's guard of honor marched in proudly. Tanis reached the platform and stood at the bottom of the stairs, as he had been ordered. The crowd quieted then and, as the last draconian filed through the door, a murmur began to sweep through the Hall. The crowd strained forward, anxious to see Kitiara's entrance.

Waiting within the antechamber, allowing the crowd to wait just a few more moments to enhance the suspense, Kit glimpsed movement out of the corner of her eye. Turning, she saw Lord Soth enter the antechamber, his guards bearing a white-wrapped body in their fleshless arms. The eyes of the vibrant, living woman and the vacant eyes of the dead knight met in perfect agreement and understanding.

Lord Soth bowed.

Kitiara smiled, then—turning—she entered the Hall of Audience to thunderous applause.

Lying on the cold cell floor, Caramon struggled desperately to remain conscious. The pain was beginning to subside. The blow that struck him down had been a glancing one, slanting off the officer's helm he wore, stunning him, but not knocking him out.

He feigned unconsciousness, however, not knowing what else to do. Why wasn't Tanis here, he thought despairingly, once more cursing his own slowness of mind. The half-elf would have a plan, he would know what to do. I shouldn't have been

left with this responsibility! Caramon swore bitterly. Then, *quit belly-aching, you big ox! They're depending on you!* came a voice in the back of his mind. Caramon blinked, then caught himself just as he was about to grin. The voice was so like Flint's, he could have sworn the dwarf was standing beside him! He was right. They were depending on him. He'd just have to do his best. That was all he could do.

Caramon opened his eyes a slit, peering out between half-closed lids. A draconian guard stood almost directly in front of him, back turned to the supposedly comatose warrior. Caramon could not see Berem or the draconian called Gakhan without twisting his head, and he dared not call attention to himself. He could take out that first guard, he knew. Possibly the second, before the other two finished him. He had no hope of escaping alive, but at least he might give Tas and Tika a chance to escape with Berem.

Tensing his muscles, Caramon prepared to launch himself at the guard when suddenly an agonized scream tore through the darkness of the dungeons. It was Berem screaming, a cry so filled with rage and anger that Caramon started up in alarm, forgetting he was supposed to be unconscious.

Then he froze, watching in amazement as Berem lurched forward, grabbed Gakhan, and lifted him off the stone floor. Carrying the wildly flailing draconian in his hands, the Everman hurtled out of the jail cell and smashed Gakhan into a stone wall. The draconian's head split apart, cracking like the eggs of the good dragons upon the black altars. Howling in rage, Berem slammed the draconian into the wall again and again, until Gakhan was nothing more than a limp, green-bloodied mass of shapeless flesh.

For a moment no one moved. Tas and Tika huddled together, horrified by the gruesome sight. Caramon fought to piece things together in his pain-befuddled mind while even the draconian guards stood staring at their leader's body in a paralyzed, dreadful fascination.

Then Berem dropped Gakhan's body to the ground. Turning, he stared at the companions without recognition. He's completely insane, Caramon saw with a shudder. Berem's eyes were wide and crazed. Saliva dripped from his mouth. His hands

and arms were slimy with green blood. Finally, realizing that his captor was dead, Berem seemed to come to his senses. He gazed around and saw Caramon on the floor, staring up at him in shock.

"She calls me!" Berem whispered hoarsely.

Turning, he ran down the northern corridor, flinging the startled draconians to one side as they tried to stop him. Never pausing to look behind him, Berem slammed into the partially open iron door at the end of the corridor, the force of his passing nearly tearing the door from its hinges. Clanking against the stone with a dull booming sound, the door swung crazily back and forth. They could hear Berem's wild shrieking echo down the corridor.

By now, two of the draconians had recovered. One of them ran for the stairway, shouting at the top of its lungs. It was in draconian, but Caramon could understand it well enough.

"Prisoner escape! Call out the guards!"

In answer came shouts and the sound of clawed feet scraping at the top of the staircase. The hobgoblin took one look at the dead draconian and fled toward the staircase and his guardroom, adding his panic-stricken shouts to those of the draconian. The other guard, quickly regaining its feet, jumped into the cell. But Caramon was on his feet now, too. This was action. This he could understand. Reaching out, the big man grabbed the draconian around the neck. One jerk of the huge hands, and the creature fell lifeless to the floor. Caramon swiftly snatched the sword from the clawed hand as the draconian's body hardened into stone.

"Caramon! Look out behind you!" Tasslehoff yelled as the other guard, returning from the stairway, dashed into the cell, its sword raised.

Caramon whirled, only to see the creature fall forward as Tika's boot caught it in the stomach. Tasslehoff plunged his little knife into the second guard's body, forgetting—in his excitement—to jerk it free again. Glancing at the stone corpse of the other creature, the kender made a frantic dive for his knife. Too late.

"Leave it!" Caramon ordered, and Tas stood up.

Guttural voices could be heard above them, feet scraping and clawing down the stairs. The hobgoblin

had reached the stairs and was waving his hands frantically and pointing back at them. His own shouts rose above the noise of the descending troops.

Caramon, sword in hand, glanced uncertainly at the stairs, then down the northern corridor after Berem.

"That's right! Follow Berem, Caramon," Tika said urgently. "Go with him! Don't you see? 'She's calling me,' he said. It's his sister's voice! He can hear her calling to him. That's why he went crazy."

"Yes . . ." Caramon said in a daze, staring down the corridor. He could hear the draconians plunging down the winding stairs, armor rattling, swords scraping against the stone walls. They had only seconds. "Come on—"

Tika grasped Caramon by the arm. Digging her nails into his flesh, she forced him to look at her, her red curls a mass of flaming color in the flickering torchlight.

"No!" she said firmly. "They'll catch him for certain and then it *will* be the end! I've got a plan. We must split up. Tas and I will draw them off. We'll give you time. It'll be all right, Caramon," she persisted, seeing him shake his head. "There's another corridor that leads east. I saw it as we came in. They'll chase us down that way. Now, hurry, before they see you!"

Caramon hesitated, his face twisted in agony.

"This is the end, Caramon!" Tika said. "For good or for evil. You must go with him! You must help him reach her! Hurry, Caramon! You're the only one strong enough to protect him. He needs you!"

Tika actually shoved the big man. Caramon took a step, then looked back at her.

"Tika . . ." he began, trying to think of some argument against this wild scheme. But before he could finish, Tika kissed him swiftly and—grabbing a sword from a dead draconian—ran from the jail cell.

"I'll take care of her, Caramon!" Tas promised, dashing after Tika, his pouches bouncing wildly all around him.

Caramon stared after them a moment. The hobgoblin jailor shrieked in terror as Tika ran straight for the creature, brandishing her sword. The jailor made a wild grab for her, but Tika hacked at him so ferociously that the hobgoblin fell dead with a gurgling scream, his throat cut.

Ignoring the body that slumped to the floor, Tika hurried down the corridor, heading east.

Tasslehoff, right behind her, took a moment to stop at the bottom of the stair. The draconians were visible now, and Caramon could hear the kender's shrill voice shouting taunts at the guards.

"Dog-eaters! Slime-blooded goblin-lovers!"

Then Tas was off, dashing after Tika who had vanished from Caramon's sight. The enraged draconians—driven wild by the kender's taunts and the sight of their prisoners escaping—did not take time to look around. They charged after the fleet-footed kender, their curved swords gleaming, their long tongues flicking in anticipation of the kill.

Within moments, Caramon found himself alone. He hesitated another precious minute, staring into the thick darkness of the gloomy cells. He could see nothing. The only thing he could hear was Tas's voice yelling "dog-eaters." Then there was silence.

"I'm alone . . ." thought Caramon bleakly. "I've lost them . . . lost them all. I must go after them."

He started toward the stairs, then stopped. "No, there's Berem. He's alone, too. Tika's right. He needs me now. He needs me."

His mind clear at last, Caramon turned and ran clumsily down the northern corridor after the Everman.

8

The Queen of Darkness.

Dragon Highlord Toede."

Lord Ariakas listened with lazy contempt to the calling of the roll. Not that he was bored with the proceedings. Quite the contrary. Assembling the Grand Council had not been his idea. He had, in fact, opposed it. But he had been careful not to oppose it too vehemently. That might have made him appear weak; and Her Dark Majesty did not allow weaklings to live. No, this Grand Council would be anything but boring. . . .

At the thought of his Dark Queen,† he half-turned and glanced swiftly up into the alcove above him. The largest and most magnificent in the Hall, its great throne remained empty still, the gate that led into it lost in the living, breathing darkness. No stairs ran up to *that* throne. The gate itself provided

Ariakas, in dedicating himself to the Dark Queen, once said that he bowed before "a might that makes puny any power on all this world."

the only entrance and exit. And as to where the gate led, well, it was best not to think of such things. Needless to say, no mortal had passed beyond its iron grillwork.

The Queen had not yet arrived. He was not surprised. These opening proceedings were beneath her. Ariakas hunched back in his throne. His gaze went—appropriately enough—he thought bitterly, from the throne of the Dark Queen to the throne of the Dark Lady. Kitiara was here, of course. This was her moment of triumph—so she thought. Ariakas breathed a curse upon her.

"Let her do her worst," he murmured, only half-listening as the sergeant repeated the name of Lord Toede once more. "I am prepared."

Ariakas suddenly realized something was amiss. What? What was happening? Lost in his thoughts, he had paid no attention to the proceedings. What was wrong? Silence . . . a dreadful silence that followed . . . what? He cast about in his mind, trying to recall what had just been said. Then he remembered and came back from his dark thoughts to stare grimly at the second throne to his left. The troops in the hall, mostly draconian, heaved and swayed like a sea of death below him as all eyes shifted to the same throne.

Though the draconian troops belonging to Lord Toede were present, their banners mingling with the banners of the other draconians standing at attention in the center of the Hall of Audience, the throne itself was empty.

Tanis, from where he stood upon the steps of Kitiara's platform, followed Ariakas's gaze, stern and cold beneath the crown. The half-elf's ears had pricked at the sound of Toede's name. An image of the hobgoblin came swiftly to his mind as he had seen him standing in the dust of the road to Solace. The vision brought back thoughts of that warm autumn day that had seen the beginning of this long, dark journey. It brought back memories of Flint and Sturm. . . . Tanis gritted his teeth and forced himself to concentrate on what was happening. The past was over, finished, and—he hoped fervently—soon forgotten.

"Lord Toede?" Ariakas repeated in anger. The troops in the Hall muttered among themselves.

Never before had a Highlord disobeyed a command to attend the Grand Council.

A human dragonarmy officer climbed the stairs leading to the empty platform. Standing on the top step (protocol forbade him proceeding higher), he stammered a moment in terror, facing those black eyes and, worse, the shadowy alcove above Ariakas's throne. Then, taking a breath, he began his report.

"I—I regret to inform His Lordship and Her D-Dark Majesty"—a nervous glance at the shadowy alcove that was, apparently, still vacant—"that Dragon Highlord To—uh, Toede has met an unfortunate and untimely demise."†

Takhisis must have still been using Toede as a game piece, because he was expected to arrive at Neraka as the White Highlord. The story of his oh-so-sad demise (at least the first one) is told in "Lord Toede's Disastrous Hunt," in Kender, Gully Dwarves, and Gnomes.

Standing on the top step of the platform where Kitiara sat enthroned, Tanis heard a snort of derision from behind Kit's dragonhelm. An amused titter ran through the crowd below him while dragonarmy officers exchanged knowing glances.

Lord Ariakas was not amused, however. "Who dared slay a Dragon Highlord?" he demanded furiously, and at the sound of his voice—and the portent of his words—the crowd fell silent.

"It was in K-Kenderhome, lord," the officer replied, his voice echoing in the vast marble chamber. The officer paused. Even from this distance, Tanis could see the man's fist clenching and unclenching nervously. He obviously had further bad news to impart and was reluctant to continue.

Ariakas glowered at the officer. Clearing his throat, the man lifted his voice again.

"I regret to report, lord, that Kenderhome has been l—" For a moment the man's voice gave out completely. Only by a valiant effort did he manage to continue. "—lost."

"Lost!" repeated Ariakas in a voice that might have been a thunderbolt.

Certainly it seemed to strike the officer with terror. Blenching, he stammered incoherently for a moment, then—apparently determining to end it quickly—gasped out, "Highlord Toede was foully murdered by a kender named Kronin Thistleknott, and his troops driven from—"

There was a deeper murmur from the crowd now, growlings of anger and defiance, threats of the total destruction of Kenderhome. They would wipe that miserable race from the face of Krynn—

With his gloved hand, Ariakas made an irritated, sweeping gesture. Silence fell instantly over the assemblage.

And then the silence was broken.

Kitiara laughed.

It was mirthless laughter, arrogant and mocking, and it echoed loudly from the depths of the metal mask.

His face twisted in outrage, Ariakas rose to his feet. He took a step forward and—as he did so—steel flashed among his draconians on the floor as swords slid out of scabbards and spear butts thudded against the floor.

At the sight, Kitiara's own troops closed ranks, backing up so that they pressed closely around the platform of their lord, which was at Ariakas's right hand. Instinctively Tanis's hand closed over the hilt of his sword and he found himself moving a step nearer Kitiara, though it meant setting his foot upon the platform where he was not supposed to tread.

Kitiara did not move. She remained seated, calmly regarding Ariakas with scorn that could be felt, if not seen.

Suddenly a breathless hush descended over the assemblage, as if the breath in each body was being choked off by an unseen force. Faces paled as those present felt stifled, gasping for air. Lungs ached, vision blurred, heartbeats stilled. And then the air itself seemed sucked from the Hall as a darkness filled it.

Was it actual, physical darkness? Or a darkness in the mind? Tanis could not be certain. His eyes saw the thousands of torches in the Hall flare brilliantly, he saw the thousands of candles sparkle like stars in the night sky. But even the night sky was not darker than the darkness he now perceived.

His head swam. Desperately he tried to breathe, but he might as well have been beneath the Blood Sea of Istar again. His knees trembled, he was almost too weak to stand. His strength failed him, he staggered and fell and, as he sank down, gasping for breath, he was dimly aware of others, here and there, falling to the polished marble floor as well. Lifting his head, though the move was agony, he could see Kitiara slump forward in her chair as though crushed into the throne by an unseen force.

Then the darkness lifted. Cool, sweet air rushed into his lungs. His heart lurched and began pounding. Blood rushed to his head, nearly making him pass out. For a moment he could do nothing but sink back against the marble stairs, weak and dizzy, while light exploded in his head. Then, as his vision cleared, he saw that the draconians remained unaffected.† Stoically they stood, all of them staring fixedly at one spot.

Draconians, being creatures of evil—and, in effect, the children of the Dark Queen—are not affected by the evil aura the goddess gives off.

Tanis lifted his gaze to the magnificent platform that had remained empty throughout the proceedings. Empty until now. His blood congealed in his veins, his breath nearly stopped again. Takhisis, Queen of Darkness, had entered the Hall of Audience.

Other names she had upon Krynn. *Dragonqueen* she was called in elven; *Nilat the Corrupter* to the barbarians of Plains; *Tamex, the False Metal,* so she was known in Thorbardin among the dwarves; *Mai-tat, She of Many Faces* was how they told of her in legends among the seafaring people of Ergoth. *Queen of Many Colors and of None,* the Knights of Solamnia called her; defeated by Huma, banished from the land, long ago.

Takhisis, Queen of Darkness, had returned.

But not completely.

Even as Tanis stared at the shadowy form in the alcove overhead with awe, even as the terror pierced his brain, leaving him numb, unable to feel or sense anything beyond sheer horror and fear—he realized that the Queen was not present in her physical form. It was as if her presence in their minds cast a shadow of her being onto the platform. She, herself, was there only as her will forced others to perceive her.

Something was holding her back, blocking her entry into this world. A door—Berem's words returned in confusion to Tanis's mind. Where was Berem? Where were Caramon and the others? Tanis realized with a pang that he had nearly forgotten about them. They had been driven from his mind by his preoccupation with Kitiara and Laurana. His head spun. He felt as if he held the key to everything in his hand, if only he could find the time to think about it calmly.

But that was not possible. The shadowy form increased in intensity until its blackness seemed to

create a cold hole of nothingness in the granite room. Unable to look away, Tanis was compelled to gaze into that dreadful hole until he had the terrifying sensation he was being drawn into it. At that moment, he heard a voice in his mind.

I have not brought you together to see your petty quarrels and pettier ambitions mar the victory I sense is fast approaching. Remember who rules here, Lord Ariakas.

Lord Ariakas sank to one knee, as did all others in the chamber. Tanis found himself falling to his knees in reverence. He could not help it. Though filled with loathing at the hideous, suffocating evil, this was a goddess, one of the forgers of the world. Since the beginning of time she had ruled . . . and would rule until time ended.†

One view of her role in the "forging of the world" is told in Dragons of Summer Flame.

The voice continued speaking, burning into his mind and into the minds of all present.

Lord Kitiara, you have pleased us well in the past. Your gift to us now pleases us even more. Bring in the elfwoman, that we may look upon her and decide her fate.

Tanis, glancing at Lord Ariakas, saw the man return to his throne, but not before he had cast a venomous look of hatred at Kitiara.

"I will, Your Dark Majesty." Kitiara bowed, then, "Come with me," she ordered Tanis as she passed by him on her way down the stairs.

Her draconian troops backed away, leaving a path for her to walk to the center of the room. Kitiara descended the rib-like stairs of the platform, Tanis following. The troops parted to let them pass, then closed ranks again almost instantly.

Reaching the center of the Hall, Kitiara climbed the narrow stairs that jutted forth like spurs from the hooded snake's sculpted back until she stood in the center of the marble platform. Tanis followed more slowly, finding the stairs narrow and difficult to climb, especially as he felt the eyes of the shadowy form in the alcove delve into his soul.

Standing at the center of the ghastly platform, Kitiara turned and gestured toward the ornate gate opening onto the far end of the narrow bridge that connected the platform with the main walls of the Hall of Audience.

A figure appeared in the doorway—a dark figure dressed in the armor of a Knight of Solamnia. Lord Soth entered the Hall, and—at his coming—the

troops fell back from either side of that narrow bridge as if a hand had reached up from the grave and tossed them away. In his pallid arms, Lord Soth bore a body bound in a white winding cloth, the kind used for embalming the dead. The silence in the room was such that the dead knight's booted footsteps could almost be heard ringing upon the marble floor, though all gathered there could see the stone through the transparent, fleshless body.

Walking forward, bearing his white-swathed burden, Lord Soth crossed the bridge and walked slowly up to stand upon the snake's head. At another gesture from Kitiara, he laid the bundle of white upon the floor at the Dragon Highlord's feet. Then he stood and suddenly vanished, leaving everyone blinking in horror, to wonder if he had really existed or if they had seen him only in their fevered imaginations.

Tanis could see Kitiara smile beneath her helm, pleased at the impact made by her servant. Then, drawing her sword, Kitiara leaned down and slit the bindings that wrapped the figure like a cocoon. Giving them a yank, she pulled them loose, then stepped back to watch her captive struggle in the web.

Tanis caught sight of a mass of tangled, honey-colored hair, the flash of silver armor. Coughing, nearly suffocated by her constricting bindings, Laurana fought to free herself from the entangling white cloths. There was tense laughter as the troops watched the prisoner's feeble thrashings—this was obviously an indication of more amusement to come. Reacting instinctively, Tanis took a step forward to help Laurana. Then he felt Kitiara's brown eyes upon him, watching him, reminding him—

"If you die, she dies!"

His body shaking with chills, Tanis stopped, then stepped back. Finally Laurana staggered dizzily to her feet. For a moment she stood staring around vaguely, not comprehending where she was, blinking her eyes to see in the harsh, flaring torchlight. Her gaze focused at last upon Kitiara, smiling at her from behind the dragonhelm.

At the sight of her enemy, the woman who had betrayed her, Laurana drew herself to her full height. For a moment, her fear was forgotten in her anger. Imperiously she glanced beneath her, then above her, her gaze sweeping the great Hall. Fortunately, she did not look behind her. She did not see the bearded half-elf dressed in dragon armor, who was watching her intently. Instead she saw the troops of the Dark Queen, she saw the Highlords upon their thrones, she saw the dragons perched above them. Finally, she beheld the shadowy form of the Queen of Darkness herself.

And now she knows where she is, Tanis thought in misery, seeing Laurana's face drain of color. Now she knows where she is and what is about to befall her.

What stories they must have told her, down in those dungeons below the Temple. Tormenting her with tales of the Death Chambers of the Queen of Darkness. She had probably been able to hear the screams of others, Tanis guessed, feeling his soul ache at her obvious terror. She had listened to their screams in the night, and now, within hours, maybe minutes, she would join them.

Her face deathly pale, Laurana turned back to look at Kitiara as if she were the only fixed point in a swirling universe. Tanis saw Laurana's teeth clench, biting her lips to keep control. She would never show her fear to this woman, she would never show her fear to any of them.

Kitiara made a small gesture.

Laurana followed her gaze.

"Tanis . . ."

Turning, she saw the half-elf, and, as Laurana's eyes met his, Tanis saw hope shine. He felt her love for him surround him and bless him like the dawning of spring after winter's bitter darkness. For at last Tanis realized his own love for her was the bond between his two warring halves. He loved her with the unchanging, eternal love of his elven soul and with the passionate love of his human blood. But the realization had come too late, and now he would pay for the realization with his life and his soul.

One look, that was all he could give Laurana. One look that must carry the message of his heart, for he could feel Kitiara's brown eyes on him, watching him intently. And other eyes were on him, too, dark and shadowy as they might be.

Aware of those eyes, Tanis forced his face to reveal nothing of his inner thoughts. Exerting all his

control, he clenched his jaw, setting the muscles rigid, keeping his gaze carefully expressionless. Laurana might have been a stranger. Coldly he turned away from her and, as he turned, he saw hope's light flicker and die in her luminous eyes. As if a cloud had obscured the sun, the warmth of Laurana's love turned to bleak despair, chilling Tanis with its sorrow.

Gripping the hilt of his sword firmly to keep his hand from trembling, Tanis turned to face Takhisis, Queen of Darkness.

"Dark Majesty," cried Kitiara, grasping Laurana by the arm and dragging her forward, "I present my gift to you—a gift that will give us victory!"

She was momentarily interrupted by tumultuous cheers. Raising her hand, Kitiara commanded silence, then she continued.

"I give you the elfwoman, Lauralanthalasa, Princess of the Qualinesti elves, leader of the foul Knights of Solamnia. It was she who brought back the dragonlances, she who used the dragon orb in the High Clerist's Tower. It was by her command that her brother and a silver dragon traveled to Sanction where—through the ineptness of Lord Ariakas—they managed to break into the sacred temple and discover the destruction of the good dragon eggs." Ariakas took a menacing step forward, but Kitiara coolly ignored him. "I give her to you, my Queen, to treat her as you believe her crimes against you merit."

Kitiara flung Laurana in front of her. Stumbling, the elfwoman fell to her knees before the Queen. Her golden hair had come loose from its bindings and tumbled about her in a shining wave that was—to Tanis's fevered mind—the only light in the vast dark chamber.

You have done well, Lord Kitiara, came the Dark Queen's unheard voice, *and you will be well rewarded. We will have the elf escorted to the Death Chambers, then I will grant your reward.*

"Thank you, Majesty." Kitiara bowed. "Before our business concludes, I have two favors I beg you grant me." Thrusting out her hand, she caught Tanis in her strong grip. "I would first present one who seeks service in your great and glorious army."

Kitiara laid a hand on Tanis's shoulder, indicating with a firm pressure that he was to kneel. Unable to purge that last glimpse of Laurana from his mind, Tanis hesitated. He could still turn from the darkness. He could stand by Laurana's side and they would face the end together.

Then he sneered.

How selfish have I become, he asked himself bitterly, that I would even consider sacrificing Laurana in an attempt to cover my own folly? No, I alone will pay for my misdeeds. If I do nothing more that is good in this life, I will save her. And I will carry that knowledge with me as a candle to light my path until the darkness consumes me!

Kitiara's grip on him tightened painfully, even through the dragon-scale armor. The brown eyes behind the dragonhelm began to smolder with anger.

Slowly, his head bowed, Tanis sank to his knees before Her Dark Majesty.

"I present your humble servant, Tanis Half-Elven," Kitiara resumed coolly, although Tanis thought he could detect a note of relief in her voice. "I have named him commander of my armies, following the untimely death of my late commander, Bakaris."

Let our new servant come forward, came the voice into Tanis's mind.

Tanis felt Kit's hand on his shoulder as he rose, drawing him near. Swiftly she whispered, "Remember, you are Her Dark Majesty's property now, Tanis. She must be utterly convinced or even I will not be able to save you, and you will not be able to save your elfwoman."

"I remember," Tanis said without expression. Shaking free of Kitiara's grip, the half-elf walked forward to stand on the very edge of the platform, below the Dark Queen's throne.

Raise your head. Look upon me, came the command.

Tanis braced himself, asking for strength from deep inside him, strength he wasn't certain he possessed. If I falter, Laurana is lost. For the sake of love, I must banish love. Tanis lifted his eyes.

This scene was interesting to write because I needed to show Tanis feeling himself to be in the presence of a god, albeit an evil one. Thus he is awed and feels reverence, even though he's horrified. —MW

His gaze was caught and held. Mesmerized, he stared at the shadowy form, unable to free himself. There was no need to fabricate awe† and a horrible reverence, for that came to him as it comes to all mortals who glimpse Her Dark Majesty. But even as he felt compelled to worship, he realized that, deep inside, he was free still. Her power was not

complete. She could not consume him against his will. Though Takhisis fought not to reveal this weakness, Tanis was conscious of the great struggle she waged to enter the world.

Her shadowy form wavered before his eyes, revealing herself in all her guises, proving she had control over none. First she appeared to him as the five-headed dragon of Solamnic legend. Then the form shifted and she was the Temptress—a woman whose beauty men might die to possess. Then the form shifted once again. Now she was the Dark Warrior, a tall and powerful Knight of Evil, who held death in his mailed hand.

But even as the forms shifted, the dark eyes remained constant, staring into Tanis's soul, eyes of the five dragon heads, eyes of the beautiful Temptress, eyes of the fearful Warrior. Tanis felt himself shrivel beneath the scrutiny. He could not bear it, he did not have the strength. Abjectly he sank once more to his knees, groveling before the Queen, despising himself as behind him he heard an anguished, choking cry.

Tiamat was a creature delineated in the first monster manual, a multiheaded dragon whose name came from Babylonian myth and who guarded the top-most level of the Nine Hells. Takhisis is a goddess of Krynn, who appears as a multiheaded dragon (among other forms) and whose domain is the Abyss, a different place in the Lower Planes.

Are these creatures one and the same?

Yes and no. Takhisis was definitely creatively descended from Tiamat, but Tracy always denied they were one and the same. There were two reasons for this. First, most of the "unique" creatures from the AD&D Rules belonged to GREYHAWK, one of the earlier shared worlds, and it had fixed (and beatable) statistics. Second, there was a little matter of a cartoon show at the time, where Tiamat would show up (usually to scare the kids into running into a cave). Neither presentation was particularly what we wanted. But the multiheaded chromatic dragon was SOOO cool.

So Takhisis showed up instead. Now we weren't tied to the limitations of Tiamat as presented in previous material and could take her in her own direction. Of course, in the years since, everyone has tried to prove (or disprove) that they are one and the same.

I'm in the former camp and point out that, to natives of Krynn, all of the lower planes are considered "The Abyss." The natives (and all those who care about DRAGONLANCE) know the chromatic dragon by her Krynnish name, Takhisis. Tiamat may be someone else's name for the creature, but not its real name.—Jeff Grubb

9
Horns of Doom.

Lumbering down the northern corridor in search of Berem, Caramon ignored the startled yells and calls and grasping hands of prisoners reaching out from the barred cells. But there was no sight of Berem and no sign of his passing. He tried asking the other prisoners if they had seen him, but most were so unhinged by the tortures they had endured that they made no sense and, eventually, his mind filled with horror and pity, Caramon left them alone. He kept walking, following the corridor that led him ever downward. Looking around, he wondered in despair how he would ever find the crazed man. His only consolation was that no other corridors branched off from this central one. Berem must have come this way! But if so, where was he?

Peering into cells, stumbling around corners, Caramon almost missed a big hobgoblin guard, who lunged out at him. Swinging his sword irritably, annoyed at the interruption, Caramon swept the creature's head off and was on his way before the body hit the stone floor.

Then he heaved a sigh of relief. Hurrying down a staircase, he had nearly stepped on the body of another dead hobgoblin. Its neck had been twisted by strong hands. Plainly, Berem had been here, and not long ago. The body was not yet cold.

Certain now he was on the man's trail, Caramon began to run. The prisoners in the cells he passed were nothing but blurs to the big warrior as he ran by. Their voices shrilled in his ears, begging for freedom.

Let them loose, and I'd have an army, Caramon thought suddenly. He toyed with the idea of stopping a moment and unlocking the cell doors, when suddenly he heard a terrible howling sound and shouting coming from somewhere ahead of him.

Recognizing Berem's roar, Caramon plunged ahead. The cells came to an end, the corridor narrowed to a tunnel that cut a deep spiral well into the ground. Torches glimmered on the walls, but they were few and spaced far between. Caramon ran down the tunnel, the roar growing louder as he drew closer. The big warrior tried to hurry, but the floor was slick and slimy, the air became danker and heavy with moisture the farther down he went. Afraid he might slip and fall, he was forced to slow his pace. The shouts were closer, just ahead of him. The tunnel grew lighter, he must be coming near the end.

And then he saw Berem. Two draconians were slashing at him, their swords gleaming in the torchlight. Berem fought them off with his bare hands as light from the green gemstone lit the small enclosed chamber with an eerie brilliance.

It was a mark of Berem's insane strength that he had held them off this long. Blood ran freely from a cut across his face and flowed from a deep gash in his side. Even as Caramon dashed to his aid, slipping in the muck, Berem grasped a draconian's sword blade in his hand just as its point touched his chest. The cruel steel bit into his flesh, but he was oblivious to pain. Blood poured down his arm as he turned the blade and—with a heave—shoved the draconian backward. Then he staggered, gasping for breath. The other draconian guard closed in for the kill.

Intent upon their prey, the guards never saw Caramon. Leaping out of the tunnel, Caramon remembered just in time not to stab the creatures or he risked losing his sword. Grabbing one of the guards in his huge hands, he twisted its head, neatly snapping its neck. Dropping the body, he met the other draconian's savage lunge with a quick chopping motion of his hand to the creature's throat. It pitched backward.

"Berem, are you all right?" Caramon turned and was starting to help Berem when he suddenly felt a searing pain rip through his side.

Gasping in agony, he staggered around to see a draconian behind him. Apparently it had been hiding in the shadows, perhaps at hearing Caramon's coming. Its sword thrust should have killed, but it was aimed in haste and slanted off Caramon's mail armor. Scrabbling for his own sword, Caramon stumbled backward to gain time.

The draconian didn't intend giving him any. Raising its blade, it lunged at Caramon.

There was a blur of movement, a flash of green light, and the draconian fell dead at Caramon's feet.

"Berem!" Caramon gasped, pressing his hand over his side. "Thanks! How—"

But the Everman stared at Caramon without recognition. Then, nodding slowly, he turned and started to walk away.

"Wait!" Caramon called. Gritting his teeth against the pain, the big man jumped over the draconian bodies and hurled himself after Berem. Clutching his arm, he dragged the man to a stop. "Wait, damn it!" he repeated, holding on to him.

The sudden movement took its toll. The room swam before his eyes, forcing Caramon to stand still a moment, fighting the pain of his injury. When he could see again, he looked around, getting his bearings.

"Where are we?"he asked without expecting an answer, just wanting Berem to hear the sound of his voice.

"Far, far below the Temple," Berem replied in a hollow tone. "I am close. Very close now."

"Yeah," Caramon agreed without understanding. Keeping a fast hold on Berem, he continued to look around. The stone stairs he had come down ended in a small circular chamber. A guardroom, he realized, seeing an old table and several chairs sitting beneath a torch on the wall. It made sense. The draconians down here must have been guards. Berem had stumbled on them accidentally. But what could the draconians have been guarding?

Caramon glanced quickly around the small stone chamber but saw nothing. The room was perhaps twenty paces in diameter, carved out of rock. The spiral stone stairs ended in this room and—across from them—an archway led out. It was toward this archway Berem had been walking when Caramon caught hold of him. Peering through the arch, Caramon saw nothing. It was dark beyond, so dark Caramon felt as if he were staring into the Great Darkness the legends spoke of. Darkness that had existed in the void long before the gods created light.

The only sound he could hear was the gurgling and splash of water. An underground stream, he thought, which accounted for the humid air. Stepping back a pace, he examined the archway above him.

It was not carved out of the rock as was the small chamber they were in. It had been built of stone, crafted by expert hands. He could see vague outlines of elaborate carvings that had once decorated it, but he could make nothing out. They had long ago been worn away by time and the moisture in the air.

As he studied the arch, hoping for a clue to guide him, Caramon nearly fell as Berem clutched at him with sudden, fierce energy.

"I know you!" the man cried.

"Sure," Caramon grunted. "What in the name of the Abyss are you doing down here?"

"Jasla calls . . ." Berem said, the wild look glazing his eyes once more. Turning, he stared into the darkness beyond the archway. "In there, I must go. . . . Guards . . . tried to stop me. You come with me."

Then Caramon realized that the guards must have been guarding this arch! For what reason? What was beyond? Had they recognized Berem or were they simply acting under orders to keep

everyone out? He didn't know the answers to any of these questions, and then it occurred to him that the answers didn't matter. Neither did the questions.

"You have to go in there," he said to Berem. It was a statement, not a question. Berem nodded and took a step forward eagerly. He would have walked straight into the darkness if Caramon hadn't jerked him back.

"Wait, we'll need light," the big man said with a sigh. "Stay put!" Patting Berem on the arm, then keeping his gaze fixed on him, Caramon backed up until his groping hand came into contact with a torch on the wall. Lifting it from its sconce, he returned to Berem.

"I'll go with you," he said heavily, wondering how long he could keep going before he collapsed from pain and loss of blood. "Here, hold that a minute." Handing Berem the torch, he tore off a strip of cloth from the ragged remains of Berem's shirt and bound it firmly around the wound in his side. Then, taking the torch back, he led the way beneath the arch.

Passing between the stone supports, Caramon felt something brush across his face. "Cobweb!" he muttered, pawing at it in disgust. He glanced around fearfully, having a dread of spiders.† But there was nothing there. Shrugging, he thought no more of it and continued through the arch, drawing Berem after him.

Not surprising considering the number of monstrous blood-sucking spiders there are on Krynn, as well as the number of times the companions have been involved in web spells.

The air was split with trumpet blasts.

"Trapped!" Caramon said grimly.

"Tika!" Tas gasped proudly as they ran down the gloomy dungeon corridor. "Your plan worked." The kender risked a glance over his shoulder. "Yes," he said breathlessly, "I think they're *all* following us!"

"Wonderful," muttered Tika. Somehow she hadn't expected her plan to work quite so well. No other plans she had ever made in her life had worked out. Wouldn't you know this would be a first? She, too, cast a quick glance over her shoulder. There must be six or seven draconians chasing after them, their long curved swords in their clawed hands.

Though the claw-footed draconians could not run as swiftly as either the girl or the kender, they had

incredible endurance. Tika and Tas had a good head start, but it wasn't going to last. She was already panting for breath, and there was a sharp pain in her side that made her want to double over in agony.

But every second I keep running gives Caramon a little more time, she told herself. I draw the draconians just that much farther away.

"Say, Tika"—Tas's tongue was hanging out of his mouth, his face, cheerful as always, was pale with fatigue—"do you know where we're going?"

Tika shook her head. She hadn't breath left to speak. She felt herself slowing, her legs were like lead. Another look back showed her that the draconians were gaining. Quickly she glanced around, hoping to find another corridor branching off from this main one, or even a niche, a doorway—any kind of hiding place. There was nothing. The corridor stretched before them, silent and empty. There weren't even any cells. It was a long, narrow, smooth, and seemingly endless stone tunnel that sloped gradually upward.

Then a sudden realization nearly brought her up short. Slowing, gasping for breath, she stared at Tas, who was only dimly visible in the light of smoking torches.

"The tunnel . . . it's rising . . ." She coughed.

Tas blinked at her uncomprehendingly, then his face brightened.

"It leads up and out!" he shouted jubilantly. "You've done it, Tika!"

"Maybe . . ." Tika said, hedging.

"Come on!" Tas yelled in excitement, finding new energy. Grabbing Tika's hand, he pulled her along. "I know you're right, Tika! Smell"—he sniffed—"fresh air! We'll escape . . . and find Tanis . . . and come back and . . . rescue Caramon—"

Only a kender could talk and run headlong down a corridor while being chased by draconians at the same time, Tika thought wearily. She was being carried forward by sheer terror now, she knew. And soon that would leave her. Then she would collapse here in the tunnel, so tired and aching she wouldn't care what the draconians—

Then, "Fresh air!" she whispered.

She had honestly thought Tas was lying just to keep her going. But now she could feel a soft

whisper of wind touch her cheek. Hope lightened her leaden legs. Glancing back, she thought she saw the draconians slowing. Maybe they realize they'll never catch us now! Exultation swept over her.

"Hurry, Tas!" she yelled. Together they both raced with renewed energy up the corridor, the sweet air blowing stronger and stronger all the time.

Running headfirst around a corner, they both came up short so suddenly that Tasslehoff skidded on some loose gravel and slammed up against a wall.

"So this is why they slowed down," Tika said softly.

The corridor came to an end. Two barred wooden doors sealed it shut. Small windows set into the doors, covered with iron gratings, allowed the night air to blow into the dungeon. She and Tas could see outside, they could see freedom—but they could not reach it.

"Don't give up!" Tas said after a moment's pause. Recovering quickly, he ran over and pulled on the doors. They were locked.

"Drat," Tas muttered, eyeing the doors expertly. Caramon might have been able to batter his way through them, or break the lock with a blow of his sword. But not the kender, not Tika.

As Tas bent down to examine the lock, Tika leaned against a wall, wearily closing her eyes. Blood beat in her head, the muscles in her legs knotted in painful spasms. Exhausted, she tasted the bitter salt of tears in her mouth and realized she was sobbing in pain and anger and frustration.

"Don't, Tika!" Tas said, hurrying back to pat her hand. "It's a simple lock. I can get us out of here in no time. Don't cry, Tika. It'll only take me a little while, but you ought to be ready for those draconians if they come. Just keep them busy—"

"Right," Tika said, swallowing her tears. Hurriedly she wiped her nose with the back of her hand, then, sword in hand, she turned to face the corridor behind them while Tas took another look at the lock.

It was a simple, simple lock, he saw with satisfaction, guarded by such a simple trap he wondered why they even bothered.

Wondered why they even bothered. . . Simple lock . . . simple trap . . . The words rang in his mind. They

were familiar! He'd thought them before. . . . Staring up at the doors in astonishment, Tas realized he'd been here before! But no, that was impossible.

Shaking his head irritably, Tas fumbled in his pouch for his tools. Then he stopped. Cold fear gripped the kender and shook him like a dog shakes a rat, leaving him limp.

The dream!

These had been the doors he saw in the Silvanesti dream! This had been the lock. The simple, simple lock with the simple trap! And Tika had been behind him, fighting . . . dying. . . .

"Here they come, Tas!" Tika called, gripping her sword in sweating hands. She cast him a quick glance over her shoulder. "What are you doing? What are you waiting for?"

Tas couldn't answer. He could hear the draconians now, laughing in their harsh voices as they took their time reaching their captives, certain the prisoners weren't going anyplace. They rounded the corner and Tas heard their laughter grow louder when they saw Tika holding the sword.

"I—I don't think I can, Tika," Tas whimpered, staring at the lock in horror.

"Tas," said Tika swiftly and grimly, backing up to talk to him without taking her eyes off her enemies, "we can't let ourselves be captured! They know about Berem! They'll try to make us tell what we know about him, Tas! And you know what they'll do to us to make us talk—"

"You're right!" said Tas miserably. "I'll try."

You've got the courage to walk it, Fizban had told him. Taking a deep breath, Tasslehoff pulled a thin wire out of one of his pouches. After all, he told his shaking hands sternly, what is death to a kender but the greatest adventure of all? And then there's Flint out there, by himself. Probably getting into all sorts of scrapes . . . His hands now quite steady, Tas inserted the wire carefully into the lock and set to work.

Suddenly there was a harsh roar behind him; he heard Tika shout and the sound of steel clashing against steel.

Tas dared a quick look. Tika had never learned the art of swordsmanship, but she was a skilled barroom brawler. Hacking and slashing with the blade,

she kicked and gouged and bit and battered. The fury and ferocity of her attack drove the draconians back a pace. All of them were slashed and bleeding; one wallowed in green blood on the floor, its arm hanging uselessly.

But she couldn't hold them off much longer. Tas turned back to his work, but now his hands trembled, the slender tool slipped out of his clammy grasp. The trick was to spring the lock without springing the trap. He could see the trap—a tiny needle held in place by a coiled spring.

Stop it! he ordered himself. Was this any way for a kender to act? He inserted the wire again carefully, his hands steady once more. Suddenly, just as he almost had it, he was jostled from behind.

"Hey," he shouted irritably at Tika, turning around. "Be a little more careful—" He stopped short. The dream! He had said those exact words. And—as in the dream—he saw Tika, lying at his feet, blood flowing into her red curls.

"No!" Tas shrieked in rage. The wire slipped, his hand struck the lock.

There was a click as the lock opened. And with the click came another small sound, a brittle sound, barely heard; a sound like "snick." The trap was sprung.

Wide-eyed, Tas stared at the tiny spot of blood on his finger, then at the small golden needle protruding from the lock. The draconians had him now, grasping him by the shoulder. Tas ignored them. It didn't matter anyway. There was a stinging pain in his finger and soon the pain would spread up his arm and throughout his body.

When it reaches my heart, I won't feel it anymore, he told himself dreamily. I won't feel anything.

Then he heard horns, blaring horns, brass horns. He had heard those horns before. Where? That's right. It was in Tarsis, right before the dragons came.

And then the draconians that had been hanging on to him were gone, running frantically back down the corridor.

"Must be some sort of general alarm," Tas thought, noticing with interest that his legs wouldn't hold him up anymore. He slid down to the floor, down beside Tika. Reaching out a shaking hand, he

gently stroked her pretty red curls, now matted with blood. Her face was white, her eyes closed.

"I'm sorry, Tika," Tas said, his throat constricting. The pain was spreading quickly, his fingers and feet had gone numb. He couldn't move them. "I'm sorry, Caramon. I tried, I truly tried—" Weeping quietly, Tas sat back against the door and waited for the darkness.

Tanis could not move and—for a moment, hearing Laurana's heartbroken sob—he had no wish to move. If anything, he begged a merciful god to strike him dead as he knelt before the Dark Queen. But the gods granted him no such favor. The shadow lifted as the Queen's attention shifted elsewhere, away from him. Tanis struggled to his feet, his face flushed with shame. He could not look at Laurana, he dared not even meet Kitiara's eyes, knowing well the scorn he would see in their brown depths.

But Kitiara had more important matters on her mind. This was her moment of glory. Her plans were coming together. Thrusting out her hand, she caught Tanis in her strong grip as he was about to come forward to offer himself as escort to Laurana. Coldly, she shoved him backward and moved to stand in front of him.

"Finally, I wish to reward a servant of my own who helped me capture the elfwoman. Lord Soth has asked that he be granted the soul of this Lauralanthalasa, that he might thus gain his revenge over the elfwoman who—long ago—cast the curse upon him. If he be doomed to live in eternal darkness, then he asks that this elfwoman share his life within death."

"No!" Laurana raised her head, fear and horror penetrating her numb senses. "No," she repeated in a strangled voice.

Taking a step backward, she looked about her wildly for some escape, but it was impossible. Below her, the floor writhed with draconians, staring up at her eagerly. Choking in despair, she glanced once at Tanis. His face was dark and forbidding; he was not looking at her, but stared with burning eyes at the human woman. Already regretting her wretched outburst, Laurana determined

that she would die before she gave way to any further weakness in front of either of them, ever again. Drawing herself up proudly, she lifted her head, in control once more.

Tanis did not even see Laurana. Kitiara's words beat like blood in his head, clouding his vision and his thoughts. Furious, he took a step forward to stand near Kitiara. "You betrayed me!" he choked. "This was not part of the plan!"

"Hush!" ordered Kit in a low voice. "Or you will destroy everything!"

"What—"

"Shut up!" Kitiara snapped viciously.

Your gift pleases me well, Lord Kitiara. The dark voice penetrated Tanis's anger. *I grant your requests. The elfwoman's soul will be given to Lord Soth, and we accept the half-elf into our service. In recognition of this, he will lay his sword at the feet of Lord Ariakas.*

"Well, go on!" demanded Kitiara coldly, her eyes on Tanis. The eyes of everyone in the room were on the half-elf.

His mind swam. "What?" he muttered. "You didn't tell me this! What do I do?"

"Ascend the platform and lay your sword at Ariakas's feet," Kitiara answered swiftly, escorting him to the edge of the platform. "He will pick it up and return it to you, then you will be an officer in the dragonarmies. It is ritual, nothing more. But it buys me time."†

Why doesn't the Dark Queen pay attention to the machinations going on?

I believe that the Queen of Darkness is completely aware of what is going on here. It matters little to her who is in charge of the Dragon Highlords—Indeed, it is the strength that she wishes to support. The fact is that the Queen is paying too much attention to what is happening here—a fact that allows Berem to go unnoticed by the Dark Queen.—TRH

"Time for what? What do you have planned?" Tanis asked harshly, his foot on the stair leading down. He caught hold of her arm. "You should have told me—"

"The less you know the better, Tanis." Kitiara smiled charmingly, for the sake of those watching. There was some nervous laughter, a few crude jokes at what appeared to be a lover's parting. But Tanis saw no answering smile in Kit's brown eyes. "Remember who stands next to me upon this platform," Kitiara whispered. Caressing the hilt of her sword, Kit gave Laurana a meaningful glance. "Do nothing rash." Turning away from him, she walked back to stand beside Laurana.

Trembling in fear and rage, his thoughts whirling in confusion, Tanis stumbled down the stairs leading from the snake's-head platform. The noise of the

assembly rolled around him like the crash of oceans. Light flashed off spearpoints, the torch flames blurred in his vision. He set his foot upon the floor and began to walk toward Ariakas's platform without any clear idea of where he was or what he was doing. Moving by reflex alone, he made his way across the marble floor.

The faces of the draconians who made up Ariakas's guard of honor floated around him like a hideous nightmare. He saw them as disembodied heads, rows of gleaming teeth, and flicking tongues. They parted before him, the stairs materialized at his feet as if rising out of fog.

Lifting his head, he stared up bleakly. At the top stood Lord Ariakas; a huge man, majestic, armed with power. All the light in the room seemed to be drawn into the Crown upon his head. Its brilliance dazzled the eyes, and Tanis blinked, blinded, as he began to climb the steps, his hand on his sword.

Had Kitiara betrayed him? Would she keep her promise? Tanis doubted it. Bitterly he cursed himself. Once more he had fallen under her spell. Once more he had played the fool, trusting her. And now she held all the gamepieces. There was nothing he could do . . . or was there?

An idea came to Tanis so suddenly he stopped, one foot on one step, the other on the step below.

Idiot! Keep walking, he commanded, feeling everyone staring at him. Forcing himself to retain some outward semblance of calm, Tanis climbed up another step and another. As he drew closer and closer to Lord Ariakas, the plan became clearer and clearer.

Whoever holds the Crown, rules! The words rang in Tanis's mind.

Kill Ariakas, take the Crown! It will be simple! Tanis's gaze flashed around the alcove feverishly. No guards stood beside Ariakas, of course. No one but Highlords were allowed on the platforms. But he didn't even have guards on the stairs as did the other Highlords. Apparently the man was so arrogant, so secure in his power, he had dispensed with them.

Tanis's thoughts raced. Kitiara will trade her soul for that Crown And as long as I hold it, she will be *mine* to command! I can save Laurana . . . we can escape together! Once we are safely out of here, I can explain things to Laurana, I can explain everything! I'll draw my sword, but instead of placing it at Lord Ariakas's feet, I will run it through him! Once the Crown is in my hand, no one will dare touch me!

Tanis found himself shaking with excitement. With an effort, he forced himself to calm down. He could not look at Ariakas, fearing the man might see his desperate plan in his eyes.

He kept his gaze upon the stairs, therefore, and he knew he was near Lord Ariakas only when he saw five steps remained between himself and the top of the platform. Tanis's hand twitched upon the sword. Feeling himself under control, he raised his gaze to look into the man's face and, for an instant, was almost unnerved at the evil revealed there. It was a face made passionless by ambition, a face that had seen the deaths of thousands of innocents as the means only to an end.

Ariakas had been watching Tanis with a bored expression, a smile of amused contempt on his face. Then he lost interest in the half-elf completely, having other matters to worry about. Tanis saw the man's gaze go to Kitiara, pondering. Ariakas had the look of a player leaning across a gameboard, contemplating his next move, trying to guess what his opponent intends.

Filled with revulsion and hatred, Tanis began to slide the blade of his sword from its scabbard. Even if he failed in his attempt to save Laurana, even if they both died within these walls, at least he would accomplish some good in the world by killing the Commander of the Dragonarmies.

But as he heard Tanis draw his sword, Ariakas's eyes flashed back to the half-elf once again. Their black stare penetrated Tanis's soul. He felt the man's tremendous power overwhelm him, hitting him like a blast of heat from a furnace. And then realization struck Tanis a blow almost physical in its impact, nearly causing him to stagger on the stairs.

That aura of power surrounding him . . . *Ariakas was a magic-user!*

Blind stupid fool! Tanis cursed himself. For now, as he drew nearer, he saw a shimmering wall surrounding the Lord. Of course, that's why there

were no guards! Among this crowd, Ariakas would trust no one. He would use his own magic to guard himself!

And he was on his guard, now. That much Tanis could read clearly in the cold, passionless eyes.

The half-elf's shoulders slumped. He was defeated.

And then, "Strike, Tanis! Do not fear his magic! I will aid you!"

The voice was no more than a whisper, yet so clear and so intense, Tanis could practically feel hot breath touch his ear. His hair raised on the back of his neck, a shudder convulsed his body.

Shivering, he glanced hastily around. There was no one near him, no one except Ariakas! He was only three steps away, scowling, obviously anxious for this ceremony to come to an end. Seeing Tanis hesitate, Ariakas made a peremptory motion for the half-elf to lay his sword at his feet.

Who had spoken? Suddenly Tanis's eyes were caught by the sight of a figure standing near the Queen of Darkness. Robed in black, it had escaped his notice before. Now he stared at it, thinking it seemed familiar. Had the voice come from that figure? If so, the figure made no sign or movement. What should he do? he wondered frantically.

"Strike, Tanis!" whispered once more in his brain. "Swiftly!"

Sweating, his hand shaking, Tanis slowly drew his sword. He was level with Ariakas now. The shimmering wall of the Lord's magic surrounded him like a rainbow glittering off sparkling water.

I have no choice, Tanis said to himself. If it is a trap, so be it. I choose this way to die.

Feigning to kneel, holding his sword hilt-first to lay it upon the marble platform, Tanis suddenly reversed his stroke. Turning it into a killing blow, he lunged for Ariakas's heart.

Tanis expected to die. Gritting his teeth as he struck, he braced himself for the magic shield to wither him like a tree struck by lightning.

And lightning *did* strike, but not him! To his amazement, the rainbow wall exploded, his sword penetrated. He felt it hit solid flesh. A fierce cry of pain and outrage nearly deafened him.

Ariakas staggered backward as the sword blade slid into his chest. A lesser man would have died from that blow, but Ariakas's strength and anger held Death at bay. His face twisted in hatred, he struck Tanis across the face, sending him reeling to the floor of the platform.

Pain burst in Tanis's head. Dimly, he saw his sword fall beside him, red with blood. For a moment, he thought he was going to lose consciousness and that would mean his death, his death and Laurana's. Groggily he shook his head to clear it. He must hang on! He must gain the Crown! Looking up, he saw Ariakas looming above him, hands lifted, prepared to cast a spell that would end Tanis's life.

Tanis could do nothing. He had no protection against the magic and somehow he knew that his unseen helper would help no more. It had already achieved what it desired.

But powerful as Ariakas was, there was a greater power he could not conquer. He choked, his mind wavered, the words of his magic spell were lost in a terrible pain. Looking down, he saw his own blood stain the purple robes, the stain grew larger and larger with each passing moment as his life poured from his severed heart. Death was coming to claim him. He could stave it off no longer. Desperately Ariakas battled the darkness, crying out at the last to his Dark Queen for help.

But she abandoned weaklings. As she had watched Ariakas strike down his father, so she watched Ariakas himself fall, her name the last sound to pass his lips.

There was uneasy silence in the Hall of Audience as Ariakas's body tumbled to the floor. The Crown of Power fell from his head with a clatter and lay within a tangle of blood and thick, black hair.

Who would claim it?

There was a piercing scream. Kitiara called out a name, called to someone.

Tanis could not understand. He didn't care anyway. He stretched out his hand for the Crown.

Suddenly a figure in black armor materialized before him.

Lord Soth!

Fighting down a feeling of sheer panic and terror, Tanis kept his mind focused on one thing. The

Crown was only inches beyond his fingers. Desperately he lunged for it. Thankfully he felt the cold metal bite into his flesh just as another hand, a skeletal hand, made a grab for it, too.

It was his! Soth's burning eyes flared. The skeletal hand reached out to wrest the prize away. Tanis could hear Kitiara's voice, shrieking incoherent commands.

But as he lifted the blood-stained piece of metal above his head, as his eyes fixed unafraid upon Lord Soth, the hushed silence in the Hall was split by the sound of horns, harsh blaring horns.

Lord Soth's hand paused in mid-air, Kitiara's voice fell suddenly silent.

There was a subdued, ominous murmur from the crowd. For an instant, Tanis's pain-clouded mind thought the horns might be sounding in his honor. But then, turning his head to peer dimly into the Hall, he saw faces glancing around in alarm. Everyone—even Kitiara—looked at the Dark Queen.

Her Dark Majesty's shadowy eyes had been on Tanis, but now their gaze was abstracted. Her shadow grew and intensified, spreading through the Hall like a dark cloud. Reacting to some unspoken command, draconians wearing her black insignia ran from their posts around the edge of the Hall and disappeared through the doors. The black-robed figure Tanis had seen standing beside the Queen vanished.

And still the horns blared. Holding the Crown in his hand, Tanis stared down at it numbly. Twice before, the harsh blaring of the horns had brought death and destruction. What was the terrible portent of the dread music this time?

10

"Whoever wears the Crown, rules."

o loud and startling was the sound of the horns that Caramon nearly lost his footing on the wet stone. Reacting instinctively, Berem caught him. Both men stared around them in alarm as the blaring trumpet calls dinned loudly in the small chamber. Above them—up the stairs—they could hear answering trumpet calls.

"The arch! It was trapped!" Caramon repeated. "Well, that's done it. Every living thing in the Temple knows we're here, wherever here is! I hope to the gods you know what you're doing!"

"Jasla calls—" Berem repeated. His momentary alarm at the blaring trumpets dissipating, he continued forward, tugging Caramon along behind him.

Holding the torch aloft, not knowing what else to do or where else to go, Caramon followed. They

were in a cavern apparently cut through the rock by flowing water. The archway led to stone stairs and these stairs, Caramon saw, led straight down into a black, swiftly flowing stream. He flashed the torch around, hoping that there might be a path along the edge of the stream. But there was nothing, at least within the perimeter of his torchlight.

"Wait—" he cried, but Berem had already plunged into the black water. Caramon caught his breath, expecting to see the man vanish in the swirling depths. But the dark water was not as deep as it looked, it came only to Berem's calves.

"Come!" He beckoned Caramon.

Caramon touched the wound in his side again. The bleeding seemed to have slowed, the bandage was moist but not soaked. The pain was still intense, however. His head ached, and he was so exhausted from fear and running and loss of blood that he was light-headed. He thought briefly of Tika and Tas, even more briefly of Tanis. No, he must put them out of his mind.

The end is near, for good or for evil, Tika had said. Caramon was beginning to believe it himself. Stepping into the water, he felt the strong current sweeping him forward and he had the giddy feeling that the current was time, sweeping him ahead to—what? His own doom? The end of the world? Or hope for a new beginning?

Berem eagerly sloshed ahead of him, but Caramon dragged him back again.

"We'll stick together," the big man said, his deep voice echoing in the cavern. "There may be more traps, worse than that one."

Berem hesitated long enough for Caramon to join him. Then they moved slowly, side by side, through the rushing water, testing each footstep, for the bottom was slick and treacherous with crumbling stone and loose rock.

Caramon was wading forward, breathing easier, when something struck his leather boot with such force it nearly knocked his feet out from under him. Staggering, he caught hold of Berem.

"What was that?" he growled, holding the flaring torch above the water.

Seemingly attracted by the light, a head lifted out of the shining wet blackness. Caramon sucked in his breath in horror, and even Berem was momentarily taken aback.

This experience later led Caramon to write, shuddering, "How can you compare a crocodile, no matter how large or powerful it is, with even the smallest dragon hatchling?"

"Dragons!" Caramon whispered. "Hatchlings!"† The small dragon opened its mouth in a shrill scream. Torchlight gleamed on rows of razor-sharp teeth. Then the head vanished and Caramon felt the creature strike at his boot once more. Another one hit his other leg; he saw the water boil with flailing tails.

His leather boots kept them from hurting him now, but, Caramon thought, if I fall, the creatures will strip the flesh from my bones!

He had faced death in many forms, but none more terrifying than this. For a moment he panicked. I'll turn back, he thought frantically. Berem can go on alone. After all, he can't die.

Then the big warrior took hold of himself. No, he sighed. They know we're down here now. They'll send someone or something to try and stop us. I've got to hold off whatever it is until Berem can do whatever he's supposed to do.

That last thought made no sense at all, Caramon realized. It was so ludicrous it was almost funny and, as if mocking his decision, the quiet was broken by the sound of clashing steel and harsh shouts, coming from behind them.

This is insane! he admitted wearily. I don't understand! I may die down here in the darkness and for what? Maybe I'm down here with a crazy man! Maybe *I'm* going crazy!

Now Berem became aware of the guards coming after them. This frightened him more than dragons, and he plunged ahead. Sighing, Caramon forced himself to ignore the slithering attacks at his feet and legs as he waded forward through the black, rushing water, trying to keep up with Berem.

The man stared constantly ahead into the darkness, occasionally making moaning sounds and wringing his hands in anxiety. The stream led them around a curve where the water grew deeper. Caramon wondered what he would do if the water rose higher than his boots. The dragon young were still frantically chasing after them, the warm smell of human blood and flesh driving them into a frenzy. The sounds of sword and spear rattling grew louder.

Then something blacker than night flew at Caramon, striking him in the face. Flailing, trying desperately to keep from falling into that deadly water, he dropped his torch. The light vanished with a sizzle as Berem made a wild grab for him and caught him. The two held onto each other for a moment, staring—lost and confused—into the darkness.

If he had been struck blind, Caramon could not have been more disoriented. Though he had not moved, he had no idea what direction he faced, he couldn't remember a thing about his surroundings. He had the feeling that if he took one more step, he would plunge into nothingness and fall forever. . . .

"There it is!" Berem said, catching his breath with a strangled sob. "I see the broken column, the jewels gleaming on it! And she is there! She is waiting for me, she has waited all these years! Jasla!" he screamed, straining forward.

Peering ahead into the darkness, Caramon held Berem back, though he could feel the man's body quivering with emotion. He could see nothing . . . or could he?

Yes! A deep sense of thankfulness and relief flooded his pain-racked body. He *could* see jewels sparkling in the distance, shining in the blackness with a light it seemed even this heavy darkness could not quench.

It was just a short distance ahead of them, not more than a hundred feet. Relaxing his grip on Berem, Caramon thought, Perhaps this is a way out, for me, at least. Let Berem join this ghostly sister of his. All I want is a way out, a way to get back to Tika and Tas.

His confidence returning, Caramon strode forward. A matter of minutes and it would be over . . . for good . . . or for . . .

"Shirak," spoke a voice.

A bright light flared.

Caramon's heart ceased to beat for an instant. Slowly, slowly he lifted his head to look into that bright light, and there he saw two golden, glittering, hourglass eyes staring at him from the depths of a black hood.

The breath left his body in a sigh that was like the sigh of a dying man.

The blaring trumpets ceased, a measure of calm returned to the Hall of Audience. Once more, the eyes of everyone in the Hall—including the Dark Queen—turned to the drama on the platform.

Gripping the Crown in his hand, Tanis rose to his feet. He had no idea what the horn calls portended, what doom might be about to fall. He only knew that he must play the game out to its end, bitter as that may be.

Laurana . . . she was his one thought. Wherever Berem and Caramon and the others were, they were beyond his help. Tanis's eyes fixed on the silver-armored figure standing on the snake-headed platform below him. Almost by accident, his gaze flicked to Kitiara, standing beside Laurana, her face hidden behind the hideous dragonmask. She made a gesture.

Tanis felt more than heard movement behind him, like a chill wind brushing his skin. Whirling, he saw Lord Soth coming toward him, death burning in the orange eyes.

Tanis backed up, the Crown in his hand, knowing he could not fight this opponent from beyond the grave.

"Stop!" he shouted, holding the Crown poised above the floor of the Hall of Audience. "Stop him, Kitiara, or with my last dying strength I will hurl this into the crowd."

Soth laughed soundlessly, advancing upon him, the skeletal hand that could kill by a touch alone outstretched.

"What 'dying strength'?" the death knight asked softly. "My magic will shrivel your body to dust, the Crown will fall at my feet."

"Lord Soth," rang out a clear voice from the platform from the center of the Hall, "halt. Let him who won the Crown bring it to me!"†

"Give me the crown. Here, cousin, seize the crown." Shakespeare's Richard II

Soth hesitated. His hand still reaching for Tanis, his flaming eyes turned their vacant gaze upon Kitiara, questioning.

Removing the dragonhelm from her head, Kitiara looked only at Tanis. He could see her brown eyes gleaming and her cheeks flushed with excitement.

"You will bring me the Crown, won't you, Tanis?" Kitiara called.

Tanis swallowed. "Yes," he said, licking his dry lips, "I will bring you the Crown."

"My guards!" Kitiara ordered, waving them forward. "An escort. Anyone who touches him will die by my hand. Lord Soth, see that he reaches me safely."

Tanis glanced at Lord Soth, who slowly lowered his deadly hand. "He is your master, still, my lady," Tanis thought he heard the death knight whisper with a sneer.

Then Soth fell into step beside him, the ghostly chill emanating from the knight nearly congealing Tanis's blood. Together they descended the stairs, an odd pair—the pallid knight in the blackened armor, the half-elf clutching the blood-stained Crown in his hand.

Ariakas's officers, who had been standing at the foot of the stairs, weapons drawn, fell back, some reluctantly. As Tanis reached the marble floor and passed by them, many gave him black looks. He saw the flash of a dagger in one hand, an unspoken promise in the dark eyes.

Their own swords drawn, Kitiara's guards fell in around him, but it was Lord Soth's deathly aura that obtained safe passage for him through the crowded floor. Tanis began to sweat beneath his armor. So this is power, he realized. Whoever has the Crown, rules, but that could all end in the dead of night with one thrust of an assassin's dagger!

Tanis kept walking, and soon he and Lord Soth reached the bottom of the stairs leading up to the platform shaped like the head of the hooded snake. At the top stood Kitiara, beautiful in triumph. Tanis climbed the spurlike stairs alone, leaving Soth standing at the bottom, his orange eyes burning in their hollow sockets. As Tanis reached the top of the platform, the top of the snake's head, he could see Laurana, standing behind Kitiara. Laurana's face was pale, cool, composed. She glanced at him—and at the blood-stained Crown—then turned her head away. He had no idea what she was thinking or feeling. It didn't matter. He would explain. . . .

Running over to him, Kitiara grasped him in her arms. Cheers resounded in the Hall.

"Tanis!" she breathed. "Truly you and I were meant to rule together! You were wonderful, magnificent! I will give you anything . . . anything—"

"Laurana?" Tanis asked coldly, under the cover of the noise. His slightly slanted eyes, the eyes that gave away his heritage, stared down into Kitiara's brown eyes.

Kit flicked a glance at the elfwoman, whose gaze was so fixed, whose skin was so pale she might have been a corpse.

"If you want her." Kitiara shrugged, then drew closer, her voice for him alone. "But you will have me, Tanis. By day we will command armies, rule the world. The nights, Tanis! They will be ours alone, yours and mine." Her breath came fast, her hands reached up to stroke his bearded face. "Place the Crown on my head, beloved."

Tanis stared down into the brown eyes, he saw them filled with warmth and passion and excitement. He could feel Kitiara's body pressed against his, trembling, eager. Around him, the troops were shouting madly, the noise swelling like a wave. Slowly Tanis raised the hand that held the Crown of Power, slowly he lifted it—not to Kitiara's head, but to his own.

"No, Kitiara," he shouted so that all could hear. "One of us will rule by day *and* by night—me."

There was laughter in the Hall, mixed with angry rumblings. Kitiara's eyes widened in shock, then swiftly narrowed.

"Don't try it," Tanis said, catching her hand as she reached for the knife at her belt. Holding her fast, he looked down at her. "I'm going to leave the Hall now," he said softly, speaking for her ears alone, "with Laurana. You and your troops will escort us out of here. When we are safely outside this evil place, I will give you the Crown. Betray me, and you will never hold it. Do you understand?"

Kitiara's lips twisted in a sneer. "So *she* is truly all you care about?" she whispered caustically.

"Truly," Tanis replied. Gripping her arm harder, he saw pain in her eyes. "I swear this on the souls of two I loved dearly—Sturm Brightblade and Flint Fireforge. Do you believe me?"

"I believe you," Kitiara said in bitter anger. Looking up at him, reluctant admiration flared once more in her eyes. "You could have had so much . . ."

Tanis released her without a word. Turning, he walked over to Laurana, who was standing with

her back to them, gazing sightlessly above the crowd. Tanis gripped her arm. "Come with me," he commanded coldly. The noise of the crowd rose up around him, while above him, he was aware of the dark shadowy figure of the Queen, watching the flux of power intently, waiting to see who would emerge strongest.

Laurana did not flinch at his touch. She did not react at all. Moving her head slowly, the honey-blonde hair falling in a tangled mass around her shoulders, she looked at him. The green eyes were without recognition, expressionless. He saw nothing in them, not fear, not anger.

It will be all right, he told her silently, his heart aching. I will explain—

There was a flash of silver, a blur of golden hair. Something struck Tanis hard in the chest. He staggered backward, grasping for Laurana as he stumbled. But he could not hold her.

Shoving him aside, Laurana sprang at Kitiara, her hand grabbing for the sword Kit wore at her side. Her move caught the human woman completely by surprise. Kit struggled briefly, fiercely, but Laurana already had her hands upon the hilt. With a smooth movement, she yanked Kit's sword from the scabbard and jabbed the sword hilt into Kitiara's face, knocking her to the platform. Turning, Laurana ran to the edge.

"Laurana, stop!" Tanis shouted. Jumping forward to catch her, he suddenly felt the point of her sword at his throat.

"Don't move, Tanthalasa," Laurana ordered. Her green eyes were dilated with excitement, she held the sword point with unwavering steadiness. "Or you will die. I will kill you, if I have to."

Tanis took a step forward. The sharp blade pierced his skin. Helpless, he stopped. Laurana smiled sadly.

"You see, Tanis? I'm not the love-sick child you knew. I'm not my father's daughter, living in my father's court. I'm not even the Golden General. I am Laurana. And I will live or die on my own without your help."

"Laurana, listen to me!" Tanis pleaded, taking another step toward her, reaching up to thrust aside the sword blade that cut into his skin.

He saw Laurana's lips press together tightly, her green eyes glinted. Then, sighing, she slowly lowered the the sword blade to his armor-plated chest. Tanis smiled. Laurana shrugged and, with a swift thrust, shoved him backward off the platform.

Arms flailing wildly in the air, the half-elf tumbled to the floor below. As he fell, he saw Laurana—sword in hand—jump off after him, landing lightly on her feet.

He hit the floor heavily, knocking the breath from his body. The Crown of Power rolled from his head with a clatter and went skittering across the polished granite floor. Above him, he could hear Kitiara shriek in rage.

"Laurana!" He gasped without breath to shout, looking for her frantically. He saw a flash of silver. . . .

"The Crown! Bring me the Crown!" Kitiara's voice dinned in his ears.

But she was not the only one shouting. All around the Hall of Audience, the Highlords were on their feet, ordering their troops forward. The dragons sprang into the air. The Dark Queen's five-headed body filled the Hall with shadow, exulting in this test of strength that would provide her with the strongest commanders—the survivors.

Clawed draconian feet, booted goblin feet, steel-shod human feet trampled over Tanis. Struggling to stand, fighting desperately to keep from being crushed, he tried to follow that silver flash. He saw it once, then it was gone, lost in the melee. A twisted face appeared in front of him, dark eyes flashed. A spear butt smashed into his side.

Groaning, Tanis collapsed to the floor as chaos erupted in the Hall of Audience.

11

"Jasla calls—"

aistlin! It was a thought, not spoken. Caramon tried to talk, but no sound came from his throat.

"Yes, my brother," said Raistlin, answering his brother's thoughts, as usual. "It is I—the last guardian—the one you must pass to reach your goal, the one Her Dark Majesty commanded be present if the trumpets should sound." Raistlin smiled derisively. "And I might have known it would be you who foolishly tripped my spelltrap. . . ."

"Raist," Caramon began and choked.

For a moment he could not speak. Worn out from fear and pain and loss of blood, shivering in the cold water, Caramon found this almost too much to bear. It would be easier to let the dark waters close over his head, let the sharp teeth of the young dragons

tear his flesh. The pain could not be nearly so bad. Then he felt Berem stir beside him. The man was staring at Raistlin vaguely, not understanding. He tugged on Caramon's arm.

"Jasla calls. We must go."

With a sob, Caramon tore his arm away from the man's grasp. Berem glared at him angrily, then turned and started ahead on his own.

"No, my friend, no one's going anywhere."

Raistlin raised his thin hand and Berem came to a sudden, staggering stop. The Everman lifted his gaze to the gleaming golden eyes of the mage, standing above him on a rock ledge. Whimpering, wringing his hands, Berem gazed ahead longingly at the jeweled column. But he could not move. A great and terrible force stood blocking his path, as surely as the mage stood upon the rock.

Caramon blinked back sudden tears. Feeling his brother's power, he fought against despair. There was nothing he could do . . . except try and kill Raistlin. His soul shriveled in horror. No, he would die himself first!

Suddenly Caramon raised his head. So be it. If I must die, I'll die fighting—as I had always intended.

Even if it means dying by my own brother's hand.

Slowly Caramon's gaze met that of his twin.

"You wear the Black Robes now?" he asked through parched lips. "I can't see . . . in this light. . . ."

"Yes, my brother," Raistlin replied, raising the Staff of Magius to let the silver light shine upon him. Robes of softest velvet fell from his thin shoulders, shimmering black beneath the light, seeming darker than the eternal night that surrounded them.

Shivering as he thought of what he must do, Caramon continued, "And your voice, it's stronger, different. Like you . . . and yet not like you . . ."

"That is a long story,† Caramon," Raistlin replied. "In time, you may come to hear it. But now you are in a very bad situation, my brother. The draconian guards are coming. Their orders are to capture the Everman and take him before the Dark Queen. That will be the end of him. He is not immortal, I assure you. She has spells that will unravel his existence, leaving him little more than thin

In fact, it's a trilogy, called DRAGONLANCE *Legends*

threads of flesh and soul, wafting away on the winds of the storm. Then she will devour his sister and—at last—the Dark Queen will be free to enter Krynn in her full power and majesty. She will rule the world and all the planes of heaven and the Abyss. Nothing will stop her."

"I don't understand—"

"No, of course not, dear brother," Raistlin said, with a touch of the old irritation and sarcasm. "You stand next to the Everman, the one being in all of Krynn who can end this war and drive the Queen of Darkness back to her shadowy realm. And you do not understand."

Moving nearer the edge of the rock ledge upon which he stood, Raistlin bent down, leaning on his staff. He beckoned his brother near. Caramon trembled, unable to move, fearing Raistlin might cast a spell upon him. But his brother only regarded him intently.

"The Everman has only to take a few more steps, my brother, and he will be reunited with the sister who has endured unspeakable agonies during these long years of waiting for his return to free her from her self-imposed torment."

"And what will happen then?" Caramon faltered, his brother's eyes holding him fast with a simple power greater than any magic spell.

The golden, hourglass eyes narrowed, Raistlin's voice grew soft. No longer forced to whisper, the mage yet found whispering more compelling.

"The wedge will be removed, my dear brother, and the door will slam shut. The Dark Queen will be left howling in rage in the depths of the Abyss." Raistlin lifted his gaze and made a gesture with his pale, slender hand. "This . . . the Temple of Istar reborn, perverted by evil . . . will fall."

Caramon gasped, then his expression hardened into a scowl.

"No, I am not lying." Raistlin answered his brother's thoughts. "Not that I can't lie when it suits my purposes. But you will find, dear brother, that we are close enough still so that I cannot lie to you. And, in any case, I have no need to lie—it suits my purpose that you know the truth."

Caramon's mind floundered. He didn't understand any of this. But he didn't have time to dwell on it. Behind him, echoing back down the tunnel, he could hear the sound of draconian guards on the stairs. His expression grew calm, his face set in firm resolve.

"Then you know what I must do, Raist," he said. "You may be powerful, but you still have to concentrate to work your magic. And if you work it against me, Berem will be free of your power. You can't kill him"—Caramon hoped devoutly Berem was listening and would act when it was time—"only your Dark Queen can do that, I suppose. So that leaves—"

"You, my dear brother," Raistlin said softly. "Yes, I can kill you. . . ."

Standing, he raised his hand and—before Caramon could yell or think or even fling up his arm—a ball of flame lit the darkness as if a sun had dropped into it. Bursting full upon Caramon, it smote him backward into the black water.

Burned and blinded by the brilliant light, stunned by the force of the impact, Caramon felt himself losing consciousness, sinking beneath the dark waters. Then sharp teeth bit into his arm, tearing away the flesh. The searing pain brought back his failing senses. Screaming in agony and terror, Caramon fought frantically to rise out of the deadly stream.

Shivering uncontrollably, he stood up. The young dragons, having tasted blood, attacked him, striking at his leather boots in frenzied frustration. Clutching his arm, Caramon looked over quickly at Berem and saw, to his dismay, that Berem hadn't moved an inch.

"Jasla! I am here! I will free you!" Berem screamed, but he stood, frozen in place by the spell. Frantically he beat upon the unseen wall that blocked his path. The man was nearly insane with grief.

Raistlin watched calmly as his brother stood before him, blood streaming from the slashed skin on his bare arms.

"I am powerful, Caramon," Raistlin said, staring coldly into the anguished eyes of his twin. "With Tanis's unwitting help, I was able to rid myself of the one man upon Krynn who could have bested me. Now I am the most powerful force for magic in this world. And I will be more powerful still . . . with the Dark Queen gone!"

Caramon looked at his brother dazedly, unable to comprehend. Behind him, he heard splashes in the water and the draconians shouting in triumph. Too stupified to move, he could not take his eyes from his brother. Only dimly, when he saw Raistlin raise his hand and make a gesture toward Berem, did Caramon begin to understand.

At that gesture, Berem was freed. The Everman cast one quick backward glance at Caramon and at the draconians plunging through the water, their curved swords flashing in the light of the staff. Finally he looked at Raistlin, standing upon the rock in his long black robes. Then—with a joyful cry that rang through the tunnel—Berem leaped forward toward the jeweled column.

"Jasla, I am coming!"

"Remember, my brother"—Raistlin's voice echoed in Caramon's mind—"this happens because *I* choose it to happen!"

Looking back, Caramon could see the draconians screaming in rage at the sight of their prey escaping. The dragons tore at his leather boots, his wounds hurt horribly, but Caramon didn't notice. Turning again, he watched Berem run toward the jeweled column as if he were watching a dream. Indeed, it seemed less real than a dream.

Perhaps it was his fevered imagination, but as the Everman neared the jeweled column, the green jewel in his chest seemed to glow with a light more brilliant than Raistlin's burst of flame. Within that light, the pale, shimmering form of a woman appeared inside the jeweled column. Dressed in a plain, leather tunic, she was pretty in a fragile, winsome way, very like Berem in the eyes that were too young for her thin face.

Then, just as he neared her, Berem came to a stop in the water. For an instant nothing moved. The draconians stood still, swords clutched in their clawed hands. Dimly, not understanding, they began to realize that somehow their fate hung in the balance, that everything turned upon this man.

Caramon no longer felt the chill of the air or the water or the pain of his wounds. He no longer felt fear, despair, or hope. Tears welled up in his eyes, there was a painful burning sensation in his throat. Berem faced his sister, the sister he had murdered,

the sister who had sacrificed herself so that he—and the world—might have hope. By the light of Raistlin's staff, Caramon saw the man's pale, grief-ravaged face twist in anguish.

"Jasla," he whispered, spreading his arms, "can you forgive me?"

There was no sound except the hushed swirl of the water around them, the steady dripping of moisture from the rocks, as it had fallen from time immemorial.

"My brother, between us, there is nothing to forgive." The image of Jasla spread her arms wide in welcome, her winsome face filled with peace and love.

With an incoherent cry of pain and joy, Berem flung himself into his sister's arms.

Caramon blinked and gasped. The image vanished. Horrified, he saw the Everman hurl his body upon the jeweled stone column with such force that his flesh was impaled on the sharp edges of the jagged rock. His last scream was a terrible one, terrible—yet triumphant.

Berem's body shook convulsively. Dark blood poured over the jewels, quenching their light.

"Berem, you've failed. It was nothing! A lie," Yelling hoarsely, Caramon plunged toward the dying man, knowing that Berem wouldn't die. This was all crazy! He would,

Caramon stopped.

The rocks around him shuddered. The ground shook beneath his feet. The black water ceased its swift flow and was suddenly sluggish, uncertain, sloshing against the rocks. Behind him, he heard the draconians shouting in alarm.

Caramon stared at Berem. The body lay crushed upon the rocks. It stirred slightly, as if breathing a final sigh. Then it did not move. For an instant two pale figures shimmered inside the jeweled column. Then they were gone.

The Everman was dead.

Tanis lifted his head from the floor of the Hall to see a hobgoblin, spear raised, about to plunge it into his body. Rolling quickly, he grabbed the creature's booted foot and yanked. The hobgoblin crashed to the floor where another hobgoblin, this one dressed

in a different colored uniform, smashed its head open with a mace.

Hurriedly Tanis rose to his feet. He had to get out of here! He had to find Laurana. A draconian rushed at him. He thrust his sword through the creature impatiently, remembering just in time to free it before the body turned to stone. Then he heard a voice shout his name. Turning he saw Lord Soth, standing beside Kitiara, surrounded by his skeletal warriors. Kit's eyes were fixed on Tanis with hatred as she pointed at him. Lord Soth made a gesture, sending his skeletal followers flowing from the snake-headed platform like a wave of death, destroying everything within their path.

Tanis turned to flee but found himself entangled in the mob. Frantically he fought, aware of the chill force behind him. Panic flooded his mind, nearly depriving him of his senses.

And then, there was a sharp cracking sound. The floor trembled beneath his feet. The fighting around him stopped abruptly as everyone concentrated on standing upright. Tanis looked around uncertainly, wondering what was happening.

A huge chunk of mosaic-covered stone tumbled from the ceiling, falling into a mass of draconians, who scrambled to get out of the way. The stone was followed by another, and yet another. Torches fell from the walls, candles dropped down and were extinguished in their own wax. The rumbling of the ground grew stronger. Half-turning, Tanis saw that even the skeletal warriors had halted, flaming eyes seeking those of their leader in fear and questioning.

The floor suddenly canted away from beneath his feet. Grabbing hold of a column for support, Tanis stared about in wonder. And then darkness fell upon him like a crushing weight.

He has betrayed me!

The Dark Queen's anger beat in Tanis's mind, the rage and fear so strong that it nearly split his skull. Crying aloud in pain, he grasped his head. The darkness increased as Takhisis—seeing her danger—sought desperately to keep the door to the world ajar. Her vast darkness quenched the light of every flame. Wings of night filled the Hall with blackness.

All around Tanis, draconian soldiers stumbled and staggered in the impenetrable darkness. The

voices of their officers raised to try and quell the confusion, to stem the rising panic they sensed spreading among their troops as they felt the force of their Queen withdrawn. Tanis heard Kitiara's voice ring out shrilly in anger, then it was cut off abruptly.

A horrible, rending crash followed by screams of agony gave Tanis his first indication that the entire building seemed likely to fall in on top of them.

"Laurana!" Tanis screamed. Trying desperately to stand, he staggered forward blindly, only to be hurled to the stone floor by milling draconians. Steel clashed. Somewhere he heard Kitiara's voice again, rallying her troops.

Fighting despair, Tanis stumbled to his feet again. Pain seared his arm. Furious, he thrust aside the sword blow aimed at him in the darkness, kicking with all his strength at the creature attacking him.

Then a rending, splitting sound quelled the battle. For one breathless instant, everyone in the Temple looked upward into the dense darkness. Voices hushed in awe. Takhisis, Queen of Darkness, hung over them in her living form upon this plane. Her gigantic body shimmered in a myriad colors. So many, so blinding, so confusing, the senses could not comprehend her awful majesty and blotted the colors from the minds of mortals—Many Colors and None—so Takhisis seemed. The five heads each opened wide their gaping mouths, fire burned in the multitude of eyes, as if each were intent upon devouring the world.

All is lost, Tanis thought in despair. This is the moment of her ultimate victory. We have failed.

The five heads reared up in triumph. . . . The domed ceiling split apart.

The Temple of Istar began to twist and writhe, rebuilding, reforming, returning to the original shape it had known before darkness perverted it.

Within the Hall itself, the darkness wavered and then was shattered by the silver beams of Solinari, called by the dwarves, Night Candle.

12

The debt repaid.

"And now, my brother, farewell."

Raistlin drew forth a small round globe from the folds of his black robes. The dragon orb.

Caramon felt his strength seep from him. Placing his hand upon the bandage, he found it soaked, sticky with blood. His head swam, the light from his brother's staff wavered before his eyes. Far away, as if in a dream, he heard the draconians shake loose from their terror and start toward him. The ground shook beneath his feet, or perhaps it was his legs trembling.

"Kill me, Raistlin." Caramon looked at his brother with eyes that had lost all expression.

Raistlin paused, his golden eyes narrowed.

"Don't leave me to die at their hands," Caramon said calmly, asking a simple favor. "End it for me now, quickly. You owe me that much—"

The golden eyes flared.

"Owe you!" Raistlin sucked in a hissing breath. *"Owe you!"* he repeated in a strangled voice, his face pale in the staff's magical light. Furious, he turned and extended his hand toward the draconians. Lightning streaked from his fingertips, striking the creatures in the chest. Shrieking in pain and astonishment, they fell into the water that quickly became foaming and green with blood as the baby dragons cannibalized their cousins.

Caramon watched dully, too weak and sick to care. He could hear more swords rattling, more voices yelling. He slumped forward, his feet lost their footing, the dark waters surged over him. . . .

And then he was on solid ground. Blinking, he looked up. He was sitting on the rock beside his brother. Raistlin knelt beside him, the staff in his hand.

"Raist!" Caramon breathed, tears coming to his eyes. Reaching out a shaking hand, he touched his brother's arm, feeling the velvet softness of the black robes.

Coldly, Raistlin snatched his arm away. "Know this, Caramon," he said, and his voice was as chill as the dark waters around them, "I will save your life this once, and then the slate is clean. I owe you nothing more."

Caramon swallowed. "Raist," he said softly, "I—I didn't mean—"

Raistlin ignored him. "Can you stand?" he asked harshly.

"I—I think so," Caramon said, hesitantly. "Can't, can't you just use that, that thing, to get us out of here?" He gestured at the dragon orb.

"I could, but you wouldn't particularly enjoy the journey, my brother. Besides, have you forgotten those who came with you?"

"Tika! Tas!" Caramon gasped. Gripping the wet rocks, he pulled himself to his feet. "And Tanis! What about—"

"Tanis is on his own. I have repaid my debt to him ten-fold," Raistlin said. "But perhaps I can discharge my debts to others."

Shouts and yells sounded at the end of the passage, a dark mass of troops surged into the dark water, obeying the final commands of their Queen.

Wearily Caramon put his hand on the hilt of his sword, but a touch of his brother's cold, bony fingers stopped him.

"No, Caramon," Raistlin whispered. His thin lips parted in a grim smile. "I don't need you now. I won't need you anymore . . . ever. Watch!"

Instantly, the underground cavern's darkness was lit to daylike brilliance with the fiery power of Raistlin's magic. Caramon, sword in hand, could only stand beside his black-robed brother and watch in awe as foe after foe fell to Raistlin's spells. Lightning crackled from his fingertips, flame flared from his hands, phantasms appeared—so terrifyingly real to those looking at them that they could kill by fear alone.

Goblins fell screaming, pierced by the lances of a legion of knights, who filled the cavern with their war chants at Raistlin's bidding, then disappeared at his command. The baby dragons fled in terror back to the dark and secret places of their hatching, draconians withered black in the flames. Dark clerics, who swarmed down the stairs at their Queen's last bidding, were impaled upon a flight of shimmering spears, their last prayers changed to wailing curses of agony.

Finally came the Black Robes, the eldest of the Order, to destroy this young upstart. But they found to their dismay that—old as they were—Raistlin was in some mysterious way older still. His power was phenomenal, they knew within an instant that he could not be defeated. The air was filled with the sounds of chanting and, one by one, they disappeared as swiftly as they had come, many bowing to Raistlin in profound respect as they departed upon the wings of wish spells.

And then it was silent, the only sound the sluggish lapping of water. The Staff of Magius† cast its crystal light. Every few seconds a tremor shook the Temple, causing Caramon to glance above them in alarm. The battle had apparently lasted only moments, although it seemed to Caramon's fevered mind that he and his brother had been in this horrible place all their lives.

The Staff was given to Raistlin Majere at the completion of his Test. The question is open on whether it portended the power that he would attain or the tragedy that would befall him.

When the last mage melted into the blackness, Raistlin turned to face his brother.

"You see, Caramon?" he said coldly.

Wordlessly, the big warrior nodded, his eyes wide.

The ground shook around them, the water in the stream sloshed up on the rocks. At the cavern's end, the jeweled column shivered, then split. Rivulets of rock dust trickled down onto Caramon's upturned face as he stared at the crumbling ceiling.

"What does it mean? What's happening?" he asked in alarm.

"It means the end," Raistlin stated. Folding his black robes around him, he glanced at Caramon in irritation. "We must leave this place. Are you strong enough?"

"Yeah, give me a moment," Caramon grunted. Pushing himself away from the rocks, he took a step forward, then staggered, nearly falling.

"I'm weaker than I thought," he mumbled, clutching his side in pain. "Just let me . . . catch my breath." Straightening, his lips pale, sweat trickling down his face, Caramon took another step forward.

Smiling grimly, Raistlin watched his brother stumble toward him. Then the mage held out his arm.

"Lean on me, my brother," he said softly.

The vast vaulted ceiling of the Hall of Audience split wide. Huge blocks of stone crashed down into the Hall, crushing everything that lived beneath them. Instantly the chaos in the Hall degenerated into terror-stricken panic. Ignoring the stern commands of their leaders, who reinforced these commands with whips and sword thrusts, the draconians fought to escape the destruction of the Temple, brutally slaughtering anyone—including their own comrades—who got in their way. Occasionally some extremely powerful Dragon Highlord would manage to keep his bodyguard under control and escape. But several fell, cut down by their own troops, crushed by falling rock, or trampled to death.

Tanis fought his way through the chaos and suddenly saw what he had prayed the gods to find, a head of golden hair that gleamed in Solinari's light like a candle flame.

"Laurana!" he cried, though he knew he could not be heard in the tumult. Frantically he slashed his way toward her. A flying splinter of rock tore

into one cheek. Tanis felt warm blood flow down his neck, but the blood, the pain had no reality and he soon forgot about it as he clubbed and stabbed and kicked the milling draconians in his struggle to reach her. Time and again, he drew near her, only to be carried away by a surge in the crowd.

She was standing near the door to one of the antechambers, fighting draconians, wielding Kitiara's sword with the skill gained in long months of war. He almost reached her as—her enemies defeated—she stood alone for a moment.

"Laurana, wait!" he shouted above the chaos.

She heard him. Looking over at him, across the moonlit room, he saw her eyes calm, her gaze unwavering.

"Farewell, Tanis," Laurana called to him in elven. "I owe you my life, but not my soul."

With that, she turned and left him, stepping through the doorway of the antechamber, vanishing into the darkness beyond.

A piece of the Temple ceiling crashed to the stone floor, showering Tanis with debris. For a moment, he stood wearily, staring after her. Blood dripped into one eye. Absently he wiped it away, then, suddenly, he began to laugh. He laughed until tears mingled with the blood. Then he pulled himself together and, gripping his blood-stained sword, disappeared into the darkness after her.

"This is the corridor they went down, Raist—Raistlin." Caramon stumbled over his brother's name. Somehow, the old nickname no longer seemed to suit this black-robed, silent figure.

They stood beside the jailor's desk, near the body of the hobgoblin. Around them, the walls were acting crazily, shifting, crumbling, twisting, rebuilding. The sight filled Caramon with vague horror, like a nightmare he could not remember. So he kept his eyes fixed firmly on his brother, his hand clutched Raistlin's thin arm thankfully. This, at least was flesh and blood, reality in the midst of a terrifying dream.

"Do you know where it leads?" Caramon asked, peering down the eastern corridor.

"Yes," Raistlin replied without expression.

Caramon felt fear clutch at him. "You know . . . something's happened to them—"

"They were fools," Raistlin said bitterly. "The dream warned them"—he glanced at his brother—"as it warned others. Still, I may be in time, but we must hurry. Listen!"

Caramon glanced up the stairwell. Above him he could hear the sounds of clawed feet racing to stop the escape of the hundreds of prisoners set free by the collapse of the dungeons. Caramon put his hand on his sword.

"Stop it," Raistlin snapped. "Think a moment! You're dressed in armor still. They're not interested in us. The Dark Queen is gone. They obey her no longer. They are only after booty for themselves. Keep beside me. Walk steadily, with purpose."

Drawing a deep breath, Caramon did as he was told. He had regained some of his strength and was able to walk without his brother's help now. Ignoring the draconians—who took one look at them, then surged past—the two brothers made their way down the corridor. Here the walls still changed their shapes, the ceiling shook, and the floors heaved. Behind them they could hear ghastly yells as the prisoners fought for their freedom.

"At least no one will be guarding this door," Raistlin reflected, pointing ahead.

"What do you mean?" Caramon asked, halting and staring at his brother in alarm.

"It's trapped," Raistlin whispered. "Remember the dream?"

Turning deathly pale, Caramon dashed down the corridor toward the door. Shaking his hooded head, Raistlin followed slowly after. Rounding the corner, he found his brother crouching beside two bodies on the floor.

"Tika!" Caramon moaned. Brushing back the red curls from the still, white face, he felt for the lifebeat in her neck. His eyes closed a moment in thankfulness, then he reached out to touch the kender. "And Tas . . . No!"

Hearing his name, the kender's eyes opened slowly, as if the lids were too heavy for him to lift.

"Caramon . . ." Tas said in a broken whisper. "I'm sorry. . . ."

"Tas!" Caramon gently gathered the small, feverish body into his big arms. Holding him close, he rocked him back and forth. "Shh, Tas, don't talk."

The kender's body twitched in convulsions. Glancing around in heartbroken sorrow, Caramon saw Tasslehoff's pouches lying on the floor, their contents scattered like toys in a child's playroom. Tears filled Caramon's eyes.

"I tried to save her . . . " Tas whispered, shuddering with pain, "but I couldn't. . . ."

"You saved her, Tas!" Caramon said, choking. "She's not dead. Just hurt. She'll be fine."

"Really?" Tas's eyes, burning with fever, brightened with a calmer light, then dimmed. "I'm—I'm afraid I'm not fine, Caramon. But—but it's all right, really. I—I'm going to see Flint. He's waiting for me. He shouldn't be out there, by himself. I don't know how . . . he could have left without me anyway. . . ."

"What's the matter with him?" Caramon asked his brother as Raistlin bent swiftly over the kender, whose voice had trailed off into incoherent babbling.

"Poison," said Raistlin, his eyes glancing at the golden needle shining in the torchlight. Reaching out, Raistlin gently pushed on the door. The lock gave and the door turned on its hinges, opening a crack.

Outside, they could hear shrieks and cries as the soldiers and slaves of Neraka fled the dying Temple. The skies above resounded with the roars of dragons. The Highlords battled among themselves to see who would come out on top in this new world. Listening, Raistlin smiled to himself.

His thoughts were interrupted by a hand clutching his arm.

"Can you help him?" Caramon demanded.

Raistlin flicked a glance at the dying kender. "He is very far gone," the mage said coldly. "It will sap some of my strength, and we are not out of this yet, my brother."

"But you can save him?" Caramon persisted. "Are you powerful enough?"

"Of course," Raistlin replied, shrugging.

Tika stirred and sat up, clutching her aching head. "Caramon!" she cried happily, then her gaze fell upon Tas. "Oh, no . . ." she whispered. Forgetting her pain, she laid her blood-stained hand upon the kender's forehead. The kender's eyes flared open at her touch, but he did not recognize her. He cried out in agony.

Over his cries, they could hear the sound of clawed feet, running down the corridor.

Raistlin looked at his brother. He saw him holding Tas in the big hands that could be so gentle.

Thus he has held me, Raistlin thought. His eyes went to the kender. Vivid memories of their younger days, of carefree adventuring with Flint . . . now dead. Sturm, dead. Days of warm sunshine, of the green budding leaves on the vallenwoods of Solace . . . Nights in the Inn of the Last Home . . . now blacked and crumbling, the vallenwoods burned and destroyed.

"This is my final debt," Raistlin said. "Paid in full." Ignoring the look of thankfulness that flooded Caramon's face, he instructed, "Lay him down. You must deal with the draconians. This spell will take all my concentration. Do not allow them to interrupt me."

Gently Caramon laid Tas down on the floor in front of Raistlin. The kender's eyes had fixed in his head, his body was stiffening in its convulsive struggles. His breath rattled in his throat.

"Remember, my brother," Raistlin said coldly as he reached into one of the many secret pockets in his black robes, "you are dressed as a dragonarmy officer. Be subtle, if possible."

"Right." Caramon gave Tas a final glance, then drew a deep breath. "Tika," he said, "stay still. Pretend you're unconscious—"

Tika nodded and lay back down, obediently closing her eyes. Raistlin heard Caramon clanking down the corridor, he heard his brother's loud, booming voice, then the mage forgot his brother, forgot the approaching draconians, forgot everything as he concentrated upon his spell.

Removing a luminous white pearl from an inner pocket, Raistlin held it firmly in one hand while he took out a gray-green leaf from another. Prizing the kender's clenched jaws open, Raistlin placed the leaf beneath Tasslehoff's swollen tongue. The mage studied the pearl for a moment, calling to mind the complex words of the spell, reciting them to himself mentally until he was certain he had them in their proper order and knew the correct pronounciation of each. He would have one chance, and one chance only. If he failed, not only would the kender die, but he might very well die himself.

Placing the pearl upon his own chest, over his heart, Raistlin closed his eyes and began to repeat

the words of the spell, chanting the lines six times, making the proper changes in inflection each time. With a thrill of ecstasy, he felt the magic flow through his body, drawing out a part of his own life force, capturing it within the pearl.

The first part of the spell complete, Raistlin held the pearl poised above the kender's heart. Closing his eyes once more, he recited the complex spell again, this time backward. Slowly he crushed the pearl in his hand, scattering the iridescent powder over Tasslehoff's rigid body. Raistlin came to an end. Wearily he opened his eyes and watched in triumph as the lines of pain faded from the kender's features, leaving them filled with peace.

Tas's eyes flew open.

"Raistlin! I—plooey!" Tas spit out the green leaf. "Yick! What kind of nasty thing was that? And how did it get into my mouth?" Tas sat up dizzily, then he saw his pouches. "Hey! Who's been messing with my stuff?" Glancing up at the mage accusingly, his eyes opened wide. "Raistlin! You have on Black Robes! How wonderful! Can I touch them? Oh, all right. You needn't glare at me like that. It's just that they look so soft. Say, does this mean you're truly bad now? Can you do something evil for me, so I can watch? I know! I saw a wizard summon a demon once. Could you do that? Just a small demon? You could send him right back. No?" Tas sighed in disappointment. "Well—hey, Caramon, what are those draconians doing with you? And what's the matter with Tika? Oh, Caramon, I—"

"Shut up!" Caramon roared. Scowling ferociously at the kender, he pointed at Tas and Tika. "The mage and I were bringing these prisoners to our Highlord when they turned on us. They're valuable slaves, the girl especially. And the kender is a clever thief. We don't want to lose them. They'll fetch a high price in the market in Sanction. Since the Dark Queen's gone, it's every man for himself, eh?"

Caramon nudged one of the draconians in the ribs. The creature snarled in agreement, its black reptilian eyes fastened greedily on Tika.

"Thief!" shouted Tas indignantly, his shrill voice ringing through the corridor. "I'm—" He gulped, suddenly falling silent as a supposedly comatose Tika gave him a swift poke in the ribs.

"I'll help the girl," Caramon said, glaring at the leering draconian. "You keep an eye on the kender and, you over there, help the mage. His spellcasting has left him weak."

Bowing with respect before Raistlin, one of the draconians helped him to his feet. "You two"—Caramon was marshaling the rest of his troops—"go before us and see that we don't have any trouble reaching the edge of town. Maybe you can come with us to Sanction—" Caramon continued, lifting Tika to her feet. Shaking her head, she pretended to regain consciousness.

The draconians grinned in agreement as one of them grabbed hold of Tas by the collar and shoved him toward the door.

"But my things!" wailed Tas, twisting around.

"Keep moving!" Caramon growled.

"Oh, well," the kender sighed, his eyes lingering fondly on his precious possessions lying scattered on the blood-stained floor. "This probably isn't the end of my adventuring. And—after all—empty pockets hold more, as my mother used to say."

Stumbling along behind the two draconians, Tas looked up into the starry heavens. "I'm sorry, Flint," he said softly. "Just wait for me a little longer."

13

Kitiara.

As Tanis entered the antechamber, the change was so startling that for a minute it was almost incomprehensible. One moment he had been fighting to stand on his feet in the midst of a mob, the next he was in a cool dark room, similar to the one he and Kitiara and her troops had waited in before entering the Hall of Audience.

I've been silent for a while now—mostly just enjoying the end of the book. Chapter 13 is the culmination of all three Chronicles books—when everything that has gone before comes to its moment of decision. More than any other place, this chapter tells us why we have come on this amazing journey.—TRH

Glancing around swiftly, he saw he was alone. Although every instinct urged him to rush out of this room in his frantic search, Tanis forced himself to stop, catch his breath, and wipe away the blood gumming his eye shut. He tried to remember what he had seen of the entry into the Temple. The antechambers that formed a circle around the main Hall of Audience were themselves connected to the front part of the temple by a series of winding corridors. Once, long ago in Istar, these corridors must have been designed in some sort of logical order. But the distortion of the Temple had twisted them into a meaningless maze. Corridors ended abruptly when he expected them to continue, while those that led nowhere seemingly went on forever.

The ground rocked beneath his feet as dust drifted down from the ceiling. A painting fell from the wall with a crash. Tanis had no idea of where Laurana might be found. He had seen her come in here, that was all.

She had been imprisoned in the Temple, but that was below ground. He wondered if she had been at all cognizant of her surroundings when they brought her in, if she had any idea how to get out. And then Tanis realized that he himself had only a vague idea of where he was. Finding a torch still burning, he grabbed it and flashed it about the room. A tapestry-covered door swung open, hanging on a broken hinge. Peering through it, he saw it led into a dimly lit corridor.

Tanis caught his breath. He knew, now, how to find her!

A breath of air stirred in the hallway, fresh air—pungent with the odors of spring, cool with the blessed peace of night—touched his left cheek. Laurana must have felt that breath, she would guess that it must lead out of the Temple. Quickly Tanis ran down the hallway, ignoring the pain in his head, forcing his weary muscles to respond to his commands.

A group of draconians appeared suddenly in front of him, coming from another room. Remembering he still wore the dragonarmy uniform, Tanis stopped them.

"The elfwoman!" he shouted. "She must not escape. Have you seen her?"

This group hadn't, apparently, by the tone of the hurried snarls. Nor had the next group Tanis encountered. But two draconians wandering the halls in search of loot had seen her, so they said. They pointed vaguely in the direction Tanis was already heading. His spirits rose.

By now, the fighting within the Hall had ended. The Dragon Highlords who survived had made good their escapes and were now among their own

forces stationed outside the Temple walls. Some fought. Some retreated, waiting to see who came out on top. Two questions were on everyone's mind. The first—would the dragons remain in the world or would they vanish with their Queen as they had following the Second Dragon War?

And, second—if the dragons remained, who would be their master?

Tanis found himself pondering these questions confusedly as he ran through the halls, sometimes taking wrong turns and cursing bitterly as he confronted a solid wall and was forced to retrace his steps to where he could once again feel the air upon his face.

But eventually he grew too tired to ponder anything. Exhaustion and pain were taking their toll. His legs grew heavy, it was an effort to take a step. His head throbbed, the cut over his eye began to bleed again. The ground shook continually beneath his feet. Statues toppled from their bases, stones fell from the ceiling, showering him with clouds of dust.

He began to lose hope. Even though he was certain he was traveling in the only direction she could possibly have taken, the few draconians he passed now had not seen her. What could have happened? Was she— No, he wouldn't think of that. He kept going, conscious either of the fragrant breath of air on his face or of smoke billowing past him.

The torches had started fires. The Temple was beginning to burn.

Then, while negotiating a narrow corridor and climbing over a pile of rubble, Tanis heard a sound. He stopped, holding his breath. Yes, there it was again—just ahead. Peering through the smoke and dust, he gripped his sword in his hand. The last group of draconians he had met were drunk and eager to kill. A lone human officer had seemed like fair game, until one of them remembered having seen Tanis with the Dark Lady. But the next time he might not be so lucky.

Before him, the corridor lay in ruins, part of the ceiling having caved in. It was intensely dark—the torch he held provided the only light—and Tanis wrestled with the need for light and the fear of being seen by it. Finally he decided to risk keeping it

burning. He would never find Laurana if he had to wander around this place in the darkness.

He would have to trust to his disguise once again.

"Who goes there?" he roared out in a harsh voice, shining his torchlight boldly into the ruined hallway.

He caught a glimpse of flashing armor and a figure running, but it ran away from him, not toward him. Odd for a draconian . . . his weary brain seemed to be stumbling along about three paces behind him. He could see the figure plainly now, lithe and slender and running much too quickly. . . .

"Laurana!" he shouted, then in elven, *"Quisalas!"*

Cursing the broken columns and marble blocks in his path, Tanis stumbled and ran and stumbled and fell and forced his aching body to obey him until he caught up with her. Grasping her by the arm, he dragged her to a stop, then could only hold onto her tightly as he slumped against a wall.

Each breath he took was fiery pain. He was so dizzy he thought for a moment he might pass out. But he grasped her with a deathlike grip, holding her with his eyes as well as his hand.

Now he knew why the draconians hadn't seen her. She had stripped off the silver armor, covering it with draconian armor she had taken from a dead warrior. For a moment she could only stare at Tanis. She had not recognized him at first, and had nearly run him through with her sword. The only thing that had stopped her was the elven word, *quisalas,* beloved. That, and the intense look of anguish and suffering on his pale face.

"Laurana," Tanis gasped in a voice as shattered as Raistlin's had once been, "don't leave me. Wait . . . listen to me, please!"

With a twist of her arm, Laurana broke free of his grip. But she did not leave him. She started to speak, but another shudder of the building silenced her. As dust and debris poured down around them, Tanis pulled Laurana close, shielding her. They clung to each other fearfully, and then it was over. But they were left in darkness. Tanis had dropped the torch.

"We've got to get out of here," he said, his voice shaking.

"Are you injured?" Laurana asked coldly, trying to free herself from his grasp once more. "If so, I can help you. If not, then I suggest we forego any further farewells. Whatever—"

"Laurana," Tanis said softly, breathing heavily, "I don't ask you to understand— *I* don't understand. I don't ask for forgiveness—I can't even forgive myself. I could tell you that I love you, that I have always loved you. But that wouldn't be true, for love must come from within one who loves himself,† and right now I can't bear to see my own reflection. All I can tell you, Laurana, is that—"

Tanis's comment, on the face of it, seems like a strange one: He appears to be saying that only narcissists are capable of love. That is not what he means here at all. His point is that only people who feel worthy of love themselves are truly capable of loving another. Throughout the story, Tanis has indulged in tremendous bouts of self-recrimination and doubt. There is no more time left for self-pity. He must now face down his own demons if he is ever to have a chance at loving and being loved by Laurana.—TRH

"Shhh!" Laurana whispered, putting her hand over Tanis's mouth. "I heard something."

For long moments they stood, pressed together in the darkness, listening. At first they could hear nothing but the sound of their own breathing. They could see nothing, not even each other, as close as they were. Then torchlight flared, blinding them, and a voice spoke.

"Tell Laurana what, Tanis?" said Kitiara in a pleasant voice. "Go on."

A naked sword gleamed in her hand. Wet blood— both red and green—glistened on the blade. Her face was white with stone dust, a trickle of blood ran down her chin from a cut on her lip. Her eyes were shadowed with weariness, but her smile was still as charming as ever. Sheathing her bloody sword, she wiped her hands upon her tattered cloak, then ran them absently through her curly hair.

Tanis's eyes closed in exhaustion. His face seemed to age; he looked very human. Pain and exhaustion, grief and guilt would forever leave their mark on the eternal elven youthfulness. He could feel Laurana stiffen, her hand move to her sword.†

At last the triangle is complete: all three elements of the personal story are brought together for the first time. We have seen Laurana with Tanis, Tanis with Kitiara, Kitiara with Laurana, but this is the first moment—at the apex of the story—when all three of them are together in the same room at the same time. The personal story has finally reached its climax.—TRH

"Let her go, Kitiara," Tanis said quietly, gripping Laurana firmly. "Keep your promise and I'll keep mine. Let me take her outside the walls. Then I'll come back—"

"I really believe you would," Kitiara remarked, staring at him in amused wonder. "Hasn't it occurred to you yet, Half-Elf, that I could kiss you and kill you without drawing a deep breath in between? No, I don't suppose it has. I might kill you right

now, in fact, simply because I know it would be the worst thing I could do to the elfwoman." She held the flaming torch near Laurana. "There—look at her face!" Kitiara sneered. "What a weak and debilitating thing love is!"†

Kitiara's motivations are entirely power-based. Love for love's sake is beyond her comprehension. Emotional attatchments, for her, are largely a means of controlling others. This springs from her "evil" nature—an embodiment of a kind of dependent love that is debilitating rather than strengthening. —TRH

Kitiara's hand tousled her hair again. Shrugging, she glanced around. "But I haven't time. Things are moving. Great things. The Dark Queen has fallen. Another will rise to take her place. What about it, Tanis? I have already begun to establish my authority over the other Dragon Highlords." Kitiara patted her sword hilt. "Mine will be a vast empire. We could rule toge—"

She broke off abruptly, her gaze shifting down the corridor from which she had just come. Although Tanis could neither see nor hear what had attracted her attention, he felt a bone-numbing chill spread through the hallway. Laurana gripped him suddenly, fear overwhelming her, and Tanis knew who approached even before he saw the orange eyes flicker above the ghostly armor.

"Lord Soth," murmured Kitiara. "Make your decision quickly, Tanis."

"My decision was made a long time ago, Kitiara,"† Tanis said calmly. Stepping in front of Laurana, he shielded her as best as he could with his own body. "Lord Soth will have to kill me to reach her, Kit. And even though I know my death will not stop him, or you, from killing her when I have fallen, with my last breath, I will pray to Paladine to protect her soul. The gods owe me one. Somehow I know that this, my final prayer, will be granted."

This is only partially true. I believe that until this moment in the story, he really had not fully made the decision between Laurana and Kitiara. —TRH

Behind him, Tanis felt Laurana lay her head against his back, he heard her sob softly and his heart eased, for there was not fear in her sob, but only love and compassion and grief for him.

Kitiara hesitated. They could see Lord Soth coming down the shattered corridor, his orange eyes flickering pinpoints of light in the darkness. Then she laid her blood-stained hand upon Tanis's arm. "Go!" she commanded harshly. "Run quickly, back down the corridor. At the end is a door in the wall. You can feel it. It will lead you down into the dungeons. From there you can escape."

Tanis stared at her uncomprehendingly for a moment.

"Run!" Kit snapped, giving him a shove.

Tanis cast a glance at Lord Soth.

"A trap!" whispered Laurana.

"No," Tanis said, his eyes going back to Kit. "Not this time. Farewell, Kitiara."

Kitiara's nails dug into his arm.

"Farewell, Half-Elven," she said in a soft, passionate voice, her eyes shining brightly in the torchlight. "Remember, I do this for love of you. Now go!"

Flinging her torch from her, Kitiara vanished into the darkness as completely as if she had been consumed by it.

Tanis blinked, blinded by the sudden blackness, and started to reach his hand out for her. Then he withdrew it. Turning, his hand found Laurana's hand. Together they stumbled through the debris, groping their way along the wall. The chill fear that flowed from the death knight numbed their blood. Glancing down the corridor, Tanis saw Lord Soth coming nearer and nearer, his eyes seeming to stare straight at them. Frantically Tanis felt the stone wall, his hands searching for the door. Then he felt the cold stone give way to wood. Grasping the iron handle, he turned it. The door opened at his touch. Pulling Laurana after him, the two plunged through the opening, the sudden flaring of torches lighting the stairs nearly as blinding as the darkness had been above.

Behind him, Tanis heard Kitiara's voice, hailing Lord Soth. He wondered what the death knight, having lost his prey, would do to her. The dream returned to him vividly. Once again he saw Laurana falling . . . Kitiara falling . . . and he stood helpless, unable to save either. Then the image vanished.

Laurana stood waiting for him on the stairway, the torchlight shining on her golden hair. Hurriedly he slammed the door shut and ran down the stairs after her.

"That is the elfwoman," said Lord Soth, his flaming eyes easily tracking the two as they ran from him like frightened mice. "And the half-elf."

"Yes," said Kitiara without interest. Drawing her sword from its scabbard, she began to wipe off the blood with the hem of her cloak.

"Shall I go after them?" Soth asked.

"No. We have more important matters to attend to now," Kitiara replied. Glancing up at him, she smiled her crooked smile. "The elfwoman would never be yours anyway, not even in death. The gods protect her."

Soth's flickering gaze turned to Kitiara. The pale lips curled in derision. "The half-elven man remains your master still."

"No, I think not," Kitiara replied. Turning, she looked after Tanis as the door shut behind him. "Sometimes, in the still watches of the night, when he lies in bed beside her, Tanis will find himself thinking of me. He will remember my last words, he will be touched by them. I have given them their happiness. And *she* must live with the knowledge that *I* will live always in Tanis's heart. What love they might find together, I have poisoned. My revenge upon them both is complete.† Now, have you brought what I sent you for?"

Kitiara has too high an opinion of herself and too low an opinion of Tanis. Tanis's devotion to Laurana, from this moment on, is one of singular fidelity. She may comfort herself with this lie, but it is a lie nevertheless.—TRH

"I have, Dark Lady," Lord Soth replied. With a spoken word of magic, he brought forth an object and held it out to her in his skeletal hand. Reverently, he set it at her feet.

Kitiara caught her breath, her eyes gleamed in the darkness nearly as bright as Lord Soth's. "Excellent! Return to Dargaard Keep. Gather the troops. We will take control of the flying citadel Ariakas sent to Kalaman. Then we will fall back, regroup, and wait."

The hideous visage of Lord Soth smiled as he gestured to the object that glittered in his fleshless hand. "This is now rightfully yours. Those who opposed you are either dead, as you commanded, or fled before I could reach them."

"Their doom is simply postponed," Kitiara said, sheathing her sword. "You have served me well, Lord Soth, and you will be rewarded. There will always be elfmaidens in this world, I suppose."

"Those you command to die shall die. Those you allow to live"—Soth's glance flickered to the door —"shall live. Remember this, of all who serve you, Dark Lady, I alone can offer you *undying* loyalty. This I do now, gladly. My warriors and I will return to Dargaard Keep as you ask. There we will await our summons."

Bowing to her, he took her hand in his skeletal grasp. "Farewell, Kitiara," he said, then paused. "How does it feel, my dear, to know that you have brought pleasure to the damned? You have made my dreary realm of death interesting. Would that I had known you as a living man!" The pallid visage smiled. "But, my time is eternal. Perhaps I will wait for one who can share my throne—"

Cold fingers caressed Kitiara's flesh. She shuddered convulsively, seeing unending, sleepless nights yawn chasmlike before her. So vivid and terrifying was the image that Kitiara's soul shriveled in fear as Lord Soth vanished into the darkness.

She was by herself in the darkness and for a moment she was terrified. The Temple shuddered around her. Kitiara shrank back against the wall, frightened and alone. So alone! Then her foot touched something on the floor of the Temple. Reaching down, her fingers closed around it thankfully. She lifted it in her hands.

This was reality, hard and solid, she thought, breathing in relief.†

Soth's touch, and his words, bring us back to one of the pillars of the DRAGONLANCE story: Evil Turns on Itself. For all purposes, the dragonarmies have self- destructed despite this transient victory for Kitiara.—TRH

No torchlight glittered on its golden surface or flared from its red-hued jewels. Kitiara did not need the flare of torches to admire what she held.

For long moments she stood in the crumbling hallway, her fingers running over the rough metal edges of the blood-stained Crown.

Tanis and Laurana ran down the spiral stone stairs to the dungeons below. Pausing beside the jailor's desk, Tanis glanced at the body of the hobgoblin.

Laurana stared at him. "Come on," she urged, pointing to the east. Seeing him hesitate, looking north, she shuddered. "You don't want to go down there! That is where they . . . took me—" She turned away quickly, her face growing pale as she heard cries and shouts coming from the prison cells.

A harried-looking draconian ran by. Probably a deserter, Tanis guessed, seeing the creature snarl and cringe at the sight of an officer's armor.

"I was looking for Caramon," Tanis muttered. "They must have brought him here."

"Caramon?" exclaimed Laurana in astonishment. "What—"

"He came with me," Tanis said. "So did Tika and Tas and . . . Flint, " He stopped, then shook his head. "Well, if they were here, they're gone now. Come on."

Laurana's face flushed. She glanced back up the stone stairs, then at Tanis again. "Tanis—" she began, faltering. He placed his hand over her mouth.

"There will be time to talk later. Now we must find our way out!"

As if to emphasize his words, another tremor shook the Temple. This one was sharper and stronger than the others, throwing Laurana up against a wall. Tanis's face, white with fatigue and pain, grew even paler as he fought to keep his footing.

A loud rumble and a shattering crash came from the northern corridor. All sound in the prison cells ceased abruptly as a great cloud of dust and dirt billowed out into the hallway.

Tanis and Laurana fled. Debris showered down around them as they ran east, stumbling over bodies and piles of jagged broken stone.

Another tremor rocked the Temple. They could not stand. Falling on hands and knees, they could do nothing but watch in terror as the corridor slowly shifted and moved, bending and twisting like a snake.

Crawling under a fallen beam, they huddled together, watching the floor and walls of the corridor leap and heave like waves upon the ocean. Above them, they could hear strange sounds, as of huge stones grinding together—not collapsing so much as shifting position. Then the tremor ceased. All was quiet.

Shakily they got to their feet and began running again, fear driving their aching bodies far beyond endurance. Every few minutes another tremor rocked the Temple's foundations. But as often as Tanis expected the roof to cave in upon their heads, it remained standing. So strange and terrifying were the inexplicable sounds above them that they both might have welcomed the collapse of the ceiling as a relief. "Tanis!" cried Laurana suddenly. "Air! Night air!"

Wearily, summoning the last of their strength, the two made their way through the winding corridor

until they came to a door swinging open on its hinges. There was a reddish blood stain on the floor and—"Tas's pouches!" Tanis murmured. Kneeling down, he sorted through the kender's treasures that lay scattered all over the floor. Then his heart sank. Grieving, he shook his head.

Laurana knelt beside him, her hand closed over his.

"At least he was here, Tanis. He got this far. Maybe he escaped."

"He would never have left his treasures," Tanis said. Sinking down on the shaking floor, the half-elf stared outside into Neraka. "Look," he said to Laurana harshly, pointing. "This is the end, just as it was the end for the kender. Look!" he demanded angrily, seeing her face settling into its stubborn calm, seeing her refusing to admit defeat.

Laurana looked.

The cool breeze on her face seemed a mockery to her now, for it brought only smells of smoke and blood and the anguished cries of the dying. Orange flames lit the sky where wheeling dragons fought and died as their Highlords sought to escape or strove for mastery. The night air blazed with the crackling of lightning bolts and burned with flame. Draconians roamed the streets, killing anything that moved, slaughtering each other in their frenzy.

"So evil turns upon itself," Laurana whispered, laying her head on Tanis's shoulder, watching the terrible spectacle in awe.

"What was that?" he asked wearily.

"Something Elistan used to say," she replied. The Temple shook around them.

"Elistan!" Tanis laughed bitterly. "Where are his gods now? Watching from their castles among the stars, enjoying the show? The Dark Queen is gone, the Temple destroyed. And here we are—trapped. We wouldn't live three minutes out there—"

Then his breath caught in his throat. Gently he pushed Laurana away from him as he leaned over, his hand searching through Tasslehoff's scattered treasures. Hurriedly he swept aside a shining piece of broken blue crystal, a splinter of vallenwood, an emerald, a small white chicken feather, a withered black rose, a dragon's tooth, and a piece of wood carved with dwarven skill to resemble the kender.

Among all of these was a golden object, sparkling in the flaming light of the fire and destruction outside.

Picking it up, Tanis's eyes filled with tears. He held it tightly in his hand, feeling the sharp edges bite into his flesh.

"What is it?" asked Laurana, not understanding, her voice choked with fear.

"Forgive me, Paladine," Tanis whispered. Drawing Laurana close beside him, he held his hand out, opening his palm.

There in his hand lay a finely carved, delicate ring, made of golden, clinging ivy leaves. And wrapped around the ring, still bound in his magical sleep, was a golden dragon.

14

The End. For Good or for Evil.

"Well, we're outside the city gates," Caramon muttered to his twin in a low voice, his eyes on the draconians who were looking at him expectantly. "You stay with Tika and Tas. I'm going back to find Tanis. I'll take this lot with me—"

"No, my brother," Raistlin said softly, his golden eyes glittering in Lunitari's red light. "You cannot help Tanis. His fate is in his own hands."† The mage glanced up at the flaming, dragon-filled skies. "You are still in danger yourself, as are those dependent upon you."

Raistlin's words merely echo a fact that has been with Tanis all along—that his fate was in his own hands. In some ways, however, Raistlin is also saying this to Caramon, and telling his brother that his fate, too, is his own—separate from his twin. —TRH

Tika stood wearily beside Caramon, her face drawn with pain. And though Tasslehoff grinned as cheerfully as ever, his face was pale and there was an expression of wistful sorrow in his eyes that had

never been seen in the eyes of a kender before. Caramon's face grew grim as he looked at them.

"Fine," he said. "But where do we go from here?"

Raising his arm, Raistlin pointed. The black robes shimmered, his hand stood out starkly against the night sky, pale and thin, like bare bone.

"Upon that ridge shines a light—"

They all turned to look, even the draconians. Far across the barren plain Caramon could see the dark shadow of a hill rising from the moonlit wasteland. Upon its summit gleamed a pure white light, shining brightly, steadfast as a star.

"One waits for you there," Raistlin said.

"Who? Tanis?" Caramon said eagerly.

Raistlin glanced at Tasslehoff. The kender's face had not turned from the light, he gazed at it fixedly.

"Fizban . . ." he whispered.

"Yes," Raistlin replied. "And now I must go."

"What?" Caramon faltered. "But, come with me . . . us . . . you must! To see Fizban—"

"A meeting between us would not be pleasant." Raistlin shook his head, the folds of his black hood moving around him.

"And what about them?" Caramon gestured at the draconians.

With a sigh, Raistlin faced the draconians. Lifting his hand, he spoke a few strange words. The draconians backed up, expressions of fear and horror twisting their reptilian faces. Caramon cried out, just as lightning sizzled from Raistlin's fingertips. Screaming in agony, the draconians burst into flame and fell, writhing, to the ground. Their bodies turned to stone as death took them.

"You didn't need to do that, Raistlin," Tika said, her voice trembling. "They would have left us alone."

"The war's over," Caramon added sternly.

"Is it?" Raistlin asked sarcastically, removing a small black bag from one of his hidden pockets. "It is weak, sentimental twaddle like that, my brother, which assures the war's continuation. These"—he pointed at the statuelike bodies—"are not of Krynn. They were created using the blackest of black rites. I know. I have witnessed their creation. They would not have 'left you alone.'" His voice grew shrill, mimicking Tika's.

Caramon flushed. He tried to speak, but Raistlin coldly ignored him and finally the big man fell silent, seeing his brother lost in his magic.

Once more Raistlin held the dragon orb in his hand. Closing his eyes, Raistlin began to chant softly. Colors swirled within the crystal, then it began to glow with a brilliant, radiant beam of light.

Raistlin opened his eyes, scanning the skies, waiting. He did not wait long. Within moments, the moons and stars were obliterated by a gigantic shadow. Tika fell back in alarm. Caramon put his arm around her comfortingly, though his body trembled and his hand went to his sword.

"A dragon!" said Tasslehoff in awe. "But it's huge. I've never seen one so big . . . or have I?" He blinked. "It seems familiar, somehow."

"You have," Raistlin said coolly, replacing the darkening crystal orb back in his black pouch, "in the dream. This is Cyan Bloodbane, the dragon who tormented poor Lorac, the Elven King."

"Why is he here?" Caramon gasped.

"He comes at my command," Raistlin replied. "He has come to take me home."

The dragon circled lower and lower, its gigantic wingspan spreading chilling darkness. Even Tasslehoff (though he later refused to admit it) found himself clinging to Caramon, shivering, as the monstrous green dragon settled to the ground.

For a moment Cyan glanced at the pitiful group of humans huddled together. His red eyes flared, his tongue flickered from between slavering jowls as he stared at them with hatred. Then—constrained by a will more powerful than his own—Cyan's gaze was wrenched away, coming to rest in resentment and anger upon the black-robed mage.

At a gesture from Raistlin, the dragon's great head lowered until it rested in the sand.

Leaning wearily upon the Staff of Magius, Raistlin walked over to Cyan Bloodbane and climbed up the huge, snaking neck.

Caramon stared at the dragon, fighting the dragonfear that overwhelmed him. Tika and Tas both clung to him, shivering in fright. Then, with a hoarse cry, he thrust them both away and ran toward the great dragon.

"Wait! Raistlin!" Caramon cried raggedly. "I'll go with you!"

Cyan reared his great head in alarm, eyeing the human with a flaming gaze.

"Would you?" Raistlin asked softly, laying a soothing hand upon the dragon's neck. "Would you go with me into darkness?"

Caramon hesitated, his lips grew dry, fear parched his throat. He could not speak, but he nodded, twice, biting his lip in agony as he heard Tika sobbing behind him.

Raistlin regarded him, his eyes golden pools within the deep blackness. "I truly believe you would," the mage marveled, almost to himself. For a moment Raistlin sat upon the dragon's back, pondering. Then he shook his head, decisively.

"No, my brother, where I go, you cannot follow. Strong as you are, it would lead you to your death. We are finally as the gods meant us to be, Caramon—two whole people, and here our paths separate. You must learn to walk yours alone, Caramon"—for an instant, a ghostly smile flickered across Raistlin's face, illuminated by the light from the staff—"or with those who might choose to walk with you. Farewell, my brother."

At a word from his master, Cyan Bloodbane spread his wings and soared into the air. The gleam of light from the staff seemed like a tiny star amidst the deep blackness of the dragon's wingspan. And then it, too, winked out, the darkness swallowing it utterly.

"Here come those you have waited for," the old man said gently.

Tanis raised his head.

Into the light of the old man's fire came three people—a huge and powerful warrior, dressed in dragonarmy armor, walking arm in arm with a curly-haired young woman. Her face was pale with exhaustion and streaked with blood, and there was a look of deep concern and sorrow in her eyes as she gazed up at the man beside her. Finally, stumbling after them, so tired he could barely stand, came a bedraggled kender in ragged blue leggings.

"Caramon!" Tanis rose to his feet.

The big man lifted his head. His face brightened. Opening his arms, he clasped Tanis to his breast

with a sob. Tika, standing apart, watched the reunion of the two friends with tears in her eyes. Then she caught sight of movement near the fire.

"Laurana?" she said hesitantly.

The elfwoman stepped forward into the firelight, her golden hair shining brightly as the sun. Though dressed in blood-stained, battered armor, she had the bearing, the regal look of the elven princess Tika had met in Qualinesti so many months ago.

Self-consciously, Tika put her hand to her filthy hair, felt it matted with blood. Her white, puffy-sleeved barmaid's blouse hung from her in rags, barely decent; her mismatched armor was all that held it together in places. Unbecoming scars marred the smooth flesh of her shapely legs, and there was far too much shapely leg visible.

Laurana smiled, and then Tika smiled. It didn't matter. Coming to her swiftly, Laurana put her arms around her, and Tika held her close.

All alone, the kender stood for a moment on the edge of the circle of firelight, his eyes on the old man who stood near it. Behind the old man, a great golden dragon slept sprawled out upon the ridge, his flanks pulsing with his snores. The old man beckoned Tas to come closer.

Heaving a sigh that seemed to come from the toes of his shoes, Tasslehoff bowed his head. Dragging his feet, he walked slowly over to stand before the old man.

"What's my name?" the old man asked, reaching out his hand to touch the kender's topknot of hair.

"It's not Fizban," Tas said miserably, refusing to look at him.

The old man smiled, stroking the topknot. Then he drew Tas near him, but the kender held back, his small body rigid. "Up until now, it wasn't," the old man said softly.

"Then what is it?" Tas mumbled, his face averted.

"I have many names," the old man replied. "Among the elves I am *E'li.* The dwarves call me *Thak.* Among the humans I am known as *Skyblade.* But my favorite has always been that by which I am known among the Knights of Solamnia—*Draco Paladin.*"

"I knew it!" Tas groaned, flinging himself to the ground. "A god! I've lost everyone! Everyone!" He began to weep bitterly.

The old man regarded him fondly for a moment, even brushing a gnarled hand across his own moist eyes. Then he knelt down beside the kender and put his arm around him comfortingly. "Look, my boy," he said, putting his finger beneath Tas's chin and turning his eyes to heaven, "do you see the red star that shines above us? Do you know to what god that star is sacred?"

"Reorx," Tas said in a small voice, choking on his tears.

"It is red like the fires of his forge," the old man said, gazing at it. "It is red like the sparks that fly from his hammer as it shapes the molten world resting on his anvil. Beside the forge of Reorx is a tree of surpassing beauty, the like of which no living being has ever seen. Beneath that tree sits a grumbling old dwarf, relaxing after many labors. A mug of cold ale stands beside him, the fire of the forge is warm upon his bones. He spends all day lounging beneath the tree, carving and shaping the wood he loves. And every day someone who comes past that beautiful tree starts to sit down beside him.

"Looking at them in disgust, the dwarf glowers at them so sternly that they quickly get to their feet again.

"'This place is saved,' the dwarf grumbles. 'There's a lame-brained doorknob of a kender off adventuring somewhere, getting himself and those unfortunate enough to be with him into no end of trouble. Mark my words. One day he'll show up here and he'll admire my tree and he'll say, "Flint, I'm tired. I think I'll rest awhile here with you." Then he'll sit down and he'll say, "Flint, have you heard about my latest adventure? Well, there was this black-robed wizard and his brother and me and we went on a journey through time and the most wonderful things happened—" and I'll have to listen to some wild tale, ' and so he grumbles on. Those who would sit beneath the tree hide their smiles and leave him in peace."

"Then . . . he's not lonely?" Tas asked, wiping his hand across his eyes.

"No, child. He is patient. He knows you have much yet to do in your life. He will wait. Besides, he's already heard all your stories. You're going to have to come up with some new ones."

"He hasn't heard *this* one yet," Tas said in dawning excitement. "Oh, Fizban, it was wonderful! I nearly died, again. And I opened my eyes and there was Raistlin in Black Robes!" Tas shivered in delight. "He looked so—well—evil! But he saved my life! And—oh!" He stopped, horrified, then hung his head. "I'm sorry. I forgot. I guess I shouldn't call you Fizban anymore."

Standing up, the old man patted him gently. "Call me Fizban. From now on, among the kender, that shall be my name." The old man's voice grew wistful. "To tell the truth, I've grown rather fond of it."

The old man walked over to Tanis and Caramon, and stood near them for a moment, eavesdropping on their conversation.

"He's gone, Tanis," Caramon said sadly. "I don't know where. I don't understand. He's still frail, but he isn't weak. That horrible cough is gone. His voice is his own, yet different. He's—"

"Fistandantilus," the old man said.†

It has been so long that it is difficult to remember when the second trilogy came to us. Indeed, it seems as I look back on it, that the story for Legends was always there for us to tell.—TRH

Both Tanis and Caramon turned. Seeing the old man, they both bowed reverently.

"Oh, stop that!" Fizban snapped. "Can't abide all that bowing. You're both hypocrites anyway. I've heard what you said about me behind my back, " Tanis and Caramon both flushed guiltily. "Never mind." Fizban smiled. "You believed what I wanted you to believe. Now, about your brother. You are right. He is himself and he is not. As was foretold, he is the master of both present and past."

"I don't understand." Caramon shook his head. "Did the dragon orb do this to him? If so, perhaps it could be broken or—"

"Nothing *did this to him,*" Fizban said, regarding Caramon sternly. "Your brother chose this fate himself."

"I don't believe it! How? Who is this Fistan—whatever? I want answers—"

"The answers you seek are not mine to give," Fizban said. His voice was mild still, but there was a hint of steel in his tone that brought Caramon up short. "Beware of those answers, young man," Fizban added softly. "Beware still more of your questions!" Caramon was silent for long moments, staring into the sky after the green dragon, though it had long since disappeared.

"What will become of him now?" he asked finally.

"I do not know," Fizban answered. "He makes his own fate, as do you. But I do know this, Caramon. You must let him go." The old man's eyes went to Tika, who had come to stand beside them. "Raistlin was right when he said your paths had split. Go forward into your new life in peace."

Tika smiled up at Caramon and nestled close. He hugged her, kissing her red curls. But even as he returned her smile and tousled her hair, his gaze strayed to the night sky, where, above Neraka, the dragons still fought their flaming battles for control of the crumbling empire.

"So this is the end," Tanis said. "Good has triumphed."

"Good? Triumph?" Fizban repeated, turning to stare at the half-elf shrewdly. "Not so, Half-Elven. The balance is restored. The evil dragons will not be banished. They remain here, as do the good dragons. Once again the pendulum swings freely."

"All this suffering, just for that?" Laurana asked, coming to stand beside Tanis. "Why shouldn't good win, drive the darkness away forever?"

This is not a warning against being good—it is a warning against intolerance, bigotry, and elitism.—TRH

"Haven't you learned anything, young lady?" Fizban scolded, shaking a bony finger at her. "There was a time when good held sway. Do you know when that was? Right before the Cataclysm!"†

"Yes," he continued, seeing their astonishment, "the Kingpriest of Istar was a good man. Does that surprise you? It shouldn't, because both of you have seen what goodness like that can do. You've seen it in the elves, the ancient embodiment of good! It breeds intolerance, rigidity, a belief that because I am right, those who don't believe as I do are wrong.

"We gods saw the danger this complacency was bringing upon the world. We saw that much good was being destroyed, simply because it wasn't understood. And we saw the Queen of Darkness, lying in wait, biding her time; for this could not last, of course. The overweighted scales must tip and fall, and then she would return. Darkness would descend upon the world very fast.

"And so, the Cataclysm. We grieved for the innocent. We grieved for the guilty. But the world had to

be prepared, or the darkness that fell might never have been lifted." Fizban saw Tasslehoff yawn. "But enough lectures. I've got to go. Things to do. Busy night ahead." Turning away abruptly, he tottered toward the snoring golden dragon.

"Wait!" Tanis said suddenly. "Fizban—er—Paladine, were you ever in the Inn of the Last Home, in Solace?"

"An inn? In Solace?" The old man paused, stroking his beard. "An inn . . . there are so many. But I seem to recall spicy potatoes. . . . That's it!" The old man peered around at Tanis, his eyes glinting. "I used to tell stories there, to the children. Quite an exciting place, that inn. I remember one night—a beautiful young woman came in. A barbarian she was, with golden hair. Sang a song about a blue crystal staff that touched off a riot."

"That was you, shouting for the guards!" Tanis exclaimed. "You got us into this!"

"I set the stage, lad," Fizban said cunningly. "I didn't give you a script. The dialogue has been all yours." Glancing at Laurana, then back to Tanis, he shook his head. "Must say I could have improved it a bit here and there, but then—never mind." Turning away once more, he began yelling at the dragon. "Wake up, you lazy, flea-bitten beast!"

"Flea-bitten!" Pyrite's eyes flared open. "Why, you decrepit old mage! You couldn't turn water into ice in the dead of winter!"

"Oh, can't I?" Fizban shouted in a towering rage, poking at the dragon with his staff. "Well, I'll show you." Fishing out a battered spellbook, he began flipping pages. "Fireball . . . Fireball . . . I know it's in here somewhere."

Absentmindedly, still muttering, the old mage climbed up onto the dragon's back.

"Are you quite ready?!" the ancient dragon asked in icy tones, then—without waiting for an answer—spread his creaking wings. Flapping them painfully to ease the stiffness, he prepared to take off.

"Wait! My hat!" Fizban cried wildly.

Too late. Wings beating furiously, the dragon rose unsteadily into the air. After wobbling, hanging precariously over the edge of the cliff, Pyrite caught the night breeze and soared into the night sky.

"Stop! You crazed—"

"Fizban!" Tas cried.

"My hat!" wailed the mage.

"Fizban!" Tas shouted again. "It's—"

But the two had flown out of hearing. Soon they were nothing more than dwindling sparks of gold, the dragon's scales glittering in Solinari's light.

"It's on your head," the kender murmured with a sigh.

The companions watched in silence, then turned away.

"Give me a hand with this, will you, Caramon?" Tanis asked. Unbuckling the dragonarmor, he sent it spinning, piece by piece, over the edge of the ridge. "What about yours?"

"I think I'll keep mine a while longer. We've still a long journey ahead of us, and the way will be difficult and dangerous." Caramon waved a hand toward the flaming city. "Raistlin was right. The dragonmen won't stop their evil just because their Queen is gone."

"Where will you go?" Tanis asked, breathing deeply. The night air was soft and warm, fragrant with the promise of new growth.

Thankful to be rid of the hated armor, he sat down wearily beneath a grove of trees that stood upon the ridge overlooking the Temple. Laurana came to sit near him, but not beside him. Her knees were drawn up beneath her chin, her eyes thoughtful as she gazed out over the plains.

"Tika and I have been talking about that," Caramon said, the two of them sitting down beside Tanis. He and Tika glanced at each other, neither seeming willing to speak. After a moment, Caramon cleared his throat. "We're going back to Solace, Tanis. And I—I guess this means we'll be splitting up since—" He paused, unable to continue.

"We know you'll be returning to Kalaman," Tika added softly, with a glance at Laurana. "We talked of going with you. After all, there's that big citadel floating around still, plus all these renegade dragonmen. And we'd like to see Riverwind and Goldmoon and Gilthanas again. But—"

"I want to go home, Tanis," Caramon said heavily. "I know it's not going to be easy going back, seeing Solace burned, destroyed," he added, forestalling Tanis's objections, "but I've thought about

Alhana and the elves, what they have to go back to in Silvanesti. I'm thankful my home isn't like that, a twisted nightmare. They'll need me in Solace, Tanis, to help rebuild. They'll need my strength. I—I'm used to . . . being needed. . . ."

Tika laid her cheek on his arm, he gently tousled her hair. Tanis nodded in understanding. He would like to see Solace again, but it wasn't home. Not any more. Not without Flint and Sturm and . . . and others.

"What about you, Tas?" Tanis asked the kender with a smile as he came trudging up to the group, lugging a waterskin he had filled at a nearby creek. "Will you come back to Kalaman with us?"

Tas flushed. "No, Tanis," he said uncomfortably. "You see, since I'm this close, I thought I'd pay a visit to my homeland. We killed a Dragon Highlord, Tanis"—Tas lifted his chin proudly—"all by ourselves. People will treat us with respect now. Our leader, Kronin, will most likely become a hero in Krynnish lore."

Tanis scratched his beard to hide his smile, refraining from telling Tas that the Highlord the kenders had killed had been the bloated, cowardly Fewmaster Toede.

"I think *one* kender will become a hero," Laurana said seriously. "He will be the kender who broke the dragon orb, the kender who fought at the siege of the High Clerist's Tower, the kender who captured Bakaris, the kender who risked everything to rescue a friend from the Queen of Darkness."

"Who's that?" Tas asked eagerly, then, "Oh!" Suddenly realizing who Laurana meant, Tas flushed pink to the tips of his ears and sat down with a thud, quite overcome.

Caramon and Tika settled back against a tree trunk, both faces, for the moment, filled with peace and tranquility. Tanis, watching them, envied them, wondering if such peace would ever be his. He turned to Laurana, who was sitting straight now, gazing beyond into the flaming sky, her thoughts far away.

"Laurana," Tanis said unsteadily, his voice faltering as her beautiful face turned to his, "Laurana, you gave this to me once"—he held the golden ring in his palm—"before either of us knew what true love or commitment meant. It now means a great deal to me, Laurana. In the dream, this ring brought me back from the darkness of the nightmare, just as your love saved me from the darkness in my own soul." He paused, feeling a sharp pang of regret even as he talked. "I'd like to keep it, Laurana, if you still want me to have it. And I would like to give you one to wear, to match it."

Laurana stared at the ring long moments without speaking, then she lifted it from Tanis's palm and—with a sudden motion—threw it over the ridge. Tanis gasped, half-starting to his feet. The ring flashed in Lunitari's red light, then it vanished into the darkness.

"I guess that's my answer," Tanis said. "I can't blame you."

Laurana turned back to him, her face calm. "When I gave you that ring, Tanis, it was the first love of an undisciplined heart. You were right to return it to me, I see that now. I had to grow up, to learn what real love was. I have been through flame and darkness, Tanis. I have killed dragons. I have wept over the body of one I loved." She sighed. "I was a leader. I had responsibilities. Flint told me that. But I threw it all away. I fell into Kitiara's trap. I realized—too late—how shallow my love really was. Riverwind's and Goldmoon's steadfast love brought hope to the world. Our petty love came near to destroying it."

"Laurana," Tanis began, his heart aching.

Her hand closed over his.

"Hush, just a moment more," she whispered. "I love you, Tanis. I love you now because I understand you. I love you for the light and the darkness within you. That is why I threw the ring away. Perhaps someday our love will be a foundation strong enough to build upon. Perhaps someday I will give you another ring and I will accept yours. But it will not be a ring of ivy leaves, Tanis."

"No," he said, smiling. Reaching out, he put his hand on her shoulder, to draw her near. Shaking her head, she started to resist. "It will be a ring made half of gold and half of steel." Tanis clasped her more firmly.

Laurana looked into his eyes, then she smiled and yielded to him, sinking back to rest beside him, her head on his shoulder.

"Perhaps I'll shave," said Tanis, scratching his beard.

"Don't," murmured Laurana, drawing Tanis's cloak around her shoulders. "I've gotten used to it."

All that night the companions kept watch together beneath the trees, waiting for the dawn. Weary and wounded, they could not sleep, they knew the danger had not ended.

From their vantage point, they could see bands of draconians fleeing the Temple confines. Freed from their leaders, the draconians would soon turn to robbery and murder to ensure their own survival. There were Dragon Highlords still. Though no one mentioned her name, the companions each knew one had almost certainly managed to survive the chaos boiling around the Temple. And perhaps there would be other evils to contend with, evils more powerful and terrifying than the friends dared imagine.

But for now there were a few moments of peace, and they were loath to end them. For with the dawn would come farewells.

No one spoke, not even Tasslehoff. There was no need for words between them. All had been said or was waiting to be said. They would not spoil what went before, nor hurry what was to come. They asked Time to stop for a little while to let them rest. And, perhaps, it did.

Just before dawn, when only a hint of the sun's coming shone pale in the eastern sky, the Temple of Takhisis, Queen of Darkness, exploded. The ground shivered with the blast. The light was brilliant, blinding, like the birth of a new sun.

Their eyes dazzled by the flaring light, they could not see clearly. But they had the impression that the sparkling shards of the Temple were rising into the sky, being swept upward by a vast heavenly whirlwind. Brighter and brighter the shards gleamed as they hurtled into the starry darkness, until they shone as radiantly as the stars themelves.

And then they *were* stars. One by one, each piece of the shattered Temple took its proper place in the

sky, filling the two black voids Raistlin had seen last autumn, when he looked up from the boat in Crystalmir Lake.

Once again, the constellations glittered in the sky.

Once again, the Valiant Warrior—Paladine, the Platinum Dragon—took his place in one half of the night sky while opposite him appeared the Queen of Darkness—Takhisis, the Five-Headed, Many-Colored Dragon. And so they resumed their endless wheeling, one always watchful of the other, as they revolved eternally around Gilean, God of Neutrality, the Scales of Balance.

The Homecoming

There were none to welcome him as he entered the city. He came in the dead of a still, black night; the only moon in the sky being one his eyes alone could see. He had sent away the green dragon, to await his commands. He did not pass through the city gates; no guard witnessed his arrival.

He had no need to come through the gates. Boundaries meant for ordinary mortals no longer concerned him. Unseen, unknown, he walked the silent, sleeping streets.

And yet, there was one who was aware of his presence. Inside the great library, Astinus, intent as ever upon his work, stopped writing and lifted his head. His pen remained poised for an instant over the paper, then—with a shrug—he resumed work on his chronicles once more.

The man walked the dark streets rapidly, leaning upon a staff that was decorated at the top with a crystal ball clutched in the golden, disembodied claw of a dragon. The crystal was dark. He needed no light to brighten the way. He knew where he was going. He had walked it in his mind for long centuries. Black robes rustled softly around his ankles as he strode forward; his golden eyes, gleaming from the depths of his black hood, seemed the only sparks of light in the slumbering city.

He did not stop when he reached the center of town. He did not even glance at the abandoned buildings with their dark windows gaping like the eyesockets in a skull. His steps did not falter as he passed among the chill shadows of the tall oak trees, though these shadows alone had been enough to terrify a kender. The fleshless guardian hands that reached out to grasp him fell to dust at his feet, and he trod upon them without care.

The tall Tower came in sight, black against the black sky like a window cut into darkness. And here, finally, the black-robed man came to a halt. Standing before the gates, he looked up at the Tower; his eyes taking in everything, coolly appraising the crumbling minarets and the polished marble that glistened in the cold, piercing light of the stars. He nodded slowly, in satisfaction.

The golden eyes lowered their gaze to the gates of the Tower, to the horrible fluttering robes that hung from those gates.

No ordinary mortal could have stood before those terrible, shrouded gates without going mad from the nameless terror. No ordinary mortal could have walked unscathed through the guardian oaks.

But Raistlin stood there. He stood there calmly, without fear. Lifting his thin hand, he grasped hold of the shredded black robes still stained with the blood of their wearer, and tore them from the gates.

A chill penetrating wail of outrage screamed up from the depths of the Abyss. So loud and horrifying was it that all the citizens of Palanthas woke shuddering from even the deepest sleep and lay in their beds, paralyzed by fear, waiting for the end of the world. The guards on the city walls could move neither hand nor foot. Shutting their eyes, they cowered in shadows, awaiting death. Babies whimpered in fear, dogs cringed and slunk beneath beds, cats' eyes gleamed.

The shriek sounded again, and a pale hand reached out from the Tower gates. A ghastly face, twisted in fury, floated in the dank air.

Raistlin did not move.

The hand drew near, the face promised him the tortures of the Abyss, where he would be dragged for his great folly in daring the curse of the Tower. The skeletal hand touched Raistlin's heart. Then, trembling, it halted.

"Know this," said Raistlin calmly, looking up at the Tower, pitching his voice so that it could be heard by those within. "I am the master of past and present! My coming was foretold. For me, the gates will open."

The skeletal hand shrank back and, with a slow sweeping motion of invitation, parted the darkness. The gates swung open upon silent hinges.

Raistlin passed through them without a glance at the hand or the pale visage that was lowered in reverence. As he entered, all the black and shapeless, dark and shadowy things dwelling within the Tower bowed in homage.

Then Raistlin stopped and looked around him.
"I am home," he said.

Peace stole over Palanthas, sleep soothed away fear.

A dream, the people murmured. Turning over in their beds, they drifted back into slumber, blessed by the darkness which brings rest before the dawn.

I really enjoyed writing this scene. I worked on it for hours, even though it's a short scene. I wanted to try to make it as dramatic as possible. The use of Raistlin as the final character in the story is a Shakespearean device that indicates that Raistlin will henceforth be the person who holds the power in the world.—MW

Raistlin's Farewell

Caramon, the gods have tricked the world
In absences, in gifts, and all of us
Are housed within their cruelties. The wit
That was our heritage, they lodged in me,
Enough to see all differences: the light
In Tika's eye when she looks elsewhere,
The tremble in Laurana's voice when she
Speaks to Tanis, and the graceful sweep
Of Goldmoon's hair at Riverwind's approach.
They look at me, and even with your mind
I could discern the difference. Here I sit,
A body frail as bird bones.
In return
The gods teach us compassion, teach us mercy,
That compensation. Sometimes they succeed,
For I have felt the hot spit of injustice
Turn through those too weak to fight their brothers
For sustenance or love, and in that feeling
The pain lulled and diminished to a glow,
I pitied as you pitied, and in that
Rose above the weakest of the litter.

You, my brother, in your thoughtless grace,
That special world in which the sword arm spins
The wild arc of ambition and the eye
Gives flawless guidance to the flawless hand,
You cannot follow me, cannot observe
The landscape of cracked mirrors in the soul,
The aching hollowness in sleight of hand.

And yet you love me, simple as the rush
And balance of our blindly mingled blood,
Or as a hot sword arching through the snow:
It is the mutual need that puzzles you,
The deep complexity lodged in the veins.
Wild in the dance of battle, when you stand,
A shield before your brother, it is then
Your nourishment arises from the heart
Of all my weaknesses.

When I am gone,
Where will you find the fullness of your blood?
Backed in the heart's loud tunnels?
I have heard
The Queen's soft lullaby, Her serenade
And call to battle mingling in the night;
This music calls me to my quiet throne
Deep in Her senseless kingdom.
Dragonlords
Thought to bring the darkness into light,
Corrupt it with the mornings and the moons,
In balance is all purity destroyed,
But in voluptuous darkness lies the truth,
The final, graceful dance.
But not for you:
You cannot follow me into the night,
Into the maze of sweetness. For you stand
Cradled by the sun, in solid lands,
Expecting nothing, having lost your way
Before the road became unspeakable.

It is beyond explaining, and the words
Will make you stumble. Tanis is your friend,
My little orphan, and he will explain
Those things he glimpses in the shadow's path,
For he knew Kitiara and the shine
Of the dark moon upon her darkest hair,
And yet he cannot threaten, for the night
Breathes in a moist wind on my waiting face.

I tried to sound Shakespearean here, but ended up more like Browning (Mr., not Mrs.). That could have been exploited nicely: With Robert Browning's monologues, people are always trying to hide something, always betrayed by their words. Problem is, Raistlin's too honest here for a Browning hero, and the result is a poem that (in my opinion) has some good early flashes, but is kind of strained and flat in conclusion.
—Michael Williams

A Last Thought

DRAGONLANCE brought me success and a comfortable living. But the dearest and best gift has been the friends I have made. These include the people who have worked and continue to work on the project, from artists and game designers to fellow authors and editors. These also include some of the fans who have become dear friends over the years. Finally and most importantly, DRAGONLANCE brought me my husband, Don Perrin. We met at Gen Con in 1989, introduced by friends who were fans of the books. (He hadn't read them!) Later he did read them and endeared himself to me by spending an evening telling me what was wrong with them! Tracy was the minister at our wedding in 1997. We were surrounded by the people we love, people we've met through this project. No wonder it has such a special place in my life.

Some Very Special People Who Deserve Special Thanks:

Ray Puechner
Jean Blashfield Black
Patrick McGilligan
Michael Williams
Roger E. Moore
Jeff Grubb
Doug Niles
Harold Johnson
Larry Elmore
Jeff Easley
Clyde Caldwell
Keith Parkinson
Laura Hickman
Mary Kirchoff
Peter Adkison
Brian Thomsen
Jonathon Lazear
Christi Cardenas

Of course, without Tracy, there would not have been DRAGONLANCE.

—Margaret Weis